C000004838

No Other Name

ROBERT BEATTY

authorHOUSE®

AuthorHouse™
1663 Liberty Drive
Bloomington, IN 47403
www.authorhouse.com
Phone: 833-262-8899

© *2020 Robert Beatty. All rights reserved.*

No part of this book may be reproduced, stored in a retrieval system, or transmitted by any means without the written permission of the author.

Published by AuthorHouse 10/30/2020

ISBN: 978-1-7283-4309-9 (sc)
ISBN: 978-1-7283-4308-2 (hc)
ISBN: 978-1-7283-4310-5 (e)

Library of Congress Control Number: 2020922061

Print information available on the last page.

Any people depicted in stock imagery provided by Getty Images are models, and such images are being used for illustrative purposes only. Certain stock imagery © Getty Images.

This book is printed on acid-free paper.

Because of the dynamic nature of the Internet, any web addresses or links contained in this book may have changed since publication and may no longer be valid. The views expressed in this work are solely those of the author and do not necessarily reflect the views of the publisher, and the publisher hereby disclaims any responsibility for them.

This is a work of fiction. All of the characters, names, incidents, organizations, and dialogue in this novel are either the products of the author's imagination or are used fictitiously.

Chapter 1

"Did I say I gave the guy a fair chance? Did you hear me say one word about giving the guy a fair and fighting chance? But I always figured that fairness doesn't have a lot to do with the way you go about killing a snake or a rabid dog. Where it came to things being fair and equal, I doubt it was a fair and equal fight between him and her. Probably took him only one twist of his wrist to snap her neck. Up to that time in my young life, I hadn't done a mean thing to anyone, except to beat up a man in a barroom brawl. I did that because I thought I was trying to protect her. But I never lifted a hand to her, my sister, or any woman. I was always respectful and gentle to any girl or woman. My father drummed it into me always to be respectful to women, even the ones who weren't respectable themselves. When I found out it was him who had killed the girl, my kind and gentle side went away, and it hasn't come back. Since then I've used my hard side all over the place on those who've had it coming to them. But I've never used it on a woman."

The night outside the trench went silent.

"My meanness started the minute I found out the girl had been murdered. From there it sank in all the way. The man who killed the girl started out mean. He was mean to the depths of his soul, which didn't have the first bit of kindness. When I found out it was him who had killed the girl, I went white-hot, raging, out-of-control mean with a vengeance. At the same time I became cold-blooded, calculating, and mean—meaner than I had ever been, meaner than I ever thought I could be.

"I waited for him in the shadows of his own barn. When he came in, I stepped out of the shadows, my newfound meanness at full cock, looking to put his meanness down for good. But my meanness from out of the shadows was only a shadow compared to his deeper meanness. He'd broken a young girl's neck. In return I blew most of his head apart with my father's shotgun."

The earsplitting blasts of the exploding shells that had showered them with sand and pulverized the beach coral had ceased. The silence following loomed in the night air around them, distant and close in, tightly wound and ominous.

"I'm a country boy. Us countryfolk know our shotguns. It's our weapon of choice. Sure does make a mess of a man's face at close range, though. When I first laid eyes on the girl, she had the prettiest face I had ever seen. When he was done with her, he didn't leave her face a very pretty sight to look at. In return I left his face a mess—a mess that his own mother wouldn't have been able to recognize. Probably turned the stomachs of the chief constable and the deputies who had to pick him up and carry him into town for the doc to pronounce him dead. I sent him off into eternity looking worse than he'd sent her out of this world looking. I don't think his entering into eternity either cleaned up his soul or made him any better to look at once he got there. The Indians used to believe that the physical condition you were in when you died carried on into eternity. That's why they would mutilate the bodies and faces of any enemies they killed. For all I know he's walking around in hell with no face."

During the shelling, the two men listening had kept the sides of their heads pressed tight against the dirt walls of the trench, their faces downward. The roar of the shellfire and the insulation of the dirt walls of the improvised trench had partially drowned out the sergeant's voice. Now the only sound in the darkened trench were the dark words of the man's remembrance.

"I don't know how quick she died or how much pain she was in when she died. From what I was told about it, she didn't die right away. The doc who wrote up her death certificate said that she was still alive and breathing when the bastard threw her in the river. She just couldn't move because her neck had been broken. She couldn't struggle. She couldn't cry out to me or anyone. She just slipped quietly under and drowned. I don't know how long she lived before the water finished her off. The murdering bastard who killed her didn't die easy at my hands, but he died quick and easy compared to the way he had made her die. But I made sure he saw it coming from me as much as she'd seen it coming from him."

In the sudden descent of silence, the major raised his head slightly. Whether it was caution or his concentrating on what his adjutant was saying, the major kept his head below the level of the trench as the old veteran sergeant continued to tell his story.

"I thought I had covered my tracks pretty well, but I wasn't near as clever or clean as I thought I'd been. It took the constable about two days to figure out that I had done it. As it was, I had splattered enough of the guy on my boots with the shotgun to give myself away."

With one hand on the dirt wall of the improvised trench, the major started to raise his head upward.

"The constable came to our house in secret with his two deputies. He could have dragged me off then and there. I thought my race was run. Instead he surprised all of us. He said he knew I had killed the man and why I had done it. He even said he might have done the same thing in my place. On the other hand, he said the town was going paranoid with fear over the killing. They thought a madman was on the loose. He said he had to calm the town and give them some kind of explanation as to why the richest man in town had been murdered, and murdered in such a bloody, ugly way. He also said that he couldn't sweep under the table his job and his responsibility as a sworn upholder of the law by turning his back. So he split the difference. He did the old-time western sheriff thing and told me to get out of town. He gave me three days to run. When the three days were up, he said, he'd come for me like he would go after any killer. I left the farm and my family behind and lit out running the second morning."

Whatever shadows were gathering in the man's story, whatever shadows of dark memory stained his remembrance, however his remembrance had darkened his mind where his memories had begun moving to the darkened horizon that lay beyond the trench and the beach, whatever shadows had dogged his path from the barn, from where he had become a killer to the narrow island that he and the remainder of the Philippine Expeditionary Force were trapped on with their narrowing fortunes, the attention of the major was focused more on the shadows out on the dark water than he was on the sergeant's story.

"I picked up running in my hometown, the town where the girl had left off with her running. She had come into town on her own run. I guess in one way or another she had been running all her life. Even when she was lying herself down and around in that house down by the river in my hometown, in her mind she was still running. In her running I was never able to really catch up with her. In her fear she was always out ahead of me. Now it looks like I'm finally going to catch up with her. I just don't know where it's going to be that I meet up with her again. She died far from her home, wherever that was. She died close to my home. She died close to my heart. But I wasn't able to get her heart close to mine. My sister said her heart was too torn for her to give it to anyone."

The smell of cordite from the exploded shells hung in the air, as did the shadows. The smoke of the exploded shells started to drift away on the night breeze. The shadows remained.

"This island is about as far away as you can get from my home on this earth. If I meet her again, it's probably going to be in an even farther away place for both of us."

The field telephone sat on the ground of the trench between the sergeant and the major. Neither of them knew whether the phone line was still intact or whether it had been severed by the shellfire.

"She had come into my hometown on the run to escape the torn-up life she was running from. She came into town running from her name as much as she was running from the hurt that had been inflicted on her in the home she had lived in. Her real name and what she had suffered under it were probably all one and the same to her. In her mind she couldn't separate the two. But she was running from the demons of her memory and her pain as much as, if not more than, the demons she had left behind. From the way she talked, you could tell her memories were like spikes that twisted her soul. I suppose her memories were demons to her soul. I guess that was why she ran from her memories and from her name. But she couldn't get away from her memories. In the end they ran her down."

The major hesitated in raising his head any farther. The gunners on the far shores had paused, but the major was wary that they meant to lure those in the trenches out of their place of relative safety and then start firing again without warning.

"I guess she thought she had found a safe home, such as the place where she took up residence. Maybe she thought she could stop running. If so, the man who killed her tore her up just when she thought she had reached a place of safety. After I killed the man who had killed her, I had to leave my home and go on the run. By one definition of running or the other, I've been running ever since. My being in the corps is just the longest stretch of my run. Looks like it may prove to be the neck-and-neck last stretch."

The major raised his head up higher and looked straight up. A few stars were showing in the rectangle of open sky above the walls of the trench.

"She died there in my hometown, far from her home. No one, me included, ever knew where she came from. I wanted to make a home for her and with her. The man who killed her put her out beyond any home in this world. She came into town with no name of her own. I wanted to give her my name. The man who killed her left her dead without a name. In revenge I left him dead without a face."

The man had just confessed to murder. In the time that they had been serving together, the officer hadn't known the sergeant to be a killer, at least not outside officially sanctioned military protocol. At the moment, the officer's mind was more concentrated on the present danger that threatened to come at them from across the darkened water.

"A lot of countryfolk, mostly Negroes, were heading to the big cities up north at that time, looking for work. I took the train to Chicago, hoping to find some kind of job. I didn't get a lot of productive work at first, but I got a taste of what the underside of Chicago was like in those days. Whether it was irony or God's sense of payback, I finally got a job in the Chicago stockyards. For all I knew, it was the same stockyard where the man I killed sent the hogs he had raised to be butchered. He kept his hands clean of the actual butchering of the animals he sent to the slaughterhouses of Chicago. In my hometown he butchered the girl I was in love with."

The major raised his head up, level with the top of the trench.

"A lot of labor trouble was going on at the time. The workers were getting organized. And radical. And angry. I got caught up in the radical labor movement. I got caught up in a bad strike. The company brought in strikebreakers. There was a big fight at the plant gate. During the fight I shot another man dead. He was trying to beat a woman striker's brains in with a length of iron pipe. I heard her scream. In my head I heard the girl scream as the man back home broke her neck. I went crazy again. Didn't give him much of a chance either. I didn't bother to introduce myself. I pulled out a rickety old pistol my father had given me and shot the SOB dead on the spot where he stood, trying to beat the woman striker dead on the ground. By then I had developed a nasty habit of just taking apart bastards who hurt women, without stopping beforehand to debate the ethics of what I was doing with the thugs I killed, with God, or with the law. Unlike the first guy, this one never even saw it coming. Now I was a killer in two towns, neither of which I could call home or remain in."

The major, raising his head so his eyes were above the top of the trench, looked toward the ocean beyond the shore that the trench overlooked.

"From the fight at the plant gate, I ran again. I ran from the cops. I ran from a lover I had picked up along the way. I ran from the slaughterhouse I had been working in. I ended up running to the corps. Since then I've been running through one slaughterhouse after another, wherever the corps posts me. Now we're all caught in what might be my final slaughterhouse, one I can't run from any better than the animals they sent out of the cattle cars to run down the chute and be butchered then hacked apart."

"Well, they've stopped," the major said. "They must think they've softened us up sufficiently. The landing barges won't be far behind. They'll be swarming all over us soon enough."

The largely ineffectual fire from the guns of the artillery batteries positioned on Bataan Peninsula across Manila Bay and on Cavity Shore on the other side of the bay had ceased. Landing craft would soon be approaching the beach on which the US force thought they had destroyed any opposition.

"I started out in my hometown as a farmer. I made myself a killer in my hometown. After that I branched out as a killer all over the world."

The officer was familiar with the phrase *battlefield confession*, in which men who are certain they will soon be killed in combat try to clear their consciences by confessing their past misdeeds to their fellow soldiers. Having never being in combat before being assigned to the island fortress of Corregidor, the major had never heard a battlefield confession. He figured he was hearing one now. But it didn't register very deep with the major as he was otherwise occupied. He partially tuned out the sergeant's dark confession as he listened intently in the tropical night, straining to hear the sounds being carried past him and away from him by the low rush of the night wind.

In a quick single move, the sergeant stood up beside the major and looked in the same direction the officer was looking. He continued to talk in the same slow, deliberate voice.

"I'm not bragging on myself. I'm not saying I'm proud of what I made myself into. I'm just not denying any of it. It's way too late in the inning to pretend I'm a choirboy now or that I ever was one."

In the distance, both men could hear the dim muttering of the engines of the approaching landing craft. The Japanese gunners on the far shore across the bay had stopped firing out of fear of hitting their own men in the landing craft. The officer imagined their movement, coming upon them in rows like an approaching swarm of square-faced carrion beetles moving toward the carcass of a dead whale washed up on the beach. The night breeze had carried away the smell of cordite from the exploded shells. Now it carried the smell of jungle forest mixed with the scent of salt water. Behind them, palm fronds and branches of other forms of the once lush foliage that hadn't been shattered and shredded by the bombardment rustled in the breeze in the eye of the storm, there in the quiet interim between the end of the shelling and the closer-order melee to come. In the night sky above, stars had become visible following the last faded glow of the sunset.

With the exception of the distant growl of the approaching assault craft engines, it would have been another warm Pacific night with all the sounds and smells that poets and writers of tropical romance and adventure stories like to go on about. It was the kind of night when people with wanderlust visualized walking on beaches of golden sand at sunset as the last of the native fishing boats returned to shore. It was an otherwise ridiculously nice evening to have to face down an invasion.

"Here they come," the major said. "We're in for it now."

"As I was ducking the cops on the streets, heading for the train station to get out of the city, I came across a Marine Corps recruiting poster and decided to put my talent with guns and killing to work. I walked right in and signed up. That's how my career in the military began. No patriotic fervor. No adventure-seeking plan to see the world. No flag-waving send-off by the town. No tearful goodbyes from my family. The tearful goodbyes between us had already happened months earlier in the quiet of a country morning. When I joined the corps, I was just a two-time gunman on the lam, dodging two police departments by hiding out in an outfit dedicated to guns with men who knew how to use them. It was also an outfit I figured would get me out of town and send me far away. I got both those things—double."

The sergeant touched the metal dog tags hanging around his neck. "Forget the name on these." He touched the cloth name tag sewn on his uniform. "Forget the name here. It's not the name I was born with, not the name my parents gave me. I made it up on the spot as I stood in front of the enlistment desk. I've lived my whole life in the corps under this name. I suppose I've violated something in the UCMJ somewhere by enlisting under a false name, but by that time names had become as interchangeable to me as they had been to her."

The major moved his head around, focusing on the sound of the approaching boat engines, trying to determine the direction they were coming from.

"It's too late to go back to my real name now. I guess I'll follow her out the same way she went. I'll go into the grave and end up buried under the name I chose for myself, the way she ended up buried under the name she had given herself. That's provided Tojo's boys don't throw all of us in an unmarked mass grave and leave no cross, let alone names on the crosses to mark where we are."

In this particular case and situation, the officer didn't challenge the sergeant's analysis of their possible fate. The major had come into the army between the wars. He had no combat experience. The sergeant had been in the service a lot longer. He had served in wars and fought in battles the major had only read about in military history class at Officer Candidate School. The sergeant had the service ribbons on his chest and the battle scar on his face to prove he had served in combat. The officer figured that with his practical combat experience, the man had a good eye for sizing up any given military situation. But a person didn't have to be a Spartan at Thermopylae or General Custer at Little Big Horn to know that this regiment was trapped with no back way out. Neither did one have to be a seasoned veteran who had seen death before to sense the mortality coming at the soldiers out of the growing darkness or to know that no help would be arriving from any direction.

"I signed up back in 1913. Now it's almost '42. Just one more year in service and I would have put in my thirty years and would be ready to retire. Like she would have said, it wouldn't have made no never mind if I had retired just before Pearl Harbor. I would have signed right back up. After all those years gone by, I was all marine and wasn't thinking of being anything but more of a marine. I wouldn't have used retirement as a back door to dodge out on my country, and I wasn't about to back off from the slimy bastards who attacked my country and stabbed it in the back."

The major tried to judge the distance from the shore of the coming landing barges. He couldn't tell, but he knew they were drawing close.

"When I was a teenage boy, I had my place in the world. It was the place I wanted to be. I thought it would be mine forever. But my world blew up on me. This isn't the first time that the world I planned on blew up in my face. As it was, when I joined the marines, I signed up just before the world blew up in the Great War. I survived Belleau Wood by making sure a bunch of Germans didn't. Used a shotgun there too. After that I fought and killed insurgents in Haiti and Nicaragua. Then I got stationed out here on the tip of the rusty spear, right in front of the Jap steamroller."

The muttering of the landing craft engines grew louder as more boats pressed in behind the front wave.

"You army boys probably think that every one of us marines grew up wanting to be nothing but a marine. That's the case for some, but it wasn't that way with me. I wasn't afflicted with wanderlust. Or adventurelust. I had no plans or desire to leave home anytime. Before I met her, all I wanted to be was a farmer like my father and his father before him. When she was alive and with me, all I wanted to be was a farm husband with her as my wife and the mother of the next generation of my family on the land. After she was killed, I became a killer myself. I haven't been much more than a killer ever since. If there are scales to be balanced and accounts to be rendered, I've got a definite feeling that it's all about to catch up with me."

Out on the darkened expanse of Manila Bay, the muttering engines were resolving themselves with the fuller sound of the approaching Japanese landing barges. The grizzled old sergeant looked over at the officer.

"Maybe you'd better not stand too close to me, Major. When the lightning strikes me down, it may take you out as well. Better find yourself a place to hide away so you're not near me."

"This island's too damned small for anyone to hide out on," the officer said. "Not in a trench. Not in the jungle. Not back in the tunnels. When the lightning strikes, it's going to land on all of us, whatever our individual backgrounds may be."

The small size of the island had more or less thrown everyone on the island together in an interservice cooperation of convenience. Though they were in different units and different branches of the service, the major and the sergeant had worked closely together, with the sergeant serving as the major's adjutant along with performing his other duties. The arrival of the Japanese juggernaut within artillery range on the main island of Luzon had forced everyone even closer together in the crowded tunnels for cover from the daily aerial bombing and artillery fire.

"Whatever secrets any of us may be carrying, we may all carry them to the grave."

The sergeant had served the major in a professional military manner since he had been the major's adjunct. Limited resources and personnel had dispelled any interservice rivalry and had brought about their alliance of convenience. But they had never shared any personal stories of their lives. The officer had wondered what the man's story was. Somehow he had always sensed that there was more to the story of the man's life than he let on. As the bombardment had grown in intensity that night—the bombardment that was the softening-up precursor to the landing that was moving in behind the cover of the shellfire—the major had been too distracted to pay much attention to the narrative his adjutant sergeant was spinning. It was the only narrative he had heard the otherwise reticent man spin. For all the major knew, the man probably thought it was the last narrative he would ever relate to anyone, so he wanted to get his life story out to someone before he died.

The bombardment had stopped, but the tension hung tight in the air. To break the tension, during the bombardment the major had asked the sergeant what his real story was. Apparently feeling the oncoming of mortality, the man had opened up. Words poured out of the leathery and otherwise closed-mouth man at a rate the officer had never heard him speak before. In its own way, it was a scene out of one of the formula war movies that Hollywood would soon crank out as its contribution to the war effort. The major figured it was the man's battlefield confession. He just hadn't expected a confession of two murders. The officer knew that some Americans used the Marine Corps the way Frenchmen used the French Foreign Legion—as a way to escape from a tragic life or to hide out from something they had done. Some joined the corps to escape from the law. Apparently that was just what this man had done.

The sergeant shook his head. "The thing of it," he went on, "the thing that messed me up with her, was that she never liked violent men. A lot of violence had been done to her by men earlier in her life. She grew up convinced all men were violent by nature. I never acted violent to her, but I beat a man senseless in front of her in a barroom brawl that I started with a man she was working up as he was working her up. At the time I looked on what I was doing as my way of protecting her. I hoped looking protective would draw her to me. All I accomplished was to make her think I was just another violent man, no different from all men. It was a stupid stunt on my part, and it cost me her. It may have very well cost her her life by driving her away from me to a really violent man in the shadows."

The major glanced down at the field telephone on the floor of the trench to see if it was still intact. Then he turned and looked across the ground behind the trench to see if the line had been cut by the shelling. In the darkness, he could see only a few feet of the black wire.

"My stupid display of juvenile male violence drove her away from me. I might have eventually won her back later, but in the meantime I'd driven her far enough away from me, long enough for her to die at the hands of a really violent man who hid his meanness under a cloak of respectability. On that day, I became the violent man she thought all men were. If she's been watching me from somewhere out in the blue, she probably figures she had me pegged right all along."

The major turned back and looked out over the ocean in the same direction as the sergeant was looking. The major figured that the man was looking across a farther gulf than Manila Bay.

"The home I left was the only home I had known or would know after that." The sergeant continued, "When I left home as a teenage boy, it felt like I was stepping into a long, dark corridor I couldn't begin to see the end of. Looks like this island is where my corridor finally lets out."

The man sort of laughed.

"Corridor Corregidor. I don't know whether it's fate's idea of a play on words or if heaven is playing a joke on me. Whether I end up buried under a false name or buried with no name at all, my story started back in my hometown with a girl who didn't have a name. Her story ended with her being buried in a town that wasn't her home and under a name that wasn't hers."

The major was getting the idea that the reason the man was seeing the past so intensely was because he didn't see much in the way of a future.

"I loved that girl like nothing else. I loved her like nothing else mattered in life. The man who killed her went and killed her like her life was nothing at all to him. I killed him like his life was far lower than nothing to me. In the process, I threw away my own life like it was nothing at all. She was all the life I wanted. After she died, my life meant nothing to me. I guess that's why I went around throwing away lives so easily after that, my own included."

From the direction the sound was coming from, it seemed the landing barges were approaching farther down the shore than they'd been expected to head for. If they kept up their deviation, they would miss the optimal landing beach. If they kept heading in that direction, they would come within range of the island's shore defense artillery.

"A lot of guys join up with the corps because they've got wanderlust. They want to see the world. Like I said, that wasn't the case for me. I never had the fever to wander. I wasn't looking to see the world. I had all the world I wanted. At least I had all the world I wanted until I saw her. Then my world seemed empty and incomplete. I wanted to fill my world with her. My trouble started when I began wanting to bring her into my world. Before she came along, I knew what I wanted to do in life. I was in the town I wanted to spend the rest of my life in. I had my life all set and worked out. Meeting her changed everything for me. She turned my life around as if everything in my life that had come before her had never existed. In return I wasn't able to do one thing that I wanted to do for her in her life. I wasn't able to soothe her soul. I wasn't able to take her away from the disreputable life she was living. As a farm boy, I didn't have a lot I could give her, but I gave her what I could. The one thing above all that I wanted to give her was my life, in the sense that I would spend it with her. She had even less to her name to give me than I had to give her, whatever her real name was. In return she gave me what was naturally hers to give as a girl."

The major tuned the man out even more as he stood trying to figure out why the Japanese were heading to a less optimal landing site.

"It's pretty corny to say, but I would have given her all the love I had in my heart. She gave me love in the open way that she knew how to, probably the only way she knew how to, the way of love that girls in her profession master early on, the way she was so easy and practiced at doing. But, like my sister said, I guess her heart was too cut up and scarred for her to give love from the heart. I guess she had been too hurt and was running too scared to trust in any kind of love from anybody. She lived openly by the ways and particulars of love, but I don't know if she ever believed in the word.

"I would have given my life for that girl. In the end, I suppose you could say that's what I did. All the times we were together in life, in all the ways we were together, dirty and clean, after all I would have given her, after all she gave me, the one thing she never gave me was her name." The sergeant paused. "I killed a man in the name of that girl. After that, after all the years gone by since, I still don't know her real name!"

"The current!" the major said. "They didn't anticipate the strength of the current. It's pulling them away from where they intended to land. Their cover on the beach won't be as optimal. If they drift far enough, they'll come in range of the six-inch guns."

The rumble of the engines of the approaching landing barges was growing louder. They were definitely slipping laterally into range of the island's shore defense artillery. The big guns of the main defense batteries had been positioned to defend against squadrons of warships sailing in the classical line-of-battle formations from an earlier era. The small, rickety landing craft would be harder targets to hit in the dark, and they fired too slow to hit fast-moving landing craft. The smaller guns were able to swivel on their fixed-position mounts, but they could barely turn far enough to hit the beach that was optimal for landing. But if the landing craft kept drifting to the side in the direction they were currently drifting, they would come within the arc of fire of the smaller guns. The guns would be firing at an oblique angle, which would make them harder to aim. Any hit the guns might make would be a random chance occurrence. But any small advantage might make the difference.

"I loved that girl like there was no tomorrow. I loved her until all her tomorrows ran out. In the end, all that my love for her got her was killed by making her run from me, off to a really dangerous man. I killed her killer, but my love for her hadn't stopped her from being killed. All that my love for her got me was out of the home and life I knew and a one-way ticket on a train heading far away from everything else I loved. Eventually it got me into the corps and into every war the corps has been involved in since the Boxer Rebellion."

From the military history of the corps that the major had learned in OCS, he was familiar with the Boxer Rebellion in China, against the colonial powers occupying parts of China at the time. He was also familiar with the involvement of the corps in suppressing the rebellion and rescuing the diplomats and their fellow marines besieged in the city of Beijing. All the wars the major was familiar with, he had read about in books. All the wars the sergeant had been in, he had been in firsthand, up close and personal. Only minutes ago he had revealed that his familiarity with killing had started not in the military, but in his hometown. Wherever it had started, the man's familiarity with killing and war was written in the set of his words, the set of his face, and the scar on his face.

"She came into my town on a cold run of fear and pain. My love for her sent me on a hot run of vengeance to kill the man who killed her. After a long and circuitous run, my love for her got me here. In that way, you could say, she made a goat out of me. For my part, my love for her made a killer out of me. But I was the one who made a killer out of myself—all in the name of a girl whose real name I never knew and still don't know."

The major turned to face the sergeant and pointed to the field telephone. "Get on the horn to Battery Morrison and Battery Hearn," he said. "Tell them to swing their guns around and target the beach at North Point. They may be able to get their licks in."

"Oh, I can remember her face well enough," the sergeant said, continuing his narrative unbroken as he picked up the field telephone receiver. "I've seen her face in more places and in a greater number of dreams than a service paymaster can add up. I can close my eyes and still see her face clearly. Maybe I didn't have my eyes fully open to her when she was alive. But even before she died, whether I was asleep or awake, I was seeing her face in my dreams. After she died, I saw her face in nightmare dreams of her being killed. At any time then or since, I could still see her face clearly in my mind. I've seen her face floating before me in every corner of the globe I've served in. I've seen her here too. Maybe it's only more of my imagination that makes me think she's here. Then again, maybe she is here, out there in the beyond, watching—not watching over me, just watching what happens to me. Maybe she's here because she knows something I don't."

He turned the hand crank to signal the switch panel operator back in the tunnel complex.

"But of late when I see her, the picture of her in my mind keeps getting covered over and darkened by the image of her gravestone standing on the top of the ridgeline in the cemetery where I left her. Makes me think that I'm not all that far from joining her in a grave of my own. Maybe I won't be so thickheaded and reckless out in the beyond. Maybe I won't stumble all over myself like the jackass I was as a youth. I only wanted her with me for the rest of my life. Instead I sent her running away from me like she was running for her life."

The major looked out, trying to see the shape of the coming armada and the shape of the future. He could barely see the beach.

"Maybe I won't send her running away from me in the beyond. Maybe we'll get on better together in death than we did in life. I didn't know all that I was getting into when I joined the corps. I didn't know anywhere near what I was getting into when I took up with her. I didn't know how much running she was coming off of or how much running she was still doing in her heart and mind. I didn't know how much running that loving her would set me out on. Maybe all our running will finally stop out there in the beyond. I don't know what's up ahead for either of us. Maybe she knows what we're both heading for."

Chapter 2

The town was up ahead, but it was the rest of his life that he was heading toward.

Samuel didn't drive the open country road the way Tony danced down the alley, singing about how he was sure something great was coming his way, as he did in *West Side Story* before he met Maria at the dance. Samuel wasn't filled with an undefined and unformed anticipation that something great was coming his way. It wasn't a day of undefined feelings or unformed longings. It wasn't a day of undefined anything. Everything around and ahead was clear and in sharp focus. In the bright horizon-to-horizon light of the spring day, even the remote trees and farmhouses, shrunk in size by the perspective of distance, stood out in sharp, clear, and distinct miniature, their details recognizable by sight and by their familiar outlines. All that appeared in his sight was familiar, known, and given. Even the horizons themselves were distinct and knowable right up to their vanishing point. It was the home area of his youth. It was the home of his family's past on the land. It was the home of his present. It was the home he wanted and that he intended to stay in and make even more his as he grew older on the land.

There was no mist or haziness hanging over the horizons to fade or distort the known landscape or obscure what might lie beyond any given horizon. The feeling of rooted certainty was reinforced by the feeling that what lay beyond the visible horizon was an extension of what Samuel could see from where he was sitting behind the wheel of the truck or from the front porch of the family farm. It was the embodiment of what he would see and be part of throughout the days of his life he had yet to see.

The sky might not have been the bluest of blues, but it was blue enough for poetic mention. The blueness extended undiminished and unadulterated to where it merged suddenly at the horizon with the crisp greenness of the slightly undulating landscape. Only a few small scattered clouds broke the uniform blue of the sky with their whiteness. In the quickness of their passing, they left only fleeting shadows on the ground.

In the near dimension of the landscape, fields of wild goldenrod exuded a faint golden aura for the few vertical feet they had sway over, until the dull gold of their color blended in with the green of the wild grass around them, the wider expanses of green beyond, and the blue of the sky above. Dandelions not yet gone to seed added their own varied shade of gold. Clumps of wild thistle interjected occasional bursts of light purple that broke up the uniformity of the green-gold hue of the land. Sprigs of Queen Anne's lace added fuzzy flattened splotches of white from the flowers at the tops of their stems. Down lower, wild buttercups added their own smaller, but more sharply defined, petals of white. In the uncultivated fields, the profusion of wildflowers made a patchwork quilt of color and life. In the plowed fields, the crops planted at the beginning of spring had established themselves and were pushing toward maturity from out of the dark, rich soil of the cultivated rows.

Long grasslike stems were quivering in the faint breeze. When full grown, they would become fields of wheat, alfalfa, barley, or oats rippling in brown undulations like waves driven by a distant storm coming in from the ocean under an otherwise clear and open sky. Rows of broader-leafed plants on more rigid stalks reached the height of a man's knee. By the end of summer, they would have transformed themselves into tall phalanxes of corn, each stalk crowding the others, holding their ripening ears up to the sun passing over head as if they were endless lines of religiously devout peasants holding their children up to be blessed by the passing overhead pontiff of the sun.

In the immediate close-in landscape, patches of water in the ditches and farm retention ponds alongside the road, between the road and the fields immediately beyond, sported stands of cattails with their characteristic thick brown heads crowning their heavy stalks and their long saberlike leaves paralleling the stalks. In some patches, red-winged blackbirds balanced on the swaying stalks, occasionally waving their red-shouldered black wings for balance, singing into the bright day, their song being both a call for a mate and a warning to male competitors to stay away from the territory of their miniature swamp.

Some of the farm fields were divided from their neighbors' by nothing more than a wood-post wire fence. Other farms were delineated from their neighbors by the one-dimensional linear forests. Freshly painted barns glowed deep red in the sun. Older barns, their paint faded, shone a deeper burgundy color. The farmhouses shone a whitewashed white color. Freshly washed clothing hung in multicolored profusion from clotheslines. Young children played in the yards of some of the farmhouses. Dogs ran parallel inside the fences along the road, barking at the rattling contraption passing the domains they defended.

The 1910 Ford pickup truck Samuel was driving didn't have a front windshield, and the side panels of the driver's compartment didn't cover the driver's side all the way, so the driver wasn't enclosed. The model was one of the lowest-priced entry-level pickup trucks in the Ford line of that day. Two years earlier, Samuel's father had finally bought a truck after Samuel had worn him down, arguing that the modern convenience of a truck would greatly increase their ability to get the produce his family grew on their farm to market more quickly than their old horse-drawn wagon. His father finally came around to Samuel's more modern way of thinking, but only as far as the truck went. His father absolutely refused to consider buying one of the steam-powered behemoths that large farms were using. He preferred the more traditional methods of planting and harvesting. He was far more familiar and comfortable with the old traditional farming methods he had learned from his father. Besides, the family couldn't begin to afford one of the megamachines that large farms of that era were staring to employ.

The minimalist design of the open-cab truck didn't do very much to keep out dust and road grit, but Samuel liked the feel of the air on his face as he passed the farms and fields outside of town. The open architecture of the truck let dust enter the cab from multiple directions. But if he could keep moving, he could stay ahead of the cloud of fine dust the truck raised as it traversed the dry dirt road. What breeze there was that day was not fast enough to cause the dust to keep up with the truck and send it into the cab. The breeze was blowing in from off to the side. It sent most of the dust out over the open fields.

The sky might not have been the bluest of blues, but it was blue enough for poetic mention. The blueness extended undiminished and unadulterated to where it merged suddenly at the horizon with the crisp greenness of the landscape. Only a few small scattered clouds broke the uniform blue of the sky with their whiteness. In the quickness of their transit high above the land, they left only fleeting shadows on the ground as they traveled past.

It was summer now. Crops were in the field, green with growing promise. In the sunshine and in the open air and open sky above the fields that stretched to the bright horizon, Samuel's growing life was bright with the promise of freedom to come. In less than a week he would graduate high school. But it would be only a relative and passing freedom. With high school behind him and no college on any horizon, he would be working on the farm full time as he father needed him. Any heady interlude of short-lived freedom to come would soon be swallowed up by the full-time responsibility of helping his father manage the farm and helping provide for the rest of the family. Whether Samuel would ever have a family of his own was a question that, as of late, was pressing in on him. When and if he would have a family was something unseen over the horizon.

On the floor of the truck there was a three-pedal arrangement. One pedal was the brake pedal. The other two controlled the two-speed planetary transmission. Along with the still prevailing cultural attitude that knowing how to drive was not ladylike, the confusing arrangement of pedals and the other quirky mechanical oddities of automobiles of that day was one of the reasons that many women did not know how to drive a car. But by nature, teenagers, with the flexible minds of youth, often tech-savvy, could pick up the latest technological innovations as if they'd been born to it. The flexibility of mind that one day would quickly make teenagers comfortable and proficient masters of the internet and iPods had made Samuel Martin as comfortable and proficient at handling the latest in mechanized equipment on the road and in town as he was at handling a horse team in the field. In quick order he had become a better driver of the family truck than his old-line, horse-and-buggy-era father was or would ever be. It was the main reason that Samuel's father had sent him into town in the truck to run errands instead of doing them himself. The arrangement gave Samuel time on the open road and mobility that he might not otherwise have had. It gave him the chance, however narrowing of a chance, that, for a short while, would allow him to feel like a footloose and fancy-free wanderer seeking adventure on the open road, under the open sky.

In the near dimension of the landscape, the unplanted areas of wild goldenrod exuded a faint golden aura for the few vertical feet they held sway over, until the dull gold of their color blended in with the green of the wild grass around them and the wider expanses of grass beyond. Dandelions not yet gone to seed added their own varied shade of gold. Clumps of wild thistle interjected occasional bursts of light purple that broke up the uniformity of golden hue. Sprigs of Queen Anne's lace added fuzzy flattened splotches of white from the flowers at the tops of their stems. Down lower, the buttercups added their own smaller, but more sharply defined, petals of white. The wildflowers in the uncultivated fields were a patchwork quilt of color and life in their natural random element. In the dedicated and designated crop fields, they were considered weeds.

In the immediate close-in landscape passing by as Samuel drove were the ditches that caught the excess rainwater coming off the fields and channeled it away so that it would not sit in puddles on the ground, which would rot the crops. In the strips of standing water in the ditches, the blackbirds sat on their swaying cattail perches and called out their longing to find a mate.

At the river at the north boundary of the town, Samuel drove over the bridge where the road turned to enter the town. The heavy wooden planks of the bridge, loosened slightly by time and wear, rattled as he drove across them. Where the road entered the town, the first landmark Samuel came to was the small-town lumberyard. Beyond that was the side road that hugged the riverbank, running past the large two-story house of the late Arthur Richardson, whose untimely death in middle age had left his widow with diminishing finances. Her reduced fortune had forced her to convert the house into a bordello that now serviced the footloose farmhands of the area and the otherwise footloose, straying middle-aged and older gentlemen of the town who took their dalliances away from their plain-faced wives to cavort with the only slightly less plain-faced women of the house. Given that the house was outside the town boundaries, the town councilmen could not force a closing of the Richardson house of ill repute. Whether they had any inclination to do so was an entirely different matter, one they kept as secret as their dalliances at the house.

Samuel Martin passed the intersection and drove toward the beginning of Main Street, where the business district of town commenced. Decreasing the engine's RPMs by adjusting the throttle mounted on the top of the steering column, he drove the Model T Ford truck on to the brick pavement of the main street through the heart of town. The brick section of road that ran through the middle of the town, past the shops, stores, and establishments of the business district, was the only paved street in the town. The rest of the roads, including the roads that ran through the residential area, were of hard-packed dirt. Except for the concrete walkways that ran in front of the businesses of the business district, sidewalks had yet to come to the town. On the far side of the town, where the pavement ended, the livery stable, the wagon repair shop, and other pedestrian country blue-collar manual labor establishments were located. Beyond them were stationed the town bar and the pool hall, which was also a bar.

In town, Samuel worked the pedals in the right sequence to slow the truck. When he arrived at the feed and grain store, he turned the truck down the side drive that led around behind the store, where the attached storage shed used for loading and unloading was located. There he shut off the truck motor, got out of the cab, and walked back the way he had come, toward the front entrance of the store. He could have gone in through the back of the store, but it seemed more polite to go in the front.

As Samuel turned the corner of the wood-framed building, he looked across the street toward the brick building that housed the town newspaper. It was the habit of the journalists there to post a copy of the day's newspaper in the main window of the building. The purpose was to give townspeople walking by on the street a taste of the latest news headlines and to whet their appetite to buy a full newspaper. Today there was a newspaper posted in the window as usual, but no crowd surrounded it. It had been only a month and a half since Samuel and his father had spotted a larger than usual crowd knotted around the paper's window and had stopped to investigate. Murmurs and conversations were going on among the crowd as Samuel and his father walked up. Pushing in between the building and the crowd, they saw the glaring headlines on the paper posted in the window: TITANIC SINKS! The upper right corner of the paper had been folded over as if the paper had been shoved into its mounting frame on the window ledge in haste. Samuel had asked his father if there had been anyone from the town on the ship. His father had answered that the ship was a "rich man's folly tub" and that no one from town could afford to walk up the gangplank, let alone afford a stateroom. In an apocryphal exaggeration, he had gone on to say that people from the town didn't have enough money to even afford to pay for the privilege of washing dishes on the luxury liner, let alone think about one of the luxury cabins, which probably cost more per night than the average citizen of the town made in one year. His attitude was somewhat borne out when the paper later printed a partial casualty list, which included luminaries of upper-upper-class America such as John Jacob Astor and Levi Strauss.

What wasn't made clear in the paper was that a large number of the casualties were near-penniless immigrants traveling in steerage class who were no richer than and, on the average, possibly poorer than most of the people in the town. The predictable comments about the economic leveling effect of the tragedy, and the working out of equanimity, and the rich dying like the poor, and human arrogance tempting the will and providence of God were heard from the crowd gathered around the window. The minister had pontificated on that specific point in his sermon the following Sunday.

The front window of the paper was empty and unattended that day. Apparently the sea-lanes had gone without human arrogance prompting another maritime tragedy, and human folly and madness had not yet caused Europe to erupt in another war. Samuel Martin turned the corner of the building that housed Harper's feed and grain store and walked in through the front door.

Inside the store he paid for the requisite number of bags of feed his father had specified and was sent out into the back, where someone would help him load them into the truck. In the back, he met his friend Ben Norton, son of the owner of the feed store and Samuel's classmate in the about-to-graduate senior class with him in the town high school. Ben was working part time on Saturdays in his father's store. At that time and in that locale, one the last major transition points in the life of a teenager was graduation from high school. Outside of entering into the institution of marriage, graduation from high school set the institution they would follow for life. After graduating from high school, Ben would start work in his father's business full time. Samuel would become a full-time farmer who would follow in his father's footsteps down the same linear path between the furrows of the same ground his father and grandfather had plowed.

College was not in the works for Samuel. Nor was it in the plans or the thinking of either him or his father. Their footsteps had been set by their station and situation in life and by their place in the world. Their stations in life, the positions they would take and not take in life, the paths they would follow and not follow in life, the place they would call home for the rest of their lives, had been set for them by their station in life, and they had tacitly agreed to this. There was, however, one transition the young men had not yet made. It was a transition that their upcoming graduation ceremony would not accomplish for them, a transition that was otherwise occupying Ben's mind as the transition from high school approached.

Together Samuel and Ben started loading the truck, each carrying one bag of oats on his shoulder at a time and loading the bags in sequence into the bed of the truck. The oats were feed for the plow horses used to work the fields on the Martin farm. As far as mechanized transport to and from the farm went, Samuel's father could afford a Model T truck. As far as mechanical means to plow the fields of the farm itself were concerned, Samuel's father could not afford one of the big steam-powered behemoths that had appeared in the 1890s. Neither could he afford one of the motorized tractors that were beginning to make their appearance.

Horses were plentiful. Horses were affordable. But horses had to be fed.

Mr. Martin had sent his son into town to lay in a supply of horse feed. Following that, Samuel was scheduled to go to the Wells Fargo receiving warehouse and pick up a new cutter blade to replace one of the blades on the disc harrow that had broken on a stone. They would replace the blade themselves. Of necessity, many farmers of the day were also good mechanics. They often had to be. Outside mechanics were often hard to find. And they were often expensive when found.

Ben slumped a bag of oats into the back of the truck. Instead of going for another bag, he paused and waited for Samuel to come up to him. They were alone in the backyard of the store. No one was there to overhear their conversation.

"Have you thought any more about what we were talking about?" Ben asked as Samuel came up to the truck with a bag of oats on his shoulder.

"What's that?" Samuel asked.

Ben hadn't chosen the moment as a deliberate act of symbolic irony. The grain they were loading was intended for horse feed. It wasn't seed grain, but the subject did otherwise have something to do with sowing wild oats.

"You know," Ben said in a sideways tone of voice, "your idea that we should sneak away early from the graduation dance and take ourselves over to Mrs. Richardson's place and lose our virginity?"

"As I recall, that was your idea," Samuel said as he slid the bag of grain off his shoulder and dropped it into the truck bed. He rested his forearm on the top of the truck side and leaned against the vehicle. "You're the one who brought up the suggestion to me, not the other way around. You're the one who keeps bringing the subject up."

"And at no time during any of those intervals did you ever tell me to take my idea and go jump headfirst in the river," Ben said. "You always said 'I'll think about it' or something like that. You never said a flat-out no. You seemed interested enough. If we're going to be doing it, we've got to think about how we're going to go about it. Graduation is on Wednesday. The graduation party is Friday night. We can sneak away and head over to the house without anyone seeing us. But we've got to set our plans. We've only got until next Friday to work it out."

"Why do you want to go to that place?" Samuel asked. The question was mostly rhetorical. The answer was mostly obvious.

"Because that's the only place of its kind in the county," Ben said. "If we wanted to go anywhere else, we'd have to drive all day to get there. We'd spend as much in gas and tolls as we would paying the ladies' fees.

Mrs. Richardson's is a short drive from the school auditorium in the dark of night. No one will see us go from the dance, and no one will see us go into the place. We can be in and out without anyone knowing what we were doing."

He hadn't meant the in-out part as a sexual pun.

"The ladies in residence are going to see us," Samuel said. "We can't very well stand outside in the dark and order them to put on blindfolds before we come in so they won't know who we are."

"The ladies in that house all have their secrets," Ben said. "They've all got a whole lifetime of secrets behind them. The ladies over there aren't going to tell anyone we were there. It would be bad for business if they snitched on anyone. It would keep customers away. As long as they get paid, they'll keep silent. Besides, they've never seen us before. They don't know us from Adam."

"There may be plenty of other people there who will recognize us," Samuel said. "They've got male customers coming there all the time. And they're from every section of town. Town councilmen frequent the place when they aren't in a back room somewhere making deals to help themselves to the town treasury while making it look like they're performing a service for the town. Besides, the dance is Friday night. Friday is payday for a lot of the hired hands and freight workers and the lumberyard workers. There could be a bunch of them there at the house looking to spend their money. We may have to wait in line with them. One way or the other, we may be recognized."

"They'll keep our secret if we'll keep their secret," Ben reiterated. "Everyone who's been through that house has secrets to keep. That house is built on keeping secrets under wraps. We'll just be nothin' more than one more set of secrets that pass through the house."

"I thought you were sweet on Molly Ivers?" Samuel asked as a way of redirecting the conversation. "Aren't you planning on escorting her to the dance? If so, how are you planning on getting away from her? Are you just going to walk away from her in the middle of the dance, saying that you have to go somewhere and scratch an itch?"

"I had a small passing interest in Molly Ivers," Ben answered, "but I'm not sweet on her. I've hardly ever said a word to her. I haven't done anything with her, and I'm not taking her to the dance. I'm not escorting any girl to the dance. Any girl around here you take anywhere would probably take the fact of being taken to the dance as a sign that they are now engaged to be engaged. If you as much as brush the side of their hand with yours, they're off in their minds thinking about a trousseau and designing their wedding gowns, selecting patterns, and planning the color of the nursery room. I'm not ready to get married, and I'm not looking for the trouble that can come from giving a suggestive and grasping girl a thirdhand idea that I'm looking to marry her. That's why I'm not escorting Molly Ivers to the dance. … What about you? Are you taking anyone to the dance? If you're taking someone, you haven't mentioned it to me."

"I'm not taking anyone to the dance," Samuel said. "I'm just going. When I'm there, I may dance with an unattached girl, but I'm not taking anyone."

Samuel had been planning on going stag to the dance. His reasons for planning on going alone had nothing to do with not wanting to be tied down squiring around one girl and keeping himself unattached so that he would be able to slip away and patronize the local bordello. His reason for attending the dance alone had been twofold. First, Ben was more or less right. Any girl he took to the dance might indeed start to get the idea that he was getting serious. In his time and place, the perception that he was getting serious would be amplified by the fact that he was starting out on his life path and was probably thinking about settling down. Girls of the day could easily see a hand extended to them in a dance as an implicit Oh-Promise-Me indication that the young man extending the hand was soliciting a partner to walk through life with. A hand extended for a single dance could lead to a whole lot of misplaced assumptions on the part of the girl.

Where it came to court and spark, the other reason Samuel wasn't taking any of the local girls to the dance was that none of them had ever sparked much interest in him. Among the limited selection of available town and farm girls, in Samuel Martin's mind and estimate a few of them managed to ascend to the level of bland and uninspiring. The rest didn't even rise that high.

"If you're not dancing with anyone in particular at the dance, then we can slip away and take ourselves over to Mrs. Richardson's house and do some dancing under the sheets with the ladies over there," Ben said.

"When you're done with that kind of woman, you can get away from her. They're made to be left behind. They expect to be left behind. When the men they're servicing leave, they move on to the next man who's going to do them and then leave them. That's the way they do it. That's the way they want it. There's nothing permanent about it. There's no demands for marriage and ever after from them. There's nothing romantic about it. After romancing those kinds of women, they aren't going to up and insist that you walk them home. They're already at home right where they are. After you're done with them and they're done with you, they're not going to insist that you take them home to meet your mother. And they're not going to tell their father to grab a shotgun and drag you to the altar because you soiled them. They're already soiled, dozens of times over."

Ben shifted his stance by the truck and shifted the direction of the conversation. "Molly Ivers isn't going to give me what I'm looking for," he went on. "None of the girls in this town are going to give us what we want unless the wedding vows have been spoken by the minister. No girl in this town will give us anything we're looking for until after they've marched us down the aisle and back. We can both get what we want and need from the ladies over at Mrs. Richardson's without any complications, as long as we pay their fee. They're not honest women. They're not going to demand you marry up with them and make an honest woman out of them."

Samuel turned and headed back to the storage shed to get another bag of oats.

"My mother says that you can pick up diseases from women like that," Samuel said as he walked away, "diseases that stay with you all your life. You may not be stuck married to them for life, but you may be stuck for life with the bugs they leave you with. Even if they only charge you the cut rate, in the end it can turn out to be a lot more expensive than you had planned if you end up rotting your pecker off or paying extended doctor bills for their services. Losing your virginity kind of loses its appeal if you lose your cock and your health in the process."

Actually he was somewhat wrong on the point about there being no treatment for venereal disease in that period. For some time venereal disease had been treated by administering inoculations of a low-concentration solution of mercury. The treatment worked to reduce the effect of the disease to some degree, the problem being that mercury is a toxic heavy metal. The doctor administering the treatment walked a fine line between treating his patient and killing him. The other problem was that mercury treatment was a palliative, not a cure. When administered in proper (i.e., less than toxic) amounts, mercury would debilitate syphilis and gonorrhea microbes to some degree, but it would not kill them and purge the body of the disease. The patient would need repeated doses of mercury for the rest of his life. As the saying went at the time: "One night with Venus, a lifetime on mercury."

"They say they've got a younger girl over there now," Ben said, following Samuel back to the storage shed. "She's supposed to be a real looker too."

"Who's the 'they' who knows all this about who's over at the house?" Samuel said without turning around as he walked. "If you haven't been there, how do you know what girls they have on call there?"

"Some of the other workers here," Ben said to Samuel's back. "They've been to the house. According to them, the new girl's only been there for the last few months. I guess she's a new recruit. If she's new in the trade, she may not have been in circulation long enough to have picked up any kind of disease. But the other workers here say all the ladies in the house, even the older ones, seem clean. At least nobody around here has come down with any kind of peter-eater disease from them. From the other men they drink with at the saloon, they say no one else they know of has come down with anything either."

At the foursquare stack of full grain bags on the floor of the feed shed, Samuel took hold of an oat sack at the top of the stack and prepared to shift it onto his shoulder to carry it back to the truck.

"If you want it so bad, why don't you just go over there by yourself?" Samuel asked as he prepared to heft the grain bag. "You don't need me to show you how to dip your wick. I'm no more acquainted in that respect than you are. If you're looking for advice on loving a woman who's made a lifetime career out of loving men, I'm not your man. There's nothing to be gained by taking me along."

"I still think it would work out best if we went together," Ben said.

Samuel still hadn't lifted the grain bag. "How so?" he asked.

"It would make it easier for me," Ben answered.

"What do you mean?" Samuel said, his hands on the grain sack, his arms prepared to lift it to his shoulder. "Are you afraid to go there by yourself? What are you afraid they're going to do to you? Are you afraid they're going to laugh at you and make fun of you? Do you want me there to take you by the hand and play big brother for you?"

"You did keep the bullies off me in school," Ben said. "They never liked the thought of tangling with the school fistfight champ. They didn't last long when they tried."

"I don't think you're going to run into any problem with bullies at Mrs. Richardson's," Samuel said as he pulled the heavy sack on to his shoulder. "They have a guard there to roust any rowdies who get out of control. I don't think the ladies of the house are going to get rough with you. Some of those ladies of the night may kick a bit under the covers, but I doubt they're going to kick you in the teeth, and I don't think they'll kick you out of bed or out of the place. Like you say, both of those are bad for business. … So what else do you want me there for? Do you want me around to be some kind of confidence builder for you?"

"I just think that you being there would complete the picture," Ben said.

"What do you mean by that?" Samuel said as he turned to walk back to the truck.

"For one, you're the most handsome boy in school," Ben said. "They'd probably open the door quicker for you than they would for a more homely looking boy like me."

"The women over there at Mrs. Richardson's work on a strictly cash-and-carry basis," Samuel said. "They don't open doors or shut them in the face of customers because of their looks. The only manly profile they're looking for is the manly countenance of whatever president is on the dollar bills you hand them."

"At least having you along would get me in the door easier than if I went alone," Ben went on. "You're not only better-looking than me, but you're also bigger than I am. And you're older and more mature-looking. If they see me by myself, they may think that I'm underage. They might not let me through the door, but I'm sure they'll let you in."

There was something to Ben's assertion. With his height, square shoulders, square jaw, and stout upper body, eighteen-year-old Samuel Martin could pass for a man in his early twenties. With his rounded face and smaller physique, Ben still had a young-boy-in-knickers appearance. He looked younger than his age.

"Once we're in, you can vouch that I'm the same age as you."

Samuel didn't answer. He hefted the grain sack on to his shoulder and headed back toward the truck. Ben picked up a sack in the same manner and followed him.

"Seventeen, eighteen," Samuel said, keeping a running total as he and his friend dropped the bags onto the bed of the truck. "Two more to go."

"In case you missed it, seventeen and eighteen are our ages," Ben said, picking up on the small piece of momentary and passing synchronicity. Samuel didn't quite see the point of his friend's comment.

"You're already eighteen. I'm going to be eighteen in two months," Ben went on. "Neither of us knows what it feels like to be with a woman yet. Where it comes to being with a woman, we're about to cross the threshold of manhood while wearing diapers. At least we'll still be wearing the same old pants we've never been out of with a woman. As far as knowing anything about women, we know less about loving a woman than a newborn whelp hunting dog pup knows by instinct about hunting pheasants. When and if we do get married, we're going to start out like dumb mules, not knowing what to do."

If we ever do find an unplain, unboring girl to get married to in this town, Samuel thought to himself. The prospect had seemed foreclosed since Samuel had started thinking about loving women, let alone marrying one of the plain, drab girls of the town.

"Those women in the house could teach us a whole lot that we could take right to our wives. At least we could have ourselves some grown man fun and do some real coming of age on the night that's supposed to mark our coming of age."

Ben's dogged insistence on the subject was starting to tap into a vein of frustration for Samuel, and it wasn't frustration at any adolescent male fixation with sex on the part of his friend. So far no hint of the woman who would be his life mate and the nexus of his own family had appeared, not even on the distant horizon. His future of a life farming the land that he had already grown long attached to was set and ensured. The woman he would be attached to for that life was nowhere in sight. He didn't even have a vision of that woman. Where affections were concerned, at least the women at Mrs. Richardson's emporium of momentary and passing affection might provide some momentary and passing approximation of what a full life with a woman would be like.

Samuel turned toward his friend and leaned on the truck again. "If you get caught, what are your parents going to say?" he asked, a weak and fading rejoinder to what his friend had been saying.

"The only thing my father would probably say is to ask me if I had used my allowance or if I had taken money out of the store till to pay my way," Ben answered. "He's been suspicious of people robbing the store ever since he caught Archie Plummer dipping into the cash register. Beyond that, he'd probably say it was my business what I did with my own money. My mother would probably just tell me not to bring the woman home for supper. … Are you afraid of what your parents might say? Is your father going to take a belt to your backside if he learns where you've been dallying and the kind of woman you've been dallying with?"

"If I were to get caught, the only thing Father would probably hit me with would be a story about what he did at my age back in his wild youth," Samuel responded. "But he'd probably keep his belt on. Mother would probably just tell me to wash my clothes in lye soap. When I reminded her that I was out of my clothes at the time, she'd probably tell me to wash myself off in lye soap. My snot-nosed little sister might stick her tongue out at me. After that she'd probably go running off to tell her friends and all the other girls in town. Some of the girls in town might pull back from me, but there aren't many girls in town whom I've ever felt much of a desire to draw nigh to."

"If nobody is going to get their nose seriously out of joint, and if I'm not going to be sent to live in the shed out here and your father isn't going to send you to live in the hayloft in your barn, then let's do it," Ben said. "If we get caught, we can get forgiveness afterward. But I don't think we'll get much permission beforehand. If we do it right, we won't get caught at all. If we do it right with the women over there, the women of the house may ask us to come back anytime we want. While we're opening the door on manhood, we may open the door for ourselves with them."

Ben didn't end his come-on pitch with a "Come on" or a "Whaddya say?" He just sort of stopped where he did and waited for Sam's response.

At that transitional moment in Samuel's transitioning mind, the prospect of being attached for the first time to a warm and immediate woman outweighed and any theoretical consideration. The immediate lure of the forbidden fruit exceeded any and all other bland, receding, and detached admonishments. The prospect of taking a real woman by the hand and feeling the warm press of a real woman's warm body against his body caused all other considerations to recede out of sight.

After another moment of silence while leaning against the truck, Samuel Martin sort of waved his hand to the side. "Okay, I'm in," he said in a quiet but considered voice. He hadn't meant the wording of his answer to be a sexual pun.

Ben didn't respond by saying "Yeah" or "Swell." Instead he looked at his friend and asked, "Will your father let you use the truck the night of the dance?"

"He's already said I can take it," Samuel answered. "He's not going to drive me in, turn around, and go back home only to turn around and come back and pick me up. And he's not going to stay at the dance and chaperone me. … What do you need the truck for? The house is close enough that we can walk there."

"If we leave the truck at the school, the principal is sure to see it," Ben said. "If he doesn't see us around, he may wonder where we're at, especially if it's still there after everyone else has left. He may grow suspicious as to what we were doing all the time we were gone. If he doesn't think we went to Mrs. Richardson's, he may think we went to hang out at the pool hall."

"What difference does it make what he thinks?" Samuel asked. "We're not going to be in school anymore after Wednesday. We won't see him much again. We'll have our diplomas in hand and be gone."

"You know what a stickler he is about clean living for his students," Ben said. "If he gets the idea that we're frequenting some less than savory establishment, he might possibly try to pull our diplomas on some kind of charge of moral turpitude and say that he doesn't allow that kind of behavior in any student or graduate of his school."

Samuel really didn't think the principal would do something like that. However, the man was a stickler for propriety. As far as the possibility of the positional disposition of the truck being a giveaway, there was a clearer and more present problem.

"Someone may see the truck parked at Mrs. Richardson's," Samuel said.

"We can park it around the side," Ben said. "It's dark enough outside the house that it won't be seen and recognized unless someone is right on top of it."

Samuel sort of missed his friend's inadvertent sexual allusion. At the moment he was a bit distracted. As far as being questioned by the school principal, in the back of his mind he wondered if they might end up running into the principal at the house. But if they did, then all three of them would have mutually offsetting secrets to keep.

"Besides, I don't want to walk all that way in the dark, both there and back home. I figure you can drop me off home after we're finished."

After discussing a few other minor arrangements, the two teenage boys, with intentions of transforming themselves into finished men, finished loading the last two bags of grain onto the truck. From there Ben went back into the store. Samuel opened the door of the truck. Without climbing into the cab, he reached up to the top of the steering column and adjusted the control that retarded the timing of the ignition spark. Then he took the manual crank out of the cab and walked around to the front of the truck. The Model T, otherwise known as Tin Lizzy, didn't have an electric starter. It was necessary to crank-start the engine by hand.

The sequencing of the ignition spark inside the cylinders also had to be set manually by a level mounted on the steering column. The timing of the spark was a function of the position of the piston during the ignition stroke and the RPMs of the engine. For maximum power at higher RPMs, the ignition spark had to come just as the crankshaft was coming around to the top of its swing and the piston was reaching the top of the cylinder. The speed and momentum of the higher RPMs would ensure that the crankshaft would carry past the top of its swing, then it and the piston and connecting rod would begin to head back down on the power stroke. When starting the engine, it was necessary to retard the timing of the spark so that the firing of the cylinders would take place slightly later in the strike cycle, when the crankshaft and the connecting rod had passed the top of the stroke and were on the way down in the correct direction of rotation.

The hand crank had a saw-toothed ratchet design that meshed with the teeth of the engine crankshaft, which protruded out in front, under the radiator. The teeth of the crankshaft extension were oriented to the crankshaft's direction of rotation. When the engine started, the rotating teeth on the shaft extension where it meshed with the teeth on the hand crank would simply cause the crank to be pushed away from the spinning shaft. If the crankshaft rotated in the reverse direction, the two sets of teeth would mesh and the crank would be spun around backward. If the spark was not retarded, it could cause the cylinders to fire too soon in the cycle and cause the engine to backfire and run backward for a short interval. That in turn would spin the steel hand crank backward with enough force to break the arm of the person trying to start the car.

It was the little inconveniences and bodily threats associated with early automobiles that dissuaded women from driving in those days. The awkward and occasionally osteopathically dangerous method of starting Ford cars wouldn't change until Alfred P. Sloan, head and first CEO of the newly created General Motors Company, started introducing different models of cars with choice of color and, above all, an electric starter. The conveniences and the variety of GM cars started to eat Ford's lunch in sales. At that point, the stubborn Henry Ford relented and introduced the Model A, which possessed an electric starter as well as other amenities. As a catchy advertising slogan that touted the Model A's advanced features went, "Ford has made a lady out of Lizzie."

Having restarted the occasionally cranky truck, Samuel retraced his straight-lined path back on the familiar roads of his hometown, back to the farm that was the only home he knew or wanted to know. To that end, he stayed on the straight and narrow dirt road he was on. The time for straying from the straight and narrow would come soon enough.

Whatever transition and change was pending in Samuel Martin's life, back on the Martin farm, his otherwise unchanged life was the third generation of sameness and continuation the farm had seen in the little-altered form of its ongoing operations. Samuel Martin had been born in the farmhouse he had grown up in. He had known his grandfather and grandmother from the same day he had been old enough to know his mother and father. At the time, his father had been the dutiful son and he had been the distant generation appearing on the horizon. When in due course Samuel's grandparents had passed away, his father and mother became the master and mistress of the farm. Samuel's life in turn had resolved itself into the third generation that would continue on the land after his father had passed from it and from him.

That his life had been resolved for him in such a manner had never been something that Samuel had rebelled against. That was the pattern that life had assumed for him, and he was both resolved and contented to follow the pattern that proceeded him, the pattern he would follow. Just where the other half of his pattern, who would provide the fourth generation of Martins, would come from was an issue that had not even begun to resolve itself.

Samuel Martin and his father kneeled on the floor of the barn, but they weren't kneeling in dutiful prayer for a bountiful harvest. That was reserved for Sunday services at the church in town. In this application of intergenerational closeness, they were both wrestling, with their two sets of hands, with the long-handled wrench they were using to set the right tension on the nuts that attached the replacement cutter disc to the disc harrow. Mr. Martin's older and more experienced hands provided the direction and the finesse. Samuel Martin's younger and stronger hands provided the balance of the power.

As a dutiful son, Samuel had already stored the grain sacks in the barn, where they would not be rained upon. As soon as he had arrived back at the farm after taking a pass on checking out Mrs. Richardson's establishment, he had unloaded the grain himself without even telling his father he was back. By reflex and rote, his father might have helped unload the grain. But Samuel had wanted to spare his father the labor. Mr. Martin was growing a little old for that kind of heavy lifting. Now Samuel and his father were completing the repair work on the disc harrow. They had the disc harrow pulled out into the open space in the front of the barn to work on it. The wide double front door of the barn had been thrown open to let in as much light as possible. The flat ceiling inside the barn was much higher than the ceilings in the house.

The expanse of the barn did not end at the high ceiling above their heads. The hayloft was located on the upper floor. There was another wide door located on the hayloft floor through which hay could be pitchforked in and out without having to first transport it inside the barn. In one corner of the barn, a single narrow wooden staircase led up through a narrow opening into the hayloft. Contrary to farm lore, Samuel had never sneaked up the stairs and into the hayloft with a girl. Neither had he ever taken a girl into an outdoor haystack to perform another bit of country legend with a farmer's daughter.

Without hardly saying a word, Samuel and his father continued working on replacing the broken blade of the disc harrow. There was really nothing to say. Both knew what had to be done. The only human sound in the barn was the occasional clunk of metal. The only other sound heard was when one of the plow horses snorted and stomped a hoof in its stall. Outside the barn, framed in the open doorway, the growing crop of corn in the north field shone a bright mottled emerald green topped off by the light green of the developing tassels. The blue sky of the still cloudless day hung over the top half of the pastoral picture framed in the barn doorway.

A momentary flash of somewhat dingy white crossed the set pattern of green and black as the family dog ran across the path at an angle. Then the dog ran into the barn and came up to where father and son were working.

Samuel's father turned around on his haunches as the dog came up to him. They had gotten the unpromising dog for free as a runt of the litter, otherwise about to be drowned to be gotten rid of. Samuel's mother had come across some farm boys about to throw the dog wrapped in a bag into the river. Having recognized what they were about to do, she had stormed over to where they were and snatched the dog out of their hands just as he was about to be thrown in. Samuel's mother had always had a heart for rescuing doomed creatures. The time would come when Samuel would hope that the trait in his mother would come to be turned toward a thrown-away girl.

The unpromising puppy had quickly developed into a friendly and faithful family pet and a useful farm dog. That day the dog once again proved his usefulness as a farm dog. In his jaws he carried a dead rat that he had caught and killed somewhere on the farm. There was now one less rodent on the farm to gnaw through the sacks Samuel had brought home and eat the grain intended for the horses and the other livestock, one less rat to multiply until the farm was overrun by the large, voracious, biting, disease-carrying rodents.

The dog wasn't as big as some farm dogs. He was some kind of unknown terrier mix, not as large as a collie or a shepherd. He was stocky for his size, along with being shorthaired and short-legged, but he was tough and wiry. When they had acquired the dog, he had proven scrappy from the start. Samuel had named the dog Teddy after Teddy Roosevelt. Teddy Roosevelt may have been somewhat short in stature, but he made up for it in toughness and tenacity in facing down the military enemies of the United States and the greedy robber barons and monied economic trusts of the period, always on the lookout for ways to make themselves into monopolies to soak the average citizens. Samuel considered Teddy Roosevelt to be a scrappy fighter. Samuel Martin liked scrappy fighters.

As if delivering a tribute to his master, Teddy dropped the dead rat at Samuel's father's feet. Then the dog came up to Mr. Martin, nuzzling his lower leg. The dog's stubby tail wagged rapidly.

"Good boy," Samuel's father said as he praised and petted the dog. "It looks like we're not the only ones doing our job around here." The dog placed his forelegs on his master's leg and stood up on his hind legs as if trying to gain enough height to lick Mr. Martin's face. He barely came halfway up to the man's knee. Samuel's father bent all the way down to let the dog give him the canine equivalent of a kiss. Samuel looked on with the wrench in his hand. He still didn't know where he would find a woman who would bring him presents and affectionate kisses, but for the moment, outside the barn the sky was clear, the sun was shining, the broken machine had been made whole, there was one less rat in the land, and everything was relatively right with the world.

At the dinner table that evening before sunset, Samuel's father slipped the dog an extra generous tidbit from his plate as a belated reward for having caught the rat. The dog would be fed his regular meal after the family had finished their dinner, but as was his habit during dinner, the dog circled around their feet at the table, quietly petitioning everyone seated for handouts. During in the summer, it was Samuel's mother's habit to serve dinner before sunset. That way they did not have to eat by the light of kerosene lamps. There was no electricity in the Martin farmhouse or in any of the outlying farmhouses in the area. At that transitional time in the history of the nation and the local area, electricity had been brought into the town, but rural electrification would not begin to arrive until the New Deal.

"I'm trying to break that dog of begging at the table," Samuel's mother complained for the umpteenth time as the dog ate out of her husband's hand. "But I can't get that one bit accomplished when the three of you"— referring to Mr. Martin, Samuel, and Samuel's little sister—"slip him something every time he whines and looks up at you with sad eyes."

They had heard it before. The tone in Samuel's mother's voice wasn't sharp and accusatory. It was more or less just quiet country farm wife pique.

"All the trouble I go through to prepare a good meal, only to see it palmed off on a dog. He gets fed well by me. I don't see why he has to get fed extra portions from the table, no matter how sweet and loving he is. You're going to spoil that dog and make a table beggar out of him."

"He earned his keep again today," Samuel's father said. "He killed off another big rat that was trying to eat up our stores. I figure that earns him an extra helping from our hands."

Samuel's mother didn't say anything more. Bringing up the issue made her feel like a fusspot. It wasn't a big deal, and she loved the dog as much as the others did.

Samuel had not risen to the dog's defense as his father had, but not because he didn't love the dog as much as the rest of the family. A different, but otherwise family-related, issue had been going through his mind. Of late, the issue had been gaining strength in his mind. Midway through the meal, he broke his silence and broached the subject, though in an indirect manner.

"Tell me again the story of how you and Mother met."

Samuel knew that it wasn't much of a challenge to set his father to reminiscing about the old days. The half-hidden point was that his father had not married a girl from town.

"I met your mother in the first town northwest of here. You can drive it in two hours now, but it was a good full day's journey when you were riding in a wagon drawn by draft horses. My younger brother and I were out on the road engaged in farm business."

"You mean the two of you were out carousing," Samuel's mother interjected. Samuel's sister, Beth Martin, was chewing on a piece of cooked carrot. The dog continued to scan the movement of their hands for indications that additional tidbits might be coming his way.

"It was after harvest. Father had sent the two of us on the big wagon to take a load of crop to the silo by the railhead in Mother's hometown. It took all day to get there. Me and my brother stayed overnight in a single small room of a boardinghouse. If the house had been full, we would have had to sleep under the wagon in the livery stable where we'd left the horses. But we didn't spend the evenings reading in the library or in the room writing home. We spent the evenings when we were in town shooting pool in the pool parlor and wetting our whistles in local saloons. Only we did more than wet our whistles. We pretty much drowned our brains until they were pickled."

Mr. Martin cut a piece of meat and prepared to eat it. Mrs. Martin listened, not moving her hands. Bethany Martin continued to chew without moving her hands. Samuel Martin held his hands still as he listened to his father's story. The dog was a bit disappointed to detect so few food-carrying motions of their hands.

"My father, your grandfather, was a strict teetotaler. He didn't approve of his respectable sons drinking. So we had to do our drinking and carousing out of his sight. We had arrived late the day before and had spent the night sober in the rooming house. It was a three-day round-trip: one day out, one day there, one day back. It was pretty much necessary to spend the whole next day in town after conducting business. If we left in the middle of the day, the sun would have set during the trip home, and then we would have had to drive the wagon on through the night.

"The next day we unloaded the crop and received the payment we were going to take back to Father. After we dropped off the crop and had received payment, we had the wherewithal to do the cutting loose we had planned to do once our business transactions had been completed. That left a small shortfall in the amount of money we brought home, but we made up for any shortfall by telling Father that prices for crops had gone down and that the price of meals and lodging had gone up."

Mr. Martin handed a scrap of food to the eager dog.

"We had sold the crop and had already started in shooting pool and drinking early that day. It was about midafternoon. Both my brother and I were approaching our limit with a loss of vision stability and the ability to stand stable vertically. At least I could still stand on my feet in a somewhat coherent manner. My brother was rapidly approaching the threshold of falling down drunk across the threshold of the saloon door. I was trying to herd him out the door. I figured we would spend the rest of the afternoon sleeping it off in the rooming house and start in later that night.

"As we crashed through the saloon door, we almost collided head-on with a young woman who was walking down the sidewalk. Even though my vision was going dim, I could see by the look on her face that she took a dim view of the two drunk roughnecks who had almost knocked her off her feet. That young woman was your mother. She lived on a farm. But at the time she was staying in town caring for her sick grandmother, who was bedridden. Your mother had been on her way back from the apothecary shop with some medicine when I almost crashed into her in a half-drunken stupor while trying to steer my brother in a full drunken stupor. But I sobered up fast when I saw your mother. My vision may have been going a bit bleary by that time, but I could see that she was about the best-looking girl I had seen in a long time. She was better-looking than any girl I knew in town."

Maybe not seeing much of anything of what interests you in the girls in this town is a trait that runs in the family, Samuel thought to himself. Samuel was possessed of the pseudoscientific country superstition that traits like that could be passed on genetically in families through breeding.

"The first moment I saw your mother, I knew I wanted to see more of her, when I was in a full sober state. Some men sweat profusely when they're drunk. I wasn't sweating profusely, but I started apologizing profusely for almost knocking her off her feet. Your mother said something to the effect that I should be ashamed of myself, acting like a jackass at my age. I wanted to say that if you can't act like a jackass when you're young and healthy, when can you? But all I did was continue to apologize. At the same time, I was trying to hold my brother up on his feet and keep him from falling on his face. My brother was too looped for anything to be registering. He didn't even remember the incident.

"I kind of lied to your mother then. I said that we weren't usually in this kind of condition, that we were just farmers letting off steam and celebrating a good harvest. That sort of took the repulsion out of her eyes and the stiffness out of her voice and attitude. We started talking right there on the sidewalk. All the while I was trying to hold up my brother. Your mother said she was a farm girl herself, so she understood. I asked her what she was doing in town if she was a farm girl. She told me she was caring for her ailing grandmother. In short order, I learned where she was staying in town and where her family had their farm.

"Later that night, I stayed sober while my brother got hammered again. I didn't want to have any lingering traces of liquor on my breath the next day. In the morning, on our way out, I stopped by the house your mother was staying in. I gave her a bouquet of flowers and apologized again for acting like a boor the day before. Then I asked her if I could call on her again and say hello when we came back into town to take another load of crops to market. She said yes. My brother sat on the wagon the whole time, nursing a hangover. When I got back to the farm, I smashed the liquor bottles I had hidden in the barn and became a teetotaler. I didn't want to lose your mother then or after. I haven't touched a drop since."

Samuel paused to reflect on the fact that his father had found the woman of his future and the life of his future, not in the town but from outside.

"When the spring came, I started up courting your mother even more seriously, traveling to her family's farm instead of going to town. Finally, in the summer, I told her that all the long-distance courting was wearing out the horses and was wearing holes in the seat of my pants. I said that it would make it whole lot easier for us to see each other if she would marry me. That way I wouldn't have to travel to the ends of the earth for us to see each other and be together. We could do that a whole lot more efficaciously if we were together in one place."

"Your father's persistence paid off," Samuel's mother said. "All that 'hang in there' determination proved to me that he was serious about wanting to marry me and carry me home with him."

"We were married in the late summer of that year in her hometown, and we moved back here to live," Samuel's father went on. "Of my brother and me, I was the first one to bring home a bride. My brother and I had started out as boys on a lark and drinking partners. In Father's eyes, I turned into the responsible son with a wife and an intent to stay on the farm. Out of the corner of his eye, he saw his other son turning into a wastrel.

"As the oldest son, I was in line to inherit the farm," Samuel's father went on. "My brother felt that he had kind of been left out of the family picture in both regards. Not long after I had brought your mother home, my brother left the farm and moved to the city. I guess he didn't want to spend the rest of his life playing second fiddle to me. He had never really wanted to be a farmer anyway. We didn't hear a lot from or about my brother after he left. He went to Cincinnati the way our older sister Alicia had. I guess he figured that if our sister could make a life in the city, he could too. For a while he sponged off Alicia and her husband. But Alicia had made something of herself and her life in the city. She had become a schoolteacher and later a mother and the keeper of her house. Our brother Ned, on the other hand, became a bricklayer and a drunkard. He never got married. He didn't have a family or a house and home to call his own. He just dissolved himself and his life into nothing in the acid solvent of hooch. Not too long afterward, not that many years later, we got a letter from Alicia saying that Uncle Ned had died from something drink related."

Mr. Martin talked about down end of his family in the form of his missing and self-destructive brother as much as he talked about the upside of how he had managed to find a life partner when the odds had seemed stacked against its happening. At the moment in his mind, Samuel was contending with the same odds. He didn't really want to go running off down a dead-end trail of family black sheep. At the moment he was focused on the dead-end trail that he saw as his own possibility of romance, marriage, and family.

"Your brother was running himself off the track of life, whereas you got on it and found a wife," Samuel said, beginning his own free wave of spontaneous association. "You just had to go outside the town to find her."

While looking at his father, Samuel, off to the side, handed a scrap to the dog, who wagged his stubby tail in grateful appreciation that the dry spell had ended.

"Maybe I should take the truck, drive to other towns, go around getting hammered at the local saloon, and go off weaving down the streets, colliding with anything in a dress. Maybe I'd meet my future wife that way."

"Now you're starting to talk as my restless brother did before he left," his father said. "Are you starting to think about leaving the farm like he did?"

"I'm not planning on making my home anywhere but here on the farm," Samuel said in a decisive tone gauged to reassure his father. "And I'm not planning to make my home in a bottle the way Uncle Ned did. It's just that when it comes to getting myself a family to go along with the farm and give Mother and you the grandchildren you both want, all the roads into the town are nothing but dead ends everywhere I look."

"Well, if you're looking to get yourself a wife, there are probably more than enough girls around here who would jump at the chance to marry you," Samuel's mother said in her country mother counselor and matchmaker's voice. Like her husband, Mrs. Martin was also country mother gratified to hear her son talking about getting married, settling down, and becoming a dutiful son.

"As far as eligible girls go, I've heard from a source that Katherine Clarke happens to be attracted to you," Samuel's mother said in a secret-revealing, name-dropping, knowing motherly voice. "And I doubt she's the only girl in line hoping you'll take a shine to her. You're the most handsome boy in your class and in the whole school. You could probably have your pick of any one of the girls in your class or the whole town."

"I assume the source you heard it from is her mother," Samuel said. "Or did Katherine put in a word for herself to you directly?"

"The last time Mrs. Clarke talked to me, she let it drop that Katherine likes you," Samuel's mother said, confirming what he had thought.

"Did she also let it drop that Katherine is on the prowl for a husband?" Samuel asked.

"Not in so many words," Samuel's mother said. "I didn't ask her, but I can surmise. Katherine is the same age as you. She's getting to the stage where a young woman starts thinking seriously about the rest of her life and if she will find a husband or else end up an old maid. She's likely wondering what her prospects for finding a husband are."

Since his mother was surmising, Samuel could surmise what Katherine Clarke was surmising: She probably saw as few inspiring potential marriage partners among the boys of the town as he found inspiring potential marriage partners among the few plain girls of the town. Samuel had an advantage over Katherine in that his youthful good looks and devil-may-care attitude made him the town's most eligible, sought-after bachelor, hoped-for marriage material. But whereas Samuel could take his good looks anywhere and find a suitable marriage partner outside the town as his father had done, Katherine Clarke would take her plainness with her everywhere she went. If he were married to her, her uninspiring plainness would be with him for life.

"You might want to give Katherine at least a polite consideration," Samuel's mother went on. "I'm sure she would make you a dutiful wife and be a partner to me around the house."

"You have Sis for that," Samuel said.

"Beth will be wanting to get married and have a family of her own soon enough," Samuel's mother said. "From what I can tell, and from what she's said, she doesn't see any eligible prospects among the boys of this town any more than Katherine Clarke does apart from you," Samuel's mother said.

"I'll join the British Foreign Legion in India and bring home a dragoon for her," Samuel quipped. "One with a fiery mustache."

Samuel's mother scrunched up her face at the quip. "I still say you should at least give Katherine a consideration," she replied.

"Katherine Clarke is as flat and plain as week-old pumpernickel bread that's gone stale," Samuel responded, using a country analogy he was sure would register on both his parents. "The rest of the girls around here are as plain and drab as an old straw-filled mattress. There's not a one of them I have any desire to take onto any kind of mattress for an hour, let alone onto a wedding bed for life."

As boys of all ages and historical time periods tend to do, Samuel spoke vulgar with his friends. But neither of his parents had ever heard him use such earthy language before, and certainly not at the dinner table.

"If I were to marry any one of the girls in this town, I would have to either spend the rest of my life pretending to her that I love her or spend the rest of my life trying to force myself to love her. I doubt I could keep up the pretense for even a short time, let alone all my life. Whoever I married would see through it in a minute. She'd know I didn't really love her. We'd both spend the rest of our dry and loveless lives in a dry and loveless hollow shadow of a marriage. It wouldn't be any kind of life that would hold much of anything for either of us. The marriage would come apart when one of us walked away from the other. If we stayed together, we would spend the rest of our lives cold and distant from each other under the same roof. Neither of us would consider it much of a marriage. Neither of us would call it much of a life. We both might turn to drink to ease our secret and not-so-secret pain."

Samuel focused on his father.

"You know what it's like. When you were my age, you were in the same predicament as I am now. You were where I am now before you went to Mother's town. There wasn't anyone here who interested you or attracted you. Nothing was coming your way around here. You had to shake loose from this town to find Mother. Before you got pickled in that saloon in Mother's hometown, you were in the same pickle as the one I'm in now. So far there doesn't seem to be any possibility of getting married shaking loose for me anywhere in this town. There isn't a single girl whom I have any interest in."

"Well, I still think you should be escorting someone to the graduation dance," Samuel's mother said. "It's not seemly for you to be going alone. You should at least show one of the local girls here a good time and show them all what a polite boy is like."

"Yes, and any girl in this town I take to the dance will start planning her wedding trousseau and pledging her troth," Samuel said. "For all practical purposes, she'll consider us engaged, or at least engaged to be engaged. And so will her parents, and so will the town. When nothing comes of it, her parents will accuse me of trifling with their daughter's emotions and of being as big of a cad as Harold Ethridge. I don't have the time or inclination to get up false hope in some girl I have no interest in and get her parents mad at me when the hopes of their little dear fall through when I don't go on to propose the next day. Besides, it's too late to ask anyone to the dance now."

And besides that, other arrangements for later in the evening had already been made.

"Is it still clear for me to take the truck? I promised to drop Ben off back home after the dance."

"You can take the truck like I told you," Mr. Martin answered. "Just

46

don't get liquored up and try to drive it drunk. I can't afford the expense of either you or the truck getting smashed up."

"Even if you don't dance with any of them, you should be escorting one of the graduating senior class girls back home," Mrs. Martin said. "You may not want to marry any of them, but at least they're your classmates. Or is the reason you don't want to escort any girl to the dance that you and Ben are planning on celebrating graduation by going out on a bender at Charlie's … establishment after the dance, like your father and his brother used to do at bars in other towns when they were out on the road together? I hope you don't feel the need to prove that you're now a grown man by draining a bottle of cheap liquor and passing out on the floor or in a manure pile in the middle of the street."

At that date, much of the transport in the town was horse drawn.

"We're not planning on going out somewhere and getting drunk," Samuel said in his decisive voice. It wasn't a lie—Not a bald-faced lie at least.

"Maybe the reason he doesn't want to take any girl to the dance is because his reputation as the handsomest boy in school has gone to his head and he think he's too good for the rest of us plain Janes in town," Samuel's younger sister, Bethany, volunteered in a sneering and taunting girl's nyah-nyah voice.

"Maybe it's that I don't want to get caught up for life handcuffed to one of your snot-nosed, backbiting, henpecking friends," Samuel answered in a snide impersonation of his little sister's voice. Beth stuck her tongue out at him. Samuel cocked back his hand, feigning like he was going to snap the piece of potato on the tip of his fork at his sister. The dog watched the bite, waiting for it to drop.

"Knock it off, the two you," Samuel's father growled in his fatherly command voice to his supposedly two mature teenage children. Whatever age and stage of thinking they had progressed to, they seemed to have retained the art of regressing themselves to sandlot age and bringing the pissy children out in each other.

"Grow up and stop acting like the bickering brother and sister you've always acted like. I don't think you're ever going to grow up when it comes to being around each other. When you're both eighty years old, you'll probably still be scrapping away at each other like cats in a bag."

"We can't both be eighty years old at the same time," Bethany Martin said. "I'm two years younger than he is. When he's eighty, I'll only be seventy-eight."

"And as snotty as the day you were born," Samuel interjected. "At least you know enough math to subtract two from a number larger than ten. When you get married, at least you will be able to balance the household budget and pay the bills, as long as your husband doesn't give you more than eighty dollars to work with at a time. If he gave you more, you'd be off buying fancy dresses from the Sears catalog."

"Be nice to your sister now," Mrs. Martin admonished her son. She hadn't noticed that, where it came to commenting on his sister's marriage prospects, at least Samuel had been relatively nice enough to say *when* his sister got married instead of *if* she ever got married. But the relative noninsult passed by unnoticed. The dog kept looking for more handouts.

"He's snottier than I am," Beth protested.

"You should take a hint from your brother," Samuel's father interjected. "He may not always act mature with you, but at least your brother is starting to think like a grown and responsible man. All this talk of his about finding a wife means he's thinking along the lines of settling down and staying home. It was the same line I started thinking along the minute I met your mother. It was the line my brother never thought along. Maybe the only place Samuel will find the girl he's looking for will be in another town, but when he finds the right girl, he's going to bring her back here and continue life with us. He's not talking about leaving and not coming back like my brother Ned, who never returned home once he had left the farm."

When his son had started talking about other towns, the senior Mr. Martin had momentarily worried that Samuel had picked up Ned's propensity for leaving home. Mr. Martin was possessed of the pseudoscientific country superstition that traits like that could be passed on genetically in families through breeding. But now he sounded reassured that his son had not picked up the wider wanderlust that had infected his brother. He looked back at Samuel.

"As to how to go about finding a wife for yourself if you can't abide any of the girls in this town, I can't help you there. There isn't one set formula for how to go about it. Meeting and marrying works different for every couple."

"He'll probably have to send away for a foreign woman," Bethany said, trying to get one more jab in. "I doubt any girl is going to put up with being married to him, whether she comes from this town or any town in the country. He'll have to marry a foreign woman who doesn't understand English and doesn't know what he's saying to her. Maybe he'll get an Irish woman who'll knock him out flat with a shillelagh if he gives her any snotty lip."

For a second Samuel thought to ask if there were still mail-order brides available, but he didn't say anything.

"One thing you'll have to do as man of the house is to look after your mother if I'm gone before her," Samuel's father said, repeating the lineage of responsibilities his father had recited to him before. "And as much as the thought may pain you, it will also be your responsibility to look after your sister if she's not married and still living at home when I'm no longer around."

Beth made a face as if to protest the idea that she would turn into an old maid. At any other brother–sister squabbling stage, Samuel might have thrown in a zinger about the inevitability of his sister's becoming an old maid, but this time he let the opening pass. His mind was otherwise distracted with what it had been distracted with since the beginning of the dinner table conversation.

"Speaking of sisters," Samuel said, before Beth could say anything, "how did your sister Aunt Alicia find her husband? He wasn't from this town either."

"How they found each other outside of this town wasn't a big trick," Mr. Martin answered. "Neither of them were here in town when they met. Alicia had gone off to Cincinnati to study to be a teacher. She's the only member of this family before or since who's ever gone off to any kind of institution of higher learning. She met her husband in Cincinnati. He's a businessman there. Now she's Mrs. Alicia Heisner of Cincinnati. She left home too, but unlike Uncle Ned, she established herself in a profession and had a family. She didn't just run off on some wanderlust impulse like my brother did. As far as brothers with wanderlust go, her husband also had a younger brother who had the wanderlust in him like Ned did. Except he went off and joined the marines."

"Wasn't he the one who marched into Shanghai, China, with the marine expeditionary force during the Boxer Rebellion?" Samuel asked.

"That was Beijing, the capital of China, they marched into," Mr. Martin said. "Not Shanghai."

In 1905, foreign diplomats and foreign nationals were surrounded and besieged in the Old City of Beijing by the ultranationalistic antiforeigner native Chinese Boxer rebels, who were determined to oust all colonialists from China. All the foreigners trapped in the compound would have been murdered by the xenophobic rebels if rescue forces hadn't reached them in time. A US expeditionary force, along with troop contingents from several other nations, had marched into the capital city of China in time to rescue the diplomats and foreign nations. As a young boy, Samuel had followed the expedition in the town newspaper.

The earlier subject of Samuel's finding a wife trailed off and was covered over by talk of things more germane to the farm. But in the back of his mind, Samuel was aware that another member of the family had found their life mate outside the town. When he added it up, he figured there hadn't been anyone in the family since his grandfather who had married someone from the town.

The dog continued to look for handouts or spillage from the table.

After dinner, Mrs. Martin and Beth cleaned up the dishes. Cooking and cleaning had long been designated women's work in the culture of the time and in the Martin household. The females also fed the dog. Mr. Martin and his son retired to the parlor to talk farming talk, discussing crops and what repairs had to be done around the farm. Afterward they read by lantern light while Mrs. Martin and Beth did some sewing by lantern light. Television obviously didn't exist at the time. Radio, the box that would later come to connect isolated rural people to the world, had not yet been commercially developed. In 1912, radio existed as point-to-point messages between message stations and ship-to-shore communications in Morse code. It was radio that a month and a half earlier had alerted the world to the drama unfolding on the *Titanic*, but it had not managed to bring rescue in time to save all the passengers. Beyond that, general audience broadcasting had not yet come about to fill in any dull and drab evenings with entertainment. Far away in another state, an ambitious young man close to Samuel's age by the name of David Sarnoff was planning on revolutionizing both radio and entertainment.

With not a lot to otherwise fill the evening, the Martin family retired to bed. Samuel Martin's room in the family farmhouse was small, but it was his. It had been his uncle Ned's room before he had left the family. The walls were painted a flat white. The floor and ceiling were bare wood plank. The only light in the room was a kerosene lantern. Before going to bed, Samuel extinguished the lantern so its flame would not attract insects. Then he opened the window in the darkened room. It was a warm night, too hot to sleep with the window closed. In that particular time and locale, what air-conditioning existed consisted of a block of ice and a fan. The Martin family farm lacked even that amenity.

Samuel climbed under the single sheet. The faint breeze stirred the barely visible curtains over the window. In the night outside the room, the sounds of crickets could be heard, the insects calling to each other. The heavy hum of a night-flying june bug droned close by the open window. From a faraway tree, a hoot owl hooted its call, announcing the darkened landscape as its domain. Moths flew silently past the open window and disappeared into the night. There was no light in the room to draw them in. The only light visible outside were the momentary and passing flashes of the light of fireflies.

The next day was Sunday. As was their usual practice when the elements allowed, the Martin family drove into the town to attend church. Given that the truck only had a single bench seat in the cab, Samuel's father drove and his mother sat in the single passenger's seat. Samuel and his sister rode facing backward with their backs to the back wall of the cab, sitting on chairs in the bed of the truck. When it was raining or the dust on the road was high, a canvas cover rigged on an improvised frame was positioned over the back of the truck to keep the rain or dust off the Sunday-go-to-meeting clothes of the riders in the truck bed.

At the church service, Pastor Russell delivered a sermon on sticking to the straight and narrow path. The text of his sermon was drawn from the passage in the Old Testament which reads: "To the left or the right I will not go." Radar hadn't been invented yet. If it had, Samuel might have wondered if the minister had somehow possessed radar given the way he and Ben were planning to stray from the straight and narrow path of chastity before the end of the new week.

It wasn't that Samuel didn't believe in God. It wasn't that he disrespected God or Pastor Russell. It wasn't that he disrespected things spiritual. It wasn't that he thought in terms of profane love or sought to profane the concept of love. It wasn't that he disrespected, disparaged, or discounted the concept of home. It was just that where love and home were concerned, Samuel wanted a real-world physical taste of love that could not be supplied by any sermonizing on the subject or any admonition to wait in limbo for the perfection of either love or home. He was aware of the biblical injunction to treat his body as a temple unto the Lord and not to join his consecrated temple body to the body of a prostitute. But a temple on a mountain can be a cold and empty structure to inhabit when you live in it alone. He had no plans to leave God or home behind. They would just have to wait on the sidelines a bit while he diverted himself for a night to play house, to play the part of a lover in a house not otherwise consecrated to God or dedicated to the permanence of love, family, or home.

On the way back from church, at the lumberyard on the edge of town, they passed the beginning of the dirt road that led toward Mrs. Richardson's establishment, close to a mile down the road outside the east end of town, where the river wound back closer to the town. As they passed the intersection, Samuel Martin did not look to the left or the right. He didn't want to give his sister any kind of tipoff as to what was on his mind or what he had planned by craning his neck to look down the road toward the house where he would take his next step into nominal manhood. Bethany may have been a snot, but she was not a naive snot. She knew what took place in the house at the end of the lane as well as everyone in the town did. Samuel didn't know if the earth would move for him during the experience that would take place in the house. Maybe it wouldn't. Maybe it would. But in the long run, he didn't think that it would be all that life-changing.

Chapter 3

It would be at least seven decades and half as many generations before Bruce Springsteen would sing the lyrics about high school days past: "Glory days, yeah, they'll pass you by. Glory days, in the wink of a young girl's eye." At the commemorative dance for the town's high school graduating class of 1912, Samuel Martin spent as much, if not more, time holding forth and exchanging stories with the members of the baseball team and the wrestling and boxing club, both of which he had captained and dominated, as he did dancing. The poets have it right: the indiscretions of youth can become the regrets of old age. And Mr. Springsteen is more or less right. The high school triumphs of teenage males can become the boring stories told by old men. The distant future notwithstanding, the knot of boys recounted their triumphs over the four years they had spent together maturing into the manhood they were now taking a step into by graduating from high school. Samuel and Ben would be taking an additional step into manhood, formal or informal, after the dance. But that went unmentioned to anyone.

Samuel did occasionally dance with some of the unescorted girls, but never with any one of them more than once. The civic band was playing at the dance. When they weren't giving public concerts from the band shell in the central square park next to the courthouse, they were available for the Fourth of July and a variety of civic-related celebrations. The band's repertoire was a long way from containing anything resembling a Bruce Springsteen song. Though they were a bit closer in chronological time, musically and conceptually they were as equally far away from Bill Haley and the Comets, who forty-plus years later would start livening up teenage school dances with their rendition of "Rock Around the Clock."

But either way it was a bit of a moot point. The conservative school administration did not allow anything with a punchier beat or any loud, blaring, sexually suggestive tunes blown out hard on loud, blaring, flashy brass instruments by musicians with sweat popping off their brows from the strain. Louis Armstrong hadn't made the pop culture music scene yet, but he wouldn't have been welcome in the town if he were on the jazz circuit. That kind of music was Negro jungle music designed to cloud the minds of pure and proper young white women and send them off on a giddy spin, inducing them to shed all inhibitions. There were no Negroes in the town. Bourbon Street music didn't make a show either. By default what the band played was mostly a collection of waltzes, stirring marches, and tea dance favorites. It was a bit hard to turn a dance in a suggestive direction or even to get a dance going particularly fast when the most spritely and very mildly suggestive tune played was "Walking Miss Molly Back Home."

Red, white, and blue bunting hung on the walls of the gym the dance was being held in. It made the dance look more like a Fourth of July celebration held indoors or a political convention hall instead of a high school graduation. The graduation ceremony two days earlier had taken place in the same gym. On the wall behind the band, a long sign, hand-lettered on a strip of canvas, read: CONGRATULATIONS, GRADS. THE FUTURE IS YOURS. The banner had been put up for the graduation and was left there for the graduation dance. It was the same banner the school used at every graduation.

When Samuel felt that the appointed time had come, he walked over to Ben and motioned with his head toward the door. Without an audible word passing between them, Samuel mouthed, "Let's go." You didn't have to subaudibly tell Ben twice. Neither did he question Samuel's timing. Ben trusted his friend's sense of organization. As captain of the baseball and

54

wrestling team, Samuel, Ben figured, had everything in hand and knew what he was doing.

The headlights on the truck were not angled up in the right direction to fully illuminate the sign painted over the door that read Bailey's Lumber and Coal Yard, but Samuel knew that they were at the intersection. The outline of the building, sheds, and lumber piles where he worked part time on Saturdays were familiar to him in the dark. Half the money he had earned had gone to help the family finances. The other half he had kept. A portion of the money he had earned at the lumberyard would come to be spent that night at the cash-and-carry establishment farther down the dirt lane that ran past the lumberyard. The difference being that after plunking down their cash at Bailey's, customers were allowed to carry away their purchases permanently. After tendering cash at Mrs. Richardson's commercial establishment, one had to utilize the product there and leave it there once one was finished. However high the usage rate of the product was, the inventory turnover rate was very low.

With several hard turns of the manual steering wheel, Samuel turned the truck more than ninety degrees down the side road, running at a diagonal past the lumberyard. Nobody was at the intersection or on the road to see them make the turn. The truck was almost indistinguishable from the many other similar-model trucks in the town. From a distance at night, it could be the truck of any farmer or tradesman in town. If anyone from the town had seen them turn, Samuel hoped that it would be too dark for them to identify the occupants of the vehicle. The only streetlights in town were the weak lights that lined Main Street where it passed through the business district. The crescent moon hanging low over the horizon in the west had turned orange as it prepared to set. Its weakening light provided little illumination to show anyone the way anywhere in the town or outside it.

There were no lights lining the side road that ran past and away from the lumberyard. The truck had headlights operated by a small magneto run off of the flywheel of the engine. But the headlights were only a little brighter than a modern-day flashlight. The illumination provided by the truck's headlights was minimal. But given the relatively slow speed that automobiles traveled in those days, it was easy to outdrive the headlights. It was also a bit hard to see the outline of the road in the dark. The black color of the dirt in the shallow ruts of the road faded to the edge of visibility in the darkness. In some ways Samuel found it easier to steer by the feel of the road, turning the wheel to put the truck back on path as he felt the tires ride up the sides of the ruts.

Mrs. Richardson was an outsider woman who had been brought into the town by her lawyer husband. He had died prematurely, before having built up sufficient savings to support his widow. They had no children to support them. Finding herself in need of funds, Widow Richardson had repurposed the big house she lived in. The nominally upstanding people in the town were scandalized that a local townswoman would open a bordello on the outskirts of their town. But they weren't terribly surprised that she had done it. Financial need aside, outsiders were associated with loose behavior. Outsiders did the sort of thing Mrs. Richardson had done. Then again, Mrs. Richardson was the wife of a lawyer. Then as now, lawyers and those associated with them were often equated with whores if not actively accused of being for legal sale to the highest bidder.

The coming of a bordello so near to the town scandalized the wives of the town. For the husbands and single men of the town and its surrounding area, their being scandalized was more of an equivocated thing. For Mrs. Richardson and the women of the house, scandal paid.

By being closer to the town than the outlying farmhouses, the house had the benefit of being electrified. A single electrical wire suspended on a pole crossed the road in the dark sky overhead. Through the windows, a steady, lighter-colored orange glow of electric lights, as opposed to the flickering darker orange of kerosene lamps, shone through as Samuel drove past the front of the house and turned off the road. The truck bounced slightly when going over the ruts. Though light shone in squares through the windows, it was a bit hard to discern the full shape and outline of the house. Such was the light that drew the two new graduates on to the Richardson house. Out beyond the back of the house, the river flowed on out of sight, heading past and away from the town.

A lot of things can go through the mind of a teenage boy when he's about to experience his first time. With no other customers apparently in attendance at the house, the main thing that went through Samuel Martin's mind as he shut off the truck motor was whether the ladies of the evening who lived in the house actually maintained more conventional daytime business hours and whether he and Ben had arrived too late after all. But there was only one way to find out. Samuel opened the truck door and quickly stepped out. His friend Ben didn't move with the same anticipatory alacrity as he did, sitting on the passenger's seat without going into instant movement. He seemed to be hanging back. The captain of the baseball and boxing team was otherwise a take-charge guy, even if it was only to state that he was not going to take charge.

"This was more your idea than it was mine," Samuel said, turning on his feet on the ground to face Ben, still sitting in the passenger's seat. "Are you getting cold feet on me? Like I said, I'm not going to play big brother and take you in hand. You may have started this, but I've been looking forward to this since I agreed to it. I'm up and running now. I'm not going to give everything up because you freeze up on me at the last minute. If you don't want to go in, I'm not going to drag you by the collar. You can sit in the truck if you want, but you'll have to wait here until I'm finished."

Sometimes teenage boys do freeze up when on the threshold of their first time. In this case Samuel's friend might have frozen up before he had even gotten out of the truck and made it to the door of Mrs. Richardson's establishment. But take-charge Samuel had long decided that he was going to have his one night of romance and marriage equivalency come rain, hail, high water, dark of night, or last-minute wimpishness on the part of his friend. He would walk through Mrs. Richardson's door and the door to manhood alone if he had to.

"Just gathering my wits," Ben said. He opened the passenger's-side door of the truck, got out, walked around the front of the truck, and joined Samuel. Samuel figured the explanation was reasonable enough. One should at least have his wits about him to some degree for his first time.

Together the two teenage boys seeking initiation into fully confirmed manhood walked around the front of the house toward the door in the center of the building. Through one of the windows, Samuel caught sight of a female figure in a dress moving along the wall on the far side of the room. At least not everyone in the house had gone to bed. There was a low wooden porch in front of the door and a stoop leading up to it. Samuel and Ben climbed the stoop and crossed over to the door. There was no sign on the door that read CLOSED of the type one normally saw on the shop doors in town after business hours. There was a big brass knocker on the door. As befitting his take-charge manner, without any hesitation, Samuel knocked the knocker several times. The sound seemed to echo off the wooden floors inside the house.

As he knocked, for a moment Samuel wondered if anyone was going to come to the door. But he did not have long to wait to be disabused of that preconceived notion. Almost as soon as he finished knocking, the knob on the door turned. A relatively tall woman opened the door. She looked to be in her fifties. She had a rectangular face and a rectangular build. From the dress she was wearing, the woman appeared to be the same one Samuel had seen through the window, moving inside the house. Either she had been walking into the central hall that led to the front door when they had been approaching or else she had seen them walking by outside and had come to the door in anticipation of their coming in. Samuel Martin had never met the Mrs. Richardson who owned and maintained the house, but he assumed he was in her presence.

"Good evening, gentlemen," the woman said in a husky older woman's voice.

"Good evening, ma'am," take-charge Samuel said in a voice that sounded like he was greeting women at a church function. The woman had opened the door for them. In return Samuel opened in a polite manner. It was both his nature and part of his upbringing to be polite. He had been trained by his father from birth to be polite to all women whatever reputation might proceed them or follow them. As part of his country philosophy, he didn't believe that any woman should be approached in a coarse manner. Samuel figured that whores had a sense of self-respect like other women and didn't like to have a man advance on them in a crude and demeaning way.

"I know it's a bit late, but we were just wondering if you were still open to receive ... callers?"

Given it was his first time at the house, as well as what would be their first time sexually, Samuel was a bit uncertain as to the right terminology to use to describe anyone associated with the house and its function.

The woman motioned for them to come in.

"We do usually have something of a rush Friday and Saturday nights," Mrs. Richardson said as Samuel and Ben entered the front hall. "But it usually happens in the middle of the evening. You're catching the tail end of the busy hours."

Mrs. Richardson stepped around behind them and closed the door. She turned and examined Samuel and Ben.

"I don't believe I've seen either of you in here before. Are you from around here, or are you passing through? You look awfully young to be transient hired hands, freight men, or truck drivers."

Samuel started to worry that the woman might turn them out because they looked too young. Maybe there was something to his friend's idea of bringing him along as an age bridge.

"I'm old enough to work my father's fields for as long of a day as he does," Samuel said, emphasizing his humble origins and the fact that he was a native son. "My friend is old enough to work in his father's business in town. We're both old enough for the school district to have just graduated us and conveyed upon us our diplomas."

Then the thought hit Samuel that it might be a different kind of maturity the woman was probing to determine—financial maturity, to be specific.

"We're both old and established enough that we can pay our way in cash. We're not here looking for you to extend us credit or asking you to carry us on your books."

Samuel just hoped the women of the house weren't big enough to throw them over their shoulders, like he and Ben had done with the feed grain bags, and carry them to their beds. Samuel wasn't quite sure what type of women became prostitutes. He assumed that women who became prostitutes came out of extreme poverty and went into the world's oldest profession because they could find no other source of income. Then again, for all he knew, they might be women who were so ugly or hefty that they couldn't find a man who would marry them. The local grapevine had not described the women of the house in terms quite that extreme, but he didn't imagine the women of the house to look like an idealized portrait of a demure and blushing Victorian beauty from a Harrison Fischer print.

"We do accept only cash here," Mrs. Richardson said in a not totally mercenary-sounding manner. "But if you're willing to pay up front, you're welcome like all good faith paying customers are."

"Then you're not saying we're too young for you?" Samuel asked.

"You are a bit younger than the men we usually get in here," Mrs. Richardson answered, "but you're not so young that I'd feel guilty of robbing the cradle. If you're here knowing what you want and are willing to say it up front without blushing and stammering, then you're old enough for both our purposes and yours."

Mrs. Richardson cocked her head slightly and smiled a little. She spoke in a kind of coy and knowing voice.

"But, as I said, I haven't seen you in here before. I would have remembered if I had. This is your first time in here. By any chance, is it your first time anywhere?"

The rest of their night teetered on the brink of possible nonfulfillment. Both of them had wondered if their callow youth and virginal state might prompt the keeper of the house to turn them away, fearing she would be accused of seducing and corrupting minors. Samuel had hoped that the question would not come up to be addressed before they started undressing. But the woman's inquiry had brought up the issue of their age, their virginal status, and whether they would be turned away from the house because they were deemed to be underage.

Ben didn't say anything. He just kind of looked at Samuel to provide the answer. Samuel kind of figured that if he made it seem as if they both had extensive experience, Mrs. Richardson would see right through his bald-faced lie. Because of this, he figured that honesty would be the best policy—equivocated honesty at least.

"Well, no one's born into that kind of knowledge and experience," Samuel said. "Everyone has to start somewhere."

Samuel put a hand on his friend's shoulder. He spoke in his best take-charge guy's voice. "My friend here is a bit nervous. I agreed to take him by the hand and walk him through it, though I'm not planning on going into the room with him and giving him instructions from the sidelines like I were his baseball coach standing at third base and telling him when to run to first base and when to run for home."

Samuel shifted his voice to a more serious tone. "If either one of us is inexperienced, would that cause you to turn us out?" he asked.

"As you said," Mrs. Richardson replied, "everyone's got to start somewhere. Someone's got to initiate things. My girls have probably initiated most of the boys who have been turned into men around here. I don't turn away any boys who are grown up enough to know what they're doing and are seriously seeking to make themselves into men. The girls don't mind it either. They actually kind of like it when they're a boy's first one. It makes them feel not quite as old and worn. If they have a young and innocent boy out on his first time, for a while they can feel like they're young and innocent again themselves."

As a farmer, Samuel's way of thinking was connected with the land. To him, the future flowed from the past in a seamless whole in the way he flowed from his family and their place on the land and in the way the future would flow on from him through his family, provided he ever had a family. To cut yourself off from your past was to cut yourself off from life and the continuation of life. To Samuel, when a woman became a prostitute, she cut herself off not only from polite society but also from her family, from her past, and from her future. She cut herself off from all that she was or ever would be. Samuel could understand how seeing herself cut off from her past for the rest of her life and how facing a future that was nothing more than a dead-end alley could make a woman feel old and worn even before she had reached that stage physically. Yet he couldn't help but wonder how much mileage the women of the house had on them, body and soul.

The moment of reflection passed as quickly as it had come (no sexual pun intended). Taking up where the take-charge Samuel had said he would leave off, Mrs. Richardson reached down and took Ben's hand in hers like she was a mother leading her bashful son up to a girl she wanted to introduce him to.

"Your friend is right that he can't hold you by the hand and walk you into manhood," Mrs. Richardson said to Ben. "I can't take you by the hand into the room either. But I can take you to meet the girls. They'll be the ones to take you by the hand and take it from there. They're waiting in the parlor. I'll introduce you to them, and you can make your choice."

Samuel wanted to make a humorous quip to the woman to the effect that having your first time with a woman is a bit like riding a horse for the first time and that he hoped she would give his friend a gentle filly who wouldn't buck him off. But he decided that neither the woman nor her girls would take kindly to being compared to horses.

Mrs. Richardson started to lead Ben down the hall with the more natural-born leader Samuel following. As far as making the first contact with the women who were going to bring them into full manhood, in one small ironic way it was the younger-looking Ben who performed that role. Samuel had wondered why the madam of the house had been the only woman in evidence. Then he remembered that he had heard that in big-city bordellos, the available women would line up for the male customer to pick from. Apparently Mrs. Richardson employed that method also.

Samuel followed the woman with his friend in hand down the hall to a transverse hall that led down the long axis in the center of the house. Near one end of the house, there was a doorless entrance to a large room that once, in the more standard design and usage of the house, had been a parlor. At the door of a large room, Mrs. Richardson turned in with Ben still in hand. As Mrs. Richardson and Ben passed through the hall doorway, they blocked the view of the room's interior.

When they walked deeper into the room, around to their sides, Samuel caught a glimpse of female figures in various states of dress. As he approached the doorway and prepared to pass through, his blood didn't start to run quicker. His high school years of leading the baseball team and the wrestling squad had left him with a sense of control born of the feeling that he could handle whatever unexpected contingency came his way. As he entered the room, he didn't have the sense that he was going to meet his destiny, but he did think that at least one reasonably memorable pedestrian transition was about to take place.

The house had been designed and built in a pre-electric era. There was no chandelier or ceiling light in the center of the parlor ceiling. The electrical system of the house looked like it had been added as an afterthought. Electrical current was brought in by way of exposed insulated wire that was held off the wall by ceramic standoff insulators. The only light came from two floor lamps on either side of the room. The long-filament bulbs in the lamps were a bit more advanced than Thomas Edison's original offering, but as far as wattage went, they weren't all that much stronger or brighter in their illumination. The lamps only half filled the room with a half-white, half-orange half-light.

The main piece of furniture in the room consisted of a large ornamental sofa done in a purple velvet covering with a curved and decoratively carved wooden frame that went around the top of the back, down the arms, and down the front to a wavy and ornamentally carved baseboard above the ball-and-claw feet. The sofa appeared to be a holdover from the Empire period of furniture design popular in the 1850s. With the exception of two small end tables, the bulk of the other furniture in the room consisted of several equally ornate high-backed upholstered chairs with similarly decoratively carved and channeled wooden framing. Six women sat on the sofa and on the chairs, dressed, so to speak, in a manner commensurate with the role they played and function they performed at the house.

"Well, girls," Mrs. Richardson said as she and Ben stopped at the focal point of the curve of women in the parlor. "We have ourselves some newcomers out on their first howl. At least the smaller one is here for his first initiation. I'm not sure if it's the bigger one's first time or not, but either way he's a paying customer."

Samuel stepped out from behind the woman and his friend and came up to the same frontal position. As he did so, he waved and uttered a polite-sounding "hello." Ben was still as speechless as he had been since he had entered the house. The women of the establishment nodded and uttered their own faint hellos.

"Show them a good time and give them their money's worth, and we can get them back as repeat customers."

Mrs. Richardson released Ben's hand and stepped to the side to afford him and Samuel a better view.

"The choice is yours, gentlemen. Just please don't take all night making your selection. It may be your first time, but don't turn choosing into a drawn-out artistic decision. You can't see the river from here at night. This isn't a grand artist's studio overlooking the Grand Canal of Venice. None of us are the Mona Lisa sent to model for you, and neither of you are another Da Vinci preparing to paint a masterwork. Make your choice and get on with things. It's getting late and the girls have to go to bed—normally speaking."

Without making it too obvious, the take-charge Samuel had been surveying the women available as soon as he had been accorded a unobstructed view of Mrs. Richardson's charges. The women lounging on the furniture were dressed in some variant of mistress-in-waiting, waiting-the-return-of-the-keeper-of-her-heart-and-body boudoir style—either tight-fitting corsets or loose-fitting silky robes.

Moving his gaze from left to right, Samuel scanned each woman in turn. The women looked older than he. From what he could tell, they appeared to be somewhere between thirty and forty years old, but he figured that the terms and trials of their profession might make them look older than their years. The women had a shopworn look about them. Their expressions weren't haggard or hangdog, but they didn't look very fresh-faced, and the possibility of having a virgin notwithstanding, they didn't look like they saw much in Samuel beyond his being another passing client. From the expression in their eyes, they didn't look to Samuel like they saw much ahead of them, either that night or in their lives, beyond another round of the same old same old they had always known.

Though not gratified to find that the women of Mrs. Richardson's cathouse were no better-looking than the women of the town, Samuel had not gone into the house assuming he would find a uniquely beautiful woman. He had gone into the house assuming that his passage into manhood with whatever presented itself and whomever presented herself would not be a rare and transcendent experience. He assumed that what began there that night would stay there after he left.

Then all of Samuel's life assumptions broke at the center and fell away to the sides.

Samuel had heard the term *a vision of loveliness* used many times before, but it had always been little more to him than an overworked poetic phrase. In an instant the phrase was more real and alive than he thought it could ever be.

The woman sitting at the end of the line of the women of the house was the most beautiful figure of femininity he had ever seen in his life. She was also the most alluring figure of female shapeliness and loveliness he had ever seen in town, far more exquisite than anything he had even vaguely suspected he would encounter in a farm town brothel.

The woman sat at the rightmost position at the end of the sofa. Her bare shoulders trailed off into slender bare arms. The color of the woman's skin was not a sunbaked leathery brown like the face of a farmer who has worked the fields all his life. Neither was it a pale and sickly alabaster white of the type that was still in favor as a holdover from the Victorian era with its emphasis on demure and retiring beauty that had never been exposed to the sun. The woman's skin had the creamy but bright flesh-tone hue of youth and vigor. The woman's left arm lay linearly and lightly along the top of the wooden arm of the sofa. The life and color of her skin shone in a bright counterpoise to the deep and sunken dull red color of the old mahogany wood of the sofa.

The woman's long fingers touched lightly upon the wooden arm of the sofa. The bright vitality of her bare upper thighs pressed downward against the velvet covering of the sofa she was sitting on. Her thighs both pressed down into the velvet covering and were pushed out to the sides. Compared to the faded and aged purple color of the covering, in the limited light of the room the woman's legs seemed almost luminous.

The woman wasn't even really even a woman. In her face, she was a teenage girl who looked to Samuel to be about the same age as he was. Samuel figured that she had to be the young recruit whom Ben had heard about through the grapevine, the women who had recently come to the house. Whatever age she was in specific calendar years, whatever relative age she appeared in her face, in her body the girl was every inch a full-grown woman and more. The girl's mode of dress and the lack of it provided all the more for male eyes to feast upon. All the women in line wore something related to the boudoir, something deliberately suggestive, something that otherwise defined their profession, something designed to be removed and put back on, on a quick-turnaround basis.

The girl was wearing some form of corset made up of alternating red and black vertical strips of shiny material woven together at the edges. The corset had been designed and structured to crimp a woman's waist in at the middle and to push her womanly features up and outward at the top. It was obvious that the corset had been designed to push the female frontal aspect forward and outward. It was more than successful in the girl's case because it had more than enough material on hand to work with.

Samuel had often heard the term *womanly figure* bandied about. But the words had always been something of a theoretical construct to him. Suddenly he found himself confronted by a more womanly figure than he had ever imagined. At the full sight of the girl, the stirrings of lust started to leap within his breast. But these were accompanied by the stir of feelings and imaginations more sublime.

There's an old country saying something to the effect of "A faint heart never won a fair lady." Whether the girl's profession would ever allow her to be classified as a lady was one question. Whether she was chronologically old enough to be classified as a mature woman instead of a teenage girl was another. At the present moment in the parlor of Mrs. Richardson's establishment, both questions were moot for Samuel. By all natural accounts and visual definitions, the girl was a full-grown, mature woman. To Samuel, any other, limiting definitions of womanhood could take a back seat to the figure of the woman sitting bare-legged and nearly bare-chested in her tight red and black corset on the purple velvet sofa. There's another country saying that he who hesitates is lost.

"Ah, is she available?" Samuel said as Mrs. Richardson finished her admonition to the boys to make their choices with dispatch. In the back of Samuel's mind, the girl seemed both too beautiful and too good to be true. Somehow he suspected that she was some kind of bait-and-switch lure used to excite male customers, only to have the madam say that she was not part of the bargain and redirect them to the other women of the house.

As he asked the question, the take-charge Samuel pointed to the girl on the sofa. As he pointed, the girl stood up. When she leaned forward to stand up, the unconfined upper hemispheres of her breasts bulged forward as if trying to overflow and circumvent their confinement below. As she stood up to her full height, the girl's womanly breasts settled back down with a liquid tinge as if they were semiliquid plum pudding spreading out into the bowl it would be served from. Her thighs went back to the full roundedness of their youth and health. The girl's delicate-looking fingers briefly touched the darkened old wood of the sofa arm and then parted from it.

The girl started to walk toward Samuel. The otherwise in-charge Samuel had always prided himself on being in control of his reactions. But his sense of control over his reactions had been developed on a baseball diamond, on a wrestling mat, and in a boxing ring. It had all been familiar territory. Standing virginal in the parlor of Mrs. Richardson's bordello, facing the girl, Samuel found himself entering unfamiliar territory (you can make a sexual pun out of that if you wish).

All that Samuel knew about reactions and the control of reactions was being knocked into a cocked hat. Make that a strategically cocked corset. As far as controlling reactions and the effect of reactions goes, Samuel was only beginning to discover the effect a beautiful, shapely half-naked girl could have on a boy.

You couldn't really say that Samuel stared in a transfixed manner at the girl's approach, but as another old saying goes, if the shoe fits, wear it. At the moment, all Samuel could see was the way the tight, constraining corset the girl was wearing fit and how her body seemed too long to be shed of it. As the girl walked toward him, her naked upper thighs brushed against each other in a manner that the fully corseted and cosseted women of the time would have considered to be a decidedly unladylike display of what shouldn't be displayed. The girl's legs moved with the suppleness and flow of youth. In a country twist, while the other women wore slippers, the girl's feet were bare.

"She is available," Mrs. Richardson answered as her star attraction approached. "But she's young. Young and pretty sells more readily. Because of this, she commands a premium around here."

Whatever premium the girl's body might have commanded, she was in full command of her body and her beauty. She moved with the casual fluid grace of feminine youth. It was a studied casualness that edged on impudence. As she walked barefoot toward Samuel, the unimpinged and unrestrained upper curves of her pushed-up breasts quivered and trembled in a liquid motion.

The girl's face was an elegantly long and soft rectangular shape that tapered at her chin. Her face was neither puffy with baby fat nor gaunt and bony. She had long and thick dark black hair with a natural wave to it. Her hair hung down the sides of her face and down the back and front of her shoulders. On the right side of her face, a wide wave of thick hair partially covered her right eye. As she came ever closer, Samuel could see that her eyes were a deep crystal-blue color. She had long and thick natural eyelashes to go with her long and thick black hair. Her nose was neither small and dainty nor too large for her face. All the features of her face were in artistically balanced proportion to each other.

In a serviceable enough country analogy, the girl's skin seemed to shine in the half-light of the room with the iridescent color of fresh buttermilk. Her cheeks had a slight blush to them. The blush looked artificial, as if she had rubbed a light coating of some form of rouge on her cheeks to give them more color. The girl had the beginning of a wide mouth. Her lips were full and rounded without being thick. The term *pouty look* had not yet been invented, but latter-day fashion consultants would say the girl had the mouth to fit the look. Her lips shone a deep and shiny cherry red that also looked to be an artificial color. Apparently she had rubbed the pulp of actual cherries over her lips or had rubbed on some form of gloss to give them their hue and shine.

Samuel had heard women of the night described as "painted ladies." The girl had obviously painted herself in a way that she thought would make her more classically attractive. The effect served to make her resemble a Rubens nude with shiny pink cheeks. The rouge-colored makeup did rather go with scarlet letter territory.

The girl stopped in front of Samuel. Without saying anything, she stood with her head slightly tilted to her left side. The angle at which she held her head caused her loose hair to fall over her right eye, further obscuring it. The girl stood silently before him with her legs slightly spread and her hands behind her back. Samuel noticed that instead of being laced down the back, the girl's pseudocorset was buttoned down the front with heavy buttons. The buttons would have left noticeable bulges if the corset were worn as an undergarment with a blouse over it. Avoiding unsightly bumps from hidden buttons was why corsets were secured at the back by laces. It was apparent that the false corset had never been meant to have anything worn over top of it. It had been designed openly without cover to show off and enhance a woman's figure as a device for seducing men.

"The two of you look like farmers to me," Mrs. Richardson continued. The woman was half right. Ben was from the town, but Samuel was a farmer's son. Just how the woman had pegged them for farmers, Samuel wasn't sure. They weren't exactly wearing manure-stained overalls. Neither of them was dressed like a farmer. Both Samuel and Ben had worn their Sunday-go-to-meeting best dress clothes to the dance. Samuel figured that they must have been giving off some kind of subtle clues that the woman had interpreted as being classic farmer.

"I know how cost-conscious farmers can be. You're always looking for a bargain. You may not want to pay the extra that she's worth."

Samuel didn't want to come right out and ask "How much?" In his sense of relative gentlemanliness, he felt that would be an impolite question, even when posed to a woman of a bordello. It seemed even more impolite, if not actively insulting, to ask the question off to the side to the madam while the woman was standing by mute as if the woman in question didn't exist or that in his eyes she was little more than meat on the hoof and he was a cattle buyer. Samuel felt he needed other language to address the woman.

"May I inquire as to what the differential is?" Samuel said, stumbling for polite words to use in a situation and a profession that almost by definition had no polite words to offer. Even in his own mind, he sounded like a suitor asking a father for his daughter's hand in marriage.

Mrs. Richardson stated the price range. The differential wasn't as large as Samuel had imagined. It was big enough, but he had enough money to cover it. The price was within reach. The girl was within his reach financially and physically. For a moment Samuel said nothing as he stood and contemplated. Ben took his friend's momentary silence as indecision.

"Well, if you're not interested," Ben started to say as he stepped forward.

Samuel clamped his hand on his friend's shoulder and squeezed in an authoritative manner. "I drove us here," he said in his take-charge voice. "I'm the one who'll drive us back. That gives me first pick."

Ben didn't argue the point with his friend. Samuel had indeed provided the transportation. But that wasn't the reason for Ben's deference. Ben found the girl attractive too, but from Samuel's emphatic hand on his shoulder, he got the definite idea that his otherwise good friend and defender seemed rather intent on having the girl for himself and was prepared to get physical about it. Ben didn't want to press the issue with the captain of the wrestling and boxing team who was a full head taller than he.

"Besides, she's too tall for you."

The girl was half a head shorter than Samuel, which made her half a head taller than Ben, who was a full head shorter than his friend. The girl's shapely torso was of average length. Her height came from her proportionately long legs. Samuel turned to look at the leggy girl.

"She looks like she could kick you off her without half trying when she gets going," Samuel said. "It could prove embarrassing your first time out. You'd be better off leaving her with someone her own size while you choose someone your own size." He took his hand off his friend's shoulder and turned to the girl.

"Ah, I choose you, ma'am," Samuel said, putting his take-charge request in before his friend could say anything more.

Without saying anything, the girl sort of smiled. She reached her hand around from behind her back and took Samuel's hand in hers. Her delicate fingers slipped softly over the back of his hand, her thumb across the palm of his hand. Samuel had spent his life and developing years on the outer fringes of a developing electric world. There was no electricity on the farm for him to encounter by accident. He hadn't yet experienced the bite and feel of electricity. The trembling surge that ran through him at the feel of the girl's soft hand sliding over his was the closest he had ever come to the feeling of electricity. He glanced at the girl's hand in his. With a slight tug, and without any further ado, the girl started to lead him away from where they were standing, heading deeper into the house. He didn't know where she was leading, but she could take him in hand anytime and walk him anywhere she was of a mind to.

Once Samuel was in motion with the girl, the knowledge of the motions that he soon would be taking with her set in fully. The electrical feeling that had passed through him at the first feel of her touch multiplied exponentially in intensity and spread out in all directions. He visually followed the trail from the girl's hand along the full length of her graceful bare arm up to where it connected with her bare shoulder, which spread across laterally to the base of her elegantly curved neck, which rose up to join her lovely face framed by her thick hair. Below, the girl's bare shoulders merged downward into the swelling curves of her full and alive body. Samuel had heard the poetic clichés about lovers thrilling and trembling at their paramour's touch, but he had never experienced any feeling like what he was feeling now, in the presence of and in the hand of the beautiful girl. The phrase *perfect storm* had not been coined yet, but he was experiencing something of the sort now, his having spent his pubescent years so far without having encountered a single girl in town who aroused his interest to any appreciable degree. His frustration at his lack of a marital future, toward which he was making no progress, the unanticipated extreme beauty of the girl, and the sudden full-scale release of pent-up and previously unutilized pubescent male hormones were combining to create a perfect storm of swirling feelings in Samuel—feelings of a kind and an intensity that he had never approached feeling before.

It would be trite to say that Samuel's feelings had gone out of his control. But his feelings were coming on faster than he could juggle them or control them. Then again, he didn't particularly have the desire to either suppress or control them.

Without speaking, the girl led Samuel across the parlor floor, away from Ben and her madam, and past the other women seated in the room. In short order they passed out of the parlor, leaving Ben to make his choice from among the remaining women. Still not saying anything, still holding his hand, the girl led Samuel down the hall. Her bare feet padded silently while the hard rubber soles of Samuel's best dress shoes clomped noisily on the hardwood floor. Samuel walked at the girl's side while she held his hand. The girl was about the same height as Ben, which meant that Samuel was a head taller than she was. As they walked, Samuel didn't try to make up the conversation deficit caused by the girl's not speaking. The silence could have used a bit of distraction, but Samuel was otherwise distracted looking over the girl's shoulder, watching her thick hair bounce and watching the unrestrained top halves of her ample breasts bounce as she walked.

Near the end of the hall, the girl led Samuel up a narrow stairway leading to the second floor. The stairway was too narrow for them to walk up side by side without squeezing each other up against the walls. With the girl still holding his hand, Samuel followed close behind her. The girl's corset covered only the top half of her hips. As they climbed the stairs, Samuel watched her hips rhythmically sway in alternating sequence, from side to side. The girl's hips were not fat, sagging, lined, or puffy. Neither were they small and pinched. They were full, firm, and rounded and as filled with the fluid motion of life as her bosoms were. Taken individually, all the separate parts of the girl's body seemed to rise and swell, challenging her corset from all angles. Taken as a whole, however many times her body had been taken by men, the girl's body seemed up to the challenge of her profession.

There were no lights in the upper hallway. The second-floor hall was a bit dark at the top of the stairs. Lights came into the corridor from the open doors of the rooms off the hall. There was a master suite at the far end. The larger room was Mrs. Richardson's room. The rest of the rooms on the upper level were small and somewhat cramped. The smaller rooms had been designed as bedrooms for the children of a large family, hence the large number of small rooms. Mrs. Richardson and her husband had never had any children to occupy the designated children's rooms. When the house and rooms had been converted to their alternate purpose, the rooms became the living quarters and business rooms for the women of the house. There were enough rooms in the house to accommodate all the working women. Their individual rooms doubled as both living space and workrooms. For the first time in their existence, the rooms were being employed as the bedrooms they had been designed to be. They were just doing double duty in that regard.

The girl led Samuel into a room at the end of the hall near the stairway. The room had a single window with the drapes drawn closed. There was a bed close to the far wall. Along another wall was a small dresser. The only other piece of furniture in the room was a nightstand with an electrical desk lamp sitting on it, turned on. The lamp provided the only light. As they entered the room, the girl let go of Samuel's hand.

"Close the door behind us, please," the girl said. This was the first time Samuel had heard her speak. He had always rather thought that prostitutes have coarse and hard voices and spoke using profane gutter language, but the girl's voice was soft and melodic.

Without turning around, the girl stepped away from Samuel and walked over to the bed on the far side of the room. The bed was made up. At least the cover had been pretty much pulled back into place after the bed's last use. When she arrived at the bed, the girl started to turn the covers down, preparing to perform her duty. Samuel dutifully closed the room door behind them at her request.

Though the house was dedicated to an impolite and obvious purpose, Samuel didn't think it would be impolite to go about being obvious in the way he undressed himself in front of the girl. While the girl's back was turned, he hastily unbuttoned the tight cuff buttons of his shirt and started unbuttoning the front buttons in order, from the top to the bottom. Samuel figured that when the girl turned around, he would already have his shirt unbuttoned. From there he could slow down his disrobing to a pace that made him seem more relaxed and sophisticated. He didn't know what the girl was used to when it came to the way men went after her. But he figured she had had more than her share of men veritably ripping her limited clothes off and their own clothes off in a fevered rush to cut to the chase. Whatever ways men had approached the girl, Samuel didn't want to come on like a hired farmhand or a train brakeman panting to get on with it.

However impolite their actions would soon become, there was another immediate politeness consideration. Though the house was dedicated to what many people would consider to be an impolite practice, Samuel had been raised believing that a gentleman should make polite conversation with a lady. Despite the fact that many people might not define the girl as a lady beyond her designation as a lady of the night, Samuel still felt that he should approach her in a way that at least somewhat approximated the way he would converse with women at a church social. Samuel didn't have a lot of experience at making small talk with girls his own age. He had zero experience making conversation with scarlet women.

"Ah, what's your name, ma'am?" Samuel asked in a friendly conversational voice to the girl's back as she turned back the sheets on the bed. Samuel didn't know what the proper sexual etiquette was in a cathouse, if there was any etiquette in a bordello. It just seemed polite to ask. He figured that knowing your lover's name, even if it was only tawdry love for one night, was the natural beginning point of any kind of love.

"I don't have no name," the girl said in a matter-of-fact voice with her back still to him.

Samuel had two buttons to go on his shirt. As fast as he was going and as anxious as he was to get on with moving things farther along, the girl's strange and unexpected answer stopped him in his tracks. He stood there with the second-from-the-bottom button in his hand. The girl offered no further clarification of her unexpected answer.

"Ah, everybody has some kind of name," Samuel said. "We all get a name when we're born. Did your parents forget to give you a name when you were born?"

He hadn't meant the question to be flippant or crude. He just couldn't quite see how something as basic as giving a child a name had been overlooked by the girl's mother. Unless she had been disowned by her mother as an infant.

"Were you abandoned as an infant? Did your mother leave you in a basket on the steps of an orphanage?"

Samuel imagined the girl growing up in a crowded orphanage for abandoned girls. In Samuel's mind, that could explain why she had become a prostitute. He figured that being an orphan wasn't the most auspicious launch for anyone. Her upbringing as an orphan could have set the pattern for her life. In Samuel's thinking, the girl might have just drifted from being one kind of orphan, living in an institution full of homeless young girls left on their own, to being another kind of orphan in a house of wayward women out on their own.

But that wouldn't explain why she had no name. Even abandoned foundlings are given a name in the orphanage on whose doorstep they are left.

"My mama gave me a name when she birthed me," the girl answered in the same flat-sounding, matter-of-fact voice, her back still to him. "Then she died before I was hardly old enough to say my name and call her 'Mother.' When she went into a hole in the ground, she left me in a hole that was my life. My given name didn't do nothin' for me but leave me in pain where I lay. My name didn't keep the hurt from comin' on me and over me when I had it. The nothin' name I had back then was only the beginning of the nothin' life that I've spent my days since then tryin' to put out of my mind. It'll be a happy enough day for me when I wake up one morning and find that I've forgotten it all the way."

The girl spoke with a country accent. It wasn't the lilting inflection of a Southern belle. Her accent was hard-edged country, sharp around the edges. Samuel couldn't place her accent directly, but it sounded deep mountain hillbilly.

"Don't go 'round tryin' to drag my name outta me. You knowin' my name won't make it any better for me. It won't make me feel any better to you in this bed tonight. You knowin' my name won't make me no more of a wildcat in bed than I am without a name."

"Pardon me, ma'am," Samuel said, "I didn't mean to be insulting. I was just wondering what they call you around here. What does someone say when they want to get your attention? Do they call out, 'Hey you, girl!'?"

The girl turned around. She stood facing him with the same partially spread leg stance she had displayed herself with in the parlor. Her body seemed as ready to go as it had seemed in the parlor. Her face was set. Her look seemed neither angry, nor lustful, nor frightened.

"If you need a name so bad, you can call me Clarinda," the girl said in the same measured voice. "That's what I call myself. It ain't my name by birth, but that's the name I go by and get by on. That's what they call me here. I gave myself the name. In that sense it's not real. But it's more real to me than the one that was tossed on me when I was born. It's real to me above the name I was born with because I gave the name to myself on my own terms."

"If you want to be called Clarinda, that's what I'll call you," Samuel said in his best agreeable voice. "A rose by any other name would be as sweet."

The name sounded as invented as the girl had said it was. To Samuel, the name sounded like something she had gotten out of a medieval romance story about knights in shining armor and fair damsels in distress. In a backhanded manner, the name that the girl had fashioned for herself fit her and outlined her well—as did her revealing corset. To Samuel, the name was a darkly beautiful name that went with the darkly beautiful girl.

"Sweet I ain't," the girl said, a tone of hard-edged agreeableness in her voice. "Available I am if you want to see me again. You just have to pay the house fee for me and agree to my terms. Far as names go, you can call me any name you want. You can call me girl. You can call me woman. You can call me bitch. You can even call me whore. That's what I am. I'm not denying it or backin' away from it. I am what I am. I've been what I've been for too long in my life to deny it. You can have me anytime you want as long as you obey the house rules and mine. But don't go tryin' to drag me through the dirt of my life by tryin' to drag my name out of me."

Without looking down, the girl started to unfasten the heavy buttons on her corset, working slowly from top to bottom. Apparently she had done it enough times that she didn't have to look. She did seem to have a practiced hand at it.

"You didn't come here lookin' for a name. You came here lookin' for a woman by any other name. That's what I am. That's what I'll be for you tonight."

As she unbuttoned the snaps of her corset, the girl started walking toward Samuel in a swaying seductive walk that seemed long practiced. In her walk, the girl was as poised and practiced as she was at undressing herself. It was obvious to Samuel that she had unbuttoned her corset many

75

times before. She had walked the walk before. Samuel figured the girl probably employed the same burlesque striptease routine as part of the endgame act she used with all her customers. He was otherwise distracted by the knowledge that the girl and her practiced ways were about to spell the end of his virginity.

"You give me my name for the night. I'll go by any name you give me. Call me by the name of a girl you wanted to have but who wouldn't have you. You can pretend I'm a girl you loved but who turned her back on you and sent you away. You can pretend I'm a proper woman you longed for from a distance but never approached because she would shun you as being a dirty-minded, presumptuous, upstart boy. To you I'll be all the women you have known. I'll be the woman you have wanted to know. Take me by any name you want to take me by. Take me with no name at all. But don't say you love me as you take me. I don't need to hear any profession of love to get me going or keep me going. I wouldn't believe you anyway. Far as names go, put any name you want on me for the night. Just don't go thinkin' of asking my born name, and don't go about tryin' to put your name on me as if you own me."

"Well, I sure won't name you for my snot-nosed, henpecking little sister," Samuel said as a way of making a lame joke to the advancing half-naked girl, who moved as if she were anything but lame. "If Mrs. Richardson needs more girls in the house, maybe I can send my sister to work here. It might loosen her up. If she was as experienced as you, she might not be such a snot."

He had meant the comment as a joke to lighten up the moment. The girl did not respond.

The girl had closed the distance and had advanced about two-thirds of the way from the bed to where Samuel was standing. She had also reached the last button, where the button row ended near the bottom of her corset. Samuel hastily unbuttoned the last two buttons on his shirt. At that point he stopped and stood in a semihypnotic state, watching the girl advance.

"Like I say, don't pry me for my name," the girl went on. "Names aren't why neither of us are here. Names tie you down. Knowin' someone's name ties you that person even if you don't want to be tied to them. Not knowing my name will make it that much easier for you to walk away from me. Names get in the way of walking away. Names trip you up. Knowing the name of your lover leads you to think that there should be somethin' more between you than just being lovers. Havin' a name ties you to other people who think they own you because you have their last name. You can't move free. Havin' a name ties you to yourself such that you can't move beyond yourself. A name in life ties you to a grave in the future."

Samuel wondered if that was some kind of hillbilly superstition.

"A girl who don't have no name is free in the wind. You can blow past each other like the wind and keep on going your way without getting caught up on nothin'."

"Not having a name makes it kind of hard for those who want to know you better," Samuel said.

To Samuel the path of life led through family. The end of life was to be buried with family under your family's name. To be buried nameless was not to exist and never to have existed.

"When my last day comes upon me, Clarinda is the name they can carve on my headstone," the girl answered. "It won't make no never mind to me if it ain't my real name. I've already left my real name behind in life. I'll lie in my grave under any name they put on me. I'll be where earthly names don't mean anything."

The girl reached up with both hands and locked her hands on the top of her corset on either side, her thumbs down on the insides. "Hey," she said. "Are you here for names or for a girl? If you're here for me, cut to the chase and cut to what you came here wantin' to get from me. Once you get what you're here wantin' out of me, you're going to want to be on your way without any complications trailing after you. You'll probably forget any name you give me as fast as you forget me."

In one smooth and continuous move that in its own way was as graceful as the motion of a ballerina, the girl pushed her corset down to the floor around her ankles, dipping slightly and bending her knees at the bottom of the curve. Instead of collapsing into a flat circle on the floor at her feet, the heavy material the corset was made of caused it to maintain some of its shape as it leaned against the bottom of the girl's legs around her ankles.

Just as quickly as she had bent down, the girl stood back up to her full naked height. Samuel's estimate that the girl's womanly figure was capable of sustaining itself without the artificial support of a corset proved to be correct. In the half-light of the room, the deep rose red of the girl's nipples shone in counterpoint to the dark black of her hair to the buttercream glow of her skin. He had neither appreciated nor quite known that a woman's body could be so full of suppleness, life, and the color of life.

If the girl's breasts had not needed her support of her come-hither corset to hold themselves in a forward orientation, neither did it seem that the girl's waist needed to be cinched in by her corset to give her the hourglass figure that in those days was considered a mark of beauty and womanliness. The hourglass shape of the girl's figure wasn't exaggerated to the degree that some litho drawings of idealized women of the day would have it, but her waist had its own natural narrowness to it. Overall the girl's body etched a smooth and tight figure without any sags, puffiness, or extraneous rolls of flesh. Her skin was smooth and free of wrinkles or stretch marks. Even in the limited light of the room, the whole of the girl's body was possessed of the glow of health and life. It also seemed to be wound up tight with the pent-up energy of youth.

At the sight of the girl-woman's now fully naked body, Samuel found that the knowledge that his own youth was only moments away from being transformed into full mature manhood in the arms of a fully mature woman set in fast and hard. At the same time, the full knowledge dawned on him that the dreary isolation of his life from the fullness of life and from the promise of love was about to be broken, if only for the night. Samuel's pent-up youthful energy ramped up suddenly like the overstoked boiler of a steam engine straining its riveted seams, about to explode.

"Knowin' each other in the dark and then being gone from each other is exactly the way both of us want it," the girl went on.

The girl stepped out of her corset with one leg. With her other leg, she kicked the corset out of the way. She started to walk the remaining distance to Samuel in a coy and practiced seductive glide.

"You came here lookin' for a woman who'll be all woman to you for the night without any questions asked. I'll be that woman for you. I'll be all the woman you want or can handle. But you also came here lookin' for somethin' where everything don't mean nothin' beyond."

Even when filtered through her hard mountain accent, the girl's voice was still soft, melodic, and calculatedly seductive. Her country vernacular was otherwise fractured and jumbled. From her chopped-up phonetics, it sounded like the girl probably hadn't received much in the way of an education. She didn't have a full grasp of English vernacular. But as far as the skills that went with a cathouse and the attitudes that defined a bordello were concerned, she had her walk and her philosophy of noncommitment-based love down quite well.

"I'll move in bed for you like a woman should. Between the two of us, we can make the earth and the sky move. Then we'll both move on in our own way."

Samuel had figured the night would be a simple in-and-out occurrence. He had assumed that the women of the house would be as plain, bland, and uninspiring as the rest of the girls in town. The girl had taken him by surprise more than he thought he was capable of being taken by surprise. He had never thought serendipity could look this good. The effect the girl was having on him went far beyond conventional teenage lust or the obvious coming-of-age clichés.

As Samuel watched the girl approach, all his life that had come before that night now seemed to be a dull and trite splotch. As a farm boy in the fields, he had seen the world around him in color. But the life he had known now seemed a flat and washed-out sepia compared to the hues and shine of the girl. As Samuel prepared in his body to take the next step in life, in his mind the life he had known before was starting to seem as if it had been little more than an imitation of life. It would be too much of a stock romantic metaphor to say that Samuel felt like he was floating above the clouds or was soaring like a hawk on the wing. But as he watched the approach of the beautiful dark-haired girl in all her unadorned womanly naturalness, Samuel Martin knew that he was never again going to look on his life in the same way. This night, he knew, would change everything.

"I'll wrap around you as tight and close as the skin on your body. Our bodies will press together as one. Our hearts will never touch. Tomorrow we'll be strangers who never met."

The girl came up to him and stopped less than a step away. Her large nipples brushed his half-open shirt.

"Up here in my room, you can have me all you want, the way you want. I won't ask you to say you love me. You don't have to say a word to me the whole time. When you're done with me, you can leave me without saying a word. Just close the door of my room behind you and walk away free."

The girl reached up through his unbuttoned shirt and placed her hands on his chest. From there she started running her hands over his chest. Samuel tried hard to act controlled and to stand as impassively as a wooden Indian in front of a cigar store, but at the girl's far more intimate touch, the trembling excitement ran through him at an exponentially increasing level.

"I'll stay here where you left me without grousing like some prissy girl that you did me wrong."

With a quick and smooth glide of her soft hands, the girl ran her hands up to his shoulders underneath his shirt. From there she ran her hands to the sides and down his arms, pushing his shirt off his back and downward so it dropped off his arms and fell on the floor behind him. Leaving her left hand on his shoulder, the girl reached up and laid the back of her right hand on his left cheek, stroking it.

"But for the time you're havin' me, you can have me like there's no tomorrow. Tomorrow you can leave me and pretend we never met. At least while you're havin' me it'll be nice to be had by someone my own age for a change."

With an equally practiced move, the girl wrapped her arms around his back and pulled herself up to him close and tight. Samuel was only half successful at suppressing the gasp he let out as he felt the girl's large breasts press against his chest and spread out. The feel of the press of the girl's warm and full chest against his own was only the first of many new sensations he had never felt before that would come in rapid-fire sequence that night. Samuel's half-controlled half gasp had just barely escaped when the girl's lips closed over his mouth.

The girl swayed from side to side, rubbing her body against his. Friction and the pressure of their bodies pressed against each other held the girl's nipples and the center of her breasts in place against his chest, while the base of her breasts moved from side to side with the undulating sway of her body. To Samuel it felt like they were both figures made of warm modeling clay and the girl was trying to rub herself into him until their bodies flowed and merged together into one. The effect on Samuel was both explosive and paralyzing at the same time. For the first few moments, Samuel stood motionless as the girl pressed the full length of her naked body against his.

Samuel kneaded the girl's hips in his hands the way he had seen his mother knead dough to make bread. The girl's hips were warm, soft, and pliable in his hands. As he squeezed her soft but tight hips, Samuel felt like he was losing control. He wanted the girl to lose all of her control for him. But in a backhand way, the girl was in full control of herself and of him.

Either way, Samuel continued to kiss the girl hard and fast on her full lips. He tried to keep up with her pace, but she seemed one step ahead of him. After several long minutes of trying to match the girl one-for-one in mouth kissing, Samuel changed directions. He broke his kiss, moved his face away from the girl's face, turned his head to the right a bit, brought his head down, and started kissing her neck just under the angle of her jaw. From there he kissed his way down to where her neck joined her shoulder. From there he kissed his way across the top of her shoulder to where her arm joined her shoulder. Samuel had heard that lovers often kissed their lovers' necks and also kissed up and down the length of their lovers' extremities.

The girl rolled her head to the side, closed her eyes, and sighed softly. Samuel reversed direction, lowered his focus slightly, and started kissing his way back across the upper part of the girl's chest. He had heard that lovers do that. As he reached the center of her chest, the girl put both her hands on the back of his neck and brought her head down to where her lips brushed the hair on top of his head. From there he kissed the rest of the way across to the other side of the girl's chest.

Samuel brought his head back to the center and started to kiss the uppermost part of the girl's cleavage. The girl rolled her head back and sighed louder. She pulled tighter with her hands on the back of his neck as if she were trying to pull his face deeper into her chest. At the same time, she pushed down on the back of his head as if trying to direct his focus lower. Samuel took the girl's lead and started moving his kisses downward into the deepening cleavage between her bosoms. He had heard that lovers do that too. Soon enough his cheeks were surrounded on both sides by the soft flesh of the girl's breasts. He caught the scent of some kind of bath oil. The girl brought her face back down to the top of his head. She started running her fingers through his hair and kissing the top of his head.

Samuel reached the bottom of the girl's cleavage. He was about to start working off to the sides when the girl broke her contact with him and backed up a step. She turned to the side, turned around, and started to walk away from him. As she did so, she took hold of his arm and started to tug him gently to follow her. From the direction she was heading, Samuel realized the girl was beckoning him to follow her to the bed on the opposite wall across the room from where they were standing. The girl was obviously ready to get on with what they were both obviously in the house for and what Samuel had been ready for since he had first seen her.

Samuel followed the girl for the few steps that took him across the small room. But just before they arrived at the bed, Samuel realized that he still had his pants and shoes on. He stopped to complete the necessary undressing. The girl dropped his arm and proceeded on toward the bed. Samuel's shoes were laced tight. He couldn't kick them off in a smooth motion while standing. It was necessary to bend down and unlace them. He hopped around awkwardly, trying to maintain his balance, as he unlaced his shoes and pulled them off. Then he pulled his socks off in turn. With nothing to put a hand on to balance himself, he almost tumbled over twice. Having removed his shoes and socks, he pulled his pants down and hastily pulled them off. One of his pants legs became stuck on his foot, turned inside out and pulled out full length inside out. As he tried to pull it off, he almost fell over a third time while doing his little dance, trying to pull his trailed-out pant leg all the way off. Having finally accomplished the removal of his pants, he pulled down his underpants and removed them. His exaggerated interest in the girl caused a lesser hang-up as he pulled down his shorts.

When Samuel had finished the final stages of undressing, he looked toward the bed. The girl had already climbed onto the bed. She was now lying down.

"Do you want the light on or off?" the girl asked as Samuel quickly approached the bed in the same end-stage nakedness as the girl. She made a reaching gesture toward the lamp on the end table next to the bed. She would have pulled the chain that would have switched off the single bulb in the lamp if Samuel had answered in the affirmative. Samuel was too distracted to answer coherently or even respond with a grunt. He clambered onto the bed, blocking the girl's reach of the light. By default the light stayed on. He did not pull the sheet up over them.

As quickly as he had mounted the bed, Samuel mounted the girl. He positioned his body over hers. At the same time, he positioned the eager and ready-to-be-initiated extension of his manhood near the entrance portal to the girl's experienced womanhood. With a little final positioning help from the girl, Samuel entered into his new life to come. He hadn't been thinking in terms of a sexual pun. He was thinking in terms of life and the life he had never entered into until the moment he entered the girl. A half-audible gasp escaped from the mouth of the otherwise controlled Samuel as he felt his soon-to-be fully initiated manhood slip down into the warm wetness of the girl, when he fully realized where he was and how deep he was penetrating both the girl and life. He had come to the house at least to get some kind of sense of what it was like to be with a woman and come home to a wife. He had no idea that coming home could feel so good.

As Samuel exploded into the girl, he exploded out of the gate like a racehorse. From the second he started in (in and out actually), Samuel abandoned all pretense of control and all pretext that he sought or even wanted control. He surged into the girl for all he was worth, physically and financially. In response, the girl arched her body up to meet his and rubbed her flesh from side to side as far as Samuel's grasp and the press of his body would allow. Her body seemed alternately to tense up in spasms and to shudder. She dug her fingernails into his back and drew long scratches down its length. Her legs thrashed on the bed. Samuel had heard that women locked in the throes of passionate pleasure did that sort of thing. Though the passion the girl seemed to be giving herself over to may have had an earthly, commercial basis, she approached her passion like she was soaring with it toward the heavens.

The girl's wood-frame bed squeaked and shuddered under their combined assault. For a second, Samuel wondered how far the sound was carrying through the house and who was hearing them, but then he dropped the thought. It wasn't like that kind of house hadn't heard that kind of sound before.

What his inexperienced, unpolished, and somewhat awkward adolescent male movements lacked in terms of the smoothness and control of a practiced lothario, he more than made up for in terms of youthful exuberance, the thrill of new territory discovered, and the rush of new life being experienced. You can label what Samuel was feeling as serendipity if you like. What Samuel was feeling was as much the surge of being taken by surprise as it was the thrill of unexpected discovery.

The take-charge Samuel threw himself into everything he did. In the girl's room on the second floor of Mrs. Richardson's establishment, he took the same approach with the girl that he applied on the baseball diamond or the wrestling mat. But it wasn't just the girl Samuel was throwing himself into. It was life itself and his sense of the future that he was throwing himself into. In that focused moment in the girl's room, life seemed to be coming together for Samuel. It was all there for him. In his body he possessed the vitality of life. In his limbs he had the strength of youth. In his arms he held a girl who possessed the strength and vitality of life and youth.

The girl seemed to embrace life with all the strength, relish, and spirit that flowed out of him for her. As an expression of life, the beautiful girl was a life that equaled his own. She was a definition of life and ongoing life that he had never experienced in a girl before and that he had come to suspect he would never find in any girl. In the minimal light of the room, all Samuel could see was the girl's lovely face framed by her dark hair spilling over the pillow, and her blue eyes alternately closed in seemingly sublime pleasure or open looking at him. The girl was all he could see. The girl was all he wanted to see.

Though he otherwise enjoyed his life on the farm and in the town, Samuel had often felt isolated and alone because his vision of the present lacked a wife. That emptiness had impinged on his vision of the future. Now the only present he could focus on was the sweaty, sighing, kissing, grabbing, stroking, scratching, shuddering girl. Until that night and the girl, Samuel's life had seemed flat and tasteless to him because he had lacked anything that he could call a real taste of the future. Now the only taste of the future he wanted at the moment was another taste of the girl's lips.

In the half-light of the room, Samuel and the girl surged on into the night as Samuel surged himself deep into the girl. Samuel's thoughts were profane and sublime toward the girl. Pastor Russell would have probably considered what Samuel was doing with the soiled dove in her soiled bed to be profane. To Samuel the whole of what he was feeling was sublime. Reality was pulling him deeper into itself as he drove himself deeper into the enfolding warmth and wetness of the girl. Where he once had held reality out ahead of him and love at a distance in his mind, he now held them both in his arms in volumes that he had never imagined or expected. It was a reality and a girl he could hold onto for life.

All of Samuel's feelings, physical and ethereal, profane and sublime, coursed and cascaded through him. His feelings merged and grew in scope and in volume, pushing the bounds of containment. Samuel could not define, organize, or control his feelings. Soon enough he became unable to hold his feelings under any restraint. About a half hour into the affair, and as deep into the girl as he could arrange, the take-charge Samuel was no longer able to hold back the single-point expression of his feelings. All the feelings that had been rushing through him as he thrust himself into the girl swelled upward suddenly to a high peak of pressure and pleasure. His body tensed along its full length. His hands gripped the girl's shoulders in a near-death grip. His body shuddered like the girl's body had been doing. All the feelings that had been surging through Samuel's body and mind surged into the girl in a free association stream of liquid passion. The take-charge Samuel let out a single uncontrollable deep groan of male release.

In sequenced response to the feeling of Samuel's releasing both inside her body and outside, as his liquefied expression of male passion and his loss-of-control groan escaped him, the girl's body tensed up. Her back arched. Her hands moved from his upper back to the back of his head. As soon as Samuel's groan was out, the girl pulled his head down to her and brought her head up at the same time. Before he could make another sound, she kissed him long and hard on the mouth. As if caught in a mutually induced muscle spasm, they held the kiss while the remainder of Samuel's male response pumped itself, throbbing, into the depths of the girl, both his narrowly focused lust of the present and his panorama hope for the future flowing into the vessel of his hopes.

When the last passion contraction was over, both Samuel and the girl's body uncoiled and relaxed. The girl's head fell back on the pillow. Samuel's head dropped alongside of hers. Their cheeks touched. Samuel could feel the moistness of the girl's sweat on his already sweaty cheek. He felt the sweaty press of the girl's now motionless body against his. For several long moments, both of them lay still and motionless. Somewhere Samuel had heard that lovers were supposed to exchange polite conversation after making love. He raised his head up and looked down at the girl. She had her eyes closed. It was Samuel who broke the silence.

"I hope you don't think that I'm finished with you," Samuel said. Whether his silence-breaker could be considered polite after-sex conversation is a matter of interpretation. But in one way the definition of polite after-sex conversation technically depended on whether sex had been completed for the night or not.

"Oh, I hope not," the socially impolite girl answered as she opened her eyes.

Samuel reached over and brushed the girl's lips with the back of his fingers. Everything he had been feeling came back into him as if it had not gone away. Whether the feelings he carried for the girl were profane lusts or the product of higher-elevated thoughts, his desire for her carried him over the gap as if the pause hadn't happened. That he was eighteen years old and in the middle of the season of teenage lust had a lot to do with it. The energy and stamina of youth was helping to carry him in the girl's bedroom.

With a quick shift, Samuel recovered his position and started making love to the girl again. She gasped slightly as he started up. She seemed a bit surprised that he was actually going for a second round. Samuel figured that most of the girl's customers were middle-aged or older men who probably just gave her a onetime pop and then paid her and left. Samuel figured she probably wasn't used to a repeat performance by a man. She didn't seem fazed by his starting up again, but the look on her face was a bit indeterminable. It was neither a look of pleasure anticipated or nor one of reluctant weariness. Samuel couldn't quite make out the look on the girl's face. It was as if she was with him and at the same time wasn't.

Samuel and the girl resumed their mutual grappling. Samuel grabbed the small of her back and pulled her lower body in closer than he had held her before. Then he grabbed her hips in his hands and pulled her waist in even closer and tighter. In response, the girl dug her fingers and her fingernails into his hips and pulled him in tight to her. She kissed him as fast and hard as she had before.

For close to another hour, the two of them flailed away at each other, sweated on each other, and kissed their wetness into each other's mouths. As Samuel surged away at the girl spread out beneath him, he managed to surge his desire into her two more times, straining hard and pumping away like a hand pump on a dry well until there was nothing more his body could bring out.

As the night crept by, dark and impenetrable outside the window with the drawn curtains, in the half-light of the room, Samuel continued to penetrate the girl, until both of them finally collapsed in exhaustion into each other's arms. For several long minutes the two of them kissed languidly as they wound down. There was no conversation, polite or otherwise.

Samuel gave the girl one last kiss. Her eyes were closed. Then he slipped his head off to the side and laid it down on the pillow next to her upturned face, his face and lips brushing her right cheek. He placed his right hand on the side of the girl's left cheek. For a long and languid interim period, the two of them lay silent, the girl facing the ceiling with her eyes closed, Samuel's eyes half open, inches from the girl's face. His thoughts hovered close to the girl as his lips were touching her cheek and drifted far beyond her at the same time.

In the space of a single night, he had gone from not knowing a single girl in town he could imagine as his wife and the mother of his children to having intimately known a girl who was far more than he had dreamed of or imagined. For the first time in his life, Samuel was able to put a face to his dreams.

In his dreamy state, Samuel imagined himself walking hand in hand with the girl out on the far edges of the farm's fields, the black of the earth beneath their feet, the green of the crops rising up to their heads and stretching out toward the horizon. He imagined himself and the girl sitting next to each other on the porch, watching the sunset. He imagined the girl leaning her head on his shoulder. He imagined the two of them watching the sky turn orange and red above the fading green of the landscape. He imagined the two of them looking at the sky in silence, lying still, watching, drifting, dreaming.

The next thing Samuel felt was a hand slapping him on the side of his hip.

"Oh, come on, wake up," he heard the mountain-accented girl say. "You're falling asleep on top of me. You've got to get up and get off of me. You're too big for me to move."

Samuel realized that he must have fallen asleep. Pleasant thoughts do have a way of lulling one to sleep. But then again, going to sleep wrapped in the girl's arms seemed both pleasant and natural. He still had to drive Ben and himself home.

"Sorry about that," Samuel said sheepishly as he started to push himself up. "But you kept saying how we wouldn't know or acknowledge each other in the light of day but how well we would get to know each other in the night. I kind of took that as an invitation to spend the night."

Samuel didn't really believe the girl had meant that when she had spoken her piece about knowing each other in the night and walking away and forgetting each other in the light of day. It was just rather wishful thinking on his part.

"You can't stay here, honey," the girl said in a half-jocular but otherwise insistent tone. "The house is still open, and I'm still on duty. I get paid by the number of men I do, not by how languidly romantic I make any one man feel. Besides, your friend needs a ride home. If you stay the night here with me in this room, he's going to end up having to sleep in the parlor or walk home in the dark."

The girl was right. Samuel's passage had been more involved and time-consuming than he had figured it would be. It was later than he had planned to stay. As it was, he might have some explaining to do. He did have to get Ben and himself back home. But in one way he felt that he had already come home.

Samuel did a half vault over the girl and landed on his feet on the floor alongside her bed. From there he stepped quickly over to where he had dropped his pants. In a way he hoped his little display of athletic ability would impress the girl. But in the male vanity lobe of his brain, Samuel sort of figured that if after an hour and a half of near-nonstop lovemaking the girl hadn't been impressed by his physical prowess, she was beyond the ability to be impressed.

"Forgive me for dressing fast," Samuel said as he put his clothes back on. "I don't want it to look like I'm runnin' out on you."

"Doin' it and running out like you was never here is what this house is about," the girl said.

Samuel looked back toward her. She had rolled over onto her stomach, still lying on the bed. Her large breasts were compressed and flattened out on the sweaty sheet that covered the mattress. Her full and rounded hips protruded up into the half-light of the room.

He sort of grunted out an agreement and said something about needing to get home. He wondered how much sleep the girl got on a normal business night, but he didn't ask the question. But the question of nights to come and how the girl allocated her time and apportioned nights was very much on his mind.

Samuel quickly put his shorts and pants back on. The naked girl pulled the pillow up closer under her chin. She laid her head down on the pillow and watched him from the bed. She made no attempt to get up or get dressed. The look on her face was neither satiated nor relieved, neither dreamy nor weary. As far as facial expressions go, the girl looked like she was there and wasn't there.

After he finished buckling his belt, Samuel reached into his back pocket and pulled out the money. "I guess this is where I settle up with you, ma'am," he said, trying not to sound too crudely commercial about it.

"You leave the money with Mrs. Richardson on the way out," the girl said in a matter-of-fact voice. "She keeps the accounts. She'll give me my half tomorrow."

Samuel had heard it said that women who work in bordellos got to keep only a small fraction of the money laid on the counter for them to lay themselves out on a bed. The lion's share of the money went to the house. Samuel figured that cathouses were like gambling houses; the house always wins. Though he didn't have comparative percentage take-home pay figures for girls working in other establishments, the 50 percent pay the women in Mrs. Richardson's establishment were apparently receiving seemed generous.

"Well, I'm glad that you're getting a fair share," Samuel said as he reached for his shirt. "I'd hate to see a hardworking girl like you get stiffed."

The girl put her elbow on the bed next to the pillow, raised her head up, and rested it on her hand. "Now that's gotta be the worst pun I've ever heard spoken in this house," she said in a wry tone.

"I didn't mean to make a bad joke," Samuel went on in an apologetic tone. "I just sort of stumbled over my words."

"Farm boys like you do tend to stumble over your words," the girl said. "And a lot of other things to boot."

The girl didn't seem to have a high opinion of the grace and poise of farmers, but the accent and inflection in her voice made her sound like she had come from farm country. For all Samuel knew, the girl was speaking from experience.

"Well, I suppose I do stumble about at times," Samuel said as he pushed his other arm through the other sleeve of his shirt. "But I sure stumbled into something good when I stumbled onto you."

It was supposed to be what pop culture would one day come to call a killer line. Samuel didn't think that it would make the girl swoon. He figured she had probably heard all sorts of lines. He also figured the girl was probably beyond swooning over any line or any man. But at least it would leave her thinking that he didn't think of her as a cheap tramp. It also might leave her with the impression that he thought of her as something special.

The girl didn't answer. She just sort of smiled.

Samuel finished pulling on his shirt, but he left it unbuttoned. He picked up his shoes and socks, walked over to the girl's bed, and sat down on the bed next to her. He started putting on his socks and shoes.

"I hope you don't mind me using your bed to put my shoes back on," Samuel said without a tone of irony, "but I need to sit down somewhere."

There was only a single chair available on the other side of the room that he could have sat down on. It would have served the same purpose where putting his shoes on was concerned. But convenience in dressing himself was just an excuse. His real reason for sitting on the bed was to position himself next to the girl he intended to position next to him for life.

The pretty sight in Samuel's mind and in his eyes was the sight of the girl on the bed. From her position lying on her front, the girl's long, dark hair flowed over her shoulders and down her back. In the half-light of the room, her body glistened with the mist of drying sweat. Her compressed breasts flowed out to the sides from under her chest. Her hips rose up smooth and rounded like the rounded tops of the distant Appalachian Mountains. The half of her face she had turned toward him had an apparent serene and untroubled look to it. Her lips shone deep red in the harsh orangish light of the desk lamp. It was a picture of all the loveliness that Samuel had ever imagined. It was a picture Samuel would carry with him in his mind when drove the empty night road back to his family house. It was a picture of the woman he wanted to carry through the door of his family's house and across the threshold of his life and live with in their house for the rest of his life.

"I hope you don't mind me taking the liberty of using your bed."

"You've already taken your liberty in my bed," the girl said. "But only because I gave you that liberty. You bought both it and me until you're done and gone for the night. If you want to sit on it and tie your shoes, that's the least of its uses. I'm not going to nitpick some little last-minute use you want to put it to. You paid for the bed as much as you paid for me. You're going to have to pay for that liberty. See Mrs. Richardson downstairs to pay up."

"I hope you don't think that I took liberty with you," Samuel said in a quasi-apologetic tone.

"Like I said," the girl said in the same flat tone of voice, "you paid for it. Payin's not takin' liberties. By definition, you aren't taking liberty when you pay for somethin'. Takin' liberty is when they take it from you for free and leave you hunched over in a corner with your arms wrapped tight around your legs, crying like a dying cat, biting down on a belt to keep from bitin' your tongue, holdin' yourself together waitin' for the pain to go away with nothin' left to do afterward but to get up and hobble away. That's takin' liberty and gettin' your liberty taken away without a 'never you mind' tossed in your face. That's hurtin'. That's havin' your liberty taken away and gettin' absolutely nothin' in return for your pain. Here, at least, in the morning I'll get half of what was paid out for me to ease any pain I might feel."

The way the girl talked of pain caught Samuel up short. He had never made love to a woman before. He had entered into it and into the girl without an instinctive feel for where the boundaries and limits were. He wondered if in the athletic intensity of his shedding his virginity, he had somehow physically hurt the girl. The thought of the girl in pain knotted Samuel up inside on its own accord. If he had hurt her, she might not want to see him again. He might find any door to the girl closed in his face from that night forward.

"I hope I didn't hurt you in any way," Samuel said. His tone of concern was both affected and real.

"You are one big ball of apologies, aren't you?" the girl said. "Stop apologizing for things you didn't do. You didn't take liberties with me beyond what I gave. You didn't hurt me. I'm older now. I'm bigger now, outside and inside. And you were a perfect gentleman, as much as any man who comes in here is or can be a gentleman. But nothin' you did hurt me. I enjoyed it all. I enjoyed what we did together. I enjoy that I'm gettin' paid for doing what I enjoyed. But I would have enjoyed it as much even if I weren't getting paid for it. Just don't go getting yourself the idea that I'm canceling your bill."

Samuel relaxed upon hearing that he hadn't hurt the girl. At least in that sense the door to her room and bed was still open to him. The door to her heart might not be far out of reach.

The girl turned her head a little farther around toward him. "I must say it was fun havin' someone my own age instead of some of the paunchy slobs that come into this place," she said.

"And you, ma'am, were the most fun I think anyone's ever had since fun was invented," Samuel said, forgetting the talk of pain. He said what he had hoping the hyperbolic compliment would help ingratiate him with the girl and leave him on her good side as he left for the night. "At least you were the most fun I've ever had in my life so far. But like the saying goes, anything worth doing is worth doing right. And you're worth doing again and again."

It was the perfect segue to ask the question that Samuel had been wondering about and readying himself to ask. All that the girl had said about making love and then forgetting about each other was her idea of a courtesan's code of love on the run without commitment and complications. He could find himself shut out behind the girl's door no matter what she thought of him or how much she enjoyed his presence or any of his physical attributes.

"Along that line, I was wondering if you allow men to come back and visit you again or whether what you said about not seeing a man again after you've seen him once holds in all cases with you."

"Most of our business is repeat customers," the girl said. "Are you thinkin' 'bout being a regular?"

"For you, yeah," Samuel said.

"Men come here lookin' for a good time without any complications comin' back to haunt them," the girl said. "They don't want to get any ideas that I'm going to be a problem to them or a hanger-on who gets in their hair. I just tell them what they want to hear. If I didn't tell them that I was going to keep quiet and be discreet, they might not want to hang around even once, and they wouldn't come back. Most men don't usually bother to ask names in here. They don't come here for names. They don't give their names. The fewer names bandied about in here, the better."

With her chin still resting in her hand, the girl looked at Samuel.

"If you want to be a repeat customer, I don't have any objections," she said in her matter-of-fact voice. "Come on back anytime you want. Like I said, you're welcome to come back here and back to me as often as you want. You can ask my favors anytime. Just don't go askin' me my name."

Samuel's initial concern melted away. The girl was welcoming him back. Now he wondered if she was doing it on a personal or professional basis.

"And don't go gettin' yourself no idea that I'm going to give you somethin' off for volume sale."

Samuel had the opening he was looking for. An extended courtship of the girl could get a bit expensive. But beyond the possible question of finances, there were no stumbling blocks in the way. He hadn't yet fully considered what strategy he would use to try to win the girl, but at least she'd let him back in through her door. He'd figure out the rest as he went along.

Without having finished buttoning his shirt, Samuel laid his hand on the girl's naked back and leaned down to where his face was next to hers. She turned her face toward his. Though the extraneous gloss had been kissed off earlier, the girl's lips were still wet.

"The only idea I'm getting is to see you again," Samuel said in a lower-volume version of his decisive, take-charge voice. "I'll meet the house price. Just don't fill your calendar all the way up to where you don't have time for me."

Samuel leaned in and kissed the girl's naked back. "As for names, I'll call you by any name you want," he said after breaking his kiss. "Just so you'll know, my name's Samuel Martin. You don't need to go blabbing my name all over town, but if someone asks, you don't have to deny knowing me. I'm not about to carve your name on every tree in the county, but if it gets out that we've been keeping time together, I'm not going to deny knowing you either. I don't particularly care if people know I'm seeing you."

Samuel leaned back up and stood up next to the girl's bed. "If people come to talk about us, let them talk. I'm not about to walk away from you because the henhouse gallery gets to cackling up a storm about us. You've got a far too rich and full body from one end to the other for me to let any single skinny old biddy with a pinched tight nose or a whole collection of pinched noses get in between me and you."

Samuel reached down and smacked the girl on her upturned buttocks. It was another first for him too. He had slapped members of the baseball team on the back in a congratulatory way when they had made a good play, but he had never smacked a girl on her bottom before. He had always rather wanted to do it, though. But he didn't swat the girl's bottom any harder than he did his friends' backs. At least he didn't think it was any harder than that. "So get yourself ready. I'll be coming back around to see you."

At the slap of his hand, the girl's body seemed to jump like the snapping of a spring-loaded trap. She gasped. In a quick move, she put both her hands on the bed and quickly pushed herself up. At the same time, she turned her upper body to the side, away from Samuel. For a moment the girl seemed like she was going to roll and push herself away from him. Her breasts came off the bed and swelled down to their full natural shape. They vibrated and swayed in their release and from the sudden acceleration of her body.

The girl turned her head to face Samuel. For a moment she seemed to have a wild look of startled fear on her face. The fingers of her right hand, the hand closest to him, tensed and curled and dug into the bottom sheet of the bed like a cornered cat baring its claws.

But almost as quickly as the look had come over the girl's face, it faded to a look of annoyed pique.

"Oh, I think I'm goin' to be havin' trouble with you," she said. The tone in her voice wasn't an angry one. It just sounded slightly put out.

"The only trouble that you may get from me is that you may find me wanting all of your time," Samuel said in a sweet and reasonable voice.

"Well, take it easy on my tail when you do," the girl said. "I can't do nothin' much for you or anyone if any part of my backside has welts all over and is too sore for me to lie down on it."

Now the moment of parting had come. For a moment, Samuel thought to repeat the poetic line that says "Parting is such sweet sorrow," but advanced and flowery romanticism like that didn't quite fit either the girl or the setting. In an anticlimax instead, Samuel just promised not to spank the girl again. She did not respond. He turned to leave, continuing to finish buttoning his shirt as he walked across the room.

"Please shut the door behind you," the girl called out to his back as he approached the door, repeating and reversing the same request she had made to him when they had entered the room together.

At the threshold of the door, Samuel turned around and looked back toward the girl. Still naked, she was completing pulling the sheet up over her. Either the girl slept in the nude or she was too tired to get up and put on a nightgown. As Samuel was closing the door, the girl reached over and turned out the desk lamp. The room went dark behind him. Apparently the girl considered her working day to have been concluded and she was tired and ready to go to sleep forthwith without any further delays. Samuel figured that all the women in the house concluded their work shifts in the same straightforward manner. That the girl apparently slept naked was an interesting sidelight to him.

Samuel pulled the door to the girl's room closed the rest of the way. He had to finish buttoning his shirt by feel in the near-darkness of the hall. From there he went back downstairs, where he found his friend Ben waiting for him in the parlor. Ben and Mrs. Richardson were the only two other people in evidence. Along with the girl, the other women of the house had gone to bed. After settling up with Mrs. Richardson, Samuel and Ben left the house together.

"Wipe that silly grin off your face," Samuel said as he threw the crank on the floor of the truck and climbed into the driver's seat in the cab. "You look like a cross-eyed donkey who's been sucking down cheap moonshine."

There were no dome lights or dash lights in the cab of a Model A truck. Samuel caught a glimpse of his friend's face in the indirect light coming through the windows of the house.

"And while you at it, make sure that you get any lipstick wiped off your face. If your mama finds lipstick smeared all over your puss, she's going to know that you've been doing more than sneaking a smooch with one of the girls at the dance."

Samuel backed the truck around, shifted into forward, and drove away from the house, out onto the darkened dirt lane that led back toward the town. There was no moon that night. The light from the house faded behind them. It faded inside the cab of the truck to the point where Samuel could no longer see his friend's face. He heard Ben rustling around in his pocket for a handkerchief.

"While we're busy cleaning ourselves up, we're going to need an excuse for why we're getting back so late," Samuel said as the house dropped away behind them. "That took longer than I expected."

"You mean you took longer than expected," Ben interjected. "The two of you were still going head-to-head when I went past, going back downstairs. For a while there, I thought you were never going to break off and that you were going to end up spending the night. As I sat there in the parlor, I had visions of having to stumble back home on foot in the dark."

Samuel didn't particularly want to say it, but he may very well have spent the night and let his friend fend for himself if the girl had asked him to.

"If you get asked what you were doing that kept you out so late after the dance, just tell them that the two of us went off to Two-Bit Charlie's saloon and had some drinks to celebrate graduating," Samuel said. "Just say we got distracted and the time got away from us. They'll believe that."

Samuel, who was employing a strategy of distraction by using a lesser misdemeanor to divert suspicion from the greater, figured that if they confessed to a lesser form of letting their youthful hair down and sowing a smaller form of wild oats, their parents wouldn't think that they had been out sowing the larger seeds of physical manhood.

"With the grin you walked away with on your face, you seemed to have had yourself a good time," Samuel said, breaking the silence about halfway to where the side road joined up with the main road that led back into town. "Which one did you have?"

"Since you cut me off from their headliner, I took the one with the big melons," Ben said, referring to the short woman with the large breasts. "You and her sure didn't stick around to see me make my choice. I'd thought the four of us would walk out of the parlor together as a couples pair, but you were so hot and bothered to get on with it that the two of you left very fast, so fast that you set up a wind in the hall."

"It was the girl who took me by the hand and led me out," Samuel said. "I wasn't about to nail her shoes to the floor and make her wait." That would have been a bit hard considering the girl wasn't wearing shoes. "Neither of us went there to wait for anything, including for each other," he said.

Samuel was looking to change the direction of the conversation. He glanced in over at his friend, whose face he could not particularly see in the darkened cab of the truck, even though he was only a few feet away from him.

"How was the one you had?" he asked, posing the typical buddies-out-together-on-their-first-time question. "She looks a bit like your aunt Frieda. She looked old enough to be your aunt Frieda."

"Her name's Polly," Ben answered. "She's the second-youngest one there. She's twenty-four. You had the youngest. She's the one who just got there."

If the woman his friend had had was twenty-four, that would make her six to seven years older than Ben, depending on what month she was born. In the culture of the time, six years was a lifetime. It was a double lifetime when the woman was older than the man. But when you're sorting around for a lifetime partner or even a one-night partner, in a small-town bordello it's bound to be a bit of a catch-as-catch-can proposition. It's a bit hard to cherry-pick from a selection that isn't particularly cherry.

The discussion of relative ages set Samuel to thinking about the girl. Compared to the pudgy and used-looking Polly, the girl he'd been with seemed fresh, unworn, alive, and vibrant. He wondered how long it would be before she grew worn and dull-looking like the other women of the house. Samuel figured that prostitutes do tend to grow a bit shopworn and old-looking before their time. He didn't find the image of the fresh and beautiful girl turning aged and worn before her time to be a pleasant one. For the girl to be a prostitute seemed to be a waste of a beautiful face. It seemed to be a waste of a beautiful life all around.

"How do you know how old she is?" Samuel asked, referring to Polly.

"She told me," Ben said. "We got to talking afterward while I was waiting for you. I asked her her name, and she told me, along with her age. She's shy. She's sweet and friendly."

"They may not be paid to be sweet," Samuel quipped, "but they're paid to be friendly. It's their stock in trade." He paused for a moment. "Well, at least you know your woman's real name," he said. "All the girl I had would give me in the way of a name was a theatrical-sounding stage name. She wouldn't tell me her real name. She was very insistent that I not try to pry her real name out of her."

"Polly's a bit chunky," Ben went on. "She's got buckteeth. She speaks with a lisp. All of that probably kept her from finding a man who wanted to marry her. She's not the swiftest woman in the world intellectually, but she's friendly and she's nice. I kind of expected all bordello ladies to be as hard and tough and coarse as a gandy dancer, but she wasn't. In her own way, she's sweet and accommodating."

At least he didn't say she was innocent.

"It's her job to be accommodating," Samuel said. "Her profession is dedicated to being accommodating to men. Did you choose her because she looked accommodating?"

"I chose her mostly because she had big jugs," Ben answered.

"I didn't know you were a breast man," Samuel said.

"I didn't know myself until I saw her," Ben said. "After you walked off with the youngest and most eye-catching of the lot, Polly's breasts were the one feature about her that caught my eye out of all the rest."

"I guess every man has to start someplace, and attraction has to start with something," Samuel said. He figured that the woman's large breasts were her calling card and the standout attraction that counterbalanced her heavy hips, thick thighs, buckteeth, and lisp.

Samuel wasn't really one to talk given that it was the girl's large, nonsagging breasts pushed up and out by her corset that had caught his eye as much as her soft and beautiful face.

"There was one other thing I liked about her," Ben said.

"What was that?"

"She's short," Ben said in a practical mode. "All the others, including the one you had, were taller than me. She's the same height as me. I didn't feel like such a pipsqueak with her."

"She may be short, but she has melons big enough to smother a man," Samuel said. "Especially a sawed-off runt like you."

"That's not a problem when you're on top," Ben said, sounding like a man of wide experience. "They spread out every which way when she lay down. Women's breasts only stick out or sag down when they're standing up. When women lie down, their breasts flatten out. It's like the foreman at the store, Murphy Hendricks, said. All women are equally flat when they're flat on their backs. Her breasts might become a suffocation hazard if she were on top. I may try it that way next time."

"Are you planning on coming back?" Samuel asked.

"Now that I know the way and the how-to, yes," Ben answered. "I just have to work out how I go about juggling the time and expense and keep what I'm doing from my parents."

Samuel again glanced in the direction of his friend. He could not particularly see in the dark. He cut to the chase. "So how was it with her?"

"It wasn't love, but it wasn't bad," the now initiated-into-physical-manhood Ben quipped, giving a classic casual male detached response. In fact, Ben seemed to have been able to detach from his first-time lover without any complications. A detached observer might say that Samuel hadn't detached from his first-time lover at all. Ignoring the obvious sexual pun, he was in deep and heading in deeper.

"How was it for you with Little Miss Premium Fare?" Ben asked. "From what I could tell, it must have been pretty good for the two of you. You were still going at it when I went by your room. I could hear her all the way down the hall, even before I got up to the room you were in. At least it sounded like both of you were enjoying yourselves."

Samuel turned his head around and looked out the back window, toward the house. His answer was both indirect and to the point. "She's the most beautiful girl I've ever seen in my life," he said as he looked back toward the house where the girl lived and worked. They were three-quarters of the way to the turn. He couldn't particularly see the house in the darkness behind them any more than he could see his friend's face in the unlit cab of the truck. Though he could see nothing definite behind in the darkness, in his mind he still held an unambiguous and undiminished image of the girl's lovely face. In his mind he carried an indelible memory of the girl's warm, alive, and surging body.

"She's about the only girl you've ever seen outside the ones in this town," Ben responded. "You don't have much to compare her with. She's quite a looker in her own right, but there are probably a whole lot of good-looking girls out there in the world. You just haven't run into them. You've just got to get out and look for them."

Provided you can get away from this town to do it, Samuel thought to himself.

"Just don't look for them in whorehouses."

Ben made one last wipe with his handkerchief to make sure he had gotten any trace, and the smell, of Polly's makeup off his face. They were approaching the turn to the road back into town. Samuel set his hands on the wheel and prepared to make the turn.

"The one you had sure looked like she fit in with a whorehouse. She looks like she was born to the job. She sure sounds like she's up to the job. At least she sounds like she enjoys her work. I could hear her carrying on all the way down in the first-floor parlor. From the way she was shouting, either she is a very good actress who throws herself all the way into the part or she was really going out of her head. Either way, she fits right into the role that nature and the house assigned to her. Where it comes to being a lady of the night, she's got the job down pat. She's going to go a long way in her field."

Not if Samuel could help it.

Samuel was far into the turn onto the main road. He gripped the wheel and turned harder. The truck started to point off toward the side of the road.

"That girl's got it in her to be a real whore's whore."

Samuel straightened out his oversteer and headed toward the streetlights of the town. Other things needed straightening out.

"I'll ask you to speak more respectfully about the girl I'm going to marry," Samuel said in a voice tinged with an underlying tone of menace.

Ben went silent for several moments.

"Ah, marry?" Ben said, regaining his power of speech. "What marry? What do you mean, marry?! Did you propose to her in the middle of thrashing around with her?"

Ben was joking. Samuel wasn't.

"She's the girl I'm going to marry!" Samuel went on, becoming more emphatic. "I haven't asked her yet. I'm going to have to work up to it and work her into it. Right at the moment, she seems to like it where she's at. But I don't think she's had much of anything or any real love in her life.

I'm sure I can convince her that I can make a better life for her. With me she can fill in the gap that's been in my life. I can fill in the empty hole of love that hasn't been in her life."

Ben went silent again. The streetlights of the town were coming up ahead. The light was starting to illuminate the inside of the cab. Ben's mouth seemed to be open.

"Are you serious about this?" Ben said, regaining his power of speech a second time. "Or are you coming up with some kind of graduation joke to outdo all the other practical jokes you've pulled?"

"I've never been more serious about anything before in my life," Samuel said. "I figure that at my age, it's time I start getting serious about something beyond the farm. At the moment, she's all I can see in life. She's all the life I can see. She's all the future I see or want."

"What happened in her room up there?!" Ben said, regaining his power of speech a third time. "Did she rope you into marrying her? Is that what was taking you so long? How did she manage to get you so dreamy-eyed in two hours that she ran away with your heart in one direction and your mind went running off in the other direction?!"

"Actually she didn't have anything to do with it," Samuel said. "Actually she had everything to do with it. But marrying her isn't her idea. She never even brought up getting married. It's my idea. I've just got to figure out how to go about talking her into it."

"You just met her a few hours ago," Ben said. "It may have been a really great time, but it was only a short time. How do you tell she's the one for you after so short a time?"

"My father knew that Mother was the one for him the moment he saw her," Samuel answered. "And he was half drunk at the time. He straightened himself up in a flash when he saw Mother for the first time. I was flat-out sober when I saw the girl. Even if I had been drunk, the sight of her would have sobered me up and straightened me out in a moment."

"And now you want to marry her on the basis of a few minutes' look at her and two hours humping away at her in the dark?"

"The lights were on," Samuel said. "She's just as good-looking out of her clothes as she is with them on."

"But, Sam, she's a whore!"

They had crossed onto Main Street in the area under the streetlights.

The illumination made it easier for Samuel to see his friend. In a somewhat more verbally serious and physically tinged replay of what had happened in the parlor, Samuel grabbed Ben by the arm.

"Don't call her that!" Samuel said in a snarled incarnation of his take-charge voice. He pulled Ben toward him slightly. The gesture was more physical than the one in the parlor had been. To Ben, getting between his friend and the girl he had apparently become instantly enamored of was starting to seem as perilous as getting between a bad-tempered mother bear and her cub.

"But, Sam, that's the name girls who do what she does for a living usually end up getting called," Ben said. "If the corset fits, wear it. Or step out of it as the occasion calls for. And it's what girls who step out of their clothing for pay with men get called. They're called … what you don't want me to call her, because she does what girls who do that sort of thing get called. All of polite society is going to call her that. Impolite society calls girls who do what she does by that name. She probably even calls herself … that."

Ben looked quickly around as if to see if anyone was within earshot. Even under the weak streetlights, the night was so dark that he couldn't see the road ahead.

"It don't mean a hill of cow flop what I call her," Ben went on. "The problem is what everybody else is going to call her. Just how do you plan to take her home to your parents? Are you going to waltz in one day all starry-eyed with her in tow, saying, 'Meet my soiled dove sweetheart fiancée, who also happens to be the star performer and top money draw at Mrs. Richardson's bordello'? They'll probably turn blue from asphyxiation from not being able to catch their breath. Your parents will be so mortified, they won't be able to show their faces in town again. Your sister will probably join a convent. Pastor Russell probably won't even be willing to perform the ceremony."

"I'll handle my parents," Samuel said. "They may both be a lot more easygoing and understanding than you give them credit for. After all, my father had to reform himself and straighten himself out to impress Mother. But he had incentive to do it. He did it and won Mother over. The girl I was with will probably win my parents over right away."

The term *a bridge too far* hadn't been coined yet, but that was what it seemed to Ben.

"If Pastor Russell doesn't care to bless our union, I'm not going to let the disapproval of one minister determine who I will or won't spend my life with. If we have to drive all the way to Cincinnati to get married, so be it. I intend to begin my life with her as soon as I can talk her into sharing her life with me. No one pastor or regiment of pastors is going to stand between me and her and between us and our having a life together."

Ben sort of shook his head. Samuel could see the gesture in the light of the streetlamps.

"Whatever she gave you must have been something damned good," Ben said, "'cause you've got it for her something bad."

It was supposed to have been a memorable evening for both of them. It had indeed been memorable for both of them in more than one unexpected serendipitous way. Especially in the light of the subsequent but related events that unfolded later, in his later years, Benjamin Harper had trouble sorting out what the more memorable part of the evening had been for him.

Still discussing the issue, Samuel turned the truck down the side street that Ben's house was located on. Samuel pulled up in front of the door to Ben's house. His parents had left a light on for him.

"There's something you may be overlooking here," Ben said as Samuel stopped the truck. "And I don't mean what the society column in the paper is going to say."

"What's that?" Samuel asked.

"You're as all fired sure as I've ever seen anyone about how much you want to marry that girl," Ben said in a serious voice that befitted his newly minted manhood. "But what makes you so sure that she's going to want to marry you? She's living over there in a house with electricity and a big coal furnace with steam heat in all the rooms. In some ways she's living better than we are. She may not have any desire to throw it all out for love and move to a farmhouse with only one fireplace and a stove for warmth, a house where it can get so cold during winter nights that water freezes in the washbasins. And that's just the start. Right now she's earning good money doing something it sure sounds like she enjoys doing. She's getting paid well to do something that comes natural for a woman—what seems double natural for her. What makes you think that she's going to want to chuck all that and go off and become a farm wife in a farmhouse where she can work her fingers to the bone washing and sewing and sweeping and cleaning all day in a remote house lit by kerosene lamps when she can lie around for a few hours a day doing something that sounds like it sends her into spasms of ecstasy, doing it and get paid for it and then sleeping it off in a warm bed in a warm house? I can see how she may be good enough in bed to make you want to take her into your bed, but I don't think no man may ever be stud stallion enough to make her want to leave what she's got going for her right now in that house. Sex may be her craft and trade, and she's good at her trade, but she doesn't seem like the kind of girl who's going to trade what she's got in that house for sex with you in a drafty farmhouse that she's going to have to clean."

Samuel listened in silence as his friend spoke. Ben's statement was a little more sobering this time around than his superficial pointing out of superficial social problems that Samuel might encounter in trying to turn a practicing prostitute into a respectable wife.

"You seem to think of women through the prism of romanticism," Ben continued. "Or you seem to think that all women see everything through their own lens of romanticism, that all women are motivated by love alone, and that they all go around ready to fall into a romantic swoon when their Prince Charming appears on the horizon. Pretty much by definition whor … ladies who do what the ladies of that house do to earn a living are in it for the money, not for romance. Women like the ones in that house make money satisfying the temptations of men who are willing to spend money on them. They don't tend to get tempted out of their houses for love alone. The only way they leave the money they get from working out of a protected house is if someone comes along who offers them more money on a long-term contract. Robber barons and millionaires keep mistresses as kept women. Farmers can't afford mistresses. They can barely afford feed and grain. You may find your romantic appeal to be quite insufficient to either move her heart or move her out of that house she's been lolling around in, making money doing what she probably enjoys doing, and into your farmhouse for a life of drudgery as a farm wife."

"Being a prostitute can't be nearly as fun or satisfying for a woman as some people make it out to be," Samuel said. "It's got to be wearing on a woman's body. It's got to be twice as wearing on her soul. After enough time, even the money probably turns stale. It's not a real life. Even a prostitute probably secretly longs for a real life with a man who will stay with her for life. I don't think it's romanticism to say that both women and men long for someone faithful and loving to spend their lives with. It's just basic human nature to want a life with someone who'll stay with you and be by your side for life."

"That sounds good in and of itself," Ben said. "But it only works if she's thinking the same as you in all respects. Short of that, you may find that you're talking for yourself and for your wishful thinking more than you're talking for her."

The engine of the truck rattled on.

"I hope you're right. I hope it works out for you. I hope she's thinking the same as you and that she turns out to be everything you're hoping for. But the old saying says not to bite off more than you can chew. I just hope you're not biting off someone who may bite you back."

The night was wearing on. The two boys who had nominally become men that evening said their good nights to each other, promising to keep in touch, even though both of them knew that given the different patterns of their lives, they would not see each other as much as they had in high school. Ben walked into the house, where the light had been left on for him. Samuel turned the truck around and headed out for the country road that led to his home out beyond the town in the darkened countryside.

Out on the open road between the town and Samuel's home, the landscape was not visible in the darkness, but he could see the whole sweep of his future. He had gone into the night figuring he would take one relative step into physical manhood. He had assumed the step would be a small linear step along a rutted path that would look the same ahead after he'd taken that step as it looked behind. Instead, the narrow path had opened suddenly onto a vast and sunlit prairie field of wildflowers and waving grain that stretched out over the horizon. He had stepped from one field of the past over a narrow dirt road onto what he had assumed would be another field, indistinguishable from the one he had crossed over from. Instead he had found himself on the threshold of a glorious and golden city, and he had been handed the keys to the kingdom.

But that night everything in his life had changed. He had come to the house with the low expectation of momentarily holding in his hand a small snippet of what a full life with a woman would be like. Instead he had found himself holding the future in his arms. He had found his future in the girl. The girl was the future. He would make the girl his life. He needed no life beyond the farm and a life with the girl.

The girl held more of a dream of love and life than he had ever dreamed. She was more real to him than every dream he had ever dreamed of a woman. Everything about the girl was more real than he had expected to find in a woman. Even the girl's contrived name was more real to him than other, plainer given names of women. He could live with the girl's name. He could live a life with the girl. He could live with the girl on his side of life, whatever side of life she had come from, whatever side of life she had been driven to by life. He could live with all that the girl was, whatever side of respectability the girl came from.

Even his friend's suggestion that the girl might possibly be mercenary to the core had only cast a momentary and superficial pall over Samuel's exulted feeling of life unfolding and horizons opening. In his heart, Samuel didn't believe that in her heart, any woman really enjoyed being a whore. He had always assumed that for a woman, prostitution was a last option when there were no other options. He would offer Clarinda a lifetime of real options.

As he drove home that night away from Mrs. Richardson's establishment, Samuel continued to assume that prostitution was a last option for a woman, an option that a woman would naturally and instinctively avoid if she were presented with any other option. The girl may have come to the house seeking refuge from a life she felt held no refuge and no future for her. Given that the girl had gone as far as to deny and reject the name she had been given and that her stated desire was to forget her name and cast away from her the name she had grown up with, Samuel figured the girl probably didn't see much in the life she had left behind. He also figured that she hadn't seen much in the way of any place for her in the world. He would provide the option that would move the girl. He would open the door to a far better future and life for her.

The moon had set. Its light was gone, but the stars were out in glory in the clear but dark night. The headlights of the truck only illuminated a short and passing section of road immediately in front of him. The distant scattered light of kerosene lamps coming through the windows of farmhouses occasionally flickered off to the side. In the starry sky above, Samuel saw a picture of the girl's face suspended over the passing landscape hidden beneath in the dark. Her blue eyes seemed to shine with the same light as the stars. The waves of her long, dark hair hung down to where they blended in with and disappeared into the darkened landscape below. In one night he had experienced more visions than he had in all his life up to that point. Whether she was a celestial vision of detached loveliness drifting among the stars or a vision of carnal desire stepping out of a corset next to a sweat-stained bed, the vision was of the girl. She was all the vision Samuel could see. She was all the vision he could want.

The visions hadn't left him. They were still growing in number. They grew in life and in the color of life. Surrounding and amplifying all his visions of life was a newfound zest for life and the expanding possibilities of life that Samuel had never felt before. Ahead of him in the dark was the farmhouse that had been the center of his life up to that night and that would continue to be one of the centers of his life for the rest of his life. It had just been displaced, knocked slightly off to the side, by the suddenly found new center of his life. In what had been the night of his coming into manhood, Samuel had come into a wider life and a wider thrill of life than a simple first-time experience with sex could provide.

Looking through the front windshield of the truck out over the landscape hidden in the darkness, Samuel felt the full coming of his life was just one sunrise away, over the horizon. The full meaning and zest of life would come into its own when the girl came to be with him and came to be his own. When he brought the girl home, the fuller journey of his life would begin—when his life as it should be would begin in full.

The land was still in darkness, but Samuel Martin could see more clearly than he had ever seen. The turnoff to the farmhouse was coming up in the darkness. The headlights of the truck didn't provide all that much illumination. But even in the dark, Samuel would recognize the familiar outline of his home when he came upon it in the distance. Only now he could recognize the outline of two homes. Home was the outline of the familiar farmhouse coming up in the distance, the house and home where he had grown up. Home was the outline of the beautiful but still distant girl who called herself Clarinda. His journey back to his first home would be concluded shortly. His journey to his second home in the girl had only just begun. When both homes were merged together, he would be home for life.

Chapter 4

The squeaking of the wooden floor of the hardware store as he walked toward the door reminded Samuel of the way the wood frame of the girl's bed had squeaked when they had made love on it—commercial love for the girl, surprising and surging love for him. The weight of the fifty-pound box of nails he was carrying with his hand wrapped around the wire that held the top of the wooden nail box on made him think of the grip he had taken on the girl's hips in the throes of their lovemaking, commercial for her, groundbreaking and direction establishing for him. Given that the railroad did not pass through the town, one couldn't quite use the easy analogy and say that Samuel had a one-track mind. But of late everything did seem to make Samuel think of the girl.

Outside, Samuel placed the new hammer and the box of nails in the bed of the truck. On his way out of town, he would stop at the lumberyard and pick up the wood needed for the extensive rebuilding that had to be done to repair the chicken coop. If the old coop grew any more dilapidated than it was now, holes would open up enough to give predatory nocturnal animals easy access to the chickens. Even the feisty Teddy wouldn't be able to counter every raid by foxes and weasels, especially at night.

But it wasn't the layout design of the renovated henhouse that Samuel was turning over in his mind. At the present moment, in his present proximity to Mrs. Richardson's establishment, Samuel was trying to determine in his mind if and how he could detour himself to the house and engage the girl in a second-stage wrestling match and, from there, move her along to the next stage of the life he was planning with her.

As he cranked the truck to life, Samuel debated whether to pay a daytime visit to the house and the girl. It wasn't like he was on a tight schedule and that workmen were waiting for him to bring back the materials for the project so they could start work. He was just laying in supplies. He and his father would start the rebuilding of the henhouse when time and other chores permitted. Samuel did have enough free time to work in another visit to the girl. He also had some cash to spare. He would make his attention to the girl and his intentions toward the girl public in due time, but that time hadn't yet fully come.

The question of whether he should or should not try going to the girl was otherwise answered for him. As Samuel opened the truck door, he looked down the street. On the other side of the street, the door to the laundry opened. A familiar womanly figure with a familiar long train of flyaway black hair emerged through the door. It was unquestionably the girl. Slung over her shoulder and down her back was a large cloth bag tied at the top with a drawrope. The scene made the girl look a bit like a sailor in port carrying his belongings over his shoulder in a wide seabag. Apparently the girl had picked up a load of laundry and was carrying it back to the house.

As Samuel watched, the girl crossed the street to his side. From there she turned the other way and started walking down the sidewalk, away from him. Despite the weight of the bulky-looking laundry bag, the girl moved quickly with the lithe speed of a teenager. To Samuel it looked like the girl was heading toward one of the side streets that ran perpendicular to Main Street. Apparently the girls of the Richardson house were familiar with side streets.

But he had to get moving before the unexpected girl and his unexpected opportunity slipped away from him. Any minute she might turn and disappear down a side street. If she reached the end of the street and headed out across open ground, he would be able to follow her in the truck. His chance that day could vanish with the quick-moving mercurial girl. The truck engine was running. Samuel tossed the crank into the cab and climbed in. The truck was pointing in the direction the girl was walking. Quickly working the pedals that shifted the truck into drive, he headed out down Main Street, hugging the side of the street the girl was walking on.

The truck didn't have one of the classic *aaaoooogggaah* horns, but it did have a squeeze ball horn mounted on the left front fender just beyond the door. As he pulled up alongside the girl, Samuel squeezed the rubber horn ball several times in rapid succession.

"Hey, Clarinda!" he shouted through the open window of the truck as he blew the horn.

The girl startled noticeably at the unexpected sound and the approach. With both hands still holding the drawrope on the laundry bag, she stopped and quickly turned her head around to face him. She kept the rest of her body facing forward as if she were preparing to run. The expression on her face was the same indeterminate look she had when he had slapped her on her behind at the conclusion of their lovemaking three nights earlier. Her expression seemed at the same time to be surprised, unsure, and slightly frightened.

"Hi, Clarinda," Samuel called out jauntily as he applied the brake. The truck squeaked to a stop. "Remember me from Friday night?"

For a moment the girl stood silent with a blank expression on her face.

"Ah … yeah … I remember you," she said, regaining her composure. Her blank look switched to one of recognition as she now realized she was looking at a familiar face, if in only commercial terms of familiarity. "You're about the only one I've had who's my own age. I remember that. And I remember you."

"Are you going someplace?" Samuel asked.

The girl was silent for a short moment.

"Ah, I was headin' back to the house with a load of clean laundry Mrs. Richardson sent me to pick up."

"Hop in," Samuel said in his take-charge voice. "I'll give you a lift back to the house. It beats walking all the way back."

The girl looked at the truck. "In that?" she asked. Her tone sounded a bit uncertain.

"It may be a farm truck," Samuel said, "but it gets you there reliably."

Samuel started to wonder whether the girl had ever ridden in a motorized vehicle before. If she was from the mountains or from deep country somewhere, she might not have ever ridden in anything run by an engine. The girl definitely wasn't a virgin sexually. She was the courtesan who had initiated him into the wider world of lovemaking. If he was about to give the girl her first experience riding in a mechanical transport, then at least in one sense they would be equal.

"Is this the first time you've ever ridden in a car?"

"Well, before I came to the Richardson house, I ain't ridden in anything with a motor in it," the girl said, "unless you count hoppin' a freight train. When I first came to the house, Mrs. Richardson took me to see the doctor in her car. My knees and other parts of me were still pretty banged up from jumpin' off a freight train. They hadn't healed all the way and needed fixin'. Now that I'm healthy and my legs work right again, I can walk into and around in town. I never rode in an auto until I got here. I still haven't ridden in no truck yet."

"It doesn't ride any different than an auto," Samuel said. Actually the suspension was a bit stiffer.

"You won't have to walk bent over carrying that bag like an old Negro toting a bale of cotton on his back. Come on. I'll give you a lift."

The girl's face brightened a bit. "Ah, sure," she said.

After Samuel had opened the passenger's-side door from the inside, the girl walked around the front of the truck and climbed into the front seat next to him. She hefted the laundry bundle onto her lap and pulled the door closed on her own. Then she sat holding the bag in her lap with both arms wrapped around it, pulling it up against her chest. Samuel didn't know if she had meant anything symbolic or expressive by the way she held the bag, but at that moment, all Samuel could think of was the girl's bare arms wrapped around his back, her bare chest pulled up next to his, and her full lips about to close over his.

Samuel turned the truck around in a hard U-turn and headed down the brick-paved street toward the side road that ran out to the house. As of that day, the dirt track road that ran to the Richardson house ended at the house. It would not be until several decades later, when the area became a commercial zone, that the road would be paved and extended to loop back into town.

"It looks like you have to do chores at your house the same as has to be done at a farmhouse," Samuel said by way of making small talk as he straightened the truck out and headed down Main Street. He figured that he was taking a chance that someone might see him driving the girl around in the family truck. Rumors could start spreading from there. But Samuel intended to start his life with the girl that day. If someone saw him squiring the girl around, and if the story of who he planned to make his life partner started that day from his being seeing with the girl in the truck, then so be it.

"Of course we do chores like everyone else," the girl answered. "We don't just lie around that house on our backs all night and day doing what we do to make a living. The house would grow real messy real fast if that's all we did. Since I'm younger and spryer, they send me into town to pick up things."

Samuel wondered if the girl meant that as a professional pun. The women of the house were known to come into the town and do direct soliciting in the two local saloons.

"Today I'm picking up the laundry. Our clothes get dirty just like everyone else's clothes. Even when we're not in them." The girl touched the full cloth bag sitting on her lap. "I've got some of our clothes in here, but what's in here is mostly sheets. That's where the difference is. Our sheets get soiled faster than usual family sheets do, unless you lie down on yours after mucking out a stall."

As far as soiled clothing went, the girl wasn't wearing her corset or anything deliberately calculated to be provocative. She was wearing a very plain and standard-looking going-to-do-chores everyday dress. Nothing about the dress was designed to specifically focus on her natural shape or enhance her figure, and from the lack of bulges and ridges showing through her dress, it was clear that she wasn't wearing a waist-cinching and chest-expanding corset underneath it. But her womanly figure enhanced her plain dress and stretched the upper seams while it pushed the limits of the dress's strength. It also pushed the girl's figure deep into the territory of full-grown womanhood. To Samuel, the girl would have looked beautiful and sensual dressed in a feed and grain sack.

"Do you get into town often?" Samuel asked, continuing his casual banter.

"Two, three times a week," the girl answered. "It depends."

"I've never seen you in town," Samuel commented. "If you get into town that much, I wonder why I haven't seen you around before."

"I ain't been here in town all that long," the girl said. "I just came into town a little under a year ago. If you're a farmer who's livin' way outside town, you probably get into town even less than I do. You may have missed me. We probably just had our backs to each other goin' our own ways in our own different directions."

The truck engine rattled. The rubber tires thumped in a fast-paced staccato as they rolled over the brick paving blocks of the downtown section of Main Street. On the corner, Mr. Kindelspire was sweeping off the front stoop of his restaurant and soda fountain. He looked up and watched them pass.

"Well, it's not like I get into town only once in a blue moon," Samuel said. "Up till this June, I was in town every weekday going to high school. But the school's over on the far side of town from here. I guess I was in class when you were in town those times. I just graduated about a week ago. What with school being over and me taking over more responsibilities on the farm, I suppose I won't be in town as much." Samuel looked over at the girl. "Except to see you. Now that I know you're here and now that I know the way."

Samuel remained looking at the girl. She looked at him, her soft face framed by the long black tresses of her hair. Her disarming soft beauty prompted a disarming confession on Samuel's part.

"The night I met you at the house, me and my friend had just come from sneaking off from our graduation dance with the intent of coming to your house. We were both looking to lose our virginity and become men that night. We got it done for the both of us."

Samuel turned his head back to look at the road ahead.

"That night was the first time for both of us. If I gave you any impression that I was experienced, it was a false impression. In that sense you're one up on me. So if you want to laugh at me for being wet behind the ears and being a first-timer, I guess you can."

The girl still looked at Samuel. The expression on her face did not shift or change.

"Now why would I laugh at you?" she said in a coy and diplomatic tone. "Everybody's got to start sometime and someplace at some age." She turned her head around and looked out the windshield. "At least you got to pick where, when, and how you got started and how old you were and how big you were when you started out. You had a good time, and you walked away with a pleasant memory and a smile on your face. You got the chance to wait till you were big enough to do your first time in a way that was pleasant for you. That's more than I can say."

Samuel didn't know if the girl was responding kindly to his confession of his loss of virginity at her more experienced hands because she was a naturally easygoing and sympathetic person or if she didn't want to discourage and drive away someone who had stated his intent to become a repeat customer. Either way, his appreciation of the girl went up a notch up higher. His love for her went one step farther.

When they arrived at the Richardson house, there were no other vehicles in evidence or any male customers coming or going through the door. As he pulled the truck to a stop with the engine still running, Samuel turned to the girl. "You don't seem to have any takers this morning," he commented.

"It's a bit early in the day for that," the girl said. "Most of our business comes at night. It gives us a chance to catch up on cleaning the house during the day. The men who patronize us are mostly working during the day and can't break away."

The girl looked at Samuel directly.

"But even when you're not married and sneaking around on your wives, you men just seem to need the dark when it comes to comin' to a place like this. It's like you're ashamed to be seen doin' what you're not ashamed to spend your money on doin'. That don't make no sense neither. You go to the horse racetrack and gamble in broad daylight, and there's no guaranteed payout like we give you for your money. You shoot dice in broad daylight, you shoot each other with guns in broad daylight, you fight wars in broad daylight, you break each other's heads with pickax handles in broad daylight. You do all sorts of mean and hateful things in broad and open daylight, but when it comes to makin' something that looks a bit like love, you feel the endless need to go sneakin' around behind closed doors in the night to do it. Why in your whiskey-sozzled brains do you young men do what you do? Especially with women?"

"I don't know the reasons men do what they do when they do it," Samuel said in a voice changing to sound coy, "but whether it's morning, noon, or night, do you think you could fit me into your schedule now? Or is your morning time taken up with doing house chores?"

The girl kind of smiled coyly herself for a moment. Her hair fell partially over one of her eyes like it had the night he had met her in the parlor of the house they were outside of now.

"We're open for business primarily at night," the girl said in her own coy voice. "But there are no rigid, set hours. In the morning and during the day, we do chores just like you farmers do. I don't have any more chores set to be done after I drop off and pick up the laundry. Doin' what you want to be doin' is my main chore at the house. If you want, I can fit you in now. I'm sure Mrs. Richardson won't give no never mind to it."

The girl reached for the door handle, opened the door, and climbed into the cab next to Samuel. She set the laundry bundle on her lap.

"Drive us there. At least that's part of the way I won't have to walk. I'm wearing my feet out walking into town."

It was what Samuel wanted all right. But at the same time he felt there should be more to it than that. At the moment, he felt that something wider and more significant than a mere commercial transaction should happen between them and pass between them. He wanted a wider life with the girl. He wanted to do something more with the girl that day, something beyond sex alone, something that looked and felt like real courting.

"I'll tell you what," Samuel said. He touched the steering wheel of the truck. "Before we get down to that, if you'd like I'll take you for a drive around the area and show you some of the sights."

The girl was silent and uncertain for a moment at the unexpected offer. Then her face brightened. "Yeah," she said, "I'd like that. All I've seen since I got to this town has been the house and the two bars in the town. Except to walk into town on errands, I don't get out hardly at all. I'll go along with you. Just don't run us off into a ditch." The girl touched the laundry bag on her lap. "Before we go, I've just got to drop this off in the house."

Together they drove off.

When they arrived at the house, the girl quickly turned the door handle and opened the truck door.

"I'll be right back," the girl said as she jumped out of the cab. "Don't go nowhere on me."

She sprinted off athletically toward the house with the bundle over her shoulder. The bulkiness of the bag didn't seem to slow her down. When she reached the door, she opened it with a quick turn of the knob. Then she disappeared inside, leaving Samuel sitting alone in the truck.

For a moment Samuel wondered if the girl had pulled a fast one in order to get away from him. He didn't know if she would be coming back out. But after only a short while, the girl reappeared at the door. Sprinting back to the truck even faster than she had left, she climbed back in. Without the large laundry bag to block his view, Samuel could get a better view of the full curve of her womanly figure. For a moment the sight of the girl's full and swelling figure made him sort of regret that he hadn't taken her up to her room right away. But he wanted her to come to think of him as something more than just another commercial customer who came to her on off-hours. Showing the girl the wider world was the first step in showing her that he had a wider interest in her.

The truck motor was running, and so was the motor of Samuel's imagination. He put the truck in gear. Together, the no longer innocent farm boy and the soiled drove back down the road that led away from the house toward the edge of town. As he passed the lumberyard, Samuel made a mental note that after he had concluded the day with the girl, he would have to stop by on his way out and pick up the wood needed to rebuild the henhouse. At the same time he also made a mental note to himself to think up an excuse as to why a simple purchase of hardware and lumber had taken so long.

"That's the town cemetery over there," Samuel said, pointing off to the left as they passed the cemetery. He wasn't sure why he pointed out the cemetery, but he had promised to show the girl the local sights, and it was the nearest landmark to the town.

"My grandparents and great-grandparents are buried in there. Our family was one of the first families to pioneer and settle in this town."

Samuel didn't say what he had because he had a morbid fascination with cemeteries. Telling the girl that his ancestors had been some of the first settlers in the area was his way of informing her in a backhanded way that his family was an established family in the town, without coming across as braggy or snooty about it.

"I saw it when I first came into town," the girl said with a flat tone. "It was the first sight that caught my eye when I came over the bridge."

"It is kind of the first sight you see on the way into town from the east," Samuel said. He was otherwise wondering what it was that had set a young teenage girl out on the road alone.

"Graveyards have been some of the first sights in all my memory," the girl said in the same flat and hollow tone. "One of the first memories I have in life is bein' in a graveyard and seein' my mother in a box bein' lowered by ropes into her grave. I was probably less than three years old at the time. I don't remember the graveyard. I don't remember any of the sights in it. All I remember was the box my mama was in and the hole beneath that she was being lowered into. I couldn't see her, but I knew she was nailed up in the box. I also knew I wouldn't see her ever again in this world. Half of me wanted to crawl into that box with her and cry on her chest for the rest of eternity. The other half of me wanted to turn and run as fast and hard as I could. But I had a hand holdin' mine so tight and holdin' my arm up high so high that I couldn't move a step."

"I'm sorry that your mother died and that you were so young when it happened," Samuel said. "I didn't mean to bring up bad memories for you."

"My memories are what they are," the girl said in a flat, fatalistic voice. "I can't change them, and I'm not going to deny them. I just don't want to go 'round runnin' through them in my mind by runnin' 'round in a graveyard. I just hope you're not planning on stopping off here sayin' a piece over the graves of your ancestors and takin' me in with you. Draggin' me into a graveyard would kinda get things off on the wrong foot between the two of us."

Getting off his feet with the girl was Samuel's eventual intention for that day. Getting off on the wrong foot with her was definitely not what he was intending to do.

"Don't worry," Samuel said in his definite tone. "I wasn't planning on dragging you into a cemetery. I brought you out here to show you a land that's full of life. I didn't bring you out here to revisit death."

Samuel said no more about graveyards. He drove the truck over the bridge, past the cemetery, and out into the expanding countryside.

It was another bright early summer day, warm but not sweltering. With the exception of a few thin and wispy high-altitude clouds, the sky was clear. On either side of them the land was a country quilt pattern of the varying greens of different crops. A wind was stirring from behind them. The breeze blew softly but would suddenly rush up into quick random gusts. The stronger gusts coming in through the open windows sent the girl's long hair flying. She pulled the hair away from her face with her fingers and continued to look around. Samuel offered to stop and pull the side windows up to keep out the wind and the dust of the road. The girl answered that she was used to the taste of dust in her mouth and that she liked the feel of the wind on her face.

Not far outside of town on the road that led away from town, they came upon the field where a mare and her foal, which had been startled by the approach of the truck, had stood when Samuel had driven past on his way into town a week earlier. The mare and her foal were standing in the same spot they had been standing, next to the fence, when Samuel had refrained from honking the horn so as not to further frighten the newborn foal. The foal was a little bigger today than it had been at that time. It was starting to look more like the young colt it was turning into.

"That's the Peterson's riding mare," Samuel said as they approached. "She dropped her foal not long ago."

The quietly reserved girl suddenly came alive. She grabbed Samuel's arm with both her hands. "Stop," she said. Her voice sounded breathless. "I want to get out and see them close up."

"They don't know you," Samuel said as he slowed the truck. "They're probably skittish around strangers, especially a mare with a young foal. They may just bolt and run away if you get close to them."

But the girl seemed insistent on stopping and getting out. She already had her hand on the door handle. Samuel steered the truck off the road and stopped on the grass strip between the road and the fence. The girl jumped out quickly and headed toward the horse and her foal. Samuel figured that the girl didn't know the first thing about horses and that she was thinking of them like newborn puppies that she wanted to pet as they lay squirming in a basket instead of semiwild creatures with the whole of an open field to escape into. By Samuel's estimate, the mare and her foal would probably take off at a gallop before the girl got halfway to them.

As she approached them, the girl slowed down from a run to a walk. The mare snorted and bobbed her head. As the girl came within reach, she held out one hand and let the mare sniff it. As the girl came the rest of the way up to the mare, she gently put one hand on the mare's long snout above her nose. She cupped her other hand under the mare's chin, beneath her mouth. The girl cooed to the mare in a soft voice as she stroked the mare's nose.

"There now, see, there's nothin' to be 'fraid of from me." The mare snorted again and shifted position but did not break and run. The horse might have been naturally friendly to people because of her familiarity with them. Then again, Samuel figured she might have a natural instinct that told her the girl was not a danger. The foal stood off to the side and behind her mother at an angle, watching.

"You're not afraid of me, are you?"

Samuel came around from the other side of the truck and walked up slowly. Having been shown up by the girl that she did know how to approach horses, he didn't want to play the rube and spook the mare that the girl had successfully made contact with. That the girl liked horses and possibly all farm animals was a good sign to Samuel. It might be that the girl just loved animals and had a natural instinct for to approach them. But that the girl knew at least the beginnings of how to handle horses suggested that she was a country girl as her accent had led him to suspect. Possibly she had been a farmer's daughter before whatever misfortune or circumstance of life had sent her out on the road and into the nonpastoral profession she now practiced.

That the girl might be a displaced and diverted farm girl was an encouraging thought to Samuel. If she had started out as a farm girl, before she had been sidetracked into becoming a lady of the evening, it might be only a small step for her to return to her roots and become a farm wife. If the girl was a farm girl at heart, a warm and loving heart might be able to win her back to life on a farm, a life with him. For both him and her it would be coming home all around.

"We have plow horses on our farm," Samuel said as he came up alongside the girl. If the girl liked horses as she seemed to, he hoped to plant a small seed by letting her know that his family had horses on his farm too.

"They're a different breed. Percherons. But they're as friendly and easy to get along with as this one is."

At the same time Samuel hoped to plant the seed of thought in the girl's mind that he was easy to get along with too.

Instead of turning her head toward him at the sound of his voice, the girl turned and looked at the foal. "And you're not afraid of me either, are you?" she said to the foal. She held out a hand toward the creature. The foal had been at least partially reassured by its mother's lack of fear of the strangers it had never seen before, but it still seemed suspicious and skittish. The foal shook its head in imitation of its mother and whinnied. It moved in a few steps closer to its mother's side and to the girl, but not close enough to where the girl could reach and touch it.

"Now you're a young one," the girl said to the foal. "He looks to be no more than a month old," she said to Samuel while she looked at the foal.

"You're right about his age," Samuel said, impressed by the girl's ability to judge the age of newborn horses. Being able to tell the age of a foal by looking at it is not something that most city girls can do right off the tops of their heads. It was another bit of evidence that the girl had come from country stock somewhere.

"The first time I saw them out together was about three weeks ago. She probably dropped her foal a few days before that. You do seem to know your horseflesh."

"I'm in the flesh business," the girl said with a flat tone. "It's just not the horseflesh business. I do get my share of horse's asses, though."

The girl continued to look at the foal. "Who's your daddy?" she asked the foal rhetorically. "Where's your daddy? I don't see him out here in the field with the two of you, stickin' close around here and lookin' after you the way your mama is."

The foal looked back at the girl. He shook his head and developing mane again.

"I don't know who the sire was," Samuel said. "It was probably a stud they brought in."

"You mean that they paid to bring in," the girl said flatly, again without looking up at Samuel. Instead she looked into the face of the mare. "That's the difference between her profession and mine." The girl went on speaking to Samuel while looking at the mare. "At least in my profession it's the stud male who does the payin'. I guess that's something of an equalizin' of things. For humans at least."

The girl stroked the sides and top of the mare's head.

"In her world, it's the stud who gets to walk away after havin' himself a good time and who gets paid for his labors in doin' it, while she's the one who's left behind to go into labor. The male don't take no responsibility for that which he starts out in the world."

"A brought-in sire doesn't have much choice in the matter of raising his offspring," Samuel said. "The breeder takes him back right after he's done. The stud couldn't take responsibility even if he was of a mind to do so. That's the difference between free men and horses."

"Which don't make the two so different after all," the girl said brittlely. "Maybe it's people who make it that way with domestic stock horses, but it's no different or better with males in the wild. Out there, the biggest male stallion kicks all the other stallions in the face and drives them away so that he can have all the fillies to himself. After he gets his team all pregnant, he walks around pleased with himself, snorting with his tail in the air. Then he stands off and eats grass while the mares do the work of birthin' and raisin' the young ones by themselves. Males in the wild don't take no more responsibility for the young they sire than barnyard males do."

"I suppose that's the way it's been with horses since the Lord made horses," Samuel said.

"I don't think the Lord don't have nothin' much to do with that kind of behavior in animals or humans," the girl said. "It's just the nature of males in the wild. And actin' wild and irresponsible don't stop with horses in the wild. Give a human male half an excuse or a quarter of an opportunity to act wild, and he'll do the same thing, taking off for the open road or the nearest bar and leaving his family in the lurch. At least women like me earn a livin' off men passing wild. We get the benefit of both their money and the fact that they're passing by, not staying around long enough to do us harm."

The girl didn't say anything more. Neither did Samuel. He walked the last step up to the mare, leaned against the fence, and started rubbing the side of the mare's neck as the girl stroked her head and mane. The still suspicious-looking foal stood back the same distance he had stopped at and looked at them. After a few more minutes, Samuel and Clarinda left the horses and walked back to the truck with its motor running. Samuel turned the truck back onto the road, and they started on their way again. The sky was open from horizon to horizon. The horizon was open in all directions. Samuel could have taken any number of the country roads around toward any given horizon, but to him there was only one ultimate horizon. All the roads of his mind led to that horizon. He would take the girl past that horizon that day. Someday in the future he would take her there to stay.

They followed a winding path past the farms along the road. Presently they passed by the farm that was Samuel's home. He pointed off in the direction of the fields and at the farmhouse set back from the road.

"This land here is our family's farm," Samuel said as he swung his pointing hand around to give the girl the sense of the sweep of the land. He used the word *our* instead of the singular possessive as a way of delivering a subtle hint to the girl that she could be part of all that he was showing her.

"We've farmed this land for three generations up through my father. I'm the fourth generation on the land. I'll be taking over the farm from my father one day. I intend to stay on the farm and start up the fifth generation of Martins to live on the farm and work the land."

The girl looked around attentively as the fields passed by. As he spoke, Samuel emphasized the continuity of his family's presence on the land. It was an indirect way on his part of showing the girl that his family was established. He also wanted to emphasize that, unlike his uncle Ned, whom he did not mention, he was solid and dependable, and he intended to take responsibility and stay on the land.

"I don't see my father in the field," Samuel went on, turning his head as if looking for his father. "He's probably working in the barn. He taught me how to plow and plant as well as he knows how. I do as much of the farm work as Father does. Now that I'm out of school, I'll be taking over an increasing percentage of the work on the farm. I have work to start later in the day. After I pick up the lumber, I'll be helping Father rebuild the henhouse."

Samuel wanted to emphasize that he was a hard worker who came from a hardworking family that could provide for its members.

"Mother's probably in the kitchen. She's a good soul. Works hard.

Loves everybody. I don't know where my younger sister is. She's out of school for the summer now. She can be a bit of a snot at times, but she's a good kid once you get to know her and she gets to know you."

As they passed the farm, Samuel went into a quick and passing history of the Martin family on the land. In a relatively quick time as they passed, he spoke of his family quite a bit, but he did not offer to take the girl to meet his family. Putting his parents' actual reaction to the girl to the test would have to wait until another time, after the ground had been better prepared.

"I'd take you in and introduce you to everyone," Samuel said as they passed the dirt drive leading up to the farmhouse. "But I don't think Mrs. Richardson would like me keeping you out that long."

"I think you'd better forget the idea of introducing me to your family entirely," the girl said with emphasis. "Now or ever. I don't think your mama would be at all happy about you bringin' a girl like me home for supper. I'd probably leave the house hearin' words like *tramp, hussy, trash,* and *slut* thrown at my back."

"You'd be surprised at how my mother might react," Samuel said.

"I don't want to be surprised or appraised like that no more," the girl said. "Better just forget takin' me into your house. Just drive me back to Mrs. Richardson's. That's the nearest thing I've ever had to a home. Nearest thing I'll probably ever find to a home."

"I mean you might find Mother a whole lot more easy to get along with and ready to accept you than you think," Samuel said in a voice deliberately laced with confidence. "She can put a whole lot more than you think behind her if the person's willing to put what they've been doing behind them. Being a bit wild and soiled doesn't necessarily mean that Mother's going to shut you off and out right away. She can see beyond the surface of a person and see what they're really like and can be like. My father was half wild-eyed drunk when he ran into Mother. But that didn't stop Mother from liking him and accepting him, after he put his drinking ways behind him, which he was willing to do in order to win her hand."

As the turnoff to the farmhouse fell away behind them and the fields of the Martin farm came to an end, Samuel recited for the girl the story his father had related to him of how he had met his mother. The girl listened in polite silence with an attentive but uncertain expression on her face.

She continued to look around at the landscape passing by outside while Samuel recounted the family story. He did mention the name of his uncle Ned, who had left his home and gone on the road, reaching a dissolute's end. Samuel didn't want the girl to think he came from a family where men left like the girl seemed to think that all men did.

They were driving through a wooded area between farms, traversing a natural feature of the landscape known as Reynold's Gorge. Reynold's Gorge wouldn't have been classified as a gorge in more mountainous lands that had real precipitous gorges, but in the local area it was the only thing around that passed for a gorge. It was actually a relatively narrow and not all that deep gully, about an eighth of a mile wide and not more than seventy feet deep, that had been cut over the ages by the small stream that flowed along the bottom. The road wound downward on a sloping curve into the bottom of the gully, where a rickety wood-framed bridge crossed the stream. Samuel had to shift into a lower gear and slow the truck on the curve. At the bottom they crossed the bridge over the stream. The wooden slats of the bridge rattled as if the boards had been worked loose.

As they were driving up the far side of the slope, a large female deer darted out of the woods on one side of the road. A less than yearling fawn followed close behind her. The two deer sprinted across the road in front of the truck. On the opposite side of the road, they went partway into the woods and then stopped and turned to look at Samuel and Clarinda.

The deer was a large doe. The small fawn still had the bright and mottled pattern of a recently gestated fawn. The fawn stopped and looked at Samuel and Clarinda like her mother was doing. Clarinda grabbed Samuel's right arm with her left hand. "Slow down," she said. "I want to see them."

Samuel slowed the truck to a crawl. At what the doe apparently assumed to be a relatively safe distance, she and her fawn stood watching them. From the distance, the large eyes of the doe seemed an impenetrable dark brown. The doe stood almost completely motionless. The fawn stood motionless too, except for the twitching of its tail and ears.

"No use getting out," Samuel said as he brought the truck to a near-stop. "They aren't going to let you get close to them the way the Petersons' horse and foal did."

The girl seemed to have known that even before he'd told her. She hadn't made any move to open the truck door. She only leaned her arm on the open window. For several moments she looked in silence at the mother and child deer. The doe looked back at them with her unblinking large eyes.

"They have such beautiful big eyes," the girl commented. She spoke in a hushed tone as if not to spook the animals. At the moment, Samuel would have liked to look deeply into the girl's large blue eyes, but she had the back of her head turned to him as she watched the deer. From the way she was reacting, it almost seemed as if seeing the deer was a magic moment for the girl. Samuel figured that it might well indeed be a magic moment for her in a life that hadn't held a lot of magic moments.

"But I guess they need big eyes out in the woods in order to see wolves sneakin' up on them," the girl said, "and human hunters comin' after them with guns, and dogs lookin' for venison."

The doe turned quickly and bounded off into the woods with her fawn close behind.

"That's a good idea, mama," the girl called after them in a louder voice. "Run off into the woods and hide. Take your baby with you. Stay in the deep woods. You'll be safer there than you'll ever be livin' 'round us humans. We'll just shoot you, and skin you, and put your hide on the floor, and put your head on a wall and your meat on a table, and leave your baby to starve without you."

"That wasn't a whitetail," Samuel started to say in his country boy informative way. "That was a—"

"Mule deer," the girl interjected. "You can tell because they don't have a white tail. They're also bigger than whitetails, and their head is a different shape. It all makes them look more like a mule than a deer. That's where they get the name from. Her fawn looks to be even younger than the foal. She's still got her fawn coat, and she ain't got her legs quite working all together yet. I'd say she's no more than two weeks old. She's probably still nursing from her mama."

Once again the girl demonstrated a detailed country knowledge that would have escaped a girl raised in the city. It only confirmed for Samuel that Clarinda was a country girl. At least she had come from someplace where the people still had game on the hoof. He resolved to learn the girl's roots and where in the country she had come from.

Before Samuel could question the girl about her point of origin, she turned to him with her own question. It was an accusatory statement more than a question: "I suppose you're a big hunter who gets your jollies by goin' 'round blasting mama deer like her and leavin' their babies without their mothers' milk."

Suddenly Samuel felt like the one in the girl's sights. The icy tone of the girl's voice and her phraseology gave him the distinct impression that she did not like hunters one little bit, especially ones who go after doe deer. He was a hunter of sorts. It would be lying to flat-out deny it. Samuel decided that minimizing would be the best strategy.

"Well, me and Father have done some hunting," Samuel said in a dismissive tone as he accelerated the truck. "But we hunt game birds mostly. I have been deer hunting a few times, but only for buck. We never shoot does."

"I suppose you've got trophy heads all over your parlor walls," the girl said. "You men just can't seem to keep from killin' somethin' just to prove to yourselves and demonstrate to yourselves and anyone who cares to listen that you're men. You especially show off that way for girls. But don't go draggin' me to your home showin' me the heads on your trophy wall. That kind of manly hooey don't impresses me none."

"We've got one pair of antlers over the fireplace," Samuel said defensively. "It's from a trophy buck that Grandfather took a long time ago. But that's all. I don't do a lot of hunting now. I've got too many responsibilities on the farm that have to be looked after. I don't have much time for diversions like hunting."

What Samuel had said about the deemphasis of hunting in his life was more or less true. He had phrased his statement about the farm's taking up most of his time as both a way to show that he didn't go hunting all that much and to make himself look like a solid and responsible provider at the same time. But he couldn't deny that he had been hunting. The girl didn't seem to like the idea of hunting at all. She also seemed to identify with animals in the wild, especially animals with young. He could especially see how a girl cut off from her home like she was might identify with a doe running through the woods alone.

It was starting to seem like he might have to give up hunting if he wanted to win the girl's affections and her hand for life. He did like a good hunt now and then, but if he had to give up hunting to win the girl, it was a small sacrifice he was willing to make.

The girl leaned back on the seat.

"Well, I suppose that if you have to hunt, I guess that huntin' bucks is a little better than huntin' does. It's not like a fawn loses its daddy. A dead buck's no big loss to any deer family. Mostly because there aren't deer families any more than there are horse families. Buck deer are like stallion horses. They just get the doe pregnant and then they don't pay no never mind to helping to raise and look after what they produce. They're just up and gone on to the next doe."

"I suppose it's been that way since the Lord made deer as well as He made horses," Samuel said.

"You mean it's been that way since God made the world and then tossed it off over His shoulder and left it up for grabs," the girl said as the truck reached the top of the rise. In a short distance the strip of woods along the stream opened up into another farm field.

"As soon as God dropped the world, the devil grabbed hold of it and ran away with it. The devil's been runnin' with it and runnin' the place his way since then. The devil's the one who filled the world up with predators. Wolves with teeth, and mountain lions with claws, and feral hogs with tusks, and human hunters with their spears, bows, and guns are the devil's doin', not God's. I just blame God for lettin' the devil have his way with His creation for so long and so total-like."

Samuel considered that he was certainly getting quite a dose of the girl's homespun, or brothel-spun, philosophy. But just where had the home that had spun her personal theology been located?

"You were right about the deer and the horse and foal," the take-charge Samuel said in an attempt to change the subject of the conversation and bring it around to the direction he wanted to take it. "That's stuff that countryfolk know. When you talk, you sure don't sound like a proper Boston lady or a big-city girl."

"I ain't a proper lady from nowhere," the girl said. "Why should I sound like a proper anything from anywhere?"

"I mean you sound like you're from the country," Samuel said. "You don't talk like a city girl. You sound like you came to the house from the country."

"Well now, I guess it's been that way since the Lord of this world made brothels," the girl said, looking straight ahead at the road in front of them. "Country girls on the loose or on the run go to work in country brothels. City girls stick with their own on the streets they grew up on. Country girls on the run go afield anywhere someone will take them in."

"Then you are from the country?" Samuel asked.

"Yeah, I'm from the country," the girl half snapped. "What of it?"

"I'd like to know where you come from in the country."

The girl turned her head partially toward him. "You don't need to know none of where I come from in the country any more than you need to know my name," the girl said with a rising tinge of annoyance in her voice. "You're not comin' to me for my genealogy. You don't need to know one inch where I come from. And don't tell me you're interested in knowing who my ancestors were. The only thing you're interested in is where you can find me when you have an itch you want me to scratch."

"I'd kind of like to know something about your background," Samuel said in an otherwise nondemanding, nonprying voice.

"You're not comin' to the house or me lookin' for background," the girl said with the same edge to her voice. "You're comin' to me to get me on my back."

"I just wanted to know something about where you come from and who your family are," Samuel said.

The modern parlance would have it: "Bad move, Sam."

"Don't ask me about my family," the girl said with a rising tone like a steel trap snapping. "Not now or ever. My family's not somethin' I'll be asked about by you. That's not somethin' I'll share with you or any man. Along with my name."

Samuel was caught up short and surprised by the girl's unexpected reaction. He quickly grew alarmed by the snap in her voice.

"I didn't mean anything by it," Samuel said in a confused tone. "I just thought—"

"Think any thought you want," the girl said sharply. She brought her head a little more around toward him. "Think any thought you want about me. Girls like me get paid to be thought of as what we are as much we get paid to do what we do. I'll give you that as my due for what I am. But no more. Don't make me think or talk about my family."

129

Farmers have a natural sense for when they've stepped into a cow pie. In a later phase of his life, Samuel would use the analogy of stepping into a minefield.

"I have no need of a past or a family that had no need for me when I was part of it or that cared nothin' for me when I was livin' in it. I live apart from my past. I live my life as I live it. I like my life just fine now. I live my life without the name I had in the past. For me the past is as deaf to me as the people in the graveyard you wanted to drag me through. My past don't have nothin' to do with me or what I am now. My past don't make me nothin' no more. I'll make myself what I will. No man makes me what I am or tells me what to be. That includes you."

Samuel Martin didn't want to get off on another wrong foot with the girl, especially the wrong foot that she apparently considered to be either the first step to a long and painful march into the past or the last step of a pain-filled march she had already sloughed through and that she wanted to put in the past and leave buried.

"I do what I do because I decide to. Nobody makes me do it, not even at the house. If you don't want to get off on the wrong foot with me, don't go about trying to get me to talk about my past. Making me look at a graveyard is the least mistake you can make with me. Trying to make me talk about my past is the real wrong way to go off gettin' on my wrong side. I just walk away from men like that and leave them by themselves by the side of the road."

"It sure didn't seem like I had started out on your wrong side last Friday night," Samuel said, hoping for some carryover from the fact that the girl seemed to like it that he was the same age as her. "You sounded like you were enjoying yourself. As far as starting off on the wrong foot, neither of us knew each other, and both of us were off our feet at the time."

From the way the girl had reacted with him in her bed, she did seem to have been enjoying herself quite intensely. Samuel figured that had to have counted for something with her.

"That was commercial," the girl said. "I turn that on and off on a whim. You're there at the house for a piece of me. You're there for my presence and for what you want out of me in my present. If you try to pry open the hard door to my past, I'll slam the door to my room shut in your face."

Samuel had a vision of the girl turning her back on him and walking away. At that moment she turned on a dime.

"I like you," the unexpected girl unexpectedly said. "I like being out here with you. I like to get out of the house now and then. Gettin' out of the house clears my head. It helps me get my mind off things. But the biggest thing I want to get my mind off of in my life is my family. Makin' me think about my family and my past for one minute will ruin the day for me. And that will ruin the day for you."

Samuel faced the girl. He took both his hands off the steering wheel and waved them apart in a sweeping gesture. Without his hands on the wheel, for a second the truck wavered on the road.

"I promise I won't make you talk about anything you don't want to talk about," Samuel said in a voice as sweeping as his hand gesture. "I won't make you bring up any names from the past that you don't want to hear, and I'll call you Clarinda or any name you want me to call you."

"Whatever you do or don't do, don't run us off the road doin' it," the girl said in alarm as the truck started to drift toward the side of the road. She pointed to the steering wheel.

"If you ever want to put your hands on me again, put your hands back on that wheel. I don't want to be the first brothel house woman in history killed in a truck wreck."

Samuel put one hand on the wheel and straightened the truck.

A lot of proper people of that day might have called wanting to marry a prostitute a counterintuitive move on a young man's part. Samuel suddenly thought of a somewhat counterintuitive idea for how to divert the girl from his mistake in asking about her family.

"Let me show you what this thing can do," he said. Soon enough it would become a stock line that teenage boys in cars would use in an attempt to impress their girlfriends. The technology was a bit limited in Samuel's day, but soon enough it would reach the point where motorized macho male displays would indeed come to leave both teenage boys and teenage girls dead in rolled-over wrecks in ditches. Or dead in the middle of the road inside the more tangled ball of wreckage left from a high-speed head-on collision with alcohol involved.

With one hand on the wheel, Samuel reached up with his free hand and pulled the throttle all the way open. The engine roared to life, as much as an uncarbureted flat-head four-cylinder engine can roar. The girl thought she had gotten the motorized situation under control. Now suddenly she found herself in a 1912 dragster as the truck accelerated. Her eyes opened wide. By modern standards the dragster truck was more drag than not, but from the way the girl's eyes had opened wide, Samuel guessed it was the fastest she had ever gone in her life. But then again, that depended on how one defined a fast girl.

"Hadn't you better slow down?!" the girl said. She was already thinking in terms of winding up on the side of the road with a broken neck. She was thinking of it even more as the truck reached the breakneck speed of thirty miles per hour. The truck with its high center of gravity set on tall wheel rims bounced and swayed on the rutted dirt road. The narrow tires had a rather limited road-hugging capacity to begin with, but the clay and gravel washboard roadbed was an uncertain and unpredictable medium for any set of tires to grip. The hammer and box of nails Samuel had bought at the hardware store clanked and thudded on the metal bed of the truck. The crank bumped on the floorboard near the girl's feet. Fence posts and the trees along the road sped by at a rate making them too fast to count, for people used to counting at a more leisurely pencil-and-paper pace. The girl looked around with growing alarm.

"This thing rocks and teeters worse than that boxcar on an uneven grade," the girl said, fear rising in her voice. "I almost fell out back then. You're goin' to pitch both of us out on our heads!"

"If you don't trust my driving, here, you drive," Samuel said. He took his hands off the wheel, put them behind his head, and leaned back.

The girl gave out a single high-pitched peep. She lunged forward, past Samuel, and grabbed the wheel in a death grip with both hands. Her long hair flew out to the sides and was carried by momentum out in front of her. Instead of steering, the girl pulled back hard on the wheel as if, in her turn-of-the-century country instinct, she was pulling back on the reins of a runaway buggy horse, trying to stop it. At least she hadn't shouted "*Whoa!*"

"How do you stop this thing?!" the girl shouted. Samuel laughed loudly. He grabbed the wheel with one hand. The tug of the girl's hands on the wheel made it difficult for him to steer. With the other hand, he turned the throttle all the way down. The truck slowed down and coasted. Samuel used the brake to bring the truck to a squeaking stop. With the divided twin expanse of farm fields spreading out on either side of them and the unified expanse of open blue sky above them, the truck stood motionless in the middle of the otherwise empty road. The engine rattled. The dust cloud the truck had raised in its relative wild tear down the road drifted past and away from them.

For a moment the girl remained frozen in place, leaning across Samuel with her hands still gripping the wheel. Then suddenly the seemingly paralyzed girl came to life. Her hands, which had been clenching the wheel in a frozen grip, flew off the steering wheel and started beating on his arm in rapid-fire, but otherwise ineffectual, staccato succession.

"Oh you!" the girl shouted at him without completing whatever epitaph she had in mind. "You could have gotten us killed!"

At the feel of his grip, the girl pulled backward as hard as she had pulled on the steering wheel. It was as if it had been an instinctive reaction on her part. The same look of fear snapped into her eyes. Samuel's immediate thought was that she had mistaken his gesture of grabbing her wrists as his being angry with her for hitting him. He immediately released his grip on her arms. To further reassure her, he lowered his hands and leaned back and to the side in his seat.

"Don't go off crazy on me like that again!" the girl said emphatically with a country-tinged accent.

"We weren't in any danger," Samuel said in a calm and reassuring voice. "I know how to handle a truck. I've been driving for years. I would have stopped it before it got out of control."

The girl was still holding her arms up in the position they had been in when Samuel had grabbed her wrists. Loose strands of the girl's long hair hung in front her face.

"Well, don't do that no more. No, never!" the girl said as she caught her breath and lowered her arms. "You may know these things, but I've hardly ridden in one before, especially with a young buck who thinks that actin' like a crazy jackass who thinks scaring the daylights out of a girl is part and parcel of being a man."

It started to dawn on Samuel how badly he had frightened his companion. He certainly did not want to leave her with the memory of a close brush with mortality as the last memory of the day and of him.

Neither did he want to see her walk away, leaving the sight of her walking away as the last sight he would ever have of her.

"I'm sorry," Samuel said in an apologetic tone. "I didn't mean to scare you. I won't do it again. I was just funning around with you."

The girl brushed the strands of hair away from her face with her hand. The look on her face had become composed and controlled. With the same hand, she reached over and took Samuel's hand in hers in the same manner she had when she had taken him in hand in Mrs. Richardson's parlor three nights ago. He felt the same electrical twinge of excitement as he had the first time she had ever touched him.

"See that you don't tease me again like I'm your little sister," the girl said. "Women like me often get to where we end up because of somethin' serious in our lives drove us to go runnin' to where we ended up. We're serious women at our trade. We don't like to be teased like schoolgirls. I like to be teased even less. Take me as a serious woman. Take me as I am or don't take me at all. If you want to play games, play with me the kind of grown woman game I'm well versed at playin'."

In a smooth and take-charge move, Samuel, wrapping his hand around the hand the girl had used to take hold of his, pulled her in close to him. The girl did not tense up or resist the force of his tug. With smooth movement equal to his, the girl fell next to him. Her face stopped close enough for them to be breathing each other's air, her lips only inches from his. In the next instant the girl had moved her lips over to where they were brushing his cheek. She pulled her hand out of his grasp and brought it up to cup the other side of his face. Her long hair fell across his chest.

"If you want to play race and chase so bad," the girl said in a hushed and husky tone, "I know how to run a race with you that's not goin' to kill nobody before we get to the finish line and that's goin' to be a lot less scary for me and a lot more pleasant of a race for both of us to run."

Samuel reached up with his hand, put it on the back of the girl's neck, and pulled her face the last few inches toward his. The girl did not act surprised. Neither did she offer any resistance. Sitting in the cab of the truck, they ran their wet lips over each other's the way they had done during their first kiss while standing next to the girl's bed in the house. The girl was no longer a snotty little sister or a flustered country girl. She was back to being a practiced bordello seductress.

For an extended timeless moment, Samuel and the girl held their movable kiss. The truck engine rattled. The green growing crops around them trembled in the breeze. No other drivers came up behind them to honk their horns and yell for the couple to move on. High above the road a lone nightingale with a long tail turned gracefully on the wind. Some country stories have it that nightingales live their whole lives flying on the wind.

The girl finally broke her kiss and moved her face back from Samuel's face by an inch.

"Where do you want to go now?" Samuel asked. He meant the question to be both geographic and symbolic.

"Well now, I think we should go getting about what you came to me to go on getting about in the first place," the girl said, running one finger over his cheek.

At that moment she pulled away suddenly and sat up quickly.

"But back at the house. Not here. I don't want to be lyin' on my backside in the back of a truck that you've probably used to haul cow manure in, and I don't have any more desire than that to be doin' it out in some bug- and ant-infested field. I'm not that country anymore. I want to use a bed like a civilized whore."

Samuel turned the truck around. They headed back toward town.

When they reached the house and got out of the truck, the girl walked around to Samuel and placed her arm in his. From there she walked arm in arm with him into the house as if they were sweethearts coming in from a stroll. As they walked, Samuel was otherwise engaged reading meaning into the girl's gesture of taking his arm in hers. In the hopefulness of his interpretation, Samuel read the possibility of a whole world into the girl's one small and limited sweetheart-style gesture.

"Well now, where have you two been all this time?" Mrs. Richardson said in a knowing-sounding tone of voice as the girl led Samuel down the main hall toward the steps up to her room. Mrs. Richardson didn't seem angry that her star protégé and money earner had been gone for a large portion of the morning. But mornings and daytime were off-hours.

"We've been for a drive in the country in style," the girl said as she walked with her arm in Samuel's arm.

As the girl walked toward her resident madam, she sashayed her body

135

a little to emphasize the point. Samuel didn't say anything, willing to leave the explanations to her. At the moment he was more focused on what was to come (no sexual pun intended). He was also still focused on the girl's having taken his arm in hers.

The girl pointed to the stairs heading up to the second floor as she led Samuel toward Mrs. Richardson.

"Now we're goin' to get on with doin' what he came here wantin' to do, before he offered to take me for a ride. I figure I owe him that much. He's agreed to pay."

The girl and Samuel went up the stairs and into her room on the second floor. For Samuel the room was becoming familiar territory. For the girl it was a return to the native.

Inside the room, Samuel closed the door behind them without being told. The girl drew the drapes on the windows. The only light in the room was the diffused light that came through the drapes and one thin band of direct sunlight that came in through the gap between them.

There wasn't a lot of conversation exchanged. They just started to undress. But in precoital situations, conversation was superfluous almost by definition.

As Samuel took off his shoes and unbuttoned and removed his shirt like he had done three nights earlier, the girl pulled her dress off over her head. Underneath her dress, she was wearing what looked like a lighter-weight corset made of thinner material. Instead of being made from bright red and black strips of heavy cloth, this corset was a flat off-white color. It looked to be less binding than the corset she had worn the previous Friday night. It looked like it had been made for reasonable support and comfort without the extreme form-enhancing tightness and the gaudy harlot colors of the presentation corset she had been wearing when the two of them had met.

The girl turned her back and started to turn down the sheets on her bed. At that moment, Samuel decided that he didn't want the upcoming engagement between them to be just another commercial transaction. He wanted it to resemble his idea of what the seduction and love scene out of a classical romance novel or epic ballad would look like—or at least what he expected an epic romantic scene from a silent film to look like.

Dropping his shirt on the floor, he rushed up shoeless and silently behind the girl and swept his arms around her waist. At the same time, he pressed his face on her neck and started kissing it. In the scene setting of his romantic imagination, Samuel expected her to give out with a gasp of pleasure, wrap her hands over his, throw her head backward, and sigh with her mouth open as he passionately kissed her neck.

Classical romance and hardscrabble existence often have a way of diverging hard and fast at the beginning. Instead of falling into a passionate swoon in his arms, the girl uttered a sudden and cut-off half scream. She spun around in the enfolding romantic embrace of his arms with the speed of a dervish banshee. In the instant he had to look, Samuel couldn't see the girl's face. Her face was blocked by her hands, which she held with her fingers clawed like a big cat about to strike.

In the next half instant, the girl drove her clawed fingers into his face. Samuel felt her fingernails dig into the skin of his forehead in semicircles, running around the perimeter of his eyes and down his cheeks. In the surprise of the instant, it seemed like the girl was intent on trying to scratch his eyes out.

Samuel had fast reflexes of his own, born of years of baseball and boxing. He instinctively spun his head back and to the side. In a sweeping motion, he swung his arm up and across, catching the girl's arms at the leverage point of her elbows, knocking her hands away from his face. With his other arm, he gave the girl a half shove backward. Then he stepped backward himself. When he looked again, he got a clear view of the girl's face. Instead of a dreamy romantic swoon with her mouth open wide and yearning for the touch of his lips, the girl's lips were pulled back tight, her teeth bared and grinding. Her eyes were wide. At the same time her brow was pulled down tight and tense. Instead of a moonlight-shaded picture of softness and surrender, the girl's face was a twisted and distorted mask of what looked like a combination of equal amounts of primal fear and rage.

Samuel backed away from the girl several steps. She held her arms steel-rod tense out from her sides and at a slight angle. Her hands were still in the clawing shape. The whole of the girl's otherwise lithe and supple body seemed to be frozen as tense and hard as her arms were. The stunned look of fear or hate, or whatever it was, remained frozen on her face. The church Samuel attended believed in and taught the possibility of demon possession. Samuel had never seen a case of demon possession and was somewhat skeptical of the whole thing. The twisted and grinding look of the girl's face was the closest thing he had ever seen to what he could imagine as being demon possessed.

"What did you do that for?!" Samuel half yelled in stunned surprise as he stopped. The girl, who had been exaggeratedly friendly three nights earlier and while they had been kissing in the truck, had turned on him with the instantaneous speed of a steel spring leg trap being sprung. There was absolutely no logic he could see to the girl's action and reaction. All that Samuel could think was that he had made some terrible mistake with her. From pointing out the graveyard to mentioning her family to scaring her by speeding in the truck, he had made several mistakes. He had been able to sidestep any bad consequences of those missteps. But now whatever misstep he had apparently made with the girl was several orders of magnitude greater, big enough to negate all the lesser positive outcomes of having avoided the bad consequences of his earlier mistakes. In his moment of stunned surprise, in face of the girl's near-hysterical reaction and the twisted face she wore, all Samuel could think was that in the next instant, the frozen girl would explode in animated fury and shout at him to get out of her room and out of her life forever. The hope for the future that he had nourished within him and that he had been trying to carefully cultivate with the girl would disappear in an instant and be placed irretrievably out beyond any horizon of hope.

For several seconds the look of near-panic and hate remained frozen on the girl's face as her body remained in its tense and rigid pose. Then it broke. Her arms relaxed. Her hands unclawed. She started to breathe heavily.

"I'm sorry if I did anything to offend you," Samuel said, not knowing what else to say. He was still at a loss to understand why kissing the girl on the neck from behind was something that she would find to be so violently offensive. But every person has their own little idiosyncrasies. Samuel was starting to realize that some idiosyncrasies can be real killers. "I didn't mean anything by it."

The girl started to move again, but not with arms flailing in anger. Her shoulders slumped a bit. She lowered her head to where he could not see her face, and she shook her head.

"No … no," the girl said. Her body seemed to shudder as she talked between heavy breaths. She almost seemed to be gasping. "It's not you. ... I'm the one. ... I didn't mean to do what I did. ... I just snapped. ... I do that kind of thing at times. I'm just wild jumpy out of my skin like that sometimes. ... It's not your fault. ... I can't always control my reactions. ... Just don't ever come up behind me like that again!"

Samuel bent down and picked up his shirt. "I'll leave if you want me to," he said ruefully. He had no intention of fighting the girl if she asked him to leave. It wouldn't accomplish anything to fight and argue with her. She would only slam the door in his face all the harder. But if he had to leave, Samuel felt that he would be leaving the only real future he had ever imagined, the only future he wanted, behind with the girl at the house.

The girl raised her head.

"No," she said quickly in a high-pitched squeak. She started looking around quickly from side to side as if she was thinking of what to do next. Then she focused on the nightstand next to her bed. She stepped over to the nightstand, opened the small drawer at the top, and reached in. For a second, Samuel wondered if she was reaching for some kind of weapon.

The girl pulled a handkerchief out of the drawer. She draped the handkerchief over the index finger of her hand and started to walk quickly toward Samuel. As she walked, she wetted the part of the handkerchief over her finger with her mouth.

The girl came up to Samuel. She placed one hand on his chest. Instead of gripping and clawing, the feel of her hand was soft and gentle again. With the other hand she started wiping the scratches she had clawed into his face using the part of the handkerchief that she had wetted in her mouth. The cleaning wasn't really necessary. She hadn't broken the skin. His face wasn't bleeding. It started to dawn on Samuel that the girl's motherly little gesture was her way of saying that she was sorry.

"I'm sorry for anything I did," Samuel reiterated as the girl daubed his face. "I didn't mean anything by it."

"I know you didn't," the girl said with only half-regained composure. "It's just me. You don't know me. You don't know how jumpy I can get at times. That's the way I am."

The girl started wiping the fingernail marks on the other side of his face.

"You're a country boy like I'm a country girl. You know how a spooky horse will kick out if someone comes up behind them sudden-like. That's the way I am. I don't know how to go about gettin' rid of it."

"I'll still leave if you want me to," Samuel said, continuing with his unfeigned magnanimousness.

The girl wrapped her arms around his sides and back and pulled herself in closer. She turned her head to the side and laid it in Samuel's chest. "No," she said in a soft voice. "Stay with me please. Just hold me for a while. I want you with me. I like you being close to me." Her softly melodic voice turned hard. "For the good of both of us, don't *ever* come up behind me like that again!"

The otherwise uncertain Samuel wrapped one arm around the middle of the girl's back. He wrapped his other arm across her bare shoulders with his hand hanging down the upper part of her arm. With both his arms, Samuel could feel trembles passing through the girl's body. He didn't quite think they were trembles of rising passion.

"You're shaking," Samuel said.

"I know," the girl answered quietly into his chest.

"Should I go and get the doc for you?" he asked.

"I don't need no doc," the girl answered. "Just stand here with me and hold me till I settle down."

The girl hadn't had to tell Samuel to hold her the first time, and she didn't have to tell him a second time. In the middle of the girl's now quiet room, Samuel held the now quiet girl in his embrace. Whatever had spooked her, she seemed to feel safe in his arms. At least he liked to think of it that way. For the moment at least, Samuel's path to the future seemed safe and open to him. Beneath their feet, the thin band of light coming in between the drapes stretched across the floor as if it were a fixed and unmoving shaft of light falling on the face of a sundial without numbers.

Samuel didn't keep track of how much time had passed. Quietly holding the girl in his arms, he could have stood there an hour as the girl kissed and nuzzled his neck. Instead she brought her lips up next to his ear.

"I've shared myself with a lot of men," the girl said softly into his ear. "But I've never shared what I'm goin' to tell you with any man. I've been on the bad side of men all my life. I've understood the bad side of men all my life. I've never had any man who cared to understand me. I've never cared to be understood by any man. You're the first man I've cared to be understood by. You're the first man I've cared to reveal myself to."

Samuel didn't know if what the girl was going to say was trivial or significant in the greater scheme of things, but to her it seemed to be significant. Samuel said nothing. He simply held the girl and listened as she spoke quietly in his ear.

"The reason I jumped the way I did when you came up behind me and grabbed me is that I've been grabbed from behind and jumped a lot of times in my life. None of those times I was jumped turned out good for me. They never led to one thing good or pleasurable for me. They all led to something painful and dirty with my back being rubbed hard into the dirt and me hurtin' and screamin' and bein' made to feel torn up and dirty all over, both outside and inside of me. None of those times when someone came up behind me and grabbed onto me didn't lead to nothin' pleasant for me. That's why I jumped the way I did when you came up behind me and grabbed me like that."

Almost as a natural reflex, Samuel squeezed the girl tighter. She said he was different. She had said he was better than other men. The rocky path through the uncharted and uncertain woods suddenly burst out into a sunlit meadow. Home was just over the next ridge.

"If you want to come back to me here at the house or anywhere, you can. I'll be to you what a lady of this kind of house is supposed to be. If you want to make me your favorite, you can do that too. But don't come up behind me like that ever again. However you come to me, always make sure you let me see you comin'."

"Maybe you should hang a bell around my neck like the mice did to the cat in the story," Samuel said. "That way you'll always know when I'm coming." He didn't mean that as a sexual pun.

But the darkness of the thought was eclipsed and rendered secondary to the brightness of the possibility of a future together that the girl had opened to him by saying that she liked him better than the other men she had known. Lovers build whole worlds on a few words casually dropped by the objects of their affection.

The girl's statement that she respected him more than all the men she had known and was willing to at least partially open up to him about her past had opened up a world of hope and possibility for Samuel. In return he would give the girl hope for a future, a hope she had never had. He would give her the world she apparently never had. He would also give her a real family, a loving family, composed of him and his parents and sister, even though his sister could be a little snot.

The girl sort of laughed at his suggestion of wearing a bell.

"It don't make a lot of sense to go 'round wearing a bell," she said. "It would be ringing all the time you were bouncing around on me." Samuel sort of laughed. "Besides, the bell would just get pushed into my chest when you sprawled yourself out full length on top of me."

The girl turned around in Samuel's arms. Samuel loosened his arms so she could turn. With a free hand, the girl pushed her long hair away from her neck on the side that Samuel had tried to kiss her on.

"Instead of me belling you, why don't you go back to kissing me where you started to, now that I know where you are and you're already close to me and you're not rushin' up on me unawares."

With the girl's back to him, Samuel retightened his arms around her waist and lower chest. He started kissing her at the base of her neck as he had started to do before her memory had snapped shut on him like the steel trap it was. This time the girl did bend her head back and start to sigh softly.

For several minutes Samuel kissed the girl on her shoulder and neck, gradually working his way up her neck to her cheek, heading toward her parted lips. Just before he got to her lips, the girl straightened up and pushed herself forward slightly, opening a gap between them.

"Why don't you unlace me?" she said in her coy voice, indicating the lacing on her corset. She reached around behind her body and pulled her long hair out of the way.

The girl was still standing close to him. The gap between them was only a few inches. Mostly by feel, Samuel reached down and unlaced the lacing on the corset. When he was finished, the girl let her long hair fall back again. Then, with another smooth and continuous movement, she reached down to the bottom of her corset with both hands and pulled it down as far as she could without bending her knees. From there the corset dropped the rest of the way to the floor by itself and collapsed around her ankles.

With the remaining impediment of her clothing removed, the girl pushed her fully naked self backward up against Samuel's half-naked male form. He felt the press and shape of the girl's naked and rounded buttocks against his waist and upper thighs. He quickly wrapped his arms around her again from back to front. He wrapped his hands around her large self-supporting breasts and started caressing them as he rubbed his fingers over her erect nipples. The same faintness and throbbing urgency he had felt three nights ago when the girl had first presented herself to him naked was rising in him again.

"Let's go over to my bed and get on with what you wanted to get on with when you honked your horn at me out in the street," the girl said. She broke away from him and started to walk toward the bed, Samuel's lingering hands following the curves of her breasts as she walked away from him.

The girl didn't have to tell Samuel twice. He just had to stop long enough to hurriedly remove the rest of his clothes. When he was finished, he left his clothes on the floor in an untidy heap and moved quickly to where the girl, who had already climbed into her bed and had assumed the pose that women and girls of her profession are known for, was. She didn't have a sheet over her.

In short order, Samuel came up to the girl in a walking stride and lowered himself onto her, preparing to resume his vertical striding from a horizontal position. Pastor Russell might have said that he was lowering himself by coming into this kind of contact with a harlot. That notwithstanding, in equally short order he lowered himself into the girl. Once again he felt the extension of himself slip into her warm and enfolding wetness. Once again the girl gasped softly as he entered her. Once again her body arched up to press against his body. In the moment before the main motions commenced, he once again felt the full-length press of the girl's warm body against his. Again he felt the girl's body tense and tremble, but it wasn't out of fear or pain. Again he felt the girl's arms wrap around him. Once again he felt as if he were both home and coming home. Once again he resolved to show the scared, scarred, wounded, homeless, nameless girl how warm and loving a real home could be.

The squeaking of the girl's wood-framed bed started out slow and quiet at first, but it soon built up in both speed and volume. The soft sighs of a teenage girl rose to the throaty moans of a grown woman's pleasure. Only a few short minutes earlier, the girl had been a terrified waif backed into a corner in her mind, trapped in a remembrance of a tortured past, fighting to hold off the coming of pain and violation. Now she was a full-grown, take-charge woman in control of herself and her immediate situation. In Samuel's mind the girl was like their dog Teddy, an orphan waif who had narrowly escaped destruction. Teddy had escaped destruction by capturing their hearts by being feisty. The girl was feisty. Samuel liked the trait of feistiness. He liked the trait in presidents and national leaders. He liked the trait in boys. He liked the trait in girls. Along with everything he found that he liked about the girl, Samuel found that he liked her trait of feistiness. She had just chosen a socially dubious way of giving vent to her feistiness.

It was the girl's dead-end life that Samuel resolved to rescue her from. Teddy's feistiness had saved Teddy, but only in that it had landed him in a loving family that took him in and accepted him. Samuel resolved again to do for the girl, half drowned by life, what his family had done for the puppy, which would have been drowned without their intervention. He would supply the nameless girl with her route of escape. He would supply the feisty girl with a far better option, a far better family, a far better way of moving on into the future, a far better definition of the future, a far better future, and a far better life than the one she had been forced into by default.

Inside the house the bed squeaked away into the late afternoon. Outside the house, the river continued to run past and away. Above, a few wispy clouds continued to drift high and detached across the blue sky. In the lower sky, the distant speck of a single flying bird headed off toward the horizon.

Chapter 5

"Is that the stuff they put cocaine into?" the girl asked. The respectable farm boy, a long-standing member of his respectable community, sat openly in a seat in a booth in Kindelspire's lunch and soda fountain with the soiled dove who had only recently come into the community, calling herself by the made-up name she had given herself. She hadn't yet spoken her real name, and she gave no sign that she ever would.

The question was a rather unexpected one for Samuel. He looked up from his drink and over at Clarinda. She had moved her face to the side. With a somewhat suspicious look on her face, she looked at the red fizzy liquid in the tall inverted-cone-shaped fluted glass in front of her.

"That's Coca-Cola you're thinking of," Samuel said, realizing what the girl was talking about. "This is just root beer. The government made them take the cocaine out of Coca-Cola several years ago. They said people were starting to get addicted to the stuff. Now they just use syrup and carbonated water like what's in what we're drinking now."

Samuel raised his glass of root beer and tipped it toward the cherry phosphate the girl was drinking. The somewhat suspicious look faded from the girl's face.

"Well, that's good to know," Clarinda said. "I've heard it said that

that stuff can make people act like real animals. It's supposed to make the natives where the stuff comes from go hoppin' around yellin', wavin' spears, and lookin' for someone to sacrifice to a snake god. I've heard it drives the Negroes wild and makes them crazy. I don't need you goin' crazy on me more than you are. You drive crazy 'nough as it is."

"I wouldn't worry about it even if they still did put cocaine in Coca-Cola," Samuel said. "I think that a lot of what they say about Coca-Cola was always blown out of proportion. I've never heard of anyone going off their nut from drinking Coca-Cola, even when they did spike it with cocaine. The concentration of cocaine they put in it was probably pretty low. It was just supposed to relax you a bit. I think that's all the stuff does. Down in South America, where they use coca all the time, it doesn't send the natives out in a frenzy to look for heads to shrink. From what I've heard, all the stuff does is relax those Peruvian natives, or wherever it comes from, so much that they fall asleep on the necks of their llamas as they ride over the tops of the Andes."

"I suppose you're right about that," Clarinda said, putting her hand back on the glass of cherry phosphate. "They put a lot more dangerous stuff in bottles and jugs right here than they do in South America. Then they turn around and sell the stuff to a lot more dangerous men than Peruvian llama riders. They use it to fill their snoots up with liquor and their heads up with alcohol, and to fill their mouths up with cursing and vomit, and to fill their minds up with ideas about what they can do to a girl when they're drunk out of their minds."

The girl drew a slip of her cherry phosphate through the paper straw. An otherwise distracted Samuel couldn't help but notice how full her lips were when they were close together and wrapped around something.

"If the government wants to forbid puttin' stuff in bottles that drives dangerous men wild and gets them to bein' more dangerous, they should listen to those Prohibitionist people and ban whiskey and liquor."

The girl pushed the straw to the side. She had chewed the tip of it. Her full lips chewed out her words.

"You men like your damned whiskey so much, even you young bucks. You think it makes an extra man out of you. Whatever you think whiskey does for you, whiskey never did a damned thing for me other than make the men around me not recognize me or care to recognize me as family and cause them to think they could treat me like the whore I wasn't at the time because there weren't no women within easy reach and they were too drunk to even walk to the door, let alone out on the road, to start lookin' for a handy woman. The times whiskey did anything good for me was when those men were too cross-eyed drunk to find where I was hidin'. The only other time was when they'd pass out halfway through and I could push them off and then go sit alone with my legs crossed hard, tryin' to make the pain go away, while they lay off to the side vomiting into their armpit."

Samuel and Clarinda could have sat on the padded seats of the tall wrought-iron-framed stools at the marble-topped soda fountain counter. They could have sat anywhere they wanted. At the particular off-hour of the day, they were the only two customers in the joint. But Samuel had chosen a booth in the side window away from the front door. It was the brightest and most sunlit place in the building. But everywhere he went with the girl, he always seemed to be falling into another dark corner of her life.

"That's why Mrs. Richardson don't allow men to come into her place drunk. It's not that they can't perform. That's the least of their problem or ours. The problem is that instead of slappin' the parts of them that don't perform, they start slappin' 'round the girl and blamin' her. Or they start slappin' the girl just for the drunken fun of it."

The girl looked at him with a serious glint in her blue eyes. Her full and rounded lips rounded her words decisively.

"So don't you come to me with your snoot full of hard liquor and your mind full of drunken thoughts about doin' hard things to me or to any of the girls in the house. If you come to me in any kind of cup, I'll just slam the door to my room shut in your face and have you locked out of the house forever."

Samuel found it to be a bit surprising to hear a whore disassociate herself so thoroughly from whiskey and drinking. In popular mythology, the hard-drinking harlot was a well-established stereotype figure. But now Samuel found himself confronted by a prostitute speaking a prostitute's version of one of the chief mottoes of the Woman's Christian Temperance Union: "Lips that touch liquor shall never touch mine."

"I'm not much of a drinker myself," Samuel interjected with casual defensiveness. "I'll drink a beer now and then, but that's about all. But hard drink is nothing I need. Father and Mother don't hold with it."

When Samuel said that he didn't drink very much in the way of anything alcohol based, he wasn't lying any more than when he had told the girl that he didn't hunt very much. Some redneck types can't imagine existence or existing without hunting and drinking. Samuel had never quite shared that kind of half-assed male redneck attitude. If it would prove to be necessary to give up drinking as well as hunting to win the girl, it was another sacrifice he was willing to make.

"My father hasn't hardly drunk anything with alcohol in it since Mother reformed him. Grandfather was a teetotaler himself."

Samuel figured that it might be a good idea to throw in the fact that he was the third generation of a family that didn't need hard drinking to feel like men.

"Too much drinking doesn't make a man into more of a man. It just turns him into a slob who can't control himself and who ends up puking all over himself and on the floor. Then he passes out face-first into what he's just thrown up. That's not being a man. That's just being a dumb jackass."

The girl didn't say anything, but she did seem to appreciate his disavowal of drinking. He could never tell what the girl was thinking by looking at her face. She didn't wear a whore's faked smile or a perpetual frown on her face, but underneath the fullness of her lips, she didn't smile all that much.

Samuel Martin and the girl he knew by no other name than Clarinda sat in a booth in the front window of Old Man Kindelspire's restaurant and soda shop and talked. Samuel deliberately tried to steer the conversation away from any mention or remembrance of the girl's past and the family she had left behind. There were no other customers in the building. But it was an off-hour of the morning. Mr. Kindelspire, the owner and proprietor, was behind the counter. The cook was in the kitchen behind the swinging double doors that led to the back. When Samuel asked Clarinda what she wanted to drink, she said she liked anything with the taste of cherries. She said something about having grown up eating wild cherries right off the tree.

Samuel ordered the girl a cherry phosphate and a root beer for himself. The girl also seemed impressed by the large crystal pull handles on the soda dispensers. She commented that they looked just like the handles behind the bar in Two-Bit Charlie's saloon, but she said that the soda smelled better than the beer they served at the saloon. She went on to say that the whole place smelled better than Two-Bit Charlie's saloon. Mr. Kindelspire didn't say anything in the face of the girl's backhanded compliment. He sort of looked at her the whole time.

Inside the restaurant, the girl was finishing her drink. Behind the counter, Mr. Kindelspire was wiping the marble top of the soda fountain counter. As the girl was finishing the last draft of her cherry phosphate, a man walked by outside the window. In a short turn of his head, the sight of the girl's long tresses and eye-catching figure framed in the window had caught his attention.

As the girl put down her glass and she and Samuel were stirring to get up to leave, a man walked into the restaurant through the front door, which had been mounted at a forty-five-degree angle to the walls at the front corner of the building. The man stopped a few paces into the store, far enough in to be able to see around the back of the booth where Samuel and Clarinda were sitting, so he could get an unobstructed view of the girl. The man was approaching middle age, but he was somewhat youngish-looking. Still, he was older and more mature-looking than Samuel. The man was nattily dressed, maybe not natty by the standards of New York dandies, but natty by the standards of the town—natty in comparison to Samuel's farmer's jeans and shirt. He had a small mustache neatly trimmed.

After he entered and paused, the man looked around. If he was looking for an open table, the gesture was meaningless. He and Samuel and the girl were the only patrons in the combination restaurant / soda fountain. The man looked around all the same. But his gaze slowed and lingered on the girl.

As soon as he saw the man enter, Mr. Kindelspire quickly came out from behind the counter, walked over to the man, and greeted him. From their booth near the front door where the man was standing, Samuel could hear Mr. Kindelspire ask the man where he would like to sit. The question was a bit moot as he could have any seat in the house except where Samuel and the girl were sitting. The man pointed to a table in the restaurant portion of the establishment across the room from the booths.

Old Man Kindelspire graciously took him to the table he requested, where the man sat down. Though the table was at the back of the restaurant, it was positioned in such a way that it gave a clear and unobstructed view of the booth where Samuel and the girl were sitting. Having escorted the man to the table he had requested, Mr. Kindelspire went back to the counter, where he retrieved a menu, which he took to the man. The man didn't seem to see the store proprietor either go or return. The whole of his glance was focused on the booth where Samuel and the girl were sitting.

As the man looked up at Mr. Kindelspire, across the room the girl leaned in toward Samuel.

"Who's that?" Clarinda said in a voice low enough that the man could not hear. "I've never seen him at the house before."

Samuel didn't have to look up or turn around. He had seen the man walk by outside and had heard him come in.

"That's Harold Ethridge," Samuel said in an equally discreet voice. "He owns the biggest farm in this half of the county. But he don't farm it himself like my father and the other farmers around here do. He's an absentee farmer. He lives here in town most of the time while his hired hands work the fields for him. He's also a commodities broker who deals in crops and produce. He owns a big portion of the bank. He's on the board of directors at the bank. He's probably the single-richest man in town. He inherited it all from his father, who was the real moneymaker. That doesn't stop him from thinking he's the biggest cheese in the crate. Half the time he acts like he owns half the town. The other half of the time he acts like he owns the other half of the town. The trouble is that when you add all his holdings up, he probably does own half the town. He's also a member of the town council. Money and position goes to money and position around here like it does everywhere."

"If he has all this money to throw around, he hasn't been throwing any of it around at the house," Clarinda commented.

Samuel figured that a girl of the house would see everything through the prism of who came through the house and who didn't come through the house. "I doubt you're likely to see him or his money at your house," he said, a subtle tone of contempt seeping into his voice. "Being caught in a bordello or being found associated with one would dirty up his public image would be too much for his taste. Besides, when it comes to trifling with women, he prefers to trifle with married women. There's been more than one divorce in this town that's come about because he led on some woman he was having an affair with, making her think that he was going to marry her. Whenever he did such a thing, after the woman would leave her husband, or after her husband got wise to what she was doing and threw her out, he'd walk away from the woman he'd been snowing and leave her in the lurch from both ends."

"What does his wife think about all the cattin' around he's doing?" Clarinda asked. The tone of her voice was more curious than Samuel's condemnatory tone. "Or is he divorced too?"

"He's never been married," Samuel said. "Though he should have been married at the point of a shotgun more than once. But it wouldn't change him none to be married. He would still play as fast and loose with all women if he were married to one of them or not. No woman could trust him any farther than she could throw a shadow. There's a problem right at the source. I don't think he could ever love any woman as much as he loves himself. He's more stuck on himself than a porcupine blown into the side of a cactus by a tornado. The point is that any woman who thinks she can trust him is a bloody fool."

At Samuel's direction, he and Clarinda stirred themselves, got up from the booth, and walked out the front door. The eyes of Harold Ethridge followed the girl's enhanced form as she walked through the door and out of sight, leaving behind a man to whom all promises of love were a lie.

Sitting in the truck where he had left it parked on a side street, out of view from the side window of Kindelspire's restaurant and soda fountain, Samuel looked at Clarinda's face. He said there was a spot of soda on her mouth, and he proposed to wipe it off for her. After having just left behind a man for whom love was pretext, Samuel's cleaning of the girl's face was a pretext. With the index finger of his right hand, he pretended to rub an imaginary spot of lingering soda off the girl's mouth, just below and to the side of her lower lip. From there he started to rub his finger over the fullness of her two lips. For a few moments she closed her eyes and pursed her lips, making them look even fuller. She sat silent and unmoving as Samuel continued to rub his finger over the soft and slippery wetness of her lips.

Then the girl opened her eyes back up. With a knowing look, she took Samuel's right hand in her left hand and stopped his motion when his finger was positioned between her lips. From there she parted her wet lips slightly, took his finger halfway into her mouth sideways, and started slowly rubbing and kissing his finger with her lips. For several moments the girl went on in like manner, licking and kissing the side of his finger. Then she slowly changed the orientation of her head, bringing it around to face him fully. As she turned her head, she took his finger into her mouth perpendicularly up to the second knuckle. From this more direct angle, the girl wrapped the fullness of her lips around his finger and started sucking on it languidly, moving her head from front to back. The warm wetness of her mouth enfolded his finger from all sides. He could feel the girl's tongue playing with the tip of his finger.

The girl closed her eyes again and continued to suck on his finger while she held his hand softly. They had become familiar enough with each other to do little spur-of-the-moment things like that. Then again the girl had made herself far more familiar with him in a spur-of-the-commercial-moment rush the first time he had met her. That had been business. What the girl was doing with his finger seemed a little more spontaneously personal. At the end of their date, they would retire to the girl's room in Mrs. Richardson's house and proceed to become far more fully personally engaged with each other, enabled by the exchange of funds as required by the house and by the girl and as agreed upon by Samuel. However commercial it would be for the girl, for Samuel it would feel like love. The soft and wet feeling of the girl's lips, moist and warm, sliding over his finger held the promise of fuller love to come later in the day.

Back inside the restaurant, Old Man Kindelspire stepped into view of Harold Ethridge. Mr. Ethridge summoned the man over. He didn't wave his hand several times in rapid succession to do so. With a gesture of studied arrogance, he held up the index finger of his left hand and then flipped it toward himself once, indicating that he wanted the old man to come to him. Old Man Kindelspire walked over to the table where Harold Ethridge was sitting.

"Can I serve you something for lunch, sir?" Mr. Kindelspire asked with due deference to the single-richest man and the richest single man in town. Given that it was just after ten o'clock in the morning, it seemed a little early for lunch.

"I didn't come in for lunch," Harold Ethridge said, pushing the menu to the side. "As for what I want." He nodded toward the door that Samuel and the girl had just left through. "What I came in for, and what I want to know more about is, that girl with the Martin boy. She's exquisite. I've never seen a more delectable-looking creature. But I've never seen her in town before. Is she a relative of the Martin family? Is she in town visiting? Has she come to live with the Martin family?"

"She's a member of a house all right," the old man said in an old man's wry and ironic voice. "But she's not a member of the Martin family household. As anyone's house goes, she's one of the women who work out of Mrs. Richardson's house. From what I've heard, she's been working at Mrs. Richardson's for close to a year now. When she's in town, she's usually to be found on the dark end of the streets she works herself on."

"She's a streetwalker?" Harold Ethridge remarked in a flat tone of voice that sounded more inquisitive than surprised, shocked, dismayed, disillusioned, or disapproving.

"One that I've heard that you pay through the nose for," Mr. Kindelspire remarked. "With her looks, I can see why she's high priced. She doesn't actually walk the streets all that much. She does most of her work out of the Richardson house. That's probably why you haven't seen her before. A man of your caliber and position wouldn't frequent a place like Mrs. Richardson's. Young buck farm boys don't seem to be possessed of the same inhibitions."

Mr. Kindelspire glanced out the window in the general direction in which he had seen Samuel and Clarinda walk away. "The Martin boy seems to have taken quite a fancy to the girl," he said. "He's never brought her in here before today, but I've seen him squiring her about the last few weeks. With her looks, I can understand why he's fawning over her and spending money on her at the house and here in town. I don't know how long it's going to last between them. I doubt a poor farm boy like him is going to be able to afford the likes of her for very long. He only bought her a soda in here. That's all the money I got out of him where she was concerned. Who knows how much money he's dropped on her over at the house."

The fact that the woman wasn't really a full-grown woman but a teenage girl about the same age as the Martin boy didn't slow the pace of Harold Ethridge's thinking. She might be only a teenage girl, but she had the full figure of a woman. She was also acting the role of a full woman. The girl had taken on the mantle of womanhood enough to enter into a profession that, in the thinking of Harold Ethridge, carried the maximum application of womanhood to its utmost degree. Harold Ethridge knew about taking things to a serviceable degree.

If the girl played the role of woman to every man who came to her with money in hand, then she was woman enough by any definition, especially his. That the woman was in womanhood for the purpose of remuneration didn't bother Harold Ethridge either morally or financially. If the girl demanded payment for services rendered like the other women of her ilk and disposition, he didn't mind and had no ethical or financial qualms. He had enough money to both attract and sustain the girl. At least he would be able to keep her in the style she was probably looking for a lot more readily than a penny-pinching farm boy like Samuel Martin. Whatever feelings the Martin boy might have had for the girl, he was sure that her feelings for him were shallow and easily transcended.

"She does come into town now and then to scare up business for herself," Mr. Kindelspire went on. "I've see her walking around in town a few times during the day, carrying laundry bundles and grocery sacks. But I guess she's not open for business then. She keeps night hours. I've heard tell that she occasionally solicits over at Two-Bit Charlie's saloon and Floyd's pool hall after dark."

Old Man Kindelspire couldn't provide any further useful information. Harold Ethridge thanked the man and left the place. If the Martin boy and the monetary girl he was trying to impress had stayed longer, he would have ordered a cup of coffee as an excuse to sit and look at the girl longer. But they had left almost as soon as he had come in. As it was, he left without ordering anything. He didn't even leave a tip.

Gustafson Lake was an irregular-shaped lake with a dogleg turn about two-thirds of the way down. The lake was about three-quarters of a mile long and no more than an eighth of a mile wide at the widest point. In later decades, houses would be built along the comparatively high side of the lake, but in 1912 the lake was isolated, secluded in woods. There was no direct drive leading to the shore. Samuel had to park the truck off the road. From there he and Clarinda followed a narrow path through the woods. At the far end, the path broadened slightly at a small clearing at the lake's edge. At the end of the trail there was a small beach of gravel and sand, which had been washed up and concentrated by some natural mechanism of the lake in one small bay or had been dumped there in order to provide a small firm surface to stand on in the mud of the bank. As they approached, they could see the greenish blue of the lake in the near distance and the glare and twinkling of the bright sunlight reflecting off the ripples on the water.

Along any of the postage stamp beaches, the trees and bushes came right down to the water's edge. Samuel and the girl stood looking silently at the lake. Out on the open water, the breeze moved across, raising irregular small ripples. Heavier gusts of wind pushed sections of disturbance in random directions across the top of the water as if the gusts were fast-moving clouds. When the wind died down, the rustled patterns disappeared. When the breeze left the open expanse of the lake, it was quickly taken in by the trees and shrubs of the forest.

On the far side of the lake from where they were standing, the land was slightly lower. The boundary between water and land was less distinct and transitioned slowly from lake to swamp to dry land behind. At the beginning of the far shore, a flat green field of lily pads, their circular leaves floating flush on the water's surface, covered the greenish blue of the lake and broke up the miniature wavelets that washed into them. Atop the lily pads, heavy flower pods pushed up into the air immediately above the water and opened into deep-yellow-colored flowers. Along the length of the near shore, the snags of fallen trees protruded perpendicularly into the lake, their bare trunks gradually slipping lower into the water along their lengths until they disappeared below the surface, leaving only bare and barkless limbs protruding above the water to show where the submerged trunk was located. Iridescent dragonflies buzzed over the pads and occasionally alighted on a floating pad, their weight not enough to disturb the vegetation. Bullfrogs grunted from the lily pads and between the snag trees. Near one shore a long-legged wading bird, either a heron or and an egret, carefully stalked its prey, its head poised attentively at the end of its long neck, its long beak cocked as if it were a bolt loaded in a medieval crossbow, the bright white of its plumage contrasting sharply with the mottled greens and blues of the forest and the lake and the brighter primary blue of the sky above. Closer in toward the concealed shore, the lily pads changed to cattails and an expanse of low-lying water-tolerant bushes where the ground beneath gradually rose upward past the lake level. Deeper in the woods resumed once again. The tops of the distant trees towered above the low-lying flora of the swamp at the water's edge. Off toward the other end of the lake, the water took a dogleg turn and disappeared around the bend of the shore.

There was no one other than the two of them on the lake or standing on the shore. They had the whole place to themselves. No one was canoeing the lake. No one was there fishing that day to possibly upset the girl with the sight of a hooked fish thrashing in its death throes. Samuel and his father had come to the spot they were standing on to fish in the past. There was a good bass shoal with the kind of aquatic plants bass prefer not far out from the beach where the couple was standing. In other words, Samuel was familiar with the ground he was standing on. The beautiful girl standing beside him was new and unexplored territory. He had made himself intimately familiar with the girl's body, but somehow he still couldn't help feeling that he was otherwise standing on unfamiliar ground with her.

Since he had not brought fishing poles, a canoe, or a rowboat with him, Samuel was sure what he would do with the girl once they had arrived at the lake. All he could think of was to take her on a walk around the lake. They could, of course, find an even more secluded spot in the already secluded woods and do what prostitutes and their clients are known to do, what they had scheduled to do upon return to the house. But on their first outing, the girl had indicated that she didn't like making love in the bed of a truck or in a bug-infested cornfield. Samuel rather assumed she wouldn't want to do it on the edge of a mosquito-breeding swamp.

"We can walk around the lake if you like," Samuel said, breaking the silence that otherwise was being broken only by the sound of the stirring breeze and the thumping call of bullfrogs. He pointed off to the right. "There are logs we can sit on if you get tired and want to rest. We can follow the shore more closely on this side. It gets swampier over on the other side. We'll have to move away from the lake and cut through the woods there. If we keep the lake on our left side, we can go the rest of the way around and end up back here without getting lost."

"Let's go for a swim," the girl countered with a practical solution, offered with impulsive spontaneity. "It's been years since I skinny-dipped."

She didn't dillydally; she just went ahead and did. Instead of waiting for Samuel's response, she started disrobing.

"Ah, we didn't bring any bathing suits with us," Samuel said, stumbling over his words as the girl unfastened her dress.

"With our clothes off, you ninny," the girl said. "It's not like I've never been naked with a man before. It's not like we haven't seen each other out of our clothes. We've got the lake to ourselves. There's no one here around to see us."

"But, ah, someone may come along," Samuel said as the girl pulled her dress off and tossed it across the branches of a nearby bush. "Men fish this lake."

"If some man comes along and sees me, he sees me," the girl said as she started removing her undergarments. "It's not like I'm shy and reluctant about men seein' me bare-assed. It's part of my job. If some fisherman sees me from a distance, he'll think he's seen a mermaid or the ghost of an Indian princess. As long as he don't try to hook me and reel me in."

In short order the girl had removed her undergarments.

"I didn't come all the way out here with you on a nice day like this just to skip stones on the water," she said as she deposited her undergarments unceremoniously on the bush next to her dress.

Actually, Samuel had been thinking of showing the girl the country art of skipping flat stones across the water. But if she was country enough to have gone skinny-dipping, then she probably already knew how to skip stones.

The girl looked out across the water. "In the back of my mind, I've always dreamed of livin' alone by a lake and havin' the lake all to myself. This is the closest I'll probably ever come to that in my life. I'm going to take advantage of it while I can."

Naked, she bolted away from Samuel's side and sprinted into the water, her feet sending up splashes of lake water and bottom sand, her breasts bobbing free in the sun. As the water deepened, it dragged against her calves and thighs, slowing her progress. Where the bottom started to drop off, the girl launched herself into a headfirst horizontal dive into the water. The last thing Samuel saw of the girl dry was the sight of the rounded twin hemispheres of her hips as the displaced water rushed back in and covered over them.

Almost as soon as she went into the dive, the girl resurfaced, touched bottom, and stood up. Her flyaway long wavy hair was now straight and slicked back down her shoulders and her back. She struggled a bit to gain footing and stand upright as her feet sank into the soft bottom. When she had stabilized herself, she turned her upper body partway around and waved over her shoulder for Samuel to follow.

"Come on," the girl called to Samuel. "Don't stand there like a lump on a log. Get your clothes off and follow me in. It's goin' to be a lot more fun for both of us with you here in the water with me than you standin' there in the woods with your mouth open, catchin' flies."

The girl didn't have to tell Samuel anything twice. He started to disrobe in like manner as she had. After all, it wasn't like he wasn't planning on getting naked with her later. As he started to undress, Samuel looked around furtively, the way the girl hadn't, to see if anyone was around to see them. He felt embarrassed at the thought of being seen in the altogether. A moment after that, he felt embarrassed that he felt embarrassed at the thought of being seen in the altogether when the girl apparently wasn't embarrassed by the thought of being seen naked by a passerby. But then again the girl made a living out of not being embarrassed to be seen naked by strangers. Beyond thoughts of modesty, Samuel liked the spontaneity and spunk the girl had displayed. She had proved herself lively enough in bed on more than one occasion. Disrobing on an impulse and diving into the lake without any inhibitions about being seen naked made her seem even more alive in Samuel's mind. He wanted a girl with spunk. He wanted a girl who was feisty. He wanted a girl who wasn't embarrassed by being alive and wasn't embarrassed about being seen to be alive and lively. Modesty had its place, but he didn't want a modest and retiring maiden who was so modest and retiring that she retired from all zest for life.

While Samuel undressed, the girl swam back and forth several yards out from the shore, but she didn't head out in a straight line across the lake. She swam both on the surface and under it. When she swam on the surface, the wet curves of her shoulders and naked buttocks would flash and shine in the sun. She wasn't a particularly graceful swimmer. She didn't swim with a smooth and gliding style, but she knew the basics. When she dove under water with her arms at her sides and kicked with her legs only, she moved with a more fluid motion. When viewed from a distance and at a shallow angle, the water of the lake appeared blue-green. Looking down into the lake from a steeper angle, the water was more of a peaty brown color. As the girl swam under the surface of the water, the flesh of her body was shown in relief against the dark of the mud and tannin at the bottom underneath her, her naked body glowing a dull gold color in the reflected sunlight coming back up through the surface of the water—a hillbilly mermaid and Loreli seductress from a deep woods stream in a mountain valley come to tempt the farm boy and lure him onto the rocks in a lake that had no rocks, only wooden snags and mud. When she broke the surface and swam there, the waves she made spread out and refracted the reflections in the still water near the shore.

Upon further reflection of the moment, as he removed his last item of clothing, Samuel was more convinced that he wanted a girl who wasn't afraid to make waves. It didn't bother him that the girl didn't seem bothered that she might be seen swimming nude. Samuel wanted a girl who was unashamed at the thought of being seen naked. He wasn't embarrassed at the thought of being caught swimming naked, and he wasn't embarrassed at the thought of being seen naked in the company of a lively naked girl, even a lively girl who had come from the dirty side of town and from a dirty side of life. Samuel was ready to embrace a certain amount of embarrassment in life to have a life with her. He was ready to embrace a wider life if he could embrace the soiled, lively girl for life. It was just that as he finished undressing, the take-charge Samuel kind of had the feeling that it was the girl who had taken charge of him and his life without even trying.

Samuel, dropping his clothes on the ground in no better order than the girl had deposited hers, entered the water. Beyond the sand and gravel the first few feet out from the shore, his feet sank into the soft mud and decayed plant material on the bottom that oozed up over his feet and around his ankles. He could easily imagine his sister and any of the other girls of the town cringing at the feel of their feet sinking deep into the slippery goo of the lake bottom. It didn't seemed to bother Clarinda at all, though. She seemed to have gone skinny-dipping like this before, possibly in a mountain hollow pool. He wondered again if she was a hillbilly like her accent seemed to indicate.

In the water, Samuel swam after the girl with the intention of grabbing her from behind. The thought of grabbing the wet, naked, wriggling girl in his arms represented something he couldn't pass up.

Samuel started swimming after the girl with all his youthful teenage baseball player's vigor. In turn the girl took his approach as if it were a relay race or a game of keep-away tag. He would get close enough to momentarily grab a leg or an arm. Sometimes he would draw close enough to run his hand across the moving muscles of her naked back and bottom, feeling his hand slip over the rounded curve of her hips. But he wasn't quite able to catch up with the swimming girl. She was proving to be surprisingly quick and nimble at keeping herself out ahead of him.

Samuel paused in midstroke and stopped chasing the girl altogether. Remembering the way she had reacted when he had come up behind her and grabbed her in her room at the Richardson house, he was afraid that if he grabbed her from behind now, she might have another panic attack and swallow water and choke. He up stood in water over his stomach and watched her swim. Standing still and just watching the naked girl swimming was as pleasant to Samuel as the thought of touching her naked moving body.

After a short interval, the girl realized Samuel was no longer chasing her. She reversed direction and swam back toward him. As she drew close, she dove under the surface of the water, closed the remaining distance between them under water in an upward bending arc, and came up in front of him with her eyes closed. Water ran down her face, over her lips, and off her head and shoulders. Her long hair was slicked straight down her back. She looked like a sleek otter with a human face.

The girl opened her eyes, standing on the lake bottom in front of Samuel. She was tall enough that her breasts came fully out of the water. The sleek otter with the human face now resembled an animated version of the wooden figureheads of well-endowed women mounted on the bowsprits of eighteenth-century sailing ships. With a quick smile, the girl walked the remaining few feet until there was no longer any distance remaining between them. She threw her arms around him, pulled herself up tight against him, and started kissing him on the mouth hard and full. It wasn't Samuel's doing. This was solely the girl's move.

You didn't have to tell Samuel twice. In this case, anything the girl or anyone would have tried to tell him would have gone unheard. In a move as quick as the girl's move had been, Samuel wrapped his around the girl and started kissing her back. Bound up in their water-bound clinch, Samuel matched the girl's passion pound for pound while their feet slipped and sank in the mud and their bodies swayed on the verge of falling sideways into the water. Just why the girl was opening herself up to him and seemingly opening a later chapter early, Samuel wasn't sure. Samuel had sort of figured that she had scheduled what was transpiring and what seemed to be on the way to transpiring once they arrived back at the house, with payment to follow. That was the way they had left things arranged when he had picked her up at the house and they had left for the soda fountain. He wasn't sure why she was deviating from her game plan. The girl's unexpected sweeping and enfolding naked embrace had caught him by surprise as much as her sudden urge to disrobe and go skinny-dipping had. Maybe it was just more of her natural spontaneity. Whatever the case may be, Samuel was starting to appreciate the girl's spontaneity more by the minute.

At this point in the day that had seen more than one unexpected development on the girl's part, Samuel no longer cared if anyone happened to see them.

Still locked in their liquid clinch, Samuel and the girl sank down into the water up to their necks. The warmth of her body next to his mingled with the coolness of the water on Samuel's flesh. Their legs were bent at oblique angles, trying to keep their heads above the surface.

The girl's hands ran back and forth all over Samuel's back. Samuel's hands ran all over her back, becoming alternately entangled in the long falls of her wet hair. He was forced to shake his hands free of her entangling hair several times. Locked in their embrace, they settled lower in the water. Their thighs and knees worked their way down into the soft mud beneath them.

When the water was about halfway up the sides of her face, the girl suddenly broke her clinch. Instead of enfolding Samuel, her arms started waving in the air and flailing the water, trying to get a platform to push herself up on.

"Well, good grief, boy, don't drown me tryin' to screw me," the girl said as she thrashed her arms in the water and mud, pushing herself up. Samuel broke his clinch and let the girl rise.

"The water's too deep here for that kind of purpose," the girl said as she pushed herself up to a sitting position. "Another inch and it would be comin' up my nose. If you want to drown me, drown me in kisses, but I don't have no desire to be drowned in water that's one step removed from a swamp."

The girl looked around for a moment. Then she pointed to one of the shoals of lily pads and cattail grass that flanked the sides of the small beach. "Over there," she said. Without any further words, the take-charge girl took Samuel by the hand and led him over and into the lily pads and tall grass, a point where the water mingled into the slowly rising mud of the shore. Without further ado; without any qualms, moral or otherwise; and without comment about the primitive setting being somewhat less than the bridal suite at a grand European hotel, the naked girl, still holding Samuel's hand, dipped her knees and lay down on her back where the water was no deeper than a shallow rainwater puddle.

There was a thin stand of tall grass with its roots in the water where the girl's shoulders and upper back went down. As she lay down, her body pushed the tall grass down like it was a mat. The ends of her legs protruded out into the lily pads near the shore. The grass gave them some concealment from the side, but the grass and the lily pads were too thin to hold the girl up off the mud beneath. As she laid herself down in the water at land's edge, with the hand she was holding Samuel's hand with, she drew him down toward her.

There were some things you didn't have to tell Samuel at all. Whether she had planned that as a conscious tool of seduction or whether it was inadvertent, long before chic fashion consultants would coin the phrase *the wet look*, the girl was applying the principle beyond Samuel's ability to resist, an ability he had no wish to employ if he could. In quick time, the girl drew Samuel the rest of the way down to her. With no noticeable pause to position himself, Samuel was inside her. In quick time they reach a mutually quick tempo. As far as pioneering new phrases goes, in an equally short time they also pioneered the more modern term *wet and wild*. At least they pioneered a new personal definition of getting wet while getting wild in the wild.

As Samuel drove himself deep into her, the girl's legs thrashed and flailed in the water, sending lily pads flying, stirring up a soupy cloud of mud in the shallow water under her legs and feet. Samuel's arms were under and around the girl as far as they could be in the mud beneath their bodies. The girl's arms went windmilling everywhere. Her hands alternately gripped the mud and gripped Samuel's back. She shouted her pleasure in no uncertain terms. On the far shore, the wading bird paused in the focused deliberateness of its stalking hunt and raised its head to listen to the unaccustomed sounds drifting across the water.

It wasn't exactly what you could call a biblical scene. But as the servant girl of the daughter of Pharaoh's house had brought forth Moses from the bulrushes of the Nile, the biblically named Samuel came into the working girl of Mrs. Richardson's house in the bulrushes of Gustafson Lake. It couldn't be said that they parted any water, but they did splash a lot of it around. And raised a lot of mud. Making spontaneous love in the shallow of the lake was a departure from the schedule for that day. This wasn't supposed to have happened until they had returned to the house and to the girl's clean bed. Making love in the outdoors also represented a departure from what the girl had insisted upon in terms of surroundings. Apparently she had overcome her inhibitions against making love in the back of a truck or in a farm field. But however much of a departure her departure from the arranged schedule represented to her, to Samuel the girl's spontaneous departure represented another major opening of a door into the future and his future with the girl. She was willing to do with him and for him something that she had stated she was not willing to do. On top of that (while he was on top of her), by making love with him in the country, she had proven herself a country girl. Only a real country girl would make love under the open sky out in the country, in the water and the mud, and on the shore of a lake no less. In one way at least the girl was coming home to her roots. In his hopeful expanded interpretation, Samuel took it to mean that the girl was coming home to him.

For some time the impromptu thrashing of the couple went on in the shallow water near the shore of Gustafson Lake. After due time, Samuel's body suddenly ceased its motion and tensed up hard. All his outward surging motion ceased and was transferred into a focused series of internal surgings. At her feel of what was happening, the girl ceased her random thrashing and tensed up as hard as Samuel. To the tune of her single drawn-out high-pitched cry, the girl's head rolled back in her pillow of mud. Samuel's elbows dug deeper into the mud than they had so far. The girl's fingers dug into Samuel's back, Samuel's fingers clenched tight in the mud. The intermingled sum of Samuel's passion, lust, hopes, dreams, and love for the girl surged unrestrained and unashamed across the short distance between them, fully into the girl, with nothing held back. For several long moments they held each other tight in their spasmodic grip. Then the seizure passed and their mutual spasm broke. The girl sagged, gasping, down onto the bed of mud beneath her, into which, in tandem, she and Samuel had sculpted the mold of their passion. Samuel sagged down on top of the girl. For several minutes afterward, they lay with their heads next to each other, gasping in each other's ears.

"I thought you said you didn't want to make love in a field," Samuel said as he raised his head.

"Not in a cornfield," Clarinda answered in a semilanguid voice through closed eyes. "The ground's too hard and laced with old corncobs. It hurts the back. Mud's a lot softer and less lumpy than plowed ground."

The girl opened her eyes and looked into her lover's face. Her upturned face and the exposed front of her shoulders were streaked with mud where Samuel had dug his hands into it in the throes of making love to the girl, having gripped her shoulders with his muddy hands and drawn them across her face.

"I'm afraid I've gotten you all muddy," Samuel said apologetically. He could only imagine how much mud the girl had on her back. He tried to wipe some of the mud off her face with the side of one hand, but he only succeeded in smearing more mud on her face.

"In one way or the other I've been dragged through the mud all my life," Clarinda said. "It's nothin' new for me. But I must say, this is the only time I've ever enjoyed the experience. You can dirty me up like this any old time you're of a mind to."

Samuel placed his muddy hands on either side of the girl's dirt-streaked face and kissed her again. He could feel her head roll slightly from side to side, working into the mud beneath as he kissed her. He tasted something in her kiss that he had not tasted before. He wasn't sure if it was the taste of lake water or mud.

When he had finished kissing the girl, Samuel again rested his cheek against her cheek, being careful not to let his head slide down far enough to where his nose would be in the thin layer of water under her head. Their bodies lay languid and quiet with their arms entwined around each other. The only movement Samuel felt was the girl's hands softly stroking his back. Above and around him he heard the stir of the breeze through the grass next to them and the trees surrounding them. Small birds flitted through the branches of the trees. On the other side of the lake, that large white wading bird, either a heron or an egret, stood in the shallow water.

The girl stirred under Samuel and softly prodded him to get up. "It's gettin' late," she said. "You've got to get me back to the house. Mrs. Richardson won't take kindly to you keeping me gone all day. I've got to get myself washed up. Mrs. Richardson won't either take kindly to me comin' in the way I am, tracking mud all over the house and rubbin' it into the sheets."

The girl placed her hands in the mud to the sides of her and started to push herself up.

"Though God knows I wasn't in much of a cleaner state the first time I showed up at the house."

They had just performed in a rustic and natural setting what they had contracted to perform in the girl's bed in her room at the house once they returned from their outing. The question on Samuel's mind at the moment was, given that they had performed by the side of the lake the standard act that the women of the house and the girl performed in their rooms, just what the girl had planned for them to do back at the house when they returned. As soon as they arrived, would the girl just request her payment for the day, saying she had otherwise lived up to the terms of their agreement, say goodbye, and then withdraw herself into the house? For a moment, Samuel wondered if the girl was planning a repeat performance with him in her bed. He wondered if she would charge him double duty if she did. Was that what she had meant about possibly dirtying up her bed? Or was she talking about dirtying up her bed with other men in further performance of her duties later that day, either after he had left or at night during normal customer hours. Samuel had known that having undifferentiated sex with men was the girl's business even before he had met her at the house, but to him the girl was different from any other girl he had ever met. To Samuel, what they had just gotten through sharing was more different and unique than anything he had done or experienced before in his life. Not so far back in his mind, he knew that the girl had been and was still servicing other men in the performance of her commercial duties at the house. Still, knowing that she would probably be going back to her designated role at the house and going to bed with other men before the footprints and body impression they had left in the mud had washed away, and while the memory of what they had shared at the lake was still fresh and bright in his mind, took some of the glow off the morning for Samuel.

Samuel withdrew himself from the girl and rolled to the side to let her get up. She stood up. He stood up alongside her. Standing up next to the girl at the altar and in life was something that he had wanted to do with her since their first night together. Their country pastoral impromptu tryst on the edge of the lake hadn't dulled Samuel's appetite for the girl or for spending a life with her. If anything, their time of spontaneous abandon in the mud of the lake had only increased his desire for the girl and his wish to have a life with her.

Having ridden on top of the girl while his weight had pushed her down into the mud, Samuel had been insulated from getting as dirty as the girl had become. His hands and forearms were pretty much covered with mud back to his elbows. His knees and the front of his lower legs were coated with mud. There was mud on his back where the girl's arms had drawn streaks and circles with her hands and arms. The girl's rear side was smeared slick with a coating of wet and slippery mud from her head down to her heels. Her hair was sticky and caked with mud, which plastered it down to her back and made it cling to her skin. Samuel had heard it said that the natives in the heart of darkest Africa often smeared their bodies with mud in order to keep biting flies off their skin. Samuel had only seen a small number of Negro men in his life, but he had yet to see a Negro girl. He had wondered what Negro girls looked like, both dressed and out of their clothes. The coating of brown mud on the girl's back made her look dark enough to be a Negro girl. From behind, the naked, mud-caked girl looked like what he imagined a buck naked African native girl would look like in the most primitive part of Africa where the natives didn't even wear loincloths.

The girl took Samuel's hand and led him back out into deeper water again. There she released his hand and dove back into the water to wash herself off. While Samuel stood and washed the mud off his knees and the front of his calves, the girl swam and splashed in an attempt to wash the mud off her back. In her efforts to clean herself up, she was not completely successful. Though most of the mud washed off, some streaks of extra-clingy mud remained stuck to her body. She walked back to Samuel, turned around, and asked him if there was any mud still on her and, if so, if he would wash it off for her. This was another thing you didn't really have to tell Samuel to do. For some time he stood there running his hands over the girl's back and legs, washing the remaining mud off her. He lingered at the task longer than was necessary, especially when it came to rubbing the girl's full hips. He rubbed some areas that didn't need to be washed at all. After that he sat down in the water at the edge of the lily pad field and had the girl sit down in the water in front of him. Then he proceeded to wash the remaining mud out of her long hair, scooping up water with his hand and running it through her hair. Using his fingers for the teeth of a comb, he combed and untangled her hair.

"I've got most of the mud cleaned out of your hair," Samuel said when he had gone as far as he could (with her hair, that is). "But it's still dirty from lake water. To really get it clean, you'll have to wash it out back at the house."

The girl didn't say anything. She leaned her body back against his, leaned her head back, and rested her head on his shoulder. With measured gentleness so as not to revive old nightmares and make the girl think she was being grabbed from behind, he wrapped his arms around her below her breasts and above her stomach and held her in front of him. Together they sat in silence in the water just beyond the edge of the field of lily pads and looked out over the lake. With the mud off her back, Samuel's vision of the girl as a wild and primal naked African faded, to be replaced with a vision of the girl as a not-so-dark-skinned but dark-haired Polynesian beauty with him as her native lover, the two of them living together alone on a small island in the South Pacific, sitting in the same pose at the edge of the water of a lagoon and looking out over the ocean. In Samuel's mind, that vision faded, to be replaced by the closer-to-home vision of them sitting on the porch of their farmhouse in the light of day watching their children play in the yard, or sitting alone at sunset watching the sky turn orange and purple on the horizon.

Sitting quiet and motionless after their moment of energetic completion, looking at the clouds drifting over the trees toward the horizon beyond, Samuel wanted no other horizon. Sitting naked with the naked girl in the lake they had all to themselves, he wanted no other throne to sit on with the girl other than the porch outside his front door. He couldn't see beyond the circle of trees around the isolated lake, but he needed no vision beyond the one he held in his arms and his heart.

In the sky above the opening in the forest that contained the lake bed, some clouds rolled by, driven by the winds aloft. The clouds shifted shape as they rolled on. Down at Samuel and the girl's level, the breeze ruffled the surface of the lake once more. The heron or egret on the other side of the lake took flight, soaring on widespread white wings over the lake they lay in the mud of, heading past and flying away.

Chapter 6

"If your friends on the baseball team want to go, they can ride in the back of the truck," Samuel's father said with firm fatherly definiteness as Samuel stood with his mouth open and his finger pointing at his sister. "It's not like any of them have never ridden in the bed of a truck or a wagon before. If you take more than one, the excess number are going to have to ride in the back anyway. Your sister wants to go to the summer fair in Ashton. She's been looking forward to it. She's your sister. She's family. You're old enough to take over the role of being the man of the house, which means you put off your childish ways and be a man and helper and protector to everyone in the family. It's high time you stop thinking like you're living in some silly boys' club shack with a sign on the door that says No Little Sisters Allowed. You can just grow up, drop your boyish exclusive ways, treat your sister like she's part of the family, and take her along with you. It's much too far of a distance for her to walk."

Bethany Martin looked at Samuel with a satisfied smirk on her face. She didn't stick out her tongue at her brother, but it looked like she was about to.

"I don't want her on the open road alone for ten feet, never mind fourteen miles, so she rides with you to the fair. And when you get there,

I don't want you to dump her off and leave her alone while you and your buddies go around on your own acting like a pack of wild Indians. You can jolly well play the proper big brother role and look after your sister when you get to the fair. I expect you to stay with her and show her around and show her a good time. If that means that you'll have to break away from your scruffy friends for a spell to treat your sister like you're supposed to, they can fend for themselves without you for a while."

As Samuel had been heading jauntily toward the door to leave that morning, his father had unexpectedly stopped him and announced his sister's wish to go with him to the Ashton summer fair. In what had otherwise seem like a straightforward and uncomplicated venture, Samuel suddenly found himself confronted with the problem faced in all periods of modern history by an endless number of older brothers: a tagalong little sister. Samuel had objected on the grounds that he had planned to take some of his former teammates from the high school baseball team he had captained. In so many indirect words, he had said that it was a 1912 guy thing and that girls would just slow them up. But that had been a spur-of-the-moment excuse he had made up to cover the real problem and his real intent.

The problem for the day, and the situation, was that it wasn't the other boys of his high school baseball team whom he planned to take with him to the fair. They could pound sand on the sandlot. It was the girl he had already arranged to take to the fair. With his bigmouthed little sister in tow, the clandestine affair he had been carrying on for the past two months would almost surely get back to his parents. The affair he was carrying on with the girl had been becoming increasingly less clandestine and more obvious to the people of the town. Whatever amount and form of gossip had been going around in the town about Samuel and the girl hadn't gotten back to his parents as of yet. But if his sister got ahold of the fact that he had been getting ahold of the girl, Samuel figured his parents would learn about it within a day and a night as surely as night follows day. His sister couldn't hold a secret much better than a hired hand could hold his water when he's drunk. But it was catty little nitpicking secrets among her friends that Beth couldn't hold. Maybe she was capable of holding a higher-level and more serious secret when it involved a family member.

Nevertheless, if his sister went along when he picked up Clarinda at the house, Samuel figured that his secret would be almost as good as out.

But he simply couldn't change plans and blow the girl off and go to the fair by himself with his sister. He had already arranged to take the girl. She was looking forward to going to the fair as much as his sister was. In Samuel's mind, taking the girl to the fair was a major step forward in his romantic campaign to win her heart and hand. It was another way of showing her that he thought of her as a regular girl and a sweetheart, not just as a paid courtesan. It was also another of his ways of demonstrating to the girl that he wanted to have an ordinary life with her. If he were to stand her up, it might do more damage than could be repaired later. On the other hand, he couldn't kick his sister out the truck door halfway to the house. Halfway across the kitchen floor, heading to the door, Samuel Martin suddenly found himself caught in a classic dilemma for which there was no satisfactory solution from either direction and no clever trick that would allow him to slip through the middle.

In one way, Samuel's whole plan had been knocked for a loop. On the other hand, his affair and his intent beyond the affair was something that would have to be kicked out into the open soon enough. If this was the day that the final stage of going public with his affection for the girl and his intent to marry her found its way back home, not just to his sister but also to his parents, so be it.

When his father put his foot down, that was that. A resigned Samuel shrugged his shoulders and pointed to the door. "Okay, Crab Apple, get in the truck," he said to his sister.

With a satisfied look on her face, Beth Martin scrunched up her nose at her brother, stuck out her tongue, and turned toward the kitchen door. Samuel followed behind her. Outside, Beth headed toward the truck with a spring in her step. Samuel followed with an uncertain gait.

"I thought you'd be meeting your baseball cronies at the school baseball field," Beth said as Samuel turned the truck down the side road at the intersection near the lumberyard. "I didn't know you were meeting them here at the lumberyard."

"I'm not meeting them anywhere," Samuel said flatly. "For your information, the information you'll probably have put in the ear of every member of your gossip group of friends before the sun goes down, I'm not taking any of the members of the team to the fair. I just made that up. The real reason that I didn't want to take you along is that for the last two months I've been escorting a girl around. We had it all arranged that we'd go to the fair together. I didn't know you wanted to go to the fair so bad."

Bethany Martin's eyes widened. "So that's why you've been spending so much time in town the last two months," she said with a teenage girl's smirk in her voice. "You haven't been playing baseball and running errands all day. You've been seeing your whoever girl."

"For various reasons that will become clear enough soon, I wasn't quite ready to tell Mom and Pop about it just yet," Samuel said. "Now I'll have to take you into my confidence. But with your gossipy mouth, you'll probably inform all your chatterbox friends in no time. I suppose I might as well paint the news on the side of the largest barn visible from the road."

"So who is she?" Beth asked in the voice of a teenage girl eager for gossip. "Is it someone I know? Is it Katherine Clarke?"

"She's a long way from Katherine Clarke," Samuel answered. That point was starting to dawn on Bethany Martin. They had passed the lumberyard and were heading past it and away down the road.

"Well, Katharine Clarke sure doesn't live down here," Beth said with growing confusion in her voice as she looked around at the unexpected turn her brother had taken. For another two-tenths of a mile she sat in silence and looked around.

"None of the other girls in town live down here. Nobody lives down here. Just who are you supposed to be seeing, and where are you supposed to be meeting her?"

"You'll find out soon enough," Samuel said. "We just have to take this road a piece."

"This road doesn't lead anywhere," Beth said. "It doesn't connect up with any other part of town."

Samuel didn't say anything more. He drove the last few tenths of a mile in silence. The Richardson house was coming up on the left side.

"Here we are," Samuel said in a flat voice as he slowed down and prepared to turn into the dirt drive leading to the front of the house.

"But this is the—" Beth suddenly stopped in midsentence. Her eyes went wide as the realization of the only logical person and only type of person whom her brother would be seeing in said establishment set in. Samuel started to turn toward the Richardson house.

"Sam, are you keeping time with one of Mrs. Richardson's girls?!" Beth blurted out as the full realization of the reason for her brother's secrecy set in.

"There aren't enough clocks in the world to keep track of the time I would like to keep with her," Samuel answered.

"But she's a painted woman!" Beth said.

"She's not painted like a barn," Samuel retorted. "She's not even a full-grown woman. She's not any much older than you are. She's had a hard life. That's why she had to come to work here. But I don't intend on leaving her here."

"But, Sam, she's—"

"Only because she's never known a better life or a real home and family," Samuel said, before his sister could say the word *whore* or a more genteel equivalent. "Between me and the rest of us, we're going to give her the family and home and life she's never had and has been starved for."

"Sam!"

Samuel slowed the truck and stopped it outside the front door. He reached for the door handle. "I'll bring her out and introduce you to each other."

"Sam!"

"You don't have to sit in the back of the truck when we go to the fair. There should be enough room for the three of us in the front. It may be a bit crowded, but it will get you used to sharing space with her. You're going to be doing a lot of that in the future."

"Sam?!"

Samuel opened the door and started to get out. "I'm sorry to have to throw it at you like this out of the blue, but I didn't know you wanted to go the fair so bad. I was trying to prepare things so that I didn't drop it on you so sudden, but the issue's been forced."

"Sam!"

"But the two of you should get on together. She's easy to get along with … as long as don't go asking any personal questions about her family. I have to warn you, that's kind of a sticking point with her. And don't come up behind her and take her by surprise."

"Sam!"

"Pastor Russell wouldn't think much about the way she behaves in the company of men, but she's behaved enough with women her age. Least I think she is. I've never been with her when there's been other girls around. This is the first time that it's been more than just her and me. But I'm sure she'll treat you with respect. You just forget the line of work she's in for now and treat her with respect, the way you would treat a relative. Treating her like a family member will get you into practice. After all, she's going to be your sister-in-law."

"Sam!"

"Once I get around to proposing."

"Sam!"

"While we're at the fair, don't let it slip and tell her that I'm planning to propose. I want to do that in my own way."

"Sam!"

Samuel stepped out of the truck. He turned around and looked back at his sister, whose mouth was still open.

"You stay in the truck, and don't go wandering about. Wait for me to come back out. If any stray men see you walking around, they might get the idea that you're a new recruit. It could lead to some embarrassing questions and offers being put to you."

"*Sam!*"

Samuel turned toward the house.

"But then again, it might be a way for you to pick up some extra spending money," he said in a wry voice, over his shoulder. "Girls your age with fresh and pretty faces like yours go for a premium at this house—"

Bethany's mouth fell farther open.

"Near twice the going rate. If you got yourself a position here, you would be able to afford those fancy dresses you're always yearning for in the Sears catalog."

"*Samuel!*"

Beth's brother left the truck and disappeared through the door of the house. The door closed behind him. Finding herself alone in the truck, Beth Martin looked around nervously to see if any men were looking at her. She was afraid that if anyone saw her sitting in the truck, they might be likely to conclude that she was indeed an employee of the house, either being picked up and transported elsewhere to perform the function performed by the women of the house or being returned from having performed the function elsewhere. Any minute she could find herself beset by a crude approach and proposition. Beth was not sure she could ever forgive her brother for putting her in the position she was in, sitting alone, exposed, in the cab of the truck. For a moment she seriously considered lying down on the front seat below the level of the windows and hiding to keep from being seen by anyone. But her brother had left the driver's door open.

Beth didn't have to wait near as long as she feared she might. In fairly short order, a youngish-looking woman emerged through the front door with her brother following. The pair veritably sprinted to the truck and around the front to the passenger side.

Samuel opened the door from the outside. Standing at an angle to the door, Beth got her first close view of the object of her brother's apparent infatuation and the source of her acute embarrassment that day. Beth hadn't been speaking all that much figuratively when she had referred to the women of the house as painted ladies. She had more or less literally expected to see an older woman with a coarse, shopworn face and a sour look, her face painted thick with garishly bright makeup.

Instead, the girl she saw standing on the ground outside the truck was a young and modestly dressed girl about her own age and the age of her brother. From the looks of her, the girl could indeed have been a girl from Beth's class in high school. But also the girl was far removed from any of Beth's classmates. Her face had the pastel beauty of the face of an idealized woman hand painted and transferred onto lithographed postcards. The sinking beauty of her face was framed and set off by her long, dark black hair. The dimensions of the girl's face could set artists to painting canvases for years and poets to dreaming and verbalizing for all time. The dimensions of the girl's front put the *Venus de Milo* to shame. Beth could easily see why her brother was smitten. She wondered how deeply smitten he was.

"Beth, I'd like you to meet my friend Clarinda," Samuel said, standing to the side of the door with no immediate trace of irony in his voice. "Clarinda, I'd like you to meet my sister, Beth."

The girl smiled and said hello quietly with no more irony in her voice than was in Samuel's voice. Beth smiled a forced and nervous smile and said a chirped hello.

"No need for anyone to ride in the back," Samuel said solicitously. "I think there's enough room for all three of us to ride in the front seat. ... Beth, why don't you slide over into the middle? It may be a little tight for all of us, but I think we can manage without any problem."

"Ah ... since ... the, ah, two of you are ... sweethearts," Beth stammered in an embarrassed manner, "the two of you sit next to each other. I'll sit on the outside."

Beth stepped out of the truck and let the girl climb in. After his sister climbed back into the cab, Samuel closed the door behind her.

"Now don't go leaning on the door in the wrong way and knock it open and fall out on your head halfway to the fair," Samuel said after he'd closed the door. "Father's ticked off at me enough about my not wanting to take you. I don't need to bring you back home with a broken neck."

"I'm not that dumb!" Beth called out in a piqued voice through the open side window of the truck, reverting to her standard little sister attitude toward her big brother, as Samuel walked around the front of the truck to the driver's side. In the forgetful moment of sibling bickering, Beth forgot who and what the girl was and spoke to her as if she were a member of her close circle of henpecking friends she dished dirt with, instead of the girl being her brother's lover and a high-priced courtesan who would be considered a loose and dirty woman in polite society.

"Big brothers can be such snots at times."

Samuel put the truck in gear and maneuvered it out of the driveway of the Richardson house, putting them all back on the road leading to the edge of town and out into the open country beyond.

There were more clouds in the sky that day than there had been in the almost completely clear skies on the days when Samuel had taken the girl on their first drive and to the lake. The clouds were lower, thicker, and more billowing than the high, thin clouds in the sky the other times. The lower clouds had more moisture in them, but they didn't threaten rain. After two months of maturing, the crops were higher, thicker, and greener than they had been the day Samuel had driven into town, where he had been propositioned by Ben Harper to go to the Richardson house.

The road to Ashton, the nearest town to the east, was a familiar one for Samuel Martin. He had driven it before. Beth knew the road as well. She had ridden it with him. On the other hand, sitting close to her brother's unexpected paramour in her unexpected profession, Beth Martin felt like she was on a road she had never been on before. She could only begin to guess at the particulars of the road the girl had traveled to get to where she was now.

For the first few minutes of the drive, the only sound in evidence in the truck had been the rattle of the engine. Inside the truck there had been a rather embarrassing silence. At least it was embarrassing for Beth as she sat shoulder to shoulder with a girl of questionable character whom her brother had only minutes earlier announced that she would be sharing space with as her future sister-in-law. Beth felt it was impolite to sit in silence. The girl might find her silence accusatory. Beth didn't expect her brother to make conversation; he wasn't a natural born conversationalist. Boys are that way.

"Have you been in town long?" Beth asked the girl, going with the only neutral and nonprovocative question she could think of on the spur of the moment.

"I've been here for a little under a year," the girl answered. "I got into town in late September of last year. It was startin' to get cold. I couldn't keep movin' anymore, and my legs were still sore from gettin' banged up."

"I don't remember seeing you in town during that time," Beth said.

"In that case, we're even," the girl answered. She continued to look straight ahead. "I've never seen you in town. I suppose that's mostly because you live on a farm. … I saw your farm from the road. Your brother drove me past your place once. Your brother also told me that you're still in high school in town. If we haven't seen each other, it's because we've been movin' in different circles."

"Sam told you about me?" Beth asked. She was a bit surprised that her brother had mentioned her to the girl.

The girl turned her head partway toward Beth. "Yes he did," she said. "More than once."

"Well, in that case, you have the advantage over me," Beth said. "I didn't know about you until about two minutes before we stopped to pick you up. Before that I didn't know you existed."

Beth was more or less winging it in her conversation. She had no idea how a churchgoing girl went about making girl talk with a fallen angel.

"When I was back home, not a lot of people knew I existed," the girl said, turning her head to face forward again. "As for me havin' the advantage over you, that's a switch and a first for me. All my life it's been other people who held the advantage over me."

"Where do you come from?"

Samuel looked across at Beth and shook his head slightly as an indication that she was touching her toes on the threshold of a subject that he had learned, and had been informed, to avoid. Whether his sister or the girl caught his gesture, Samuel wasn't sure.

"West Virginia originally," the girl answered. There wasn't any tone of rising anger or objection in her voice even though the question was the entryway into the subject of the girl's family, a subject she had put firmly off-limits with Samuel. Apparently she was willing to open up to another girl her age in a way she wasn't willing to reveal herself to him.

"Other than that, I don't come from anywhere in particular other than a place that held a lot of pain for me. I wasn't goin' anywhere in particular when I landed in your town. I guess I'm still not goin' anywhere in particular."

"How did you happen to hear about our town?" Beth asked. The question was an indirect ruse. What Beth was really trying to get at was the story of how and why the girl had become a prostitute.

"What I happened to hear," the girl said, "was the sound of a gang of darkie hoboes walkin' across the top of the boxcar I was ridin' in, comin' down the ladder on the car, and slidin' their way alongside the car to the open door of the empty car I was in by myself. I'd heard all kinds of stories 'bout what darkies do to white girls they catch alone. I didn't want to find out if any of those stories were true. So I jumped. I landed not far outside your town. Hurt my legs and feet doin' it."

The girl was still looking at the road ahead. Beth was still looking at the girl, but she would have felt more comfortable looking elsewhere.

"I was all banged up from the fall. But I was used to being in a banged-up state. Spent half my developing life in a state of being banged up and ripped up. … My leg and feet hurt, but I kept goin'. I went 'round on foot for days, sleepin' in barns, stealin' eggs and whatever else I could find to eat."

The girl looked over at Samuel.

"One day a nasty old farmer caught me stealin' from his barn. He had me trapped in there, but I guess he was too old to do with a young girl what men like to do to girls when they have them cornered and have a ready excuse, like catchin' a girl thievin' from them. I had my hand on my brother's jackknife. I was ready to fight if the man came after me. I figured I would probably lose if I went after him with the knife. But I wasn't about to be taken down hard and done dirty and painful again."

The girl looked back ahead.

"Instead of forcin' himself on me, he just called me a tramp and ran me off. As he did so, he said that if I wanted to be a tramp, I should go and live in the bordello in your town. That's how I came to know that Mrs. Richardson's house was here and what it was. I was all dirty and ragged-lookin' by the time I got there, beggin' to be taken in. Mrs. Richardson took one look at me and was shocked. She took me right in, cleaned me up, gave me a good meal, and called a doctor to fix me up. Later she took me all the way in and made me a girl of the house."

Beth looked at the girl.

"When my brothers weren't forcin' me to play the whore with them, slammin' me down and ripping themselves into me, they said that with my looks and the form I had, a whore is what I was cut out to be. I took them up on that and used it to open the door at Mrs. Richardson's house. I sure didn't see any other doors opening for me anywhere else at the time."

Beth looked away.

Samuel wished he had been the one who had caught the girl stealing out of their barn. He would have opened up a much better door for the girl without her having to go knocking on Mrs. Richardson's door.

"That's ... quite a story," Beth said with polite indirection.

"It ain't much of a story as I see it," the girl said. "But it's pretty much the only one I've got."

The girl turned her head partially around to look at Beth again. "I suppose you know what kind of place the house is and what function I perform there," she said in a quasi-rhetorical tone.

"Ah … yes," the otherwise proper Bethany said in a strained voice. "The reputation of the establishment has preceded you."

"I met your brother there when he came to the house one night with a friend. What did your brother tell you about me? But it don't make no never mind. I am what I am, and that's all I'll ever be."

"He didn't tell me anything about anything," Beth said with entry-level pique in her voice. "Not until the last minute, when he got out of the truck to knock on your door. He left me sitting there in the truck worried that some sweaty mule driver was going to come along and think that I was fresh blood being delivered and who'd want to get his licks in first, ahead of everyone else."

The girl got a laugh out of the image of proper and retiring young woman left dangling at the fringes of a den of vice.

"I know about sweating," the girl said. "I've sweated a lot of myself out in a lot of beds. But not in the bed of a truck."

Samuel leaned forward and looked past Clarinda to his sister. "Far as any objections or complaints you might have go," he said to Beth, "keep them to yourself. Don't you go complaining to me, Mom, or Dad about anything about this outing, including who I'm bringing along apart from you. I'm taking you like you wanted. Do me the favor of not being your usual snotty self and tattling. I am taking you like you want."

"Only because Father threatened to hit you over the head with a rake if you didn't take me along to the fair," Beth said in the voice of an annoyed little sister. "Otherwise you would have gone on your own way and not told anybody about your secret traveling companion. You're secret's out now, at least with me. Now you'll probably swear me to secrecy and make me not tell Mother and Father what you're doing and who you've been seeing in secret. I'll have to walk around biting my tongue with the secret inside me."

"You keeping a secret means it will be all over town before the engine on this truck cools," Samuel said.

Beth reverted to form and stuck out her tongue at her brother. The girl sort of smiled at the sibling bickering going on around her. She kept looking at the road ahead.

"I'm not surprised he hasn't told anybody about me," Clarinda said without any noticeable hint of resentment or rancor in her voice. "I'm not the kind of girl a respectable boy, even a respectable farm boy, dangles on his arm like a charm on a charm bracelet. The likes of me don't get brought home to meet the folks too often. So I suppose it don't make no difference if your folks find out about me or don't. He's not going to be bringing me home to meet them."

To Beth it seemed apparent that her brother had been keeping his intentions secret from the girl as well as from their parents.

"He said he's going to …" Beth stopped speaking. She was going to say that her brother had stated his intent to marry the girl, but she remembered that he had told her to keep it mum until he was ready to propose in his own time. Now Beth found herself the keeper of secrets from the girl and from her parents.

"Does your brother treat you right?" Beth heard the girl ask. Beth had been looking forward. At the unexpected question, she turned her head around and looked over at the girl. The girl had turned her head around all the way and was looking at her.

"Does he look out for you? Does he take care of you? Does he protect you?"

"Well … yes," Beth stammered again. "He can be quite a pill sometimes, but he's a good brother."

"Well, at least there's one family in this world that does things right," the girl said. She glanced ahead and then looked back at Beth. "Do you care for your brother?"

"Ah … yes," Beth said. The girl was still looking straight at her. Beth hadn't thought that blue eyes could be so penetrating.

"Are you thinkin' that I'm going to end up hurting him?" the girl asked.

"Well, I don't know," Beth said evasively. "I don't know what you're thinking."

"You're probably thinkin' that because I'm a fallen woman, I don't have any kind of heart myself, that I'm not capable of love, and that I'm going to break his heart," the girl said. "Is that what you were thinkin' of me and what I might do to your brother?"

"I don't know what you think of or about my brother," Beth said, giving another diplomatically evasive answer. "What the two of you think of each other is your business."

"Do you think I'm capable of hurting him?"

Samuel winced a bit and touched the now healed scratches on his face where the girl had scratched him when he had accidentally crossed the trip line and had come up behind her unexpectedly. But the direction the girl was taking was an encouraging sign for Samuel. The girl hadn't said that she loved him with heart love, but the fact that she was asking questions related to love of the heart was a hopeful sign that she thought in terms of love of the heart.

"I don't know," Beth replied, not quite knowing how to answer the question. "He's no milquetoast. He's beyond the age where I can take him in hand. Whatever he gets into with you is his own doing. He's old enough to stand on his own. I guess when it comes to affairs of the heart, he's old enough to know what he's doing."

"In that case, you don't have to worry about me hurting him in any affair of the heart. The establishment I work in isn't dedicated to affairs of the heart, just affairs of the body."

The girl looked over at Samuel.

"As far as affairs of the body go, your brother knows what he's doin' quite well."

Beth looked down, blushing, more from shock than embarrassment. The girl was a teenager, hardly much older than her, but there was no tenderness of youth in her. In her years, she seemed to have taken in and absorbed all the hardness of the world.

The girl turned her face back to Beth and resumed her questioning. The blush hadn't faded from Beth's face.

"Are you here putting all these questions to me because you're lookin' out for your brother's interests?"

"I'm here because I wanted to go to the Ashton summer fair and he said he was taking his baseball buddies, but Father badgered him into taking me along," Beth answered curtly. "He didn't tell me that it was you he was really planning on taking along. I didn't come here with the idea of guarding his virtue from the blandishments of wayward women."

Beth caught herself. She had no idea how hard a hardened girl might react to being declared less than virtuous.

"Are you afraid that your brother's getting caught up with a tainted woman of vice and sin?" the girl asked in a tone that was half joking and half serious.

"Well ... no ... not exactly," Beth answered in an embarrassed tone that didn't sound very convincing. "He's never gone this ... far with any girl before. I never could tell him anything about girls. But then I never was able to tell him much of anything."

"Not that you don't try," Samuel interjected, "every two minutes."

"With all your questions," Clarinda said to Beth, "you do sound a bit like a doting mother checkin' up on what kind of girl her son is gettin' himself mixed up with. Don't get me wrong, it's kinda nice to see a sister so concerned for her brother. I never had a sister be concerned with me. Or any brothers concerned for me."

When it came to the subject of age and womanhood, Beth did have a question.

"If you don't take the question as being impertinent," Beth said, "do you mind if I at least ask you how old you are?"

"I'm seventeen," the girl answered in a matter-of-fact voice. "Least they tell me I was born in '95."

"Didn't your mother tell you when you were born?" Beth asked the obvious. "If anyone would have known what year you were born, it would be your mother. She's the one who gave birth to you. Women tend to graphically remember the year they give birth."

"My mother didn't live long enough to tell me much of anything I can remember," Clarinda said. "The biggest impression my mother left me with was her dyin'. When they buried my mother, I wanted to crawl into the coffin with her, but they wouldn't let me." The girl looked at Beth. "Since you asked me how old I am, how old are you?"

"Sixteen," Beth said.

"That's a good age to be if you've got a good life to live out your years in—not too young to be naive, not too old to have picked up much hurt."

The girl's story of her earlier life was starting to make Beth feel as cold and distressed as her story of being a starving tramp girl with no future and no option other than to present herself to a madam and enlist herself in service at a bordello. She wondered if the girl had anything approximating a single warm story in her life to tell.

On the other side of the truck, Samuel was getting nervous that the line the girl had drawn was being crossed. She had made it clear to him earlier that her past and her family of the past was poison ground that she had no desire to revisit. It could ruin their day at the fair.

"Now hold on, Sis," Samuel said. "You're getting into territory that's painful for her and that she doesn't want to talk about. Let's just both of you leave all that where it lies and talk about something else."

Samuel looked over at Beth.

"Why don't you tell Clarinda about where you are in high school and what you're doing in school," Samuel said, trying to turn the conversation onto a blander track.

"Mrs. Richardson's educated," the girl said. "But I never got educated beyond learning to read and write. It weren't done where I come from. My father pulled me out soon after I learned just 'nough to not be completely illiterate dumb. He said I had more important things to do at home, like doin' cleaning and lookin' after him when he was falling down drunk. Far as school education goes, about all I know is how to read and write my name. I don't read that much, and the second part of it don't do that much for me as I don't use or even want to remember my name, let alone write it."

"Then Clarinda isn't your real name?" Beth asked.

"I just took the name from a tale I heard once that had a princess in it by that name. It was a romantic story. Though I never particularly thought romantic-like, I took the name into my head. When I left home with only my ragged clothes on my back, I left my real name behind. I don't want to go back for it."

Samuel was afraid that Beth was taking the girl and the conversation back into dangerous territory. But Beth didn't ask anything more. Largely in silence, they drove the remaining miles to the fair.

"I know what Father said," Bethany Martin said. "I was there. I know he told you to keep an eye on me and look out for me. But you don't have to keep me at your side and lead me around like a lamb on a rope."

The three of them stood on the grass in a small group of their own just inside the entrance to the fairground, fenced in by a split rail wood fence. Samuel had dutifully paid the nominal entrance fee for all three of them. Adults dutifully paid to enter the fair, but the fence was minimal and penetrable enough that young children could easily hop over or slip through the rails. Immediately beyond them, the booths and attractions spread out in only nominally organized form.

"I know the two of you want to be alone together without a little sister tagging along. I'll be all right by myself. You don't have to look out for me. I'm capable of looking out for myself. You two just go on your way. I'll walk around on my own. I'm a big enough girl to do that."

For his part in the matter, Samuel was conscientious enough in following his father's wishes and concerned enough for the well-being of his sister that he would have followed the instructions given him and would have kept his sister with him. At the same time, the independent-thinking Samuel wanted to be alone with the girl without his little sis hanging on to his belt. It bothered his conscience, but he split the difference.

"Okay, we'll split up," Samuel said to Beth. Then he pointed his finger at her. "But don't you go outside the fair, especially if someone promises to show you some kind of exotic and forbidden thing he says they wouldn't let on the fairground. Stay with the crowd inside the fairground. Don't let some carny barker lead you off into a tent alone. And don't let anyone offer you anything to drink that you haven't bought yourself." He pointed at Clarinda and resumed talking to Beth. "I don't need you getting kidnapped by a white slaver, shipped off to a house in another state, and made to do by force what she's had to do out of necessity in order to get away from her bad family. Father and Mother would never forgive me if I let something like that happen to you. I'd never be able to forgive myself."

"Sam, it's only a small-town county fair," Beth said. "It's not Coney Island in the big city. This isn't a pirates' lair, and the people here aren't Saracen raiders looking to kidnap girls for a sultan's harem. Most of the people here are from this town and the other towns in the county. They're not white slavers."

"Maybe," Samuel said. "But you just keep your wits about you. When you're not a little snot off in a snit, you're a good sister. I don't want to see you get hurt. You don't know the first thing about the kind of tricks men pull in order to fool a girl and have their way with them."

Clarinda had a tell-me-all-about-it look on her face.

"I don't want any slimy man getting his slimy way with my sister. I'll lay out any man who tries to mess with you flat on the ground in a bloody heap."

"Oh, Sam," Beth said, "stop being so juvenile and melodramatic. You're thinking like you're still on the school boxing team. You can't solve every problem with your fists. Now nothing is going to happen." She held out her hand, palm up. "Just give me some money that I can spend myself. It's not like you're being drained of funds you wouldn't have spent anyway. If I was with you, you would have spent the same on me just the same. You two go your way, and I'll go mine."

Beth's mind added, *And never the twain shall meet.*

Beth was starting to get the feeling that, where the girl was concerned, she was possibly dealing with something beyond her meager ability to work out. The question was whether or not it would prove to be something beyond her brother's ability to sort out.

Beth pointed to the nearest booth with its jars of honey and homegrown fruit preserves on display for sale. "I'll meet you over there when it's time to leave. Until then, you two go off and have a good time on your own."

Samuel handed his sister some spending money, and she walked off on her own path. Once the two of them were alone, Samuel turned to the girl and asked her what she would like to see or do. Almost as soon as he asked, the girl took his arm and turned him in the direction she was looking.

"I want to ride that," she girl with almost childlike eagerness, pointing to the merry-go-round set up on one side of the fairground. "I've always wanted to ride one of those. I've seen them from a distance, but I've never had the chance to ride one."

Off at the far side of the fairground, the merry-go-round was turning, its bright colors flashing in the sun. The calliope sound of the ride floated in the air above the murmur of the crowd and the stir of the breeze. The girl grabbed Samuel's hand and led him toward the merry-go-round at an excited half run. Her womanly form and her long hair bounced and swayed as she ran with Samuel in tow. The darkly beautiful and mysterious courtesan was acting like a delighted seven-year-old girl at a circus for the first time.

The merry-go-round wasn't near the biggest-sized one in operation in 1912. It had been retained by the town for the fair and brought in by sections on wagons. To Samuel, merry-go-rounds were something for little children. It kind of surprised him that the girl wanted to ride it. But if she wanted to ride it, he would buy tickets for them. The things he was willing to do for love of the girl. At least they could sit together on the same mechanical horse, where he could hold her tight to keep her from falling off.

Samuel and the girl stepped onto the wide circular wooden platform of the merry-go-round. The merry-go-round sported the usual collection of wooden horses painted bright garish colors that one never sees on a real horse. The horses proved too small for two people to sit together on. He boosted the girl up onto one of the wooden horses. Instead of mounting a different horse, he climbed on the same horse and sat behind her. He wrapped his arms around her to catch her if she started to fall. He hoped the girl would see it as a protective gesture on his part.

The merry-go-round creaked and started to turn slowly. As it did so, Samuel stepped around to the other side of the wooden horse behind the girl, put one foot in the stirrup the girl wasn't using, put his hand on the pole just above the girl's hand, stood up in the stirrup, wrapped his other arm around the girl's waist, and held her steady next to him, holding her steady in place on the back of the wooden horse. If the girl had asked why he was leaning forward so close, Samuel would have simply said that he was leaning forward in order to keep his balance and to prevent himself from falling off backward. But it was just an excuse to draw himself close to her and pull her closer to him. Some observers might have considered the couple to be putting themselves into what could be considered a compromising position. But the girl lived by putting herself in compromising positions.

The merry-go-round started to turn. The horses started to move up and down on their drop rods. Samuel held the girl tighter. The ride began to pick up speed.

In short order the merry-go-round was up to speed. Standing on one leg with all his weight on it and the other leg dangling, with one hand on the metal pole and his other arm wrapped around the girl, Samuel leaned forward slightly, pulling himself up against the girl's back. With his arm tight around her waist and his chest pressed against her back, he could feel little trembles of excitement pass through her as the merry-go-round turned and the horse rose and fell.

The girl was excited to be on a ride she had never been on before. It was a sensation and a feeling she had never experienced.

Since the girl was sitting higher in the carved saddle on the wooden horse, her head was at the same level as Samuel's head. Using his position and forward leaning as an excuse, Samuel nestled his head next to the girl's. He could feel the softness of her hair on the side of his head and cheek. From the close-in position of his ear, above the rattle and grind of the moving merry-go-round, he could hear the little subvocal pipes and sighs of enjoyment the girl made in her throat.

For a reasonably long time given the small admittance fee they had paid, the merry-go-round ride continued to turn. The same visual themes repeated themselves in sequence, the familiar territory of home and the people and the world Samuel was familiar with. Sitting behind the girl, feeling the press of her body against his, Samuel wanted to spend the rest of his life going around in circles with the girl. The girl kept her head straight ahead, looking out over the passing scene. She leaned back against the support of his body, but she didn't turn her head back or around to look at him.

Samuel wasn't feeling dizzy on the merry-go-round. The only thing that came close to making him feel dizzy was his thinking about the life he would share with her. Though the merry-go-round was turning in circles and the horizon was moving, Samuel saw only one horizon. As the simple act of taking the girl on her first ride on a merry-go-round had shown the girl a new experience and a new world she had never known before, he would take her from the old world of pain and fear she had known and the world of false love she knew now and transport her over the horizon into a new world of love, one she had never known or experienced before.

Samuel leaned his head down farther over the girl's shoulder and tried to kiss her on the neck, but he stopped. There were other people on the merry-go-round at the time, some with small children. They might have considered Samuel to be putting on an improper public display for young children to witness. If they were to complain to the operator of the merry-go-round, it could prove to be a problem. For Samuel the real problem was that the girl's long hair got in the way.

The fair didn't possess anything resembling a tunnel of love where he could kiss the girl frontally or at least from the side when they went through the darkened section. Most of the booths were open-air booths with no tent covering. Despite his warnings to Beth of a slimy carny barker luring her off into the back of a dark tent, there wasn't even a tent large enough to have a secluded section, or that even had a loose flap that he could walk the girl behind and kiss her.

Of course a county fair of that day or most any day would not be complete without one of those test-of-strength machines where one uses a wooden mallet to hit a lever, which in turn drives a slide up a pole graduated in measurements of height, the height the slide rises to on the blow being the measure of strength of the individual swinging the mallet. It was basically a man thing. Women of the day were considered to be too demure to engage in displays of strength or even to consider swinging a mallet. The strongest man was supposed to send the slide up all the way to where it would strike and ring a bell at the top. The only reward offered was that the he-man who rang the bell would be able to show off to his girlfriend or the other males in his company.

The operator of the game commented that Samuel looked like a strapping lad who could knock the bell off the top of the pole. Samuel stepped up to the challenge. All contestants got three tries per ticket. As the girl looked on, Samuel took what he considered to be a reasonably hard swipe at the impact head that drove the lever that propelled the slide. The slide rose a little over halfway to the top. Samuel was a bit chagrined. He comforted himself by thinking to himself that the thing was probably rigged such that only John L. Sullivan could ring the bell. But his thinking of himself as the girl's protector was a big male thing for Samuel. Having put his relative strength on display with the juvenile test, he was afraid that he might end up leaving the girl with the idea that he was physically unable to protect her.

He tried again with a measure of focused concentration that he thought should be enough to make up the difference. This time he sent the slide up somewhat over three-quarters of the way. He had assumed that the curve of exertion it would take to ring the bell was a linear one, but it was starting to seem that the curve was one of exponentially increasing difficulty. It was starting to look like it was going to be harder to reach his goal than he thought. He had come close to employing almost all the power he had on hand.

With a drive that was more of a personal internal explosion than a focused external effort, Samuel wound up and bent himself over double in his body and mind. His effort sent the slide up to the top, where it just barely touched the bell at the apex of its fixed vertical trajectory. Technically he had scored, but the bell gave an uncertain ring. Samuel walked away smoothly and confidently, but there was low-level pain in his back and elbow joints from the hard and spasmodic wrenching effort.

Being a baseball player with a sure arm and an accurate eye, Samuel did better at the baseball toss booth, where he knocked over enough wooden pins to win a prize: a bar of candy, which he gave to the girl.

Of course a county fair wouldn't be complete without live animals. The fairground had permanent constructed pens with live animals ranging from prizewinning bulls to sheep with their young lambs. In a near replay of their first drive in the country, when they had stopped so she could see the foal, the girl crouched down and reached between the rails of the pen so she could pet the lambs. The lambs were more animated than the ewes, which stood around placidly, acting like they had seen it all before. Their lambs moved around, making bleating sounds. They sniffed at the girl's hands as she reached to pet them.

For a while the girl petted the lambs. As she did so, she seemed to have a satisfied and contented look on her face. Then suddenly the look passed, to be replaced with one of troubled uncertainty. Still kneeling, the girl turned her face to look at Samuel.

"Are these lambs going to be raised for their wool?" the girl asked. "Or are they going to be sent off to be cut up for lamb chops?"

The area wasn't a wool-producing region. Unless they became someone's pet, the baaing lambs with their inquisitive noses were destined to end up as mutton or lamb chops on someone's table. Samuel reluctantly started to open his mouth to so inform the girl.

Before he could answer, she turned her head back toward the lambs. "Don't tell me," she said in a flat and hollow tone. "I don't want to know."

Samuel didn't answer. He didn't have to answer. The girl seemed to know in advance what he was going to say. Maybe she had caught the look on his face. For a moment she continued to pet the lambs.

"Looks like we're all in the same pen in life," the girl spontaneously said to the lambs. "Little brainless, wobbly legged, wet-nosed things set out to be meat on someone's platter to have the good part of them chewed up and their gristle spat out by someone who don't care that they once lived or that they died to provide the meal they're eating."

Samuel ached to tell the girl that wasn't the way with him and that it wouldn't be the way with them the rest of her life when they were married and living at home on the farm. But the time wasn't right to ask her for her hand, the hand she was using to pet the lambs, in marriage.

The animals in the next pen over had a more secure, if not pedestrian, future as farm animals. They were goats. Given that goat meat was not big on American tables, the goats in the pen were not in immediate mortal danger. Given that goat cheese wasn't a big seller either, the female goats in the pen weren't even facing a future of hard milking.

There were several mature goats in the goat pen with a variety of types of horns on the males. Some were straight, and others were twisted. As with the lambs in the sheep pen, there were also several young goats in the pen. The young male goats had buds on their heads that would later turn into mature horns. In their way, the baby goats were as endearing as the young lambs. The kids were weaned off of their mothers' milk. Samuel bought a small bag of dried corn that Clarinda could feed the baby goats with. She held handfuls of the corn down for the kids to eat. The kids swarmed as the girl's hand extended over the fence. They greedily devoured the corn from her hands, pushing each other's heads away as they jockeyed for position and a share of the grain. The girl laughed softly at the feel of the lips and tongues of the young goats licking her hand, wiping their saliva over her palms as she held out the grain for them to eat. She didn't seem to mind getting her hands dirty. Some people would say that the girl lived to dirty herself up.

The girl had neglected to bring a handkerchief along with her. When she was finished feeding the goats, she found her hands coated with goat slaver that had to be removed. There were no modern full-service washrooms at the fairgrounds. She could have been conveniently expedient and wiped her hands on her dress, but she wanted to spare her dress, of which she had only two apart from her work uniform corsets. Instead she reached over and wiped her hands on the lower leg of Samuel's trousers.

As they walked away, the girl looked back, but not at the goats. She looked again at the pen that held the doomed lambs.

"I wish I could buy one of them and make it a pet and take it home with me," she said with a tone of fatalistic resignation in her voice. "At least I could keep one of them off the butcher's block. But I don't think Mrs. Richardson would allow it. We've got no place at the house to keep one."

The girl looked at Samuel.

"I don't suppose you could buy one for me and keep it on your farm. I might not get to see it very much, but at least I'd know it's alive."

Samuel balked inwardly. "I don't know if those ones are for sale," he said. "And I don't think I have enough money on me to buy one."

The other problem was that if he did buy a lamb as a pet for the girl and brought it home, he would have to explain to his parents whom he was keeping it for. Many people there were who would not consider the girl to be an innocent lamb.

A diversionary idea came into Samuel's head. He took the girl by the hand. "Come with me," he said as he started to lead the girl away from the pens. "I think I know a way to get you a pet that isn't any kind of work for anyone at all, one that Mrs. Richardson will let you bring into the house without any problem, one just as cuddly as a live lamb but that doesn't leave droppings all over the place, one you can keep in your room but that you don't have to feed or water."

Samuel led Clarinda to where they had a shooting gallery set up on the edge of the fairground, on the opposite side from where the merry-go-round stood. Samuel was a very good shot. If he had been at the fair alone, the shooting gallery was one of the first places he would have headed for. Since the girl had said that she didn't like hunting and wasn't impressed by shooting skills, he had avoided the shooting gallery. But now the opportunity presented itself to impress her with his shooting skills without killing a living thing. In the process, he could win the girl's heart by winning for her a prize that would serve as a replacement for the lamb she wanted to save.

One of the prizes they gave away at the shooting gallery were stuffed animals that resembled bear cubs. The soft stuffed toy bears were inspired by the apocryphal story in which, as an attempt to ingratiate themselves with the newly elected president they knew to be a hunter, the city fathers of a city somewhere offered Teddy Roosevelt the opportunity to shoot a live bear that had been tied to a tree by a rope that was looped around its neck. The sportsman and conservationist Teddy Roosevelt was incensed by what he considered a cowardly and cruel act and ordered the animal released. Inspired by Roosevelt's gesture of kindness to the trapped and helpless animal, toy manufacturers started making plump stuffed animals that resembled bears but that were more child-friendly. Thus the teddy bear was born.

The shooting gallery was a long counter set up several yards in front of a wall of hay bales designed to stop the bullets. In front of the hay bales, lines of clay targets the size and shape of smoking pipes were set up as targets. On the shooting counter were several Winchester pump-action twenty-two-caliber rifles. Samuel paid the fee, picked up one of the rifles, and fired at the first clay pipe at the end of the line of targets. He missed. Rather the shot missed, but Samuel saw the small spurt of dust where the bullet entered the hay bale behind the target line. He knew he had aimed right. He also knew that shooting gallery proprietors had a reputation for setting the sights on their guns wrong as a way of preventing shooters from hitting the targets and winning the prizes. Samuel leaned toward the girl, who was standing beside him.

"The sights are off on this gun," he whispered to her. "Distract the supervisor while I reset them."

Now Clarinda knew all about distracting men. Being a distraction to men was what she and those of her profession were dedicated to. As Samuel pretended to prepare to fire again, Clarinda sort of sashayed in a calculated and rather obvious lady-of-questionable-virtue suggestive way over to where the manager of the shooting gallery was watching, close to the far end of the counter. She walked past the man all the way to the end of the counter just beyond him to where he would have to turn his head away from Samuel to look at her. Having arrived at her calculated position, Clarinda stepped in close so her lower body was in contact with the counter. A proper young woman of the era would not have advanced that close to a man in such a forward manner. Clarinda leaned over the counter in a suggestive way. The angle of her lean and the press of the counter holding her stomach back enhanced her full and obvious womanly figure, causing it to bulge and bringing it more to the forefront. She laid her arms down on the counter and leaned farther forward. The man turned his head around to look at the obvious figure of the attractive young woman acting in an obvious manner. The man was leaning against the counter with one hand resting on it. Clarinda reached over and ran the tip of one finger in a circular pattern over his hand.

"Now a big, strong man like you must have more to do at night than just sit home and clean his guns," Clarinda said in a hushed but otherwise obvious tone. "You should come by and see me some night over at the Richardson house down by the river in the next town down the line west of here. We women at the house know all about taking care of strong and handsome men like you and how to show them a good time."

The man shifted his stance, stood up straighter, and turned around the rest of the way to face the girl. From his new position, he couldn't even see Samuel out of the corner of his distracted eye. He sort of cocked his head back slightly once to indicate the boy he could no longer see. "What about your friend over there?" the man asked about the teenage boy, who had a loaded gun in his hand.

"He's something of a special friend and customer of mine," Clarinda said. She continued moving her finger back and forth in slow, suggestive figure-eight pattern on the counter as if it were the man's hand. "But with me friendship does take a back seat where business is concerned. When it comes to what he is to me, he's a payin' customer just like all the rest. Just like you could be if you were of a mind to. I go for a little more than the other girls in the house. But you pay for what you get in life. And when you pay for me, you get what you pay for."

"So where is this house of yours?" the man asked. Clarinda gave him accurate instructions on how to get to the house. In this way, she kept the conversation and the diversion going.

Distracting the man while Samuel fixed the crabbed rifle was only part of the reason for her display of obviousness. Samuel was something of a special friend to her, but he was still a customer, and customers were what she and the house were about. The merry-go-round operator and the game and sales booth proprietors were all at the fair promoting themselves and soliciting their wares. The girl didn't see why she shouldn't do a little promotion of her own. Special friendships on the side notwithstanding, Clarinda wasn't reticent about promoting her wares and soliciting some extra business outside her customary territory.

With the man duly, obviously, and thoroughly distracted, Samuel quickly reached into his pocket and pulled out a small screwdriver with a small blade that he carried with him to make adjustments to the truck carburetor. With it he reset the rifle sights the two clicks his marksman eye estimated it would take to bring them back to straight and true.

With his task accomplished thanks to the aid of the girl's accomplished skill at distracting men, Samuel shouldered the rifle again and fired. The first clay pipe target in line shattered from a direct centered hit. He had set the sights just right. From there he started breaking the small clay pipes in rapid sequence. Targets were disappearing at an alarming rate. Soon even the distracted shooting gallery operator became conscious of what was happening downrange. When the rifle Samuel was using ran out of ammunition, the operator tried to hand him another loaded rifle with equally jehawed sights. Saying he was used to the rifle he was using, Samuel made the operator reload that one. From there he proceeded to turn the rest of the shooting gallery into a veritable Gettysburg for clay pipes.

Samuel cleaned out the target row sufficiently to win a large stuffed bear for the girl. When he handed the stuffed animal to her, she gathered it in her arms and hugged it as if she were holding the lamb she had not been able to save.

They walked away from the shooting gallery with the girl holding the teddy bear in her arms up next to her chest as if she were carrying a child. Samuel noticed a large manufacture's tag on the back of the stuffed bear. "If I had a knife, I could cut that tag off for you," he said. "But I didn't think to bring my jackknife with me. We can do it back at the house."

The girl stopped in her walk, reached into a pocket in the side of her dress, and pulled out an elongated brown rectangular object that seemed to have metal caps on the ends. Without saying anything, and still holding the teddy bear in her other hand, the girl raised her hand in the air in front of her, up to the level of her neck. With a sharp snap of her wrist, she brought her hand down. A five-inch knife blade snapped out of its handle and locked into place. The unidentifiable object in the girl's hand proved to be some kind of flip-blade knife. The decidedly unladylike instrument resembled something an alley fighter would use instead of being a dainty fingernail trimmer out of a woman's manicure set.

Without saying anything, the girl handed the knife to Samuel. In turn she handed him the teddy bear. As if being confronted by a girl carrying the functional equivalent of a switchblade was an everyday occurrence for him, Samuel took the knife from her, along with the bear he had just won for her.

"Now don't go cuttin' a hole in it," the girl said as Samuel proceeded to cut the tag off the stuffed animal.

Samuel finished cutting the tag off the teddy bear. Then he handed the teddy bear, now shorn of its manufacturer's identity, back to the girl. The nameless girl took the now nameless stuffed animal back in her arm. In turn, Samuel handed her back the knife he had not known she was carrying. She pushed a small metal stud in the handle near the base of the blade, which released the catch that held the blade out forward, and folded it back into the handle. Samuel was a bit chagrined that he hadn't noticed the weight in the girl's pocket that would have told him she was carrying the knife. But he hadn't suspected that she would be packing a knife, especially a knife built for quick deployment and surprise use. Like other males of his era, Samuel held the prejudice that it was an improper thing for a proper young woman to be familiar with a weapon of that sort. Then again, most people of the day would not find the girl herself to be particularly proper.

"Where'd you get that?" Samuel asked casually as the girl put the concealed weapon back in her pocket. "Did you buy it at the hardware store in town?"

"I stole it from one of my brothers," she said flatly. "He came lookin' for me later with a snoot full of liquor and a head full of wantin' to get at a girl—any girl. He and his brother had been comin' at me that way and more as I had grown older and more womanlike. By then I had had enough. All I was thinkin' was that I wasn't going to take it anymore. I surprised him by pulling his own knife on him. He was surprised that I had had it with me. He was surprised, but he wasn't worried about it none. He didn't think I knew how to use it. He didn't think I had the strength to use it. He didn't think I had the guts to use it. But you'd be surprised what you can do when you've got nothin' but fear and anger runnin' through your veins. … I gave him his knife back. Across the face, not in his hand. I could feel the knife cut his face to the bone. Probably scarred him for life. He can count himself lucky that I didn't give it to him in his heart."

In the midst of the cheerful pastoral scene of a county fair in the sun, Samuel caught a darker vision of the girl slashing out wildly and desperately; a man falling back, his hand covering his face, blood surging out around and between his fingers; and the girl turning and running.

"Father and my other brother came after me. I didn't have enough room in my head to imagine what they would do to me if they were to catch me. They probably would have killed me. ... I hid in the woods. They flushed me. I went runnin' again. Got to the tracks ahead of them. A freight was comin'. I jumped across the tracks just feet ahead of the steam engine. The train cut them off. As soon as I had the train between them and me, instead of goin' on straight, I turned right around and grabbed the ladder on the first open car I saw. Just about pulled my arms out of their sockets, but I managed to haul myself up and into the car. When the train passed them, I was nowhere in sight. They probably thought I had gone on runnin' straight into the woods on the other side of the track. They probably went on lookin' for me in that direction."

Samuel had another vision, one of vengeful males in angry pursuit of the girl. They were a dark vision for a sunny day.

"Along with the clothes on my back, the knife was the only thing I carried away from home. When those Negro hoboes started comin' into the car I was in, I figured I couldn't handle them all with a knife in such a small place. So I jumped. You heard me tell your sister the rest of the story."

Samuel had no way of telling whether the girl's story was true or not. But truth has a way of being hard and dirty. Too much of the girl's story had the ring of hard and dirty truth about it. Apparently the story of the girl's flight from home was even more intense than the cryptic partial story she had told him and Beth in the truck on the way to the fair.

The girl fell silent. She offered no further explanations, and Samuel asked no further questions. In her arms the girl was holding the substitute for the doomed lamb she had not been able to save. Samuel looked at the girl he now thought of more as the lost lamb he would save.

Over the course of the rest of the day, Samuel and the girl walked around the rest of the fair. As they explored the rest of the entertainment, the dark mountain gothic of the girl's past faded into the pastoral frivolity of the county fair. In Samuel's mind, the course of the rest of his life was set. In Samuel's heart, he was convinced that the course of his love would deliver the girl from the pain of her past. As he watched the girl embrace the stuffed animal he had won for her, he hoped his love and attention would win her to him. He hoped she would come to accept and embrace a life with him, a country life in which they would become a country couple who would fit in with the kind of countrypeople around them at the fair.

When the day had run its course for them and the appointed time for them to leave arrived, Samuel and the girl headed back to where Samuel's sister had said that she would meet them. As they approached the booth by which Beth had indicated they should meet, Samuel saw his sister standing there talking with a boy. From a distance, Samuel reckoned that the boy was a teenager about their age. He was dressed in the same kind of country clothes they were wearing. One thing Samuel could see as they approached was the way his sister looked at the boy and the way the boy looked at her. In his sister's expressions, she was more animated and lively in her communication with the boy than she had ever been with him or that he had ever seen her be with any other boy her age.

"There you are," Beth said as Samuel and the girl walked up to them. She pointed her finger at the boy she was standing with. "I'd like you to meet William Howard. We met each other here at the fair today." She pointed to Samuel and Clarinda. "Bill, this is my brother, Samuel, and his ... friend, whom I just met today."

The boy said a friendly hello. Samuel nodded his head but said nothing. They were too far apart for either the boy or Samuel to extend a hand to shake. Beth turned back to look at the boy she had just introduced. From the angle of his sister's head, Samuel could tell that she was looking into his face and eyes.

"That makes two new friends that I didn't know existed whom I've met today."

The boy looked at Beth and smiled. Even without a mirror to view him in, by way of his newly discovered personal experience, Samuel knew the way a boy looks at a girl when it's becoming personal for him. The way the boy looked at his sister gave Samuel the distinct impression that it was the start of something personal for him.

"Your sister and I have become fast friends in the space of just having come to know each other here at the fair," the boy said. Samuel didn't quite know what to make of the boy's use of the word *fast*. But he wasn't sure he liked it.

Beth turned back to look at Samuel. "Bill has been showing me around the fair," she said.

"And precisely what have you been showing my sister, sir? And where is it that you have you been escorting her?" Samuel said with an ominous tone rising his voice.

Beth Martin caught the tone and implication in her brother's voice.

"Now don't start that, Sam," Beth said. "He's not a slimy carny barker who came in from outside with the fair. He lives here in this town. Outside the town actually. His father is a farmer like our father is. He comes from a farm family just like we do."

The boy pointed off in a general direction. "We have a farm about six miles northeast of the town," he said.

"He's not a white slaver come to drag me off to a bordello in New Orleans," Beth went on. "He's just like us. We've just never met before because we don't get here hardly at all except for the fair. So you don't have to play that you're one of the Rough Riders come to rescue me."

Beth turned quickly to the boy. "I must apologize for my brother's behavior. He can be rude when he gets the idea that he's going to protect me."

The announcement that the boy was a farm boy from a farming family like his set Samuel's mind partway at ease, but only partway.

"My behavior is what it is when and where my sister is involved," Samuel said to the boy. "The specific nature of my reaction to the interest any man shows in my sister depends on the specific nature of his intent toward my sister. You said that after knowing my sister for only a short time, you consider yourself her fast friend. What exactly do you mean when you use the word *fast*? I'm not sure I like any definition of the word when it's applied to my sister. May I ask exactly what your intentions are toward my sister, sir?"

Beth had a look on her face that made it seem that she was positively chagrined.

"My intentions are to meet your sister here during next year's fair," the boy answered. There was neither fear nor apology in the tone of his voice. "I will be out of school and established by that time." The boy looked at

Beth. "In the meantime, I have asked your sister's permission to write to her now and then."

Beth looked at Samuel. "Bill is only a year behind you in high school," she said. "When he graduates, he is going to take over running the farm from his father the same way you have been taking over running the farm from Father. So you can stop acting like Father and stop asking questions about his intent. You're embarrassing me to no end."

"He's only asking the questions I would ask of any boy who showed an interest in my sister Agnes," William Howard said to Beth in an "I don't blame him for doing what he should rightly be doing" voice. "It's only right that a brother look out for his sister."

Clarinda held the teddy bear tighter.

"It's just that I've never seen him quite like this before," Beth said to the boy in a voice bordering on being pleading. "It's not every day that I meet someone new whom I like, and here he is acting like Cotton Mather running some kind of witchcraft trial. I just met you, and he's probably going to drive you away. You'll probably avoid me like the plague from now on. You probably won't come to the fair next year. I'll probably never see you again."

Samuel was caught up short by his sister's reaction. At the same time he was caught up short by his own situation, the situation that had sent him to Mrs. Richardson's house so he superficially address (undress actually) it. There were no girls in the town whom he had any interest in. He had given up all hope of ever finding a girl in town he wanted to marry. For all he knew, his sister had come to a similar conclusion that there was no boy in town that she was interested in or wanted to marry. For all Samuel knew, in her mind his sister might have been looking at spinsterhood, and here he was going around slamming in her face the only door that had opened even a crack for her.

"I didn't say you can't see him again." Samuel backed off. "I just want to know more about him. Just like Mother and Dad would. Nothing more than that. It's only natural that I'd want to know just like they would. We all care about you and don't want to see you hurt."

"Stop treating me like a kid sister," Beth said, voicing the age-old complaint girls have leveled against big brothers. "I'm not a baby in diapers.

I'm a grown-up girl, old enough to choose my friends without having to beg your approval."

Clarinda had been stroking the teddy bear's head with her hand. She stopped stroking it.

"If you drive away any boy or man who comes my way, the only thing you're going to protect me into is being an old maid. That's going to hurt as much, if not more, than being caught up with a trifler. Don't come at any boy you see me talking to like a railyard bully with your fists clenched. Stop treating me like that."

"What's he done to you so bad for you to chew him up like you are?" Clarinda unexpectedly broke in. Samuel looked at her.

"He's embarrassing me in front of a friend I just met," Beth said in the voice of a peeved sister.

"That makes him such a mean-ass brother in your wet-behind-the-ears little girl's eyes?" Clarinda answered, a growl growing in her voice.

"That's bad enough," Beth responded in a defensive voice. She was taken aback by the harshness in Clarinda's voice, as well as by the language she was using. Samuel was used to the girl's bordello language. The seeming intensity of her words gave him pause as it had his sister.

"He shouldn't treat me that way," Beth said. "He's being a bad brother—"

"Hey, missy!" Clarinda cut her off sudden and hard in midsentence. "Did your brother ever rape you?!"

Beth fell instantly into a stunned silence.

"Don't you go tellin' me nothin' 'bout bad and bad brothers," Clarinda snapped in a voice more savage than Samuel had ever heard her use. "You don't know the first thing about badassed brothers and what they do to a girl. Did your brother ever drag you into a shed and rape you there on the ground?"

Under her breath, Beth gasped.

"Did he ever cinch a belt across your mouth to keep you from screamin', cinched so tight that you could hardly breathe like my brothers did to me as they took turns with me? Did you have no one to come to help you like I had no one who would stand protector over me, my mother dead and gone, my father drunk and not knowin' or carin' what his boys were doing to me, his mind made numb and damped down by the white lightning he brewed in his still in the woods, the same rotgut that fired up my brothers to rape the life out of me?"

Beth's mouth fell open.

"Did your oh so bad brother leave you torn and bleedin' because you're not old and developed enough inside to handle him? The damage my brothers did inside me made it sure that I wouldn't never have no children. That don't otherwise matter much to me. I don't want to bring no child, especially a girl-child, into this world."

Beth's lips moved slightly as if she wanted to talk, but no words came out.

"Did you ever lie in bed torn up and hurtin' so bad you could hardly stand it, holding yourself together on the outside, feelin' like you've been torn asunder on the inside? Did you ever cry and cry and try to stop cryin' because you knew it would do no good and it wouldn't buy any sympathy or a promise not to do it again from your brother? Did you ever lie hurtin' like you felt the hurtin' wouldn't stop, scared into more tears, knowin' that they would do it to you again whenever they got their hands on a new jug and on you again?!"

Now it was Samuel's turn to fall into a stunned silence. Looking at Beth, the girl, with her left arm, pulled the teddy bear tighter up against her. As the girl's words sank in, Beth started to shake visibly.

With a sudden fast move of her hand, Clarinda reached into the pocket of her dress and swung out the long-bladed jackknife she was carrying, the same knife Samuel had used to remove the tag from the teddy bear. With an equally fast flip of her wrist, she snapped the blade open. The three others took an instinctive half step backward. Beth's mouth fell farther open. Clarinda looked harder at Beth.

"Did you ever have to slash your brother's face to the bone from one side to the other to stop him from rapin' you again because you couldn't take what he was doin' to you no more, and you weren't goin' to take it no more, but you couldn't think of any other way to stop him? And you were so mad that you were ready to cut him apart if he did try it again?"

Beth remained silent, but the shocked look on her face grew more shocked. Bill Howard furrowed his brow. Otherwise he didn't seem to know how to react. None of them, including Samuel, knew what to say or how to say it.

"Did you have to go jumpin' into a passin' freight train because you knew your father and your other brothers would probably kill you if they caught you for the way you cut your brother up? Did you have to jump out of a train car in the middle of nowhere because you were found alone by a bunch of Negro hoboes who you figured would probably have raped you all across the country until the train got to its stop? Did you ever have to sleep in the rain and steal eggs out of a barn to eat? Did you have to beg to be taken into a bordello to be given shelter and to work because gettin' laid by men was all you knew about, but at least you had a roof over your head, and protection, and some control over the way men went about slamming themselves into you?"

Beth seemed too stunned to form any words. Her life and the life of her family in a small farming town had been borderline hardscrabble, but it had been a polite, loving, and otherwise sheltered existence. She had never known or heard of anything even close to the kind of life Clarinda was describing. She had no words or thoughts of response that seemed even vaguely adequate.

"You think you've got yourself a bad brother on your hands because he stands up for you in the face of another boy and because he's clumsy at it."

Beth was still too stunned to respond. Clarinda pointed at the ground with her knife.

"Instead of yammering like a snot-nosed child, you ought to go to your knees and give thanks to the Lord of All in front of the heavenly host and the whole world that you've got a brother who looks after you and protects you the way a brother is supposed to think of and protect a sister," she snapped hard at Beth. "Even if he does act like a jackass when he's doin' it. You should give thanks in full all the days of your life together now, and all the days apart and to come, that you have a brother who looks out for you and protects you instead of treating you the way my brothers treated me. If I had had one brother who looked out for me, I wouldn't be holed up here, hidin' out in a whorehouse. If your brother was anything to you like mine were to me, you'd be somewhere farther down the train line, a nameless whore girl working in a whorehouse somewhere far from here with no home you dare to go back to."

As fast and sudden as it had started, Clarinda's torrent of words came to a stop. She quietly folded the blade of the knife back into its handle and put it in her pocket. Then she looked at Samuel.

"You keep sayin' you want to know me better so much," Clarinda said to Samuel in a voice that was neither angry and accusing nor soft and pleading, just flat and biting. "Well, know me now. That's my story. It is what it is. I am what I am. My story don't get much cleaner or nicer. You probably won't want to know me none after today. But for better or worse, now you know 'bout me from what I've just told you. I am what I made myself. I am what's been made of me. I am what I am. What I am ain't no Sunday-go-to-meetin' girl. While you're knowin' me better, just know that it don't get much better 'bout me any more than it got any better for me in my family back then."

The girl looked back and forth at Samuel, Beth, and Bill Howard.

"Now that you know I'm nothin' but a dirty little trash tramp who is the way she is because I was raped into bein' what I am, you probably think that I deserve the life I'm livin' now. I don't suppose neither of you will want to be meeting me again at any fair anywhere in any state of the union. That's up to you. That's for you to choose. But I didn't choose what was done to me or the life it sent me running off to. And I can't change what was done to me by my so-called family."

The girl looked over at Samuel and then back at Beth. Her whole demeanor changed. Her jaw seemed to relax. The scowl on her face faded. The cutting edge to her voice grew softer. The raging moment seemed to pass as fast as it had come on.

"I'm sorry for lettin' myself run off and run on the way I did about what I was runnin' on about," Clarinda said in a subdued and apologetic tone. "Sometimes my mind is like a dog that can't keep from lickin' its own vomit. When my mind gets itself on the subject of my past, it just runs away on me and runs me right back into the mud of my past, even though the biggest thing I want out of life is not to think about the past."

She looked back and forth between Beth and Beth's newfound friend, who gave every impression of being on the way to becoming more than just a friend to her.

"I don't mean to rain on your day. This was probably a happy day for both of you. For you it was probably one of those red-letter days people like to remember for the rest of their lives. I just rubbed dirt all over it for you. … As days go, this day's been probably been the best day of my life. I enjoyed this day better than I've ever enjoyed any day ever. I suppose I've ruined it for you now, the way I've ruined it for myself. Just forget about the way I flew off the handle like that. It just happens to me that way when I get goin' on my past."

Her voice fell an octave. She looked at Beth and back to William Howard. "The two of you just go on seeing each other and enjoying each other's company. Enjoy each other's company for the rest of your lives. Just forget about me or how I darkened the day you met."

She looked between William Howard and Samuel and nodded toward Beth. "The two of you just go on looking out for your girls the way men are supposed to look after women."

She looked up and over at Samuel in particular as the proper brother of the moment. "You just go on being protective of your sister, and don't apologize to her or anyone for doin' it. Protect her till the right and proper man for her comes along. But when the right man does come along, let her go to him so he can take care of her and they can be together like it's supposed to be. In the process, all of you can go on with your lives and forget about me. You'll all do a lot better for yourselves if you forget about me."

The tearing bitterness in her voice a few minutes ago was gone. The girl's tone was soft, almost sweet. It was as if a wave had swept over her and passed, and now she was trying to make up for what she had said. In a way it was almost a replay of what had happened in the girl's room in the house where, in a sudden reflex, she had tried to claw Samuel's eyes out and immediately after, realizing what she had done, had acted shaken and contrite.

"I promise both of you that I won't stop being protective of my sister," Samuel said as if taking a solemn vow. "But I refuse to forget you for one minute any more than I intend to forget my sister. You're stuck with me and my clumsy protective instinct and nature as much as my sister is."

Hearing the story of the girl's early life in more graphic detail, Samuel was doubly determined to make up for what life and the world had done to her.

Samuel didn't know whether the girl believed him or not when he stated in front of witnesses that he had no plans to desert her. What she might doubt in the way of his intentions was irrelevant. By his subsequent actions, he intended to prove to her that he meant what he'd said.

The girl didn't say anything in response to Samuel's magnanimous oath of continuing fealty toward her and his proclamation that he wasn't going to leave her, even in the face of her revelation.

By her magnanimous apologies to Beth and William Howard, the girl had diffused any bad feelings that might have developed. Nevertheless, given the girl's revelation, there was a certain amount of awkward feeling left hanging in the air. Neither Beth nor Bill Howard voiced any feelings or questions. But then again, neither of them quite knew what to say.

Bill Howard took his leave, promising to meet with them all at the fair next year. From the way she smiled, Samuel's sister seemed to appreciate the promise and the prospect. Samuel, his sister, and the girl turned their backs on the fair and walked to the front entrance. Neither Samuel nor the girl would see the Ashton county fair again. Beth and William would indeed meet again at the appointed time next year at the Ashton county fair as they had arranged. They would indeed become more than just fairground and fair-weather friends. Samuel would not meet William Howard again.

Just outside the fairground entrance, Samuel did the polite male thing. Instead of making them walk to where he had parked the truck, he told Clarinda and Beth to wait by the road for him, saying he would bring the truck around. While Samuel went off to start up the truck and bring it around, Beth and Clarinda stood and waited. As the start of their journey that day had been marked by a certain embarrassed silence, Beth and the girl stood in silence now, waiting for Samuel's return. Clarinda stood motionless, holding the teddy bear in her arms. She looked straight ahead.

It had been a strange day for Beth. At the same time it had been an arguably momentous day for her. In the space of one day, she had met two quite different people, both of whom might very well become people close to her in the future.

The silence stretched out. The truck wasn't far away. Samuel would be back with it soon. Beth felt that there should be some sort of conversation between her and the girl alone without her brother being there to hear. She just wasn't quite sure what form of conversation fitted both the uncertain and undefined situation she and her brother were in and the uncertain and undefined person she was standing next to. Somehow she felt that any conversation between her and the girl should involve more than just girl talk.

"You do know my brother is in love with you?" Beth said, turning her head toward the girl. "Really in love with you. Not the kind of love you've been getting at the Richardson house."

It was the only thing of import she could think of to say at the uncertain moment. Beth had had numerous chatty and occasionally catty conversations with her friends, but never on the multitude of subjects she had just embarked on. Thus began what would prove to be one of the strangest woman-to-countrywoman conversations of Beth Martin's life.

"Are you an expert on love?" the girl said, looking forward, away from Beth. "Do you know real heart love when you see it? 'Cause I sure don't. I doubt that kind of love exists outside of fairy tales."

"I don't know fairy tales, but I do know my brother," Beth said. "I've always been able to tell everything he's thinking and feeling. I can tell he's in love with you, even if he doesn't fully know it."

"If he is in love with me, he hasn't said anything about it to me," the girl said. She continued to look forward, away from Beth.

"He doesn't have to say it," Beth said. "I can see it in the way he looks at you. I can hear it in the way he talks to you."

"At your young age, are you an expert at spotting the signs of true romance in a man?" Clarinda reiterated her earlier question in an equally flat voice.

"Not really," Beth said. "But he's said as much to me directly that he loves you."

Beth came about as close as she could without violating her brother's wish that she not to tell the girl that he was planning to ask her to marry him.

"As far as spotting signs of romantic feelings in a man, I thought that women in your … profession were far more practiced at spotting those kinds of signs of love."

"My profession isn't dedicated to romance," Clarinda said, turning her head a touch toward Beth. "And it ain't dedicated to love from the heart. My profession is pitched to a superficial resemblance of romance that is actually a negation of romance. My profession is dedicated to a lie that looks like love on the surface of the skin but that has nothin' to do with real love beneath it. My profession is dedicated to anything but romance. You look at it that way long enough, it kind of comes to blind you to real romance and recognizing it. It goes with the territory. You lay yourself down under lying love so much you can't see real love when it's lying on top of you. You can't hear real love when it's whispered in your ear. And your brother hasn't whispered or said anything out loud to the effect that he's in love with me from the depths of his heart."

"My brother isn't that big on words," Beth said of the communication-challenged Samuel. "He can also be a bit slow and deliberate in the way he gets around to doing something big. But when he gets rolling, he goes on to the end. He just told me he loves you for the first time today. He just told me about you for the first time today. I assume he's going to get around to telling you soon enough."

"I wouldn't worry about it too much," the girl said in a flat and dismissive voice as she continued to look out ahead. "After what I told all of you about my life before I came here, I don't think he's going to be much interested in seeing me anymore after today. Your worries about me will probably be gone as soon as he drops me off at the house and takes you back home. He probably won't want to give me the time of day, let alone my pay fare anymore, now that I've told him what I just told him and all of you."

"I'm not at all sure of that," Beth said quietly. "I know my brother better than you do. He's not a liar by nature or temperament, especially when it comes to love. He's not like Harold Ethridge, the town Casanova, who has loved half the women in this town but doesn't have a heart for anyone but himself."

"Your brother mentioned him once," the girl said, still looking away from Beth. "I suppose you don't think that a prostitute is capable of love or any good intent. I suppose you think that double about a girl who's been with more men than she can remember. You probably think that I'm beyond any good intent to anybody. You probably think my soul is as twisted and deformed, shut down, and away from love beyond that which I give in the dirty bed I lie in."

To tell the truth, Beth was somewhat disposed to think that way because of the culture of the time. But this had been a day of at least nominal transcendence. At present, Beth was already thinking out ahead of that. At the transcendent moment, standing with the damaged girl beside the road they would both ride back to town on with Samuel, Beth knew instinctively that she needed a response that went beyond the kind of whip crack prejudice the girl was probably expecting from both her and her brother.

"Whatever other people may think of you, I know my brother doesn't think that way. He doesn't blame you or hold what was done to you against you. I don't think anything you've said today, on the way here, or just a few minutes ago has made a dent in the way he feels about you."

Beth rolled the biggest pair of dice she had. "Though he hasn't said it in glossy words, he's planning on asking you to marry him."

The girl gave Beth a hard look.

"If you care anything for your brother, missy, you'd better talk that idea out his head and do it quick-like. I ain't the marryin' type. Especially if all that getting married means is exchanging a mountain shack for a flatland farm; cookin' and cleanin' and doin' chores by day; and being tied to him and the same thing for the rest of my life. Maybe I wouldn't have my brothers rapin' me, but in the overall it's not much of an up trade."

The girl turned her gaze ahead again.

"Besides, I don't go along with men very much. I tolerate what they do with me in Mrs. Richardson's place. But after they're done with me, they go away and leave me alone. All that is just fine with me the way I've got it. I don't think much of men in any category, and I sure don't see myself being tied to one and tied down in his shack for the rest of my life. I never met a man who was good to me, and I doubt any man will ever be good for me. Men are all so … men. They all seem mean and violent at the core. … If I was tied to your brother in marriage and tied down in that house of yours, there wouldn't be nothin' to keep it from comin' out and comin' out all over me."

"Other than calling me a snot now and then and playing a few harmless practical jokes, my brother has never done anything mean, cruel, or disrespectful to me," Beth said.

"You're family," Clarinda said, still looking straight ahead. "Maybe family means more in your family than it did in mine. But I'm not family, and I'm not what anyone in your family circle or in this town would call respectable. Soon enough he'd stop respecting me, if he ever even started out respecting me. Then his bad side would come out on me. I don't think any man has any good side to him."

She looked back at Beth.

"So you tell him right up front, and tell him right away, not to go askin' me to marry up with him. I'll tell him no to his face, and I'll say it hard. If you're worried about his feelin's bein' hurt, you tell him not to even think of askin' me. You'll probably say it a lot more gently than I ever would. You can tell him that what you're sayin' isn't your idea. You can say it came directly from me. If it's going to hurt him, it will probably hurt less coming from you."

"I'll tell him what you said," Beth responded. "It may put off his asking you to marry him, but I don't think it's going to slow the time down by an hour when he finally gets around to telling you he loves you."

"I still say he'll be over me soon enough," the girl said, still looking straight ahead. "Women like me are meant to be put aside and put behind when a man is done with them. I haven't known love any other way from any man. If your brother is a lover who loves for real, more power to him. But I'll believe that only when I see it, and I don't expect to see any real love from any man. When he gets over the novelty of me, he'll be over his puppy love for me."

"He may be all over you in bed back at the house," Beth said, "but I don't think he's going to be over you anytime soon in the bad way you're thinking. My brother isn't like that."

The girl turned her head back slightly in Beth's direction. "Of the two of us, I thought you were supposed to be the polite and proper one," she said of Beth's first foray into a double entendre. "Now you're talking like a woman in my … profession."

"The situation requires it," Beth said, without pausing to blush at the possible sexual pun she might have stumbled into. "And my brother deserves clarification of what you feel for him."

"Do you still think I'm out to hurt him?" the girl asked, continuing to look at Beth at an angle.

"I don't know what to think," Beth said after a few moments' silence. Whatever part the girl might come to play in her brother's life, her thought at the moment was for her brother and the girl who was making his world spin. She didn't know if the girl was some form of vengeful harpy who was conspiring in her mind to deliberately wound him as a way of taking revenge on men for having wounded her so badly. She didn't know if her brother needed defense against the girl. Beth only felt that she should offer some form of defense of her brother. She also knew that it had to be a finessed defense, one that wouldn't turn her brother away from her and drive him farther into the arms of the girl.

"I'm not accusing you of planning to hurt him," Beth said. "I just want you to know that he can be hurt. I don't know what your intentions are toward him, but I can tell you that he doesn't harbor any bad thoughts or intentions toward you. I know you've been treated horribly bad by your brothers, but my brother isn't like yours were. You said as much yourself a minute ago."

"I'm not out to take vengeance on all brothers of the world," Clarinda said. "The only thing I'm out for is to get by one day at a time. I'm not out lookin' to set your brother up for a fall. And I don't know anything about him lovin' me as much as you say, not beyond what he's been doin' with me at the house and other places. Are you sayin' that I've got to love him just because he's your brother?"

"I'm not ordering you to love him," Beth answered. "I doubt I can order you to do anything."

The girl gave Beth a silent *You've got that right, sister* look.

"I'm not even asking if you love him. I'm just asking that if you don't love him, let him know up front that you don't. Don't lead him on. If you don't love him, be truthful with him. We're farmers. Farmers get used to dealing with a lot of hard truths. It may hurt Samuel some if you don't share the same affection for him, but he can live with that hard truth. What will hurt him a lot more is if you play games with him and make him think you love him when you don't."

They both looked away from each other and out to the road as they heard the familiar rattle of the motor as the truck approached.

"My brother probably feels more love and respect for you than women in your profession will usually ever get from any man. I'm not going to say that a prostitute is beyond respect or is incapable of love. But if you can't love him, at least be honest with him. In and of itself, honesty may be a poor substitute for love, but it's the threshold of love. Being honest with someone is the first and most basic form of respect."

Beth fell silent as the truck approached. She didn't know what, if anything, further she could say. She had defended her brother and had done so without acting like a harpy herself, shouting at the girl that she was a tramp, slut, floozy, hussy, and so forth. Beth assumed her brother had arrived at maturity in the arms of the girl, probably more than once.

Samuel pulled the truck up to where the two girls were standing. He could see that his sister was saying something to Clarinda, but he couldn't hear her words. The two got in the truck. The trio drove back to the house in polite silence. On the return leg of their trip, Beth didn't try to force any conversation. Then again, she really didn't know what more she had to say to the girl or what she could say. She didn't fully know what to say to her brother either. She only knew she had to say something.

When they arrived back at the Richardson house, Samuel escorted the girl to the front door, while Beth waited in the truck again. At the door, the girl turned around to face him, but she didn't say anything. The question was and wasn't on her face. Not a lot of words were subsequently exchanged between them. It wasn't particularly a time for words.

"Wait for me," Samuel said. "I'll return as soon as I take my sister back home."

"Are you sure you still want to see me again after today?" Clarinda asked. The question was half rhetorical and half genuine surprise at his statement.

Samuel brushed the back of his hand on the girl's cheek.

"Nothing's changed," he said simply and quietly. Samuel assumed that what he had said was enough to reassure her. He really wasn't sure what more he could say.

From the house, he took his sister on the road that led back to the farmhouse they shared, the house that, the thought was forming in Beth's mind, she might be sharing with the girl as her sister-in-law. There wasn't any conversation, polite or otherwise, for most of the ride. But then again, neither of them particularly knew what they had to say to each other at the juncture.

When they arrived at the turnoff that led to the farmhouse, Samuel stopped the truck without turning down the drive. "Do you mind walking the rest of the way back home from here?" he asked. "I have a few things I have to do back in town. If Father sees me, he might grab me and set me to doing something else. He won't be able to do that if I'm already gone when you come back in the door."

Beth didn't mind the short walk. But she had a definite idea what the unspecified thing was that was really on her brother's mind to do.

"You're going back to see her, aren't you?" she said in a nonaccusatory voice, cutting to the chase she knew her brother wanted to cut to. As an element of timing, Beth knew that at that moment Samuel would have otherwise been at the Richardson house chasing the girl around in the manner in which she was used to being chased after, that is, if he hadn't have been sidetracked by having to take his little sister back home. Some things are too obvious to be denied. In response to his sister's question, Samuel said nothing. Beth saw no reason to pretend.

"You don't have to worry about me," Beth volunteered. "I'll keep your confidences. If Father asks where you are, I'll tell him that you went back into town to take your baseball team friends back home and that you and they were planning on doing something in town."

It was a ready and serviceable cover story.

"Are you planning to tell Mother and Father about her?" Samuel asked.

"I'll keep your secret about her too," Beth said with a the-things-I-won't-do-for-my-wayward-brother tone of distaste in her voice. "But don't ask me to become any more involved than I am or try make me into some kind of go-between for you and her. I don't like lying to Mom and Dad. Keeping your secret from them is going to be distasteful enough for me as it is."

"I take it you don't like her?" Samuel said.

"I'm not sure what I feel about her," Beth answered. "I don't know if I'll ever be sure what I think or feel about her. As far as what I like or don't, I don't like lying to Mom and Dad. So don't ask me to lie more than you have already. Don't try to make me into an even more involved liar. I won't go beyond what I told you or do anything more scurrilous for you when it comes to keeping your secrets."

"I won't ask you to do more," Samuel said. "It won't be that long that you'll have to keep silent. I'll be asking her to marry me shortly. I just have to wait a little longer, until the time is right."

The realization that the bitter and wounded girl might actually soon become her sister-in-law was starting to settle in fully upon Beth.

"Do you think she was telling the truth when she told us about herself?" Beth asked spontaneously. "Especially about what her brothers did to her?"

"I don't see why any girl would want to make up a story like that," Samuel said in his real-world voice. "People usually try to cover up things like that that have been done to them. They don't let it out unless it hurts more to keep it in. If she was going to lie about her past, she would be more likely to tell a story that would make her look better, such as that she was the princess child of a deposed European monarch or that she was the wayward daughter of a rich robber baron who had been turned out of her rich home."

"I take it that what she said hasn't made her the least bit untouchable to you," Beth said.

"I don't blame her for what was done to her," Samuel said, the tone of his voice rising slightly. "If she was raped, she's not to blame for anything. Being raped doesn't make a girl dirty, despite what you might have heard and what the old wives' tales say."

In Beth's mind it was obvious that, in his mind, her brother had taken the question all the way to its end. Beth figured there was no need for her to take it any farther.

"I hope you know what you're getting yourself into," Beth said as she reached for the door latch. "You may be letting yourself in for a lot more with her than if you were to marry Katherine Clarke."

"Why?" Samuel asked with a rhetorical snap to his voice. "Why should she be any more of a problem child to marry than any other girl or woman? Because she's not presentable or acceptable to polite society? Because she's a prostitute?"

Beth paused with her hand on the door latch. All of that was a problem enough in itself. But just as Beth knew that it would have been counterproductive to have said as much to the girl's impassive face, she knew it would be doubly counterproductive to say it to her brother's tense face. Besides, all those problems weren't the real problem as Beth saw it.

"It's not that," Beth said, looking for a diplomatic way to express something for which there was little diplomatic language available. "She's … she's …" The problem for Beth wasn't only that delicate and tactful words were limited with regard to the particular problem of the girl. Beth wasn't even sure how to define the particular problem of the undefined and probably unknowable girl. "She's all torn up inside her soul as well as in her body. If you get too close to her, you could find yourself torn up by her. If you try to love her and pull her in, you could wake a demon and bring it out from her past. Her mind is like a crown of thorns. You might find yourself cut up by her no matter how and from what direction you try to embrace her."

Beth hadn't meant what she said as a crude reminder of how the girl had slashed her own brother's face with a knife.

"Whatever it is she's carrying around in her memory, she's carrying as big a load of it in her heart. There may be nothing left of her heart but shreds and scars. I don't know if she has a heart left for anybody. Not even for herself. If you try to give her your heart, she may lacerate it. Her soul almost seems too damaged to recognize love, receive love, embrace love, or give love. I don't know if she even wants love. She pretty much said so herself while we were talking before you came with the truck. She said enough to all of us at the fair. There was pain and biting in just about every word she said. There wasn't anything soothing in anything she said. I don't think you're going to be able to soothe her soul. I don't think anyone can soothe her soul."

Though he didn't like what his kid sister was saying, Samuel was impressed by the maturity with which she had spoken it. In that moment his sister sounded more mature than he had ever heard her be. She was growing up. She was on the cusp of becoming a full-fledged woman. He never thought of her as a snot-nosed little sister again.

"She's had a very hard life," Samuel said in his measured voice. "She's been knocked around by one thing or the other, by one person or the other, as far back as she can remember, starting with the death of her mother when she was barely three. That left her stuck with a family who treated her worse than we'd treat a goat. That kind of thing can't help but scar a girl deeply. Yes, she's carrying a lot of pain from her past, but we're going to help her put all that in the past and leave it there to be forgotten. I intend to show her what real love is. I'm going to show her what a real brother is like. Between us we're going to show her what a real family is like. We're going to balance all the bad she's been through with good. We're going to be as good for her as much and more as life's been bad for her. We're going to make it up to her for everything that's happened to her."

Now this was a switch. Beth had more or less thought of her brother as being the hard-edged realist and herself as being the proverbial incurable romantic. Now Samuel was the one touting love as the cure-all for a lifetime of a girl being raped like a backwoods whore and living the life of a whore.

"I'm not sure I share your ready confidence that we can cure her and wipe away all that's been done to her," Beth interjected, sounding even more mature. "Apparently what's in her mind and soul has been burned into her from the first years of her life and all her days since. I don't know if she can think in any other terms. She may not be able to drop her burden by the side of our road and walk away as clean and easy as you think just because you offer her romance and the rest of us offer her friendship. She's been hurt most of her life. She may not know anything else but hurt. All she seems to feel is pain. Pain is all she may end up giving you."

"And we're going to show her that there is more for her in life than hurt," Samuel interjected. "And we're going to show that there are people in life who will do more than hurt her. We're just the family to do that."

"She may end up carrying what's in her for life," Beth went on in the same vein. "You may find yourself having to carry more of her hurt on your shoulders, longer and farther than you suspect, maybe all the way to her grave."

"I'm sure we can all change her once we bring her into the house," Samuel said.

"She's not exactly the kind of routine girl you bring home every day," Beth said, stating the obvious, which she thought her brother should at least acknowledge.

"And we're going to treat her to more than the routine cruelty and abuse that she's known all her life," Samuel countered. "We're going to be a family to her the way a family should be."

"In some ways this just isn't like you, Samuel," Beth said, not knowing which way to take the conversation. "I'm afraid you're being awfully reckless by trying to save that girl and by the way you're proposing to bring her into the house."

"The reckless thing would be to leave her in that house where she would continue to be a whore and would be treated like a whore," Samuel said. "We'd also be leaving her in a place where she would probably eventually catch a venereal disease that will kill her."

In the pre–penicillin era were incurable afflictions that killed people in an often long and painful wasting-away process, Samuel's fears of mortality staring the girl in the face in the form of venereal diseases weren't misplaced fears. In the pre–antibiotic era, upward of forty thousand prostitutes a year died of complications from syphilis and other then-untreatable venereal diseases. Syphilis was the AIDS of the nineteenth century and the early twentieth century, a slow and incurable killer. The isolation of their small town had protected the girl so far. But Samuel knew it was only a matter of time before the statistics caught up with her. Even in their small and isolated town, the girl was dicing with looming mortality.

Samuel fell silent on the subject. The thought of the girl's beautiful face and the currently smooth skin of her body coming to be pockmarked and covered with ulcerated sores, which was one of the more visible and garish attributes of syphilis, only drove him to push up his timetable to marry the girl as reasonably soon as he could.

"Did you know the details about her earlier life and the way she was treated by her family before today?" Beth went on.

"I got a good hint from what she said to me over the times we've been together," Samuel answered. "This is the first time she's said anything about having brothers, let alone being raped by them. It's also the first time she said that she cut up one of her brothers trying to get away from him."

Beth fell silent and asked no further questions. At the juncture, her instinct, shaped by the culture of her time, was to blurt out something like "Oh, Samuel, what are you thinking?!" but she felt like a dove throwing itself against a boulder. Her brother was obviously resolved to marry the girl. She seriously doubted that any nagging ninny sister would either budge or dent her brother's determination to marry, clean up, and save the soiled and broken-winged dove he was in love with.

"Sam, I just hope you're thinking this through carefully," Beth said in a more gentle way than a proper women's tea set would probably conjure up. "There are a lot of pitfalls to marrying a girl with her background. There are a lot of sharp edges to her." Beth hadn't meant that as a pun about the way the girl had slashed her brother with a knife. "You might not find out how sharp-edged she can really be until you marry her."

"You're starting to sound like Ben Harper," Samuel said. "I thank the both of you for your solicitous concern in this matter. But all you'd doing is pointing out that she's not perfect. I know she's not perfect. None of us are perfect. If I wait till I find the perfect girl, I'll be waiting for the rest of my life for something that won't ever come along, something that can't ever come along. ... I know she's got sharp edges to her. You can't help but come away with some sharp edges if you've lived the life she has. Given what she's been through, she wouldn't be human if she didn't pick up some sharp edges along the way. I think that between all of us in the family, we can smooth out her edges."

In his vision-prone mind, Samuel caught a vision of the girl gently touching the mare and speaking softly to its newborn foal. He caught a more recent vision of the girl's sympathy for doomed lambs. He remembered the way she hugged the teddy bear he had won for her.

"But under it all she's got a more loving heart than I've seen in most girls. We've just got to get past the thorns to find the rose in her."

The truck engine rattled as Samuel held the truck in place at the turnoff on the road to his and his sister's home, the home he intended to take the girl to in order to be a part of.

"The moment I saw her, I knew she was the one I wanted to spend my life with and share my future with." Samuel pointed in the general direction of the fair they had returned from. "You had your own taste of that today. You just met someone who might be your future. At least you think that he might be your future enough that you're planning on meeting him the same time next year. ... How long were you in his company before you started thinking of him in terms of the future?"

"A little less than two hours," Beth answered.

"That's just about as fast as it took me to know that I wanted to spend my future with her. We're both neck and neck out of the gate when it comes to knowing who we want to spend our futures with."

"But, Sam, I'm not going to meet him till next year," Beth said. "In the meantime, we're just going to write to each other. You've only known her about a month, and already you want to marry her."

"I knew I was going to marry her by the end of our first night together."

Beth sort of winced at her brother's frankness and at what he was alluding to regarding what he and the girl had been doing that first night.

"But we're not neck and neck in how we're going about this," Beth said. "You're way ahead of me. If I'm a racehorse, then you're moving like a bullet."

"You didn't much like it when I started picking apart the boy you think may be your future," Samuel said. "She is my future. I've known that for some time now. Don't pick her apart on me. I'll respect your sense of the future. You respect mine."

Beth felt rather trapped. She liked the boy very much, more than she'd ever liked any boy. She was definitely thinking of the boy in terms of a possible future together. She had been rather put out when her brother had started questioning the boy as if he were an outraged father with a shotgun in hand, going after someone he thought was trifling with his daughter. For a while she had indeed felt almost terrified that Samuel would drive Bill away and she would never see him again.

In the back of her mind, Beth was a bit afraid of the possibility that the girl might turn into a wicked stepsister. But the girl seemed more haunted victim than actively wicked. She was more of a Jane Eyre or a Catherine from *Wuthering Heights* than a wicked stepmother from "Cinderella." "Cinderella" was a fairy tale that had a happy ending. *Wuthering Heights* was a tragic failed love affair that ended in pain all around, pain that carried into the next generations of Earnshaws and Lintons. The question for Beth was not so much what the girl might do to her. The question was what sadness and betrayal might the girl bring to her brother, who seemed determined to play Heathcliff to her Catherine.

"Well, I'd better get back in the house," Beth said, going for the quick breakaway. "Father is waiting for me. Clarinda is probably waiting for you back at the house. We'd better get on about our own ways."

Beth opened the truck door and started to get out.

"I'll keep your secret like I promised. But I won't lie to Mom and Dad for you forever."

"While you're at it, don't tell anyone that Ben Harper is keeping his own time with one of the other girls over at the Richardson house," Samuel said. "Especially don't tell your circle of henpecking gossipy friends what I told you."

Beth paused getting out of the truck. "Am I to become the keeper of secrets for the whole town?" she asked.

"You probably won't have to keep my secret for that much longer," Samuel answered. "I'm just waiting for the right time to ask Clarinda to marry me. It won't be tomorrow, but it will probably be soon enough."

Beth got out of the truck, closed the door, and turned to walk to the farmhouse. Samuel turned the truck around and drove off toward town. Beth stopped and turned to watch her brother drive away, heading to the Richardson house and the arms of the girl.

Like a tulip bulb in dry earth growing into a beautiful flower once it is watered, would they see the scarred and bitter girl blossom into a beautiful soul in the garden of love Samuel had it in mind that the Martins would provide for her, or at some point would Beth find herself shouting at Samuel for having brought the devil woman into their house? The girl's spirit could become as soft and beautiful as her face. She could just as easily turn mean, contentious, and slashing as the girl who claimed to have slashed her brother's face with a knife. To Beth it seemed the girl could go both ways, and she had no measure by which she could sort out which outcome was the more likely one. If the girl turned out to be a problem child who turned into a problem woman under their roof, Beth figured that it might not be a permanent problem for her. She may have very well met her method of escape from home that very day in the form of Bill Howard. It was her brother who would be closing the door behind him.

With the truck, her brother, and the future out of sight and down the road, Beth Martin turned and walked back to the familiar door of home.

Samuel Martin, turning the knob on the door of the Richardson house, opened the door and walked in. He didn't knock anymore. He had become a regular at the house. As he walked down the front hall, which ran perpendicularly away from the front door, Mrs. Richardson appeared from around the corner in the long transverse hall that he and Ben Harper had first walked on their way to the parlor two months earlier.

"She's waiting for you upstairs," Mrs. Richardson said simply to Samuel.

Samuel thanked her and headed for the stairway to the second floor and the rooms of the women of the house. Mrs. Richardson's hair had grown slightly whiter in the two months since he had first met her. Soon enough it would complete its transition from the hair color of relative youth to the white of a mature older woman. Though her hair was approaching that of an old woman, in the form of her body, Mrs. Richardson had not developed the stooped and frail form of an old woman. Her stance was still erect and strong-looking. Her shoulders were still straight and square. While her chest was not as full as the chest of Polly or Clarinda, it was full enough to give a womanly counterpoint to the otherwise manly squareness of her body. In her square-shouldered older woman way, Mrs. Richardson was a handsome enough specimen. She was forceful in appearance. She was also forceful but restrained in demeanor. She looked like and sounded like she had made a good lawyer's wife as she had once been. In her current situation and station in life, she made a good madam.

In his now familiar way as a regular customer, Samuel didn't knock on the door of Clarinda's room. He just turned the knob and opened the door. When the door opened, he found Clarinda inside the room, sitting on the bed. The teddy bear was sitting on the single chair. The shades in the room were drawn, and the electric lamp on the end table was turned on.

Samuel stepped into the girl's room and closed the door behind him. The girl rose up off the bed. She was dressed in a shiny red robe that looked as if it was either silk or satin. The robe was tied just above the waist by a golden-colored rope of some kind that looked like sash cord, but the robe was otherwise open to her navel. From the sight of flesh showing through the extended opening and the way the girl's chest swayed and vibrated as she moved, Samuel could tell she wasn't wearing any kind of foundation. Below her waist, the robe hung casually open. Her legs and feet were bare.

As Samuel approached her, the girl brushed strands of her long hair off her face.

"I got undressed to wait for you, but I didn't know if you would be coming back to me or not," the girl said as Samuel closed the distance between them. The tone of her voice was neither surprised nor relieved, nor was it bubbly, but she seemed gratified. "After what I told you and your sister, I thought you probably wouldn't want to give me the time of day any more than you'd want to give me your hard-earned money. Half of me thought you would come back to me. Half of me thought you wouldn't."

"I'll tell you now what I told you at the fair," Samuel told the girl in his best no-nonsense tone. "What happened to you in the past, what was done to you in the past, doesn't mean anything to me. I still want you. I want all of you, both halves and the middle."

As Samuel walked close enough to reach her, the girl untied the sash cord. Her robe fell open from top to bottom. Samuel cupped his hands on her neck.

"I told you I'd be back. I always come back to you. I always will."

He ran his hands down to where her neck joined her shoulders. "Are you happy that I came back to you?"

Clarinda didn't answer directly. She leaned her head back to look directly into Samuel's face. She pressed her body softly against his.

"Your sister told me that you think you love me," the girl said in a soft half whisper. "Do you?"

"My sister can be a little snot some of the time," Samuel said. "But she has a way of being right about important things. And when she's right, she's right."

With his hands on her shoulders, Samuel pushed the girl's robe to both sides. It fell loose on her to where it stopped, then it hung in place by the press of her chest against his.

"If you think you love me so bad, then tell me you love me while you're lovin' me."

Before Samuel could say anything, the girl raised her now half-bare left arm inside the sleeve of her robe and pointed in the direction of her now familiar bed behind them. The robe had slid so far down on her that her forearm and hand were just halfway inside the sleeve when she pointed. The front part of the sleeve hung straight down like the empty arm of a scarecrow.

"Take me into that bed and tell me you love me while you make love to me. Tell me you love me over and over and over again. Don't stop telling me you love me the whole time you're goin' about lovin' me."

The girl stepped back, allowing the robe enough room to fall all the way to the floor. Then she stepped back in and pressed herself against Samuel tighter than before.

"Keep telling me the whole time that you're in love with me. Even if you don't mean a second of it, keep telling me that you love me every minute that you make love to me. … I go for a premium at this house. That's the premium I'm charging you today. If you want to make love to me, you've got to tell me you love me the whole time you're lovin' me. Plenty of men have made love to me, but none of them have ever once told me they loved me. I just want to hear it from someone. It would mean double to me to hear it from you."

Wordlessly, Samuel gathered the naked girl into his arms and started kissing her hard. As was her habit, she kissed him back hard and fast. For several minutes they held the clinch as Samuel kissed the girl and ran his hands over her bare back and sides. Then, at the girl's prompting, he paused to remove his own clothing. In the meantime, she stepped over to the nightstand and turned off the light. Then she turned down the bed and climbed in.

The otherwise noncommunicative Samuel was as good as the word he had promised to say to the girl. He said "I love you" over and over and over to her in cadence with his stroking. In response, she moaned and gasped, giving out little cries of pleasure. She undulated her body underneath him and wrapped her arms around him, alternately moving her hands over his back and then freezing them in place and grasping in miniature seizures. Some male egos can suffer enough damage simply by saying "I love you" to a girl. Their egos can be damaged all the more by doing so at a girl's request and direction, especially if it makes it look like the girl is in charge. Of all the macho words employed by macho males, communicative or otherwise, the words *I love you* together are the most closely guarded and least employed of all.

Samuel didn't know whether the girl would have denied him her bed and body if he had not carried out her instructions, but he didn't want to take the chance. A knife-wielding girl might prove to be a bed- and favor-denying girl. Both are ways of cutting men down to size. But then again, Samuel would have followed the girl's instructions and said that he loved her anyway, even if it had been a simple request by the girl and there was no denial or danger factor involved. Samuel didn't mind employing the word and employing it over and over and over again, even though in one way it rather put the girl in charge of the scenario that day.

Telling a girl you love her at her direction might not be a macho thing. It makes a macho male think the girl is trying to wrap him around her little finger. But as Samuel lay in bed, locked in his intimate struggle with the girl, machismo could take a back seat and watch. The girl was probably right that love wasn't a word too often spoken or a concept too often honored in the Richardson house or in any bordello. In Samuel's mind, the fact that the girl had asked him to say she loved him meant that she was moving closer to being in love with him. For all Samuel knew, and for all he hoped, the girl had arrived at loving him.

The girl was warm, beautiful, and alive as he felt her and experienced her in his arms. The girl and her love was the future as Samuel saw it. Macho doesn't mean a lot where your future is concerned. Even though the girl had made speaking the words of love to her a condition of making love with her that day, the words did not stick in Samuel's throat. The words came readily up from within him and flowed freely from his lips. It's not hard to say the right word or words when you're speaking the truth.

Oh, he didn't shout that he loved her. No one could hear him outside the house. It was an off-hour. There were no male customers at the house. The only other people present to hear him and the girl were Mrs. Richardson and the female residents of the house. Samuel figured that at the volume he was employing, the women inside the house might be able to hear him if they happened to pass by the closed door to the girl's room. Once, in the interval between his own vocalizing and the girl's, he heard the distinctive clop of Mrs. Richardson's high button shoes walking past the door. Her pace seemed to slow as she passed by. There seemed to be a conversation going on in the next room. Samuel could hear the sound of at least three distinct hushed female voices coming through the wall. Mixed in with the conversation, Samuel could hear the sound of Polly's distinctive girlish giggle. They were apparently talking quietly so as to not disturb their colleague at work. But if their lowered voices were penetrating the wall, Samuel figured his professions of love were traveling the other way back through the wall at the same level of audibility as the next room.

Samuel didn't consider being overheard professing his love for the girl who made her living practicing a physical approximation of love to be a problem. It would be only the first outward profession of love for the girl he planned to soon make to a wider public.

After his second coming, Samuel and the girl fell into an exhausted slump with Samuel on top. Samuel placed his head on the pillow beside the girl's head with his lips beside her ear.

"I love you," Samuel whispered one more time in the girl's ear as she softly sighed. She did not respond.

Presently, Samuel stood up. The girl followed him off the bed and put her robe on.

"How would you like to go on a picnic?" he asked.

"Now?!" the girl said. With both hands she held her robe open. "Like this?!"

Samuel caught a vision of the two of them sitting naked by the lake with him feeding her grapes by hand.

"With our clothes on this coming Sunday," Samuel said. "I thought the two of us could take the truck and go on a picnic out in the country somewhere. I thought we could take Polly and Ben along with us. Maybe if she and Ben can get away together, it will help out poor Polly's love life."

"That sounds good," Clarinda said affirmatively. "Beats staying around the house and washing clothes. I like getting out of the house and into the open. Makes me feel free."

Samuel outlined his plan. Clarinda seemed to be in agreement with everything he had in mind. A surge of exhilaration went through Samuel. With the girl having agreed to go on a picnic with him, the main element was going his way. If Ben or Polly couldn't come, he would still take the girl and be alone with her. As the girl turned around to walk to where she had left her clothes on the chair, in the exuberance of the moment, Samuel gave her a swift boyish smack on her butt the way he had done at the end of their first time together.

The girl spun halfway around, her arms out to the sides and down at an angle. The smoothly practiced seventeen-year-old courtesan was once again a frightened sixteen-year-old hillbilly girl standing in the open door of a retreating boxcar, her eyes filled with fear and anger. Samuel realized that he had stumbled again.

"Sorry," he said quickly, holding his hands up to indicate that he had meant no harm. "I forgot. I didn't mean to come up behind you like that. I'll try not to let it happen again."

For the girl, the moment passed almost as quickly as it had come on. Her arms lowered. The look on her face went from one of fight or flight to one of annoyance.

"You and your boyish antics are going to be the death of me yet," she said in a piqued tone. Samuel sort of smiled apologetically. But what he felt was mostly relief. The girl hadn't grabbed for a knife, and she hadn't angrily said that the picnic was off. She turned back on the path she had been taking and walked over to the window with the shades drawn.

Instead of turning on the electric lamp on the nightstand next to her bed, the girl opened the shades partway to let in the sunlight outside. It was enough light to see to get dressed by. The girl dropped her robe, preparing to put her clothes back on. For a short while she was naked once again. Looking at the girl in her natural state, in the natural light coming in through the window, Samuel felt natural and at home with her and with the life he wanted to have with her. He also felt that he was on his way to a natural future with her.

To Samuel it was all a natural picture of a right and natural future he would spend with the girl for the rest of the time they would have together. As to the girl's prediction that his boyish antics would be the death of her, in light of what would happen later, Samuel would blame a reckless antic of his for indirectly causing the girl's death. In the light of objective truth, the girl's own recklessness would be as much or more the cause of her own death as any blunder Samuel would fall into. But in the darkened world he would come to inhabit after her death, you wouldn't be able to tell Samuel that.

Chapter 7

"And it came to pass that one of the Pharisees invited Jesus to come to his home for a meal, so Jesus accepted the invitation and sat down to eat. A certain immoral woman heard that He was there and brought an alabaster jar filled with expensive perfume. She knelt behind Jesus at His feet, weeping. Her tears fell at His feet, and she wiped them off with her hair. Then she kept kissing His feet and putting perfume on them."

Pastor Russell's voice was a bit gravelly so as to lend full poignancy to the scene, but Samuel sat in respectful stillness and silence on the hard wooden pew as the pastor related the story from the seventh chapter of the Gospel of Luke about the unnamed immoral woman who spontaneously anointed Jesus's feet with her perfume and her tears. Whether it was love for Jesus or fear for her soul that had sent the woman running to Jesus, her love had been greater than her fear.

In Jesus's first century, about the only option open to a single woman was to be a wife or a prostitute. One way or another, through marriage or harlotry, about the only immorality that a woman could easily and naturally fall into was the one she carried with her in her body, her form and function as a woman. Being a harlot was a trap, a trap that marriage could free her from.

Sitting in the pew on a summer Sunday morning after he had washed out the girl's hair in Gustafson Lake the day before, Samuel had a vision of himself sitting on a big chair back at home on a winter's night in front of the fireplace, the girl sitting on the floor next to him, leaning her head on his leg, her long hair falling down her back and over his leg.

"When the Pharisee who was the host saw what was happening and who the woman was, he said to himself, 'This proves that He is no prophet. If God had really sent Him, He would know what kind of woman is touching him. She is a sinner!'

"Then Jesus spoke up and answered the Pharisee's thoughts. 'Simon,' He said to the Pharisee, 'I have something to say to you.'

"'All right, teacher,' Simon replied. 'Go ahead.'

"Then Jesus told him a story: 'A man loaned money to two people, five hundred pieces of silver to one, fifty pieces to the other. But neither of them could repay him, so he kindly forgave them both, canceling their debts. Who do you suppose loved him the more after that?'

"Simon answered, 'I suppose the one for whom he canceled the larger debt.'

"'That's right,' Jesus said. Then He turned to the woman and said to Simon, 'Look at this woman kneeling here. When I entered your home, you didn't offer me water to wash the dust from my feet, but she has washed them with her tears and wiped them with her hair.'"

Samuel didn't really expect or require that the girl wash his feet with her hair. It was enough that she let her hair fall across him when she laid her head down on his chest. It wasn't necessary that the girl beg his forgiveness for the life she had lived in the past. It was enough that she join her life to his for all the future, with all her past put behind and forgotten.

"'You didn't give Me a kiss of greeting, but she has kissed My feet again and again from the first time I came in. You neglected the courtesy of olive oil to anoint My head, but she has anointed My feet with rare perfume. I tell you, her sins, and they are many, have been forgiven, she has shown Me so much love. But a person who is forgiven little shows only little love.' Then Jesus said to the woman, 'Your sins are forgiven.'"

The pastor paused to let Jesus's words and his words sink in.

"The men sitting at the table said among themselves, 'Who does He think He is, going around forgiving sins?'"

In the near-enough future, Samuel could imagine more than a few people wondering who he thought he was, brazenly bringing what they considered to be a reformed tramp into church like she was a respectable country girl and farm wife. But as he had visualized the girl sitting quiet and contented at his side by the fire on a winter's night, Samuel visualized her sitting demurely next to him on the same pew in church.

For Samuel the sight went over as well in his mind as his vision of the girl sitting beside him in front of the fireplace. Just how well the vision of him sitting in church with an ex-prostitute might or might not go over with other members of the congregation once he had brought the vision to life was another question. But to Samuel, his still mute and yet to be openly spoken vision was a moot question. When he finally made clear his intentions and cleared the air by marrying the girl, he would bring her into church even if that made the air in the sanctuary a bit thick.

Samuel liked feistiness. He liked the trait in their dog Teddy. He had liked the feistiness of President Teddy Roosevelt, for whom the dog was named. To Samuel's way of thinking, Jesus may have been a little quieter in His feistiness, but in His own way, Jesus had been just as feisty as the Rough Rider Teddy Roosevelt as witnessed by the way He had stood up to a crowd of men with rocks in their hands about to stone to death the woman taken in adultery and sent them skulking away with only the force of His courage and the penetrating sting of His words following them at their backs. To Samuel, that took guts. In that unfolding moment, Samuel vowed that he would do the same for the girl. He would stand with the girl and protect her verbally and physically. He would stand by the side of the girl for life, even if he had to stand in the face of everyone in the town to do it. In that moment, the shape of the forming die to be cast developed another edge.

"And Jesus said to the woman, 'Your faith has saved you. Go in peace.'"

The girl wasn't with him in church that day. What the women of the Richardson house did on Sunday, Samuel didn't know, but he did know they weren't open for business on Sunday. The girl had told him so. Whether this was their backhanded way of showing respect for the Lord or whether they just needed a day of rest like everyone else, Samuel didn't know either. At least he had the consolation of knowing that on Sunday, other men were not further soiling the soiled dove he intended to make an honest woman of.

"The Pharisee deemed the woman to be fallen," Pastor Russell thumped on. "But in his smug hypocrisy, he was the true fallen one. In God's eyes, he had fallen farther than the woman."

Hearing the words *woman* and *fallen* spoken together, Samuel snapped back to the present. He had been drifting. He had not fallen asleep in the pew, but he had drifted into his visions to the point that in his imaginings of the future he had detached from the present.

"In his shriveled soul, the man who lived by and for his inflated sense of self-righteous spirituality didn't realize that he was in the presence of true spirituality," Pastor Russell intoned on. "He didn't realize that he was in the presence of true spirituality on two accounts. He didn't realize that he was in the presence of the Son of the living God. He didn't realize that the woman knew that she was in the presence of the true Spirit of God. If he did know, he would have honored Jesus in his own way as much as the woman was and would have repented of his own sins as intensely as the woman was repenting of hers. That's why Jesus repeatedly slapped down the scribes and Pharisees almost every time He spoke of them or to them. On more than one occasion He told them to their faces that tax collectors and harlots would enter into the kingdom of heaven before they did."

Samuel's church wasn't the kind of church where the audience acted like a chorus, shouting, "Preach it, brother!" Proper Baptists frowned on that kind of spontaneous emoting. That form of call-and-response vocalizing was something Negro congregations did.

"By her faith, the woman proved that she was spiritually closer to heaven and to the heart of God than the Pharisee ever could be with all his outward shows of righteousness. By her tears she proved her love more real than all the religious incantations that the Pharisee and all his ilk could offer. The Pharisee's proclamation of the woman's fallen state was meaningless. All the religious rituals he would put the woman through if he had a mind to declare her redeemed were meaningless tripe. The woman didn't need his folderol to be redeemed. Her faith and her tears had redeemed her beyond any power the Pharisee had to add or subtract."

Samuel didn't want to subtract anything from the girl. He wanted to add her to his life and add his life to hers. At the same time, he wanted to add a real life and authentic love to the girl who had known neither so far in her life. In Samuel's mind and life plan with the girl, he would redeem the girl's heart and soul through his love for her and his standing beside her and bringing her into true love and true life. He would redeem the girl's body by taking her away from the house and the life where she casually gave her body to be used by every man who came her way with a few loose dollars in his hand. The girl had known only false love all her life. Possibly as her way of compensating for the love she had never known and the options she never had, the girl had given herself over to the false option and the false love practiced in the Richardson house. Samuel would be the girl's real lover for life. He would be the girl's option for life and for a life of real love. He would forever alter the girl's definition of love. He would redeem the girl and restore her ability to know and give real love. He would replace the false love the girl had immersed herself in with his true love.

"It's not clear what happened to the woman in the story in Luke's Gospel after she left the party at the Pharisee's house and went on her way and after Jesus had moved on to another ministry in another city," Pastor Russell went on in his stem-winding sermon.

For all Samuel knew, the woman had returned to her former life on the street simply because she had no other options and no one in the town would accept her despite the fact that Jesus had forgiven her. It would not be the same with the girl. Jesus had left the woman and moved on. Samuel wasn't going anywhere. He wasn't planning on leaving the farm, and he wasn't planning on leaving the girl. Wherever he was going in life, he planned on bringing the girl along with him. More properly stated, he would keep the girl with him for life on the farm he would not leave.

"There is no name other than Jesus's by which we may be saved," the pastor intoned in a rising voice, heading for the wrap-up.

Samuel snapped back to attention. He realized that he had been drifting again and had missed another chunk of the sermon. Samuel assumed the statement was from the Bible, but he had missed the chapter and verse. But when it came to no other names, that brought up another small problem. He knew the girl by no other name than the romance novel name she had given herself. He still didn't know her real name. He only knew not to press her for it.

"Sin is an offense to the Lord, but in His grace and in the sacrifice of

His Son, sin can be forgiven and the record of what we have done and the bad ways we have lived wiped away as if it never happened. Life as it should be lived can be granted anew here and in the life to come. Be it known for all time that the Lord's forgiveness is for all eternity. We have but to call upon the Lord in faith, and He will forgive us our sins and cleanse us from our unrighteousnesses here on earth, making us one with Him and keeping us one with one another together in heaven for all eternity."

In the story just concluded, Jesus had given the woman equal measures of what she both needed and wanted: forgiveness and acceptance. Samuel accepted the girl. He accepted her for who she was and what she was. As he sat in the pew that Sunday, Samuel stood ready to forgive the girl for what she was and what she was continuing to be over at the house. In his mind he had already forgiven her.

As far as forgiveness for the past went and continuance into the future, there was one small problem brewing on the horizon. In the story of the woman taken in adultery, after saving the unnamed woman from the stone-waving mob, Jesus turned to the woman and told her to go and sin no more. Samuel had already forgiven the girl for being a woman of ill repute. He was ready to forgive her for the rest of their lives together for being what she was still out there being at the Richardson house. At the present moment, both in church and out, the knowledge that the girl was seeing and sleeping with other men was growing increasingly large and increasingly distasteful to Samuel.

Pastor Russell finished the sermon. The collection plate was passed. Samuel passed his hand over the plate and dropped in his tithe. He kept his hand down on the plate so that the other members of his family would not see the amount that he was contributing. It wasn't that Samuel was following the biblical injunction of Jesus not to let the left hand know what the right hand was doing and not to make a hypocritical show of being charitable. Samuel didn't have as much spare change to contribute to the upkeep of the congregation's spiritual shepherd and to the physical upkeep of the church itself. He had been contributing a good deal of his spare change to the upkeep of the girl.

That having been accomplished, it was time to wrap up both liturgy and ritual and bring the service to a close.

"For our final hymn today, we'll sing the old favorite hymn 'Abide with

Me,'" Pastor Russell said. "That's hymn number one hundred seventy-eight in your hymnals."

Samuel vaguely remembered having heard the hymn sung only once in the church, but he remembered neither the tune nor the words. He found the choice of hymns was a bit of a departure for Pastor Russell. Given that the pastor and the congregation were Baptist, Pastor Russell was a bit more partial to hymns like "On Jordan's Banks the Baptist's Cry," which was one of the pastor's favorites. Samuel wondered what had prompted the departure from the usual fare on the pastor's part. For a moment he wondered if the pastor was again trying to play on the maritime tragedy recently concluded in the North Atlantic in order to make a comment on the brevity of life and the moment-to-moment possibility of sudden and unexpected death by having the congregation sing the hymn that was supposedly being played on deck during the last minutes as the *Titanic* floundered. As Samuel opened the hymnal book to the appropriate page, he wasn't aware that the hymn played on the sinking *Titanic* was "Nearer My God to Thee."

Mrs. Herkheimer, the church organist, cranked the wheezing and otherwise limited organ to life. On Pastor Russell's cue, the congregation started singing. Samuel usually found most hymns to be a bit stilted-sounding with language that seemed forced, but he found the tune of the hymn that he and the congregation started singing to be surprisingly simple and melodic. To Samuel's thinking, the lyrics of the hymn were simple, poignant, and gripping at the same time. In its own way, the hymn contained all the longings of the human soul. It covered the whole of the journey of the soul. Played on the limited organ, with its few lyrics, the hymn covered the whole of the human journey to God. It also followed the whole of the human journey from life to death. But then again, Samuel figured that was what a well-written hymn was supposed to do.

> Abide with me, fast falls the eventide,
> The darkness deepens, Lord, with me abide.
> When other helpers fail and comforts flee,
> Help of the helpless, O abide with me.

The hymn "Abide with Me" could have worked as well as an epitaph for the *Titanic* and the souls on board who had stepped off the sloping deck to meet their Maker when no rescue appeared on the horizon. Just as quickly, it set Samuel to thinking about the girl who had appeared on his horizon and how he was going to be her rescuer.

Darkness had been with and followed the girl all the days of her life, almost since birth. The darkness had deepened for the girl, deepened enough that she had been forced to flee her home by jumping on a passing freight train. Even before she had been forced to flee, all comforts had fled her. Those who should have most been her helpers and protectors, the members of her own family, had turned into her tormentors. As the lyrics of the hymn unwound, Samuel vowed that where others had failed the girl and had become her oppressor, he would not fail her. He would be the true helper of the helpless girl. For the rest of their days together, he would abide with the girl as the true helper and protector she never had. Samuel poured himself into the song with more conviction than he had ever sung a hymn in church.

> I need Thy presence every passing hour;
> What but Thy grace can foil the tempter's power?
> Who like Thyself my guide and stay can be?
> Through cloud and sunshine, O abide with me.

Through the lyrics of the hymn, Samuel came to know his part in the girl's life. He would be her guide and stay. He would be the steady and loving presence that would guide her away from the torment of her past and the dead-end life she had been forced to live in the past. He would dispel the clouds that had hung over the girl's life since her life had begun. He would dispel the bleak sky that hung over her life now. He would bring into her life the first sunshine that she had ever known.

> Come not in terrors as the King of Kings,
> But kind and good with healing in Thy wings;
> Tears for all woes, a heart for every plea.
> Come, friend of sinners, thus abide with me.

Samuel was assured in himself that the girl's days of terror were over.

No longer would she have to pull a knife on a man to defend herself and keep herself from being torn and violated, especially by the very men who were supposed to protect her. Never again would she be forced to flee in terror of her life into the night, into a boxcar and out onto the open track to escape pain and degradation and the threat of death. She would suffer no degradation at his hands. He would be her protector. Her days of pain, fear, and flight were over. He and his family would answer all the silent pleas he was sure she was making inside her heart. He and his family would heal all the hurt she had felt since the beginnings of her days. He would be all that a man should be to a woman: friend, lover, protector. He would be all that a proper man should be to a woman, even if she wasn't a proper woman.

> Swift to its close ebbs out life's little day;
> Earth's joys grow dim, its glories pass away;
> Change and decay in all around I see;
> O Thou who changes not, abide with me.

Samuel resolved again in himself that he would be the changeless lover and protector of the girl for the rest of their lives together.

> I have no foe with Thee at hand to bless;
> Ills have no weight and tears no bitterness.
> Where is death's sting? Where, grave, thy victory?
> I triumph still if Thou abide with me!

In that moment, in Samuel's mind, his future, the future he had already decided on and had set for himself, was set in place again. He knew his place in life. His place was on his father's farm at the girl's side, walking through life with her, giving her a better life than she had ever had in her backwoods shanty, the house of, and at the hands of, her abusive family. His place was to give her a better life than she could ever have in Mrs. Richardson's house. He knew his future. The future was the girl. His future and calling in life was to be the girl's lord and protector, but more protector than lord. The girl had been lorded over by the wrong kind of men for all her days. She didn't need another hardhanded lord. He would be the man who would make up for and set right all the wrongs that had been done to her. He would be the one who would take the sting of hurt out of her life. He would be the lover of the girl's life and soul as well as of her body. He would be the healer and redeemer of her spirit as much as he would be the redeemer of her reputation and her place in society. Like Jesus with the many less than proper women He had redeemed, Samuel would redeem the girl's life and soul from the pit she had begun her life in and was currently living in. His love for her would triumph over all the ills that had befallen her since her life had begun. Together their love would triumph through their lives together and into the life beyond.

As lyrics of the hymn swelled to the concluding stanza and the volume of the singing rose with it, the volume of Samuel's singing swelled to match the swelling of his heart and soul for the girl. The lyrics of the hymn swelled up from darkness toward the promised light.

> Hold Thou Thy cross before my closing eyes;
> Shine through the gloom and point me to the skies.
> Heaven's morning breaks, and Earth's vain shadows flee;
> In life, in death, O Lord, abide with me.

As the hymn ended, Samuel saw his future clearer than he had ever seen it before. He saw his path in life clearer than he had ever seen it before. He saw his path through the rest of his life as clear and unequivocal. The life of his future was the girl. His future was with the girl. His path to the future and into the future was with the girl.

In life, in death, O girl, I'll stay with thee, Samuel vowed to the girl and to himself as he closed the hymnal.

As the service wound to an end, Samuel was now able to see everything clearly. He thought it was too early to ask the girl to marry him, but in the interim he could start to make her see how he felt about her. Hopefully the day would come soon enough when, instead of sneaking off to see the girl behind closed doors, he could walk with the girl in the open under the sun. Samuel figured that if he waited until the town accepted the girl, he would have to wait forever. Instead of waiting for acceptance of his love and lover to come to the girl from the town, he would grab her by the hand and bull his way through the town's reluctance to admit a "soiled dove" into society. He would take her as his wife and present her to the town as his wife and his partner for life, and that would be that. In the meantime, he would have to find a personal way to deal with the fact that the girl was sleeping with other men.

The girl had once casually said that if he came to meet her at Charlie's saloon, he might have to wait in line for her if he didn't get there soon enough to catch her as she came in the door. All Samuel knew at the otherwise churchy moment was that he didn't want to stand in line waiting while the girl made love to another man, even if she was just doing her job and there was nothing personal between her and the man, any more than he wanted to wait to have a life with her. The only other thing he knew was that the girl would be back to going to bed with other men as if the love they had shared at any given moment or in any given place was completed. He had heard her say what her schedule was outside the house. He hadn't heard a lot of the rest she had said.

As Samuel continued listening to the hymn, his thoughts took proverbial flight. But they didn't soar over the horizon as they had before. They more or less just circled around in a tightening circle inside his head. He had seen the girl's face in the sky. In his more truncated vision, he saw the lights of Charlie's saloon. In his imagination, he stood outside the window of Charlie's saloon looking in. He saw the girl standing in front of the bar talking to a man. She smiled at him with the smile all women in her profession give the man they are working up, the same smile she had often smiled at him. In his vision he saw her take the man's hand. In his vision, they turned to leave.

As Samuel rose to leave the church, the only thing that he could see in the immediate future was that as soon as any times of loving they shared together were over, the girl would be back to her profession of sleeping with other men as if the time they had spent loving together hadn't happened or had happened but had meant nothing. The real love, the real home, and the real hope he hoped to share with the nameless girl still seemed as distant and out of sight as her real name.

Chapter 8

The site Samuel had chosen for their picnic was a clearing along the shore of the river a few miles east of the town, not far off the road that he, the girl, and Beth had taken earlier to the fair in the next town over. Samuel wasn't sure who owned the land, but it wasn't near a farmhouse or an open farm field where they could be seen by someone. The turnoff was half hidden in the trees. To get to the clearing, they had to drive over a rutted and ill-defined path about a quarter of a mile through the woods. They bounced a bit getting to the clearing, but the woods around the clearing gave them concealment from prying eyes.

The clearing was an area about the size of a small public park in a small town. It was free of heavy underbrush and had only a few scattered trees in it. The grass was a bit tall for a picnic ground, but they had brought blankets to sit on. The sunlight easily penetrated to the ground of the clearing. The few trees in the clearing gave shade against the sun. At the same time, the lack of trees gave an open view of the sky above. At the edge of the river, the view opened up even more. Across the river on the other side was the open expanse of a farm field that was becoming obscured at ground level by the maturing crop of corn growing in it.

Clarinda and Polly sat cross-legged on the blankets spread on the grass and chattered away like magpies. And they did it without talking shop. Samuel didn't think that small-town prostitutes would have that much to talk about, but the girls found a seemingly endless range of pedestrian subjects to discuss. A lot of it was gossip about the other women in the house. Samuel figured his sister, Beth, could fit right in as if the social divide between small-town gossiping girls and the kind of girls who lived the kind of lives and practiced the profession that made them the subject of major gossip didn't exist there in the sun in the clearing by the flowing river. To Samuel it was a good and hopeful sign that the girls could so easily sound like average farm girls on their way to becoming farm wives. That Polly was technically already a woman, being over twenty-one, was somewhat lost in her bucktoothed grin and her tongue-tied speech, which made her seem younger and more relatively innocent than her years and professional involvement allowed.

As the girls sat on their haunches on the blankets, Samuel and Ben reclined casually on the grass alongside the blankets. They left the blankets to the girls and didn't try to crowd onto them too. After all, they were boys turning into men. They weren't bothered by a little grass. Together the four of them ate the picnic lunch prepared by the girls at the house and drank the (cocaine-free if not yet sugar-free) bottled soda that Sam and Ben had bought from Mr. Kindelspire's soda fountain. Behind the scenes, the scene hidden in the woods wasn't exactly a "Tom Sawyer with Becky" vignette of youthful pastoral river bottom innocence. But for the moment, all that anyone peeking through the trees would see was an imitation of a Currier and Ives print of turn-of-the-century youthful innocence in the sun with no clouds in the sky or on the horizon.

Having finished eating, Ben and Polly got up and walked off, heading to the riverbank. Samuel reached over and took Clarinda's hand, preparing to get up and follow them to the edge of the river. Instead of standing up, Clarinda scooted on her knees across the blanket over to Samuel. You couldn't really say that she threw herself on him, though a much more proper woman would say that she threw herself at him. She pulled herself up to Samuel, wrapped her arms around him, and started kissing him. Samuel fell backward in the grass, taking her with him. Clarinda stretched herself out full length on top of Samuel. The two of them lay on the grass with Clarinda on top, kissing each other long and wet. While proper observers of the period might consider a picnic shared by young couples to be a Currier and Ives scene of pastoral innocence, they would probably be scandalized by the display Samuel and Clarinda were putting on. Proper young people just didn't do that sort of thing. But then again, none of the four who had come to the clearing by the river's edge that day could exactly be called proper. Neither were they exactly innocents. Innocence was relative that day, and some were less innocent than others.

To Samuel, the move the girl had put on him was a spontaneous display of easy and natural affection equal in significance to the way she had swum up out of the water of Gustafson Lake and wrapped herself around him. It was even more spontaneous as they had not discussed lovemaking and remuneration. In its spontaneity, the girl's action held out for Samuel the possibility that she was thinking in terms of love and loving and of being in love with him in a way that went beyond fee-for-service. He could read a whole future into her easy and natural display of affection. Then again, she was well versed in the art of making love seem easy and natural.

With his arms wrapped around her back, for several long minutes Samuel clench-kissed the girl. She kissed him back just as decidedly. The long grass was underneath them. The breeze whispered through the treetops above them. The green woods were all around them. The river flowed by quietly close to them. The girl he wanted for life was in his arms with her face in front of his face and her lips pressed to his. The future and the life Samuel wanted was just a short distance away over the horizon. All proper observers were out of sight. For a dreamily long interval, the length of which Samuel did not measure and which he did not want to end, the girl kissed him and he kissed her. Then she broke the kiss and pulled her head back and away a short distance. For a moment she looked into his eyes in silence.

"You've got that look in your eye, boy," Clarinda said in a coy and suggestive voice, their faces separated by just a few inches. She twirled his hair as she spoke. "Just what is it you're thinkin' 'bout? What you got on your mind?"

What the girl was referring to was obvious. The girl was thinking that Samuel was thinking the obvious. Samuel did have his own obvious coefficient, but his thinking wasn't as shallow and formulaic as some might imagine a farm boy's thinking to be. Though obviousness wasn't that far away over Samuel's shoulder, what Samuel was thinking at the moment wasn't quite what the girl was thinking he was thinking.

"I was thinking of the pioneers," Samuel said, looking up into the trees of the natural setting they were lying together in.

Lying spontaneous and natural in the clearing with the girl in his arms, it seemed to Samuel like they were the only two people in the world. Lying alone in each other's arms, Samuel imagined that he and the girl were a homesteader pioneer couple, one of the first pioneer couples to come into the area. In his mind they were out beyond the edge of civilization in the open wilderness of a new land. They had just arrived in the place they would clear and settle. They were alone together and on their own. They had the forest and the land around them. They had the future and a new life in a new world ahead of them. Soon they would build a home and start clearing the land. For the moment they were together alone in the woods celebrating their arrival, celebrating their love, and celebrating the future and the life they would make for themselves, christening the new land and the new life that would be theirs with their bodies and their love.

"The Martins were some of the earliest pioneers in this area. They helped clear the land and bring civilization to the state before it became a state. My grandparents taught me a song that the pioneers used to sing. My singing voice isn't much, but I can sing part of it for you if you like."

"Go ahead," Clarinda said, still running her fingers through his hair. "Don't ask me to sing along though. My singin' voice ain't much better 'n yours."

The girl actually had a soft and pretty voice. It seemed to Samuel that if she could get past her hard-edged hillbilly accent and her garbled syntax, she would have a singing voice as soft and beautiful as her face.

Samuel couldn't remember the whole song, just what he recalled as the most memorable lines. Those were the lines he sang to the girl. What resulted wasn't exactly turn-of-the-century karaoke, but the simple words meant a lot to Samuel historically. Now they meant even more to him as a symbol of the future he hoped for:

> Come, come, there's a wondrous land
> For a hopeful heart and a willing hand.

Come, come, come away with me,
And I'll build you a home in the meadow.

Samuel's foray into musical nostalgia ended after only those four lines.
The girl's expression did not change. She offered no comment on either
the words of the song or the quality of his singing voice. Samuel took one
of his arms off her back and brought his hand up to the side of her face.
With the top sides of his fingers, he stroked the girl's cheek.

"I'd love to build you a home in the meadow," he said. "I'd love to
build you a home anywhere. I would most love to build a home with you
on the farm. We could live there close to each other, as close to each other
as we would live close to life, close to our family, and close to the land. I'd
build you a home where you would be happy and safe and wouldn't feel
the need to run."

Along with his first foray into singing for the girl, Samuel's comment
about building a home for her was his first foray into hinting at marriage.

"In my house you'd never be threatened, and you wouldn't ever again
think that you were threatened."

"Are you proposing to take me away to live in some magic fairy-tale
castle where I'll be a princess with you as my handsome Prince Charming,
where we'll live happily ever after?" Clarinda asked in a skeptical tone at
best.

"I'm not talking about a magic castle," the real-world Samuel answered.
"I don't believe in magic castles."

Actually he did sort of believe in magic. Finding the girl had pretty
much been more magic to him than he had ever expected to find in life.
The girl was more magic than he had imagined. She was all the magic he
wanted.

"But I do believe in real love," Samuel replied. As he spoke, he stroked
the side of her cheek with the palm of his hand.

"I believe in real love in the real world. Real love may not be fairy-tale
magic like in the stories, but I believe that real love lasts."

"I doubly don't believe in fairy tales," Clarinda said with a bite in her
voice. "And I have quadruple reasons not to believe in fairy tales. When
it comes to fairy tales, I grew up on the far side of hell, far away from
anything resembling a fairy tale."

Clarinda stopped stroking Samuel's cheek with her finger.

"You talk like you think you're my Prince Charming. Prince Charmings were in real short supply where I grew up. They're in just as short supply at Mrs. Richardson's house. A long time ago I stopped believing that any Prince Charming was going to ride up on a white horse and sweep me up off my feet and take me away to live in some magic fairy-tale castle somewhere. I sure didn't take any romantic fairy-tale notions along with me when I ran away from home. And I don't see a lot of fairy tales coming to me through Mrs. Richardson's door."

The girl ran the tip of her finger in a figure-eight pattern over Samuel's cheek. Her touch was soft and teasing, but her voice was hard.

"I learned the hard way to keep myself movin'. That way I keep myself ahead of trouble. I travel light. When I left home, the only things I took with me were the clothes on my back and the knife I cut my way out of my home and out of my brother's drunken grasp with. I shed just about everything when I ran away from home. That goes for storybook romantic notions. The only romantic notion I carried with me when I left home was the name I gave myself. So whether you get your romantic notions from a fairy-tale storybook or from pioneer history, don't go trying to talk far-fetched romantic notions into me. Men who hand a girl those kinds of romantic notions are just trying to snow her so they can get what they want out of her for free by puttin' stars in the girl's eyes and pullin' the wool over her eyes while they're pullin' her dress off. For the most part, those kinds of notions are just flat-out lies told by men to get a girl to do for free what we do for money."

With her lips a few inches from his, Clarinda redirected the conversation to a more immediate application.

"I've never been one for fairy-tale romantic notions, not one little bit. At the very best, those kinds of notions are nothin' but a snare to me or any girl."

Midstream in her free association, Clarinda suddenly switched subjects. She also switched from her hard voice back to her coy voice.

"But where it comes to getting practical about things, on the other hand, I do know about practical romance. Where it comes to getting down to practical, Polly and I have worked out a little surprise for the two of you. Back in the house, before we came here, Polly and I got together and talked. We decided that since you and Ben were so nice to take us on a picnic, to show our thanks, if you want to take us into the woods like you did with me at the lake and like we do what we do at the house, we won't charge you for it this time. It's a fair enough trade all around. We get a free picnic from you; you get a free bounce from us. Even Mrs. Richardson agrees. I told her my idea. She said we could go ahead. She just doesn't want us to be making a regular thing out of it with the two of you, even if you are our regular customers. She'll make this exception for the two of you this one time, but she doesn't want us to start trading our services for nonmonetary intangibles with our other customers. Intangibles like picnics or gifts given to us don't bring in money for the house or pay the house bills."

The prospect of making love to the girl was a pleasant bonus for the day. Not having to pay for it was another plus. The high-priced girl was getting to be a drain on Samuel's savings. But paradoxically, he was a bit irked at the interruption. Not that he didn't enjoy the prospect of feeling up the girl, so to speak, but one of the reasons he had wanted to be alone with her on the picnic was to indirectly feel her out on the prospect of marriage. To that end, Samuel had thought he had seen an opening (no sexual pun intended). His talk of pioneers and homesteading had been his way of touching on the edge of the subject of marriage and home without bringing it up directly. In Samuel's estimate, the girl hadn't said anything directly or given him any hint as to what she might feel about marriage and family. He wasn't sure how he could go about bringing up the subject again without her catching on to what he was trying to hide.

"Will making love to me on the ground in the bushes next to this meadow be practical-romantic enough for you, honey?"

Making practical love to the girl well practiced in lovemaking was practical enough for Samuel. Making love to the girl in a clean room in laundered sheets under a canopied bed was all right for the dandy in Samuel. Making love to the girl on the mudbanks of a lake or on the ground in the woods under a canopy of branches was equally acceptable and natural to the rustic Samuel. It was just that at the rustic natural moment, Samuel was thinking in terms of a wider love. While the girl was pinning him to the ground and proposing to let him pin her to the ground, Samuel still wanted to pin her down as to what she thought in terms of wider love. The girl had made herself a home in Mrs. Richardson's house and employ. Samuel still wanted to know what she thought of in terms of a wider home, in a meadow or in a farmhouse.

"I thought you didn't like doing it on the ground with sticks and bugs under you," Samuel said. He supposed he could let her be on top, but he didn't like the feel of sticks and bugs under him either.

"The mud on the riverbank is as soft as the mud at Gustafson Lake, but there's a lot more vegetation around the shore of Gustafson Lake. The riverbank is open and exposed. Someone may see us. All some farmer has to do is come by with his team in the field on the other side, and our secret will be all over town by the time we get back. We could go into the trees in the woods, but then we're back on the ground with the twigs and bugs. I thought you didn't like that."

"We can use the blankets," Clarinda said, pausing her finger on his cheek. "That's why I had you bring two of them along. It wasn't just so we could sit ladylike on the ground without getting our dresses dirty. I'm long beyond that or any kind of ladylike behavior. I don't care about getting my dress dirty. I just don't want to get my back dirty and full of cockleburs."

Samuel was still as far from knowing whether the girl would marry him as he'd been when he made love to her the first time in her room in Mrs. Richardson's house.

"If you'd rather do it back in Mrs. Richardson's, she'll make you pay. It's only out here today that you'll be gettin' it for free. … If you prefer to use my bed in the house, you can meet me there. You just may have to wait in line. But I'll be there all week." The girl paused for a second. "Except Wednesdays and Thursdays. Those are the nights I work Charlie's saloon. If you want to meet me, you'll have to meet me there. But you'll have to arrive early and catch me before some other man gets his dibs in first. Otherwise you'll have to cool yourself off playing pool until I'm finished."

Samuel had always known that the girl wasn't a fairy-tale snow-white princess. But in outlining her itinerary and schedule for the week, she had only emphasized and brought home the fact that the girl Samuel wanted to bring home and make a home with was sleeping with other men. In copious numbers. When she hadn't answered his hidden question as to how she might feel about marrying him, Samuel hadn't felt himself any closer to home. After she had so blithely reminded him of how much and how far afield she was sleeping around, Samuel felt even father from home than when he had started.

The girl ran her finger across his cheek one more time. "But I'll do it for you here and free like I promised."

The girl suddenly pushed herself up and off of him. In a quick second the quick and lively girl was up and standing over him. "But first I want to go for a swim." She held out her hand for him to take. "Come on."

The fact that the girl would be off and sleeping with other men like their time together had never happened was still weighing on Samuel's mind. He wasn't quite sure how to react, but he wasn't about to tell her to get out of his sight. He stood up as quickly as the girl had and took her hand. Holding his hand in hers, the girl pulled him off in the direction of the river.

Polly and Ben were sitting on the riverbank, splashing their feet in the water and laughing like a pair of young children, when Clarinda and Samuel came up alongside them.

"Come on, we're all going for a swim," the take-charge girl said to the couple. Polly and Ben looked a bit surprised by the suggestion. Clarinda focused on her coworker and in-house sister. "After that, we'll perform the other thing we promised them we would. But first I want to cool off in the river before I get heated up again. We can all cool ourselves down in the river afterward."

Without further comment of her own and without soliciting further comment from the rest of them, the girl started to pull her dress off over her head. Samuel looked across the river to the empty field beyond. Ben and Polly looked in the same direction.

"Ah, we don't have the same wraparound cover here we did at Gustafson Lake," Samuel reminded. "The ground is open on the other side. If someone comes along on the far side of the river, like a farmer driving his team, he'll see us."

"Today is Sunday," the girl said through the cloth of her dress that she had halfway over her head. "Farmers aren't in the field on Sundays. If they're not in church, they're home in the barn oiling their thresher machines. I don't think anyone's going to come along."

The girl finished pulling her dress off. As she had tossed off her sexual mores a long time ago, she tossed her dress off behind her on the riverbank.

"Even if someone see us, that don't bother me none. Everyone 'round here pretty much knows me and what I am. Seeing me naked in the river won't tell nobody what they don't already know about me. And Polly. The only ones who have to worry about keeping your reputations clean and your secrets secret are you and your friend."

The girl started to remove her undergarments.

"The pioneers you were bragging about being part of your stock swam naked in the lakes and rivers they pioneered by. Like you said, they took the dare of a new land. Don't you have enough of their spirit left in you to take the dare of swimming naked with a girl in a place where there's only a small chance that you'll be seen? If the two of you want to hide in the woods and watch us swim, you can. I won't drag you in with me. But if you have any adventure about you, if you don't mind being a bit daring, and if you aren't afraid to take my dare, come in and join us."

In the same quick order she had shown at Gustafson Lake, the girl had her clothes off. With a sprinting dash, and without looking to see if anyone was looking from the far shore, she rushed into the water and dove headlong into it. As the girl disappeared under the water, Samuel started taking off his clothes. Polly and Ben followed. As they disrobed, all three of them took the precaution the girl hadn't and looked across the river and up and down the far and near shores to see if anyone was watching them. From what they could see, no one was present and watching. They had the stretch of river to themselves. Soon enough they would have each other to themselves in the woods next to the river.

For some time the four frolicked and splashed in the water like children half their age, swimming after each other, splashing, and ducking each other. They could feel the sun on their faces and the mud of the river bottom beneath their feet. Samuel used the occasion of their being alone without benefit of bathing suits to grab various parts of the girl's naked body under the water. In return the girl would grab him back. When he had a full grip on her, he pulled her in toward him. For a moment the girl responded by pulling herself next to him and kissing him. Before the clinch could begin in full and the act be consummated, the girl would push herself away. The expression on her face was alternately laughing and teasing. She even stuck out her tongue at Samuel in a girlish manner. In one way it was almost like swimming with his sister, the difference being that he had never gone skinny-dipping with Beth or grabbed her naked body under the water.

After a length of time spent in childlike capering, the girl's expression changed. As she had at Gustafson Lake, she came up from under the water just in front of Samuel. She stood facing him with wet hair on her face. Rivulets of water ran down her chest. Her breasts were half out of the water. As she pulled a length of wet hair off her face, her expression had changed from the previous teasing, playing, and distance-keeping look to the set look of a mature woman that said the time had come. After brushing her hair off her face, using the same hand, she took Samuel's hand and led him out of the river, away from the riverbank, and into the clearing where they had left the blankets. With Samuel's hand still in hers, she used her other hand to pick up one of the blankets. From there she turned and led Samuel into the woods beyond the edge of the clearing. Polly and Ben followed suit, gathering up the remaining blanket and heading off in the opposite direction into the woods on the other side of the clearing.

Far enough into the woods so as not to be seen readily by anyone who happened to walk into the clearing, the naked couple stopped. In the shade of the dense tree cover, not a lot of light reached the forest floor. Not much underbrush grew. Between the standing and fallen trees, the dirt of the ground was as bare and uncovered as they were. The girl chose a reasonably long enough stretch of ground between the trees. She continued to clear the spot by kicking away the loose branches lying on the ground with her bare foot. Then she proceeded to spread the blanket out on the ground.

After spreading out the blanket, the girl turned, wrapped her arms around Samuel, pulled him in tight against her body, and started kissing him hard and wet. Samuel responded by wrapping his arms around her and pulling her to himself as much as she was pulling him to herself. He felt the warm wetness of the girl's naked body as it pressed against his. He felt the smooth slip and slide of her wet skin under his hands and arms. When he brought his hands up her back, he could feel the tangled wetness of her hair between his hands and the skin of her upper back and shoulders. For some time the couple stood there pressing against each other, pulling each other in tight.

The wrestling star Samuel was stronger than the girl. He could have pinned her down under him on his own terms in a minute. But he waited

249

for her to give the next clue and set the direction. Soon enough she started slowly lowering herself to the ground. As she did so, she continued to kiss Samuel, pulling him down along with her. Samuel jockeyed to keep his balance while he continued to kiss the girl as she lowered them both toward the ground, dropping first to his knees and then to his hands and knees, with the girl's arms still wrapped around him. The position was getting rather awkward for Samuel to hold a kiss in. It was also a bit of a strain on his back. Just before becoming fully horizontal, the girl broke her kiss. She proceeded to lie the rest of the way down on the blanket. Now fully on the ground on the blanket, she wriggled around, positioning herself. As she did so, Samuel positioned himself above her.

What happened next is too proverbial to go into depth about. The girl gasped softly and tensed up as Samuel went deep into her. She arched her back as Samuel's motions began to flow within her. Inside, Samuel's feelings began to both tighten hard and flow faster as he felt himself deep in the girl he wanted to spend his life with. His feelings flowed faster and warmer as he felt himself slip deeper into his feelings of love for her.

Though the girl was on the bottom, underneath Samuel, it had been her show all the way. She had taken Samuel down in her own way and in her own time. The girl was in control. Samuel didn't feel that his masculine ego had been otherwise damaged by letting the girl take the lead and set the pace. There on the ground in the woods, he was right where he physically wanted to be with her. In that immediate sense, Samuel felt that he was holding the world and the future. In any sense beyond the immediately physical, Samuel felt like he was trying to hold a will-o'-the-wisp that shimmered and glowed before his eyes in a deep woods but that vanished when he tried to gather it to himself.

In his arms the girl was fully real. In his heart the girl was the only reality Samuel could see. In his heart she was the only future and the only future of love he wanted. In his body on top of hers, Samuel's heart was only inches from the girl's heart, but he still didn't know how close her heart was to him really. In Samuel's arms, in his life, and in her life, the girl was a contradiction in terms he couldn't unravel. She was an enigma he had no desire to unravel or even understand fully. The girl was all girl and all woman. She wasn't a naive innocent like his sister, wide-eyed on the brink of womanhood, shuddering under the feel of new sensations, afraid she would be swept away by them as if caught in the current of a running river. The girl was a practiced sensual seductress in full command of her passion as she gave in to that passion.

The girl unfolded her sensuality as she unfolded her arms. She wrapped her sensuality tight around Samuel as she wrapped her body around him. The girl was demure, soft, and stroking in the sweetness of her love. She was sweaty, heaving, and shameless in the intensity of her need. She was sweating hard in the heat of her passion, but she was sweating the way she wanted to sweat.

The naked girl in his arms was an orphan who had been stripped of everything she had in life. At the same time, she was a regent of herself who held her life and the realm of herself in her own hands. The girl wasn't a lost and unsure waif trembling in his arms. She was a full and certain woman in control of herself and her situation. At least that was the way she saw it—and the way she saw her life.

The girl had no name she wanted other than the name she had given herself. Beyond the obviousness of his desire for the nameless girl, Samuel had no desire other than to give the girl his name for life. Whatever first name she wished to call herself, Samuel didn't care. He would marry her under the name of Clarinda as well as under her real name.

On the ground in the woods with the girl in his arms, Samuel was as near the girl as had ever hoped he would be. At the same time, she was as far from him as she had been at the start.

For the remainder of their time together on the ground, hidden from Ben and Polly and anyone else, Samuel and the girl rolled and tussled with one another. She alternately went into spasms, during which she tensed her arms, drawing them tight across his back in an X or in a parallel motion down his sides, and dug her fingers into his shoulders. When she wasn't tightening up, she ran her arms and hands in wild random patterns over his back. Beneath Samuel, she rolled her body against his and heaved it up and down under his body. She pushed the fullness of her chest up against Samuel and rubbed her chest against his. She kept the fullness of her lips pressed against Samuel's mouth. The girl was well versed in handling her body in a full, womanly way. An observer spying on them unseen from the woods could say that the girl certainly looked and acted like she was in love with the boy. But then again, it was part of the girl's profession to be well versed in the bodily techniques of love and to make the way she handled her body look and feel like fuller love. To a detached observer, it also looked as if she were fully abandoning herself to love. But as Clarinda kept up her end of the performance, she also held her opinions of romantic love unchanged.

Samuel still had no clear idea of whether she loved him or whether it was a crafted professional performance on the part of a girl for whom all love was an art form leading not to love for its own sake but to a paycheck. That the girl wasn't charging him her going house rate for their joining that day was something of a hopeful sign for Samuel that she thought of him as something more than just a paying client. But he wondered if she was just looking to secure him as a friend as much as a lover. The only thing that Samuel could see in the immediate future was that as soon as their day together was over, the day Samuel felt so special, the girl would be back to her profession of sleeping with other men as if their time together had meant nothing to her.

Samuel broke off kissing the girl. He slowed down and stopped moving on top of her. She stopped moving underneath him. Samuel lifted his head and looked at the girl. The girl looked back at him. With a free hand, Samuel started toying with a lock of her hair.

"If we lie here much longer, we're both going to get chiggers," Clarinda said.

It wasn't the most romantic response ever spoken by a woman in an intimate encounter, but not a lot of turn-of-the-century hillbilly girls were Madame Bovary.

"I still want to take you into my life," Samuel said, returning to his original theme.

"Personally I've had enough of livin' out in the weeds in the woods where there ain't no roads, and the ones they have don't lead nowhere except from one hollow to another hollow and back to the nowhere hollow they start out in. Or from farm to farm as the roads do here. I started out in life in a place like that and a woods like this. I ran from that kind of life as much as I ran from my drunken brothers who had their caps set to rape me for the rest of my days. Now you say you want to live with me out in the brush. Why do you want to keep draggin' me out to the country so bad?"

"So I can have you all to myself," Samuel said. "So I could be close to you all the time."

So, okay, it wasn't the greatest romantic comeback that a man ever gave a woman during an intensely intimate moment like the one they were currently experiencing, but country boys of his era weren't exactly known as natural-born Romeos.

"It's enough that you're talking on top of me," the girl said, her hillbilly accent growing more pronounced. "Don't go talkin' down to me. And don't go talkin' your romantic treacle to me about wanting to get closer to me as if that's going to make me swoon. As for getting close to me, you're about as close to me as close comes. But it ain't going to get no closer or deeper than it gets here or back at Mrs. Richardson's."

The girl shifted as if she were uncomfortable.

"As a lover, you're startin' in learnin' the basics pretty good. But you've hardly been around the block. I've been around enough blocks to build a city out of. A city is where I should be; Chicago or New Orleans is what I've got in mind. I've advanced about as far in my profession as I can advance in a whistle-stop town out in nowhereland like this place. While I've still got days left of my life to spend, I don't want to spend 'em in a small-town nothin' nowhere any more than I want to go back to the hills and spend my life in the nothin' nowhere I started out in."

She still hadn't told him the name she had started out with. It didn't sound like she was going to tell him that day.

"And I don't want to do more getting close with you or anyone out in a briar patch. I'll do you one here, but from now on, when it comes to us getting close, I want to get close on a bed with clean sheets. If you just have to do me out in the wild like this, at least find a spot with softer ground."

The girl wrapped her arms around Samuel. Her voice and her hillbilly accent softened to her coy turn-of-the-century come-on voice.

"If you want to get close to me, you can get close to me anytime you want without having to drag me off into the deep woods to do it. You can come to the house and get close to me up in my room like we've done already. It's easier on my backside, and if I'm off duty, it won't cost you. If I'm not in town, you can find me there. If you want to come to me, come to me at the house. I'll be there most any time." The girl paused. "Except for Wednesday and Thursday nights. Those are the nights I work Charlie's saloon. If you want to get close to me those nights, you'll have to meet me over there. But like I said, you'd better get there early, before the other men at the bar get a claim on me. Otherwise you'll have to wait in line to take a turn with me."

Not knowing what to say at that juncture, Samuel went back to kissing the girl. The testimony of love he had hoped to hear from her hadn't happened.

The girl still held herself close to him. Whatever she might have felt, she held tightly inside. His heart belonged to the girl. Her heart belonged to her. That day by the river, she held her body against him, but she held her heart out to the side, out of his reach. Beyond him she held her body in reserve for any man who would pay her fare.

"Charlie's got a bed upstairs for patrons and us house girls to carry out our business in. But it costs extra. If the man doesn't want to pay the extra fare, we go outside and find ourselves a place where there's grass and the ground is soft. And the ground out beyond Charlie's can be as hard on the back as the ground here."

The girl had said a lot that day on her back by the river. Samuel had heard her say what her schedule was outside of the house. Beyond that he hadn't heard a lot of the other things she had said.

As Samuel continued making love to the girl, his thoughts took proverbial flight. But they didn't soar over the horizon as they had before. They more or less just circled around in the clearing and faded into the air above the river. He saw her face in shadows as he kissed her in the shadows of the woods. In his mind's eye he saw the lights of Charlie's saloon. In his imagination he stood outside the window of Charlie's saloon looking in. In his imagination he saw the girl standing in front of the bar talking to a man. She smiled at him with the smile all women in her profession give the man they are working up, the same smile Clarinda had often smiled at him. In his vision he saw her take the man's hand. In his vision they turned to leave.

Western movies usually portray saloons in Wild West frontier towns as being populated with hard-drinking cowboys and saloon girls in tight corset-like Floradora outfits dancing the hootchy-cootchy on a cramped stage. When they weren't dancing for the leering, boozed-up, rough-riding cowboys and miners, they were sidling up to them, coming on to them, plying them to buy more drinks or give them money, or picking the pockets of drunks who had passed out. That picture of saloon hall girls is somewhat misleading. Most of the time, women in Old West towns weren't even allowed into saloons. It was somewhat the same in Charlie's bar and pool hall. The patrons just were dressed in farmhand overalls or workers' clothes instead of western chaps.

As a whole, women weren't allowed to enter. That didn't present much of a feminist nondiscrimination, equal-access issue in the only bar in Samuel's wild Ohio farm town. None of the good, stay-at-home, churchgoing, respectable women of the town wanted to be caught dead in or even near Charlie's establishment. The ambience was bad. The reputation was even worse. The liquor wasn't imported from France. It was imported from a lower-end warehouse distributor in Cincinnati. The saloon didn't cater to women of the Woman's Club tea party set, nor would those types of women be allowed to enter. The only woman who would voluntarily enter Charlie's bar would be Carrie Nation with a hatchet in her hand.

There was only one class of professional women who were allowed, even solicited, to come into the bar at the far end of Main Street and be active in the bar: women otherwise active in the world's oldest profession.

As Samuel pushed the door open and looked past the pool tables toward the actual bar, the vision he had of Clarinda plying her trade, taking the hand of a male patron she was soliciting and walking him away to a back room where she would carry out the function Mrs. Richardson had dispatched her there to perform, became translated from unpleasant vision to gritty reality. From the moment he had seen her in Mrs. Richardson's parlor, he had had a vision of love with her. Now he saw her pursuing her own vision of love. It was a commercial vision of love. It was a vision of love that didn't include him at the moment. In the fleeting moment as he stood still watching, before he went into motion, he wondered if she had any vision of love deeper and more abiding than the one she was engaged in. He wondered if she even wanted a deeper vision of love, with him or anybody.

At one end of the bar he saw the girl standing talking to a man a little older-appearing than he, probably a farmhand or a passing-through freight man. Clarinda was smiling at the man. The man was smiling at Clarinda. She was obviously soliciting. The man was obviously interested in what she was suggesting. He hadn't taken her hand. But any minute he might take her hand, or she would extend hers to him, and then they would go off to one of the rooms on the second floor. But the man would have to pay extra for the rental of the room. If the man did not have the extra money or did not want to pay the additional fee, they would leave and find a dark, secluded place, probably in the alley that ran behind the bar, where the agreed-upon transaction would be consummated, not on silk sheets but on the ground.

Samuel knew what the girl's profession was. He had known it from the first night he met her. There was no shocked surprise involved in finding her where both Mrs. Richardson and the girl herself had told him she would be that night. He had known from the first second he had seen her in her corset in the parlor of Mrs. Richardson's establishment that she wasn't an innocent shrinking violet. He knew tongues would wag until they dropped off once he announced that he intended to marry her. However long and winding the road to redemption, he would bring the girl to redemption. If the town couldn't see it or accept it, they could go to hell. He would marry the girl. At the point of tight-wound thinking he had arrived at when he had arrived at the door of Charlie's saloon, he could not imagine marrying any other girl. She was the girl he would love for life. At that transition point of his life, he could no longer imagine life without her.

But to redeem the girl and to love her for the rest of his life and her life, he first had to save her—save her from herself and from the men she sold herself to, starting with the man she was smiling so coyly at next to her in front of the bar. As Samuel pulled open the door of Charlie's saloon on the far side of town, his anger reached a near-fever pitch, not at the girl but at the man she was working up. As he strode through the door, his anger surged into his arms. The muscles of his arms tightened until his arms felt like the baseball bats he swung in the baseball games he played. The tension in his arms made his fists curl up hard. In the baseball games he played, he always swung for the fences as the saying goes. When he played baseball, he gave baseball his all. He would give his all to save the girl. She had been dirtied up enough in life. The man she was smiling at would not dirty her up further.

Picking up speed, Samuel strode past everyone and came up next to them. Neither Clarinda nor the man saw his approach. Clarinda was extending her hand to the man. The man was reaching to take her hand. Though it could be considered a preromantic moment, the look on each of their faces was not exactly romantic in nature. It wasn't exactly a tender, dreamy romantic interlude they were preparing to head out for, but they were about to leave, either for an upstairs room or for the alley. Focused as they were on what was in their minds, they didn't see Samuel coming. He stopped no more than three feet in front of both of them.

"If you don't want your jaw broken, don't put a hand on her," Samuel growled from a short distance in front of them. Their hands stopped moving toward each other. Clarinda turned her head toward Samuel with a quick, startled look on her face. The man turned his head toward Samuel with a confident, unbothered look on his face.

"Sam!?" Clarinda said in a startled and confused voice.

"You know this guy?" the man said in an unbothered voice, looking at Clarinda with an unbothered look on his face. Clarinda's mouth moved, but no words, startled or otherwise, came out.

"Yeah, she knows me," Samuel said, the gravelly, threatening tone of his voice not abating. "What she's not going to get to know is any part of you. Not unless you want to be known in the obituary column of tomorrow's newspaper. So get your flea-ridden, mule-skinner hide out of here and away from her. Now!"

The man could have reacted with wounded pride at the insult. At the moment, though, he felt more amused than threatened.

"Are you telling me to leave?" the man said rhetorically.

"You can leave on your heels or be dragged by them," Samuel said. "But if you don't get leaving fast, I'm going to hasten your departure— through the window if necessary. So get humping, or I'm going to pull you apart like a greasy fried chicken."

The man was in his early twenties to midtwenties. When he looked at Samuel, though Samuel was big and well-developed for his age, strong enough to throw hay bales around like feed bags, the man saw a teenage boy. He otherwise didn't see much of a threat in Samuel. But the light in

Charlie's saloon was kind of dingy, and the man had been looking only at Samuel's face. Had he looked more closely and seen the strength in Samuel's shoulders and upper arms, along with the tight clench of his fists, he might have backed off a bit. But he was calm in his assessment of Samuel as a threat-spouting, wet-behind-the-ears bumpkin. The man's look was confident and unafraid. Samuel's arms began to tremble slightly with the tension building in them. Clarinda looked at him but said nothing.

"Is this about her?" the man said, glancing at Clarinda.

"It's all about her," Samuel said. "All about her for as long as it can be. It's not one inch about you with her."

"Do you have your brand on her?" the man asked with a smirk on his face and sarcasm in his voice.

"I don't have a brand on her," Samuel said, "but you aren't going to put a hand on her."

"What's she to you?" the man asked. "Is she your high school sweetheart or something? Is she betrothed to you? Did you give her a ring out of a Cracker Jack box? Do you think she's going to swoon at the prospect of you taking her hand and pledging your love and fealty to her? Did you come here to ask her to marry you?"

He had actually planned to ask her to marry him on the shore of Gustafson Lake, where they had first made love outside the house, but he had gotten distracted by more immediate things.

"If you take her outside and ask her to marry you, she'll hand your engagement ring back to you and turn right around and come back in here, or else go back the whorehouse she works out of."

"She is what she is to me," Samuel said. "But she isn't going to be anything to men like you anymore."

"Open your eyes, boy," the man said. "Look at the romantic setting you came looking to have a romantic interlude with her in." The man waved his hand around to encompass the seedy bar, the pool tables, and the seedy patrons. "This isn't the tea party social room of a big-city hotel, and she isn't the high-society virgin daughter of a robber baron or the child of a duchess. And she isn't a lost innocent looking to be rescued by you as if she were a kidnapped princess."

The man looked at Clarinda. Clarinda was silent.

"Look at what she is." The man fixed his look on Samuel. "She's a whore, boy!" he said with punctuated barroom rhetoric. "Are you totally dense or just dumb as a mule with blinders on? You may think she's your sweetheart. You may imagine she's sweet on you. But the only thing she's sweet on is money. She's sweetheart to any man who brings her money."

She was also the girl Samuel had come to find to ask her to marry him and spend her life with him.

"Do you think you're going to sweep her off her feet and carry her away to marry you in front of a preacher and then carry her over the threshold of your sodbuster shack, where she's going to spend the rest of her life happy to cook your grits and mop your floors and wash your manure-covered overalls?"

Samuel was silent. Clarinda said nothing. The man leaned back against the bar with an insouciant, unthreatened, taunting pose.

"She's not a lost innocent. She's not lost at all about anything she is or what she's doing. She knows why she's here. It don't bother her none to be here. She wants to be here. She ain't going to leave here and go off with you to fold doilies downstairs and service you exclusively in your bedroom upstairs with no money profit. This is where the money's at for her, and she's not about to turn off the spigot to chase after some fairy-tale romance that she knows doesn't exist and never will exist for her if she's hooked up with a sodbuster like you. Are you so dense that you can't see that, can't see what every other man can? How dumb are you sodbusters?"

Samuel found himself caught in a crude echo chamber bombarded by the reverberating words of the man, Clarinda, his sister, Mrs. Richardson, and his friend Ben.

"She's here because she's a whore. She wants to be a whore. She's content to be called a whore. She's content to be a whore as long as a whore's money comes to her. Beyond that she isn't the least particular about love, or who she loves, or how many men love her."

Clarinda didn't seem shocked by the man's words. Neither did she raise a single word of her own in objection to the man's assessment of her character.

"If any number of men bring money to her, they can all have her in turn. If you've got the coin, you can have her tonight after I'm done with her. That is, if sodbusters like you have more than two nickels to rub together. If you don't have the cash she's got itching palms to get her hands on, you might as well leave now and go back to your plow. If you didn't bring any money with you to tickle her real fancy, for her and you it's a washed-out proposition."

Samuel wanted to relate the many times Clarinda had made spontaneous love to him outside of the house, but now that seemed somehow meaningless. It was made more meaningless by Clarinda's silence.

"Even if she has given you a freebie to pique your interest and get you coming back for more, it was probably what stores call a loss leader, what they put in the front display window. If she gave herself to you anywhere along the line, she probably gave herself as a free sample to get you to come back to her again, the next time with money in your hand. But she's all business tonight. If you don't have the cash, you might as well leave right now. But when you leave, you'll walk out of here alone. She isn't going to take one step after you. Not because I'm going to hold her here. Only money holds her."

Samuel was silent, but the words echoed in his head, growing louder. Clarinda was silent.

"I hope you don't think she loves you or even particularly thinks of you. I hope you don't have some dumbass romantic fool notion that she's going to up and leave the house she works out of, kiss off the money, and run away with you to live on some backwoods jerkwater dirt farm. You ask her to do that and the only thing she'll kiss off is you. She's not romantic, and she's no fool. You may wear your love for her on your sleeve. You may carry her around in your heart, but she doesn't carry enough around in her heart for you or any man to feed an ant. The only love she carries around is the folding green she carries pushed down between her jugs when she's upright and not flat on her back earning more green. That's where the extent of her love for you or any man begins and ends."

The way the man was denigrating his love and lover was hurtful to Samuel. But it didn't hurt nearly as much as Clarinda's silence and the way she continued to stand alongside the man, not separate herself from him and moving toward Samuel. Sometimes the worse hurt is when you ask someone you love to come with you, but they stand where they are and don't come to you.

The man pushed himself up from his backward lean against the bar.

"So stand aside, boy, and let her earn her keep. That's what she's here for. I'm first in line tonight. Let me and her do what she came here to do. We'll be right upstairs. Hang around down here and have a drink. After I'm done with her, you can move right in on her. She won't even have to put her clothes back on. She'll probably be only too happy to make a double fare tonight. Keep your ears open. You may hear the sound of the bed squeaking through the ceiling as I put it to her. But don't worry. She's done this before, probably far more times than you've done it to her. Probably more times than she can remember. She's tougher than you think. She won't be hurt by it none. She's probably beyond being hurt by anything. She's no tremulous virgin princess. She's a real trouper. She'll come through none the worse for wear. Yeah, I'll use her, but I won't use her up. The truth is that she wants to be used and she's ready and willing to be used. She lets herself get used every time she beds down with a man. One more time ain't going to hurt her none. You can't really hurt a woman like her."

In one way Samuel knew the man was speaking the crude truth. The truth can hurt. But thinking of someone you love being hurt can hurt more than any truth or hurt done to you. Inside of Samuel, the pain of thinking of the girl being used and hurt, even if it was in the line of duty, tore full length through him like a saber blade. For a second Charlie's place disappeared and he caught a vision of the girl in her backwoods shack crying and twisting in pain as she was being raped by her father and brothers. Whether she married Samuel or not, there would be no more hurt done to her, no matter whom he had to hurt to prevent it. The tension in his arms became spring steel.

"She won't be hurt by nothing any man will do to her in a bed as long there's a buck in it for her."

The man took Clarinda's arm in his hand to lead her away. As he did so, he turned to see what he assumed would be the distressed look on Samuel's face. The only thing he saw coming was a savage rabbit punch coming at his face.

The punch, coming as it was from someone the man had dismissed as a wimp farm boy, took the man by total surprise both in the fact of it and in the intensity of the blow. The punch split the man's nose and drove his head backward. Blood splattered. With both hands, Samuel grabbed the man by his shirt and yanked him away from the bar and from Clarinda so that she wouldn't get caught up in the maelstrom. Clarinda gasped but didn't scream. Neither did she shout Samuel's name or intervene to try to pull the two combatants apart.

Samuel spun the man around and heaved him backward toward the pool tables. With speed, dexterity, fast reflexes, and aim born of many years of playing sandlot baseball, he windmilled blows to the man's head, alternately and rapidly with both fists, swinging hard from one side to the other. Already stunned and disoriented from the opening blow, the man tried to block the punches and hit back, but Samuel's assault was too fast and furious for the man to mount any kind of defense. Clarinda pushed back against the bar and froze there. On her face she wore an expression of shock and fear but not one of surprise.

Unable to mount any kind of effective defense, and as the stunned patrons of Charlie's bar watched, the stunned man was driven backward, closer toward the pool tables. No verbal response was raised by any of the patrons of the bar. None of them moved to intervene and pull the two pugilists apart. Some of them didn't move to intervene because they didn't want to mix it up with the seemingly demented whirling dervish that Samuel had become. Other patrons were enjoying watching the fight. The brawl added an unexpected bit of stimulation and entertainment to what had been another dull and boring night at the bar. From behind the bar, the bartender shouted for someone to get the police. A patron ran to the door and exited to do just that. Samuel neither heard the call for police assistance nor heard the patron run out of the bar.

The outcome of such an unequal contest was not long in doubt. Twisting from the waist up, slamming punches at the man's head with both arms from both sides and all forward directions like a professional pugilist, Samuel drove the man farther backward. The man tried to block and ward off the blows, but he was not very successful against Samuel's onslaught. Samuel drove him backward until they ran up against a heavy pool table. There Samuel shoved the semiconscious man backward once more. The man bent at the waist and went down onto the pool table. From his upper-hand position, Samuel continued to slam blows at the man's head.

Samuel had more than vindicated the girl who had been seeking neither vindication nor protection from him with regard to the man she had been about to leave with and do duty with when Samuel had come out of nowhere to confront him. Samuel had more than vindicated himself and his protective love for the girl by effectively battering the man unconscious. Yet somehow it wasn't enough.

Driven by an impulse of anger at the man who would have used and defiled the girl he had gone to find in order to draw closer to himself, Samuel grabbed a loose pool ball off the table. Holding it in his hand, he swung it like it was an Indian war club, driving the hard ball against the side of the man's head. He reared back, raising the ball higher for a blow that would be magnified by angle and momentum.

A split second before he swung, a counterimpulse of restraint that would not particularly come to characterize Samuel at later times kicked in. He remembered a story he had heard of a teenage baseball player who had died from a cerebral hemorrhage after being hit in the head by a line drive. A pool ball is far harder than a baseball. At that cautionary moment, Samuel came to realize that he could easily kill the man if he delivered the blow his anger was driving him toward. The law would not consider his attack upon the man as a harmless teenage scrap over the favors of a girlfriend. The law wouldn't take it as a barroom fight over the favors of a prostitute. The law would take it as murder. As part of the judgment, Samuel would forfeit his home and family. He would forfeit the girl. He would forfeit his life, either in jail for life or dying at the gallows.

Samuel lowered his cocked arm and threw the pool ball back onto the table. He released his grip on the man with his other hand and stepped back. The unconscious man bent backward at the waist, slipped off the table, and collapsed in a heap at Samuel's feet.

"When the swelling in your face goes down, don't show you face in here again," Samuel growled. Without looking at her, he pointed toward Clarinda, still cringing at the bar. "And don't show it to her again. It won't be pretty to look at anyway." He looked around at the other men in the bar. "That goes for the rest of you."

The other patrons of the bar did not respond. Clarinda said nothing. She just stood in place when Samuel came up to her, breathing heavily, a look of fear on her face.

At that moment the front door of the saloon swung open hard and the police sergeant and one of the four uniformed officers of the town police force strode in. The sergeant looked around quickly and saw Samuel standing over the fallen man. It took him only an instant to assess what had transpired. He pointed at Samuel with his drawn billy club. "Stand your ground!" he shouted at Samuel in his command voice.

The sergeant looked at the policeman and pointed to the crumpled man on the floor.

"Check him out," the sergeant said to the officer. The officer moved over to where the man lay. The sergeant looked back to Samuel. "Stand your ground!" he ordered Samuel. "Don't get belligerent, and don't try to leave or resist.

"What happened here?" the sergeant said, looking around at the patrons.

Samuel started to open his mouth.

"The two of them got into a fight over her," the bartender said from behind the bar. He pointed to Clarinda.

The sergeant looked at the only woman in the saloon. He had seen her before in the town and knew she was a resident of the Richardson house and a practitioner of what all the girls in the house practiced. He assumed that she was in the saloon soliciting. In the cultural milieu of the time, unescorted women in saloons at night were there for just one purpose, the purpose that Clarinda was there for.

"Everything in here was quiet and natural-like," the bartender said. "No one was making any trouble." The bartender pointed to Samuel. "Then he comes barging in with a head full of steam." He pointed at Clarinda. "He came up to where she was standing with the guy on the floor, talking like he knew her, talking strong and belligerent-like. I didn't see or hear all that transpired between the three of them before the fight started, but she was probably playing one young buck against the other, trying to bid up the price. It probably got out of hand. That's when it came to blows. She probably provoked it."

"I didn't do nothing!" Clarinda snapped defensively, falling into her backwoods double-negative verbiage. "I didn't start no fight. I was conducting myself without making no trouble. Me and the man on the floor were about to walk out all quiet-like and do our business"—she pointed to Samuel with his hands on the pool table—"when he comes stormin' in, swinging up a storm with his fists at the guy I was about to leave with. He broke the deal I had goin' with the guy, and then he broke up the guy. Cut me out of a night's work and pay. I didn't do nothin' wild. It was him who went crazy on me and on the other man. Now you're probably blaming me for everything, lookin' to drag me off for somethin' I didn't do and only had a second hand in. It ain't fair."

"You can cry about it on Constable Harkness's shoulder tomorrow," the police sergeant said. "Maybe if you cry in your hankie for him, he'll let you off with time served. Until then, both of you can spend the night in the lockup in the basement to cool off."

Clarinda's mouth started to open in protest. The sergeant pushed the end of his nightstick against Samuel's back.

"The two of you are coming in with us," he said to Samuel. "You and your floozy are both under arrest."

Clarinda threw both her hands up in the air in a gesture of anger and frustration.

"On what charge?" Samuel said.

"Drunk and disorderly to start," the sergeant replied.

"I'm not drunk," Samuel said. "I haven't had a drink all night."

"Then try public brawling," the sergeant answered. "Public brawling. Assault and battery causing bodily injury." The sergeant looked at the bruised and battered fallen man on the floor. "Possibly attempted murder. Murder if the man dies."

The sergeant looked over at the officer who was completing his examination of the unconscious man on the floor. "Is he dead?" the sergeant asked.

"No," the officer said. "He's just cold-cocked. But he may need medical attention."

"Someone go wake up Doc Simpson and bring him here with his bag," the sergeant directed.

The town didn't have a hospital. It wouldn't even have a medical clinic until the 1970s. Back in those days, doctors still made house calls. Some even made saloon calls.

The sergeant looked hard at Samuel. "I'm taking you to the station house. Come along peaceful-like. Don't try anything wild, and don't try to run. Even if you get away from us tonight, we know where you live. We can find you anytime we want."

The sergeant looked at the officer and pointed at Clarinda with his nightstick.

"Bring his doxy along. When we get them in custody in the station house, come back here and check on the condition of the other man. If he's in any shape to talk, bring him back to the station."

The officer went to take Clarinda's arm to lead her, but she turned and pulled her arm away in spitting disgust. She started walking toward the door of the saloon with the others following. They exited through the saloon door and started walking down the street in the direction of the station house, about two blocks away.

The police station was marked by two white globe lights at the top of iron lamp poles on either side of the entrance. As the foursome approached the front entrance, a car was coming down the darkened street, which it had all to itself. To the extent that cars were capable of looking high performance in 1912, the car was lower slung and racier-looking than the boxy Model T. That the car didn't have a top wasn't a problem on a warm summer night. Like teenage boys of all automotive generations, Samuel was fascinated by fast cars. He would have turned to look as the car passed, but he was otherwise too distracted to take notice.

As the foursome stood in front of the station, the driver turned and looked at the procession. The figure of the girl he had considered so exquisite when he had first seen her framed in the window of Kindelspire's restaurant and soda fountain was as much of a standout in the subdued orange-tinged light of the gas-fired streetlamps on Main Street. The girl seemed agitated and angry. One of the two policemen tried to take her arm in a gentlemanly gesture to assist her up the front steps of the station, but she yanked her arm out of the officer's hold and stomped up the stairs unaided. The driver watched them go inside the station.

After the door of the station house closed behind the group, the car headed down the street slowly as if the driver were weighing and considering options. Then the car turned up a side street and slowed to a stop. It reversed and backed down Main Street. After another shifting of gears, it started to move slowly back down the empty street in the direction of the police station.

"What do you need to know my real name for?" Clarinda snarled at the night duty sergeant sitting behind the front desk in the lobby of the police station, where offenders were checked in. The desk itself was built upon a platform. The police officer behind the desk had to step up onto the platform to sit down behind the desk. It was positioned high like a judge's bench with the top just above eye level. It had been built that way to be intimidating and give the impression of the law looking down upon you. The sergeant sat behind it with pencil in hand.

"You've got me. You've got my body. That's all that the men who come to me are there for. They don't need to know my name. You don't need to know it. You've never inquired about the names of the other girls at Mrs. Richardson's. You let them alone without slapping them in jail or slapping their names all over the place. Just use the name I use at the house."

The six men of the town's police department had long looked the other way at the existence of Mrs. Richardson's bordello, which contained more working girls than the police department contained cops. One of the reasons they looked the other way was because the house was technically outside the town limits and hence beyond the jurisdiction of the department. The main reason they looked the other way was because the town council told them to (behind the scenes, of course). Council members and town elders were some of the biggest patrons of the house. Hence the house was allowed to continue quietly in its function. The girls in it were allowed to continue in theirs. That included soliciting in town. But quietly soliciting for prostitution was one thing. Public brawling was quite another.

The sergeant looked over at Samuel, who was standing next to the mouthy girl. He knew Samuel and the members of the Martin family by sight. The girl was a mystery, new to the town.

"Do you know her name?" he asked. "Who's her family?"

"My family, my so-called family, my family that gave me my name that I'm not going to give you, is totally of no account," Clarinda said. "They're far away in another state. They wouldn't lift a finger to come and get me, and if they did, they'd probably kill me on the spot for cutting up one of them because he raped me once too often."

The sergeant figured he had a wild one on his hands. He looked at Samuel for the answer to her identity.

"I don't know her real name," Samuel answered truthfully. At that point Samuel remembered the story the girl had related about how she had been abused by the male members of her family. For all he knew, she might be frightened that if her name went out on some police file list, her father and brothers might somehow learn where she was and would come after and drag her home, possibly never to be seen again. For all Samuel knew, for the girl, keeping her name suppressed might be a life-and-death issue to her. Then again it could be what she had said it to be, an attempt to separate herself from a life of pain and leave it all behind, her name included.

"A lot of … bad things have been done to her under her given name. So much so that she wants to leave her name and her past behind. … You don't need her name. She's got no family she wants to come for her. The only thing she has resembling a family is Mrs. Richardson and the girls at her house."

The girl didn't look at him. The sergeant dropped the formality of getting the girl's full name. It wasn't necessary. He wrote down the name she used at the house.

"What are you arresting her for?" Samuel asked as the sergeant filled out the form.

"Partaking in a public disturbance," the sergeant said. "I'm charging both of you with causing the disturbance."

"You mean the fight?" Samuel said. "She wasn't in the fight. She was standing off to the side. Me and the other guy were fighting over her."

"For all we know, she provoked it," the sergeant said.

"She didn't," Samuel protested. "She was just there. I was the one. I came in there."

"Constable Harkness will determine that in the morning," the sergeant said, cutting Samuel off. "Along with what charges might be filed. Until then, I'm going to hold both of you overnight." He looked at Samuel. "Your parents will be contacted in the morning and informed that you're here." He looked at Clarinda. "Mrs. Richardson will be informed in the morning also. Until then, both of you will be held in custody here, where neither of you can cause any more trouble."

Miranda rights were few and far between in those days.

"Until then you can cool your heels, as well as your passion for soliciting and your passion for bare-knuckle boxing, in the lockup downstairs."

The sergeant stood up and motioned with his hand toward a stairwell on the other side of the room. In his hand he held a set of keys that looked like the cell door keys in the western movies that would be produced in a later decade.

"Let's go."

With Sergeant Plechathy in the lead and Officer Warner bringing up the rear, the sum total of the night shift at the town police department was walking down the dark narrow stairway to the holding cells in the basement. Even by the standards of the day, the police station was old and obsolete, having been built in 1860. The detention area was a dimly lit room with three small cells along the outside foundation walls made of masonry. The cells were separated from each other by interior brick walls. The furnishings in the cells consisted of a single cot with a thin, straw-stuffed mattress and a bucket for sanitary purposes. The front doors of the cells consisted of standard iron prison bars. The cells were so narrow that the doors covered half the width of the barred fronts. The entire area was lit by a single electric bulb hanging from the ceiling. There were no windows, not even ground-level ones, to let in sunlight during the day. To say the whole arrangement was claustrophobic was an understatement.

The sergeant perfunctorily ushered Samuel into one of the cells, closed the door, and turned the key in the lock. Then he did the same for Clarinda. Samuel had gone to the saloon to deliver the girl from what he considered sexual servitude. Instead he had delivered both of them to bondage in the dingy lockup of the local police station.

The police officer turned and walked back up the stairs, leaving them alone in their cells. Given the arrangement of cells and the brick wall separating his cell from hers, Samuel couldn't see Clarinda. He could have reached through the bars and around the ends of the wall to extend his hand into her cell, but somehow he didn't think she would take his hand.

Samuel sat down on the cot. The straw mattress was so thin, he could feel the metal slats of the cot through it. A moment later, an inarticulate female bellow of fury came from the next cell, accompanied by a metallic rattling sound. Samuel took the sound to be Clarinda shaking the cell door, not in an attempt to break out but in order to blow off steam.

Another moment later the sound changed to one of thumping or rattling. Samuel took it to be the girl kicking the cell door in frustration and anger.

"Thank you very much, Samuel Martin!" the girl's exasperated voice came from out of sight in the cell next to his, the hillbilly accent she had worked to free herself of coming back into her voice by her anger. "When they let me out of here, if they ever do, they'll probably tell me to get out of town and take my lovin' self somewhere else and be quick about it. I came into this town with nothin'. I'll be leavin' with just as much of nothin' as I came here with, before I'm ready to leave. And I owe it all to you being a dumbass farm boy actin' like a typical jackass man."

"Sorry," Samuel said in a low voice, not knowing what else to say.

The rattling of the cell door stopped. For a moment there was silence. Samuel didn't try to say anything. He doubted the girl would entertain anything he had to say.

"Where does that rail line I rode into this area but had to jump off go to?" the girl asked in a flat voice from the next cell. Samuel paused in answering. He wasn't fully sure where the rail line went, and he wondered why she had asked the question. It didn't seem germane to their immediate situation.

"Chicago, I guess," Samuel said in his own flat voice. "Chicago's not a whistle-stop. Chicago's a rail hub. All the railroads in the Midwest branch go into and come out of Chicago. Why?"

"If they tell me to leave town, I'll get back on the rails," the girl said from the next cell over. "I'll ride the train all the way to Chicago. That's where I was heading. On the way, I got sidetracked and ended up in this town. If I can get together enough money, I'll head the rest of the way to Chicago. I'll look for work there. They probably have all sorts of houses like Mrs. Richardson's in a big city like Chicago, fancy ones looking for fancy women. I could get a job in one of them. Mrs. Richardson keeps telling me I'm good-looking enough to land a job there. I could go to work in one of those houses. They've got a lot more work for a girl like me and a lot more fancy stuff and fancy livin' in a big city than they do in a bare-ass town like this. If they don't have room for me in Chicago, I can take myself down south to New Orleans."

"I don't think they're going to run you out of this town like that," Samuel said. His voice didn't sound particularly confident.

The girl didn't answer. In the silence that followed, Samuel remembered how he had planned on asking the girl to marry him. From the sound of her voice, he didn't think she would be very receptive to a proposal of marriage from him. She didn't even sound like she wanted to see him again in a professional capacity at Mrs. Richardson's. Now she was talking about possibly moving to another bordello in a faraway city. As he sat on the thin mattress in the cramped cell, unable to see her, contemplating what he had done, the realization was dawning more fully on him that he had seriously complicated everything from every angle.

"Chicago's a big city," Samuel went on in a cautioning voice. "It's got a reputation for being a town as rough as it is big. You could get into a lot of trouble in a place like that."

"I'm in enough trouble in this small one-horse town," the girl said, out of sight in her adjoining cell. "Thanks to you. At least in Chicago I won't have you to get me into trouble."

Samuel fell silent again.

When the station door opened, Sergeant Plechathy thought it was Officer Warner returning from the saloon after checking up on the condition of the other man involved in the fight, the one Samuel had beaten unconscious. When he looked up, he was surprised to see the town's most prominent citizen walking toward the main desk.

"Ah, good evening, Mr. Ethridge," the police sergeant said in a bit of a confused tone. "What brings you here at this hour? Did a pickpocket lift your wallet on the street?"

"What brought me in here," the man said in a smooth tone, "was that I was driving home and I observed you apparently taking two young people into custody. One of them I recognized as the Martin boy. I didn't recognize the girl. Are they sweethearts? If so, what are they being arrested for? Is there an ordinance against kissing in public on the streets, even at night?"

"The Martin boy was picked up for brawling in a public tavern," the sergeant answered. "He beat another patron unconscious. It was the girl they were fighting over."

"She was in the bar too?" Harold Ethridge answered in a feigned tone of surprise. "From what I could see of her, she looks so young and innocent."

"The girl is hardly a sweet innocent getting stars in her eyes from her first kiss," the sergeant replied in a wry voice. "She's one of the working girls over at Mrs. Richardson's bordello. As sweethearts go, she's a sweetheart equally to any man with the money to buy her favors."

The sergeant wasn't telling Ethridge anything he didn't already know. Harold Ethridge had known the girl was a hooker since Mr. Kindelspire had so informed him the day he had first seen her in the window of the soda fountain. He had spent a lot of his time since thinking of ways to make contact with the girl without being seen patronizing a bordello. Suddenly he found her available to him as a captive audience, so to speak.

"The Martin buck isn't such an innocent choirboy either," the sergeant went on. "Not so innocent that he can't get himself into saloon fights over a whorehouse tart. He's under arrest for assault and battery. He beat the other man so bad, they had to call in Doc Simpson to treat him. They were fighting over the girl. She probably caused the fight by flashing herself around to both of them. We're holding her for probable incitement and being the cause of a public disturbance."

"What do you plan to do with them?" Harold Ethridge asked. "What will they be charged with?"

"I plan to hold them here until morning," the sergeant said. "I'll see what Chief Constable Harkness wants to do when he gets here. Cooling their heels in a basement cell overnight might make both of them think before they let their youthful blood get to running so hot again. But then running her blood hot and heating up men's blood is how the girl makes her living. Hopefully she'll stick to one client at a time and not get more than one man on her well-experienced tail again."

"What will the girl be charged with?" Harold Ethridge asked.

"I doubt she'll be charged with much of anything," the sergeant answered. "She says she didn't start the fight. She may be covering for herself, but the other patrons in the bar seem to back up her story. They say that she was there plying her trade quietly when the Martin boy burst into the saloon and went after the man. We don't have much actual proof that she egged either of them on. It would be hard to make a charge of incitement to riot or fighting stick on her."

"What will be done with her?" Harold Ethridge asked.

"We'll probably just send her back to Mrs. Richardson's with a warning to stay away from her hotheaded would-be swain boyfriend while she's in town. In the morning we'll call Mrs. Richardson and have her bail out her chief house protégé. Meanwhile, spending a night on a hard bed in one of our drafty basement cells with bugs and mice running around might make her more amenable to keeping herself out of trouble and keep her from being quite as provocative as she has been."

"Will she be publicly charged with solicitation?" Harold Ethridge asked.

"I don't think the town is going to charge her with prostitution for working in a cathouse the town has tolerated and let exist outside the town limits for years," the sergeant answered. "They'll probably just tell her to keep herself around the house for a month or two and to keep herself more discreet when she does come back into town."

"What are you going to do with the Martin boy?" Harold Ethridge asked.

"We'll keep him overnight the same as her," the sergeant responded. "In the morning we'll contact his father and have him bail his son out. If he takes a belt to his boy's backside out behind the barn, it will cool him off. Beyond that, Chief Harkness will probably tell the boy to stay out of town for a while until he learns to comport himself better in public."

Harold Ethridge reached for his wallet, which hadn't been lifted by a pickpocket. "I wish to post bond for the girl," he said in a straightforward manner. "But only for the girl. Like you said, maybe a night spent in custody will serve as an object lesson to the boy and will prompt him to control his temper in the future."

The sergeant was a bit surprised by the unexpected gesture, but he had no reason to object.

"Bring the girl up here," Harold Ethridge said after posting the bail money. "I'll take her back to her … place of residence. Maybe the whole experience will serve as an object lesson to her to choose her profession and her friends more carefully."

"As you wish, sir," the sergeant said, reaching for the cell keys.

"When you release the girl, don't mention it to the Martin boy who it was who posted her bail. I don't need a hotheaded jealous juvenile saloon brawler with fists cocked coming after me later in a fit of jealous anger, thinking the worst of my intentions."

273

The police sergeant nodded and headed to the steps to the basement lockup without asking any further questions. If a leading citizen wanted to perform a public-spirited gesture, who was he to object or question the man's intent?

"Your bail has been posted," the sergeant said as he turned the key in the lock of Clarinda's cell. "You're free to go."

Clarinda had been standing when the sergeant had come up to her door and unexpectedly opened it. She figured that it was Mrs. Richardson who had made her bail. She was surprised that it had happened so quickly.

Clarinda wasn't a girl to look a gift horse in the mouth. Offering no words of her own, she exited the cell. Without saying a word, she crossed the floor ahead of the sergeant. From the oblique angle view through the bars of his cell, Samuel caught a glimpse of the girl as she headed toward the steps leading up from the basement cell room. Clarinda didn't look in his direction as she passed. Neither of them said anything to the other in passing.

At the top, where the stairs opened up into the dim wood-floored main floor of the police station, Clarinda looked around. She had expected to see the familiar face of Mrs. Richardson, but the only other person besides the sergeant was a dapperly dressed, dapper-looking early-middle-aged-looking man. His face seemed somehow familiar, but it wasn't from the house or the saloon. She didn't recognize him. But a man was a man, especially one coming to her with money in hand to get her out of a jam.

"Mr. Ethridge saw you being brought in," the sergeant said. "He was kind enough to post your bail. He'll drive you back to your … residence."

The sergeant didn't say *You should thank the man*. Women like her had their own way of showing their appreciation to a man.

Without further prompting, Clarinda walked over to Harold Ethridge. She walked in the easy manner she used to approach men in general.

"I must thank you for getting me out of that rathole, which even the rats don't want to live in," Clarinda said. "I might have had to stand on my feet all night. The only thing they have to sleep on is a filthy cot. I had the distinct impression that I would have been swarmed by a whole colony of cockroaches mad at me for having displaced them from their ancestral home. If I fell asleep, they might have me picked me clean to a skeleton by morning."

"Allow me to introduce myself," Harold Ethridge said in a dapper voice, using a standard opening line from the nominally more polite period. "I was driving by and observed your plight and felt compelled to intervene. No lady should be forced to endure the facilities, or dismal lack of them, in this station house. Those cells are more properly suited to corral roughnecks like your boyfriend. They're not intended to give comfort or solace to a lady."

"I thank you again," Clarinda said. "But I should inform you that around here, I'm not what most people would consider to be anything of a proper lady. I might as well tell you right away. You'll probably find that out about me soon enough. I haven't been in town very long, but everyone in town has pretty much got a handle on who and what I am. … Given my luck, now that you know how unladylike I really am, you may send me back down to the cell you found me in. I'm not any kind of lady a man of your quality thinks of as a high-up lady. I'm just a trouble-prone alley cat of a girl."

It wasn't a girl Harold Ethridge was seeing in the half-light of the station. It was a woman he saw, more of a woman than he or Samuel had ever seen in the town. The half-light of the station house made her long black hair seem darker and more sensual. The fullness of her figure was not distracted from or hidden beneath the shabby dress she had on. The upper part of her dress pulled tight over where her swelling chest pushed out against it. The strain on the limited material of her dress caused by the fullness of her chest pulled the dress in around her waist, giving her the wasp-waisted appearance so popular in those days. In the right tight-fitting chorus line dancer costume, she could put most other Floradora girls to shame. Harold Ethridge could only imagine how provocatively she dressed for work in the Richardson house. He hadn't yet seen her in her corset the way Samuel had.

"The sergeant explained your … proclivities and your method of livelihood," Harold Ethridge responded in a smooth diplomatic voice. "He also outlined the particular situation with your explosive boyfriend and how it came to bring you in here. Whatever your social and life situation that has brought you to where you presently are and what you are today, no woman should be forced to endure the kind of degradation she would experience in the limited confinement facilities they have here."

Clarinda wanted to say something to the effect that she had been degraded far worse in far dirtier ways, but she didn't want to go into details. It might dirty up the moment.

"On the other hand, maybe spending an indefinite time down there will take some of the eruptive steam out of your hotheaded would-be suitor."

It was Harold Ethridge's way of hinting to the girl not to ask him to bail out Samuel. At the moment, Clarinda was not predisposed to do so anyway. Any thought of doing so disappeared from her mind as she remembered where she had seen the man before.

"Now I think I remember where I saw you," Clarinda said. "I thought you looked familiar. I believe I saw you when you came into the soda fountain when I was there with Samuel some time back. Sam mentioned your name."

At the same time, Clarinda also remembered that Samuel had said that Ethridge was the richest man in town. She forgot that Samuel had said that he was the biggest womanizer in town. But servicing womanizers was what she and her sisters at the house were about.

"I suppose it was fortunate that I didn't introduce myself to you in his presence," Harold Ethridge said. "It might have triggered an incident of fisticuffs on his part right then and there. From the way you and the arresting officer describe him, he, along with being possessed of a violent temper, is possessed of the strength, ability, and tendency to assault and do damage to anyone who gets between you and him. Apparently that's how the fight in the saloon started. I don't see how you put up with him. I don't see why you should put up with that kind of behavior on the part of any man. He doesn't have the first quality of being a gentleman or the first instinct of a gentleman. You should make a decided effort not to see him or fraternize with him again."

The girl looked away from him and across the station house. The look on her face seemed both confused and pained.

"I don't know what happened to Sam tonight," she said in a softer voice that sounded both confused and pained. "He's never acted that way before. Not to me. I just don't know what got into him tonight. He's usually so polite. Mostly he's actually rather sweet and considerate. Tonight he was a different boy altogether. He came chargin' in from out of the blue like he was out of his head, swinging his fists at the guy I was doin' my job with, makin' a deal with, shoutin' that he wasn't going to let no more men dirty me up. He beat the guy cold, scaring the piss outta me, and got us both arrested. Kept me from earning my keep for the night. He's probably spooked all the other men in town offa me. I started out thinkin' he was so nice. Now it looks like he's got a mean streak in him I didn't know about."

To Harold Ethridge, that the girl was able to speak of the Martin boy using his name in the first-person familiar in a soft voice brought up the possibility that she still felt affectionate toward him. Women could be so fickle like that. In the next minute she might change her mind and ask him to bail the boy out as well. His open opportunity to get the girl separated from the boy would be lost then. He had to get the girl out of the station and away from the boy and keep her distracted so she stays away from him.

"Maybe it's like I've thought all along: all men are just naturally violent. I guess there's a mean streak that runs through them all by their nature," Clarinda added.

"Whatever the case, it's not going to do any good standing around in a dingy police station waiting for him to repent and reform, if he ever does," Harold Ethridge said. He took the girl lightly by the arm. "I'll drive you to the Richardson house so you won't have to walk home in the dark." With a sweeping gesture, he pointed toward the station house door. "Shall we go?"

"At least that's one more chance I've got in life than I had when I got brought in here," Clarinda said. She walked toward the station house door. As she did so, she pulled herself free of Ethridge's hold on her arm and walked away on her own with him following her. He caught up with her at the door.

Harold Ethridge held the door open for the girl. They walked out into the warm August summer night, down the front steps of the police station, and to his car parked in front. Even in the flickering light of the gas lamps, the car looked a lot sleeker, a lot racier, and more energetic than the boxy family truck Samuel drove. To Clarinda, the car had one obvious unusual feature to it: it didn't have a top.

"What kind of car is this?" the automotively illiterate Clarinda asked. "It doesn't have a top on it. Did you drive under a low-hanging tree limb and rip the top off?"

"It's called a Stutz Bearcat," Harold Ethridge said of his rolling status symbol. "It's a sports car, not a truck built for carrying hay bales and cow flop like your would-be swain Samuel Martin drives. I had to go all the way to Cincinnati to get it. There aren't any others like it around here. It doesn't have a top because it's built that way."

The Stutz Bearcat was the top-end sports car of its era. In a way, the Stutz Bearcat could be called the Maserati of its day, though it's a bit hard for a car to be Maserati-like when powered by a four-cylinder sixty-horsepower engine. But the model was light in weight and had plenty of get-up-and-go, relative to more pedestrian, utilitarian modes of transportation like Samuel's truck. It was the hot car of its era. Some people of the day would say it was the bee's knees.

"Haven't you ever seen one before?"

"I've only been out of the mountains less than a year," Clarinda answered. "Most of the territory I grew up in, there weren't no roads you could drive much of anything around on, even if it was pulled by a mule. Mrs. Richardson's big touring car and Sam's truck are the only things with motors I've ever ridden in, unless you count the freight train I hopped to get here. When I rode in the country with him once, Sam drove his truck so fast, it liked to scare me to death."

For Harold Ethridge, the girl's accent, tortured syntax, and jargon, along with her description of the primitiveness of her place of origin and her statement that she had ridden the rails to get to where she now was, only confirmed what he had thought: that she was a hillbilly from some other state, probably Virginia or the closer state of West Virginia. That placed the girl's family at a safe distance away. If they even knew where she was.

"I promise not to drive like that," Harold Ethridge said. He opened the passenger door, took the girl's hand, and helped her into the front seat of the car. Bearcats had only one seat. She got in, sat down, and looked around.

"Sure is a lot fancier than Sam's truck," Clarinda said. "You don't sit up as high. But it's got nicer seats. They're as comfortable as the sofas in Mrs. Richardson's house."

Harold Ethridge came around to the driver's side and got in. After he sat down and closed the door, he looked over at the girl, who still looked every inch a woman. She wasn't looking at him. She was looking away into the dark. She had the same uncertain look on her face.

"I got put upon by a lot of violent men before I ran away from home," she said out into the darkness, not looking at him. "I was starting to think Sam wasn't that way. I was starting to think of him as someone I could trust. Then he goes and blows up on the other man tonight. Now I'm afraid he'll bust up any man who gets near me, even if it's one I'm just doin' my job with. I'm starting to get afraid that he'll turn on me and bust me up for getting close to any man, or if one gets close to me. I thought I could see a violent man coming down the road at me. But Samuel took me by surprise. I guess I'm not as smart as I thought I was at spotting a dangerous man. And here I was startin' to think of him as a friend. Not just a friend, but a lover. A regular lover lover. It got so I wasn't even chargin' him for some of the times we rolled around together. I even made love with him in the mud down by a lake and in the woods by the river."

"Is the specter of Samuel Martin to follow us everywhere?" Harold Ethridge asked, looking at the girl, who was still looking away. "If you continue to dwell on him like you're doing now, you'll only ruin the rest of your evening. If you dwell on him for the rest of your life, you'll cast a pall over the rest of your life. You have to think about the rest of your own life and not let Samuel Martin disrupt it."

"In my life so far, I've never really thought about my life in the long run kind of way," Clarinda answered, still looking out into the dark. "I never had much of a chance to do so. I've been too busy livin' one day at a time to think about any days or the rest of my life beyond. I just do what I have to do to get through the day I'm in at the moment. My life's been a blur to me since it began. What's ahead is an even bigger blur to me. So I don't look out ahead. I just look sideways at where I am. I don't think none about the past at all, and I don't think much about the future."

"Well, right now your tumultuous roustabout would-be possessor is safely locked away from you," Harold Ethridge said. "He can't get to you tonight. I'm here with you. I can take you away from here and from him to an even safer distance."

"Just take me to Mrs. Richardson's," Clarinda responded. "That's far enough away."

Harold Ethridge reached for the ignition but stopped. "Instead of taking you straight back to the house, if you would like, I could take you for a midnight drive," he said. "The air is cool, and the stars are out. I'm sure you would find it more enjoyable than sitting in that jail cell or sitting in a barroom with the Martin boy and the other patrons. We can go out in the open country on an open road. I could show you what my vehicle can do."

"Sounds okay, I guess," Clarinda said, still looking away. "I'm not on a clock at the house. The house doesn't have a check-in time that women have to be back in by like more proper boardinghouses do. The house is hardly for proper ladies. The door is always open. I don't have to be in by a certain time like the proper young lady I ain't."

Harold Ethridge paused a moment, still in position to engage the ignition. "As an alternate," he said, "if you don't want to go back to Mrs. Richardson's house, I could show you my house. It's one of the finest in town."

Clarinda turned her head and looked over at him. "And what, pray tell, sir, do you have in mind for us to do at your house?" she asked in a hillbilly-accented wry, ironic voice. "Do you intend to introduce me to your parents?"

"Both my parents are dead," Harold Ethridge answered. "I live alone in the house."

"Are you then intent on showing me the furnishings in your house?" Clarinda asked in a continuance of her ironic, knowing voice. "Is all you have in mind for me to show me your sainted mother's tapestries and wall hangings?"

Harold Ethridge continued to look at the girl without saying anything further. He didn't have to say forwardly what the girl knew full well what he meant.

Clarinda reached over and started toying with his collar in a coy manner. "I guess I should have known that you weren't doing what you did for me out of the goodness of your heart or because I look like your sainted mother or your sainted aunt or a saint anybody," Clarinda said in her coy mountain voice. "You're a regular man after all, not one of those Boy Scouts out to do his good deed for the day."

Clarinda took her hand off his collar.

"Okay, so let's be off to your place and what you have in mind for doin' with me there. After all, it is my given profession." She pointed at him with the index finger of the hand she had tweaked his collar with. "I do have to inform you that I will be charging the going rate. I don't give out free samples any more than you give anything away for free. If you had any thought that I owe you a free ride because you bailed me out, you'll have to forget it and let me go on my way. So far I haven't fetched a dime out of this night. I can't go back empty-handed. I have to have something in hand that I can give Mrs. Richardson to keep the house and us girls in it. She's not keeping me around for free so I can give it away for free. I've got to come back with somethin' to help her and the other girls in the house. We're all in this together. We're like sisters. We all depend on one another. I gave some free rides to Samuel, but he's a poor country boy. That was also when I thought he was a friend, before he went crazy on me."

She leaned in a bit toward Harold Ethridge. "So am I right in assuming that you're assuming of me what I assume you want of me when we get back to your place, the same thing all men want to get offa me when they get me alone in any place?"

"I didn't want to be presumptuous and come right out and state it directly," Harold Ethridge started to say. "It wouldn't be proper to address a lady, even a lady of the evening, in such a blunt and direct manner."

Clarinda held up her hand, palm forward, to cut him off. "You don't have to be gentlemanlike with me. If you wish to engage me in the profession I'm engaged in, just come out and say it straightforward. Just call me by one of the improper names of the improper profession I'm part of. It won't offend or embarrass me. I'm not ashamed to be called what I'm not ashamed to be."

She lowered her hand.

"I'm the top money earner there. I don't work cut-rate anywhere. Paying full price shouldn't make no never mind to a rich man like you. Payin' out a little extra money for your pleasure should come easy for a man in your position. If you can afford to ride in a high-priced car like this, you can afford to ride high-priced women."

Harold Ethridge sort of smiled.

"They say you're a man who knows how to pay good money for good value. They also say you're a man who bargains. I'm not a bargain-basement item. Men don't negotiate price with me. They pay what I say, or they take themselves away from me. You work the way you work. I work the way I work. I don't give credit. I work on a cash-in-hand basis. Before we go any farther, do you want to hear my rates?"

"There's an old saying that says that if you have to ask how much it costs, you can't afford it," Harold Ethridge said. "I'm sure I can afford you, as long as you keep it reasonable and don't try to gouge me in an obvious manner. We can discuss your remuneration when we get to my place—my place in town. I actually maintain two residences, one here in town, the other at my farm. I switch back and forth depending on what business I'm transacting or managing at the time. I think you'll find both my residences more amenable than your room in Mrs. Richardson's house. You'll find them far more amenable than the jail cell you were in or the Martin family barn."

"Lead on," Clarinda said.

Harold Ethridge started the car. As he reached to release the brake, he looked over at the girl. "Is the ghost of Samuel Martin going to be following us everywhere I take you?" he asked. The semiaffectionate way she talked about the boy made him wonder if she was still inwardly sweet on him despite her apparent superficial anger with him.

"I forgot about him the minute I walked out of the cell," Clarinda said in a decided voice. But to Harold Ethridge, the hotheaded boy could still possibly prove to be a problem.

"Before we proceed any further, I want you to give me your word that you won't inform him that I've become one of your clients," Harold Ethridge said. "He might become incensed. I don't need a crazed farm boy coming after me with a pitchfork."

"I never discussed any of the other men I've serviced with him," Clarinda said in her decided voice. "I won't never mention your name to him. I'll probably never talk to him again."

The girl's anger was real, and her statement satisfied him. He put the car in gear, swung it in a wide arc, and headed back the way he had come, back to his house in town, the girl riding with him. He found that he liked the girl. She was straightforward and businesslike in making deals and arranging things her way. He worked the same way in business. He hadn't been actively engaged in looking for a mistress to be a kept woman, but this one would certainly fill the bill. With a little fixing up, she could make an intriguing addition to his other possessions. But somehow he had a nagging feeling that he might not be able to control her.

Samuel sat on the thin mattress on the cot, looking at the floor. Outside the cell, the filament of the single light bulb glowed a dim orange. The light of the bulb shining through the bars of the cell cast long parallel shadows across the unswept dirt on the floor. The shadows seemed to trail off and disappear into the larger shadow at the far end of the cell. Hidden in the shadow in a far corner was the bucket that served as a toilet.

It wouldn't be hyperbole to say that Samuel felt more alone than he ever had in his life, mostly because it was true. It was literally the first time in his life that he had been separated from his family at night. He assumed that his parents and sister had gone to bed and didn't know what had happened and what he had done to gain the incarceration that kept him from his home.

Samuel looked up and looked over through the bars to the empty steps leading up to the lobby of the police station. The girl had passed by him in a huff without looking at him. Just who had bailed her out, he didn't know. He assumed Mrs. Richardson had been informed and had driven over to procure the girl's release. That it had happened in seemingly no time wasn't the thought that occupied Samuel's mind, though.

The girl was gone entirely from him. Now he didn't even have her angry in the cell next to him. For all he knew, she was angry enough with him that she would be gone entirely from his life, yet another separation brought on by his impulsive, reckless thoughtlessness. Along with his parents and sister, a thoroughly chastened Samuel knew he would have to apologize to Clarinda as well. He wasn't even sure that she would accept his apology. His family more or less had to accept his apology and restore him to themselves. The girl didn't have to. For all he knew, she might see in him the violence that her brothers had inflicted on her. For all he knew, she might see in him the violence she saw in all men. His explosion of violence may very well have brought up in the girl a memory of pain and thrown her up against a wall of memory that he would not be able to breach.

Samuel lay down on the cot. Through the thin straw-filled mattress, he could feel the metal strap slats of the bunk. He tried to formalize the words of apology he would use to try to allay the girl's anger and fears and convince her to take him back, but in the half dark, the words did not form up. In the back of his mind was the fear that no words could allay the fear driven deep in the girl's memory. His separation from his family would end with his release the next day. But he might emerge to restoration with his family only to find himself separated from the girl forever.

Chapter 9

"I don't see why you're going to need all this secrecy and slipping around to backdoor meetings," Clarinda said as she stood in front of the mirror over the dresser, trying to run the brush she had gotten out of the drawer through her hair. "If you want to make me a regular, why do I have to gather myself up and come sneaking all the way over here on foot at night? You could easily drive over to the house and pick me up. The way you've got it, I don't get no more rides in your fancy car. My feet are going to get worn down to a nub with all this runnin' back and forth to here and back home. The way you want to set it up, not only do I get a workout in your bed, but also I have to do the work of hoofing it all the way across town to get here—and in the dark. Why here? And why do you always want me to come to you in the dead of night? You don't have to meet me here. You don't even have to meet me at Charlie's saloon. Just come over to Mrs. Richardson's house and avail yourself of me there the way the mayor and your friends on the city council do. They aren't bothered by takin' the chance they'll be spotted comin' to the house. Mrs. Richardson and the girls at the house keep their secret. They'll keep yours."

From where he lay naked on the four-poster bed with the ornately carved bedposts, Harold Ethridge looked over at the naked girl as she attempted to brush her long black hair. Her full unbound breasts swayed and undulated with the physical exertion of her arms and upper body as she brushed uselessly at her hair. In the half-light of the room, the thinness of her waist expanded below into the rounded fullness of her hips—a long-tressed backwoods Renoir nude in a classical still life painting come to life.

"It don't make no never mind to the mayor and his cronies on the city council, the same council you sit on, that they might be seen at the house. They run into each other all the time there. I suppose they hide their comings and goings at the house from their wives. If their wives ask where they're going, I suppose they make up a story that they're going to a town meeting or something, but they don't take no elaborate precautions beyond that. They just walk into Mrs. Richardson's house as big as life."

Harold Ethridge looked over at the grumbling girl fighting with her tangled hair. The tall corner posts of the bed framed her image. The effect made it appear that she was onstage. He had wondered how Lillian Russell would look naked. Now he was getting an idea.

"Let's just say that there are those in town and on the town council who might try to use the knowledge that I'm seeing you against me in some way," Harold Ethridge answered. "What they don't know, the knowledge they can't be trusted with, is something they don't need to know."

"Do you guys on the council blackmail each other?" Clarinda asked. "When you're not screwing us girls in the rooms of the house, are you busy trying to screw each other in the back rooms of the town council?"

"Close enough," Harold Ethridge said.

"Seems to me that if they tried to blackmail you, you could blackmail them right back equally."

"The point of politics or anything is not to be equal, my dear," Harold Ethridge said from the vantage point of the bed, where he had just finished having the girl. "The point is to have the advantage. The point is to be out ahead of those who would get the better of you and to keep yourself out ahead of them. If the town council members don't know that I'm seeing you, then I have something on them that they don't have on me. If they try to pull some clumsy stunt on me, I can shut them up and shut them down by threatening to expose them. But they won't have anything they can counter me with."

"I think it would be pretty stupid of them to try to blackmail you,"

Clarinda said. She looked at the brush in frustration and went back to trying to run it through her hair.

"Blackmail is a clumsy tool for rubes who don't know how to handle themselves and can't think of any other way to get the advantage," Harold Ethridge answered. He sat up and swung his legs off the bed. "Using blackmail is as clumsy as your farm boy friend using his fists to try to hold onto you," Harold Ethridge said, reaching for his pants. "He's probably as clumsy in bed with you as he is in a saloon. Another reason for you not to see him again … provided that Constable Harkness doesn't send him off for assault and battery."

"Sam may be clumsy in a saloon, but at least he's not clumsy in bed," Clarinda answered. "He's unsure of himself. He needs practice to get himself seasoned. He's naive in more ways than one. But he's not clumsy in bed." She paused in her brushing efforts and looked at Harold Ethridge.

"When it comes to clumsy in that manner, your mayor sure is. With his paunch, being had by him is like being jumped by a prizewinning sow. Of us girls in the house, given the way she's built, Polly is better suited to handle him. She's less expensive too. But he keeps coming to me."

Though Harold Ethridge otherwise held his possessions closely, he was not possessed of a deep and abiding respect or concern for women. But he was not without a sense of beauty defiled. The thought of the large and oily mayor lying heaving on top of and coming inside the girl was something he found repugnant.

"Talk about casting pearls before swine," Harold Ethridge said. "You giving yourself to our bloated mayor is like using the Da Vinci painting of Venus rising on a half shell to line the floor of a hogpen." As the biggest livestock breeder and dealer in several counties, Harold Ethridge knew about hogpens. "The mayor and the other council members are a collection of leering jackanapes. You're draining your beauty by your letting them use you. The same goes for your brawler boyfriend. They're dragging your beauty through the mud."

Samuel could tell him a few things about being down in the mud with beauty.

"You're sullying yourself by being with men like that and letting them use you."

"Now you sound like Sam," Clarinda said. She stopped brushing her hair and looked at the brush. "I can't get nowhere with this brush. It won't sink in. The bristles are too short and too close together."

"It's a man's hairbrush," Harold Ethridge said as he fastened his pants. "It's made for short hair. I don't have any women's hairbrushes lying around to be used."

Clarinda put down the brush and started running her fingers through her tangled hair. It didn't work all that much better.

"I guess I'll just have to brush it out when I get back to the house."

"When you get back to the house, don't tell them you were with me," Harold Ethridge instructed. Clarinda looked over at him.

"What am I supposed to say?" she asked. "They're going to wonder where I've been all this time. They'll probably be worried about me."

"Tell them you were with a client," he suggested. "Which you were. I'll pay you what I promised. Show them the money, and that will end it and clinch the deal. It works that way for me."

Harold Ethridge gathered up his shirt and started to put it on.

"Before we can go any further in the days to come, I want you to promise me here and now that you won't tell anyone that we're keeping time together. As I said, this includes not revealing my name to Mrs. Richardson or any of the other girls in the house."

"I promise," Clarinda said casually. She dropped the brush on the dresser and pointed to her dress, lying crumpled beside the bed. "Would you hand me my dress?"

He reached down, gathered up the girl's fallen dress, and handed it to her. With moves as smooth and supple as the ones she had used in bed, the girl slipped back into her dress. As her womanly figure disappeared under her shabby dress, Harold Ethridge caught an almost involuntary vision of the girl's naked body being pressed down beneath the sweaty, corpulent bulk of the town's mayor. The vision prompted him to speak.

"I still say that you're sullying yourself by being with men like the mayor and the town council members and all the dirt-faced, dirty-bodied farmer rubes like your would-be boyfriend and the manual workers in this town. Stay away from them. You're better than that."

"Now you sound like Sam again," Clarinda said, her head appearing as she pulled her dress down over her body. "Those were his words near exactly. Are you going to start pulling yourself in on me the way Sam tried to pull me into himself?"

Harold Ethridge said nothing. Clarinda pulled her dress the rest of the way on and positioned it.

"Just how am I supposed to go about getting by in this town not doing what I do in the house? All I can do in this town is be what I am or marry a farmer and be a farm wife and spend half my life workin' the fields and the other half of it cookin' and cleanin' a farmhouse. I was a dirt-coated mountain girl all my life before I came here. I don't 'tend to be a dirt-coated and manure-tainted farm bride for the rest of my life."

"Do you plan to stay in Mrs. Richardson's house for the rest of your life?" Harold Ethridge asked.

"I've got plans," she said, "ones that'll get me to a better house with big-paying clients, in Chicago or New Orleans. I'm about ready to make my move."

Harold Ethridge could appreciate that. He knew all about making the right move at the right time. Given the girl's looks and proficiency in bed, he figured she might be able to pull it off. It all sounded like a gamble against long odds, but he figured that just about everything in a whore's life is a gamble against long odds.

"When do you plan to make your big move to Chicago or the Big Easy?" he asked.

"I don't know," Clarinda replied. "Like I said, when I'm feelin' up and ready for it. When I've saved up enough money to tide me over till I get settled. Then I'll just slip away one day without Sam, the mayor, the constable, or anyone in this town, except Mrs. Richardson and the rest of the girls, knowing I'm gone or where I went so that none of them will try to hold me here. When I'm gone, I won't be comin' back. I've got plans. The plans I've got are for myself. Nobody's going to hold me here and substitute the plans they have for me for my plans for myself."

The girl was certainly businesslike in the way she was going about setting her plans. Harold Ethridge appreciated that. He, too, went about his business, including the shady aspects, in a businesslike manner. The girl was crafting her plan around money. Harold Ethridge knew all about dealings and making plans that involved money.

"My plans don't involve any romantic notions of looking for love or falling in love. After what I've been put through at the hands of men, I don't think I could ever love any man. I can make up a storm of love with my body, but I don't give my heart to anyone. My body is an open door to men who bring money to buy me with, but my heart belongs to me."

In likewise manner and sentiment, Harold Ethridge was not a man given to romantic notions. In the back of his mind, there was no romantic notion that he loved or was falling in love with the wayward girl. Oh, he intended to marry someday, but he had long resolved that it would be a socially advantageous marriage, possibly to the daughter of a rich man whom he had business dealings with in one of the larger cities he frequented in his line of work. The right marriage to a rightly positioned daughter would not only cement his business dealings but also enhance his social position in the town even more. Marriage to a local hooker, even a fetchingly attractive one, would be a social disaster.

"My plans don't involve romantic notions about falling in love, marriage, having children that I can't have, or love for a lifetime. Along with the notion of falling in love with any man, my plans sure don't involve falling in line with any notion that men might have about holding me and keeping me. And they don't involve any romantic notions that Sam may have about me."

"In the interim, before you take yourself off to parts unknown, may I call upon you and have you come to my house to join with me in your … capacities?" Harold Ethridge asked.

Clarinda was neither surprised nor fazed by the man's revelation of his desire to employ her in her capacity. He was, after all, a man, a man typical of all men, just one who could afford to pay a premium for the services sought.

"Sure," Clarinda answered in her let's-get-down-to-setting-terms voice. "My rates will be the same in this house as they are in Mrs. Richardson's house. I don't suppose there's any chance of you picking me up at the door of the house in your spiffy car?"

"As I specified earlier," Harold Ethridge responded, "any dealings between us, at what remuneration you set, must be conducted in a way that I remain anonymous. That does entail you coming here at an agreed-upon time."

"I suppose that time will be at night?" Clarinda asked.

"Continuing anonymity will require it," Harold Ethridge said in a set voice.

"That means that I'm going to have to hoof it all the way over here in the dark," Clarinda said. "A girl don't feel safe out on the streets at night."

Harold Ethridge noted to himself that the girl apparently felt safe enough to walk to the local saloon at night to do her soliciting there. "You needn't worry, my dear," he said. "There aren't any Jack the Rippers prowling around the dark in this town. Alienist killers like that are found in the fetid streets of cities, not in small-town pastoral landscapes. Neither are there any back-alley thug muggers such as they have in the big cities you will be off to. You needn't worry about anyone cutting your throat after dark in this town. … When you come, don't use the front door. Use the alley entrance. I'll leave the gate and the back door unlocked. You don't have to knock on anything. Just quietly come in without letting anybody see you."

"I don't suppose you could drive me back to the house afterward when it's later and even fewer people are about?" Clarinda asked.

Harold Ethridge shook his head. "To get to the road that runs by Mrs. Richardson's house by automobile, you have to drive down Main Street," he said. "That takes you right past the front of Charlie's saloon. There are people going in and coming out till all hours. I might be seen driving you in my car late at night. If we're seen, even if the ones who see us are inebriated, they'll put the obvious two plus two together in their rum-sozzled brains. They'll start talking. The patrons of the saloon can't control their mouths any more than your friend can control his fists in a saloon. When they get liquored up, they talk and keep on talking. I don't want to be seen by the boozers in Charlie's saloon any more that I want to be seen by members of the town council, often one and the same. You, on the other hand, can cut between the buildings on foot before you get to Charlie's and take the shortcut back to the house without anybody seeing you in the dark. But, as I say, once you're back in the house, don't use my name there either."

"As you want it," Clarinda said. "As it works, to keep your name out of it, I'm going to be walking all the way both ways to keep your secret. I should charge you extra for wear and tear on my feet."

"So where do we go from here?" Harold Ethridge asked rhetorically as he continued dressing.

"Where we go to from here is obvious," the girl said in an obvious tone of voice. "You pay me." She paused and looked at him in a decided way. "Just don't go using that I'm keeping your name quiet as an excuse to stiff me and not pay."

She hadn't meant the part about stiffing her to be a sexual pun.

"If you try that, now or anytime in the future, I'll tell all the girls in the house that you're a deadbeat and not to do business with you because you're not to be trusted. Not only will you be cut off from all of us, but also the girls at the house can't hold their talk much more than the hooch hounds in the saloon can. Your name will end up all over the town as a patron of the house, including in the ears of the town council, just where you don't want your name to be."

Harold Ethridge bristled inside at the girl's quasi blackmail. He wasn't above possibly blackmailing members of the town council if the need should arise, but he didn't like being threatened with the incipient threat of backdoor blackmail and exposure, especially from a petty, impudent hooker putting on airs as if she thought she was the equal of him.

"I'll pay you as promised as long as you keep my name out of your itinerary as you promised," Harold Ethridge replied. "I'm even willing to pay you a little extra, within reason, for your troubles in coming here. Just remain discreet at all times."

"I'll be glad to perform service to you and take payment from you for services rendered anytime you want, any way you want, for as long as I'm around," Clarinda said. "But when I'm ready to go, I'm leaving. I'm not talking about this house. I mean this town. Even you aren't going to hold me here. When I want to move on, no man's going to hold me where I don't want to be held or hold me in any way that I don't want to be held in. Not Sam. Not the constable. Not you. Not the mayor. Not anyone."

"I've already pledged that I'm no threat to you in that manner," Harold Ethridge said. "I won't try to make you stay in this town like your saloon-brawling friend."

"Well and good," Clarinda answered. "See that you don't."

"Is Clarinda your real name?" Harold Ethridge asked, though he didn't know why. It didn't particularly sound like a hillbilly mountain name.

"My real name is no longer part of me," Clarinda answered. "My real name is gone from me. My real name, I left far behind me. My real name is only a memory of pain to me. I gave myself the name when I came here. I'll give myself a different name when I get where I'm going. But it won't be a name in the shadows. It will be a name out in the sun. I've been in the shadows all my life. Whatever city I go to, I'll move around out in the sun. I won't be lingering in the shadows around here. I'm not going to bury myself in this town."

Over in the basement cell of the jail, Samuel had not yet fallen asleep. When he finally fell asleep, it was to a vision of the girl standing on the edge of the bank that overlooked the river that ran by Mrs. Richardson's house. In his vision, the girl was looking away from him.

Chapter 10

"Well, well, if it isn't the great John L. Sullivan," Mrs. Richardson said, making ironic reference to the famous turn-of-the-century bare-knuckle pugilist whose name was still remembered and revered. "What brings you here? A paddy wagon?"

"I'd like to see Clarinda," he answered in a subdued voice.

"She's off duty now," Mrs. Richardson said, standing in the doorway of the house. "All the girls are. It's too early."

"I'm not here to see her that way," Samuel said.

"What are you looking to do exactly, give the girls boxing lessons?"

"I want to talk to her. I want to apologize for the way I behaved and for getting her in trouble."

Mrs. Richardson paused for a moment.

"I don't particularly think she wants to talk to you at the moment," Mrs. Richardson said. "She was pretty angry at you for getting her arrested. She told me that if you came around to tell she didn't want to see you. You threw one hell of a scare into her, not by getting her arrested, but by the way you went crazy. When she got back, she told me all about it."

Mrs. Richardson didn't say that before returning to the house, Clarinda had picked up a new client, a new client whose name she didn't reveal, a name she didn't know.

"You shook her up her so bad, I don't think she wants to see you at all again, as a client or as a friend."

In his mind, Samuel caught a vision of the door of the house closing on him. But it wasn't Mrs. Richardson closing the door. It was the girl closing it.

"Please, ma'am," Samuel said in a farm boy's plaintive voice, "I don't intend to scare her. I don't want to rile her up any more than I've done already. I just want to talk to her quiet. I want to apologize to her for what happened. I didn't intend for it to turn out the way it did. I want to tell her from my heart that I didn't intend to do anything to her."

"But what happened did happen," Mrs. Richardson said. "Where your heart was concerned, your fists were way out ahead of your heart. She didn't see your heart beating for her, just your fists pumping. I don't know if she'll ever see you or think of you in any other terms again."

"That's why I've got to talk to her, before that feeling sets in on her forever. I need to tell her I'm sorry. I want to tell her I won't do that again. She's been scared and put upon all her life. I don't want to scare her any more than she has been scared already. I need to convince her that I'm not going to hurt her."

"You think you can convince her of that?" Mrs. Richardson asked in a skepticism-tinged rhetorical voice. It was a both good faith question and a doubt.

"I don't know," Samuel said. "If I have to grovel at her feet, I will. But I've got to try, or else I'll lose her forever."

Instead of a jealousy-crazed possessive male maniac poised to rush in swinging violence from both fists, what stood before her outside her doorway was a distraught farm boy afraid he was going to lose his sweetheart. In spite of his outburst of violence in the saloon, to Mrs. Richardson, the boy was an endearing contradiction. Of all the men who had ever come through her house, this boy-man had the largest heart and most sincere soul of any boy or man who had come for a taste of pedestrian love. Of all the erstwhile "lovers" who came into her house to make erstwhile love, the boy was the only one who seemed capable of deeper and real love—love for a lifetime. If she were Clarinda, she would have left the house for the boy. If she had been a young girl of the town the same age as the boy, having recognized those qualities in him, she would have thrown herself at him shamelessly in order to win his deeper and more enduring love.

Even as a woman old enough to be his mother's older sister, Mrs. Richardson rather thought she would like to know what it would feel like to share the physical working out of the kind of deeper love the boy had to offer.

"I've got to make it right with her, or I may spend the rest of my life never finding or knowing real love and knowing it was my reckless stupidly that separated me from her and from love forever. … Please let me see her. At least tell me where she is."

Mrs. Richardson had thought she had stopped being a romantic when her husband had died and she had opened the house she inherited to far less than romantic applications of love. But the boy's unfeigned plight of unfeigned love opened a narrow window to the past she had left behind and an even narrower window onto an idea of romanticism she had not even thought of since she had been a romantic-minded young girl about to ascend the first step of womanhood. With all that romanticism, past and present, in mind and standing before her, she could not close the door in the boy's face.

Mrs. Richardson glanced to the corner of the house and to the river beyond. "The last I saw of her, she was going to take a walk along the river like she often does."

Samuel turned to head in the direction Mrs. Richardson indicated. Before he started, he stopped and turned partly back to face her.

"Thank you for bailing her out as soon as you did," Samuel said. "She didn't like being in that jail."

"I didn't bail her out," Mrs. Richardson replied. "I didn't even know she was in jail until she came back to the house and told me what had happened."

Samuel looked at her with a puzzled look. "If you didn't bail her out, who did?" he asked.

"She didn't mention his name," Mrs. Richardson said. "I guess he wants to remain anonymous. But she now has a new client. At least she came away from the fight and all of what went on with something other than a black eye."

Samuel didn't inquire further. He had more pressing concerns on his mind. Besides, if Clarinda accepted his proposal, she wouldn't be seeing any more clients. He turned and started walking toward the riverbank.

"Don't go rushing up on her," Mrs. Richardson called to his retreating back. "That will just scare her more. Come up to her slowly and respectfully, like you've got your hat in your hand."

That would be a bit problematic as Samuel wasn't wearing a hat.

"Don't tell her it was me who told you where she was. That might make her mad at me. Pretend you found her on your own."

Mrs. Richardson didn't know if the boy had heard anything she had said or not.

The one-story-high embankment along the river dropped off at a steep angle to a flat muddy beach, then sloped slightly to the water's edge. At the crest of the embankment, Samuel saw Clarinda where Mrs. Richardson had said she could be found. She was walking slowly along the riverbank, heading away from him. He thought to call out her name, but he didn't. He was afraid a loud shout might scare her and send her running. With her back turned to him, he walked silently along the crest of the ridge, closing the distance between them, until he came to a shallow gully cut by rainwater in the side of the embankment. There he scrambled down the embankment wall, slipping and sliding as he went. From where she stood, the girl heard the sound of his approach. As he reached the bottom of the embankment and stepped on to the sand and clay of the low-level riverbank, the girl turned around to face him.

Following Mrs. Richardson's admonition not to rush at her, Samuel walked toward the girl slowly and respectfully. If he had had a hat, he would have held it in his hands, both of them. The girl watched his approach. She did not look frightened. She did not look around quickly as if casting about for a direction in which to run. She did not back away from his approach, but she did not move toward him.

Samuel approached the unmoving girl with the look of a religious penitent on his face. The girl did not pick up stones from the riverbank and throw them at him. Neither did she rush forward to throw herself into his arms, sobbing in relief to see him out of jail and unmanacled. Her face wasn't tightened in anger. Neither did it brighten and flash as an animated surge of joy swept across it. The girl's eyes neither narrowed to slits of focused anger nor well with tears of joy. Her eyes followed his approach, neither glowering in a patina of anger nor filling with a rush of love.

"I see they didn't pack you off to Devil's Island or a chain gang in Leavenworth," Clarinda said. Her voice had no emotion in it, but at least she was talking to him.

"My father bailed me out," Samuel answered. "Constable Harkness said he's going to let me off with a fine for being disorderly in public and for brawling. Beyond that, he said I could come into town, but he told me I had to keep myself out of any saloon for six months."

The girl's body tensed visibly.

"And what did he say he's going to do about me?" she asked, the tone of her voice tensing up. "Did he tell you to tell me to get my slutty self out of town?!"

"Harkness didn't even mention you. I don't think he's even thinking about charging you with anything. He blames me for the fight. With me under police orders not to go into any saloon, you don't have to worry about me coming in and scaring away your customers, even if only by reputation."

"Fat lot of good that will do me now," Clarinda answered. "No man around here will probably want to get close to me for fear that you're going to beat the stuffing out of him. They'll all think I'm a jinx. I'll lose all my clients. I'll have to leave this town and go back on the road before I'm ready."

The part about leaving and going on the road didn't quite sink in on Samuel. He had other thoughts on his mind.

"I'm sorry I caused you so much trouble," Samuel said in his hat-in-hand voice. "I came here to apologize to you."

"Fat lot of good your apology is going to do me now. Men are probably going to steer clear of me for fear that you're going to go after them—if not in the saloon, then somewhere else—when you find out that they've been with me."

"I never attacked any of your other customers," Samuel protested weakly.

"You never saw me with a customer before that night. When you saw me with one the first time direct, you went crazy. If you saw me with another one, you'd probably go crazy again. Craziness has probably been building up inside you. It broke out into the open when you saw me in the bar with the guy I was dealing with. The jealousy building up in you blew up like the overloaded boiler of a steam engine. You lost control there on the spot and started swinging. You'll likely do the same thing the next time you see me with a client. Even if you don't see me with a client, the pressure will probably keep on building up in you just knowin' that I'm doing it, your jealousy getting hotter by the day. One day it'll explode and you'll explode all over me. I'll be the one who gets beat to a pulp. For all I know, I'll die from the beating."

The allegation surprised Samuel.

"I never hit you," Samuel said. "I couldn't hurt you."

Clarinda's hand moved down to the pocket in her dress.

"Have I ever hurt you as much as once?"

"Nothing's ever done till it's done," the girl snapped. The edge of her voice became sharper. Her words started coming faster.

"No man ever beats a woman until he beats her for the first time. After that it comes natural to him. He goes on beating her every time the spirit moves him, and it moves him more by the day. Men think it makes them a man to beat a woman senseless and leave her on the floor as much as it makes them a man to beat another man down flat and leave him unconscious on the floor of a saloon. A woman's weaker than a man— nowhere near the equal of a man in a fight. It makes a man feel more of a man proper when he beats a woman. He thinks she deserves it. He thinks all women deserve to be beaten just on principle. He thinks they deserve to be beaten all the more if they wound and offend his pride."

Samuel had heard the story of the abuse that had been inflicted upon the girl at the hands of her father and brothers, but he had not realized the depth to which it had penetrated her soul. His sister, Beth, had guessed at it, but he hadn't listened. He hadn't wanted to listen.

"What you did to that man, you'll probably get around to doin' to me when me bein' what I am gets around to offending your manly pride and causes you to want to have me to yourself and control me."

Samuel had come down the bank to talk to the girl on the riverside.

Instead he found himself talking to the girl across the divide of a river, a river and a gulf he might never be able to cross.

"With your temper, like I saw in the bar, if I got you mad, you'd probably bust my neck and throw me in the river."

It wasn't a surprise revelation to Samuel that Clarinda saw all men in terms of what her father and brothers had done to her. Given that she had come from a very isolated environment with few outside contacts, in a way it was predictable that she saw her father and brothers' abuse in terms of all males. The problem for him was that she saw what he had done to the man in the bar as a prelude to what he would inevitably do to her.

"Not all men are violent to women like that," Samuel said, pushing his words out ahead of him. "Don't judge all men by what your father and brothers did to you. Don't judge me by what they did to you. I'm not that way."

Clarinda's blue-green eyes looked directly at him. Her gaze didn't flinch, but her expression didn't soften. Samuel couldn't read her set expression, but it didn't look like she believed him.

"My father and mother have been married over twenty years. He hasn't hit her once. I've never even heard him raise his voice to her. Talk to her. She'll tell you that. I learned how to treat women from him, not from your brothers."

Introducing the girl you intend to marry to your parents is an uncertain enough prospect in a conventional situation. Taking home a prostitute who makes her living picking up clients in bars and introducing her to your conventional parents as the girl you intend to marry and bring into the house is a far trickier meet-the-parents arrangement.

"As I was growing up, from the first that I can remember, my father taught me to respect my mother. From there he taught me to respect all women."

"He apparently also taught you to be a good boxer and saloon fighter," the girl said. "If you can flatten a man with just a few punches like you did in the saloon, you could break my jaw with one punch."

"I never hit you," Samuel reiterated. "I'll never hit you. I love you."

It was his first open profession of love for the girl. For her part, the girl didn't respond with a gasp of surprise like she was a live-for-love romantic girl waiting with a trembling heart and trembling lips to hear a word of love spoken by the master of her soul. The set of her face didn't change. His words and profession of love faded out over the river, heading past and away.

"You love havin' me," Clarinda said back at him. "But all the while, the jealousy's been building up in you. It burst out on the guy in the bar. If your jealousy beats up on any man who gets near me, eventually it's going to start beating up on me anytime I'm near another man or you even think I'm near another man. That's the way jealousy runs, and the hell if I'm going to let your jealousy run all over me and run me down."

Exposure to the more sophisticated and polished Mrs. Richardson had taken some of the hillbilly accent edge off Clarinda's speech. As she started talking faster, her hard-edged hillbilly accent started coming back.

"If you're of the type who can break a man's head just because you see him near me, someday you'll up and break my neck if you see me with another man. Jealousy and wantin' to possess a woman gets a man to that stage eventually. If it's goin' to start, it's going to start someplace. Last night in the bar was just the start of it. Your jealous rages will just go on gettin' worse from here on out till they end up gettin' turned back on me in short enough order. In the end, your jealousy is going to smash me up as bad as you smashed the man in the saloon. Probably worse."

"I was trying to protect you," Samuel said. "I suppose I did go off half-cocked. But people can get crazy when they're protecting the ones they love."

The set of Clarinda's face broke and dissolved, but not into a look of gratitude for Samuel's solicitous concern. As much as a hillbilly can look incredulous, a look of incredulousness came over the girl's face.

"Protect me?!" she snapped, her face becoming more animated. "He wasn't comin' hard at me. I weren't in no danger from him. He wasn't workin' me. I was workin' him. I was just doin' my job. You went after him 'cause your jealousy blew your brains out and made you want to beat his brains out. The only thing that needed to be protected against in that place needed to be protected from you! Don't run at me with no bull that you went crazy because you thought you were protecting me. It was just your exploding jealousy that set you on that man and beat him down. Next time, which there ain't going to be, it will be me they find lying bloody on the floor."

In his mind, Samuel paused a moment to analyze what his motivation had been in attacking the man. At that point, he didn't know if it had been some form of protective instinct or whether it had been jealousy and possessiveness. It was probably a mixture of both. But for the rest of his life, Samuel would wonder what the percentage of that mixture had been. At the present moment he had too much else on his mind to do an in-depth analysis.

"I promise to behave in a more gentlemanly manner when I'm around you and any of your clients in the future. I won't be any more trouble to you."

"Oh, you ain't goin' to make no more trouble for me or around me again all right," Clarinda said, biting in anger on her words, "because you ain't goin' to be 'round me again. I don't want to see you no more, Samuel Martin! Not professionally. Not as a picnic goer. Not as the friend you never really were."

At that point, Clarinda could have gone on and told him about what had happened after she had been taken back upstairs, about the cooler-tempered and level-headed gentleman who had salvaged the evening for her by bailing her out of jail, who had taken her for a ride in his modern car to his well-appointed two-story house in the respectable part of town, who had paid a premium for her to service him in his big four-poster bed. But she didn't say what she could have said. She was afraid that it might send him off again, grabbing at her, shaking her, demanding to know the name of the man whose name she hadn't even revealed to Mrs. Richardson. But the man wouldn't be there for him to turn on. It would be only her and the boy alone, out of sight behind the bank down on the river shore. She was afraid that in another jealous rage he might turn on her, beat her, and throw her in the river.

Samuel wasn't moving, but what the girl said stopped him in his tracks. "What do you mean you don't want to see me again?" he asked in a confused voice.

"Just exactly what I said," Clarinda answered. "Should be plain enough. No more. No less. You got more education than me. I shouldn't have to spell it out for you none."

"Why?" Samuel asked, the full effect of what the girl had said starting to sink in.

"Because you're dangerous," Clarinda answered decisively in her hillbilly accent. "I came here runnin' from men who would have killed me and dumped by body in the woods. I didn't ride the rails and sleep in barns so I could hook up with an equally dangerous man who'll break my neck and throw me in the river. I ain't run all this way to get to a place of danger equal to what I left. I intend to keep on goin' till I find me a place that is safe for me for all time."

"If you want a place where you can feel safe and be safe, come home with me," Samuel said. "I'll bring you into the family and make you part of it. You'll be safe there. You won't have to live the life you've been living. You won't have to do the kind of work you've been doing in the places you've been doing it."

With his hope trembling on the edge of becoming a fully realized dream, Samuel waited for Clarinda's response.

Once again the girl's face didn't blossom into an expression of ecstatic joy at an unexpected dream realized. Instead she sort of sniffed.

"Your mother ain't going to want to take in a wayward midnight rambling girl she'll think of as a back-alley floozy," Clarinda said in a dismissive tone. "Neither is your father. I doubt your sister is going to want to bunk with me either. She's probably filled your parents' ears with all kinds of stories about me. They'd all slam the door in my face, bar it, and tell me to take my dirty lovin' self back to the alley I came out of."

The girl stood on the mud of the riverbank, one foot on the mud, the other at the place where the water touched the shore.

"They wouldn't treat you that way even if they caught you stealing eggs out of the barn," Samuel said in as reassuring of a voice as he could muster. "Mother doesn't think that way. She's always been charitable to those in need. She'd probably take you in and feed you. If she knew you were without a home and on the run from people who treated you as bad as you've been treated, she might even want to bring you into the family and make you a member."

At that point Samuel saw an opening to do what he had determined to do the minute he had first seen the girl. He hadn't imagined it happening this way. It pushed his plans up. Given the way the girl felt about him, it was a chancy prospect at best. Most outside observers would say the time was not right—nowhere near right. He suspected that he had a lot more smoothing things over to do with the girl. But it could make the difference and make it fully right now. Either way, Samuel felt he had to try.

"If we were married, you would automatically be a member of the family."

Clarinda looked at him with a quizzical expression on her face as if she hadn't heard him right.

"I want to marry you. I wanted to marry you the first time I saw you. I want to marry you and take you into my family and make you part of it. I want to give you the family you never had, a family as it should be. I want to be to you what a man should be to a woman. I want to make up for all the hurt in your life. I want to make up for all the hardness of life you've been through. I want to make up for all the love you've never been given."

Instead of gasping in ecstatic grateful surprise at an unanticipated dream unexpectedly realized and throwing herself into his arms, crying with joy, the girl stood her ground, unmoved, at the river's edge.

"Marry me?!" Clarinda scoffed louder. "That's a crazier idea than all your other ones put together. But I'd be the really crazy one if I took you up on it. Instead of staying away from your temper and violence, I'd be walkin' myself right in the front door of it.

"There are all sorts of people around Mrs. Richardson's house. I've got friends there and witnesses. That gives me a measure of safety, more than I'd have livin' out and away at your place. When I lived in the mountains, I was cut off and isolated. There weren't a lot of women around in our hollow. I was about the only thing in the way of a woman for them to lay hands on. My brothers could do with me as they liked. With me developing the way I was, with Mother gone and not there to look after me, and with my father not carin' for what his sons were doin' to me, even when he was sober, they started turnin' on me to get their jollies with a woman. The way was all clear for them, no one to see them, no one to stop them."

Clarinda shuddered visibly.

"If I came out to your farm, I would be cut off and isolated again the way I was then. If you wanted to beat me up out behind the barn, there would be no one there to stop you or even see. The rest of your family would look the other way because you're family and I'm just a trick you brought in from a cathouse. If they feel themselves to be right and proper upstanding folks, they'll probably think women like me deserve to be beat up on."

"I wouldn't treat you that way," Samuel protested once again. "Neither would my family."

"Even if you didn't do all that, you still live on a farm," Clarinda said in response. "If I came into your family and became part of it, I'd spend the rest of my life doing farm chores and workin' at farm drudgery. I've spent most of my life up till now in a hovel in the mountains. I don't want to spend the rest of it in a farm hovel workin' every day till my youth and looks are gone, myself down to a shriveled, worn-out nothin' of a nothin' woman, dyin' from work and tiredness before my time, bein' buried in the back of a churchyard cemetery without ever havin' been out in a wider life in the wider world."

Samuel paused momentarily to remember that on the night he had first met the girl, his friend Ben had said she would probably think that way.

"That's all nowhere anyway. Where it comes to marrying, I ain't going to be marrying any man anytime anywhere, not in this town and not in the biggest city. When a woman marries a man, she ends up held by him. I'm not going to be held by any man, poor or rich, on a farm or in a mansion. I intend to hold to myself alone. Men can come to me in the bigtime house I'm in. At the end of the day or the night, they'll be gone. I'll have their money, but they won't have me. I'll have my life to myself to live it my way."

Samuel had come to Clarinda with the hope of convincing her of his love for her and establishing a life for her and a future with her. But instead, the situation was deteriorating. Now she was talking about leaving the town and taking herself off to a bigtime bordello in a city far away.

As the old saying goes, a faint heart never won a fair lady. And it doesn't begin to win the heart of a cynical, hard-bitten girl with grit in her teeth and a knife edge to her soul. The only thing Samuel could think of to do at that juncture was to sweep the girl into his arms and hug her tightly. Maybe a direct, personal, enveloping display of love on his part would break the icy sheath around her heart, convince her of his love, and win her over to love. Samuel abandoned the position he was standing in, abandoned Mrs. Richardson's caution about not rushing the girl, and stepped quickly forward, moving toward her with the full intention of wrapping her in his arms.

As Samuel stepped toward Clarinda, the unflinching set of her face fell away. Her expression became animated. A palpable look of fear came over her face. As he stepped toward her, she stepped back from him with a stumbling, frightened step. With a quick motion, she reached into the pocket of her dress and pulled out the knife she always carried, the knife she had stolen from her brother and later used to slash his face when he had tried to rape her again. With an equally quick motion, she snapped out the blade. She stood in an upright defensive posture and waved the blade at Samuel. Though he couldn't tell through the loose-fitting dress she was wearing, her body was trembling.

"You stop right where you are, Samuel Martin!" the girl said in a half shout. "You stay back from me now, you hear!"

Samuel stopped in place just beyond the point of the knife blade, stunned by the unexpected intensity of the girl's reaction. Despite all she had said, he had underestimated her fear of him. But it was dawning more fully on Samuel that he wasn't just faced with her fear of him; he was also dealing with her deep-seated and consuming fear of all men. At that point, and at the point of the girl's knife, he realized that he was only starting to see how long of a journey he would have following the girl, trying to turn her slashed heat back to him, back to the home and life he wanted to make with her. From where he was standing on the river shore facing the girl and her life of fear, he couldn't see the end of the path he would be taking.

"Oh, Clarinda, put down the knife," Samuel said. "I didn't come to hurt you."

"For all I know, you're lookin' to wring my neck."

"I just want to hold you."

Clarinda crouched a little more. She pushed the knife out a little farther. "I don't want to be held or held down or held back, not by you or by any man! No way, no how. That's what I've been sayin' all along since the day we met. But you haven't been listening. No man listens to what a woman says when he's out to get somethin' he wants off of her."

"I don't mean that way," Samuel said. "I just want to hold you in my arms and show you I don't mean to hurt you."

Samuel leaned his body forward a small degree. Apparently the girl interpreted the motion as if he were intending to resume forward motion toward her. She jabbed at the air in his direction with the knife.

"You stay where you are!" she said in a loud voice. Her arm and body seemed to tremble as if in preparation for fight or flight. For all Samuel knew, she was drawing herself up to lunge at him with the knife. After all the time they had spent together and all they had done together, Samuel found it hard to think that she would try to attack him with the knife. It wasn't as if she hadn't gone after a man with a knife before. She had slashed her brother's face when he had tried to rape her once again in a drunken rush. At the time it had been her only option. For all Samuel knew, she felt she was back in the same situation with no other option. From the fighting crouch of her body, she seemed on the verge of sending herself rushing at him slashing. Her fear seemed real enough to send her.

Samuel held his hands up in front of him, palms out, to show he was not going to attack her. "I promise I won't come any closer," he said in a reassuring voice.

A standard formula, then and now, would have the hero rush in, sweep the girl in his arms, and hold her tight in a hard kissing embrace that sweeps away the heroine's reticence and resistance and causes her to melt in the hero's forceful arms. It was a formula that the embryonic movie industry would come to apply in formulaic movies for generations to come. But all simple formulas are simple and formulaic. They also have a way of backfiring. Samuel had recklessly acted on his own simplistic formula the night before. It had blown up in his face in more ways than one.

"You see you do stay back from me," Clarinda said in a gravelly voice. "Don't you come no closer."

From where he was standing just beyond the reach of the girl's knife, Samuel calculated that he could lunge suddenly forward and slap the knife out of her hand. But any kind of charging grab at the girl, even one that ended in a romantic clinch, would probably only provide the final proof to the girl that all men, especially him, were innately aggressive. Even if he could get the knife out of her hand, stripping her of the only protection she felt she had, that would probably send the girl running away in a panic. He might be able to catch up with her and throw his arms around her, but she would probably only take it all as an attack on her, sure that she was about to be brutalized again as she had been at the hands of her brothers. The now more clearheaded Samuel figured that if he behaved as impulsively as he had in the saloon, he would never be able to convince her of his love for her and his good intentions toward her. If he triggered the girl's deep-seated fears, she would retreat from him and take herself beyond his reach. Everything would be lost. If he were to keep her near him, he would have to approach her in the least threatening way. At this point, the point he had brought her to by his reckless, impulsive violence toward the man in the saloon, the point she had been brought to by the depth of her fear, he just wasn't sure there was anything he could do that she wouldn't take as a threat.

For a moment Samuel stood in his place in silence. The girl stood in her place in silence.

"So why are you here comin' at me again?" Clarinda snapped, still holding the knife up and pointing it at him. "What is it you're lookin' to get off of me? What do you want from me?"

"I just wanted to say I was sorry for what I did and for scaring you like I did," Samuel reiterated, trying to make his voice sound as reasonable, apologetic, unaggressive, and nonthreatening as he could. "I also wanted to say again that I love you."

"Love?" Clarinda scoffed. "So now you're back at me talkin' love words to me again. I didn't particularly believe your words when you were payin' for it. I believe them less now that you're trying to get me back for free. I don't think you've got enough words of love or anything that is ever going to make me think you love me or can love a girl without beating her down."

"I don't know what words I can use other than the ones I have," Samuel said. "I'm not a grand poet who writes the kind of words they print in books of poetry and literature. All I've got are my own words."

Clarinda stood with the knife still raised. A strand of her long black hair had fallen across her eye. With her free hand, she reached over quickly and brushed it away.

"Your jealousy and your fists were talkin' a whole lot louder than your words were in the saloon," Clarinda responded. "But then you weren't using words. You were just bellowing in threats and anger."

"But it wasn't directed at you," Samuel answered. "I don't believe in violence against women."

"You sure were doing a damned good imitation of violence in the saloon," Clarinda said, holding the sharp edge in her voice, pointing the sharp point of the knife blade at him. "It may have been against a man, but if you'll do violence against one of your drinking buddies, its's only a small step to doing violence to the women around you. When nobody's lookin', that is."

At that moment Samuel stopped. They were going around in the same circle again. It was a circle without end. It was a circle that would never convince the girl. A change of direction was needed.

"Talk to my sister," Samuel said. "She'll tell you I never did anything to her that way. She told you as much herself at the fair when you asked her. You seemed to believe her. She and her henpecking friends will tell you that I've never done anything physical to any of the girls in this town. There have been times I wanted to spank Beth's snotty bottom, but I've never hit her, and I've sure never raped her. I'm her brother, a brother the way brothers are supposed to be. I'm not your brothers."

What Samuel said seemed to have an effect on the girl. She continued pointing the knife at him, but she seemed somehow more uncertain. She glanced down and then out over the river. She seemed to be casting around for a response. Samuel took her uncertainty as a hopeful sign. It was as if he had made one small inroad. Maybe it would be a road that took him back to her.

"Like I say," Clarinda said in an elevated voice, "what is it you want from me? What is it you're lookin' to get off of me? You took away any trust I had in you. I don't have any of that left to give."

"What I want is for you not to turn me away," Samuel said. "I want to keep seeing you. I want you to give me the chance to prove what I say, that I love you and don't want to hurt you. I want to show you my heart."

"Oh, so now it's your heart you want to show me," Clarinda scoffed again. "Leading out with the heart is a rarity for any man. Half of all men think with their peckers. The other half think with their fists. They all think that's the way a real man thinks and acts. Precious few, if any, think with their hearts like you claim to be wanting to do for me."

The opening Samuel had imagined seemed to be closing again.

"Don't go tellin' me about this great and abiding love you have for me. Don't tell me what you're incapable of doing to any woman. In the saloon, I saw what you're capable of doing when you get riled up. That's the way men go after each other when one man offends another man's pride. Their pride is their all in all to them. Their pride is more all in all to them than the women who are supposed to be their be-all and end-all. It's no different when a woman offends a man's pride and vanity, although a woman does make for an easier target.

"I've only begun to tell you what men have done to me. Don't tell me what you can't bring yourself to do to me. Don't tell me to trust you and regard you as harmless after what I saw you do in that saloon. I don't trust any man, and I don't trust you!"

Samuel's hopes for a grand tearful reunion and reconciliation faded away over the river as it flowed past and away. The only hope he had left was to salvage some small part of what he and Clarinda had shared together. Maybe, given time and opportunity, he could rebuild their affinity and regain her trust.

"You were the one who came into the saloon bellowing and swinging your fists like a typical male. I'm not the one who was swinging their fists around like a Negro on cocaine."

"And I'm not the one waving a knife around like an Apache warrior out for scalps," Samuel countered. "I said I wasn't going to do anything to you, and I mean it. I'll stay in this spot like I promised. Now please, put down the knife."

Samuel didn't know if what he was saying had finally convinced Clarinda or whether her arm had grown tired from being held out so straight and tense, holding the knife leveled at him. She wavered a moment and then lowered her arm to her side, the knife pointing down. But she didn't fold the blade into the handle and put it back in her pocket.

"You hold your ground and stay where you are," Clarinda instructed. "You say you're not angry or dangerous? Prove it by holding yourself where you are. If you make one move toward me, fast or slow, I won't believe you or even listen to one more word you ever say."

Samuel complied with Clarinda's directive. She seemed to have regained enough trust in him to let her guard down the partial way she had. Samuel reasoned it might be the only positive response he would get out of her that day. He didn't want to throw it away.

It would be rather lame to say that Clarinda was pretty when she was angry, but the partially faded anger that still simmered in her did not distract from her backwoods sensuality or pastoral beauty. Her full chest moved under her dress as she breathed. The liquid blue-green of her eyes contrasted with, and stood out when surrounded by, the almost midnight black of her hair. Only a slight breeze stirred the embankment top that day. The air seemed even more motionless down at the river bottom. The look on her face was a tangled and interwoven knot of anger, suspicion, and uncertainty. In their separate stances, Clarinda and Samuel stood their separate ground, facing each other across the gap that Samuel wished to close and that the girl demanded he maintain. In the sky above, some distant clouds hung suspended, seemingly motionless. At their feet, the river moved slowly by them.

"So what do we do now?" Clarinda said after several long moments of silence.

The take-charge Samuel didn't know where to take things. That Clarinda had used the term *we* was a hopeful sign, but he had no coherent idea of where to go next. He had proposed to take her into his family's home and he had proposed marriage to her, only to have her toss both those things aside. Samuel still wanted to take the girl in his arms, but in the fragile moment he was afraid that if he broke his promise not to move any closer, and if he advanced on her and tried to take her in his arms, she would snap back into the depths of her fear and would slash at him with the knife. The fragile progress would be shattered as badly and permanently as the girl had said it would be if he moved on her. To maintain anything with her, Samuel knew he had to maintain his distance from her. He only hoped he could find some way to salvage something between them.

"All I can do is apologize again and tell you again that I love you and don't intend on doing you any harm," Samuel said, struggling in his own way to say something convincing. Though not all that poetic by nature, he decided to up the romantic ante.

"The first time I lay with you in my arms, I knew I had found the girl I wanted for the rest of my life. I should have said it right then and there. I knew just the same that I wanted to spend the rest of my life with you the other times and places we made love. Nothing has changed in me toward you. You're the future I see. You're my life as I see it."

The look on Clarinda's face didn't turn totally hostile and explode again as if she thought she was hearing another postured lie. Neither did her expression melt into a romantic swoon. Her expression remained unchanged.

"Men have been known to say all sorts of endlessly romantic things and make any number of flowery-sounding promises of love and goodness to a woman to make her swoon and fall into their arms and under their control," Clarinda said, still holding the knife at her side. "Their male pride is tied up in controlling the woman. Once they've got her under their control, if the woman they promised their all in all to somehow steps on their arrogance or violates their manly virtues, they slap her silly or beat her black and blue. If their pride is easily offended to the worst degree, they beat her within an inch of her life. Sometimes they kill her. What starts as a romantic promise of love and fealty ends with the crumpled body of a dead woman found in an alley or floating facedown in a river."

"Pride and control and possessiveness may be everything to some men," Samuel said, "but pride and arrogance and possessiveness aren't the things I'm looking to live my life for. A prideful man is only an inflated shadow of what a real man is. A real man loves the loved ones around him more than he loves himself or loves his pride. Pride isn't the way life's supposed to be lived, and pride isn't what life's supposed to be lived for. Loving others, not yourself, is the way life's supposed to be lived. The Bible says that. I don't want to run my life on pride, and I don't want to run your life into the ground. I don't want to add to the pain and loss of your life. I want to give you love and life as it should be, not as you got it at home, not as you're getting it in Mrs. Richardson's house."

Almost without conscious effort, the words formed inside him. They poured out in a continuous stream.

"A life spent loving a woman is the way I've always thought life should be lived. Since I first saw you, all I wanted was to spend my life with you. You were the future as I saw it. You were the future I wanted. Now the future I wanted and hoped for has been threatened by my reckless stupidity. That's why I came here, not to exercise my pride or possessiveness, but to say I'm sorry, try to make up for what I did, and put things back like they were before I blundered and frightened you the way I have. I only pray that I can make it up to you somehow and correct the mistake that I've made."

Though Samuel did not hold back on his words, he held his position and did not move toward her. As he spoke, Clarinda stood in silence, still holding the knife at her side.

"Well now, those were some pretty words all right," Clarinda said in a tone as edged as the knife she held. "But they're just words. Words are like the spots on a fawn or a white coat on a rabbit in winter. Words are just a protective cover for a liar. And the bigger the liar, the bigger, better, and more flowery are his words. You talk a talk that would make most girls melt." She pointed at herself with the knife. "But I'm not most girls. And I'm not a girl who turns to oatmeal at the sound of words of love, especially when the words sound like the words of a lie. … Like the saying goes, actions speak louder than words. It's the actions of men that have made me what I am, not their lying words. Words are like raindrops on a roof. They pitter and patter. They sound harmless. They are harmless if you keep yourself sheltered from them. But you can get soaked to drowning if you go out and dance in them. If the rain comes fast and hard enough, it can turn into a gully washer that can sweep you away. Your words are like a rainbow. They're all sparkly and colorful. But a rainbow is nothin' but the sun shining through distant rain. Your words are sparkly, but they're just words sparkling in the air."

The thin sliver of light that had shone through the door of hope that had seemed to open disappeared as the door shut again. To Samuel, the dark tunnel that had been Clarinda's life before she had come to him was just too long and dark for him to bring a light to and lead her out of. In the vision in Samuel's mind, the girl he thought of as his future faded and disappeared into the dark corridor of her past.

"If you ever hope to make me believe a single word you're saying, you're going to have to do more than spit watercolor words at me. You're going to have to prove your love to me through your actions."

As quickly as it had closed, the door was back open. She had said she would love him if he proved his love. That meant she was not sending him away as she had seemed to be saying since they had started talking down by the river. Hope leapt in Samuel's chest. As if he were jumping off a sinking ship onto a life raft, he jumped on Clarinda's words.

"That's what I want to do," Samuel said enthusiastically. "That's what I've been saying I want to do for you, prove myself and my love for you. But I can't prove myself to you if you send me away and won't see me. I can't prove myself from a distance. You have to let me stay close to you to prove myself. If you let me stay close to you and you stay close to me, I can."

Clarinda held up the hand she wasn't holding the knife with, palm forward, cutting him off. "That ain't particularly the way I meant it," she said in a set voice.

Samuel paused, confused. "What do you mean?" he asked.

"I mean that if you want to be with me, you're going to have to prove that you can stay away from me," Clarinda answered. "If you don't want me to get the decided idea that you're obsessed with having me, you're going to have to prove that you can back off from me and that you're not going to strangle me with your possessiveness. You're not going to move one inch toward convincing me of that all the while you keep after me, crowding me all over the place all the time. You can't prove nothing to me if you keep pressing in on me, tryin' to see me and be with me every minute like you're wantin' to do. That would be easy—easy for you. Too easy. And that wouldn't prove nothin'. Whatever is too easy don't prove anything. If you want me to believe any part of what you say is this great love you have for me, you have to prove it's me you love and not yourself and your own wants. The only way you're going to be able to convince me that your love isn't the grabbing, grasping, and holding kind is if you take yourself away from me and keep yourself away from me for the time I set. If you can't do it like that, you're not a real lover. You're just a grabber and a taker and a holder who holds for his own gratification, not for love of, or concern for, the woman he's grabbin' on to. Men like that aren't lovers; they're takers. They want what they want when they want it. They want it the minute they want it, and they aren't willing to wait as much as a day for it. If you can't stay away from me for the time I set, the only thing you're going to prove to me is that you are not in love with me but are in love with yourself, in love with your pride, and in love with your wants. That ain't love as I see it. That ain't even love as you called it to be. If you can't do it my way, I'm gone from you, and no amount of flowery words is going to lure me back, 'cause your actions will have proved those words to be nothin' but a lie."

"How long do you want me to stay away from you?" Samuel asked.

"How long did Constable Harkness say you have to stay out of the saloon?"

"Six months. He says I can come into town to buy farm supplies and household goods. But when I'm in town, I have to keep myself out of the saloon even if I'm not in there drinking. He didn't say that I have to keep myself away from Mrs. Richardson's place or stay away from you."

"Sounds fair enough," Clarinda said. "Six months it is with me too. If you ever want to see me again at all, you'll have to show me you can stay away from me for six months."

The door that had swung open now swung partway closed.

"Does it have to be that long?" Samuel asked. "It's going to be hard for me to be away from you and not see you for that long."

"Oh, Samuel, drop that 'every minute without you is torture' romantic crap!" Clarinda snapped back. "That's just an excuse men give for not being able to control themselves. That's just an excuse men give for not wanting to control themselves. That's just one more line men use to maintain control and dominance but also make themselves sound like wounded heart romantics when they're doing it. That's all just more self-love, not real love. … They say that true love waits. Love that can't wait, love that has to have its way every moment, isn't love. It's greed and grabbing and having and possessing for the purpose of having and possessing. It's love from pride. It's love of pride. For the prideful, their pride is their real love. It's pride they can't control. It's pride they don't want to control. But it ain't love nowhere along the line. It ain't healthy love from the man. It's even less healthy for the woman caught up in it. I've done all sorts of love that a lot of folks would say isn't Christian or healthy. When I've done it, I haven't let myself get caught up in it for a minute. I'm not about to start now, no matter how much you say you love me."

Clarinda pointed at him with the point of the knife.

"You do it my way or it doesn't get done, not now or ever. If you can't control yourself, if you break down even once and come to me before the time I say is up, your one chance is over then and there and you'll never see me again, no matter how much you cry and moan and mope around and come beggin' after me."

She pointed the knife at the mud beneath their feet.

"You either agree to do it the way I say, or you take yourself away from me, right here and now, and don't come back, either tomorrow or in six months. Do you agree to what I say or not?"

Only a thin shaft of light was coming through the door that was almost closed. But Samuel knew he had to accept what Clarinda wanted or else the door would be slammed shut in his face, never to be opened again.

"I'll do it your way," Samuel said in a resigned voice.

"Well and good," Clarinda answered. "Don't say any more. Now let's end it here and now and not drag things out any longer. We both said our piece. No use sayin' anything further. Don't go tryin' to make me change my mind or trying to get me to change my mind with a long, tearful goodbye. I cried in the night when I buried my daughter in secret. I ain't going to cry no more over anyone or for anyone."

Samuel started to turn to leave, but he stopped. "When and where do we meet again?" he asked in a straightforward, nonpleading voice.

"Come back six months from today," Clarinda said. "If you don't find me in the Richardson house, look for me here down by the river."

With nothing more he could do or say, Samuel turned and walked toward the embankment. He didn't say anything like "I'll be thinking of you the whole time. Will you be thinking of me?" or "I'll remember you. Will you remember me?" He figured she would take it as him using more oily words on her. Pushing one more inch or uttering one more word might have put Clarinda's attitude and the situation beyond reach. He was still sure that his love would make all the difference in her damaged and pained life, but if there was any chance that she would ever share her life with him, he would have to do it her way.

The river made soft lapping sounds as it flowed past and away.

The girl stood watching Samuel walk away from her. She felt neither a tug of sorrow to see him go nor any lingering anger toward him. If anything, she felt relief that he had accepted her terms and had gone away without causing a serious scene. That he had accepted her terms and was willing to walk away as she had said brought up the possibility that he was sincere in his words and that his stated love for her was real after all. She also warmed to the idea he actually didn't present a threat to her, other than the threat of her ending up as his drudgery-laden farm wife. That he might actually keep the terms of the bargain she had set and would keep his agreed-upon distance for six months was all a rather moot point to the girl. She didn't plan to be around in the town six months later. She didn't plan to be in the same state.

Samuel climbed back up the embankment. He stopped at the top and looked back the way he had come. The girl was standing where he had left her. She was looking at him. She didn't move or wave.

Samuel didn't wave either. Instead he turned away for the last time and started walking toward the truck. He had come to the girl with an expanded offer in hand to share a life with her. He was walking away with only a thin, faint, and faded possibility of realizing that hope and that life. He was walking away with the echo of the girl's voice in his memory, his hopes for a life with her only an echo of the hope he had come there with. Any hope beyond that was in the form of a deferred chance on the horizon.

Samuel started up the truck and drove away from the house slower than he had come. When he had driven away from the house after first meeting her, he had seen the girl's face silhouetted in the night sky out ahead of and above him. As he drove home in the daylight, all he saw were the open fields and the horizon they stretched toward. No farmers were working in any of the fields. The home Samuel had to make with and for Clarinda was farther away, around the curve of the road and out over the curve of the horizon. The home he had seen in his mind seemed horizons farther away than it had when he had first driven home from the house. The familiar fields of his youth were a hollow landscape around him. It was a long and empty drive back home.

Chapter 11

It was definitely a better crowd than the one at Two-Bit Charlie's saloon. The scene at the yearly community social and potluck dinner was almost pastoral—pastoral enough that Constable Harkness felt relaxed. His presence at the social was required, along with that of the other town fathers. Two of his police officers were there in uniform, not to keep order but to reinforce his department's and the town's commitment to law and order. The most trying thing about the evening was that, as the representative of the law enforcement contingent of the town, he would have to sit at the head table with the mayor and other members of the town council and listen as they speechified. The only thing that might come about to disrupt the evening was the remote possibility of a food fight developing between factions of the more rowdy boys in attendance during the cleanup afterward, with handfuls of leftover German potato salad and stuffed peppers being thrown about.

It seemed that most of the town was in attendance that evening. Everyone had been invited—everyone except the women of the Richardson house.

There was no hint of tension in the air. The conversation around him was light and friendly. No outsiders, transients, passing freight men, or rowdy members of the community were there. Constable Harkness smiled to himself at the evenness and even temper of the crowd. Everything was peaceful and pastoral with the scene and with the people. There were no troublemakers to disrupt the pleasant gathering.

The constable did, however, spot one known troublemaker in the crowd. He was busy at the main buffet-style serving table, doing the pastoral task of helping his mother and sister set out and arrange the various dishes of food and the pies. The scene was hardly a threatening one, yet the constable felt the need to deliver one small word of caution to one person helping with the serving setup. He walked over to the serving table.

"Good evening, Mr. Martin," the constable said to Samuel. He wasn't addressing Samuel's father, Mr. Martin. Samuel's father was off talking farming with the other farmers of the area. "I trust you've been adhering to the terms of the agreement you made with my department to stay out of certain specified establishments."

"I am presently in a double confinement agreement to avoid certain places and people," Samuel said, "the one I have with you to stay out of Two-Bit Charlie's saloon and pool hall—I don't think I'll ever be going back there—and the one I have with Clarinda to stay away from her for the same period. I am quite content to abide by your terms. I agreed to her terms reluctantly, but I will keep them as I keep yours."

The constable didn't say anything negative or threatening, such as "See that you do." He nodded his head and walked away.

Constable Harkness stopped in the middle of the floor and looked around. It seemed that everyone in the town was there.

"I don't see why you're not at the social," Clarinda said as she straightened her dress that she had just finished putting back on. "All of the bigwigs of the town are supposed to be there. You're one of the biggest. As the richest man in town, you're probably the biggest man in town, bigger than the mayor and any of your cronies on the town council. Why aren't you there?"

"The mayor is a fathead," Harold Ethridge said as he buckled his pants in preparation for putting his shirt back on. "The members of the town council are all fatheads. I see enough of them in town council meetings. I don't need to seem them more. Besides, potluck socials bore me. Only unsophisticated hicks like potluck suppers. All the members of this town are unsophisticated hicks. That includes your barroom brawler and would-be lothario, Samuel Martin. Unsophisticated hicks bore me. I'm better than all the hicks of this town put together. Especially him. At least you had enough brains to put him away from you. That puts you one up on the two-bit tramps who work in the Richardson house. Along with getting away from Samuel Martin, you also have enough brains to get away from them. They'll all be no-account, low-level trash-tramp whores for the rest of their lives. They'll never rise above what they are now. They'll never be able to make it outside the house. They'll all just hold you down and hold you back. You've got the ability to make a real high-tone whore out of yourself once you get to wherever you're planning on taking yourself."

At hearing Ethridge running down Samuel, Clarinda paused momentarily from smoothing her dress. She wasn't sure she liked what he had said about her erstwhile friend and lover, the friend and lover she was holding at arm's length. Neither did she particularly like the way he was running down the other girls in the house, the girls she had come to think of as erstwhile sisters. Like the vines that creep and grow between the stone blocks of a wall, second thoughts and second feelings about leaving were starting to creep in around the edges of her otherwise decidedly set mind.

"How are your plans for leaving coming along?" Harold Ethridge said as he buttoned his shirt. "When are you going to make your big move?" Harold Ethridge knew all about making big moves at the right time.

"I'll make my move when I'm ready," Clarinda said, "when I've got it all thought out in my mind."

"Well, don't take too long to make your move, or the decision to leave won't be yours to make and you won't have a house to make it out of," Harold Ethridge said cryptically.

Clarinda stopped and looked at him. "What do you mean?" she asked.

"I've got it all worked out and ready to go," Harold said. "As head of the town council, I'll propose that the town annex the land between the present town boundaries and the river, the section of land the Richardson house stands on outside the town boundaries. The Richardson house will then fall under town jurisdiction and control. At that point I'll move that the Richardson house be closed as a blight on the town and the inhabitants be evicted. When that is accomplished, I'll move to buy the land. The town needs money so bad, they'll probably sell it to me for dimes on the dollar. Then I'll have the house torn down. Once the land is cleared, I'll either sell the land to an industrialist to build a factory on—as close as the town is to the railroad, it will be a prime site—or build my own business or industry on the land and cut the town out. By the time the dolts on the town council figure out how much I've put over on them, it will be far too late for them to do anything about it."

"Is this what they call a land swindle?" the girl asked, nominally aware that a lot of swindles were going on in what was an era of swindles with classic swindlers like Boss Tweed and Ponzi.

"I don't consider myself a swindler, my dear," Harold Ethridge said with a small smile on his lips. "Where it comes to land, business, and women, I consider myself a player. Swindlers are clumsy. They trip over themselves and their clumsy swindles. Players are more skillful and subtle. They arrange things more carefully. The rubes they take for a ride don't know they've been taken until after they've been took and the player is out ahead of them and gone, so far ahead of them they can't get him back. That's the way I'm going to work it with the town council. They'll think I'm giving them a deal, a deal they won't see through until after it's done—if they ever do."

"You can't just take someone's house and land like that," Clarinda said, anger rising in her voice. "It's not yours to take."

"By myself I can't," Harold Ethridge said. "But the town can. It's called eminent domain. Cities and towns use it all the time to clear out blighted areas and open them up for more productive use and enterprise."

"Is that legal?" Clarinda asked.

"It's been legal for a long time," Harold Ethridge said. "If you're smart and everyone else around you is dumb, you can use it to your advantage."

"Mrs. Richardson won't like it one bit," Clarinda said. "Her husband was a lawyer. She knows the law. If I know Mrs. Richardson, she'll sue to stop you."

"Mrs. Richardson may take it to court to challenge the eminent domain action by the town," Harold Ethridge said, "but courts tend to side with governments when they are seeking to clean up their environs and close down low-class establishments. In those cases, they usually approve eminent domain. Mrs. Richardson is not very likely to prevail in court if her attempt to block eminent domain is done to preserve a house of prostitution. It's almost a foregone conclusion that she'll lose in any and all courts in the land. The money she once had is all but gone. That's why she turned her house into a bordello."

"What's going to happen to Mrs. Richardson and the girls of the house?" Clarinda said.

"Mrs. Richardson will be paid something for the place," Harold Ethridge said. "The law says you have to give fair market value for property taken in an eminent domain action. But it's a bit hard to establish a fair market value for a whorehouse. But this far from a big city, with the land unsuited to agriculture, the payout will be minimal."

Clarinda's jaw started to tense.

"With her background, maybe she can land a position as a madam in another whorehouse somewhere. Or maybe she can find work as a seamstress. But her future is dim. You should separate yourself from her and the house and head out for greener pastures while you're at the peak of your form."

"What about the girls?" Clarinda said.

"They'll probably move off to different whorehouses," Harold Ethridge said. "If they can't find a house, they'll end up walking the streets, selling it there, or peddling themselves in bars like you did in Two-Bit Charlie's saloon. The lucky ones may get work as cleaning ladies or washerwomen. But they'll have to clean up their own act and bury their pasts to do it. Not a lot of rich or middle-class people have much interest in employing ex-whores under their roofs."

"Those girls are like sisters to me," Clarinda said.

"A sisterhood of whores," Harold Ethridge said.

"They may not be blood sisters, but they're the only sisters I've ever had," Clarinda said, the tension of her anger spreading to all sections of her mind and all quadrants of her body. "Mrs. Richardson and the girls of the house have been good to me," Clarinda said. "You're planning on dumping them out on the streets like they was trash!"

"They are trash!" Harold Ethridge said, the pique he started with growing toward anger of his own. "Street trash. They came from off the streets. They can go back to the streets. They won't be losing a home.

They'll be returning to the home they started out from: the streets. It may not be a joyous homecoming for them, but they'll be back where they started."

"Whatever you and anyone in this town thinks of them, they deserve better than that," Clarinda said. "You can't do that to them."

"No cheap whore, not even an expensive one, tells me what I can or can't do to a cheap whore!" Harold Ethridge snapped. "Or what I have to do for them. Or that I have to respect them in any way. When you go back to your sisterhood house, tell your whore sisters to get out of the house and get out of my way! I don't stoop, bend, or back off for trash. I walk over it."

"I'll stop you!" Clarinda snapped, her anger reaching a high level of intensity.

"Just how do you intend to do that?" Harold Ethridge scoffed.

"I'll tell all the members of the town council that you called them fatheads," Clarinda said. "I tell them that you think they're suckers and you're trying to sucker them. I don't think they'll vote for one idea you'll ever come up with after that. I'll tell that constable man the same thing. I don't know if you're breaking any laws by your idea, but if he starts sniffing around, he may find other things you've been doin' behind the town's back. But that's just where I'll start in on you."

Harold Ethridge stopped talking and stood with his mouth starting to open. He hadn't anticipated that the girl he considered a cheap floozy, easily manipulated, would react the way she was reacting. Things were not going the smooth way he had expected.

"But that's just for openers. I'll rake muck all over you. When you was braggin' on yourself, tryin' to make yourself sound like a real smoother operator, you told me about some stock and bond type deals you were workin' in Columbus the times you went up there. I'm no stockbroker. I can't tell a straight stock deal from a crooked one. But from the way you described them, they sounded shady to me. Maybe the constable can take it to the authorities up there and they can dig in deeper. Who knows what they might come up with."

Harold Ethridge suddenly realized that the girl he had taken as an empty-headed strumpet and had underestimated was a potentially dangerous liability and a threat to him.

"Are you trying to ruin me?" Harold Ethridge seethed. The question alone revealed that he was afraid that she could.

"You're tryin' to ruin the other girls of the house," Clarinda said. "If I have to ruin you to stop you from ruining them, I'll do it in a minute."

For Harold Ethridge, it wasn't just his toes the impudent tart girl was stepping on. It was his world and the place he had forged for himself in the world. It was his position and status in life, as well as his status in the town. It was his view of himself and everything he considered himself to be. He couldn't let all he had achieved and all he was be destroyed by an insolent piece of trash. Something had to give way between him and the girl. And it wasn't going to be his sense of self.

Harold Ethridge grabbed Clarinda's face in his hand, his thumb on one side of her mouth, his fingers on the other side. He gripped her face hard, the force of his grip multiplied and driven exponentially by the force of his swelling anger.

"No cheap tramp bed bouncer mouths off to me like that," he hissed through clenched teeth. "And no two-bit, two-timing slut threatens me and gets away with it. Shut up and stay shut up, or I'll wring your scrawny neck for you. I could kill you in a minute and dump your body where it will never be found. No one in this town outside the Richardson house will know you're gone. No one will miss you. Even if they know you're gone, no one will care."

He had forgotten about Samuel. But he had discounted Samuel from the beginning.

The term *flashback* wouldn't come to be widely use until several decades later. At the feel and pain of Ethridge's grabbing and clamping his hand over her mouth, Clarinda noted that the memory of her brother cinching a belt tight over her mouth in preparation to rape her in the woods next to the mountain shack she had grown up in, the mountain shack she had fled from when the abuse became too great to bear, flooded back into her and washed through her. To Clarinda it felt like Harold was going to force her jaw open and push his gripping fingers inward until they met in the middle of her mouth. With a hard twisting effort, Clarinda pulled her head back and broke out of his grip.

"Get your hands off of me, you filthy pig!" Clarinda shouted from where she stood in the middle of Ethridge's well-appointed bedroom.

Ethridge did not at all like being compared to the animals he raised as livestock and sent off to be butchered in the slaughterhouses of Chicago.

"I'm going to break your neck for that, whore!" Ethridge bellowed. With a one-handed shot, he slapped Clarinda hard across her mouth. Clarinda recoiled at the force of the blow, but she didn't collapse on the floor, and she didn't start crying. With the same hand he had slapped her with, Ethridge reached for her throat. Clarinda didn't know if he was talking metaphorically or literally about breaking her neck, but to her, his fury seemed easily great enough to do what he had threatened to do.

Psychologists call a juncture like the one she was in the "fight-or-flight stage." Given that she was in the middle of Ethridge's bedroom and that he could easily grab her if she were to try to run, flight was not an option.

Driven by her fear and anger to the final depth of the flashback state she was in, Clarinda quickly stepped back from Ethridge. With a quick move, she reached into the pocket of the dress she had put back on and pulled out the long-bladed jackknife she had used to slash her brother's face with when he had tried to rape her the time that had been the last straw for her. With an equally quick move, she jerked the knife in a downward direction and snapped out the blade. A second later she swung the knife at Ethridge, aiming for his throat. Being in his thirties, Harold Ethridge was still a relatively young man with his reflexes still intact. He jerked his head backward, turning it to the side to avoid the knife that was being swung at him.

His defensive move was successful, but only partially. He wasn't able to get full distance. The tip of the thin-bladed knife scribed a slash horizontally across his neck, cutting a shallow slice in the skin. The knife was so thin and sharp that its passage didn't cause any immediate sensation of feeling. The pain would come later.

His reflexes fully aroused, Ethridge rushed the girl. With a quick blow, he struck the knife from her hand. It flew and landed several yards away. Standing in front of her, he threw a savage right cross at her face. The punch landed on Clarinda's jaw. The blow didn't knock her out, but it was hard enough to stun her into immobility. She collapsed onto the floor.

Before she could rally or even react, Ethridge bent down over the fallen girl. Seething with anger at the effrontery of a whore pulling a knife on him, he smashed his fist into her face repeatedly, the force of his blows amplified by his anger. Not satisfied with that, he grabbed her by the neck and pulled her up bodily to where her head was at the level of his chest. From that position, he twisted her head savagely around, almost one hundred eighty degrees. He was gratified by the muffled cracking sounds that told him he had broken her neck. Flashes of light seared through Clarinda's field of vision. Then the room and the world went black. The girl's body went limp as a rag doll.

Certain that he had killed her, Ethridge let the girl's body drop. It landed in a crumpled heap at his feet. Other than a few gurgling sounds that Ethridge took to be her death rattle, the girl showed no sign of movement or indication of life.

Satisfied that she was dead, Harold Ethridge walked quickly to the washroom, where he washed the blood oozing from the shallow gash off his neck, cursing the girl all the while he did so, mindful that an inch or two deeper and it might have severed the jugular vein or the carotid artery.

To staunch and catch any further flood of blood, he wrapped a thin, moist towel around his neck. That having been completed, he went back into the bedroom. The girl's body was lying in the same spot in the same configuration. He was gratified that he had accomplished the killing without creating any flow of blood that would have stained the carpet. On the off chance that the police came to the house asking questions, there would be no telltale stains anywhere to show the girl had ever even been to the house. She was planning on leaving town, looking to find a better bordello. If she went missing, he assumed that anyone familiar with her would think she had left early in search of a more lucrative whorehouse to plant herself down in. That would explain her sudden disappearance. He doubted anyone would miss her anyway.

But if he wished to leave the question of why she had disappeared so suddenly and totally an open-ended one pointing in no direction, her body would have to disappear.

"Okay, bitch," Ethridge said to the motionless figure on his floor. "You said you were planning to leave town. I'm going to help get you on your way and complete the journey you planned, and your passage won't cost either of us a penny."

Ethridge gathered up the limp body and carried it downstairs. At the back entrance to the house, he opened the door and peeked outside. No one was around to see. From there, still carrying the girl's body, he dashed quickly across the open space to the garage and went inside. From there he carried the girl's limp body over to his car, where he encountered his second problem in disposing of her body.

Along with having no roof, the 1912 Stutz Bearcat had no trunk or back seat. The only things behind the driver's seat were the gas tank and the spare tire. There was no closed compartment or convenient place to conceal a body for transport. But it was night, and the roads of the town were deserted.

Inside the garage, Ethridge unceremoniously dumped the body of the girl on the floor of the car and pushed it up against the front seat, leaving his legs and feet enough room to reach the pedals.

Having completed that, he manually opened the garage door, holding it steady, raising it slowly so as not to make too much noise. Then he started up the car and drove out, leaving the garage door open for a quick return.

Harold Ethridge drove the long way around the town, heading for the bridge. He knew that most of the town would be at the potluck supper social. No witness saw his passing in the dark. One person did hear him in his passing, but no one would hear the girl's passing.

In the middle of the bridge over the river that ran beyond the town's northern boundary, he stopped the car, leaving the motor running. There he looked around to see if anyone was in sight. The bridge and the road in both directions were empty. The darkness prevented any vision for more than a few yards either way.

Ethridge quickly gathered up the girl's body again and took it to the guardrail of the bridge. He held the body suspended above the guardrail.

At that moment Clarinda became conscious. She didn't fully remember what had happened. She wasn't sure where she was or how she had gotten there. There was darkness around her. She didn't whether she was alive or dead, but her body didn't seem to be with her.

At that moment Harold Ethridge saw that her eyes were open. Her eyeballs seemed to be moving as if she were looking around.

"I see you're still alive," Ethridge said. "You whores are more durable than I gave you credit for."

Ethridge moved closer to the guardrail. He stood holding the girl's body suspended in the air above the river.

"This river eventually flows through tributaries into the Ohio River," Ethridge said in a contemptuous voice. "The Ohio River flows into the Mississippi River. The Mississippi flows all the way to New Orleans. That's where you were going to take yourself to find the bigger and better whorehouse you were looking for. I'm prepared to facilitate your journey. Just stay in the center of the rivers, stay in the main current of all the rivers along your journey, and eventually you'll find yourself washed up on the levies of New Orleans. There you can be buried with all the other dead whores of the city. They just won't know your name there either."

Actually he expected the body to become waterlogged and sink to its final resting place on the bottom of the river, somewhere off the shore in southern Indiana.

"Bon voyage," Harold Ethridge said.

Without further ado, not wanting to linger in case someone might see, Harold Ethridge let the girl's body fall. The plunge might have been sickening if her body had been intact. But since her spinal cord had been severed, she felt nothing from her head down. She hit the water with a thudding splash. Lights flashed before her eyes again as the impact further twisted her torn spinal cord.

The girl's body sank quickly out of sight beneath the water, in the dark. As soon as she felt the water close over her face, she instinctively clamped her mouth shut and held her breath. Respiration was one part of her body that still functioned. For a moment Clarinda wondered if Ethridge was trying to drown her in his bathtub. Then she realized that she must be in the river. Either way she knew she was under water and was going to die.

The old adage is that when someone is about to die, their life flashes before their eyes. Only two thoughts flashed through Clarinda's mind as she held her breath, settling on the river bottom. One was that she was about to die with her soul unshriven. In that moment she remembered the small backwoods school she had attended as a child in the mountain hollow near her home when her mother had been alive. Her mother had insisted that she receive at least a lower-grade education, at least enough to read and write. She did so often, against the complaints of her husband that book learning wouldn't do the girl any good. He otherwise disparaged book learning, but mostly he had just wanted to keep the girl around home to help do chores.

The school doubled as a Sunday school on Sundays. Her mother had also insisted that she attend Sunday school to learn the Word of the Lord. As she touched bottom, Clarinda remembered the stories of the woman taken in adultery and the woman at the well. Jesus had forgiven them both for their sins. Clarinda knew that there would be no salvation for her in the present world. But salvation waited for her in heaven, provided by the sacrifice of Jesus on the cross. Her father and her brothers never attended church of any kind. As far as unshriven souls were concerned, her father and brothers had no more respect for God than they did for women and sisters.

"Jesus forgive me!" Clarinda cried out in her mind, not able to open her mouth. In that moment, instead of throwing the love and forgiveness of God away, she clung to it with a death grip.

There was a second love that had surrounded her, a love she had thrown away. He had loved her more than any man had, more than she thought any man could love or was capable of loving. Suddenly she wanted that love back, though she knew she would never have it again in life.

"*Samuel!*" she shouted out into the dark water that enveloped her. The word rose as bubbles no one would hear. Water rushed into her lungs, filling them with their dirt, choking off any other words. She went spinning down into the darkness surrounding her.

Chapter 12

It takes only a quick twist of the wrist to break the dried ear of harvest corn off its brown stalk. With a smoothness and economy of motion that bespoke practice and a settling in to the ways of farming, the boy tossed the ear to the side without really looking where it was going. The ear of corn struck the vertical bangboard in the center of the wagon and dropped down into the growing pile of ears of harvested corn. Without breaking stride, the boy moved on to the next stalk of corn, where with the same quick and grooved movement, he broke the ear off and tossed it into the wagon. His father was doing the same on the other side of the wagon. Together they moved at a reasonably fast pace down the rows. Soon they had moved out ahead of the wagon. The boy's father clucked to the horse team pulling the wagon. The horses stirred out of their catatonic stance. They walked forward the distance they knew by instinct their master wanted them to move, and then they stopped and fell back into their torpor.

The boy was a high school classmate of Samuel, only two years behind. Like Samuel, he was on track to become a farmer like his father. As was Samuel, he was fast becoming an experienced hand at sowing, plowing, planting, and harvesting. At that moment in time, his immediate focus was on the row of corn he was harvesting. The only thing that broke the monotony and sameness was that the particular row was the outermost row in the field. While working the outside row, he could at least see the open country beyond and the river that bordered the field.

As they moved down the row, the boy broke his focus on the long row ahead and glanced off to the side toward the river. The bank along the stretch of river that ran past the farm wasn't nearly as high as it was by the Richardson house. Only a low and gentle slope graduated from the field down to the river shore. It was all familiar territory to the boy. He had fished the river from the side of the field before. He had seen it before.

Except this day he saw something he hadn't seen before. That is, in the quickness of his glance, he almost mistook something he had never seen in the river before for a familiar object he had seen many times. A dark-colored object floated near the shore. It had a central trunk with four lighter-colored protrusions coming off it. From his peripheral glance, the boy assumed that it was a tree trunk with bark still on it, with the extending branches that the bark had come off of exposing the lighter-colored sapwood beneath. In that instant of recognition, the boy figured it was the trunk of a dead tree that had drifted down the river and had temporarily run aground on the bank. You see those kind of snags in rivers all the time. The boy gave it no mind. He turned back and reached for the next ear of corn on the next stalk. Just before his hand closed on the ear of corn to break it off, he stopped. It had just registered that something was decidedly different about the wooden snag. Unless that particular snag had managed to pick up a trail of weeds along the way, the particular tree had a head of long flowing hair.

With his hand still in the air, the boy turned back to look at the object in the river. The flowing, floating black streamers weren't elongated willow-type leaves from a leafy branch still attached to the trunk. It looked like long black hair. The dark color of the trunk wasn't bark still adhering to the trunk. It was a dress. What he had first taken for lighter-colored branches stripped of their bark were arms and legs. As his vision focused more, the boy saw fingers at the ends of the arms and the lighter color of a face between the darker color of the dress covering the torso and the long flowing hair coming off the head.

The boy abandoned the corn row and broke into a run toward the riverbank. Stopping where the outer edge of the field started to angle down to the river, he looked again at the figure in the water. The body was floating on its back with the arms and legs at random angles a few feet from the shore, where it had grounded on the shallow mud of the river bottom. The head was turned to the side. The long hair drifted out to one side as if drawn in that direction by the faint current near the shore. As the boy watched he could, see no movement of the silent floating figure.

"Where are you going, boy?" the boy's father called out, wondering what had gotten into his son.

The boy turned and called out to his father, "Dad, there's a woman in the river here! It looks like she's dead."

"You must be seeing a dead deer," the boy's father said skeptically from among the corn rows on the other side of the wagon. "Or a dead dog or something."

"This is the first time I've ever seen a deer wearing a wig and a dress," the boy called back.

There was no immediate verbal response. A few seconds later his father appeared around the back end of the wagon, heading out of the field and toward where the boy was standing. When the father came up alongside his son, he stopped and stared down into the river where his son was pointing. He knew instantly it wasn't a deer.

"O sweet Lord," his father said in a half whisper. Then he broke into a half run down the bank toward the river's edge with his son following.

At the river's edge, the father paused momentarily. The body was lying in shallow water on the river bottom where it had washed up, but it was just touching bottom. The father could tell right away it wasn't a stable position. A rise in the river level could float it away, or a hard wind from off their side of the bank could push it out into the current at the center of the river.

"Grab her other arm," the boy's father said as he splashed into the water. "We've got to get her up on the bank."

The boy followed his father into the water. The water was only a few inches deep, but their feet pushed down into the mud. The boy grabbed the woman's arm at the wrist as his father grabbed her other wrist. The body had passed through the rigor mortis stage and had gone limp. Fortunately for the boy, he didn't end up taking hold of a stiff and rigid limb, but the sensation of touching death was bad enough. The boy cringed at the clammy feel of the dead limb in his hand. The flesh was indeed cold and clammy. There was no warmth or hint of life in the limp, cold arm.

By lifting up on the arms, the father and son raised the upper half of the body out of the river. From that position they dragged the body out of the water and up onto the bank, where it was no longer in danger of washing away. The head rolled to one side, almost twisting all the way around. The face was the same sickly pale white color. As the head hung down, the boy saw water flow out of the open mouth. He quickly looked away, up toward the open sky and out toward the familiar cornfield.

Not knowing what to do next, they paused and looked at the body. For the first time they could see the face fully. The mouth was open. The boy could still see water in the mouth. The eyelids were half open; the eyes beneath were glazed and clouded. There were dark marks on the face that the father took to be the marks of lividity or the beginnings of decay. The cold water of the river had retarded decomposition enough that the body did not have the smell of death.

"Is she dead?" the boy asked. There was still no sign of any movement or life.

"Sure looks that way," the father said. "From the looks of her, I'd say she's been in the river a couple of days."

They looked in silence a few more moments. The girl's age was apparent even through the sickly pale death mask.

"She's about your age," the father said to his son. "Is she someone from your school?"

"I never saw her before," the boy said.

"She may come from somewhere way upriver," the father said. "Who knows how far she may have drifted downstream before she ended up here."

"What do we do with her?" the son asked.

"Well, we can't leave her here for the flies to start in on," the father said. "I'll take her arms. You take her legs. We'll put her behind the seat of the wagon. We'll take her back to the barn. We'll put her in the truck and take her to the police in town. They'll know what to do with her. They can also embalm her in town. She's going to start to go sour real fast out of the cold water in the open air."

The father moved toward the girl's head and motioned to his son to pick up her legs.

"You mean we've got to touch her more?" the son said.

"Don't go squeamish on me now, boy," the father said. "You've seen death before. When your grandmother died, you saw her lying dead in her bed at home."

"But the undertakers came and picked her body up," the boy protested. "I didn't have to carry it."

"She's not about to oblige us by walking to the wagon herself and getting in," the father said. He motioned again for his son to help in the grim task. The son reluctantly moved into position.

"We can't just let her float away down the river," the father said as he took the girl's arms in his. "She's probably someone's daughter or sister or someone's wife. Right now they may be going crazy wondering what happened to her. The police will be able to find out who she is and who her next of kin is. Knowing she's dead will be sad enough for them. But at least they'll know what happened to her and can bury her. I don't know if it will ease their loss very much, but at least they'll have her grave to mourn over."

With little relish for the task, the boy did as his father asked and took the girl by the legs, which were as wet and clammy as her arm had been. But there were two legs, and the boy had to wrap his arms around both of them. Together he and his father hoisted the girl in the air and carried her like hunters would carry a deer they had killed. Before the body came off the ground, from his forward-looking position, the boy was looking the girl's face. He didn't particularly want to look into the sallow dead face again. He would have bad dreams about it for weeks after.

At the wagon, they wrestled the body into the narrow space behind the driver's seat. When they had the body halfway into the wagon, the father climbed in to pull the body the rest of the way in. The boy helped by raising up the dead girl's legs so that they could move her body the rest of the way into the wagon. But this only brought the girl's legs up to the level of the boy's shoulders, closer to his face than ever. He turned his head away and worked by feel as he helped load the body the rest of the way. He felt a bit queasy, worried he might get sick.

The father turned the horse and wagon around and started back toward the farmhouse and the barn. All the way back to the barn, the boy could feel the girl's lifeless body pressing against his back as it shifted and tried to roll forward with the motion of the wagon. The wetness of the girl's dress had soaked through their shirts. The teenage boy was old and mature enough to have had thoughts about being alone in the back of a wagon with a girl his age. This was definitely not the way he had imagined it, and it certainly didn't wish to repeat the experience.

As was the usual routine for a usual day, Sergeant Plechathy was sitting officially at the front desk of the station house, trying to look busy. Chief Constable Harkness was in his office catching up on some paperwork. The other two officers on duty were out walking their see-and-be-seen foot patrol beats. The routine was as grooved and worn in as the wear pattern of the old wood just inside the front door, on the threshold, where all traffic entering and leaving over the years had been concentrated.

As the door opened, Sergeant Plechathy looked up to see a man dressed in farmer overalls come in. In an unneeded gesture of deference to the enforcers of the law, the man held his hat in his hand. He walked up to the desk.

"What can I do for you?" Sergeant Plechathy asked before the man spoke. He was giving his own deference to a citizen whom the law was there to serve and protect. As for what the man wanted, given that he was a farmer, Sergeant Plechathy assumed he was probably there to complain about boys stealing melons out of his melon patch or to ask them to keep an eye out for a mule that had gotten away. It was a pedestrian day, and the sergeant expected another pedestrian complaint.

"My son and I found the body of a young woman in the river," the farmer said, still holding his hat in his hand. "We brought it in to you figuring you would know how to go about finding out who she is."

The sergeant's look of surprise turned to a frown. Bodies turning up at random times and locations was an everyday happening in other parts of the country at the time, but in this small Ohio town, it wasn't the pedestrian occurrence the sergeant had expected to hear about. He got up from his chair and came around the desk.

"Where is this body?" he asked.

"I have her outside in my truck," the farmer said.

The sergeant started to head to the police chief's office. Constable Harkness met him coming out of the door of his office.

"I heard," the constable said. Then he turned to face the farmer. "Take us to the body if you please, sir."

The farmer led the two minions of town law outside, to where his truck was parked across the street. Like the Martin family, the farmer also owned a truck, but he didn't own a Ford Model T. He owned a 1909 Haynes. The man's son was standing by the truck.

The farmer pointed to the bed of the truck. In it, a figure lay covered by a blanket that had been pulled up over the head and face. Shoeless human feet protruded out from under the blanket. As the four gathered around the truck, the farmer pulled the blanket back to reveal the girl's blanched white face. Constable Harkness moved closer to the girl's head to get a better look at her face.

"My son and I found her washed up on the bank of the river by my field when we were out harvesting," the father said. "We didn't just want to leave her there, so we brought her to you."

"I don't recognize her," Constable Harkness said, looking at the face intently. He turned to look at the farmer. "Do you know her?" he asked. "Is she someone from your area?"

"I've never seen her before," the farmer said. "From the looks of her, she's been in the water for some time. For all I know, she could have drifted on the current from the other side of the state."

They all looked back at the unidentified face. It was starting to look like they had a real mystery on their hands, complete with a real mystery woman. Sergeant Plechathy leaned in to take a closer look.

"I recognize her," the sergeant said unexpectedly. The other three turned from viewing the body and looked up at him. "She's one of Mrs. Richardson's girls. She's the one the Martin boy got into the fight over." The sergeant pointed off toward the edge of town. "She lives in the Richardson house not more than half a mile from here."

"Then she's someone's daughter like I was afraid," the farmer said. "At least she didn't float so far away that her body would never be found and returned home to her parents. There's going to be some real sadness in the house though. She looks so young."

"She may be a daughter of the house, but she's not a family relative of anyone in the house," Constable Harkness said. "Though she does maintain quite a number of relationships there, so to speak."

The constable continued to study the face of the dead girl.

"She was probably walking along the bank and lost her footing and tumbled into the river," the farmer said.

"I don't think she slipped on mud and took a header," the constable said. "This doesn't look like a violation of the law of gravity. From the marks on her face, it's starting to look to me like her death may be in violation of human law."

"She's the one I arrested along with the Martin boy about a month ago, the night he got into a fight over her in Charlie's saloon," Sergeant Plechathy said to the constable. He wasn't sure what the constable had meant by the girl's death being in violation of the law. The constable was still looking at the girl's face. The sergeant turned to look at the farmer.

"Whoever's daughter she originally was, she was an active prostitute at the Richardson house," the sergeant went on. "So I wouldn't worry about there being a lot of crying and family mourning for a lost loved one going on in the house. All they're going to be mourning is the passing of a money earner. Her being a prostitute is probably the biggest part of what contributed to her death. Prostitutes are loose living all around. She probably got drunk and fell into the river and drowned."

"I beg to differ with you," the constable said. While still looking at the girl's face, he pointed to the dark marks he saw there. "Look at the bruising and lacerations on her face. They weren't caused by a drunken stumble. She's been beaten." The constable pointed to a circular bruise that ran around her neck just below the jawline. "Looks like she's been strangled too. She may have filled up with water after she was thrown in, but she was strangled first. It wasn't an eel wrapping around her neck that made those marks. Those were made by human hands. Strong hands. A man's hands."

The constable looked up at the others. "It looks to me like we've got ourselves a homicide on our hands here."

It was turning out to be something other than a small-town pedestrian day all around.

"Maybe she fell headfirst and landed on rocks," Sergeant Plechathy said, offering an alternative theory. "That could account for both the bruises and the broken neck. She may have fallen from the bridge. That could be why she did so much damage to herself."

"There aren't that many rocks in the river," Constable Harkness said. "And the ones that are there are worn smooth and rounded." He pointed to the bruising and the cuts on the girl's face again. "It would take sharp-edged rocks to make cuts like these. And the cuts themselves aren't that big. A fall from a height as high as the bridge onto sharp rocks would have left bigger gashes than these, and there aren't any sharp-edged rocks around the base of the bridge or anywhere nearby in the river."

He looked back at the marks on the girl's face.

"In my life, I've seen plenty of bruises left from fistfights. The size and shape of the bruises on this girl's face look like those left by fists, not rocks." The constable looked at the sergeant. "We saw the same kind of bruises on the face of the man the Martin boy beat up in his fight over this very girl." He pointed again to the cuts intermingled in the bruises. "The difference is these cuts. They weren't on the face of the man the Martin boy beat. They look like they were made by something the attacker had in his hand or was wearing on his hand—brass knuckles or a big ring."

The sergeant didn't dispute the constable's observations and hypothesis. After all, he was the chief of police, such as the police were in the town. The farmer figured the chief of police must know what he was talking about.

"Prostitutes do run with a rough crowd," the sergeant said.

For the next moment the four of them looked at the face of the murdered girl. The moment hung motionless in the air.

"Well, if it was murder, we're not going to solve it from the back of a truck," Constable Harkness said. "We need a full medical exam to start with, and we can't do that out here. Let's get her inside. We can put her on the table in the back room. The doc can do a preliminary exam there. If he wants to do an actual autopsy, we can have the body taken from there to his office or the funeral home."

He made a circular motion with his hand, indicating for them to spread themselves out around the body.

"All of us will grab a limb, and we'll carry her inside. Take the blanket with her. We need something to cover the body." Constable Harkness looked at the farmer. "I'll have it returned to you when we're done with it."

"We got to touch her more?" the boy said.

"Just this one last time," the father said. "Don't go getting squeamish on me again. Not in front of others."

"There's a sink inside," Constable Harkness said as he took one of the girl's limp arms. "You can wash your hands afterward if you're afraid of catching the plague."

The four of them lifted the girl and carried her across the street and into the station house. The four men carrying the sagging body made for an odd-looking procession as they crossed the street. But there were few people in the street at the time to observe their passage.

Inside the station house, they carried the body into the back room and laid it on the wooden table. Having completed that, Constable Harkness turned to the sergeant.

"The first thing I want you to do is go over to Doc Simpson's office and have him come over here when he gets the free time. We'll have him examine the body," Constable Harkness said in an official voice. "After that, he'll have to take her to his office and embalm her. He's the only one in town who knows how to embalm, and she's going to get ripe real fast in the heat of the stuffy basement."

He looked at the other policemen.

"I want one of you to go over to Mrs. Richardson's and bring her back here to identify the body. After that, I'm going to have you round up Arthur and Hanley and go over to the Martin farm and bring in the Martin boy for questioning. If you can't find him, leave word for him to come in on his own."

"Why do you want to talk to the Martin boy?" Sergeant Plechathy asked.

"He was the one who got into a fight over her," the constable said. "Men who beat up other men who are having their girlfriends behind their backs often end up beating their girlfriends who are fooling around behind their backs. We know the boy got violent over her. Maybe he finally got violent with her. She's had violence done to her, and he's the only trail of violence connected to the girl."

The constable turned to the farmer and his son.

"I may want to come out to your farm and view the spot where you found her. There may be a clue to be found there. But I doubt that will

produce much of anything. She was most likely killed elsewhere and her body thrown into the river. The actual scene of the killing was somewhere else. I doubt we're going to be able to trace from where the body was found back to the actual site of the crime."

"Are you through with us then?" the farmer asked. "We've got to get back to harvesting." The father looked at his son. "Provided he doesn't find a whole 'nother string of bodies to be brought in."

"If I see any more bodies in the river, I won't say anything," the farm boy said. "I'll keep my mouth shut and let them drift on down to the next town. They can handle them there. Least I won't have to."

Soon enough Samuel Martin would stand in the same room and accuse the whole town of wanting to keep their mouths shut about the killing of the girl.

Constable Harkness nodded that the farmers could go.

Before they went, the father and son did in fact use the washbasin to wash their hands. After them, the constable and the sergeant used the sink to wash their hands. Soon enough, Samuel Martin would be standing in the same station house next to the girl's body, accusing all there of washing their hands of her death.

"Must the fact that she was a prostitute in life follow her in death?" Mrs. Richardson snapped at the duly designated administer of the law. "She was what she was because life didn't leave her a lot of choice in the matter. I don't care what you think of any of us. Any loss of revenue on my part is the last thing I'm here with on my mind. She's lost everything. I've lost someone whom I had come to think of as the daughter I never had. So I'll thank you to keep your snide comments that I've lost my biggest money earner to yourself, sir. The crudity of your remarks isn't doing anything for her, and your remarks are not doing anything to apprehend the man you say murdered her. Or do you intend to just write her off as a hussy and shovel her under the sod with no thought to giving her the benefit of either your words or the benefit of the law and justice?"

Constable Harkness didn't care if Mrs. Richardson was a sassy and impudent bordello madam being disrespectful toward the law. Offenses to one's petty pride have been known to lead to murder, but the murder of a young girl had placed the constable beyond any offense done to his petty pride by an uppity woman. He wasn't about to arrest Mrs. Richardson for being uppity with him. Neither was he about to arrest her for being angry and gnashing because one of her charges had been killed on her watch. Neither was he about to be convinced of the woman's cloying sentimental story of having loved the girl like a daughter. He still rather assumed that the woman's interest in the girl had been more commercial than quasi familial. The exact nature of the love the woman had for the girl was irrelevant. The girl was beyond the reach of the law and any kind of love now.

"If she was so much like a daughter to you, why didn't you report her missing as soon as you discovered her absence?" Constable Harkness snapped back. "You said she didn't return to the house Wednesday night. Her body was found today, Saturday. That's close to three full days, but you hadn't said anything to us about her being missing. Any other parents would be frantic with worry when their child didn't return home after dark and was still missing the next day. The first thing they would do would be to run to the police. But you remained silent the whole time. That's not showing much concern for someone you claim to think of as a daughter."

Looking on the spectral white death mask of the girl's pale and battered forlorn face made Mrs. Richardson bold to speak. "Sometimes men who patronize prostitutes will ask them to spend the whole night with them," she said. "It's as if they're fantasizing that they're married to them. They're willing to pay extra for that. At first I thought that might have been what had happened, that the man she had been seeing in town had asked her to spend the whole night with him. When she still hadn't come home by Friday morning, I started to get worried."

"But even then you didn't contact us," Constable Harkness said. "We didn't know she was dead or even missing until a farmer brought her body in to us. If she had drifted all the way to the Mississippi, or if she had sunk out of sight in the river and disappeared altogether, would you have ever informed us that she was gone at all? Or were you just as ready to write her off and forget her because she was a whore as much as you're accusing me of being willing to do?"

"And if I had come to you and told you she was missing, would you have dropped everything and started a house-to-house search for a missing whore?" Mrs. Richardson spit back. "Would you have stirred yourselves from anything you were doing to look for her, or would you have just dismissed her as a two-bit slut not worthy of your time?"

"Would you have ever come to us?" Constable Harkness asked.

"I can't really say," Mrs. Richardson said in an otherwise defiant voice. "I'm not sure what I would have eventually done if she had remained missing. But at the time, telling you about it wasn't the first thing on my mind. Whether you would have given us anything resembling satisfaction, whether you would have given us as much as the time of day, is an open question. I still suspect you would have dismissed her, me, and all of us as being beneath your concern or undeserving of your involvement."

"You might have given me the benefit of the doubt by coming to us when she disappeared," Constable Harkness said. "It seems to me it would have been the least you could do for someone whom you claim to have thought of as a daughter."

Mrs. Richardson stiffened inside. Her teeth clenched inside her unmoving jaw. The constable's insinuations that she was thinking of the girl only as a revenue source and that she had failed to treat the girl like a daughter by not reporting her as missing stung Mrs. Richardson harder than his policeman's opinion of ladies of the evening. The sting of his comment was magnified in Mrs. Richardson's mind by the thought that she had failed the girl in that and other ways. In her passing, Clarinda would leave more than one person feeling they had failed her.

The constable glanced over at the girl quickly and then back to Mrs. Richardson.

"But given the type of men she was keeping time with and running with, she was probably dead and in the river before you knew she was missing. She had most likely been killed before the night was out. Even if you had informed us the next day, it would have probably been after the fact, when she was already dead. So in the end I guess it's all a moot point."

"And just how moot of a point do you intend to make of the case, and how moot do you intend to leave her?" Mrs. Richardson asked in a voice not snappish but with a sharper cutting edge. "Do you have any intention of trying to find the man you say killed her? Given that he was probably a rich man, do you even have any interest in going after the man who killed her?"

"I don't like murder in my town," Constable Harkness growled the proverbial sheriff's line in an official-sounding voice. "Whatever side of town the dead come from. So keep your street woman class-consciousness to yourself. I don't have time for it. I have a killer to catch."

"You mean to tell me that you actually intend to go after her killer?" Mrs. Richardson said in a voice as heavily loaded with skepticism as it was with grief and anger. "You're going to stand there over her body and tell me that you would drag a rich man into court for the murder of a cheap little tramp?"

"If I thought of her as nothing more than a dead alley cat the way you say I do, I would have had the farmer put her body back in the river," Constable Harkness said. "Leave the investigation to me, and spare me your muckraking. You're no closer to Ida Tarbell than I am to Teddy Roosevelt."

Mrs. Richardson pointed hard to the girl's body lying on the table. "All right then, Mr. Investigator," she said in a hard and explosive voice, "tell me who killed her!"

"That's what I brought you here to possibly help tell me," Constable Harkness said. "You knew her. As the madam of the house, you knew her activities. You knew where she was going. Other than the killer, you may have been the last one to see her alive. If anyone would have any direct or indirect relevant information, it's you. I didn't call you here just to identify the body. Sergeant Plechathy already did that. And I didn't call you here so I could gloat in your face that one of your strumpets is dead. I want to know what, if anything, you can provide that might give us a clue as to who her killer is."

"All I can tell you is what I've already told you," Mrs. Richardson answered. "For the last month she was seeing someone in town. She didn't give me his name. She said he wanted his name kept quiet, even inside the house."

"You didn't find that unusual?" Constable Harkness asked.

"It's not all that unheard of for a man in a high position in society to patronize a prostitute. It's not that unusual for him to want to keep his name free from the scandal that would be caused if people found out he was doing it. But it's usually higher-up men who try to keep their names quiet. Hired hands and street men don't go through the trouble. She didn't say where she was meeting her mystery man, but one time she did let me know that she was meeting him at his house. She wasn't lying herself down in an alley with a blacksmith or garage mechanic or between lumber piles with a lumberyard worker. I assume she went to his house the other times. Though she didn't describe the house in exact words, she made it sound like a fancy house. Fancy houses are owned by rich men. At the time I assumed the man she was seeing was a rich and fancy man. I still do. She was on her way out to see her fancy man the night she didn't come back. I can't help you by giving you his name because she didn't give me his name. She wasn't big on names at all. She never even gave me her real name. I say find the man she was seeing and you'll find the man who killed her."

"She may very well have been seeing someone in town," Constable Harkness said. "But I'm also working on the assumption that she might have been on her way in to see the man she was seeing or was on her way back when she was grabbed and accosted by an unrelated man. Her attacker was probably a rough man like a hired hand or a laborer, one of the rougher breeds of men she was servicing. He killed her and then threw her body into the river. Rough and hard men do things like that routinely."

"That doesn't make much sense," Mrs. Richardson said.

Constable Harkness was starting to get a bit griped. First the woman had lectured him on his class-consciousness, and now she was criticizing his investigative techniques and assumptions. Constable Harkness didn't consider all women to be ipso facto stupid and empty-headed, but however nuanced his period views of the limitations of the mental abilities of women were, he didn't have as high an opinion of whorehouse madams as he did police inspectors.

"At least not the part about a man on foot throwing her in the river. If a man intercepted her in town and killed her in the shadows, I doubt he would have thrown her body over his shoulder afterward and carried her on foot halfway through town, all the way to the river, and thrown her in. He would have left the body where he had killed her. But if the killer had killed her in his house, he would want to get the body out of the house and leave it somewhere else. A man rich enough to own a house would probably own a car or a buggy. He could have loaded her body in it and driven through the town at night with the body out of sight and thrown it into the river somewhere he thought he wasn't being seen. A street thug would have left her body in the street or an alley."

Constable Harkness had to admit that she had a bit of a point there.

"The killer may have been lurking around your house," Constable Harkness countered. "He may have grabbed her and killed her in the dark, out of sight of anyone in the house but within sight of the house from outside. After that he may have dragged her body the short distance to the river and put her in."

The constable made a mental note to have the uniformed policemen look for drag marks through the grass heading for the river near the house.

"I think you should leave the investigative work to the police," he said in a semipatronizing tone. "For the moment, I just want you to keep your ears open. If you or any of your girls hear anything from their clients that sounds like it might have a bearing on the case, I want you to bring it to me."

Before Mrs. Richardson could respond, he shifted gears to the only suspect he had. "As far as men prone to violence goes, the only man directly associated with both the girl and violence is the Martin boy. He got into a saloon fight with another man over the girl because the other man was trying to pick her up for her usual purposes. The Martin boy might have possibly decided that he had had enough of the purposes she was performing behind his back and decided to end her purposes and end her cheating once and for all. Jealous men have been known to do things like that to women they have come to consider their own. The Martin boy knew where she lived. He had an idea of her schedule. He could have guessed at her approximate time of leaving or return. He might have been waiting for her return in the dark outside the house. He could have beaten her silent and broken her neck without anyone in the house hearing."

To the constable it seemed to be the thread that tied it all together. In the next second, when he pulled the string, it became the thread that caused everything to unravel.

The boy had been in town the night the girl had disappeared. He had been at the potluck supper at the high school Wednesday night, the night the girl didn't return. The high school was on the other side of the town from the Richardson house. But it still placed him in proximity to where the crime had been committed, at least as far as being in town went. At the same time, Constable Harkness realized that it placed him in the presence of dozens of witnesses who had seen him there the whole time, himself included. He had seen the boy there with his parents and sister. He had spoken to him in an attempt to ascertain whether he was keeping his nose clean. The boy's presence in town the night the girl went missing held out the theoretical possibility that he had slipped out of the party, killed the girl, dumped her body, then slipped back in, his absence unobserved. As an element of opportunity, the boy's being in town worked. As an element of timing, it was almost impossible to make it work.

The constable's thoughts trailed off into a blank open space and into silence.

"I've never seen the Martin boy become violent with her once," Mrs. Richardson said, throwing in the first of her own set of complications. "He may have punched out the man in the bar who was trying to procure her, but he never struck her, and she never claimed that he did. Besides, she had gotten pretty mad at him for starting the fight for which your sergeant arrested both her and him. She had put him under restriction and forbade him to come and see her for a month. Last I saw, he was respecting her wishes. He hadn't been around the house for the whole month. I really don't think he was spending the time plotting to jump out of the dark and kill her a few short days before her restraining period was over."

Constable Harkness mumbled something. He was still trying to sort out in his mind whether the boy's being at the potluck supper the night the girl was probably murdered spelled the beginning or the end of the boy as a suspect.

In the constable's silence, Mrs. Richardson looked at the girl's body. Then she looked back at the duly designated officer of the law. "What are you going to do with the body?" she asked.

"Doctor Simpson is going to examine the body," Constable Harkness said in a distracted tone, still trying to determine if his theory of Samuel Martin as the killer of the girl still stood.

"Doctor Simpson's already examined her," Mrs. Richardson said. "He was the one who said that she was so badly torn up in her female parts that she would probably never have children. I took her into see him after she first came to the house with her legs all battered up. Now he gets to see her again, this time with her face all battered up and her neck broken. She's dead. Isn't it a little late for medical examinations?"

"The examination is to determine cause of death," Constable Harkness said. "Hopefully it will give us a clearer picture of how she died and the time of her death. That may help provide a clue as to who her killer was."

A less than visually, as well as less than conceptually, pleasant thought came into Mrs. Richardson's mind. "Is he going to do an autopsy on her?" she asked. She had a picture of the girl being disassembled piece by piece like a butcher taking apart a steer. "She was chopped apart by life. Her face was chopped and disfigured by whoever killed her. Must she be chopped apart in death too?"

"That's up to the doc," Constable Harkness said. "I don't know what he'll want to do. Don't you want to learn more about how she died?"

"Not if it means getting her back in pieces or gutted like a fish," Mrs. Richardson said. "Knowing in gory detail how she died won't change anything, and I doubt it will give us the name of the killer."

"I'll pass on your thoughts to the doc," Constable Harkness said. "An autopsy may not be necessary. Right offhand, you can pretty much say what was done to her just by looking at her. Maybe he can leave it there without having to dig any deeper."

They both stood in silence for a moment.

"After the doc's finished doing his examination, whom do I release the body to?" Constable Harkness asked. "Did she have any next of kin?"

"All I know is that she claimed to come from somewhere in West Virginia," Mrs. Richardson said. "From mountain folk stock, I gathered. Her family treated her frightfully mean and cruel. That's why she ran away. She refused to talk about them beyond that. She never gave me her family name. She never would even give me her first name. I guess she was just either so ashamed or so angry, or both, that she didn't to want to speak her family's name again. She didn't even want her real first name spoken. She went by her made-up name. Now she's dead, and I'll never know what her real name was. I have even less of an idea what her last name was. But I have the distinct impression that she wouldn't want to be released back to her family, even in death."

"Then I guess she'll go to the township," Constable Harkness said by default.

The killer had had his way with the girl. He had given her no consideration in life. Mrs. Richardson figured that if the town had its way with her, they would bury her with all the dignity and consideration they would give a dead stray dog. They'd probably just give her a small stone with nothing on it at all to mark her grave in the back corner of the cemetery. For all anyone whoever glanced at the stone would know, it could be the row's end marker or the grave of a dead cat. People wouldn't even know for sure if there was a human being under the stone, let alone know her name.

Mrs. Richardson looked at Constable Harkness. "When you're done, release her body to me," she said in a definite summing-up voice. "We were the closest thing she had to a family. In the end we were probably more of a family to her than her birth family ever was. I'll pay for her burial."

Constable Harkness nodded his head. "As you wish, ma'am," he said. It seemed the best solution all around. Constable Harkness rather suspected that if the town buried the girl, they would accord her less honor than they would a dead firehorse.

Both Constable Harkness and Mrs. Richardson looked over at the body of the girl on the table. For the girl it was over and done. Whatever the girl's story had been, her story in this world had come to an end. Wherever she had come from, wherever she might have gone, she had come to them from somewhere over the horizon out of their sight. Her journey through this world had ceased within their sight. It was proverbial enough to say, but she had come to them as a solitary wanderer without a name. She had passed from them as a wanderer, receding from sight still without a name. She would be buried under no other name than that of a wanderer.

"Is that all you need from me?" Mrs. Richardson asked, turning back to face the constable.

"For the moment," Constable Harkness said. The case was still as open as it had been when she had come into the station house. The killer was still unknown. But for the time being the meeting was over. As far as crime detection and solving went, there was nothing more the woman or the women of her house could provide. The girl had come to her final end. Constable Harkness saw no reason to drag the meeting out past the natural end it had come to.

"If you happen to remember anything or hear anything that sounds like it might have a bearing on the case, let me know."

Mrs. Richardson turned and started to walk out of the room. "Like I said," she remarked as she cleared the doorway, "find the man she was seeing, and you'll find the killer."

Constable Harkness didn't respond. In the space of the meeting, he had developed a bit of respect for the woman. But he still didn't think any more highly of her as a detective.

"I'll have one of my men drive you back to the house," Constable Harkness said to Mrs. Richardson's back as he stepped out of the back room after her.

"Don't bother," Mrs. Richardson said. "I'll walk. I have to stop at the funeral home and make arrangements anyway. When you're done here, call the funeral home and have them pick her up. We'll take it from there. The town won't have to pay anything."

Mrs. Richardson had no reason to prolong the meeting. There was nothing more she could provide and nothing more she wanted to say. She still had doubts, serious doubts, about how far the police chief would take the investigation. She had equally serious doubts about how much desire he had to take the investigation anywhere. But she saw no reason to stand and argue any point with the constable any longer. Mrs. Richardson figured the police probably figured the girl had gotten what she deserved because she had left herself to lie in the beds she had lain in. She had little choice but to leave justice for the girl where it lay: with the police.

Mrs. Richardson walked out through the front door of the station house and down the steps. The fall day was still bright. But the girl would see no more days on earth. Soon she would lie in the unchanging twilight world of the grave. Whatever definition of life and love one applied to the girl, whatever love she had nominally achieved for herself, her life had ended cut off and unfulfilled. Whether justice for the girl would be accomplished, Mrs. Richardson didn't know, but she had her suspicions that justice for the girl would buried as deep and unfulfilled as her murdered body would be. Whether anyone beyond her and a handful of others would ever know the girl's story was something else Mrs. Richardson couldn't tell. She rather figured that the girl's story would come to an empty and unknown end in the cemetery, where the girl's wandering would also come to its final end.

"The last time I saw his girl, she was alive and kicking," Doctor Simpson said, looking up from the blanched face of the now dead girl. "At least she was kicking as far as the damage to her legs would let her. She had severe contusions and lacerations to her knees and legs."

"Mrs. Richardson said that she had taken her to see you soon after she had come to the house," Constable Harkness said.

"At the time the main thing she was suffering from was mostly was malnutrition," the doctor went on. "The damage to her legs was painful but largely superficial. The present damage to her face is also largely superficial, but the trauma to her neck is deep and catastrophic."

"Was it the cause of death? And was it accidental, or was it intentionally inflicted?" the constable said, getting down to the critical peace officer question.

"Well, you've got most of it right," Doctor Simpson said of the constable's forensic exam done on the fly out of the back of the farmer's truck. "Her neck appears to have been subjected to an extreme and violent twisting motion far in excess of the normal range of flexibility. It looks to have been turned around almost one hundred eighty degrees."

The doctor ran his fingers behind the silent and inert girl's neck.

"From the dislocation I can feel, she seems to have suffered a twisting fracture in the area of the second and third cervical vertebrae. The extreme twisting of the neck bones would have stretched and torn the spinal cord by itself. The fracturing of the bones could have produced sharp edges that could have cut the spinal cord. I can't be entirely sure by performing a visual examination. If you want more exact information on the extent and the precise dimensions of the damage, that will require a detailed autopsy."

"But without opening her up, you can say that the cause of death was a broken neck?" Constable Harkness asked.

The only police chief of the town and the only doctor of the town stood on opposite sides of the table. The girl lay on the table as still as when she had been put there. The doctor had pulled down her dress to examine the body for other signs of violence. Mercifully for onlookers, he had closed her eyes. At least in that one small symbolic way, her modesty had been preserved. Whether the girl appreciated the gesture was unknown. She was well past the modesty stage. But then again, she had lived her professional life beyond the bounds of being modest in terms of men seeing her with her clothes removed.

"I would say that her broken neck was the prime contributing cause of death," the doctor said in a medically equivocated voice, "and a rotational break like this wasn't caused by a fall. If she had fallen vertically and struck her head, there would be signs of trauma to the head. There aren't any signs of damage even to the skin of the cranium. She would have been left totally paralyzed by the severing of her spinal cord. She would have eventually died from complications of that."

The doctor waved his hand over the girl's neck and pointed to the bruises and cuts on her face. "However, neither the fracturing of her neck nor the blows to her head were the immediate cause of death."

Constable Harkness looked at the ghostly white body of the girl. He could see no other marks on her body. "What else is there?" he asked.

"From what I can see down her throat, her chest seems to be filled with water," Dr. Simpson answered. "Without a formal autopsy, I won't know if there is water in her lungs, but from what I can see, there probably is. The immediate cause of death was drowning. She may have been paralyzed, but she was still alive when the killer threw her into the water."

"Thoughtful bastard," Constable Harkness growled.

For a moment the constable looked again at the body. Then he pointed to the girl's face. "What do you make of the marks on her face?" he asked.

"I'd agree with you," the doctor said. "It looks like she was beaten. I would say it looks like the killer first beat her unconscious and then proceeded to twist her neck. There wouldn't be any need to beat her after he had broken her neck. She would have been incapable of resistance or movement from that moment on."

"Then in your medical opinion, would you say for the record that this was a homicide?" Chief Constable Harkness asked in a formal voice, looking for a formal opinion.

"From what I can see, I would say that all the elements point to deliberate killing," the doctor said. "I can't tell you whether it was premeditated or was something that happened on the spur of the moment. Death by beating is not generally something done in a premeditated manner. It usually arises out of spontaneous heat-of-the-moment passions, and it involves the use of the hands. Premeditated murder generally involves some form of weapon. There are cuts on her face associated closely with the bruises. That may point to the use of some kind of weapon, but if it was a weapon, it was a small one."

The constable looked at the bruises on the girl's face again. "What can you tell me about these cuts on her face?" he asked.

"As you can see, the cuts aren't peripheral," the doctor said. "They're centered in the bruises. That would tend to indicate a smaller weapon. Your speculation that it was something the killer was wearing on his fingers makes as much sense as anything. Like you said, they could have been made by brass knuckles or a large ring. If not that, they might have been made by some kind of tool or implement." The doctor pointed to the cuts on the girl's face. "If you look closely, you can see that they left a rather distinctive pattern, sort of a hexagonal shape."

The constable looked closer. Some of the cuts did have a straight line shape that took angular turns on either end as if a small and hard item with sharp edges and a definite angular shape had been driven into the girl's face at a downward angle.

The doctor pointed to a spot on the girl's lower left jaw. "You can see the pattern better here."

The constable had to walk around to the side of the table the doctor was on in order to get a better view. He looked at the spot the doctor was pointing to. At the tip of his pointing finger, there was a uniquely shaped mark driven into the skin of the girl's jaw by the force of the blow. If the girl had lived, the mark would have eventually healed up and closed over. Death had stopped the healing process, leaving the mark imprinted in the flesh of her face.

The pattern was of a three-sided box with sides that came off the ends at forty-five-degree angles. The sides appeared to be bending back at the same angle. But that was where the bottom of the jaw turned under. If the lower part of the pattern were to be carried out the same as the upper part, it would form a hexagon with the two center sides a bit longer than the end angles. The pattern sat at a partially turned-back angle to the girl's jaw. Inside the outline, centered in the pattern but disconnected from the surrounding sides, he could see what looked like an inverted *V* with the open ends pointing downward and forward at an angle. The *V* was at a perpendicular angle to the long side of the hexagonal box.

"What do you make of it?" the constable asked.

"Like the other marks, the killer appears to have hit her with something small and hard," Dr. Simpson answered. "From the position at the center of the bruises, it may have been something on the killer's finger. Your theory that he was wearing brass knuckles is plausible. That could account for the shape of the cut."

"If it was a pair of brass knuckles, I don't know what the center mark is supposed to be," Constable Harkness commented. "It almost looks like an initial. I've seen brass knuckles, but I've never seen brass knuckles that were monogrammed."

"It and the bruises themselves could have been made by the butt end or the extension of some kind of tool. If it was a tool and you find it, you might be able to identify the tool from the pattern embossed in it."

The constable stood back up.

"If it was brass knuckles or a tool of some kind, that points to a hired hand or a laborer … or a farmer if it was a common farm implement."

And that pointed back to the Martin boy. But as far bare-knuckled men who might be inclined to use brass knuckles to reinforce the power of their bare knuckles went, it also pointed to half the girl's clientele. The sergeant was right: whores do tend to run with a less than refined and genteel crowd.

The doctor pointed to a vertical extension of the bruise on the girl's jaw running perpendicular to the mark at the base of the jaw.

"Whoever he was, and whatever he hit her with, it looks like he hit her hard enough to break her jaw," the doctor said. "From the pattern of this bruise, it looks like she has a hairline fracture at the point of impact."

"To the best of your ability, can you pinpoint the time of death for me?" Constable Harkness asked, getting down to what could be the critical piece of information where murder and suspects entered into consideration.

"Not down to the hour," the doctor said. "But from the condition of the body, it looks like she's been in the water for two days. The cold water kept her from bloating."

Constable Harkness looked off toward the wall of the room, not looking in any particular direction. "From what Mrs. Richardson said, she went out and didn't return to the house this Wednesday night," the constable mused to himself as much as for the doctor's benefit. "She was missing Thursday and Friday. She's found today, Saturday morning." He looked back at the doctor. "There are your two days. If she didn't come home Wednesday night and she's been dead for a full two days, that would mean she was killed that night."

"Does that narrow it down for you?" Dr. Simpson asked.

"Actually it blows things wide open," the constable said. "It more or less tosses my first suspect out of the window. Now I'm left with a whole field of suspects, none of them for whom I have a name to go with the face. It doesn't narrow anything down. It just opens things up and leaves it less clear than before."

"Do you want me to perform a full autopsy on her?" the doctor asked, offering the only medical solution he could.

The constable looked at the girl's body and battered face. "No," he said. "She's been taken apart enough. I doubt a formal autopsy is going to tell us anything we don't already know about what killed her, and it's not going to give us the name of the killer. Let's just let her rest in peace. It may be the first time in her adult life that she's been able to get any rest lying on her back."

"Is there anything more you want me to do here?" Doctor Simpson asked.

"You can start by re-dressing her," the constable said. "Granted that she made her living out of her dress. But I think we can afford her at least a bit of dignity in death. After that I'll have you fill out the official death certificate. Beyond that, we're pretty much finished here. … Mrs. Richardson said she's going to have her buried. When you're finished dressing her, I'll tell the funeral home to come and pick up the body."

"What name should I use on the death certificate?" the semiofficial town coroner asked. The official chief constable had to think about that one.

"Good question," Constable Harkness said. "Nobody seems to know her real name. Not even her madam knew what her given birth name was."

He thought for another moment. "Just put down 'Girl known as Clarinda,'" the constable said. "I suppose that's the closest anyone's going to get to her real name now. … What name Mrs. Richardson puts on the girl's tombstone is up to her."

Constable Harkness paused for a moment. "There is one other medical-related thing you can do for me."

"What's that?" the doctor asked.

"I assume you have experience in doing medical drawings?" the constable asked. "At least you probably received some training in how to do medical drawing in medical school."

"I'm hardly a Rembrandt," the doctor said, "but I have some experience at it." This was in the days before cameras had become small enough to be extensively used in forensic recording work.

The constable pointed to the impression driven into the girl's jaw. "I want you to make a drawing of the pattern of that wound. Two drawings, one an expanded scale drawing, and the other drawn as close to the exact size and shape of the mark as you can make it. If by chance we ever find the weapon used on her, we might be able match the weapon to the wound. It's a long shot, but I'd still like to have it for the case record."

"I'll have to go back to the office and get pencil and paper and a ruler," Dr. Simpson said. "I didn't bring anything with me to do a drawing with."

"Got that all for you right here, Doc," Constable Harkness said.

They were otherwise finished. The doctor nodded. Constable Harkness exited the room to procure drawing material and a fine graduated ruler to take the measurements with. The doctor turned again to the body of the dead girl who had been effectively nothing to the man of the family she had grown up with, less than nothing to the man who had killed her, and all the future of life to the one young man who had loved her beyond his years and beyond his own life. With reasonable medical respect for the dignity of those beyond dignity, the doctor started to re-dress the unknown girl who had lived on the fringe of the town and on the fringe of town consciousness and consideration, the girl without a name who had passed beyond them, leaving behind few to grieve for her and no name for the grieving to bury her under.

"The Martin boy wasn't home," Sergeant Plechathy said, walking back into the station house. "He's out with his father someplace. I left word that you wanted to see him. The boy's mother didn't know when they would be back. I can't say when he'll be in."

"Can the boy's mother vouch for his whereabouts for the last few days?" Constable Harkness asked.

"She swears that he's been home with them the whole week," Sergeant Plechathy said. "She said the only time any of them were in town this week was for the potluck supper Wednesday night. And she said they were all together at the supper and that they went home together after. According to the boy's mother, he hasn't been off the farm or out of the area since."

"Did she sound like she was telling the truth?" Constable Harkness asked.

"She seemed to be," the sergeant said. "She sounded sincere enough. But I suppose she could just be a convincing liar. As you said, the Martin boy is our most likely suspect."

The constable pointed into the back room. Inside the room Dr. Simpson was bent over the face of the dead girl, taking measurements of the wound with a ruler.

"Mrs. Richardson said the girl didn't come back Wednesday night," the constable said. "Doc Simpson says that the girl was most likely killed Wednesday night. That was the night of the potluck supper and social. The Martin family was there all the time that the doc said that the girl was being killed. Dozens of people saw them there. The same people saw the Martin boy there. All those people can alibi him."

The constable touched his chest.

"I saw him there. I talked to him to see if he was keeping himself out of trouble. I can alibi him myself for that night. That's a whole lot of alibi going for him. The only way the boy could have killed her is if he snuck back into town that night, caught her on her way back from whoever she had gone out that night to service, and did her in then. That's why I asked whether you think his mother was lying. It's the only way he could have been the killer of the girl."

"I suppose the family could be lying to protect one of their own," Sergeant Plechathy said.

"It's still a rather awkward and unlikely scenario," the chief constable of the town said. "There's little or nothing that ties him in directly or even circumstantially with the killing. The timing makes no sense. I think we're going to have to wash him out as a suspect."

"Who does that leave us with as a suspect then?" Sergeant Plechathy asked.

"Mrs. Richardson said the girl was seeing someone in town, someone the girl didn't name because he wanted his name kept free of scandal. She thinks he's the killer. But I don't put much stock in that. I doubt that a genteel and refined citizen is going to kill a young girl and kill her in that manner. You need someone more coarse and prone to violence. With the temper the Martin boy demonstrated in the bar fight he got into over the girl, he fits that mold. But there's almost no way he fits the time frame."

It has long been an adage of police work that the most likely suspect is the one who usually turns out to be guilty. If the Martin boy didn't have such an airtight alibi with so many witnesses, Constable Harkness would have considered the case against him to be pretty much open and shut. But far too many people, himself included, had seen the boy at the potluck supper during the time the girl was being killed elsewhere. The fact that he himself was an integral part of the boy's alibi was the beginning of complications for the constable.

"Her killer was probably one of the types of men she ran with the rest of her time, someone who wouldn't get invited to the dinner. I'd say we're looking for a hired hand or a day laborer. Whoever killed her probably either caught her on a dark street on the way in to see whomever she was seeing in town or caught her on the way back. Most likely he jumped out of the dark, grabbed her as she passed by, dragged her into an alley, and killed her. Afterward he dumped her body in the river."

"Why did he kill her when he could have had her for the going price?" Sergeant Plechathy asked.

"Why does any man kill a whore?" Constable Harkness asked a return question. "Maybe he didn't have the money. She was supposed to be high priced. Maybe he didn't want to pay when he thought he could have it and her for free. She may have put up a fight and the man went out of his head with anger and killed her for being an impertinent hussy who wouldn't submit to his demand. Then there are some men who just enjoy killing whores for the sport of it. That was Jack the Ripper's game. And whores oblige men who play that game by making themselves easy game the way they run around on the streets after dark and out of sight. No law of human nature says that kind of psychological aberration is confined to big and dirty cities. We may have a man like that on our hands. That's why I told Mrs. Richardson to keep her girls in the house."

"If the Martin boy is washed up as a suspect, why are you calling him in for questioning?" Sergeant Plechathy asked out of curiosity.

"I had him called in before I remembered he was there at the potluck supper," the constable said. "They were sweethearts, as sweet as the heart of a hooker can be. He ran with her. Maybe he knows something that can give us a clue that will point us in the right direction." Constable Harkness looked off in the direction of the back room, where Doctor Simpson was still doing his forensic drawing. "I just have a feeling that he's not going to be too happy about this, though."

At that point the he remembered that Mrs. Richardson had said the girl had put the boy on probation and that he hadn't been seeing her in the month prior to her disappearance. It was possible that she was lying to protect the boy, but he couldn't see why she would want to lie to protect someone who had killed one of her girls, a girl she thought of as a daughter. It was another complication in a case that stubbornly seemed to defy being brought to an easy conclusion.

The constable rubbed his fingers over his forehead in an unconscious gesture of perplexity.

"If he can't provide us anything, then we go around talking to all the hired hands and manual laborers in the area to see if they've heard anything or if any of them comes across as evasive and suspicious."

The constable ended it there, mostly because he had nowhere else to go. With professional dispatch, he broke away from the sergeant and went on as if he were pursuing a pressing professional issue. He had ended the outline of the direction he planned to take the investigation and left it hanging in a functionally positive but otherwise open-ended direction. If the truth were to be known, beyond that he didn't have any clear idea of where to go from there. But he didn't particularly see any reason to dwell on the point or even reveal that to his professional colleagues in law enforcement. The condition of the girl's neck and face showed it to be a clear-cut case of murder. But nothing else about it was a clear and open case of anything. It was a case with any number of beginnings that trailed off and disappeared into the nothingness beyond. But then again that's what a whore's love life was all about.

The constable and the sergeant went their own ways in the station house. The investigation was afoot, albeit on feet stumbling over themselves as they went to rise up.

Chapter 13

It was a pastoral posed picture in what would prove to be the last pastoral day in Samuel Martin's life.

Samuel's mother stood in the middle of parlor, the fingers of her hand curled over, her hand up in front of her mouth. She had heard the truck pull up and had gone into the parlor to finish delivering the news that the police sergeant had brought. The truck had pulled up by the barn, where her husband and son would be unloading it. From the direction of the barn, Mrs. Martin could hear Teddy's excited yapping because his two masters had returned. She didn't know how long it would take, but she figured they would use the back door to come into the house when they were finished. Instead of going out to the barn, Mrs. Martin stood in the parlor waiting for one of them to eventually come back into the house. She would stand there and wait however long it was before they came into the house. What she had to say wasn't exactly the kind of cheerful pastoral message she wanted to bring out to them.

It was sooner than she had expected when Mrs. Martin heard the sound of footsteps on the wooden stoop of the back door. At the sound, her heart sank. Instead of the slower and heavier step of her husband, she recognized the lighter and quicker tread of her son coming up and across the stoop. She had sort of hoped her husband would come in first. That way she could tell him the news, and he could deliver it in a strong father-to-son way. Now she would have to tell her son directly that the girl he loved had been slain. She didn't know if she could handle it. Beth was up in her room sitting on her bed with her knees drawn up to her chest. She knew she couldn't handle it.

The door opened, and Samuel walked in with a bolt of cloth in his hand. He was a bit surprised to see his mother standing in the parlor, but he waved the cloth in her direction.

"Here's the crinoline cloth you wanted," he said. He put the cloth down across the arms of a chair. "I have to help Father unload the truck. We'll be back inside after."

Unable to say anything immediate, Samuel's mother waved her son over toward her. Puzzled by his mother's strange look and gesture, Samuel walked over to her. As he got closer, what he had taken for a strange look on his mother's face resolved into a look of anguish.

Like a lot of close-knit families, the Martin family members had learned to read each other's nonverbal communication. The look on Samuel's own face fell as he saw his mother's face.

His mother reached out with one hand and touched him on the arm. Her breath came heavily. Her chest almost seemed to shudder. It was as if she was fighting to speak. She didn't seem to be able to bring the words up or put them out. At this point Samuel didn't need the subtleties of nonverbal communication. He could plainly tell something was wrong—badly wrong.

"What's wrong?" Samuel said without wasting time or words.

As if turning the handle on a vise, his mother jammed herself internally and forced the words out. Her words were as much gasps as they were words.

"Oh, Sam," she said. She pushed the words out in a forced and disjointed manner. She seemed to stumble over them, only to rise and stumble again. "Sam … you've got to listen to me. … I have bad news. … Something terrible has happened."

Samuel grabbed his mother's arms in his hands. That kind of shuddering anguish on his mother's part could only be produced in her when it involved someone close and dear. He had heard her react this way at the death of his grandfather and when she had received word of the passing of her own mother. She had also reacted the same way when the news of the death of his uncle Ned had arrived. The set of her face and the wrenching in her voice could only mean something bad had happened to a family member. But who was it? Most of his grandparents were already dead. He had just left his father alive and fine only a minute ago. She could have been about to announce that the family dog Teddy had died, but Teddy was alive and yapping. There was only one person left. He gripped his mother's arms tighter.

"Has something happened to Sis?" Samuel asked, his own breath and fear rising in him. All he could imagine was that some kind of accident had befallen Beth. In that instant he was already sorry for every time he had called her a snot.

His mother shook her head. The gesture didn't readily shake the words out of her. Neither did it shake the look of tightly coiled sorrow off her face.

"Sam," she said, pushing hard at the words jammed, seeming to tear her throat as she forced them past her lips.

"Sam … it's the girl … the one you're in love with … Mrs. Richardson's girl. … There's something I have to tell you about her …"

At the mention of the girl, Samuel relaxed somewhat. He released his grip on his mother's arms and dropped his hands. In his mind, Samuel figured that the cooling-off separation period that Clarinda had required of him as a term of seeing her again would soon be over was the catastrophe she saw looming. Samuel figured that now the story was out, his mother figured the family would be the talk of the town when he started seeing the girl again, openly this time. Samuel figured that the thought had been brewing in his mother's mind for some time and that her fear of the social stigma of her respectable son's keeping time with a disreputable prostitute had finally broken through to the surface.

"I suppose you know that the separation period she put me under will be over in a few days," Samuel said, sure he was on the right track of his mother's fears. "You know I'll start seeing her again as soon as she'll let me."

"That's not it, Sam," his mother said, still fighting to get her words out.

Samuel figured that it had to be it. He assumed that his mother and father had gotten together and talked about their son's scandalous behavior and decided they had had enough. He also figured that they had decided among themselves to forbid him to see the girl anymore. Samuel figured that was why his mother was having so much trouble talking to him about it. He figured that she figured that he would take it hard. He figured his mother was tense and afraid to tell him of their decision to order him to stop seeing the girl because she feared it would lead to a family fight.

"I don't intend to rub your nose or anybody's nose in it," Samuel said in a calm, quiet, yet firm voice, "but I don't intend to stop seeing her just because some old biddies in town might get their noses out of joint about it."

Where it came to what is and what would be, to Samuel the girl was about everything there was. He wasn't about to give up the girl no matter the public rumormongering. Neither was he about to give up the girl because his parents had decided between themselves to order him to stop seeing her. His loss of control in the saloon notwithstanding, he would show them that he wasn't going to lose control over her. He would show his parents that he wasn't going to get into a family argument with them about her. At the same time, in a calm but forceful way, he would make it plain to them that he wasn't about to give up his dream of a future and a family with the girl. If it became necessary to defy his parents' edict, he would do so to keep the girl. He would do it in a calm and reasoned manner. He would do it without shouting and rancor. He would do it without splitting the family he intended to make the girl a part of. But he would do it. He loved his parents, but the girl was his dream of love and family for all his future to come. He wasn't looking to split the family, but he wouldn't give up his dream of love and a future family to prevent any and all disagreeable feelings for his family of origin. There was some family that you just didn't put behind you for anyone, not even other family members.

"I love her. I still do. I always will."

"Sam ..."

"As soon as I can, I intend to get her out of that house and out of the life she's been living."

"Sam ..."

"I intend to get her into this family as soon as she'll let me."

"Sam ..."

"I don't give a damn what anyone in any ladies' sewing circle or men's beer and cigar circle thinks about any of it."

"Sam …"

"I don't mean to be disrespectful to anyone, but I'm not about to give up the one girl I've ever loved, the one girl I probably ever can love, for the sake of some dried-out definition of respect and respectability."

"Sam, it's not that."

"If it's respectfulness and properness you want, I'll make her a proper woman."

"Sam …"

"There may be more than a few people who will never respect her no matter how much she reforms, but I'm not living my life for them, not one minute of it."

"Sam."

"I intend to live my life for her and with her."

"Sam …"

"The whole town can take a header into the river if they think I'm going to throw her over for their dried-out sense of proper respectability."

"Sam …"

"I don't meant to be disrespectful of you or Father, and I don't mean to be disrespectful of this family, but Clarinda is the family I want. She's all the family I can see. She's all the family and future I can imagine or want to imagine."

"Sam, please listen to me …"

"I'm not looking to cause a break in this family. I only want to bring her into the family. I want to make her a part of this family. I'm not looking to scatter us. I want to make the family bigger. I want to give her the family she never had."

"Sam …"

"I'm not looking to start a family fight. I'm not looking to split us up. I want all of us to be together."

"Sam …"

"If you won't accept her, it will be you who puts a split in the family. It won't be me."

"Sam …"

"I don't intend to walk away from this family, but I don't intend to walk away from her."

"Sam, please."

"She's my future and my life. I'm not going to leave my future and my life behind. I'm not going to leave her behind."

"*Sam!*"

His mother slapped him hard across the mouth. Samuel stopped talking and stood there, shocked and stunned. In his whole life his mother had never slapped him.

"What?" Samuel said in a half breath with his mouth open. For an instant he wondered if his mother could really be so angry about his defiant instance that he was going to marry the girl and bring her into the family.

His mother balled her hands up into fists and held them out in front of her. But her face wasn't angry. If anything, it only looked more anguished than before. She closed her eyes and tensed up as if she were straining to bring the words out. Then she opened her eyes again. There were heavy tears in her eyes. "Sam, she's dead!" she said in a half-crying, strangled voice.

For what perhaps could be called a merciful moment, what his mother said didn't fully register on Samuel. His mouth opened a bit more as comprehension started to settle in.

"What do you mean, dead?!" Samuel said in a gasp-sounding voice.

His mother fought again to bring out the words.

"Sam, the police were here," Mrs. Martin said. To Mrs. Martin it was like childbirth. Her words started to flow even through the contracting pain that would have held them back and kept them inside her. Though her words flowed, the tone of her voice tore in her throat as the words came out.

"They found her body in the river. … Sam, somebody killed her! They say she was murdered. They think you had something to do with it. They want to talk to you at the police station."

For a moment Samuel stood unmoving in stunned paralysis. Then the paralysis broke. "You're making this up," he said in a tone edged with both disbelief and desperation. "You're just saying that because you don't want me to see her again!"

His mother raised her head and looked at him. The sorrow was still

366

on her face. Samuel knew his mother's expressions. She wasn't feigning sadness. The knifepoint for Samuel was that she didn't seem to be feigning anything.

"Oh, Sam, in the name of merciful God, why would I make up a cruel and vicious lie like that just to keep you away from her? I'd sooner cut off my hand than hurt you like that. I'd sooner cut off my other hand than see her dead. But someone killed her. That's what the police said." Samuel's mother raised her arm and pointed in the general direction of the town. "The sergeant said they've got her body down at the station house. They want to talk with you about it right away. They also want you to help identify the body."

Quicker than Mrs. Martin could catch her breath, her son turned on his heels and headed for the door. He kicked the chair that was holding the bolt of cloth out of his way as he passed and broke into a run. In a few short steps, he banged through the back door. He left the door open as he charged toward the barn and the truck. Inside the barn, Samuel's father heard the truck motor race to life and the sound of the starter crank being thrown onto the floor of the driver's compartment. A moment later he heard the motor race and the truck pull away fast from where they had parked the car near the front door of the barn. Mr. Martin had only begun to unload the truck. The bed was still mostly full.

Mr. Martin went to the side door of the barn and looked out to see the truck pulling away fast with his son at the wheel. The truck was already too far away from him to call out to Samuel and ask him where he was going. He could only wonder what had gotten into his damned fool son and where he was heading off to. In the not too distant future, he would have cause to wonder the same things in aching sorrow.

It's a bit hard to drive a pre–Model T Ford truck like there's no tomorrow. Thirty-some miles an hour tops is not breakneck, nothing-to-lose, death-wish speed by modern standards, but at the time it was fast enough.

In the mind of Samuel Martin, if what his mother had said was true, then for him there was no tomorrow that held any meaning. As he drove, gripping the steering wheel with the throttle pulled all the way open, the thoughts in Samuel's mind spun in as fast a blur the wooden spokes on the wheels of the truck were turning. No one thought stayed in one place long enough for him to see it and hold its outline. The only fixed thought that kept repeating itself in Samuel's mind was that there must have been some mistake. The police had gotten their identification wrong. They really didn't know the girls of the Richardson house. It hadn't been the girl. It had been another woman of the house. It was a totally different girl whose body had drifted downriver from far away. She only looked like the girl. The girl was probably sleeping late from a hard night's work. The police were being totally stupid, or they were playing a crude practical joke on him. It just couldn't be her. It just couldn't be the end of his world. His future couldn't end like this. His life just couldn't end this way. The girl had come through so much in her life. Her life couldn't just end this way.

As Samuel drove, he focused on the road passing in front of him. In times past when he had driven the same road going the other way, he had seen the girl's face in the sky. Now he was frantic to see her face anywhere again, even pointing a knife at him on the river's edge, just so he could see her face again somewhere.

Samuel took the final turn onto the road leading into town not only too soon but also too tight. The truck bounced over the grass at the edge of the turn. The back fender caught the corner fence post at the edge of the McReady farm, jarred it at an angle, and bent the front of the fender. Samuel kept on driving. As he approached the town, the cemetery came up on the side. He turned his eyes forward, unable to look at it. That couldn't be the final location of the girl. He was going to take her home. She couldn't end up buried away from him forever in there. The cemetery couldn't be the final end of his future. The silent and unmoving rows of markers couldn't mark the final end of the girl.

The door of the police station exploded inward. A figure full of the energy of male youth and the energy of fear of what he might find behind the door charged in without shutting the door behind him. Constable Harkness happened to be on his feet when Samuel surged into the police station house. He turned around at the sound of incoming calamity.

"You say you have the body of a girl here you want me to identify?" Samuel half shouted at the standing constable.

"Any further identification is pretty much a formality," Constable Harkness said in an official, formal voice. "Sergeant Plechathy and Mrs.

Richardson have already identified her. It's other things I want to talk to you about."

The floor beneath Samuel opened up to the breadth and depth of eternity. The door he had swung open in his passage had hit the doorstop on the other side and was swinging back to close behind him. Ahead of him, the door of his love and the door of his future closed hard in his face. All coulds and couldn'ts dropped away from him, leaving only a faint smear of hope that faded quickly. There wasn't any wishful hope of a mistake left to be grasped at. If Mrs. Richardson had identified the girl, then it had to be her. If it was the girl, her world had imploded on her. His world would follow.

"Where?" Samuel said in a half-uttered near-gasp.

The constable pointed to the door of the back room. From two different angles the two different men converged on the door.

At the door, Constable Harkness motioned Samuel to go into the room. Samuel entered with the police chief behind him. In the tight confines of the back room, surrounded by storage shelves crowded with boxes, stretched out unceremoniously on a table, Samuel saw an unfamiliarly pale white face showing over the neck of a familiar-looking dark-colored dress. Some men would have frozen in the spot, unable to go any farther. By instinct, the take-charge Samuel, captain of the baseball team, wrestler with an eye to his opponent's moves, was used to moving to resolve whatever situation and factors he was facing. He paused for a half second, then he moved quickly to the edge of the table, to the fallen and prostrate side of the girl he had wanted to stand with for the rest of his life.

Most of his denial had deserted him when he had heard that Mrs. Richardson had identified her. Now denial and hope pulled back from him and disappeared over every horizon on every side and left him standing on a floor he could not see in a dark void with no boundaries and no light from any direction.

The head of the girl on the table was turned with her face slightly toward him. Once warm and right with the colors of life, even without the makeshift rouge of cherry juice, the girl's beautiful face was now the grim ghostly white of a corpse drained of blood in a ritual sacrifice to a demon god. The only color to the girl's face was the purplish-black of the bruises that stood out at random locations from the pale whiteness of her otherwise undamaged skin. Death had fixed the color of the bruises in their shade and had fixed the swelling around them. Some of the bruises stood alone. Others merged together.

There was no question, hoped-for misidentification, or distant wish remaining. It was her. The amateurishly rouged but compellingly lovely face he had seen rising up off the sofa and coming toward him in the parlor of Mrs. Richardson's, the angelic face he had seen in the sky when he had driven home the night he had met the girl, the streaked wet face he had seen rising to meet his face as she had pulled herself up tight to him in Gustafson Lake, the radiant and happy face he had seen on the girl while she had ridden the merry-go-round at the fair, the makeup-lacking but otherwise pastorally beautiful country girl face he had seen looking down on him with her hair hanging wet around her face and down on his face during the time they had made love on the shore of Gustafson Lake, was gone. All the faces of the girl he had known were gone, to be replaced by the blanched white death mask of her battered face. The final traces of her life, a life that he still had no name to attach to, the life that would never be attached to his in this world, had come to a drained and broken end on a wooden table in the dingy storeroom of the police station. The face of the girl he had once seen in the sky above him, he would never see again alive in this world.

At the point of recognition, some men would have said "Oh God" or something like that. For several long moments, Samuel stared at the body in frozen silence.

"What …?" Samuel finally said. The words started to push out of his mouth but stopped halfway. Constable Harkness assumed the boy was trying to say "What happened?" or something like that.

"No weapons were employed," Constable Harkness said, recounting his and Doctor Simpson's forensic analysis in a blow-by-blow manner. "Whoever killed her used his hands and beat her with his fists. Then he deliberately twisted her neck hard enough to crack it. After that, he threw her body into the river, where she drowned because she was paralyzed and unable to move due to her spinal cord's being severed."

"Who did this?" the boy said in a voice that some people might have called a barely audible whisper. Other people might have likened it to the hiss of a coiling snake.

Constable Harkness began, "The theory I'm going on—"

"*Who did this to her?!*" Samuel exploded, shouting at the top of his voice. He raised both his arms with rabbit punch speed and slammed his fists down on the table next to the motionless girl with enough force to jar the table.

"That's what I was hoping you could tell me, boy," Constable Harkness said, his own voice rising. The boy's shock and anger seemed real and spontaneous enough. If he was acting, it was a good act. "You wouldn't happen to know anything about this, would you?"

"No!" Samuel said at a volume only slightly lower than before. "Why would I know anything? I haven't been with her for some time."

"You were keeping a whole lot of time with her," Constable Harkness said in his confrontational policeman's voice. "That by itself puts you close to her and within reach of her. As it turns out, more often than not most murder victims are killed by people they know, people close to them. They're often the first suspects that police look at, especially when the suspect has a history of violence connected with the dead person."

"I never raised a hand to her," Samuel said in his still raised voice.

"You sure raised more than one hand to the hired hand you got into a fight with over her in Two-Bit Charlie's saloon," Constable Harkness said. "You didn't take kindly to the idea of her seeing other men back then. Any chance that you were hanging around outside the house after that, watching her take on man after man, getting madder by the moment? Did you watch from the shadows as she went out of the house to pick up more clients in town? With your temper, it's not all that hard to imagine you coming to a slow boil over her activities and then finally snapping. The last time she went out, were you waiting for her? Did you grab her and have it out with her? Did she end up with a broken neck and jaw at your hands, because of your temper, the way the other man ended up with a broken nose and beaten-in face like hers?"

"No!" Samuel said.

"Somebody gave her a good beating with their fists," Constable Harkness went on. "Someone strong enough to inflict a lot of damage. Someone with a lot of strength. Someone with enough strength to twist her neck until it snapped. You're a wrestler; you know wrestling holds and moves."

"I've never done any violence to her," Samuel said, his voice hardly lower from the peak volume it had reached just prior. "Ask Mrs. Richardson."

Mrs. Richardson had already said that he hadn't been physically abusive to the girl. Constable Harkness just didn't say that at the moment. He didn't want to give the boy a false sense that he was in the clear.

"Well, somebody did violence to her," Constable Harkness said in a tone laced with obviousness. "There are only two men I know of who've been involved with violence associated with her: you and the man you got into a fight with over her. And you're the one who started that fight. The main, and just about the only, past violence that's been around her has come from you."

"I haven't been near to her for close to a month," Samuel said. "She got mad at me for starting the fight in the bar. She told me not to come around her for a full month until I cooled myself off. I haven't been at or around the Richardson house for that long."

That was another thing Mrs. Richardson had already corroborated. If the constable was trying to draw a net around the boy, the threads kept fraying and the ends wouldn't reach and connect.

"Mrs. Richardson said she didn't come home Wednesday night," Constable Harkness said. "Doc Simpson said that from the condition of her body, it looks like that was the approximate time of death. Can you account for all your time Wednesday night?" The question was largely rhetorical. He pretty much knew the answer he would get.

"I was at the potluck supper with the rest of my family Wednesday night," Samuel said, giving the answer the constable expected. "You saw me there. You talked to me."

Samuel stood bent over the table with his back and side to the constable. He alternately pounded his fists silently on the table and ground them on the top of the table next to the girl's body. He tried not to look at her face. He had seen the girl's face in the full color of life. He had seen her face greater than life size projected outward and upward into the night sky by his full-blown imagination. That same imagination had projected the girl's face and an image of him standing with her for life down into the depths and across the breadth of his soul. Now the face that had been so imbued with life and that had come toward him so often, full of beauty and life, was lifeless. The girl's face had held the image of love and life for him. The face that had looked into his with all the promise of love, life, and a future, the face he wanted to see for the rest of his life, now lay beaten, cadaverous, cold, and unmoving. He didn't know if he would ever be able to get the death mask image of the girl's face out of his mind.

"Where did you go after you left the dinner?"

"I went straight home with my parents and sister."

"Did you leave the dinner anytime while it was going on?"

"No."

"Can you prove that?"

"Ask my parents. I was with them all the time when I wasn't talking with friends. Ask the guys I talked with. You saw me there part of the time. Ask yourself. Ask everyone who was there if they saw me sneaking out. I didn't know her schedule. If I wasn't around the Richardson house, how did I know what the girl was doing that night? How would I know when she was coming or going or where she'd be going so I could be waiting for her?"

The questions had crossed the constable's mind.

"Mrs. Richardson said she knew the girl had gone into town to meet a client there," Constable Harkness said, taking it in a different direction. "She claims the girl hadn't given her his name. But she thinks the girl was seeing a rich man. She called him a fancy man."

The constable thought so little of the madam's power of deduction and detection and her theory that he felt free to mention it to the boy.

"Mrs. Richardson says the man the girl was seeing is probably the man who killed her. It's her idea that a poor man who killed the girl in the street would have left her where he killed her, but a rich man who killed her in his house would have had something to transport her to the river in, say, a car or a buggy."

Samuel stopped grinding his fists on the top of the table. He raised his head. He seemed to be looking straight ahead, over the girl's body, and toward the wall, but he was looking down every street in town. The murder of the girl had made no sense. Mrs. Richardson's theory was the first thing he had heard that made any sense.

Constable Harkness leaned his words in at Samuel. "You have a truck. Bodies can be carried in the back of a truck."

"My father owns the truck," Samuel said. "I drove the family to the potluck supper in it and back. I didn't take it out again that night. Ask my parents and sister."

Constable Harkness said nothing. However he looked at it, the boy could not have been involved the night of the killing of the girl. He had hit a wall.

"Do you mind if I take a look at your truck?" Constable Harkness asked.

"Have at it," Samuel said. "It's outside. It's not a crime to own a truck."

"No it's not," Constable Harkness said. "But what I'm investigating is."

With as little warning and with as almost the same speed as he had slammed his fists on the table, Samuel spun around to face Constable Harkness directly. "You expect me to believe for one minute that you actually have any intention of investigating her killing?!" he said in a half shout, almost as loud as the voice he had used to ask who had killed the girl.

In his own way, Samuel had hit the wall and gone over. He had no more ability to control his voice than he had when he hit the table. He had no more desire to control his voice, the words of his voice, than when he had hit the table. His love and his future were gone. Gone with them was any need he otherwise felt to be circumspect with officers of the law, a law he didn't expect would ever be brought to the service of the dead girl.

"You and the rest of the town didn't give one damn for her for one damned second. Now she's just a dead whore to you. She was just a whore to everyone in this town. You're probably glad enough to be rid of her. You don't care that she's dead. You don't care that someone killed her. You wouldn't have lifted a finger to help her if you knew she was in trouble and someone was after her. You won't do anything to help her now that's she's dead." Samuel pointed hard at the girl's body behind him on the table. "The only thing you want to do where she's concerned is get her body out of your station house and dump it in an ash can in the alley. You'd bury her in a second to be rid of her. You'd bury her in a spittoon as soon as you would look at her."

"Mrs. Richardson is presently making funeral arrangements for the girl," Constable Harkness said in a steady voice intended to show that he was in control and could not be easily provoked. "You can talk to her about that."

"I mean you won't do anything to get justice for her," Samuel went on with his free association without any intention of stopping. "Whoever buries her, you'll bury any investigation you don't intend to make along with her. I doubt you have any intention of going after the man who killed her. You wouldn't trouble yourself to trouble any man by arresting him for the murder of a whore—a respectable man above all else. If by accident you happen to learn the killer's name, you'll probably just put it out of your mind as fast as you can, and you'll keep it out of any criminal record book forever. Most likely you'll never know his name because you'll never spend a minute of your time looking for it."

"You might give me the benefit of the doubt, boy," Constable Harkness said, his control of his voice slipping slightly. "I'll tell you what I told Mrs. Richardson: I don't like murder in my town, especially the murder of young girls, disreputable ones included. Whenever I find out who killed her, I intend to go after him to the full extent of the law."

"And *whenever* probably means never for you," Samuel said at half of full volume. "Especially if you get the sense that the killer was a rich and respectable man from the town, the town she headed into that night and didn't come back from."

"She was more likely killed by someone on her own street level," Constable Harkness said. "Someone with an explosive temper. Someone with a temper like yours. Maybe you didn't kill her. Maybe there isn't any evidence against you. If I arrest you, a judge will be the judge of that. But the killer was most likely someone with a temper like yours. That by itself puts you close enough in the circle to being a killer."

If the constable had meant his veiled innuendo about arresting Samuel as a way of cooling the boy off, backing him down, and rendering him a bit more respectful of and deferential to the law, it didn't work. The volume of Samuel's voice didn't tone down as much as a quarter octave. The inclination of Samuel's voice and words didn't alter an inch or deflect a degree.

"And while you're so busy trying to nail me for her murder, the real killer is getting farther and farther away," Samuel said. "But straining your eyes looking at me or some low-class man like a hired hand is probably just your way of not looking anywhere else because you don't want to take the chance of finding out that it was a rich man or one of the town fathers who killed her. Mrs. Richardson is probably right: it probably was a fancy man who killed her, the same fancy man she had gone out that night to see."

"Whores run with a rough crowd," Constable Harkness said. "It was probably a man of her own level who got her."

"Whores run with whoever pays them," Samuel corrected, "including otherwise respectable men. But rich and respectable men can be just as rough of a crowd as farmers and hired hands, even worse in their own way …"

The constable figured the boy fancied himself another Teddy Roosevelt–style crusader against corrupt corporate tycoons like Andrew Carnegie who sent in goons to break strikes. Apparently in his scaled-down class-consciousness, he saw conspiracies among the rich of the town around every corner.

"If you find that she was killed by someone rich and respectable in town, you'll probably run away from him faster than the girl was able to."

Samuel steadied himself and looked at Constable Harkness. "Did you call me in here to arrest me for her murder?"

"The first thing I called you in for was to help identify the body, though it's mostly a formality now," Constable Harkness said in an official voice and in an official capacity. "Is that her?"

"Yes," Samuel said, pushing the word out before it could catch in his throat. "But you didn't need me to identify her. Mrs. Richardson could have done that like you said she did. If you aren't going to arrest me, why have me come in? Did you just want the satisfaction of seeing my face when I saw her dead?"

The constable's reasons for calling the boy in had largely disappeared when he had remembered that he had seen the boy at the potluck supper the night and in the time frame that Doctor Simpson said the girl was murdered. Now he found himself having to think up an alternate justification for having brought him in.

"The main reason I brought you in here was to see if you had heard anything," Constable Harkness said.

"I didn't know or hear anything about her being dead until my mother told me less than an hour ago," Samuel said. "If she's been in the river the whole two days that she's been dead and her body was just discovered today and brought straight to you, how the hell could anyone know she was dead to chat about it over tea?!"

"What I meant was that, whether it's out of guilt or they're just bragging, criminals often talk to others of their kind about their exploits," Constable Harkness said. "If the killer was a lowlife hired hand, he may have told other hired hands what he did. But he may not say it in so many words. He may beat around the bush about it. Being a farmer, you have contact with hired hands. I thought that maybe you might have heard something from one of them, or perhaps one of your friends heard something that on second look might sound like someone talking about murder."

"It's only been three days since she was killed," Samuel said. "Not even three full days. I've hardly been off the farm the whole time to be able to talk to anyone. I thought that when killers start talking about their crimes, it's usually years later. I doubt that whoever killed her is going to start talking about it in the first two days after the killing."

When Constable Harkness thought about it, the time frame involving the boy did start to seem a bit unlikely.

"All this stuff of yours about her having likely been killed by a hired hand or a manual laborer is probably just your way of deliberately looking in a different direction and looking away from the possibility that a man of the town killed her. You'll bury justice with her and bury it as deep as her body. Then as soon as you bury her, spitting on your hands to clean them, you'll walk away spitting on justice for her. You'll carry buckets of water for the bigwigs of this town on both shoulders, but you won't bring up one tear for her. You'll bury her without a single tear shed and then walk away, glad she's out of your hair. But you won't lift a finger to find her killer if you think a respectable man of the town killed her. You'll blame me or some other farmer or a hired hand for killing her, but you'll turn a blind eye if you get a hint that a respectable man from the town killed her. You'll keep that man's secret because he's respectable and she was just a low-class whore."

Being circumspect with those in positions of power is a reasonable caution, but it's a caution that applies to the living. The dead have no reason to be circumspect. Badges of respect applied to the living by the living don't register much on the dead. With the girl dead a few feet away from him, Samuel felt dead himself. With the hope of his life dead, Samuel felt no particular reason to be circumspect with anyone living, even if they were wearing a badge.

"I told Mrs. Richardson, and I'm telling you, to save that stuff for Karl Marx," Constable Harkness said. "You can save your class-conscious speeches for the Farmers Grange. As for both you and her saying that I won't go after the girl's killer, I'll go after any killer as long as I have a clear evidence path that takes me to the real killer. I'm not writing her off or saying she was trash that didn't count the way you think I am. In her own way she wrote herself off."

A sharp twinge ran through Samuel. All he could think at that juncture was that the girl had been out on the street alone the night she had been taken and killed. Whatever street she had been going or returning on, like the road she had taken when she had run away from home, that street was only another road she had walked alone because she had little other choice in life and because she had no one to walk with her. Whatever house she had been killed in, on whatever street the house stood on, she would have been safer if she had remained in Mrs. Richardson's house.

A new wave of anger crested in Samuel. But only the smaller part of it was anger at the constable for suggesting that the girl had brought her death upon herself. A greater part of Samuel's anger was at himself for having driven the girl away from him and into the arms of the man who had killed the nameless girl he had loved beyond all names.

"She was what she was because she had to be," Samuel said in a voice cresting again to a near shout. "Life didn't give her much choice. She had to take herself on the road to save her life. The man who killed her had probably been given more by the left hand of life than life had ever given her. The bastard who killed her probably killed her because he was afraid that she might cause him some embarrassment! He took everything she had in life to protect some small corner of his own life. He took what little of anything she had in life. And I don't think you're going to do one little bit of anything to find the man who killed her!"

Samuel steadied himself, but only a little.

"For the whole of her life, someone was always taking what little she had and leaving her nothing. Her own family did it to her, and now he's done it to her worse. Whoever the son of a bitch was, he took her life. Now she doesn't even have that. All she has left to her now is for someone to seek justice for her. Leaving justice for her to you and this town would be no different from leaving her to the worms in the grave. You'd probably think a horse thief running off with someone's mule to be a bigger crime than killing a whore could ever be!"

"Don't raise your voice with me, boy," Constable Harkness said.

"If you want to hear a muffled voice out of me, cover your ears, stick your head in a rain barrel, and listen from the inside," Samuel said. "That's the only way you're going to hear a lower tone of voice from me. Someone killed the girl I was planning to marry. I don't have the beginning of any reason to be calm and collected about it, and I don't have any desire to hold my tongue."

"If you don't want to look like a suspect, I would control your temper if I were you," Constable Harkness said. "Whoever killed her seems to have had a bad temper. Losing your temper only—"

"Only what?!" Samuel snapped. "Only makes me look guilty the way you say that starting the fight in the saloon makes me look like I can't control myself? In your theory of criminology, is my being angry that someone killed the girl I wanted to marry some kind of proof that I'm guilty of her murder?! That's hog manure."

Having grown up on a farm where his father had kept hogs, Constable Harkness could relate to that.

"If I'm losing my temper, it's because someone killed the girl I loved. Men have been known to get mad as hell when someone kills their wife or sweetheart. If a man can't get mad about that, what can he get mad about?"

The constable had to admit the boy did have something of a point there.

Actually, in the constable's mind the boy's anger was doing more to prove his innocence. In a backhanded and reverse sort of way, both the intensity and the spontaneity of the boy's anger was additional proof of his innocence to the constable. Real killers don't usually put on such a detailed and free-flowing show of pretend anger when they're trying to direct suspicion away from themselves. When they do feign anger, their performances generally ring hollow and are unconvincing. Or they try to soft-soap you. By instinct alone, you can often see through the fake show. To the constable, the boy would have to be one hell of an actor to put on the performance he was putting on and make it look as spontaneous and real as it did. Frankly, he really didn't think the boy had the brains or wits about him to do that.

"I think your trying to blame this on me or a hired hand is just a way to avoid looking at who her real killer was—as Mrs. Richardson said, some kind of fancy man in town."

Constable Harkness pointed in the general direction of the girl's neck. "It wasn't a pantywaist who broke her neck like that," he said. "That was done by somebody strong, possibly somebody young, strong, and athletic. That puts you in the ballpark, Mr. Captain of the Baseball Team. It was done by someone who knows how to use their hands and fists. That fits you as a boxer, wrestler, and barroom brawler. At least it fits someone who's used to physical labor. That puts you in another ballpark, Mr. Farm Boy. It takes someone who can throw around hay bales and throw around men in a saloon to throw down a young girl and beat her and break her neck."

"Then I take it that I'm still your prime suspect," Samuel said.

"You fit several of the molds right on down the line," Constable Harkness answered, "starting with the fact that you were acquainted with the girl and moving down to the fact that you committed violence over her. It's not that big of a step from there to committing violence against her. And you're strong enough to have done the kind of damage done to her. In that sense you fit right into the pattern at several points."

"If my feet fit Jack the Ripper's boots, would that make me him?" Samuel asked. "If I fit into Lizzie Borden's bustle, would that make me her?"

"You fit enough of the criteria. You just don't fit the time frame," the constable acknowledged.

"Sorry to leave you hanging when you wanted to leave me hanging from a gallows," Samuel said dryly.

"Like I say," the constable intoned, "I'm looking for a killer. I'm not looking to do a cover job for anybody. All the evidence pretty much eliminates you as her killer. If you want to find her killer, if you want the justice for her you say you do, you're in a position to help me find her killer."

"How so?" Samuel said at the constable's surprise change of direction.

"What I want you to do is keep your ear to the ground," Constable Harkness said. "You know Mrs. Richardson and the women at the house.

They hear things from their clients. They talk about what they hear. You know the hired hands around here. They talk too. If you hear anything that might point to who killed the girl, bring it to me."

The constable wanted any word heard on the street or in the bars. Samuel reflected that his words hadn't kept the girl safe. His words hadn't held back the night from overtaking the girl. Samuel saw no reason to hold back his words.

"If I find out who killed her before you do, if you ever look at all, the only thing I'm going to tell you is where to come and pick up the body and how many men to bring, along with how many shovels and mops you'll need to clean up!" Samuel growled. "She's not going to get any justice from you or from the law in this town. If I find her killer, I'm not going to hand you the name. I'll hand you his head!"

"I think you'd best leave criminology and the execution of law enforcement to us, boy," Constable Harkness said. As the constable had discounted Mrs. Richardson's acumen as a detective, he discounted the boy's threat. To him it was just the typical noise of male youth. Romantically inclined boys are forever swearing oaths where their sweethearts are concerned, including blood oaths. To the constable it was all more of the same. His voice trailed off with no particular alarm and no more warnings.

For a moment there was silence between them.

"If you're not going to arrest me, are you finished with me?" Samuel asked.

"You can go," Constable Harkness said in his official-sounding voice. In the constable's mind, an end had been reached. He had nothing he could hold the boy on, and he couldn't see anywhere else he could go with the interview. They would just be going over the same ground.

"Just don't leave town," Constable Harkness added, uttering the policeman's ultimate proverbial directive. "I may want to question you again later."

"I live on the farm," Samuel said as he stirred himself to leave. "I've never been outside the state. I've hardly ever been outside the county. Where do I have to go?"

Samuel broke away from the constable and headed to the door. "If you want to find me in the next hour, I'll be at the Richardson house sharing my sympathies with the few people who cared for Clarinda," Samuel said as he passed the constable and exited.

After seeing the dead body of the girl he had put his love and hope for the future in, Samuel found himself in the same situation as Scrooge in the company of the Ghost of Christmas Future. After seeing the graphic beaten face of his dead lover, and after being grilled by the cold and unsympathetic police chief, who probably thought no more of the dead girl found in the river than he would of a dead stray dog found in his streets, Samuel had wanted to see some tenderness connected with the girl's death.

At the door, Samuel did not turn around and take a longing last parting look at the girl on the table. He didn't want to look at her broken and cadaverous face again. It was not the face he had known. When he walked out of the room, all he would have left of her would be his memories. He didn't want to remember her that way.

For Samuel it was an ending. It was the ending that he had not expected or made any preparations for. It was an ending he didn't know how to approach in any other way than in burning anger and with a seething desire for vengeance. Without stumbling or hesitating, he walked out of the room at a quick pace. The reason for his speed of departure wasn't so much that he did not want to see the girl in the condition she was in; it was just that he didn't want to delay the letting go that had to come. The quicker he moved, the less he felt that his leaving the girl would tear at him. He had started the day thinking of the closeness he would soon begin again with the girl and the life he would begin with her after that. Now he had to let go of all of life as he saw it. He would have to let go of the world and the future as he had come to define it. He would be left holding nothing of the life and the world he had wanted and had thought would be his. He knew he had to let go of the girl. There seemed to be nothing ahead of him but an endless stream of letting go.

Samuel crossed the floor of the police station quickly, heading for the front door. As the constable came out of the back room, Samuel burst back out through the door. He didn't bother to close the door behind him this time either. The constable stood in the interior doorway watching Samuel leave. Sergeant Plechathy had to get up from his desk and close the door. As he walked back from the door, he stopped a few yards away from the constable. "You're not going to hold him?" he asked.

"Got nothing to hold him on," Constable Harkness answered. "Can't hold someone just for what they might have done without some kind of evidence that they actually did it. We've got no evidence against the boy, and the only evidence I can supply myself puts him solidly somewhere else at the time the killing took place."

The constable waved the sergeant over.

"Call the funeral home and have them come and pick up the body," he said as the sergeant stepped closer. "Mrs. Richardson should have finished making her arrangements by now. We have no reason to hold the body any longer."

The sergeant nodded and started to walk toward the desk and the phone, leaving the constable standing where he was in the middle of the floor. The constable would have normally moved off in his own direction, but this time he stood in place thinking. The girl had made her living off her connections with men. There was one connection that might need further clarification.

"Who was it who bailed the girl out the night you arrested her and the Martin boy in the saloon?" Constable Harkness asked as the sergeant stared to pick up the receiver of the candlestick-style upright phone.

"Harold Ethridge," Sergeant Plechathy said. "After I had the two of them locked up, he came in saying that he had seen me taking them both into custody. He said that he felt sorry for the girl and wanted to pay her bail as a public-spirited gesture toward a 'less fortunate young girl'—something like that."

"What about the Martin boy?" Constable Harkness asked. "If Ethridge felt so much toward wayward youth, why didn't he bail him out too?"

"He said that I should leave the boy in his cell as a way of cooling him off," the sergeant said. "He didn't even want me to tell the boy who was bailing the girl out. He said he was worried that it might set the boy off on another jealous rage."

"Did Ethridge and the girl leave together?"

"They walked out the front door together. Where they went afterward, I didn't look to see."

Constable Harkness was silent for a short moment.

"I think maybe we should have a word with Mr. Ethridge about this," he said. He still didn't put much of any store in Mrs. Richardson's bordello madam's social class suspicions and theories, but he didn't quite know where to pigeonhole Harold Ethridge's class-lines-crossing act of public-spiritedness toward a wayward girl who lived on the wayward side of the town and the wayward side of life.

"That happened over a month ago," the sergeant said. "I doubt there's any connection to what has happened now."

"But it's a connection," the constable said. He had a far-off look on his face as if he were looking over a far horizon. "This whole affair may not be as random as it seems. It may be about connections—connections seen and connections unseen."

The constable broke his train of thought and went about other business.

Though the faint light of lingering twilight was coming through the window, Samuel didn't look at it. He lay in bed in his darkened room staring up into the full and undifferentiated darkness as he looked at the ceiling. Samuel had resisted going to bed. He had gone to bed because everyone else in the family had, but he didn't think that he would get much sleep that night. It wasn't that Samuel was somehow afraid that the dead girl was going to emerge from the darkness to pay him a ghostly visit in his own bedroom. Like Heathcliff tortured by the death of Catherine and begging her to come to him as a ghost even if she drove him mad, Samuel would have actually welcomed the ghost of the girl coming to haunt him. At least he would have her with him in some manner.

As he lay silently in his bed staring into all the darkness around but at no darkness in specific, like Heathcliff, Samuel would have preferred ghostly visitations even from a gaunt and faded white spectral figure of the girl to the emptiness and nothingness that pressed in around him and expanded out into a seeming eternity in all directions. He would have gladly opened his heart, mind, and soul to let the soul of the dead girl possess his soul for the rest of his life, even if she drove him mad. Either way, no ghostly female figure materialized out of the darkness of his room or his soul.

To the side of his bed, the door to Samuel's room swung open in the dark. A figure shrouded in the dark of the hallway stepped into the room.

The figure walked softly. As much as from the feel of the silent presence as from the faint outline of the shape, Samuel could tell it was a female presence. The soft and unidentified female presence kneeled down beside his bed and took his hand in hers.

"Samuel," a female voice said in the darkness. From the tone of the voice, Samuel could tell it was his mother. Knowing it was harder for his older mother to kneel than his younger sister, Samuel started to object and tell his mother to stand up and not kneel, but before he could say anything, his mother spoke again from down at his level.

"Before I go to bed, I just wanted to tell you that I'm sorry for what happened," she said, taking his hand in both of hers. "I'm sad for both of you. I know you loved her. I know how much you loved her. I just wanted to say that I'm sad for both her and you for what happened. I'm especially sad for her. She deserved better treatment and a better life than the one she had. I'm sure you would have given her that better life. I would have too. I would have opened our house and home to her if she had left her former life and married you. I would have ignored her past and what she was. I would have accepted her as your wife and my daughter-in-law. I would have loved her because you loved her. I don't know if what I have to say will make you feel any better, but I wanted you to know that I would have taken her into my heart and into our family."

Samuel and his mother exchanged a few more words. Samuel's mother assured her son that she wasn't hypocritically saying that she would have accepted the girl because the girl was dead and safely out of the way. His mother didn't have a hypocritical bone in her body. She sincerely meant what she had said. Samuel believed her.

There was nothing more either could say. Samuel thanked his mother. She got up and left as silently as she had come. Samuel could hear the quiet padding of her slippers as she walked back down the hall toward her and his father's bedroom.

After Samuel's mother left him to go back to her room, he went back to staring into the darkness that both encroached on him and receded from him into eternity. When one loses a loved one, one tends to think about what they had shared and what they wouldn't share again. The two natural directions of thought pulled hard in Samuel's mind. At one and the same time they made him remember what he and the girl had shared and caused him to acknowledge the life he would not have with her.

Any thought along either line was instantly too painful to bear. He felt like he was wrapped by leather harnesses, being stretched out between two teams of draft horses pulling in opposite directions. It seemed to Samuel that if he allowed himself to think either thought, he would be overwhelmed by both and would be pulled apart mentally. Therefore, he did not allow himself to think either thought. In the enforced vacuum left behind, all he could think of were the words he had said to the girl. But as he allowed himself to think of the words he had spoken to her, in his mind the words were overridden and blanked out by the words that he had not spoken. All his words to the girl were buried under the weight of the words that he wanted to speak to her but never would. The saddest words ever spoken are the words that might have been.

With the girl dead, Samuel felt he had nowhere to go into the future. The future was as dead to him as the girl. He had gone to bed thinking that he probably wouldn't be able to sleep at all that night. At some unmarked point in the timeless night that seemed it would go on forever, Samuel fell into a fitful sleep. Entering into the land of dreams in his state of mind was not the best idea.

Samuel stood alone looking out over a formless, shapeless void hidden in the dark. He knew he was standing on ground because he could feel it under his feet. From somewhere out in the dark, he heard the sound of a girl screaming. From the tone of the scream, it sounded like Clarinda screaming. In a gripping panic of fear for her, Samuel started running in the direction he thought the scream had come from. The dark ground under his feet didn't seem to shift. He couldn't tell if he was covering ground or even moving. He ran all the harder. Presently he awoke from the dream, his legs flailing wildly in the dark room, kicking the covers off. Realizing it had only been a bad dream, he lay back down, hoping he would not have the same dream again. Soon he fell back into his fitful sleep. Mercifully the dream did not recur that night. But his sleep was fitful. His fitful sleep seemed to swirl around him, carrying him everywhere and nowhere. When Samuel opened his eyes again, the first light of dawn was gathering over the land outside his window.

When Clarinda's eyes opened, it was into the full light of a full day. Almost instantly she was up on her feet and running. Clarinda ran quickly along the river's edge down at the base of the riverbank. She ran under the ridge where the road into town crossed the river. From there she kept running along the river's edge, to the point where she knew Mrs. Richardson's house sat on the land above. She couldn't see the house from down at the river bottom. It was obscured behind the riverbank. But soon she came to the familiar cut in the bank where she had climbed down to the river and up from it before. It was not far from the place where she had had her knife-brandishing confrontation with Samuel.

At that point, Clarinda turned and tried to climb the bank. All she could think of at the moment was that she had to get back to the Richardson house. She would be safe there. But when she tried to climb the path, her feet kept slipping on the clay of the embankment. Try as she might, every time she tried to climb the bank, she slid back down to the riverbed. She had climbed it many times before. She didn't remember the bank being this slippery and impossible to negotiate. Finally she stopped trying to climb the bank she wasn't able to climb.

Clarinda stood there at the bottom of the embankment, looking up toward the house she could not see on the land, out of sight above the riverbank. Clarinda stood in her bare feet in the soft soil of the riverbed, trying to figure out why she was unable to climb the bank. The river flowed behind her, heading past and away.

Chapter 14

"Gentlemen, don't make any more out of it than what it was," a steady and sculptured-faced Ethridge said. His smile was as polished as his teeth, which half showed through his half smile. The conversation was amenable and agreeable as it is between gentlemen of like minds.

"More properly stated, don't make any more out of it than she did. I saw Sergeant Plechathy here leading her and the Martin boy into the station house that night. She seemed quite put out about the whole thing. At the same time, she looked fragile and vulnerable. What I saw was a veritable picture of misguided youth without supervision reaping the fruits of their wild behavior. In her case, I also saw an unfortunate girl who had drifted into the life she was in because of her background and lack of upbringing. I was moved by her plight and decided on the spot to be a good citizen and helpmate to the girl. To that end, I paid the girl's fine and bailed her out as the sergeant here can testify. It was a small sum for me, but gaining her release proved to be a big relief and point of gratitude for the girl."

Harold Ethridge spread out his hands in a nothing-to-hide gesture.

"And yes, gentlemen, I readily confess that I had relations with the girl afterward. She was so grateful to me for having gained her release that she practically threw herself at me, saying that I could have her for free as payment for getting her out of your lockup facility. I've seen the cells in your basement during the tour you took the town council on, and I can understand why she would be all too happy to be released from there."

Harold Ethridge brought his hands back down and laid his arms across his legs in his seated position.

"Gentlemen, I don't claim to be a saint, plaster or otherwise. I won't say that I was powerless to resist the charms of a practiced seductress and that she had me in her spell from the first moment I was alone with her. I pride myself on having more control than that. I readily say that I found her quite desirable. I accepted her version of showing gratitude to a man for the reason that I found her desirable and that I wanted her because she was desirable. In her back-alley way, the girl was quite alluring. She didn't have the shopworn look that soon comes to overcome so many prostitutes. The girl still had the freshness of youth about her. She was extremely attractive and vivacious. In many ways she was the most beautiful girl I'd ever seen. She certainly could have made a high social presentation wife to any man if she hadn't been born into such humble beginnings that provided her with so poor of a foundation an upbringing and if she hadn't from there drifted into such a socially disreputable position. If you wish, you can say that I was sowing some late wild oats. ... For your records, gentlemen, I readily confess that I readily took her up on her offer. Along with being young and attractive, she was also quite experienced at her amorous craft and quite openly shameless in her passion. But women in her profession lead lives of open shameless passion."

Constable Harkness and Sergeant Plechathy sat in the stuffed chairs in the living room of the Ethridge house, the biggest single house in town, and listened without interrupting and without making any comment as Harold Ethridge revealed the story of his contact with the nameless girl he had known only by the name Clarinda. The constable and the sergeant nodded their heads in an amenable and agreeable way as is the custom between men of like minds.

"I took her to my house in town. Afterward I drove her back to the Richardson house and left her off. From there we both went our separate ways and returned to our separate lives, such as hers was. I didn't see her again, and I had no further contact with her after that night. From the description in the newspaper, I assumed that the girl I bailed out and the one you found in the river were one and the same. It was a tragic end to a tragic life all around. I'll help you gentlemen of the police all I can, but my only contact with her was limited to that one single night with her a month ago. I never patronized the Richardson house before I met the girl. I didn't patronize the house after meeting her. I have no idea of what she did in the interim between when I met her and the time of her death. I have no idea who or what kind of men she was meeting and servicing during that interval. I only assume that she was taking care of many and varied men. After all, it was both her inclination and her profession to do so."

The light in the room was filtered through the curtains on the window. Books filled the bookshelves on one side of the room. Having been gathered by his father, most of the furniture in the house was earlier-era furniture from the Empire period. The sofa that Harold Ethridge sat on and the high-backed chairs the policemen sat in all had intricately carved arms and legs in the sections where they weren't covered by the satiny fabric that bulged over the thick stuffing and padding beneath. The chairs were ornate but comfortable. The setting was a refined and amenable and agreeable place to have a conversation between men of like minds. Everything in the room seemed in place, including the three amenable and agreeable men of like mind. The one small item that seemed a bit unusual and out of place was the somewhat large bandage-like piece of cloth that Mr. Ethridge had on one side of his neck.

"Can you give me any idea who, in your opinion, might have killed the girl?" Constable Harkness asked a policeman's background question. The question was largely rhetorical. He wasn't even fully sure why he had asked it.

"I would say your best bet would be the Martin boy," Harold Ethridge responded right away with certainty and without any noticeable pause to muse about the question. "He flew into a jealous rage and started a barroom brawl because the girl was soliciting other men in a saloon, as was the wont of her profession. For a violently jealous man, it's only a small step from turning violent against other men who are beating his time to becoming violent toward the woman he feels is two-timing him. In this case the girl was cuckolding him and doing so openly—and parading a long line of men before his eyes as she did it. His damaged and already fractured ego most likely finally snapped all the way and he went after her."

Constable Harkness scratched the side of his neck slightly.

"For the reasons you mentioned, we thought along the same lines from the beginning," he said. "Initially the Martin boy did seem to be the most likely suspect. We've already called him in and spoken with him. Unfortunately he was demonstrably elsewhere at the time that was most likely the time of the girl's death. I myself can place him there at the time. As likely of a suspect as he may be on the basis of circumstance, unless he's the quickest boy on his feet in the world, the element of timing pretty much eliminates him as being the killer. For all the boy's demonstrable temper, the killer pretty much has to be somebody else. We're thinking it was a hired hand or a manual laborer, someone as rough and acquainted with violence as the Martin boy, just not as well-known to the girl or as directly associated with her as the Martin boy was. Sometimes in crime detection, things don't present themselves to you as easily as you think."

"I maintain that if it wasn't the Martin boy, it was a hired hand," Harold Ethridge said. "That's the direction you should take your investigation in."

"A properly conducted investigation shouldn't jump to any a priori conclusions or directions," the constable said. "You can miss a lot of things that way. We intend to keep our investigation open and flexible."

The look on Harold Ethridge's face was hard to interpret. It was too controlled to be called a look of obvious disappointment, but it wasn't exactly what one could call neutral. Around the edges he seemed to look a bit like a man who has glimpsed a complication or at least has seen a small thing that he hoped would go in a certain direction not quite going the way that he would have liked it to go.

"Well, at least it looks like you and the police are already out ahead without me having to point out the direction," Harold Ethridge said. "If the Martin boy is not the killer, then it could be any number of the kind of men she was seeing. After all, she wasn't out seeking her patrons in the halls of a missionary society. She was soliciting in a saloon. You don't find the most genteel cut of men in locations like that. She could have run into any number of low-class men with low thoughts of women who thought they could do anything they liked with a two-bit tramp. One of them might have thought he was entitled to have his way with her without paying her fare. Prideful men think they can use any woman to their pleasure and bend any woman to their will."

"Mrs. Richardson has the idea that the killer may be a socially prominent member of the town," Constable Harkness said. He was making conversation more than anything. "It's part of her class-consciousness. She also wants votes for women."

Harold Ethridge smiled an oily smile. "I don't want to tell you how to go about doing your business," he said. "I think your most profitable line of inquiry is to proceed along the lines that you are pursuing. The killer will prove to be a violent and brutish man from the girl's own lower class as you suspect. I don't think there's really any reason to look beyond the level that the girl lived at."

The constable hadn't especially wanted to come there, not seeing much reason to look beyond the level at which the girl had lived and the kind of man who came from the bottom-rung social level as she had. He was satisfied that was where the answers and the killer lay. He was satisfied with Mr. Ethridge's account of his onetime encounter with the girl. He was satisfied that there was no reason to circle back and probe a prominent citizen who inhabited a social realm far above the tawdry world the girl inhabited. He asked no further questions concerning her.

For a short while longer, the three men of the town sat and chatted amiably and agreeably, mostly concerning other town issues. Having satisfied himself that Harold Ethridge had nothing to offer the investigation and was not going to take it in any alternate direction beyond the one they had amiably and agreeably agreed that it should continue in, Constable Harkness stirred himself to leave. As he went to rise from his chair, the constable's gaze and curiosity was again drawn to the bandage on Harold Ethridge's neck. He pointed to it.

"What happened to your neck?" he asked in a friendly, agreeable, and nonprobing way.

"I nicked myself shaving with a straight razor," Harold Ethridge responded. "After all these years, I still haven't gotten the full knack of it. A straight razor can be a tricky and unforgiving device to employ."

The answer satisfied the constable. For an instant it did seem to him that Mr. Ethridge was wearing the bandage rather low on his neck. The position was almost below the level at which there would be any beard hairs to shave. But it was a minor point. He saw no reason to ask him more about it.

The constable and Sergeant Plechathy left the house of Harold Ethridge. For a moment, as he left, Constable Harkness thought to ask Ethridge if he had asked the girl to keep his name quiet the one time they were together. But he decided that the point was trivial and unrelated, not the thing to be asking a respected member of the town council and a prominent citizen.

Chapter 15

"I had to go all the way to the Henderson Monument Company in Chillicothe to have it made," Samuel said. "It's one of the better monument companies in the area. A lot of people use it. They had a lot of other work to do at the monument company. That and all the carving I had them do on her stone is why it took all this time to have it done and get the stone placed. But here it is."

Mrs. Richardson looked at the newly placed gravestone that Samuel had brought her to the graveyard to inspect.

"The stone's not as fancy as granite, but it's just as hard and weather resistant as granite. A stone this size cut out of granite would have cost twice as much. As it is, this stone took most of my life savings to prepare. The carving costs as much as the stone itself. I had the letters cut deep so that it will carry her name for as long as it stands. I just wish I knew what her real name was."

Mrs. Richardson ran her hand over the curved top of the stone. It was almost a loving caress.

"I might have been able to afford a little bigger stone if I hadn't had so much carving done on this one," Samuel went on. "But that would have limited what I could have had put on it to just her name and dates. In some way I wanted to tell her story. I suppose I did get a bit wordy. But I wanted to tell her story, if only in some poetic way. This way someone who sees this stone in the future will wonder who she was and what her story was."

Mrs. Richardson looked at the words of the epitaph carved into the stone:

UNKNOWN GIRL, APPROX. 17 YRS.
1895?–1912
CALLED "CLARINDA"
REAL NAME UNKNOWN

I DIED ALONE FAR FROM MY HOME.
NOBODY KNOWS FROM WHERE I CAME.
THIS STONE AT MY HEAD
WILL SAY I AM DEAD
AND KNOW ME BY NO OTHER NAME.

"It says well enough what you felt for her," Mrs. Richardson said. "Anyone who sees this will probably stop and take note of all that's said here."

"But they won't know her real name," Samuel said. "She took that with her to this grave."

"She never told me her real name either," Mrs. Richardson said. "She came to me with her real name already buried."

They were both silent for a moment.

"I appreciate what you've done for the girl," Mrs. Richardson said. "This tombstone is very nice. It's more than nice. It tells her story in a few lines. In many ways it does sum up her life. At least it sums up what she lost in life. At least people who see this stone will know that she lived and was loved."

Mrs. Richardson looked down the low slope of the graveyard toward the more populated central section.

"I was never sure why you chose this spot up here on the ridge near the trees at the back of the cemetery," Mrs. Richardson said. "If I was doing it, I would have put her down there in the center, where more people would see what's written on her tombstone. Why did you place her here on the edge of the cemetery, on the edge of the woods?"

Samuel wanted to say that the girl had lived on many different edges, but he felt that saying it would be disrespectful of the girl who had died on the edge of life.

"She came to us from out of the woods," Samuel said, "the woods of West Virginia and the woods around here. She came to us out of the fringes of life. She lived with us on the fringe of polite society, out beyond the fringe of this town. We buried her on the fringe of the world she lived on and looked out on. People in this town looked down on her. Even those who paid to use her services looked down on her. Up here, she can look down on the town and on the people who looked down on her."

Mrs. Richardson assumed the boy had chosen the spot in order to give the girl a small symbolic victory over everyone who had used and abused her and over the low-order life that had abused her all the more.

"It's a nice grave," Mrs. Richardson repeated.

"But she's in a grave," Samuel said with noticeable choking bitterness in his voice. "And when the sun rises tomorrow and all the days of eternity on this earth, she'll still be in her grave. The man who killed her is still out there nearby somewhere. He's probably gloating to himself about how he got away with killing her like the piece of trash he thought of her as. I intend to find out who it was if it takes me the rest of my life, the life I won't have with her."

"I've heard it said that you've been all over the town asking if anyone knows anything about who killed her," Mrs. Richardson said, continuing to look at the tombstone. "You may be a good farmer, but you're no Sherlock Holmes. Shouldn't you be leaving this to the police?"

"Harkness probably dropped the case an hour after Frank MacKenzie and his son dropped the girl's body off at the police station," Samuel said. "He probably stopped looking for her killer before he even started. It's like I told you at the house the day Harkness called us in to identify the body: Clarinda was probably nothing more than a dirty little whore to him, a whore whose killer he probably has no intention to try to run down."

Mrs. Richardson turned and took Samuel's arm in her hand. "Come with me back to the house," she said, in an attempt to direct the conversation away from all the subjects at hand. "I thank you for providing her with a big headstone. It's more than we at the house would have done. But if I stay here any longer, I'm going to start crying again."

Still holding Samuel's arm with her hand, Mrs. Richardson started leading him down to where her car was parked in the lane at the foot of the slope leading to the top of the ridge and the girl's now completed grave.

In her life, the girl had seemed to be in constant motion, both physically and in her spirit and emotions. Neither Samuel nor Mrs. Richardson had ever been sure from one day to the next what she was thinking or where she might go next. Now she was forever motionless. On earth at least. Samuel didn't know where the girl had started her journey from. He had never been fully sure where the girl saw herself going in her journey. Now her journey had come to an abrupt and unexpected end that no one had seen coming. The girl indeed wouldn't be going anywhere further. He especially knew that the girl would never be coming home with him. Not in this world.

At the front door of the house, where the uncompleted story had started, Mrs. Richardson climbed the two short steps up to the small front stoop. Samuel climbed to the stoop himself but stopped just after the top step. That was the spot he had chosen from which he would say goodbye to the woman. After he had said his goodbyes and Mrs. Richardson had passed through the door, he would turn and walk away from the house and not ever return. Mrs. Richardson put her hand on the knob of the front door, but instead of opening the door, she turned to Samuel.

"Somehow I have a feeling we won't be seeing any more of you around here now that she's buried and her marker set," Mrs. Richardson said in a matter-of-fact tone of voice.

"I don't suppose you will, ma'am," Samuel said in a matter-of-fact voice. "I met Clarinda here. We parted down by the river outside this house. Good and bad, there are just too many memories associated with this house for me to abide if I were to come back in any capacity. Coming back here would only remind me that she will never come back here. It's best that I just stay away."

"Well, I thank you again for all that you've done for the girl," Mrs. Richardson said, putting her hand on the knob of the front door once again. "You've done quite a favor for her and for all of us. If it's not too forward of a thing to ask, before you go, there's one more little favor. It won't cost you a cent."

"What's that?" the gentlemanly and ever agreeable Samuel asked. Mrs. Richardson paused in turning the knob of the front door.

"Before you go from this house, never to return again, would you take me up into my room and make love to me?" Mrs. Richardson asked straightforwardly in her madam's matter-of-fact voice. "This is not a house of deep love from the heart. You're a boy who loves from the heart. If only for a short while, I want to feel a heart that can love for real and hold it close to me."

Samuel stood at the bottom of the front stoop with his mouth open, not knowing what to say or how to respond.

"Just like that?" Samuel asked.

"All love in this house is on a 'just like that' basis," Mrs. Richardson answered. "This house and all houses like it are dedicated to love just like that."

In the bright sun and cool harvest season air of an early October country day, the shadow of a moving cloud crossed behind the house on the other side of the road, behind where they were standing, heading past and away.

"We won't be doing anything faster and more detached than you and Clarinda did the night you met her and had her for the first time. Afterward you can forget me the way you would have forgotten any of the other girls."

"You don't have to do this," Samuel said weakly, not being able to think of anything else to say.

"Do you think that, even for a short while, you could feel love for me the way you felt love for the girl? I just want to feel the kind of love she felt from you, even if it's her and not me you're feeling that love for."

"I'm not sure what I feel about anything anymore," Samuel said. "I'm not sure how much I'll ever feel again, or whether I'll ever love again or be able to love again. … I just don't think that I'll ever love any woman the way I loved her. Right now I can't think beyond the fact that she's gone."

"Would you at least sit with me in my room for a while?" Mrs. Richardson asked. "We can talk or just sit quietly."

Samuel couldn't say no to the sad-faced woman. "Lead on," he said.

Mrs. Richardson held out her hand. Samuel took her hand. Rather, she took his. Mrs. Richardson turned the doorknob, and they walked into the house together.

With Mrs. Richardson holding his hand, they walked through the front hall, heading toward the stairs to the second floor. The only girl of the house in evidence passed down the long hall holding a bundle of rumpled clothes in her arms. Apparently she was doing laundry. The other girls of the house were either off doing chores, in their rooms, or outside on the lawn that overlooked the river. It wasn't a Currier and Ives poster, but it was pastoral enough for a portrait of a small-town bordello.

"Is it because I'm not the girl that you can't make love to me?" Mrs. Richardson said as she sat down on the edge of the bed. "Are you so still in love with her that you can't make love to any other woman?"

"It's not that or that I find you unattractive," Samuel said as he walked toward the window of Mrs. Richardson's second-floor room. "It's just too soon. Right now half my mind is filled with the thought that I'll never see her again. The other half of my head is filled with wanting to find the man who killed her. I'm not sure I'll ever get her or what happened to her out of my head. Right now there's not a lot of room in my head or heart to think of anything else."

Samuel stopped at the window and stood looking out. But he wasn't looking at anything in particular.

"I suppose you're thinking about her," Mrs. Richardson said to the boy, who was gazing out the window with a faraway look on his face, "still loving her no matter how far away she is, dreaming of her even though you know you'll never see her again, wondering what life would have been like with her, and sure that you could win her over and take her to be with you."

Samuel didn't say anything. He just kept looking out the window through the gap in the drapes.

"You may call me a liar. You may get angry with me. You may storm out of here saying you're not coming back …"

Samuel was planning to do none of those things. He continued looking out the window.

"But you would never have had a life with her."

Samuel continued looking out the window.

"She wasn't planning on staying here in this house or in this town, with me or you."

Samuel continued looking out the window.

"Once she got herself a little more seasoned as a prostitute, she planned to leave and go to one of the big-name bordellos in Chicago or in the Storyville district of New Orleans. I know she was because she told me that's what she was planning to do. She talked to me about it more than once. She had saved up travel money. She just didn't tell you that's what she was going to do."

Samuel looked slightly toward Mrs. Richardson. Then he turned his head back to looking out the window.

"She was still young enough and good-looking enough that she would have been taken right in. That's one of the reasons she put you on restriction against seeing her after you had the fight over her in the bar. It wasn't that she was afraid of you so much. It's that it would make it easier for her to slip away. One day you'd just find her gone, and you wouldn't know where she had gone, so there would be no way you could get her back."

Samuel continued to look out the window.

"I'm not trying to turn you against her. I'm trying to say she would have never turned toward you, and she was planning on turning all the way away from you."

Samuel continued looking out the window.

"You wanted to make a home for her. The home she wanted wasn't here in this house or with you. The only home she wanted was at the end of the road to a bigger and better brothel."

Samuel looked at Mrs. Richardson.

"Sam, she was never with you. She was already long gone from you before she died. She came in from off the road. In a way she had always been on the road."

"I guess I kind of always knew that," Samuel said in a quiet, almost desolate voice, looking out the window. "I guess her hard life had hardened all her thinking and heart to where she couldn't believe in much of anything, including love. Not any kind of love beyond what she gave in here."

With a quick snap like ice breaking, Samuel's voice went from dissolute to being edged as sharp as a hunting knife.

"Some murdering bastard took away the time she might have had. He took the possibility of a better life away from her. He took what chance she had to get beyond the hard life she had lived and get to a real life, a life with the love she never had. He took her away from me and the future I could have given her. He took her away from me as much as he took away her life. When I find out who he is, I'm going to take him down to hell, if I have to drag him down there myself!"

"There are plenty of girls in this house who've had lives as hard as hers," Mrs. Richardson said, in an attempt to direct him away from wherever he was heading. "If they had better lives to turn to, they wouldn't be here. If you want to save a woman from a hard life going nowhere, take up with one of the other girls here and give her the home and love for a lifetime you wanted to share with Clarinda."

The trouble being that the other girls of the house were up to and over a decade older than Samuel, and they weren't much better-looking than Katherine Clarke.

Samuel turned his face back to the window and looked out. He spotted a familiar face. "There's one of your girls now. It's Polly."

Almost as soon as Polly appeared in his field of view out the window, from around the same corner a familiar short male figure appeared, following Polly. Samuel recognized his friend.

"And there's Ben Harper," Samuel went on in the same breath. "I didn't know he was here."

"Either he was busy when we arrived or he arrived when we were busy," Mrs. Richardson said. "That's why you missed him. By design and intent, those who come to this house end up behind closed doors. People in this house tend to pass by each other in more ways than one."

Out on the lawn in back of the house, Ben caught up with Polly and walked at her pudgy side. As Samuel watched, they walked to the edge of the embankment and went down the slope. Whatever they had been doing before or would do after, at the moment they were apparently going for a walk by the river as he and Clarinda had.

"Well, there's at least one romance in this house that's still alive and intact," Samuel said as his friend and his friend's social-conventions-defying prostitute sweetheart disappeared from sight behind the top of the embankment. He turned his head to look at Mrs. Richardson.

A feeling came over him. He didn't know if it was romantic boldness, cold fatalism, or the fear that fate might in some way repeat the cold and empty end of his own failed love story.

"If he holds back too long the way I did, he may find himself like me, outside of love and unable to get back in." Samuel straightened up and moved away from the wall and the drapes he had been leaning against. "Someone's got to tell that lunkhead to get moving before he loses her like I lost Clarinda." For all Samuel knew, Ben might lose Polly to murder at the hands of the same man who had killed Clarinda. "I do believe that I'll have a word with him on the matter."

Samuel left the window and headed across the room. In the process, he walked past a confused Mrs. Richardson, who was still thinking of getting him into bed with her. As Samuel passed by Mrs. Richardson, he neglected to tell her when and if he would ever be back.

Outside Mrs. Richardson's room, Samuel headed down the upstairs hall, down the stairs, and out the front door. Several of Mrs. Richardson's girls on the first floor saw him pass. If his secret with Mrs. Richardson had been an actual secret up to that point, it was definitely out now. Samuel definitely didn't care. All he wanted to do at the moment was save one small semblance of the kind of love he had known, even if he made a fool of himself doing it.

Samuel crossed the north yard of the Richardson property and stopped at the edge of the embankment. Down at the bottom of the embankment he could see Ben and Polly with their backs turned, walking slowly away, side by side, on the shore of the river. Ben wasn't even holding her hand.

From where he had stopped, Samuel moved to the place on the bank he had gone down the day he had met Clarinda and tried to apologize. He scrambled down to the bottom of the bank and set off on a run after the couple. It was quiet down by the river. Ben and Polly heard the sound of someone coming up behind them at a run. They turned around as Samuel came up to them and stopped in front of them. They stood facing each other at a spot along the river that was only a short distance beyond the place where Samuel had faced Clarinda.

"Sam!" Ben said in surprise. "I didn't know you were here today."

Samuel looked straight at Ben. "I came here after I set Clarinda's stone," he said. "I said my final goodbye to her at the same time. I won't be back here again. There's nothing more for me here."

A month earlier, Samuel had gone down to the river in an attempt to save his love for the girl. He had failed that day. This day he had come back down to the river bottom in an attempt to save love again—vicariously, for his friend.

"But there's something here for you, provided you don't fumble it like a stupid jackass the way I did." He pointed to Polly. "You've been coming here to see her as much as I came to the house to see Clarinda. I can tell you're in love with her even if you don't know your own mind." He looked at Polly and pointed at Ben. "The day I came to the house after they brought Clarinda in dead, I told you to tell him to stop hiding and come out into the light and make his feelings for you plain. I don't know if you did." He looked at Ben. "But somebody's got to tell you to do it before another love story out of this house gets buried forever."

Samuel looked back into the surprised face of his friend.

"If you're in love with her, you'd better get off your duff, boy, and tell her and do something about it. If you keep on holding back like you've been doing, like I did with Clarinda, one day you're going to wake up and find her gone one way or the other, either dead or off to another house or another man. If I can save one thing out of the mess I made of my chance at love, I'm going to salvage love somewhere for somebody, even if I have to kick your ass to do it."

Ben's mouth was still open in the face of the unexpected verve he was hearing from his friend. Polly was as silent in her surprise as Ben.

"I loved Clarinda, but I lost her by waiting too long and by going crazy when I did finally take my love to her. I have nothing left of that love now, nothing but to try to see that your love gets fulfilled, nothing but to see that some kind of real love gets saved. Maybe if I can save love for one of her friends and make sure that her friend gets that love, it will in some small way make it up to Clarinda."

Polly's mouth closed. Her pudgy girl face softened.

"Like I told you up in her room," Polly said with a lisp that was filled with real sympathy, "we were all so sad at w'th happened to her. We were all sad for you. You were good to her and good for her. All of us felt that you and her should h'f been together."

"She didn't think that we should have been together," Samuel said in another extension of his self-flagellation. "She sent me away from her because I had acted violent in her presence. I scared her off and lost the love she might have come to."

"But you w's never violent to her," Polly said with her signature lisp. It was the same observation that Samuel had tried unsuccessfully to convince Clarinda of.

"It w's the oth'r man she w's seeing who w's violent to her. But he must h've hid the way he w's from her till it w's too late for her to see. He had her fooled right to the end. Near the end there, when she went out to see him one of the last times she did, she called him her Mr. Teddy Bear or s'methin' like that. He m'st have sweet-talked her to the end."

"I was the one who gave her the teddy bear," Samuel said. A double pang went through Samuel as he thought that the girl had not only transferred her affections for him to the other man but also that, in her mind, she had transferred the gift he had given her into a nickname for the secret man she was seeing. A third and worse pang was the thought that the man had who killed her had advanced in Clarinda's mind behind the soft and harmless symbol of love Samuel had given her.

"Well, it w'sn't Mr. Teddy Bear she called him," Polly said. "Now that I remember it, it w's s'methin' like that but d'ff'rent. It w's s'methin' to do with a bear. I think she called him Mr. Bear Cub."

Samuel froze at the sound of the name.

"But it w'sn't a bear cub she called him. It was some oth'r strange animal. I remember that it sounded like two animals put together."

Polly screwed up her bucktoothed mouth like she was thinking hard. Samuel figured that at her level of mental acumen, it was probably a struggle for her to remember what she had for breakfast.

"I remember now," Polly said. "It w's Bearcat."

A bolt of black lightning fixed Samuel to the spot where he stood. His body tensed as his arms straightened and froze at his sides.

"What was that name?" Samuel said.

"Bearcat," Polly repeated. "She'd been seein' someone in town regular-like for close to a month. She started seeing him right after you and she had your fight. But she wouldn't give out h's name because he didn't want her to. She kept his confidence, even with us. One time when she w's goin' out, I ask'd who she w's goin' to see. She said she w's goin' to see her Mr. Bearcat. I assumed it w's the man she w's seein'. I heard her call him that the one time only. It w's him she was on her way to see the night she didn't come back."

Polly's lisping words cut off sharply at that point when she found her arms grabbed and held hard by Samuel's hands. The force of his grip pulled her forward to the point that her heels came up off the ground. As he held her in a hard grip, Samuel leaned forward and looked hard into her pudgy, bucktoothed face.

"Are you sure about that name?" Samuel said, his words as intense as his stare and his grip. "Mr. Bearcat?"

Almost pulled off-balance by Samuel's grasp, Polly gasped in surprise. Her lisp became worse.

"Ah … y'th," Polly stammered. "Now that I think about it, I remember it. … It w'th Mr. Bearcat. I couldn't make up a nickname like that, but she could."

"Damn!" Samuel growled as the full realization burst in on him like a battering ram. "Damn him to all hell here and below!"

Samuel pulled harder on Polly's arms, pulling her forward more. An alarmed Ben stepped in to protect the girl he was in love with.

"Sam," Ben said. He grabbed Samuel's nearest arm with both his hands. The muscles in his friend's arms seemed as taut and hard as steel. He had no clue what was going on in Samuel's mind.

Polly wasn't sure why he was reacting the way he was. In Polly's limited mind, she figured her working sister in the house had made up the name for herself as a way of describing the man's sexual prowess. Polly figured she had combined the names of two large, powerful, and virile animals, a bear and a wildcat, to describe the man's sexual power and energy. At the same time she figured that Samuel recognized that the nickname meant that she had found a man whom she considered more sexually virile and potent than he and that she preferred the man to him. Polly knew that men have a way of getting really angry when they think some other man is beating their sexual time, especially when their woman finds the other man to be more of a man, and especially when the cuckolded man is known to be hot-tempered.

"I'm sorry she had the nickname for him," Polly said with a tone of alarm slipping into her voice. "But it d'sn't necessarily mean that she preferred him over you. He may h'f just been athletic or something and run her ragged. She may still h'f loved you more than she did the man."

"That's not what she meant!" Samuel said, shaking Polly's arms once. The tone of his voice rose exponentially.

"It's not a man she was referring to …" His lips pulled back, baring his teeth like a snarling dog. The rising curve of his voice flattened out and transformed into a grisly-sounding hiss. He looked to the side. His eyes had a sharp-edged crystalline glare like the surface of freshly broken cast iron. His fixed gaze seemed to be looking through and past both of them. "It's a car!"

Samuel brought his iron gaze back and looked into Polly's eyes. Polly didn't know what he was seeing through his eyes. She didn't know what she was seeing in his eyes. Whatever it was, it frightened her.

"A fancy, expensive car. There's only one man in this town who has that kind of car," Samuel said, grinding his words between his teeth. "He's already a real lady-killer when it comes to playing fast and loose with women and then dropping them. Looks like he's graduated to killing women for real and dropping them in the river!"

Samuel slid his words back and forth inside his jaw as if grinding something in his teeth. He reached around behind him and pulled out the hunting knife he carried in its sheath. He held the knife up, twisting it. The sun glinted off the blade. Both Polly and Ben gasped.

"I do believe I'm going to have a word with him on this matter!"

Without saying anything more, Samuel released his grip on Polly's arms and turned to go. Ben had both his own hands on one of Samuel's arms, but Samuel pulled away from Ben's grasp as if Ben hadn't been holding him at all. Ben couldn't hold Samuel or slow him down. As Samuel started to walk away, Ben tried to grab his other arm as it came around. With one hand, Samuel pushed him out of the way so hard that he fell backward and off his feet. Before Ben could get back up and grab him again, Samuel took off running in the direction he had come.

At the truck, Samuel jarred the engine to life with a furious turn of the crank, jumped in, and shifted gears hard. As the truck started to roll, he gritted his teeth so hard that he felt the enamel would crack. He held the steering wheel in a death grip, broken only by his attempt to pull the throttle beyond the maximum to make the truck go faster.

When Samuel arrived back at the farm, he drove the truck in through the open door of the barn where it was kept, shut it off, and jumped out, leaving the door half open. There were no interior lights that stayed on with the open door to run down the battery. There was no battery. Inside the barn, instead of heading into the house, Samuel went quickly over to the workbench in the corner. A variety of tools hung from nails driven into the wooden wall above the workbench. Samuel reached up and pulled a hunting knife with a seven-inch blade off the wall.

For several minutes Samuel stood nearly motionless, looking at the heavy blade of the knife in his hand, breathing through his teeth in hissing anger. Visions of the girl's death throes were replaced with visions of the knife in his hand slashing in spiral motions like the sails of a windmill whirling out of control in the vortex of a tornado. In his frenzied imagination, strands of flesh flew like strips of bacon in the same high wind. Guttural male screams and gurglings pushing up through a thick blanket of blood replaced the sounds of the girl's last screams and her drowning gurgles coming up from under the surface of the river. At any given moment he could have easily exploded back into the truck and driven away with the knife stuck in his belt.

But with all the fire in his mind and heart, Samuel held himself in place. In the back of his mind he remembered a line from a Wild West adventure pulp magazine he had read once. In the magazine's main story, the grizzled old veteran gunfighter counseled the hotheaded young gunslinger who was out to take revenge on the bandit gang that had murdered his family: "Revenge is a dish that must be eaten cold or you'll choke on it."

In police work of all ages, the most likely suspect is the one who usually turns out to be guilty. Harold Ethridge was most likely the killer of the girl. But being the most likely suspect isn't proof of guilt. Constable Harkness's theory that it could be someone else could be right after all. Clarinda might have been attacked by a transient worker or a farmhand on the way back from Ethridge's. If Samuel were to kill Ethridge but Ethridge hadn't killed the girl, Samuel would be summarily executing an innocent man while the guilty man walked around free in his lower-class world, free in his squirming toad soul.

Samuel needed some kind of proof that Ethridge had killed the girl. It didn't have to be proof that went beyond all reasonable doubt and would survive any legal challenge. It just had to be one thing that pointed out of the dark in a way that let him know he was in the presence of a killer.

Samuel lowered the knife and looked around. Farther away, at an oblique angle to him, Samuel saw light coming into the barn through the open side door. Beyond that, across the open space that separated the two buildings, was the farmhouse and the back door. The back door was unlocked. Inside the house the gun rack was unlocked.

Chapter 16

As was his habit when he was spending the night on his farm, Harold Ethridge did a walk-around inspection of the farm facilities before retiring for the night to see if anything was amiss. At that particular time on that particular night, he was finishing up his inspection routine by walking through the inside of the hog barn. The hired hands who worked on the farm had gone to bed. That night the inspection was mostly a perfunctory and passing affair he could have dispensed with. There was nothing wrong or out of place that he could see. Harold Ethridge was otherwise satisfied with the way things were going for him. In his managed disposition of agriculturally conventional problematic matters that arose from time to time, or in his disposition of unconventional problematic women, by his own definition he had handled all problems that had come his way. Not even a hint had developed that would indicate that the problems he had dealt with in the near past would return to haunt him in any way. Everything was turning out the way he had wanted it to. But it is when things seem to be going the best and going your way that things can fall apart completely. Both Samuel and the girl could testify to that.

It was the beginning of fall. Days were growing short all around. Outside it was close enough to a crisp autumn night. In the chilled night sky above, a few stars twinkled. In the lower altitudes the air was still. No breeze or wind stirred in restlessly across the chilled and dark landscape like a lost specter looking for rest. Everything in the darkened shadows of the countryside seemed set and frozen in place by the chilled hand lying on the land. On the ground there was the possibility of a frost that night. If so, it would be the first frost of the approaching winter season. The deepening cold wrapped itself around the remaining standing stubble of the harvested corn crop. With tops rounded or cut off square, row upon row, the stumps of the cornstalks stretched beyond, quickly vanishing into the darkness. Though frost usually starts near the ground, the stubs were so short that there really wasn't much for any approaching frost to get ahold of. Something taller was needed. Now devoid of most of their leaves, the trees around the perimeter of the farm held their skeletal limbs motionless in the unmoving air as the sky slowly turned above.

Inside the barn, the hogs stirred and grunted quietly in their pens as Harold Ethridge walked the length of the elongated hog barn and back. At the front end of the hog barn, at the completion of his inspection, he turned with his back to the closed main door and looked back the way he had come. Here too he was satisfied.

"Sure does smell in here," he heard a voice say from behind him and to the side. Harold Ethridge didn't jump in startled surprise at the sound of the voice behind him. At first he simply thought it was one of his hired hands making a quip. There wasn't any other logical source for the voice. But he didn't recognize the voice.

"But I guess one does have to consider the source."

He turned and saw a teenage boy standing just inside the small side door to the hog barn. The boy had his hand on the doorframe as if he had just stepped into the barn.

"A pig walks around ankle deep in his own manure all his life. I guess he does become accustomed to it to the point where he can't even notice how bad he smells."

The boy pushed off of the doorframe and started to walk into the barn toward Harold.

"I guess the same thing can happen to a man who tends pigs. After a while he gets so he doesn't know how bad he smells to others, the smells that permeate the air around him and become part of him. He gets to a point that he doesn't even think people can notice his smell. He just goes on thinking everyone thinks he's clean. A man finally gets to the point that he doesn't know how bad he and his world smells until someone outside tells him."

The boy walked slowly toward him.

"We don't have hogs on our farm. I supposed I'd have gotten used to the smell of them by now if we did. But all we have on our farm are a few milk cows."

The boy glanced around at the hogs in their pens.

"I suppose all these hogs are going to be sent out to a slaughterhouse. … We keep our animals around. They're kind of like family to us. We don't drag our animals out by the neck to be butchered."

"You can't milk a hog," Harold Ethridge said. "About the only thing you can do with hogs is fatten them for the slaughter."

Harold Ethridge recognized the boy as the Martin boy. In a small town where everyone knew everyone else, he knew the Martin boy. He had seen him around the town at various times. Of late it seemed that his contact with the boy was growing closer. The closest he had been to him was in Kindelspire's restaurant and soda fountain, where he had seen him sitting with the girl. He had seen the boy from almost as close of a distance the night he had seen police bring the boy and the girl into the station house after the boy had gotten into a fight over the girl. Now, inexplicably, the boy was standing in his barn after dark.

"You are Frank Martin's son, aren't you?" The question was more or less rhetorical.

Samuel's answer was less than rhetorical. "That's right," he said. "I'm surprised you recognize me, sir. I didn't know you knew me."

"In one way or another, I know everyone in this town," Harold Ethridge answered. "I may not be on a first-name speaking basis with everyone, but, by sight if nothing else, I know just about everyone who lives in this town, especially farmers like me and their sons. If I remember correctly, your name is Sam. Do I have that right?"

Samuel stopped moving. From his position he looked Harold Ethridge straight in the face. "Right as can be, sir," he said. "Right as any of the names people go by in this town. Right as any name a given name can be. But then you're probably familiar with the names of people who never gave you their real names. From what I've heard, you're a lot more intimately acquainted with the names of women in this town than with the names of men."

Given that the girl hadn't informed him that Clarinda wasn't her real name and he hadn't asked, Harold Ethridge wasn't sure what the boy meant about knowing people who didn't give their real names. He figured that the boy's comment that he was more acquainted with the names of the townswomen rather than the names of the townsmen was apparently a snide reference to his reputation as a womanizer. Mind you, it was a reputation he had never taken pains to deny. The boy's bringing it up in such a manner seemed a rather insolent way to start off a conversation. But at the moment, Harold Ethridge was more puzzled by the reasons for the boy's strange appearance in his barn after dark than he was offended by his curt manners.

"Either way, I have seen you around town many times before," Harold Ethridge said. Harold Ethridge was a man who kept his edges carefully concealed. Nevertheless, a certain edge came into the tone of his voice. "I've just never seen you around here on my property before. And I've never seen you walk openly into one of my barns before, especially at this time of night. What, may I ask, is the reason for the pleasure of your visit to me here at this late hour?"

Samuel started walking again. Instead of walking toward Mr. Ethridge, he walked around him, toward the hogpens.

"My father and I were thinking of possibly going into the hog raising business ourselves," Samuel said, looking toward the hogs in their pens. "I wanted to come and take a look at the way you did things. I thought maybe I could learn a thing or two about the way you do business when it comes to raising hogs, butchering them, and disposing of the carcasses."

"I just raise them till they're the right size and weight to bring the best price on the market," Harold Ethridge said. "Then I ship them off. I don't do the butchering and processing. That's done at the slaughterhouse."

At this juncture, Samuel could have said something to the cryptic effect that this place was a slaughterhouse, but for the moment he held his tongue.

"Then they're alive when they leave here, heading wherever it is you send them?" Samuel asked. He bit his tongue twice as hard so as not to make a less than cryptic comment about a body leaving the premises accompanied by Mr. Ethridge, still alive and breathing but unable to move.

"Yes," Harold Ethridge answered, as puzzled by the boy's question as he was about his comment about his knowing people without names. "I would be only too happy to show you and your father my operation," he went on. "But you should bring your father with you and come back during the day. This is a rather unusual and awkward hour to try to explain the hog farming business to you."

But wanting to learn the livestock breeding business did not even begin to explain why the boy was there at night asking him for advice. It seemed to Harold Ethridge that there had to be more going on than a one-farmer-to-the-other friendly exchange of information on how to go about entering a new and unfamiliar agricultural market. The boy's father could have done that with a friendly visit during the day at any of his places of business on the farm or in town, or over drinks at a bar. The boy's request for information didn't fit with the primary source who apparently wanted the information. The boy's request for information fit even less with the timing of his appearance.

"Did your father send you here to ask me about hog farming at this time of night?"

"No, it was my idea," Samuel said in a leading tone. "I came here on my own. Father doesn't even know I was coming here."

Neither did a friendly request for information fit with the sour and brittle tone of the boy's voice.

"Well, if you came for my advice at this late hour, I would say that you should forget the whole idea," Harold Ethridge commented. "Hog farming can be an expensive thing to get into if you're starting from scratch. It's not like growing the standard farm cash crops on a small piece of land. It takes a lot of land and specialized facilities. That all takes a big outlay of capital. I've got almost four times the amount of land as your father's holding. I have enough room to do both. I don't think a small farm like yours could afford to turn over enough of your land to livestock raising and maintenance to make it pay. You'd lose a good deal of your tillable land on a speculative venture that could blow up in your face."

Samuel walked closer to one of the hogpens. "Are you afraid of the possible competition?" he asked in a tone that was as loaded as it was leading.

"The meatpacking industry is growing right along with the population of the country," Harold Ethridge said. "Demand for processed meat is constantly rising. There's plenty of room for all of us in the business. But like I said, you need capital, land, and know-how to pull it off and make it pay. Neither you nor your family have enough of either of that to put it together from nothing."

"From what I've heard, your father started out as a straight farmer," Samuel said. "You're the one who expanded into livestock raising and into the livestock commodity trade. If you started from scratch, why can't I?"

"I congratulate you on your forward thinking," Harold Ethridge said. "It shows that you have ambition. But you shouldn't use me as a model. We're not starting out on the same plane. Other than being farmers, we don't share at lot in common."

"Oh, we have shared one marketable, salable commodity in common," Samuel said. Harold Ethridge assumed he meant the standard corn crop they had both grown that year.

"What commodity is that?" Harold Ethridge asked. The tone of the boy's voice made him wonder if he was jealous because Harold's total yield had been four times that of Samuel's father's farm.

Samuel walked a step closer to the hogpens. He waved his hand toward the hogs. "Are all these hogs going to be sent out?" he asked, not answering Harold Ethridge's question.

"Yes," Harold Ethridge answered.

"Where do they get sent?"

"That depends on what packinghouse I sell them to. Here in the state, some of them go to the original fast-line scientific slaughterhouse in Cincinnati. In the Midwest, just about all the rest go to one of the big packinghouses in Chicago. That's where all the big meatpacking companies are located—Armour, Swift. I can tell you something about raising hogs, but if you really want to know the meatpacking business, you have to go to Chicago and take a tour of one of the big packing plants. I did once. It's really quite fascinating. They have it down to an assembly line system. They can take a full-grown live steer down to processed cuts of meat in less time than it takes for a cow to give birth to a calf."

"Well now, a skillful hand can always take a weakling creature in his power down into death in less time than it took a mother in her hours of pain and labor to deliver," Samuel said in a spit-choked voice. "Sometimes all it takes is a sharp crack of the wrists. But being so familiar with the inner workings of a slaughterhouse, you, I guess, should know all about that and how things get done there. You probably came home with your head full of knowledge about how to kill fast and quiet—like I said, with just a twist of the wrist."

What Harold Ethridge knew at that point was that this wasn't about either the hog raising business or the meat processing industry.

"What did you really come here for, boy?" Harold Ethridge asked, his tone changing from one of veiled condescension to one of rising and less than veiled suspicion. "And don't tell me you want to know about raising hogs. You're not here to ask me about how I go about disposing of my animals. There's more to you than that. Why are you here?!"

Samuel stopped dead in his tracks. And it wasn't because Harold Ethridge had seen through his story of wanting to learn about the hog raising business. More specifically it was Harold Ethridge's words that had stopped him in his tracks. Even more specifically, it was one particular word that stopped him in his tracks. Samuel wasn't even sure why he had started in with the charade about wanting to learn about hog farming in the first place. He had just wanted to put Harold Ethridge at ease and get him started on talking. At the time, the story of wanting to go into the livestock commodities trade had seemed like the best story to lead in with. But the real story of why he was there would be just as dicey to get into from any angle or starting point.

Starting points no longer meant anything to Samuel. In his mind he had known only endings since the girl had died. Only end points held any meaning for him anymore. The coldness set in when the final realization set in that the point where was standing was not far from one of the two probable places where the girl's story had ended. The coldness set into Samuel double, to the final degree, as he knew he was standing just out of reach of the man who had brought her story to an end. Before she had taken the road to his town, the girl's life had been nothing but an endless road of pain and fear. While the girl had been alive and with him, Samuel had wanted to turn the story of her life from one of pain and fear to one of love, joy, and family triumphing over the pain and fear. Instead of escaping from pain and fear, she had died in pain and fear. When the girl's story had ended, her chance for love had ended. When she had been killed, Samuel considered that more than his lover and his love had ended; he considered his ability to love had ended.

It was the time and place for endings all around. The first thing to be ended was his charade of wanting to learn the hog raising business. Nevertheless, Harold Ethridge's hogs had one more small role to play. Samuel turned back at an angle to face Harold Ethridge. At the same time he kept himself angled toward the hogpen he was closest to. Harold Ethridge's words had run through him like a steel blade thrust downward from the base of his neck. They had stopped his heart as cold in its track as they had stopped his movement across the barn floor. Earlier that night, Samuel had provided himself with one half of the ending. Harold Ethridge had just provided the other half.

Samuel stood with his side and back to the hogpen in the Ethridge barn with Harold Ethridge between him and the side door. In one way it was an awkward position to be standing in. Samuel was standing in place in the barn in the same mind as he had walked to Harold Ethridge's farm in: his lover dead, all love in him dead. The grinding rage in Samuel racked up to the sticking point as he held in his mind that the smug and self-satisfied man standing across from him was the man who had brought the perverse end to the girl's life in pain and violence as it stood on the verge of hope, love, and safety. From where he stood, one way or the other, Samuel was determined this was where all stories would end. From where he stood, Harold Ethridge saw the boy's eyes narrow.

"Sometimes you find the answer in the question, sir," Samuel said, looking straight at Harold Ethridge. "In your reply, you didn't ask why I had come here tonight asking you about the livestock business or how to get into it. In your own specific wording, you asked me why I'm here questioning you about the way you go about 'disposing' of your livestock. Disposal of what you're done with seems to be on your mind, sir. At least it's not far from your thinking. Otherwise your mind wouldn't have gone to the word so easily and so naturally. The way disposability and disposable commodities comes to your lips so easily makes me think that you sent another disposable market commodity out of here recently, or at least something that you considered to be a disposable commodity. It was a top-dollar market commodity too. The difference was that this commodity cost you money instead of bringing money to you. For all I know, the expense to you may have been the reason you decided to dispose of the commodity without having to pay the final fare. Unlike your animals, which you send out alive, you sent her out only half alive. Unlike what we don't have in common as farmers, this was one commodity that you and I held in common."

"What is all this about?" Harold Ethridge interjected, his voice growing as edgy as Samuel's.

Samuel turned to the side. As if pacing at random, he started walking toward the fence of the hogpen he had been angling toward.

"About a month ago, one of the girls at Mrs. Richardson's house was found dead in the river," Samuel said as he approached the hogpen fence, the tone of his voice growing more brittle. "Do you happen to remember the incident?"

"I vaguely remember reading something to that effect in the newspaper," Harold Ethridge answered. A cold knot of suspicion started to form in his chest.

"Were you by any chance personally acquainted with the girl?" Samuel asked.

"No," Harold Ethridge answered. "I do not patronize any of the women in Mrs. Richardson's employ."

"She may have been a woman if you measure being a woman by the degree of jaded worldliness and being beaten down by life," Samuel said. "But in years, she was a girl one year younger than I and only about a year older than my sister. Life may not have granted her a lot of opportunity or reason to be tender of heart, but she was of a rather tender age to die. But no woman, innocent or jaded, deserves to die the savage way she died."

"From the way you describe her, you seem to have known her personally," Harold Ethridge said.

Samuel reached the fence of the hogpen he had been walking toward in his seemingly distracted random walk. At the pen he stopped and put his hand on the rail. He looked away at an angle as he addressed Harold Ethridge.

"Oh, quite intimately, sir," Samuel said, "in all senses of the word. But then again you should have known her just about as well as I knew her. At least you should have known her as well in bodily intimacy as I had if you didn't take the time to know her soul. Where lower-level intimacy came into it, she was the salable commodity I alluded to that we both held in common."

The coldness set in on Harold Ethridge. As he had started to suspect the minute the boy mentioned her, it was the girl he was there about. Apparently he knew they had been seeing each other. He had made the girl promise not to reveal his identity to anyone, even to her sisters in the house. The cheap little tart must have broken her word. Harold Ethridge figured he should have known better than to trust a whore for anything. At some point the little tease must have told the boy that she was servicing him. Or she had told her coworkers in the Richardson house and the word had gotten back to the boy. But what was it that the boy had come to him for in connection with the girl? Harold Ethridge weighed everything by cost and profit. Whatever the boy wanted, somehow he had the feeling that it was going to cost him.

"The difference being that she lived and died as the market commodity she always was to you. She otherwise happened to be the girl I was in love with and was planning to marry and have a family with."

With his hand still on the top rail of the hogpen, Samuel Martin turned from looking into the distance to look at Harold Ethridge directly. "It's not a whore I'm here to talk to you about, Mr. Ethridge. It's the sweetheart I was in love with and planned to marry that I came here to discuss with you."

Given the way the girl had talked about the boy, Harold Ethridge had gotten the idea that the boy had more than just a passing customer's interest in her. And jealous boyfriends can be a problem. That was one of the reasons he had tried to dissuade the girl from seeing Samuel again. If he had hoped to marry the girl, apparently the boy was far more enamored of the girl than he had thought. But he wasn't otherwise all that surprised to hear that the boy wanted to marry his soiled dove sweetheart. Small farm rubes do country bumpkin things like fall in love with hookers.

"Then that's why you came skulking here in the dark of night," Harold Ethridge said.

"This hour of the night may be as much of an awkward hour to talk about a dead prostitute as it is to talk about hog farming," Samuel retorted. "But she was the light of my life. There's been nothing but darkness in my heart, in my soul, and in my mind since she was found dead. There's been nothing but darkness in front of my eyes everywhere since. It's been dark of night everywhere I've looked since then, no matter what time of day it is. Day or night isn't a lot different for me anymore. So coming to you in the dead of night is no different to me than coming to you in the light of day. Besides, I wanted to talk with you alone. That's why I came at night. I can't talk to you alone when you're surrounded by your farmhands who run this farm for you or by your business associates in your office in town. It could also be quite embarrassing to you to have me bring up the subject of her in front of your other associates. Let's just say that I'm doing you a social favor by coming to you to talk about her in private instead of at noon in the middle of the town square in front of the whole town."

There's nothing for us to talk about concerning her," Harold Ethridge responded. "I didn't know the girl. I'd never seen her or heard of her before she was found dead in the river."

"How did you know she was found in the river?" Samuel asked with another edge to his voice as if drawing a knife across a whetstone.

"The newspaper article said so," Harold Ethridge answered. "But I had never been with her. I've never been inside Madam Richardson's establishment."

"Oh, you've never been in Mrs. Richardson's house all right," Samuel clarified. "That much is true. A man of your social standing and position wouldn't be caught in a bordello. That puts you above the mayor and some of her other clients on the town council. But you've been with her on the grounds of one of your holdings, either here or in town. I'm just not sure which one was the last one she saw."

"Who says I was with her?" Harold Ethridge shot back in an attempt to change the direction the boy was taking. "Her? Was she the one who told you I was with her?"

At no time had Harold Ethridge ever shown up at the door of Mrs. Richardson's house. In that sense he knew he was safe. From there it was just her word against his.

"She was a whore. Whores lie about anything and everything. Whores brag about their exploits the way sailors and gandy dancers and saloon toughs do. They make up their stories. She probably told you or her house sisters that she was seeing me as a way of impressing the lot of you and building herself up by bragging that she was being kept by the richest man in town." Harold Ethridge huffed out a short sneer. "You can't take the word of a whore one inch farther than you could slide the Rock of Gibraltar. Whores are liars from the beginning to the end, and their ends aren't very good, whether you're talking about the ends of their intents or the physical ends they come to."

Only half under his breath, Harold Ethridge sneered another little sneer as he tried to turn the subject back on the boy.

"But you wanted to marry a whore. She was probably lying to you the whole time you knew her. If you had married her, she would have lied to you just as frequently and just as casually. Did she promise you she would reform after you married her? Did she promise to be faithful to you in marriage once you were married? What makes you think she would have been faithful to you if you had married her? She probably wouldn't have remained any more faithful to you than she was to any of her clients."

"Well now, I'll grant you that you do have a pretty practiced eye and a natural practiced instinct for picking out women who are weak on keeping their marriage vows," Samuel said in a tone of acid sarcasm, alluding not very subtly to Mr. Ethridge's reputation for being a seducer of married women. "At one time or another, you've put half the women in town to the test, including married women like Sally MacGregor and Sarah Perceval, whose marriages you broke up not because you had a grand passion for any of the women involved but because it amused you to do so and for no reason beyond."

"I didn't wrench either of those women away from their husbands," Harold Ethridge said. "If they succumbed to temptation, maybe the simpler reason was that those women were just natural-born sluts."

"They may have had an innate moral weakness in them enough to make them fall for your slippery and oily ways," Samuel answered, "but the blandishments and lies and promises you waved at them to seduce them were all your own. You invented the lies they fell for. That is, they fell for your lies and blandishments and promises until after your affairs with them were completed and their husbands' divorcing of them was completed. Then all your blandishments and lies evaporated in their faces.

Once you had them where you wanted them and had the satisfaction of having broken up their marriages, you dropped your lies and promises to them as fast as you broke it off with them and withdrew your affections, which had been another lie from the beginning, and dumped them out your back door."

Samuel was forced to stop there. Not because Harold Ethridge cut him off or because he was out of words that could have been said. He practically had to bite his tongue to keep from adding something about the way Ethridge had broken it off with the girl by breaking her neck and dumping her in the river. But the time hadn't quite come yet. Much more had to be elicited.

"And what makes you think your strumpet had any more moral fiber than she did?" Harold Ethridge went on. "By definition, all women like her don't have the beginnings of moral fiber, and they don't strive for what they don't have. Your doxy had less moral fiber than the women I was involved with to begin with. But unlike them, she didn't make any pretense about it. What makes you think a walk down the aisle and into marriage with you would have put any moral backbone in her? For that matter, what makes you think that she would have wanted to give up a life of lolling around in Mrs. Richardson's establishment, getting paid top dollar for it, so that she could take up the life of a farm wife, cooking and scrubbing and milking cows and husking corn with you? She didn't strike me as being the kind of woman inclined to do that. Do you really believe that your country bumpkin boyish affections could have turned around her natural orientations and made a snow-white princess out of a whorehouse floozy? Do you think that your boyish professions of love could have purified her behavior or would have even won her affections? Do you think your manly behavior could have in the least influenced the intentions of a woman like her?"

With little visible movement of his hand, Samuel's fingers gripped the top rail of the hogpen fence. But it wasn't Harold Ethridge's impugning of the girl's moral character or his assessment of Samuel's ability to reform her that had notched the tension up in Samuel. Harold Ethridge had uttered the keyword when he had said that she didn't strike him as being a faithful woman. The question wasn't the kind of woman she had struck him as being. The question was whether she had struck him as being the kind of woman he felt he could strike down with impunity, and how had he gone about striking the life out of her, and how far away both he and Samuel were now standing from where he had struck her down.

"Nobody will ever know how her affections may have turned out or what she could have turned into," Samuel said, turning the final corner. "Given the distance you put her affections away from me, I'll never know what her affections could have become for me or any member of my family. You put her affections beyond me. You put her affections beyond her or beyond any ability she otherwise might have had to have any affections."

"Are you accusing me of alienation of her affections?" Harold Ethridge scoffed. He was still thinking in legal terms and in the language of divorce petitions from the divorces his affairs had initiated. "A whore doesn't have those kind of affections. A whore's affections are her stock in trade. They're extended with the money handed them and then withdrawn until money is traded for them again. A whore's affections have no meaning beyond the money she receives for the service of her affection. That girl had no affections for any man beyond what she gave in exchange for money. She had no more affection for you than she did for me."

Samuel's eyebrows raised.

"She had no more affections for any man than she did for either of us. The difference was that I knew that from the beginning. You're the one who went starry-eyed and convinced yourself that her affections for you were anything more than the momentary tool of convenience that they were for her. Maybe you could have married her, but I could have had her again anytime I wanted."

"Then you did have her after all." Samuel snapped down like a trap spring. "Despite your protestations and lies of not having known her, you did know her."

Harold Ethridge was caught up silent.

"You weren't talking in an abstract construct about the way whores think and the cheapness of a whore's affections. You were talking about her in specific. Or you were talking what you thought of her. Whether your estimate and opinion of the depth or lack of depth of her affections was accurate or not, you were disparaging her personally. You would have phrased it differently if you were talking in general and had never known her the way clients know their whores."

"Yes, I knew her," Harold Ethridge said.

"Then why did you lie so ardently that you didn't know her?" Samuel said.

"Because my associations, business or social, clean or questionable, are nobody's concern but my own," Harold Ethridge said decisively. Maybe he had stumbled and had given away his denial of having known the girl, but Harold Ethridge figured it was a minor point easily dispensed with. What difference was it if a farm boy knew that his prostitute sweetheart was servicing other men in the course of her employment? He figured he had given away nothing. As for any objections the boy might have, Harold Ethridge figured that the best way to move beyond and forward was to move through.

"And I certainly don't feel compelled to share the details of my private life and my female associations with a simpleminded farm boy, especially when it comes to sharing a girl who made her living sharing herself with all comers. But, yes, we shared the same girl whose livelihood was to share herself. From the moment I saw her with you in Kindelspire's restaurant, I found her to be a fascinating creature. I wanted to know her better. Shortly after the two of you left, I was informed that she made her living over at Mrs. Richardson's house by making herself available to being known by men."

"But if you never put in an appearance at Mrs. Richardson's house, how did you go about making your first contact with her?" Samuel asked. "Did you manage to get yourself to the head of the line on a night when she was soliciting in Two-Bit Charlie's saloon? I thought a man of your social caliber avoided going into establishments such as Charlie's saloon as much you avoided Mrs. Richardson's establishment. I didn't think you would want to be seen in public anywhere picking up a public woman. If you didn't meet her in either Mrs. Richardson's or Charlie's saloon, then how did you manage to make contact with her?"

"In fact my meeting with her had something to do with Charlie's saloon," Harold Ethridge answered. "It just wasn't quite in the way you went about meeting and impressing the girl in the saloon. I happened to observe the two of you being taken into custody the night you lost your juvenile hotheaded temper and started your jealous juvenile barroom brawl over her in Charlie's saloon. It seemed the least I could do to procure the release of a poor benighted misfortunate girl who got caught up in your infantile antics and tossed into a dismal cell in the police department cellar. That night she wasn't particularly grateful to you for getting her arrested. On the other hand, she was grateful enough to me that she offered her services to me free for the night."

It hadn't happened exactly that way. Clarinda hadn't volunteered herself for free. But Harold Ethridge wanted to rub the boy's nose in the dirt by claiming that the hooker he had taken to heart as a sweetheart had offered herself to him for free as a reward for springing her from jail.

"Then you were the anonymous patron who bailed her out that night," Samuel said. The ramping anger in Samuel went to the final notch and froze in place. But it was not because of Harold Ethridge's attempt at a sexual one-upsman dig. He was now face-to-face with Mrs. Richardson's maxim in light of the case: Find the girl's mystery man and you'll find the killer. "But I pretty much knew that already. I just wanted to hear it from you."

"And you probably heard my name from her," Harold Ethridge said. "I asked her not to reveal my name to you or anyone, not even her sister whores in Mrs. Richardson's house. I especially wanted you left out of it because I didn't need a jealous hotheaded boyfriend who started a saloon brawl making an issue out of it and coming after me. Apparently she told you despite my request. Like I said, she probably bragged about it to you. Shows you how far you can take the word of a whore."

"Actually she didn't tell me or anyone in the house," Samuel said hollowly. "For what it's worth to you—and it wasn't worth anything to her—she did keep your confidence. It was a whore's honor. But she was more honorable than you."

Harold Ethridge didn't seem very impressed by the revelation that the girl had kept his name quiet after all. But then he was distracted wondering what it all meant to the boy one way or the other.

With his hand still on the top rail of the hogpen, Samuel turned his body so he was facing Harold Ethridge a bit more directly. The hogs grunted and ambled around in the pen. They must have been full because they showed no interest in their food trough. They had eaten their fill for the night. Harold Ethridge fed his animals well. They were being fattened for slaughter.

"But all faith-keeping aside," Samuel went on like a snarling dog circling the pole he's tethered to, "tell me this, sir. After you became her patron saint of the bail bond, how many other times did you patronize her?"

Harold Ethridge quickly debated in his mind how many times he should confess to having had sex with the girl. At first he thought of telling the boy the same thing he had told Constable Harkness, that it had only been once. But even once might set the boy off. Harold Ethridge decided to avoid the subject altogether.

"What do you want to know that for?" Ethridge asked. "What difference does it make to you? Are you trying to boost your ego and feel like more of a man by seeing which one of us had her the most? Are you here to compare scorecards with me? As far as keeping score, the only thing she was keeping score of was the money coming in. Or are you trying to find out which one of us she had the most affection for? The only thing she held close in her affection was the money she was getting from both of us. If you're here looking to do some sort of man-to-man competition with me to see which one of us she liked best, it's a waste of time. She wasn't juggling us to see who was the manliest. She was juggling with us to shake the money out of our pockets. The only thing she held in esteem was the money she was getting from us. It's no use trying to find out which one of us she put on a pedestal. In her eyes we were all on the same level. She went with neither in order to get either manliness or affection. She went with both of us for what money she could get from us. Money was the only terms she wanted from either of us."

"Well now, you do think in terms of money, don't you?" Samuel said. "But money and the number of turns either of us had with her was kind of a moot point for her during her last month. More moot for me actually than for her. You see, the last month of her life, she had me sitting on the bench." As captain of the baseball team, Samuel did tend to use baseball analogies. "She put me on suspension as penalty for my having started that fight in Charlie's saloon. She had told me to stay away from her until I cooled off and grew up. My little stunt not only cost me a month with her, but also in the end it cost me her. It also cost her. Not in money. It cost her in the fact that she met you. If I hadn't started the fight that landed us in jail, you wouldn't have bailed her out and she would have never met you. In the end, the end for her, knowing you cost her a lot more than money."

Samuel laid the rest of his forearm down on the pen rail and leaned in against the pen.

"But the suspension she put me on started the night of the fight, the night she met you. So any measure of how many times we had her in common doesn't have any meaning. The measure doesn't exist because I was on the sidelines when you knew her."

"Then what's the point of you being here discussing it with me?" Harold Ethridge asked.

"The point is that you were the unnamed mystery man she took up with while I was waiting for her to take me back. For the next month I didn't even know she was seeing you. For a month after her death, neither I nor anyone at the Richardson house knew the identity of the mystery man she was going off into town to meet. Your name came up only when one of the other girls at the house inadvertently remembered a clue the girl had inadvertently dropped the last time she went out. That's why I'm here now and why I didn't come earlier. Believe me, if I had known your name a month ago, I would have been here a lot sooner."

Given the terms in which he thought, Harold Ethridge figured that the boy was on the verge of getting down to business.

"And just why are you here at all?" Harold Ethridge asked in his let's-get-down-to-business voice. "Have you come trying to extort money out of me by threatening to blackmail me, and if I don't pay, you'll make it public that I was seeing a prostitute? Is this your country clod's way of trying to get money out of me?"

"Like I said," Samuel commented, "you do think in terms of money, don't you?"

Samuel leaned against the hogpen fence a bit more. The tone of his voice dripped with a combination of something. Harold Ethridge just couldn't quite pull apart the combination of elements in the boy's voice. They were too closely intertwined to be separable.

"Don't worry about any attempt at blackmail on my part, sir. I'm not here for the first part of your money. I'm just here for one last part of her."

Harold Ethridge wanted to comment something to the effect that a lot of men, including him and the boy, had had a good part of the girl and that no man would be having any part of her again. But something in the boy's voice kept him from saying it.

"I wanted to live my life with her. But as it was, fate intervened. Not only didn't I get to live a life with her, but also I wasn't with her or even around her when she died. If you want to know why I'm here so badly, let's just say I'm here on a sentimental journey to say goodbye to her. But in order to say a proper goodbye to her, I need to learn about how she lived her last days on earth. That's why I've come to you. After all, you were with her during her final days. I wasn't. You were there. You should be able to tell me how she lived her final days and hours. … You know a lot about women. You've had far more experience with women than I've had."

Samuel turned more fully to face Harold Ethridge. Without bending over backward, he leaned his back against the top rail of the hog fence. His hand was still on the rail.

"You've especially had experience dispensing with women when you're done with them. I assumed you were done with and had dispensed with the girl by the date that she died. You must have been done with her and had dispensed with her by the time of her death. I certainly haven't seen you around town with a long face mourning for her. I haven't seen you lighting candles in church for her. I haven't heard any account that you've been going around carrying a hopeless torch for her the way I have. You haven't demonstrated any lingering pain of bereavement to me here tonight. So you must have dispensed with the girl in your mind, if not in body, before she met her end. You said you found her to be fascinating. I wonder why you were so ready to dispense with her and dispense with her so emotionally completely when you found her so fascinating?"

Samuel's voice grew dryer. At the same time his hand and fingers gripped the fence rail again.

"But in your own words you called her a fascinating creature. Calling a woman a creature of any kind is a revealing bit of wording. After all, creatures are creatures. They aren't humans. When you call someone a creature, it signifies that you don't quite think of them as being fully human. … In your experience with women, you've found more than a few to be dispensable after you've had your way with them."

Samuel glanced partway at the hogs in the pen behind him and then turned back to Harold Ethridge.

"But then you are man who deals in dispensable creatures all around.

When the fascination wore off, just how did you go about dispensing with her?"

"Now just what are you implying by that?" Harold Ethridge asked.

"It's a straightforward enough question, sir," Samuel said. "I just said that you are as practiced at disposing of women as you are at seducing them. But the other women you've disposed of have all had at least some measure of social standing and visibility in this town. You dispensed with them emotionally and socially. On the other hand, the girl had no social standing in this town. She existed on the shadow edge of town. In dispensing with her, you were dispensing with someone beyond the pale. Even superficial social niceties could be dispensed with. Shortcuts could be taken."

Samuel nodded his head toward the hogs in their pens. "When the time comes, you dispatch with these hogs by sending them out without any reservations, any pity, or any lingering emotional attachment. When it came time to dispense with her, in just exactly how brusque of a manner did you send her out from you?"

Now it was Harold Ethridge's turn to find himself riveted in one spot by a head-to-foot stab of coldness as he suddenly realized that he was facing a much bigger problem than a clumsy farm boy with a harebrained blackmail scheme. "Are you accusing me of being the one who killed her?" he said in a tightening voice.

"Did I say that you killed her?" Samuel said in a voice like ether. "Did you hear me say anything about your having killed her? I didn't even say that she had been murdered. Why are you saying that she was? Where did you even get the idea that she had been killed?"

"The newspaper article," Harold Ethridge said. "It said that foul play was suspected."

"That makes two things about the article in the paper that you recall in detail," Samuel said, "the fact that she was found dead in the river and the fact that foul play was suspected. It's been a month since the story appeared in the newspaper, and it was just a small piece at the bottom of the page. But you remember two main elements. Obviously you have more than just a vague memory of the piece in the paper about her death. Beyond that, the subject of killing seems to be on your mind or else you wouldn't have jumped to it so fast."

When Harold Ethridge had disposed of the girl's body in the river, his hope had been that the current would carry her as far as the Ohio River, possibly even as far as the Mississippi River. At least he had thought that the river would carry her body to another county where no one would know her and where she would remain, buried as a nameless, unidentified mystery girl who nobody knew where she had come from. But the snotty and uncooperative little tart had washed up onshore hardly a mile downstream. He thought he had dodged a bullet on that one. Now her country rube lover was standing before him in his own barn accusing him of having murdered her. However easy (if expensive)a lay the girl had been when she was alive, the ghost of the girl was proving a hard ghost to lay to rest.

"Where the hell did you get the idea that I killed her?"

"Now there's no need to go about invoking hellfire, sir," Samuel said. "Though hellfire might easily come to be invoked on any man who kills a young girl he has in his power, especially after she's kept his confidences."

Samuel shifted back against the hogpen fence again.

"As for where I got the idea, I got the idea from Mrs. Richardson. The night the girl disappeared, Mrs. Richardson said, the girl claimed she was going out to see her mystery man. She just never came back. Mrs. Richardson said that if you find the mystery man, you'll find her killer. And you, sir, just confessed to being her mystery man."

"If you're crazy enough to love a whore, I guess you're crazy enough to believe what her madam says." Harold Ethridge snorted.

"Mrs. Richardson said what she said about the girl's mystery man being the killer long before she or any of us knew who the mystery man was," Samuel said. "And it wasn't Mrs. Richardson who put it together and figured out that you were the girl's mystery man. The girl herself accidentally let it slip who you were. It just didn't register on anyone in the house at the time. The last night the girl went out, she told one of her sisters in the house that she was going out to see her Mister Bearcat that night."

Harold Ethridge noticeably twitched.

"Now, as you probably think, whores can be a bit dumb. The girl who heard her say it thought it was some kind of appellation about the sexual prowess of the man she was seeing. Whores think in those terms. But the girls in that house don't know anything about cars. Even Mrs. Richardson, who owns a car, isn't aware of the latest models. But we men know cars. … You're the only one in town who owns a Stutz Bearcat. The second I heard the other girl say the name 'Mister Bearcat,' I knew it couldn't be anybody but you, sir. Logically it can't be anybody else. It was the last name on the girl's lips as she left the house that night. She didn't return to speak any other name. The last words a person speaks are usually considered significant. They're remembered. The girl's last words identify you as the mystery man she was going out to see as she left the house the night she vanished, to turn up dead in the river. It just took awhile for the name to be remembered by the house sister the girl had spoken it to. All the words I ever spoke to the girl weren't enough to save her. But the name she spoke was enough to identify you as her mystery man. They may be the last words of a whore, but they're words enough to put your neck in a noose."

"For your information, Constable Harkness questioned me about the girl's death," Harold Ethridge said in a mostly confident voice. "He interviewed me in my house in town two days after the girl had been found and brought in."

Now that was something new. Samuel didn't know that Constable Harkness had interviewed the man about the girl's death. But had Constable Harkness been digging for the truth, or had he been there to spread a protective berm over someone he knew to be a killer? Dirt had been shoveled. Which direction had it been shoveled in?

"Well, that is interesting," Samuel said in a voice dripping with calculated exaggerated irony. "Now why would Constable Harkness be interviewing you, of all people in town, about the murder of a common street tramp? What could be the possible connection between a man of your stature and a girl like her?" His tone went wooden flat again. "But then she worked in a profession intended to be obvious. The connection between you and her is obvious and self-explanatory. At this juncture I suppose I really don't have to ask what your connection with her was, now, do I?"

At that juncture, Harold Ethridge caught himself. He had told Constable Harkness that he had employed the girl's service only once, the night he had bailed her out of jail, and that he hadn't seen her in the following weeks preceding her death. Although he hadn't told the boy exactly how many times he had been with the girl, he had been letting on to the boy that he had seen her more than once. If the boy got together with the constable and gave his account of the number of times he had implied that he had seen the girl, to the constable it could smell like a rather large inconsistency in his story of having seen the girl only the one time. Depending on whom the constable believed, it could prove trouble for one of them. At least it could bring the constable back to Ethridge with a lot more questions.

"He interviewed me because I was the one who bailed the girl out," Harold Ethridge said. "It was just a matter-of-course interview, trying to learn if I might have an idea who her killer might have been. I told him it was probably a drunken farmhand or worker whom she ran into on her way back to the house."

"Then for the record you're saying that she was at your house that night," Samuel interjected. "Which is another way of saying that you were her mystery man. And that's just another way of saying that you were the last one to see her alive. The last one before her killer, that is. It's funny how in murder the next to the last and the last one to see someone alive often have a way of being one and the same. But then I guess it isn't so funny after all, now, is it?"

"When he interviewed me, Constable Harkness told me he thought she was probably accosted and killed by a rogue farmhand or a day laborer she encountered on her way back from seeing me," Harold Ethridge said. "The constable's theory makes more sense than any of your wild-eyed ruminations. You should listen to him and go back to your farm and do something useful like plow your field and clean the mud off your boots instead of sitting up in your attic room mooning for a dead whore and dreaming up all your fetid conspiracy theories."

"She wasn't killed by a farmhand or a street thug whom she happened to cross paths with when coming back from seeing you," Samuel said as if he were talking from deep within a tunnel. "Any man on foot who caught her on the street on her way back and killed her there would have left her body where he'd killed her. He wouldn't have carried her to the river and thrown her in. He especially wouldn't have carried her through the streets of the town. She was transported all right, but it wasn't over the shoulder of a farmhand or roustabout running on foot. She was taken to the river in a conveyance in which she could be concealed from the sight of anyone on the street at night or anyone who happened to look out their window as the killer passed, a conveyance where her body, her still living but paralyzed body, could be kept low and out of sight, a conveyance that wouldn't attract attention if seen on the road at night, the conveyance of a respected man, a man whom people wouldn't be surprised to see out and about after dark, a man with a reputation for being a midnight rambler."

With his right hand still on the hogpen fence rail, Samuel reached up with his left hand to the pocket of his shirt.

"I didn't come here directly from home. I must confess that I have been sneaking around your grounds here since before sunset. As for the nickname the girl gave you, Mr. Bearcat, I clued in on it and spent some time examining your car. Guess what I found? I found strands of her hair in your car. I have one right here."

Samuel reached into his shirt pocket and pulled up the hair he had found on the floor of Harold Ethridge's car. In the dim light of the barn, Harold Ethridge's eyes seemed to follow the direction of his hand. Samuel doubted that Ethridge could see the hair from the distance he was standing away in the dim light of the barn, but it was the threat effect Samuel was after.

"Doesn't that beat all that I would find her hair in your car? But then it came from a head that had been beaten senseless."

"So you found one of her hairs in my car," Harold Ethridge retorted. "I took her for a ride in my car once. That proves nothing."

"If you took her once, you took her twice," Samuel said. "Whether it was in your bed or in your car. If you took her for a midnight car ride where she was sitting up, you later took her for one more ride where she wasn't in a sitting position.

"I always liked the way the wind blew through her hair. I didn't find this hair in the front seat. If it had come off while the wind was blowing through her hair and her hair was flying, the wind would have blown it over the back of the car and away. I found this hair along with others down low on the floor in the rear. That means her head wasn't held up proudly for all to see. It was down on the floor. Now that's kind of a rough position to ride in. Did you tell her to keep down so neighbors wouldn't see her with you from their windows? Kind of spoils the fun of a midnight ride for a girl."

Samuel pushed the hair back into his shirt pocket.

"But it's right where her head would have been if you had thrown her body in the back where she wouldn't be seen so you could drive from here or through the town unseen at night to the river, where you threw her in while she was still alive and breathing. I don't know whether you took her from here or from your house in town. In the end, the end for her, I guess it doesn't make a lot of difference where you and she were that night and where you started from. She ended up in the river. But she ended up in the river because you had already disposed of her in your mind. Wherever it was that you killed her, before you threw her in the river, you threw her out of your mind. You took her out from your own personal slaughterhouse and threw her in the river"—Samuel rolled his thumb over toward the hogs in their pen—"as casually and as surely as you send these disposable creatures out on a train to the slaughterhouse waiting for them down the line."

Samuel put his hand back on the hogpen fence rail.

"You do have a vivid imagination, boy," Harold Ethridge said, the frustration in his voice winding tighter. "You'd make a great scriptwriter for plays. Or for the new medium of film. Too bad they're silent. Your talent for words would be wasted."

"If I had any talent at words, she would be alive with her hand in mine and my ring on her finger," Samuel snapped in a rising tone. "Not dead in the river and in her grave with her face battered black by your fists!"

"The point is that Constable Harkness didn't see any cause to arrest me at the time," Harold Ethridge said in his mostly confident voice. "And he hasn't seen fit to arrest me or question me further for nearly a month since then. He's apparently satisfied that I had nothing to do with her death. Why don't you take the chief of police at his word? Do you fancy yourself a better investigator than he is, or do you fancy our chief of police to be an idiot?"

"I fancy that he could be covering for a wealthy man at the top of this town's social ladder as much as I fancy he has much of any interest in finding the killer of a tramp girl out of a bordello," Samuel said. "Especially where the trail of the killer leads back to the richest man in town. Besides, that was a month ago. At the time, nobody knew who the girl's mystery man was. We do now. But only because one of the girl's less than stellarly bright sisters at the house recently remembered the nickname the girl had used the last night she went out to see her mystery man. She just didn't know what she knew. But at times these prostitutes can be rather dense about things."

"Who was this other girl who you say identified me?" Harold Ethridge asked.

Since he had left the farmhouse, Samuel had been focused totally on Harold Ethridge. He hadn't been thinking in terms of what would one day come to be called "collateral damage" or whom that damage could be done to. Suddenly Samuel realized that if things didn't turn out the way he had planned, he could be putting all the women of the Richardson house in grave danger.

"Why do you want to know?" Samuel asked. "What do you want to know her name for? So you can arrange it that she ends up being found dead in the river too? Or so that all the women of the Richardson house mysteriously disappear one at a time to wind up in the river somewhere, or in a hole under one of your fields, or under the floor of this barn?"

Samuel actually hadn't told Polly what the name really meant. He had stormed out of the riverbed that day shouting to Polly and Ben that it was the name of a car. He hadn't been back to the house or talked with Ben since then. He didn't know if what he had said had registered with them or not. They might eventually put it together, if they hadn't already. The real danger was that Harold Ethridge would put it together in his mind that they had put it together and that he would want to remove all possible sources who might know. Samuel had no idea what Harold Ethridge was thinking or how far he would go to keep his murder of the girl secret. But for all Samuel knew, a man who thinks and kills like Harold Ethridge just might try something like that. If things did not turn out the way he planned that night and Harold Ethridge came out on top, the women of the Richardson House could end up disappearing one by one or dying under mysterious circumstances.

It was no longer just him and the girl and his vengeance. Now the stakes possibly included the lives of all the women of the Richardson house, even Mrs. Richardson's. To keep the danger away from the women of the Richardson house, Samuel now had double reason to take it to the end he had planned. Samuel had come to the Ethridge farm with his rage focused on Harold Ethridge to the exclusion of others. Now in Samuel's mind, to protect the women of the Richardson house, he had to get to the end he planned on. To do that, he had to keep the rage of Harold Ethridge focused on him.

"For whatever reason in your twisted mind, you found the girl to be a mortal problem for you," Samuel continued. "In turn, you made yourself a mortal threat to the girl. But the women of the Richardson house aren't a threat to you. I don't even know if they know what they know. I'm the mortal threat to you now, Mr. Ethridge. Like I said, if I had known earlier you were her mystery man, I would have been here a lot sooner."

"And why are you here at all now, boy?" Harold Ethridge asked. "Did I have it right earlier, just for the wrong reason? Instead of blackmailing me for a lesser dollar amount by threatening to disclose that I was seeing a prostitute, have you come here with an invented story of my having killed the girl to try to blackmail me for a much larger sum?"

Harold Ethridge figured that now the boy might get down to business. But that left the problem of how much the boy would want. It also left the problem that there was someone who knew about his killing of the girl, and possibly a lot more problems if all the women of the Richardson house knew. Even big problems could be solved. He had solved them before. But how big was this problem?

"I see you're still thinking in terms of blackmail," Samuel said. "Your mind just naturally goes to the subject quite a bit. The threat of blackmail and losing money seems ever on your mind. Is that why you killed the girl? Did she try to blackmail you by threatening to make your liaisons with her public? Did she start asking you for more money? Did she become too expensive for your tastes? Did you decide to cut your losses by cutting off the life a woman who was already cut off from the life of the town and from membership in the town and whom you considered easy to dispense with?"

The boy wasn't taking the bait of Ethridge's dropped hint of blackmail. Harold Ethridge couldn't figure the boy out. He wasn't responding the way he had expected. He just kept talking about the dead snitty little bitch. Just what did the boy want? How crazy was he?

"Or is there an evil in you that goes beyond money? Did you kill her to cut expenses, or did you kill her for the thrill of killing? Is it no longer enough of a stimulation to you to seduce a woman and cut her off emotionally and then dump her away from you? Have you graduated to the larger thrill of cutting women off physically and dumping them in the river? Of course that's something a lot more easily done to women who exist on the fringes of society and who aren't missed, and whom polite society doesn't care about to begin with. If that's the case, then all the women in the Richardson house are in danger from you whether they know anything about your killing of the girl or not. If you've gone from seducing women for sport to killing women for sport, then, dense or insightful, knowledgeable or not, any one of Mrs. Richardson's girls could be the next one you choose to get the greater thrill you've come to need. But then again, I guess it doesn't have to be prostitutes. You could just as easily start going after the everyday women of the town. You'll probably just be more careful about not disposing of the bodies in so clumsy manner as you did hers."

The thought hit Samuel that his sister could be the next victim.

"You're not just a dumb country yokel," Harold Ethridge said. "You're as mentally unbalanced as you say I am. You'd better not go about spreading that kind of stuff around town. I'll bring a suit for libel and defamation of character that will take your whole farm. You'd better watch your words."

"I had a whole lifetime of words I wanted to say to her," Samuel said. "I wasn't able to do much good for her with my words while she was alive. Now, thanks to you, words are all I have left. But I've got plenty of words. And before I'm done with you, you're going to eat every one of my words. ... Don't threaten me with libel, sir. By definition, truth isn't libel. You can yell about libel all you want, but everyone in town is going to hear the ugly truth about you. Constable Harkness is going to hear what I've got to say, right along with everyone else. I don't know if he's going to want to hear what I've got to say, but one way or the other he's going to hear what I know and see the evidence I'm going to hand him. If he's not covering for you, he may appreciate and make use of the information that helps him crack the case of the girl's murder. If he is covering for you, he may be forced to act anyway, even if he doesn't want to. Either way, everyone in this town is going to know that you're a snake who kills young girls. At least every parent in town will be forewarned to snatch their daughters off the street when you walk by or when you drive by with the body of another young girl dead or dying on the floor of your Bearcat."

As the boy ratcheted up his rhetoric, the frustration was ratcheting up in Harold Ethridge with no release valve and no way he could see of getting to the boy. His threats hadn't moved the boy one inch from where he was standing. Neither had they apparently changed, softened, or held back one word the boy was saying. He wasn't able to intimidate the boy or back him down. He didn't know where to take it next. He didn't know where the boy was taking it. And he still didn't know what the boy wanted.

"You keep asking why I came here. You keep thinking I want money from you. I just want the truth out of you, and I'm going to take the truth out of your hide any way I can get it. Like I said, I don't want money out of you, sir. I just want what you did to her taken out of the soul you don't have. The only payment I want is justice for her. At the end she lived and died what you put her through. I had to live through her end. Now all I want is to live to see your end. I want you on the gallows with your neck in a noose. I want you to see the end coming toward you with no escape. I want you to see your end coming with no way out like the girl did. I want you to feel what the girl felt just before you killed her."

"You think you can take me on, boy?" Harold Ethridge said in as direct a voice as he could muster. "She was a nameless little tramp. I'm not about to let my name and reputation be dragged down into the mud because a two-bit farm boy wants to defend the name and honor of a nameless tramp and give his name to a whore who had neither name nor reputation. I'll do whatever I can to stop you from spreading your poisonous lies over the town. If you want that kind of satisfaction out of me, you should have brought a pair dueling pistols with you. And I don't have any intention of giving you the satisfaction of me incriminating myself by confessing to the town or the constable that I was the one who wrenched the neck of your midnight slut."

Now it was really over. Samuel's hand took a death grip on the top rail of the hogpen.

"Did you hear me say anything about how she died?" Samuel said in a low growl. "Did you hear me say one word about how she was killed? I didn't say anything about her neck having been broken. So how did you know specifically that her neck had been cracked?" Samuel held up his other hand. "And don't tell me you got it from the newspaper. The article about her death was short enough. It just said she was dead and that it was probably foul play. It didn't give any medical description of how she had been killed."

"You just said she was buried with the marks," Harold Ethridge began.

"I said she was buried with the marks of your fists on her face where you beat her," Samuel cut in. "I didn't say anything about the marks of your hands on her neck. Did you see her body?"

"No."

"Well, I did. I saw her body when they brought me in to identify it the day she was found. I could tell her neck had been broken by looking at it. Doc Simpson said her neck had been broken. If you didn't see the body, how did you know her neck had been twisted to the point of snapping? As they say, that's something only the killer would know."

"Constable Harkness told me," Harold Ethridge said in an uncertain and unconvincing tone. "He told me when he interviewed me in my house in town."

"Investigators working a fresh case don't give out information like that," Samuel said. "They don't voluntarily hand detailed but hidden information about a crime they're investigating to a suspect in the case. They keep details like that close to their vests, hoping the killer will reveal himself by slipping up and blurting out information that only the killer would know. Just like you did. My words didn't help the girl very much. I'm sure the constable will find your words revealing."

Harold Ethridge gritted his teeth to near the breaking point. His slipup had cost him all the crafted denials he had been advancing. As it was, he hadn't been making much headway trying to either put the boy off or back him off. His threats hadn't worked. Even his implicit hint at paying blackmail money hadn't had the slightest effect. The boy seemed obsessed with getting his confession. Offering to pay hush money to keep his killing of the girl quiet would only be a further confession of murder.

"You may protest that it was only a slip of the tongue. But slips of the tongue are the first and realest of confessions. Either way I take it as a confession. After the beating she took from you I'll take your confession any way you deliver it. It's one small bit of justice for her. I thank you for that, sir. I makes what I have to do all that much easier."

Harold Ethridge wasn't fully sure what he was dealing with in the boy. But in a moment of clarity in the half-lit hog barn, he knew that everything was at stake. The boy could ruin him in and out of court. The boy could take everything from him. The threat was total. It necessitated a response as total as the threat. In his mind, Harold Ethridge searched quickly for a way to get the advantage over the boy. There is an advantage to having your opponent alone and isolated on your ground.

"You took everything she had from her when you took her life. You took everything I wanted out of life and the future from me when you killed her. You might say it's only fair that I return the favor for the both of us. Fairness didn't mean anything to you as far as she was concerned. Fairness doesn't have much of any meaning at this point. Evening the score for her is about all that's left to or for either of us. Evening the score is about all that's left of either of us. I don't even know the name of the girl I'm evening the score in the name of. But it's all I've got left out of everything you took from both of us."

"Oh, how very nauseatingly romantic," Harold Ethridge said in a molded tone of rising anger. "You snivel and moan and carry on that she was your everything. She was a two-bit saloon crawler who would have reached her hand into a full spittoon to retrieve the nickels thrown to her. She put the rest of herself into equally dirty beds for the dollars that men threw to her afterward. This was your everything. She was nothing!"

"And you killed her like she was nothing," Samuel said, not holding back his words while he held his position by the hogpen fence.

"And you're a bigger fool and a smaller nothing for having loved a soiled nothing like her. You wanted a life with her. Do you really think you would have had a life with a tramp like that? She wouldn't have honored your name or the straw-filled mattress on the farmer's bed in your house any more than she honored the silk sheets on the four-poster canopy bed in my house."

"I take it then that it was your house in town where you killed her," Samuel said. "Actually that was where you broke her neck. You finished the job when you threw her in the river to drown."

Harold Ethridge liked to consider himself in control in all things large and small. But he wasn't in full control of the small detail of his facial expression. As he closed the distance, even in the half-light of the hog barn, Samuel could see the muscles of Ethridge's neck and jaw tense up.

"I don't hear you rushing to deny it."

"Is that what you're planning on telling everyone?" Harold Ethridge said. "You think anyone is going to believe you?"

"They won't be thinking about who to believe or not," Samuel said. "They're going to be too busy trying to figure out who cut you down on your own property."

There was a moment of silence as the words of Samuel's concluding sentence hung in the air.

"She was a nothing, and you're nothing," Harold Ethridge reiterated as he went on down the narrowing path of the corridor they were both standing in. "You say I took everything from her. You can't take anything from nothing. And I'm not going to take everything I've have built for myself and throw it all away for having killed a sleazy little tart."

"You should mind your words, sir," Samuel cut in, using a grating voice, next to the hogpen fence where he continued to stand. "You didn't say that I was trying to force you to confess to a false charge of killing her. You used the phrase *having killed*. That's an open confession."

Harold Ethridge could have protested that his use of the words was being misinterpreted by the boy, but at this point he was functionally unfazed and unmoved by his third slip of the tongue for the night. The boy stood unmoving in the same spot besides the hogpen.

"I take it you intend to dog me with the shadow of your accusations for the rest of my life?" Harold Ethridge asked more or less rhetorically.

"I don't intend to dog you with any shadow," Samuel said. "Shadows don't have any bite to them. I intend to leave you in the shadow of her grave. If I leave you in the shadow of your own grave, so much the better. You made sure that I'll never have a life with her. I'll live the rest of my life in the shadow of her death. In return, I intend to leave you in the deepest shadow hole I can manage."

Samuel stood motionless in his position by the hogpen. Though he stood outwardly motionless himself, Harold Ethridge had reached the brink of visibly trembling with rage. Only the self-control he prided himself on kept him from losing control of his faculties.

"It is not my intent to let you drag me through the mud over your dirty girl," Harold Ethridge said as his body started to twitch. "I want to lead a public life, and I intend to lead a public life free of your mad ravings. And any part of my life, public or private, is worth more than the life of any insolent gutter tripe or hick farm boy."

The previously motionless Harold Ethridge went into motion. In a movement that was both shuddering and smoothly controlled, he turned and quickly walked over to the side door of the barn through which Samuel had entered. When he reached the door, instead of passing through it, he slammed it shut from the inside. With a quick motion, he pulled the padlock off the latch hook, set the inside latch on the door, put the padlock on the latch, and locked it, sealing Samuel and himself in the barn. The other doors were locked from the outside.

"You're insane, boy!" Harold Ethridge said as he quickly put the padlock key in his pocket. He spun back around to face the boy. Samuel hadn't moved from his spot by the hogpen.

Harold Ethridge stepped quickly over to a section of the wall where tools were hanging from hooks.

"That's exactly how you came here tonight," Harold Ethridge went on. "You came here raving insane, wild-eyed out of control, shouting that I killed your tart. You were out of your mind. I couldn't talk to you. You couldn't be reasoned with. You just kept coming at me shouting that I had killed her and that you were going to kill me. At least that's what everyone will think. After all, you already have the reputation of being insanely jealous and of going crazy and starting fights in a pool hall where you almost beat a man to death over her. You came charging in here at me tonight wild-eyed with rage the same way you went charging after that hired hand you beat senseless in the saloon. Whose account of the fight you started here tonight do you think people are going to accept? Whose word are they going to take, my word or the word of a boy already known to be an explosively violent, jealous hothead?"

Harold Ethridge reached up and pulled the brush knife off its hanging pegs on the wall. The brush knife was a short-bladed machete made with a blade of thick metal about as wide as a butcher's knife but three times longer. Instead of being squared off at the end like a butcher's knife, the blade of the brush knife was rounded, ending with a pointed hook curved backward. With a quick close-quarter swing, it could lay a man's chest open from front to back, practically slicing him in half on a diagonal.

With the knife in his hand, Harold Ethridge spun around and started walking toward the boy. Samuel's expression didn't change. He stayed glued to the spot where he had stopped by the hogpen.

"Everyone will understand why I had to defend myself against a raging insane boy who came at me at night yelling that he was going to kill me."

It would be easy enough to claim that the crazed boy had attacked him and that he had been forced to defend himself. Conveniently he even had a knife in his pocket to place in the dead boy's hand to make it look like he had come at him with it. "Everyone in this town will know how insane you were when I describe the way you came at me tonight. You came here insane all right. It just isn't quite the insanity that I'll describe. You're insane to have loved a tramp like her. You're doubly insane to come here thinking that you could talk me into confessing to killing your slut."

Samuel continued to stand by the hogpen fence, unmoved and unmoving, seemingly unaffected by anything Ethridge said.

"You're trying to ruin me the way she threatened to ruin me. I wasn't about to let myself be ruined by a two-bit backwoods hussy harlot, and I'm not about to let myself be ruined by clod-headed sodbuster. You're insane if you think I'm going to let you do that. You're doubly insane to think that you could come here and talk or threaten me into throwing my life away over a two-bit tramp like her. You're triply insane to come here alone and unarmed and telling me that you told no one where you were going!"

At the moment, the illogicalness of the boy's coming at him alone and unarmed was overshadowed by Ethridge's inability to understand the boy's lack of reaction to his approach with the brush knife. The girl had been more animated in the face of approaching death than her farm boy sweetheart was.

Harold Ethridge considered himself a sporting man. The seed idea of a possibly new sporting thrill of hunting and killing whores had been taking shape at the edge his mind. One could call it open season on women who made it their business to be open season game for men on the prowl. It could be a whole new sensation for him in a life that, despite his wealth, was growing stale.

But first things had to be attended to first. As for the disposition of any bodies that might arise on any occasion, the one at hand or any that might arise in the future, he would just have to avoid his previous mistake and find a method and place of disposal more reliable than the river.

"You and your gutter sweetheart were equally matched where it comes to be empty-headed. She said I was dealing dirty with all women. She said I was dealing dirty in my business. She lived her whole life dealing herself dirty to any man who would pay her, and she said she was going to expose what she called my dirty dealings. Your brazen little bordello tart thought she could extort me. After laying herself down for money, she stood up in front of me in my room as bold as brass and said she was going to expose me to the mayor the next time she serviced him. The two-bit little tramp thought she could dictate my dealings and my life. She stood up and told me to my face that she was going to expose me in a way that would have ruined several profitable deals for me. No two-bit lowlife gets away with getting the better of my life—not her and not you."

"You said she stood up in front of you in a room in your house in town," Samuel said. "Is that where you killed her?"

The two last small pieces had fallen into place. Harold Ethridge had had the girl alone in his room, unseen in his house. That gave him opportunity to kill her. Criminologically speaking, opportunity isn't trivial. Now he had just revealed his reason for killing the girl. Now Samuel knew the motive. Motive isn't trivial. Harold Ethridge had had the girl alone when he killed her. He had motive and opportunity. Samuel wasn't Sherlock Holmes, but he was about to teach a lesson on having your victim alone with both motive and opportunity.

"Is that why you killed her? Because she stood up to you?"

"I killed the little tramp where she stood because she thought that, even as the tramp she was, she was better than me!" Harold Ethridge said. He had finally spoken the first-person past-tense word that Samuel had wanted. Given what Samuel knew, what had been said, and where the two of them stood, it didn't make much difference now.

"She was a whore, but she stood there in front of me thinking she was better than me. Just like you're standing there thinking you're better than me."

The boy was still standing in the same spot by the hogpen. He still wasn't trying to get away from Ethridge, and he still didn't seem to be getting ready to fight him. For some reason the boy's fight-or-flight mechanism didn't seem to be working.

"She was a cheap little caricature of a woman. Women, especially women like that, exist for the pleasure of men, even when the man's pleasure in her causes the woman pain."

"Well, I must say this for you, sir," Samuel said. "You are forthcoming about what you think about women." Samuel stirred from where he was standing in front of the hogpen fence. "But I think I've heard enough out of you about your philosophies on how to treat women. I've certainly heard all I want to hear. … Oh, she was far from social graces. Pastor Russell would probably pronounce her far from divine grace. She was a sinner all right. I don't know where she stood in the sight of heaven when she stood before you the night you murdered her, but Jesus found prostitutes to be closer to the kingdom of heaven than the Pharisees who would eventually kill Him. You say she thought she was better than you. I don't know if she thought she was better than you. I don't think she thought she was better than anyone. She never had much time to think about being superior to anyone. She was too busy staying alive to be bothered by measures of social position and breeding and by superiority thinking. In my humble thinking, a girl who deals in love, even if it is dirty love for sale, is a far better person than a psychotic alienist who kills young girls."

Harold Ethridge continued his slow advance on the boy, calculating the angle at which, the manner in which, and the moment when he would rush the boy.

"Do you think you're going to back me down with your mouth, boy?" Harold Ethridge asked. "I don't back down in front of anybody. Backing down isn't in me."

Harold Ethridge wasn't able to understand the boy's apparent lack of fear. But these country yokel farm boys could be pretty dense at times when it came to not seeing the obvious.

Harold Ethridge had paused about twelve feet from the boy. He tipped the brush knife toward him slightly. "You seem to be missing the wider picture here. Just what and who do you think you're looking at here, boy?"

"I think I'm looking at a man who likes to kill young girls," the boy said with ice in his voice. "I think I'm looking at the man I'm going to kill. I think I'm looking at the man I'm going to kill as casually and as with as little bother to my heart, soul, or conscience as you killed her. I'm looking at the man I'm going to butcher as thoroughly as the men at the slaughterhouse dispatch the pigs you send down the line to them. I think

I'm going to leave you dead in the midst of the pigs that you were planning to send out. You'll be found dead among your hogs. The setting will be both poetic justice and poetically symbolic. Ashes to ashes, dust to dust. Like to like. A dead pig among living pigs."

Samuel steadied himself against the hogpen fence. Then he loosened himself. "You may not consider it to be a fair fight between us. Did you hear me say I would be giving you a fair and fighting chance? But then I never figured that fairness comes into the way you go about killing a snake."

"And just how do you plan to go about doing that, boy?" Harold Ethridge asked in a jeering voice. "All you've got is mouth. It's kind of hard to kill someone with lip."

Samuel took his hand off the top rail of the hogpen fence. He leaned over the top of the fence, thrust his hand down into the hog feed in the trough inside the pen, and drew his hand sideways across the trough a few inches below the surface. He hadn't seen anyone else come into the hog barn while he had been watching for Harold Ethridge to arrive. But there was still the possibility that feeding hogs had exposed what he was searching for or that a hired hand had come into the far end of the barn, unseen to him, and had discovered it. But in only a second or two, his hand made contact with it at the point where wood and metal joined.

"What are you going to do with that, boy?" Harold Ethridge scoffed. "Do you plan to mow me down with a handful of hog feed?"

Samuel pulled his hand up sharply. In his hand he held an ominous-looking object that needed no introduction or explanation. As he spun the object around, it sent an arc of hog feed flying out. As he brought the object around, with a quick push of his thumb, he clicked off the safety.

"Actually I was thinking of using this," Samuel said.

Harold Ethridge stopped in his tracks, his mouth open in surprise. The boy he thought had recklessly come to him empty-headed and empty-handed was pointing a double-barrel shotgun at him, the fierce anger in his voice spitting at him, the equally fierce anger in his eyes poised above the twin barrels of the gun.

In the same instant Harold Ethridge realized the boy had drawn a gun on him, he was hit by the double realization that the farm boy he had

447

considered so dumb had walked him into a clever trap by sneaking into his barn and hiding a shotgun where he could easily reach it.

"You called her impertinent," Samuel said. "She wasn't one one-hundredth as impertinent as you, killing a young girl because she mouthed off to you. I knew you killed her. I just wanted to hear it from your own mouth. You arrogant egomaniacs are so much chattier when you think you have the upper hand."

Harold Ethridge was decidedly anything but chatty.

"What's the matter, sir?" Samuel said in a tone of strangled fury. "Why are you so suddenly silent when you had been so gregarious only a moment earlier? You had so many words for me but a minute ago. Where are your words now? What were the last words you spoke to her? All I have left of her is the words I'll never say to her."

Samuel continued his slow walk down toward the motionless Harold Ethridge.

"To paraphrase the Bible, there's a time for words and a time to refrain from wording. My words didn't save her. Maybe they could have if I had spoken enough. I'll never know now. As far as any words left to say, consider and speak your next words carefully. They're going to be your last."

At the boy's words, Harold Ethridge became animated enough to glance around quickly. There was only open space around him. There was nothing close by for cover that he could jump behind. The boy could pivot and fire in any direction he chose to run. If he rushed the boy, he would run right into the barrels of the shotgun. The doors were locked. He had locked the last one. There was no way out. No one was coming. No ideas were coming.

"Hold your tongue and save all the words you have for the judgment seat. You're going to need every last word you can get up there."

Samuel twisted his hands on the barrels and put his finger inside the trigger guard of the shotgun. He fought to control, or at least channel, the surging hate within him. When the girl was alive, he felt that he could see beyond every horizon. Now the only relevant distance that meant anything to him was the range of the shotgun. For him it had all ended when the girl had died. In the semidarkness of the hog barn, in the darkened corridor of Samuel's mind, the rest would end there that night.

"While we're on the subject of last words, what were her last words? Did she beg you not to kill her? What were the last sounds she made? Did she cry as you killed her? Did she gag as your hands crushed her throat? Was any sound she was making cut off and drowned out by the crack of her neck? The doc said she was paralyzed but still alive when she went into the river. As you drove her there paralyzed, did she beg you all the way there from the floor of the car not to kill her? Did she scream as you dropped her into the river? Did you hear her gurgle and gasp as she went under?"

Samuel waved the shotgun up and down a bit, but not enough to take its aim off the center of Harold Ethridge's torso.

"I would have held her in an embrace for the rest of my life. Now all I have left to hold onto is this. I would have been her lover for life. I would have made her my lover for life. But you took her from me. Now the only lover I have left to me is this. You wanted to have my lover so bad. You had her your way right up to the end. Now you can get acquainted with the only lover I have left. I'll arrange the bridal suite for you. Except that this lover is going to be the one who has you in her own way."

Samuel stopped moving. He was close enough to see the veins in Harold Ethridge's neck pulsing with rage, but the man was at least three arm's lengths out of range of his reach.

"I was going to make myself into a world of love for her. Now all my love is poured out on the ground and into the ground with her. All I have left is to put you in the ground with her."

For one of the first times in his life, words and ideas deserted Harold Ethridge.

"This is the only thing I have that can hold my love and my hate. It's the only lover I have left. You're so versed at taking other men's lovers. Come and take my new lover away from me."

If the boy would only come closer to him, Harold Ethridge calculated, he could rush the boy suddenly. If he could take the boy by sufficient surprise and close the distance quickly enough, he might be able to swing the brush knife fast enough to knock the gun out of the boy's hands before he could react. Then he would have the advantage again. But the boy had stopped maddeningly at a distance just far enough away that he couldn't be certain that he could reach him in the natural reaction time interval. To make up for the difference, Harold Ethridge figured that if he moved fast enough and suddenly enough, he could possibly throw the knife at the boy. The throw might not hurt the boy seriously. He might even duck. But it could cause him to pivot out of the way. That would swing the shotgun out of the way and throw his aim off. It might give Ethridge just enough time to rush the boy and grab him by the throat with his hands. After all, Harold Ethridge was an experienced killer with his hands. Harold tensed all the muscles that he would use for either move.

Come on, boy, Harold Ethridge said to himself. *Just keep talking and start coming again. Just one more step.*

"Let's put it this way," Samuel said. "An eternity of hell won't pay you back for what you did to her, but it's all I can offer you."

He pulled the first trigger. The right barrel of the gun fired. The blast spewed a geyser of orange flame in the gap between them. The wooden walls of the barn concentrated the sound inside and muffled it outside. Harold Ethridge felt like he had been slammed in the stomach by a sledgehammer. With a heavy grunt, he fell backward onto the floor of the hog barn. As he fell, the brush knife dropped out of his hand, landing within easy reach beside him. Startled by the sudden loud noise, the hogs in the barn squealed and grunted in alarm. They milled about in their pens, not knowing what was going on or where to turn to escape.

The smoke of the black powder hung in the air, obscuring the already semidarkness of the hog barn. Without wasting much time or motion, Samuel broke open the action on the gun, pulled out the expended shells, and reloaded. From there he walked over to inspect his fallen target.

Harold Ethridge lay on his back on the ground. The center of his stomach was riddled with a pattern of buckshot pellet holes the width of his torso. His eyes were open, but they didn't seem to look at Samuel as he approached. They just seemed to stare off at the ceiling, glazed and uncomprehending.

Samuel came up to the side of the body and stood looking down impassively for a moment.

"After you broke her neck, did you stand over her and watch her die, sir?" Samuel asked rhetorically as he stood looking at Harold Ethridge's fallen form. "Since you broke her neck instead of using a gun, no one would have heard you kill her. Alone in your house, you certainly would have had enough time to stand around leisurely and watch her until you thought she was dead. My grandfather was in the Civil War. He said that gutshot men often took hours to die. You watched her die. Maybe I'll just return the favor and watch you die."

Samuel turned his full back on the fallen Harold Ethridge and started to slowly walk away from him without looking at him.

As Samuel continued to walk away, still without looking, Harold Ethridge's hand reached out and again took hold of the handle of the brush knife. With a quick rush, the wounded man was back on his feet behind Samuel. He raised the knife and lunged toward Samuel's back. In the second before he could bring the machete-like knife down, Samuel spun around.

"Point and pull!" Samuel shouted, using an old trapshooting phrase, as he threw the shotgun up to his shoulder. Samuel had done trapshooting. He had also hunted fast-moving upland game birds like pheasants that would flap up suddenly from the brush of an open field and fly away fast at an oblique angle. Samuel knew how to rapidly shoulder a shotgun and swing it toward a target. Unlike with a clay pigeon or a live pheasant, Samuel didn't have to lead this target.

The second barrel of the double-barreled gun blasted into the acoustically confined space of the hog barn. Hit harder in the upper chest at closer range by a more confined pattern, Harold Ethridge was knocked off his feet backward and fell harder on his back this time. The brush knife flew farther away from his hand. Samuel had deliberately turned his back on the wounded Harold Ethridge, knowing he would jump up and charge him. Killers are that way.

The hogs, which had started to quiet down after being frightened by the first shot, started squealing and grunting again.

Samuel quickly pushed the lever and broke open the action of the shotgun. The ejectors threw two smoking spent shotgun shells over Samuel's shoulder. With a move just as quick, Samuel reached into his pocket, brought out two more shells, and reloaded the gun. With a hard jerk of his hands, he slammed the gun shut again.

"I knew you'd do that," Samuel said as he started walking back toward Harold Ethridge.

There wasn't any pretense left for Harold Ethridge. There wasn't any pretending to be dead. Hit harder in the upper chest, Harold Ethridge lay on the ground, the brush knife out of reach of his hand, his eyes half closed, a thick pool of blood forming over the wound pattern on his upper right chest, his breath coming in ragged gasps. Samuel walked up to the side of the fallen object of his seething hatred. Though the gesture was more symbolic than cautionary, he kicked the brush knife far out of reach. Then he turned.

"I see you still don't have any words for me," Samuel said in a voice like the jaw-grinding sound a trapper makes when he pushes open the jaws of a heavy bear trap and sets the trigger. "How many words did you spare for her?"

The hogs were starting to quiet down after their second alarm of the night.

"I loved that girl like there was nothing else in the world for me. I would have loved her for a lifetime. In a few minutes of your meanness, and with a twist of your hand, you took all the love we would have shared away from both of us. She was everything to me. You killed her like she was nothing at all to you."

Samuel pulled the muzzles of the shotgun back.

"I see you still don't have any last words for yourself. But you've already spoken your mind and heart. So you might as well hold your words, Mr. Ethridge. There's nothing you have to say for yourself or to me. Where last words are concerned, I don't care to hear any words you have to say to me. I just thought that maybe you might have a few words left for her. Do you at least now have an idea of what she felt? Do you know what it's like to know death is coming and there's nothing you can do to stop it—the way she did? Do you feel the least bit sorry for what you did to her?"

The hogs had almost quieted all the way down.

Samuel raised the barrels of the gun and leveled them so they were positioned about two feet from Harold Ethridge's head.

Harold Ethridge's eyes fluttered. He seemed to be trying to open them.

"When you open your eyes next, you will be in hell. Just without a face."

Both barrels of the shotgun blasted together into the confined space of the hog barn and through the confined distance between the shells and their target. Harold Ethridge's face exploded into a triangular vortex of red spray mixed with bits of shredded flesh. At the doubly loud sound of two barrels being fired simultaneously, the hogs started squealing and grunting a third time, louder than before. As if he were facing into the wind during an approaching rainstorm, Samuel felt droplets of mist strike his face.

Samuel stepped back from the scene he had created. He brushed a shred of wet flesh from his cheek, where it had splattered. Then he brushed another splotch of red off one of the barrels of the shotgun. Decades hence, forensic investigators would make a systematic science out of blood spray patterns. The pre-*CSI*-literate Samuel wasn't thinking in terms of blood spray patterns. He was actually surprised that blood would spray that far. He would find a small piece of flesh caught in his hair when he got home.

One could say it was over. Samuel considered it over. The killer of the girl lay definitely dead on the floor this time. The handsome face that had turned so many women's heads to his fancy was a blasted-out, unrecognizable red crater of jumbled and mangled fleshy shapes that someone trained in anatomy would have difficulty sorting out. Samuel didn't grow sick when he saw the results of his handiwork. Neither did he freeze in place, gripped with horror at the sight. He didn't run a series of self-justifying thoughts through his mind. Neither did he justify what he had done as self-defense. Samuel would have drawn his shotgun and killed Ethridge even if he hadn't come at him with a brush knife in hand. The immediate thought on his mind was that some of the hired hands might have heard the shots and the squealing of the hogs and would come to investigate what was wrong. Samuel's only instinct at the moment was to get out of there.

Samuel backed away from the body. He quickly looked around behind him until he found the two spent shotgun shells he had fired first. Leaving the two other fired shells in the gun, he shoved the shells he had picked off the floor into his pocket. That way, if anyone came to his farm to question him, nobody could compare them to the shells in the box in the gun cabinet. Samuel figured the precaution should be sufficient to cover his tracks.

The next thing was to get out of the barn. Since the main doors to the hog barn were locked from the outside, in order to get out he would have to open the small side door that Harold Ethridge had locked. Samuel had made a mental note of the pocket into which Ethridge had put the key.

He stepped quickly back to the body. Holding the shotgun in one hand, he crouched down on his haunches and reached into Harold Ethridge's pocket with the other hand, looking for the key. If he couldn't find it, he'd have to blow the lock off the door with the shotgun.

Samuel's fingers found the key, but there was another item in Harold Ethridge's pocket. It was larger and longer than the key. In his haste, Samuel pulled both items out. The other object proved to be a large pocketknife of a very familiar look and configuration. Samuel stared at it for a moment, then he flipped the blade open. Every muscle and sinew in his body, every fiber in his soul, seemed to tense up as tight as it could contract.

"This was hers!" he shouted at the dead man, his voice exploding beyond control. "She carried it because she thought it gave her protection. She wouldn't have given you this. You took it off her when you killed her! You kept it as a souvenir of killing her, like an Indian warrior who keeps the knife of the brave he kills. The only thing you didn't do was scalp her with it!"

A total fury that went beyond any consideration of who might be coming or of getting away swept through Samuel. He dropped the shotgun and grabbed the knife in both hands.

With a swift and savage swing, teetering on his haunches, Samuel raised the knife high over Harold Ethridge's body. At the apex of the thrust, he drove the knife down into the body with all the force that lost love and fully founded hatred could muster. The blow drove the knife into the center of Harold Ethridge's chest deep enough that it stopped only where the handle of the knife smacked into the bone.

Samuel fell to his knees, but it was hardly to pray or beg forgiveness. The total fury gripped him and carried like he was caught in midstream in a raging canyon rapids at flood tide. Like Captain Ahab astride the back of Moby-Dick, Samuel repeatedly raised the knife high and drove it into the chest of Harold Ethridge in the area below the rib cage. As he did so, he shouted imprecations about cutting out the heart that Harold Ethridge never had and how Ethridge had cut out his heart.

Samuel didn't stop to count how many times he drove the knife into the area beneath Harold Ethridge's already stilled heart. Finally the spell broke. The imperative to get away before someone possibly came into the barn and discovered him slashing away with maniacal intensity finally caused him to regain control. As the fury passed, with one last concentrated thrust, Samuel drove the knife into Harold Ethridge's chest one last time. Instead of pulling the knife out, he unwrapped his hands that had gripped it so tightly and left it sticking out of Harold Ethridge's chest. To Samuel it was one small symbolic act of vengeance for the dead girl.

Samuel grabbed the shotgun and stood up. With the shotgun and padlock key in hand, and with his anger at least partly back in hand, he walked quickly to the side door that Harold Ethridge had locked on him when he had thought he had him trapped. He opened the lock and opened the door. From inside the barn, Samuel glanced around. There was no one outside the door. He heard no sound of anyone coming. Samuel quickly stepped through the door and took off running toward the edge of the Ethridge farm and the road beyond. Finding the truck where he had left it, he cranked the engine to life.

Samuel didn't drive directly back home. As he passed the road into town, he detoured down the road until he came to the bridge over the river on the edge of town. In the spot where Harold Ethridge had thrown the dying girl into the river, Samuel stopped, unloaded the empty shells from the shotgun, and threw them and the other two empty shells he had picked up from the hog barn floor into the river. He was fairly sure they would sink and wouldn't wash up on the bank of a farmer's field like the girl had inconveniently done for Harold Ethridge. Then he took the remaining unfired shells out of his pocket and jammed them back into the cartridge box in a haphazard manner.

Having completed what he considered the covering of his tracks, Samuel Martin turned the truck around and drove back home in the night. In the dark, he saw neither the image of the girl's face in the sky nor the sight of Harold Ethridge's shattered face in the back of his mind.

When Samuel arrived back home, no lights were showing from the windows. The rest of his family had gone to bed. He parked the truck in the barn and headed toward the house with the shotgun and shell box in his hands. He opened the back door quietly and walked into the house as silently as he could, closing the door as silently as he had opened it. In the darkness inside the house, he could only see the outlines of the furniture in the parlor. Being careful not to make noise by bumping into any furniture, Samuel walked through the parlor to the adjoining room. There he put the shotgun back into the gun cabinet and the shell box back into the storage section beneath it. It was too late and too dark in the house to clean the gun. As he left the room, he made a mental note to clean it later. At the foot of the stairs, he detoured into the mudroom, where he unlaced his boots in the dark and took them off, leaving them there.

Samuel climbed the stairs as quietly as he could. Several of the old stair treads squeaked when stepped on them. He kept to the side of the stairs so as not to cause them to squeak. Samuel wasn't afraid of waking up his parents and sister. But Teddy had much more sensitive hearing. The dog slept in his parents' room. If he heard the stairs squeak in the night, he might wake up and start barking.

When Samuel had fired the final fatal volley into Harold Ethridge's face at close range, he had felt splatters hit his face. He had brushed off the largest piece of flesh he felt hit him, but still he figured his face probably needed washing. Inside his room, Samuel lit the kerosene lamp and took it over to the table where the washbowl sat beneath the mirror on the wall. By the light of the lantern, he discovered that he had more small but nevertheless noticeable splatters on his face.

Samuel began washing his face by the swaying light of the kerosene lamp. It was there that he discovered the small splatter of flesh caught in his hair. He washed it out. When he was done, he opened the window and threw the wash water outside. Then he took off his shirt and pants, balled them up, and dropped them in the corner. He didn't have time to inspect them for blood spots, but they would probably have to be washed too.

Samuel put out the lamp and got into bed. Outside, the chill of a fall evening was setting in. Lying in bed, Samuel looked up into the darkness toward the ceiling. He felt no distress, horror, regret, despair, elation, satisfaction, or justification at what he had done. None of those feelings would bring the girl back. If he felt anything in the surrounding darkness of his room, Samuel felt like he was drifting through the darkness without anything to grab and hold on to. In the surrounding darkness of the room, Samuel didn't have any reference points to orient himself. His body seemed to drift sideways as well as in a straight line. It seemed to turn as if caught in eddy currents of darkness.

Though he tried to put the thought out of his mind, for some time Samuel wondered if that had been what the girl had felt as she had floated on the current in the darkened river, paralyzed and unable to move with her neck broken. Finally she had drowned. Samuel could have assured himself that he had extracted specific and deserved revenge for the girl's murder, but the vengeance that had burned and flowed in him like molten iron coming out of a blast furnace in a foundry had cooled in him into jagged, unmoving slag. His soul was neither tormented nor gratified by what he had done. Samuel neither reflected with vengeful indulgence on his act nor remembered with fondness the times he had spent with the girl.

"Well, girl, I settled the score for you," Samuel quietly intoned, soft enough that no one in the house could hear. "It won't bring you back, but he's not after you. At least you won't have to run from him anymore."

Clarinda opened her eyes. The light was bright all around her. In a flash she was up and running, her feet splashing in the river. Across from the Richardson house, she crossed the river and came to the embankment that ran in front. She knew she would be safe in the house.

But when she tried to climb the embankment like she had done so many times before, she slid backward on the slippery clay. She tried to climb again. Once again she slid backward to the shore of the river. Every time she tried to climb the bank, she only slid back to where she'd started. She kept trying to climb the bank, her frustration growing every time she failed. She just couldn't understand why she wasn't able to climb the bank.

Samuel eventually fell into a dreamless sleep. When he opened his eyes again, the light from the sun rising on the far side of the house was filtering through the window into his room.

When Harold Ethridge opened his eyes, he was in hell.

Chapter 17

"If any of you feel you're going to vomit, please take yourself outside and do it there," Constable Harkness intoned. None of the policemen with him had seen a crime so bloody and graphic in its detail. They were starting to look a bit queasy.

"With all the hogs, it smells bad enough in here. Puke will only make it smell worse. If you can't make it to the door, go over to the far side and do it there. If you heave right here, it may cover up the one footprint that might solve this case."

As he concentrated on the figure on the ground, Constable Harkness waved the men behind off to the side. They stepped wide and gingerly, trying not to step on any footprints. Nobody vomited, but none of them had a ready tension-breaking quip to offer.

"Try to stay out of the footprint pattern around the body, and try not to step on any preexisting footprints. Footprints may turn out to be all we have to have to go on."

The constable looked from the door to the body and back. Moistened by hog urine and mixed with hog manure, the wet dirt of the hog barn floor had acted like a thin layer of mud or clay, deepening and preserving the footprints in it.

459

"It looks like we've got three separate sets of fresh footprints leading from the door to the body and back to the door." Constable Harkness looked at the soles of Harold Ethridge's shoes. "One of those sets of prints looks like his." The constable looked over at the foreman. "I take it one of the other sets of prints is yours."

"I opened the door in the morning like I always do and saw him lying there like he is now," the farm foreman said. "I couldn't believe what I saw. I ran up to him. Then I turned and ran back out. I went straight to the house from here to get word to you at the station."

"The third set of footprints may belong to the killer. Unfortunately, by coming in here, you may have partially obliterated the footprints of the murderer."

"Sorry, sir," the foreman said. "I was so shocked to find him lying there like that. I couldn't believe it. I just ran in to see what had happened. Then I ran out again to call you. I didn't think."

"May I see the soles of your shoes, please?" Constable Harkness asked, cutting off the foreman's apology. The foreman lifted one foot and then the other. The constable looked at the man's soles and then back at the ground.

"I can recognize your tracks from the others. Fortunately there aren't too many of them."

It did look like the man was telling the truth. The footprints of his shoes led straight in and straight back out, almost on top of each other.

"I didn't mean to mess anything up," the foreman said.

"There's plenty of the other footprints to work with," Constable Harkness said, glancing around at the widespread footprint pattern. He looked back at the foreman. "Has anyone else been walking around in here since you found the body?"

"No, sir. I told the other farmhands to keep out until you got here."

"Well, at least someone around here was thinking," the constable said. He turned to the body and got down on his haunches. "The question is, what was the killer thinking?"

Constable Harkness looked at the human carnage that was the body of the late Harold Ethridge. Flies, drawn by the combined scent of hog manure and death, were starting to gather around the mangled crater that had been the upper half of Harold Ethridge's face.

"Jeez, what a mess," the constable said. "This is as bad as anything

I've seen or heard of. He may have been a gentleman, but his killer sure isn't gentlemanly about the way he goes about killing. The last homicide in this town was one farmhand stabbing another in plain view of witnesses in a saloon. That was six years ago. Now we've had two homicides within a month of each other. When it rains, it pours."

Constable Harkness stood back up. He continued to look around. "I don't know why the killer killed him, but at least there's no big mystery as to how he killed him." The constable pointed to the patterns of the wounds. Even through the pooled blood and mangled flesh that had been the center of Harold Ethridge's face, the multiple pellet holes were visible.

"The gunshot wounds in the stomach and upper chest were made by a shotgun. That's plain enough. Same for the damage to the face. It's too big to have been made by a single bullet. That was done by a scattergun at close range." He pointed off toward some small white lumps lying on the ground. Two of them were close to the body. The others were out beyond the body. "We've got shotgun wading all over the place. He was shot repeatedly from different ranges."

Constable Harkness looked at the knife protruding out of Harold Ethridge's chest. "He was killed with two weapons, a shotgun and a knife. Now why would the killer have used two entirely different weapons on him? And which did he use first? Probably the gun. But why did he stab him too? Did he stab him to make sure he was dead after shooting him? Did the killer run out of ammunition and switch to his backup weapon to finish the job?" The constable looked at the innumerable stab wounds around the knife. "And why did he use both weapons so much?"

The constable turned to the foreman. "Did you or any of the other hired hands hear anything that sounded like shots being fired last night?"

"The servant house where the hired hands live is off in the other direction, on the other side of the main house," the foreman answered. "The hog barn is over here, about as far the other way. It's a pretty good combined distance. If all the doors on the hog barn were closed, the sound wouldn't have carried very far. All the doors were closed when I came to open the barn in the morning. It was cold last night. The doors in the hired hand quarters were closed to keep out the cold. We were all inside. With the distance, and the barn doors being closed, and the doors and windows of the hired hands' quarters being closed, it is quite possible that the sound of the shots was too muffled to be heard or taken note of."

The answer seemed logical enough to Constable Harkness.

The constable went back to looking at the footprint pattern on the hog barn floor. "We've identified two sets of footprints as being yours and Mr. Ethridge's," he said to the foreman. "There's a third set here."

Constable Harkness pointed to the third set of footprints, which looped around in an arc to the edge of the hogpen fence. From there they led in a straight line toward the body. Close to the body, the prints stopped and went in all directions, crossing over each other as if they were milling around aimlessly like the hogs in their pens. From the body there was a single line of the same patterned prints leading straight toward the door.

"They're all around this end of the barn and all around the body. They don't look like shoe prints. They look more like boot prints." He turned to the foreman. "Do these prints look familiar to you in any way? Have you seen them anywhere before? Do you recognize them as the prints of any of the boots of any of the hired hands?"

The farm foreman shook his head. "No."

Constable Harkness looked at both the foreman and Sergeant Plechathy. "I want to see every pair of boots and shoes worn by every hired hand on this farm." He turned back to the foreman. "Including yours."

Before the foreman could say anything, Constable Harkness turned back to the sergeant.

"Before we go, I want you to get a pad of paper from somewhere and draw as careful of a picture of the pattern of those boot prints as you can. We may need it for comparison later."

The constable turned back to the foreman. "Did Mr. Ethridge fire any hired hands recently?"

"Not within the last year," the foreman answered.

"Right offhand, do you know if there was bad blood between Mr. Ethridge and any of the hired hands on this farm? Did any hired hands hold a grudge against him in the past? Do you know if any of the hired hands holds a grudge against him presently?"

"Not that I know of, sir," the foreman said.

Before the foreman could say anything further, Constable Harkness looked back at the wounds on the body. He looked at the foreman again. "Do any of the hired hands here own a shotgun?"

"None that I know of, sir. If they do, they don't keep it here."

"Are there any guns kept in the house?"

"A few. There's just one gun rack in the house."

"Can you tell if any of the guns are missing? Could you identify the missing gun if we found it?"

"Yes, sir."

Constable Harkness turned to the other policeman with him. "You and the foreman go into the house and check to see if any of the guns have been taken. If they're all there, check and see if any of them have been fired recently. The killer might have snuck a gun out of the rack, used it on Ethridge, and then snuck it back. But I doubt he would have taken the time to clean it. If the killer used one of the guns in the house, it's a good bet that he was familiar with the house and what's in it. That would point to one of the hired hands, past or present, as the killer. While you're in there, you and the foreman go through the house and try to determine if anything has been taken. Look at the drawers and cabinets to see if any look like they've been rifled through. The killer may have been a thief looking for easy pickings. Mr. Ethridge may have surprised him in the act."

The officer and the foreman turned to leave. As they walked away, the sergeant stepped over to the police sergeant.

"If he confronted an ordinary house burglar, he would have been killed in the house," the sergeant said, "not here in the barn. I don't think this is a case of him stumbling onto a cat burglar."

The constable glanced around at the hogs in their pens. "He may not have had cats to burgle, but he did have hogs. He may possibly have come upon a small-time livestock rustler trying to make off with some hogs, either to sell on the market or to keep for himself."

The constable looked at the markings in the dirt floor again, looking in a wider arc this time.

"I don't see any drag marks, so he wasn't killed elsewhere and dragged in here. He was killed right here. That would possibly indicate that the barn had something to do with it. That could point to a rustler."

The constable glanced at the hogs again. "These hogs are the only eyewitnesses there are to the crime. There's dozens of them. We just don't know how to make them talk. And beating them with a rubber hose isn't going to work. They're already facing a death sentence in a slaughterhouse somewhere. Mr. Ethridge's death will give them some length of reprieve until his will is read or a probate court determines whose property they become."

"There hasn't been any theft of livestock around here for a long time," Sergeant Plechathy said of the constable's only working theory of the moment. "And I doubt that a hog rustler would go on a job armed with a shotgun. You need your hands free to rustle any kind of livestock animals. A rustler might carry a pistol in his pocket, but a long gun would just get in the way and would fill up his hands. He might carry a jackknife. He might use it if someone caught him in the act. But the killer used two different weapons. If he was surprised by Mr. Ethridge, why would he use both weapons to kill him? You would think he would have used one weapon on him once and then run away quick-like before anybody else came along. I doubt a common rustler would linger to kill him over and over again the way the killer did."

"I'm thinking the same thing," Constable Harkness said. "The fact that the killing took place in this barn may have nothing to do with a rustler out to get himself a pork dinner. It may have everything to do with the killer ambushing his target in an isolated and soundproof location."

The constable glanced around again. This time he was looking at the barn itself instead of the hogs in it.

"The other possibility is that the killer was lying in wait for him and followed him into the barn looking for an isolated opportunistic place to kill him where he wouldn't be seen or heard. This barn fits that description well enough. It's a good place to finish what you came here to do. Along with no drag marks, there are no signs of a struggle. The killer may have had the drop on Ethridge from the beginning. That means he may have come here with the premeditated idea of killing him. ... Harold Ethridge may not have encountered his killer. His killer may have come here to encounter him."

Constable Harkness continued to study the body of Harold Ethridge.

"There's way too much damage done here to be explained by a startled thief firing once and then running away as his victim slumps over," he continued. "The killer made a shooting gallery and a pincushion out of him. It takes a lot of meanness to do that amount of damage to a body. But it also takes time. This was a case of sustained contact, not a panicked shoot-and-run. It takes a lot of personal hate to bring a killer this close to his victim and kill him over and over again, and in more ways than one. There's more heat than light to this killing. The more I look at this, the more it's starting to seem like a crime of passion, not a robber surprised in the commission of a robbery. I doubt we're going to find any gun missing from the house. It's starting to look more like the killer came here stalking Ethridge and brought his own gun with him. That smells of premeditation. And that smells of a bad grudge working its way out."

"Who might have carried a grudge that bad that would make them come out here and kill him like they did?" The sergeant had asked the rhetorical question that had become a real-world homicide question.

The constable looked off to the side. "Far as Mr. Ethridge's business ethics goes, some of Ethridge's business deals were a bit on the shady side. It could be a former business partner he got the best of or a rival farmer who thought Ethridge cheated him somehow. But all the men in town whom he did business with are old men. They wouldn't have the strength, let alone the courage, to do something like this."

Constable Harkness looked off to the other side. "As far as his other lack of ethics goes, Mr. Ethridge here had quite a reputation as a lothario. I don't know if anybody really knows how many women he dallied with or lured into adultery with the implicit promise of marrying them after they divorced their less than wealthy husbands. Most of the ones he dallied with were married. That kind of thing can make a husband real mad."

The standing Constable Harkness looked back down at the bullet- and knife-riddled body of Harold Ethridge. "That looks like the kind of thing an enraged husband who's been cuckolded would do to the Casanova who's been bucking his wife behind his back." He looked back at the sergeant. "There are a lot more people in this town than ticked-off, no-account small-time would-be rustlers who might be looking to do Mr. Ethridge in. If nothing turns up out here, we're going to have to go back into town and talk with everyone and anyone he did business with."

The constable turned and started to move. He motioned for the sergeant to follow. "Let's look around in here to see what more we can find. Then I want to follow those boot tracks and see where they lead outside. If they don't belong to any of the hands on this farm, then we've got an outside killer who came in. Maybe we can track him back to where he came from."

"There's some kind of bolo knife over here on the floor," the sergeant said, pointing to the brush knife. The pair walked over to where the machete-like knife lay on the ground.

The sergeant bent over and started to reach for the knife. Constable Harkness grabbed his arm and stopped him.

"Leave it where it lies," the constable said. "The position may mean something."

The constable stared at the knife for several moments.

"Now did that fall off the wall, or was it used in the crime?" Constable Harkness wondered out loud. "It's closer to the barn wall than to the body. It might have fallen off its mounting on the wall. But the distance from the wall looks too far for it to have fallen and slid over here."

The brush knife had left small skid marks in the dirt where it had landed after Samuel had kicked it. Constable Harkness focused on the slide marks in the dirt. "There are sliding marks on the ground behind it. It looks like it was thrown here."

The constable turned around and looked back at the body of Harold Ethridge. "Why did the killer bring two different weapons with him—a shotgun and a knife? If he did, he sure believed in coming prepared. And why did he leave his knife in Ethridge's body, a knife that might be traced to him?"

He looked at the sergeant. "When Harmon and the foreman get back, ask the foreman whether this knife came from here. If he doesn't recognize it, that means the killer brought it in. Maybe we can track it back to who bought it."

The turn-of-the-century small-town local law enforcement pair examined the interior of the barn for several minutes more. Finding nothing of further note, Constable Harkness and Sergeant Plechathy followed the boot prints out through the side door of the barn.

The pattern of boot prints outside was as confusing as the pattern inside. There seemed to be four sets of similar prints, maybe more. The prints both came and went from the side door of the barn. Though the sole patterns were the same on all, one set was noticeably different.

"These tracks are all fresh," the constable said as he tracked with his head down. The sergeant followed to the side, looking on. "They all look like they were made no more than a day ago."

With his head still down, the constable pointed to the set of prints that was different. "Look at this set of tracks. They're wider spaced than the same ones going in. The toes and front edges are also driven deeper into the ground. You can hardly see the heel print. He was walking when he left those tracks going in, but he was running when he left these going out. And he was running away from the barn."

The constable straightened up and looked in the direction in which all the tracks either originated from or headed toward.

The constable looked at his sergeant.

"Coming and going, walking or running, all these tracks lead in one direction. Let's see where they go."

With a motion for the sergeant to follow him, Constable Harkness followed the tracks away from the barn. Together they followed the tracks to the edge of the farm, where a low clay embankment rose up to the roadbed. The boot prints continued up the clay embankment. One print was driven deeper into the clay than the others as if the person making the print had hit the bank running. Other prints weren't prints at all; they were scrapings in the clay. The drawn-out and sliding shape of the scrapings made it look like the runner had scrambled up the bank, partially slipping back down as he lost his footing on the slippery wet clay surface.

"Our runner went up this bank and kept on going," Constable Harkness said as he and the sergeant came to a stop at the embankment at the boundary of the farm. "That just convinces me more that these are the tracks of the killer." He looked out over the road and the landscape beyond. "If the killer was a farmhand here on the farm, he wouldn't have been likely to head this way after killing Ethridge. He would have tiptoed back to the hired hand quarters. I doubt he would detour this far out and circle back."

The constable glanced around in no direction in particular. "It's both what I thought and what I was afraid of. The killer is probably an outsider who came in to the farm from the town or another farm or somewhere else, someone who came here last night bringing his own gun with him. We can grill all the farmhands as a matter of course, but I don't think we're going to wrap this up here on the farm. Things hardly ever go that simple and clean. Who knows where this is going to lead or where we're going to end up following it."

The constable turned to the sergeant. "You go back and see if Harmon found anything. While you're at it, find out from the foreman whether that sling blade on the floor is from this farm or not. When you're done, meet me back here. I'm going to try to see if I can track where these prints are heading."

Sergeant Plechathy turned and headed back toward the farmhouse. Constable Harkness climbed the low embankment onto the road. He stood looking in the direction the boot prints headed. Then he started following the boot prints. They were plain and easy to see in the open dirt of the road, but then they turned off and disappeared in the grass and brush alongside the road. It was as if the killer had realized he was leaving footprints and decided to walk where he wouldn't leave any. Constable Harkness proceeded from there down the road a ways, but the boot prints did not reappear. He turned and headed back to the Ethridge farm.

"All the hired hands have the same story," Sergeant Plechathy said from the edge of the low embankment by the side of the road, where he had caught up with the constable. "They all say they were together in the hired hand quarters and that none of them were gone during the time the killing took place. None of them heard any shots. The foreman backs up their story. He was in the hired hands' house with them at the same time. Either they're all in it together or none of them were involved. All the guns in the house are still there, and none of them have been fired. The foreman says that the brush knife we found in the barn has been there for years, along with the other tools in the barn. The killer didn't bring it."

"Well, that buries one clue," Constable Harkness said as he started down the low embankment from the road. "At this point we'd better call the funeral home to pick up Mr. Ethridge and prepare him for burial before he starts going rank on us. When they take the body to the funeral home for preparation, we can have Doc Simpson examine him and give us an official medical report. Maybe there's something there we've missed that isn't obvious by looking at him. Then you draw up or trace out the pattern of that boot print." He pointed down the dirt road in the direction in which the boot prints went. "If those are the footprints of the killer, it looks like he came from that direction—from the town or one of the other farms. It looks like we're going to have to take the investigation wider from here."

"Do you still want to interview the hired hands on the farm?" Sergeant Plechathy asked as the constable walked up to him.

"We might as well, just to be thorough," Constable Harkness answered. "But I don't think it's going to give us anything. I'm pretty sure the killer came in from outside." He glanced over his shoulder in the direction he had just come from. "The tracks head up to the road. From the direction of the one or two partial prints at the top of the rise, the killer seems to have headed to the west. But I lost the tracks on the hardpan of the road surface. Either that or the killer left the road and walked on the grass alongside the road. I lost the trail pretty quick and couldn't pick it up in either direction. I'm sure this is the direction the killer left in. I can't tell which way he went from here, but if he came from the town, he's probably back there by now, covering his tracks further."

"Are we going to give the story to the newspaper?" Sergeant Plechathy asked.

"Of course we're going to tell the paper," the constable said. "You can't keep something like this under wraps."

"A killing like this could possibly set off a panic in the town," the sergeant said, "especially if we say that the killer is in the town somewhere."

"We don't have to emphasize that the killer is in town," the media-savvy-enough constable countered. "We don't have to say it directly. We just say that the killing was done by a person or persons unknown. But we don't go around telling people that the killer may be standing behind them on the street."

"The townspeople will get that idea on their own," the sergeant said. "If they don't, the paper will give them that idea. Newspapers just naturally love to blow any story up into as big and splashy a piece of yellow journalism as they wring out."

"You've got that right," the media-aware constable concurred. "The paper and the town will be calling this the crime of the century in the town. The thing is that it is more or less the biggest crime ever committed in this town. At least it's the most sensational and glaring killing ever committed in the history of the town. The last killing was six years ago, and that was a simple fight between two saloon toughs. The identity of the killer was known before the body of his victim hit the floor. The case was closed before it was written up. Now the killings are coming in twos. But the identity of the killers and their motives is unknown. That leaves people scared. ... Within a month we've had two brutal and senseless killings in this town, neither of which were anything like what has happened before around here. First that young prostitute, now Ethridge. The prostitute was the first girl ever murdered in the history of the town. That by itself should have caused a stir. But people in the town let it slide by like it was nothing. Like the Martin boy said, they probably thought the girl was a dirty little nothing who had gotten what comes naturally to a dirty girl who hung around with the kind of men she hung around, of which there are plenty. We've got our work cut out for us."

"Where do we go from here?" Sergeant Plechathy asked.

"The first thing we do is finish questioning the hired hands on the farm and check their boots for a match," Constable Harkness said. "We should ask whether they saw anyone suspicious lurking around the farm. If we don't come up with anything, then we go back into town and pick the place apart looking for any kind of suspect or motive. The first people we call in are the husbands of the women Ethridge was playing around with, past and present. They're the primary ones who might have enough passion to kill a man the way Ethridge was killed. Then we talk to the business partners Ethridge dealt with and any hired hand whom he had any dealings with in the past. We should also interview everyone who lives around the Ethridge house. The killer may have been stalking him at both places, looking for an opening. If anyone saw someone suspicious lurking around his house in town, it could give us the clue and the opening we need to find the killer."

The constable paused for a moment and looked at the police sergeant. Then he turned and looked back out over the road and the land beyond. "He's out there somewhere," he said with gravitas. "We don't know who he is or why he killed. All we're probably going to be able to say to anyone at the end of this day is that the killer is out there and that he's probably closer to the town than he is to this farm. ... I don't know what drives this guy. I don't know how smart he may be. I don't know what mental state he's in.

I don't know if he's looking to kill again. But where it comes to killing, we can see how mean he is. He's already put distance between himself and us. The longer he keeps away from us, the harder it's going to be to apprehend him and get the town back to normal. The quicker we can catch him, the quicker the fear will be put to rest. If there are no more killings, one way or the other the fear will fade with time. But I don't know if the fear will ever go totally away until everything in the town is like it used to be and this never happened. Even if we catch the killer, I don't think that anything is ever going to be quite the same in this town again."

The constable turned and walked past his sergeant. "Come on. Let's talk to those hired hands."

Chapter 18

"Somebody gave it to him in spades, so don't give it to me in Latin," Constable Harkness said, looking at the body on the mortuary table. "Don't try to impress me with your knowledge of medical terms, Doc. Just give me the verbs. Tell me in plain English what killed him and how he died."

He looked again at the exploded and mangled remains of the face of the man who used to be the richest man in town and the leading citizen.

"As if that isn't obvious. You can see how he died by looking at him. I just need an official coroner's report for the record."

The town's single physician, Doctor Simpson, doubled as the town coroner. The Evergreen Funeral Home doubled as the town coroner's office. The mortuary table in the funeral home where the bodies of townspeople were prepared for burial had been pressed into service as a forensic autopsy table.

"The immediate cause of death was gunshot wounds by a shotgun fired from close range," Dr. Simpson responded. "I've extracted as many of the pellets as I can find. That goes along with the shotgun shell wads you found at the scene. They're in that mason jar over there." The doctor pointed to the glass jar sitting on an auxiliary table. Constable Harkness picked up the jar and looked at the small pile of rounded lead shot inside.

"Double-aught buckshot," Constable Harkness said by sight, recognizing the ammunition without having to measure the actual shot size. "You don't hunt ducks with this. This is meant for bigger game. Whoever went after him didn't just grab any old box of shells out of the closet at random. He planned it out in advance, and he meant to get the job done."

The constable looked back at the body of Harold Ethridge.

"I would say these wounds were delivered first," the doctor said, pointing to the shot patterns clustered in the abdomen and the upper right chest and shoulder area. "From the degree of spread of the shot, I would say both shots were fired from a distance of between seven to five feet. From the angle of penetration, the victim seems to have been standing when the shots were fired. Both wounds were serious in themselves, but they missed vital organs. He could have survived either. Taken together they were life-threatening, but he might possibly have been able to survive both." Dr. Simpson nodded toward the shattered head and face. "It was the shot to the head that was definitely fatal. From the tight grouping of the pellets, it appears the shots were fired from a much closer range, no more than three feet. From the number of pellets, I would say that the shotgun was a double barrel."

"The diameter of the wadding indicates the gun used was a twelve-gauge," Constable Harkness said.

"The patterns had only begun to overlap when they struck," Doctor Simpson went on. "Together they formed a figure-eight pattern. From the tight side-to-side patterns, I would say that the killer fired both barrels at the same time. If he had fired separately, the two impact patterns would be more random and overlapping. The angle of penetration wasn't straight in. It was at a much steeper angle than the other two shots. If I were reconstructing the sequence of the murder, I would say the killer probably approached with his gun leveled and fired the first shots into the chest and torso in rapid but separate succession, knocking Mr. Ethridge off his feet. Once he had him down and incapacitated, he probably approached to a closer position."

474

The doctor held his hands out as if holding a long-barreled gun downward at a forty-five-degree angle.

"Once he got up close, he fired the next two shots simultaneously from a near-point-blank range. The shots shattered the mastoid process and the ocular orbits."

"You're back to medical Latin again," Constable Harkness said. "I don't know what either means any more than I know what's on a lawyer's bill."

"Stated in plain English, the shot blew open the front of the skull and shredded the brain," Dr. Simpson went on in street English. "I haven't seen gunshot wounds this bad since I was an army field doctor in the war with Spain. And this goes beyond typical combat injuries. The final shots were focused and deliberate. As I said, he might possibly have survived the other shots, but there was no way he could have survived the final barrage. The killer knew that. The third and fourth shots were fired together for maximum effect. That was the execution shot. That was how the killer delivered the coup de grâce. That's not Latin; that's French."

Doctor Simpson pointed to a glass-bottomed petri dish with a glass cover. "I found gunpowder grains in the wound and embedded in the face around the wound. Given that the killer fired from such a close range, the grains were still traveling with enough velocity to drive them into the surface of the skin. I extracted as many as I could and put them in that dish."

Constable Harkness picked up the petri dish, examining the gunshot residue for several minutes. "These look like black powder grains," he said, lowering the glass dish. "Whoever killed him used an old gun, old ammunition, or both."

"You're the gun expert," Doc Simpson said.

The constable picked up the knife off the side table. "When we examined the body in the field, the killer had left this rammed in his chest," the constable said. "What can you tell me about it?"

"The killer stabbed him repeatedly with that knife," the stand-in coroner said. "So many times the individual wounds merged together, making it difficult to count the exact number of stab wounds. I'd say that the killer stabbed him at least three dozen times, maybe more. There was some seepage from the wounds but no bleeding or edema. The heart had stopped beating when the stab wounds were administered. Mr. Ethridge was already dead when he was stabbed. There was localized bruising around the stab wounds where the knife was driven in with so much force that the front of its shaft impacted with the body. All the stab wounds were close together in the area just below the heart."

"Now why would the killer go to all that trouble to kill a man who's already dead and obviously so?" Constable Harkness mused out loud to himself as much as to the doctor. "And why did he hang around to do it? Somebody might have heard the shots and could have been coming. If the killer was thinking straight, he would have wanted to get out of there as fast as he could in order to avoid being seen and identified. Why did the killer stick around and play mumblety-peg with his victim when he should have been on his heels running?"

"The number of the blows and the force of the blows indicate they were delivered in heated passion," Doctor Simpson said. "It parallels the way the killer deliberately sought to obliterate Mr. Ethridge's face. I'd say the killer was trying not only to make sure Mr. Ethridge was dead but also to obliterate Mr. Ethridge's identity. It points in the direction of someone with a seething hatred of Mr. Ethridge."

"I'll go along with you on that," Constable Harkness said as he examined the knife. "When you blow off someone's face then stab him several dozen times in the heart, even though he's dead, and leave the knife stuck in him as a calling card, it's about as personal as it gets. The killer did a lot more than necessary to ensure he was dead. A simple thief or burglar caught in the act wouldn't have gone to all this trouble to express his disdain for the victim. And we couldn't find any evidence of forced entry at either of Mr. Ethridge's residences, and nothing was taken from anywhere. Right offhand I'd say we're looking for someone with a grudge against him, possibly a farmhand who considered himself ill-used by Mr. Ethridge or someone he had bested in business."

It made as much sense as anything to Constable Harkness, the one small potential problem with the theory being that not a whole lot of itinerant farmhands owned and carried double-barrel twelve-gauge shotguns around with them.

Constable Harkness folded the blade of the knife back into its handle and put the instrument in his pocket. "I need this for the investigation right now," he said by way of explanation. The doctor didn't question why the chief of police was walking off with evidence.

Constable Harkness stepped back toward the body on the mortuary table. "Is there anything else you can tell me?" he asked.

Dr. Simpson pointed to Harold Ethridge's neck. Where the doctor was pointing, the constable could see a fading reddish line drawn in the flesh that looked like a healing scar.

"The only other thing of note would be this cut on his neck," Doctor Simpson said. "It looks to be somewhat recent, but it's partially healed over. The original cut looks like it was made by a long- and sharp-bladed instrument, but it wasn't made by the same knife that was found in the body. From the advanced healing stage, it looks like it was made several weeks ago, which eliminates it as a part of this crime. It couldn't have happened when he was killed, or it would be fresh with no signs of healing."

"I remember now," Constable Harkness said. "He had a bandage on his neck in the same position when I interviewed him about the killing of that young prostitute you wrote up the report on."

"That was about a month ago," the doctor said. "The amount of healing of the wound is consistent with that amount of time elapsed."

"When I asked about it, he said he had cut himself shaving with a straight razor."

"That's a bit inconsistent with the wound," the doctor said.

Constable Harkness looked up at the doctor. "How so?"

"Well, a straight razor is long enough and sharp enough to make a cut like that, but men usually shave the neck in an up-and-down movement from the base of the neck to the bottom of the jaw. The shape and length of the wound is not consistent with a razor nick made by a razor being worked in a vertical direction. The razor would have to have been drawn horizontally across the side of the neck from front to back to make a cut of that length."

"Well, maybe Mr. Ethridge was the world's biggest incompetent when it came to handling a razor or anything with a sharp edge to it," Constable Harkness said in a subtle, dismissive manner.

"The last time we had a murder in this town was six years ago," Doctor Simpson said. "That was an outsider farmhand killing another outsider farmhand. Now we've had two murders within a month of each other. One of them was a low-level hooker. The other was a leading citizen of the town. People are going to say no one in this town is safe anymore."

Constable Harkness felt he was getting his first taste of the chorus he would be hearing soon enough from alarmed citizenry of the town. At the moment he had no more of an answer for the doctor than he did for the rest of the town.

"I wouldn't make too much out of the close timing of the two cases," Constable Harkness said, trying to deliver at least a small bit of diversionary reassurance through some homespun country philosophy. "Sometimes things just follow close on the heels of each other by coincidence. But it doesn't mean the whole world has suddenly come unraveled and is going to hell in a handcart."

The constable did believe in coincidence and unrelated random chance. Sometimes groupings like this did just occur at random, he thought. But then again, sometimes a coincidence was just too much of a coincidence.

The constable had a lot to do that day. He turned and motioned to Sergeant Plechathy. They started to leave. The constable spoke half over his shoulder to the doctor as he left. "You finish up here. If you find anything else, let me know. When you're done examining the body, turn it over to the funeral home and let them go to work embalming it. He's not getting any fresher, and I'm sure the mayor and the town are going to want to get on with giving him a big send-off funeral service without holding their noses."

As he walked out of the mortuary preparation room, Constable Harkness figured it would be a closed-casket service.

Chapter 19

"God knows," Horace Thompson went on, "if an upstanding citizen like that can be killed in such a cold-blooded and vicious manner, ain't none of us safe. We could all be murdered in our beds. I don't think that Helen and I have had a proper night's sleep since this happened. We're going to worry ourselves into an early grave. At our age we don't have all that many days left to worry away."

Constable Harkness sort of laughed at the old man's comment. He didn't mean any disrespect by it. Old people were forever making comments about how few days they have left before forever catches up with them.

"At my age I'm too old to be crazy," the old man said. "The craziest thing I do now is to make myself a double bourbon instead of a single. I'm not the 'crazed killer' who the newspaper and everyone is saying is supposed to be on the loose in this town or hiding in the woods outside the town. I don't own a shotgun. The only gun I have is my old Remington forty-four-caliber cap-and-ball revolver that I carried all through the War between the States when I was a young man in the cavalry. I've still got powder, shot, and caps for it. I'll use that on any crazed killer who tries to enter this house."

The small bit of bravado on the old man's part brought a half smile to the face of Constable Harkness—and more than a little worry.

Constable Harkness raised both his hands, palms forward, in a gesture for the old man to slow down. "Now, Horace, you just put that old horse pistol of yours away," Constable Harkness said in a steady, calming voice. "If you keep it loaded and at the ready, for all I know you'll wake up hearing a sound in the dark at night and panic and end up shooting Helen here as she comes back from the bathroom. You've been together too long for it to end in such a way."

He pointed at the old woman standing next to the old man. "I'd hate for that to happen as much as you would, and I'd hate to have to write up the report. You just leave that gun right where it is in the drawer. Unloaded. Let the police in this town look for any crazed killer who might be on the loose. Or else everyone in this town is going to be blazing away at every sound that goes bump in the night."

"Are you here to caution me that?" the old man asked. "Or are you thinking that I may have snapped in my old age and that I'm the crazed killer supposed to be loose?"

"Nothing of the kind," Constable Harkness responded diplomatically. "I'm just asking around to see if anyone saw anybody suspicious lurking around the Ethridge house. I've checked with the people in the houses around his. They didn't see anything suspicious. Now I'm just expanding my search for possible witnesses to the houses farther away."

As it stood, the killing of Harold Ethridge was still without apparent and obvious motivation. That it wasn't a case of a simple attempted robbery gone bad was also evident. The savagery and apparent fury of the killing, combined with the seeming deliberate mutilation of the body, indicated a darker and more personal passion behind the killing. Tensions were rising. Guns were being loaded. As the chief of police, Clarence Harkness had the law enforcement duty of investigating the killing and the political duty of trying to tamp down public hysteria such as the madman theory. The trouble was that, in the absence of any clear motive, the theory of a madman on the loose was by default as credible as any.

"For someone to kill someone like that, the someone who did the killing has to be a madman," the old man went on. "Whatever reason he killed him, the way he killed him had to have been driven by some kind of madness. I've seen men crack and go mad under the strain of combat. Men do all sorts of crazy things when they go mad. Sometimes they couldn't even recognize their own friends. They think that everyone around them is out to get them."

Constable stood in the living room of Horace Thompson's house, a veritable picture of a turn-of-the-century small-town policeman acting the role of small-town politico. Smiling, his thumbs in his vest pockets, he was the very picture of unruffled official officiousness.

"Which is why I think you should put away that old Colt of yours and don't leave it lying around primed and loaded," Constable Harkness reiterated in his experienced policeman's advisory voice. "A lot of people end up shooting someone they have no intention to hurt and who are the last persons they would want to shoot just because it's dark and they're jittery, thinking that someone's coming to get them. I'd hate to see you shoot your wife after you've fallen asleep at night and she goes to the bathroom. You wake up when she's coming back into the room, and in a half-asleep state, you mistake her for a madman on the prowl. I'd hate for her to shoot you in the same way. Let's be careful not to add a senseless tragedy to a senseless murder. You just leave the defense of the town and your person to the police. With our investigative methods, we can work out what happened and who did what." He wished he could be as sure himself that it could be worked out as he was telling the old man.

Any chief of police can be made nervous by the thought of a nervous and trigger-happy local population, armed to the teeth and sniping at shadows. When it came to old Horace Thompson, any danger of the old man's potential gunslinging might prove to be a moot point. Constable Harkness figured his ammunition was so old that it might not fire if he tried to use it.

"It's the senselessness of it all that's got all of us worried," Mr. Thompson responded in his same track. "I've been going over this in my mind, trying to figure out who the killer might be, why he did it, and why he killed Mr. Ethridge the way he did. It's the way the killing was done that makes it seem like the work of a madman. You even said so in the newspaper article about the murder."

"I didn't say that," Constable Harkness responded with clarification. "I didn't personally say anything about a madman being on the loose in our midst. The newspaper said that. But newspapermen are out to sell newspapers, and yellow journalism and lurid speculation sells newspapers the way plodding police work doesn't."

As soon as he had said what he said, Constable Harkness felt that he had used the wrong word. He should have said *methodical* instead of *plodding.*

Constable Harkness still figured that the girl had met her fate at the hands of a bad-tempered farmhand or a bad-tempered something or other she had been servicing in her profession. They figured the girl had made her own bed and had died in it. It was the grisly murder of a leading citizen that had set the town's teeth to chattering in fear and their mouths chattering about being murdered in their beds.

"Helen and I have been trying to figure out the whys and the wherefores of his murder," Horace Thompson went on. "We don't know if we've got a Jack the Ripper in town killing people for the fun of it or whether it was done by some crazed anarchist who wants to kill people just because they're rich. Either way, we seem to have a crazy someone or something running around the town. Who knows who they're going to take out next."

"Jack the Ripper only killed prostitutes," Constable Harkness said. But right off the bat he had trouble with that one. Someone had killed a prostitute only a month earlier, and so far he hadn't been able to crack the case. That didn't give him confidence that the case of the murdered girl would ever be closed. The case of Jack the Ripper had never been broken.

"And I doubt any anarchist would come all the way out here to kill a rich man. He'd be much more likely try to kill a big-city industrialist or banker like Andrew Carnegie or J. P. Morgan. President McKinley was shot by a crazed anarchist ten years ago, but that happened in Washington, DC. I doubt an East Coast anarchist would come all the way out to our little out-of-the-way town gunning for the richest man in town when there are fatter and richer targets elsewhere. I wouldn't worry about either of those ideas."

"But to kill someone the way the killer killed Mr. Ethridge sure seems to speak of a madman of some kind on the loose around here," Horace Thompson said. "If the killer isn't a madman, who and what do you think he is?"

Constable Harkness was starting to appreciate all over again the old adage that more than half a policeman's lot consists of trying to calm a jittery public, who were always out ahead of the police department with their imaginings and conspiracy ideas. Already the public of the town seemed irretrievably out ahead of him in lurid speculations.

"From what we've observed at the crime scene, several aspects of the crime seem to indicate a personal motive for the crime," Constable Harkness conceded in his best logical, methodical, speculation-disarming voice. "Given the seeming personal nature of the crime and the passion it seems to have been committed with, we in the police department are currently treating the crime as a personal grudge killing, probably committed by someone Mr. Ethridge knew. Our main suspicion is that the crime was committed by a disgruntled hired hand who felt that he had been somehow shortchanged or mistreated by Mr. Ethridge. Or possibly by the husband whom Ethridge cuckolded by seducing his wife. Either way, the killing was probably focused and personal, not the work of a mad random killer."

The constable had never really liked Ethridge. He could see how a lot of others could have liked him even less.

"For now, please leave the speculation and the police work and any gunplay to those of us in the police department."

"But you're saying that the killer may have been here, lurking around in our backyard!" Horace Thompson said. "Your being here and saying that the killer may have been lurking around in the shadows is what's got me thinking about us being killed in our beds. You're the one making me think that. My worry about that doubled the minute you said that the killer might have been here. If the crime and the killer are out there in the country, what are you doing looking for him here in town?"

"What I said," Constable Harkness tried to say in his most professional voice, "was that there is a possibility that the killer may have been stalking and hunting Mr. Ethridge for some time before the killing, looking for an opportunity and an opening. All I came here today for was to ask you if in the last few months you ever observed anyone suspicious-looking loitering around, especially anyone you may have seen go into the alley that separates the lots on North Street from the lots on Grange Street, which your house is on. If you saw someone who looked strange and suspicious, someone who looked like they might be casing the Ethridge house, especially someone looking at it from in the alley, then you may have possibly seen the killer."

There was another reason Constable Harkness was coming to the old man. Old men like to sit on porches and in windows and reminisce about days gone by and watch the world go by. Sometimes they see things. If the oldster is old and senile, sometimes he or she imagines things. But if their minds aren't completely gone, they often do observe useful things that other, more active people miss or don't see at all because they are off somewhere doing something else. An old man sitting around with nothing to do but sit around on the porch or look out a window and observe can often be a very useful source of information.

"So far nobody in the other close-by houses reported seeing anyone suspicious coming or going. It seems that if someone was stalking Mr. Ethridge from the brush, they did it all out there in the country. That's consistent with our theory that it was a disgruntled farmhand who did the plotting and carried out the killing. But he did it all from out there. So it looks like you don't even have to sweat that the killer was ever even around your place or is intending on coming back."

That seemed to ease the old man's worries somewhat. Horace didn't scratch his head, but he did seem to be thinking.

"Can't say that I've seen anything that I could call suspicious," Horace Thompson said after a few moments spent ruminating. Constable Harkness had sort of figured he would say that. No one else had heard or seen anything out of the ordinary in the days immediately before the most famous killing in the town's history. After talking with Mr. Thompson, he planned to shut down that branch of the investigation. It had produced no important information or sighting. In a few minutes he would excuse himself, thank the old man for his time, say a polite goodbye, and leave with a parting instruction to the old man to come and see him if he remembered anything. The constable's feet were already inclined toward the door.

"The only person I can think of who seemed out of place would be that woman I saw going into the alley behind the Ethridge house some time back."

Serendipity. You go looking for one thing, you find something you didn't expect, and then you have to start from the beginning. Constable Harkness stopped in his tracks.

"Woman?" Constable Harkness said with a puzzled tone. "What woman?"

"Some woman I saw going into the alley at night about a month ago," Horace Thompson answered. "She's been the only person I can even remember seeing going into the alley at a time when respectable women are supposed to be home. I don't know who she was, but she couldn't have been a respectable woman. Respectable women don't go sneaking into alleys in the dead of night. Unless they're in their natural element in an alley at night."

"What happened?" Constable Harkness asked, his feet now far less inclined to departing.

The old man pointed out the window toward a tree on the parkway of the main street that ran by the front of the corner lot house.

"I was outside walking our dog Banjo on a leash. I was over there by that tree trying to get him to empty himself out for the night before I went to bed. If he don't pee himself out for the night, he'll empty himself on the kitchen floor. The dog was sniffing around the tree roots. It's his favorite spot to go. I looked up."

The old man pointed out the side window and toward the street that ran perpendicularly to the street that went in front of the house. The old man was actually pointing to the end of the central alley that emptied out from the next block over.

"I saw a woman come out of the alley on the other side of the street." He swept his arm back. "After crossing the street, she didn't turn and go down the sidewalk. She crossed the street and headed right into the alley on this side of the street. That's why I got the idea that she was probably one of the girls from the Richardson bordello."

"How so?" Constable Harkness said.

"No respectable or proper woman is going to be out alone and unescorted after dark," Horace answered. "And no proper woman is going to be taking herself through an alley to back doors. Any woman who goes down back alleys that lead past back doors is a backdoor woman and a back-alley woman. When I saw her, I figured that she must be one of the women who works at the bordello over by the river. No proper lady would be sneaking down an alleyway after dark as if she's trying to keep from being seen. When I saw her, I figured she must have been out and about doing the chasing around those kind of women live by."

"Can you describe this woman?" Constable Harkness asked.

"Like I said," the old man commented, "it was dark. I couldn't get a good look at her. All I can give you is a vague general description, more impression than actual description."

"Give me what you can."

"Well, from what I could tell, she seemed to be young. She moved with a sprightly step. She was about the average height for a woman, a bit taller maybe. She seemed to have long hair."

"How long was her hair?" Constable Harkness asked. His thumbs were starting to come out of his officious pockets.

"It seemed to be almost halfway down her back," Horace Thompson said. "She was moving fast at a half-run pace. I could see her hair sway and bounce while she went on."

"What color was her hair?"

"The only time I got an even partially good look at her was when she crossed under a streetlight. From what I could tell, her hair seemed to be dark. That's all I can remember of what she looked like."

Constable Harkness's thumbs were all the way out of his officious pockets. "When did you see her? Can you remember the exact date?" He didn't really think the old man could remember the exact date. Old men Horace's age had trouble remembering what they'd had for breakfast by the time they get to lunch.

"I can remember exactly when it was," the old veteran said. "I don't remember the exact calendar date, but what I do seem to remember is that it was the first Saturday in September. I remember it because it was the night of the big church social potluck supper. Helen wasn't feeling very good that night, so we didn't go. I was out with the dog and saw the woman while the dinner was going on. That's one of the other reasons her being on the street seemed strange to me. I thought most of the people in town would be at the potluck dinner. But if she was one of the bordello women, I guess they don't live much of a social life or get invited to functions in proper society too much. … Is there something to it?"

Sometimes serendipity works in murder investigations too. Scratch at the door to one case that won't open, kick open the door to another case you thought was closed. In the serendipity of crime, there is, however, the proviso that you might not like what you find.

"Why didn't you come to me tell me this when it happened?" Constable Harkness said, all fingers out of his pockets, all his studied officiousness gone. "If it was the same girl, she was in this neighborhood that night and was found dead the next day."

"I didn't think nothing of it at the time," the old man said in unfeigned innocent confusion. "Is it important?"

"What you've just described is the girl from the Richardson house who was murdered and whose body was dumped in the river," Constable Harkness said. "You've described her to a tee, and you saw her on the exact night she disappeared. The story was in the paper. It only happened a little over a month ago. Didn't you read about that in the newspaper?"

"I vaguely remember reading something along that line," the old man said. "It was on a back page. I didn't make any connection between the woman I saw and the one who was killed. I didn't know it was the same girl until you told me just now."

The old man's unawareness of the story could simply be the forgetfulness of old age. Then again, it could have been that the girl found dead was a prostitute who lived on the fringe of respectable society and died and was found dead outside the fringe of the town, not a respected icon of society who was killed in the center of the supposedly secure town. At the time he had glanced at the article about the girl's death, Horace Thompson had dismissed it as the girl's having come to lie in the bed she had made for herself and ending up dead in it. It was the murder of a fellow citizen who lived only a few doors away that had started him and so many other citizens of the town thinking in terms of being murdered in their beds.

"I don't know what it means to the Ethridge case," Constable Harkness said, "but it could possibly mean quite a lot to her case. Other than the killer, you may have been the last person to see her alive. Policemen do often find little things like that to be a point of interest."

"Does what I told you give you the name of her killer at least?" Horace Thompson asked.

"By itself it doesn't tell us who her killer was," Constable Harkness answered. "But if the girl you saw that night is the same girl who was found in the river, and if she was around here the night before she was found dead, it changes the whole direction of the investigation."

It was an investigation that had already started to go cold and that Constable Harkness hadn't been shoveling coal onto the fire of, mostly because in police work, the most likely subject is usually the guilty party and the most likely explanation is usually the right one. Like Horace Thompson and the rest of the town, Constable Harkness had more or less assumed that the girl had been killed by a farmhand, a roustabout, or some other thug from outside the town. He had more or less left the case there to go cold.

The new line of causality the old man had just revealed was not straight or clear, but now, suddenly, the arrow of direction had been turned around from the outside of town and an outsider doing the killing to the veritable center of town.

Constable Harkness didn't want to say that openly to the old man. He had managed to get him calmed down a bit and had hopefully given him reassurance enough to keep him from shooting at everything that went bump or passed his house in the night. He didn't want to set the old man off again. Who knew what shadow in the dark he might shoot at out of paranoid fear. Who knew which one of a pair of sweethearts out for a moonlight stroll, or which inebriated husband and father coming home from the saloon, might end up dead. Sometimes and in some places, the measure of a good cop is how well he keeps his mouth shut before a jittery public and how well he explains things to them.

But two points do still determine a straight line. The trick is to decipher the points correctly. The two unspoken points that Constable Harkness had weren't fully clear in and of themselves, but already in his mind, they were evolving in a direction that was not the most pleasant one to contemplate. But a good cop rides the evidence like a hobo taking a freight train, to whatever destination it leads to. He doesn't try to ride the evidence like a bronco and bend it to his will, forcing it to go in his direction.

Constable Harkness pointed off to the side. "Do you mind if I use your telephone?" he asked. "I have to call the station house."

Horace Thompson agreed. Who was he to impede an investigation by the duly appointed minister of the law in the town?

Constable Harkness cranked the phone the number of times required to contact the police station house.

"Police department," Sergeant Plechathy's familiar voice said over the line.

"Come over to Horace Thompson's house," Chief Constable Harkness said with professional dispatch into the line. "Bring the key to the Ethridge house. Don't walk over. Bring the department squad car. We may have some other places to go afterward that could involve a lot of walking. As Sherlock Holmes would say, the game is afoot. But I don't want to do this all on foot."

For the next several minutes, Constable Harkness asked Horace Thompson to try hard to remember anything else about the night he had seen the girl cross from alley to alley—a sight, a sound, or anything, no matter how small and apparently insignificant. All the old man could remember was hearing the sound of Harold Ethridge's car passing by outside late that night and returning later. In that day, the garages of the houses were not attached to the house. They were located on the alley. Horace said he could tell it was Mr. Ethridge's car because it made a distinctive sound. When he said that, Constable Harkness's face seemed to darken a bit. He asked the old man to think carefully. Was he really sure it was Harold Ethridge's car he had heard? Mr. Thompson restated what he said about the car's having a distinctive sound to it. The constable asked him how long of an interval had separated the leaving and the return. Horace Thompson commented that it seemed to have been less than half an hour. He didn't know why that particular bit of information would mean anything to the police chief, but he figured the constable knew what he was doing.

As they talked about the familiar sound of Harold Ethridge's smooth-running car, they heard the familiar rattle of the department's Model T squad car as it pulled up outside the house. Constable Harkness directed Horace Thompson to meet with him on the front porch of the house. There he had the old man relate the story of seeing the late-night rambling girl. When he finished, the constable let him go back inside. He didn't want the old man to hear what he was saying. It might set off another round of rumors.

"Leave the car there," Constable Harkness said to the sergeant. Then he motioned for him to follow. "Let's take a walk."

Without another word, the constable and the police sergeant stepped off the porch and walked away. With the constable leading the way, they headed down the street that ran along the side of the house.

"She came out of the alley there," Constable Harkness said, pointing to the alley across the street. "She was walking fast, but she wasn't running. No one was following her. No one came out of the alley in hot pursuit of her. And she wasn't heading in the direction of the Richardson house. She was heading directly away from it. That would tend to indicate that she was heading out to meet and service a client. She wasn't returning to the house when Horace saw her on the night she didn't return to the house. The next time she was seen by anybody, she was a body that washed up on the riverbank."

He swung his arm around and pointed down the alley behind the houses on the block they were standing at the edge of. "She crossed the street and went directly into this alley. She didn't turn and use the sidewalk. She stayed in the alley." His voice shifted to a rhetorically sarcastic tone. "Now why would a lady of the night and a lady of the alley be out at night walking through alleys? Could it be that she was out performing the function that ladies of the night perform at night? Alleys lead to back doors. And alleys are a way to get to a back door of a house unseen. What houses might there be that would draw our little miss of the alleys to this particular alley? Let's see what we can find down here."

At Constable Harkness's direction, they started to walk down the alley.

"When I interviewed her about the murder of the girl, Mrs. Richardson said that she had been seeing someone," Constable Harkness said as a point of clarification as they walked down the alley. "Someone she wouldn't name, even to her madam. Someone who didn't want his name to get out even among the rest of the whores at the house. At the time she was found dead, we went on the assumption that she had been killed by a hired hand or by some other street-level lowlife thug. We more or less left it there, leaving her dead and leaving the case dead on the assumption that she was killed by some outsider we would never be able to trace."

The backs of the houses on both sides of the block went by as the two men walked. The likely scenario of what had happened had fallen into place in Constable Harkness's mind the minute he had first heard the old man's story. Now the story was completing itself in his mind. More properly stated, the story of the first murder was wrapping itself up and completing itself in his mind. In the newly dawned light of the first murder, a story of a second murder was starting to take form out of the darkness.

"But what if we're wrong on both counts?" the constable said. "Mrs. Richardson said that the girl had withheld the name of the mystery man she was seeing and that she had done so at his request. A hired hand she was meeting to roll in a hayloft with wouldn't have taken such elaborate measures to ensure that his name was withheld. That's something that a well-known and respectable man would do if he didn't want the news to get out that he was frequenting a prostitute, the kind of man who wouldn't want his neighbors to see prostitutes coming and going out his front door in broad daylight, the kind of man who would instruct the prostitute to come to him after dark and use the back alley and his back door in order to keep his liaison secret, the kind of man who lives in a respectable part of town with an alley conveniently behind every back door and in a house that could be on the very street we're walking down the back side of right now."

Constable Harkness stopped at the third house down from the entrance of the alley. "And guess whose house we find here?" While still looking forward, he pointed at the house on the left that they had stopped behind, the biggest house on the block. In fact, it was the biggest house in the town.

"You should recognize it right away, from both sides. Of late it's become quite familiar ground to us. We interviewed the owner in this house. We put the seals on the doors ourselves after he was killed."

The sergeant looked over at the back of the largest house on the block. It wasn't that familiar from the back, but he was well aware of the ownership of the house. They had searched the house and then posted legal notices on the doors that sealed the house off as a possible crime scene to keep people out of it until the distribution of the estate could be adjudicated.

"The Ethridge house," Sergeant Plechathy said.

"Give that man a big cigar," Constable Harkness said.

The constable turned and walked over to the wooden picket fence that separated the backyard of the house from the alley. At the fence he stopped and put his arms across the top rail. He leaned in and looked at the house. He could see the legal Keep Out notice on the back door. Sergeant Plechathy came up alongside him and stopped. For going on what seemed like two minutes or more, the constable said nothing. He just kept looking at the house. The sergeant looked at the house and then back to the police chief. He couldn't tell what the chief constable was seeing. But he was the chief of police. The sergeant figured he must be seeing something.

"They say two points determine a straight line," Constable Harkness said, still leaning on the fence, looking at the house of the man whose murder they were actively investigating when they had stumbled onto the trace of an older murder. "But the line exists before the points become visible. The trick is to be able to tell if the two points and all other points are on the same line. In this case we've suddenly found ourselves with a whole lot of points trying to crowd onto the same line. You have to do more work to push them off the line than you do to squeeze them onto it."

The constable paused a moment and continued to look at the house. Following the unknown lead of his superior officer, the sergeant looked back at the house.

"Point number one," Constable Harkness said at the end of his pause. "It was Ethridge who bailed the girl out of jail the night you brought her and her hotheaded swain in for starting the brawl in Charlie's saloon. You said that he said that he felt sorry for the plight they were in and that he wanted to be a public-spirited benefactor. But he bailed out the girl alone. He didn't bail them both out. In that respect, his public-spirited compassion was limited—limited to the girl."

The sergeant looked back at the police chief.

"Point number two: Ethridge said that he had had sex with the girl afterward but that she didn't charge him because she was grateful to him for getting her out of jail. But I've never known any whore to ever give it away free as a way of thanking a man for anything. Point number three: Ethridge said he had no further contact with the girl after that. But if the girl whom Mr. Thompson saw going into the alley that night was the murdered girl, and if she was heading to this house, then Ethridge lied. He was seeing her afterward. Point number four: Mrs. Richardson said the girl had been missing for two days. When the girl was found dead, the doctor said that she had been dead for about two days. That would mean that she was killed the night she disappeared. Point number five: She was last seen alive heading in the general direction of this house the night she disappeared."

"Could Mr. Thompson be making up the story of seeing the girl?" Sergeant Plechathy asked.

"Why would he?" Constable Harkness answered. "He has no reason to invent a story like that. He wasn't involved. He didn't even know there was a story there to invent a story of his own around. On the other hand, if Ethridge was involved in the girl's death, he'd have every reason to lie. The first and foremost reason would be to save his neck."

"Maybe Horace Thompson just imagined it," Sergeant Plechathy said. "Old men's minds do get to wandering in that way. Maybe his mind was subconsciously making up something he thought might help us close the case."

Constable Harkness shifted his look from the Ethridge house to the sergeant. "We weren't talking about her case," Constable Harkness answered. "I was talking about the Ethridge case. It was his story about the girl that changed everything and opened her case up again. As for whether he's gone senile and imagining things, he was sharp enough to remember the exact night he saw her, which, as it happened, was the night she disappeared. And he was sharp enough to describe the girl in detail though he had never seen her before and her description wasn't in the newspapers. The story sounds too real to be the product of senility or dementia. If there was a demented mind in play that night, it wasn't Horace's."

Constable Harkness looked back at the sergeant. "Point number six: Mrs. Richardson said that while the girl didn't give out the name of her secret client, she made it sound like she was keeping time with someone who was bigtime. We took that to be a whore's bragging. But if she was keeping regular time with the richest man in town, she wasn't bragging. Point number seven: Mrs. Richardson said that the girl left the house saying she was going to meet her secret man the night she disappeared. Point number eight—more like point number seven and a half: Horace Thompson says he remembers hearing Harold Ethridge's car both leave the alley and return a short while later in the night, within a half hour. The river isn't far from here. It would be just enough time to drive the girl's body to the bridge and throw it in the river."

Constable Harkness looked back at the Ethridge house. "Point number nothing, because it's nothing but a madam's speculation that would probably be taken as a mere guess in any capital murder trial: Mrs. Richardson said she was sure that it was the girl's secret man who killed her. She told us that if we find the girl's secret man, we would find her killer. We may have just found the killer and the crime scene. If two points determine a straight line, we've got a whole freight train of connected points. They make for a sloppy train, but taken altogether, all the points make for a line that curves right back to this house."

While still leaning on the alley fence, Constable Harkness pointed at the house. "We may have interviewed the killer face-to-face in the same house where the killing took place, but we were too dense to recognize it. We were there having pretty much already made up our minds that the girl had been killed by a farmhand. What we were right in the middle of was out of sight and over our heads because we were thinking that only a lowlife man would kill a lowlife prostitute."

Constable Harkness turned to the sergeant. "Did you bring the key to the Ethridge house?"

"Yes. I've got it here in my pocket."

Constable Harkness stood up quickly and opened the back gate in the fence. "Come on," he said as he headed through the open gate at a near-run. "We've got to get back in that house."

The sergeant followed him into the backyard. "What are we looking for?" he called out to the constable's back as he headed for the back door of the house.

"Blood spots," the constable called out. "Strands of hair pulled out. Things broken. Dented spots in a wall that might have been made by a girl's head being slammed into it. Signs of a struggle."

He reached the small platform stoop at the back door and climbed it.

"Harold Ethridge was found dead out at his farm, which is probably where his killing took place. The last time we were here, all we were looking to see was if the house had been broken into and whether anything had been obviously taken." He stopped at the locked door with the posted legal notices. "We were thinking in terms of a crime that had taken place elsewhere. We weren't looking for evidence of a crime having been committed here."

Police Sergeant Plechathy came up alongside the constable.

"We've got to look for signs of what we weren't looking for the last two times we were in this house. ... Where's the key?" the constable asked.

The patrolman took the key out of his pocket and handed it to Constable Harkness.

"He's had a month to clean up after himself," Constable Harkness said as he fitted the key into the lock. "The doctor said the girl didn't bleed much when she was killed. There may not be any bloodstains to be found. There may not be much of anything we can find in the way of direct evidence." The lock turned, and the door opened. "But if we look close, maybe we can find evidence of evidence."

Constable Harkness entered the back door. He wasn't at all sure what he was looking for. He wasn't even sure what evidence of evidence would look like. Sergeant Plechathy followed him in. He wasn't sure what the constable meant by "evidence of evidence" or what evidence of evidence would look like, but he assumed that the chief of police would know it when he saw it.

.

Chapter 20

Someday they may have a magic chemical that when sprayed onto a crime scene will give future police the perpetrator's complete DNA profile, height, weight, hair color, eye color, name, address, social security number, religion, favorite pro sports team, sexual preference, and beer preference. In Constable Harkness's day, they didn't even have luminol to highlight blood traces, DNA hadn't been discovered, and CODIS was something in Latin at the end of a will stipulating that the lawyers handling the estate got half of everything.

The search of the Ethridge house had gone on fruitlessly for over an hour. No obvious signs of violence were evident—no blood spatter, no out-of-place or suspicious stains of any kind, no bits of flesh stuck on the arms of chairs or in the corners of desks, no depressions in any wall where a head had been slammed into it, and no gouges in the wall where it had been hit by things that had been thrown. Nothing easily grabbed and thrown was cracked, broken, or dented in a suspicious pattern. The whole house was spotless, undamaged, and neatly cleaned. All the loose knickknacks that might have been thrown by a desperate girl grabbing for anything to defend herself with were intact and in place. But then it was impossible to tell if anything was missing. There was no inventory of items taken before or after the girl had been found murdered. Anything that might have been broken in the house during the girl's still unexplained murder could have been sent out with the trash before the house was searched following Mr. Ethridge's own as yet unsolved and unexplained murder.

Halfway through the search, Constable Harkness had sent the patrolman to look through the other rooms while he concentrated on searching the master bedroom. It had started out in the bedroom. The bedroom or a substitute was where things usually started with whores. Constable Harkness figured that if it had started in the bedroom, it had probably ended for the girl in the bedroom.

For half an hour, Constable Harkness searched the room. He started by pacing the room on his feet, looking for wider clues. Then he went to his hands and knees looking in every corner and under the bed and furniture. As he searched, he wasn't looking for evidence of bloodstains. On the surface they were already bucking a death that by its nature hadn't left any fluid traces. According to the doctor, the only thing that had even broken the girl's skin was a single hard blow that fractured her jaw and had left the unusual inverted V-shaped impression driven into the skin of her face. But it had drawn little, if any, blood. In the end, the girl had died from strangulation and a savage twist of the head that had broken her neck. All the fatal damage was internal. Even if they had had luminol, there hadn't been any blood flow to look for.

He concentrated his search on the floor. If the girl had died in the room, she would have ended up on the floor before she ended up in the river.

At one side of the bed near the head, he found a single strand of long black hair. As soon as he found the hair, Constable Harkness reared back up on his knees and held the strand of hair up to the light coming in through the window. Given its length and color, the hair must have come from the girl. But any exaltation that policemen feel in finding the one critical piece of hidden evidence that cracks a case didn't come. In itself the hair proved that the girl had been there and had been in the bedroom. But Harold Ethridge had already confessed that the girl had been there and that she had come in her usual capacity, which involved the bedroom. But the single hair strand couldn't say that she had been there more than once. It couldn't say what trip it had been lost on, and it couldn't say that she had died in the process of losing it. Sitting on his haunches in the bedroom as he had gone into the house sitting on his hunches, Constable Harkness knew the discovery didn't take him any farther than where he was at the moment.

An extended examination of the floor while standing revealed more long dark hairs in front of the bureau. But that was where a woman would naturally stand because it had mirror where she could brush her hair. Constable Harkness turned back the bedcovers, but he could find no hairs or evidence of sexual use of the bed. The sheets had obviously been changed.

For Constable Harkness, time was wearing as thin as his speculation was. He had nowhere further to go with his search for anything more related to the girl's presence in the house. He had nowhere else to go in the room for evidence of the end of the girl's life, like no one had anywhere else to go to find the girl's name while she had been alive. For several minutes Constable Harkness paced the room, looking at the floor. The room had provided evidence that the girl had been there, but it provided no evidence of trespass—at least no evidence of violent trespass. Finally, more out of frustration than any methodical thinking, he went over to the dresser across from the end of the bed and examined it. Nothing seemed out of place on the surface. He opened the top drawer and looked in. The inside of the top drawer was subdivided into several smaller cubicles filled with male things like cuff links, stickpins, and tie tacks. On one end of the end cubicle, a large ring sat by itself, not surrounded by other examples of period male jewelry.

When he saw the ring, in a recess of his mind somewhere something like a flash of recognition happened. It had something to do with the design of the ring. A second look at the ring revealed the familiar configuration of a Masonic order emblem with dividers and builder's square raised in silver-colored metal above the hexagonal body with the two central sides elongated. The ring sat next to the divider in the drawer, the band up against the divider, the face of the ring facing Harkness with the ends of the builder's square pointing down. Constable Harkness figured that it was the familiar Masonic symbol that had caught his attention. But somehow, out on the edge of undefined consciousness, there seemed to be some unformed recognition that went farther than recognizing a simple Masonic ring.

Constable Harkness was a practical man. He had no time for belief in precognition, and he had little time to stare vacantly at a drawer of vacant objects left behind by their vanished owner. He closed the drawer and opened the other drawers below it in turn. There was nothing but clothing in any of the other drawers.

Constable Harkness closed the last drawer then stood up and glanced around the room. He was looking for where to go next as much as he was looking to see if there was anything he had overlooked. In the silence of the empty room, the constable could hear Sergeant Plechathy stirring in another room on the same floor. But in the silent room there was no stir of echoes that spoke of terror and death. No ghost whispered in his ear telling of the girl's murder. Constable Harkness wasn't surprised that no psychic communication came to him out of the blue. He believed in an afterlife; he just didn't particularly believe in ghosts.

As he stood nominally surveying both the room and the situation, Constable Harkness tried to fit in the missing piece that couldn't be found. His theory that it had been the spectacularly murdered Harold Ethridge who had committed the far tawdrier murder of the young prostitute girl hadn't been dispelled, but nothing in the house had advanced it one step further.

The practical-thinking Constable Harkness was a bit reticent to start prying away at the good name facade of a leading town citizen who was not there to defend his name and honor. The dead cannot defend themselves against wildly spun allegations, and the spinner of wild allegations can find himself caught up in a sharper-spinning and slashing backlash with no way to defend himself if he lacks the defensive armor of proof. Sometimes the measure of a good cop is that he knows when to keep his mouth shut.

Constable Harkness took one more look around the room. That was an end to it. What he would do with his theory in his mind, he didn't know, but he would not take it any farther than he had with Sergeant Plechathy, and he would not take it public. He just didn't have enough evidence to show on the face of it.

The constable started to walk to the bedroom door. He would gather up the sergeant, close up his speculation, and go back to the investigation of the murder of Harold Ethridge. Ethridge's was the public face the public remembered, not the blanched white face of a dead outsider girl. His murder was the one they wanted to see the public face of law enforcement busily working on. The constable would leave the Ethridge house as he had found it on the face of it.

As Constable Harkness was halfway from the dresser to the bedroom door, the face of recognition cracked open wide. He stopped in his tracks. His eyes were wide open, but he wasn't seeing the face of a ghost. But then again maybe he was. The chief constable of the town turned around and stood staring at the dresser he had just come away from. From the way he looked at the dresser, someone observing the scene might think that he had seen the face of the devil in a dresser drawer. Maybe he had.

Constable Harkness walked quickly back to the dresser and pulled the top drawer back open. He reached in and pulled out the large Masonic order ring that had caught his distracted attention earlier. The recognition had been pushed just below the level of consciousness when he had seen the ring lying inverted in the drawer with the ends of the builder's square pointing down. The final recognition had broken through when his thoughts of what was on the face of things had taken his mind back to what was on the face of the ring.

For several minutes Constable Harkness stared closely at the face of the ring, rolling it around in his hand and in his mind. At that transitional moment, the murky darkness cleared and light flooded in.

"Harmon, come here!" he called to the sergeant, wherever he was within earshot in the house. "I've got what we're looking for!"

In short order he heard his fellow police officer's footsteps coming down the hall. As Sergeant Plechathy came into the room, Constable Harkness held up the ring with the tips of the fingers of the hand of his extended arm.

"What does that look like to you?" he asked in police rhetorical language.

The sergeant squinted at the ring face. "It looks like a Mason's ring," he said, thinking on the face of things. "Harold Ethridge was a member of the local order of Masons. What's unusual about him having the ring? Probably all Masons have one."

"Forget about what fraternal order the ring symbolizes," Constable

Harkness said in his getting-down-to-the-real-world voice. "Look at the outline pattern of the ring itself."

The sergeant looked more closely at the ring. All he saw was the overall hexagonal shape of the ring with the embossed and raised dividers crossed over by a builder's square, which had been the main symbol of the Masonic order for centuries. The constable was holding the ring with the open ends of the square pointing downward. He wasn't sure whether he was holding the ring with the right side up or whether it made any difference which side one wore up.

"Think of it as a signet ring that is used to stamp a personal seal into the hot wax of a letter. Now reverse the pattern in your mind. Do you remember seeing a pattern like this stamped into anything connected to any crime we've dealt with in the last month? An extra clue for you: Let's just say that as a stamp seal, it sealed someone's doom."

The little extra verve and embellishment the constable had added to the end of the question was a bit unusual for the plain-talking police officer. To the small-town police sergeant of the six-man police department, the Teddy Roosevelt impersonator was now talking like the newly popular fictional detective created by the British author Sir Arthur Conan Doyle, Sherlock Homes, directing his colleague Doctor Watson to examine a critical piece of evidence at a critical turn in the case. He hadn't seen his department head playact since he had assumed the position of police chief. But then again, the opportunity to play the role of grand crime sleuth didn't come along too often for them.

The sergeant looked at the ring more closely for several more moments. The blank expression on his face told Constable Harkness that he was drawing a blank.

"It's not that far from us right now," Constable Harkness said, filling in the blanks for his blank-faced Dr. Watson. "And we're probably not more than a few feet from where she died. ... I'm talking about the prostitute whose last steps we've been chasing since old Horace told us she came chasing this way the night she vanished and turned up in the river. You were there when Dr. Simpson gave us his findings on the autopsy. Remember the strange miniature pattern that had been driven into her jaw? It was the only puncture wound on the body. She had been hit with something with enough force to break her jaw. Remember the pattern, an inverted V-shaped center mark surrounded by a half-hexagonal frame? We all scratched our heads trying to figure out what would make a pattern like that. We assumed it may have been a pair of brass knuckles that the owner's initials were engraved in or that it was made by the butt of some kind of farmhand's implement or worker's tool."

The sergeant stood in silence, looking at the constable.

"Look at the ring. Look at the shape of the body of the ring, and then look at the pattern in the center. The shape and size is almost exactly as the half-hex shape of the body of the bruise indentation. The downward *V* was at the center of the indentation driven into the girl's jaw. The builder's square of this ring is in the same relative position at the center of the ring. The dividers were too small to leave any impression; that's why only the *V* shape remained."

The constable pulled the ring back and held it up close to his face. "This is what created the strange pattern left by the blow. This ring. Men in barroom brawls and street fights get their faces scratched and torn by big rings worn by their opponents all the time. The exact same thing happened to the girl. It just didn't register on us."

The constable started to slip the ring on the ring finger of his right hand. "Ethridge was right-handed. I saw this ring on his finger when we interviewed him."

Given that his fingers were thicker than Harold Ethridge's fingers, he couldn't get the ring past the second knuckle.

"Normally I guess you wear it with the *V* of the builder's square up like this." He held the ring out in a clenched fist for the sergeant to see. Then he pulled back and delivered a slow-motion roundhouse punch at the sergeant's jaw. "But when you throw a right cross punch, the wrist twists around and over." As he swung, he rolled his wrist in the natural motion it would follow at the higher speed of an actual punch. "Instead of facing up, the *V* made by the builder's square ends up facing to the left."

He stopped his demonstration punch an inch short of the sergeant's jaw. "If he was facing her and hit her with a hard right cross, he would hit her just about there on her left jaw, right where the contusion was. The force was strong enough to break her jaw. Probably knocked her out too. I doubt the blow was enough to break her neck by itself. After he knocked her unconscious, he probably proceeded to strangle her and wrench her neck for good measure."

The constable pulled his fist and the ring back. He waved the ring to emphasize another point he had just remembered.

"I remember Ethridge wearing this ring before the girl turned up dead. He had it on at all the town council meetings I attended when he was there. When I interviewed him after she was found murdered, he wasn't wearing it. The impression of the ring was still visible in the skin of his finger. It looked fairly fresh, like he had removed the ring only a short time before. I didn't think much of it at the time, but now I think he removed it after he killed the girl. He probably saw the mark it left and figured that someone might make the connection if they saw it on him."

The constable looked closer into the face of his fist and the ring. "Whatever I failed to see then, this ring was probably the last sight the girl saw coming at her in life."

In a quick motion, Constable Harkness pulled off the ring and put it in his pocket. "Come on, we've got to get back to the station house," he said as he started walking to the door of the bedroom. "Doc Simpson left a to-size drawing of the impression on the girl's chin. We've got to do a comparison, but I've got the feeling they're going to fit together far better than Ethridge's story and better than Harold Ethridge and the girl ever did."

Constable Harkness passed the sergeant on the way to the door. The sergeant turned and followed him. In the once again silent and empty room, the form of what had happened that night remained silent and hidden. In Constable Harkness's mind, the second half of the story was taking its final shape.

Constable Harkness and Sergeant Plechathy left the upstairs room and headed for the staircase. As they crossed the landing, heading for the stairs on the far side, Constable Harkness slowed and let the sergeant pass. As the sergeant headed down the stairs, the constable slowed up more. He turned to the railing of the second floor landing and stopped. He put his hands on the railing and looked at the back of the sergeant heading down the stairs.

"Harmon, we bungled it," Constable Harkness said in a voice that was both hollow and factual.

The sergeant stopped and turned to look at the constable. "How so?" he asked in a surprised voice.

"By not doing the first job that policemen are supposed to do," the constable said. "By not particularly wanting to do the job. When we questioned Ethridge, we turned off our ears and our minds. We let Ethridge write the score and create his own ticket out. My father would say Ethridge hornswoggled us. We didn't do our job when we talked to Ethridge in this house about the death of the girl. Having bailed the girl out, he had the most direct contact with her. He had brought her to this house that night. He said he had seen the girl once but that he hadn't seen her after that. He lied to us. In hindsight, his story about the girl throwing herself on him out of gratitude is pretty weak, but I took it at face value. I also took at face value his story about having cut himself when he was shaving, even though the bandage he had on looked a lot larger than the covering for a simple razor nick."

"We really didn't have a lot to suspect him of then," Sergeant Plechathy said. "We didn't know then what we know now. As an investigator, I don't think you can hold that against yourself."

"What I can hold against myself as a policeman is that I soft-pedaled him because he was rich and influential," the constable said. "I looked at what he claimed once on the surface and pushed any suspicion aside quickly because I didn't want to think of him as guilty. I didn't think in depth. I didn't look in depth. I didn't dig. I didn't push. I didn't do what a good policeman is supposed to do."

"I don't know if it would have made any difference at that point if you had," Sergeant Plechathy said.

"Maybe not," Constable Harkness said. "But maybe it would have. Maybe if I had gone the extra foot, maybe if I had turned over one more rock, I might have found the snake under it. I walked away from him and walked around him easy because of his wealth and his position in town. I was doing just what the Martin boy and Mrs. Richardson said I was doing. I just didn't quite know I was doing it. I let the killer of a young girl go unexamined. In the end I let him go free. Now we've got another killer on our hands, a vigilante who is as much of a cold-blooded killer as Ethridge. Or who became one when he found out it was Ethridge who killed the girl."

The constable joined the sergeant on the stairs. The two duly designated upholders of town law walked the rest of the way down the stairs and out of the house.

Constable Harkness's heavy brogan shoes clomped across the wooden floor of the police station. While still in motion, he called out to one of the other policemen in the station: "Arthur, bring the case box with the evidence on the Ethridge killing into my office." While still in motion, he pointed to the storeroom. "While you're there, bring me the file on the last homicide before."

"You mean the knifing in Charlie's saloon six years ago?" the uniformed policeman asked, a little confused as to why his superior officer would want to examine evidence on a solved case that was so old.

Sometimes dumbness will stop you in your tracks. Constable Harkness stopped in his tracks and looked at the man.

"No, dodo," the constable said, "I mean the file on the prostitute who was found dead in the river a month ago. In case you don't remember the case or don't have the inclination to think about it, she's dead too. And it wasn't from a drunken stumble into the river."

The chastened officer turned and headed toward the storeroom.

"We're still treating it as a homicide," the constable called to the retreating man's back. "At least I am, if the town doesn't care. I'm reopening the case here and now, and I'm reopening it as a demonstrable homicide."

Constable Harkness figured that his fellow officer's omission was an inadvertent pickup on the public attitude of the town toward the death of the girl. Since the day her death had been reported, the town had more or less considered the girl to have been a two-bit whore doing what comes natural to a whore and who in the process had gotten what comes natural at the hands of the class and kind of clients she dealt with. Even before she was buried in the ground, the town had written her off on that ground—written her off even to the point of forgetting her death had been a homicide.

The relevant evidence files were procured and brought into the chief's office. On his desk, Constable Harkness laid out the sheet of paper with the drawings Doctor Simpson had made of the wound on the girl's face. With Sergeant Plechathy looking on, he fitted the ring to the actual scale drawing. With only a simple turn for adjustment, the raised three-dimensional surface of the ring melded into the two-dimensional drawing below it and covered it like a shoe covers a footprint it made. Constable Harkness took his hand off the ring. The two small-town policemen bent over the desk, examining the picture that was emerging out of obscurity into reasonably plausibility.

"Almost like it was traced," Sergeant Plechathy said.

Constable Harkness moved his head around, examining the ring and the drawing from every angle that he reasonably could.

"I can't say they're like peas in a pod," Constable Harkness said, giving his relative opinion. "But allowing for swelling, expansion, rounding, and filling of the wound before and after death, and allowing for random variations in freehand drawing, there's a lot more points of similarity than of difference. The right-angle shape of the main body of the wound is the same. The size of the *V* is the same and is in correct relative alignment with the sides."

Constable Harkness straightened up from his bent-over position and pointed at the ring. "If I was called on to testify on the stand, I'd say that ring inflicted that wound," he said in his best on-the-stand, testifying-in-assurance voice. "I'd say we've got our man and that we've got the murder weapon. At least we have the beginning of a murder and the initial murder weapon. If you want the full arsenal of murder weapons he used, you're going to have to exhume Harold Ethridge and take a closer look at his hands."

He paused and looked down at the ring and the drawing beneath.

"As far as exhuming anybody goes, if we want to do a real test, we would have to exhume the girl's body and fit that ring to the wound directly. But after a month in the grave, there's probably been some degree of decomposition, possibly enough to make any comparison unreadable."

"I don't think the mayor and the town is going to want to go to the expense of digging up a dead whore," Sergeant Plechathy said. "And they'll probably be less happy about it if all it may accomplish is to dirty up the name of a respected citizen—a murdered respected citizen whose murder we're supposed to be investigating."

"We don't have to do any exhumation," Constable Harkness said after a short weighing of the evidence in his mind. "We've got both hard physical evidence and nearer-term evidence. We have the ring, and we have a true copy of the wound made closer to the day of death. We'll have to get Doc Simpson to look at what we just did, but he'll probably testify that in his opinion the ring is what inflicted the mark on the girl's face."

"There are other Masons in town," Sergeant Plechathy reminded. "They probably all have rings."

"I've never seen any of them wearing a ring of that size and shape," Constable Harkness said. "I've seen Ethridge wearing that ring before. He wasn't wearing it when we interviewed him before he was killed. That's suspicious enough on the surface. Combine that with the testimony of Horace Thompson that he saw the girl heading in the direction of the Ethridge house the night she vanished. None of the other Masons in town live on the same block that Ethridge did. Unless the girl was taking a very circuitous route to some other Mason's house, she was heading for the Ethridge house the night she didn't come back. But Harold Ethridge went out and came back later that night. Horace Thompson heard him go out and come back in his car that night, all in a short time interval that made it seem like he was performing a chore, a time interval just long enough to take him to the river and back."

"It's all kind of thin evidence to try a man for murder on," Sergeant Plechathy said. "If he was alive, would you put him on trial with circumstantial evidence like this?"

"We're not putting him on trial," Constable Harkness said. "He can't be put on trial. Not in this world."

"You're going to be putting his reputation and the public memory of him on trial if you start telling everyone that he killed the girl in the river," Sergeant Plechathy said. "What is indicting him posthumously for the death of the girl going to accomplish anyway? They're both dead."

"Ethridge is probably the killer of the girl," the constable responded. "The killer of Harold Ethridge is still out there alive somewhere, and the whole town has the bejesus scared out of them by the thought that there's a crazed killer stalking around in their midst."

"The mayor and the town council sent us to find out who killed Harold Ethridge," the sergeant said. "I don't think they're going to be either impressed or particularly happy if, instead of handing them Ethridge's killer, we come back with a story saying he killed a cheap floozy. It don't make him look good. It don't make the town look good. Provided they don't fire the both of us on the spot, they'll probably tell us to keep looking for Ethridge's killer and to let sleeping tramps lie. As if she didn't lie around enough in life."

Constable Harkness picked up the ring and nominally examined it again. "I say we should drop the whole thing with the dead girl from both ends—and she's been handled from both ends—and go back to looking for the killer of Harold Ethridge. That's what everyone in town wants us to be doing."

"As Hamlet said, 'Therein lies the rub,'" Constable Harkness said in his ironic leading voice. "And the rub for the town and the rub for us is that revealing Ethridge as the killer of the girl gives us the killer of Harold Ethridge, the killer whom everybody wants brought in so badly. The dead girl the town chucked out of its collective mind the minute she was found dead, the girl you want to chuck now, is the key to the killing of Harold Ethridge. To get to the killer of Harold Ethridge and why he went through Ethridge so brutally, you have to trace it back through the girl and the way Ethridge went through the girl."

In his talking about hidden connections and traces, Constable Harkness was back to his Sherlock Holmes imitation. Sergeant Plechathy didn't know what connection his superior officer was talking about, but the tone of his voice seemed confident enough in whatever he was confident about.

"The death of the girl is one point. The killing of Ethridge is the second point. Except our two points didn't determine much in the way of a straight line. As points, they seemed separate and unconnected. But as the Good Book says, 'The lightning flashes in the east and shineth unto the west.' In the same way, the discovery that Harold Ethridge killed the girl illuminates the third point, which was hidden. Now we have three points. Except those three points don't determine a straight line. In this case I do believe they determine a triangle."

The constable focused on the sergeant's blank stare.

"Old Horace and most of the town think the killing is the work of some kind of madman. Well, in a way they're right. We do have a madman running around in our midst. A madman did kill Harold Ethridge. It just depends on whom you consider as a madman and what he's mad about."

Sergeant Plechathy's blank stare didn't grow any less blank.

"As far as raving madmen go, if you remember back to when the girl was killed, we had a madman right here in the station house, and he wasn't a quiet madman either. He was storming all over the place, ranting and raving about how we didn't care nothing about her because she was a prostitute, and that we weren't doing anything to find her killer, and that we probably didn't want to know who her killer was, and that we probably thought she deserved to be killed, and that we were just making a show of trying to find her killer, and that we weren't going to try to find her killer at all. He sure sounded like he believed what he said."

The sergeant's look started to seem as if it was pushing toward a breakthrough. He just needed a little extra push.

"And that wasn't the first or only time our madman was in here for being mad and violent concerning the girl and what other men were doing with her. You brought him in about a month before that for beating the tar out of a man who had gone after the girl over in Charlie's saloon."

"You mean the Martin boy?" Sergeant Plechathy said.

"Give yourself a great big cigar," Constable Harkness said dryly. "Now you're getting the drift. One thing just follows the other like the cars of a freight train or the links of a chain. The chain here doesn't lead you as much as it drags you by the heels."

The constable bent toward the sergeant as if he were about to make an emphasized point. He pointed past the evidence box, pointing in no particular direction other than outside.

"That girl wasn't just another expensive piece of ass to the boy. She was his sweetheart. More than sweetheart. From the crazy way he was reacting to her death, even a mule could see that he was crazy in love with her. When someone butchers a young man's sweetheart, the young man often has a way of going mad over it. He didn't know about the girl being dead until the day we called him in. He came in already spinning wild and out of control. He probably went out swearing all kinds of bloody vengeance on whoever killed the girl if he ever found out who he was."

The constable straightened back up. He was speaking not directly to the sergeant but to no one in particular.

"And that's just what he did. Somehow he found out ahead of us that it was Ethridge who killed the girl, and he took out after him with a shotgun."

The constable focused back on the sergeant. "There was a lot of personal anger apparent in the way Ethridge was killed, more anger than a disgruntled farmhand who thought Ethridge had shortchanged him would have had. There's enough passionate anger in it for the kind of roaring personal insanity that results when a man sees his lover murdered in cold blood. ... Ethridge erased the girl. In his fever of vengeance, the Martin boy erased Ethridge by erasing his face. I'd probably do the same thing myself in the same situation."

"That makes sense by itself," Sergeant Plechathy said. "But that doesn't mean that's the way it happened. Jealous men are known to turn on and do violence to the women whom they think are betraying them. It could have been the boy who killed the girl herself because she was seeing Ethridge, a rich man he couldn't compete with. Love triangles work that way too. Everything he said in our presence afterward might just be a big act to divert suspicion from himself."

"The girl disappeared Saturday night," Constable Harkness recapitulated. "She was found in the river Monday morning. The doctor said she had been dead two days. That means she was killed Saturday night, the night she vanished, the night she was seen heading toward Ethridge's house. The Martin boy was at the supper Saturday night. I saw him there. I talked to him, checking up on him to see that he was keeping his nose clean and out of the saloons. There were plenty of other witnesses who saw him there. His parents said he came home and stayed home with them after the dinner. Half the town can alibi him. I can alibi him. He couldn't have been the one who killed the girl. Ethridge is an entirely different matter, though. I have no idea where the Martin boy was when Ethridge was killed. The Martin boy is a farm boy. He would know when Ethridge would be out at his farm and when and where he could catch him alone. But the Martin boy was at the party with the rest of his family. The key person who wasn't there that night was Ethridge. He wasn't at the supper for any length of time. In one of his books, Conan Doyle's master detective Sherlock Holmes says that the dog that didn't bark in the night was the clue. Now we know who Ethridge was home dallying with. We also know that it went wrong that night. We just don't know why. Nor do we know how the Martin boy found out about it. Somehow he got out ahead of us in finding out who had killed the girl."

In the back of his mind, Constable Harkness knew the boy would only question how hard they had been out looking. In the farther back reaches of his mind, he wondered how much truth there was in what the boy thought. The feeling started to steal over him that he owed the boy one.

"That's still not proof," Sergeant Plechathy said. "All we have is a theory, nothing physical. Far as the Martin boy goes, all we have is circumstantial evidence and speculation."

Constable Harkness tossed the ring into the box of evidence for the Ethridge killing. "Maybe," he said. "But I have a hunch that we'll find the answers where it all started. At least where the girl started out from that night. I also have the feeling that's where the source of information that the Martin boy had, and that we didn't have, came from. I do believe that the ladies of the establishment have been holding out on us. To determine that, it's going to be necessary to sweat the ladies of the house a bit. As women of their profession, they're used to sweating up a storm in bed. They can be pretty tight-lipped. But if we lean on them hard enough, I think we can sweat it out of them."

The constable reached into the Ethridge evidence box and took out the knife that had been found in Harold Ethridge's chest. He and the sergeant walked out of the station house and to the car.

Chapter 21

"Don't think that the fact that this house is outside the town limits and exists on the fringe of the town will protect you. I am the law in the town in an area where the law exists on the fringe. I assure you, I can find ways to extend the law to cover this house and have you ejected bodily from here and then have this house legally sealed and put off-limits, pending further investigation, the way I have had the Ethridge house sealed and put off-limits until the estate is adjudicated. I also assure you that in the case of this house, any further legal action against you and this house can be extended indefinitely by law, especially where homicide is involved."

Constable Harkness paced slowly and methodically back and forth in front of the assembled group of women of the Richardson house, who were seated in the parlor. Sergeant Plechathy stood silently in uniform behind him for added effect. It was a moving, talking, intimidating cop / unmoving, silent, intimidating cop routine they had worked out and practiced. Constable Harkness paused in his officious, postured, and intimidating pacing of the parlor floor to focus on Mrs. Richardson in specific. Applying another calculated intimidating posture, he leaned in toward her a bit.

"You can legally challenge my actions as is your legal right. You can apply any knowledge of legal appeal procedure you picked up from your late husband, having been a lawyer, and use it to file an appeal. You might even be able to have my actions overturned by a higher court. But all that is a long and involved process. In the meantime, I control the situation from here. What the situation for you is, will be the situation I'll make. And I can make a whole lot of trouble for all of you. You will be out of this house and will remain out of this house. Which means that you will have to write your appeal to the state supreme court from the middle of a cornfield or from out of whatever deserted barn you and your ladies of the house find to set up shop in."

Constable Harkness straightened up. He held up one hand as if to cut off what they might be thinking. "And don't gamble on the mayor or any of his or the town's good offices intervening to bail you out. I know the mayor has patronized this house in the past, but I doubt he will prove to be much of a patron to you if doing so will reveal the breadth of his involvement with this house to the wider public. The degree that this town has patronized this house has been a minor and disregardable point to me and to the law up till now. But capital murder is hardly a minor legal matter in my eyes or in the eyes of this town. The mayor will not step in to shield you in such a weighty matter if I make a case that you were involved even tangentially in the murder of Harold Ethridge. That will be just the beginning of abandonment for you. No one will raise a finger in defense of you, nor will anyone in town at any social level, low level or high, especially high level, want to be associated with this house or touch it with a ten-foot pole if it is revealed that this house or anyone in this house was in any way part of or connected with the murder of a leading citizen."

"You mean the leading citizen who you just said may very well have killed one of my girls?" Mrs. Richardson asked in an accusing tone. "The youngest one of us?"

Constable Harkness leaned in toward Mrs. Richardson again, closer this time. It was another practiced intimidation gesture. Cops of that day knew how to get in your face. "I mean the man you may have sent a lovesick, heartsick, vengeance-crazed farm boy out to kill for you and do your dirty work for you!" Constable Harkness said in a controlled rumble that was building toward to a controlled bellow when he leveled his voice off. "The boy you handed the name of the girl's killer to. The boy you were willing to let get blood on his hands and take the fall for you. The boy you sent out to take the law into his own hands instead of you coming to the law with what you knew. The boy you made as much of a killer out of as Ethridge made out of himself. The boy whose neck you may have stuck into a noose or whose butt you may have stuck into an electric chair. The boy you sent out to cut down Ethridge for having cut down the youngest soiled lamb in this house."

Mrs. Richardson tensed into the end of the sofa where she sat with the town sheriff, now known by the title of chief constable, pressing his inquiry into the house and pressing his face into hers. This wasn't just some periodic and superficial moralistic rattling and harassment by the town. It was starting to dawn on Mrs. Richardson that she and the house could be in serious trouble, trouble she was sure the constable would soon elaborate on even more.

"Could you be a little more specific about who you are referring to as the assassin you suppose I dispatched?" Mrs. Richardson said, trying to remain studiously unruffled while she hemmed and hawed, wondering where the constable would take things next.

"Could you be specific with me as to which one of the girl's clients was in love with her?" Constable Harkness came back in a leading rhetorical voice. "In love with her enough to take hot-blooded personal revenge on her killer if he ever found who the killer was? I'll give you a little clue. I had him in the station house asking him about the murdered girl the day she was found dead. He couldn't have been the killer of the girl, though, because I and half the town saw him elsewhere at the likely time she was being killed. He freely admitted that he patronized her and this house frequently. He also freely admitted that he was in love with the girl. In the mental state he was in, he held nothing back. So you've nothing to gain by denying you know whom I'm referring to or saying he wasn't here. I'm not going to believe any denials or feigned ignorance on your part."

"I assume you're talking about Samuel Martin," said Mrs. Richardson, trying to keep her voice steady.

"Give that lady a big cigar," Constable Harkness said. "Whether she smokes or not." He hadn't meant the cigar comment as an allusion to a Freudian phallic symbol.

"Not only was the boy in love with her, but also, from what I saw of the way he took her death, I'd say he was crazy in love with her. Men as crazy in love and as crazy in grief as he was do crazy things like go after the killer of their loved one. He acted all sorts of crazy in front of me. He did a lot of ranting and raving, saying we weren't going to do anything about her killing. He kept wanting to know who killed the girl. He seemed to think that I knew who the killer was and that I was holding back the name because I thought whores were two-bit trash and that every man in the town was better than she, so I didn't want to send the killer up for killing her. I wouldn't have given him the name of the killer if I had the name at the time, but I didn't have the name to give. I didn't have the name of her killer until today."

Constable Harkness liked to think that he was confronting the madam of the house with the evidence. Actually he was confronting her with what he figured was the likely scenario, hoping the weight of the story and the weight of his personal gravitas would carry him over the holes and force a confession out of the woman.

"At the time you claimed you didn't know the name of the girl's killer. But I'll bet you better than even odds that you had the name all along. I'll bet you the same odds that you gave the name of Harold Ethridge to the boy because you figured that in his wound-up condition, he would go after the girl's killer. In his mental state, he was a stick of dynamite with a short fuse ready to go off. I think you used him for exactly that purpose to exact your own revenge on the killer of your charge because, like the Martin boy, you were convinced that I wouldn't pursue her killer because Ethridge was a leading citizen and I and the whole town thought the girl was trash."

"I didn't know the name of the killer," Mrs. Richardson protested, holding a dignified tone. "I didn't know the name until you gave it to me when you came here today."

It wasn't exactly a lie, and it wasn't exactly the truth. It was a bit closer in time and detail to her side of the story than it was to Constable Harkness's take on it.

"When you were at the station house identifying the girl's body, you told me that in your opinion she had most likely been killed by the client she was going to see that night," Constable Harkness said. "You said that if I found the man she was going to see that night, I would find her killer.

You sounded pretty confident on that point. I found a witness who saw your girl apparently on her way to the Ethridge house that night. The witness just didn't know who and what he was seeing. And he didn't know whom she was going to see. I found evidence in the Ethridge house that links Ethridge to the crime directly. But I think the reason you were so confident that the man she was seeing and the killer were one and the same because you knew the name of the man she was seeing that night. You knew the name of the man all along. Everything you said about finding the man and finding the killer was just wordplay on your part, designed to put me off and make me think you didn't know. You're trying to cover your part in this by hiding behind the thin claim that you didn't know the name of your star attraction's mystery man."

"If I knew the name of the man she was seeing and thought he was the killer, I would have given you the name in a minute at the time," Mrs. Richardson said in a raised voice. "I loved that girl like she was my daughter. I wanted her killer caught. Why wouldn't I have told you his name if I knew it?"

"Probably because, like the Martin boy, you thought I and the law wouldn't go after him because he was a rich man and a leading citizen. You planned to set the Martin boy on him to do the job because you were sure he would kill him. Which he's done a very thorough job of. The men who utilize this house may not choose their companions well, but you chose your assassin well enough."

"I didn't know the name of the man Clarinda was seeing because she didn't tell me his name," Mrs. Richardson said with emphasis. "She said that the man asked her to keep his name secret because he didn't want his name to get out and for it to get around the town that he was seeing a prostitute. Only rich and influential men with their reputations to lose if their dalliances are uncovered do that. Hired hands don't go to that kind of trouble to keep their names quiet. If Harold Ethridge was the man she was seeing like you say he was, I can understand why he would want that information kept secret. He was young and up-and-coming. He had a lot more reputation to lose. He might even have become mayor one day."

"You whores may indeed keep secrets from those outside the house," Constable Harkness came back, "but I doubt you keep any secrets from one another inside the house. Every one of you probably knows everyone else's secrets. This house is a house of secrets kept from only those outside the house, not inside it."

"She didn't keep it a secret that she was seeing someone," Mrs. Richardson said. "She told me every time she went out to see the man. She brought me the money back every time, and in full amount. But she never gave me his name, like he told her not to. Maybe you don't think the word of a whore is worth anything, but we keep our word to each other in this house. Maybe you don't think a whore has an ounce of honor, but in this house we honor each other's privacy. When one of us chooses to keep a secret from the others, we don't badger her about it. We don't even inquire about it to each other."

"I suppose you deny having any knowledge or idea that the Martin boy may have been angry and was seeking revenge?" Constable Harkness asked, changing the direction of the conversation.

"I knew he was angry," Mrs. Richardson said. "After you questioned him, he came here breathing fire about what he was going to do to the man who killed her if he ever found out who he was. He went on badgering me for the name of the man she was seeing or for anything I knew that would be a clue to the identity of her killer. He acted like he was running his own investigation. Or a one-man lynch mob."

"Then you admit the boy was here in an agitated mental state and that he was looking for information leading to the identity of the girl's killer," Constable Harkness said in a raised tone as if he had just caught the woman stumbling into revealing a critical piece of confirming evidence.

"Yes," Mrs. Richardson conceded. "But I couldn't give him the name of the man she was seeing any more than I could give you the name. I didn't have it." There was a slight catch in Mrs. Richardson's voice. "I didn't have it until you told me today."

"Well, if it was the Martin boy who killed Harold Ethridge," Constable Harkness said, "and there aren't a lot of other suspects on the horizon who make much sense as the killer, then somehow the Martin boy found out ahead of me. In that he's a better detective than I am. Now I wonder how he managed that. Maybe I'm dumb when it comes to detective work and he's a country boy Sherlock Holmes. But the simpler explanation is that he just had better information from a source close to the case, a source who knew the name of the killer all along."

"It's been a month since Clarinda was found dead," Mrs. Richardson said, reaching for the first bit of defensive logic she could think of. "If I knew all along who the girl's killer was, why would I wait a month to tell the boy?"

"You waited to tell the boy so that there would be a gap between the killing of the girl and the killing of Ethridge, in the hope that a connection wouldn't be made between the two killings," Constable Harkness said by way of counterlogic. "Or you told the boy right away and he waited a month for the same reason. Just because he may have been consumed with grief and anger doesn't mean he was totally out of his head and illogical in how he went about plotting his revenge. He may have had a hard time holding back, but he waited for what he thought would be a long enough time so that people wouldn't see the connection between the death of the girl and his killing of Ethridge."

"Constable, that's just a lot of conjecture," Mrs. Richardson said, trying to answer the way her late lawyer husband would have. "You may have this new evidence of yours linking Ethridge to the killing of the girl, but you don't have any solid evidence linking this house to the killing of Ethridge. You don't have anything but conjecture linking the Martin boy to Ethridge's killing."

"I may not have any direct evidence yet linking the Martin boy to the killing of Harold Ethridge," Constable Harkness said, "but short of that, I've got more than just conjecture. I've got connection. In some criminal cases, connection speaks louder than small and dry pieces of disconnected evidence." And sometimes a credible-sounding threat can more than fill in the gaps where dry evidence is lacking.

Constable Harkness leaned in toward Mrs. Richardson. "And in a court of law, I can make a connection that will tie this house and everyone in it up in a balled barbed wire knot that you'll never be able to cut your way out of. In a contest between the law and a whorehouse, you'll be starting way down the line and with a heavily loaded disadvantage going in. I'm sure I can make something stick against the house and everyone in it. I'm not just talking about shutting this house down on some morals charge. I'm talking about charges lodged against you for withholding evidence, conspiracy, and accessory after the fact to murder. I can more than get you put out on the street. I can probably get everyone in this house sent up for long stretches in prison. None of you will be in much shape to either run a house or serve in one by the time you get out."

Mrs. Richardson sat and listened in composed, stony-faced silence. The other women of the house looked at the constable with uncertain expressions on their faces. One woman of the house was starting to sweat and tremble.

"And don't give me any lawyerly talk about presumption of innocence. This house isn't based on innocence, and a jury isn't going to think and presume in terms of innocence when they think about this house and those in it and the way women in whorehouses think and act. In a courtroom, the presumptions are going to run against this house, and that could both run you out of here and run all of you into prison. I think I can reasonably guarantee all of you a rough time in court and a rougher time afterward. The only way it's going to go easy on you is if you tell me what you know and tell me right now. ... The person I want is the killer of Harold Ethridge. If I can get that and prove it, I might even be willing to turn my back and forget who gave the boy Ethridge's name. But if I have to go through you to get the killer, I'm going to go through you the hard way. Once I get the law up and running against you, it's going to get harder by the minute to slow it down, turn it around, and keep it away from you. So if you have anything to tell me, you'd better do it now before it gets too late to call it all or any of it back."

There was a sort of strangled half sob from the line of women seated in the parlor. Constable Harkness looked over to the side. In the middle of the seated women, he saw a short, plump woman sitting with one hand over her mouth. Tears were starting to fall down her face. Her upper body was trembling, the trembles extending downward and spreading out into the depths of her large liquid breasts. She seemed to be gasping. Constable Harkness could easily see that the woman was in visible distress. He figured his gambit might be about to break something loose.

"She didn't do it," the plump woman said in a half gasp, half wail.

"Polly," Mrs. Richardson said. Constable Harkness held up his hand to cut her off.

"Is there something you want to tell me, girl?" Constable Harkness said.

Instead of answering him directly, Polly looked over toward Mrs.

Richardson. "I can't let all of you take the blame for something I did," the twenty-eight-year-old said to her madam and mentor. She turned to face Constable Harkness. "I'm the one who gave the Martin boy the name of the man who killed Clarinda." She threw her arms and hands out toward him. "But it was an accident. I didn't know what I was doing. I didn't even know I was giving him the name when I did it. I didn't know the name. I just said something related. He picked the name out of what I said."

"Do you want to tell me about it?" Constable Harkness asked in a loaded but not directly threatening tone.

The woman brought her hands back in and held them in front of her face. She half gasped as she spoke, seeming to be on the verge of breaking into full sobs. Under the strain, her speech impediment became more pronounced. The combination made what she had to say a little harder to hear, but it was clear enough.

"He w's here," Polly said, her lisp coming back into her half-strangled voice. "The Martin boy w's here … a few days before Ethrich w's killed. … We w's all outside together. He still didn't know who killed her, but he w'sn't askin' who killed her right then. … I w's talkin' to him, trying to make him feel better. I said something about how when Clarinda was going off to see the man she w's seeing, the man Mrs. Richardson said probably killed her, she said she w's going off to see her Mr. Bearcat. … That w's the third time she had gone out to see him. … When I said that, Samuel turned around sudden-like and grabbed me by the shoulders. I thought he w's mad that she had a nickname for the secret man she w's seeing but that she didn't have a pet name for him. … I figured that it made it look to Sam that she liked her secret man more than she liked him. … I figured he w's upset about it. She said he had a temper about her being w'th other men. … But instead of saying anything about being mad at her, he started shouting that it wasn't a man she w's talking about; it w's some kind of car she meant."

"A Stutz Bearcat," Constable Harkness said. "There's only one man in town who owns a Stutz Bearcat—Harold Ethridge. I've drooled over that car many times. But on a policeman's salary, I couldn't afford the front seat."

"Sam said the same thing about only one man in town owning a car like that," the tongue-tied woman went on. "After that he went stormin' out of the house. No one could stop him. After we heard about Mr. Ethrich bein' killed, we figured he must haf been the one Samuel w's talkin' 'bout. So I guess I gave him the name. But I didn't know I was givin' him the name when I let it slip without knowin' what I had done."

"Why didn't you tell me about the nickname the girl used when I was here investigating her death?" Constable Harkness asked.

"I didn't think about it at the time you w's here," Polly said. "I just remembered it when Sam w's here the day or so ago before Ethrich w's killed. I didn't know it w's a car she w's talkin' about when she said it. I don't know nothin' about cars."

To Constable Harkness it had been a strange day in the annals of crime in the town. It was also a strange day in the annals of crime solving in general. Horace Thompson solved the murder of the prostitute girl in the river with a single and earlier unshared remote recollection of a fleeting glimpse of the girl the night she died, an observation that had meant nothing to him at the time. Then a knothole-brained woman inadvertently solved the murder of the girl for the Martin boy. In the process she set off the killing of Harold Ethridge with a single forgotten and belated remembrance of a single dropped nickname uttered only once in passing by a girl doomed to a lifetime of passing.

Constable Harkness turned to Mrs. Richardson. "Is what she said the way it happened?" he asked in a straightforward voice.

"Pretty much so," Mrs. Richardson said without volunteering a whole lot more. "Polly came to me after Ethridge was dead and told me what happened and what she had said."

"Then you confess to knowing that the Martin boy had a name in mind and he was going out to settle scores?" Constable Harkness asked.

"Only in that I found out about it just before the killing of Harold Ethridge," Mrs. Richardson said. "I wasn't sure whom he was thinking about."

"And you say that the day the Martin boy went out the door breathing bloody vengeance against the girl's killer, you had no idea whom he was gunning for?" Constable Harkness asked in another rhetoric-edged tone. Mrs. Richardson was silent.

While looking at Mrs. Richardson, Constable Harkness pointed to Polly. "Maybe she doesn't know a Bearcat from her bare bottom. But as the only independent woman in town who owns her own car and knows cars and is aware of who in the town owns what car, you probably knew the girl was talking about Harold Ethridge as soon as this woman here told you the nickname. Why didn't you come to me with the story when it happened? I could have stopped the boy if I knew what he was planning. At least I would have had Ethridge in protective custody. Now one man is dead and the Martin boy is facing murder charges as the only logical killer. It was two days afterward that he killed Ethridge. Why didn't you come to me with all this the minute he went out the door shouting of revenge? This all could have been prevented."

Instead of pushing the point of moral and legal complicity further, Constable Harkness pulled the knife found driven into Harold Ethridge's chest out of his pocket and opened the blade. "Did any of you ever see the Martin boy with this?" he asked, holding up the knife for Mrs. Richardson and the rest of the women of the house to see.

Mrs. Richardson looked at the knife for a moment. "That was hers," Mrs. Richardson said. The constable stopped in his tracks.

"Who do you mean when you say 'hers'?" Constable Harkness said with a puzzled tone in his voice. "You mean it was the girl's?"

"Yes. She said she had used the knife to slash her brother's face when he tried to rape her. She always carried it with her for protection when she went out."

"Did she have it with her when she went out for the last time?" Constable Harkness asked.

"I assume so," Mrs. Richardson said. "She always carried it in the folds of her dress. I didn't see it in her nightstand drawer after she was found dead. That's where she kept it when she didn't have it with her. I assumed you found it in her pocket when you found the body."

"Where we found it was stuck in Harold Ethridge's chest when we found him with his face blown off," Constable Harkness said. "We all assumed it was a little personal calling card left behind by the killer. If it was her knife and not the boy's, then how did it end up in Ethridge on his property a month after she was found dead in the river?"

Sergeant Plechathy had been standing as still and silent as a wooden Indian in front of a cigar store. He seemed to come to. "Maybe she was the one who cut him with it," the sergeant said.

Constable Harkness turned to look at his sergeant, an expression of incredulity beginning on his face. Sergeant Plechathy held up his hands as if he had just snapped his fingers. "Remember the cut that Ethridge had on his neck the day we interviewed him about the girl's death? He had it covered with a bandage. He said he had cut himself shaving. We couldn't tell the length of the cut because it was covered by the bandage. The wound wasn't fully healed when Doc Simpson examined the body."

The light snapped on. Constable Harkness looked at the knife.

"The doc said that the wound looked like it had been made by a—"

"By a long, sharp-bladed instrument," Constable Harkness said, still looking at the knife. "We took Ethridge at his word and assumed he had cut himself shaving with a straight razor. But with the bandage off, it was a pretty long cut to have been a made by a razor nick. You have to be awfully careless with a straight razor to do that much damage to yourself. Looks to me more like a desperation swing of a knife by a girl being strangled. It's another nail in the coffin of a killer already in his coffin."

"But how did it end up rammed into Ethridge's chest a month after the girl was killed?" Sergeant Plechathy asked, recapitulating the police chief's question.

"If Ethridge took it from the girl the night he killed her, he might have kept it to conceal evidence," Constable Harkness said, still looking at the knife. "He may have had it on him the day the boy went after him. The knife was driven into his chest all the way to the tang and left there after being driven into him several dozen times. That denotes anger. Not just anger—flat-out rage. But the doc said Ethridge had been stabbed after he was dead. Maybe the Martin boy found the knife on Ethridge after he'd shot him. If the boy found it on him after shooting him, he might have gone out of his head even more and driven it into his chest in another burst of frenzied rage."

Constable Harkness folded the blade of the knife back into the handle. The stories of the women of the house were plausible, but they couldn't be proven one way or the other. He was just going in circles talking to them. And they were bit players anyway. To even start in the direction of final resolution, it would be necessary to confront the principal suspect directly.

"We're just walking around in a puddle here," Constable Harkness said to Sergeant Plechathy. "If we want to get to the end of this, we're going to have to go out to the Martin farm and have a word with the Martin boy directly."

The constable motioned to the sergeant, and the two minions of the law turned to leave. That was apparently that. They were leaving without taking anyone away in handcuffs, and they weren't leaving behind any order to close the house and vacate the premises. A wave of qualified relief came over Mrs. Richardson. Apparently the limit to the jeopardy to the house had been reached, leaving them, for the moment at least, intact. The feeling of relief made Mrs. Richardson relatively bold, but only so far as boldness could go in the situation.

Constable Harkness pointed at Mrs. Richardson. "We've tolerated you in this town because you've become a fixture here and a lot of the town fathers otherwise enjoy the … midnight entertainment options this house offers," he said in a half-growling voice. "But I don't tolerate murder in my town, especially when they come almost back-to-back. I know that Ethridge killed your … house sister, whatever her name was. It has to be the Martin boy who killed Ethridge in revenge. Everything about the way Ethridge was killed reeks of anger and vengeance. It has to be the Martin boy. I just want to hear it from you. I want to hear what you knew, and I want to hear all of it, with nothing held back."

Constable Harkness fixed Mrs. Richardson and the assembled women of the house with a hard stare. Along with Constable Harkness and the policeman, they were assembled in the parlor of the Richardson house where Samuel had first seen Clarinda. With her death, a light had gone out of the house and out of Samuel Martin's life.

"If you try to play it coy, if you don't divulge everything you know, I'll close down this house and run the lot of you out so fast and so far that you'll wear out the leather of your shoe soles beating it on down the road."

"This house isn't within the boundaries of the town," Mrs. Richardson said. "And it's not within your jurisdiction. You can't run us out." She had said what she said without flinching. But she didn't seem all that confident.

"I'll find a way," Constable Harkness retorted. "The town council can annex the land and have you run out as undesirables engaged in moral turpitude. … I'm engaged in the investigation of a murder. Two murders. If I catch the slightest hint that any of you are lying or withholding evidence, I'll run the lot of you out, even if you didn't know what your sister held back. You'll be gone and as far removed from here as last year is from today. One lie, one attempted lie, by any of you and it will ruin it for all of you, whether you were involved on not." He swept them all with a quick, sharp gaze. "So don't try to be clever with me. Don't try to be clever liars. Don't even think to be clever. Whores aren't very clever to begin with. If they were cleverer, they wouldn't be whores."

Mrs. Richardson looked at him. The other women of the house looked down or appeared to be nervous. Polly seemed the most unsettled of all, but she had always had a tremulous demeanor.

"I know the Martin boy cut down Ethridge," the constable went on. "The only question still open is how the Martin boy found out that Ethridge killed the girl. I didn't tell him. I didn't know then who had. Somehow he found out, and he found out ahead of me and the rest of the force. How did he do that? The only thing I can figure is that you knew or figured that Ethridge killed the girl before I found out. Then you told the Martin boy. That means that you must have known where the girl was going that night. Assigned rounds and all that."

He fixed his look on Mrs. Richardson. Mrs. Richardson didn't flinch or look away, but she looked like she had nowhere to go.

"When she left here, did you send her to Ethridge's house?"

"In their dealings outside this house, my girls function as independent contractors," Mrs. Richardson said in her professional madam tone. "When they go out on their own, mostly to the bars, they don't have to tell me where they're going, and they don't have to file a written report with me in advance like they're railroad schedulers."

"So then you say you didn't know where she was headed when she left the house?" the constable asked.

"I did not," Mrs. Richardson said. "I didn't even see her go." She pointed to Polly. "Polly was the last one she spoke to in this house."

"Apparently you give your girls a lot of leeway in their dealings," the constable said. "I thought madams called all the shots and directed all their girls' footsteps."

"All I ask of my girls in their dealings outside the house is that they give an accurate account of what they earn and surrender half to the house when they return."

"But you otherwise deny that you knew the girl was headed to Ethridge's house the night she left and did not return," the constable said.

"I already have," Mrs. Richardson said.

"At any time afterward, did you tell the Martin boy where she had gone that night?"

"I did not," Mrs. Richardson repeated.

Whether she was lying or telling the truth, the constable figured he wasn't going to get anywhere with her. Maybe the lesser women of the house might prove more pliable. The constable looked at the other women. He focused on Polly, whom he had already marked as the weakest of the women. Polly put her head down.

"And what might you know?" he asked the trembling woman in his commanding voice. "Before you say anything untruthful or evasive, let it be known by you that lying to an officer of the law engaged in a criminal investigation is punishable, not just by expulsion from the town but also by prison time for withholding evidence, lying under oath, and aiding and abetting a criminal."

Mrs. Richardson opened her mouth in start of a protest that he was browbeating and frightening her most emotionally fragile girl. Constable Harkness caught the gesture out of the corner of his eye. Still looking at Polly, he held up his hand and cut off Mrs. Richardson.

"So how did the Martin boy learn that it was Ethridge who killed his erstwhile sweetheart? Did you have anything to do with it?"

Polly trembled more. She started to cry quietly. Tears ran down her downturned face.

"I ... I ... I didn't know," she half sobbed. "After she w's killed ... when he asked me if I knew where she had been going. ... I saw her leaving the house the night she didn't come back. ... I asked her who she was going to see. ... She said something to the effect that she was going to see her Mr. Bearcat. ... She didn't give any name, she just called him Mr. Bearcat. ... I thought ... she meant that whoever she was talking about was good in bed ... that w's why she compared him to something wild. ... I thought it was her nickname for him.

"We met down by the river. Sam was all broken up and beside himself with grief. When we tried to comfort him, nothing we tried worked. When Sam asked me the same question you asked, if I knew whom she had gone to see, I remembered what she had said. … I didn't think anything of it. I didn't think the name would mean anything to him. So I told him the name she had used. At that moment, Sam went wild, shouting that it wasn't a nickname, it w's the name of a car."

"A Stutz Bearcat," Constable Harkness said. "It's a very expensive sporting model car. Ethridge had one. It's the only one in town. There may be only a handful in the whole state. I drooled over that car every time I saw it. But on a constable's pay I couldn't even afford the hood ornament."

"Sam went out of his head, absolutely furious, mad with rage. He stormed away, shouting that he was going to, in his words, 'have a word' with the owner of the car. Ben tried to stop him, but he couldn't even slow him down. He pushed him away and headed out running. Two days later the paper said Ethridge had been killed."

The constable pulled the long-bladed jackknife that had been left rammed in Harold Ethridge's chest, the item that he had stopped at the station house to pick up, out of his pocket. With a quick flip, he snapped the blade out and held the knife up.

"Is this Samuel Martin's knife?" he asked.

"It was her knife," Mrs. Richardson said.

"Did the Martin boy give it to her?" the constable asked.

"No. She had it with her when she first came to the house," Mrs. Richardson answered. "She carried it in a hidden pocket of her dress. I assume she carried it as a means of protection against any man who got out of hand with her."

"A rather contradictory point," the constable said. "She was a practitioner of a profession where men tend to get out of hand with women."

"I mean seriously out of hand," Mrs. Richardson said, "violently out of hand. In her earlier life, she had been seriously manhandled by the men around her. She came to think all men were violent by nature. She was fearful and distrustful of all men."

"If she was so frightened and mistrustful of men, she sure picked a peculiar and conflicting profession as her trade," the constable said.

"She didn't have much of anything in her life to trade on," Mrs. Richardson said. "She traded on the only thing she had to trade on. She traded on herself. She had known nothing but hurt in her life. That's one of the reasons I took her in. I felt sorry for her."

"When she met Ethridge, she probably thought she had traded up," Constable Harkness said. "Instead, she traded a house of sisters and a halfway life for a house of death and a man who thought women were sluts to be traded off. Ethridge thought all women were nobodies to be dealt with the way he saw fit. In the end he thought the girl was a nobody who could be dealt all the way out because nobody outside this house would miss her or care that she was gone. He just didn't know that there was one boy who thought more than the world of her …"

Mrs. Richardson was more than a bit surprised that the constable saw it the same way she did.

Constable Harkness waved the knife a bit. "And would come after him, looking to rip him apart." He looked at the knife. "She didn't have this knife on her person when her body was examined. I'm just not quite sure how, if she kept this knife with her all along and didn't give it to the Martin boy, it ended up in the Martin boy's hands and, from there, got buried in Ethridge's chest. For some reason she must have given it to the Martin boy shortly before she was killed. She should have held on to it. It could have come in handy when Ethridge went after her."

A look came over the policeman's face. "Maybe it was with her that night," the policeman said. "Maybe that's when it first came into play."

The constable looked at him. "How so?" he asked.

"Remember the first interview we did with Ethridge after the girl was killed?" The policeman pointed at his neck.

"Ethridge had a partially healed cut on his neck that ran from under the front of his jaw to close to the back of his neck. When we asked him how he got the cut, he said he had nicked himself while shaving. But the cut was a lot longer than a simple nick. Even using a straight razor, when he first felt it cut, he would have dropped it. He wouldn't have continued drawing it across his neck. Besides, a man shaves up and down, not from front to back at an angle. Now that I think about it, it looks more like"— the constable held up the knife and focused on it—"like it was made by an instrument with a long, thin, sharp blade." The constable lowered the knife slightly and looked away as if looking across the horizon of time, visualizing an act of violence that had taken place behind the closed doors and walls of a closed-off house.

"Harmon, I think you've got it!" the constable said, still looking away.

He looked back at the policeman. "That's probably how it went down. Ethridge had called her in for another of the late-night dalliances he had been having with her. But that night something went south. They had a falling-out. Maybe Ethridge, tired of shelling out money to a girl he considered a two-bit tramp, didn't want to pay her. He probably thought that a low-class girl like her should be giving it for free to a high-class man like he thought of himself as. Maybe he got rough with her. She pulled the knife, trying to defend herself. At that point, Ethridge lost it completely. He wasn't about to take any lip from a cheap floozy, and he wasn't about to take one pulling a knife on him. He took it away from her. Then in his rage, he proceeded to break her neck. Then he drove her to the river in his fancy car and threw her in."

The policeman looked at the constable. Mrs. Richardson looked down. The constable tipped the knife again.

"After he killed the girl, Ethridge must have put this knife in his pocket and kept it to conceal evidence that he was her killer. Or he kept it as a souvenir of having escaped being slashed. He probably had it on him when the Martin boy confronted him in the Ethridge barn. When the Martin boy discovered it on him after shooting Ethridge with a shotgun, he went even more berserk and used the knife to give back to him many times over what he had given the girl. He left it sticking in him out of rage and vengeance and as a final curse on Ethridge. Then he ran off, thinking nobody would know he was the one who had killed the killer of his soiled sweetheart."

The constable folded the blade back into the body of the knife. Then he pointed with the folded knife at Polly.

"When the Martin boy ran off shouting that he was going after the man who killed the girl, why didn't you come to the police and tell us what he was going to do?" the constable said in a hard voice. "By not informing the police about what he was planning on doing, you could be held as an accessory to the crime."

At the not so veiled threat, Polly started to cry again, harder this time.

"I didn't know he was going to kill anyone," Polly sobbed. "He didn't say he was going to kill anyone. He just said he was going to have a word with someone. … A word isn't killing."

"From the way he was acting, you must have figured that it wasn't going to be a friendly word," the constable said. "Did he say anything about whom he was going after? Did he give a name?"

"He didn't give no name," Polly said in a sobbing tone that was almost inaudible. "When he asked me if I knew who Clarinda was going to see that night and I said that she had called him 'Mr. Bearcat,' he went crazy and stormed out. He didn't say any name, but he must have known whom Clarinda was talking about."

The constable looked a bit skeptical, but the girl didn't look or sound as if she was lying. She sounded too frightened to lie.

"Why didn't you come to us at the time this happened?" the constable asked pointedly. "If you had come to us right away in time, we could have stopped him before he killed Ethridge. By your not saying anything, Ethridge ended up dead, and now the Martin boy is wanted for murder. Your silence in the matter didn't do either of them any good."

"And your police department and the town's justice system didn't do either of them much good," Mrs. Richardson said in her own hard voice. "You did the girl even less good. You're here all afire to catch the killer of the richest man in town, but you hardly did any investigating into her death. But then she wasn't a rich, prominent citizen. To you she was probably a disposable whore you were happy to be done with and out of town. If the Martin boy didn't come to the police, it was probably because he felt that you would have swept it under the rug and would have done nothing because Ethridge was a first citizen and she was just a tramp who had come into this town from outside. Samuel probably didn't come to the police because he was convinced he wouldn't get justice for the girl from you."

"Did he tell you that?" Constable Harkness asked.

"When he found out from Polly's inadvertent disclosure that the girl had gone to Ethridge's house that night and that it was Ethridge who had probably killed her, he stormed away," Mrs. Richardson said. "He didn't stop here and tell us or anyone."

"If that's what he thought, he was mistaken about me," Constable Harkness said. "If he had come to us with what he had learned from your girl Polly, I would have investigated the case and done a full job of investigating."

"As I recall, the only person you questioned in her killing was the

Martin boy," Mrs. Richardson said. "You yourself said the investigation you did wasn't very thorough. That's where the Martin boy probably got the idea that you weren't going to do anything. He probably figured at that point that if he wanted justice for the girl, he was going to have to take justice in his own hands."

"As I recall, we did investigate her killing," Constable Harkness said in response. "As I also recall, you weren't very much help there either. We didn't even learn until just today that she was seeing Ethridge. We found out about the connection when Horace Thompson told us he had seen her going to the Ethridge house. If you wanted justice for the girl so bad, why didn't you tell us who she was seeing that night?"

"I've already stated that I didn't know where she was going," Mrs. Richardson said. "I told you that at the time when you first questioned me after her body had been found."

"That you did," Constable Harkness said. "But as I remember, when I questioned you for what you might know, you otherwise seemed to hang back. You didn't seem to want our investigation to go anywhere."

"That was a misinterpretation on your part," Mrs. Richardson came back hard. "To begin with, I didn't have anything I could add to your investigation. As I stated, none of us legitimately knew where she was going the night she left and didn't come back. She didn't tell any of us where she was going or give the name of whom she was going to see, except for the cryptic nickname she gave to Polly. I suppose Ethridge told her not to mention his name to anybody because it might dirty up his public image in the town."

"I can easily imagine Ethridge doing that," the constable said.

"For all practical purposes, Ethridge was the town," Mrs. Richardson said. "You're the head of the town police force. You work for the town. This house and all of us in it, including the girl, are from out in the dark, on the wrong side of town, though plenty of the town fathers have no trouble finding this house in the dark when they're out looking to do some midnight rambling. If you misinterpreted my reaction and you thought I was being reluctant to help you investigate her killing, I may have given you that impression because I doubted that you had much interest in rigorously pursuing an investigation of the killing of a nameless girl you considered to be a tramp to begin with and who you probably felt got what she deserved for the way she was living. At least you probably felt that she was asking for it. I doubted you had much of an interest in pursuing anybody as her killer, even if it was a man from the same lower level of society as her. I assumed that as soon as your perfunctory interview of me was over, you'd walk away, forget the whole thing, and blame the killing on a person or persons unknown. I don't believe you would have sent the leading citizen up for the murder of a girl he and you probably considered to be a no-account slut."

"You might have swallowed your surly class-consciousness long enough to give me the benefit of the doubt," Constable Harkness said.

"I'm still rather doubtful that you would have sent Harold Ethridge, leading citizen, richest man in the town and maybe the county, away to the gallows or to jail for killing a small-time prostitute with no name of her own," Mrs. Richardson said in a doubtful tone.

"Oh, I would have sent him up if I had known at the time it was him who had killed the girl," Constable Harkness said. "I'm the head of the police. I serve justice in this town, not any one person of this town."

"That's easy to say now that Ethridge is dead," Mrs. Richardson said. "But if he was alive, I don't think you would have as much as even touched him."

"I would have touched him all right," Constable Harkness said.

"I doubt that all across the board," Mrs. Richardson responded. "I doubt you would have started anything or said anything. You'd probably have been afraid that Ethridge would sue you for libel or would have the town council fire you. You would have left him standing and untouched. Now that he's safely dead, you probably won't still won't say anything. No reason to go about raking up muck about anybody in this town where a nameless tramp is concerned. Now you'll probably keep silent and do whatever you can to keep Ethridge's name and legacy clean."

"On the contrary," Constable Harkness said, "I'm going to smear this all over town in no uncertain terms. I'll make them listen. I'm going to shove this down the throat of everyone in this town. If they choke on it, that's their problem."

Mrs. Richardson did not quite know what to make of the unexpected direction the constable was taking things. "Sounds good in itself," she said. "I'll believe it when I see it." She fell silent, still unsure if she believed him.

Constable Harkness looked at Mrs. Richardson. "You stay here," he said, pointing to her. With an encompassing sweep of his finger, he motioned to the rest of the women of the house. "The rest of you go back to your rooms or about your business. I need to talk to your mistress alone."

The women rose up and filed out of the parlor. Polly's cheeks were still streaked with tears. Both Constable Harkness and Mrs. Richardson waited until they heard the last of the house girls go into their rooms.

Mrs. Richardson wondered if he was going to demand sexual favors from her or one of the house girls as a price for not further involving them.

"Now that you know it was the Martin boy, what do you intend to do?" Mrs. Richardson asked, stealing a march on the constable.

Constable Harkness looked at the madam of the house. Mrs. Richardson was middle-aged, about the same age as he was. In her middle-aged way, she was a fairly handsome woman. Under her blouse, her breasts were rounded and full. She wore a narrow dress with little flare at the bottom, stretched a bit at the middle by her full hips. On her feet she wore high button shoes with pointed tips. Her brown hair, pulled tight into a bun in the back, wasn't showing any hint of going gray.

"I was about to ask you what you think I should do," Constable Harkness said.

The statement took Mrs. Richardson by surprise. It wasn't what she had expected. She had expected a stern lecture about the letter of the law and yet more words about how he didn't tolerate murder in his town.

"Since when does a constable of the law ask the advice of a madam of a bordello on the disposition of a murder case?" Mrs. Richardson asked. "Either the murder of a small-time, small-town prostitute with no name, or the murder of a big-name town ward healer with a name synonymous with the town?"

"You have an emotional connection to the girl," Constable Harkness responded, again going in an unexpected direction. "You're the one who felt sorry for the girl. You're the one who took her in to give her shelter and a life, such as it was. The Martin boy loved the girl. He had his own emotional connection to her, one strong enough that it drove him to kill the man who killed his lover."

"I loved her in my own way, even if it was partially that I felt sorry for her," Mrs. Richardson said.

"I fully understand how the Martin boy felt and why he did what he did," the constable went on in his unexpected direction. "If I had been him and his age, I probably would have done the same thing."

"Now there's a strange revelation from one supposed to be the sworn and pledged enforcer of the letter of the law," Mrs. Richardson said.

"The Martin boy loved the girl. Because he loved her, you probably have as much affection for him as you did for the girl."

"Oh, he loved her," Mrs. Richardson said, still wondering where he was going with it. "Really loved her. It would be the easy and romantic formula to say that she loved him. Whether she loved him to the same degree as he loved her, whether she was capable of giving or receiving love, I'm not fully sure. At times she seemed so hard-bitten and knotted up inside, I wondered if she could ever escape what had been done to her and what she had become because of it. Now I guess I'll never know. I don't know if the Martin boy knew either. But he loved her nonetheless. Because he loved her, I had an affection for him."

"I also have the distinct feeling that if you were in my place, you would cover up and cover over what he did and would let him go without charging him or even naming him as a suspect," Constable Harkness said.

"You're damned straight I would let him go," Mrs. Richardson flared. "I wouldn't send him or anyone to the gallows or the new electric chair for killing a butcher like Ethridge who killed young women. If that's what you looking to hear from me, I confess that I would let him off and keep it a secret. If that's what you're waiting for me to say, I just said it. If in you legal estimate that constitutes aiding and abetting, then arrest me."

Constable Harkness did not answer. Mrs. Richardson stopped and looked at him. "Why are you telling me any of this? Why are you asking me what I would do? Are you trying to get me to confess that I would aid and abet a killer so you can use it as an excuse to close down this house and run all of us out of town?"

"I've already said I'm not going to do that," Constable Harkness answered.

"Why then are you even asking me at all if I would let him go?" Mrs. Richardson asked. A light went on in her head. Maybe it wasn't the light of justice. Maybe it was. "Is it because you're thinking of letting him go yourself?"

"My first duty is to the law," the constable said. "But for the first time in my career as a lawman, I find myself in conflict with the letter of the law, and it's not a small conflict. I know you probably don't believe me, but my sympathy went to the girl. My sympathy goes to the Martin boy. I haven't the least bit of sympathy for Ethridge. My instincts, my nature, and my extrajudicial sense of justice tell me to hold what I know, keep it concealed, and keep the law away from the Martin boy. But I find myself stuck between a rock and a hard place. Or should I say a rock and a hard case? There's an old saying that hard case makes bad law. Yes, I'm a sworn deputy of the law. I tend to give deference to the letter of the law. In this case I find myself clinging to the edge of the law by my fingernails."

Mrs. Richardson looked at the constable, who appeared to be looking beyond her and out beyond the house.

"With two killings coming almost right on top of each other, the citizens of this town are going over the edge with fear. They think there's an anarchist assassin or an alienist psychopath loose in their midst. Earlier today I had to persuade Horace Thompson not to load up his old blunderbuss pistol and keep it loaded under his pillow. I don't know if I succeeded. If I didn't and he wakes up in the night and something is moving in the room, he'll shoot his wife or his dog. Or someone else just as jumpy will shoot someone in their family, or one of their neighbors walking past the house at night. The town could become an armed camp with a hair trigger. If the situation isn't damped down, the whole town could degenerate into a free-rolling ball of paranoia with everyone looking over their shoulder at everyone else, wondering if they're a mad killer. Every little eccentricity on the part of anyone will be misinterpreted and misconstrued as being a sign that the person is a closet madman and insane murderer. Suspicions will be aroused at every turn. Fingers will point. False charges will be leveled. The town could become as jumpy and fear filled as Salem during the witchcraft trials. The town could come apart at the seams. There's no way of saying when or if everything or anything in the town will ever get back to being at least the reasonable way it was."

The constable looked at Mrs. Richardson. "I can't sit on my hands and say nothing. Sitting here in your removed house, you don't know what's going on in the imagination of the town. They think there's a crazed killer lurking in every shadow. I've got to give the public something.

I've got to explain to them that, even though it's murder, the reasons for both murders have low-level, pedestrian explanations: a sexual encounter that went bad, vengeance exacted on the killer of a sweetheart. I have to show them that it isn't a case of there being a seething madman out there somewhere who might rise up and strike again. I have to show them that it's over. To do that, I have to give them the story. To give them the story, I have to give them names. Both stories are down and dirty in their own way, but they're understandable, and they end where they ended. There's no hidden dimension of madness, no crazed killer lurking in the shadows who may strike again at any time. At least there's no madness beyond the background madness of human nature."

"Can't you just stick with your 'person or persons unknown' explanation and leave it there?" Mrs. Richardson asked.

"The town council wants answers," the constable said. "If I can't provide them with one, they may come to consider me to be an incompetent nincompoop. They'll send me packing and hire a new chief of police."

"Is that the point of it then?" Mrs. Richardson said in her sour, now-we're-getting-down-to-it voice. "It's not the boy and not the letter of the law, but your job?"

"The point of it is that if the town council gets a different police chief, he'll probably work out what happened as quick as I did," the constable said. "But he won't have any inclination to cut the Martin boy any kind of break. Along with that, he may not go anywhere as easy on this house, on you and your girls."

Mrs. Richardson furrowed her brow.

"I've got to give them a story. That story has to make sense. The runaway fear the killings have created has to end. To wrap it up, the story has to give them a name."

"Then you are planning to send the Martin boy up," Mrs. Richardson said.

Constable Harkness was silent for a moment.

"I've been working on that, and I think there's a way to split the difference," the constable said. "I've got a way that it can be worked out at least halfway for the boy. He may not find it the most preferable or pleasant of options. It may be a hard option for him. But it's better than the electric chair or life in state prison. It's just not an option that can be worked out in this town."

Constable Harkness and the policeman turned and started to walk away.

"Constable," Mrs. Richardson called out to the officer's turning back.

Constable Harkness stopped and turned to look at the madam. "Yes?"

"If you had had the information you say you now have against Harold Ethridge, would you really have used it to arrest him and send him up for killing the girl? Or would you have spiked the evidence and kept quiet because he was a rich man and big-name citizen and she was a prostitute, and you and the town wouldn't want to send a prominent town member up for killing a girl you probably all called a tramp?"

"I can only tell you what I told the Martin boy when I talked to him after the girl was killed," Constable Harkness said. "I don't like murder. I don't like murder in my town, whether it's of a high-rolling citizen or a street girl. I had to make sure my ducks were in more of a row before I accused Ethridge. He could have hired a lot more lawyers than the Martin family can. The case would have been more of an uphill fight, but I would have gone after him."

"You sound like you're trying to convince yourself more than you're trying to convince me," Mrs. Richardson said in a skeptical voice.

The charge of favoritism toward the rich and the law looking the other way when a member of the poor classes was killed was standard fare for Progressives and Socialists of the era. In her calling and day-to-day function, Mrs. Richardson wasn't a period political activist, but she was possessed of a period skepticism of the willingness of the law to take any action against a rich and influential man vis-à-vis the killing of a lower-class prostitute, a lower-class worker, or a lower-class anybody.

"However inadequate job I may do of convincing you, I have only you to convince, ma'am," Constable Harkness answered. "I know what I think."

"I have only your word for that," Mrs. Richardson said. Both the wording and the tone of her response carried the implication that she didn't particularly believe him.

"Just like I have to take your word that you didn't have anything to do in egging the Martin boy on to kill Harold Ethridge," Constable Harkness answered in an even tone. The tone and structure of his response carried the implication that he didn't particularly care much one way or the other what she thought.

"Your word is as much conditional and doubtful to me as my word is to you. For whatever either of our words are worth, we're just going to have to take each other at our word and leave it there. That's the best we can do for each other."

The woman wasn't simpering, and she had a certain amount of backbone and bravery to her. As a policeman, Constable Harkness liked brave and stalwart women. Whatever the convictions of a bordello madam might happen to be, the woman had the courage of her convictions. Constable Harkness found himself actually starting to like her. If the woman's part in and the bucktoothed, tongue-tied girl's part in it had been inadvertent and unintentional, it was a part he could otherwise overlook for the both of them.

"Do you intend to put the Martin boy away for killing Ethridge?" Mrs. Richardson asked in passing. She didn't add "whether he's guilty or not." She figured it might only set the police officer off. Besides, it was a moot point. She knew as well as the constable that the boy was guilty. Mrs. Richardson still cared for the boy. In her relative class-consciousness, she didn't want to see him get sent up for killing the man who had killed the girl he had been so deeply in love with. When it came to keeping quiet, she would have kept quiet about the boy's having killed Ethridge.

"I intend to follow the evidence where it leads," Constable Harkness said in proper but unspecific and evasive police rhetoric. "I'll put the Martin boy where the evidence puts him. If perchance he gets put away anywhere and escapes, my reach beyond this town is limited."

Mrs. Richardson said no more about it. She said no more at all. She had reached both the limit of what could be said and the limit of her boldness for the day. The two official representatives of the law turned, walked out of the parlor, and exited the house.

"Before we go to the Martin house, drive back to the station," Constable Harkness said as he and the sergeant got into the car. "I want to pick up Arthur."

Sergeant Plechathy drove back to the station house. None of the riders in the car said anything.

"Harmon," Constable Harkness said in a coldly cautious and bottom-line voice to Sergeant Plechathy after they had parked what passed for a squad car and walked to the door of the station house.

"Yes?"

"Before we leave for the Martin house, strap on your pistol. Tell Arthur to do the same. I'll get mine too. They're a family of farmers. All farmers have guns, often a whole rack of guns. At least we know they have one shotgun. The boy is hotheaded, and he's already used a gun on a man once. No telling how this is going to go when we get there."

The caution having been delivered, the two minions of the law walked into the station house.

Chapter 22

"Pull wide around the house. I want to see if there's anyone in that barn," Constable Harkness instructed the policeman who was driving the squad car. "No use having someone hear us and come out of the barn to come up behind us while we're armed."

Arthur did as he was instructed. If the chief of police thought the precaution was necessary, who was he to say otherwise?

The trio of the town's finest drove the squad car, such as the squad car was in the town in that day, in a wide arc around the house, approaching the open door of the barn on the far side. As they pulled up to the open door of the barn, Constable Harkness looked intently through the windshield of the car and into the barn. He didn't see anyone or any motion in the barn or the hayloft above.

"Take us wide around the far side of the barn and then around to the house," Constable Harkness said next. "Pull up to the corner near the kitchen door. Stay tight to the side of the house."

As the car rounded the back of the barn and headed toward the Martin farmhouse, Constable Harkness leaned out of the passenger's-side window and scanned the second floor of the house to see if there were any gun barrels sticking out of any windows. Bonnie and Clyde had yet to make their debut as heavily armed crazed country killers, but Constable Harkness was aware of the story of the Hatfields and the McCoys. He knew well enough that countryfolk and farmers could get quite crazy at times, especially when you come to arrest one of their own, especially when that one of their own is a family member. And the one they were coming to question and probably arrest had already proven himself a crazed killer with a gun.

The policeman stopped the car out of the line of sight, around the corner from the kitchen door, where he'd been instructed, and the three armed men got out.

"Maybe one of us should go in the back door while the rest go in the front," Sergeant Plechathy said as they assembled at the font of the car. "It might be best to come at them from both sides at once."

"No," Constable Harkness said. "Don't split up. One of us may run into the Martin boy alone. I don't know what he might be likely to try if he thinks there's only one of us."

The constable turned to face the corner of the house. "We'll all go in at once. Take them by surprise and in numbers. If we appear forceful, hopefully it will be enough to intimidate them. That may be our best chance to keep things from getting out of control."

The constable touched the pocket of his jacket, inside of which he carried a concealed revolver. He started to head toward the kitchen door of the Martin house. The other officers followed in close train. He knew the way. He had been there before. The Martin house was becoming familiar territory to him.

"Don't knock," Constable Harkness said as they approached the door. "Just go in."

"Wasn't that the truck I just heard pull up?" Mrs. Martin said to her daughter as they stood folding clothing in the laundry room at the back of the house.

"Sounded like it," Beth said.

"I thought your father was upstairs," Mrs. Martin went on. "I didn't hear him leave."

Mrs. Martin's husband was forever going and coming on the spur of the moment in pursuance of something having to do with the farm. She assumed that while she and Beth had been working in the laundry room, he had remembered something he wanted to do, had gone out unnoticed, had taken the truck somewhere, and had returned.

"I didn't hear him come down the stairs," Beth said.

"Then it must be Sam," Samuel's mother said. Her son was forever coming and going, doing some boyhood thing by himself or with his friends. He had been coming and going from the house quite a bit while he had been secretly squiring around the girl from Mrs. Richardson's establishment. Most of his unknown comings and goings had ceased after she had been found dead.

"Last I saw of Sam, he was moping around in his room," Beth said. "When I passed by his room, he was just lying there on the bed, staring off into space. He's been acting very strange lately."

"He's still getting over the shock of that girl being killed," Samuel's mother said. "Seeing the sweetheart he wanted to marry turn up murdered can take a lot out of any man and change them. He'll have to get used to and live with the fact that he's going to be this way for a while."

"I mean the last couple of days," Beth said. "He's really seemed to be out somewhere else the last few days."

"Well, it has to be one of them," Mrs. Martin said. She figured it was probably Sam. He was being as moody and unpredictable as his sister said. In his moody unpredictability, he had probably jumped off his bed and gone somewhere that made sense only to him. Now he had returned. It was as simple as that.

"I didn't hear either him or father come down the stairs," Beth said.

At that moment they both heard the kitchen door openly heavily and bang against the corner wall. That sound was followed in train by the sound of heavy male feet walking across the wooden floor of the kitchen.

"Whoever it is, they're back," Mrs. Martin said. She left her work folding the clothesline-dried wash they had brought in earlier and headed toward the sound of the footsteps. From the heavy clomping sound of the footsteps, she assumed it was her husband returning.

"Frank, where have you …"

As she rounded the hall corner and walked into the parlor, she stopped in her tracks, her mouth falling open. Instead of the long familiar form of her husband, Mrs. Martin saw a man she had only recently become familiar with standing in the middle of the parlor, a man wearing a badge. That was only the beginning of her surprise. Standing behind him and to either side were two men in police uniforms, also wearing badges.

"Hello again, ma'am," the uniformed leader of the uniformed officers said. "We seem to keep meeting under less than auspicious circumstances. But then police are usually called out when something less than auspicious happens."

The man looked at her directly. At the same time he also seemed to be warily surveying the room. His attention seemed especially directed to the hallway beyond.

"Pardon me for barging in here like this," the man went on, "but we're investigating a matter of extreme seriousness and concern. I felt it necessary to dispense with formal polite entrances."

"You're the sheriff, aren't you?" Mrs. Martin said redundantly.

"They gave me a fancy title," Constable Harkness said, "but basically a sheriff is what I am."

"I remember you. You were here looking to question my son about the death of the girl he was in love with. Is this about that matter again?"

"Yes and no, ma'am," the constable said.

"The last time you were here, you knocked on the door," Mrs. Martin said. "Has it since become your investigative practice to enter into someone's house unannounced?"

"Pardon the impertinence, ma'am, but we're investigating a crime where someone walked in unannounced on someone else and did so with far less than benign intentions. Given the gravity of the case, I thought it would be best for all concerned to temporarily put aside the extra degrees of polite manners and proceed more directly."

Curious about the strange voices coming from the parlor, Beth came into the room. She stopped just inside. The constable looked at the girl and then back at Mrs. Martin. "Are your husband and son here?" he asked.

"I believe they're both upstairs," Mrs. Martin said.

"Would you call them down here please?" Constable Harkness said. "I have to talk with them both on a matter of utmost importance."

"I'll get them," Beth said quietly. She turned and headed up the stairs.

"May I ask what this is all about?" Mrs. Martin asked after Beth had disappeared from sight.

"I think it would be best to have everyone assembled before we go into that," the constable said.

Mrs. Martin opened her mouth to ask something, but she stopped before any words came out. It was at this less than auspicious moment that Mrs. Martin noticed that the two uniformed policemen were wearing holsters with pistols in them.

"Call your son down, please," Constable Harkness said to Samuel's mother.

"I'll get him," Beth said.

As Samuel lay on his bed looking out the window and the blue of the sky beyond, once again the window and the light behind it seemed to stretch out and recede into a narrowing rectangular tunnel leading nowhere, to an undefined end over an unknown and unspecified horizon. The window was a door to a corridor beyond. It was a door he didn't want to take leading into a corridor he didn't want to be in. But as he looked, instead of standing on the threshold, it seemed to Samuel that he was in the corridor. It was as if through no action of his own he had crossed the threshold without noting the bump or transition, and now he was in the middle of the hollow blue undefined corridor that had neither a definite nor visible end.

Samuel was jolted out of his blank reverie when he heard his name called from the door of his room. He turned his head toward the sound. The body of his sister filled the doorway.

"Sam, get up and go downstairs quickly," Beth said in a voice half breathless from running up the stairs, in a tone clearly filled with worry. "The sheriff is here with the police. They want to talk to you and Father."

As quick as she had appeared, Beth disappeared from the doorway and headed down the hall to her parents' room, where her father was.

A gnawing feeling came into Samuel's stomach. A cold pit of undefined shape but seemingly bottomless dimension opened under his feet. But Samuel had no time to analyze the shape of the pit or to speculate on why the police were at his house again. All he could do in the time not allowed him was to get up and walk to the stairs. As he started down the stairs, behind him he could hear the footsteps of his father coming down the hall.

As Samuel came into the parlor, he felt the floor drop out from under him. Shortly enough he would feel the acceleration of his world dropping out from under him.

Samuel's father came into the room and stopped off to Samuel's side. "Good afternoon, Officer," Mr. Martin said tentatively. "I'm a bit surprised to see you out here. The last time I saw you was at the potluck supper in town. I remember the mayor had you say a few words after his speech."

"I remember that night too," Constable Harkness said. "It was a peaceful and friendly enough night. But now in hindsight, I'd say that was the night the town started to fall apart. It all started quite literally that night and went downhill from there. While everyone was enjoying themselves at the festivities, things were happening, things that set in motion a chain of events that resulted in a lot of unpleasantness for a lot of people. In fact, I'm here pursuing an extension of that night. As I said to your wife, forgive me if I'm blunt about things, but I'm here investigating a crime that was rather blunt. Homicide is about as blunt of a crime as it gets."

"Is this about the dead girl from the Richardson house?" Samuel's father asked.

"As I told your wife," Constable Harkness said, "yes and no."

"You've already questioned our son about her death," Samuel's father said.

"It's not her death I'm here about."

The thin film of hope that the police chief was at his house with half the musterable police force to talk further about Clarinda's death broke in the pit of Samuel's stomach like the skin of a balloon.

"Before I get down to specifics, I have to ask you if you or anyone in your family owns a double-barrel twelve-gauge shotgun."

"I do," Samuel's father answered. He pointed to the next room over. "It's in the gun cabinet in the reading room."

"Would you please bring it to me, sir?" Constable Harkness said. He motioned to the younger-looking officer. "Arthur will accompany you."

The policeman crossed the room and came up to Mr. Martin. The two walked close past Samuel and out of the room. From the next room, Samuel heard the sound of the gun cabinet door being opened. After that he heard some other indistinct noise as if someone were rustling around.

"Can't you tell us what this is about?" Samuel's mother asked the constable.

"I will make everything plain in due time," Constable Harkness said. There was a hint of heaviness and reluctance in his otherwise gravelly voice. The heavy tone of his voice frightened Samuel's mother.

"Is it necessary for you in your investigation to go about armed as you are?" Samuel's mother asked. She had seen the police in town at random times before. But unlike the western sheriffs of old, they wore no sidearms in the usual course of their daily rounds. This was the first time she had seen any of them armed. And they were armed in her house.

"In this case, we have to go about armed because the perpetrator we're looking for felt it necessary to go about armed," Constable Harkness said. "He also felt it necessary to employ the firearm he was carrying in a most emphatic manner."

Samuel didn't have any time to analyze the nuances in the police chief's voice. His father and the police officer came back into the room, the officer in the lead. In his hand he carried the shotgun. He handed the gun to the constable. With his other hand he passed him another item. "I found this too," the policeman said. Constable Harkness looked at the small, nearly square cardboard box. It was a box of shotgun shells marked double-aught buckshot.

The constable opened the box and looked inside. His face seemed to set. The top row of shells was gone. Without saying anything, he closed the box and set it down on the end table by the big chair, at which point he turned his attention to the shotgun. He turned the gun around in his hands, looking at it from different angles.

"This looks like an old gun," the firearm-familiar Constable Harkness said.

"It's a Purdy," Samuel's father said. "I got it from my father. He bought it a long time ago. It's more of a keepsake than anything."

"Does it have the old-style Damascus twist barrel?" Constable Harkness asked.

"Yes," Samuel's father said.

The constable's question was rhetorical. He had known the likely construction of the barrels just by looking at the gun and knowing its age.

Beyond that he had found half the answers he needed when he had seen the box of shells. He rotated the gun in his hand slightly.

"I assume you know that modern high-velocity smokeless powder is too powerful for this gun," the constable went on in a rhetorically cautionary vein. "This gun will blow up in your face if you use modern shells in it. That's why you have to use less powerful old-style black powder shells"—the constable nodded to the box of shells on the end table—"like the ones in that box."

Constable Harkness pushed the lever on the action and opened the barrels. He held the gun up with the barrels facing the light coming in from the window and looked down the barrels. "These barrels are dirty," he said. He brought the gun up and sniffed the breech. A faint scent of burned gunpowder lingered. "This gun has been fired within the last few days."

He closed the gun and looked at Mr. Martin. "Have you been hunting with this gun recently, sir?"

"I haven't used that gun for years," Samuel's father answered. The innocent answer was the first step that set the shape of Samuel's future for the rest of his years. "I keep it more as a reminder of my father than anything else. Nowadays when I hunt game birds or crows, I use the single-barrel pump-action shotgun."

Constable Harkness turned to face Samuel directly for the first time. "Then that leaves you," he said. "Your mother and sister don't look like the hunting type to me. But you neglected to run a cleaning rod and an oil patch down the barrels. If you leave a gun barrel uncleaned like that after firing it, after time it can cause the barrel to rust up. Didn't your father teach you to clean you gun after using it, boy? And just what particular game were you out hunting with your father's family heirloom?"

"I saw some pheasant in the field," Samuel said weakly. "I thought that maybe I could bring one or two in for dinner."

"Do you have a hunting dog trained to flush birds out of the bush?"

"No," Samuel said. "Teddy knows how to catch rats, but he's not an upland game bird dog."

"Then you must have flushed them yourself," Constable Harkness said. "How many did you spot?"

"It was just a pair," Samuel said. "They saw me coming and spooked and took off."

"You obviously fired at them," Constable Harkness said. "How many did you bring down?"

"I missed with both shots," Samuel said, his voice sounding as weak as before. "I guess I need more practice. I'm afraid I'm getting rusty."

"Or maybe you were using the wrong load," Constable Harkness said. "What kind of shot were you using?"

"Bird shot," Samuel said.

"Were you using newer smokeless powder shells in this old gun?" Constable Harkness asked. "If you were, you were risking your head."

Samuel was silent. Constable Harkness turned to the boy's father. "Do you have any old black powder bird shot shells?"

"No," Samuel's father said, answering again in honest innocence. "We just have the newer ammunition. That's why I don't use that old gun."

"Then you must have grabbed that box of buckshot by mistake without noticing what you had done so," he said. "They're older black powder shells. Given that the residue in the barrels of this gun looks like black powder, I'd say that these were the shells you used. The oversight on your part kept you from blowing your head off, but no wonder you didn't bring down anything—anything on the wing, that is. There are so few pellets in a buckshot load, you have to be a real crack shot to hit a flying bird with it. Buckshot is made for bigger game. It's made for what walks on legs, not for what flies on wings."

Constable Harkness looked at the box of shells on the table and then looked up at Samuel's father. "How many shells were in that box?" he asked.

"I never used any of them," Samuel's father said. "They came to me from my father along with the gun. It's a full box."

The constable reached over and opened the box, this time in a way so that all could see. Instead of being filled to the top, a complete layer was missing.

"Well, there's four of 'em gone now," Constable Harkness remarked. He looked back at Samuel. "Looks like you didn't take the box with you when you went on your hunting expedition. Looks more like you just opened the box and grabbed a handful of shells without looking what you were grabbing and then headed out the door with them loose in your pocket. You must have been in a hurry. But once spotted, pheasants don't stay in one spot too long. They move around quite a bit. I can understand your haste to be out and after them. I suppose that's the reason you grabbed a handful of shells from the nearest box without looking to see if they were the right kind for the game you were going after or even if they were safe to use in the gun you'd also grabbed out of the cabinet without thinking. Having the wrong ammunition naturally caused you to miss."

Constable Harkness looked back into the open box. He pointed to the remaining shells inside it. Instead of being arranged in neat alternating order, two of the shells sat with the brass ends of their shell cases side by side.

"The shells in this box are out of order. Looks like you just jammed the unused ones back in the box without placing them in front-to-back order. That stretches the box out of shape. Kind of looks like you shoved them back in the box in a hurry. Was that when you discovered that you had grabbed the wrong ammunition? But I can understand your anger with yourself. So many shots fired and nothing accomplished. Then you find that you've made a dunce out of yourself by taking the wrong ammunition. If I considered myself to be a crack hunter and I had fanned four shots to the wind and later found out that I was using the wrong ammunition, I would be pretty mad at myself too."

The constable looked back at Samuel. "But didn't you just say that you only fired two shots? According to your father, there are four of these shells missing. You must have tried to make another kill later."

"I saw another pair later," Samuel said, his tone no more convincing than it had been at the outset. "Or maybe it was the same pair come back to earth."

"I take it you went after that pair with no better results," Constable Harkness said. "Apparently you still hadn't discovered that you were using the wrong cartridges. ... When exactly was it that you embarked on your abortive hunting expedition to put dinner on the table?"

"It was in the afternoon," Samuel said.

"I was in the field that day at that time," Samuel's father said with a puzzled tone in his voice. "I don't remember hearing any shooting close by."

Constable Harkness looked at Samuel again. "Now that's kind of reckless of you, boy," he said before Samuel could say anything. "Shooting wild like that with heavy shot in the same field your father is in. You could have knocked him off the thresher and killed him dead on the spot."

Samuel hadn't stopped to think where his father had been that day or if he had been in the field. Samuel's father hadn't thought there was any reason to lie about where he was that day. Samuel found himself trying to fly a story that made him sound totally stupid about guns, too stupid for a country boy who'd been raised with firearms.

He also found himself walking into a hole left by his father's statement that he had not heard him or seen him in the field that day. Later generations might say that Samuel's story about spontaneously going out to hunt pheasants, coupled with the constable's suggestion that he had inadvertently grabbed the wrong shells, didn't "have traction." In his time, at the present moment, Samuel knew his story was washed up before it had begun. He had to think of something else and think it up on the fly. He needed something more convincing, something bigger, something that went with buckshot.

"I wasn't hunting pheasants that day," Samuel said. Given that what he'd just said was a negation of everything else he had said up to that point, the tone of his voice couldn't help but come out sounding hollow.

"Then, pray tell, what in specific were you hunting, boy?" Constable Harkness asked in a gravelly voice that was more rounded and deeper-sounding in its hollowness.

"I was out by the barn. I saw what looked like a pair of wolves in the tree line out on the western border of the farm. They weren't on the move. They were just standing there looking this way. From the looks of them and the way they were standing around looking, they seemed to be eyeing the barn. I thought that maybe they were looking to go after the horses and the chickens. If they did go after our farm animals, Teddy would have gone after them and would have gotten himself killed."

Samuel's father looked at him with a growing quizzical look on his face. Constable Harkness looked at him with a set and unchanging look.

"I ran inside and grabbed the gun and a pocketful of shells like you said and chased out after them."

"You chased a pack of wolves alone on foot, with no help, only a shotgun in hand?" Constable Harkness asked. His voice sounded more dubious than it had since he had entered the house.

"Our horses are plow horses," Samuel said. "They're not fast cow ponies that cowboys ride. I couldn't ride one of them. The pack was too far off the road for me to drive after them in the truck. I had to chase them on foot. … Wolves know by instinct when a man has a gun in his hand and that they're in danger. They saw me coming toward them and took off, loping away. I chased them into the wooded section past the far side of the Jorgensons' farm. Once they got into the woods, they probably thought they were safer. They turned around. I was able to get in at least a little closer to them. That's when I started shooting."

"I haven't seen any wolves around here since I was younger than you," Samuel's father said, seeing no reason to claim that his farm was infested with them. "My father's generation cleaned them out a long time ago. I didn't think there were any wolves left in the whole state. After all this time, where would wolves come from around here?"

"Maybe they came up from the heavy forest area down south near the Ohio River," Samuel said. "Or maybe they weren't wolves at all. They might have been a pack of large wild dogs. I didn't get all that good of a look at them."

"But you got close enough to shoot at them," Constable Harkness said.

"I fired four shots at them," Samuel said. "That's where the four missing cartridges went."

"Apparently you scored no more success against your pack of errant wolves than you did against your hypothetical flock of pheasants," Constable Harkness said sourly. "You didn't manage to bring back a wolf pelt any better than you did pheasant for the table. Where it came to hunting wolves with a shotgun, you were using the right gun and shot size, but you should have used a rifle. You can bring down a wolf at a lot longer range with a rifle than with a shotgun, and with less danger to yourself."

"I thought I heard one of them yelp," Samuel said. "I wasn't trying to kill them as much as frighten them enough so that they wouldn't come back. When I started shooting, they scattered and took off running in two directions. They moved too fast for me to chase them after that."

Constable Harkness turned to Samuel's father. "Did he tell you about his abortive wolf chase any more than he did about his futile pheasant hunt that never happened?" he asked.

"No," Samuel's father answered, seeing no reason why his son would keep that from him, not any more than he saw any reason to claim that he had said something when he hadn't.

Constable Harkness turned back to Samuel. "So why didn't you tell your father that you spotted wolves moving back into the area?" he asked in a voice more cynical than inquisitive. "Given that he's the head and master of the farm, you would think that, as something that would influence the operation and future of the farm, he would want to know about the wolves. Why did you keep silent about a serious threat to local livestock like that?"

"I suppose I thought the wolves wouldn't come back," Samuel said, his voice and answer sounding as weak as everything else he had said. "I guess I didn't want to worry him."

"Yet you put your life in possible danger through your quixotic quest to kill the wolves," Constable Harkness said. "Why didn't you tell your father what you had attempted to do? Why didn't you tell him while you were on your way what you were heading out to do?"

"I suppose I was afraid the he would tell me to stay away from dangerous animals and wouldn't let me go," Samuel answered. "The wolves may have come back later and killed something on our farm or on someone else's farm. They might have even gone after a farmer's child somewhere. I figured that the only way anyone on a farm around here would be safe was if the wolves or whatever they were had been killed or driven off to where they wouldn't come back."

"And you were willing to risk paying with your life by chasing after a pack of dangerous animals alone, but without any credit and honor accruing to you by not telling anyone afterward what you attempted?"

"I suppose so," Samuel said weakly.

"All very noble of you, boy," Constable Harkness said dryly. "But why would you stand where you are and lie to me as you just admitted you have, saying you had been hunting pheasant when you had been hunting wolves? Why would you lie to your father? Why would you lie to a duly appointed enforcer of the law about your noble gesture? Didn't your father and the minister teach you that there's nothing right about lying and nothing to be gained from it?"

"Running like I did across someone else's property with a gun in my hand, shooting it off, I guess I thought that what I had done might have violated the law somewhere," Samuel said. "That's why I lied to you."

"Well now, I am investigating an illegality," Constable Harkness said. "It does have something to do with the discharging of firearms, but none of it has anything to do with violating hunting season laws or game laws." The constable looked down at Samuel's feet. "Are those the shoes you were wearing during your lone wolf hunt after you spotted the wolf pack that your father out in the field didn't see and nobody else apparently saw?"

"No," Samuel said. "I was wearing my hunting boots."

"Where are your boots now?"

"They're in the laundry room. I usually leave them off at the door when I come in. Most of the time they have too much dirt and mud on the soles to wear them in the house."

The constable turned to Samuel's mother and sister, standing off to the side. "Would one of you ladies be so kind as to bring me his boots?" he asked.

"I'll get them," Samuel countered, stirring to leave.

The constable held up his hand. "Not you," he said definitely. He pointed over to Samuel's mother and sister. "One of them." He turned back to Samuel's mother and sister. "If you please."

Being the closest to the laundry room, Beth turned and left the parlor.

"Bring me any and all pairs of your brother's footwear," the constable said as Beth exited.

As Beth walked away, Constable Harkness leaned the shotgun up against the end table. After that he reached into his pocket, brought out the knife Clarinda had carried, the knife Samuel had left protruding from the base of Harold Ethridge's chest just below the heart, opened the blade, and held it up for Samuel to see.

"By any chance, have you ever seen this knife before?" the constable asked.

"No," Samuel said weakly.

"Well now, that's unusual for you not to recognize a personal possession of your sweetheart," the constable said. "Especially a sweetheart you were so personal with and about. Mrs. Richardson said that this knife once belonged to the girl of hers who was found dead, the girl you were in love with. Mrs. Richardson said she carried it in her pocket everywhere she went. Strange that in all the time you and Mrs. Richardson said that you and the girl were together, she wouldn't have taken this knife out of her pocket and shown it to you."

"I spent a good deal of the time we were together endeavoring to get her out of her clothes," Samuel said. "After getting her out of her clothes, I didn't spend a lot of time going through her pockets."

Samuel hoped his candor would deflect whatever point the constable was alluding to and heading toward.

"Well now, that's interesting," the constable said. "Supposedly the two of you were a lot more to each other than just a woman of ill repute and a client. According to Mrs. Richardson, you and the girl did a lot more and varied things together than her other women and their clients did in the upstairs rooms of the domicile she maintained for them for those purposes. She said that the way the two of you behaved in each other's presence was far closer to sweethearts than to a woman of the night and a customer. It's strange that in all the more than standard times you were together with the girl, she never revealed to you that she carried this knife. Why would she keep a thing like this from a friend? Hadn't she come to trust you by that time?"

Samuel said nothing.

"Whatever the girl herself may have thought about you, at least Mrs. Richardson said that you seemed to think of her that way. When I called you in to the station house, you sure as hell took her death like a bereaved and vengeful sweetheart, as opposed to a Johnny-come-at-night who'd lost a good piece of ass. You were shouting all over the station house at the top of your voice that someone had killed the girl you loved and that I didn't have any intention to do anything about it." The constable lowered the knife slightly. "Which is something else beyond your questionable and otherwise in vain hunting expeditions that doesn't add up here. You've said nothing about the girl today. You would think that given the way you felt about the girl, you would be all over the place asking me how the case was going and whether I was closing in on her killer. At least you would be accusing me of continuing indifference to the finding of her killer. But you haven't said a single word about the girl since I got here. In the station house you were shouting loud enough to blow open the door and crack the leaded glass windows in the church four blocks down and one block over. Here you haven't raised your voice one single note or pitch. For that matter, you haven't raised your voice to say word one about the girl. Have you forgotten her so soon? Or in your mind has the question of finding her killer and establishing justice for her been put somehow beyond reach?"

Beth came back into the room with Samuel's boots. The constable motioned her to hand him the boots. Holding both the knife and the boots, Constable Harkness examined the boots closely, starting out at the top and then turning them over. For several long seconds he looked at the soles of the boots.

"Seems to me that I've seen the pattern on these soles pressed into the mud somewhere outside the grounds of this farm," he said hollowly, "coming and going. It was at a point some distance from here, but not so distant that the traces of where you had gone have had enough time to wear off the boots you walked the ground in."

With the point of the knife, he pried a small piece of clinging dirt out of the tread of the boot sole.

"Wherever you were, you seemed to have gotten your boots dirty with the soil of the ground you walked on. Didn't you mama tell you not to come into the house with dirty shoes on? But then I guess that's why she has you take off your field shoes at the door and leave them in the laundry room. Makes for a lot more cleaning work for her if you track dirt in all over the floor."

Samuel was silent. His parents and sister were silent. The constable held up the fragment of dirt on the tip of the blade. "But this isn't dirt. It's clay. And from what I can see, you don't have any exposed clay on this farm. The question being, if you didn't pick this clay up here at home—the only clay I know of around here is along the riverbank, and on the floor of hog barns—whose ground did you pick it up on?"

The constable looked at the traces of clay on the soles of Samuel's boots. "This clay is lighter than the dirt on this farm is. For that matter, it's lighter and chalkier brown in color than the clay around here, which, where you can see it, is a bit redder in color. Just what the long-vanished geological process was that imparted the subtle differences between the clay of the two areas was, I'm not aware of. I assume you will tell me that you must have picked this clay up on your boots during your private and unobserved, and otherwise failed, campaign against that group of marauding wolves that entered our area from points unknown."

Samuel remained silent.

"But then again you said that you pursued the wolves past the far boundary of Jorgensons' farm. The Jorgenson farm is to the west of here, not the east."

Samuel remained silent. The other members of his family remained with puzzled looks on their faces.

"And to my knowledge there's no exposed clay on the Jorgenson farm either. So the clay on these boots isn't consistent with the soil on your farm or the Jorgensons' farm. It is, however, consistent with the clay east of here." Constable Harkness waved the boots once slightly in Samuel's direction. He focused his gaze on Samuel's face. "More to the immediate point, it's consistent with a bank of exposed clay along one side of a particular farm east of here."

He waved the boots again.

"Even more to the point, the clay on these boots is consistent with the spot where I found boot prints identical to these in the clay of the bank where someone had climbed the bank. When you climb a bank, the exertion of climbing conveys more force into the foot, which makes for a deeper footprint. It also tends to force dirt deeper into the cracks of the boot. Soft clay holds a shape quite well. That's why potters make pots out of it and sculptors make statues out of it. Even wet, it holds its form until fired."

With the tip of the knife blade, the constable pointed to a spot on the sole of one boot where a chunk of leather had been gouged out by normal wear and tear.

"Climbing the bank not only left the imprint of the sole of these boots, but it also managed to drive the print deep enough into the clay that it left the imprint of the gouge in this boot. The malleable clay held all the details of the boot driven into it, down to this nick in the sole."

The constable focused his immediate attention back on the boots. "In the right medium, boots have a way of leaving behind impressions of their passage. At the same time they have a way of carrying away impressions of the ground they've passed over."

Before Samuel or anyone could say anything, Constable Harkness brought the boots up to his face and sniffed the soles. He then pulled the boots away. For a long moment he looked at the soles of the boots. On his face he had the look that people get when they know that they've found the final piece of what they've been looking for. At the same time he had the look that people get when they don't like what they've found.

"Ah yes," Constable Harkness said in a low tone, "the wonderful lingering smell of pig manure." He looked at both Samuel and Mr. Martin. "For what it's worth to anybody, I grew up on a farm myself," he said. "I know the difference between the scent of cow manure, the scent of horse manure, and the scent of pig manure. They each have their own distinct signature."

He pointed to Samuel's boots. "There's the faded but definite trace of pig manure lingering on these boots. It's not fresh, but it's still there. From what remains, I'd say the smell is about as old as the scent of gunpowder still in the gun."

Constable Harkness looked at Mr. Martin in particular. "Do you raise hogs on this farm?"

"No, sir," Samuel's father said.

The constable turned to Samuel. "But the scent of hog manure is all over your boot soles," he said. "The only way you could get the smell of pig manure on the bottom of your boots enough that it would linger this long is if you walked through an area with pig manure spread out on the ground. Pray tell, where did pick up the grounded scent of a type of animal that you do not maintain on your farm?"

Samuel did not have anything to say. It was otherwise a moot point as the constable didn't allow him enough time to answer.

"Maybe you don't raise pigs on this farm, but they do raise pigs on the Ethridge farm. It just so happens that the Ethridge farm is the place where we found the impression of your boot soles in the clay of the slope on the small ridge on the edge of the property. It is also the place where we found similar footprints in the droppings in the hogpens. Instead of hunting either pluck pheasants or wolves trying to reestablish themselves in this territory, by any chance were you at the Ethridge farm hunting pork?"

The tone of Constable Harkness's voice had become a sour and hollow shell of sarcasm. Samuel was silent. Mr. and Mrs. Martin were growing both increasingly confused and increasing alarmed.

"If that was what you were there doing, I can see why you would want to lie about it," Constable Harkness went on, the sarcastic tone in his voice remaining unchanged. "There's no law against shooting pheasants in season, and there's no law against running off prowling wolves. There is, however, a law against poaching livestock. The law carries some stiff penalties for making off with another man's stock. In the Wild West, up until a short time ago, they used to hang men for cattle rustling. So I can see why you would want to keep any pig shooting on your part a guarded secret. But then again, I suppose the degree to which you would want to keep your pig shooting activities covered up depends on your definition of a pig and the kind of pig you shoot."

Samuel hadn't stopped to think that his boot prints might be unique among the footprints of the other hired hands who worked the Ethridge farm. In a literal sense, he had discovered that he hadn't covered his tracks as well as he had thought. Indeed, he hadn't covered his tracks at all.

"Were you over at the Ethridge place hunting sows?" Constable Harkness asked in a rhetorical tone that was a continuance of the sour tone he had been using.

"No," Samuel said as weakly as ever. He could have confessed to attempted poaching and livestock rustling as a way of explaining his presence at the Ethridge farm, but that would only place him at the murder scene with his only defense being a claim that he had been there at a different time and that someone else had killed Harold Ethridge later. That would be far too risky of a tactic. The only fallback strategy that seemed open to him was to lie and deny it and say that someone else must have the same boots as he and that he must have picked the smell of pig somewhere else. At least he decided not to invent another, even more implausible story like the story of his phantom wolf hunt, a story that would put him at the scene of the crime.

The constable rolled the boots back over in his hands and held them upright. "Well, whatever you were hunting, your efforts weren't as fruitless as you indicated," he said. "From the looks of these boots, you apparently drew blood after all."

With the tip of the knife blade, the constable pointed to one of several small brown spots on the tops of the boots. "If I don't miss my guess, these are dried blood spots on your boots."

The spots weren't rounded, and they didn't stand above the surface of the boot leather like spots of dried mud would. They were flush with the surface, where they looked like they had sunk into the leather.

"They aren't splatters of mud, clay, or even manure. They look like dried blood to me. Along with shooting hogs on Harold Ethridge's land, were you dressing them out there too? Or did you bring them back here?"

Constable Harkness had been looking at the boots while he was talking. At that point he stopped in the middle of his narrative and stared down at one of the boots. He quickly wiped the clay off the point of the knife on his vest and then started probing down in the hidden part of the boot between the two flaps, where the boot was still laced. What he was probing at looked like a small dried strip of outer skin over a dried brown layer of underlying tissue that was red when it had been fresh.

"And that doesn't look like pork rind or a piece of old fatback to me."

Constable Harkness held up the boot for Samuel to see. He pointed with the tip of the knife to indicate the undefined piece that looked like dried flesh.

"I don't know what kind of medical detective tricks Doc Simpson has up his sleeve or in his black bag, but he has a microscope. I'll bet you if he puts this under his microscope, he will identify this for what it looks like: a piece of shredded human flesh. He was an army doctor in his earlier years. He knows very well how far pieces of the human body can go flying in all directions when you blow a hole in someone at close range with a big-caliber gun."

The other members of Samuel's family looked quickly at each other. Samuel didn't move his head; he looked straight at Constable Harkness. The constable looked at him.

"Constable, just what is this all about?" Samuel's mother said, the rising tone of her voice following along with her rising alarm.

"Let me tell you about another hunting expedition that took place around here recently," the constable answered by way of indirection, momentarily turning his head only partway toward Mrs. Martin, "a hunting expedition that has a lot in common with the hunting expedition your son has just elaborated two conflicting versions of. This hunting expedition also involves exactly four shots from a shotgun firing black powder."

Constable Harkness focused his look squarely on Samuel. "The difference being that, unlike your excursion after wily pheasants, the expedition that never took place, or your equally futile chasing after the pack of ghost wolves that no one else seems to have seen or reported, this hunting expedition found its mark and brought down its target. And there wasn't any waste of ammunition involved. All four shots found their target. And all four shots were needed as the target involved was big game. Bigger than a wolf even. But then I guess that depends on what the hunter involved was defining as a wolf."

Constable Harkness turned to look at Mr. Martin. In his mind the investigation was over. The final evidence was in, and it was there in quantity. At this late stage, his confidence was as high as it would ever be. He saw no reason to be coy any longer. That being said, he took no pleasure in having solved the case or in what he would have to say next. Neither did he see any reason to put off what had to be said.

"I assume you've heard the news about the murder of Harold Ethridge?" Constable Harkness asked in an economy of opening words. "If not from the paper, then by word of mouth. The news has been all over town for the last few days. It seems there hasn't been any other topic of conversation in the town itself since the killing."

"Yes, I heard the news," Samuel's father said. "But the paper and everyone else says the killer was either a hired hand with a grudge or a madman. My son is neither. What does the killing of Mr. Ethridge have to do with my son?"

"As far as the killer being a madman goes, I guess that depends on what you're mad about and how mad you are about it," Constable Harkness said. "What it has to do with your son is that the prints of your son's boots were found both leading to and going away from the Ethridge farm. They were found all over the floor of the hog barn, where the killer had crouched in wait for Mr. Ethridge." Constable Harkness elevated Samuel's boots. "But your son's boots turn up back here smelling of pig manure, when you don't maintain hogs on this farm."

The expression on Mr. Martin's face remained frozen in its suspended position. Samuel's mother's mouth was starting to open. Her face was growing increasingly worried. An increasingly alarmed-looking Beth took a step closer in. The tone of Constable Harkness's voice was rising in timbre and certainty.

"What are you implying?" Samuel's father asked.

"Harold Ethridge was killed with a double-barrel twelve-gauge shotgun firing double-aught buckshot black powder shells," Constable Harkness said in reply. "We know it was a twelve-gauge by the size of the shotgun shell wads left at the scene. We can pretty much tell it was a double-barrel gun by the pattern of the two final wounds. We know it fired double-aught buckshot by measuring the size of the shot. We know that four shots were fired because we can count the number of pellets and the number of wads left at the scene. We know it fired black powder shells because we found black powder grains embedded in Mr. Ethridge's face, what was left of it." He pointed to the shotgun leaning against the end table. "Your shotgun turns up smelling of having been fired recently, when you claim it hasn't been fired in years, except for your son's abortive hunt for phantom wolves, which he didn't tell you about. At the same time, a box of black powder double-aught buckshot shells turns up with four shells missing. You can't explain the use of the gun, but your son offers a story of how he went hunting for pheasants with it, a story that he later changed to one of hunting after wolves that haven't made an appearance in this area since the days of the first settlers."

The constable waved the boots again. "He claims to have hit nothing, yet his boots turn up with drops of dried blood spray on them." Constable Harkness pointed with the tip of the knife blade at the small strip that had dried intertwined in the laces of the boot. "His boots also turn up with fragments of what I'm quite sure will prove to be the remains of Harold Ethridge's face, which splattered on his boots from where he stood over him and fired into his head from near-point-blank range!"

The alarm among Samuel's family became complete. Samuel's mother and sister gasped with their mouths open. His father's face and brow became more furrowed than it was already from a lifetime of farming. Samuel's face drained the rest of the way.

"Why the hell would he do something like that?!" Samuel's father exploded, his voice rising suddenly from a tone of respectful deference toward designated authority figures to one of steel trap defense of a son accused of a capital crime. "We don't even know Harold Ethridge. We have no contact with him. My son doesn't work for him. He never has worked for him. My son has no grudge against him. There isn't a family rivalry between us and him. We haven't crossed paths or crossed swords in any way. My son has absolutely no reason to do Mr. Ethridge any harm. And he has no reason to kill him in the way you're saying that he did."

"I beg to differ with you, sir, on almost all those points," Constable Harkness said. "As you say, there may not have been a blood feud family rivalry between your family and Mr. Ethridge like often happens between backwoods mountain families, but your son had a blood issue with Harold Ethridge that was as big as they get. He had a grudge as big and primal as any grudge can be. That grudge drove him into a state of uncontrollable anger and lust for vengeance. It was the passion of that anger that led to the passionate way in which he killed Mr. Ethridge."

"What could Mr. Ethridge possibly have done to my brother that would make him so bloodlust mad?" Beth jumped in with her own defense. "It's just not in my brother's nature to think like that or to do something like that. Why would he kill Ethridge?"

Constable Harkness looked back full into Samuel's face. He spoke into Samuel's face as he answered Beth's questions. "Harold Ethridge butchered the girl he was in love with!" he said, the tone and rumble of his voice rising rapidly. "He broke her neck and threw her into the river to drown. He took the life of the sweetheart whom your brother loved more than his own life."

Constable Harkness glanced back at Beth Martin. "An offense like that done to a man can drive a man out of his mind. It can change his very nature to the core and drive him to do things he wouldn't have considered the day before. In your brother's mind, Harold Ethridge took everything he had. From the minute he found out he was the killer, your brother became obsessed with taking as much from Harold Ethridge as he had taken from him and the girl. Maybe he didn't show it to you, but I saw that passion tearing out of him and tearing him apart when he saw the girl's body. At the time he just didn't know whom to vent it on yet."

Constable Harkness looked back at Samuel. "When you were in the station house identifying her body, you had enough fury in you for a dozen men. You had enough hate in you to kill a dozen men. You just didn't know who killed her any more than I did. You vented most of the anger you spilled that day by yelling at me and accusing me of not being interested in finding who killed her. You didn't quite storm out of the station house shouting that you were going to exact bloody vengeance the way Mrs.

Richardson and her pumpkinseed girl said you did in front of them. I guess you figured that wouldn't go over very well and would make you a suspect if you ever did find the girl's killer and kill him in retribution. But you made your anger plain enough, and it was plain enough that you had it in mind to break the neck of the man who had murdered the girl."

"Oh, so now you're saying that she was murdered!" Samuel said. "It's a bit late for justice on her behalf, but now you're willing to admit that she was killed by someone. At least you're not sweeping her killing under the rug just because she was a whore and you think whores aren't worth anything."

"I always said she had been murdered, boy. The doc said she had been killed. I never denied that. If you had listened to me instead of to the sound of your own accusations, you would have heard me say that. I just didn't know who had killed her at the time any more than you did." He leaned back as far as he had leaned in. "But you found out ahead of me, didn't you? You found out when that pudding-headed, tongue-tied girl of Mrs. Richardson's remembered that the girl had once referred to the man she was seeing by the nickname of Mr. Bearcat. You knew right away that it could only have been Harold Ethridge she had been referring to as he was the only person in the county who owned a Stutz Bearcat car. According to the girl, you charged out of there with enough fury in you to kill a dozen men."

Mrs. Martin looked at her husband. Mr. Martin looked at the constable. Arthur the policeman and Sergeant Plechathy looked on silently.

"But instead of either you or Mrs. Richardson coming to me with what you knew, you both went your own way with what was inside you. You went running off like a raging lion to grab the first gun you could get your hands on in your father's gun cabinet. You should have come to me instead of taking the law into your own hands. If I could have brought Ethridge to trial, I might have been able to prove that he killed the girl. Now he's dead. You've put him beyond any possibility of being tried and formally convicted. What he did will never be aired in public. People will probably never be convinced that he was a killer. But now you'll be branded a killer for the rest of your life. In the end the girl is just as dead. But you've thrown your life on an ash heap. Is this what you call getting justice for her?"

"And what the hell would you have done?!" Samuel exploded, the intensity of his voice as high as Constable Harkness's. "You weren't doing anything about her killing. You probably didn't think a dead prostitute was worth your time and effort, and you probably didn't want to convict any man who killed a prostitute."

"You said all that back then," Constable Harkness snapped.

"And it still stands!" Samuel said, his voice on the brink of a shout. "You probably didn't have the slightest interest in finding and convicting the man who killed a girl you considered to be a two-bit whore, especially if it was a rich and influential man. For all I know, you probably knew from the first day who killed her, but you didn't want to send him up because he was the richest man in town and you thought a prostitute was beneath him and beneath you!"

Mrs. Martin was growing more alarmed at the rising tone of the exchange between the police chief and her son. Mr. Martin was growing alarmed that his son was vehemently protesting the constable's attitudes toward the girl and the slowness and inconclusiveness of his investigation of her death instead of vehemently protesting his innocence of the crime the police chief had come to arrest him for. His son's angry focus on the girl, to the exclusion of denying his involvement in the crime at hand, was only making him look guiltier.

"I'm getting a little tired of having people accuse me of turning my back on murder like I didn't care about the killing of a young girl because she was a prostitute any more than I would care about someone killing a spider," Constable Harkness growled. "I got the same crap from Mrs. Richardson. Now I'm getting it in spades from you. It seems that before either of you jumped to your anarchist class-conscious conclusions, and before you jumped to your shotgun, you could have given me the benefit of the doubt. I would have arrested him then for her murder if I had the information and evidence I have now."

"I have only your word on that," Samuel said, echoing what Mrs. Richardson had said earlier that day. "As for evidence, I didn't see any evidence of you moving toward pointing the finger at anyone for killing her. You sure as hell weren't burning the midnight oil and burning up the trail looking for her killer. It was a month and you still hadn't made an arrest. You hadn't even said one word about the case after you gave the story to the newspaper. You were probably sitting back, not doing one thing about investigating the case."

Samuel pointed over at the other two town law officers. "You and they were probably sitting around the station house playing cards as her body went cold. You probably deliberately let the case go cold. You dumped her case as fast as the killer dumped her body in the river. You were probably just as happy to be rid of a trashy and bothersome little whore as he was."

"I hadn't moved on the case because I didn't have any evidence that pointed conclusively to anyone," Constable Harkness growled defensively. "If I had wanted to arrest someone for her killing just to make myself look good, I would have arrested you. You were the hothead getting into fights over her. Hotheaded men have been known to kill girlfriends they know are seeing other men. But I knew you couldn't have done it because I saw you at the potluck supper at the time that Doc Simpson said Ethridge had been killed. I didn't arrest you because I was going on evidence. I would have made an arrest if I had conclusive evidence. But I wasn't looking to make an arrest just to build a public record for myself."

"For the public record, the public in this town probably didn't give a damn about her or that she had been killed any more than you did," Samuel interjected. "To the men in this town, she was just something to be used and discarded. Someone took that to the final stage. The fact that she was killed didn't cause one-tenth as much of a stir in this town as the killing of Harold Ethridge has. They would have let her float away down the river like she was a dead alley cat. An alley cat was what they thought of her when she was alive. It's his killing that's got everyone boiled over and sweating about around here. It's his killing you've got to make an arrest for."

"It's his killing we've got the evidence for," Constable Harkness said with official confidence. "And all that evidence points right at you from a dozen directions."

"So now you turn up here saying that Harold Ethridge was a murderer after all," Samuel went on, unsure where he was going with it. "Now that Harold Ethridge is gone, you acknowledge that he did kill her after all. You made a ringing affirmation out of it. But it's all first-time news to me. You didn't say one word to that effect or even hint at the possibility of him being a killer while he was still alive and the richest and most influential man in town."

"I didn't say anything about it before because I didn't have the evidence," Constable Harkness reiterated. "I didn't have evidence that pointed to anybody in either case until just a few hours ago. It all came together for both cases today. The one case pointed to the other. The one solved the other. At least it pointed to the likely killer." Constable Harkness's voice lowered a notch. "The trouble was that it was the death of Harold Ethridge that shook loose the evidence that solved both killings, hers and his."

"And what was this evidence that you didn't have then?" Samuel asked, a tone of sour skepticism still in his voice.

"The fact that the girl was seen heading to the house she was probably killed in," Constable Harkness said as he started to lay out his case. After his self-confessed blundering in the matter, he felt he owed the boy at least that much. "The Ethridge house. The fact that Ethridge was the secret man she had been seeing. The fact that it was Ethridge who bailed the girl out the night you and she were arrested for the brawl you started in Charlie's saloon."

Samuel's head picked up. He hadn't known that.

"The fact that Ethridge said that he had relations with the girl that night. The fact that he lied and said that he hadn't seen her after the first time, but she was seen heading in the direction of his house the night she disappeared three weeks later. The fact that the girl was calling her secret client 'Mr. Bearcat' weeks after Ethridge said he'd stopped seeing her. The imprint of Harold Ethridge's ring driven into her jaw and frozen in place by her death that followed shortly after."

The constable elevated the knife in his hand.

"The fact that Mrs. Richardson said that this knife belonged to the girl and that she carried it with her everywhere she went. That it disappeared the night she disappeared, so she must have had it with her. The fact that it turned up in Harold Ethridge's possession, as well as his chest, proves you must have found it on him. The fact that when Doctor Simpson examined Harold Ethridge's body, he found a month-old healed cut on his neck, a cut made by something with a blade like this knife. All of that came out today."

It registered on Samuel that one piece of the evidence had to be older than this same-day evidence the chief constable was laying out.

"You said that Harold Ethridge was the one who bailed the girl out of jail the night she was arrested with me?" Samuel asked.

"Yes," Constable Harkness said. Future generations of judges in more formal legal settings would probably have instructed him not to discuss a pending case, but in the more informal setting of turn-of-the-century small country town law enforcement, he considered both cases closed.

"When your sergeant came down and let the girl out of the cell that night, nobody told me who had bailed her out," Samuel said. "I thought it was Mrs. Richardson who had paid her bail. I didn't think to ask."

"I was the one at the desk that night," Sergeant Plechathy said. "Mr. Ethridge didn't want you informed that it was he who bailed her out. He said he was afraid that you might take out after him in a jealous rage the way you took after the man she was propositioning in the saloon."

"We weren't sitting on our dead butts as you think," Constable Harkness said. "We interviewed him after we found out the girl was going to his place in secret at night."

"You had Ethridge in your hands as a suspect the day the girl was found dead?" Samuel said. "And you let him walk?"

"We had other suspects who were suspects from that same day," Constable Harkness said. "At the time we couldn't connect him directly to the crime any more than we could connect him."

"But you had more of a connection between him and her than you did between her and some hypothetical hired hand or back-alley thug whom you didn't even have the name of or a shadow of," Samuel said. "But apparently you didn't dig any deeper than Harold Ethridge's name or his position on the town council, or the balance in his bank account. You say you would have arrested him for killing the girl if you had known then that he was her killer. But when you had him in your hands, you soft-pedaled the investigation and headed it off into a dead-end alley. The question is why. Were you trying to protect him, or was it just incompetence on your part? Did you bungle the case, or did you let him go knowing what he'd done because you thought that any established first citizen and dandy from the town was worth more than the life of a soiled woman from outside?"

Constable Harkness was silent for a moment. He disliked the charge of incompetence as much as he disliked the charge of favoritism and turning a blind eye to murder. Yet they were dealing with mortal issues that day in the parlor of the Martin farmhouse. The boy was facing capital charges that could put him in mortal danger. Constable Harkness wasn't by nature a big mea culpa man. At the same time, he felt that he owed the boy at least some explanation and some degree of apology for his partial failure.

"I suppose I haven't been the best cop in town or in the world," Constable Harkness said in a subdued voice. "I missed things I should have picked up on. I should have looked closer when I knew that he had bailed the girl out. He was wearing a bandage on his neck when we talked to him about what he knew about the girl. I should have made him take it off and looked closer at the cut on his neck instead of taking at face value his word that he had cut himself shaving. I should have asked around more as to whether anyone had seen the girl the night she disappeared. Maybe I could have jogged old Horace Thompson's failing memory earlier. I didn't get around to thinking like I should have. I didn't get around to asking the questions I should have asked about her murder until after the murder of Harold Ethridge made me look where I should have been looking. I was looking out a back window, when his murder kicked open the front door."

The constable gave Samuel a slight nod. "And, yes, I suppose one of the reasons I didn't drill him like I should have, one of the reasons that I didn't suspect him any more than I did, was because I couldn't believe that a respected and respectable member of town society would be involved with murder, especially the murder of a young girl. I just went off suspecting that she had been killed by one of her own kind from the wrong side of town and the wrong side of respectability. Whether you believe me or not is up to you. I can only tell you that I would have gone after Ethridge if I had known that he had killed the girl, whore or not. As far as class roots and distinctions go for me, I was a poor farm boy myself before I became a law enforcement officer. I prefer poor farm boys who love girls, even dirty ones, over rich upstanding members of the community who kill them. But as it is, it's all moot now. ... I don't know if the evidence I have now would have been enough to convict him in a jury trial. I think the evidence is solid, but a jury might not have found it so, especially if they didn't want to find it that way. The jury might have taken that cut on his neck as evidence that the girl attacked him and that he had killed her in self-defense. Given his social position, I don't know if a jury would have been willing to convict him even if they believed the evidence."

Constable Harkness wasn't sure in his own mind what he was trying to accomplish. He wasn't sure whether he was trying to empty his feelings that he had failed, or was trying to make the boy feel better, or was hoping just to make him feel more fatalistic. All he managed to accomplish was to convince Samuel that Harold Ethridge would have never been brought to justice for the murder of Clarinda. In Samuel's estimate of the situation, one way or the other, Ethridge would have walked free of killing the girl. If the constable had been trying to empty his soul of the feeling that he had failed as a policeman, that part of it escaped Samuel. All he left Samuel with was the conviction and the final justified feeling that his personal vengeance had been the only justice that could have been procured for the girl. In Samuel's view of the moment, there had been no other option back then any more than he could see any option before him now. Standing motionless in the parlor of his home, facing the actions of his past that he had taken with his own hands and facing his future in the form of Constable Harkness and his arresting officers, Samuel felt both the future and the past were closing in on him and down around him.

"Maybe I could have caught on and caught him without his murder's having shaken loose the evidence that put it all together. Maybe I wouldn't have. Maybe I could have convicted him in a court of law, or maybe I wouldn't have been able to. I suppose neither of us will ever know now."

"If you wouldn't have been able to convict him in a court of law, then what good is your vaunted law?!" Samuel said, biting hard at his words. "And what good is all this vaunted evidence you say you now have? You said yourself that you wouldn't even have the evidence if ..."

Samuel's words froze in his mouth. He had been about to say *If I hadn't killed him for you.* That wouldn't have exactly enhanced what little of the evaporating defense was still left to him. Instead his words ended, silence hanging in the air.

"If what, boy?" Constable Harkness said in a rising tone, jumping with both feet into the silence left by Samuel's sudden pause.

"If someone hadn't killed him," Samuel rallied. "You said that you gathered most of this evidence just today. Now you're willing to say that it points to Ethridge. It all comes a little late for Clarinda's purposes. None of it or your law could have brought justice for her. None of it could have saved her life."

"By definition, all evidence of murder comes too late for the person killed," Constable Harkness said. "Evidence of murder is generated while the murder is being committed. It's all seen after the fact. There wasn't any evidence that Ethridge killed the girl until he killed her. That should be obvious enough to you. It wasn't my lateness in acquiring evidence that killed her. Having the evidence I have now wouldn't have saved her life back then. She didn't die because I was slow on registering on the evidence. My postmortem blundering didn't leave her out there to die. She died because she walked into danger on her own."

All of which reminded Samuel that the girl had been killed because he hadn't been walking with her, and now he would never walk with her again in this world.

"Now you're saying it was her fault that she was killed," Samuel said in growing anger.

"I'm saying Ethridge killed her before anyone knew he had it in him to be a killer," Constable Harkness said back in a voice just as hard. "She put herself in harm's way, in the way of the kind of men who think to use women and then be done with them. He just went one step further. That was her doing, her choice. Policemen can't readily stop people from making stupid and dangerous choices in advance. We get called out to clean up the mess left behind after people make their bad choices. And she made as bad of a choice as they come when she handed herself to Ethridge. She would have done a lot better for herself if she had stayed with you and been home in this house fixing dinner for you and your family, instead of handing herself over to men like Ethridge for a handful of dollars."

Samuel gritted his teeth and twisted internally. The constable might as well have driven the knife he was holding into his chest and twisted it the way Samuel himself had done to Ethridge. Saying the girl should have been with him in his house as his wife and a member of the family went to the heart of the life he wanted and the dream that he had dreamt of the girl, the life and dream that had died with her. Whatever his feelings of having bungled the investigation of her killing were for the constable, he was right that he probably couldn't have prevented her death. He hadn't been the one close to her. He hadn't been the one for whom her life meant more to him than his own. Samuel felt that he had been the one far better positioned to protect and deliver her. The constable was right that the police could only clean up after her death. At that moment in time, Samuel was sure he could have saved the girl from having been killed if he had only acted better—and the less he felt that he had been better positioned to do that recklessly. She had died in the interim of the moratorium she had placed on their seeing each other after he had started the barroom brawl that had driven her away from him. In his mind he had blundered far more than the police had. And he had blundered from a position where he could have prevented her death. That the girl had been killed went straight to the heart of his own feelings that he had failed her and that she had died as a result of his failure, not the constable's. A trembling and almost uncontrollable rage rose in him. Not rage against the constable, but an equal amount of rage against Harold Ethridge for having killed the girl and against himself for having driven the girl away from him and having sent her into the path of the man who killed her.

"And now, after she's dead and cold, you finally get around to admitting that Ethridge was the one who killed her!" Samuel said in a voice trembling with anger. "Now you say you have all the evidence you need. Now that it can't do her a damned bit of good. You might as well carve your evidence on the back of her tombstone for all the good it will do her and for all the justice your evidence would have provided her."

"At least I have evidence that is halfway credible and points directly to murder," Constable Harkness responded, his own voice rising again. "Like the ring that made the cut on her face. What evidence did you have? All the evidence you had was another of Mrs. Richardson's girls telling you that your girl had called Ethridge by the nickname of Mr. Bearcat. That was all you had to go on. On the basis of that and that only, you went charging out with a loaded shotgun in your hand to blow a man's head off, a man who, for all you knew or cared to know, might have been innocent. Ethridge lied when he said that he had patronized the girl only once and hadn't seen her after that. But he may have just been lying to limit damage to his public image. By itself that lie isn't proof of murder. But that was all you had. And you acted on it in an irreversible way. When you went charging out of your door in a mindless fury and into Ethridge's door in the same fury, did you ever stop anywhere along the line to think that you may be shooting an innocent man?"

"Oh, he wasn't innocent," Samuel snapped back, whiplashing himself past the brink of control. "When he thought he had the upper hand and thought he had the best of me, he confessed all over the place with a sick smile on his face."

Samuel's words froze in his throat again, but this time his voice froze on the wrong side of his words. Samuel's mother gasped. The alarm doubled on his father's face.

"Oh really!" Constable Harkness pounced. "He made a full confession to you, did he? Congratulations on your detective work, boy. Once again you're out ahead of me. And just when and how did you extract this confession?" He pointed to the gun leaning against the end table. "While you were waving that shotgun under his nose?"

Samuel didn't say anything. His mind raced, trying to think of a way out of the tar pit he had just stepped into.

"Well, come now, boy," Constable Harkness went on, pushing deeper into the breech, "don't be modest. You've accomplished a great feat. You've solved the second murder in the history of this town; you did it all on your own without the help of the police; and you got a confession out of the perpetrator to boot."

Samuel's words had failed him with the girl. Now they failed him entirely. He was still unable to say anything.

"That must have been one hell of a convincing and graphic confession. You summarily executed him the minute he got the words out of his mouth. As a policeman you're an effective interrogator, but as judge, jury, and executioner, you don't waste any time or allow for much of any appeal process. Or did you make him beg the way the girl may have begged him not to kill her?"

Constable Harkness knew it was over. But the boy's blurted-out confession was otherwise incidental. He had him on evidence. He could convict him on evidence even if the boy had remained as closemouthed as a clam. He had dropped the ball where it had come to the girl, but his hunch about the boy had been right on the money from the start. The boy had only handed him the final ribbon to tie it all up. It was the story he had suspected from the beginning, but not the one he wanted or would have chosen.

"If he confessed, you must have been the one there to take the confession. Before you took his head off. So tell me all about his confession. We might be able to tie the ribbons on two cases in one day, the killing of the girl and the killing of Harold Ethridge. While you're at it, tell me how you extracted the confession. It is rather germane to whether his confession actually wraps up the girl's murder or not. Confessions extracted under duress or threat are often, if not usually, discounted as being invalid. Ethridge might have just been saying anything to keep you from killing him. Give me the details of his confession so that I can see if it jibes with the evidence I have. If you want any kind of justice for the girl, even if it's only me pronouncing to the town and to the world that it was Harold Ethridge who killed her, you're going to have to first convince me that his confession was real and not coerced. So tell me all about it, boy. But don't try to take back what you said. Don't tell me that you stumbled over your words and they came out backward. Don't tell me you meant to say *white* and it came out *black* instead. Don't tell me that you didn't mean what you just said about him confessing."

Constable Harkness held up the boots once again. "Don't try going back on your confession. I don't need your confession that you were there. These boots speak as loudly."

Samuel knew it was over.

"Yes, I was there!" Samuel exploded in the only direction he saw open to him. "Yes, I killed him! If it's a confession you want, I'll give you that. But I won't give you my regrets. Ask me why I killed him, but don't ask me for repentance!"

Samuel's mother's eyes went wide open. Her hands flew up and covered her mouth. A strangled sound that was half "no" and half moan escaped around her hands. With the shocked look unchanged on her face, she slumped into the nearest chair. Beth quickly came around to her side and put her hands on her mother's shoulders. Mr. Martin's face went ashen.

"I assume you killed him because he killed the girl," Constable Harkness said redundantly.

"Yes, I killed him because he killed her," Samuel said. "He didn't waste an ounce of sympathy on her, and he didn't hold back an ounce of his strength when he broke her neck. I didn't hold back on him, and I haven't wasted a single tear on him. The only thing I regretted not wasting on him was more ammunition. And I won't shed any phony tears in front of any judge or jury you care to drag me in front of, trying to get them to go easy on me. He sent her headfirst into the river, crippled with a broken neck, to drown. I sent him to hell. It will be a frozen-over day in the place I sent him before I will feel even the beginnings of sorrow for sending him there."

"So you just walked right in on him and drew down on him," Constable Harkness said.

"Oh no," Samuel said in an end line sour and hollow voice. "It wasn't that way at all."

"Then just how was it?" Constable Harkness asked.

"I didn't charge in there shouting and shooting. I knew as well you did that someone else might have killed her in the night on the street and that there was a chance Ethridge might be innocent. I didn't want to kill an innocent man. I had to know for myself that he was guilty. So I arranged things in such a way that he would go running off his mouth about her. Which is exactly what he did when he thought that he was going to go running over me the way he had run over her."

"That was the confession you say you got out of him?" Constable Harkness asked.

"Oh, he confessed all right," Samuel said, still operating under a full head of steam. "Before I spilled his pig brains on the pig room floor, he spilled his arrogance and his contempt for her all over the place. He didn't think any more of her than he did a stray cat. That's the way he thought of all women, respectable or not. And he thought of her as little more than trash he could dispose of at his whim. He killed her with as little thought as he would have killed a field rat he found in his barn. He didn't say it in quite those exact words, but the words he used were close enough."

"And I suppose that after he confessed, you ran home to get your father's shotgun?" Constable Harkness scoffed. "And he was still there waiting for you when you returned?"

"I had snuck in earlier and hidden the shotgun in the hog barn ahead of time," Samuel clarified. "I walked in on him through the main door like I had come straight there. When I walked in on him, I wasn't carrying anything in my hands. The shotgun was already there, hidden where he couldn't see it, on the other side of the barn. But I knew where it was. I wanted him to think that I was there alone, accusing him of murder, without any witnesses seeing me and knowing what was going on. I doubt he would have confessed anything if there was anyone else looking on. I had to make him think he was in charge and on top of the situation the way he had felt in control and on top of everything when he killed the girl. I also wanted him to think that I was crazy enough to go up against him alone with only my fists."

"I suppose after confessing murder to you, h turned and showed you the door, asking you politely to leave?" Constable Harkness asked with deliberate skepticism.

"I told him I was going to the police with what I knew," Samuel said. "He didn't want that getting out. He took it into his mind that he was going to kill me to keep me quiet. But I figured he would probably try something like that. That's where the second part of the way I made him think I was crazy came in. He really thought I had come there unarmed. That's when he grabbed the brush knife and said he was going to try to kill me with a brush knife and then claim that I had come at him raging crazy jealous the way I had with that hired hand in Charlie's saloon. He said he'd say that he had been forced to kill me in self-defense."

"Did he say that to your face?" Constable Harkness asked.

"He said that to my face while his face was still intact," Samuel replied. "That's when he started coming at me with his knife. I let him back me up to where I had the gun hidden. He thought he had the best of me. He thought he was in charge. That's when I pulled the shotgun out from the trough of hog feed, where I had hidden it earlier. I was in charge then. His tone and the smug look on his face changed real fast when he saw the gun. He knew he was finished."

"Are you saying that shooting him was an act of self-defense?" Constable Harkness asked.

"In the sense that he would have killed me to shut me up if I hadn't been armed."

"Did he stop coming at you when you pulled the gun on him?"

"Yes. That's when his expression changed, when he knew it was all over for him."

"Doc Simpson says it looks to him that you shot him twice while he was in a standing position. Had he started coming on again when you fired the first time?"

"He was still stopped when I fired," Samuel said. "When he went down, I turned my back on him. He tried to jump up and rush me again, this time with that knife in his hand. I knocked him down again with the second shot. He didn't get back up after that."

"Doc Simpson says you fired the last two shots both barrels at the same time, standing over him at close range. Is that the way it happened?"

"Pretty much so. I told him I was going to send him to hell, and then I sent him there."

"If you're planning on arguing self-defense, I don't know if a jury is going to buy it," Constable Harkness said, giving his estimate of how it would play out in a courtroom. "He didn't come into your house with an ax. You went into his place with a gun. You had the drop on him. They probably won't see it as self-defense. They'll probably see it as a summary execution. Especially firing into his face at close range the way you did."

But then a summary execution is what it had been.

Constable Harkness held up the knife. "You say he pulled this on you before you fired the second time?"

"No. He came at me with a brush-blade knife like I said. I pulled the shotgun out of where I had hidden it. He stopped, and I started walking toward him. He looked like he was planning to throw the knife at me when I got closer. At that point I fired. I knew the first shot hadn't killed him. I turned my back on him and gave him a chance to jump up at me and come at me again. I figured he would try something like that. He did—and I finished him."

"The way you killed him, you've got the whole town thinking there's a madman on the loose in everybody's midst. Is that why you also stabbed him and left the knife in his chest? Were you trying to make people think there was a Jack the Ripper running around the town so they wouldn't suspect you?"

"The knife used to be hers."

"Oh, then you do recognize it."

"Yes. She carried it everywhere. She said she had used it to escape from her brother who was trying to rape her. I don't know if she thought of it as a good luck charm or, after what had happened to her, she was just afraid to walk around unarmed. When I saw it fall out of his pocket, I recognized it right away. He must have taken it from her when he killed her. That was the final piece of proof that he was her killer. All I could think of was how she must have panicked when she realized that something even worse was about to happen than what her family had done to her. At that point I lost control and went crazy. In my mind, all I could hear was her screaming. I just kept driving her knife into the heart Ethridge didn't have over and over again. I kept stabbing him until I couldn't hear her screaming anymore. I left the jackknife sticking out of him as one small bit of justice and triumph for her. I didn't think anyone would know where it had come from."

"I figured it was something like that," Constable Harkness said. Then he shifted directions in a way that was a bit of a surprise to Samuel.

"Did Ethridge say why he killed the girl?" Constable Harkness asked.

"Not exactly word for word," Samuel said. "At the time he was distracted, concentrating on how he was going to kill me. But from what he did say about her, it was obvious that he considered her beneath contempt. In the short period of time when he was still talking before I drew down on him, he went on about her in a way that sounded like she had done something to offend his arrogant, superior self. He thought no more of her than he did of the pig manure I left him in. All he was saying was like both she and I were bothersome pieces of trash he could dispose of anytime or in any way he cared to."

Samuel fell silent. Constable Harkness offered no direct response. For a moment he too was silent.

"The one question I have left is whether you did this on your own or whether you had help," Constable Harkness said, taking it in his final direction. "It's all pretty clever how you went about tricking Ethridge into the confession like you said you did. Did you think it all up, or did someone help you with the idea?"

"It was Ethridge's own arrogance and sense that he was on top of things that led him to confess and confess smiling the way he did," Samuel said. "He confessed casually, arrogantly, and openly. He confessed because he thought he was going to get away with killing both her and me."

"Did you have help from anyone in implementing your plan?" Constable Harkness went on. He pointed to Samuel's father. "Did he know what you were planning on doing? Did he give you the gun?"

A wave of alarm as great as any his parents were feeling swept through Samuel. When they took him away to jail, the farm would lose its youngest and strongest worker. But his father would still be there to work the farm and keep it going. If they arrested and jailed his father as an accessory to the killing of Harold Ethridge, he would probably spend the rest of his declining years in jail. There would be no men left in the household. Samuel's mother and sister would be left to run the farm on their own. Samuel didn't think they had the ability to manage it by themselves. They would be forced to turn to outside help to run the farm. In the process, they would probably end up swindled by every shyster and crook in the world and taken advantage of by every two-bit cheat and sneak thief of a hired hand they took on to run the farm. The farm would be swindled whole away from them or be stolen piecemeal out from under them. The family would disintegrate and disappear. His mother and sister would eventually be thrown off the farm and end up in poverty on the street.

"He didn't have anything to do with it!" Samuel exploded as loudly as he had when he had confessed. "I didn't tell anybody what I was planning to do. I snuck the shotgun out of the house without anybody seeing. I did it all by myself. I did it all on my own without any help from anybody." He pointed to his father and the rest of his family. "They didn't know anything about this. You've got me. I pulled the triggers. You don't need anybody else. I'll confess in front of any judge you want, but leave them out of this!"

"Fair enough," Constable Harkness said.

At that moment, for Samuel, fair didn't have a lot to do with it on either end of the scale of justice. That he had possibly saved his father from prison and the rest of his family from dissolution was something he was thankful for, but it didn't change anything for him or the girl. To avenge her murder and vent his anger, he had set his course and set himself on that course. That he had been caught after the act of murder was neither fair nor unfair to Samuel. It was as it was.

With one hand, Constable Harkness closed the knife blade and looked at Samuel. He spoke in a voice neither hard with pretrial judgment nor moderated by sentiment. "For what it's worth to you, boy, if I had been in your place and someone had killed the sweetheart I loved as much as you loved her, I probably would have done the same thing." He put the knife in his pocket. "But from the personal and legal sides of it, I just

579

can't forget about this and pretend like it didn't happen. The whole town thinks they've got a madman in their midst. People are arming themselves and going around in a nervous Saint Vitus's dance looking over their shoulders at everyone who's an outsider or who looks the slightest bit suspicious. They want the killer caught, and they want proof of who he is and why he killed. I have to give them the killer, and I have to give them the evidence and the reasons. Beyond that, I am also a peace officer and a sworn upholder of the law. I can't sweep all that under the rug and walk away from it just because I understand how you felt and why you did it."

Samuel felt the last part of his world fall out from under him. Having wrapped up the investigation, they would wrap up the remainder of his life and take him into custody. Whether they would put manacles on his hands and feet, Samuel didn't know. But they would march him out of the parlor and out of the house he had grown up in, the house that had been the center of the only life he had ever known. He would go quietly. From the small cell in the basement of the station house, he would be eventually transferred to a state penitentiary. Provided he was not hanged for the murder, he would spend the rest of his life in the narrow corridors and confined cells of the prison. The stone floor halls of the prison would be his home for the rest of his life. He would not walk the familiar halls of his own house. He would not return to the halls of Mrs. Richardson's house. He would not be a farmer. He would not have the family he had grown up with. He would not have a family of his own. He would not marry the girl. He would not marry any woman, not even Katherine Clarke. In the earlier days of his youth, he had seen the world in terms of the open farm fields around him stretching to the horizon. In his more recent and advanced youth, he had seen the world and the future in his wide-open love for the girl and in terms of the wide-open future he saw himself living with her. That future of open horizons had shrunk down to a narrow and empty hallway when she died. Now, for the remainder of his life, he would see the world through small squares covered by iron bars. He would finally die in obscurity in the confined obscure world of a prison somewhere.

After he had come home to the house that would not be his home after having contributed his identification of the girl's body, he had walked aimlessly down the road toward the horizon that he would never arrive at. On his way back, he had walked westward into the setting sun that marked the setting of his hopes for the life he had seen with the girl. It was an empty-seeming life and an empty-seeming home he had come back to, but he had come back home. Shortly he would march out of the house that was otherwise his home. He would not return to the house again.

Samuel assumed the constable's next act would be to tell him to hold out his hands so he could put the manacles on his wrists. He prepared to hold up his hands.

Constable Harkness held up his hand with three fingers raised. "You've got three days, boy," he said. "I'll give you three full days to run. On the fourth day, I'll come back to make the formal arrest like I had just finished working out all the details of the crime. If you're here, I'll arrest you. If you're gone, you're gone." Constable Harkness looked at the other members of Samuel's family. "As far as any of us are concerned, this meeting never took place." He turned and looked at his two deputies standing by silently. "That goes for the two of you."

Sergeant Plechathy and the other policeman nodded their heads silently. The constable turned back to Samuel.

"If you choose to stay, I'll arrest you and start legal proceedings against you as if I had planned to do so all along. Those legal proceedings will involve a murder trial. At that time I'll release the story."

Constable Harkness looked over at Beth. "If your brother's not here anymore, I'll just say that before he left, he revealed to you what he did and why he did it and that I got his side of the story from you." He looked back at Samuel. "If you choose to stay and fight the charge in court, that's up to you. You can try some kind of 'grieving loved one' defense or a temporary insanity plea. I'm not a lawyer. It might work. But I would say that given the time interval between when the girl was killed and when you killed Ethridge, and given the calculated and premeditated way you went about killing him, I don't think a jury will buy temporary insanity. Given Ethridge's social position, I don't know if they'll buy the story or buy any reason for your killing him, not even a broken heart over the murder of your sweetheart, especially a sweetheart from that far over the wrong side of the tracks. If you're convicted, you'll probably draw life. Given the mood of the jury, you may be sentenced to execution."

The constable spread his hands out. "If, on the other hand, you've skipped town and you're not here, there's not a lot I can do to track you

down. I'll have to explain how you found out in advance that I was on to you and was closing in. But it shouldn't be hard to think up something. …
If you leave town, that solves your problem of going to prison and possibly the electric chair. It solves my problem of arresting someone for doing what I might have done if I were in your shoes."

He still held Samuel's boots in his left hand.

"It will be a less than full victory for me, but it will calm the town. I won't have been able to present the town with a prisoner in chains, but at least they'll know who the killer was and why he did it and that it didn't involve any of them. They'll stop looking over their shoulders for a madman. Having a reason they can understand for your killing Ethridge, they'll rest easier in their beds, not thinking that they may be the next ones to die.

"If you go, I'll just say that you didn't tell your parents or your sister where you were planning on going. You could have gone anywhere on the face of the earth. I'll put out the requisite reports to other police departments in the state to be on the lookout for you, but I'm not going to go turning over every rock in the county searching for you, and I won't issue repeat summons."

The constable held up Samuel's boots. "You'll have to buy yourself a new pair of hiking boots. I'm keeping these as evidence."

With quick dispatch, the constable turned and motioned to the other two officers to leave. "Seeing how this meeting never took place, I see no need to draw it out any longer," he said over his shoulder as the other policemen turned and started heading toward the kitchen and the door beyond.

"So okay," Samuel said at this juncture to the turned backs of the town policemen. "You're going to let me slip out the back door. I guess I should thank you for that. But what are you going to do for her?"

Constable Harkness paused and turned around. "There's nothing I can do for her now, boy," he said. "She's dead and buried."

"I mean, if I leave, how are you going to explain to the town and everyone why I did what I did?" Samuel asked. "Are you going to make up some kind of story that I killed Ethridge because of some kind of farm business rivalry, or are you going to tell everyone that he killed her? What are you going to do for her memory? What are you going to do for the truth?"

"Since when have you become such a big worshipper of the truth?" Constable Harkness said. "Have you become a country Diogenes lifting his lamp looking for truth? If out, the truth will send you to a prison cell for life or to a short ride in the electric chair."

"I mean the truth about her and what he did to her," Samuel said. "Or are you planning to whitewash his memory and not tell them that he killed her? While you're giving me a chance to get away, are you planning to let Ethridge off just because he was a rich man and she was a whore? Are you going to bury the fact that he killed her? That would be like burying her all over again. It would be burying her deeper than Mrs. Richardson buried her. It would be burying her at the bottom of a lie as well as in her grave. If you cover over the story of what really happened just to preserve the reputation of a rich man by burying the memory of a prostitute, she won't receive any justice at all, not even the small belated justice of people knowing the truth. People probably think she wasn't anything more than a cheap little tramp whose life didn't mean nothing."

"Are you ready to stand your ground here and stand trial for murder yourself just so that the truth can be publicly aired?" Constable Harkness asked in a rhetorical tone.

"Maybe not," Samuel said. "But I don't see much of a life for me wherever I go from here. Whatever future she may have had, I lost any sense of the future when I lost her. There's not much future I can see for me without her, in this town or outside it."

The constable looked at Samuel a moment. He still didn't quite know how to take the boy. "For what it may or may not mean to you now," he said, "when I give out the story, I'll tell everyone that it was Ethridge who killed the girl and that I have conclusive evidence that he did so, which I do. I don't know if it will make any difference in what anyone thinks about you or the girl. I don't know if it will make any difference in what they think about Ethridge. But then I don't particularly give a damn what they think of him. He was a bigger pig than the ones he raised and sold. I don't know if getting the truth out will do much of anything for the girl or what people in this town think of her. I'm afraid it's the only justice I can muster for her."

The constable turned again. He and the other two police officers walked out of the parlor, through the kitchen, and out the kitchen door, leaving a surprised Samuel, who had expected to be arrested, standing free and unfettered in the house he had expected to be taken from for the last time in his life.

The kitchen door closed behind the constable and the uniformed officers, bringing to an end the meeting that the duly appointed chief enforcer of the law said had never happened. As the door had closed, Samuel's silent father had silently crossed partway across the room in the direction that the departing duly appointed officers of the law who officially hadn't been there had taken. He stood silently and listened as the police car started up outside. As he heard it pull away, he turned quickly around, facing his son, who in three days' time would be officially arrested by the men who hadn't officially been there. Both his arms were upward, both fists clenched in the air. His jaw was clenched. The whole of his upper body seemed to tremble.

"Whatever good God there is in heaven, you've done it now!" Mr. Martin shouted to his son across the short distance between them. "This isn't stealing melons. This isn't even beating a man senseless in a barroom brawl. My God, you're a murderer!"

A lifetime of being a farmer living at the whim of the forces of nature that he could not control had taught Samuel's father self-control. For the first time in his life, Samuel saw his father trembling on the brink of losing control. His father almost gasped his words. It was as if there wasn't enough air in the room for him to catch his breath or that there wasn't enough of anything in the universe that could make him believe what was happening. Samuel kept silent in the face of his father's unaccustomed raging. Samuel's mother remained seated in her chair, trembling, with her hands still over her mouth. Beth was still standing by her mother with her hands on her trembling shoulders.

"You're the first murderer who's ever been in this family. And you didn't just kill some hired hand or drifter. No! You had to go that even one better. You killed a town bigwig! The biggest wig in town! And it wasn't just him you killed." Samuel's father pointed over at his wife, who was shaking in silence in her chair. "You practically murdered your mother. She's never going to be the same after this. … You've killed your own future. … You might as well have put the gun to your head after you put it to his. You've torn this family in half down the middle. There isn't going to be any more of this family in the future. You've killed the future of this family! You spent all that money to write the girl's epitaph on her tombstone. You've written the epitaph of this family in blood! You've written your own epitaph in Ethridge's blood. You've written the epitaph of this family in his blood!"

Mr. Martin waved his arm hard in the air, indicating no direction in particular. "All for some …" He gritted his teeth. Samuel braced for the worst form of epitaphs from his father about the girl. "For some nameless drifter girl who blew in on the wind from outside."

"I would have done the same to any man if he killed Mother or Sis or any member of this family," Samuel said.

"And by your actions you have killed this family!" his father said. "You've ruined your own life. You might as well have doused this house and all in it with kerosene and set a match to it. You might as well have done the same to yourself at the same time. You've left your mother, me, and your sister in a pit here in this town. You've left yourself in a pit somewhere outside this town for the rest of your life. You've made a killer of yourself. You've ruined this family. All for the love of some alley-cat girl whose back-alley ways you probably would have never gotten to change."

"Well, I'll never know now if she'd ever have left the Richardson house for me or any man," Samuel half shouted back at his father. "He killed her before she had a chance to come away with me."

In the back of his mind he knew that his chance of being able to convince the damaged, skeptical, and bitter girl into leaving the life she felt she had a modicum of control over and moving onto the farm with him was an uncertain probability even if she had lived. He was shouting in defense of both the girl and his hope that he could have talked her into marrying him.

"He never even gave her the consideration of letting her go on living her back-alley life. He never gave her the chance to get a better life from us or get a better life for herself. He never gave her any kind of chance at all. Why should I have given him any kind of chance?!"

Samuel pointed to his mother the way his father had done. "You tell me. If someone had killed Mother a month before you were going to marry her and you didn't think the law was going to do one damned thing about it, what would have done?!"

"For all I know, I would have done the same damned thing as you did," his father said. "But who you did it to and who you did it in the name of changes everything. You didn't kill some grimy thug who struck down a minister's prim daughter putting on her lace gloves as she was leaving the church at night after choir practice. You cut down the most influential citizen of the town. And you didn't confront him in the middle of the town square and challenge him to a duel. You ambushed him in a pigpen and shot his head off! Nobody's going to see you as a gentleman avenger for that. And they're not going to see the girl as a wronged and ravished fair lady who needed avenging. Most of the people in this town are going to see her as a tramp drifter. Nine in ten in this town will probably think that she deserved what she got and that she probably brought it on herself. When you found out that he was the killer, you should have taken what you knew to the police. But no! You just had to go running off with a shotgun in your hand, howling for blood like a Comanche on the warpath. Your maniac juvenile lust for vengeance has blown this family to pieces as totally as you blew him to pieces."

"I don't believe the constable would have done anything if I brought him the evidence, even if he did believe me," Samuel said weakly. "He would probably have covered for Ethridge because he was the richest man in town and a member of the town council, and she was just an outsider whore."

"Good God, boy, you might have given the constable the chance!" Samuel's father shouted, his voice returning to its peak. "You should have given him the benefit of the doubt. He just might have been honorable enough to arrest Ethridge for killing the girl. He has enough feeling in him to give you a chance to get away. Maybe he would have had enough honor in him actually to arrest Ethridge for killing the girl. But we'll never know that now, because you went gun-crazy and shot Ethridge up worse than Jesse James ever killed anyone. Now your mother and I are about to lose our only son to prison, or the gallows, or the open road. This family has been brought to an end. Without a son to carry on the family name and produce the next generation that won't be, this family will wither and die when your mother and I are dead and gone and your sister marries and moves away to live somewhere else under a different name."

"I was afraid that if I told Harkness that I had information that might convict Ethridge, along with doing nothing about it, Harkness might tip Ethridge off that I was on to him," Samuel said weakly. "I was afraid that he might possibly come after me and the rest of us in order to shut all of us up."

It was more or less a lie. Samuel hadn't really thought about that scenario before. He had thought it up on the spot as a way of defending himself by invoking a danger to the rest of the family.

"Besides, Harkness said that the evidence I had might not have been enough to convict Ethridge or even bring him to trial. The defense lawyer probably would have said that what Polly had said the girl told her was only secondhand knowledge, hearsay from a whore. Harkness might not have been able to do anything even if he wanted to. Ethridge would have walked out of the court laughing and would have walked over the girl as he laughed. Most likely he would have never even seen the inside of a courtroom for killing the girl. He would have snuffed out her life like she never lived."

"And you snuffed out the future of this family!" Samuel's father interjected. "You were the future of this family. You blew the future of this family out the window, farther than you blew Ethridge's brains out through his ears! With you gone, there won't be a next generation of this family under our name."

"He snuffed out my family," Samuel protested. "She was the one who was going to give us the next generation of Martins. She would have given me and us the children who would have carried on the Martin name."

Samuel caught himself and stopped as he remembered that Clarinda had said that she might not be able to have children. He hadn't told his family what she had said down by the river. It just didn't seem like the best of times to mention the point now.

"You may have children elsewhere under a different name, but you won't have any here under the Martin name," his father said. "You've cut off the Martin name. You've cut yourself off from the Martin name. You've cut the name out from under yourself and from under all of us. All in the name of a girl who had no name."

"Ethridge took whatever name she had and took what little she had to her name away from her," Samuel said, his voice losing the weak edge it had started with. "Because of him, she won't have any name, hers or ours. He took everything she had from her. He killed her like a stray raccoon he'd caught raiding his grain and disposed of her like a dead cat. He would have disposed of me in the same way, and then there wouldn't have been any male Martin to carry on the family name anywhere. While he thought he had the upper hand over me, before he found out that I was the one who was going to kill him, he made it quite plain that he thought himself perfectly entitled to kill both me and the girl because both of us were a problem and a bother to him. He walked away from killing her thinking that she was nothing more than a little piece of dirt that he had kicked off the sole of his shoe. He left her dead. He would have left both of us dead, thinking he had the right to dispose of a pair of bothersome tramps like he was wiping pig stains off his boots. Any jury from the town would have probably agreed with him, at least as far as the girl went. Even if they believed he killed the girl, most of the town would have probably agreed with him behind the scenes and would have let him walk."

"Which shows that the constable had enough consideration for you to give you advanced warning that he would come after you, so that you could slip away," Samuel's father said. "Which is what you're going to have to do, or else you're not going to have any name to your name. All you're going to have for a name is a prison number."

In the short time between the leave-taking of the duly appointed officers of the law and his father's ensuing explosion, Samuel hadn't had time to begin to consider the option the constable had offered him or the question as whether to stay and take his chance on a trial or to run.

Samuel looked at his father. "Do you think I should leave?" he asked. His father's words did seem to leave little other room.

With her hands still at her face, Samuel's mother looked up at her husband.

"Well, you sure as hell can't stay here, boy!" Samuel's father said, looking hard at his son. He pointed in the general direction of the departed officers. "You heard what the constable said. He said the same as you. Even he doesn't know if he has enough evidence to conclusively prove that Ethridge killed the girl. If you take that into a trial and try a temporary insanity defense or a bereaved lover defense, the jury probably won't buy it. All they'll see is that you tore apart the most prominent and respected citizen of the town over a whore. They'll probably pack you off to death row at a quick time march. Even if you do manage to convince them that Ethridge killed the girl, they'll probably convict you of a lesser degree of murder and of taking the law into your own hands. Instead of the death penalty, they may only give you life imprisonment. Even if they don't give you full life imprisonment, you'll probably end up spending a lot more years in jail than you've spent on the earth so far. You'll be an older and more doddering man when you get out than I am now. Your mother and I will be gone. Your sister will be an old woman. The farm and family will be gone. You'll have no family anywhere to go back to."

"If I leave, where do I go?" Samuel asked. Hollowness and emptiness had clamped on to Samuel and had not released him since he had seen the girl's body on the table in the back room of the police station. A second-stage hollowness was starting to settle down over him. It would never fully leave.

Samuel's mother looked from him to her husband and back to her son.

"I don't know," Samuel's father said, throwing his hands in the air. "I've hardly ever been out of this state more than once in my life. I don't have any idea where you should go. I'll have to think about it."

"Does he have to leave us?" Samuel's mother said in a mother's plaintive quivering voice. "You're practically pushing him out the door. We may never see him again. Isn't there some way we could keep him here at home with us?"

"I don't see how he can stay here," Samuel's father said. "If he stays with us, he'll be dragged away from us in chains right away. We'll never see him again that way either, unless it's on visiting day at the prison. If he ends up executed, all we'll have left of him to visit will be a grave with a number on it in the back of a prison yard."

Whether he would be staying or going, it was starting to dawn on Samuel that he would never be able to visit the girl's grave in the cemetery again.

"The constable said that when three days are up, he's going to forget what just happened here, and forget that he gave Samuel a chance to run, and is going come after him like any criminal. The farm is the first place they'll come to look for him, and they will keep coming back to look again. We can't very well hide him in the attic for the rest of his life. At least if he's alive and out of jail somewhere, we can slip away and visit him. But if he lets himself be taken in, the last time we'll see him is when they walk him past us in the hall of the state prison on the way to the electric chair."

"Oh, Sam," Samuel's mother lamented as she put her face down into her hands again. Seeing his wife's distress, Mr. Martin said the only thing he could think of in an attempt to momentarily ease her sorrow.

"We don't have to run him out the door in the next five minutes," he said, hoping that the thought of having their son around for one more day would put off a certain degree of the sadness of the parting that had to come. "Harkness said he wouldn't come back after him for three days. At least we can keep him here for one more day while we get him prepared to leave. When he goes, he'll have a two-day head start. We can have him here with us for another day and still leave him enough time to be out of the state before anyone starts looking for him."

The thought of a one-day reprieve didn't bring any visible sign of relief to Samuel's mother. She continued to cry quietly into her hands.

Samuel's father pointed at his wife. "Go comfort your mother, boy!" he said in a hard and bitter directive uttered in a bitter, ironic voice. "This is your doing as much as anyone else's. You brought this on her. You brought this on all of us. She's lost her son as much as you've lost your tart. For what little good it's going to do, for what little time you have left here with us, you can at least tell your mother you're sorry for tearing this family in half and taking her son away from her."

Samuel walked numbly over to his mother and put a hand on her shoulder next to his sister's hand. His mother immediately grabbed his hand in both of hers and pulled it up to her face. Samuel could feel the wetness of the tears on her cheek.

"I'm sorry, Mother," Samuel said, saying the only thing that came into his mind. But at the moment of his mother's pure sorrow, nothing he could have said would have seemed adequate. "I didn't mean to cause you any sorrow. I didn't mean anything against you or Dad or Sis. When I found out that Ethridge had killed the girl, I just went crazy. All I knew, all I could think, was that I had lost the girl and that he was the one who had taken her from me."

"And your mother has lost her son," his father repeated, his frustration breaking into despair. "I've lost my son. Your sister has lost her brother. You've split this family down the center. You've taken a large portion of the love out of this family for the love of a girl who gave you love in only the crudest physical way and probably would never have given you any kind of love beyond that. This family has lost a member as beloved as any it ever had. This family has lost its future. You've thrown away the son and the family the Lord gave us. You've thrown away the life and the future that the Lord gave you. You've thrown away everything that's been given you, all in the name of a girl who never even gave you her name!"

The point of bitter irony having been spoken, Samuel's father fell silent. The four members of the family that soon would be a memory stood or sat silently in the room of the house that would soon be a home absent one member who had been a part of the family since birth. Samuel's father stood apart from the rest in silence and watched as Samuel and his sister faced each other with their mother seated between them as she cried silently on her son's hand.

The sky was overcast that night. Samuel could see no stars in the sky. The only light he saw in his room was the leaden rectangle of dim light coming in from the outside that was slightly lighter than the darkness in the rest of the room. To Samuel the rectangle of dim light became a door. It was a door that was closed tight in his face. At the same time it was an open door that would close behind him before he could scurry back through it. It was already closed tight behind him in two ways, one past and gone, one yet to come.

Even before he had erased Harold Ethridge's face, it had become increasingly harder for Samuel to remember the girl's face. It's not that his memory of her was fading so soon in his youth. In that sense his memory of the girl's face was still sharp and distinct. When his mind wasn't drifting and he could focus his memory, he could easily call up all the lines and angles that had made up the girl's face. He could just as easily remember in detail all the moods that had shaped the expressions on her face. But of late it had gotten that when Samuel had tried to remember the girl, he had

591

trouble seeing her face clearly. When he had looked to see her face down the lengthening corridor of separation, all he could see was her gravestone at the end of the darkening corridor.

But where his life had narrowed down to the end of the girl, he could at least see something at the end of the tunnel. The life he had imagined and hoped for had come to an end under the tombstone he had purchased for her. The girl and everything he had hoped for ended at her grave. The image of her stone standing alone at the crest of the ridge on the edge of the cemetery had become as deeply ingrained in his mind as the words he had had engraved on the stone. The corridor of his memory of the girl ended in the vision of her stone because there was nothing beyond. As Samuel lay in his bed looking through the window at the night sky, he could see nothing, not even a tombstone, at the end of the tunnel of what remained of his life, because he had no idea where the tunnel led and what lay at the end of it.

Though he knew the door led nowhere and could lead nowhere, in his mind Samuel drifted pointlessly out through the door into the dim and uniform grayness beyond. Once he was inside the corridor, the corridor itself disappeared, to be replaced by an empty and dimensionless void that expanded in all directions, until all direction and distinctions of direction became lost and meaningless. Though he was nominally outside his room above the open ground around the farm, from his position drifting in limbo he could not see the ground. Neither could he see the sky above. In the starlit sky on his ride back from Mrs. Richardson's house after the first night he had seen the girl, he saw her face in the sky above him. He could not see the girl's face in the drab, lifeless, and barely lit grayness around him. He could not see any familiar shapes or sights of the farm to orient himself by. He was adrift on an empty sea that had no name. The girl was gone from the future and the life that had narrowed down so suddenly around him. He didn't have the beacon of the girl to draw him on. He didn't have the dream of the girl to center his future and life on. He didn't have the familiar landscape of the farm to anchor himself to. In the corridor of the future, which the door behind him would soon close and lock him into, the farm would be gone from him as the girl was gone from him.

Samuel pulled his mind back into his room and back to the world that would soon be pulled away from him. The emptiness closing in on him from all quarters served to pull his mind out of the void and concentrate it on saving what he could of his vanishing life. The world he had imagined had been taken from him. The whole future he had imagined had disappeared from him. Soon he would be forced to leave the only tangible real world he had known behind. He had lost the girl. She had been his life and his future as he had imagined it. In short order he would lose his family and the farm. They and it had been the only world he had known. He knew no other life or world outside the family he had grown up with and the farm he had grown up on. To Samuel it spelled the loss of everything he had wanted and everything he had known. All he could see outside the window of the room he might be spending his next to last night in, all he could see in the long and endless corridor waiting for him, was that the two everythings of his life were slipping from his grasp. The one everything he had wanted for the future was gone. The everything he had known for all his life up to that time would soon be gone.

Samuel's mind went back and forth inside the narrowing corridor, trying to think of a way to both maintain his freedom and stay on the farm and with his family that had been the only home he had ever known and the only family he had ever known. A doorway to safety and escape from prison or the gallows had been provided by Constable Harkness. But the hard price was that he would have to leave behind everything that had accompanied and encompassed his life.

The girl was gone. Soon the life he had known, the only life he had wanted, would be as far gone. Having lost the girl, and now faced with losing his home and family, in the narrowing corridor of his mind and the fading light of his hopes, Samuel tried to think of some way to at least hold on to the life and family he knew. Somewhere within him might lie the way to hold off the long years of parting that made up the only horizon that the closing door of the future seemed to hold for him. But as he moved down the corridor of his thoughts, the corridor closed off behind him. At an unknown hour of the night, after an undetermined length of time spent reviewing his undefined plans in his mind, Samuel fell into a fitful sleep.

At some later, undetermined point in the undefined night, Samuel woke up with a start. He thought he had heard a woman's voice calling his name. The voice had spoken his name only once in a cried-out tone of loss and fear. In the uncertainty of his suddenly wakened state, Samuel didn't know if the voice had spoken in a dream or if it had been a real voice that had come out of the darkness and had awakened him. In a quick motion, he raised up partway off the bed and listened. In his fully awake state he heard no further sounds.

Samuel could not identify the voice. From the inflection, the voice had sounded like the girl's voice, but he couldn't be sure. If it was the girl's voice, Samuel assumed that he had been dreaming. It would not be the first time he had heard the girl cry out in fear in his dreams. Then again, the voice could have been his mother's, crying out her own sense of loss and her fear for him in a dream of her own.

A romantic supposition would have it that the voice Samuel had heard was the girl crying out to him from whatever limbo of the lost she was in. Samuel had always thought romantically where the girl was concerned. He had gone straight to end-stage romantic in his thoughts of the girl almost from the moment he had met her. So in that sense it was easy for Samuel to imagine that he had heard his lost love calling out to him from a world beyond.

Samuel laid his head back down on the pillow in the dark and silent room. In the dark of the unknown hour, with the darkness of his unknown days to come on his mind, Samuel wondered if the voice he had heard had been a dream or whether it had been the voice of the dead Clarinda calling to him. He discounted the idea that the voice had been the lost girl calling to him. He believed in an afterlife, but he didn't particularly believe in ghosts.

Even if the voice he had heard had actually been the girl calling to him from out in the dark, trying to find her way back home to him, it was an ironic act and a meaningless gesture all around. Soon enough he would be the one outside in the dark trying to find his way back home.

"Well, I can't sit here all day," Samuel said, standing up from the breakfast table. "I have chores to do, and I'm running late. I've got to get myself going."

On what was possibly his last day in the company of the family he had sat around the same table with all his life, Samuel acted as if he were beginning another day on the farm. He hadn't literally forgotten that he would be leaving home the next day. It wasn't denial born of desperation. His desire to maintain a semblance of normalcy was both an attempt to symbolically hold off what he knew must come the next day and an expression of his hope of preserving some form of continuation of the only life he had known and the only family he knew. As he left the breakfast table, Samuel wasn't thinking of the distant horizons he would soon be forced to leave for by default. He was thinking in terms of continuance of the farm and family, even if was continuance at a distance. The others, gathered around the table, looked up at Samuel and watched him go silently.

Samuel exited the kitchen door, rounded the house, and headed toward the barn. There were actually chores that needed doing that day. Chores are more or less a daily occurrence and necessity on any farm in any era. The family dog Teddy followed Samuel out the door. In the both the direction and the intensity of his loyalty, the dog was actually a bit more bonded with Mr. Martin, probably because with a deep-seated male dog instinct developed over eons in the wild, Teddy saw Samuel's father as the leader of the pack. Nevertheless, the dog loved all the other members of the family equally. He bounded alongside Samuel, eager to begin his day of patrolling the grounds and guarding the farm from rats and weasels. By the barn door, Samuel slowed down in his steps as the remembrance came back to him of how he had failed to keep the girl safe from the vermin she had walked with and kept her time with.

By the door of the barn, Samuel stopped and looked down at the dog. At least there was one feisty orphan alive in the world that he and the family had managed to deliver from destruction and give a home to. Teddy stopped when he did and looked up, wondering why his second master had stopped and wasn't going into the barn as was part of the normal routine. The dog was accustomed to a familiar pattern of behavior by the members of the family and had adapted the steps of his routine to follow along with the usual pattern of the male members of the family he lived with. Working days always began with a trip to the barn. Teddy couldn't see any reason why this day heading toward the barn should be any different. He couldn't think of any reason why Samuel should stop short of the door.

All Samuel was thinking was that this might be the last day he would ever walk to the barn with Teddy at his heels. The other thought that came into his mind was a remembrance of how much he had wanted to make love to the girl in the hayloft of this barn. As he looked down at the dog while Teddy looked up at him, wondering why he didn't enter the barn as he usually did, the other thought on Samuel's mind was that he would never walk into the barn with the girl for any reason, sensual or commonplace.

Samuel bent down and scratched the dog behind his ears. Teddy looked like he appreciated the gesture, but he still looked as if he didn't know why they had stopped outside the door. Despite his take-charge attempts to control his thoughts and keep them focused on his plans for continuance, a wave of empty loneliness and sorrow came over Samuel as he petted the dog that had been part of his life longer than the girl had been and who had been a member of the family from the first day they brought him home, whereas the girl had never been through their door once and had never been part of the family. Samuel fought to hold down the feeling that he was going to miss Teddy as much as he was going to miss his parents and sister. At the moment of relative weight, Samuel felt he would miss the feisty dog he had helped to save and had named as much as he would miss the feisty and wounded girl he had not been able to save and whose name he would never know.

Samuel didn't cry, but he was only partially successful in controlling the feelings coming over him. He broke off petting the dog and walked quickly into the barn. With the return of the normal routine, Teddy bounded into the barn in keeping with his younger master.

Whether a life-changing event comes up on you unawares or is seen from a day out, the lives of farm horses continue on a set routine by necessity. They have to be watered and fed. Having less of an instinct that the routine of their lives and the persons in their lives would change forever the next day, the plow horses stood impassive in their stalls. Samuel filled a bucket with oats and set about putting the feed into their feeding troughs. Having finished that, as he had for unnumbered days of his life, Samuel drew water from the well and filled their drinking troughs.

Biology may not always be destiny, but digestive biology is inexorable no matter how much your destiny is set to change in the near future.

Whatever event would overtake Samuel the next day and in the day to come after that, the remains of what the horses had eaten the day before were sitting where the horses had deposited them on the floors of their stalls. As was part of the age-old routine of caring for the farm horses, Samuel raked out their stalls with a long-handled rake. When he completed drawing the horse droppings into a manageable single pile, he would shovel the end products of the equine digestive cycle into a wheelbarrow and take it out to a manure pile located at the edge of the field. There it would be later distributed to whatever section of field or garden was deemed to be in need of fertilizer. Farm economy in that day was what it had always been. Nothing went to waste on the farm. Nothing major would be carelessly and heedlessly wasted, nothing it seemed but his life.

As Samuel was finishing raking the horse droppings into a pile, he heard his father's footsteps coming into the barn. When he looked up, he saw his father standing beside the truck. Teddy broke away from his inspecting the barn for rats and came up to Mr. Martin's feet with his stubby tail wagging. Instead of looking at the dog, Samuel's father was looking at Samuel. From the look on his father's face, Samuel could tell he had something he wanted to say to him. Samuel leaned the rake against a stall. Wordlessly he walked over to his father.

"I'm going into town," his father said quietly and straightforwardly as Samuel came up to him. "I suppose you would want to come and say goodbye to your friends, but I think it would be best if you stayed here. It might complicate things for the both of us and for Constable Harkness if you were to be seen in town anymore, especially now. I'm going to draw some money out of our account at the bank to help tide you over until you can find work. I also intend to close out your savings account at the bank and give you the money in there too. Provided there's anything left in it after what you spent buying the girl's favors and buying that headstone for her."

Samuel's father opened the truck door. "When I get back, we're going to have to talk and decide on what your plans should be," he said as he climbed into the driver's seat.

Without comment or a word of any kind, Samuel took the crank and cranked the motor to life. He stood silently and watched as his father backed the truck out of the garage, reversed direction, and drove off.

Samuel watched him go. Soon enough it would be his family watching him go, never to return to life and love on the farm. His abrupt departure would leave a lot of things unknown to him and to others and a lot of loose ends unattended to. But his abrupt leaving was necessitated by the abrupt and violent way he had attended to the man who had brought an abrupt end to the life of the nameless girl whose life had been one long unattended loose end.

Samuel was in the garden hoeing it as a make-work project to keep himself busy until his father returned from town. Some people might consider tending the garden to be woman's work, but that distinction had never been a rigid beginning-to-end thing on the Martin farm. It was the male Martins who planted the farm garden, where they grew the vegetables the family ate. Samuel's mother, in turn, was the one who did most of the tending of the garden as the vegetables grew. But as she had grown older and her strength had declined, Samuel and Beth had increasingly taken over the task of tending the garden. As mentioned, Samuel was hoeing the garden; it didn't even need tending or hoeing that particular day.

Of all the particulars pending that day, again, the garden didn't particularly need hoeing. But the ground he was hoeing was the soil that he had walked over and tended since he had been born on the land and born to the land. Every inch of dirt he turned reminded him of an event on the farm, a year on the farm, the steps of a life spent on the farm. To Samuel the garden was the farm in miniature. Tilling it was his function in life in miniature. To walk the garden was to review the days of his life on the farm. Every piece of soil he turned with the hoe was an affirmation, so to speak, of the connection he had with the land and the farm he lived on, a connection that would soon be broken forever. The garden of the farm wasn't nearly as big or lovely and bright as the Garden of Eden, but it had been the garden of his youth and part and parcel of his love for the land, for his home, and for his family.

After the Fall in the Garden of Eden, God had directed Adam to till the land and live off it. After the Fall, God had sent Adam and Eve out of the garden to walk and work the earth. Samuel figured he made for a pretty scruffy Adam. The Eve he had originally sinned with was dead. He would wander the earth without her. It hadn't been the Lord Himself who had ejected him for his home garden. Constable Harkness didn't strike much of a pose as an angelic being, but he was the one decreeing his separation from his garden. Just how big the flaming sword that barred his return to the garden would be was yet to be known.

As Samuel worked in the garden, he continued to think of ways he could preserve contact and closeness with the farm and his family. Mostly what he thought of was just a continuation and extension of what he had thought of the night before. But as he thought, a new element was added. The thought (wishful as it was) came over him that maybe there was a way to arrange for him to stay on the farm, just without ever going into town. The thought was mostly a fantasy, and Samuel knew it. But as he looked down at the dirt of the land he was tilling, he knew he would be willing to stay within the boundaries of the farm and never go into town again, and never even venture off the farm again, if it became a necessary price to stay on the farm. Staying on the farm for the rest of his life was a life sentence Samuel could live with.

Samuel looked up as he heard the familiar rattle of the truck coming up the dirt drive that led past the house toward the barn. His father was returning home. He had spent more time in town than Samuel had figured it would have taken to draw money out of the bank. The garden was on the far end of the backyard near the end of the field. It was somewhat removed from the drive. Samuel didn't know if his father had seen him standing in the garden working, but if his father had seen him, he didn't wave to him and didn't slow down as he drove past. His father turned the corner by the door to the barn. Teddy ran after the truck, yapping at his master's return. Though Samuel couldn't see his father directly, he assumed he had pulled the truck into the barn. He also assumed that this would be the time when his father would want to talk about setting his plans. With the hoe in his hand, Samuel left the garden and walked to the barn.

At his normal pace of movement, Samuel estimated that his father would have met him by the barn door as he came out of the barn. When Samuel got to the barn, his father had just finished getting out of the truck. He hadn't even closed the truck door. Samuel was a bit surprised that his father hadn't proceeded any farther.

Samuel walked up to his father, standing with his hand on the open door of the truck. His father's face looked weary and worn.

"I have the money for you," he said in a quiet tone. "It should last you a reasonable length of time if you don't spend it wildly on whiskey and gambling. Or on street women like you did with the girl. It might be a good idea not to keep it all in one place or carry all of it on you at any one time. A robber could roll you and take it all. What you do carry on you, keep a small amount of it in your pocket. If a mugger comes after you, give him that. Keep the rest of what you carry on you in your shoe. There are a lot of muggers on the streets of cities."

Samuel thought his father's precautions made sense, but he didn't see why his father was talking about cities and city streets.

With a weary gesture, his father pushed the truck door shut. With a hollow metallic bang, it closed only partway. "We've got to talk about where you're going to go," he said in a hollow voice. "This is as good a time and place as any."

"I've given that a lot of thought myself," Samuel said in a confident voice that came out sounding more ironic than anything. "I think I know the best way to handle this. I'm a farmer. I know farming. I could move to a close county and go to work as a hired farmhand."

Samuel outlined for his father his idea of changing his name and getting a job as a hired hand. He went on to outline how this would allow him to stay close to home and how it would make it easy for him to keep in touch with the family and for the family to keep in touch with him. Samuel laid out his ideas for his father in a crisp and complete manner. He was sure his father would see the logic in his ideas. He was sure both his father and mother would find the idea of having him at least reasonably close to home to be appealing. The problem for Samuel was that his father face hadn't seemed to brighten or his countenance to rise during the whole time he had been speaking to him. Samuel was starting to go over his ideas again, when his father held up his hand to cut him off.

"I appreciate your idea and all your thoughts of us, Son," he said in a quiet and tired voice. Samuel's more immediate problem was that his father's voice seemed to be tinged with sadness. "I'm sure both Mother and I would like to know that you're close by where we can stay in touch with each other. But I'm afraid that's not a very good idea."

Now it was Samuel's face that fell. It was the only idea he had going.

He couldn't see why his father was rejecting it out of hand. Samuel started to ask what his father meant, but his father spoke before he could.

"When I was in town getting the money, I slipped into the police station and talked with Constable Harkness."

Samuel froze. At least now he knew why his father had taken as long as he had to get back from town. But what was it they had talked about, and what opening to retain his family did it leave Samuel? And why did his father seem so sad and downcast?

"I don't think you understand the position Harkness is in, Son. He's going to have to tell the town who killed Ethridge. He can't sweep that under the table and leave the whole town thinking there's a raving maniac running around in their midst. He has to give them the killer and the reason he killed, even if the killer has skipped town."

Samuel went to say that the constable had already said that, but his father held up his hand again. "Like I said," he remarked, "if you get caught somewhere nearby, it could put him in a position. It could put the rest of us in this family in a position. If you get picked up and the story gets out that he let you go, that's not some minor misdemeanor. That's aiding and abetting the flight of a criminal. That's a serious charge. And that's just the start of it. If they catch you, even if they don't sweat the story out of you, they may work it backward and guess what happened. If the whole story gets out, then it will be known that everyone in this family helped you run. Your mother, your sister, and me, all of us could be held guilty of aiding and abetting your flight. There's going to be enough questions asked of us as it is. If we're found guilty of helping you run like we are, I don't know how that will work out for us. It could go hard on the whole family."

Samuel thought he had it all figured out. But then again he thought he had it all safely planned out when he had killed Ethridge. At least he thought his family was out of danger. Now they were back in potential danger, and once again it was he who was putting them there. He had been willing to confess to Harkness and have him walk him away to jail then and there to keep his family out of a potential charge of being accessories to murder. Now it looked like he was going to be forced to put distance between himself and them to keep them out of a charge of aiding and abetting the flight of a capital criminal.

"Harkness said it would be best for all concerned if you left the state entirely. He won't be sending descriptions to every police precinct in every state. If you're across state lines, it would put you a lot farther out of reach. There would be a lot less chance that someone might get a whiff of who you are and that you'd been arrested. … If you were to disappear across the line into another state, there would be less chance that you would get caught and less chance that all of us would get dragged in."

In that moment, all of Samuel's plans for staying close to his family just over the horizon in the next county faded and disappeared. Whether he liked it one little bit or not, he had to agree with his father and Harkness. In order to keep the truth of his flight from getting out, he would have to go to another state. He had little in the way of another choice. His love for the girl had driven him to kill Ethridge. His fear for his family now trapped him into leaving.

"The first place they'll look for you in this state or any state is as a hired farmhand. To make it harder for them to find you and keep them off your track, you should avoid farming altogether. Instead of looking for employment on a farm, it would be a better idea if you went to a large city and took up some kind of city work. You'd be better able to hide there. The best place to go would probably be one of the big cities up north— Chicago or Detroit."

Samuel's father rapped the side of the truck with his knuckles. "Detroit's where they make these. You might be able to get a job in Ford's River Rouge plant, where they make all their cars and trucks. But the Ford plant is the one main employer they've got in Detroit. They don't have a lot else. It might be your best bet to go to Chicago. It's a bigger city. They have more industries there. They've got the stockyards there and all kinds of meat processing plants. From what I've heard said, they're hiring all over the place. All the Negroes in the South are supposed to be heading north, especially to Chicago, to get jobs and keep from being lynched by the Klan down home. You'd probably have a better chance of finding a job in Chicago than in Detroit or some other big city."

At that moment in time, comparative employment statistics of faraway cities were lost on Samuel. In that moment of time, Samuel went numb with the thought of losing and passing from the home he had grown up in and the family he had grown up with. He had thought he had found love and the future in the form of the girl, but he had lost that love and that future. He had grown up with love and security in the house he had been raised in and the family he lived with, but now he would lose all of that over a farther horizon than he had expected. In his mind at the moment, Chicago wasn't a place of refuge. To Samuel, Chicago might as well have been a mountain range on the other side of the world separating China from Mongolia. To Samuel, everything he had and wanted was on his home on the farm. The next day he would leave everything he had known behind. He would leave everyone he had ever loved, living or dead, behind and travel alone to a city that some thought of as a mystic Xanadu and that others saw as an antechamber to hell.

"What about Cincinnati?" Samuel asked, his mind still fighting for an option that would allow him to remain closer to home. "Cincinnati is a big city. Big enough to hide in. Maybe you could talk Aunt Alicia into taking me in. I could get a job in Cincinnati and still stay in touch with you, Mom, and Sis."

Samuel's father thought for a moment. His expression didn't brighten as he did so.

"Cincinnati is still in the state," his father said. "They also have a big police department. If your wanted posters get sent there, they might spot you. I don't know if Alicia is able to put you up to begin with, and I don't know if she and her husband would want to take you in given what you're running from. If they take you in and help hide you, then they become accessories, aiding and abetting. If you get caught in Cincinnati, it could make trouble for Alicia and her family. It could make trouble for all of us right on down the line back to here. Moving in with my sister could put her in legal danger. I don't think it's my place or yours to ask her to put herself and her family in the dock like that. She has a social reputation to think of, as well as her family. I don't know how she'd feel about taking in and sheltering a black sheep relative who's wanted for murder. The thought of having a killer under her roof could make her more nervous than the thought of the police coming through her door."

Samuel spun off to the side and threw the hoe lengthwise with the spontaneous verve of a Spartan warrior throwing his spear. It traveled along a horizontally oriented arc across the inside of the barn to where it thudded with a hollow sound against the base of the wooden barn wall. Wordlessly,

Samuel turned on his heel and strode quickly toward the barn door and the open country beyond.

"Don't get mad at me!" Samuel's father called out to his son's retreating back. "I'm not the one who …" Mr. Martin stopped in midsentence. He had intended to say something to the effect that he wasn't the one who had beaten one man half to death and had killed another man in a fight over the same slut. But he caught his words and held them. His boy was hurting enough without him cutting deeper into him by venting his bile over the girl his son had loved enough to have killed to avenge. Beyond that, for all the beyonds to come in both their lives, it didn't mean anything anymore. The future Samuel's father had seen with his son at his side would be gone from him the next day. No words, however angry or accurate, could make up for the loss of two futures already gone beyond the horizon.

As Samuel rounded the corner outside the barn door and disappeared from view, Mr. Martin turned and grasped the top of the truck side with both hands. He didn't cry openly. He was too much of a hardened and fatalistic farmer to do that. But there was no thought in his mind other than a vision of an endless landscape of empty sadness. He chewed on the inside of his stiff lower lip as he held fast to the side of the truck, shaking inside and out.

Beyond the barn, Samuel walked at an increasingly fast pace until he got to the edge of the field he and his father had recently harvested. At the edge of the field, he stopped and stood to look out over the dry brown stubbly remains of the once living crop. The autumn breeze stirred the dry leaves on the ground. They made a faint and dry crackling sound. The sound was as hollow and mocking to his ears as his hopes of staying within easy reach of his family now seemed to him. A stronger gust of wind picked up some of the parched and dead leaves and carried them out and across the field, heading for the distant side. His dry hopes of remaining close to his home and family followed them out and blew away.

Samuel stepped into the now empty field and started walking at an angle toward the far end. One more time he wanted to walk the field that had been his grandfather's and his father's but would not be his. The girl may have had a hand in the loss of her own life, but there was no one with whom to share the blame for the loss of the farm and of his life and future on the farm. His loss of the farm, his home, and his family was all exclusively his own fault, the work of his reckless vengefulness. As his recklessness had put the only girl he had loved away from him to where she would not return to him, his reckless vengeance had put the only home he had known, the only family he had known, and the only life he had known behind him, to a point where he might never be able to get close enough to see them again, let alone get back to them. The girl had started out on the path she walked because others had driven her onto it. Once on her path, she had walked it alone. He would walk his path as alone as the girl had.

Samuel walked down the center line of the field he had helped plow, plant, and harvest since he had been old enough to help his father with that sort of work. As he walked the land he would not walk again, the last of his thin, false hopes that he could stay close to home and still stay out of the reach of the law fell away from him and crunched underfoot like the dry stalks he was walking on. With each step, the hope and life seemed to drain from him, until his inner landscape became a field of sadness as dry and empty of life as the empty field. As he walked and felt the draining away of his spirit, Samuel found himself wishing he could drain his life away into the familiar land that had been his life. He wasn't contemplating suicide; he didn't believe in it. On the last day he would have on the land, instead of leaving the land, Samuel wished he could drain himself out like rainwater soaking into the earth and become an eternal part of the land. From there, as some kind of ghost or spirit of the land, he could observe and be a part of the land forever. He imagined himself uniting with the spirit of his grandfather and all those who had walked the land before him. When his parents died, he imagined pulling their spirits in to join with his on the land. Together he and all his ancestors on the land would watch how the next generation of whomever came to possess it worked it and treated it. But he wasn't sure he wanted to see that.

At the far end of the field, Samuel stopped. The end of the field didn't mark any notable change in the landscape. There was a small uncultivated end strip of ground just wide enough to turn a plow team and a riding plow around on. At the end of that was a wooden rail fence. On the other side was the field of the neighboring farm, a field otherwise indistinguishable from the Martins' field. To Samuel the sameness and continuation of the adjoining fields had represented the continuance of life. For him, arriving at the end of his father's field marked the end of continuance of him on the land. When his father passed away, it would mark the end of the continuance of the Martin family on the land. The land had given Samuel his identity and place in the world. His family had given him his name. With his leaving and his father's passing, the Martin name would come to an end. The farm would be known by some other name. Samuel would spend the rest of his life under another name. While the circle of continuance on the farm would be broken, out in the wider world an ironic line through the world, a line that had come to an end, would start up again and continue on into the world.

The girl had left her home and gone off to wander the world under a name she made up for herself. Her wandering had come to an end outside of town, outside of respectability, out of reach of Samuel's protective grasp. Tomorrow he would leave the only home and family he had known and go out wandering in the world under a name he would make up for himself. He had no idea where or when his life would end or what name it would end under.

Samuel turned around and looked back across the field to the farmhouse and the barn. His distance from them made the buildings of the farm seem smaller. From his distance and his angle, he was able to see the house and barn together. From where he was standing, the scene was just the right composition and right size for a rustic artist like Andrew Wyeth to capture on canvas.

Samuel stood there taking in the familiar but remote scene that would soon enough disappear from his sight, over the horizon. The house and farm was the home of his youth. It had been the only home he had known. His family had been the only family he had known. The land beneath his feet had been the only path he had known and followed for all his life since its beginning. Tomorrow he would follow a new and unknown path to a far place. Unlike the prodigal son, Samuel would not return to his father or the rest of his family. The farm of his youth would be gone from him. The family he had known for all the days of his life would be removed from him, or he from them. They would be removed from him and would remain as far from him as the girl was.

The girl had been the future of love, life, and family-to-be as he had seen it. Being together with the girl on the farm had been his future and his place in the world as he had seen it. He had wanted it. That future had been separated from him. The future of his love and life was gone from him and could not be brought back in this world. His home and his family were now the past of his love and life in the world. Soon he would separate himself from his past and go into the empty world beyond, devoid of the love he had known and the love he had hoped for, and try to create for himself a life, the shape and form of which he could not imagine. Both his past and his future would be separated from him. Like the girl when she had commenced her wandering, he would leave past, future, place, and name behind and become a single-point wanderer existing in the immediate present. Instead of having a set place in the world and knowing his place in it and in life, he would be a lone ragged figure moving on a road that he could not see the end of, trying to find both place and name in a world that held neither for him.

In his short number of years, Samuel had become too much of a fatalistic farmer to cry out loud. He had become too much of a hardened killer to cry out loud, too. As he stood looking at the only home he had known, the home of the only family he had known and the only love that had held onto him when he had not been able to hold onto the love he had wanted, Samuel chewed the inside of his stiff lower lip. With nothing within reach to hold on to, he had to steady himself alone as he trembled inside and outside.

What does a family who have sat around the same dinner table for all their lives together talk about around the table when in all probability it will be the last time they will ever sit together at the table as a complete family? Do the members of the family that is soon to shrink dwell on what cannot be changed or held back beyond the next day? Do they reminisce wistfully about happy casual times in the past when their being together was taken as a given and it was taken that they would always be together? Do they talk about what will not be? Do they cry with every bite? Do they say nothing and pretend that the parting that will come with the light of the next day will not happen? As Constable Harkness had split the difference between his sense of being an agent of the law and his personal moral code, the Martin family more or less split the difference between silence and ignoring the coming loss of one of their members and dwelling on it, with the balance going to silence.

The parting to come couldn't be avoided. Their last supper together before Samuel's last parting from them couldn't be avoided. A family still has to eat. A boy has to keep his strength up to run. A family needs nourishment and fiber to say goodbye to each other without falling apart.

Mrs. Martin and Beth had prepared the dinner as they always had, acting outwardly like it was just one more dinner together in the usual fabric of their lives. The meal was about the same size and composition as it usually was: corn bread, ham, and sweet potatoes with the potatoes coming from the garden that Samuel had been hoeing when his father had returned. Their motions in preparing the meal were the same as they always had been. The place settings and silverware were the ones they used for all their meals taken together. Nothing was done outwardly different as to give an indication that the next day the fabric of their lives together would rip down the center.

The only mention of Samuel's leaving the next day came at the beginning of the meal, and it sidestepped the likely permanence of the parting as much as it sidestepped the reason for the parting. As was the Martin family custom, they always said grace before the evening meal. They followed the custom that night as if nothing was about to change, a statement of continuance in the face of continuance soon to be broken. Mr. Martin asked who wanted to say the grace that night. Samuel's mother quickly volunteered. Prayers for the departed had been offered around the table before on scattered occasions, usually following the death of a relative either living at home with them, such as the Martin family grandparents, or one living at a distance, such as Mrs. Martin's parents and Uncle Ned. As was their unofficial custom, it had always been Mrs. Martin who offered the prayer for the departed. As was their custom, all the members of the family closed their eyes, folded their hands, and bowed their heads. An otherwise uncomprehending Teddy sat on the floor by the table and looked up attentively as Mrs. Martin offered her altered prayer for the departing:

"O Lord, our son, Samuel, will soon be going out into the world," she began, crafting her words as if Samuel were going away to college or seeking his career in another profession in the outside world. "Be with him in his journey. Be with him on his journey. Guide the steps of his life apart from us. As the author of the Twenty-Third Psalm asked the Lord to guide him in the path of righteousness for Your name's sake, guide the steps of our son in the path he should take. Keep him safe for Your name's sake, for his sake, and for our sake. For we love him and hope You will guide him in Your way as we love You and seek to follow Your way, and as we hope he will follow in Your way apart from us. Keep all of us ever in each other's memory. Keep all of us ever close in our hearts, and bring us back together as can be. Amen."

The others echoed her amen then settled down to eat. The nonstandard prayer was the first of the nonstandard differences around the table that night. It was the biggest, but it wasn't the last. The other difference was that they ate mostly in silence. Gone was the usual review of the day's activities. Also gone was the usual banter and sibling rivalry that had seen Beth stick out her tongue at Samuel, and Samuel threaten to launch half-eaten vegetables into Beth's hair. Very soon Samuel would never see his sister stick her tongue out at him again. Of all the sights of his youth, along with the sight of the land, it was the one he would miss most.

Mrs. Martin had prepared the sweet potatoes in her usual manner by cooking them in a brown sugar and honey glaze. Samuel ate a good portion.

"I always love the way you fix sweet potatoes," Samuel said.

Mrs. Martin started to express a small bit of gratitude at her son's compliment on her cooking. As she went to speak, she realized that it might be the last time she would hear her son say anything about her cooking. It might very well be the last time she would hear him say anything to anyone in the family around the table again. The family had always sat foursquare around the table, one member on each side of the closed square. The next dinner would find one side of the table open. The closed square would be a hollow shell, perhaps forever open on one side. The square of the table and the circle of the family would be broken.

Before her words had a chance to come fully out, they caught in her throat. Mrs. Martin quickly brought her hand up with her napkin in it. She pushed a napkin-wrapped finger between her lips and stifled a sob. She shook quietly, in obvious emotional distress. Samuel looked at her and then down at his plate.

After dinner, Samuel and his father sat in the parlor discussing some operation of the farm. Maybe an outside observer would call it denial, maybe they wouldn't. What it could more or less be called was one last small and fading attempt to pretend that tomorrow would be a day no different from any of their days together. Their words were dry and shallow husks of that had been spoken between them and would not be spoken again.

The internal contradiction finally broke inside Samuel. He quickly stood up and walked through the kitchen, where his mother and sister were finishing cleaning up after dinner. He pushed through the kitchen door onto the stoop outside and closed the door behind him. He walked across the stoop and down the step to the ground beyond. He walked two or three steps—he didn't count—and stopped to stand on the ground with the house to his back. The autumn sun had already set. For several long minutes he stood on the ground two steps beyond the stoop and looked out into the darkness that hid the front of the farm and the land beyond from his view. Presently he heard the sound of the kitchen door open and close. Then he heard the sound of his father's footsteps on the wooden stoop. His father stopped at the edge. Samuel didn't turn around to look him in the face. He knew his father was standing a short way behind him, but he didn't know if he was looking at him or was looking out into the encroaching darkness as Samuel himself was. The darkness obscured the familiar landscape of the boy's past. In the darkness, the shape of his life to come was hidden, unknown, and unformed.

"I just can't leave you like this," Samuel said to his father without turning around. There was a pause of several moments.

"Are you thinking of staying here and standing trial?" he heard his father say in a measured voice. His tone sounded neither hopeful nor worried.

Samuel really wasn't sure what he was thinking. All the ideas he had been coming up with kept getting cut off before they became fully formed. All his hopes for staying at home, all his ideas to accomplish that end, were being swirled around in a tighter and ever-diminishing circle like dry leaves in a whirlpool in the river, where they were sucked under and disappeared. Later generations of the Stephen Hawking era to come would say his hopes were being sucked into a black hole, where the gravity of the situation crushed them out of existence. It was seeming to Samuel that hope itself, and even thought itself, was being cut off and removed from him.

Of all the partially formed ideas that had been going through his mind, Samuel had considered the idea of staying home and standing trial, using some form of insanity defense. If he were found to have been insane at the time of the killing, he might end up being sent to an institution for the mentally disturbed for a few years, after which he would be pronounced cured and sent home. It had worked that way for Harry K. Thaw. But Harry K. Thaw had been really mentally unbalanced. He had also been rich and socially prominent himself. Constable Harkness had said that a jury probably wouldn't buy an insanity defense on Samuel's part, especially given Harold Ethridge's wealth and social position. Samuel's father had echoed the thought. It seemed to Samuel that his options were begin snuffed out one by one like candles in a liturgy come to an end. In a world where all his options were dying, standing trial for the grisly murder of a rich and preferred member of society did not seem a hopeful or serviceable option.

Standing and looking out over the landscape shrouded in darkness, in the night of disappearing options and unformed thoughts, Samuel found that the only thought taking shape in his mind was the unformed thought that he didn't want it to end this way. In the dark boundary between his known past and his unknown future, all Samuel wanted was to preserve some measure of the closeness he had known and lived with his family.

"I mean, I can't up go away from you and never look back like I were some pioneer boy heading out west with no thought of ever coming back," Samuel said. "I don't want to go that far away from all of you and stay that far away. I'll stay out of the state while the heat is on and they're still looking for me, but when the hunt cools off and the wanted posters come down and my face isn't on them to be seen and recognized, I should be able to move back a whole lot closer to you and Mom and Sis. Besides, my face will change as I grow older."

There was another few moments of silence from his father.

"Well now, if your picture isn't plastered on post office walls and pinned up on telephone poles, it might open things up a bit for you and let you move around more freely," Samuel's father said in his quietly considered voice. He had clearly thought through the proposition. "You might even be able to get back into the state without being spotted."

There was another short pause. When Mr. Martin spoke again, his voice was a little more quiet and hollow. "But you still aren't going to be able to move back here to the farm. People in this town are going to recognize your face. Even if it's years later and you're older and your face has changed, people around here are still going to know it's you. If you try to take up residence on this farm again, you'll be spotted right away. Even if you're my age."

His father paused again. When he spoke again, his voice had completely drained of everything, past and future. "As much as I want to keep you home here with us, as much as I like the thought of you coming back to us, I'm afraid that this farm is something you're never going to be able to come back to. I'm afraid that you're just going to have to turn your back on this farm and on us."

In the years to come, Thomas Wolfe would pen the immortal words "You can't go home again." Samuel Martin hadn't left home yet, and already he was hearing the words pronounced to his back. Mr. Martin wanted to say something to the effect that for all practical purposes, the farm was as far out of his son's reach and lost to him as was the girl he had loved and lost; they were both dead to him now. But he didn't think that was what his son wanted to hear at the moment, on either account.

"You should just treat this like going out into the wider world to seek your fortune. You'll hardly be the first farm boy to do that. This country was founded and settled by pioneers who pulled up stakes and left what they knew behind. You should just think of what you're doing as that."

His father was technically right. Lots of farm boys had left the farm looking to create different lives for themselves. Lots of them had gone to cities seeking fortune or whatever they could find in the way of a different life. A good number of cities in the country had been founded by farm boys looking for a different life. But beyond pioneering a nonstandard departure from a socially proper life by loving and wanting to marry a socially improper girl, in his heart Samuel had never been a pioneer. Though his family was a continuation of the original pioneer stock that had settled the area, where continuance went, the only continuance Samuel had wanted was continuance of the life he had known and with the family he had known. The only continuance he had wanted beyond that had been with the girl and the family he would make with her on the farm that would one day be his. He had never considered himself as belonging to the pioneer class. All Samuel could think of at the moment was that he belonged together with his family and that all his family belonged together with each other more than the world needed a third-generation pioneer or than Chicago needed another fortune seeker, especially one who would come to them as an orphan. He figured the city and the world had enough fortune seekers and orphans to keep it busy.

"The only fortune or treasures I've ever wanted have been this farm, this family, and the girl," Samuel said. "Now it seems that fate and the law have conspired not to let me keep any of them."

Samuel's father could have qualified his son's statement and said that it had been his trigger-heated vengeance that had separated him from home and family. Samuel himself could have made the same observation. But at the moment, in the face of the moment of parting to come, it didn't make any difference to either of them.

"I may not be able to come back to the farm," Samuel went on, conceding what the inexorable formula of the situation required he concede, "but I don't intend to turn my back on you. If it's within my power, I will come back and live somewhere close enough that we can see each other regularly. When it's safe to return to the state, I'll try to get back and live as close to you as I can. I may have to live in another part of the state, where I won't be seen by someone from the town. I'll do it in a way that I can slip in to visit you when I can. But I don't want to just cut myself off from you, go off over the horizon, and pretend like you don't exist or never existed. This family has been the world to me. It's been the only world I've ever known. Other than the girl, this farm and this family has been the only world I've wanted. I don't have any desire to forget about you and go to the other side of the world like you mean nothing to me. Maybe I'll never be able to get everything back that I threw away, but I intend to hold on to what I can even if I have to hold it from a distance."

Samuel could say that he knew all about trying to love and hold onto people who were distant from him. Having loved the girl, he certainly knew about trying to hold onto people who were over the horizon. In the girl's case, she had come to him from out over the horizon. Even when she had seemed the closest to him, she still was well away from him, over the horizon.

At the same time, Mr. Martin remembered and reflected on how it had been his son who had paid for the girl's headstone. He wanted to say that, given that the girl was dead, his son certainly knew about trying to holding onto love that was far out of reach, but he didn't think that at the particular moment his son particularly wanted to hear that either.

"I thank you for the thought and for thinking of us that way" was all his father said in response to Samuel's stated desire to remain close and keep the family together, even if only by proxy. He said no more.

The rest of the words that Samuel did not have drained away from him and out into the darkness of the night and into the sad darkness in his heart. He stood looking out into the night for a minute, then he turned, walked back, and joined his father on the stoop. He looked at his father silently for a moment. Then he turned and looked back out into the night.

"We should get an early start tomorrow," Samuel's father said after his son turned around on the stoop to look back out into the dusk. "We have a long way to go to get to the train station in Columbus. If we get you an early enough train, at least that way it may still be light when you get where you're going. You should go to bed and get your sleep now so you'll be rested for the journey."

"I just want to stay here with you for a little while like we used to," Samuel said.

His father did not take issue with that. Together they stood in silence on the stoop and looked straight ahead, but in no particular direction, out into the darkness. The sky was too hazy that night to see the stars. In happier times of the past, they had cut a pastoral scene as they sat on the stoop on warm summer nights, looking at the stars in the night sky and talking about things such as farm operations and life in general.

Multigeneration, extended-family farm life is often punctuated by natural transitions and partings. They all knew that the parting of death must come. Samuel had seen his paternal grandparents die. He had heard the news arrive of the death of his mother's parents and of Uncle Ned. The death of grandparents had been a natural and expected part of the cycle of life. Even the early death of Uncle Ned had been expected and natural in its own way. None of them had ever experienced or anticipated a parting so premature and under such unexpected circumstances.

It was usually Samuel and his father who had sat on the edge of the stoop and talked. Sometimes Samuel's mother would come outside and stand with them and talk. She was too much of a proper lady to plop herself down in an undignified spread-legged position on the low stoop. Occasionally even Beth would join them, at which times the family would be complete together on the small stoop. That completeness was not there that night in either body or soul.

During the times they had sat and talked together on the stoop under the night sky, they didn't know they would come to see the times they had sat together as the embodiment of pastoral happy times. But then again, if they had known that this parting was to come, even in the dim future, it would have taken the edge off the happiness of the moments when they were happening. Back then it all seemed more of an everyday occurrence, not worth jotting down in the journals none of them kept anyway. At the time it didn't seem to be likely that the pedestrian occurrence of sitting on the stoop would one day be magnified by the lens of distance and separation into a remembrance that would be the equal of all remembrances. A prophet is often not honored in his own country. Happy times in the past are remembered more in times of loss. They are often seen in painful and cutting sharpness only through the prism of irrevocable loss.

Proverbial as it was, proverbial as it would be, proverbial as it couldn't help but be, taken in little individual twinges of memory and reminiscence over the remainder of his life, the sum total of Samuel's memories of sitting on the stoop with his family, and the pain of having lost it, would by itself come to equal the lump-sum pain of losing the girl. For Samuel, the pain of losing the family he did have would always equal the pain of losing the family he never had had with the girl.

When Samuel Martin had driven home after meeting the girl for the first time, he had seen her face suspended at a distance in the night sky. As he looked out into the night this evening, he didn't see the girl's face in the sky. The faces he saw in his mind were the faces of the family he would leave tomorrow, to see them again only from across a distant landscape or maybe only from the distance of memory.

In the darkness of the room the night before, Samuel had allowed his mind to slip into a long and empty imaginary corridor that expanded into an empty void without end. In the darkness of his room that night, Samuel didn't allow his mind to drift out the window and into the long corridor waiting outside for him. He otherwise kept hold of his mind and imagination, holding both of them tight in the room of the house at the center of the life that he wanted to hold tight to. The empty corridor he had drifted into the night before had been a corridor of his imagination. The corridor he would go out into the next morning would be a real one. The ending of the corridor would still be out of sight as had been the end of his imaginary corridor the night before. Not allowing his mind to drift away on him was as much an act of mental discipline on Samuel's part as it was an act of desire not to drift into a mental void. Samuel figured he would need all the self-control and clear thinking he could muster to keep on his feet in the unknown corridor and in the unknown and probably hard world he would be going into.

The thoughts going through Samuel's mind were too varied and jumbled to be easily sorted out and classified. His thoughts ran into each other. They merged and flowed together for a while. Then they would separate and go their own ways as he would separate from his family in the morning and go his own way. His thoughts were composed of equal parts denial of hope and denial that hope had been lost, coming close to crippling his mind, bringing it to a halt, and leaving it suspended over a dark pool of nothingness, only to have those thoughts of loss replaced by lively and innovative ways to sidestep that loss.

The thought that overlaid all others in Samuel's mind that night was that this might very well be the last night he would spend in the room that he had slept in for all his life in the house he had lived in all his life. He had been given that room when he had grown big enough to be taken out of his crib. He had known no other room for all his life. The shape and confines of the room were measured and familiar to him in the light. The outlines of his room were familiar and reassuring to him in the dark. After the morning of the next day, he would know its familiar and reassuring shape no more. After the next morning, he would not know the familiar shape and borders of the farm anymore. After the next morning, he would no longer know the shape of life as he had known it. The farm had been the only life he had known. It had been the only life he expected to know. It had been the only life he had wanted to know. On the farm, his life had been set. He had known what his life would be from its beginning to its end. The farm and his life on it gave him place in life. Place gave meaning.

Meaning to life gave life to him. On the farm he knew his place in the world and in life. He knew his path in life. He could see all the days and the path of his life. He knew the end of his path from the beginning. His path in life would be the same as his grandfather's had been. His path in life would be the same as his father's would be. As his father had carried on the work of his grandfather, Samuel would carry on the work and life of the generation before him. He would live out his days and die on the farm in the company of the generation around, and he would leave the farm to the generation after his. That part of his life had been set for him from the beginning. From his beginnings, he had accepted the life given him. That life had been natural and acceptable to him. In and of itself, and by itself, it was a life complete to him. For a while he thought he had glimpsed a fuller and more complete life with the girl, a life he would live on the farm with her.

Within a space of time that had been a veritable heartbeat in life, both his worlds, the world that he had grown up with and had grown into willingly into and the world he had wanted more than anything to enter into and live with the girl, had been snatched suddenly from him, and the door had slammed, immovable and unopenable, on both of them. Harold Ethridge had slammed the door on Samuel's hoped-for expanded and outward-looking world as well as on the girl's narrow and turned-inward world. He himself had been the one who had slammed the door on his first world and his life. That he had been the one who had slammed the door on his first life and world when he had slammed the door of life and a coffin lid shut on Harold Ethridge didn't change the fact that his two worlds had been placed out of his reach and now he would be forced to flee into a world totally apart. It would be a world without any set and ensured place for him, a world where paths ran in all directions but where no path was set for him, and all paths were uncertain and had no clear direction or end to them. The next morning would see and bring about an abrupt and absolute change between the world and life he had known and whatever awaited him beyond the vale. It would be an abject change from the world he had known, the world he thought he would always know, to a world whose shape, and what place it held for him, was something he could not see at all. It might be a world that would welcome him. It could be a world waiting in ambush for him the way he had waited in ambush for

Harold Ethridge. Either way, he would walk into the world alone without anything familiar and comforting accompanying him from his past. He would take almost nothing of the world he had known with him when he went into the unseen world that waited for him. He would leave all the world he had known behind. He would leave all the love he had known and the two worlds of love he had known behind. That was only the beginning of what he would leave behind. In Samuel Martin's mind was the possibly ultimate ironic thought that when he went into the world, he would go by a different name than the name Samuel Martin. He wouldn't even take his own name with him. Like the girl in her flight, he would take a different name when he walked out the front door of the home and family that had given him his name.

In her short life in town, the girl had rejected her own name. But she had had the option of keeping it or not. Samuel didn't have that open option. If he wanted to stay free from prison and off death row, he couldn't hang onto his real name. In that sense he was going on the run into the world with one less option than the girl had when she had run from her home. For quite possibly the rest of his life, he would be known by a name other than his own. In the end, whenever and wherever the end came for him, if for whatever reason he wasn't able convey his real name to anyone as he died, he might end up with a false name on his tombstone. He would follow the girl into eternity under a name he'd made up for himself. In that sense the girl would be one up on him. Anyone who saw her grave would know that she was buried under a name she had made up for herself. He had seen to that himself by the way he had worded her tombstone. People could speculate endlessly on what her real name was. In a way it would sort of keep the girl alive. At least people would know there was more to her that went beyond her name on a stone. If he ended up buried under a false name, no one might ever even know that it was false. Anyone glancing at his tombstone would think the alias he had used was his real name. No one might ever know his real name and his real life. He would be known by no other name than the one he had chosen for himself. The girl didn't seem to care what name she had gone by. She hadn't cared about what name she went under in life. She seemed not to have cared what name she was buried under. To Samuel, being buried under a false name would make it seem like he had never existed.

What name would go on his tombstone was a minor point to Samuel that night, however. The name he would be buried under could be addressed by a last will he could carry around in his pocket or leave where someone could find it. If he ever did have a family somewhere, he could tell them to bury him under his real name. If they weren't of the mind to do that, then at least he would have some kind of family name to his name. Again, holding on to his name was the least of the thoughts going through Samuel's mind. Holding on to the life, home, and family he had known all his life was the thought that concentrated his mind.

The one organizing theme to Samuel's disjointed thoughts and feelings was that he couldn't just let it end like this. He had to find a way back to the farm. It was the only home he had known or wanted. It had been the source of all the love he had known in his early years. It had been his view of the future, and his assurance of a future and a place in the future and in life. Even his love for the girl and his imagined future with the girl had been imagined in the context of the farm and a home with her on it. The world beyond was the real void in the dark, a void that bore no promise of love, place, home, or the future. Somehow Samuel had to find a way to return home and regain the home, the love, the past, and the future that had once been his. On the night before he was to leave home and seek his new life somewhere else, the life Samuel had known was more than ever the only life he wanted. No exuberant pioneer spirit or spirit of wanderlust held any meaning and drawing power for him. The unknown world beyond, all worlds beyond, meant nothing to Samuel compared to sitting on the stoop talking with his father about planting and harvesting, and sitting with the family around the dinner table talking about who he would marry. The world beyond meant nothing to him compared to hearing his mother fussing in the kitchen and clucking her tongue at him, and seeing his sister stick out her tongue at him. He had failed to win and hold the love and trust of the girl. As the day of parting approached, through the darkness outside the window and inside himself, Samuel struggled in his mind to find a way to hold on to at least some semblance of the love, the family, the home, and the life he had known.

For an undetermined length of time in the undetermined darkness in the room of his youth, all the varied jumbled thoughts ran through Samuel's mind. His spinning thoughts and feelings broke apart by centrifugal force into separate strands, only to coalesce back into an unformed ball. All his thoughts and feelings were monitored by the overriding feeling that he had to somehow hold on to his home. Somewhere in the undetermined night, he fell into a fitful and dreamless sleep. When he opened his eyes again, the faint light of morning was starting to show through the window. Samuel shut his eyes to keep out the light of what at least for an undetermined length of time to come would be his last day on the farm.

In a short enough space of time, the remaining ties with his family would be broken. Perhaps with that in mind, Samuel lingered over tying the laces of his boots. As his father had instructed, he had placed a portion of the money his father had given him on the inside bottom of each boot and put the boots back on. Samuel sat on the chair lacing up his boots, which would now come to double as money belts. Next to him was a heavy cloth laundry bag that contained a change of clothes: an extra pair of pants, two extra shirts, a few pairs of socks, and an extra pair of shoes. The bag had been packed by his mother. Before that she had fixed a breakfast for the family. A traveling boy needs a good breakfast to keep his strength up. Technically the breakfast was their last time together around the table. It had been another mostly silent meal. Samuel's mother and Beth were cleaning up in the kitchen as Samuel's father gave him the money in final preparation for the departure that would come shortly. Samuel's mother and sister stayed in the kitchen during this time. They didn't want to see the final preparations for Samuel's departure.

The clothing and the money constituted the only provisions that Samuel would be taking with him. He would be traveling light, but hoboes travel light. Beyond the first train ride, which his father would pay for, he would essentially be traveling through life in a manner little different from that of a hobo. The cloth laundry bag made for a funny-looking hobo bundle. Hobo bundles are supposed to be carried at the end of a wooden pole. The laundry bag had a drawstring at the top that pulled the top of the bag closed. It also allowed one to carry the bag over one's shoulder by the drawn rope. Carrying the laundry bag over his shoulder would make him look more like a sailor carrying a seabag than a hobo. Given that Chicago was a port city, Samuel's father figured that the appearance of the bag might lend people there to think that his son was a sailor off a lake steamer instead of a hobo off a freight train. That way he might be able to blend in with the city better. He also figured that the people of the city might have more respect for what they took to be a working sailor in port than a vagrant hobo who had walked out of a train yard.

As per his father's instructions, Samuel had distributed the rest of the money into the various pockets of the clothes he was wearing, and in the pockets of the clothes he was taking with him, and in the carrying bag itself, the practical provision being to spread out the money so that a snatch-and-run thief would not get all the cash he was carrying. Samuel had put the portions of money that he would keep in his boots in last. The only provision remaining to take himself on the road was to lace up the boots. Now the drawrope of the carrying bag was the final tie that would bind him to the house and family.

When Samuel finished lacing up his boots, he stood up numbly and took the drawrope of the laundry bag in hand. He looked at his father, who was standing by, silently watching him. Samuel assumed his father would motion him toward the door. He thought his father had given him all the provisions he considered necessary for his journey. He was wrong on both counts.

Instead of motioning him toward the front door, Samuel's father silently motioned him to the smaller reading room next to the parlor. Inside the room, he led Samuel to the gun cabinet from which Samuel had drawn the shotgun he had used to kill Harold Ethridge.

"There's one more thing that you should probably take with you," his father said, pulling the keys to the locked gun cabinet out of his pocket.

Instead of unlocking the tall and narrow top portion of the cabinet, which contained the long guns, Samuel's father crouched down and unlocked the smaller bottom portion, used for storage of ammunition and gun cleaning supplies. He reached under some boxes of shells and brought out an old and worn-looking small, flat box.

Mr. Martin opened the box. Inside was a short-barreled derringer-style pistol with over-and-under barrels. Though the gun was a derringer-style weapon, instead of being the usual low-caliber pistol small enough to be concealed in a waistband or in the palm of the hand, it was a heavier-caliber pistol on a somewhat larger frame. The larger size made concealment more difficult, but the larger caliber gave it more stopping power when fired at an opponent.

"You remember this, don't you?" Samuel's father asked. The question was mostly rhetorical.

"Isn't that the pistol that Grandfather carried during the War between the States as a last-ditch backup gun for close range in case he found himself out of ammunition and caught in the middle of a Confederate bayonet charge?" Samuel asked. The question was mostly rhetorical. He had seen it before. He had even fired it once.

"Yes," his father said. He took the gun out of the box. "You may possibly find that you may need it more where you're going than I'm going to need it here on the farm."

He handed the gun to Samuel. It felt solid in his hand.

"There are a lot of bad streets in big cities. Whatever job you get in whatever city you end up in, you may find yourself having to walk some bad streets around you. When you're out on whatever bad street you find yourself on, it might be a good idea to have that with you. Just keep it out of sight so the police don't see you carrying it. If they pull you in for carrying a weapon in plain sight, they may make the connection between you and what went on here. What with the telephone becoming more modern and new phone lines going in every day, police departments are talking to each other more."

Samuel's father reached into the cabinet drawer and pulled out a box of cartridges. "Here's the ammunition that goes with it. The box is only half full. I don't have any more shells for it. I hope you're never forced to use it."

Both Mr. Martin and Samuel could have uttered a caution to the effect that he had made enough trouble for himself by his impetuous use of firearms. Actually Mr. Martin had a secondary point on his mind concerning the old gun.

"Those shells are old. If you have to use the gun, right offhand I don't know how well they'll work."

Samuel's father could have said something to the effect that his son had a pretty good success rate with old guns using old ammunition, but he just didn't feel like saying anything along those lines.

"If a robber comes at you on the street, maybe all you'll have to do is pull it and wave it. That may be enough to make them turn and run. I didn't want your mother to see me give you this. It might just make her more worried. She's worried sick about you leaving and going off to the city as it is."

Without saying anything, Samuel opened the top of the bag, took the gun and the shell box, dropped the gun and box of bullets into the bag, and closed the bag again, using the drawrope, so his mother would not see what he had added to the items he was taking with him on the road, the road that neither he nor his mother trusted. The girl had left home with only the clothes on her back and the knife she had been forced to use to escape. Samuel was leaving a little more prepared with money, a change of clothes, and more firepower. But the road ahead didn't seem much more comforting to him than the road the girl had taken had probably seemed to her.

"We had probably better get ourselves going," he said in a quiet voice on the brink of breaking. "We've got a long drive ahead of us."

Samuel stood up. As he did so, he used the drawrope to pull shut the bag that contained his mother's gift of extra socks to keep his feet warm on the cold streets he might have to walk, and his father's gift of the handgun to preserve his life on those same streets. With his father in the lead, Samuel walked through the parlor, heading for the kitchen. He looked straight ahead, not wanting to see the only house and home he had ever known passing by as he left. In the kitchen, they walked past his mother and sister, who turned to watch them pass. Samuel did not look at the familiar kitchen or look at his mother or sister. He continued to look straight ahead. Samuel and his father passed out through the kitchen door. Samuel's mother and sister turned and followed them out of the house.

As Samuel's father stood by the truck with the motor running, Samuel hugged his mother.

"I intend to keep in touch all I can," Samuel said to his quietly crying mother. He held her head to his chest as she cried on the clean shirt she had provided for him. "I'll write you whenever I get the chance. I'm going to miss you all. But I won't be as far away from you as you think."

Beth came up and pressed close to both of them. She was crying too. Samuel wrapped his arm around her and pulled her in closer to him, next to their mother. As Beth cried, he rubbed the top of her head in a gesture of big brother affection. "I'm going to miss you too," Samuel said in a strangled big brother tone of voice. "You're not such a little snot after all. You're on the way to becoming quite a woman."

For several more minutes they held each other in silence. Then Samuel turned and walked to the truck without looking back. He didn't want to see them receding behind him. As he rounded the front of the truck, he heard his father speak to his mother and sister: "I don't know how often the trains run," Mr. Martin said. "It may be necessary for me or for both of us to stay overnight in a hotel. If I'm not back by sunset, don't go thinking the worst."

All in all, it was not the best thing to say to a mother and sister who feared that nothing but the worst might come of the venture their son and brother, respectively, was about to embark on.

Samuel's father put the truck in gear and drove down the dirt drive. As his father drove, Samuel held his bundle on his lap and looked straight ahead. He did not look back. He did not want to see the farm receding behind him. In a quasi superstition he had developed on the spot, Samuel felt that if he did not see his home fade from his sight, it would somehow make it more likely that he would return to it one day. His father turned the truck off the dirt drive and onto the dirt road that bordered the farm, following the road that led past and away.

"Your best bet is to go to the churches there," Mr. Martin said as the landscape slipped past them. "The churches in big cities are probably bigger than any we have in this part of the state. Hopefully big-city churches haven't let their wealth and bigness go to their heads and that they retain the Christian biblical commitment to helping poor strangers wayfaring in their midst. They might be able to help you with charity if you need it. At least they can point you to charitable institutions. They might also be able to help you find employment somewhere in the city."

They were about halfway between the farm and Columbus, heading on the road that led to the city. The land they were driving through was farmland. In the form of the fields and farmhouses passing by, the landscape slipping past them was familiar, differing only slightly in detail from the landscape both of them were familiar with. It was unfamiliar to Samuel in that he had never seen the area they were driving through before. He had never been this far away from home before. Passing through the unfamiliar yet familiar landscape, he felt both close to home and far away from it at the same time. In his mind, Samuel peopled the farms he was passing by with people sitting around the dinner tables together, happy and secure in the thought that, other than the end of life, they were facing no partings to come. He peopled the farm with people who walked the land that defined them and held a place for them. These people would continue to walk their land while Samuel walked somewhere undefined, alone on faraway streets that held no affection for him and held no place for him. As he watched the familiar yet unfamiliar landscape pass by, Samuel got a feeling of distance and closeness at the same time. The feeling of seeing familiar farms, combined with the feeling he was getting of distance from Harkness and the bloodhounds of the law, set him to thinking anew of looking for a job as a farmhand and moving back closer to home once the heat of his killing of Harold Ethridge receded.

Samuel's father turned to look at him. The question as to whether his son would have to leave home had been decided upon and put behind them. The automatic corollary question was still pending.

"As far as cities go, have you decided yet where you want to go yet?"

Figuring that his son was going through enough, Mr. Martin had not pressed him to make up his mind about what city in particular he wanted to go to. But they would arrive in Columbus soon enough. Destinations would have to be chosen and a train ticket purchased.

"Detroit, Chicago, New York, Indianapolis. For that matter, San Francisco. I suppose they're all on the same line, somewhere on the line. I'll buy you a ticket to anywhere you want to go."

It would be a one-way ticket, but Samuel didn't feel like commenting on that fact.

"Have you given it final thought where you want to head for?"

Samuel had never really considered New York. He had never even thought about California. He rather dismissed considering it now even though it was supposed to be warmer. At the moment, passing through landscape both familiar and unfamiliar, Samuel wasn't thinking of either New York or California. They were too far away. Going that far away would make getting home more difficult whenever the time and opportunity came, if it ever did.

"Chicago, I guess," Samuel said in a blank and disconnected voice. It wasn't an enthusiastic choice on his part. Neither was it a deeply considered or reasoned choice. The primary reason that he chose Chicago was because he was still influenced by his father's statement that Detroit was a one-industry town where, if he couldn't get a job on an automobile assembly line, he might not be able to find work at all. Indianapolis didn't mean that much to him. Along with a country reputation for other unsavory things, Chicago had a reputation for being a booming commercial and industrial center with many different industries open and hiring. He had no sense of Indianapolis as being an industrial city with thumping factories and an insatiable need for workers to man them. He didn't know if he could find much, if any, work there. Given that Indiana was just one state over, he could find his wanted posters posted on the bulletin boards of the city police department. Two states removed seemed to offer the best safety margin. Iowa and Des Moines had more of an image of a farm state and a farm city, respectively. It might be something to consider and a place to head for if he decided that he wanted to be a farmhand instead of a slaughterhouse worker.

Samuel's father offered nothing in response to his son's choice. He said nothing further, and Samuel offered nothing further.

The choice having been made more by default than anything, Samuel went back to looking ahead by default. He occasionally glanced off to the side to look at the passing farms, at most any of which he would have preferred to have taken a job as hired hand as opposed to being a meatpacking worker or steelworker, or a bricklayer as his Uncle Ned had become after his one-way sojourn to the city of Cincinnati.

"Wherever I go, I intend to keep in touch with you," Samuel said, spontaneously repeating what he had said to his mother as they had said goodbye. "Like I told Mother, I'll write to you."

"If you write to us, don't put your name or a return address on the envelope," his father said. "Even in the letter you should use an assumed name. They may possibly open and read the mail that is sent to the house, trying to find out where you are. I don't know if they'll do that. I think that's illegal. But it's better not to take the chance. On the chance that they may try to read your letters, in your letters you should claim to be a cousin of some sort. Pretend like you're from the family of a distant relative. Use a name we don't recognize, something that we know is not the name of any of our relatives but that they don't know isn't one of our relatives. You can put other clues in the letters that we will recognize but they won't. Just tell us what you're doing. Don't talk about what happened with you here in town. That way, if they're reading the mail, they won't put it together and figure out it's you. Print our address on your letters. Type the letters if you can so that someone won't recognize your handwriting. I hope you do keep in touch with us. I know your mother would especially appreciate that. But I wouldn't want your doing it to give you away."

To Samuel, his father's ideas were a bit distasteful, especially the part about using a false name. In a way it would make him feel like he was someone else. To Samuel, writing under a false name would be a bit like being buried under a false name. It would also force him to hide any expressions of love or eliminate them altogether and write under the cover of the kind of banal banter that a relative would use. Pretending to be someone else and avoiding talking about good times they had shared in the past would also reduce the sense of closeness he was trying to retain. But he otherwise agreed with his father's precautions.

"I will," Samuel said, looking straight ahead.

Having conveyed all his cautions to his son, Mr. Martin stopped talking. Both of them sat in silence as they drove, Samuel's father holding the wheel, Samuel holding his makeshift travel bag. As they drove, Samuel kept his head mostly straight ahead, but he looked out of the sides of his eyes at the farms passing by. He fantasized again about getting a job as a hired hand on a farm close to home. If he had seen a sign by the entrance to any farm saying "Farmhand Wanted," he would have had his father stop the truck so he could walk in and apply for the position. But none presented themselves.

The autumn day was bright and clear. Samuel could see the horizon. He could see the road ahead as it vanished into the horizon. He could see the faces of the people he imagined together and safe from separation in the farmhouses he was passing by. But he did not see the girl's face in the sky over the landscape he was traveling through.

They passed through several small towns similar to his hometown on the road they were traveling. As they did so, Samuel would look for signs seeking employees of any kind. He would have impulsively had his father stop if he had seen any, but there were none. Quickly enough, the towns fell away behind them, and they found themselves back in farm country.

The people in the streets of the towns didn't look much different from the people from his own hometown. If he had to go on the road and live as a hobo, Samuel would have rather wandered the back roads and towns of the land they were passing through than the back alleys of any large city.

In the towns they passed through, Samuel saw no buildings that resembled Mrs. Richardson's house in size and shape, or with obvious employees standing on display outside the front door with a line of obvious clients lined up outside. His father would have only admonished him that his troubles had all begun in a similar establishment back home. Samuel still wondered how Mrs. Richardson had taken his sudden departure from her bedroom and company the day he learned who the killer of the girl was. He wondered how she would take the news that she had made love that day to the boy who would become a killer himself to avenge the girl. Samuel didn't know if Mrs. Richardson ever felt dirty because of her profession. He didn't know if she felt dirty about propositioning a boy almost one-third her age. He didn't know if she would feel dirty when it came out that she had made love to a killer-to-be. But she had already more or less found that out from Constable Harkness.

The farm landscape had left Samuel with a residual sense of familiarity and connection to his life. For a short length of time, and in a small way, he was able to hold off the feelings of separation, isolation, and emptiness he knew had to come. But eventually the far wider dimensions of the outskirts of the city of Columbus came into view on the horizon. As they did so, the residual feeling of familiarity and continuance he had gotten as they had passed through the countryside and small towns drained away, leaving again a feeling of an empty void where familiarity and continuance had been. Cities, bigger ones than this, would be his future now, at least for the short term.

Streets would also be the shape of his future. Within the boundaries of the city, Samuel and his father pulled onto streets paved with brick and other solid paving material. Columbus was a relatively big city for its day. The buildings in the commercial district were larger than the ones in Samuel's hometown, which were no more than two stories high. The buildings in the city were often several stories high and mostly made of brick. Samuel's father wasn't familiar with the city. He drove around looking for the train station. In his doing so, they wove around several streets of what looked to be the central business district. The streets were filled with the relative bustle of people going about their commercial and personal functions. It was also filled with cars and trucks similar to theirs. Samuel's father wasn't familiar with city driving. More than once he misjudged the distance to a slowed automobile in front of him or pulling out from a side street and had to stop hard, just short of colliding with the other automobile. Samuel figured he should have driven. He wasn't familiar with city traffic either, but he figured his reaction time was better.

Mr. Martin finally was forced to stop at a gas filling station and ask for directions. He also had to fill up the gas tank the driver's seat was positioned over. The Model T wasn't a gas-guzzling SUV. It was pretty fuel-efficient by modern standards, but it ran its tank down on long hauls.

The station attendant gave them instructions on how to get to the train station. Samuel's father pulled the truck out of the filling station and headed in the direction given him. As Mr. Martin drove, Samuel looked around the city.

"Maybe when the heat dies down and the wanted posters disappear, I can come back and live here in Columbus," Samuel said of the city. "It isn't that far from home. If I learn a trade in Chicago, I might be able to bring it back with me and work in that trade here. That way we won't be so far apart."

It seemed a new and hopeful thought to Samuel. Samuel's father didn't answer.

Samuel had set the bag down on the last seat of the train car and turned around to talk with his father. They stood with Samuel in the train car and his father in the entranceway, with his back to the platform between the car Samuel was in and the next car. The final moment of parting had arrived. Samuel's father had earlier gone over everything he could think of to tell his son about what he should be aware of and look out for in the city waiting for him at the end of the train line. Given that he knew so little about big-city life, Samuel's father otherwise felt he had done an inadequate job of preparing his son for his new life away from home. At this juncture, there wasn't a lot left to be discussed. But instead of dismissing his father and sitting down to wait for the train to start rolling, Samuel had kept his father standing close to him and talking, even as the inbound and outbound passengers sorted themselves out, disembarked, and embarked and went their separate ways. Given the interval between the train's being in the station and all the passengers' having finished leaving and boarding, they both knew that the train would depart in short order. But Samuel kept talking with his father. He just had to hold on to the last visible remnant of his family until the end of the last minute they had together.

"Well, Son, I guess this is it," Samuel's father said as, out of the corner of his eye, he saw the conductor outside the train on the platform, looking around to make sure that all relevant passengers were either off or on.

"I knew we would come to a parting someday, but I had always thought it would be when I died. I never thought it would end like this."

A sharp two-edged twinge of both sorrow and desire to deny the parting went through Samuel from head to foot. It almost felt like he was being cut in two. But then the family had been cut in two. And he was the one who had cut it in two.

"I said I'm going to do everything I can to stay as close to you as I can," Samuel said with hollow-sounding decisiveness. "I meant what I said. I intend to come back and be closer to you soon enough in the future when the heat dies down. Like I said, I might live here in Columbus. Maybe in a town closer to home."

Samuel's words drifted past his father into the space between the train cars. For all practical purposes, his words were inaudible when they past the steps of the train car and blended in with and were lost in the hissing sounds of the resting train about to come back to life.

"Let's not fool ourselves, Son," Samuel's father said in a quiet voice. "Things can never be the way they were with us again. I'm not trying to knock you down or say that you can't do it. I know you. You can do a great many things you set your mind to. You may come back closer to us someday, like you said. But you'll always have to live in the shadows and see us from there."

"Then I'll live in the shadows and love you from there," Samuel said in quiet defiance of fate and the distance to come between them. "I had to give up the girl. I didn't have any choice there. I would have fought to save her. I'm going to fight fate and distance to stay close to you however I can. I'm not going to forget you or give you up."

"And we're not going to forget you," Samuel's father said. "You and your sister have been the real joy of our lives. I'm going to hate losing you more than anything I've ever lost in my life. I'm sure your mother and sister feel the same. At least we have the consolation of knowing that your leaving doesn't have anything to do with us and isn't a rejection of us and the family the way Uncle Ned's leaving was."

Another twinge of equal magnitude went through Samuel. He felt a near-desperate urge to grab and hold onto anything within the landscape or in his life that wouldn't move the way the train would soon move, but he was too manly to break into even symbolic hysterics.

"I'm sorry for splitting up the family," Samuel said, speaking quickly. He had a lot to make up for. He had a lot to say and little time left to say it. "I'm sorry I caused any of you pain. I didn't mean to split the family. I never meant to cause you or anybody in the family any pain. I'm sorry we can't be together the way we once were. I'm sorry to have split up our lives together. I'm sorry I caused loss to you and Mother. I'm sorry I caused any loss to this family. I'm sorry that I caused this family to be lost."

"I'm sorry you've lost the family you had," Samuel's father said. "I'm sorry you lost the family you wanted to have with the girl." He looked away out the window of the train for a moment and then looked back at his son. He knew his son loved him and the rest of the family. He had a lot to say on one point, about whom his son loved, and little time to say it.

"I don't know if it means anything to you now," his father said. "I don't know if it makes any difference now or if it can make any kind of difference at all. But I was wrong in a lot of things I said about her. I blamed her for breaking apart this family. But she wasn't at fault for that. I blamed her being the way she was as the cause of everything that happened to her and for what you did after she was killed. Maybe both of you could have made much better choices and done things different. In that sense you're both to blame for what's befallen you both. But she wasn't at fault for everything in the way she had to live her life. She wasn't at fault for what was done to her before she came to our town or what was done to her in our town. I can fault you for what you did in her name, but I shouldn't and can't fault you for loving her. I know now it was a real enough love, more than a lot of men have for any woman. Like Constable Harkness said, in a backhanded way you must have loved her enough to have killed for her. I suppose there are a lot better ways of showing love, even for the deceased, than killing for them. But if it means anything to you now, you and she should have been married. She should have been part of the family. You can't take her with you where you're going, but if it means anything to you, I say you should have brought her home to all of us. I don't know if that will mean anything to you where you're going. I don't know if it will mean anything to you in any family you will ever have, but you should have had a family with her, despite what we and the town might have said about it. We all should have been a family together. I can see clearly now that you did love her. A love like that has got to mean something, wherever it might or might not lead. A man should have something to sum up his life. Our love for you pretty much sums up my life and your mother's life. Your love for that girl pretty much sums up your life. Maybe all our sums taken together don't add up to all that much. But loving someone as strongly as you loved her puts some kind of mark of meaning on a life."

From outside the train, the familiar conductor's cry of "All aboard!" sounded. Samuel's father glanced out through the window and then back at his son.

"I've got to get going, or I'll end up in Chicago with you," he said. "I suppose we could do all right together on those streets, but someone has got to look after your mother and sister."

Mr. Martin turned and quickly walked down the steps of the train car. The train jerked to life and started to move as he stepped off onto the platform. Samuel walked to the top of the steps and looked at his father as the train started to pull away. Mr. Martin turned around and looked at his departing son.

"Never forget that all of us love you, Son," Samuel heard his father say as the train started to slowly pick up speed. Samuel didn't say anything. He started to raise his hand to wave a numb goodbye, but his father put his head down to an angle where he would not have been able to see him wave. Samuel couldn't tell in the widening gap between them, but his father seemed to be crying.

As the train pulled away from the platform and the station, Samuel watched the figure of his father recede into the background. As his father started to disappear around the side of the car in the increasingly oblique angle, Samuel leaned forward so he could continue to see him. He did not walk down to the bottom of the stairs, where he could have leaned out past the side of the train. He did not want to see his father shrink and finally disappear into the landscape falling away behind. In another quasi superstition, he thought that if he watched his father vanish all the way, it would somehow jinx the possibility that he would be able to come back to him and the rest of his family. He was already wondering if he would ever see his father again.

When he no longer could see his father from where he was standing, Samuel turned and went back to his seat. There were only a few other people in the train car. They all sat facing forward the way the train was going. None of them looked at Samuel. He didn't look at them. He sat down and took a grip on the top of his improvised travel sack. The fabric of the seat cover was going threadbare and had a rip in one place. Samuel didn't pause to notice the repair work that his seat and others in the car needed. He sat with his head partway down and looked nowhere in particular into the close-in distance with a blank stare.

Everything drained out of Samuel as it had never drained out of him before. Unlike the feeling he had in his room the night before, the emptiness wasn't a corridor with walls that could be brushed. It was a void expanding faster than he could reach out and grab by the fringe to hold back the expansion. This was it. This was the real and final parting. In the two days before he had left, he had still been in the house. His parents and sister had still been nearby. He had said goodbye to his mother and sister earlier. They had passed behind him when the truck had driven away from the house. At least he had had his father with him on the trip to the train. Sitting in his seat in the moving train, he felt totally alone, more alone than he had been at any time in his life. He felt even more alone than he had after the girl had been killed. The feeling of emptiness and being disconnected from his past and the future was total and absolute. There wasn't anything to hold on to and no way to fool himself into thinking that he hadn't yet separated from his family and the life he had known. This was the end of all his yesterdays and the beginnings of an unseen tomorrow.

It was the end of the only home he had known and the beginning of a long veiled road that might never touch again on his yesterdays or on any home. The last thin and frayed tether had been cut. There were no horizons of the past left open to him. The horizon of the future he was heading for was uncertain at best, ugly at worst. Like a child's kite lost on the wind, trailing a long frayed and broken string behind it uselessly, he was flying on the wind toward a horizon he could not see and had wanted no part of. He could not see his past. He could not see his future. He could not see his home. He could not see his family. He could not see the worn areas of the seat he was sitting on or the dirt and grime ground into the floor of the train car he was staring down blankly at.

When the train conductor came by punching tickets, Samuel handed his ticket to the conductor without looking up at him. The conductor didn't ask him where he was going, and Samuel made no attempt to engage the man in friendly conversation about what it was like where he was going. Samuel sat with one hand on the top of the bag and the other arm across his leg, looking down at the floor. The coat he was wearing, the clothes he was wearing, and the items in his makeshift traveling bag were the few items of his past that he was carrying with him into his makeshift future.

His home, his family, the girl, and all the times of his life, were locked away from him and receding deeper into the past with every mile traversed. In that interval between what had been for him and what could never could be again, Samuel made no attempt to measure the passage of time. The passage of distance he measured numbly by the creaking, clacking, and swaying of the train car. For a length of time he didn't know, somewhere between an hour and two hours, he didn't look out the window of the train. He just stared at the floor. Several times he tried to remember the happy times of his life on the farm. But every time he would think of anything from his past, a pain of remembrance and a piercing stab of loss would shoot through him. The pain would be so sharp that he would have to drop the remembrance as soon as he'd started it. Trying to think about the happy times of his past was like stabbing himself deep with the girl's knife. The exercise of trying to think about the life he had lost was just too painful of an exercise for him. It brought him nothing anyway. He could spend the rest of his life torturing himself to no avail or useful purpose by remembering the life, the family, and the love he was leaving behind. Samuel figured that he could cripple himself with the self-inflicted pain of memory. In the end he could render himself ineffectual and leave himself knotted up in a fetal ball of pain with memories of a past that was gone from him. He didn't have a lot of choice in the matter. If he were to function, he simply couldn't spend all his time thinking about the life he had lost. He would fall apart and live in pieces in a world that was probably merciless on those who fell apart under its heel. To be able to continue in any manner in the world ahead, he would have to stop slashing himself open with memories that would and could do nothing for him. Fate, it seemed, demanded everything from him as a price of entry into the world ahead of him. The vacuum of the void around him had now sucked in and submerged his memories of his home and family.

Nature, it seems, abhors a vacuum. Amid the void in his emotions created by his separation from all he had known and the pain of trying to remember it, a new and functionally different but otherwise functional set of thoughts slowly took shape in Samuel's head. From out of the void of what he could not get back to and what he could not think about, a new Samuel Martin started to emerge to fill that void and give it substance. It was a change born of anger, anger at all the things and persons, himself included, who had taken his past, home, family, and lover away from him. It was a change born of necessity. He simply could not go into a world whose roughness he could not gauge as a sorrow-crippled pantywaist who could not stand in the world.

Actually it wasn't a totally new Samuel Martin that emerged. It was the Samuel Martin that had emerged briefly for a savage moment and then ducked its head back into a world he had still thought secure. As he sat with his head down, Samuel's thoughts became focused and sharp-edged. The focused Samuel Martin, the captain of the baseball team and wrestling team, came back with a wider mandate conferred by the wider need of survival. He would not go into the world of the big city as a crippled ball of mush living forever in memories and wallowing in homesickness. He would walk into the world ahead with all the focus in him and all the hardness that focus could provide. The world ahead would not see Samuel Martin, lonely farm boy, walking the streets of his exile, endlessly longing for his home and family. It would see the hard and focused Samuel Martin that had walked out gunning for Harold Ethridge. It might not be the Samuel Martin that others had found to be winsome and fetching. Winsome and fetching had died in him with the girl. Being a tender and callow fellow hadn't gotten him much of anywhere. Being a head-buster and a head-shooter hadn't exactly gotten him where he wanted to be with the girl or in life either, but at least he was the one who had remained on his feet. He had the definite feeling that where he was going, a man was more recognized by his ability to stay on his feet than by the way he loved his family or orphan girls he found in an alley.

Like the tide of a rising river in a flood covering a pleasant meadow that was part of a floodplain, the rising anger in Samuel gradually submerged the soft and mossy shapes of his warm and fond but useless memories of his earlier life that was disappearing behind him down the receding track. It also came to submerge his love for home, for family, and for the girl he would not have a family with. It didn't reduce or alter Samuel's determination to try to find a way to get back to and somehow be close to his family he had left behind. As he rode with his head down on the swaying, creaking train, Samuel knew he wouldn't put that overriding desire away from him. But in its present form, his nostalgia and his emotional attachment to home and family could functionally impair him to the point that he would not be able to function in his new life and in his new world. He pretty much figured that functionality and the ability to think on his feet would be the watchword of the day and all the days ahead where he was going. If the world wouldn't let him be a lover, then the world he was going forth into would know him as a close-order proxy to the Samuel Martin who had gone forth in iron-cold blood after the man who had killed his lover and killed the love in him. Compared to the sight of a cow-eyed, lovestruck boy with a faraway look on his face as he lay on the grass under the blue skies of summer, dreaming of love and the future while he stroked the hair of the girl he was in love with as she lay with her head on his chest, the new functional Samuel Martin wouldn't be a pretty or fetching sight. If life and the world wouldn't allow him to be Samuel Martin, giddy and callow farm boy lover of a young girl he was so in love with that her voice was the same to him as the spinning of the world; if the world wouldn't let him be Samuel Martin, lover of home and family, then the world would get the hard, functional Samuel Martin. If necessary, it would be the functional equivalent of the Samuel Martin that Constable Harkness had found with blood on his boots. That would be the Samuel Martin the world would get. But then again, Samuel didn't think that a world that could produce Harold Ethridge was deserving of much better. The stirring new Samuel pushed his hand down on the bag. Inside the bag he could feel the hard form of the pistol his father had given him. Ahead lay the unseen form of a life that could prove hard and unyielding.

The newly emerging Samuel raised his head from his downcast position and looked out the train window for the first time since the train had left the station. By that time the train had long left the city of Columbus behind. It was now traveling through the same kind of farmland as he and his father had driven through. The same type of farmhouses at the corners of the same kinds of fields were passing by. Like the farms they had passed in the truck, these fields were largely empty. Most of the crops had been harvested. But the scene was basically the same as the one they had driven through in the truck. The difference was that they had had the windows open in the truck. The train windows were locked shut. The extra degree of isolation made Samuel feel more cut off and disconnected from the land and the life he had known.

In his mind Samuel filled the farmhouses the train was passing by with people like himself whom he knew. His situation gnawed inside him. The people in the farms he was passing hadn't had to go running out their back doors. They weren't heading into some great and empty unknowable. They had their place in the world. They had their families intact around them. They had their love and those who loved them. He had none of those things, no place, no home, no family, and no love. He couldn't see many people outside in the chilly autumn weather, but it wasn't hard for him to envision the landscape he was passing through as green and fertile as if it were in the middle of summer.

In the corners of the fields, out of eyesight from the farmhouses, Samuel imagined boys his age lying on their backs on the grass looking up at the blue sky above, their sweethearts lying with their heads on the boys' chests the way he and the girl had done during the picnic he and Ben Harper had snuck off to have with their improper sweethearts from Mrs. Richardson's house. A lover was something the world didn't seem to want Samuel as. If the world didn't want him as a lover, the world would get him hard and unloving, equally able to stand up to any hard unlovingness the world had to offer. If the world didn't want to know him as Samuel Martin, lover of family, home, land, place, and wayward girls on the run, then the world would know him as Samuel Martin, angry, iron-souled, revenant, reduced product of all the love that had been wrenched from him. But it would know him by some other name than Samuel Martin.

Samuel looked up into the autumn sky. He saw the face of the girl suspended in the sky over the landscape he was passing through. Her hair was half over one of her eyes. The disembodied face in his imagination had a sad and distant look in both her eyes. The face traveled with him as the landscape moved beneath it. As Samuel felt the sway of the train car, the irony hit him fully. The girl had been forced to run away from her home in possible peril of her life. She had jumped and ridden a railroad freight car with no clear idea of where she was going. She had stopped in his town long enough to die there. In the end, and as the result of her death, she had sent him running out of his town as an orphan in possible peril of his freedom and his life to ride the rails as she had. For all Samuel knew, he was going to the destination where the girl might have ended up if she had not jumped off the boxcar she had been riding in beyond the distant fringe of his town. He might have a bit of a clear idea in mind where he was going, but in another way he was completing the girl's journey for her. In the end, the end they had both created for themselves, the path of the girl's life had become the path of his life.

Samuel would and could never hate the girl. He had reserved his love for her and had extended it unequivocally to her. He had reserved his life and future for her. He just hadn't imagined that he would ever come to recapitulate her life so completely. Still, he could never hate the girl he had loved and whom he still loved as totally as he had loved her in life. But the new emerging Samuel Martin was able to reserve a small measure of anger for the girl.

I see you've decided to come with me, he said in his mind to the image he saw there. *Are you going to come all the way with me to whatever comes? This is a bit of a switch for you. When we were together in life, other than the fair and Gustafson Lake, you never wanted to go any real distance with me. Why do you want to come along with me now, when I don't even know where I'm going myself? Are you thinking differently of me and going with me now that you're dead? Do the dead think differently in death than they do in life? Is leaving and distance different to the dead than to the living? Or is there no one back home whom you care to haunt? Now that I've lost my way, have you found your way, and your way is to go with me on mine even though I don't know where I'm going?*

It was the first of many one-way conversations he would have with the far-flung ghost of his mind.

Damn you, Clarinda! Samuel thought as he saw her face in the sky. *This is as much your fault as it is mine or Ethridge's or your family's. Why couldn't you have believed me? We could have all been together in one place. We could have put all the pain of your past behind us. We could have all been one family, one love. Why couldn't you believe that I loved you? Had your soul been hurt so bad inside that all the love in you had been cut out of you? Had the ability to believe in love been cut out of you like a deer being dressed out by a hunter? I may have acted stupid and frightened you, but sometimes loving a person makes you do stupid things.*

He continued to look at the ghost in his mind.

You just wouldn't believe that I loved you and didn't want to hurt you. You just had to go your own way with your pain and fear. Now both of us are on a road we can't get off, a road taking us somewhere we don't want to be. Neither of us can ever get back to what we were and could have been. Without my family, I'm alone now. I don't know if I'll be alone for the rest of my life, but the two worlds I wanted most of all are gone. When you lose two worlds, it's hard to believe that there will ever be a world for you. If you had believed me and trusted me, we could have put those two worlds together and been sitting together in the middle of love and life. Now you don't have your life, and I don't have the only two definitions of life I ever had or wanted. I still have a hollow shell of my life, but I don't know if anything ever will or ever can fill my life the way you and my family did.

The train continued to rattle and sway.

Now I'm following you out on an empty road of my own. I don't have much more choice in the matter than you had. But I can chose what I take with me, and I will take your memory with me. I will take your memory with me wherever I go. I'm going to have to travel light from now on. I don't know if carrying your memory is going to be a blessing or a burden to me, but I don't have a lot of choice in the matter. I will always remember you, no matter what comes and where I am. I'll remember you no matter what your real name was or what name I will be using. Maybe we will meet again someday in a land where names don't mean anything.

The face of the girl had no answers for him. In life she had had no answers for herself. She had come into town as an orphan on the run and had lived there under a name she had made up for herself. She had sent Samuel out of town as an orphan on the run to live under a name he would make up for himself. It had been quite a feat of self-replication for a girl who might have remained childless and barren for the rest of her life. But in her sequential self-duplication, she hadn't managed to create any companionship for herself on her journey, and Samuel figured that her memory would be a thin companion for him. They were both alone on the road. But they were on different roads, where they could not touch each other.

When Samuel finished his silent soliloquy to the silent girl, he did not put his head back down. He turned and looked ahead, down the length of the train car. At the same time, he kept the passing landscape in view from the corner of his eye. The world behind him was growing small as he got farther away from it. The world ahead was as uncertain as it had been when it became clear that he had no choice but to seek a different life. The life he had known was fading behind him. The rest of his life was everywhere ahead of him and nowhere to be found. In Samuel's mind the girl was in the sky and everywhere around. But she had no road map to offer him to guide him into his future. Then again, she had come to his town and had come to him with no road map to guide herself by.

As Samuel's home and the life he had known receded away from him down the track, he knew that his parents and his sister would be in his heart and memory forever. At the same time, he knew the girl would be in his heart and mind forever. She would be with him everywhere he would go. He would only have to look into his heart, mind, and memory to see her. At the same time, she was nowhere to be found outside her grave, which he was leaving behind and might never see again. He had no choice but to leave her behind along with his home and family. At the same time, he could not put her memory away from him and leave her memory behind, not even if he had wanted to. In that sense he had no choice but to take her with him. He would always carry her with him. As Samuel looked ahead and in no direction in particular, he remembered the last line of the last stanzas of the hymn that had been sung in church the Sunday he had gone on the picnic with the girl: "In life, in death, O Lord, abide with me."

"In life and death, O girl, please stay with me," Samuel said to himself as he looked back at the life and lives he had left behind, the life and lives he had once called his own, and looked forward to a place he might forever be a sojourner in, in a life he might never be able to call his own again.

At the time there was a yet unpublished poem about coming to Chicago:

> Mamie beat her head against the bars of a little Indiana town and dreamed of romance and big things off somewhere the way the railroads ran. She could see the smoke of the engines get lost down where the streaks of steel flashed in the sun, and when the newspaper came in on the morning mail she knew there was a big Chicago far off, where all the trains ran.[1]

The train he was riding on swayed and bumped and clacked off the miles. Whether the fictitious Mamie had ever made it to Chicago, Samuel didn't know. Clarinda had dreamed of getting to Chicago and a better bordello than Mrs. Richardson's but had died before her journey could begin. The irony that he was completing in hard, cold, unwished-for reality the journey the two girls had dreamed of taking crushed Samuel under its weight as if he had fallen under the wheels of the train.

The once familiar and loved world he had known was gone completely. It was a totally new and threatening world he saw lying ahead of him. It was a world he had no idea how to face. He had left all the certainty of his former life fading away behind him down the track, disappearing behind the train. He had left all the loved ones of his life behind, either alive or dead. Leaving home and his loved ones was something he had thought he would never do. He had no real idea how to go about doing it or if he could handle it. It was all new and alien and threatening to him. In that sense he kind of had to take the girl with him as a spirit guide on his journey that would not lead back to home. Wherever the girl was now, she had taken the same path he was now following when she had left her home. The girl had gone only forward from there. She had known about only going onward and not being able to go back.

---

[1] Carl Sandburg, "Mamie," in *Chicago Poems* (New York: Henry Holt, 1916).

Chapter 23

It had been a long night's journey, but it wasn't a journey that had ended in day. It was in the middle hours of early morning and still dark outside when the train pulled into the station. Samuel had tried to sleep on the train but had been able to grab only a few fitful moments. He had sat awake for most of the night wondering what awaited him in the city, trying to imagine what he would encounter or be confronted with, figuring that what he would encounter would probably be larger and more involved than he was imagining.

Out of the corner of his eye, he had seen some of the lights of the city as the train had approached the station. Farther away he had caught distant glimpses of lights coming out of the windows of skyscrapers, monumental buildings he had heard of and had seen in pictures but hadn't seen in their towering muscular reality. The tallest structure he was familiar with in his hometown was the town grain elevator, its weathered exterior stretching five stories high, on the outskirts of town. But the grain elevator hadn't been built for human habitation. The human-scale structures designed to be inhabited were no more than two stories high, such as the farmhouse that was the home he had left behind and the house of Harold Ethridge, bigger than his, where the girl had met her end. The biggest two-story house in his hometown was Mrs. Richardson's house, converted to a bordello, where he had met the girl going in and had lost her coming out. But most of the time on his journey to a world he could not imagine, he had kept his face straight ahead and hadn't looked to the side.

As the train pulled into the station, the lights that were farther out and higher up as the it toward its final stop. It is one of oddities of Chicago architecture and land ownership that the railroad owned the ground level that Union Station was situated on while the air rights, starting at the second floor above the ground, were owned by other conglomerates. Those corporations had built office buildings and warehouses above the track, the structure held aloft by heavy iron girders. It made for a practical and efficient utilization of limited space. It also made for a train station from which riders could walk right into the heart of city. Between the rows of train tracks and girders were cement walkways that passengers would disembark on and use to walk to the main station building.

With a screech of brakes, the train rolled to a stop. As the conductors went about pulling down the fold-up disembarkment steps between the cars, the few other passengers on the postmidnight train got out of their seats and moved to the doors at the ends of the cars. Samuel waited until they had all passed before he slowly got up from his seat. For a moment he thought seriously of staying in his seat in the hopes that eventually the train might head back the way it had come and that he would get off back in Columbus, Ohio, where he would live, near to his home. Columbus was a world not quite so far away. In Samuel's estimate, according to his feelings, Columbus was another country. According to the way he felt standing in the empty train coach, Chicago was another planet.

Samuel quickly abandoned the idea of riding the train back home. He only had a one-way ticket. A conductor would roust him out before the train headed back east, which it might not do for days, depending on the schedule of its runs. Reluctant to face the new world waiting for him out in the dark beyond the station, reluctant to step into a world that might prove to hold nothing for him but darkness and further loss, Samuel walked out of the train coach and down the steps between cars. Carrying his bedroll backpack, he stepped onto the rust- and tobacco-juice-stained concrete of the walkway. He followed the retreating figure of the last person who had gotten off the train, making his way to the main station.

The inside of the station was more inviting than the walkway alongside the place where the train had parked. Samuel stopped and looked around. The main station area was wide with a high ceiling. It was roomy and well lit with a number of wide, high-backed benches where passengers usually sat and waited for their train to be called. Given the lateness of the hour and the fact that no trains were departing at night, there were no people sitting in any of the benches. There were ticket booths along one wall, but no one was manning them. At the far end of the main station area, there were several doors that opened onto the street beyond. The unknown street was cloaked in the darkness of the night. The last of the departing passengers who had come in on the night train exited through the front door, leaving Samuel alone in the station.

Facing the unknowns, uncertainties, and possible dangers of the city was going to be daunting enough in the full light of day. Samuel had absolutely no desire to face whatever dangers presented by low-level street denizens of the night and thugs lurking down every alley and waiting around every corner in the dark city he couldn't see the outline of. He decided that he would wait for dawn before he even ventured to the front of the station.

Samuel sat down on one of the benches in the back and leaned against his backpack for support. At first he stared across the empty station. Then he shifted his focus and stared inside himself, trying to formulate his strategy for the coming day, which seemed as many hours away as number the miles he was away from home.

While he sat running over what he would do, not having even a clear outline of what he was facing or what he would do, one strategy Samuel ran around in his mind with increasing seriousness was that he would take some of the money he had brought with him and buy a ticket back to Columbus, Ohio, where he would get off the train. He would live in Columbus and slip back home from time to time. It had been his first idea, but he had rejected it because, while Columbus was far closer to his home, it was also closer to the Ohio legal system and police. He could get picked up for the murder of Harold Ethridge. Columbus was too close for comfort. He wasn't even sure if Chicago was far enough away for safety. From his love of western lore, Samuel knew that Billy the Kid had fled all way from New York to the Wild West to escape a murder charge for killing a man in New York. But the law had finally brought him down.

Reluctantly, Samuel pushed away his idea of returning straightaway to his home state. It was far too risky, at least for now. In his mind, he ran through alternate ideas of how to proceed and make his way forward in Chicago. None of those ideas were as pleasant to consider as his original idea of returning to the outlands of his home. But the situation forced his direction on him. Like the cold and empty feeling that had settled in on him like a cold, wet shroud when it had finally dawned on him that Clarinda didn't want to see him anymore, the possibility, if not the probability, that he would never see home again pressed down upon him as if it were the weight of the train that had taken him from his home to the distant city he did not want to go out into. From where he sat looking out into the dark, his view of his future was dubious at best, as dark and foreboding as the darkness outside the door of the station.

As he sat in the semidark of the station, contemplating the unknowns of the city outside and the unknowables of his life beyond, Samuel fell asleep on the bench. In his sleep on the bench, he saw the girl in a dream image. In his dream, her face floated in the darkness outside the glass of the front doors of the station. The expression on her dream image face was neither welcoming nor beckoning, neither alarmed nor cautionary. It was more blank and uncertain. Her eyes seemed to be focused elsewhere. He wasn't even sure she was looking at him.

"Well, girl, I see you made it all the way here with me," Samuel said in his dream narrative. "I'm kind of surprised that you came all the way here with me. Outside of doing what you did so well in bed, you weren't very much inclined to go anywhere with me, anywhere that involved sharing a life with me. But here you are with me now. I just wish you would have thought more of going my way with me and staying with me when you were alive. If you had stayed with me and gone with me instead of running away from me and wanting to leave me behind at every turn, if you had cleaved yourself to me, then both of us would be together at home, together in a place we know instead of in the faraway places we both find ourselves separated in, places where we can't get to each other. But you just had to go your own way. It was your own way that got you to where you are now, wherever that place is, and finally got me to where I am now. I blame myself for that as much as I blame you. But I blame you as much as I blame myself. But then I guess the time has arrived that the assignment of blame is irrelevant."

In his dream, the girl did not move toward him like he imagined a haunting spirit would.

"If you're a ghost following me to haunt me, why do you hold yourself away from me, outside the door? If you want to haunt me, move in close to me. Move into my soul. Take over my mind. Possess me until all I can think of or remember is you. Drive me mad. Leave me a babbling madman in the alleys of this city. I may find more comfort in being mad than I will find walking the streets of this city as a sane man sojourner remembering the home he has lost, the family he has lost, the love that he has lost, and all the other things that he has lost in life."

In his dream, Samuel looked again at the image of Clarinda suspended in the air above the sidewalk outside the station door.

"Why are you holding yourself away from me? Is it your way of trying to tell me to stir myself and go forth into the city boldly and make my way there? Is it your way of trying to be with me and help me from the beyond? Is it your way of telling me that you'll be with me in spirit? Or is it just more of your way of keeping your distance from me while you keep company with me? Are you following in death the pattern you followed in life? What does that do for you in death? What does that do for you now? What does that do for either of us where we are now?"

In his dream, Samuel paused and looked at the image of the girl beyond the door.

"What are you trying to tell me? What are you here with me to say? Are you trying to say that I behaved recklessly? All right, I behaved recklessly and brashly, even violently, around you, but never to you. I loved you too much to ever hurt you. Why couldn't you believe that I loved you? Or by that time had all belief in love been beaten out of you? From the moment I met you, was love and the ability to love already dead within you? Is that why you're here now? To try to make up for not loving me back when we were alive together in the town we've both left, the town that I can never return to and that you'll be buried in forever? Are you sad that you lost my love when you left it behind and went on your headstrong way to lose your life? Have you come after me with your hat and your heart in hand to say you're sorry you didn't love me the way I loved you? Does love mean more to you now that you're in the great beyond, where everything is clear and dear to you now, especially love, but you can't give or receive love where you are now? What does love mean to you out there? What can love between us mean to either of us where we are now, both of us far away from home, both of us lost and alone?"

In his dream, the girl moved toward him. Holding both her arms out toward him with her palms open, she slowed as she approached. She seemed to strain at the effort. It was as if she was trying to reach him but couldn't fully cross the gap. Yet she managed to reach her hands out to him. Samuel thought her intention was to cup his face in her hands. Instead he felt her tug on his shoulder.

"Wake up, son. You can't sleep here," the voice said. Samuel jolted to wakefulness. The morning sun streamed through the glass of the front doors from the street beyond. People were walking on the sidewalk outside. People were moving inside the station, crossing the floor and standing at ticket windows. Ticket clerks were standing behind the counter windows.

"Be thankful that I found you and not some of the roustabouts from the train yard in back. They would have dragged you and tossed you unceremoniously out a back door into the alley. This is a train station, not a flophouse, and they don't want it being used as one."

Samuel looked up to where the voice came from. He saw an older-looking Negro dressed in a clean starched uniform tugging on his shoulder. He assumed the man to be a Pullman porter or a train announcer.

"I don't remember seeing you here during the day. You must have come in on the last train during the night."

"Ah, yeah," Samuel said in an apologetic voice. "I'm sorry to have fallen asleep on your bench, but I didn't get any sleep on the train. I was dead tired, and I didn't want to go out into the city at night, so I sat down to wait for day. I guess I fell asleep."

"Stayin' off the streets of this town at night is generally a better idea than walking them in the dark," the man said. "Especially when you don't know the streets and where the danger is." The man looked at Samuel's backpack bedroll. "You look like a farm boy. Did you leave the farm and come to the city looking to find work?" he said in a friendly voice. "A whole lot of men are comin' up from the South for the same reason. Are you up from the South? You don't sound like you're from Dixie."

"I'm from Ohio," Samuel said. "Of late I've been through a lot of reverses in life. I thought that I might be able to start over here in this city."

It was the first time Samuel had ever spoken with a Negro. He had seen them riding through town on freight wagons, but he had never talked with one. He had heard it said that Negroes didn't have enough sense to wear shoes or come in out of the rain and that they were lazy and shiftless. But the porter seemed reasonable and intelligent. Samuel felt it would be a good idea to emphasize that he wasn't lazy himself. If the man knew the city, he could prove to be a valuable source of information on how to get started there.

"You look young to have been through that many reverses in life that it would drive," the man said, his voice still friendly and sympathetic. Samuel wondered if the man was suspicious of his story.

"You don't need a long series of unfortunate events to send you away from home. Just your mother being dead, your father dying, and the bank foreclosing on your mortgage," Samuel said. It was the first iteration of the story he would give for the rest of his life to explain why he was where he was and not back at home. The details would change slightly. The location and state of origin would vary, but the basic story would remain: a tragic story of teenage boy driven from his home and onto the road by a series of unfortunate events. The real story of his reckless love of a reckless girl and his vengeance-crazed killing of the man who had killed her was something he would carry forever in his heart like he already carried the girl's image permanently etched in his mind. He would bring the real story out only rarely and only to those he would come to trust implicitly. Or when he felt he was going to die.

The porter or train caller had heard the story before: everything gone at home, the city promising all the wayward soul could hope for. At times the city was seemingly being inundated by economic and racial refugees swarming to the city, drawn by the promise of work and high pay and all forms of opportunities not available in the stagnant and hidebound worlds they had left. The boy on the bench was not the first white farm boy type the porter had seen come through the station. But the largest number of hopeful sojourners coming to the city were Negroes like himself, up from the Deep South of dirt-floored shanties in dirt-poor shantytowns with poverty and sharecropping, punctuated and accented by Jim Crow, iron-sheathed segregation, and white-robed Klansmen. They were drawn to the city by stories of big corporations hiring and paying wages that would be veritable fortunes back home in the shantytowns they had escaped from. They also came running from hooded night riders and beatings, burnings, and lynchings done at the slightest provocation or done just for entertainment on a Saturday night. At the time and in years after, in the history of the era, the movement of Negroes from the South to the relatively safer, relatively open, and relatively more opportunity-promising environs of cities like Chicago and Detroit would come to be called the Great Migration. Such was the moment and the movement Samuel had stepped off the train and into.

At the moment, Samuel thought it might be best to give assurance that he wasn't lazy and that he was in a working city looking for gainful work. He also was worried that city dwellers might think that farm people were unskilled in city work and were essentially useless at it. If that was the local prejudice, he had to dispel it, or it could make finding work problematic.

"Yes, I was a farmer," Samuel went on. "I may be a farmer, but farmers are workingmen. You can't be lazy and be a successful farmer. When you're a farmer, you grow up working and knowing how to work from birth. I'm a workingman. I'm not a layabout. I didn't come here to panhandle or live by begging. I came here to work."

The one definite thing Samuel had come away with from his night of wondering what to do was the knowledge that he would have to find work quick, before the money he carried hidden in his shoes was gone.

"I did hard work where I came from. I can do hard work here in the city. I just need to find work. Do you happen to know who in the city might be hiring?"

"Right offhand I don't have the latest information on who's hiring," the man said. "The three biggest industries in the city are the railroads and the Pullman train car building company, the farm implement manufacturers, and the meat-packers. They're always looking for workingmen, and they're not particular. There are plenty of small businesses and shops, but they're all in ethnic areas. The Irish, the Polish, and the Italians pretty much deal with their own and hire their own."

"Is the railroad hiring here at this station?" Samuel asked. For a second the hopeful notion dawned in him that if he could get a job on the rail line he'd ridden in on, he might be able to ride it back to his home state and slip off and sneak home to visit his family from time to time.

"We're not hiring here at the station," the man said. "We have all the people we need here. I don't know about the railroads in general. You'll have to check at one of the main freight yards. I'd say your best bet is to look for work in a factory or at one of the meatpacking houses in Packingtown. They pull in a lot of workers from all over."

The man glanced toward the front door. "There's work out there. The city's growing by leaps and bounds. They need all kinds of workers to keep up the pace. Especially the packinghouses. The hours are long—twelve-hour shifts, some of them. They don't always pay all that much of a living wage, especially if you've got a family to support. But they hire across the board. Just do your work and don't give them any trouble, and they'll keep you working."

At that moment Samuel remembered that it was the meatpacking factories of Chicago that Harold Ethridge sold his hogs to and where he sent them to be butchered.

When he wasn't busy butchering young girls.

"I'm going to need a place to stay," Samuel said. "Are there any rooming houses or boardinghouses that take in transients? And how much do they charge? I have some money with me, but if they charge an arm and a leg, I'll be broke before I can find work."

"There are flophouses around the city that are reasonable in price," the man said. "Nickel a night or so. You don't get much beyond a space on the floor and maybe a blanket. But it's out of the rain and snow, and it keeps you apart from the muggers and jackrollers. Some of the churches will take you in on a night-to-night basis, but they don't want you taking up residence there. Some of the restaurants make up and give out sandwiches to migrants like you. The cops can tell you better which ones."

"Can you tell me where these flophouses are?" Samuel asked.

"Not right offhand," the man said. "But they're probably all in the poorer parts of the city, which are also the rougher parts. If you want the address of one, you'll do better to ask a policeman. They would know.

They're the ones who get called on to break up fights outside the flophouses and pick up the dead bodies in alleys."

The man paused and gathered his thoughts.

"As far as working and living near where you work goes, the meatpacking houses have a whole work district and workers' district of their own. It's called Packingtown. The packers' business has been growing as fast as the city has. Your best bet to find a job is to look there. Just don't be particular where you live and room too far away, or else you'll spend the other half of the day you aren't working getting to and from where you work, and you'll burn up all your spare change riding streetcars and trolleys. And don't be late for work, or they'll fire you on the spot and hire someone else the same day. They've got a long line of men waiting at the side door looking for work."

"What's it like there?" Samuel asked. "Is it as dangerous as the other bad parts of the city?"

"From what I hear, it's not all that much different," the man said. "The streets can be as rough there as any in the other bad parts of town. If you find a place to stay there, don't go wandering the streets at night. There isn't all that much to wander to at night except saloons and bordellos."

In that sense Samuel found himself partially back on home ground. He didn't have a good track record of comporting himself in bars, but he was a practiced bordello crawler. Somehow he had the feeling that the bordellos of the city weren't as genteel as Mrs. Richardson's house. The ones in the poor sections of the city, that is. Chicago in that era also posted some of the highest-class bordellos serving a well-heeled clientele. Houses like the one run by the Everly sisters were as classy (in a relative sense) as the bordellos of the Storyville district in New Orleans. It was the high-class bordellos in Chicago or New Orleans that Clarinda had been slouching toward and had been preparing herself to depart to before she died.

"Couple of years back, a muckraking author by the name of Sinclair something wrote a novel about Packingtown. He called it a jungle. That's a good enough description. A lot of people, outside the town and in, say it's a good enough description of the city as a whole. A lot of other people say this city is first in violence, deepest in dirt. That description fits well enough as any other."

Chicago in that day had a vaguely, if not definitely unvaguely, unseemly and unsavory reputation. It had a history of violence in the streets. It had a history of gangs, usually ethnic based. It had a history of political corruption as the norm, not the exception. It had a history of the rule of corrupt political bosses. It was the city in which Clarinda had been looking forward to becoming a high-tone courtesan at the high-tone bordellos.

"This is a big city, boy, as big as the big country and even bigger world it's part of and connected with. As a farmer, you were part of the land you lived on. But there you would always have been a farmer. You would never have risen above being a farmer. In this city you can leave your roots below and rise farther than you ever could on the farm. But you can fall just as far down and as hard as you can rise."

Samuel assumed that, though he was a Pullman porter who would be a Pullman porter for the rest of his life, the man knew the streets of the city that lay beyond the station doors where the trains he rode terminated, the city Clarinda had seen as a shining gateway to her future, the city she had died trying to get herself to.

"It all depends on you and how able and willing you are to rise and merge with the good of the city and not get pulled down by the bad. This city can take you to the heights, but it can bring you as low as it can elevate you."

Samuel reached and took hold of his knapsack.

"There are two entry-level things you're going to have to know how to do in this city. One is how to run, when to run, and what to run from. The other is how to fight. Don't rely on one option only; keep both options open. You'll need them both to stay alive and stay out ahead in the city. Then again, the best option you might find to deal with the city is to leave the city, go back to the farmland you came from, and get a job as a hired hand doing what you know. Whatever pitfalls there might be in being an itinerant farmhand with no place to call home, you might find it more amenable than being alone on foot in this city, which can be a lot deeper pit to fall into."

Going off to live in hiding in farm country had always been alive in the back of Samuel's mind. If the city proved to be too tough of a row to hoe, he might very well exercise that option. For the moment he would stick with the city. It wasn't that Samuel had never mythologized the city as a wondrous place where he could easily make his fortune and rise to heights that could never be reached in his hometown. That was the city as Clarinda had imagined it. But he figured that if he played his cards right, he might gain the skills he needed and craft a new identity well enough that he might be able to return to the city of Columbus, Ohio, where he could be closer to the home he had not wanted to leave. He just didn't have the first idea of how to go about it any more than he knew about the city that lay just outside the doors of the station house he was in.

"You might find sleeping in barns or in hired hands' shacks to be better and less hard on body and soul than sleeping in the alleys and flophouses of this city."

Where it came to sleeping in places far from home, Clarinda hadn't found sleeping where she had in the capacity she had to be inordinately painful to her soul. If she could do it, Samuel figured he could be as strong and enduring in doing it as she had been.

Samuel again reflected on the irony that he had arrived in unwilling exile in the city she had died hoping to get to and had hoped to rise to the top of her trade in. He also reflected that when he walked out the door of the station and into the city, it would have to be under a name as made up as the one she had devised for herself. More than ever, he probably never would know what her real name had been. Names had meant little to her. Now his name would have to be as open and in flux as hers had been.

Samuel gathered up his knapsack and stood up. "Either way, I'm not going to rise anywhere sitting here," he said. "As much as I'd like to sit here, I've got to get going if I'm going to get anywhere."

Actually he would have liked to sit on the waiting room bench a little longer. In a way, the high-backed, polished wooden railroad station waiting room bench reminded him of the older and more worn pews in the church of his hometown. If he sat on the bench any longer, he would probably start getting homesick. He had to get moving, if only to forget that his life had become a life of movement.

"Head to the north and east from here," the Pullman porter said. "Just follow the streets. They're all lined up north–south and east–west. But don't go all the way to the lake. The only thing along Lake Shore Drive and Michigan Avenue are the fancy shops. They're probably not hiring transients who just came into the city, and there's no place to stay except the big-name, big-price hotels. The flophouses and boardinghouses, the ones a poor boy like you can afford, are in the western and southern parts of the city. Like I said, find a policeman. He can tell you better than me where to find lodging at a rate that won't drain you the first night. He might even be able to tell you who's hiring."

Samuel thanked the man, turned, and headed toward the front door. Behind him, Samuel heard the man say "God go with you, son." He did not turn and thank him again. Instead he headed across the wide expanse of the waiting room, heading forward to what he knew not what. He reflected on the man having called him son. He had always liked the way his father had called him Son. Samuel figured he might not hear the name spoken to him again.

As he approached the exit of the train station, Samuel did not feel the exhilaration of a new life beginning. All he felt was the void of his old life passing, the life he had been happy in where he was living it, the life he hadn't wanted to leave. As Samuel pushed open the door and exited the train station, he was gripped by an almost suffocating feeling of being alone and having left all that he had been and all that he had wanted to be irrevocably behind him, never to be returned to. The city outside was the city the girl had hoped to get to in life and employ her body to rise in. She had shared her body with him in life. Samuel didn't even know if she was there with him in spirit.

In the world he had come from, moving from planting to harvest, Samuel had been able to see the end from the beginning. Now he was a stranger in a strange land where he had no idea where any of his steps would take him. In his hometown he could stand on one side and pretty much see to the other side. He could see from one end of his family's farm down the rows of corn to the other end. He knew the boundaries of his world and of his life.

At least the girl had an initial plan in mind when she had come into his hometown and had sought refuge and employment at Mrs. Richardson's. From there she had expanded on her plan and exchanged it for an extended plan to take herself to a bigtime bordello in a big-name city. Her plan may have been half-baked, but she had held it full and formed in her mind. Alone in the city the girl had died before she could get to, Samuel had no plan. Other than the Pullman porter's vague suggestion of looking for work in the meatpacking factories in the place he had called Packingtown, he didn't have a clue where to look for work.

Samuel slowed in his pace even more. People walked past him as if he wasn't even there. The feeling came over him even more that he wasn't anywhere and wasn't likely to be anywhere anytime soon, unless it was on a police blotter as a nameless John Doe found dead in an alley, the victim of criminal violence, and from there to a pauper's grave, buried under an unknown designation.

Samuel wandered the streets for the better part of the day, looking for signs that anyone was hiring. He didn't see any help wanted signs, but he was seeing a lot of the city. It just seemed to go on forever in its constantly changing sameness. At one corner, Samuel turned to what he assumed to be the east. A few blocks ahead of him, down a wide street, he saw another wide street that looked like a main thoroughfare. On the far side of the street was a wide area of green that he took to be a park. Beyond that a strip of deep blue ran from the strip of green to the horizon. Samuel figured he had arrived within sight of Lake Michigan. Despite his resolution not to think of anything out of his past and near to home, the sight of the lake instantly made him remember the time he had taken the girl to Gustafson Lake and how he had made love to her in the soft mud on the bank. The memory hit so hard, it almost took the breath out of him. He quickly turned his head and averted his gaze. He turned around and walked back into the city.

It was getting on toward later afternoon. Samuel hadn't eaten since he had left home early the day before and was decidedly growing hungry. He had passed several restaurants, some of them with ethnic names, some with names in obvious foreign languages. He had crossed several ethnic neighborhood boundary lines. He hadn't gone into any of the restaurants because he didn't know how much a meal in any one of them would cost or whether they would serve him. He didn't even know if they spoke English inside.

What Samuel felt he needed was a source of local information. He spotted a uniformed policeman standing on a corner, looking around, swinging his nightstick by its carrying strap. Though leery of police of any kind and fearful that information about fugitives on the run might be passed from one department to another, Samuel figured that the man might be the best immediate source of the kind of information he was in need of. He decided to take the chance and ask. He just hoped the outline of the pistol his father had given him didn't show through his knapsack. But he had placed it deep among the spare clothes he had brought.

Samuel walked up to the local cop and, in the most polite voice he could muster, asked the man if he knew where he might go to look for work. For a moment the policeman looked at him with a sour expression. For a fleeting moment Samuel wondered if he had violated some local ordinance or taboo against poor-looking people addressing uniformed officers. The man's look went from hostile to inquisitive.

"Are you from around here?" the policeman asked. "I know most of the people on my beat by sight. I don't remember seeing you before."

"I just came into the city," Samuel answered, wondering if the admission would mean trouble for him.

"What country are you from?" the man asked in a still inquisitive voice. "You don't look or sound like a Polack, bohunk, dago, or kike."

Samuel was getting his first experience and familiarity with the ethnic tensions that were filling parts of the country against the immigrants who were crowding into the cities, displacing the original inhabitants from the neighborhoods that had been their legacy, and taking the jobs that had also been safely theirs, often taking those jobs at half the wages that the natives had negotiated for themselves through unionization. Corrupt businessmen would often simply fire their union workers and replace them with poor immigrants willing to work for near-starvation wages because they had families to support and because half wages and long hours were better than an eight-hour day of unemployment at zero wages. Labor protection and wage protection laws were not widely on the books at the time, and what laws there were, were not always obeyed or enforced.

"They've been flooding the city up, back, down, and sideways, squeezing the old-timers and regular people out. You can tell immigrants and where they come from by their accent—if they can speak English at all."

Samuel noticed that the man did not include the Irish in his list of immigrant miscreants he apparently thought shouldn't have come over. Though not an expert at identifying accents and their ethnic origins, Samuel thought he detected a hint of Irish brogue in the policeman's voice.

It wouldn't be long before he found out that most of the Chicago cops of that day were Irish. The Irish kind of had an ethnic lock on the Chicago police force.

"But I can't hear any accent on you. What country are you from, and where did you learn to speak English so well?"

"I'm from a country called Ohio," Samuel said, slipping up on his strategy of never saying the state he was originally from. "Unless you in the city don't consider farm country to be part of the United States."

Samuel caught himself wondering if the cop was going to take what he'd said and the tone he'd said it in as backtalk and sass. Instead of glowering and turning angry, the man smiled and sort of laughed.

"Well, my my," the policeman said. "How about that. An all-American, in-country immigrant. That's a switch. What brought you from farm country to here? All the immigrants from across the sea have some kind of hard-luck story about what happened to them back in their home country and why they pulled up stakes and came here; there was famine or pestilence in the land, the landlords were robbing them blind and kicking them around, the Cossacks were after them. Was some local boss demanding the right to sleep with your sweetheart?"

The cop was referring to the old medieval tradition of "first night," in which the local landlord demanded and had the right to sleep with a newlywed bride on her wedding night. The legally cuckolded husband had to sit home and chew his knuckles. The irony was that something vaguely like that had happened with Clarinda, with Harold Ethridge as the demanding first citizen of the shire, the difference being that Clarinda had actively sought out and embraced his sexual exploitation of her as long as he was paying—up until the time it all went sour. Samuel just didn't want to tell the police officer any part of the real story, especially when he might have become suspicious that there was more involved and his department might have the resources to check out the real story.

"I left the farm because Mother was long dead, Father died, and the bank foreclosed the mortgage on the farm and sent me packing," Samuel said, speaking the second incarnation of the story he had given the Pullman porter. "If I had stayed on in the area of my home, about the only kind of work I would have been able to get was as an itinerant farmhand. But I didn't want to spend the rest of my days as a hired hand slopping other farmers' hogs and slouching my way through their fields planting, hoeing, and harvesting crops that weren't mine. The only other kind of job I would be able to get would be as a ditchdigger. I figured there was a lot more, and better-paying, work in the city. So I came here. But it's my first day in the city. I don't even know where to look. You're on the streets all day. Do you know anyone who's hiring?"

"I'm just on the streets of my beat," the policeman said. "I don't know of anyone who's hiring around here." He looked off to one side, seeming to be looking away, over the canyon of buildings. "The only companies that might be hiring are the meat-packers in Packingtown."

Again with Packingtown. The Pullman porter had said the same thing.

"They run one of the biggest, if not the biggest, operation in the city. They've got men coming and going all the time. That's the place most of the immigrants swarm to looking for work. Most of the workers there don't speak English. But you don't have to have a college degree or even know the language in order to swing a beef carver's knife. Where it comes to all the languages of the world, it's kind of the Tower of Babel. But the foremen all speak English. You being an American to start with, and the fact that you speak English, might give you an in. But I don't know right offhand if they're hiring now. All I can say is go there and try." He looked away again.

"But it's on the far south side of the city. You'll have to take trolleys to get there. If you get a job there, there are rooming houses in the area you can live in. … But it's getting late. If you leave now, you'll probably get there after dark. Packingtown isn't the kind of place you want to be out on the streets in after dark, especially if you're a greenhorn. You'd better spend the night around here and get a start early in the morning. For that matter, you don't particularly want to be on the streets around here after dark either. You'd better find a place to stay for the night."

"Are there any rooming houses or boardinghouses around here?" Samuel asked.

"There are plenty of hotels in the city," the cop said. "But they all cost money. How are you fixed for cash?"

"I have a little, but not much," Samuel answered. "The train porter I talked with in the station said to find a flophouse. Are there any around here? He said they were a whole lot cheaper, a nickel a night."

"That's about the going rate in a flop," the policeman said. "For a dime they'll let you sleep on a cot. Otherwise you have to sleep on the floor. They're not very warm in the winter, and the clientele isn't always the most genteel. Don't let anyone know you have any more money on you—not if you want to keep it."

"Is there a flophouse nearby where I can get a room?" Samuel asked.

"If you can't afford a cot, the only room you'll get is whatever room you can scrounge on the floor," the policeman said, "if you don't mind sleeping next to winos, alkies, and pickpockets. Like I said, if you have any money to spare, don't let them see it."

The policeman gave him an address, pointed in the direction, and told him which streets to take. He also gave him the names of restaurants that gave out free sandwiches to unemployed men and the names of churches and charitable organizations that served meals to the poor.

Thus informed, Samuel set off in the direction of his first objective, which was to fill the hole that had grown to appreciable size in his stomach. Stretching out around him in all directions, to all horizons of the city, the actual horizon was blocked from view by the buildings. As he went, thoughts swarmed into and swirled around in his mind: What would become of him in the foreign, unfamiliar, unknown city that was possibly unknowable to him? What would be his fate in the unknowable days ahead? Would he be able to adapt to the new world he had reluctantly journeyed to? Would he survive in the polyglot, jumbled, driving, thrusting new land that was to become his home by default, the new home that he had been driven to by his fault, the new home that he was not at all sure would provide anything resembling a new home or a new hope?

The girl had seen the distant city as a bright horizon to be gotten to no matter whom she had to leave behind. Samuel was now in the center of that distant horizon, which was now near to him and all around him. The girl wasn't with him. His prior life wasn't with him. His family wasn't with him. His memories were with him, but he had to work hard to hold his memories in check and keep them at arm's length. If he indulged himself in his memories of home, family, and his prior life, his memories would eat him up and submerge him in despair and loss.

The Bible describes the Word of God as a sharp two-edged sword that divides asunder body and soul. That he had known the girl whose name he still didn't know, the girl he had killed to avenge, was a ragged but razor-sharp iron blade that had divided his life into two separate lives that could not be fused back into one. As Samuel progressed down the streets of the alien city that he already knew would never be his home, he felt neither the presence of God nor the girl with him.

Samuel located the restaurant that the policeman had said gave out free sandwiches to unemployed men. It was only one sandwich per customer, but the sandwich they gave him was fat and filled with sliced meat, cheese, and lettuce. It was the only thing he had eaten since the day before, when he had left home. He devoured the sandwich to the last morsel as he headed in the direction of the flophouse that the policeman had told him about. It was getting dark and, as per the warning of both the Pullman porter and the policeman, he did not want to be out on the streets after dark.

The flophouse was a lumped-brick structure several stories high with no external or internal decorations. All the buildings on the block were of the same minimalist architecture. They all had the same dispirited and defeated look to them.

The actual flophouse was on the basement level of the building. The floors above were apparently apartments. The entrance to the flophouse was on the side and was accessible from the alley that ran between the buildings. In the alley Samuel saw a litter of empty whiskey bottles, paper scraps, and what in the fading light looked like puddles of dry vomit.

The apparent night manager was an older man as lumped and chunky-looking as the building he worked in. For a nickel he gave Samuel a ragged blanked. He directed him to a room and told him to pick any empty spot on the floor. The room had no light of its own in the ceiling and was dimly lit by only the light from outside in the hall shining in through the doorway that had no door.

The room was already nearly filled with men sleeping. Some men slept quietly. Others snored. Others grumbled in their sleep. Samuel found a place next to a wall. That way any thug who had the idea of shaking him down and robbing him could not get at him from the side without stepping on the sleeping men, but could only approach from the direction of his feet.

Using his backpack as a pillow, Samuel lay down on the hard floor and pulled the blanket over him. Under the cover of the blanket, he pulled the double-barreled pistol his father had given him out from the small of his back and held it under the concealment of the blanket. As he lay on the floor in the dim light, Samuel couldn't help but remember how he had lain in wait to ambush Harold Ethridge in his barn back on the outskirts of the hometown that was no longer his and could never be his home again, the town that held the grave of the girl who wasn't with him and who had never really been his.

As Samuel lay on the floor of the flophouse trying to sleep, using his knapsack as a pillow, a ragged and rough-looking middle-aged man walked up to where he was lying and stood at his feet. "Hey, boy," the man said in a gruff and threat-laced voice, "you look like you got more than the others in here. Do you have anything worth anything in that pack bag of yours? You got anything in there for me? Let's see what you got. Hand it over to me, and there won't be any trouble."

"Oh, I got something for you," Samuel said. "In fact I've got two things for you." He pulled his arm up and out from under the blanket. In his hand he held the derringer pistol. As he brought it up, he cocked it. The cocking gun made a menacing metallic sound that was amplified as it echoed off the bare walls. "I'm willing to share what I got with you. I'll give you two of what I got right here. I'll give you one in the stomach and the other in the teeth. At this range I can't miss. Where do you want it first?"

The man looked at him with a surprised and put-out look. "You really think you're going to shoot me with that thing?" he asked, not quite knowing what else to say.

"There's one way you can find out," Samuel said. "And I assure you, it's the hard way. You may think you can take me, but before you try, stop and ask yourself if you can afford to be wrong."

The man said nothing. He had taken Samuel to be a timorous immigrant boy who would be an easy mark to frighten and shake down. Instead he figured that the boy was from Chicago. Some of the worst Chicago street boys of the day were known to pack rods. The more things change, the more they often prefigure the future.

The man turned and walked away quickly, muttering something under his breath about hoodlum boys. None of the other men sleeping on the floor had come to Samuel's aid. They hadn't even awakened.

"And don't come back!" Samuel shouted at the man's back as he disappeared down the hall. "I'm a light sleeper." The man didn't come back that night or any subsequent night.

One could say that the incident was a triumph for Samuel. He had beaten the city on one if its own operational terms: intimidation and threat of violence. He had beaten the city on one of its dark streets, in one of its dark corners. He had routed a mugger and had kept himself safe.

But Samuel felt neither triumphal nor safe. Neither did he feel he was anywhere he wanted to be. The incident only impressed upon him again, harder this time, how completely alone and far from home he was. Homesickness started to well up in him again, but he fought it off. If it got any stronger, it might bring him to a point where he could not function. He figured that anyone who could not function in the city was as good as dead.

As Samuel drifted off to a fitful sleep, he wondered if maybe the girl had had the right idea, however inadvertent: die before you go any deeper into a world and farther into a life that was taking you nowhere and that, in the end, would leave you broken and nowhere. Maybe the girl was in a better place. Since she wasn't there with him, he fingered the gun and wondered if he should join her in the place she was in.

With the unseeable outline of his unseeable, unknowable future in the city going round in an endless spiral in his mind, Samuel Martin drifted off to sleep still holding the gun under his blanket. His first day in the city was over. Tomorrow would be another day—another day in the city that would probably never be home for him.

Chapter 24

The darkness was being lessened by the promise of a dim dawn under a sooty sky. Farther back in the yards, the cattle may have been milling around in their pens. The men gathered by the door weren't milling, though the expended energy of milling around might have kept them warmer in the winter chill. If they had milled around, they would have only bumped into each other like the cattle. For the most part they stood silent and largely unmoving, numb in face and hands, numb in hope. There was a light dusting of snow on the ground. The light of morning had come over the scene to find it the same as it had appeared the morning before. The light of the next day's morning would probably find the scene the same. There was no clock on the outside wall over the door, and Samuel had no watch, but he judged the time to be approximately half past eight o'clock. That was the time the door would open and the announcement of any openings in the plant would be handed out as one or two of the waiting hopefuls would be pointed to. Samuel and the others had been standing in the snow and the faint light of approaching dawn since before six o'clock.

Now that it was lighter, Samuel did a quick perusal of the men around him. Technically they were his competitors, jockeying with him for whatever position may have come open in the plant. But they didn't have the faces of the leering and cocksure boys his age he had faced on the wrestling mat or across the baseball diamond in his hometown. Some of them may have called the city home longer than he had been alive. Some of them might have just come off the boat. However close or distant their points of origin, they bore the same distant stare of the kind of castaway Samuel felt himself to be.

To Samuel's estimate, all the other men by the door were older-looking than he. He didn't count that as an advantage in his favor. They all looked like experienced workers who had worked as meat-packers before, perhaps in a different plant, perhaps in the same one whose employment door they were standing outside of. Samuel figured they had been fired for some small infraction or had been laid off for some reason and found themselves orphans trying to find their way back into the only employment and world they knew. It would be easy enough for Samuel to say that he knew the feeling, the principal difference being that the men standing around him were standing in their own backyard. There are different degrees of being a refugee from one's world. The world the men were estranged from was just on the other side of the door. When Samuel had arrived in the city of immigrants, he had felt like an immigrant just off the boat with his home far away across the ocean. Of late Samuel had come to feel that his home and world was out beyond the outer planets of the solar system. He knew as much about the outer planets as he did about meatpacking.

When the men around him spoke, they so often spoke a foreign language that Samuel couldn't begin to decipher. When they spoke English, it was often with an accent so thick, it could be only marginally discerned as English. With their babble and the multitude of strange-sounding accents that Samuel had never been exposed to before, coming from countries with strange-sounding names, some of which Samuel had never heard of before, the men around him might as well have been from the outer planets.

Whatever degree of estrangement any of the men at the door knew, it didn't look like the barrier was going to be breached that day. The door opened, and a gaunt-faced, middle-age-looking man stepped to the threshold. "Sorry, boys," he said tersely. "We got nothing open today."

The other men turned silently and started to shuffle away. Samuel looked at the snow on the ground. As the others moved away from him, he started to turn to follow them.

"I might have somethin' for you, boy," Samuel heard the man say. He figured the man was addressing one of the older and more experienced-looking men, who would naturally be the first ones to be hired. Samuel continued to look at the ground as turned to go, but then he looked up to see the man unexpectedly pointing at him.

"You've been around here before, haven't you?"

"Two, three times," Samuel said.

"Are you the one who told me that you're the farm boy who used to throw hay bales around like you were playing dominoes with them?"

Samuel hadn't put it quite that way, but in an earlier interview at the hiring door, he had described how he had hefted and stacked hay bales. Not being able to testify to any prior experience working in a stockyard, all Samuel had to offer was his emphasis on having done hard physical labor in the course of his life on a farm. He figured that might be the only inducement he could offer that an employer might be interested in. It hadn't worked. Until now.

"I handled hay bales all the time," Samuel said. "It's part of farm life."

"Then you've done a lot of lifting work?" the man asked. "You're used to lifting and heaving?"

"Farming is a lot of hard work," Samuel said, "including lifting. Not all of it is lifting, but a good deal of it is as hard. I know hard work."

"Then come with me," the man said. "I can't promise you nothing, but I just might be able to fit you in."

Samuel started to move toward the man, but apparently he wasn't moving fast enough for the man's taste.

"Be quick about it, boy," the man snapped out of the depth of his gauntness. "We don't got all day, and there are plenty behind you who will take your place in a heartbeat."

Samuel quickened his pace and left the men he had been standing with behind to follow the man into the plant. He had grown used to leaving people behind on short notice. In a world that now seemed like it had been in another life, he had left his home and family behind. Some of the other disappointed job seekers looked over their shoulders as Samuel walked through the grimy-looking open door into the semigrimy-looking building.

The hallway inside the building was only half lit by indirect lighting coming in from distant and unseen windows. Samuel followed the man down the short corridor to another corridor that ran perpendicular to what apparently was a longer internal hallway running the length of the building. The man led him to a small internal office with a window that didn't open to the outside. The window didn't open at all. Instead it looked out over what Samuel took to be the main floor of the plant. At a small wooden desk sat a man whom Samuel took to be the straw boss of the shop floor. The man at the desk was a study in contrast to the thin and gaunt-looking man, who was probably his assistant. He was thick and heavyset. His thick build and bulldog face reminded Samuel of Constable Harkness. But Samuel didn't have time to dwell on the past. It was hardly the time or place for old home week.

The assistant stepped inside the door and stopped a few paces from the seated man. Samuel stopped in the doorway.

"I've got someone you might want to take on," the gaunt man said as he rolled his thumb over at Samuel. "He can start out doing menial jobs on the floor and work into something better as he learns the work. He looks young and strong enough. He's not half worn out to start with like the others we've been getting. We should be able to get a lot of good years out of him."

The seated man shot a glimpse at Samuel and then looked back to his underling. "We don't have anything open," he said. "I got no place for him."

Samuel figured that was that. It had been only a temporary diversion. He would return to the street the other turned-away men were spreading out on to.

"I was thinking we could put him on the loading dock with Rufus," the thin man said. "You had to fire the other nigger because he was getting drunk and was showin' up hungover or with a snootful. Or he wasn't showin' up for work at all. Right now we've got Cerkanowitckz filling in. He's one of the best beef boners we've got. He's just being wasted toting and loading. Besides, he's old and can't do heavy lifting work very well. If we wear him out till he breaks down, we won't have him as a beef boner or anything. This boy looks big enough to do the work easy."

The seated man studied Samuel for a moment. "You don't look like a Polack or a bohunk," he said to Samuel. "You don't look Slavic or like anything out of Eastern Europe. Are you Irish or German? They're the only other immigrants we get here in the yards who aren't from some backwater Slav land. What country are you from, boy?" The seated man looked at his underling. "Does he even speak English?"

"I'm from the country I was born in," Samuel said in plain Midwestern farm English, before the other man could speak. "This one."

White Anglos held all the positions in the boardroom and corporate offices of the company. On the killing and packing floor, white Anglos or at least second-generation English-speaking immigrant descendants held the shop management positions. Immigrants, many of them newly arrived off the boat, stood on the line, quickly rending the animals that came their way down the line, slowly rending themselves over the years in a more prolonged manner. The man had dealt almost exclusively with heavily accented workers, those who could actually speak a smattering of English and didn't require a translator, for so long that he had almost forgotten that there was a straightforward English language he didn't have to strain his ears and wrap his mind to understand.

"Well, how 'bout that," the thick-faced man said in a thick but unaccented voice, recapitulating what the policeman had said on Samuel's first day in the city. In his own thick-faced way, the man seemed surprised and gratified to hear a voice that wasn't accented, a voice like his. "A real born American, one who sounds like his family was here before all the immigrant hordes started coming. He even speaks English you can understand without an accent so thick you can cut it with a beef-boning knife."

"I come from a long generation of farmers," Samuel said, jumping into what might have been the first small opening he had seen since he had come to the city. He didn't stop to analyze whatever national origin dynamic or prejudice might be going on in the man's mind. If the man liked American pedigree, he would give him pedigree. "My grandfather was in the Civil War. Before him, our family were pioneers. We were on the land for generations."

"He says he's a farmer," the gaunt man interjected. "He also says he grew up juggling hay bales. From the looks of him, he can do loading without any problem."

"If your family was on the farm so long, how come you left it?" the floor boss said.

"It was never that big of a farm," Samuel said quickly, recapitulating the lie he had formulated as the cover story he would use for the rest of his life. "My mother died when I was eight years old. My father died less than a year ago. We were in debt. The bank got the farm, and I got the gate. I came up here looking to find work. I'm willing to work at any job you can give me."

"All I've got open is on the loading dock," the floor boss said. "That's nigger work. It's beneath a white man. Even a foreigner. You'll be working face-to-face with a darkie. Given that's he's been here longer, he'll be telling you what to do. Do you want to swallow your pride enough to do the same work as a nigger and take orders from one?"

For all Samuel knew, the man might actually think he was doing him a favor by turning him away from a job he felt to be too lowly and insulting for a white man. All Samuel could see at the moment was that the man's racial solicitousness was going to leave him out in the snow on the street.

"Hunger is beneath everybody," Samuel said before the gaunt man could speak for him. "Whatever Negroes you've got working here, they probably go home at night to a roof over their heads and eat off what they make working. I've been sleeping my white ass in churches, basements, alleys, and flophouses since I got here. I've been eating free lunch sandwiches when I can get them. When I can't, I've been eating in soup kitchens and charity lines in churches. I've been scrounging half-eaten steaks out of the garbage cans of the swankiest restaurants in the city. Starvation, cold, and hunger may kill my white ass, but it ain't going to kill my pride to work with a Negro. Race pride makes for pretty thin soup when you're hungry. Race pride don't fill your stomach none. You can't even taste it at all."

The straw boss looked at Samuel for a moment. The world, such as it was for Samuel that day, hung in the balance. Then the man looked at his underling and flipped his thumb at Samuel.

"Get him signed up, get him a check tag, and take him to the dock," the seated man said to his underling. "Have Rufus teach him what to do."

"Like I said," the gaunt man commented, "he's young and strong. He can work his way into something better. The nigger will be where he is in this plant forever."

"When you set him to work, send Cerkanowitckz back to the cutting floor," the floor manager, or whatever he was, said as he turned back to his desk.

Such were the inauspicious beginnings of Samuel Martin's career as a meat-packer. Any thought of the racial component of his employment wasn't in Samuel's mind. The point was that he was employed. He had finally secured a job. It was his first handgrip in his new life in the new world of his exile. For his part, the floor boss figured that if the boy didn't mind doing darkie labor, who was he to object and put the boy back on the street with his race dignity intact and his stomach empty? Getting the work done took precedence over any objections Jim Crow might have. In the end, practicality carried the day for both Samuel and the shop foreman. Beyond that, the two hadn't even exchanged names.

"Name?" the gaunt man said as he sat in his smaller office farther down the hall and filled out the card.

Now that was a bit of an issue for Samuel.

"William Howard," Samuel Martin said. He gave the false name he had been using with a straight and set face. His days on the streets had given him a practiced straight and set face. The set of his face didn't make any difference, though. The man wasn't looking at him as he filled out the card. As his alias, Samuel gave the name of the boy his sister had met at the county fair. It was the name he had been using on the street. Names had already become an interchangeable commodity for Samuel Martin as they had been for the girl.

As it turned out, his name was about the only information the foreman's assistant asked him. After he finished getting Samuel signed up, the gaunt man took him to a machine shop, where they punched him up a check tag on a small piece of rounded brass with a hole near one side and a number stamped on it. Then the gaunt man showed Samuel, a.k.a. William, to a wall with a large board with rows of small hooks mounted on it. Hanging on the hooks were dozens of similar tags with different numbers on them. The man showed Samuel how to hang his tag on the board to indicate that he was at the plant working. If a worker found his check tag turned over with the number facing the wall, it meant he had been fired.

"Sign your name here," the gaunt man said, handing Samuel a pencil and the employment card that was his first toehold in the city that, for a while at least, while he plotted his return to a place in closer proximity to his old home, would be his new home. Samuel bent over the desk and started to sign the card. The trouble was that he started to sign his actual name with an *S*. He caught himself and quickly erased the letter with the eraser on the pencil, signing "William Howard" instead. He stood up, assuming he was finished. Instead the man handed him another piece of paper. Instead of the smaller employment card, this paper was the size of standard office stationery. Nearly the whole page was filled with printed and official-looking type.

"Sign this too," the gaunt man said.

"What's this for?" Samuel asked in curiosity as he bent over to sign the second paper.

"It's an ironclad agreement that you won't join a union," the gaunt man said. "We don't tolerate unionism or union radicals and insurrectionists in this plant. Any attempt on your part to join a union will result in your immediate dismissal. Not only will you lose your job here, but also you will be blackballed in the industry. You won't be able to get a job in any meatpacking house in this city or anywhere in the industry. And don't go listening to any of the radical outside agitators who have been skulking around talking union talk and strike talk. If you do, you'll be gone before their words stop tickling your ears."

Samuel, now tentatively employed as William Howard, did as the man directed and signed the paper. It was too late in the day of his life to quibble over abstract principles.

After the second paper had been signed, the man led Samuel down a half-lit inner hallway. When he had been in the gaunt man's office, off in the distance Samuel had heard the squealing sounds of terrified animals confronting their own mortality. After being thrust down a narrow shoot into a dark and completely alien world, their instinctive panic began when they caught the thick scent of blood, which pooled like river mud on the floor they were headed toward. At the far side of the room that would be their last view of the world stood a man dressed in leather and covered head to foot in blood. With the exception of not wearing a leather face mask, the man could have been an executioner for Henry the Eighth. The squealing of the animals exploded and reached a crescendo when they suddenly found themselves lassoed by a cable, upended, and swung into the air by their back legs. As he followed the gaunt man, Samuel didn't pause to consider the animals' plight. If he had, he might have thought the plight of the doomed animals to be at least somewhat analogous to his own. Samuel knew all about being upended and thrust into an alien world. For the moment at least, he had managed to stay on his feet.

As he followed the gaunt man down the hallway, the sounds grew fainter and farther away. The gaunt man finally led Samuel into a long room. Inside was a forest of the dead. Rows of skinned, headless, half-legged, laterally bisected half carcasses, which only a short time ago had been the living, bellowing cattle Samuel had heard beginning their last journey, hung silent from metal hooks on wheels suspended beneath the metal tracks that they ran on. As if still twitching in the last throes of death, the carcasses pressed in on each other and jostled each as a new arrival would come down the line to bump into the backlog of the cadavers of their fellow bovines. The walls of the terminal room were windowless. Only a few scattered incandescent bulbs lit up the central axis of the departure chamber of the dead. Light otherwise shone in upon the grim scene through a large open door at the far end of the room. The room was the same cold temperature as the outside. The coldness saved the meat from spoilage. It allowed management to save on electricity. In the summer, the room was refrigerated.

There were two men in the room. The gaunt man called to them both to come over. One of the men was a Negro. From the other end of the room, he looked to Samuel to be about the same age, height, and build as he. The other one was a shorter and more stooped-looking middle-aged white man. Both men were dressed in shoulder-to-knee leather aprons.

"Hey, Rufus," the gaunt man said to the Negro as the pair approached. "I've got someone more your age and size to help you out. He's a farm boy just like you. But he's from the farmlands of the North, unlike you, being up from the cotton patches of Dixie."

The gaunt man turned to the older man and spoke a few words to him in a language unknown to Samuel. Apparently the floor foreman's underling had some foreign-language skills, at least in the language of the older man. Samuel figured that any kind of knowledge in one or more foreign languages probably came in handy in the polyglot language soup of the plant.

Without saying anything in any language, the older man turned and walked past Samuel and out of the room. Apparently the foreman's assistant had told the man to return to the position he had held farther up the line, before he had been pulled off to fill in on the loading dock. As he passed, the man did not look at Samuel, but from what Samuel could see, his face was creased with age and years of toil. But it was the man's hands that caught Samuel's attention. The man held his hands with his fingers partially curled back in an unclosed and incomplete fist. From the glance that Samuel caught of him, the man's hands seemed more gnarled than his face. What had only marginally registered on Samuel was that the gaunt man had called him a beef boner. Samuel would later come to learn that beef boners stood on the line slicing meat off the passing carcasses.

It was skilled work. Given the speed of the line, it was also fast-paced work. It was especially fast-paced and pressing work when one is working on a piecemeal basis. One often found oneself working at maniacal speed on the ragged edge of control where one's hands got ahead of caution. The knives used were large enough and sharp enough to bring a grunt of approval from a ninja warrior. Both the knives and the cutter's hands were slippery with blood, grease, and fat from the carcasses. Gloves didn't help. They just reduced the sense of touch and feel. Get distracted, let your mind wander in a different direction to where your hands are going faster than your head, and hit a bone the wrong way, and your hand can slip on the knife or fall under the blade, and you can slash your own hand seriously and painfully. In the biological hothouse of the rending line of the day, infection could set in quickly, followed by blood poisoning. The effect of the infection could further cripple and gnarl hands. If the pain and blood poisoning drove a worker off the line and sent him home to recover, when he returned he could easily find his job gone and find himself standing out in the snow by the hiring door with dozens of other desperate workers, trying to get himself back in.

The gaunt man followed the older worker out of the room. As he left, he turned to the Negro and pointed to Samuel. "Show him what to do, Rufus."

The gaunt man passed out of the room behind the other man, leaving Samuel and the Negro looking at each other.

The Negro looked to Samuel to be a bit older than he. He was as tall and sturdily built as he. Samuel figured that he and the Negro had both been hired for what the foreman and his assistant had calculated to be their strength. The man was solid ebony black, so black that his coloration had a faint purplish tinge. There had been no black people in Samuel's hometown. Since his arrival in Chicago, he had seen them at a distance walking on the streets. But he had never seen one this close up before. In his days that had been colored by the pleasantness of his childhood, Samuel had always more or less imagined Negroes to be a pleasant sort of people colored a pleasant sort of light coffee brown. He hadn't known that a man could be so black. Then again, he was finding that a lot of things in Chicago were of a different color, more intensely colored than he had known back home.

Instead of launching into a job description, the big Negro went in an unexpected and unrelated direction. It was a direction rather closely related to the direction and past he had come from.

"He says you a farm boy like me up from somewhere," the Negro said, looking at Samuel suspiciously. "Where you up from? Are you up from the South?"

The big Negro talked in a wary and ironic tone. His voice had an edge to it that made it sound like he thought that fate was chasing him when he thought he had gotten away from it and had put distance between himself and the lynch mobs. Samuel knew about running from fate.

"I'm not from the South," Samuel said. "Not unless you count southeastern Indiana near the Ohio border as being Dixie."

Samuel had picked an out-of-the-way spot in a neighboring state as his point of origin, figuring that if by chance someone had a notion to trace his story, no one would bother trying to look for evidence of him in an area as remote and isolated as that. At the same time, Samuel thought it best not to claim to be from the South. He remembered that his father had said that a lot of Negroes had been heading up north to get away from Jim Crow and the Ku Klux Klan. For all Samuel knew, the Negro might be

675

afraid that some kind of southern cracker who was used to busting Negro heads or lynching Negro people as entertainment had ironically followed him up from the South all the way to Chicago, where he had gone to get away from lynch-minded southern types.

"I ain't from Klan territory," Samuel said. "And I ain't from the Klan, if that's what you're worried about," he added for good measure.

The Negro sort of smiled. "Well, I guess that's one thing goin' my way," he said. "Or at least not comin' my way with a lynch rope in hand."

The Negro pointed with his thumb at the sides of beef hanging behind him. "Least I don't have to go back to looking over my shoulder and worrying about being left hanging out dead on a beef hook like one of these. You don't gets a lot of favors 'round here. You not bein' a southern cracker is one small favor goin' for me."

Samuel never considered that he had used the right words with the girl. But at least here he seemed to have used the right words with the big Negro. The moment seemed to relax for both of them.

"You goin' to mind workin' with a Negro?" the man asked in a still wary-sounding tone. "Even the poorest of poor white trash often get their backs up about workin' with a nigger."

"I find walking around on the street hungry with only my white self for company to be of little comfort to my pride, racial or otherwise," Samuel said in a repeat of what he had told the floor foreman. "The point I came here for today is to be working. To that end, I don't care who I'm working for. The only point for me beyond that is what the man I'm working for is like. Are you hard to work for?"

"I ain't no straw boss," Rufus said. "You work with me, not for me. We all work for the company. They the hard boss you don't want to get on the wrong side of. And around here you can slip off onto their wrong side easier than you can slip off a slimy log with muddy shoes."

Samuel could relate to the countrified simile from a fellow country boy.

"Workin' and keepin' the company happy is the real end we're both here for," Rufus went on. "So, to that end, we'd better get to gettin' down before the floor boss fires us both 'cause he says we're slackin' off. And I've got to get to teaching you."

The big Negro put his hand on a hanging side of beef. "All right, farm boy, let's put you to work," he said, getting right down to what they were both there for. "They'll start yellin' at us both if they catch us standing around any more than we have so far. We gots to start you workin'. You just won't start gettin' paid for your work till the clock rolls 'round to the top of the hour. They pays by the hour here, and they don't pay for part hours. Be sure to be here on time in the morning. If you start work one minute after the hour, they dock you for the whole hour. If you leave one minute before quitting time, they dock you for the whole hour too. If you spend too much time wandering off from the job even a short distance, or if they catch you daydreaming on the job too much, they dock you for the whole job."

The Negro pointed to a full-length leather apron like he was wearing hanging on a peg on the wall. "Put them overalls on, 'less you want your clothes to smell like a dead cow. These sides are heavy. When you carry them without the overalls on, the fat and grease rubs into your clothes, and it don't come out."

Samuel walked over to the wall and started to put on the leather apron. It tied in the back and had flaps that went over the shoulders.

The Negro pointed to the sides of beef hanging from the hooks. "These are the sides dat get sent out whole for other butchers to cut up without the cutters on the main floor cuttin' them up into smaller cuts of meat." He pointed to the open door. Outside the door, directly across a short platform made of heavy wood, a boxcar sat with its side door open. "All we do 'round here all day is take these sides and load them as they tell us to into the refrigerated boxcars they pulls up outside there. From there we hangs them up on the hooks inside the car just like they're hangin' here. Same thing for the hogs and the sheep. They don't weigh as much though."

Samuel glanced out the door to the open boxcar. As he finished putting on the apron, he remarked to himself that before the start of her life in exile at Mrs. Richardson's house, the girl had jumped into a similar passing boxcar with an open door on her way to becoming a side of meat on men's platters.

"Don't carry a whole side from the far end of this room. That makes for more work than necessary. The man who just left was too old for this kind of liftin' and carryin'. He fell half the time. At least he's back where he can stand still in one place and don't have to heft nothin' heavier than a big knife."

The Negro grabbed a hanging side of beef and pulled it along on the overhead trolley as a demonstration of how easily they rolled.

"Use the trolley to bring the side right up to the door. Let the trolley do as much of the work as possible. It's a long day, and we pushes a lot of beef out through these doors. You gots to save your strength and spread it out and make it last as much as possible. You'll be back here the next day doin' the same thing over and over again. Seein' you is a white man, they might someday find somethin' better for you to be doin', something more big payin', somewhere else deeper in the yard. I'll probably be doin' this the rest of my life. You're one up on me on that."

Rufus demonstrated to Samuel how to squat down, place his shoulder in the center of the side of beef, and lift it off its hook by pushing up with the legs instead of the back. Done properly, it was necessary to lift the side only the few inches needed to disengage it from the hook it was hanging on. With the same motion, the lifter would rotate the side over the top of his shoulder, using his shoulder as a fulcrum at the balance center of weight of the mass of beef. From there he would carry it into the boxcar. With a reverse motion, he would hang it back on one of the hooks suspended from the racks on the ceiling, all with a minimum of lifting and without letting the side touch the ground. Samuel could see why they had chosen him and the big Negro for the job. Some of the sides weighed over two hundred pounds. Strength and youthful energy were a necessity for performing the work all day long.

With management disfavor for any kind of delay hanging over their necks and weighing heavy like a side of beef on their shoulders, Rufus and Samuel got down to the work described. Samuel was used to repetitious lifting and moving of heavy bulk. Repetitious lifting and moving is what farm life was about. He got the hang of the job almost from the first load he carried. With few motions and fewer words wasted, they moved sides of beef into the boxcar and hung them up. In sequence they repeatedly passed in and out of the doors of the loading room and the boxcars. For the foreseeable future, the doors of Samuel's life would consist of the plant door he would pass through in the morning and out of at night, the door at the far end of the room through which the sides of meat would be shoved into the shipping room, the door at the near end they passed through carrying the sides, and the door of the boxcars they carried them into. Despite the

Negro's speculation that the foreman might move Samuel up to a better position someday, for all Samuel knew, he might end up doing the job for the rest his life as much as the Negro would. He could very well spend the rest of his working life passing through the doors he was passing through now with a side of beef on his shoulder.

But at least he now had a door. From this door he might be able to force other doors open for himself. He had employment. He had a handgrip to hold onto that he could use to pull himself up to a higher level. In his own right, Samuel was as much of an immigrant refugee as most of the men who worked at the packing plant. For the first time since he had arrived in the city, his foot was on something solid. As a floundering shipwreck survivor, he had grabbed a rock and pulled himself up on to an alien shore. It was a rocky shore with high cliffs around, but he had a rock ledge to stand on as he planned his climb back closer to home. He couldn't say he had arrived in any kind of promised land any more than the other immigrants around him. He was still a sojourner on the streets of a foreign land. But at least the street he was standing on wasn't quicksand. It was still necessary for him to stay out of sight of the law. But he was no longer in quite the same danger of sinking out of sight and disappearing completely on the streets of his exile.

In the summer they would have sat outside on the loading dock in the warmer sun eating lunch. That day of winter, it was equally cold inside on the loading dock as it was outside. The plant wasn't heated anyway. At least it wasn't heated beyond the protection that the factory walls gave from the winds of a Chicago winter and beyond the lingering and dissipating warmth leaking out of the cooling carcasses of the dead animals and the body heat of the men chopping them up to where they lost their remaining heat quicker. The difference being negligible all up and down the line, that particular day, a day of beginning for Samuel, another undifferentiated day for Rufus, the unlikely pair of wayfaring strangers to both the city and each other sat inside the building and ate lunch. At least Rufus ate lunch. Samuel just sat.

"Didn't you bring no lunch with you?" Rufus asked, looking over at Samuel.

"Didn't have no time to stop and get myself a free sandwich," Samuel said. "That's where I've been getting most of my meals. And it's usually been either lunch or dinner, but not both."

That was a bit of exaggeration for dramatic effect. Some of the money Samuel's father had given him still remained. He had been using it sparingly where necessary for food. That usually had meant one paid-for meal a day on a shifting basis. To Samuel, breakfast, lunch, and dinner had become interchangeable as much as his name had become. "Now that I've got a job, I'll probably be able to eat more regular."

"Don't expect them to give you no advance on your pay, though," Rufus said. "You'll have to wait for your first payroll to eat regular-like. They don't pay nobody nothin' in advance out of the goodness of their heart, not even so a man can eat or feed his family."

Rufus took the other half of the sandwich he was eating and handed it to Samuel. "Here, take this. I can't do this for you every day, but it will tide you over for today. No use in you gettin' weak from hunger and have them fire you on your first day because you don't have the strength to do the job. When your pay starts comin' in, you can buy lunch in the commissary they's got here."

The gesture of friendship warmed Samuel more than the heating system they didn't have at the factory. Samuel thanked his newfound colleague and unexpected benefactor. The sandwich was some kind of pork. It was a bit dry, but it beat an empty stomach any cold day.

"So why did you leave your farm and come here, farm boy?" Rufus asked, making unexpected conversation as they both ate. Samuel went into a slightly longer version of the story he had given the floor foreman about his parents both being dead and the bank having repossessed the farm and turned him off the land. Samuel knew enough about Negroes being kicked off their meager landholdings, especially down in the South, where attitudes hadn't changed since the days of the Civil War and Negroes owning land that had once been owned by whites was considered a sacrilege to God and the proper social order. For all Samuel knew, the fake story he had made up of being evicted from his deceased father's farm to explain why he had come to Chicago might have actually happened to his coworker.

"I came up here because there was supposed to be all sorts of work going on and all sorts of jobs open for everyone," Samuel said, wrapping up his story. "Took me all this time to get this. I probably should have stayed in farm country and become a hired farmhand. Farming is all I really know. It gets cold enough in Indiana in the winter. I came up here where the wind blows in harder across the lake with even less to stop it than in Indiana. I probably should have traded places with you and gone down south, where it's warmer, and farmed down there."

Samuel looked at the big Negro. "So why did you leave your farm?" he asked reciprocally. "Why would you want to come to a city that's an icebox in winter and work in a refrigerator all year? Must be warmer down in Georgia than it is up here. Or did the bank take your farm too?"

"I comes from Alabam'," Rufus said. "And no bank took no farm from me. We lived on land that we never really owned for it to be taken away from us. We were sharecroppers. We worked the land we was on for a share of the money from the crop. But every year Old Man Furgeson would come up with a long list of expenses that he said Pappy owed him for. When the expenses he made up were tallied up and taken out of what we would have got, there wasn't hardly anything left over for us. We was poor all the time on the land we worked but couldn't get nothin' out of. Finally Father couldn't afford to keep all his own children. We ate too much. In the end he had to turn me out. He told me to come up here and look for work. ... Pappy's still alive and livin' on the land last I heard, for whatever he's ever goin' to get out of it."

"Is what you've got here better?" Samuel asked.

"What I've gots here is what I've got," the big Negro answered. "I'm not walkin' no street paved with gold, but here I don't have to jump off the sidewalk and into the gutter in the street when a white man walks by me. The South ain't no pastoral promised land, if that's what you think. It wasn't for me or those who look like me, at least. Here they may work you till your back breaks, but at least you can take somethin' home for breaking your back. Here dey fire you if you complain too much for their tastes. But here there ain't no Klan boys to put a rope 'round your neck and drag you behind a horse till you're dead if you complain about anything a white man does to you. ... Things got a long way to go to bein' perfect here, but nothing's perfect anywhere you go in this world. It's hard to ask for perfection of anybody or anything anywhere here in this world. Don't even try."

In her own way, Clarinda had said as much.

681

"Least they didn't run you out of here or not let you in in the first place, saying you couldn't work here just because you're Negro," Samuel said in his own relative voice. "They seem to have accepted you well enough."

"People here in this plant and in the city is what they is," the Negro said in another installment of his relative voice. "There are all different kinds of people 'round here, and they've all got their own ways and minds about things, The Poles, the Lithuanians, the Jews. We've got a few of them too; they're not so bad. Some of them will even have a friendly word for you. The Germans are the snootiest of the bunch. They don't talk to many others apart from themselves. They think they're better than everyone else goin'. They're like their kaiser leading them back in their old country. They stomp around and growl a lot. The Irish like to drink every chance they get, and they fight when they're not drinkin'. They's been kicked around a lot themselves, so they make up for it by kickin' around darkies and anyone they feel like pickin' a fight with at any given moment. The ones to look out for are the Italians. They're the ones to avoid. They're just mean all the time for the sake of bein' mean. In the old days, when they was marchin' for Rome, they used to kill everyone around them with swords. Since Rome went and gone away, they took to killin' each other in feuds that go on forever in the name of their honor. But they don't have a lot of that. Seems like the Italians run most of the crime here in the city."

Samuel hadn't expected a lecture on the characteristics of the various ethnic groups in the city and the plant. He figured that the Negro was just trying to be helpful to a wet-behind-the-ears newcomer to the city by telling him whom to watch out for.

"The Irish and Germans don't like each other very much. Nobody likes the Italians. The Irish are spittin' at everybody, their own included if they're the wrong part of the Christian religion. All the races dump on the Jews. A lot of groups have it in for each other 'round here. The bosses of this place use that to set the groups against each other. By doin' that, they keep the unions busted down."

"You the only Negro in the place?" Samuel asked out of curiosity.

"Hardly," Rufus answered. "There are more workin' in other parts of the plant. Used to be they didn't have any Negroes in the plant. They is bringin' Negroes in to have another group they can set against the others and keep the unions off-balance. ... They tried to strike a couple of different times back in the eighties and nineties. The company just brought in strikebreakers and busted up the strikes. They busted up the union and the strikers at the same time. Around 1900, the Amalgamated Meat Cutters was able to organize the shop for a while. Back in '04, they tried to strike again. The results were the same as they had been ten years earlier during the strike of 1894. The company just brought in strikebreakers and broke up the strike and the organization. After that they brought in other immigrants to take the place of the strikers. That's when they started takin' in southern Negroes. To them we is just another group they can use to pit against the older groups that start gettin' big ideas about fairness and a livin' wage and unions and strikes."

"Now that I've got wages coming in, I can afford a place of my own to stay, and I can get out of the flophouses and basements I've been sleeping in," Samuel said, avoiding the subject. "Where do the men who work here live?"

"You got a wife and family?" Rufus asked.

"No on both counts," Samuel said.

"Just as well. You wouldn't be able to keep her or your kids on what we make, unless she has some kind of work of her own she can do, washing or sewing or the like, or working here in the canning department. Lots of men 'round here can't afford their families any more than my pappy could. ... As for where you can find a place to live, there are plenty of run-down tenements in Packingtown that you can rent a room in. They charges you more than the room is worth, but if you're single, you'll be able to afford it and have somethin' left over for yourself to live on. They don't let black folk live in Packingtown. We may work our fingers to the bone in the plant here, but we is segregated from living there. I lives over in what white folk of the city calls Darkie Town or the Black Belt. People who lives there are taking to calling it Bronzeville, I suppose because we're supposed to be bronzed from the African sun. There are rooms available there too, but you'd stick out like a sore thumb there. Bronzeville is a longer way out than Packingtown. No use you living there when you can live in Packingtown."

As part of his general background knowledge of the world and how the country worked in his day, Samuel was vaguely aware that things were heavily segregated in the Cotton Belt South. He had even heard the phrase

Jim Crow, though when he had first heard it as a young boy, he assumed it to be some kind of southern whiskey. He wasn't aware that segregation of the day extended to the large industrial cities of the North.

"How do I go about finding a place to stay around here?" Samuel asked.

"The plant's got what they calls a real estate office," Rufus said. "They don't sell no houses or real estate, but they knows where there are places that have rooms for rent. They can tell you where to go to get a room. It's about the only service the company gives out to any of the workers here. I guess they wants to keep their workers close by so they can gets to work on time. The rooms 'round here aren't often worth whats dey charge for them. But you can gets a roof over your head."

"Beats sleeping in an alley," Samuel said. They fell silent and went back to eating.

"Since you're not married, if you're lookin' for female companionship to fill your needs, there are plenty of whores 'round the town to service you," Rufus said in a local information vein. "All races of 'em. Like the rooms, they charge more than they're worth, but you can have some fun with them and be gone after that. The main trouble they can cause is that they gives you the clap. But other than that, they don't cause you the trouble or the expense that trying to keep a wife and family can cause you."

Whether he would get married or even look for a wife after losing the girl was something Samuel hadn't thought about much. After the girl's murder he had been too consumed with grief to think about the question. After he had learned that Harold Ethridge had been the man who had murdered the girl, he had moved too fast, too hard, and too far to have given the question any thought along the way.

As he finished the half sandwich Rufus had given him, Samuel looked out the open door at the far end of the loading dock room. The half-filled boxcar on the other side of the loading dock and the city beyond were the far end of the journey that had started down on the riverbank when Polly had remembered the nickname the girl had called the man who killed her. Rufus's comment about a packinghouse worker not being able to afford a family was a halfway moot point for Samuel. Samuel, going under the different name he had taken, didn't know if he would ever be able to find a girl who could take the place of his dead lover Clarinda, who had lived and died under the invented name she had taken. Most of his thoughts of wife, home, and family had died in his heart and mind along with the girl. The idea that he might not be able to love again after the girl's death was a romantic notion in a city where a lot of romantic notions died every day.

"I'm not looking to take on a family right now," Samuel said.

The short lunch period the company allowed their workers was over. They both had to get back to work if they wanted to be able to keep their jobs to pay for the single room in a run-down tenement that Rufus had and that Samuel hoped to find before the snow got deeper. Samuel got up and took hold of another side of beef hanging from the trolley.

"And where it comes to whores," he said as he started to move toward the door, "I didn't have to come to this town to get myself in trouble over a whore."

"You shall find them about six miles from the city," the celebrated novelist Rudyard Kipling had written of the stockyards years before Samuel's arrival. "And once having seen them, you will never forget the sight."

But Kipling had been on a guided tour of the plant at the time he had passed through the area Samuel was walking through, casting around for a place to call his own. Kipling probably hadn't been on foot. He had probably been riding in a gilded carriage reserved for visiting worthies. He hadn't been looking for a roof over his head, and he hadn't been planning an extended stay in any of the areas where more genteel visitors held their handkerchiefs to the their noses as the stench set in around them.

Samuel was on foot on the dirt roads rendered slippery by the wetness and sewage that mingled together beneath his boots. Like Kipling, he considered himself a sojourner who was just passing through. Samuel had no intention of walking the dirt streets he was on for the rest of his life, until he was an old man and melted away like a puddle of grease, sinking into and merging with the sewage-soaked dirt beneath his feet. He resolved not to let himself become one of the worn and dispirited workers sharing the dirty streets of the district. At the same time he resolved not to allow himself to become trapped and melt away into a futureless future in and on the margins of the slaughterhouse.

"Never a hill and never a hollow," the noted author of the exposé book *The Jungle* by Upton Sinclair said of that section of Chicago. Though the description applies to the whole of the industrial district where the packing plant was located, Sinclair was referring mainly to the lumped and fetid dwellings in the lumped and fetid section immediately adjacent to the packing plant, the wood-framed tenement slum crammed with two-story framed cottages, stores, and saloons that was home to the lumped and worn immigrants who worked in the slaughterhouse and related industries. "But always the same endless vista of ugly and dirty little wooden buildings."

As Samuel walked, he crossed over a never-ending succession of busy rail crossings passing over bridges that spanned creeks and canals lined with smaller slaughterhouse-associated factories that ran off the by-products of the dominant, central showpiece industry of the area, the packing plant. The smaller factories sent up curling streamers of smoke. The smoke of the lesser industrial concerns rose to where it converged and merged with the smoke from the packing plant itself. The combined sooty emissions hung over the area as if they were anchored in place, darkening the entire sky. The rail crossings and bridges broke up the landscape a bit. "But after each of these interruptions, the desolate procession would begin again, the procession of dreary little buildings."

At its inception, the packing plant had been attended by skilled butchers who could perform a variety of butchering and meat preparation functions. These craft-proud butchers, mostly Irish, Germans, and Bohemians, lived in well-kept cottages in neighborhoods north and south of the yards. As the meatpacking industry increased its production pace and speeded up the lines, pushing the speed of the workers toward the biological limit, the skilled workers were replaced with semiskilled and unskilled workers who performed one repetitive task over and over again. These workers were mostly miserably paid East European immigrants. By the time all-American farm boy Samuel had come upon the grimed-up scene, poorly paid immigrant labor from south Dubrovnik to south Dixie made up over two-thirds of the industry's labor force. Taking whatever they could find, whatever they could afford to live in close to the plant, they moved into the deteriorating neighborhood just behind the stockyard that the butchers and their families were fast abandoning. Once a pastoral settlement in the 1870s, by the turn of the century, Packingtown, or the "Back of the Yards" as it was also called, was the vilest slum in Chicago.

The Back of the Yards was a plagued island that was veritably surrounded by a circle of stench, smoke, disease, slime, and putrefaction. To the east were the yards and slaughterhouses themselves with their own attended stenches and thick soot clouds from the in-house furnaces and the coal-burning locomotives that came and went at all hours. To the west lay the largest municipal garbage dump in Chicago. The more polite term *landfill* hadn't come into popular usage yet. To the south, the district was hemmed in by a maze of railroad tracks servicing the yards. To the north was Bubbly Creek.

Bubbly Creek was a dead arm of the Chicago River so named for the carbolic acid from decaying refuse that bubbled to its surface. Every year the creek absorbed pollution that was equivalent to a city of a million people. In the summer, a hard brown scum formed on its surface. The scum would become hard enough for cats and chickens to scurry across. But cats and chickens are lightweight. Any human trying to traverse the creek would fall through because of his own weight. If the hapless individual managed to escape drowning by pulling himself out, he wouldn't have necessarily escaped danger. Possible chemical burns and possible death by any number of poisons could have followed in train, especially if the victim swallowed any of the water. The banks of Bubbly Creek were reasonably well-defined, but the scum often became thick-looking enough to hide the water and make the brown scum appear to be a passable road. To the uninitiated and unwary, the seeming surface solidity could prove dangerous.

Bubbly Creek wasn't the only scum-coated body of water in Packingtown with a crust thick enough to hide its existence and give a deceptive appearance of solidity. There was another, similar hazard only a few feet to either side of Samuel as he walked the mud streets of Packingtown. Most of the streets in Packingtown were mud streets with drainage ditches dug on the sides. Most of the houses were wood-framed cottages and two-story wood-framed tenements. They all lacked sewers. Human waste and garbage, mixed with drain water, collected in the ditches alongside the roads. Instead of the water going crusty brown on the surface, the stagnant water would stand for so long that a thick, green leathery scum would develop on the surface. In Upton Sinclair's seminal exposé on conditions in the meatpacking industry, the toddler son of the main character in the book, Jurgis Rudkus, falls into one of the sewage-filled ditches and drowns. Though the scene is rhetorical and a plot device, the scenario it depicts wasn't as far-fetched a possibility as it might seem. In the history of Packingtown there was at least one actual incident where a young child walked into the solid-looking muck, thinking it was part of the street, and fell through the crust, drowning in the deep ditch, where the water was over the head of the short child.

"No other neighborhood in this, or perhaps in any other city," wrote the contemporary housing investigators Sophonisba P. Breckenridge and Edith Abbott, "is dominated by a single industry of so offensive a character." It was an industry whose atmosphere, figurative and real, of blood, death, and disintegration permeated everything. Directly and indirectly it had a demoralizing effect, "not only upon the character of the people, but [also upon] the conditions under which they live." The paltry wages paid by the packinghouses for the frenzy of flat-out, full-charge effort expended didn't otherwise do much to counter the miasma of disrepair and disintegration in the workers' district and the lives of the workers' families.

A 1911 study of Packingtown by investigators at Mary McDowell's settlement house found that the average weekly, that's weekly, wage for male heads of households was just over $9.50. Money went farther in those days, but at the same time the estimated weekly wage needed to support a family of five was $15.40. To make up the deficit, entire families were forced to work. Children were pulled from school and sent to local factories. Wives worked in the canning department or took in boarders of the type Samuel, sloughing down the mud and sewage-slippery street, was looking to become. They also did housecleaning and sewed clothing at home. Or, if left on their own or if they developed a drink or drug habit, they became prostitutes to survive.

As Samuel walked toward the center of Packingtown that Sunday, he couldn't see the garbage dump on the western edge of the town. But the smell of it commingled with the other smells that came in from the plant to the east and the smells that were native to the district. In summer the dump provided an extra resource to the financially strapped families of Packingtown. Women would scavenge the dump, looking for pieces of wood to use as kindling for cooking and looking for old mattresses, discarded clothing, and even edible pieces of food. The dump was both resource and hazard. One out of every three infants in the households facing it died, often from disease that had probably been incubated in and by the festering garbage.

In this "necessarily unpleasant place," as the bosses called Packingtown, upward of thirty-five thousand people lived in the wooden shanties Samuel was walking past.

Perhaps as much as anything, the nature of the work done within the confines of the packinghouses translated into the treatment of workers. In a way it kind of went with the territory. If one is a corporate higher-up in an industry that reduces millions of animals a year to component parts, it's not that much of a leap in one's mind to reduce one's workers to ruin. As Upton Sinclair wrote, there was something in the industry "that tended to ruthlessness and ferocity." And since the packing companies were personal, pride-centered concerns that the founders of the companies had built from the ground up, there was the strong feeling amid first- and second-generation owners that no one but the owners should have a voice in how things were done in their domain.

Successive generations of Middle Europeans and Eastern Europeans had been lured in to the stinking square mile of stockyards by labor agents of the packing companies who spun grand stories of the high wages to be had in the packinghouses. Germans, Lithuanians, Poles, Slovaks, and blacks from the South, they came in sequential waves of nationality, brought in by the bosses to take the jobs of those who had come before them. The ongoing and oncoming pool of immigrants provided the packinghouse owners with readily available replacement manpower in sufficient numbers that allowed them to brush off any union organizing attempt or strike threat. The immigrants kept coming in like the trainloads of cattle and hogs they were hired to slaughter. The two sacrificial groups combined, confabulated, and were consumed together at the packing plant: cattle and hogs from the West, immigrant men and women from the East.

Chapter 25

Samuel found the ramshackle two-story wooden house the real estate office had said had an open room. The box-shaped building was about the same square footage under roof as the farmhouse Samuel had grown up in. It looked to have less space under roof as the family barn. The house did have a second floor, but from the relatively low height of the roof, it looked as if there was little headroom to spare on the upper floor. Next to the door was a sign painted on a flat piece of board that read, Boarder Wanted—Single Room Available. Samuel paused for a moment, reflecting on the ironic point that elsewhere there might be wanted posters with his original name on it declaring him wanted for murder. The main tenant, Samuel figured, was probably looking to take on a boarder and sublet a corner of the house in order to help defray the rent on the place or to acquire a little extra money for necessities. Samuel figured he would just never reveal how widely wanted he was in the world he had come from.

Samuel didn't stop long to reflect. In short order the open room could be filled. He walked up quickly to the door and knocked on it. The sound of his knocking reverberated inside the house with an equally hollow, if not more hollow, sound than his footsteps had made on the wooden floor of the front hall in Mrs. Richardson's house the day he had walked in without closing the front door, having come from the police station, where he had identified the girl's body. For a short while there was no response. Samuel knocked again. Then he heard footsteps inside the house.

A tall, somewhat heavyset man with hair gone almost white opened the door. The man was wearing work overalls of the kind most of the workers in the plant wore. He looked to be in his early fifties, but his age was uncertain. Samuel was aware that men did tend to age quickly on the slaughterhouse lines. When the man looked at Samuel, his expression seemed to be a bit puzzled.

"They told me at the real estate company that you have a room for rent," Samuel said, answering the man's question before he could ask it. "Your sign says the same thing. I've been sleeping in flophouses in the city, but it's a long way to get to work. I need a place to stay that's close to the plant. Packingtown is a lot closer to here than where I'm staying now."

The man's puzzled look left his face. Put in terms of one workingman to another, he seemed to understand.

"Oh, then you work at the plant," the man said in a somewhat thick Eastern European accent that Samuel couldn't identify but that he would later learn was Polish. The man still seemed a bit surprised by Samuel's youth.

"Yes," Samuel said.

"I never see you at the plant before," the man said.

"I haven't been there very long," Samuel said. "I'm on the far end of it."

"Where you work in plant?" the man said. "Are you on the cattle line or the hog line?"

"I work on the loading dock," Samuel said, "with Rufus from Alabama. I just started a few days ago. It's a long way from the flophouses I've been staying in, and streetcar fare eats up a lot of money when you have to ride them every day. Now that I'm working, I can afford a place closer by where I can walk to work. I was hoping you would be willing to take me in."

"You must be just starting like you say," the man said. "You seem so young. Most men who work the packinghouse don't look so young. They all look old before their time. That's why I didn't know who you were and why you here. I thought maybe you were some young social worker just out of college."

"I just came off a farm," Samuel said, reverting to his cover story. "My mother died when I was young. Father just died, and the bank foreclosed on the mortgage. I had to leave home and find work in the city. I've been living on the streets of the city and sleeping in flophouses for some time. I was fortunate to get the job I did in the plant."

Samuel laid it on a bit thick, figuring that if he could win the man's sympathy, it would help his chances of renting the room. Apparently it worked. The man motioned him inside.

"You have family?" the man asked as he closed the door. "The room barely big enough for one man. It's not big enough for family or even for a man and wife."

"I don't have any family," Samuel said, "either with me or waiting for me to send for them. I have no living family." It was a lie, of course, but Samuel had become as easily flexible with the truth as he had become name flexible.

"Come. I introduce you and show you room," the man said.

In many ways the house was like the wood-frame farmhouse Samuel had grown up in. In a Walden Pond setting, it could have been considered snug and pastoral. In the dirt and stench of the Packingtown slum, from the outside it looked as if it was sagging in a dispirited heap into the mud around it.

The inside of the house looked cleaner and less like the extension of the rot creeping over the district outside the house like a spreading mildew. But it wasn't what one could call pastorally bright and cheery. The downstairs of the house consisted of only three rooms. The living room was about the size of the parlor in Samuel's farmhouse home. Off to the far side of the room in the front was a small bedroom. From what Samuel could see through the open doorway, the room behind that looked like a small kitchen.

"I'm Anton Kraznapolski," the man said as he led Samuel into the house and across the front room. "My wife and I rent this house for years. We live down here. My sister is a widow. She lives here with us since her husband was killed. There are two rooms upstairs. She has one. The other room is the one for boarders. It's not very big. But if you have no family, then maybe it fit you and you fit in with us."

The man led Samuel into the kitchen of the house, which was about the same size as the kitchen in his farmhouse, slightly smaller. Like the kitchen in his home, the kitchen in this house had a plain wooden dining table in the center. It also had the same kind and size of woodburning stove that was in the kitchen of his home. A low wave of sadness went through Samuel as he saw the familiar scene. In one way it was like he was coming home, only it was a shadow of home he had come to. He would later find out that in its own way, the house was as much of a shadow home to the people who lived there as it was to him.

But Samuel did not have time to dwell on shadows. Inside the kitchen were two women, one of whom looked to be the same age as the man. Her hair had originally been black, but it was turning gray. The woman was short, rounded in that Eastern European way, and somewhat stocky. She had large breasts that sagged under her plain and worn-looking blouse. She had a rounded and somewhat thick Slavic face and thick Slavic lips that fit with her rounded and semiheavy Slavic body. Her face and expression were smiling and pleasant. In her own way, the woman reminded Samuel of Polly. In a way it was old home week, or new home week, for Samuel all around. At least the woman reminded him of the way he imagined Polly would look when she reached fifty. The sight of the woman made him wonder what Polly would look like and whether she would still be at Mrs. Richardson's house when she reached that age.

The other woman was also an older woman, but she appeared younger than the first woman, by Samuel's estimate by as much as ten years. Her hair was dark and hadn't started to turn yet. She was taller than the first woman and as tall as the man, and almost as tall as Samuel. The woman was somewhat stocky, but her build was spread out over her longer rectangular frame. She had square shoulders and breasts as large as the first woman, but instead of being rounded and sagging like full wineskins, as were the breasts of the first woman, her breasts were more full and rounded. Under her worn and drab patterned dress, in their fullness her breasts were almost pendulous. She had a more rectangular face than the other woman. Her face had the same large eyes and the same thick Slavic lips. In her face she was neither ugly nor exceptionally pretty. Like Mrs. Richardson, the woman was attractive in her own older-woman way, but like so many of the people Samuel would see in Packingtown, her face had a shopworn look to it.

"This lad here wants to rent our room," Mr. Kraznapolski said to the

694

women by way of introduction. Samuel was used to straightforward names like Smith, Jones, Harper, and Martin. He would always have trouble with long and rambling polysyllabic Eastern European names that individually contained half the vowels and two-thirds of the consonants of the English alphabet. But he figured he would get used to it. To get off the streets and have a roof over his head, he would have learned Latin or Mandarin Chinese.

"He just started at the plant. He doesn't have a family, so a single room is right size for him. He must be the youngest we've ever had looking to rent a room."

Samuel nodded a hello to the women and told them his invented name.

"Old Man Warschoski used to rent the room," the second woman said in a Polish-accented voice not quite as accented as Mr. Kraznapolski's. Her voice carried a tone of sour truth and an attitude that she didn't care if she spoke it. "He was a widower. He didn't need a bigger room either. But he got too old to work as well as he used to be able to work, and the company fired him because he had slowed down. The company gets rid of those who can't work or don't stay working up to their speed. You may be starting out your work life here at the plant, but you ain't going to finish it here. Don't expect to retire from the plant like some beloved grandfather. They won't give you a big send-off party and a gold watch and a pension. We'll all be gone from the plant and out of this house after the company's had the best of all of us. You'll be sent out the door too when your youth and years are gone and the company has squeezed all it can get out of you."

The second woman's sour little commentary tapered off without comment. Mr. Kraznapolski and the first woman neither disagreed with her nor admonished her in fearful voices to keep silent.

"Since he wasn't working and wasn't getting paid, Mr. Warschoski had to leave us after he get fired," Mrs. Kraznapolski said. "We don't know where he went off to after that—another job, or maybe a charity home for the old somewhere. He just went. That left us with a room to rent."

Mr. Kraznapolski went on with introductions. "This is my wife, Anna," he said, indicating the first woman. He pointed at the second woman. "This is my wife's sister Mara Anton."

The other woman was middle-aged, maybe slightly younger than Mr. Kraznapolski's wife. She had the same thick body and the heavy Eastern

European woman's physique. She had heavy breasts like her sister. She also had black hair that was starting to become streaked with the gray.

"They both work in the canning department of the plant. Mara lives with us because her husband was killed in an accident five years ago and she couldn't afford the place they were living in on her earnings alone. So she come here to live. If you want the room, it's upstairs in the loft next to hers. For the price of the rent, you can take meals with us."

Depending on the price, that sounded like the better part of the deal to Samuel. He wouldn't have to spend money going to restaurants or buying his own food and preparing it in a room that didn't have a stove. Small-sized portable personal microwave ovens were decades off in the future.

"I can't promise you that the room is warm. We have no furnace here. Except for the fireplace and the kitchen stove, none of the rooms in the house have any heat in them. It can get real cold here in city because of the lake." Mr. Kraznapolski pointed to the stove in the small kitchen. "When it gets bad cold, we bring out mattresses here and sleep at night by the fireplace or the fire in the stove. You can keep warm by sleeping with us on cold night."

"I grew up on a farm in a farmhouse that didn't have a furnace in it," Samuel said, which was the truth. "I'm used to sleeping in a cold room in the winter." Which he was.

"Sometimes on a hot and windless day in summer, when the air don't move, the smell from Packingtown hangs thick and heavy in the air like a mattress and presses down over the whole town," Mr. Kraznapolski went on. "But you get used to it."

Rental price was discussed. It seemed reasonable to Samuel. It would be a chunk out of his weekly salary, but then Samuel figured that rent for the house they were living in was a big chunk out of the combined salaries of the Kraznapolski household. At least it wasn't as near exorbitant as the rent charged for some of the crumbling wooden shacks in Packingtown.

"Come, I show you the room," Mr. Kraznapolski said. He led Samuel up a narrow flight of wooden stairs at the back of the kitchen that ascended to the loftlike second floor of the house. At the top of the stairs was a narrow corridor under the slope of the roof. Only a single small window gave any light in the hall. The corridor led past the doorways to two rooms.

Both rooms were about the same size, but one was one slightly bigger than the other. Mr. Kraznapolski led Samuel to the smaller of the two rooms.

Inside the door was a bare wooden floor. In many ways the room was reminiscent of Samuel's room back home in the farmhouse, which was a narrow room with bare wooden floors and a single window. But the attic room in the Kraznapolski house was a few feet narrower than his room at home had been, and it wasn't as deep. Some walk-in closets in modern luxury homes are larger. The servants' rooms for live-in servants of the rich in those days were larger. At the front end of the room, there was a single window. The inside wall of the room was higher than the outside wall. From the inside wall to the outside wall, the ceiling slanted down with the slope of the roof. At the point where the ceiling intersected the outside wall, it was low enough for Samuel to bump his head against. There was a single wood-framed bed without a headboard or footboard with a thin and lumpy-looking mattress on it. At the foot of the bed was a small table with a washbowl sitting on top of it. On the other side of the room, where the ceiling was lowest, there was a small, cheaply built chest of drawers and a single wooden chair. One would be bending over to look in the drawers or sitting down so the lowered ceiling on that side of the room wouldn't be a factor. One would just have to remember not to bend all the way back up after going into the drawers or not stand up all the way out of the chair; otherwise, one would risk a collision with the ceiling. The girl's room at Mrs. Richardson's house had been larger and better appointed, and had had more headroom.

In a village of people one step above beggary, the beggar who comes begging with his hobo bundle over his shoulder can't be a chooser. After quickly glancing around once, Samuel agreed to take the room. The deal set, Mr. Kraznapolski left the room. Samuel unpacked the few things he had in his bundle and put them in the drawer of the dresser, the gun hidden under his few articles of clothing. For the first time since he had left home, Samuel found himself with one small corner of the world that at least on the surface he could call his own.

After Samuel finished his short-order unpacking, he stood and looked out the window at the front of the room. All he could see outside were more run-down wooden shacks and the dirt streets that ran past them. He turned and looked toward the door to the room. The narrow wooden room still reminded him superficially of his room in the farmhouse. But it didn't feel quite like anything he could call a homecoming.

The sight of the small room that would now be his home only served to remind him that there were two small portions of the world that he had wanted more than the rest of the world but that would never be his.

In the room, Samuel lay on the bed, looking out into the undefined darkness. A faint light came in through the window. Out of sight above him was the sloping ceiling. It would still be the dark of a winter's morning when he would have to get up to go to work. It was the first time since he had left home that he would be sleeping alone and not in the company of homeless men. The room felt something like his room back home. Then again, it didn't. Even with its small and cramped size and the head-bumping limitations of its architectural design, at least he wasn't forced to step over rows of men smelling of urine, vomit, sweat, and whiskey to get to an open smell and fluid-soaked blanket on the floor.

That isn't to say that there weren't smells in the room. The stench of the slaughterhouse and the reek of Packingtown itself flowed back and forth through the landscape in the dark as well as it did in the light. Sometimes the smells contended with each other, one stink driving the other out. Other times they mingled to produce a stink whose whole was greater and more complex than the sum of the parts.

The smells from the yards and the town could be overpowering at times. It was winter now. The cold suppressed the stench to a degree but did not eliminate it. In the summer, the hot air rendered the stink more volatile and penetrating. Residents of Packingtown were able to recognize the smells and tell them apart or in combination. There were the smells of the sewage of the streets of the town and the smell of the garbage dump. Then there were the smells that came in from the packing plant, little reduced by the distance they traveled and over which they dispersed. In the night, residents of Packingtown would often be awakened by a choking sensation. One night it would be the odor of burned animal flesh. Another night it would be the smell of feathers. Another night it would be the smells of the pens and sties the animals were kept in. To add to the alchemist combination of fumes, the smoke of the smokestacks of the packing plant and the other factories, and the smoke coming from the trains, hung over the area day and night, dimming the sun and providing their own sooty assault on the lungs.

As nauseating as it often was, the multifaceted, multipronged assault of the smells was a minor inconvenience compared to the potentially deadly single front thrust of the winter cold. People who lived in the packinghouse district feared the cold more than they feared the disease that was so prevalent. On winter nights, families would sit around the kitchen stove and eat supper with their plates in their laps to hold the warmth of the cooked food close to them. They would go directly to bed with all their clothes on, including their overcoats. "The cold which came upon them was a living thing, a demon-presence in the room," wrote Upton Sinclair. It tore through the cracks in the wallboards, "reaching out for them with its icy, death-dealing fingers; and they would try to hide from it, all in vain. It would come, and it would come."

Samuel was used to sleeping in a farmhouse without central heating. The experience wasn't all that new to him. The water in the bowl on the washstand might have a frozen crust on it in the morning, but back home Samuel was used to breaking the ice in a washbowl to wash up on a winter's morning. In that one small sense, he was back home.

The cold that night wasn't particularly bitter, but it was cold enough. Samuel slept in his clothes that night wearing the coat he had brought with him. Through the single-board layer of wooden wall that separated the two rooms, he could hear Mara stirring in the next room and the creak of the wood-framed bed as she climbed in. The sound reminded Samuel of the sound the girl's bed made in Mrs. Richardson's room when he had made love to her in it. This was the first time he had thought about sex in any significant way, or in any way at all, since he had come to the city. But back when he'd first arrived, he had been preoccupied with finding shelter and employment. In the hierarchy of needs, sex had been far down the list compared to survival.

When he was living on the streets, Samuel had found nothing sexually stimulating about the hard-faced, hard-bitten prostitutes who had propositioned him. Even though he now had money coming in that would allow him to afford professional female companionship, he was still put off by the thought and the remembered faces of the hardened prostitutes he had encountered. Even though she had a bit of a hardened look of her own, he found the full-figured, straight-talking Mara to be more alluring in her own way than any of the streetwalkers he had seen and had rejected.

In the darkened room, in his mind, Samuel looked beyond the far-end wall, which he couldn't see, out into the wider darkness beyond. Out there in the darkness, his family was sleeping in the house he had grown up in, on the land he used to call his own. He could visualize his parents in their bed together in their room and Beth alone in her bed in her room, his room standing empty as if waiting for his return.

Samuel had found himself something of a replacement family. But it served to remind him that there was one family he would never have and one homecoming that would never be his in this world again. The gap between the past world he once knew and his new world was total and uncrossable. There was no bridge to his home and his world far away in the dark. Samuel figured there were few bridges out of Packingtown.

Chapter 26

The darkened bridge Samuel was walking narrowed down in perspective the way all corridors and roads do as they stretch toward the horizon. The far end, where the covered wooden walkway let out, was otherwise lost and uncertain in the faint first light of a winter's morning. That the far end couldn't be seen or fully grasped made no difference to Samuel and the other workers who had funneled onto the bridge. They had all walked the same bridge before in both dark and light. There were only two ways to go on the walkway: in or out. And the bridge led to only one of those two ends. The walkway wasn't lighted, but wooden railings kept one from falling off even in the darkness. The elevated walkway was more of a chute than a bridge, conveying its moving herd members to their assigned positions in the moment of relative calm before the whirling frenzy commenced at the blast of the steam-powered whistle. At least the workers had their one dimension of linear movement. Below them, the animals milled around or stood numbly in their square wooden enclosures that were often packed so tightly that they allowed no movement at all. Soon enough they would be led down a chute of their own. The unmoving animals and the moving workers would meet shortly inside the low, lumped square buildings Samuel and the other workingmen were slouching toward in the dawn that was just beginning to show a hint of light. Ahead, the square-shouldered sleeping Grendel monster was stirring to wakefulness. Soon it would begin again its fast devouring of both the animals waiting to be fed into it and the workmen shuffling toward it. They would just be devoured at different rates.

Off to Samuel's left, the working buildings sat shoulder to jaw in their low linear flatness with their slant-peaked roofs. The buildings were not the skyscrapers the city was already famous for. (It would become more famous for its skyscrapers as more were added.) Like those of other plants designed for assembly line operation, the buildings were long and low as befitted the moving assembly lines contained within them, the difference being that their moving internal lines were disassembly lines as opposed to assembly lines. The buildings presented no architectural treasures that future generations of preservationists would try to spare from the wrecking ball or would mourn the passing of. The internal architecture of the buildings was unenviable in its grim function. The external features of the buildings were unenviable in the architecture of their design. In their time, the only thing they were envied for by the existing generation was the profits they turned out.

The only vertical features that could be made out in silhouette in the dark, reaching upward to the heavens in the light of day, were the smokestacks of various heights. They soared just high enough to vent their gritty black smoke to an altitude where it fell back to settle on the gritty ground around the factory boundaries. From there it would spread out on the wind toward the city. Rivaling the tallest smokestacks in height was the plant's water storage tank, which sat high in the air at the top of a thin spiderweb metal frame like an elongated and distorted skull with drooping jawbone perched atop a spire of long bones and dangling ribs at the center of a cannibal tribe's primitively constructed sacrificial altar. The water tank was a necessary feature of a factory that needed furnaces and their attendant smokestacks, not to keep their workers warm in winter conditions, but to boil the water drawn from the elevated tank, to be used in an important step of the plant processing cycle. The tank also provided water for the in-house fire department in a plant that also had its own railroad and chemical laboratory.

Off to Samuel's right, a full story below, stretching to the borders of the factory grounds, were the pens filled alternately with cattle, pigs, or sheep. Hanging in the air over the plant, as if it were the disembodied spirit of a carnal world, was a thick stench made up of the combined smells of mangled meat, animal blood, dung, and urine. Even in the winter, the cold and heavy dampness of the air did not suppress the smell or hold it on the ground to any appreciable degree. As Samuel walked, the smell drifted through the wooden frame way of the elevated walk like a thick fog off the lake. In the summer, the lake winds carried the stench toward the city.

From whatever direction one approached the plant, the stink announced that one had arrived at the most mechanized killing machine that existed in the world at the time. For visitors touring the plant, the sickly sphere of bad smell became the boundary where they would press handkerchiefs to their noses. For the workers, it announced they had arrived back at the workplace where their stay could prove as quickly passing and transitory as an animal's if they happened to offend a boss or the hireling of a boss, or if they did not demonstrate sufficient alacrity in performing their jobs. For the animals, it announced the end of their journey. It was the point where the hogs sent out by Harold Ethridge to be rendered came to the end of their journey of life.

As he traversed the walkway on his uncertain journey of exile, Samuel did not glance down into the pens below. They were a bit hard to see in the winter morning darkness. He had seen it all before anyway. Back home he knew every one of their farm animals by sight, name, and personality. There was no reason to try to come to know any of the animals below him on an individual basis or to try to pick any particular animal out to recognize again. He wouldn't see any of the animals momentarily occupying the pens ever again, not in their present incarnation at least. At the end of his march across the bridge to the interior of the factory, within a day's march inside the plant, he would see them again in unrecognizable form. Almost every animal in the vast mass of animals in the pens below had arrived earlier that night and had been unloaded under the lights of sputtering arc lamps. By the end of Samuel's working day, almost all of them would be dead, the pens empty, and then the ritual of arrival, collection, selling, and killing would begin all over again.

In Samuel's day, upward of twenty-five thousand men, women, boys, and girls processed over fourteen million animals a year. The value of the packinghouse products equaled upward of two hundred million dollars in the money of the day. In the words of the contemporary muckraker Charles Edward Russell (no relation to Pastor Russell from Samuel's hometown), the combined livestock and meatpacking industry of the city comprised, at that time, the "greatest aggregation of labor and capital ever gathered in one place," an economic power "greater than courts or judges, greater than legislators; superior and independent of all authority of state or nation." To Samuel and the workingmen he walked with across the elevated walkway, it was the beginning of another undifferentiated working day in the square-mile empire of order and blood that was Packingtown, later to be named the Chicago Union Stockyards.

Samuel crossed the walkway, entered the building he worked in, and walked through the interior to the far end and the loading dock, where he worked with Rufus. At the beginning end of the line, the doors were being opened for the first batch of cattle that were being brought in from the pens as the killing cycle quickly geared up to the speed that would be sustained for the day. Unlike the line where the hogs were butchered, in the beef house all the work was done on a single floor. There was an overhead visitors' gallery down the center of the dimly lit building from where guests and people taking tours of the plant could look down into an inferno of blood, steam, and sweat.

The cattle were led up a limewashed gangway by a "Judas" steer that was allowed to exit ahead of the charges it was betraying, down an escape gate. The rest of the cattle were driven into narrow chutes, one or two steers to a chute, penned in so tightly that they were rendered immobile and unable to escape their fate or even duck the coming blow. On a platform above and next to the chutes, ironed muscled men in shirtsleeves guided the steers into the stalls, caressing them with the tips of their sledgehammers to calm the animals, which had by now picked up the scent of blood. Then with a sudden movement, the men lifted their sledgehammers high into the air and slammed them down with a thud into the steer's forehead. The animal would sink down into a lifeless, or at least unconscious, heap, breathing heavily and bleeding from the nose and mouth. One side of the pen was raised, and the unconscious animal was pulled by chain into the killing beds. Its hind legs were shackled. With the press of a button, the huge beast was lifted by a steam hoist and placed on an iron railway. From there it was sent down the line to a "sticker," who plunged his knife into the steer's heaving chest, severing its principal arteries. The animal was left hanging to bleed out. Then the headsman decapitated it with a few well-aimed blows.

After touring the killing floors, Rudyard Kipling wrote, "If the pig men were splattered with blood, the cow butchers were bathed in it. The blood ran in muttering circles." The blood on the floor would accumulate as much as an inch deep despite the work of unskilled immigrants, who shoveled it into drainage holes in the floor.

The cutting-up process was frenzied and fast-paced. Instead of one line of carcasses going past the workers as it was in the hog butchering section, there were many lines, and instead of the hog coming to and past the workers on the line, here the men moved from carcass to carcass working with "furious intensity, literally on the run." Each man had a specialized task to perform on the suspended carcass. When he was done, he would rush on to the next carcass in line, to be followed by a different kind of specialist performing a different operation involving the removal of something from the dead animal: intestines, hide, hooves, etc. The final operation was "splitting," where a worker wielding a large butcher knife in a two-handed, over-the-head, downward-slashing motion, like a berserk Viking swinging a battle-ax, would, cutting along the spinal column, hack the gutted steer into the two literal sides of beef.

In this way, a gang of almost two hundred men could stun, kill, gut, clean up, and core out over eighty head of cattle per hour. The sides would be delivered first to the large cooling room and from there to the loading dock for Samuel and Rufus, and other loading dock workers when needed, to load them into outbound refrigerated railcars. Given the size of the cooling room and the number of sides of beef often hanging in them at any one time, an in-house joke of the period said it was possible for a stranger who did not know his way around the plant to find himself lost in a forest of frozen sides of beef.

From beginning to end, steer butchering in the packing plant took place on one level. Hog butchering started out on a higher level, but what followed was hardly a more ethereal sight to witness. A long line of hogs was driven up an inclined chute, a chute called the Bridge of Sighs by packinghouse wags, to a small opening in the top story of a boxlike building that, when entered, gave off an overpowering stench. Ahead in the catching and holding pens were the pigs, "alive grunting and screaming, as if they had a vision of the approach of the horrible machine, from which they [could] no more escape from than a doomed man whose head lies on the guillotine."

The infernal machine the hogs were confronted with was an immense spokeless metal-framed wooden wheel appropriately called a hog wheel. The wheel had chains attached to its rim. As the wheel turned, the chains dragged across the floor. While the chain was on the ground, a man would fasten a hook on the end of the chain around the hind leg of a pig. As the wheel turned and the chain was lifted up, the hog would be jerked into the air upside down, screeching, squealing, kicking, and biting. The snared hog was carried by the movement of the wheel to an overhead railway that ran the length of the building on a descending angle from the top to the bottom floor. For the hapless and helpless hog, it was the beginning of a descent on a sloping path through the waiting sequence of death, dissection, and refrigeration.

Hanging by its feet from the trolley on the overhead railway, the pig was carried to where another sticker waited with an equally large and sharp knife. With a quick thrust, he would cut the soft throat of the pig, at which time a stream of blood, "jet-black and as thick as your arm," spurted out, some of it hitting the butcher even though he dodged to avoid it. That was followed in quick turn by another hog, then another in endless sequence.

After having its throat and jugular vein severed, the animal gravitated downward for ten yards or so, bleeding into a catch basin that preserved the contents for fertilizer. When the hog, still twitching and perhaps still alive, passed over a vat of boiling water, it was released from the guiderail and disappeared with a splash, silenced forever. The scalding water softened and loosened the hair and bristles. The pink carcass was then scooped out of the tub by a rake-like device and lifted onto a table. An endless chain was attached to a ring in the animal's nose, and it was pulled through a scraping machine, emerging ten seconds later shaved from nose to tail. Any remaining hair was scraped off by workers with fast-moving hands. The head was then partially severed and left hanging only by a flap of flesh. The body of the hog was hitched up again to the overhead conveying rail system, where it was carried by gravity and its own weight to a lower level of the plant. There it passed over a table flanked by workers, six men on each side, who would set in upon the diminishing animal. Each man, working in an almost frenzy "as if a demon were after him," performed a series of cuts and scrapes as the carcass glided past him. The head was removed the rest of the way. The tongues were cut out. Tongue is a delicacy to some. Animal parts flew everywhere in a whirligig of disembowelment. As they further rendered the animal, all the workers were rendered blood red from head to foot.

As the cleaned hog carcasses passed down the final stretch of the railway of death, as happened with the carcasses of dressed steers, they were cut down the middle by another crew of splitters. The halved carcasses were then pushed into enormous chilling rooms, thirty to forty acres of them under roof, where they were suspended for twenty-four hours to cool and become firm. It was a room where a stranger could get lost in a forest of dangling hogs as well as he could get lost in a forest of dead steers. The entire operation from killing wheel to the death lockers took less than ten minutes.

But not every carcass ended up dangling whole (halved whole actually) in a refrigerated room, to be shipped out in a refrigerated railcar, to be reduced to the final small cuts of meat that ended up on the dinner plates of the nation. The plant was its own source of the final cuts that befell the carcasses and often the workers doing the cutting.

Carcasses that did not end up whole (half whole) in the freezing rooms were pushed along the ubiquitous overhead rail system to the cutting-up rooms with long rectangular wooden chopping tables surrounded by human cutters. Two men lifted the carcass on to the table and turned it into position. The other workers would fall upon the carcass like demon goblin swordsmen in an army of the damned, wielding cleavers that had glistening blades two feet long. In a proverbial orgy of chopping that would make a modern producer of slasher movies feel like an unimaginative incompetent, the workers would lay into the lying carcass. Chop, chop, chop, chop, chop, chop would fall the cleavers in a veritable rapid-fire wave of further dismemberment. In approximately thirty-five seconds, the once whole carcass would be reduced to sorted assorted parts and the table would be clear for the next carcass in line. Decades after the days that Samuel walked across the wooden walkway and walked the lines of the plant, Norman Mailer would write, "They cut the animals right out of their hearts—which is why it was the last of the great American cities, and people had faces, carnal as blood, greedy, direct, too impatient for hypocrisy, in love with honest plunder."[2]

The cutting created hams, steaks, chops, bacon slabs, and racks of ribs. These were sent through other chutes to pickling, salting, and smoking rooms below. From there they were put in boxes and barrels and sent to the loading platforms, where the huffing freight trains were waiting to be loaded with the full and intact sides by Samuel, Rufus, and other loading dock workers. The full sides were destined for the meat cabinets of butcher shops. The final processed cuts of meat were bound for the dinner tables of the homes and restaurants of the United States.

German chancellor Otto von Bismarck once commented something to the effect that those who respect the law and like to eat sausage should not watch the process by which either is made. The owners of the packing plants did not feel quite the same way about things. Proud of their world-class operations that were feeding the country, they conducted tours of the packing plants and their operations from beginning to end. The meatpacking plant owners were not men who were faint of heart. Watching the full beginning-to-end process by which the meat the companies produced was not for the faint of heart either. The noise and uproar, and the sights of animals being dissected on the fly with the attendant flying body parts and spurting blood, proved too much for some of the visitors invited in by the plant owners to witness the spectacle. Men looked at one another and smiled nervously. Women wrung their hands and grew faint.

Whether one was squeamish or not about the kind of things that went on in the slaughterhouse, the direct effect of the processes employed on the animals was immediate and easy to see. The effect it had on the workers was often not quite as immediately seen and was often overlooked. With the technological limits existing at the time, the level of modernization and mechanization did not extend much beyond the immediate and obvious innovations such as the hog wheel and the overhead trolley system. Unable to mechanize operations beyond that, in an era when the Industrial Revolution was hitting a faster mechanized stride, the packers

---

[2] Norman Mailer, *Miami and the Siege of Chicago* (New York: Random House, 2016), 88.

built mass-production engines that were powered by hand labor. Desired levels of efficiency and productivity were often pushed toward by driving the workers as fast as a steam or electrical drive mechanical arm. Long before fighter planes developed speeds that could subject pilots to G forces, which pushed the human body to the limits of consciousness, the speed demanded of the cutters often pushed workers to and beyond the biological barrier of the work they were performing. The Socialist writer A. M. Simons wrote at the turn of the century, "That marvelous speed and dexterity so much admired by visitors is simply inhumanly hard work."

Lacking a stream of new technology constantly coming online to increase production through mechanization, and in their unrelenting efforts to cut costs, the builders of the meatpacking industry would simply increase the pace at which the animals, dead and alive, would be run past the workers of the lines. The faster the line of carcasses moved, the faster the knives flew in order to keep up.

Samuel worked out on the loading dock, which was directly outside the cold storage rooms. There was no change of seasons in the refrigerated storage rooms. He was exposed to the cold year round. But slipping off deeper into the interior of the pant to find a moment of warmth in winter was not an option. The plant was not heated. Workers on the fast-moving lines would tie up their feet with old newspapers in an attempt to keep their feet warm. The newspapers would become soaked with blood, which would freeze. When their foremen were not looking, men would sometimes thrust their freezing feet into the still hot carcasses of the eviscerated steers to warm them. But there was little way that one could keep one's hands warm. Workers were unable to wear gloves. Gloves reduced the feel of the work and slowed your hands down. Fingers and hands would go numb from the cold. The only point on the line that offered any escape from the cold was in the areas immediately adjacent to the tubs of scalding water used to loosen the hides. There the room could become so thick with steam from the hot water and the hot blood that men carrying razor-sharp knives often could not see more than a few feet in front of their faces.

The frenetic pace, the restricted vision, and the lack of sensation in the hands would combine to produce accidents. In the frenzied whiplash of high speed slashing at the carcasses, workers would cut themselves. Fingers would be severed—sometimes a whole hand. Any cut could easily become infected from the grime all around the workplace. A man with a cut or infection severe enough to be sent home to recuperate would find his job given to a worker waiting in the cold outside the plant door for an opening. On all the lines, foremen would walk up and down like slave drivers in a Roman galley, barking at the workers to keep up the pace. All that was missing were the whips. Of the meatpacking plants and the bosses who ran them, it was said that they got every last drop of blood out of the animals and every last ounce of work out of the workers.

Of one of the only slightly more unusual dangers facing workers on the slaughterhouse lines, Upton Sinclair wrote: "Sometimes in the haste of speeding-up, they would dump one of the animals out on the floor before it was fully stunned, and it would get up on its feet and run amok." Men would shout warnings and scramble to put the nearest pillar between themselves and the frantically charging animal with horns and sharp hooves that often weighed several hundred pounds. The retreating men would slip on the blood-wet floor and fall on one another in the path of the gyrating animal. "And then, to cap the climax, the floor boss would come rushing up with a rifle and begin blazing away!" Not only did the workers in direct line have to dodge a frenzied rampaging steer, but they also found themselves having to dodge live ordnance.

The sympathies of many of the visitors went out to the doomed animals. But Giuseppe Giacosa, a visiting Italian dramatist and journalist, could think only of the workers. In the book of his impressions of the United States, he wrote: "These men have neither the face nor the body of humans." A mixture of blood and animal grease, red and shiny, stained their faces. Blood darkened and hardened in their hair and beards. It caked on their overalls, forcing them "to walk with long stiff strides." This and "the abrupt and rapid movement by which they [threw] severed pieces to neighboring workers ... gave them an appearance altogether ahuman, and rather like the animals they destroy[ed] with such dispatch." By comparison, the section Samuel worked in was squeaky-clean, all the available blood in the animals having been spilled and drained farther up the line. A British correspondent told Upton Sinclair: "These are not packing plants at all; these are packing boxes crammed with wage slaves."

An expanding pool of job-hungry immigrants and desperate laborers gave the packers more than enough manpower to run the system on their labor terms. It also gave them the easy ability to casually replace workers who could not keep up the pace, or who complained about working conditions at the plant, or who considered unionizing. Replacements for any given worker were readily available on a daily basis. Unemployed workers showed up at the gates of the big packinghouses every morning at dawn. The strongest-looking ones, such as Samuel had been the day he had bucked the odds and gotten hired, or those who could afford to pay bribes were picked out by company guards or a foreman and ushered quickly into the plant. Then a policeman would wave his club, and the rejected workers would walk away.

Samuel and Rufus had managed to move from the greater uncertainty of employment outside the plant to the relatively lower but still uncertain uncertainty of holding on to their jobs inside the plant in the face of management poised and ready to fire at the drop of a hat. To keep ahead of that, they kept plant protocol close to their vests. Presently they had their routines down such that they had their tags in place and themselves clocked in when the whistle starting the day's work blew. That way their clocked time started when the clock hour started, not at an in-between time that would not be counted until the next clock hour integer rolled around, time they wouldn't be paid for. At least they would not be forced to work an hour or part of one without pay.

The work rolled on. The days rolled forward. The months rolled by. Samuel rode on in the place where he was, carried forward by the heedless current of time. Samuel didn't grow any taller, but all the heavy lifting on the loading dock broadened his chest and caused the size of his muscles to increase in a way that riding passively astride a plow pulled by a team of horses hadn't. He never forgot the girl. He never forgot his family and his home. In the Kraznapolski house, he had found something rather resembling home. He stopped thinking about the future and lived only day to day, with the next day something that he didn't think about until he was halfway into the given day. The future was something far away over the horizon. For the animals brought into Packingtown in heavily loaded cattle cars, the future ended there for them. For the men and women of Packingtown, the future was sometimes a dream better left undreamed.

Chapter 27

Christmas was fast approaching. The place Samuel was looking at wasn't exactly Santa's workshop, and it wasn't imbued with the holiday spirit.

It was not exactly a place to be quixotic about or in. If this was the place Clarinda had missed by having jumped off the freight and by not having made it to Chicago, she hadn't missed anything. She had actually done better by having had her journey interrupted and landing in Mrs. Richardson's house instead of the establishment he was looking at. Samuel stood outside the building on the late December pre-Christmas Sunday and looked at the slip of paper in his hand to confirm the address. After confirming that the address of the building was the same as the one on the piece of paper, he folded the paper back up and put it in his pocket.

A hollow and empty feeling came into the pit of Samuel's stomach as he looked at the run-down facility that his landlady's daughter had taken up residence in. As bordellos went, Mrs. Richardson's house was positively cheerful-looking compared to the three-story wood-framed tenement building with a brick front that Samuel was looking at. The brick of the building had gone dingy from having been impregnated over the years by the ambient soot in the atmosphere. The neighborhood had gone dingy at the same time. If the three most important words in real estate are *location, location, location,* the location principle didn't apply to quite the same degree when it came to bordello placement. Given that the patrons of bordellos tended to come and go (or arrive and come) in the dark of night, they were not as concerned with Club Med scenic backgrounds. An unimpeded Côtes du Jura view was not the draw that brought them there.

As far as scenic views went, the view from Mrs. Richardson's place overlooking the river and the green expanse of farmland beyond was positively pastoral compared to the view from the bordello Anna Kraznapolski's daughter had left her home to take up residence in. It was unpleasant to imagine any woman opening up her body and soul to the dingy, confined world he saw. Samuel had become accustomed to the dirt of the city. He had grown used to the dirt roads of Packingtown that had marked a no-exit dead end for so many. What he was looking at marked another dead end in a subcity of dead ends.

The girl's room in the Richardson house had looked out to the north, over the river behind the house, the house that he and Ben had tentatively approached seemingly a lifetime ago. Samuel had always enjoyed the view of the river from the girl's window. On the far side of the river, the view from the girl's second-floor room looked out over the green, open farmland stretching to the horizon over the kind of ground he had plowed with his father. Any remembrance of the view of the river that ran past the house had been since spoiled for Samuel by remembering that the girl had been thrown into the quietly flowing river to drown.

Instead of a diver, behind the dingy bordello the Kraznapolskis' daughter had exiled herself to run a local spur railroad track. On the other side of the track was a fence. Backed up to the inside of the fence was the windowless brick wall of the back of some kind of factory or warehouse. The factory wall was about two stories tall itself. Perhaps from the third floor of the building one might be able to see over the roof of the factory, but from the angle of his perspective in the street, Samuel couldn't see anything beyond. Besides, any sliver of view over the roof of the adjacent building probably wasn't any more choice.

Either way, Samuel had arrived at the house of ill repute in the city of ill repute that Katrin Kraznapolski, daughter of Anna Kraznapolski, had left the house of her parents to make her home in. One night at dinner, Mrs. Kraznapolski had let it slip that she had an estranged daughter who had left home and was working and living in a bordello. She said her daughter had left home to work in the bordello because she had grown disillusioned and cold and couldn't see any other options for her in Packingtown or in life. Her perceived lack of options had caused her to leave her home and family and go to work as a prostitute. As family oriented as he had always been, Samuel had felt bad for both Mrs. Kraznapolski and her absent daughter who'd felt she had no choice but to become a prostitute. Always the empath, Samuel had imagined how he would have felt if his sister, Beth, had left the family and had become a prostitute. When he had heard the story, he chided himself for the way he had ribbed Beth about going to work in the Richardson house.

Filled with simple hope of bringing about a reunion of mother and daughter, the home- and family-oriented Samuel was not aware of the degree and depth of the division and the defeat he thought he could brush away with a few words and an emotional appeal to home and family. Mrs. Kraznapolski's daughter had been in the house longer than he had been in the city. As of the date of the approaching Christmas, she would have been in the house for two years. She had been in the house longer than Clarinda had been in residence at Mrs. Richardson's abode. Whatever dreams Mrs. Kraznapolski's estranged daughter may have once had, she had shed those dreams and entered the house before Samuel had entered Mrs. Richardson's equivalent house and before he had entered his dream of making a home and life with the girl.

The whorehouse Samuel was looking at spelled the quiet and despairing end of the Kraznapolski daughter. But however her end had come, it was an end formed of despair and consumption. The streets had triumphed over the once unified and whole Kraznapolski family. Knowing that the woman in question inside, the girl he had never met, was the daughter of the friendly couple who had welcomed him into their house as a replacement for the children they had lost to the streets made the spirit of the scene Samuel was looking at even bleaker to his soul than the visual picture ahead of him.

As Chicago grew in prominence as a commercial center, so did its central business district grow. Along with the commercial growth of the central business district came a growth in the desire to at least keep the highly visible symbolic center of the city respectable. However corrupt and disreputable some of the business practices going on in mainline commerce may have been, more classical disreputable establishments were pushed in stages southward of the realm of reputable commerce. By 1900 the houses of prostitution had become concentrated in the "Levee," the district bordered by Eighteenth and Twenty-Second Streets, State and Armour (Federal) Streets. The district became Chicago's version of New Orleans' famous red-light district, Storyville. In the years just before Samuel's arrival, the Levee was one of the nation's most infamous sex districts. In 1910 the Chicago Vice Commission identified five thousand prostitutes alone working in one thousand twenty "resorts."

Twenty-Second Street in the Levee district contained a diverse variety of houses of ill repute ranging from the most extravagant brothels such as the Everleigh House to small and unadorned houses of prostitution located in boardinghouses and the backs of saloons. The vice was so flagrant that Mayor Carter Harrison Jr. appointed a commission to investigate vice throughout the city. In 1911, the publication of *The Social Evil in Chicago* prompted a flurry of reforms. Not long after, the US attorney launched an attack on the Levee that cleaned out the highly visible and thriving concentrated prostitution. Along with other, lesser houses, the district's most famous brothel, the Everleigh Club, was also closed. If Clarinda had arrived in time to be taken on by the Everleigh madams, it would have been a short stay before she would have been forced to move on with the rest of her coworkers. If she hadn't transferred to New Orleans, more likely she would have ended up a hard-bitten entrepreneur plying her trade on the streets alone like the hard-case women Samuel had run into before he had found his job in the slaughterhouse. Or she would have wound up in a facility in the back of a saloon or in a tacky street corner tenement of the kind that Samuel stood in front of with a crumpled piece of paper in his hand, the building Katrin Kraznapolski had gone into when she had left her house and moved out of the room Samuel now rented, leaving her family behind, the family that Samuel stood outside the run-down building with the quixotic idea of trying to put back together.

Samuel crossed the street and walked into the saloon that occupied the first floor of the dingy bordello. The interior of the saloon was somewhat reminiscent of Two-Bit Charlie's saloon back in his hometown. There was a wooden bar, booths along the interior wall, and tables in the middle of the floor. But there were no pool tables. The limitation of space was probably the reason for the absence of pool tables. The inside the saloon was about half the size of Two-Bit Charlie's, and pool tables take up a lot of room. Besides, pool players can be a rough crowd at times. They have even been known to get into fights, especially when hotheaded youths come in looking for a particular woman.

As for women in residence, there were a few women fraternizing with the male customers of the saloon. They didn't look like settlement house workers trying to talk the men in the bar out of their wastrel lives and convince them to go back to their families. Neither did the women in attendance appear to be acolytes of Carrie Nation, about to take the place apart with hatchets. The purpose the women were there pursuing was obvious enough without one's being aware of the double front room / back room function of the saloon. With the exception of the lack of pool tables, the scene was little different from the one Samuel had seen when he had gone into Charlie's saloon and found the girl soliciting.

Samuel walked up to the bar and waved the bartender over. He didn't ask the bartender anything corny like where the real action was. He simply asked where one went to meet the women he had heard were available there. The man pointed Samuel toward a door on the far end of the inside wall.

When Samuel walked through the door, he saw several women sitting around on benches inside a small room that apparently functioned as an antechamber to what lay (no sexual pun intended) beyond. The room was not nearly as spacious or as well-appointed as Mrs. Richardson's parlor. Then again, Mrs. Richardson was a lawyer's widow living in a lawyer's house. As a whole, the women in the room were as plain-looking as most of Mrs. Richardson's girls, just more haggard in appearance. Unlike the scene in the parlor the night Samuel lost his virginity and became convinced he had found his way in life, there were no single standout beauties who captured his glance, his heart, and the direction his life would take from that night on. Samuel stood for a moment, silently surveying the women in the room. An older-looking woman stepped over to him. Samuel figured that if the woman wasn't the madam, she was the floor foreman for the owner of the brothel. As older women went, she wasn't as good-looking as Mrs. Richardson. Or Mara for that matter.

"Are you looking for anything in particular?" the woman asked as the seated women looked at Samuel.

"Actually I am," Samuel said. "But I'm not looking for a woman by looks. I'm looking for a woman by a particular name." Samuel glanced at the seated women looking at him. "I was told that Katrin Kraznapolski may be found in here. If so, is she available?"

"That's me," an uncertain voice said from the side.

With an uncertain look on her face, one of the women stood up off the bench and started walking toward Samuel. If he had met the woman at random on the street, he would have never guessed she was his landlady's daughter. The woman didn't look very much like her mother at all. She had a plain face and short blondish hair that was a bit unkempt. In her figure, she was thin. You couldn't call her emaciated, but she did lack the Polish plumpness of her mother. Neither did she have the heavy and rounded chest of her mother or the heavy pointed chest of her aunt. She looked to be in her mid to later twenties, but like the other women in waiting with her, she had a tired and haggard look that made her appear older than her years.

The woman walked up to Samuel. "This way," she said in an economy of words, indicating for Samuel to follow her to the room where she performed the economy of her function. Or the function of her economy. Unlike the self-named Clarinda had done in Mr. Richardson's parlor, Katrin Kraznapolski, so named by her mother, did not take Samuel's hand.

As Clarinda had done, Katrin led Samuel to a stairwell and up the stairs toward the second floor. Samuel followed her not because he was intending to utilize her services in an upstairs room but because he wanted to be able to talk to her alone. He figured it might embarrass the woman if he tried to persuade her to return home in front of the others.

"I never see you before," Katrin said as they climbed the stairs. She spoke with a Polish accent that was apparently no more washed out than her mother's. "How is it that you know me by name? You're not a regular customer. I don't have no regular customers who ask for me above all the rest. Do I have someone out there singing my praises and recommending me to all he meets in the street?"

"I know your parents," Samuel said as they turned on the landing and headed up the rest of the stairs. "I work in the same plant as your parents, and I rent a room in their house. I have your old room upstairs."

"Oh, that's how you know me," Katrin said. "I thought Old Man Warschoski had my room."

"He did until the company fired him because he was too old to do the work as fast as they wanted him to," Samuel said as they approached the top of the stairs.

"That's the company," Katrin said flatly, without further comment.

"He had to move out because he couldn't pay the rent to your parents. I came in about a month ago. I needed a place to stay. The room was open."

"I'm surprised my mother told you about me," Katrin said as she reached the top of the stairs. It was almost as dark at the top of the stairs as it had been in the stairwell. Two weak electric bulbs lit the whole length of the second-floor hall.

"She's not exactly proud of me or what I do. I didn't think she even mentioned me anymore to anyone, let alone discuss me with strangers."

"You sort of came up in conversation," Samuel said as he stepped into the hall. "I got the address of this place from your aunt."

"Why you come looking for me by name when there are so many girls like me in city?" Katrin asked as she headed down the hall. "Even though I'm not a proper girl, you feel you need some kind of proper introduction in order to keep time with a hooker? Does my mother know you're here with me doing this? Are you doing it behind Mother's back? Or did she tell you to look me up and throw some money my way?"

"I'm here because I hoped to persuade you to come back home to your parents," Samuel said. "At least I hoped to try to get you to visit home for a few days during Christmas."

Katrin stopped walking and turned around to look at Samuel. Samuel stopped just before he ran into her.

"Did my mother send you here to say this?" Katrin asked.

"Your mother doesn't even know I'm here," Samuel said. "It was my idea to come here and talk to you. Your parents, especially your mother, have been very nice to me since I came into Packingtown. I wanted to give them a Christmas present to show my appreciation, but I don't have much money to buy them anything. I had the idea in mind that it might make a nice surprise Christmas present for your mother if I could take you out of here and bring you home. I figured that would be a gift greater than anything I could buy them with money."

Samuel had always been impressed and moved by the classic sentimental O'Henry short story "The Gift of the Magi," in which a poor couple, unable to buy each other gifts at Christmastime, end up exchanging greater gifts of love. Separated from his family, Samuel had wanted to emulate the story in an even more sentimental way by putting a family back together again, at least partially.

Katrin looked at him closed-mouthed for a moment.

"At first I thought you were a babe in the woods who's never been with a woman, thinking you needed some kind of an introduction to or reference for a prostitute as if she were a governess," Katrin said, regaining her power of speech. "Then I thought you were a dirty boy who likes sneaking around doing dirty things behind the backs of people he knows. Now I know you aren't either. You're just crazy! You don't have the mind you say you have to hold the idea you say you have."

"I know your mother and father both love you and are sad to think of you living this way," Samuel said. "I was hoping I could persuade you to go back home to them. They don't have a lot in life that gives them much of any meaning. If you were to go back home, it would make them happier than anything else. You could have your old room upstairs back."

"If I come back home and take my room, then where you go?" Katrin asked in a flat tone.

Samuel hadn't thought about that. But it was a sacrifice he was willing to make to put at least one-half of the second-generation Kraznapolski family back together again.

"I could go back to the flophouses if necessary," Samuel said. "I could live there until I find another corner to rent somewhere in Packingtown. I survived on the streets when I first came to this city. I didn't know anything about life on the streets then. I know a lot more now. It's something I would be willing to do for all of you if I could see you and your mother and father reconciled to each other."

Samuel figured that pulling at her heartstrings was the only way he could get through to a prostitute, provided the strings of her heart hadn't snapped a long time ago. Trying to pull heartstrings hadn't worked well with Clarinda down by the river. He had tried to reach for her heart that day. She had reached for a knife.

"I know what it's like to be separated from family. I lost my family. There's a gap between me and them that's bigger than the one between you and your parents. That's why I'm here in the city. The gap is too big to be crossed from my side or theirs. I can't go back to my home. Not now. Not the way you can. This is the first Christmas I have ever spent away from my family. If I could get you back with your parents, then in some small way I would be going back home to the family I can't return to. You can start a new life over with your family the way I can't with mine. It would be the best Christmas present and the best Christmas they ever had."

Katrin shook her head. "I can't go back," she said in a resigned and hollow voice. "Any life I once knew is gone. There's nothing for me to go back to. There's nothing much of me left to take back to anyone, myself included. What would I do? Where would I work? No one will have me other than the way they have me now. I'd end up lying around home with Father getting mad at me for being an expense without bringing in any money. This way I can lay myself around and get paid for it."

"You could get a job in the canning department of the plant with your mother and aunt," Samuel said. "There's other work for women outside the plant."

"I don't know any work other than this," Katrin answered. "I wouldn't be able to hold any other job. Nobody, respectable or not, wants to employ an ex-whore. I'm no good for anything other than what I'm doing here."

"You could put all that behind you," Samuel said. "Family love is stronger than drink. The love in a family is stronger than the streets."

"If that's what you think, then you're more of a babe in the woods than I thought," Katrin said. "You ain't been in the city or in the real world half as long as you give yourself credit for."

"Actually I'm a babe out of the woods," Samuel said. "I came from a farm in, oh, Indiana. I would have stayed there, but the life and family I knew is gone. Gone more than yours is. You can get back to your family. I can't get back to mine."

"Maybe you are off the farm and in the city, but you're still thinking like a wet-behind-the-ears farm boy dreamer," Katrin answered. "Life and the streets don't respect no man or woman, and they don't make way or make exceptions for no romantic view that love and family will conquer all. The streets eat you up like a junkyard dog eating garbage. I used to think that there was something out there ahead of me and that someday I would put all the past behind me and get to the future out there for me. Now I know that the only thing out ahead of me in the future is more of what I've lived in the past coming up behind me and catching up to me."

The thought came upon Samuel that his own life was trending that way. With a close enough simile of his life, he had started out thinking there was a whole future as he imagined it and that it would take shape for him out ahead of him. Now he was living the serious question as to whether there would be much of anything different in his future from the life he was living now.

"You're young like I used to be. You probably think that you're going to escape life here. You'll end up trapped in your own corner somewhere, worn out and unable to get out as much as me or my parents or anybody in Packingtown except the bosses. I gave up thinking I was going to escape a long time ago. It may not be all that long in years that I gave up thinking I was going to escape, but it feels like it was an eternity ago. I gave up any hope of family. I gave up any thought of family or any connection with family from the past. I don't have no past. I don't have no future. I accept that now. I don't have no family, and I don't have no idea that family is going to save me from where I am or what I am."

"Must the street win everything?" Samuel asked rhetorically.

"The streets always win," Katrin said in a reductionist voice. "The streets win because they've been there longer than either of us have been alive. They'll be there and be the same after we're both gone. They'll always be there. The streets win because they're bigger and meaner than anyone on them. That makes them stronger than everybody. Around here the streets pull the life out from everyone who walks on them. There's no life for me other than what I've got here. When I'm all used up, they'll turn me out of here. By then my family will be used up and gone. I'll die begging on the streets."

If it could happen to the whores of Packingtown, Samuel wondered if the same would have eventually happened to Clarinda if she had managed to get to her intended final destination.

"You may not stay on the streets in this city for all your life, but you'll stay in the life that life made for you until any dreams you have of getting yourself on top of life and coming out on top of life have come up empty. Eventually you'll end up as worn out on the inside and outside as I am. Or any of the men on the line. In the end, whatever your end will be, you'll become resigned to what life hands you, where life hands it to you. You'll stay where life drops you down and drops you off just as I will stay here. You'll become and be what life makes you, the way I've become what life has made of me. And my family won't save you anymore than it saved me or can save me."

"Can't you at least come home for Christmas?" Samuel said. "Even if it's for one day only? Like I said, it would make your mother happy to see you."

"No it wouldn't," Katrin answered. "Mother's unhappy enough knowing what's become of me. Seeing firsthand what's become of me won't make her feel any better. I send Mother money now and then when I don't drink it up. Maybe the money doesn't do much to fill in the gap that's between us, but my going home would only tear the gap wider. My showing up at home would just make things worse for all of us. You're not doing any of us a favor by bringing me home. Where there is no future to be had, it's best to just leave the past lying out of sight."

Samuel assumed she hadn't meant that as a pun.

"There's no use talking about it. I won't go back with you or on my own. There's nothing to be accomplished by my going home, even for a day. There's nothing left to be said between Mother and me. There's nothing left between us. What's gone between us is gone. There's no way any of us can put back what's gone from us forever."

The light from the dim bulbs hadn't grown any brighter as Samuel's eyes had become accustomed to the half dark. He and Katrin had the hall to themselves. No one came up the stairs or came out of any of the closed doors of the rooms. From one or more of the rooms came faint sounds of the function being performed in the room. Bodies were stirring behind some of the doors, but none of the sounds stirred Samuel's heart.

"There's nothing that my going home would do for Mother, for Father, or for me. There's sure nothing it would do for you. There's nothing it could change. Best to just leave things the way they are. Best to just let all of us go on the way we are, on our separate paths, without any of us knowing what's happening to each other. Best to not know. That way we won't be all twisted up inside, knowing what's happening when there's nothing that can be done. Best not to think of what was or any of what could have been. Best not to have any dreams of something better. If you have any dreams, the streets of this place eat them up even faster than they eat you up. They leave your dreams dead and gone and leave you an empty shell."

You didn't have to tell Samuel about dreams that hadn't been and possibly never could have been. Where it came to could-have-beens that probably couldn't have been, he was on home ground. Katrin's gloomy street philosophy and fatalistic advice wasn't much different from anything he had told himself a hundred times over, starting on the train ride to the city. Best not to think of lovers and love that never could have been. Best not to think of family left behind and families that never could be. What he was hearing was the death knell of another family.

"Best to just drift off toward the mist on the horizon without thinking of what's behind you or ahead of you. Eventually we all reach our own ends. It won't matter one way or the other once we're there. I'm dead enough to myself already. Mother and I are dead to each other. Best to leave the dead lie."

In the silence that fell in the hall as Katrin ended her monologue, Samuel said nothing. His dream of partially reuniting the broken Kraznapolski family died stillborn. There was nothing more to say.

"Well, do you want to do with me what you pretended you came here wanting to do?" Katrin asked the silent Samuel. She pointed to a room farther down the hall.

"No," Samuel said in a flat tone that matched hers. "I would feel like I was stabbing your mother in the back. Let's just say that you were another prostitute whom I wasn't able to talk out of the life and leave it there."

The worn-faced woman nodded her head slightly.

"Here," Samuel said. "That's half what your fare would have been. It's payment enough for a simple conversation."

The girl folded the money back into Samuel's hand.

"If you want to do something for my mother, give her this and the rest of the money you would have paid for a turn with me. It will do more for her than seeing me again would ever do. I'm not so far gone that I can't do that for her. She has you. I think you do more for her than I ever can."

Without saying anything in passing or in parting, Katrin Kraznapolski, the wayward daughter of Anna Kraznapolski, the wayward daughter of despair and resignation whom Samuel saw no future for where she was, got up and walked back into the house of no future. Feeling a failure in general and a failure at saving women in particular, a feeling reinforced for him once again, Samuel got up and prepared to leave the house of no happy tomorrows to return to a house he had hoped to bring a measure of happiness back into.

His altruistic, arguably naive mission to bring Mrs. Kraznapolski's daughter home in time for Christmas a failure, Samuel turned and left the house of no returns. To keep from embarrassing Katrin or possibly costing her her job, such as it was, Samuel left by a back staircase. Outside, he turned and looked quickly at the drab and dull building where Katrin was being consumed by the life she had chosen, thinking she would never have any other life. The bitter sting of the thought made Samuel turn away from the view of the dead-looking building. He walked quickly away without turning to look back.

Chapter 28

"I was hoping to bring her back here at least for Christmas, hopefully forever," Samuel said to Mrs. Kraznapolski, who was sitting across from him at the dinner table. "I was thinking of making it a Christmas for you as a way of thanking you for taking me into your house and your family. But I failed. I couldn't convince her to come back home here. I'm sorry. Back home I tried to talk another prostitute girl into leaving the life she was living and to come home with me. I couldn't convince her either. I guess I'm just not very good at convincing wayward girls to come home with me."

"It was nice and thoughtful of you that you tried," Mrs. Kraznapolski said. "But I'm not surprised it didn't work. I tried, but she didn't come home. If her own mother couldn't convince her to come home, I'm not surprised that a man she has never seen before and doesn't know wasn't able to convince her, especially one as young as you. She's more than ten years older than you, but she looks like she's in her forties. She's come to look hard and shopworn. A woman gets to looking that way in Packingtown, especially those who give up. But Packingtown is a place where a woman gives up everything. Men who work here aren't far behind. They just burn out from standing on their feet on a line instead of lying on their backs in a bed."

Apparently the conditions and the life in the house she was in were harder and more wearing than the conditions and the work in Mrs. Richardson's house had been on the girls there. But even there the older women had a shopworn look to them. Having a shopworn look and shopworn face probably went with that kind of place and the lack of future to be seen from inside a shopworn soul. Samuel had always hated the thought of the same shopworn look overtaking Clarinda.

"She gave up thinking there was anything better for her or that there could be anything better for her. She's resigned and settled into her fate. She doesn't think there's anything better for her in life. She doesn't see anything better for her in life here in Packingtown. But she doesn't think there is anyplace for her to go. She gave up thinking there is anything better for her in life here or anywhere. She doesn't fight her fate. She just drifts with it where she is in life and in the house she's in. She sees no way out coming anytime from anyone. Here in Packingtown, she may be more right than she is wrong. Packingtown is no kind of life for a woman."

"Packingtown is no life for a workingman either," Mr. Kraznapolski said. "Unless you're a boss. The bosses aren't detached and uninformed about what work and life is like here. The bosses know what it's like. You can be sure that none of the big bosses of this place live here in Packingtown."

The dinner was breaded pork tenderloin prepared by Mrs. Kraznapolski. The pork had been processed—where else?—right there in Packingtown. Samuel sat with his fork in hand, thinking about what Mrs. Kraznapolski had said about her daughter's seeing no way out for her coming anytime from anyone. In the back of his mind, an idea was pushing forward of how there was a possible way to change that. It was a bit radical, but no more radical than what he had been prepared to do in order to save Clarinda.

"You say you got family back in your hometown?" Mrs. Kraznapolski said rhetorically. "If you do, don't bring them here. You go back to them there. Go back to your family and wipe the muck of this place off your feet."

Samuel was about to say "I can't," but Mr. Kraznapolski spoke before he could.

"You said once—I don't remember exactly what you said, just one line, but it was something about your having left a sweetheart behind in your hometown. You said nothing more about her. Are you going to bring her here?"

Having seen Katrin and the life she was living had brought back a flood of memories of Clarinda, memories Samuel had tried to suppress. As if they had festered in their suppression and grown more potent in their ferment, his memories flooded back in on him, too strong to be held back, denied, or abridged. He couldn't control himself or his pouring words.

"In order to bring her here, I'd have to hire several men with picks and shovels back in my hometown to dig up her coffin, load it on to a freight train, and bring her out here," Samuel said, holding his fork upward. "I doubt she'd be in a very presentable condition. I'd rather leave her buried where she is instead of burying her in the mud and sewage of this place. The ground is a lot cleaner back there, and my sister can put flowers on her grave."

"I'm sorry that she died," Mrs. Kraznapolski said in an unfeigned sympathetic voice. "Was it fever that killed her?"

Another wave rushed through Samuel, more aggressive than the first rush, heading hard outward.

"No!" Samuel half snapped, his voice rising. He stiffened his back. His voice became a growl. "She was murdered! She was murdered by a boss! A local boss. The town boss. The mayor was a buffoon. The man who killed her was the real power in town. He was arrogant. In his arrogance and power, he thought he could dispense with a girl he considered beneath him and of no account. He killed her and thought nothing of it the way he thought nothing of her. He thought nothing would come of it. I found out what he did. I took my father's shotgun and killed him. I made as much of a dead nothing of him as he made of her. After that, the law was looking for me. I had to go on the run. That's why I'm here and not back in my hometown, which I would never have left if it weren't for him."

The uncontrollable rush of emotion left Samuel. He laid his fork back down on his plate.

"So there it is," Samuel said after a moment's silence. "I'm a killer. I'm not trying to threaten you with the knowledge. I'm just not denying it. It would have come out eventually. Might as well get it out now. Now you know that I'm a killer on the run, I suppose you're going to want me to leave. ... Like I said, I'm not threatening you. If you want me to leave, I will go. I can go back to a boardinghouse in the city to live, or I'll find another room here in Packingtown." He looked at Mr. Kraznapolski. "If you want to tell the company about me, I won't threaten you or try to stop you. They'll probably fire me."

Mr. Kraznapolski sort of laughed. "If you tell them you're a killer, they'll probably sign you on as a Pinkerton agent or a company guard," Mr. Kraznapolski said. "Or they'll keep you on the side and call you in as a goon to break heads and break strikes. They have a whole small army of street thugs they can call up and pay to break up strikes and break up strikers. If they take you off the loading dock and put you on anywhere, it will probably will be as a hired thug. We'll meet on a strike line, just on opposite sides."

"I'd quit before I'd do that," Samuel said.

"We're not going to tell you to go," Mrs. Kraznapolski said. She looked at Samuel. Mr. Kraznapolski looked at Samuel. Mara looked at Samuel.

"We've known you long enough to know you're an honest boy, a good boy. We believe you. You're not mean. That kind of mean you can't keep hidden for long. Mean finds its way to the surface soon enough. If you were mean, one way or the other it would have come out by now. So don't go packing your bags. You stay here with us. We won't go turning you in."

The others went back to eating. Samuel guessed that for them the issue was settled, and it had been settled in his favor. To him it was the first thing that had been settled in his favor since Clarinda had been killed.

"What was your sweetheart like?" Mrs. Kraznapolski asked. "Was she pretty? Was she shy and gentle? Country girls are supposed to be that way."

Irony can catch up with you in Packingtown as well as anywhere.

"Actually Katrin and her would have gotten along quite well," Samuel said. "She was a prostitute like Katrin. She worked out of a house out on the edge of my hometown. She was thinking of moving to Chicago. She wanted to get a position in one of the bigger, fancier houses here. If she hadn't found work in one of the fancier houses, she might have ended up in the same house as Katrin. They would have been housemates. She was also talking about going to New Orleans and finding work in one of the bigtime houses there. She probably would have done it too. She was as beautiful as she was fancy-free."

"What was her name?" Mrs. Kraznapolski asked.

"She called herself Clarinda," Samuel said. "That wasn't her real name. She pulled the name out of the air or a fairy-tale book and gave it to herself. I wanted to marry her and give her my name. I was going to ask her to marry me. I like to think that I could have talked her into marrying me. But I waited too long. I thought I had time enough to get closer to her and ask her. I thought we would have all the time in the world together. But then she was gone."

In his mind, Samuel glossed over to the Kraznapolskis, as well as to himself, the fact that the girl had resisted the idea of marrying him.

"I wanted to love her forever. I wanted to tell her how much I loved her, but I don't know if she believed in love. I guess she had been hurt too bad to believe in love. I wanted her to trust me, but she didn't seem to trust anyone but herself."

"Sounds like Katrin," Mrs. Kraznapolski said.

"Did it bother you that she was a prostitute?" Mara Kraznapolski asked.

"It didn't bother me to the point that I didn't want to patronize her as a prostitute," Samuel said. "I was ready to accept her as my wife. Despite her background, my parents had been ready to accept her into the family. But she kept the thought of marrying me at arm's length. I wasn't able to talk her out of the house and into my parents' house on the farm. I wasn't able to talk Katrin into coming home to you. I guess I'm not very good at talking prostitutes into coming home with me."

Talking about taking prostitutes out of the life and bringing them home brought back to Samuel's mind the idea that had been forming in his head since he had left Katrin behind in the bordello. The Kraznapolskis' acceptance of him after his confessing to being a killer made Samuel bold to speak. He put his fork back down on the plate. He paused and formed his words.

"I don't like the thought of Katrin being where she is any more than I liked the thought of the girl being where she was. In order to bring Katrin back home here, I'm willing and ready to marry her and bring her home. I was ready and willing, and wanting, to marry the girl back home and take her into my home and life there. I'm willing and ready to marry Katrin in order to bring her home here and make a home with her and you here. I was willing and fully ready to make a home for the girl back there. I stand fully ready to make a home for Katrin here, where we can all be together. Maybe that will persuade Katrin to leave the house she's in and come back home."

All the Kraznapolskis stopped eating and looked at Samuel in surprise. Mara seemed to be the most impressed by his proposal.

"With your permission of course."

For a moment everyone around the table was silent.

"You are the complete savior of women, aren't you?" Mrs. Kraznapolski said.

"If I was such a great savior, I would have saved the girl," Samuel said. "If I had been able to save her, I would be back in my hometown with her and not here. Maybe I can do better with Katrin."

"I don't think you're going to do any better trying to save Katrin," Mrs. Kraznapolski said in a flat, quiet voice. "Not that I don't appreciate the thought. Not that I don't love my daughter. Not that I'm ashamed of her. Not that I don't want her to come back. Not that we wouldn't take her back. I just don't think that she'll ever come back on her own, and I don't think anyone, even a decent and deep-feeling boy like you, or any man, is going to be able to bring her back. You can ask her to marry you if you want. I won't forbid you to try. But I don't think it will work. She's defeated. She's given up—on Packingtown, on this family, on life. Man or woman, life in Packingtown will do that to you. It grinds you into the dirty soil under your feet until you lose the strength to leave. You just go on walking numbly down the dirty streets until you can go no farther. You stop in place and give up, no matter how dirty the place you're standing in is. That's what happened to our daughter. Packingtown defeated Katrin. Once she was warm and alive. She's gone cold and dead inside. Like I keep telling you, leave this place. Leave here while you're still young, before the places ages you beyond your years. Leave before this place defeats you like it defeated Katrin. Leave while you still can. Leave before this place defeats you like it defeats everyone who stays too long."

"It happened to our son," Mr. Kraznapolski said. A quizzical look came over Samuel's face. "Though he never stepped into the slaughter lines, in its own way, Packingtown defeated him too."

732

Samuel paused at the mention of a family member whom he had not heard them mention before this. "You didn't tell me you had a son," he said.

"His name is Stanislov," Mr. Kraznapolski said. "We call him Stosh. He was trapped here too, only in a different way."

"Does he work at the plant?" Samuel asked.

"No," Mr. Kraznapolski answered. "He never worked in the plant. He didn't even want to try. He said the plant was just a place where they work you into the ground before your time. He always said he wanted nothing to do with the place."

"Where does he work?" Samuel asked.

"He doesn't," Mr. Kraznapolski said. "Except maybe on a chain gang. He wanted money, but he wanted it quick. He's in Joliet prison. Will be for a long time to come. He became involved with a gang of punks. We couldn't get him to leave the gang any more than we've been able to get Katrin out of the house she's in. One night the gang robbed a liquor store. In the process, they shot and killed the store owner. The gang was rounded up and put on trial for murder. Even though it wasn't him who pulled the trigger, Stosh was convicted of murder with the rest and sentenced to life with them. He might possibly be paroled someday, but it most likely won't be for a long time. Both Anna and I will probably be dead by that time. Mara too. He will have no one to come home to."

"You make mistake by running to this place," Mrs. Kraznapolski said. "This is place to run from, not to. Just run from here. Save yourself while you still can and while you have the strength to do so. If you wait too long, this place will eat you up like it eats up everyone who comes here. Go back into the country you know. Go find yourself another farm on clean land under a sky not filled with ash and soot. Walk the roads or ride the rails away from here. Become a footloose hobo on the open road. Go out west and become cowboy like you once mentioned you might do. Get job on ship and sail far away from this place and this city. If you can, go back to your hometown. If you can't, find another town like it where nobody knows you. Farm the land under the open sky again. Start over in the kind of life you knew. Don't try to make a life here. No one can make a good life here in Packingtown. The only people who make a good life in Packingtown are the bosses who run the place. They don't live here in Packingtown. They live far from here in fancy houses on clean streets. They live where they can see the clear sky and count their money in the sun."

They all fell silent for another moment, a longer one this time around.

"Even if you could marry my daughter and bring her back here, it wouldn't be much of a life for you," Mrs. Kraznapolski spoke up again. "You'd be married to a woman near twice your age, a burned-out, hard woman. Your love for her wouldn't make her any less hard. You'd be in a hard marriage with a hard woman. You would eventually come to dislike her. You'd come to regret marrying her. You would want to be out of the marriage. Married to her or not, if you stay here, you would be stuck here in Packingtown, working your life away under the soot-dripping clouds instead of living under the sun somewhere far better. They don't pay enough in Packingtown to have a life in Packingtown. They don't pay enough to keep a wife here in Packingtown. They don't pay near enough to keep and raise children here in Packingtown. Everyone here must work. Still it isn't enough for a real life. Go away from here while you still have strength to escape."

"Maybe there's something I can do to make it better for you here," Samuel said. He just wasn't sure what that something was. The group fell silent again, for a longer time. Mr. Kraznapolski looked at Samuel.

"If you really want to make it better, not just for us but also for everyone here, maybe there is something you can do," Mr. Kraznapolski unexpectedly said. "It might not be an easy row. You will need to stand strong. But you cannot stand alone. They are too strong for any one man. You will need to stand with others. But if you stand with others and we all stand together, it could make a real difference for everyone here."

Mr. Kraznapolski was silent for a moment as if he were pausing for effect. He seemed to be building up to something. Samuel sat and listened.

"There are plans to form a union," he went on. "The company isn't going to like that one bit. They'll probably try to break the union. If the company won't negotiate with the union, there will be a strike. The date hasn't been set, but it will probably be sometime in the spring or early summer, when you can walk the picket line without freezing. If everyone walks out together and stands together, it will close down the plant."

Samuel continued to listen in silence.

"The bosses will like that even less. They may bring in goons and strikebreakers in numbers to try to break the strike. Things could get very rough. … I don't want to presume upon you. I won't put pressure on you. I'm not going to throw you out if you don't want to join the union. But if we succeed, it could make things better for everybody in Packingtown. If we fail, the company will probably double down on their hard treatment of the workers. In the end it will be worse for everyone."

Mr. Kraznapolski looked at Samuel. "You're not a full-grown man. You're kind of young to be involved in something like what may be coming. Like I said, I won't push you into anything you don't want to go into. But if everyone sticks together, it gives us and the union more strength and brings a better day closer for all of us. One man might make a difference." He looked at Samuel again. "Are you in?" His words ended in silence. But the silence didn't last very long.

"The days of my youth and my youth itself ended the day I learned the girl had been killed and I saw her dead body lying on a table in the basement of a police station. I lost my innocence then. I lost my lover. I lost the wife and family I would never have. I lost the family I had. I lost my youth and my life then. None of them have come back to me or will come back to me."

All the Kraznapolskis listened in silence.

"As I said, the girl was killed by a boss. She may have tried to run from him, but he caught her and killed her. I didn't run from him. I closed in on him and killed him. I felt neither satisfied nor sorry I had killed him. I felt as empty as I had been since the girl had been killed. Later I had to run because the law was after me. But I don't intend to run from any boss anymore. … Count me in."

Chapter 29

In his early boyhood years, every Christmas Eve, his father would read him and his sister the classic children's book *A Visit from Saint Nick*. After reading them the story, he would instruct both of them to go to bed and go to sleep as Saint Nicholas would not visit a house where he knew children were awake and waiting up for him. Contrary to his father's instructions, Samuel would lie awake in his bed and listen for the sound of reindeer hoofs on the roof as the story described. He would fall asleep straining to hear the sound indicating the arrival of Saint Nick at their house. In subsequent years, Samuel determined that Saint Nick didn't exist. The reason his father had prompted him and his even more impressionable sister, Beth, to go to sleep and not sneak downstairs was so that his father and mother could set out the few meager presents they could afford for their children.

For Samuel it was a strange and singular separate Christmas indeed. He had never spent a Christmas away from his family before. That night marked the first Christmas he had ever been separated and distant from his family, especially the long and insurmountable distance by which he was separated from them. It was the first Christmas that he had ever confessed murder to anyone. But then again, it was the first year of his life that he had killed anyone.

Samuel sat on the single wooden chair beside the single wooden table with the single light across from the narrow single bed in the narrow room on the night of the first Christmas he had spent away from his family. He was trying to read the western adventure dime novel he had bought. But after a few minutes of not being able to concentrate on the pulp narrative, he closed the book and tossed it on the table.

In the winter chill of the unheated upstairs room, Samuel looked across to the bed along the opposite wall, less than ten feet away. He wasn't thinking of anything in particular. He didn't attempt to think of anything in particular. His mind wanted to remember the happy and close Christmases of his childhood. At the same time, his mind wanted to visualize what his family was doing back home and how they were celebrating Christmas without him. For a short moment he visualized his mother, father, and sister sitting silently around the table in the kitchen. In his mind they were eating Christmas dinner together, but there was no joy in the celebration of home and family togetherness.

In Samuel's vision of his distant home, his distant and removed family ate in sorrowful silence, an empty place at the table, Teddy sitting beside Samuel's empty chair, wondering where a familiar member of the family had gone and why he hadn't come back. Samuel shook his head to shake the vision out of it. It was too painful of a vision for him to bear anytime.

At that moment there was a knock on his door. No one had knocked on any door of his after he had left home. Samuel wondered who would be knocking on his door. Since he had heard no one enter the house through the front or back doors, it pretty much had to be a member of the Kraznapolski family. None of them had knocked on his door before. But then again, he hadn't confessed to murder in front of them before. Despite what Mr. Kraznapolski had said, for all Samuel knew he had become squeamish at the thought of having a killer under his roof and had come to turn him out.

"Come in," Samuel said without getting up. He half expected Mr. Kraznapolski to come in saying that he'd thought it over and he didn't like having a confessed killer in the house. He'd tell Samuel to leave in the morning, if not then and there.

The door opened. Instead of its being either Mr. or Mrs. Kraznapolski, Mara walked into the room. That by itself was surprising enough to Samuel. Whatever the circumstances might be, Mara was the last person of the three he had expected to see coming to pay him a nighttime visit. Mara had always been more distant and standoffish compared to her more naturally outgoing brother and sister-in-law. Her brother had been the one who had rented him the room. Had he changed his mind about renting him the room but didn't want to cause a scene by confronting him directly? Had he sent his sister to put him out of the house?

"May I come in?" Mara asked in a soft voice. "You're alone. I'm alone. We're both alone. It's almost Christmas. No one should be alone this close to Christmas. No one should be away from family at Christmas the way you are. I keep you company."

"Sure, come on in," Samuel said. He was farther from home than he ever had been, farther from home than he thought he would ever be. In the vast and expanding distance between him and all he once held so close and dear, he was ready for any company. He was not about to ask any questions as to why company was coming to him. In the dark of a Packingtown winter night, any family would do.

"You seemed so lonely at dinner not being with your family," Mara said in her heavy Polish accent as she walked through the door and closed it behind her. "I thought maybe you like to have someone to talk to. Maybe it make you feel better."

"I'd like that," Samuel said as Mara walked toward him. Her heavy breasts vibrated and swayed under her dress, which Samuel took to be a Polish-style peasant dress. She didn't seem to be wearing anything under her loose-fitting apparel. Having someone to talk to just might take his mind off the warm memories of Christmases past and the family he had lost that threatened to weigh him down and crush him.

Mara didn't pause inside the closed door and wait for permission to advance further. She continued to walk toward Samuel down the narrow corridor of the room. "I just want to say that what you did trying to bring Katrin home for Christmas was real nice," she said as she closed the door behind her.

"I'm sad I failed," Samuel said.

"You didn't fail," Mara said as she walked toward him. "You may have failed with her, but you didn't fail in heart. Katrin failed. What you tried to do was a nice thing. You are a nice man."

Mara sat down on the bed across from him. It was the first time he had been alone with a woman in an upstairs room since Mrs. Richardson had tried to seduce him into an afternoon of nonmonetary lovemaking in her room in her house of commercial seduction.

"Is this really the first Christmas you spend away from your family?" Mara asked. The tone of her voice was sympathetic. Samuel didn't know why she opened the way she had. He had stated specifically that this was his first Christmas away from home when he had explain why he had been forced to leave home. The question seemed to be rhetorical. But then again, it may have just been her way of being friendly.

"It is as much as I said," Samuel said quietly. "I've never known Christmas anywhere except back at home on the farm. But when and where it comes to being away from home, this is the first time I've been not only away from home at Christmas; it's the first time I've even been out of the state."

"Does it make you feel sad to be alone and without family the way you are?"

If the woman had come into his room with the idea of trying to cheer him up, it wasn't the best opening line. Then again, Packingtown didn't have a lot of cheerful opening lines.

"I sure didn't leave my home and family and come to Chicago for the exhilaration of being on the dirtiest streets of a big city," Samuel said. "Let's just say that if things had worked out differently, I would still be back on the farm with the family I had been born to, having our first Christmas dinner with the girl I wanted to bring into the family. But everything blew apart. I blew it apart and my family apart more than anyone. I deserve what happened to me afterward. I deserve where I am now." He didn't specify that one of the things that had been blown apart was Harold Ethridge's face. "I really don't know what I feel or how bad I really feel. I'm afraid to think about it. It may hurt more than I know. I'm afraid that if I stop to measure my sadness, I may drown in it." Samuel looked away from Mara and down the narrow corridor of his room. "I guess I should have kept my mouth shut and not brought the whole thing up. I probably made everybody's Christmas sad."

"Christmas ain't been very happy for none of us for a long time," Mara answered, "not since we got to Packingtown. Back in Poland, even if we didn't have much there, Christmas was a happy time. Then we come here. Even here in this city and in Packingtown, when my brother and Anna had the children home here, when my husband was alive, Christmas was a happy time. Now the children are gone. Stosh is in prison and ain't going to come back home. Katrin is in the low house where you talked to her. She said she ain't going to come back home either. My brother and Anna used to have a family. Now they've got a big hole where their family used to be. We all imagine Christmas be better for us when we come to America. But all those dreams fell apart. My brother's family fell apart with them. I never had any children, and now I'm a widow living in an attic. None of us ever imagine Christmas would come to this for us."

Samuel looked at Mara. Then he opened one hand and looked down at it. "I once thought I had the future in hand," he said. "I thought I had the world and all I wanted out of life in my hand. Then in an instant it was gone. One second the girl and the future I was going to have with her was alive in my mind. The next instant she was dead. My dream family disappeared. After that, my real family disappeared behind me like they had never existed. It was like they had all been a dream."

Samuel looked back up from his hand and back to Mara. "An evil man killed the girl I loved like she was nothing. In return I killed him like he was nothing. The sheriff who let me run said he understood why I did it. I don't feel bad about killing the man. My real badness was in putting my family through what I did. That's where I was bad. All bad."

"I don't think you're bad," Mara said.

Samuel wasn't sure why Mara was being so solicitous toward him any more than he knew why Constable Harkness had been solicitous toward him. But on Christmas night, far from home in a hard city, Samuel would take any unexpected gift he could get, be it a gift of the Magi or the gift of solicitousness from an older Polish woman with a worn face and big breasts.

"The law thinks I'm bad," Samuel said. "Even though the police chief of my hometown gave me a three-day head start, he and the law will still arrest me for murder if they catch up to me. I'm a killer in the wider eyes of the law." He looked at Mara. "Are you sure you want to be talking to a killer?"

"You kill the man because he killed the girl you were in love with," Mara said in a voice that was both matter-of-fact and solicitous. "I can understand why a young man would do that."

Mara paused.

"But I am a killer," Samuel said. "However nice I may have been to you doesn't change the fact that I am a killer."

"I mean, you're not a mean killer who kills for fun or just to be mean and bloody," Mara said. "Not like the men Stosh ran with. ... You may be a killer, but the man you killed was a worse killer. He murdered your sweetheart. You killed out of wounded love, not out of meanness. That is a difference."

"How do you know I didn't make the story up?" Samuel said.

"Like you say," Mara said, "why would you make up the story at all—so we love you more? So we charge you less rent? You're too nice and kindly to be the kind of killer like the mean men whom Stosh got involved with. You proved that you're not mean by the way you've been kind around us and the way you tried to be kind to Katrin. You haven't been mean and violent with us. You may have killed the one who killed your sweetheart, but you have far more love in you than meanness. You proved you have love in you by the way you tried to talk Katrin into coming home. No mean man would bother to do a thing like that even for someone he knows well, let alone someone who is a stranger he has never known."

It was a nice endorsement to get on close to Christmas night, but it didn't change any of the facts on the ground.

"I'm still mean enough to take a shotgun and blow the head off the man who killed the girl I wanted to marry," Samuel said.

"He deserved it," Mara said, continuing her qualified endorsement. "If you are mean, it's only to mean people who deserve it; you're mean to those who are mean to others. But you still love despite that. Shooting a mean killer is not the same as being a mean killer. It's not something I would send you to jail or run you out of our home for."

"Well, the chief constable of my hometown went along partway with you on that one," Samuel responded. "At least he went along with you far enough to give me a head start to run. But it doesn't change the fact that I'm effectively living under an indictment and sentence for murder. I'll never be able to get back home to my family any more than Stosh can come back home here."

"I think that's why my brother and Anna like having you here," Mara answered. "You're about the age Stosh was when he was sent to prison. Having a young man around the house is like having Stosh home. It's like they have their son home again. It's like a Christmas present for them."

"I'm a rather dubious Christmas present," Samuel said in an ironic tone. "I've lost too much to be a present to anyone."

"I know how you feel," Mara said. "You live in Packingtown long enough, and you lose pretty much everything. Despite what you did back home, you're like a gift to this house. Maybe you're not a saint. If you are not a saint or the son of a saint, what of it? None of us in this house are saints. Saints are in short supply in Packingtown and in this city. Maybe we don't deserve a saint as a gift. If you're not a perfect gift, what of it? A gift is a gift. Why look at the store tag? Who knows, maybe we're a gift to you as much as you are to us."

Samuel wondered if the woman was trying somehow to make him feel guilty over his plans to leave and find a different job, a job closer to home, once the heat died down.

"Eventually you'll be putting all sorts of distance between us. If you are going to go someday, why do we have to have distance between us now before you go? You don't need be so distant with me now." Mara patted the top of the bed beside her. "Come over and sit here next to me," she said quietly. "We live in same attic. No need to sit so far from me in your room. We know each other. We can know each other all the better now. We ain't got nothing we have to hide or put on with each other. You don't have to sit across the room from me like I'm some stiff and stuffy old churchgoing aunt with a Bible under her arm. We're both far away from what we knew and from those we loved. We're two lonely people living in an attic. There's a wide distance we can't get across and get back to, a place where we once were who we once were. We're both far apart from those we loved and who loved us. No use in us being so far apart from each other up here."

Having a woman ask him to come over and sit beside her on a bed can be a distracting and provocative thing for a man. It can cause him to forget the confines of the situation around him. Without remembering the architecture of the room, Samuel stood straight up from the chair he was sitting in and promptly bumped his head on the lowered angle of the slanted ceiling. "I'll never get used to that ceiling," he said, rubbing his head. Mara sort of laughed. But she seemed to be thinking of something else. The thump on his noggin didn't stop him from walking over and sitting down beside the older Polish woman with the heavy breasts, however.

Given the narrowness of the room, it took only two steps for Samuel to walk over to where Mara was sitting on the bed. He sat down next to her, as close to her as she had indicated.

"That was a nice thing you try to do for Anna," Mara said after Samuel sat down, "trying to talk Katrin into coming home. It shows you care for all of us."

"What it shows is how useless I am," Samuel said in a flat tone. "Like I said at dinner, I'm afraid I'm not very effectual at trying to talk prostitutes into coming home with me. If I had been better at it, the girl wouldn't be dead and I wouldn't be here now."

"Don't blame yourself because you couldn't bring Katrin home," Mara said. "So many women here in Packingtown are as dull and burned out and defeated as Katrin. Or they're on their way to it." Samuel wondered if Mara included herself in that category. "But it shows you love and are capable of love, or else you wouldn't have tried. … You must have loved her very much."

"I didn't meet Katrin before the night I saw her at the bordello where she works. I can't say I loved her. I just hate to see a family torn apart. I felt sad for her mother. I had the crazy idea that I might be able to give her a real Christmas present beyond anything I could buy for her. But I failed a second time."

"I didn't mean Katrin when I said you must have loved her. I meant the girl in your hometown. The one you killed for."

"I killed the man who killed her in the heat of vengeance," Samuel said. "But I wasn't able to save her from being killed by him. If killing to protect her and going on the run was the price of saving her life I would have killed him to save her and gone on the run even if I couldn't take her with me."

"I can respect a man who loves a woman that much. Even if you killed in her name, I find you to be a far better man than a mean street killer. ... As far as her name or anybody's name, is the name you use your real name?"

Samuel wasn't sure if Mara was perceptive and had picked up on subtle clues that told her he was using an assumed name or whether she just figured that all criminals on the run used aliases.

"No it's not," Samuel answered. "It's a name I made up on the run. Then again, I guess you could say that I got the idea of changing my name from the girl. She was on the run herself. She was a prostitute like Katrin. But Katrin is hiding from life. The girl was on the run for her life. She never did tell me her real name. But I would have loved her as much by any other name."

Mara held up her hand. "I'm no snitch. You don't have to tell me your real name. It make no difference to either of us. I don't need to know your real name any more than you needed to know hers. I would respect you and respect your love for her by whatever name you use. Your love for her was real love by any other name."

"Whatever you think of me, however much you respect me and my love for her, fate and irony didn't respect me or my love for her. As it turned out, for all my love for her, I lost her anyway. In the process I lost my home and family and ended up on the run."

"Do you miss her?"

"Yes, I miss her. I always will. I'll remember her for the rest of my days, however long they may be or whatever they may be. But where it comes to missing, what I remember most is that I missed my opportunity to save her and that I failed to protect her. If I had done a better job of protecting her, she might still be alive and with me. In my own way I'm as much responsible for her death as the man who killed her. I hold it against myself for not protecting her as much as I hold her murder against the man who killed her. I'll hold not being able to save her against myself for the rest of my life."

"If you blame yourself for her death as much as the man who kill her, you'll either be running after yourself in anger like you ran after him or be running away from yourself for the rest of your life."

Mara put her hand on Samuel's wrist and wrapped her fingers around it. "If you blame yourself forever, you'll poison yourself. You'll poison your memory of her. You'll poison your love for her. In the end you'll poison your ability to love at all. If you treat yourself blameful and mean in your own mind, soon enough you'll become hard and mean to yourself and to others. You'll become as mean as the streets you walk. The streets make too many people hard and mean like they did Stosh and the gang he ran with. The streets make too many people cold and dead inside like they've done to Katrin. A love like yours and an ability to love like you loved your girl is rare. I wouldn't want to see it lost to you or taken over by ordinary meanness."

"My love for the girl may not have been lost on me, but it was lost to me. All my love for her didn't do her any good. It didn't do me any good."

"But you still know how to love," Mara answered. "You're still capable of real and high love of the kind you showed when you tried to bring Katrin home. I think you're a better man than all the men in this city."

Samuel had been wondering why Mara had come into his room to talk to him. Somehow it had felt to Samuel that she was there for something more than to make him feel better by having a friendly chat with him. Somehow it seemed that she was there for some other reason than to preserve a small trace of true and higher spiritual love in the low-case world of Packingtown.

"Along with my brother, you're probably the only man in Packingtown capable of high love." She squeezed his wrist. "You're the kind of man I want to know."

Samuel didn't say anything.

"You say girl you love back home was a prostitute like Katrin," Mara said. "You still loved her. Weren't you afraid that people of the town point fingers if they know you loved the wrong kind of woman?"

"I didn't care what anyone thought about her. I was ready to put my thumb in the eye of everyone in town to marry her."

"Maybe you fall in love with a prostitute here. There are plenty of them in city," Mara said. Her voice had an almost exploratory tone to it. Samuel wondered if she was trying to get him to make another attempt to bring Katrin home.

"I've been approached by enough of them," Samuel said. "But the ones here aren't the same as the girl. They're all so hard-bitten and cold. I don't want to be near any of them, let alone think I could love any of them. They're as hard, cold, and sharp-edged as broken glass from a beer bottle."

With her hand still on his wrist, Mara listened quietly. She seemed to be weighing each of his words in turn as if looking for an overall pattern to emerge.

"But you weren't afraid to love a woman who might have been an embarrassment to you," Mara said. "That's still what I call real love. That's what I call good love."

"I loved the girl in spite of the fact that she was a prostitute," Samuel said. "If that's what you want to call real love, I won't argue the definition with you. If it was good love, the goodness and realness of my love for her didn't break through to her heart. She kept her heart closed to anyone but herself."

"You think you can ever love another woman?" Mara asked a repeat of her earlier question. "Even if others might call her shameless in loving?"

She tightened her hand on his wrist. Samuel started to open his mouth to say he didn't know, but before he could speak, she went on.

"If it don't bother you, I have another lonely woman you could save from being lonely with your love. At least you could save some love for her and make her feel like a live woman instead of a dead and buried one."

"Someday I might be able to find another girl I could love the same as the girl I lost," Samuel said. "But if I do find another, it will probably be somewhere other than Packingtown."

"I guess that will have to do," Mara said. Her voice sounded a bit far away. The wording of her response seemed a bit inexplicable in itself. "But everything here in Packingtown is pretty much on a 'that will have to do' basis."

Samuel didn't respond to Mara's cryptic response. Mara squeezed her hand on his wrist again. "So much in this city is built on dishonesty," she said quietly. "I'm being sort of dishonest with you. It's time I be honest to you. … Everyone in this city and this town wants something. I confess I want something too. I didn't come up here just to try to make you feel better by talking all night. I want something that make us both feel better. I want something deeper and more real for both of us."

Mara moved her hand off his wrist and placed it on his hand. "I want to feel better myself. I figure after all you've lost, you might want to feel better yourself. I thought maybe we could make each other feel better. In that my motives aren't pure. You say girl wasn't pure, but you loved her anyway. That's why I asked if you could love a woman who wasn't pure."

Samuel didn't say anything. He sort of looked at Mara. Mara sort of looked down.

"When you tell story tonight about death of girl, you sound so sad. Sadness and sorrow nothing new around here. All of us in this house know sorrow. My brother and Anna have a lot of sorrow. They've lost their children and family. They've lost most of what they had. They lost most of those they loved. But at least they have each other in their sorrow. Both of us have lost our family and those we love. We've lost almost everything we have. But we don't have anyone to be with and share our sorrow and loss with. Since we have no one to share our sorrow with the way my brother and Anna have each other, I think maybe we can do like my brother and Anna and share our sorrows. Since we've both lost ones we love, maybe we can make ourselves feel better by sharing our love together."

Mara talked in a matter-of-fact voice. But as she would say, everything in Packingtown existed on a matter-of-fact basis. There was otherwise a slight edge of embarrassment in her voice. Not really embarrassment; more like a quiet fear.

"Everyone in Packingtown has some kind of sorrow of their own. Only the bosses and the mean men in the streets don't have no sorrow. I hear you stirring around in your room at night, and I wonder what you're thinking and feeling. I knew you were carrying some kind of sorrow. I wondered what your sorrow was. Tonight I know your sorrow is for your lost love. But I also know you, and I know you can love. You prove you can love by the way you tried to bring Katrin back home. That is love I want to know. I hear you in your room and wonder what it would be like to feel you make love to me. I think of you and I wonder if you could love me back."

Mara continued to look down. Samuel looked at Mara and listened silently.

"Like I say, we're two lonely people living in someone else's attic. We live right next to each other, but we don't know each other. It's like we don't know the other is there. If we get to know each other and get closer to each other, maybe we can keep away some of the sorrow we both live in. At least we can keep each other warm on cold nights like this. I came to you thinking that maybe, if you like me, if you want me, if you accept me for what I am, if you aren't insulted by me or think that I'm cheap, if you don't think of me as a silly or desperate woman, if you take me as I am and don't laugh at me or treat me with scorn, I could offer myself to you as a lover."

Samuel didn't say anything. He kept looking at Mara. Mara kept looking indirectly away.

"We could be lovers to each other. We could make each other feel not so lost and alone. All you would have to do to call me when you want me would be to rap on the wall. I could come to you when you want, anytime you want. I would not demand anything of you for it. You wouldn't have to pay me like Katrin or your girl in bordello back home. I don't want your money. I just want love and the feeling of love from you. I would come to you as much as you want or as little as you want. After we're finished, I would stay with you quiet for the rest of the night if you want or else go back quietly to my room if you tell me to. We could be a closer part of each other's lives until you leave to find another life. When it is over, it is over. I will not demand that you take me with you when you go."

Samuel didn't say anything, but he acknowledged to himself that his suspicion that there had been more to the woman's motives in coming to him than just to have a motherly chat to cheer him up had been correct.

"I thought we could keep each other for a while for the time that you're around us. I don't really expect that you would want to keep me any closer than a part-time woman and lover of convenience. I pretty much know and accept that at your young age, you wouldn't want to make a life with an older woman like me. And I know you wouldn't want to take me with you when you go. Even though any love between us would leave when you leave, I just want to feel loved for as long as you would love me. When you go, I will let you go without saying anything. There would be nothing either of us could say to each other anyway. When you go off to your new life, I will let you go. In my mind I will live with the memory of the love you gave me. I will live knowing that for a time I had real love from a man who loved deeply, even if he didn't love me deeply."

Mara squeezed his hand with hers. "I'm not saying you'll have to marry me. You say you'll be leaving someday to go somewhere else and do something else. When you go, I won't make a scene. But until the day you go, we could be close to each other and keep some of the cold air of our rooms and some of the cold sorrow of our lives away from each other. When you go off to become a farmer again, I won't carry on like a woman seduced and abandoned. You can go without a word from me. I'll go on from there, knowing that it wasn't going to be and that it couldn't have been from the beginning."

Samuel remembered another night in another upstairs room and another similarly worded speech about what couldn't be between a woman and a man from different sides of the street and about moving on without looking back. That night the speech had been delivered by a girl in a hillbilly accent. Now he was hearing it delivered by an older woman in a Polish accent.

"I'm not asking you give me a wedding ring. I'm not asking you take me for your wife. You can take me as your lover for as long as you're around. If you take me, for however long you take me and for whatever you take me for, all I ask is that you don't take me for a joke. You say irony played a big joke on you. I don't want to be treated as a big joke. Take me as a woman. Just don't take me for a silly and desperate old woman. … I won't beg you to be my lover. That might only make you laugh. I don't beg. I just ask please that you don't take me for a joke. I want to be your lover, but I don't want to be laughed at. If you're going to call me a silly old woman, if you're going to laugh at me, just tell me to go away, and I will. I don't have much to my name. Laughing at me will take from me what little I have left to my name."

"Why do you want me for a lover?" Samuel asked in a quiet, accepting, and nonsneering tone.

First it had been the older Mrs. Richardson who had propositioned him. Now it was Mara Anton, younger sister of Anna Kraznapolski, a middle-aged woman. It seemed to Samuel that he had more than his share of older women who thought of him as loving and, hence, as a lover.

"I want you for a lover because you loved your girl deeply," Mara answered, still looking away from him, still holding his hand. "I want to be loved by you because you're a man who is capable of loving deeply and with real love. I don't expect that you will ever love me the way you loved her. But even if you don't love me the way you loved her, for once in my life I want to be loved by a man who has loved deep all the way to the bottom of his heart. I think that maybe if I am loved by a man who loves to the bottom of his soul, it will bring my soul back to life."

"I may have been a lover once," Samuel said, "but I'm a killer now. Do you want a killer for a lover?"

"The reason you killed is because you loved her so much. You killed because you loved. That you killed the killer of the girl you loved proves that you loved deeply. That you can still cry about her death tells me that you can still love. Though you will never love me like you loved the girl, I would like to feel some of that love from you to me."

"Saying that the fact that I'm a killer proves that I'm a lover is a pretty backhanded way of looking at it," Samuel said. "It's also a rather backhanded way of defining love."

"Here in Packingtown everything is backhanded," Mara said. "Everything is secondhand and used. In a backhanded place like Packingtown, most love is backhanded before it begins. Here love can be the most backhanded thing of all."

With her left hand, Mara reached down and pulled the bottom of her dress up to the top of her right leg. With her right hand, the hand she was using to hold Samuel's hand, she brought his hand over and laid it on top of her naked thigh. Samuel felt his fingers sink into the soft flesh of Mara's upper thigh. The chill of the room didn't mask the warmth of her leg. If anything, it emphasized it.

"I don't mind backhanded love. I would take backhanded love from you just to know love from you. I will give you backhanded love if you take it from me."

Samuel felt the chill of the room. He felt the warmth of the woman's leg under his hand. He felt the warmth of her body next to his. He felt the swell of her middle-aged woman's full body.

"Maybe you think I am forward woman," Mara went on.

Maybe it was the closed-in feel of the small room, maybe it was the closeness of their bodies, maybe it was because in her mind she was reverting to the time when she was a younger woman, or maybe it was just her way of further letting down her hair, which she had already let down. Whatever the reason, in the closed room, in their closeness together, Mara's hard edges were softening. Her openness to Samuel was growing more open to him with her every word. Her Polish accent was becoming thicker.

"Maybe I am forward woman. But we are alone in attic on a cold Christmas night. No Saint Nicholas is coming in sleigh to give us presents. We have only what we have in our hands, in our hearts, and in our bodies to give each other."

Placing his hand on her bare thigh in such an obviously suggestive manner could certainly be called a forward move on a woman's part in any era, post-Victorian, postmodern, or Packingtown present. If it was a forward move on Mara's part, it was a forward move that Samuel made no attempt to reverse.

"Maybe I am forward woman. Maybe you think I am shameless woman. All I know is I am not woman getting younger. All I know is that I have lost most of what I once had and what I once thought I had. All I know is I am secondhand woman now. All I know is everything is secondhand and backhand to me now. All I know is that I would take backhand love from you if you would give it. All I know is that I would give you backhanded love if you would take it from me."

All Samuel knew was that he was far away from home. All Samuel knew was that the love he had known and those who had loved him were far away across a divide he couldn't get back across. All Samuel knew was that he was sitting in a cold attic in someone else's house far away from home in a world far from anything he would call love or loving. All Samuel knew was that the woman was offering to share with him whatever definition of love they could scrape together.

Samuel hadn't said anything or made any kind of motion since the woman had pulled up her dress and laid his hand on her bare thigh. Mara more or less took Samuel's inaction and lack of direct response to her moves and what she was saying as evidence that he wasn't interested. She looked away from him again.

"But it probably makes no difference. I probably get nowhere by asking. I probably am just what you probably think of me: a silly old woman gone sillier with age to think you would want me at my age. A young man like you probably don't like older women like me. You probably don't want to make love to a woman who you think is old enough to be your mother."

At that juncture, Samuel wanted to comment that he had almost made love to an older woman before and that he didn't find the prospect objectionable.

"Inside you probably laughing at me already, or you just thinking that you want me to go away."

Whatever Mara figured was going on inside his mind, inside the cold loft room in the dark of a winter's night in Packingtown, at the moment, the only thing going on in Samuel's mind was that he liked the feel of sitting close to an older, full-figured woman with heavy breasts who was pressing his hand onto the bare flesh of her thigh.

"If you don't want me, I understand. Why would young man want old, tired woman like me? If you reject me, I just go back to my room and don't bother you again. I am used to being alone. I have been alone for a long time. I can be alone again. Being alone don't hurt me like it used to. But since you come here, I realize how alone I am and how much I don't want to be."

Call it a weakness. Say that Samuel was a soft touch for lost girls and women. Call it any old lover in a storm of sadness and loss. Call it not knowing if anyone knew. Call it not caring if anyone knew. Call it low-order love of convenience. Call it transcendent love, but Samuel just couldn't stand to think of the sad-faced woman being hurt again. He took his left hand off Mara's leg. Mara took his move as the beginning of his final rejection.

"If you don't want me, I go away and leave you."

Before Mara could get out her second statement of resignation, Samuel wrapped the hand he had taken off her leg around the back of her neck, pressing her hair between his hand and her neck. With a silent and quick movement, her pulled her head and face toward his. At the same time he brought his head and face in toward hers. Mara had only enough time to let out one small gasp of surprise before their faces split the distance and met halfway in between.

Before Mara could say anything more, Samuel's lips pressed full against her full, shopworn middle-aged woman's lips. Mara didn't melt in his arms, but she didn't let out one peep of objection. Living in the upstairs room next to a new boarder who was a young man had awakened feelings in Mara that living across from Old Man Warschoski had never awakened in her. For many nights, almost since Samuel had come into her brother's house, Mara, lying in her bed listening to Samuel stir in the room next to hers, had dreamt of what it would be like to have him make love to her. She had more or less convinced herself that he would never be interested in her and that it wouldn't happen. The story Samuel had told at their Christmas dinner had prompted Mara to abandon caution and propriety and try.

Poetry and poetic words of love were kind of lost in Packingtown. Without either of them wasting time with any further words, they kissed each other hard and wet in the silence of the upstairs room. The only sounds in the room were the small gasps and grunts of surprise and expectant pleasure Mara made. The sounds in Mara's throat were muffled by the press of Samuel's mouth on hers. As they embraced, Mara wrapped both her arms around Samuel and pulled him in close to her, to the point that her large, pointed breasts flattened and spread out against Samuel's chest. Samuel kept his left hand behind Mara's neck and used it to keep her face and lips pressed against his. He placed his right hand where Mara had placed his left hand earlier and started rubbing her bare leg. Having gotten started with that, using the same hand, Samuel pulled Mara's dress the rest of the way up and started rubbing both her bare thighs. This went on for a while. Finally Samuel abandoned rubbing Mara's legs. Leaving her dress pulled up to her waist, he brought his left arm down and moved his right arm up to wrap them both around Mara's back the way she had done to him. In this way they continued kissing for several long minutes. They remained unspeaking.

On a cold night in an attic, time wasn't something that could be wasted, and foreplay was time wasted. With both his hands, Samuel reached down to where he had left Mara's dress, pulled up to the top of her thighs, took hold of it, and pulled it up. Mara obliged by raising her arms to allow him to pull her dress the rest of the way off, over her head. Mara's hair had been a bit stringy and uncombed when she had come into the room. Her hair, reemerging as her dress was pulled over it, was even more tangled and messed up.

Mara was still wearing her undergarments, but now her shoulders were bare. Samuel started running his hands over her bare shoulders while he went about kissing her shoulders and her neck. At the feel of the warmth of his lips on her shoulders and neck, Mara rolled her head back. She sighed and gasped more openly in the chill of the room.

"When you love me, you can pretend that I am your girl back home," Mara said with a mixture of anticipation and resignation in her voice.

Given the way the boy felt about the girl, Mara rather assumed he would be fantasizing that he was making love to the girl while he was making love to her. Mara figured that in a sense he would be making compromised love to her. But a whole lot of the love in Packingtown was compromise and compromised love.

"I don't make love to ghost women," Samuel said, moving his lips a few inches off the base of her neck. "I make love to real women. When the girl was alive, I made love to her in her compromised state. I did not make love to some vision of snow-white and pure chaste love. I made love to a compromised woman in the there and then. When I make love to you, it will be to you in the here and now, not to a memory out of my past. I made love to the girl however imperfect she may have been in the real world. I will make love to you as imperfect as you may be in the real world here and now, as far from perfect as it may be."

Sitting on the bed, Samuel and Mara continued to kiss and run their hands over each other's backs and sides. Then Samuel settled down and regained his focus. With his hands, he tried to undo the snaps and bindings on Mara's undergarments, but the complexity made it too difficult for him. Mara lent a helping hand by standing up. With a beckoning touch and a tug of her hand on his, she prompted him to stand up with her.

Once she was on her feet and had her unexpected lover on his feet in front of her, Mara undid the remaining constraints holding her undergarment in place. She let her undergarment drop to the floor as the girl had let her corset fall down around her ankles on Samuel's first night with her, which had been his first night with any woman. In the half-light of the single light bulb, Samuel saw Mara naked for the first time. She didn't have the tight and sleek body the girl had. Her body was the body of a middle-aged woman. It was a fuller body, somewhat rounded and chunky. She had the skin of a middle-aged woman in her forties. Her skin wasn't as smooth and clear as Clarinda's had been. Over the years of her hard life in Packingtown, Mara's skin had developed a few moles and age spots, but it wasn't wrinkled, and it didn't sag off her in flaps. Her breasts were as large and relatively pointed at the nipple as they appeared under her dress. The fullness and shape of her breasts hadn't been a manufactured artifact of her underclothes the way Clarinda's corset had added extra lift to her breasts. The removal of the last of her clothing had left Mara's hair even more mussed up.

"I suppose you laugh at me and my body now that you see me naked," Mara said as she brushed the hair off her face.

"I don't laugh at women," Samuel said as he stepped back to take off his own clothes. "I have never laughed at a woman. I don't intend to start now."

It was a true enough statement. Mara appreciated it. Women appreciate little things like not being laughed at.

Samuel's clothes were somewhat simpler and easier to remove. With only a little help from Mara, he had them off in quick time. After having discarded his clothing as thoroughly as he had discarded his inhibitions, he stepped over to the single lamp and turned it off. There wasn't much light coming in through the single small window, but it was enough for him to see his way back to Mara. What they had left to accomplish could be accomplished by touch.

Samuel stepped the two steps back to Mara. He wrapped his arms around her naked body and pulled her up firmly next to him. Without clothes between them, Samuel felt the expanse of Mara's heavy Polish woman's breasts spread out against his chest. He felt the warmth of her body on the front of his body as he felt the chill of the room at his back. In what an observer watching from out of the darkness could call a passion frenzy, Samuel and Mara started rubbing their arms over each other's backs and sides fast and firmly. Standing bare and barefooted on the wooden floor of the unheated and darkened room, they rubbed their bodies together. They kissed each other in a fast-paced random swirling pattern until their faces were wet from the warmth of each other's mouths.

However proverbial it might be, however poetic it may be, however much an example of Americana it might be, many people would find a spring or autumn romance between a displaced midwestern farm boy in the city and a middle-aged Polish immigrant woman to be a strange matchup, an even stranger matchup than one between a local-yokel farm boy still on the farm and a small-town hillbilly prostitute down from the mountains. The gaps were much wider. Some observers might find the romantic passage they had come to in a Packingtown night to be a strange ending to the story that had started in a small town far away in Ohio.

But endings weren't on Samuel's and Mara's minds. From the moment of their beginning, beginnings weren't on their minds either. The only dimension in play was the here and now. The future was out of sight, over the horizon in the night. Their pasts were out of sight and unreachable behind them. In the attic of a small room next to the sewage-filled dirt streets of a mean world where love was in little consideration, all they could reach for and grasp was hidden love in a small hidden upstairs room. For Samuel and Mara, the future and the past blended together and disappeared into the here and now of each other and the love they would share.

With no further ado and with no further words exchanged, Samuel entered into his unexpected affair in the strange and distant world he had come into (no sexual pun intended) by entering bodily into relative love with the woman who unexpectedly had come to him looking to find love, even cold love, on a cold night, seeking to become his lover. Mara gasped and arched herself up against him as Samuel pressed home his relative love for the woman and pressed home the affair they were having in an attic room far from either of their original homes.

Some might say he was cheating on Clarinda—at least on her memory. But all thoughts of the girl were far away, over a horizon that Samuel was not thinking about. The only thing he could see, taste, or embrace was the woman who had unexpectedly come to him. The only thing he could feel was the warmth of the woman's thick body and his now rearoused manhood deep inside the warm, wet universe inside the big woman's body. At least one woman in Packingtown was still warm inside.

It was not the Christmas that Samuel had imagined back in June when he had first met the girl. Though some social commentators had predicted that Christmas gift giving would become a thing of the past, Christmas was fast becoming a time of exchanging presents. As gift giving went, it was an unexpected Christmas present that Mara had presented him with. In return she seemed quite satisfied with the present he was giving her. But as far as any gift of the Magi was concerned, they were both Magi and the gift they gave each other. No Saint Nicholas arrived to bring them presents, or to chide Samuel for being a bad boy, or to hector Mara for being a bad old-enough-to-be-the-boy's-mother woman. The only Christmas presents they received and exchanged that night with each other in the crowded bed in the small unheated room in the attic of a Packingtown shanty were the ones they brought to each other.

Outside a few stars shone through the soot-choked sky overhead, which was relatively clear that night as the factories had been largely shut down for the Christmas holiday. In the street, the sewage was frozen and the smell held down. In the quiet darkness outside the house, no creature was stirring, not even a mouse. Inside the small upper room, neither Samuel nor Mara had deposited their clothing with care because neither of them expected that Saint Nicholas soon would be there. For an extended time in the silent darkness of a Christmas night in winter in Packingtown, the unusual winter- or spring-relative love affair was energetically consummated. Neither Samuel nor Mara was a timid person, and their joining was not a timid and quiet affair, The warmth of their bodies, the covers over them, and the energy of their lovemaking provided the warmth that the lack of central heating or a space heater failed to supply. The bed shuddered and squeaked. Mara gasped and shuddered, crying out only half quietly. In the throes of the affair that she had sought out and in which she had promised to be discreet and to hold her tongue, she was only partially able to keep her promise to keep her mouth shut.

Under the thermal protection of the blankets, the warm and intimate struggle between Samuel and Mara continued on into the night. Poetic-minded observers of the scene might allegorically liken the unusually paired couple to two castaway survivors of a shipwreck, gasping as they pulled themselves out of the surf and onto a small island of safety. Some observers of the struggle going on between them might say that the two of them were struggling with the demons inside themselves. Others might say that they were trying to exorcise the demons in themselves. As far as demons on the loose were concerned, there were and had always been far more demons afoot in the factories and on the streets of Packingtown than in the attic room, so there were few in the backstreet attic love that Samuel and Mara were sharing for the night.

What the unexpected couple was energetically engaged in may have been only relative love, but it wasn't demon love. Oh, there were demons of memory in Samuel, ready and waiting to be invoked. But at the moment the only thought filling Samuel's mind was the sad-faced older woman filling his arms who had come to him offering to fill his bed for the night and to fill his life for the small amount of time they might have left between them before any demons inside either of them or in the world around them might conspire to pull them apart.

And so it went with them. And so it was for them, all social distinctions of age, ethnic origin, and social propriety put away, unseen and untouched, in the grasping strain of their embrace. All passed out of sight in the darkness of the room and the darkness on the streets outside. All lovers of the past were out of sight and not brought to mind. There was no other name of love known other than the love they were sharing at the moment. No other name of love was sought or wanted. No higher definition of love was invoked. As relative as it may be, their love of the immediate present was all the love there was to be had in the world. The future would be what it would be, as much of a future as could be invoked or had been invoked for anyone living in the Back of the Yards.

With all demons, past and present, put to the side, along with all lovers of the past, in the closed-in and closed-off space of the small attic room, wrapped tightly in each other's arms, Mara and Samuel wrestled with each other, their bodies generating a heat that held off the cold. Locked in each other's arms and locked in their definition of love, their possibly stolen, definitely opportune, definitely sought and accepted, relative but energetically embraced, bounding and binding coming together went on amid the limited space of the room and the bed. It wasn't the case that Samuel found the idea of marriage creeping around the edges of his thoughts about the woman.

The bed on which they made their opportunistic love squeaked away into the depths of a Packingtown night.

"If you want me anytime, all you have do is knock on the wall and I come to you," Mara said quietly into the darkness of the now quiet room. The two age-disparate members of the unexpected couple were lying on their sides, facing each other. Even though her face was directly across from his, in the darkness of the room, Samuel couldn't see Mara's face clearly.

"If you knock for me on any given night, I come to your room to you. If you don't want me any night, don't knock. I don't come and bother you."

Mara paused for a second in the darkness.

"I may knock on your wall from time to time to see if you want me. I have feeling that I be knocking on your wall more than you knock on mine. If you want to come to me, don't bother to knock. Just come. Anytime. I won't turn you out."

Samuel had his arm draped over Mara's side and angled up to her head. With his hand, he toyed with her hair as she toyed with her words, describing the simple procedure to call her anytime he wanted to have her again. He wasn't quite sure what it would mean if she were to rap for him. Was he supposed to come to her room as quickly as she promised to come to his?

"You don't even have to knock on wall. If you want me in the night, you just come into my room. It bigger room, but the bed squeak as loud. And it's closer to my brother's and Anna's room below."

What Mara had said touched on another potentially touchy subject.

"What will your brother say if he finds out?" Samuel said, his face and lips only inches from Mara's. "For all I know, he'll throw me out of the house for taking advantage of his sister or something like that."

Samuel could only imagine what he would have done if he had caught some boy, like the one she had met at the county fair, fully naked in flagrante delicto with his sister, Bethany. He would probably have tossed the boy out of the second-story hayloft door even if Bethany had protested that the affair was consensual, even if Beth had said that she was the one who had initiated the affair.

"They probably already know," Mara said in tone of dreamy unconcern. "The way bed squeak, if they didn't hear it, they're deaf. Sound and news carries everywhere in this house. There are few secrets we keep from each other. There are few secrets that are kept in Packingtown."

"What are they going to think?" Samuel asked.

"They think what they think," Mara said. "But even if they didn't hear us, it's no surprise to them. I told them I was going to do it. I didn't ask their permission. I just said it. They shrugged and didn't say anything. They would say they always knew I was no nun. They would just go about their business and let me go about mine."

How very Bohemian, Samuel thought.

"Anna may cluck her tongue at me and say no more. They may not care one way or the other. Anna may congratulate me on getting myself a young lover. They probably feel that I am old enough to know what I'm doing and that, after what I've been through, I deserve something good. Either way, my brother won't throw you out of house. I won't let him do it."

Samuel let it go at that. There really wasn't a lot that could be said either way. For several minutes there was silence between them.

"You want me to leave?" Mara asked, breaking the silence. "If you do, I go. I'd rather stay here with you though."

"I'd rather you stayed," Samuel answered. "It's a lot warmer this way. If they catch us in the morning, so be it. They'll probably figure it out soon enough. Like you say, no secret stays hidden for long in Packingtown. I don't even particularly care if they or all the Back of the Yards finds out."

Mara didn't respond, but she kind of liked what Samuel had said. Women appreciate it when a man doesn't run them out of bed or take off after making love. Spending the rest of the postcoital night together makes it seem more like real love, no matter how relative it may be. Women also often rather appreciate it when a man declares that he doesn't care if the world knows about them as a couple.

No more words were exchanged or spoken by either one. Given that the combined warmth of their bodies helped hold off the chill, they moved their bodies as close to each other as they could. With the future drifting out of sight in the fog of a winter's night in Packingtown, Samuel and Mara drifted off to sleep.

Chapter 30

"Even back home in the old country, back in imperial Europe of the czars and kaisers and arrogant kings and bloated nobility, I have never seen such real suffering and want as I have seen in this country and this city!" the proverbial outside agitator thundered from the raised improvised speaking platform on the bed of a flatbed truck. Actually he screeched more than he thundered.

The place where the rally was being held was the less familiar historical Chicago landmark known as Bughouse Square. It was so named because of the mental institution that was located next door. Many listeners for the class threatened by name with lynching, throat cutting, and evisceration might think the insane asylum that stood there had opened its doors and turned out its patients, who had then taken control of the streets around them. Given the drift (headlong screaming charge, actually) of the often maniacal rhetoric in the air, coupled with the maniacal glare in the eyes of the speakers and the organizers of the rally, a detached observer could be given to wonder if the locks on the asylum door hadn't been broken and the inmates were now in charge of the asylum. This was Samuel's first full-scale encounter with the full-tilt radicalism of the day.

"I say an end is to be made of this! I say an end is to be made of hunger

763

and oppression and hopelessness. I say an end is to be made of overwork and underpay. I say a long-overdue end is to be made of the capitalist system that promotes the exploitation, impoverishment, and ruin of the workingman and the poor classes. I say an end is to be made of the rich who run the capitalist system from on high as they sit in luxury in their gilded domes while they keep their feet on the poor down in the dirty streets and the filthy hovels they live in. I say in the words of one of our spiritual founding fathers, Johann Most, that the best thing that could be done with the Jay Goulds and the Vanderbilts and the other robber barons is to hang them from the nearest lamppost. And I say the same for the modern-day second generation of bosses who are no different, or better in kind, or any kinder than the old bosses. They should be drawn and quartered with their gold-handled letter openers and their engraved silverware. We should cut the throats of all the capitalist bosses who have a stranglehold on the throats of the workingmen!"

Bughouse Square, located in Washington Park on the city's north side, was the favorite rallying and rhetoricalizing point for the Chicago chapter of the International Working People's Association (IWPA). The IWPA was an anarchist-dominated radical labor organization that abjured electoral politics and demanded a war to the death with capitalism and the sweeping away of all organized government and previous social orders. Their core political philosophy was often largely unfocused and incomplete as to both what the new order would look like and how it was to be achieved. While easily and fluently explicit in the violence of their rhetoric, the Chicago anarchists, the largest group in the IWPA, were never explicit in the details of how they hoped to engineer their social revolution. Instead of clarifying their ideology, they polished their Luddite edge and concentrated on winning the support of the city's trade unions, unions that often felt threatened by modern laborsaving technology, and on organizing confrontational rallies and parades, and confrontations in general with management, all designed to arouse the city's workers and terrify the capitalists and bourgeois politicians. In the end their unfinished philosophy was as nihilistic and violent as befit their anarchist roots and their nihilistic and violent rhetoric. In the end their inchoate philosophy and vision was as nihilistic and violent as their anarchistic roots and as their nihilistic and violent rhetoric.

Somewhere along the line, the IWPA and its members came to be known by the nickname of the "Wobblies." Just exactly what the origin of the nickname was is uncertain. One apocryphal story has it that the name developed from Chinese supporters of the movement who demonstrated their enthusiastic support for and identity with the movement by shouting in pidgin English: "I Wobbie! Wobbie!" Others found the IWPA's political philosophy to be rather wobbly.

"The rich and the arrogant bosses and power brokers should be dragged from their gilded mansions and made to walk the filthy streets of the Back of the Yards and stand exposed in the cold and wet shanties of the poor working people they keep in dank poverty. They should be made to look the children of the poor in their faces and see the lines of hunger on their faces and the despair in the eyes of their parents. In the faces of those children, in the faces of everyone here at this rally, they will get a good look at their future executioners."

The reference to the Back of the Yards district, where Samuel lived in Packingtown, was the first direct connection Samuel had heard to the meatpacking plant he worked in. It was the first indirect hint given of the strike that was brewing. Up to then it had been all venting about the capitalist system and the depredations visited upon the poor by the rich and upon working people by the monied classes and the bosses.

Newspaper cartoon drawings of the time depicted anarchists as dark, sinister figures wearing pointed Mephisto beards, skulking around in long black capes, holding bowling-ball-shaped bombs with lit fuses in their hands. Looking back in time, modern-day observers often think of anarchists as deranged and undisciplined protocommunists, wild-eyed men with wild, flyaway hair and unkempt Karl Marx beards standing on soapboxes, spouting wild-eyed class warfare rhetoric. As far as the image goes, it is accurate enough. At least modern observers see old-line anarchists as incendiary figures from a bitter, incendiary, and divisive era of history. Either way, modern pop culture views often reduce anarchists to quaint figures more like secondary characters in a comic opera than serious players on the landscape of their time.

Any Gilbert and Sullivan image aside, in their day, anarchists could be seriously dangerous people. They preached violence as much as they preached against the social ills and inequalities of their day as they saw them. They preached violence as prime and the only way to end the social oppression they saw, and they saw both the social oppression and the violence as the way end social oppression in exaggerated terms. Anarchist rhetoric and anarchist newspapers and publications were often filled with predictions of and calls to violence, either in the form of grandiose and apocalyptic, but otherwise improbable, class warfare or in the form of exhortations to lower-level immediate acts of violence against the propertied classes and the governments they saw as supporting the robber classes. Anarchists were fond of "dynamite talking." Along with calls to eliminate anything they defined as the oppressive classes and anyone in those classes, anarchist publications, the internet of the day for anarchists, often contained instructions for making dynamite bombs that the anarchists saw as the great equalizer between the rich and the poor.

Anarchists practiced the violence they preached. In Russia, anarchists assassinated Czar Alexander II. In Europe, anarchists were responsible for the assassinations of and attacks on a number of members of royalty and government officials. In the United States, a self-styled anarchist assassinated President McKinley in 1902. Anarchists were the al-Qaeda and ISIS fighters of their day, complete with a nebulous, nihilistic, and apocalyptic philosophy of violence as a cleansing force to purify the world and bring about a completely new world order, coupled with the stated and practiced willingness to blow up anyone who stood in the way of their religious mission or at least the mission they thought of with near-religious fervor.

At the height of its influence, the IWPA never had more than five thousand members. Like any terrorist movement or terrorist-minded movement, the impact of the anarchist movement was impressively greater than its size. That influence was due to its extremist rhetoric and tactics, which emboldened its supporters and was designed to strike fear in the hearts of its enemies.

The United States of the late nineteenth and early twentieth centuries was beset by labor violence. Given the men whom the city attracted on both sides of the labor divide, Chicago seemed to have a disproportionate share of the labor violence in the country. More often than not, it was management that brought violence to the labor scene and the workingman.

But when and where violence was brought to the labor movement from labor's side, anarchists were often the motivating force.

To one degree of culpability or not, anarchists were intimately involved with one of the single most focused and intense bursts of labor-related violence in the city's history and in the history of the labor movement. On the night of May 4, 1886, during organized labor's campaign for an eight-hour working day, at a rally called to protest the killing of two workers the day before, a tense and volatile but otherwise peaceful crowd of workers stood in an alley just off Haymarket Square, listening to haranguing speeches by anarchist speakers. As the last speaker was winding down, even though the meeting was already breaking up at the approach of a rainstorm, a confrontation-minded police commander sent in several columns of police determined to break up the meeting. As the police marched in with their revolvers drawn through the three hundred stragglers listening to the conclusion of the speech of the last speaker, from out of the dark on the workers' side, a sputtering, sparking trail arced through the night and landed directly in front of the line of policemen. The next second there was a blinding flash, followed by a thunderous explosion loud enough for the mayor to hear as he was getting into bed for the night. Someone in the crowd of workers had taken dynamite talking to the higher level of shouting.

Police close to the blast were mowed down like tenpins. Those not hit began firing their pistols wildly into the crowd of workers from which the bomb had been thrown. Some workers in the crowd began firing back with pistols they had brought. Seven policemen were killed, and sixty more were injured (mostly by friendly fire). At least an equal number of, if not more, workers were killed and injured. Though it lasted only a few minutes, the wild melee later known as the Haymarket Riot became perhaps the most violent and most well-known incident of violence in the history of the US labor movement.

It was never determined who threw the bomb. The identity of the bomber remains unknown to this day. Nevertheless, eight anarchist leaders were put on trial for conspiracy, complicity, and incitement in the bombing, even though six of them had not even been at the rally that night. All eight were found guilty. One was sentenced to fifteen years in prison. The others were sentenced to be hung. To the conservative classes, the men were diabolical fiends and wanton killers who had received exactly what they deserved and should have received earlier. To the radical labor movement, they were martyrs to the cause. To the rest of the country, the Haymarket Riot solidified the image of Chicago as a city of trigger-happy cops and hard and bitter labor strikes.

Samuel wasn't aware of the details of the history of anarchism. He didn't know the pedigree of the radicals taking turns on the truck bed that day, whether they were older-line anarchists or newer-line Marxists. He wasn't aware of the benchmarks where the history of the two groups of radicals had converged. Neither was he familiar with the dialectic details of where their two political philosophies diverged. Whatever the evolved and blended dialectic may have been, however revisionist or diversionist the rhetoric was, all Samuel knew was that he was hearing unvarnished radical rhetoric. He neither liked what he was hearing nor saw much of anything in it that was of any immediate benefit or use to anyone on the line at the packing plant or their families at home. In his own way, Samuel found the bellowing of the radicals who claimed to be speaking for the workers that day to be, in their own way, as bloodcurdling as the final screams of the dying animals before their throats were cut and they started their trip down the disassembly line.

As he stood there in the Sunday sun of a brightening spring day, Samuel would have traded all the high-volume, high-intensity radical rhetoric he was hearing to be back at home for five minutes, spending it leaning on a fence, looking at the green shoots coming up out of the spring soil, and listening to his father talk in a pedestrian farmer's monotone about what the crop would probably be like that year. He would have traded all day spent standing on his feet listening to all the fire of the rhetoric for one minute spent back at the picnic he and the girl had gone on together, lying on his back under the sky with the girl lying on top of him while he sang a pioneer song to her and as she whispered sweet nothings in his ear.

But when Samuel reflected on the words and thoughts that had passed between him and the girl that day, he discovered that some of the words were not fully sweet around the fringes. However lightly the girl had taken the ideas he had talked around the edges of that day, those ideas she'd dismissed were far more than nothing to him. It was the knowledge that his words had meant so little to the girl, as well as her keeping time with other men, that sent him to the bar to explode in anger and violence at the man she was with.

"I say an end is to be made of the mockery of the ballot box. Democracy run by the bourgeois class only serves the interests, and the function of protecting the profits and the privilege, of the bourgeois class. The sycophantic politicians who keep themselves in office by licking the boots of the bourgeois power brokers, the phony reformers who pretend to reform the system but are on the payroll of the system to protect it, will all be swept away with the monied class who carry them in their vest pockets in the coming revolution. The day of the dictatorship of the proletariat is about to dawn!"

Many years hence from that day, in the midst of their own radicalism-influenced era, the rock group the Who would sing a song titled "Won't Get Fooled Again." One of the catch lines from the song goes, "Meet the new boss. Same as the old boss." In an era when hand-cranked gramophones were the iPods, Samuel was getting his own taste of the cranky sentiment of the song to come.

A country-and-western song from about the same period said: "When you're running down America, you're walking on the fighting side of me." Samuel's grandfather had fought in the Civil War for the freedom of the slaves. George Washington, who freed the country, and Abraham Lincoln, who freed the slaves, were Samuel's favorite presidents from history. His favorite modern-day president was Teddy Roosevelt, the scrappy little fighter who led the charge up San Juan Hill to free Cuba from Spanish oppression. When you were running down freedom and democracy, you were walking on the fighting side of Samuel Martin, whatever name he was using at the time.

"And who the hell is going to run this dictatorship of yours?!" Samuel yelled back spontaneously at the speaker on the podium. Soapbox speaking was on its way to becoming a long and storied tradition in Bughouse Square. Audience response would also become a Bughouse Square tradition. "You and a coterie of your radical friends? You'll probably turn out twice as mean as any king or system or class you replace. My grandfather fought in the War between the States to remove the dictatorship of slavery. My cousin fought in China to save people from being murdered by radicals over there. I don't like dictatorships, and I don't like radicals who preach dictatorship of any kind, even dictatorship of the proletariat, which means dictatorship of radical labor organizers. I don't want your damned dictatorship any more than I want the dictatorship of the bosses!"

Samuel's outburst was the first and only coherent sound out of the crowd, whose main verbal contributions had been grunts and bellows. Some of the other workers in the front line turned their heads to look at Samuel. Some of them knew him as Bill Howard. For all Samuel knew, some of them who didn't know him might think he was an agent of the company letting his cover slip.

That the speaker was spouting and touting any kind of dictatorship was bad enough for the non-Socialist-initiated, all-American (otherwise name-altered) farm boy Samuel Martin. But if the plant went on strike and the company sent in strikebreakers like they had done in the past, things could turn quite ugly quite fast. That the strike could easily turn into a head-busting affair made Samuel bold to speak.

"I didn't spend money on streetcar fare to come all the way up from Packingtown to listen to you bitch at the rich. I came here because I thought this rally was supposed to be about improving the lot of the workers in the packing plant and their families. You're just wasting my time and theirs blowing off with your class warfare rhetoric. Unless you have something to say about conditions at the plant and what's to be done about it, get off the platform and let someone talk about what they're going to do for the meatpacking workers and their families."

If the radicals were to come to know his identity, that was the lesser danger for any plant worker speaking out that day. It was widely assumed that the company had spies at the rally who were taking names. Granted, Samuel was speaking against the radicals, but at the same time he wasn't saying anything complimentary about the plant bosses. Just being at the rally could possibly cost an identified worker his job. Speaking out in favor of a strike would definitely cause him to be fired and would probably cause him to be blacklisted in the industry.

"That's what I'm here to do," said a resonant voice with a slight German accent.

The words hadn't come from the speaker. They came from August Werner as he walked to the front of the improvised speaking platform on the bed of the truck. Mr. Werner had been sent to address the rally once the other speakers were finished. Samuel had disrupted the speaking order by cutting short the speaker who wanted to overturn the existing social order. Without having given any response, the other speaker was more or less elbowed to the side. Whether he was happy about it or not, Samuel couldn't particularly tell and didn't particularly care. At least somebody would be directly addressing the issue of the workers at the plant.

Mr. Werner came to the fore with the air and speaking stance of a veteran stump-speaking politician. Samuel went silent and listened for what he would say. He was the man who was trying to organize the plant workers. He was the one directly related to the issues the packinghouse workers were facing. He was the one who would lead the strike that the rally had been called to gain support for. He was the one Samuel had come to the rally to hear. The man had a plan and a direction the other radicals lacked.

"I know this boy here," Mr. Werner said. He pointed at Samuel like a German schoolmaster. Samuel wondered if he was going to take him to task for having interrupted the first speaker. But when Samuel looked closer at the man, he saw that Mr. Werner wasn't looking at him; he was looking out over the crowd.

"He's not a company agent. He works at the plant. He knows the conditions at the plant. He has the spirit and the spunk of youth. He has the fire of youth. I have spoken to him before. I know he is telling the truth when he says he is on our side. I know that in his heart he is with us."

It seemed to Samuel that Mr. Werner was trying to eliminate any suspicion on the part of the crowd that he was one of the spies everyone assumed the company had probably sent to the rally. As Constable Harkness had done almost nine months earlier, Mr. Werner was letting Samuel off the hook.

"But there is one thing I know that this lad does not know and has not come yet to fully knowing," August Werner said rhetorically from the truck bed platform. "For all his spirit and youth, he cannot bargain with the Beef Trust alone." Mr. Werner brought his arm back and pointed at himself. "I know I cannot bargain with the Beef Trust alone. None of you can."

He waved his hand to include everybody. From there he was off and running with the speech he had intended to give. Like a skilled politician, he could turn any occasion into an occasion for a speech.

"None of us can bargain with the bosses by ourselves. Unless we organize and act together as one, in unison, they will pick us apart one by one as thoroughly and with as little thought of you as you on the line pick apart the hapless animals sent down to be disassembled. They will do what they've always done. They will continue endlessly to pit one nationality against the other, one race against the other, to keep us off-balance and keep us down as low and subservient as they can. That strategy has worked well for them in the past. It will continue to work well for them only as long as we make it work for them through our lack of organization and our internal divisions. It is our divisions and our ethnic rivalries the bosses use as cracks that they thrust their pry bars into and break us apart with."

Mr. Werner pointed briefly at Samuel again. "This lad spoke of the workers' families as well as the workers themselves. The future of your families is in question at the plant as much as your own futures are. The bosses care for the future of your families and the quality of your families' lives even less than they care for the quality of your lives and futures."

The Samuel Martin who had once thought of little more than the future and the quality life and future he had imagined with the girl listened in silence without interrupting as August Werner spoke of the workers' families. When you spoke of family, you were speaking relevance to Samuel.

"You packinghouse workers work for the bosses of the plant interminably long hours—hours so long that you don't have any time left over to see your families. You work for them for starvation wages that don't allow you to feed the families you can't hardly get away from work to see. You work for them without any improvement in your condition or any hope of improvement in the conditions of your life. You slave away the best years of your life until you're prematurely old and worn down to nothing, too old and feeble to work at all, at which time they turn you out the back door without a job or even a thank-you. They hand us nothing but starvation wages and the backs of their hands. Through our divisiveness and lack of organization, we hand them control and dominance over us in perpetuity. Must we hand them the primary shovel that they use to bury us with again and again? I'm not going to say that the bosses won't try to beat you down if you go out on strike. They may send in strikebreakers like they've done before. Those strikebreakers may try to beat you down with clubs. But through our lack of cohesiveness and our disorganization and our ethnic rivalries, we hand them the biggest club they have beaten us with repeatedly and will continue to beat us with again. With all the work you do for them for the very little they give you, for all the work we do for them that breaks us down into the nothings they treat us as, must we do the work of breaking ourselves apart and keeping ourselves divided so they can more effectively keep us crumbled and broken down?"

There was a wave of throaty grumbles and catcalls.

"I've been there. I've stood on the line and worked sunup to sunset like you have. I know what it's like. You men and women who work in the meatpacking industry know what it's like. You know what your future will be. You live the future every day on the line. All your tomorrows will be like all your yesterdays. They will work you down to the bone like you work the animals on the line down to the bones. Like you take apart animals on the line, they will take you apart and reduce you to nothing. As they have you take every last thing you can get out of the animals you render, they will work you until they get every last little bit they can get out of you, and then they toss what is left of you away like you toss away the bones that are left of the animals you have taken apart. They will grind you down to nothing to squeeze the last breath of your productive life out of you in order to squeeze every last profit dollar they can out of you, the way they squeeze every last useful piece and dime of profit they can out of the animals you work down to nothing for them as they work you down to nothing for nothing wages. At the end of your productive life, when you reach the end of your line on the line, they discard what little is left of you the way you discard what little is left of the animals that reach the end of your processing line."

Samuel thought again of Harold Ethridge, who had sent animals to the plant to be broken and who had broken the girl.

"In their processing line of greed, the bosses of Packingtown grind the workers down till the workers have nothing left for themselves. They grind your lives down to become the feedstock of their profits as you grind the offal of the animals you process. The bosses take everything from the worker, down to his last breath, the way the butchers on the lines of the plants you work in take everything from the animals that come to you. They grind the bones of the workingman down to become the glue that holds together their empires the way you grind the bones of animals for glue."

Actually it was the horns, hooves, and sinews they made glue out of.

"They work the life out of the workingman. They work the body of the workingman to death. They work the soul of the workingman to deadness. They take not only the strength of your bodies and the breath of life of the workingman but also your joy of life, even your very sense of life. They take from you the sense of being alive. At the end of the line of his life, they leave the workingman nothing in either body and soul. They leave the used-up workingman ag nothing as the animals that are left as nothing at the end of a slaughterhouse line. They work your body to frailty and death. They work your soul to deadness and emptiness. They take from you the joy and hope that otherwise sustain the life of the soul. For all that, they hardly pay a lone man enough to sustain the life of his body."

That fit Samuel well enough. Even as a single and unmarried worker, after paying rent and other necessities, he had barely enough money left over to buy the inexpensive pulp novels he read for diversion in his empty room in the empty hours before falling into a cold and empty sleep in his small, cold room, before rising early in the morning to spend the day moving around refrigerated sides of beef. Cheap books were something he could afford at a dime apiece. They served to remind him that there was a world outside his life in Packingtown. That and walks in public parks. The parks were free, even if the streetcar rides to them were not.

"They certainly do not pay workingmen enough to sustain and feed their families. Your wives and your children have to work to make ends meet, often for the same packinghouse bosses, who pay them even less than they pay the primary breadwinner fathers. Fathers go hungry to feed their children. Children go hungry because, even with their earnings added in, it is not enough to properly feed and clothe a family. The bosses rob the workingman of his dignity. They rob the workingman of his function as provider by not paying him enough to provide for his family. The bosses rob the families of workingmen of their fathers by keeping them at work so long that they are home with their families only a short while. They rob families of their fathers by rendering them so tired at the end of the day that they can hardly talk to their families, let alone do anything with them. In that they rob the working family of their father. At the same time and in the same manner, the bosses rob the workingman of his family when they deny him the wherewithal to support his family and deny him the very time and energy to be with, and be a father to, his family. They deny the workingman any leisure time of his own so that they can live a life of leisure. They deny the workingman even the small luxury of being with his family so that they can maximize their lives of leisure to the last dime. The bosses empty the workingman of his life and the substance of his life in order to maximize the profit of their lives. All they leave the workingman, where the members of his family are concerned, is an empty void that he is not able to fill."

In the alternative political zeitgeist and terminology of the day, Samuel didn't know dialectic materialism from diet cola, which hadn't been invented yet. To Samuel, all the heated hyperventilating of the radical speakers had been the screeching of cats fighting on the other side of a fence and the growling of alley dogs ready to go for the throat of the first person who passed by. The politics of the people he was listening to were the hallway howling of the mental ward for which the square he was standing in was named. Up until August Werner had taken the podium, Samuel had not heard anything much spoken that he had liked or could relate to.

That changed in a moment when Mr. Werner started referring to the families of the workers. Samuel related strongly to family and caring for family, and the pain and emptiness of being separated from family or seeing them hurt. Mr. Werner wasn't describing anything Samuel hadn't seen since he had come to work at the plant. Samuel wasn't hearing any condition described that he hadn't seen at the plant or in Packingtown. At last the family-oriented Samuel was hearing something that he could relate to and understand. It was something that fired him up the way he had become consumed by the fires of vengeance when he had seen the girl lying dead on the table. Now, instead of hearing blitherings, Samuel felt he was hearing the iron nexus of truth. He felt the truth in his heart. He felt the truth in his soul. He felt the truth in his hands the way he had felt the shotgun he had used to kill Harold Ethridge.

"His wife and children become strangers to him and he to them.

His sons go off and learn to become criminals on the street because he is not home to correct them and be the guiding influence that fathers are supposed to be to their sons."

Samuel could relate to the collapse of a family and to criminal sons on the run on the street. Not because his father had failed to be to be a guiding and shaping influence, but because he had—and because Samuel had loved his father so deeply.

"His wife and daughters drift away from him and become prostitutes because it is the only way they can support themselves."

Samuel could also relate to girls who left home to become prostitutes because their fathers and family had failed them or betrayed them. He had related to one in body and soul more times than he was sure he could remember.

"Out of the goodness of their hearts, the bosses aren't going to pay the workingman a decent wage. They aren't going to pay you enough to support your families. They aren't going to allow you a living wage. They aren't going to allow you a wage that you can keep your families living on. They aren't going to afford you your dignity. They won't afford you enough of their money for your work to be able to afford anything for yourselves or for your families. They aren't going to afford you your destiny. The only destiny they will afford you is a destiny that shouldn't happen to a dog. The only future they'll leave to you will be a slow-motion version of what you do to the animals on the packing line."

There were grumbles and muttering of agreement. Samuel didn't make any sounds, but unlike the times the radicals had held the podium, he wasn't hearing anything he disagreed with.

"The bosses won't afford you anything but an endless future of penury so they can keep themselves in the lap of endless luxury. By themselves, by their instincts and their nature, the bosses won't give you anything more than the barest minimum they must pay to keep the line moving. They won't allow you your destiny. They won't allow you your dignity. They won't allow you your families. They won't allow you a life worth living. On their own, and by their own sweet favor, the bosses won't allow you a future worth contemplating. You're going to have to take your future out of their hands and take your life and future into your own hands!"

Whether they were finding Mr. Werner's oratory to be spellbinding or whether at this point they instinctively recognized that a critical juncture had been arrived at, the crowd listened on in silence.

"But we will have to do it together as one. As I said, as individuals we cannot bargain with the bosses of the meatpacking industry. Neither can we bargain with them as Germans, Poles, Lithuanians, Slavs, Irish, and Negroes. We can only stand up to them as unified workingmen demanding our rights and fair treatment. The only chance we have of winning or gaining anything from the bosses, wrenching anything from their hands, is if we organize and present a united front. We must put aside all thoughts of nationality. We must put aside nationality itself. We must put aside race itself and think of ourselves as workers only, workers demanding our rightful share of the bounty of this country and the industry we work in. But we must do it together. We must do it organized if we are to have any chance that it will be done for us and done for our children at all."

For one sublime moment, as sublime as any moment that could have existed amid the company he was with that day, facing the pending situation he might find himself facing a few days hence, Samuel caught a glimpse of himself back on the farm, outside in the sun in some grassy field, with the girl in the life he would never have with her, with the children they would never have, the children they might not have had even if they had been married, running through the grass and playing in the field of his vanished dream. He saw the girl's beautiful and smiling face approach as she walked up to him. He felt the soft touch of her hand on his arm. He felt the softness of her lips on his. Beyond the girl he saw the fields of his home and the horizon stretching past and away.

The vision was gone almost as soon as it had come, and Samuel found himself again in the company of raggedly dressed, muttering men in the middle of Bughouse Square.

"If you decide to go on strike, you must walk out together. You must walk off the line together. You must stand on the picket line together. If you decide to go on strike, I beg each and every one of you to stay with your brother and not walk away, hoping to leave the task to someone else. If a strike is called, every one of you who walks away because you want to placate the company in hopes of ensuring your job or because you don't want to face what the bosses might throw at you leaves a hole for the bosses to drive their ripping bars into. If you go on strike, it must be a total commitment to the cause. It must be as much a total commitment to your fellow workers. It must be a total commitment to the strike. ... And it can't be a strike where you go home and sit down in your shacks and tenement halls. The bosses will just bring in replacement workers. You must shut down the plant and hold it. You must occupy the plant."

Now Samuel was hearing a plan even more radical than he had thought of doing.

"The bosses have little concern for the workers. The plant is the bosses' only concern. It is the source of their profit, which is their only other concern in life. You must take the source of their profit away from them and hold it. You must use your occupation as the source of their profit to deny the bosses their profit. The bosses have used their plant to deny you a living wage and a living for your families in order to maximize their profits. You must take the instrument of their profit and hold it away from them to make them realize what poverty is and what it feels like to have little or nothing coming in. You must hold their profit-making plant away from them to make them realize that it is you, the workers, who generate their profits for them. That is the formula for making them respect you."

It seemed a reasonable enough formula on the surface. At the same time it was also reasonable to expect that the corporate bosses would want their plant back at all costs. To Samuel it also seemed a formula for the company sending in strikebreakers as they had done in industry strikes in the past.

"If you elect to go on strike, I will join you on the line to show you that I am not one who sends workers out to a fight while he holds back and keeps himself in safety. It may be a hard fight. It may be a long fight. But if we stay together and stand our ground as we stand for each other, we can triumph against the thugs and the calamity they send against us."

From the rising curve of Mr. Werner's tone of voice, it was obvious that he was winding up his speech. Though he had remained mostly focused and had not been all over the board with detached and unrelated incendiary rhetoric like the old-line hard-core anarchists who had spoken first, in the end his verbiage took off to its own detached heights.

"If we triumph against the machinery of their oppression, we will set the standard that will rally other workers to our standard, the standard of fair treatment of the workingmen of this city and the world. We will light the torch to show the way for all the downtrodden workingmen in this industry and in other industries to follow. Our example will lead to a flood tide that will sweep out from us and around us to all the outraged and ground-down workingmen of the city, the country, and the world! It will be a tide that cannot be slowed or turned back. In the end the plant will be ours. The city will be ours. The future will be ours!"

The crowd erupted into cheers and whistles. Though the speech ended on a bit of a grandiose note, it hadn't on the whole been as wild-eyed and far-flung as the speeches of the more radical radicals. Even Samuel was impressed. Being in the city had taught Samuel something about triumphing over thugs. But then he hadn't had come to Chicago for that experience. He had triumphed over a thug back in his hometown, but that triumph had ended in his flight from his home.

The rest of the rally consisted of various other speakers giving some pointer tips on conducting a strike. There were more exhortations. After the rally ended, some members of the crowd milled around, talking, while the rest dispersed. Mr. Werner and the other radicals stood around holding forth with the small groups of men who would listen to them. From the looks of concentrated intensity on their faces, Samuel figured they were dispensing with the finer points of radical political philosophy. Samuel chatted briefly with a few of the workers from the plant, but he soon left. He wasn't interested in delving into radical Socialist philosophy. He had other agendas on his mind. The first was to find a quiet bar to have a quiet drink in a secluded indoor spot where all he could see was the bottle in his hand and was able to see no farther than the other side of the bar. After that he would go out to find himself an open space of sky where he could see to the horizon.

Chapter 31

"So, Mr. Farm Boy, why did you leave the farm?" the man asked his rhetorical question, expecting an ordinary answer.

"My mother was dead. My father died," Samuel said, repeating the story he had given others. "The bank foreclosed the mortgage and took the farm in payment of debt. It's gone now. The bank got the farm. I got a train ticket here to find a job."

It was a proverbial story after all: a proverb of rich, acquisitive, callous bankers profiting from the misfortune of poor country people and turning them off their land in order to turn a profit from their misfortune. It was a proverb that radicals of the day spoke of when they referred to greedy rich bankers as much as they denounced the higher-level greed of higher-up capitalist bosses. It was a proverb the man was also familiar with.

"What are your feelings for the rich?" the man asked, a sound journalist's question. "What do you think about the rich? After losing the farm that your father had tried to leave you to a rich banker, what might you want to do to the rich?"

Oh, Samuel had a story he could tell about the rich all right. If the man was a radical, Samuel could tell him a story that would affirm his radicalness and affirm for him everything he thought and felt about the rich. Samuel could tell the man stories about the meanness and cruelties of the rich. He could tell a story as proverbial as they came. But while his hatred for Harold Ethridge had hardly cooled a degree, where it came to the rich in general, the real Samuel was somewhere in between.

"I don't care if people get rich," Samuel said. "As long as they don't step on others and chop them up doing it. I don't hold it against anyone simply 'cause they're rich, and I don't fault people for working to make themselves rich. If you can't get rich, what's the purpose of ambition, and taking personal initiative, and attempting to improve your lot in life? What's the purpose of working hard? What's the purpose of working at all if it isn't to make yourself a place in the world and improve your lot in life? A rich man is just a common man after he's worked his way up and successfully applied all that stuff they tell you about working hard and pulling yourself up by your bootstraps. But rich men often make themselves rich by making things that common people want and need to make their own lives better."

Samuel took another swallow of his common man's working-class beer.

"The only thing I've got against the rich is that so often they just can't seem to keep from beating up on those below them while they become rich and as they become richer. They create the factories and jobs that employ and feed the common man. The average people benefit from the goods and services they provide as they get rich. But they don't want to share any of the prosperity they create. They want it all for themselves. They want every last dime for themselves. They keep on beating up on the common people to keep themselves rich. Too often they seem to beat up on the poor, but not as a way of getting rich and staying rich. Sometimes they seem to do it just for the joy of beating up on those beneath them, with no other discernible reason. They just can't seem to keep their hands off the throats of the poor beneath them. They break the backs and break the necks and break the hearts of the little people who service them and make them rich."

"Now you sound like a radical," the man said.

"I'm not out to hang anyone for being rich," Samuel said. "I'm not out to throw any bombs at anyone for having more money or a better home than I do. I'm not even out to stand in the way of or stop anyone from becoming rich. I just want a little fair play for working people who help make the rich, rich."

"That's all I'm looking for too," the man said. "If that makes me a radical, then we both stand convicted in absentia, and we're both on the run together."

Poets like irony. Poets live by irony. Sometimes unpublished poets just aren't aware of it when they're looking irony in the face.

"I don't bear the rich any great and abiding hatred," Samuel Martin, a.k.a. William Howard, who still bore a great and abiding hatred for Harold Ethridge, said. "Neither do I bear any great and abiding love for the rich." Samuel turned back to his beer and looked straight ahead. "But the radicals have nothing in them but their hatred and vengeance. They have nothing to offer but hatred and vengeance. They have no answers beyond hatred and vengeance. Any world they create or come to rule would be a mean, empty, barren place where they would rule with an iron hand as mean as the meanest rich man."

Samuel took a drink of his beer. Then he set the bottle down and looked at the man. "So, whoever and whatever you are, if you're a company spy, tell the bosses who hired you that it's a stupid farmer who beats and mistreats and won't feed his plow horses who work the ground and produce his crops for him. If you're a radical, go back and tell your radical friends that it's a stupid plow horse who threatens to kick his farmer at every turn. If you're a journalist, go back and tell your readers that an ex-farmer told you both."

"And who shall I say said this?" the man asked. "What's your name, Mr. Displaced Farm Boy who lost his farm to a banker?"

Samuel looked at the man suspiciously. The man held up his hand. "I promise I won't use your name in any column I write," the man said in an earnest-sounding voice. "I'll just say I got the story from an anonymous source. I just wanted to know your name on the basis of one common man to another common man."

"William Harper," the name-flexible Samuel said. The name he used was a modification of the name he used at the packing plant, combining it with the name of his back home friend Ben Harper, whom he had grown up with in his hometown and who had been with him the night he had met the girl. "If you want to be common man informal about it, you can call me Bill."

"That's a good American farmer's name," the man said.

"I told you who I am," Samuel said to the stranger next to him. "So tell me who you are, Mr. Stranger at the bar. As far as pegging people goes, I had you pegged for a Norwegian. But you don't have any accent. You sound as everyday American as you say I do."

"My parents were Swedish immigrants," the man said. "You were one country off and one generation off."

"With the exception of the guys running around in the forest or riding bareback around the plains with paint on their face and feathers in their hair, we're all immigrants or the sons of immigrants," Samuel said in response.

Still holding his beer bottle, Samuel looked at the man. "So what's your name, Mr. Second-Generation Swede?" Samuel Martin, a.k.a. William Howard, a.k.a. Bill Harper, asked.

"Sandburg," the man replied. "Carl Sandburg."

"I guess that's a good enough Swedish name," the name-relative Samuel Martin said. "Provided that is your real name and you really are a journalist and not a Pinkerton agent."

"If you don't believe I am what I say I am, you're welcome to come down to the *Chicago Daily News* any day and look me up. There aren't any Pinkertons working at the paper."

"So if you're not a Pinkerton, and if you're not a radical even though you talk like one, what are you?"

"Like I said," the man replied, "I'm a journalist."

"I mean, what's your philosophy?" Samuel asked. "You've been pumping me for my political philosophy. What philosophy do you hold to? If you're not a radical like you say you're not, and if you're not a company man, which side are you on?"

"I believe in the common man," the man sitting next to Samuel at a common man's bar said. "Where it comes to the common man, I'm a lot closer to Walt Whitman than I am to Karl Marx. I believe in the innate nobility of the common man. I believe in the nobility of the common man more than any idea of the nobility of the rich. Being rich doesn't make a man good and noble. More often than not, riches and richness are just a trapdoor that leads to meanness. You know that well enough dealing with the bosses of your plant. I have faith in the persistence and endurance of the common man—common men like you. The common man will be around long after the rich have strangled themselves or are strangled by the radicals, one of whom I'm not."

"If you're looking for a common man, I'm common enough," Samuel said in a wry tone as he turned back to his beer bottle. "I just can't say it's made me particularly noble."

In the anonymity of the moment, in the strange bar he was in, talking with man he would probably never see again, in the passing anonymity his life had become, Samuel's thoughts almost couldn't help but drift out past the boundaries he could not see anymore.

"At least in my common man's life I was common enough to have loved a girl a lot of people thought was common in the worst sense," Samuel said, slipping into his own form of barroom free association. "My innate common man nobility didn't do her much in the way of any favor. My common man goodness didn't do her any good or keep the meanness of the world from breaking her neck." Samuel took another swig of his dwindling beer. "As far as meanness goes, there are a lot of things in this life that can make people mean. Being rich and wanting to get rich is definitely one of them. The lust for wealth can make a man mean as a snake. But power and the lust for power can make a man just as mean. So can a lot of other things, like sex and vengeance, and crazy political ideas."

Samuel took the last swallow of beer in his bottle. His free association deepened and went wider.

"As far as the rich being mean goes, you don't have to tell me that the rich can be mean, Mr. Journalist, radical or not. I know the rich can be mean. I didn't have to come to this city to find that out. Back home I knew a rich man who broke a girl's neck as quick and as casually as he used her body. He brought her down in cold blood like she was nothing to him. I brought him down just as casually as he did her. Though I did it in hot blood." Samuel stood up. "I had to come to this city because I killed a man who killed a prostitute. I didn't have to come to this city to get in trouble over a prostitute. If I'm going to get myself in further trouble, it will be for something a lot bigger and more meaningful, like taking on the bosses."

Samuel put the beer bottle down on the bar. "Now if you will excuse me, sir, I have to get back to the hole I live in and prepare myself to become part of the story you'll probably be covering in the next few days, the one about the strike."

Samuel started to walk to the door, but he stopped and turned back to the man. "I know plenty of places in this city to get a drink in," he said in a sarcastic tone. "Do you happen to know of any place where I can find clean air and an open view of the sky without any higher view being blocked by smoke from the factories and without smelling the smell of animals being rendered and sewage festering?"

"Take a walk through the parks along the shore of the lake," the man said. "Far-thinking men in the City Planning Department held in check the factory owners and robber barons who would have crowded out every inch of available land to the water's edge and established a series of parks along the shore of the lake, where people could find green grass to sit on and trees to walk among. There you can see the blue of the sky and feel the cool of the breeze coming in off the lake. It may not be paradise with the city at its back, but from there you can catch a small view of what heaven might be like."

Without either of the strangers who had passed in a bar and would not pass each other's way again saying anything more, Samuel turned and walked a straightforward common man's walk out the door of the bar and onto the street. He figured his departure might have been a bit abrupt, but he had a lot on his mind he needed to think about. Though the man had a lot of good things to say about the common man, little of it had provided any guidance concerning the confrontation to come. Samuel didn't think that a Walt Whitman clone or a Ralph Waldo Emerson wannabe would be of much help to him if it came to blows on a picket line.

The man went back to his apartment. He wasn't sure why, but the boy had inspired him. He just wasn't sure what the inspiration was, but it was connected to the city he lived in and to which the boy had come as a refugee. The man sat down and started to pen a poem that would become his most recognized work, a work that would define Chicago both to itself and to the world:

Chicago

City of broad shoulders
Hog butcher to the world …

The flow of his words momentarily stopped there. But the rest of the words would come later.

Unbeknownst to the man, Samuel took his advice. He didn't go straight home, as much home as his one room was, to prepare himself in mind and body for the coming confrontation. Instead he used the money he hadn't expended in transitory pleasure with one of Chicago's fairest street blossoms to ride the trolley to Jackson Park on the lakefront. The park, along with the chain of parks on the lakefront, was the legacy of visionary civic planners Frederick Law Olmsted and Calvert Vaux. It was Olmsted and Vaux who had designed New York's Central Park. From the day it opened, Central Park in New York had attracted large crowds. The success of Central Park became the impetus for influential city fathers to expand on Daniel Burnham's dictum of keeping development and building back from the lakefront so as to keep commercial buildings and commercialization from crowding to the water's edge, providing a clear corridor from which people could view the lake and walk its shore.

Unfortunately for purveyors of the ideal of an uncommercialized open and natural space along the shore of Lake Michigan, the terms of an 1852 agreement seceded much of the lakefront land on the southeast side of the city to the railroads, which at the time dominated the commercial life of the city. At first the railroads came into the city from the east and swung north by crossing a causeway built several hundred feet out into the lake itself. Instead of becoming a picturesque and useful man-made harbor, the lagoon between the original shore and the causeway on which the railbed and track were laid became a fetid swamp filled with garbage, sewage, and the carcasses of dead cows and horses.

Eventually the artificial and stinking man-made lagoon was filled in with landfill, much of it rubble from the Chicago fire of 1873. In keeping with Burnham's original vision, the newly created land would not have commercial buildings erected on it. The view of the lake would stay open and unimpeded by skyscrapers, which the developing technology of steel-frame construction were making larger and taller. But anyone looking over the scene from the city toward the open expanse of lake on the south side had to look over long rows of parallel railroad tracks and parked freight trains.

Before the Chicago park system was initiated, the only place for Chicagoans to go for a picnic or just to breathe some fresh air and walk amid something resembling green and open country was to go into the city's new parklike cemeteries, Rosehill, Calvary, and Graceland (not Elvis's Graceland). To find a moment of peace and quiet, to breathe some fresh air, citizens of the city of the living had to spread their picnic blankets on the ground of the gardens of the dead.

The open and undeveloped land for parks, especially parks that would abut onto the lake itself, lay from the central part of the city northward. It was there that, under the vision of city planners and visionary and urban design architects not wedded to any vision of wringing the last dollar they could out of every last foot of land, the city would get its green and recreational spaces. For the people of the city, the parks would become what they were set aside for: a place to walk on green grass under an open blue sky. For the narrow thinkers who thought in commercial terms only, those with landholdings close to where the parks would come to be built, the park system increased the value of their land in ways that being next to a stinking sewer swamp did not.

The Chicago park system came to surpass the park systems of many other large US cities. To that was added in sequence the Chicago Board of Trade, the Auditorium Theater and Hotel, skyscrapers, and a host of cultural institutions including libraries, museums, concert halls, the art museum, and a distinguished university, the University of Chicago. In thus manner, the movers and shakers of Chicago set out to prove to London, Paris, and New York that their city was something more than a center of pigsticking and grain-handling.

The crowning achievement of this building and the beautification effort was the celestial White City of the Columbian Exposition, the Chicago elite's vision of what a great city should look like and be like at a time when the country's large cities were often thought of as being ugly, dangerous, and ungovernable. This civic movement had as much to do with what Chicago had become as it had to do with a detached and esoteric vision of what a city should be.

On weekends, especially Sunday afternoons, the park's lakes and lagoons were filled with canopied small boats and canoes "paddled by gentleman in high stiff collars, their ladies holding dainty parasols and trailing their fingers in the water." On dirt diamonds, young men in shirtsleeves would play the American game that Samuel Martin had left behind him in his hometown he had fled and that he had not taken up since coming to the city. As many as twenty thousand people would be in the parks on sunny weekends and Sundays, many walking with children and big wooden picnic baskets. Young couples walked hand in hand along the lake promenades or sat on blankets, eating from picnic baskets. The sight reminded Samuel of how he and the girl had taken a picnic lunch along the river of his hometown. He tried to put the image out of his mind but couldn't.

In fulfillment of the hopes of civic planners and would-be tamers of the boisterous and often tumultuous lower classes, many of the walkers and picnickers in the parks came from the working-class neighborhoods that were starting to spring up north and west of the parks. The parks became a quite pleasant family affair. Drug dealers were several generations off in the future. Electric lights were added in the 1880s, which allowed people to stay on after the sun had set. Wooing couples could walk the paths of the parks and along the shore, the moon throwing a silver trail across the black water.

The parks, however, remained largely alien and inaccessible territory to the city's inner immigrant neighborhoods, including the Back of the Yards district. A round-trip trolley ride for an entire family could easily eat up a Polish mill hand's daily wage. Even the upwardly mobile Germans often stayed away from the parks on Sundays because beer drinking, dancing, and cooking out were forbidden in the parks, as were political gatherings and speechmaking.

Samuel didn't have a family, and he didn't spend the small amount of money he had left over from his pay on inordinate drinking or on flowers of the street who offered to share the long-faded flowers of their hardened femininity with him for the extra money he had on his person. As a result, that day Samuel could afford to travel to Jackson Park, where he walked the encapsulated, manicured country and remembered how as a younger boy he had walked a wider country not bound by the brick of buildings and the steel of trolley track, where he stood amid the closeness of the families around him and looked homeward like an exiled angel over the open expanse of water to a home, family, and life he could not return to.

His mental picture of swimming together with the girl in the clean and cool water of Lake Michigan was quite fetching to Samuel. But all fetchingness now seemed a world and a life away. All vision behind was closed off. Ahead all he could see was the tumultuous confines of the slaughterhouse killing line and the increasingly tumultuous labor politics of Packingtown.

The girl was out over a horizon beyond him. He could not cross over to her. His past life and his family were apart from him, over a horizon that he could not cross and that he might never be able to close the final distance of. Samuel figured that if he had to be a homeless wanderer for the rest of his life, at least he should be able to wander the horizons of open sky above him and the open space around him that had been a part of his life on the farm and that went with the open unrootedness, the emptiness, and the uncertainty of his life now and in the darkling possibility of what was to come.

Chapter 32

Samuel rotated the ax handle off his shoulder and held it ready, but it wasn't the jaunty gesture of one duelist tipping in salute to another. With his one hand, he brought the ax handle down to where he'd taken hold of it with his other hand. He stood with it across his chest at an angle like a sentry standing guard duty with a rifle. Samuel was a country boy. Country boys know ax handles like they know shotguns. Rufus held a four-foot-long piece of two-by-four lumber. It was threatening-looking enough, but a two by four is a bit of an awkward weapon. It's hard to get your hands around it and get the feel of it the way you can with an ax handle.

The poet Matthew Arnold had been in his grave for twenty-five years. Though Samuel wasn't widely familiar with the works of the English poet and social critic, in literature class in his hometown high school he had briefly read three of Matthew Arnold's better-known and most evocative lines:

> And we are here as on a darkling plain,
> Swept with confused alarms of struggle and flight,
> Where ignorant armies clash by night.

It wasn't night. It wasn't even yet noon on the otherwise sunny day. But the poetic lines fit the situation well enough in the abstract. Detached and cultured observers, the kind who read abstract poets like Matthew Arnold, might consider the two groups closing in on each other, one group standing their ground in no recognizable rank and file behind the high iron gate of the plant they had occupied, the other group in disordered motion toward it, to be hordes of ignorant street rabble, as opposed to even minimally organized and disciplined armies. But the two scruffy mobs didn't exist in the abstract. The grimy steel of the plant behind the strikers didn't exist in the abstract. The grimy lives lived by the workers on the line were anything but abstract to them. The iron gate in front of them, the iron gate between them, and the approaching mob wasn't abstract. The hickory ax handle in Samuel's hands felt anything but abstract to him. Broken bones and fractured skulls would not be abstract pains.

As a young man and one of the strongest men in the plant, Samuel felt it was his place to be in the front of the line. His friend and coworker Rufus was next to him at the front of the line.

After lowering his makeshift weapon to a more serviceable level, Samuel stood there twisting the ax handle in his hands. For Samuel it would be his second all-or-nothing personal confrontation in less than a year in a life that was coming to seem like a string of mortal confrontations. All his past was dead and buried behind him. All love and lovers seemed dead and buried. There was no future he cared to pause and consider. There was nothing ahead of him he could see but the coming confrontation that would shake him and pull him like a rag in a dog's mouth.

"Here they come," August Werner said. He was only stating what could be seen through the high iron bar fence and the high gate around the front of the plant the strikers occupied. Mrs. Kraznapolski was there with her thick Polish accent and her large Polish breasts. Many striker wives who worked in the plant were there on the line with their husbands. Most of the women in the ranks of the strikers worked in the canning department like Mrs. Kraznapolski did. Samuel wasn't sure why they were there. Maybe some of them considered themselves to be fierce labor Hadrians of the type that ran amok in the city during the labor riots of 1877. Maybe their being there was their way of showing solidarity with their husbands and coworkers. But it was their plant they were on strike against as much as it was their husband's. The corporate Brahmin who had sent the ragtag street mob to eject them all from the plant thought in terms of everyone in the plant as being members of the howling classes. The gender of the mouth doing the howling made little difference to them, as did how hard any given striker's mouth got broken. They also thought in terms of absolute control of their property and in terms of absolutes when it came to breaking any strike that challenged control of their property. The gloves were off when it came to any striker, and the gloves didn't go back on where it came to any woman strikers whom they considered unfeminine harpies who didn't wear dainty gloves or carry parasols.

Mara was not there with them. It was not that she was a coward. Mr. Kraznapolski had given her instructions to remain home. She might be needed to tend the wounded when they arrived back home.

Mrs. Kraznapolski was in the front of the line with her husband. Other striker wives stood at different parts of the line. However hardened the women in the strike had become from years of working at the plant, in conditions hardly much better than their husbands', Samuel didn't think they should be there. It wasn't that he considered meatpacking or striking to be man's work. He just didn't think that facing down strikebreakers, many of whom were little more than alley thugs who would rape a woman in an alley and leave her in the alley bloodied with her neck broken, was proper woman's work. Besides, as a wrestler, Samuel had learned to size up opponents at a glance. In Samuel's estimate, Mrs. Kraznapolski's build limited her as a fighter. Though they might provide a certain amount of cushioning for blows aimed at her chest, in Samuel's estimate, Mrs. Kraznapolski's large Polish breasts could slow her down in a fight and throw her off-balance. Samuel figured that, like Molly Pitcher, some women could be good in a fight. If the girl's story was true, she had carved her brother a new profile with his own knife. Even though she had an appreciable chest size herself, the girl had been quick and wiry. Mrs. Kraznapolski was more matronly than Amazonian. In Samuel's view, Mrs. Kraznapolski was too much of a motherly woman to be involved in a street brawl.

In the approaching moments, in the face of the street thug faces of the approaching strikebreakers, Samuel imagined his mother and his sister, Beth, on the strike line, facing the band of head breakers. What the strikebreakers would do to them was not a pretty thought. What they might do to even the more hardened women of the plant wasn't any prettier a thought to think about. But pretty and abstract poetry existed somewhere else that day, not on the grounds of the striker-occupied meatpacking plant. For Samuel, resolves were the only things on his mind. Be they pretty or less than pretty, before any strikebreaker could get to any of the women on the line, Samuel resolved to leave their faces a less than pretty sight.

"They probably hope they can get us cleaned out by noon so they can get the plant reopened and get at least a half day's worth of work out of it."

The strike line wasn't actually a line. It was a disjointed assemblage of people, mostly men, gathered behind the front gate of the plant they had closed and locked with a chain and padlock when they had shut down the plant on the opening day of the strike. The body of the strikers formed an amorphous mass with a slightly concave center around the front gate, the central depression of the crowd centered on the front gate that the throng of strikebreakers were converging toward. They would have to force it open to gain entry to the plant.

Outside the gate, the strikebreakers oozed out of several streets, where they converged and moved toward the front gate of the plant like a slow-motion mudslide. The strikers behind the gate didn't stand in any rank and file. The strikebreaker army didn't advance in any rank and file. They milled as much as they marched, weaving in and out, crossing in front of each other. In a way they looked like another shipment of cattle approaching the chutes where they would take the final steps of their lives. The difference was that cattle would often balk and try to turn around when they caught the scent of the blood ahead. The strikebreakers seemed to have the scent of blood in their noses. Instead of causing them to hesitate or turn around, the smell of blood seemed to draw them on.

With the exception of not having any women in their ranks, the advancing crowd of strikebreakers were dressed like, and looked no different from, the strikers inside the gates. Their ranks consisted of unemployed immigrants and jobless, homeless men who had been promised the jobs of those the strikebreakers would eject from the plant grounds. Their numbers were augmented by street thugs and criminals hired to do a job for the day and paid for their talents at intimidation and extortion and their skills with a blackjack. Whatever the shabbiness of their clothes, whatever the color of their shabby motivations, all those in the oncoming crowd seemed to be carrying one form of club or another in their hands. As Samuel looked more closely, at the back of the jumbled ranks of strikebreakers, he saw a more coordinated-looking line of men in blue uniforms.

"They've got the police backing them up!" Anton Kraznapolski shouted. "It's going to be '94 all over again."

His reference was to the strike of 1894, when the company sent in strikebreakers backed up by the state militia. No one in the ranks of the strikers was surprised by the fact that management had prevailed on the city government and city police to serve as backup to the strikebreakers. The owners of the plant were some of the richest and most influential men in the city. Where their interests were concerned, they were active in city governmental affairs. In some ways they were the city government. The police force wasn't on their payroll, and neither were the police in their back pockets, but the police were close to the pockets where the money was kept. The front ranks of the actual strikebreakers would do the dirty work of actual strikebreaking. The police would only come in with their official throw weight if the strikebreakers got into trouble or were failing to carry the day and carry the plant back to its owners. The presence of uniformed police in the background was also a calculated way of demoralizing the strikers by letting them know they were beaten from the beginning.

"Just pretend they're Klansmen," Samuel said out of the side of his mouth to Rufus as he watched the approach of the strikebreakers. "Here's your chance to get back at them where things are on more equal terms."

The balance of forces was more or less illusionary that day. The number of strikebreakers was roughly equal to the number of strikers. The police were the wild card that tipped the balance in favor of the strikebreakers. If the police went in, the outcome was more or less already decided.

Most of the strikebreakers were on foot. At the center of their mass, a large flatbed truck moved with them. Several more men rode in the bed of the truck. As the disjointed mob of strikebreakers converged on the front gate of the plant in a haphazard manner, the driver of the truck specifically maneuvered the vehicle into a position where it was facing the center of the front gate, directly perpendicular to it. When the truck stopped, the men riding in the bed jumped out. It looked to Samuel like the company strikebreakers intended to use the truck to ram the gates open when the rest of the mob had sufficiently assembled in a tight enough mass to rush in after the gates were broken. The rest of the strikers had a similar idea. The concave gap in the strikers' ranks started to widen and deepen as strikers moved out of the direct line of the path where the truck would come crashing through.

As the crowd of company hirelings approached the gate and drew near to the fence on either side, a guttural half roar, half shout of defiance started going up from the strikers. No one in the ranks of strikers shouted *scab* or *thugs* or other labor terms at the strikebreakers. No recognizable words were contained in the verbal howl of discontent and anger of the strikers. The time for words was past. Any words that arose would have only been carried away on the wind like the smoke that wasn't rising from the smokestacks of the plant. The strikebreakers uttered no discernible sounds at all. No one in either group on either side of the fence shouted, "Solidarity forever!"

From out of the rankless mass of strikebreakers, several men ran forward, dragging a long chain, heavier chain than the one securing the gate. On the end of the chain was a large steel hook. The men pushed the jaw of the hook into a slack loop of the smaller chain the strikers had wrapped between the abutting ends of the closed gates. Once the hook was in place, they pulled the chain tight so that the strikers couldn't run up and pull the hook out of place. Keeping the chain taut, they wrapped the far end of the chain around the front bumper and the bumper mounts of the truck.

The motor on the truck raced. As the strikebreakers closest to the gate backed away, the truck backed up with a jerk. The heavy-gauge chain snapped out fully straight. The gates of plant started to pull open but were stopped by the chain holding them closed. The metal bars of the gates bent and flexed forward at the point of constriction. For a moment it looked as if the gates were going to buckle completely and be pulled off their hinges. The strain looked as it if might even pull the movable iron gate, hinges and all, out of its moorings in the imposing stone arches and bring down part of the stone gate that, like the Pullman factory compound, would one day come to be considered a lesser Chicago landmark.

Just short of complete collapse of the gates, the smaller-gauge chain that held the gates shut snapped. As the heavy chain and hook fell away, the strikebreakers rushed the gates. They quickly pulled away the remnants of the broken chain. With the chain and lock gone, the strikebreakers threw themselves against the gates, pushing them backward and fully open on both sides. As the gates opened, the main body of strikebreakers surged into the gap.

"Don't let them in the gates!" August Werner shouted.

The strikers surged forward, toward the horde of strikebreakers, who had breached their first limited defense. It was more or less too late for that though. The strikers had started out having drawn back from the gates in anticipation of the truck being rammed through the gate and slamming into them. This gave the strikebreakers an advantage in that they were able to swarm in through the now open gates and gain ground inside the plant before the strikers could close with them. It wouldn't have made a lot of difference if the strikers had been closer to the gates. The strikebreakers had momentum and a single direction of thrust. The gates were too wide for the spread-out crescent of strikers to hold against the surging throng of strikebreakers the way the Greeks had held the pass at Thermopylae against the far larger Persian army. Neither were the strikers hardened Spartan warriors who had been trained since early boyhood in the art of being professional warriors.

As the two groups closed in on the darkling plain inside the front gate of the plant, a hail of bricks, rocks, and bottles went up from the strikers into the crowded mass of strikebreakers. One strikebreaker went down after being hit in the head by a brick. After the opening salvo, the hail of rubble more or less ceased. The strikers had brought their own projectiles to throw. There were no paving blocks to be pulled up and tossed. There were no loose broken concrete chunks to be turned into succeeding volleys. After the initial volley, there was nothing more on hand to be thrown. From there on, the issue and the day would be decided at close and personal range.

Starting from the center and moving down the lines on either side, the two groups merged together into a wild melee of flailing arms and swinging instruments of battery. As the strikers rushed forward, the closing yards on Samuel's part of the line opened up a bit, allowing Samuel more room to swing around in. Probably most of the hired alley thugs Samuel was rushing toward were experienced in street-style assault and battery. For all he knew, a few of them were experienced in the act of murder. The only one on the side of the strikers experienced at killing and who had an instinct for killing was Samuel.

Samuel didn't flail away with his ax handle, swinging it over his head like a sledgehammer or a baseball bat with his hands close together on one end. Instead he held it with his hands apart as if it were a jousting staff. Samuel had always been inspired by the story of Robin Hood standing on the log over the stream, fighting it out with Little John with walking staffs. In the story, the heftier-built Little John clobbers Robin Hood and sends him sprawling into the stream. The outcome, with Robin being vanquished by Little John, was acceptable to the story as both Robin Hood and Little John were proverbial good guys who became fast friends afterward. The men Samuel was facing were not noble outlaws robbing from the rich to give to the poor. If anything, they were helping to rob from the poor and give to the rich bosses who had hired them. Samuel had no desire to make friends with any of them. Neither did he particularly think of himself as a noble industrial-era Robin Hood. That day, all the not so little Samuel Martin wanted to do by any other name was to be a head-cracking Little John.

As a baseball player, Samuel, it was said, had an arm like a rocket. He also had the reflexes for fast plays. He could field a ball in the air with the ease of a swallow catching an insect in flight, and he could scoop up a ground ball with the ease of an eagle snatching a fish off the surface of a lake. In almost the same motion, he could pivot and throw a runner out while he was still a length from reaching base. And he never balked in a pinch.

A strikebreaker swung a club made from a long piece of iron pipe over his head in a high sweeping arc, aimed at Samuel's head. The strikebreaker apparently thought that the long arc of the swing would allow him to build up momentum and deliver a smashing blow. But the wide and sweeping motion was too long for close-quarter fighting. It gave Samuel all the time he needed to react and counter the move.

Still holding his ax handle staff in a wide grip, Robin Hood style, Samuel, in a quick defensive move, brought the ax handle up in front of him, holding it out at an angle over and in front of his head. The iron pipe club bounced harmlessly off the ax handle. The only force Samuel felt from the blow was a slight sting in his hands when the pipe hit and bounced off. The feeling reminded Samuel of the sting he felt in his hands when he hit a pitched baseball on some part of the bat other than the sweet spot, where the physics transferred all the force of the swing into the ball and none of it wastefully down the length of the bat. That's how home runs were hit.

The failed blow left the strikebreaker with his hands near the bottom end of the pipe, too low to be in a good defensive position. Before the man could raise his hands to strike again, Samuel swung the ax handle around horizontally in single-staff fighting style. He caught the strikebreaker hard on the side of his head, in the area of the temple, with a smashing blow that spun the man's head to the side. Stunned to the edge of consciousness, the man dropped his pipe club; took one staggering step to the side, trying to turn away; and collapsed on the ground between the feet of his fellow strikebreakers who were trying to press in. The man behind him had a billy club in his hand. Before the man could raise it, he tripped over his fallen alley fighter comrade and partially lost his balance.

Samuel used the opening to swing the ax handle back horizontally in the reverse direction. With an equally well-aimed swing, he caught the strikebreaker with an equally hard shot to the side of his jaw. The man dropped his billy club and fell back, holding his broken jaw in both hands. Like he had done with the street thugs who had tried to rob him, Samuel pressed his attack on the others around, pressing forward to attack and then falling back to the line of strikers when his aggressiveness threatened to carry him in too deep and leave him isolated and surrounded in the line of strikebreakers.

For his part, Rufus held his 2×4 board and swung it from side to side the same way that Samuel held and swung his ax handle. But the heavy board was unwieldly and couldn't be swung as quickly and precisely as Samuel's ax handle. Rufus was only a few years older than Samuel. He had the agility of youth and the strength of one who had built up his muscle by hefting and moving heavy sides of beef. The strikebreakers in front of him ducked and moved back. He didn't connect as much as Samuel did, but the strikebreakers facing him were more than a little surprised and disconcerted by his show of resistance in standing his ground and by his apparent fearlessness. They had rather assumed that a nigger would always run away from a white man.

In one small area of the otherwise hard-pressed line of strikers, a concave bulge developed in the line of strikebreakers. They were held back in the face of the two whirlwinds flailing away at them. Elsewhere the line was faltering in the face of the onslaught of the toughs and the professional headbreakers the company owners and plant foreman had sent in to break up the strike and route the strikers. That part of the line, gathered to the side of the Kraznapolskis, was made up of older workers, mostly cutters and beef boners. They knew knives, but knives weren't the weapon of the day. Clubs, bats, and lengths of metal pipe were. Neither were they adept at street fighting like the street punks the bosses had organized and paid to break the strike. Unseen by Samuel, standing his position and flattening strikebreakers along with Rufus, that part of the line was flexing and being pushed back.

Anchored on one end by Samuel and Rufus, the strike line was holding. An extra measure of fierceness was added to the power of Samuel's arms when the thought came to his mind that the bosses who ran Packingtown, sitting safely in their boardrooms, dressed in their crisp, tailored business suits, keeping their hands clean, keeping their distance, keeping themselves safely out of the fray they had called down through the strong-arm punks they had called in, were little different in kind from Harold Ethridge, the one difference being that Ethridge had done his own killing. The bosses kept themselves out of sight, relying on their Fagins in the form of the street thugs they had hired to break the strike.

By splitting the heads and breaking the jaws of their paid muscle, Samuel felt that he was doing justice for the strikers. He also felt that, by extension, he was vicariously delivering one small extra bit of justice for the girl, belated as it was, belated as everything he had tried to do for her had been. He had tried to win the girl's love, but her love had been buried too deep under a thick layer of scar tissue. Like his sister, Beth, he had come to wonder if there was anything in her heart but scars.

He had loved the girl. He had extended his love toward her with his hand out to her, but she had kept her hand lowered and had turned away. He had tried to defend her physically, but he had gotten his one act of physical defense of her backward, and it had blown up in his face. In the end it had driven her farther from him. The one critical time his defense of her would have made the difference, he hadn't been there with her. He couldn't have prevented her death, but he still blamed himself for his bumbling that had put the distance between him and her and had allowed Ethridge the opening to kill her. He didn't prevent her murder. All he had been able to do was avenge her killing. Even that he had bungled. The result was that he had to leave her buried, leave the home he had hoped to have with her behind, leave the home and family he had, and go on the run, a run that had taken him away from the home he had known and that had brought him to the possibly mortal slaughterhouse yard fight he was in. As he cracked the heads of strikebreakers and sent them sprawling and staggering, Samuel had to admit to himself that he hadn't been very good at protecting women in mortal danger.

In the next instant, Samuel found himself having to defend a woman in mortal danger.

Not far off to his side, Samuel heard a short but piercing scream. It was a woman's scream. He looked over to see Mrs. Kraznapolski go down, struck on the side of her head by a strikebreaker swinging a four-foot length of iron pipe. As she fell, Samuel heard Mr. Kraznapolski cry out her name in alarm. He was involved in a close-quarter slugging and blocking match with another strikebreaker and couldn't move to help his wife. If he turned to help her, he would be instantly knocked down himself.

In the fast-moving instant as Samuel watched, the strikebreaker raised his pipe and swung it at the head and upturned face of the fallen Mrs. Kraznapolski. In an instinctive move, she partially blocked the blow with her wrist, but part of the swing landed on her forehead. The blow looked strong enough to have broken her wrist. The next blow would fracture her skull.

As Samuel watched, transfixed, a strikebreaker rushed at him from the line. Seeing the move coming, Samuel delivered a savage straight-in side kick to the man's stomach. The strikebreaker fell backward, giving Samuel opportunity and room to move. In a quick move, he pulled the big derringer-style gun out of his pocket. He had brought it with him but had not intended to use it unless one of his friends was facing an imminent threat. The strikebreaker standing over Mrs. Kraznapolski raised his iron pipe, quickly gathering strength to deliver a shattering blow. As he did so, Mrs. Kraznapolski screamed. But it wasn't her whom Samuel heard scream. It was the girl he heard scream as Harold Ethridge broke her neck. As the strikebreaker reached the apex of his swing, Samuel leveled the gun.

The blast of the short-barreled heavy-caliber gun ripped through the melee, even louder than the noise of the fight. A spurt of blood and goo erupted from the man's left eye socket. Encountering little resistance from the eye itself, the bullet passed through the eye socket and entered the man's brain. The soft tissue of the brain provided little resistance either. The bullet passed through the brain and exploded out the back of the man's head with a larger spray of blood, gore, and cranial material. The man crumpled and fell backward. He was basically already dead when he hit the pavement.

Samuel quickly releveled the gun and fired the second barrel of the over–under barrel arrangement at the man behind the man attacking Mr. Kraznapolski. For a second time the blast of the gun sounded above the verbal din of battle. Though Samuel had aimed at the man's head as he had aimed at the first man, this time his aim was a little lower, so the result was not quite as deadly. The bullet shattered the man's lower jaw, smashing a gap in his jawbone, blowing out several of his teeth and gouging a large gash in the man's jaw, disfiguring him for life. The man grabbed his smashed jaw then turned and ran into the crowd of strikebreakers.

Realizing they were coming under close-range gunfire, the strikebreakers turned and ran. Their line crumbled, unzipping and scattering in both directions from the center, where the two strikebreakers had been shot. Though he had more bullets in his pocket, Samuel didn't stop to reload. Instead he ran over to where Mrs. Kraznapolski lay on the ground. With the retreat of the strikebreakers, Mr. Kraznapolski and Samuel were able to help Mrs. Kraznapolski back to her feet. She held her wrist as if it was painful. Possibly it had been fractured by the blow the strikebreaker had aimed at her head and that she had blocked with her arm. If Samuel's timely intervention hadn't stopped the strikebreaker from hitting her in the head with his iron pipe, she might not have gotten up ever again.

Both Mr. Kraznapolski and Samuel started to ask the standing Mrs. Kraznapolski if she was all right. Before either of them could say anything, a fusillade of gunshots ripped through the air behind them. Samuel looked down the line of strikers, expecting to see people dropping on all sides around him, but no one fell. He turned quickly and looked in the direction from which the shooting was coming. The police were moving toward them, walking forward in a line, firing their pistols in the air.

The strikers turned and ran, heading toward the back of the yard. Samuel ran together with the Kraznapolskis. It was them he was afraid for. Samuel assumed that it was the shots he had fired at the strikebreakers who were beating the Kraznapolskis that had prompted the police response. He was facing the opposite way and didn't see that the policemen were firing into the air. For all he knew, a bullet might lodge in his back any second, or in the backs of other strikers. Samuel was deathly afraid that his actions may have set off another Haymarket Square massacre of strikers.

With the routing of the strikers, the police fired no more. Their directive had been to act as backup for the strikebreakers as the latter did the job they had been hired to do and to step in and make arrests of strikers if the strikebreakers found themselves being hard-pressed and it looked like they were losing. The police otherwise were under strict political orders not to fire into the crowd unless they themselves were under imminent threat of frontal attack. Their only interest was in clearing the strikers out of the main grounds of the packinghouse plant if the strikebreakers were unable to do so. That having been accomplished, the police stopped at the back end of the yard and did not pursue the fleeing strikers any further. No one was shot in the back. When the police returned to the front of the yard, they found two men dead: a striker who had been killed by a hard blow to the head, and the man Samuel had shot. They would be the only murders recorded that day.

The running strikers passed through the back of the plant, going past the cattle pens, past the railyard, and out the back of the plant. Once beyond the back boundary of the plant, they started to disperse, everyone heading to his own home or apartment of residence. Samuel stayed with Mr. and Mrs. Kraznapolski. Somewhere along the line he lost track of Rufus. He didn't see which way he had gone. He assumed that Rufus would circle back to where he was living in Bronzeville. But Samuel would never find out where he had gone or what subsequent fate befell him. He never saw Rufus again.

"Is it broken?" Mr. Kraznapolski asked as Mara wrapped his wife's wrist with a heavy dishcloth used for a bandage. They had made it safely back to the Kraznapolski house without being followed or seen.

"Not broken," Mara said as she finished wrapping the makeshift bandage. "Perhaps cracked."

She finished tying off the dishtowel bandage. When she was done, she looked at her sister-in-law. "Don't try to use it until it heals all the way and there is no more pain. If you work it before then, any break will just get worse."

"I don't think either of us is going to be working it at the packing plant anymore," Mr. Kraznapolski said. "They'll be on the lookout for anyone who was in the strike." He looked at Mara. "Mara here wasn't in on the strike. She may still have a job. But for all I know, they may fire everyone on the rolls now and start all over, hiring all new workers. They won't have a whole lot of trouble with that. There are plenty of unemployed people and former workers at the plant who were fired in the past but who will jump to get a job there at any wage."

"I'm sorry," Samuel blurted out. "I shouldn't have done what I did when I shot the man."

"If you didn't, my wife would be lying dead on the ground in the front yard of the plant, where the breaker would have beaten her to death. You kept my wife alive and brought her back to me. I thank you for that." He looked at Samuel. "Did you kill the man you shot?"

"I think so," Samuel said. "The shot hit him in the head. I assume it killed him." Samuel was becoming something of an expert at head shot kills.

"Do you still have the gun?" Mr. Kraznapolski asked.

"Yes."

"Get rid of it," Mr. Kraznapolski said. "Don't let them catch you with it. If they catch you with it, they will know it was you. They will try you for murder. Throw it in the river on your way out of the city."

Mara looked at her brother. "What are you saying?" she asked. "Are you throwing him out?"

"He's right," Samuel said, before Mr. Kraznapolski could answer. "I have to get out of the city. I especially have to get out of this house. I don't know if they know who fired the shot. I don't know if they know who I am or where I live. But if they work it out, they'll come here looking for me. If I'm not here, you can say that I never came back after the strike."

Mara looked at him and then back to her brother. "Can't we hide him here?" she asked. "No one has to know."

"I can't stay and hide out here forever," Samuel said. "If they work out who I am and if I stay anywhere around here, I'll eventually be spotted. If they catch me here, they'll bring all of you in as part of it. I'm not going to get all of you involved. The sooner I go, the less chance they'll know who I am and the less chance that they'll put me together with you."

"Where is he going to go?" Mara asked, looking from Samuel to her brother. There was more in her tone than just curiosity.

Mr. Kraznapolski looked at Samuel. "Go to the west side of the city," he said, "to the railroad tracks. Get on a train going north. Go up to Milwaukee and live there." He paused as if reconsidering. "That might be too close to Chicago. The police here might give your description and tell the police in Milwaukee to be looking for you. Better still, go to Texas like I said and become a cowboy. They say Billy the Kid did the same after he killed a man in New York and had to run out of the city. If the West was far enough for him to go, it will be far enough away for you. Go to California and work the goldfields there, if there's any gold left in the state. Go to the forests of Washington State and become a logger. Go to Alaska and become a gold miner. Go to sea and become a sailor."

Samuel had already considered the option of becoming a sailor on the Great Lakes and had decided against it. The ocean was a whole lot bigger. And rougher.

"Go somewhere so far away, they'll never find you or even think to look for you. I'll give you some money for train fare."

Samuel caught a vision of his father standing outside the train, hanging his head in sorrow as the train pulled out of the station.

"I have some money," Samuel said. "You don't need to give me any. If you can't go back to the plant, you're going to need all the money you have to tide you over until you get work somewhere."

It was sort of a lie. Samuel did have a few dollars in his pocket and to his name, but he doubted it would be enough to buy him a train ticket to Milwaukee or even Kenosha, let alone California. The financial limitations that had dogged his every step since he had run away from home and that had led him to Packingtown now threatened to chain his feet to the streets of the city he might have to go back to living on. But that was the only reality that Samuel could see in the narrowing prism of the moment.

"I give you money anyway," Mr. Kraznapolski said.

In a day when reality had come down like a hammer all around, another hard thought came down on Samuel. "What's going to become of all of you?" he asked. "If you can't get work, especially if you're blackballed and put on a list, how are you going to live?"

"If that happens, we'll work it out somehow," Mr. Kraznapolski answered. "We've worked it out before. We'll do it again. Don't worry about us. Worry about getting yourself away to somewhere they can't find you."

"You say I'm like a son to you," Samuel went on. "You've become a family to me. Family members stay with one another. They help one another. If I leave, I can't help you in any way."

"You can't help any of us in this house," Mr. Kraznapolski said, "yourself included, if you're in prison. Especially if you're on death row. Better to ride a freight train than ride the electric chair."

Mara looked at Samuel again. "You have been like a member of the family. I hate to see you go. But I'd hate far more to see you go out that way. Or go on locked up in prison for life. But you can't do anything here. What you going to do if the police come, shoot it out with them with two barrels and hold them off forever? You can't take on the whole world with a gun."

Mr. Kraznapolski glanced toward the front door as if he expected it would burst open the next instant and a flood of police would come surging through it and into the house. "I'm not trying to run you out in order to save our skins," he said, turning back to Samuel. "But you'd better go now before the word gets all over the city and they will be watching for you."

"I'll grab my extra pants and shirt," Samuel said, resigned. "It won't take me more than a minute." When it came to running, he already knew how to travel light.

"I have an old suitcase you can use," Mrs. Kraznapolski said.

"No," Mr. Kraznapolski said. "If you use a suitcase, you will look like someone trying to leave town. It might arouse suspicion. Carry what you take in a cloth bag. That way you will look like a hobo or a migrant worker coming into town. You can slip out of town with less chance that you'll be reported if the cops start asking if anyone saw someone suspicious-looking trying to leave the city."

Up in the attic room where he had lived in the Kraznapolski house, in the room where he had dreamed of his home in Ohio, in the room where he had dreamed of a home of any kind, in the room where he had dreamed of Clarinda and had seen her face in the dark, in the room where he had made love to Mara, Samuel gathered up his single change of extra clothes and put them in the cloth bag Mrs. Kraznapolski had given him. He concealed the gun under the clothes at the bottom of the bag. He left behind his collection of dime novel Wild West stories printed on pulp paper. At the door, he turned and looked at the room that had been one more temporary way station of his life on the run. Then he turned and left the room for the last time.

"Though we'd love to have you stay with us forever, if you're going to have any future of your own, a future without cops on your tail, a future without jail, you're going to have to get going and put distance between you and here," Mr. Kraznapolski said when Samuel came back down the stairs.

"Wouldn't it be better if he waited until it was dark?" Mara asked. "That way he wouldn't have as much of a chance of being seen."

In the short moment he had to think about it, Samuel wondered if she was just being cautious or if she wanted to keep him with her a little longer.

"Not as many trains run at night as during the day," Mr. Kraznapolski said. "He would have to walk the streets until day. Robbers and muggers walk the streets at night. If he was seen walking around in the dark, it might arouse more suspicion than if he was seen in the day. Those who see him at night may report him to the police at first light of dawn. They might start looking for him and find him before he can board a train."

"He's right," Samuel said. "Though I'd love to stay with you forever, if I stay here and the cops find me here, you might get dragged in as accessories to a crime and for harboring a fugitive. I can't let that happen to you. I have to go now."

"May God be with you," Mrs. Kraznapolski said. "May He one day bring you back together, if not with us, then with those you love."

Without any further words exchanged or offered by anyone, Samuel turned and walked out the door. Mr. and Mrs. Kraznapolski turned away and went deeper into the house. Mara stood there a while longer, looking at the door.

Samuel walked quickly away from the Kraznapolski house. As he went, he didn't look back at the house that for him had become the closest thing to a home and at the people in it, who had become the closest thing to family since he had left his home and family in Ohio. Once again Samuel found himself leaving his home behind and heading out to somewhere he didn't know. He didn't even have a fixed destination in mind. He didn't even have a vision of where he would be going.

Once again, Samuel was leaving a lover behind, the difference being that this time he was leaving a live lover behind. For Samuel and Mara, their love had been an affair of convenience, a passing love affair carved for a moment in time out of the hard necessities they were caught up in. Their love hadn't been an epic. Their love hadn't been sublime. Their love hadn't been a profanity. That the love they had temporarily shared had come to an end the way it had wasn't a tragedy. It was what had to be in the face of what was and what couldn't be.

But Mara had been a lover to him, a lover he had welcomed into his heart as much as into his bed. Now he was a lover departing. She was a lover left behind. Their parting wasn't a grand lovers' parting scene. It wasn't a sorrowful scene out of a cloying romance novel that romantically minded women readers, holding handkerchiefs in their hands, would cry over as they read. It was the quiet and wordless parting of two disparate lovers who knew they would never see each other again.

Samuel left Packingtown heading east on Forty-Ninth Street, skirting the south side of the dangerous Irish slum of Canaryville. When he came to the Penn Central railroad tracks, he followed them north. He stayed with the tracks, figuring far fewer people would see him walking down a rail line than would see him walking a major street or even a side street. The tracks skirted the western side of what was then known as the Black Belt, the area that hemmed in the bulk of the Negro population. It was also known as Bronzeville, the area where Rufus lived. As Samuel passed by, he wondered again what had become of Rufus.

Where the tracks left the Black Belt, they crossed the south fork of the

Chicago River. The tracks crossed the river over a railroad bridge. There was no footbridge over the river in that area back then. There still isn't. Samuel moved quickly across the bridge, hoping a train would not come by and possibly knock him off the bridge and into the river. Fortunately no train appeared rumbling toward him down the track. Halfway across the bridge, following Mr. Kraznapolski's instructions, he pulled the gun out of the bottom of his ditty bag and tossed it into the river, along with the extra ammunition he was carrying. If he was nabbed by the police for some reason, at least they wouldn't find the gun on him.

Once over the bridge, Samuel turned west for a short distance to Canal Street. At Canal Street he turned north, intent on getting to Union Station, west of the city center. His thought at that moment was to jump a freight train heading north to Milwaukee. But as he went, the idea of going to Milwaukee started to seem a chancy one. The Chicago police could have wired the Milwaukee police by telegraph or called them on the phone to be on the lookout for anyone who matched his description. He could end up being picked up in a short while.

Samuel dropped the idea of going to Milwaukee, but he kept on pushing to get to Union Station, from where he had first entered the city. He didn't know whether he could hop a freight to anywhere from Union Station. He didn't even know if they ran freights out of Union Station or whether it was purely a passenger station. He would find out when he got there. If it was a passenger terminal only, he didn't think he could easily hop a passenger train, what with sharp-eyed conductors punching tickets. If it was a passenger terminal only, he would have to backtrack and find a freight yard somewhere to hop a freight train going to somewhere, anywhere far from the city where he figured he would soon become a wanted man, if he wasn't already. As for jumping a freight, Samuel had no experience. He had ridden into the city on a passenger car on a ticket his father had bought for him. In all his exile, he had never jumped a train. He had no experience at being a hobo. He figured he could learn, but at the moment he didn't even know where the hobo jungles were located.

As he proceeded to where he knew not, Samuel ran Mr. Kraznapolski's suggestion that he should go to Texas and become a cowboy around in his mind. Several problems with that presented themselves right away. Though he knew horses, the horses he had known and grown up with were plow horses. He hadn't ever ridden them. He didn't think he could reinvent himself as a cowhand skilled in fast-paced horsemanship, riding, and roping. To be good at it you have to start learning at a young age. He more or less believed the old saying that true cowboys learned to ride before they learned to stand. Samuel figured that he was too old to start learning cowboy skills and that, if he tried, he would never become proficient in them.

But Texas had farms as well as cattle ranches. They probably needed farmhands in Texas and Oklahoma as much as in Ohio and Illinois. Halfway through the city and halfway through his deliberations, Samuel more or less figured that this would be an efficacious time to put his idea of going back to farming and becoming a farmhand into practice. Illinois was a wheat-producing state. Along with corn, his father and he had grown wheat on the family farm. Samuel knew wheat and how to grow it. Along with Texas and Oklahoma, Samuel considered Nebraska, Kansas, Missouri, and Iowa. They were all farm states that were also big wheat producers.

The question was where to go to become a farmhand. That translated to what state he should go to. Samuel initially thought to go to downstate Illinois, but that was in the same state as Chicago. He had just killed a man in Chicago. If his name and description got out in the big city and state newspapers, he could be spotted in Illinois and arrested. With the proliferation of newspapers and police information outlets disseminating information and wanted posters across state lines, Samuel figured that to be safe, his better bet would be to look for a farmhand job in a collar state such as Indiana, Wisconsin, or Iowa.

But Indiana and Wisconsin shared common borders with Illinois, borders that information and arrest bulletins on police department boards and wanted posters flowed across. They were too close for comfort. Even Michigan, whose shores he had looked wistfully toward over the lake and where he had considered going the day of the prestrike rally, might have been too close for safety.

As he walked his calculated course toward the place from which he intended to depart the city, Samuel calculated that to be safe he would have to head for a state farther away from Chicago or any of the midwestern states. Ohio especially. He still didn't want to venture too far from his home, which he still had hopes of sneaking back to, but the concern of the moment was to put at least a reasonable distance between himself and Chicago.

The song "On the Sunny Side of the Street" hadn't been written as of yet. As he walked to the west, Samuel kept himself in the shade on the south side of the street. He got the idea of going all the way north to Canada. From his high school geography classes, Samuel was vaguely aware that the central provinces of Canada, like Alberta and Manitoba, were also wheat-producing regions. Maybe he could get a job on a farm there. Maybe Canada was far enough removed from the police force of Chicago and Ohio for him to be safe enough to relax and unwind. Maybe he would be far enough removed from his past and his past life that he could go back to using his real name. If he eventually came to end his life there, at least he could be buried under his own name, unlike Clarinda, buried under a name that wasn't her own. He still didn't know her name, and now he probably never would. She had come in from somewhere unknown outside of his hometown. She had walked the streets of his hometown under a name that wasn't hers. She had died and been buried under that name.

Now it was Samuel who was walking unfamiliar streets under a name that wasn't his. He didn't even have his identity as a packinghouse worker anymore. The only identity he would leave in Chicago would be as an unknown gunman who killed a strikebreaker, that is, if he managed to get out of the city.

When he had come to Chicago, he had walked through a big door. What he had found on the other side of the door hadn't proven to be as friendly or kindly as the promise. But there had been something there to hold on to. When you slam a big door shut behind you, you often find yourself outside of anything recognizable, alone in a barren land. Now Samuel was on the barren streets he had started out on. The road ahead might prove to be narrower and rockier than the streets he had survived in the city.

For the moment, the city street he was on was becoming problematic in its own way. Ahead of him, Samuel saw a cop standing his beat on a corner. Two-way police radio hadn't been invented yet. Samuel didn't know if the policeman had even been informed that there had been a riot at the packinghouse gate and that there was a rogue union gunman on the loose he should keep a lookout for. Not willing to risk any chance by passing close to the policeman, Samuel changed direction at the nearest corner and walked west down the block. He figured that at the next intersection he would turn back to the resume his path to Union Station. Whether he could exit the city from there, he didn't know. Whether he exited the city or not, where he would go from there, he still didn't know.

When the cop was out of sight and behind him, Samuel turned north again and headed up the nameless block he was on, a nondescript-looking block of small businesses and first-floor shops with tenement apartments on the floors above. The street was a random street in what for Samuel had become a random walk through life. But, as the man who had encountered Samuel in the bar had found out, as Samuel learned when he had met Clarinda, sometimes random encounters can set the tone and direction for your life.

In the middle of the block or thereabouts, out of the corner of his eye, Samuel caught sight of a ground-level wall sign. The sign was brightly colored. It was the single brightest collection of colors amid the drab colors of the block, bright enough to catch Samuel's otherwise distracted eyes. He stopped moving and stood in place, looking at the picture. The sign was a colorful full-sized lithograph of a smiling soldier dressed in a clean, creased natty dress uniform. At his waist, the figure wore a dress saber. The upper left corner of his tunic was filled with medals. Above the man's head, printed in bold letters, was an exhortation to join for the prestige, for the adventure, and for the opportunity to see the world.

Samuel looked up from the colorful poster to the door it was mounted next to. Above the nondescript-looking door in the nondescript and bland-looking building was a long rectangular sign announcing that the office behind the door was a United States Marine Corps recruiting center.

In Samuel's years as an Ohio farm boy, for all practical purposes, Chicago had been a distant foreign country to him. Ironically, the US Marine Corps hadn't been as foreign to him. His distant cousin had been in the marines. His marine unit had been part of the international contingent that had been sent in to rescue the diplomats and foreigners besieged by fanatical Chinese nationalists in the old imperial city compound in the Chinese capital of Beijing during the Boxer Rebellion.

Samuel had never seriously contemplated leaving the farm he had been born on to see the world by joining some kind of foreign legion or mercenary outfit. Now he found himself standing outside the door of an organization that promised to be just exactly that to him. Looking at the recruiting poster, he didn't see the Marine Corps as a vehicle that would take him on an adventure to see the world. But it did present itself as a vehicle that he could hide out in, a vehicle that could take him far away, away from danger and from his memories.

It was also a way to put a great deal of distance between himself and the justice systems of two states.

For some time the otherwise motion-oriented Samuel stood looking at the recruiting poster. In a city where all roads led either to jail or out of the city, he found himself looking at a way out. The idealized marine in clean clothes in the lithographed drawing seemed well-fed and well provided for. The picture the poster presented seemed appealing. In the service, Samuel would have a guaranteed three square meals a day. Maybe it would be a sour mess sergeant slapping beans down onto a metal dinner plate, but it would be a set dinner. In the service he would have a roof over his head and a bed to sleep in. Maybe it would be a bunk bed with a thin mattress in a barracks, but it would keep the rain off and enough of the cold out for him to be able to sleep. As a hobo on the open road, he would be back to sleeping in alleys and basements, back to eating out of charity lines when he could find one and out of garbage cans when he couldn't find one. The Marine Corps would take him away from all that. It would also take him away from sharp-eyed cops who recognized his description. The only price he would pay for it would be that he would have to put up with a few bellowing sergeants and an endless regimen of drill and inspection.

The other price he might have to pay would be that he might find himself being shot at. The corollary price to that was that he might find himself having to shoot back and possibly kill someone. But Samuel figured he was already an expert at that. That particular skill was exactly what the corps was looking for. He was already self-trained in the art of killing. In that sense, the corps could save themselves the cost of training him.

Whatever immediate material needs being in the corps might provide, it otherwise could provide very useful cover and concealment. Samuel figured that the US Marine Corps would be one of the last places that police would look for a labor radical. Being in the corps would probably take him far from the city. It might even get him out of the country. Samuel didn't know how long a term of enlistment in the Marine Corps was. He assumed it was for several years. That just might be long enough for the heat to die down from his killing of the strikebreaker and Harold Ethridge. After that he could go back to his original plan to return and live in hiding on the periphery of his home and near his family.

As Samuel looked at the bright colors of the recruiting poster, all other paths seemed drab, dark, and fraught with danger of discovery, without form or end in their endlessness. He wondered if that had been the same thing Clarinda was feeling when she had come into the town and first looked at Mrs. Richardson's house.

Samuel saw no sufficient reason not to check it out. At least being inside the recruitment office for a short while would keep him off the street and out of the prying sight of cops. Samuel shifted the makeshift carrying bag on his shoulder and walked through the door and into the building.

Inside the door was a small wood-floored office with another door that led to a back room. Except for being smaller, the recruiting office reminded Samuel of the police station in his hometown. A middle-aged man dressed in what looked to Samuel to be an officer's uniform sat at a desk on one side of the room. A younger-looking man in what looked to be an enlisted man's uniform sat at another desk across from him. Without further ado or any ado, Samuel walked up to the desk of the officer type.

"Are you looking for men to sign up at the moment?" Samuel said as if he were back at the packing plant, asking if they had any openings. For all Samuel knew, the military had their off-seasons when things were slow and they weren't currently hiring.

"The corps is always on the lookout for good men who want to join up," the officer said in a friendly PR voice. He looked Samuel up and down as if he doing a troop inspection.

As the officer gave him the once-over, Samuel wondered about his appearance. He was disheveled from his fight at the plant gate. But fortunately he had avoided being hit in the face in a way that would have left telltale indications that he had only recently been involved in a fight or had just come from committing some form of violence. Which he had. It might have made the officer suspect that he was trying to enlist because he was a fugitive running from the law. Which he was, on two counts. It could prompt the officer to call in the police. What Samuel hoped the officer saw was a strong and healthy-looking late teenage boy who otherwise appeared to be a bit down on his luck but was anxious for adventure and to see the world. Prime recruiting material. But he didn't know what the officer was seeing. The issue hung in doubt.

"You look like just the type we're looking for," the officer said. Samuel relaxed a bit. "How old are you?"

"I just turned nineteen not long ago," Samuel said.

"Why are you thinking of joining the corps?" the officer asked in a rhetorical tone. Samuel tensed again. "I'm not trying to talk you out of enlisting," the man went on. "I just want you to be sure that enlisting is something you've made up your mind about all the way, that it's not something you're doing on a lark and it's not an impulse decision that you may regret later. Marine Corps training can be tough. Marine Corps life can be tough too sometimes. It's designed to be so. Neither you nor the corps will benefit if you become a soldier who deserts. … We in the corps consider ourselves to be an elite fighting force with a long history. Are you looking to join the corps because you're looking to be part of an elite fighting unit and for the chance to see the world, or are you just looking for a meal ticket?"

The US Marine Corps is generally not given to disarmament, but Samuel figured that a little disarming honesty would be the best way to get around the question.

"I can't deny that's part of it," Samuel said. "I'm broke and alone. I originally came from a farm on the western side of the state of Wisconsin. My mother has been dead for a long time. My father died recently. The bank took the farm because neither Father nor I could pay the debt. I don't have any living relatives I could go to live with and work for. I tried to find work in both Milwaukee and Chicago, but I wasn't having a lot of luck. I admit that one of the reasons I'm looking to join is because I'll have more in the way of something to eat and a place to stay than I've been finding walking the streets."

The officer believed him. He had heard other similar hard-luck stories before.

At that juncture, Samuel thought it might help if he claimed to be a bit of a marine legacy.

"I do have a distant connection to the corps. One of my distant relatives was in the Marine Corps during the Boxer Rebellion. I forget what unit he was in, but he marched halfway across China with the corps."

Samuel was exaggerating for effect. The marines hadn't marched halfway across China. China is a big country. The march was a relatively short march from the port of disembarkation on the shore of the Yellow Sea to Beijing, which is a comparatively short distance inland. The term *gung-ho* was originally a Chinese term. It hadn't been picked up by the corps as of that date. Samuel wanted the man to think he was ready and willing to duplicate his distant cousin's feat.

"I think I have a lot I can offer the corps. I'm the right age. I'm ready and able to go the distance. And I'm a country boy. I know the outdoors. I know guns. I know how to shoot. I figure the Marine Corps is looking for men who know how to shoot." Samuel did know how to shoot a variety of guns, shotguns and derringers in particular.

"The corps will teach you how to shoot the marine way," the officer said.

"Where do they send marines for training?" Samuel asked. "That navy base north of the city?"

To Samuel that could create a problem. If he were to be stationed so close to Chicago, where he had just killed a man not more than two hours earlier, he could be discovered and arrested.

"Parris Island," the officer said.

"Is that in France?" Samuel said, catching a vision of a quick time march around the base of the Eiffel Tower.

"Not quite," the officer said. "That's Parris with two *r*'s. It's in South Carolina. It's near the ocean, but I can assure you it's nothing like the Riviera."

Samuel figured he'd never see France, but South Carolina was a long way from Chicago. It seemed as far away as California. He doubted the Chicago police would find him or even look for him there.

As part of his enlistment pep talk, the officer outlined how marines were stationed all over the world. To Samuel, the idea of putting an ocean between himself and Chicago was a more comforting thought than just putting a single state or Lake Michigan between him and the Chicago cops.

"If I sign up, how long do I have to wait before I ship out?" Samuel asked. "A week? A month? I don't have anyplace to stay or much of any money to eat with. If you only take an allotment once a month, I'm going to be chewing shoe leather by then."

Samuel figured he could live on the streets for a few days if he had to. But he also figured that if the police identified him, they would launch a massive search for him, including the flophouses and charity houses. If he had to knock around for several days trying to stay out of sight, he could be spotted. To get away he would be forced to resume his flight on foot. He would be right back where he had started.

"Actually we have a contingent that's scheduled to leave from here today in a couple of hours," the recruiting officer said. "You could go out with the detachment scheduled to leave today. You'd have sign up right now. Are you ready to go, or do you want to think about it?"

The die had been pretty much cast before Samuel had seen the recruiting station or had even thought about joining the service. Then again, there weren't a lot of promising dice within reach for him to grab and roll.

"I've got nothing to go back to and nothing to go forward to," Samuel said. "If the corps wants me, they've got me."

It wasn't exactly the biggest display of gung-ho spoken or witnessed in a marine recruiting center, but the recruiting officer looked gratified. "Okay," he said, pointing to the younger-looking soldier at the desk across from his. "See Corporal Prescott. He'll sign you up and administer the oath."

Samuel nodded and walked over to the other desk. The corporal behind the desk motioned to Samuel to sit down. From a side drawer in the desk, he produced an official-looking form larger than the employment card Samuel had filled out at the packing plant.

"Name?" the corporal asked.

By that time Samuel had become quite proficient at making up names for himself. It was a skill he had picked up from the girl. Whether the corps would appreciate him enlisting under a false name was something that Samuel, a.k.a. whatever he would make himself known to the corps as, didn't know or particularly care.

"Heisner," Samuel said. "Martin Heisner." Heisner was the name of his distant cousin who had served in the marines. Martin was his last name transposed as his first. At least he would hold on to part of the name he was born under and grew up with.

"Home address?" the corporal asked.

"Just put down Milwaukee," Samuel answered. "The farm I grew up on is gone. I started out living on the streets of Milwaukee before I came here. I just didn't live on any one particular street."

"Next of kin?" the corporal asked.

"None that are alive," Samuel answered. He lied. He could have claimed his parents as distant relatives, but he was afraid that if their names were recorded on his official papers, it could possibly raise questions that could get back to his real identity. That could be trouble for both him and his parents. As much as he wanted the one small connection to his former home and family, as much as he wanted to be sent home for burial in his family plot or next to the girl in the cemetery of his hometown if he was killed in action in the Halls of Montezuma or on the shores of Tripoli, or marching into China, Cuba, or the Philippines as earlier marines had done, Samuel did not want to take the chance of bringing trouble upon his family back home for helping him flee the law.

Then and there, Samuel resolved that if he died in the service, he would be buried as the girl had been, away from home and under the false name he had chosen for himself as she had died away from her home and had been buried under a name she had chosen for herself. He had hoped to transform the girl into a member of his family as well as being his lover. Instead she had transformed him into a version of herself. With his declaration of his name as Heisner, only the latest in a list of aliases he had gone by, the transformation was more or less complete. But this was where the finding of new aliases would probably stop. As Clarinda had lived out her short life in his hometown, then had died and been buried under the name she had given herself, he would probably carry the name he had given himself for the rest of his life and be buried under it—however long his life in the corps would be.

"If I get killed in action, the corps can just bury me where I drop. It will be no skin off either of our noses."

The corporal didn't press the issue.

"Where do I go now?" Samuel asked after the oath had been given and he had taken it.

"You can wait here," the officer said. "Or you can leave and walk around for a while if you like. Just be back here by four o'clock. At that time, a contingent of recruits will arrive from the Great Lakes naval base, led by a sergeant sent up from Parris Island, to escort you to camp. You'll ride out on a midnight run of the *City of New Orleans* train. ... Like I said, you can walk around until then. Just remember that you're now officially a recruit in the US Marine Corps. If you don't return, you'll be considered a deserter as much as if you ran away in battle.

For Samuel Martin, now Martin Heisner on his enlistment form, the timing of his leaving was good and soon enough. The less time spent in the city, the better. That he was going out by train could be a possible problem. Mr. Kraznapolski had cautioned him against going to train stations as the police might be watching them for wanted felons trying to leave the city. Though there might be a small risk of that, Samuel figured that being in a group of recruits being led by a sergeant would give him cover and concealment. Once through the train station, he would be gone and wouldn't be back.

In a way, Samuel had hoped that, instead of going south, the train would have headed east on the first leg of its run and would have passed through Columbus, Ohio. It wasn't that he was thinking of jumping off the train and deserting and running back to his hometown. It was simply that he would have sort of liked to backtrack in the direction he had taken the day he had left home for Chicago. In a way it would be like coming home. But he decided that, having been that close to home, it would be too painful when the train pulled out of the station, taking him away from home for the second time.

"If you want to stay here until the truck arrives, you can wait in there," the officer said, pointing to the back room. "It will be a couple of hours' wait. But you're going to run into that in the corps. It's the same in any branch of the service: Hurry up and wait. In the service you're going to find yourself standing in a whole lot of lines."

Until the military transport arrived, Samuel thought it would be best to stay off the street.

"Now you're ready to see the world courtesy of the United States Marine Corps," the corporal said.

"As far as getting into or getting a grip on the world goes," Samuel responded, "I once thought I had the world in my hand. Now the world belongs to somebody else, and I'm just standing in line."

Samuel turned and walked into the waiting room in the back. There was one other boy about his age in the room. They smiled at each other as Samuel sat down on one of the wooden benches along the wall, but neither of them said anything. Samuel didn't try to engage the boy in conversation. He had a lot on his mind. He figured the boy had a lot on his own mind.

The plain bare room wasn't all that different from the one in the bordello where he had met Katrin Kraznapolski. Both rooms served the same function: waiting rooms for those in a service in which lives were in limbo and bodies were extended and expended.

Samuel heard the familiar sound of a truck pulling up outside. A short while later he heard the front door open. From the front room, Samuel heard an unfamiliar voice say, "Got anyone for me today?" The officer indicated the back room. A moment after that, a proverbial bulldog of a sergeant dressed in a marine uniform strode into the room.

"All right, gentlemen," the sergeant rumbled in a drill sergeant's voice, "you're in the corps now. You're not on a milking stool or on your mama's lap. In the corps you move on your feet, not on your butts. So get off your dead asses and form up outside!"

Samuel rather assumed the sergeant was the one sent to escort them to the marine camp with the French-sounding name in the Dixie state of South Carolina.

Samuel and the other boy got up and walked out the back room door, and from there out the front door. Outside was a truck painted in a drab military color driven by a man in what looked a navy seaman's uniform. The sergeant motioned for them to get into the back of the truck. There were several more recruits sitting inside the truck.

"Don't stand there slack-jawed like a bunch of cows chewing their cud," the sergeant went on. "You're not ladies lined up for tea and cakes. Let's move like you've got a purpose here."

Samuel climbed in and sat down on the truck bed with the others. The sergeant climbed into the truck after Samuel and the other boy. The truck had canvas sides and a canvas roof cover. Only the back was open. At least the police wouldn't be able to spot him as they drove to the train station.

"For the information of you crowd of pansies, my name is Sergeant Arnold," the sergeant said as he walked between the rows of seated recruits. "I'll be escorting you namby-pamby mama's boys to the boot camp that will be your new home, where the corps will whips your butts into military shape. If you don't like me yelling at you and calling you names, know that I'm a choirboy compared to what you're going to be getting from the drill sergeants at camp. They'll turn you pissant maggots into marines. They'll work you down into a puddle of grease and put you back together as marine devil dogs. So let's get this show and you petunia-plucking pantywaists on the road."

At the front of the truck bed, the sergeant rapped on the back of the cab as a signal for the driver to go. The gears of the truck ground to life, and then the truck started moving. Samuel watched as the recruiting center, such as it was, fell away behind him. As the truck went down the street, he watched as the streets of Chicago dropped away. As the streets of Chicago fell away and receded out of sight, the dimensions of the price he might have to pay for his decision remained out of sight.

When the truck arrived at the station, the sergeant barked them all out of the truck. To impress the sergeant, Samuel hopped out of the truck in a lively manner. When he looked around, he recognized the train station. It was the station he had gotten off at when he had first arrived in the city. The circle was complete.

"Okay, gentlemen," the sergeant said to the group assembled outside the station door as the truck pulled away. "Now let's see if you can follow one of the first principles of the corps, which is to stick with your sergeant. If you can't do that much, then you probably can't find your ass with both hands. You'll go nowhere in the corps. You'll spend the rest of your enlistment cleaning latrines."

He pointed to the door of the station. "We're going to go in there together. You don't have to march in single file. You'll be doing enough of that soon enough. But stick with me. Don't go wandering off like a bunch of snot-nosed children."

Samuel reflected on the number of times he had called his sister, Beth, a snot-nosed twit.

Samuel had been looking around nervously to see if there were any policemen outside the station. He didn't know why the sergeant had to give his lecture outside the door when he could have done it inside.

Samuel didn't see any police standing vigil outside the station, but he still wished the sergeant would finish his harangue so that they could get inside, out of sight from the street and out of the sight of any policeman looking for a gunman who matched his description. He didn't know if any bulletins had been put out by then. He hoped to be out of the city before they were posted.

To Samuel's relief, the sergeant led them through the station doors and up to the ticket counter. At the counter he produced a roll of cash that looked bigger than a sergeant's pay for the month. He assumed the money to be government funds. The sergeant bought tickets for all of them.

While the sergeant bought the tickets, Samuel looked around to see if there were any policemen inside the station. He didn't see any. He wondered if all the spare cops in the city were involved in cleaning up after the fight at the Packingtown plant. If they weren't doing that, Samuel figured they were combing Packingtown, looking for the gunman who had killed one strikebreaker and wounded another. He also figured they were browbeating the Kraznapolskis and other strikers, or beating them with nightsticks.

After finishing buying the tickets, the sergeant handed them out and told the recruits not to lose them. Then he led them over to the pew-like wooden benches in the waiting area that Samuel had slept on the first night after he had arrived in the city. It would be over an hour before they could even board the train, let alone see the train pull out. More hurry up and wait.

Samuel took a seat with his back to the front station door in case a policeman happened to stick his head in and look around, scanning the crowd. By Samuel's estimate, the police should have started fanning out from Packingtown by then, looking for the gunman at the yard. He was a bit surprised that they weren't covering the train stations already. But that didn't mean they wouldn't be there soon. Samuel's estimate of the ability of the police department to mobilize that quickly was a bit ahead of its time.

The recruits sat and talked jauntily as they waited. Samuel joined the conversation so as not to seem withdrawn and suspicious. While trying to look relaxed and natural, he occasionally glanced at the station doors. Any minute he expected to see a phalanx of police burst through the doors and sweep through the station like a wave, searching every face. He figured that, the way his life had been running, it would be just his luck to get caught one short hour before he was to board the train that would take him out of the city to safety. He had thought he had been out ahead of Constable Harkness, but he had been wrong.

No wave of blue uniforms appeared during the seemingly interminable wait. Finally a Negro conductor or train caller appeared at the far end of the waiting room. In a deep and resonant voice, he called out, "City of New Orleans now boarding on track number four. All aboard!"

"All right, gentlemen, that's us," the sergeant said in his own resonant voice. "Stay together and follow me."

Samuel got up, not quite believing it was working out after all. He half expected a rush of blue-uniformed hands to grab him just as he went to step on the train. As he stood up, he looked around one more time. He still didn't see any police.

The sergeant led them down the half-lit corridor of the cavernous train depot under the building built above it. When he had arrived in Chicago, Samuel had walked inward toward the city. Now he was walking the other direction, away from the city. One could say he was closing the circle. But Samuel wasn't thinking in terms of closing circles. He didn't consider himself particularly good at closing circles. He had tried to close the circle with Clarinda and had failed.

The sergeant picked a nearly empty train car and motioned his charges to climb aboard.

"Here we go, gentlemen," Sergeant Arnold said. "This train is called the *City of New Orleans*. But we're not taking it to New Orleans. We change trains in Memphis. That train will take us to South Carolina and your new home in the corps."

The sergeant's words only reinforced Samuel's sense that he was moving yet again, this time farther from any home that he ever had.

"This may be the first train ride for some of you. If you get trainsick, the windows do open. Just hang your head out and let fly. But don't fall out. It would wreck both of our days."

Samuel and the others climbed aboard the train car and spread out, looking for a seat. Samuel took a window seat at the head end of the car, not because he wanted the view, but so he could see any policemen walking along the side of the train, looking into windows.

"You'd better get some sleep while you can, gentlemen," the sergeant said. "You won't be getting a whole lot of rest in boot camp."

For some time the train sat hissing but motionless. Hurry up and wait, even on a train. Samuel kept his head turned forward, but out of the corner of his eye he kept looking out over the platform. He still half expected to see a squad of police suddenly appear, running down the platform to stop the train and drag him off it in handcuffs.

With a sequential jolt, the train started to move. No policemen appeared on the platform, waving their arms for the train to stop. As the train pulled out from under the building that had the air rights above the station, the late afternoon sun appeared through the windows. At that juncture, Samuel could have breathed a sigh of relief that he was safe. But as the train picked up speed, the only thought in Samuel's mind was that not only was he back on the road again, but also he was heading out for a destination even farther away than the one he had been heading for when he had left home the first time.

He had gotten away from the police, who he didn't even know if they were looking for him, but he had done it at the price of putting himself farther away from home and family both in geographical terms and in the possibility of return than he had been at the start of his run. Instead of inwardly exalting that he had given the cops the slip, in his mind he remembered the last lines of the song he had sung to the girl during the picnic they had together:

> Come, come, come away with me
> And I'll build you a home in the meadow.

Samuel knew he wouldn't be building any homes in any meadows anywhere for any woman anytime soon, if ever. Not for his lover and fateful love, Clarinda. Not for his upstairs lover Mara. Not for the sad-faced Katrin Kraznapolski. Not for the plain-faced Katherine Clarke. Not for his sister. He would not become the kept man of Mrs. Richardson in her house by the river. He would not be setting up a home of any kind with any woman anytime in the foreseeable future. Neither would he be back home helping his parents maintain the home and farm and carry on with the family he had started out in. He would be farther away from home and from family of any kind. The Marine Corps would become his hiding place and refuge, but he doubted he would ever call it home.

At first the regular metallic rattle of the train wheels as they traversed the sections of rail beneath them made Samuel think that he would probably soon be marching to an equally regular and regimented cadence. In their own clacking, clanking way, they seemed to be mocking him. Soon enough he was back thinking about the temporary family he had found in the bleak confines of Packingtown. He remembered how he had found a lover in Mara Kraznapolski. He remembered again his failed attempt to bring Katrin Kraznapolski out of the shadow existence of the bleak bordello she had resigned herself to. He remembered how her mother had said that even the promise of marriage wouldn't have been able to bring the defeated girl back home or into any family.

At that moment a stab went through Samuel. He didn't know if it was a stab of guilt, but it felt something like it. In a way it was starting to dawn on him that his offer to save Katrin by marrying her and bringing her to her original home had been something of a lie. In the hollow rhythm of the train, in the emptiness of leaving, Samuel wondered if he would have really gone through with his proposal to marry Katrin, and if he did marry her, if it all would have turned bad as Mrs. Kraznapolski had predicted. Would it have been any different if he had married Mara? Would the love he felt had developed in time really have come about, or would what little love there was inside him for any woman have faded and turned into sour resentment as Mrs. Kraznapolski had foreseen? In a stabbing instant of self-accusatory clarity, Samuel wondered if he was capable of really loving any woman.

As the orange light of the setting sun reflected off the walls of the building the train was passing and flashed in his face, Samuel wondered if he could ever love any woman other than the girl, and if he tried, would he only be lying to himself and to whatever woman he was pledging himself and his love to.

At that point of poisoned clarity, he more or less resolved never to lie to a woman again by professing love that he could not bring up in himself and bring out of himself any more than the girl had been able to bring any real love out of herself. After his manifest failures, he no longer believed that he was capable of saving any woman.

As the train creaked and clacked and swayed, Samuel resolved to himself that he would not allow himself to be enamored of any woman or allow himself to be drawn to closeness with any woman, be she soft and romantic as his sister was, as open to him as Mara had been, as needful as Katrin, or as hard-bitten as the girl. He himself would go on, though he was not sure in what direction, to what purpose, or to what end.

The train picked up speed. As it did so, the buildings it was passing fell away faster as the train headed south into the late afternoon light going orange as the sun sank toward the horizon to set. Samuel did not look out the train window. He sat motionless in his seat and thought of the ones he had left behind in both the city and his life. He wondered what would happen to the Kraznapolskis and to Rufus. He wondered what kind of empty horizon the failed strikers and their families would look out upon in the hollow light of the morning of the next day. And the days after that. He figured he would probably never know. He had left them all behind as much as he had left the girl, his parents and sister, and Mara behind.

By the time the sun rose again in the morning, the train would be closer to South Carolina than to Chicago. With all his regrets at all the leavings he had done, he didn't regret leaving the slaughterhouse behind. He just wasn't quite aware that in the not all that distant future, he would find himself immersed in another soulless killing machine and slaughterhouse that, by exponential degree, would make the slaughterhouses of Packingtown seem like a candy factory. It would be a place that would make him even willing to return to Packingtown. Because, like millions of other men who would find themselves caught up in the maw of the great grinding, rending machine of mechanized war, he would want to be anywhere else but where he was.

Samuel sat in his seat and looked straight ahead without looking at the city he had no desire to look upon any further. The sights of Chicago dropped behind as the train headed past. He didn't reflect any further on the horizons of the past he was leaving behind, but he could not see the shape of the horizon ahead. The only horizon he could see from his seat on the moving train was growing darker.

Horizons had always been a large, expansive, and complete vista for Samuel. In his earlier youth, he could see the sweep of all his horizons from one end to the other. When he was a callow youth on the land, he could see the horizon of his life on the farm, the only life he had wanted. He had seen, felt, and lived the sweep of his love for the land, his home, and his family to the depths of his soul. He had seen and felt the depth of his love for Clarinda. Together they had made up the sweep of his life and his horizons. Now he was no longer able to see the horizon of his life beyond the shopworn seat of the train he was sitting in. He wasn't at all sure that there were any horizons left to him. Once he had felt like the world belonged to him. Now it belonged to someone else, and he didn't know where to go to stand in line to get back in.

There was little left to him of the world he once knew. The only immediate thing left intact of the self he once had been was his conflict- and flight-driven body and mind. After the next chapter of his life played out, he wondered what, if anything, would be left of his heart and soul. That was a horizon he could not see beyond.

Chapter 33

In the gathering darkness over the ocean, horizons were fading from sight. The gray, restless infinity he was looking over was nothing but empty horizon in an unbroken sweeping circle of jumbled clouds and jumbled ocean waves in all directions, broken only by the lumped forms of the other ships in the convoy. Where it came to horizons of empty sky touching horizons of roiling water, Samuel would have gladly traded the empty horizons of darkening water around him and stretching away from him in all directions for the much smaller but life-infused view from the shore of Gustafson Lake.

As broad and endless as the horizons around him were, in Samuel's mind, the vast open horizon left little room for presumption or any sense of superiority. Personal bravery and fortitude, and the ability to bust heads on a strike line, means little when you're a gnat on the back of an elephant ready to surge at any random moment. Samuel figured that the ocean had rolled over men more stalwart than he. Even the iron-riveted ship he was on would be nothing but a tiny bit of flotsam the sea would sweep away without noticing if it were to decide to go mad. The eternal danger of the sea was doubled by the fact that there were other storm-tossed men huddled deeper in danker surroundings with steel horizons pressing in from all sides.

Some of the troop transport ships of the day were ocean liners pressed into military service. The ship Samuel was on was a creaking troop and cargo transport ship that had always been a transport ship. It would never cruise the idyllic seas or visit the idyllic islands of the Caribbean or the Mediterranean. If it wasn't sent to the bottom by a torpedo, it would eventually retire to a scrapyard.

Samuel stood by the railing at the position where the side of the ship started to curve inward, leading to join the other side of the ship at the point of the bow. The water was relatively calm for the North Atlantic, but it was rough enough to send swells several feet in height rolling across the open and unrestrained seascape. Generations of sailors had learned the hard way just how unrestrained the North Atlantic could become in a heavy nor'easter. Overhead, the evening sky was the leaden gray so prevalent in the North Atlantic. On the western horizon behind the ship, the last dim orange glow of the setting sun faded into the dark of the sea and met the arriving night. There was still enough light to silhouette the convoy against the horizon.

A moderately stiff breeze blew scud foam off the tops of the waves. As the ship plowed through the waves, the irregular but otherwise uniform swells rolled against the bizarrely shaped random irregular-angled patches of black and gray colors the ship's sides had been painted. Known as "jazz painting," the turn-of-the-century attempt at camouflage was designed to break up the silhouette of a ship and make it harder for an enemy observing the ship at a distance to determine its speed and direction. The sharp-edged zigzag pattern of the different-colored painted sections gave the ship something of a visual impression that it had already been torn apart by explosions, reduced to a floating scrap heap. The weird paint job was yet another small comedown for the once stately ship, sort of like putting camouflage paint on the face of Lillian Russell. But after the Allies had lost a prodigious number of ships painted in more standard uniform marine colors, painting ships in that manner did seem to cut the losses of Allied ships. Not many ships in jazz paint would be sunk. But then the newly adopted convoy system helped too.

The only part of the convoy escort in Samuel's immediate sight was the four-stack destroyer about a thousand yards off the starboard bow of the ship. At that distance, the size perspective made the destroyer live up to its nickname of Tin Can. Compared to the size of the ocean and the swells it was proceeding through, the destroyer seemed like a tin wind-up toy. Behind the small warship, the vast ocean closed in and remained spread out to the empty horizons that seemed worlds away. Beyond the empty horizons that he could see, Samuel knew that only more empty horizons waited. Though there for protection of the convoy, the destroyer, with its small size, the distance it kept, and the way it surged and disappeared on the waves wasn't particularly reassuring to Samuel. As a boy, Samuel had never played with toy boats in a bathtub, but a toy boat on a rapids was what the destroyer reminded him of. The earlier-era design of the destroyer made it seem quaint, antiquated, and plodding. As a supposedly protective outrider, the comparative expanse of space around and behind the destroyer left Samuel feeling as vulnerable as a pheasant being stalked by hunters on a plowed open field.

Straight out from the side of the ship there was nothing but the open ocean, dwarfing both the destroyer and the ship he was on. Samuel wasn't a navy man, but he could easily imagine a submarine slipping into the gap and sending a torpedo streaking far behind the stern of the destroyer, straight toward the side of the ship he was on. From his vantage point, Samuel imagined seeing a torpedo angling right for the side of the ship just below where he was standing. Looking out over the unfriendly, disinterested sea, which might conceal a wolf pack of enemies focused on his destruction, in the cold of a North Atlantic sunset, looking for the silver flash and track of a torpedo, Samuel had some small sense of what Harold Ethridge and the girl must have felt seeing death coming at them with nothing they could do to prevent it.

Off to Samuel's side and behind him in the west, occasional streaks of orange from the setting sun shone just about one celestial degree above the North Atlantic horizon. By his estimate, Samuel figured that it would be midafternoon back in Ohio. For a moment he wondered what farm chores his father and mother would be performing. He wondered what chores his sister would be settling into in her new role as a newly married farm wife. But Samuel put the thoughts out of his mind almost as fast as they had formed. At this moment in the mid-Atlantic, Samuel didn't want to think about the farm. He had left three people he loved behind in the farm world he had come from. He had left three people dead behind him on the fringes of that world. He might end up leaving his bones in a foreign field half a world away from the world he had known. He just didn't want to think about any kind of fields at the moment.

The sky behind Samuel was turning orange in the fading light. Soon enough the dark would wrap itself around the convoy, giving it the relative protection of a moonless night. When the sun rose ahead of them in the morning, the convoy would be a half day closer to the shores of France. When they arrived, at least they would be safe from the specter of death on dark water, caught in the freezing grip of water cold enough to kill a man in a few minutes while he swam frantically to get away from the searing heat of the flames from the burning oil towering behind him as the fire scorched the back of his head and the cold drained the life out of him. The trenches of France were far inland from the sea. One didn't have to worry about floating in a life jacket and going numb with the cold while waiting for rescue that might never come, or about finding oneself trapped in the final darkness as the lights went out on a ship as it rolled over. Whether the trenches would prove to be relatively safer was quite another question entirely.

Chow was over. Instead of returning to his bunk, Samuel had walked out onto the deck of the ship. The cold of the North Atlantic night wasn't pleasant, but at the moment Samuel preferred the open air to the confined and crowded ward his bunk was in. He stood leaning on the railing, looking out into the gathering night. The only things fixed and solid to concentrate on were the ships of the convoy and their escort vessels on the perimeter. Samuel looked at the destroyer off the starboard bow. Instead of plowing through the swells as his ship was doing, the destroyer rose and fell with the swells. When the destroyer was in the trough between waves, Samuel could see only the upper superstructure of the ship topped off by the four stacks. Arranged in a straight row down the center of the ship, the four smokestacks of the destroyer reminded him of the line of smokestacks on the meatpacking plant he had worked at in Chicago and at whose front gate he had received his baptism in combat. When the destroyer went into a deep trough, only the stacks would show above the wave tops. The sight made Samuel imagine the packinghouse sinking into Lake Michigan like some kind of mid-American version of Sodom or Gomorrah sinking into the Dead Sea under the judgment of God. Standing by the ship's rail, he was alone.

Suddenly Samuel found himself not so alone.

"Hi, Corporal," said an even younger-looking soldier as he walked up to where Samuel was standing. "What are you doing out here by the rail? Puking up that chow they fed us?"

Soldiers just had to have something to gripe about. They wouldn't be troops if they didn't gripe. Samuel recognized the private. He was one of the new recruits who had been assigned to his company and his squad shortly before his unit had shipped out. To Samuel, the boy didn't look much older than he had been when he had enlisted four years earlier.

"The grub on this ship ain't much different or worse than what I've been eating for the last four years in the corps," Samuel said in defense of service food. "You get used to it after a while. I suppose the food in the corps ain't nothing to write home about, but then I don't have a home to write home to."

Actually that wasn't true, either in terms of not having a home and family or in terms of not writing. Since he had left home, Samuel had been writing to his sister under the name and identity of the fictitious distant cousin Martin Heisner that he had assumed when he had enlisted in the corps. Beth would relate the information to his parents.

Rank hadn't been easy to come by in the turn-of-the-century prewar Marine Corps. Promotions were rare in the numerically limited force that had been without a mission since the Boxer Rebellion and that was suppressing the insurgency in the Philippines, which had become a US possession after the Spanish-American War. But the same natural leadership ability that had made him captain of the baseball team back home had separated Samuel from the other recruits and had impressed his superiors. As a result, Samuel had been promoted to corporal without his even bucking for promotion.

Before the war had started, the Marine Corps had largely been a small and insular organization that lived within itself and its way of doing things. Rising from the ranks was a bit of a feat in the prewar Marine Corps, which had been otherwise mostly static. With the US entry into the war, the corps had been quickly expanded with recruits and volunteers.

The now swollen Marine Corps was composed of mainly new recruits. This was the case with Samuel's unit. Older prewar soldiers had been mixed in with the younger enlistees to give leadership and stability and to instruct the newcomers in the art of war. The trouble was that they were all heading into a war that was beyond both reason and art with everyone from the lowest private to the highest-ranked and bemedaled generals being instructed in what war gone mad was like.

Samuel and the other corporals and the sergeants who had enlisted in the marines before the war were a different group. With the United States' entry into the Great War, they had effectively become the old guard of the corps. Though he was only a few years older than most of the new enlistees, Samuel, to the new recruits recently enlisted and just out of training, along with the other prewar marines, were the closest thing to hardened old veterans they knew.

"I'm out here because I wanted some air," Samuel said. "Other than the suction of shells flying overhead, this may be the last free wind any of us may feel for some time. When we get into the trenches, we're all going to have to be keeping our heads down behind the trench we're in. So enjoy the breeze while you can. This may be the last time you'll be able to stick your face up into it without a sniper trying to put a bullet between your eyes."

"I just wanted some air too," the private said. "Walking the deck is about the only thing to do around here. All there is to do on this tub is eat and lie in your bunk or get skinned by card sharks in a rigged card game. If the seasickness don't make you heave, the food will. The boredom's the worst. It drives you crazy."

The private was like many of the new recruits: a fresh-faced naïf just out of high school or fresh off the farm, eager and ready to do his patriotic duty. He might even be thinking of being a soldier in war as some kind of grand adventure about to unfold before him. Samuel figured the private probably wasn't thinking about the possibility of the ground opening under him in the form of a soldier's grave. He would be directly commanding the boy in action. The problem for Samuel was the boy's possible naivety about war. The other problem for Samuel was that the boy seemed straight off the farm. If the boy was killed, it would be like watching himself die.

"Enjoy the boredom while it lasts too," Samuel said. "The boredom on this ship is going to seem sweet compared to the wide-ranging insanity of combat in the field over there. At least in camp and on this ship we've got a roof over our heads and dry beds to sleep in. You'll spend a lot more time sitting around in the trenches than you will on this ship. The trenches are open to the rain and snow. If you're bored lying in your bunk on this ship, in the trenches you'll be bored sitting in mud up to your knees. You'll look back on this ship with fondness. If you think the food tastes rotten on this barge, the food in the frontline trenches is literally rotten half the time. And it all goes on day after day, week after week. The only thing that breaks the days of boredom are the moments of sheer terror when charging across no-man's-land with the Krauts firing everything they have at you, from machine guns, to artillery, to poison gas."

"My name's Chester Hollingsworth," the private said. Samuel already knew the boy's last name. He wore it on the name tag on his chest the same way Samuel wore the false name he had given himself.

"Where you from, boy?" Samuel asked. Sergeants and officers tended to ask young recruits that kind of question.

The private responded with the name of a town in Iowa. Samuel had never head the name before, but then again, other than Des Moines and Dubuque, Samuel didn't know the names of any Iowa towns. To Samuel it sounded like a small town. It could have been his town.

"That sounds like a farm town," he said.

For a second the boy's face brightened. "Yes. It's near the middle of the state. It's not a very big town, only a couple of hundred people. I live on a farm about fifteen miles outside the town. Being in the corps is about the first time in my life that I've been outside the state."

At that point the boy started to wonder if the corporal, who for all he knew might be a career soldier, thought all farm boys were hicks who didn't know how to be soldiers and wouldn't be a credit to the corps.

"I can't say that I come from a military family, but my grandfather was in the Civil War. Fought at the Battle of Shiloh. I may not be an experienced marine like you, but I have what it takes to be a marine. I think I can learn to be a marine. Farm boys can be a credit to the corps."

Samuel held up his hand. "Don't worry," he said. "I don't have anything against farmers or farm boys. I was an Indiana farm boy myself, until my father died and the bank took the farm to pay off the mortgage."

"Is that why you joined the marines back when you did, before the war started?" the private asked. Before the war, the Marine Corps had a bit of a reputation for being a US version of the French Foreign Legion, a home for adventurers, mercenaries, those looking to escape from some form of unhappy past, and/or those looking to escape trouble with the law. The private had figured that Samuel, Martin Heisner to him, had had some kind of personal reason for joining the peacetime corps.

"Did you join the corps because you lost the farm?"

"That and other reasons," Samuel said as he looked out over the ocean.

"What happened to your mom when you lost the farm?" the private asked. Samuel was lying in terms of broken families. The boy was thinking in terms of whole families.

"My mother died when I was eight," Samuel said, fleshing out his lie. "She was long dead when I lost Father and the farm. She never saw that. I guess you could call her lucky that way."

The pair were silent for a moment.

"Are your parents still alive?" Samuel asked, almost in spite of himself. "Do you have any brothers and sisters?"

"Both my parents are still alive," the private said. "I'm the oldest son. I've got two younger sisters in the middle and a brother younger than them."

Samuel clenched his hand on the railing. A farm boy. A farm boy with a family, an intact family, a family that Samuel might have to write a letter to expressing condolences at the death of their oldest son and his burial in a foreign country. Samuel was starting to curse himself for having asked the boy where he came from. He could be a farm boy who would not be going back to his family, a family that would be diminished by his absence. Then again, they both might not be going back. But whatever the individual consequences of the war to their similar lives, if the boy lived, he could get back to his family. Even if Samuel lived through the war, he still couldn't get back to his family.

The private pulled out a pack of cigarettes and put one in his mouth. Then he took a cigarette lighter out of his pocket and prepared to strike it. Samuel grabbed the cigarette from the boy's mouth. "Don't light that up out here," he barked in a noncom's hard tone. "We're running on blackout protocol. If some hotshot U-boat skipper is looking through his periscope and sees the flare from your lighter or the glow from your cigarette, it may be all he needs to range us. He'll pop a torpedo into us faster than you can say, 'Lafayette, we may be a little late arriving.' They'll be gunning for the troop transports first. Careless smoking can sink ships as fast as careless talk. If you forget the blackout rules and reveal the location of the ship, we may all die out here on the ocean before we set one foot on the killing ground over there."

The sun had set. The twilight was fading fast. Blackout procedures went into effect at dusk. It wasn't quite fully dark, but the private thought it best not to argue with a hardened noncom. He put the cigarette pack away. For a few minutes they both stood in silence, looking out over the darkening ocean as the light faded on the horizon. Samuel turned his head toward the young soldier. Looking out over the endless, muttering ocean, Samuel felt the sudden need to talk to someone who could respond on a human level, not the silent level of a disembodied vision.

"Did you leave a sweetheart behind when you enlisted?" Samuel asked the proverbial soldier-to-soldier question.

Samuel wasn't sure why he had asked the question, but the young soldier was a proverbially fresh-faced boy. Proverbial fresh-faced boys were usually the ones who left sweethearts behind. Wet-behind-the ears fresh-faced boy soldiers were also the first ones not to return to their sweethearts.

"Actually I sort of did," the newly enlisted private just out of basic training said. "Her name is Caroline. She lives on the farm next to ours. We've sort of been childhood sweethearts for a long time. I was getting ready to ask her to marry me, but America went into the war before I had a chance to. I wanted to do my duty to my country, so I enlisted. I figured that being in the service would make a more mature man out of me when I got back home."

Provided he got back home.

Samuel silently gripped the rail of the ship. *Oh great. Just great,* he thought to himself. A farm boy just like him with a family just like the one he had been an integral part of once, a family the private had left behind but that he could go back to. The boy also had a sweetheart. A live sweetheart. If that weren't bad enough, she even had a name that sounded like Clarinda's. Was fate or God playing a crude jest on Samuel by bringing the boy to him, or was the boy somehow being prepared to take over Samuel's place in the world and live the life he would never have? At that moment in the middle of the open ocean, far from the life and world he had known, Samuel wondered if he was looking at the replacement who would be left in the world to vicariously take over his life from a distance if he was killed in action.

"What about you?" the private asked. "Are you leaving a sweetheart behind?"

"Actually I sort of did," Samuel said blankly as he looked out over the ocean. "Actually I sort of didn't. I suppose you could say she was my sweetheart. At least I thought of her as my sweetheart. I ran after her, trying to make her my sweetheart, but I ran at her too hard. It just made her run from me. If she had run to me, right now I wouldn't be here. I'd be back on the farm I started out on like yours. But the way I ran at her just made her turn and run from me. I never could catch up to her."

Samuel paused and looked out over the fading light across the ocean. "She left me behind. In the end I left her behind."

Samuel looked back at the boy. Something compelled him to speak the harder story. It was almost as if fate or something in the beyond was pulling the story out of him.

"I left her behind dead, dead at the hands of a man as mean as any Kraut we're going to run into in the trenches over there."

Samuel's decidedly nonproverbial response stopped the boy's proverbial question in its tracks.

"Gee. What happened?" the boy soldier asked.

"Don't want to talk about it," Samuel said, giving the proverbial reticent soldier's answer. "Don't make no never mind now. At least that's the way she would have put it. I ran after the man who put her in her grave, and I put him in a grave of his own. I've been running ever since, first from the law, then from home, then to the streets of Chicago. From there it was to the marines, then to Haiti. Now it's to wherever we're headed for on the front."

Samuel threw the boy soldier's cigarette over the side. "The usual order of things is that the boy soldier marches off to war, leaving his sweetheart behind," he continued. "She spends her life wandering in mourning for him. I kind of reversed that in more ways than one. She was the one killed. I cut down the man who killed her. I went on the run to get away from the law. I've been running since I was your age. She died when she was seventeen. I was eighteen."

The younger soldier said nothing. He was only seventeen himself. He had heard apocryphal stories of how professional soldiers often had lived hard-case lives, which they joined the service to get away from. He had also heard that they were often running from something, sometimes from the law.

"So how's that for a turnabout? Instead of me ending up in a grave in a foreign land and her mourning for me at home, she's the one who ended up in a grave back home and I've been out wandering around mourning for her. What we're heading into may put an end to my wandering once and for all. That would put both me and her beyond mourning for each other. At least it would put me out of mourning for her. Just how much she would have mourned me if the situation were reversed, I guess I may never know for sure. Not in this world at least."

The boy's tone turned quieter and more mournful. "I was thinking that if I don't make it, maybe you could write a letter to my parents and my girl," he said, to change the subject from the memories pressing on the corporal's mind to a matter pressing on his own mind. "They might like it better if they got a letter from someone who knew me instead of just a telegram from the War Department. I can give you their address."

"Don't start thinking like that," Samuel said, cutting off the boy quickly. "If you start thinking about dying and start planning for your own death, you may bring it down upon yourself. Not that you'll tempt fate or anything superstitious like that. But if you let yourself get fatalistic, you won't concentrate. You'll get careless. You won't be thinking or looking. You'll forget to duck. That's when it will happen to you. Not when fate draws your number."

In a backhanded way Samuel, was trying to cheer the boy up by reassuring him that, at least to some degree, his fate was in his own hands and that he could control his fate, something Samuel was not sure the boy or he would be able to do on the battlefield.

There is a certain amount of truth to the proposition that alert and focused soldiers survive. At the same time, Samuel knew that is was as much of a lie as it was a truth. When you're exposed to fate and enemy fire in no-man's-land, no matter how alert you keep your mind, a random shell or random machine-gun burst can put an end to the sharpest and most focused mind. The war they were heading into had been going on for several years now. He knew they were heading into a random and raging whirlwind, a maelstrom that cut down the innocent and inexperienced and the hardened and proficient in equal measure.

"You just concentrate on keeping your head down, and don't start writing your own epitaph."

Samuel was starting to worry that the boy might come to attach himself to him in the hope that if he stayed close to an experienced veteran, it would increase his chances of survival. Samuel didn't want to depress the boy by saying that all combat is usually so chaotic and unstructured that there is no easy formula for surviving it, not even in the shadow of one experienced in combat. At the same time, Samuel didn't want to seem like he was cold and uncaring by telling the boy he wouldn't write a letter home if he was killed.

"When we get there, write down your name and home address. If anything happens, I'll write a letter to whoever you want. But as your squad leader, I'm going to do all I can to keep you alive while we're running Kaiser Bill's boys off the field and back to the alleys of Berlin."

If the boy was killed, he particularly didn't want the emotional burden of writing to his family and sweetheart. He still hadn't fully figured out who would be informing his parents and sister in case he was the one killed. As his designated next of kin, he had listed his sister as his cousin. But he couldn't remember if he had updated the information with Beth's married name and new address.

"Is it really as bad as they say over there?" the private asked, the tone of his voice more sober. Samuel had the feeling that this was what the boy had really come to talk to him about. Maybe like so many green recruits, he wanted to talk with an older, experienced soldier about what it was like in action. In his years in the prewar marines, Samuel hadn't been in combat, not in the marines at least. He had, however, come into the corps as an experienced man-killer.

"You don't talk about it very cheerfully. You've been in the military for several years and in combat. Being a military man, you've probably watched the war a lot more closely than I have on the farm. From what you've heard, what's it like over there?"

"I'm afraid I can't give you any hearts and flowers," Samuel answered. "I don't have any hearts and flowers to give myself. And I can't tell you that it's going to be some grand and glorious whooping charge up San Juan Hill. That kind of derring-do may have worked for Teddy Roosevelt in the war with Spain, but that was just one hill he charged up. They've got a line of fire and steel from the shore of Belgium to the Swiss border. You don't break the jaws of a death machine like that by throwing the bodies of men against it, but that's the only answer anybody has been able to come up with so far."

The generals on both sides of the trenches weren't dullards or stupid. They were as smart as any generation of generals who had made the rank. They just found themselves up against a new and unexpected form of warfare they had no familiarity with, so they did not know how to respond to it beyond doing what they knew had worked in wars of the past.

"What's going on there isn't glory war out of adventure novels. It's nothing but one big killing machine. I know killing machines. I worked in a slaughterhouse before I joined the corps."

Samuel jerked his head in the general direction the ship was sailing. "Those guys over there have killing men down to as much of a mechanized art form as the packinghouse bosses I worked for where it came to butchering steers and hogs. All I can say is that the Brits, the Frenchies, and the Gerrys have ground up an entire generation of young men our age, and the lines have hardly moved a mile closer to Paris or Berlin since the war began. Nothing has changed over there in over three years. The names of the dead just keep piling up faster and deeper than snowflakes in a snowdrift. If we think we're going to go in there and casually brush the Krauts aside like flies just because we're Americans, we're crazy. Maybe by the time we get there the Krauts will have gone through all the young men in their country and won't have anything left to fight with but a bunch of tired old men."

Despite the way bodies were piling up in no-man's-land between the trenches, so many of the upper echelons of the General Staff sent men out the way it had been done in the Napoleonic era, as if machine guns and fast-firing artillery hadn't been invented. Fast tanks, which would make future wars more mobile and give breakthrough ability, were still on the drawing boards.

"I hope that at least our commanders have enough intelligence between them to come up with a smarter strategy than just sending us charging headlong into machine-gun fire."

The boy's expression didn't get any darker, but it didn't get any brighter either.

"The Limeys, Frogs, and Huns have been doing that for three years to no avail," Samuel went on. "That's why they've lost so many men. And nobody on any side seems to have learned anything from it. I hope our generals have enough sense not to repeat the mistakes every general in Europe has made."

Samuel looked into the private's questioning face. "It may seem like a grand adventure to you now, but the scale of killing going on over there now made a joke out of any kind of glory, leaving glory dead with its face in the mud, a long time ago."

Trench warfare favored defense and doomed the attacker by several orders of magnitude.

"Glory dies as fast as your friends around you when the first wave of machine-gun fire rips through your ranks. Glory dies just as quick when you get your first whiff of phosgene gas. Glory is usually the first casualty of any war. Even killing the enemy, provided you get close enough to him to see his eyes, doesn't bring the zest back. But the war goes on. War goes on long after the thrill of killing is gone."

Samuel knew something about killing a man when you're close enough to look him in the eyes. It hadn't been a particularly zestful experience. His anger had submerged all other feelings at the moment. He just didn't want to go into detail about it with the private.

"I wish I could tell you that this is going to be a cakewalk. But I've got to be honest. The only way any of us are going to be able to handle this is if we go in knowing what we're up against and what to expect. If you go in thinking it's going to be a picnic or cakewalk, you'll come apart when reality sets in. Or you'll forget to keep your head down and get it shot off."

Samuel continued to look out over the water. The private continued to look at him.

"You're sure not seeing it from the most cheerful of angles," the private said after a moment's silence.

"I haven't seen life or the world from much of any kind of pleasant angle since I saw the girl I was in love with lying dead on a table with her neck broken," Samuel said, still looking out over the ocean. He didn't fully know why he had invoked the girl like he did, but then he didn't fully know why he had walked out onto an empty deck in a chilly North Atlantic evening to look at an empty ocean.

"I put a stop to all my dreaming then and there. I've made it a habit to look at reality only from that day on. My dreams didn't do her or me any good. My dreaming of a better life for her and the dream life I hoped for myself didn't bring either of us anything. All my finer thoughts and feelings only landed me on this ship. If I talk a bit sour, know that my sour view of reality came about long before this war or even before I joined the marines."

From the tone the corporal spoke in when relating the subject matter, the private figured that there might be more to his personal reasons for enlisting in the peacetime marines than just losing his farm to a bank after it foreclosed on a mortgage. From the tone in Samuel's voice, the private figured that he might be stepping on a subject that it might not be wise to pursue.

"Hopefully my heightened sense of reality will help get us all through this war. When we get there, don't start thinking grand like you're Teddy Roosevelt or General Custer leading the charge. Don't try to win this war by yourself. You just keep your head down and follow my lead. I'll do all I can to get you back home to that sweetheart of yours. I may have buried myself in the marines, but if it's in my power, I'll keep you from ending up buried in a foreign country."

The boy seemed to appreciate the sentiment. "After the war, do you intend to go back to farming?" he asked. "Or are you going to stay in the marines?"

"I don't really know," Samuel said, grateful for the change of direction in the conversation. "I don't have a farm to go back to. When I first signed up, I didn't intend to stay in for life. Outside the military, farming is pretty much all I know. I always kind of figured that after my enlistment ran out, I might look for work as a hired farmhand. I sure don't want or intend to go back to that job I had in the slaughterhouse."

And the Chicago police could still be looking for him after the war.

"I have a hard time imagining you as a farmhand," the private said. "Somehow I can only imagine you as being a marine for life."

Samuel figured the boy had meant the remark as a compliment, but the comment caught Samuel up short. Had he come to look the part? Had he fallen into the role so completely that it seemed natural for him? Did being a soldier fit him in the eyes of others? Did it fit him in the eye of fate?

"Well, that may be the way you see it now," Samuel said, "but before my life fell apart on me, I never wanted to be anything but a farmer. When the girl was alive, I never wanted anything but the farm and her as my farm wife. Life ended in a flash for her. In the same short flash I became a vengeance-crazed killer. Just goes to show that life can change on you in the twinkling of an eye."

Samuel caught himself. After all, they were headed for a place where life could both change and come to an end in the twinkling of an eye, or the pull of a trigger, or the screech of a shell you don't hear coming in. But Samuel already knew how fast life can change with the pull of a trigger.

"Like I said, the only two things I know are farming and being a marine. Whether I'll stay in the corps or go to being a hired farmhand after the war is over, I haven't decided yet. Who knows? Maybe I'll be coming by your place after the war is over, looking for a job as a hired hand. You'll be the one in charge there."

Samuel didn't particularly want to take his growing familiarity with the boy any farther, a familiarity that a German machine-gunner or sniper could bring to an end with the twist of a finger.

"For the moment, we'd both better get inside before some officer or cranky old topkick sergeant or navy chief petty officer yells at us for being out on deck after lights out. You go on ahead. I'll be along in a short while."

The private nodded and went back inside the ship. Instead of following him, Samuel turned back to look again at the ocean in the fading light of a mid-Atlantic evening.

Samuel didn't know if he had made a mistake by getting to know the private like he had. In the back of his mind was the idea that a soldier and commander shouldn't become too familiar with the other soldiers around him or under his command. Knowing someone only makes it harder for you when they get killed, especially if you're the one who gives the order that sends them to their death. The next time he saw the private close up, he might see him dead in shell hole in no-man's-land as he crawled his way back after a failed frontal assault on the German trench lines.

Samuel was already aware of the reality of the war they were sailing toward. Knowing the private only made the reality more personal. The private was real. The cold ocean they were on was real. The continent they were sailing toward was real. The killing fields were real. The war that had been going on for three years was mind-numbingly real for the millions of soldiers who had seen their friends and comrades dying around them. It was tearingly real for the millions of families who had received word that their sons had been killed in the maw of a war that ground up men like wheat in a thresher. The difference being that a thresher moves across a field. In the Europe of that day, men obliged the thresher by charging across the field into the jaws of the thresher while the thresher didn't move and hadn't moved for three years. The war was all too real and seemingly endless and hopeless to a lot on men on both sides.

The girl had run away from her home after having violence done to her and having done violence. Samuel had fled from his home after doing violence. He had actually fled from two homes after doing violence. The girl's violence hadn't killed anyone. To date he had killed two men. The girl had crossed a state line to die in a neighboring state and be buried under a name she had given herself. He was crossing an ocean and multiple time zones to a continent on the other side of the world, possibly to die and be buried in a foreign country under a false name he had made up for himself and had used for years. So many of the dead of the war lay unburied in no-man's-land until they rotted away into decrepit skeletons. When the final remains of all the dead were collected, if they ever were, he might very well end up in a pile of disjointed bones in a charnel house or buried under a designation of Unknown Soldier the way so many of the dead from the War between the States had. At least they ended up buried in their home country. He could end up both dead and unknown in a foreign land.

The girl had died under a contrived name. Before she died, she had been known by more than a few people. Some of them had loved her for herself beyond the physical approximation of love that was her stock in trade. She had been buried by people who loved her, Samuel included. Those who had buried the girl had honored her and her name, such as it was. He could die and be buried in a foreign country by people who didn't love him and didn't know him in the least. He might end up without even a superficial name on his headstone, only the eternally cold and impersonal designator Unknown.

If so, his last name, or lack of name, would read Unknown on his tombstone until even that empty name finally eroded away to where it was unreadable. He had run as fast as the girl, but he had run farther. Though he was now officially traveling at the directive of the US government and the US Marines Corps, in a way he was still running. He had no idea if or where his running would stop or how sudden and finally it would stop.

With the girl on his mind to the degree she was that evening, Samuel looked up. In the fading light of the mid–North Atlantic evening, he saw the face of the girl in the sky. It was the same face he had seen in the night sky outside his hometown as he had driven home after having met her. They hadn't reached the fatal shore yet, and already he was having visions of the dead. The face he had seen in the sky over his hometown that night had smiled at him. The face he saw in the sky over the empty sea was neither smiling nor sad. Her expression was more of a blank, disconnected gaze.

"Well, girl, you are a far-flung wanderer now, aren't you?" Samuel said softly to the image of the girl. "I've seen your face before me in every state I've been in, in America. Now I'm seeing you out in the middle of the ocean. It looks like you can cross oceans as well as state lines."

He looked out over the ocean again. When he looked back, the girl's face was gone. All he saw above was the thick gray of the North Atlantic sky.

"Oh, I know that's not really you up there. I know you're only in my mind. But so much of what I saw in you was all in my mind. I don't know how much I was on your mind when you were alive, but you've been in my mind since I met you. Looks like you're there still. I may never get you out of my mind. But then I don't particularly want to get you out of my mind. … For all I know, I may be on my way to join you wherever you are. France is supposed to be a country of love and lovers. I guess it's a good enough place to meet up with an old lover. Even a dead one. Who knows, you may get the chance to duplicate yourself in me. You left your home to die far away and be buried under a half name. I may die even farther away and be buried under no name at all."

Standing at the ship's railing, Samuel once again saw the girl's face interwoven with and partially hidden in the leaden sky.

"I don't know what you are now, whether ghost, angel, or lonely wanderer in the great beyond. I don't know how the dead think. I don't know what you think now. I was never sure what you thought back when you were alive. Maybe you'll consider it to be some kind of personal triumph if I follow in your footsteps and die far away from home without my real name the way you did. If I do, I don't know if it will prove anything to you or mean anything to you. Wherever you are, whatever you know, at least I hope you will know that someone loved you enough to do what I did in your name, whatever your name really was. But wherever the dead meet, wherever you are in the land of the dead, O girl, wait there for me. I may be along presently."

With all the death ahead of them on the continent they were heading toward, Samuel had had enough of communing with the dead. He turned away from the image and walked to the steel companionway door leading to the interior of the ship. Blackout procedures were in effect, remember. The inside of the bridge was darkened. Navigation lights were kept off. All unnecessary lights outside and inside the ship were turned off. All portholes and windows in lighted wardrooms were covered over to prevent light from showing. Doors to the lighted interior of the ship were supposed to be kept shut after dark. The momentary flash of light showing when an exterior door is opened to a lighted interior passageway on a ship on a dark ocean can give away the position of a convoy to prowling submarines.

Samuel opened the door and closed it behind him as quickly as he could. From there he headed down the narrow corridor and down the interior gangway steps to his bunk on a lower deck of the ship.

Chapter 34

Samuel Martin, a.k.a. Corporal Martin Heisner, Fifth Marine Regiment, Fourth Marine Brigade, Second Division US Expeditionary Force, wasn't looking at the open sky visible in a straight-line channel above. His mind was focused by default on the mud beneath his boots. Either way he ended up going in the coming minutes, the mud beyond the trench could be the lowest and final common denominator. If he was hit while advancing, his own forward momentum would carry him forward such that he would fall on his face in the dirt. If he was hit in the back while retreating, the momentum of his retreat coupled with the impact from behind could send him sprawling forward on his face.

Trench warfare wasn't a face-to-face duel between individuals on a field of honor where the defeated combatant falls on his back to die, looking toward the heavens. Unless he was sent flying end over end by the explosion of an artillery shell landing at his feet and sending him flying in a random spiral to land on his back, that was the only trajectory of death Samuel could see that would leave him lying on his back. That way, at least he would be left facing the sky as his body turned black in the sun like so many of the other dead Allied and German soldiers he had seen. Then again, if it was a big shell that landed at his feet, his body might simply disintegrate into shreds, mixing in with the dirt thrown by the shell. Unlike the girl, he wouldn't even be left with a gravestone that proclaimed him dead in a field in a country far from home that didn't know his name.

When he lived on the farm and had assumed his life would end on the farm, he had occasionally imagined himself as an old man dying from a heart attack in the field. He assumed he would fall on his back between the rows of corn or wheat he was cultivating and that his last earthly sight would be of the sky seen between the walls of green around him, a far more pleasant trench to die in. The thought of death that way on his own land had always seemed a reasonable enough way to end a life dedicated to the land. If the coming attack would write out the last chapter of his life, if death it was to be that day, then it would be death facedown in the dirt of someone else's field in a foreign land far from home. On his face seemed to be the only position in which he was likely to come to the end of his diverted life.

As far as the mud at his feet was concerned, Samuel was careful to keep from sticking the open end of the barrel of his shotgun down into the mud as he shoved shells into the magazine. Countryfolk knew shotguns. If the barrel became plugged with dirt, it could cause the gun to explode when he fired it. No use handing Kaiser Bill a cheap victory.

When the magazine below the barrel was full, Samuel put a shell in the open breech and carefully pushed the hand slide forward, closing the breech. As he had chosen the load of his shells for mortality five years earlier, the shells he was using today were loaded with double-aught buckshot. The difference this time was that instead of the old black powder shells left over from his grandfather's era, the shells he was loading in the gun were modern and used the more powerful smokeless powder. The added kick could prove useful as the range he would be firing the weapon from wouldn't be as up close and immediate as the distance at which he had shot Harold Ethridge. But then again it could all turn out to be a moot point. Most men who died in no-man's-land never got within accurate rifle range, let alone shotgun range. He could be found the next day dead with his face in the dirt with the shotgun flung out to one side uselessly and his rifle still slung across his back, held by its strap.

Samuel wrapped his thumb around the hammer and pulled the trigger, carefully lowering the hammer back down onto the firing pin. The shotgun had a carrying strap like his rifle did. Samuel usually carried his rifle alone and slung over his right shoulder as he was right-handed. That day he had his rifle slung over his left shoulder. He slung the loaded shotgun over his right shoulder in the ready-to-go position and leaned his back against the side of the trench, where he sat listening. In the near distance he could hear the crump of shells hitting the German trenches. But the gunners were firing largely by guesswork, trying to saturate the general area, hoping for a lucky hit. No one was sure of the exact positions of the German trenches in the woods or how many there were. Closer to home, Samuel could hear the blast of the German shells straddling the trench they were in.

"Why are you taking that along with your rifle?" Private Hollingsworth asked from his position next to Samuel. "It's twice the weight to carry. You can't shoot your way across no-man's-land with a shotgun."

"You can't shoot your way across with a rifle either," Samuel said in his practical soldier's voice. "Trying to hit a man who's down in a trench while you're bouncing around out in the open, running full speed at him, is a next-to-impossible shot. To hit a man in a trench, you have to be right on top of him. There's going to be a lot of close-quarter fighting in there. For close-in work, a shotgun is a lot handier."

Samuel knew about close-in work with a shotgun.

"You can fire a pump gun faster than you can work the bolt on a rife, and you can nail more than one Gerry at a time with a single shot."

The single-barrel twelve-gauge pump-action Winchester Model 97 military shotgun had been designed as a riot gun to dominate crowds in deadly riots such as the kind Samuel had taken part in at the gate to the packing plant. The battle at the packinghouse had seemed apocalyptic enough. When the police had charged, Samuel was in the back of the retreating crowd, trying to help move the battered Mrs. Kraznapolski to safety. If the Chicago police had had rapid-fire riot shotguns and had fired into the retreating crowd, his story might have ended then and there in the lesser apocalypse. As it was, Samuel sat at the bottom of a hastily dug trench in the midst of a boiling apocalypse that made the fight at the plant gate seem like a nose-bloodying squabble between choirboys.

Transported to use in the Great War, the type of gun Samuel had requisitioned had been dubbed the "Trench Broom" for its ability to sweep trenches with a hail of close-range fire and to mow down soldiers trapped in the narrow confines of the trench below with nothing to take cover behind. The Germans appreciated the potential of shotguns being used against them, and they didn't like it. They tried to get shotguns banned in war, saying it was a cruel weapon. These were the same people who had introduced poison gas into warfare. On the front, they threatened to shoot on the spot any soldier caught carrying a shotgun. Samuel faced possible summary execution if he were captured with the gun in his hands, but he didn't intend to be captured in retreat. He had resolved that if he was going to die, he would die going forward with the gun's trigger in his hand and the barrel in the face of the Germans.

"The trick with any gun is to get close enough to the Gerry trenches to use it," Samuel said. "We've got ourselves some degree of cover going in. The woods between us and the Heime lines will give us something to hide behind and will break up their aim. At least it won't be like the earlier big battles such as the Somme and Verdun, where there was nothing but open ground between the lines and the guys had nothing between them and the Gerry guns. As you move up, just try to keep a tree between you and any machine gun they're spitting at you. They just started cutting that trench a day ago. If we catch them before they get their defenses firmed up, it might make it easier to roll over them."

Samuel supposed that the military advice he was giving wasn't much comfort in and of itself. But open ground or otherwise, on the battlefields of the Great War, comfort was as limited as cover and concealment.

"They say our generals are taking orders from the French now," Private Hollingsworth went on.

GI rumors were notoriously inaccurate. However, in this case the scuttlebutt was somewhat correct. In the developing crisis on the Western Front during the spring and summer of 1918, the situation had become so critical that the normally recalcitrant and obstreperous Allied supreme generals had laid aside their egos and their differences and had united under a single commander. Even crusty General "Black Jack" Pershing, commander of the US expeditionary forces, was directed to take a side seat and put his forces under the command of the supreme Allied commander, French general Marshal Foch. When the US contingent built up to full strength, General Pershing got his back up and told the other Allied commanders to go scratch; he was going to lead his troops and attack the way he wanted to.

"What the hell are the Frenchies sending us out into the woods to die for? We're not defending a city. We're not defending a town. There isn't a railroad line out here. There isn't even a dirt road running through this place. Our guys are getting chopped to ribbons for a grubby little woods with nothing in it but trees, bushes, and stumps with a German behind every one of them. A third of the company got cut down crossing that truffle patch to get to these trenches."

The field they had crossed under fire the day before had been a wheat field under cultivation, not a truffle patch. As a farmer, Samuel had recognized the crop he was trampling down with his feet while his fellow soldiers were flattening it out with their falling bodies. He assumed the Iowa farm boy Private Hollingsworth recognized the crop too. He was probably just talking sarcastically when he had called it a truffle patch. Sitting in the trench that yesterday had been the German trench they had overrun after crossing the now largely defunct wheat field, Samuel felt a certain affinity for the French farmer whose crop they had trampled with their feet while they had watered and fertilized it with their blood. It seemed that half the crop had been trampled down underfoot. The other half had been churned up by artillery fire. Whether there would be much salable crop left for the absent French farmer to recover when he returned from being a displaced refugee, Samuel couldn't tell. Either way, too often it was that farmers' fields of pastoral peace became the killing fields of war.

Raw courage and the same tactic of advancing in straight-line ranks that had proved disastrous for all sides in the earlier part of the war had carried the day and carried them into the enemy trenches. The attack could have proven to be yet one more meat grinder battle to no effect and with no ground gained in a war that had been four years of useless meat grinder battles. Samuel knew all about standing on a line facing an endless moving line of ground meat. Instead it had been an almost classic victory, the triumph of will and fighting spirit over an entrenched enemy seemingly impossible to dislodge.

They had gotten where they were so far on determination and courage, but it had come at a stiff price. Machine guns in the hands of seasoned German gunners had exacted a terrible price. In the first day of fighting alone, more than a thousand marines had been killed or wounded, a toll more than the marines had lost in all the corps' previous battles. Samuel's squad had been in the second wave to advance. The fact that they had been in the rear of the advance that day is what had spared Samuel and his squad from the worst of it.

But they had paid enough of a price. More than enough. Samuel had brought killing to Harold Ethridge and the strikebreaker. The war had brought the killing close to Samuel in the form of a large German shell that landed virtually at the feet of the man the second from his side. The man's body had disintegrated, showering him with strips of flesh and splotches of blood. As gruesome as a first-timer might find it, the experience wasn't all that new to Samuel. Samuel had already been exposed to the feel of being sprayed with blood and flesh from his shooting of Harold Ethridge at close range. The shrapnel from the shell missed Samuel, but the explosion drove a shower of dirt into the side of his body and face, covering the side of his body with a sheet of dirt. The force of the blast peppered small pieces of dirt into the skin of his face. While he hadn't been disintegrated, the man closest to his side had been between him and the explosion of the shell. His body had blocked most of the shrapnel that would have hit Samuel. The man had been blown off his feet, horribly torn up by the blast and the flying steel shards. There was nothing Samuel could do for him. He had been forced to leave him where he fell and continue the advance as the man withered in his death throes.

The dead of their hard-hit depleted unit still lay in the field behind them where they had fallen. They had thrown the dead Germans they had killed out of the trench and piled their bodies up in a line in front of what had been the back of the trench but now was the front, to give themselves added cover from the incoming artillery fire and small arms fire from skirmishers the Germans had sent to snipe at them from the edge of the woods. Being in the second wave of yesterday's attack might have worked to spare Samuel's life. This time there wouldn't be an orderly two-wave attack. There weren't enough men left to spread out in two echelons. This time they would all attack together. Everybody would be in the first wave at the front of the line.

"Now we sit here licking our wounds and sticking cigarettes into the bullet holes in our sides, and all that's out there beyond are trees and more damned trenches. Now we've got to go in and get our heads blown off in the middle of some nowhere woods. If you get killed in that tanglebush, they'll probably never find your body. What the hell are we doing chasing Gerry into the woods for?"

"Don't knock it all that much," Samuel said in a relative tone. "At least we're not charging across open ground like we just did. We've got a lot more cover in the woods than we do out in the open. The woods will make it a lot harder for the Germans to see us coming."

"It will hide the Germans just as well," Private Hollingsworth said. "We won't be able to see where they are down in the weeds until they shoot us from the blind side. We should just leave them there on their bellies in the brush to pick spiders and chiggers out of their ears."

The private's comment about chiggers made Samuel think of the time he had lain with the girl in the brush, being more than tempted by her, while their position on the ground tempted an attack by chiggers. The pleasant vision faded quickly.

"What the bloody hell does this place have to do with winning the war?"

"The Krauts are trying to do what they failed to do in 1914, when the French stopped them at the First Battle of the Marne," Samuel said in his military analyst voice. "Now that Russia has pulled out of the war, they've got themselves a big infusion of manpower."

After Russia pulled out of the war following the Bolshevik Revolution, the Germans had been able to transfer large numbers of troops from the Eastern Front to the Western Front. On March 21, 1918, the Germans opened a concerted drive to break the Allied lines. Backed by the additional manpower from the former Russian front, the Germans had succeeded in breaking the stalemate that had held the lines frozen in place for four years, and replaced the bloody stasis of the trenches with bloody gains of the kind that neither side had scored since the lines had hardened in place in the first months of the war. In late May, the tired French divisions gave way to a massive German offensive. German forces reached the Marne River at the French city of Château-Thierry. The road to Paris seemed open. The city hung in the balance, exposed and ripe for taking. The German drive was advancing steadily toward Paris. The Germans were shelling Paris with the long-range supergun called Big Bertha. Refugees were fleeing ahead of the German advance.

"The French are worn down to a nub. The Brits aren't in much better shape. They're both exhausted. We're the only new boys they've got to put on the line. If the Germans can punch through the lines, they'll pick up momentum and be able to roll over Paris. If the Krauts win in Europe, all the people here will be under the Prussian jackboot, maybe for generations. That's why they've got to be stopped before they can go any farther and get going any faster. These woods are on their flank. Now that we've stopped them on the road to Paris, they may try to make these woods into one of their kicking-off points to try to flank us. I guess that's why they want them so bad."

The woods in which the overarching Allied endeavor and the lower-level immediate lives of the men in Samuel's battalion hung in balance were not far off the Paris-to-Metz highway that crossed the Marne River at the city of Château-Thierry. It was a patchwork of forest and cultivated fields about a square-mile in size. The local French knew the place by its local name of Belleau Wood. Before the war, the place hadn't been known to hardly anyone anywhere in the world except those few who lived around it and farmed the land. Afterward it would be burned into the annals of marine lore along with the Halls of Montezuma, the shores of Tripoli, Guadalcanal, Iwo Jima, Okinawa, Inchon, and Fallujah.

"They're throwing us right up against the spearhead of the Kraut advance. The woods the Gerrys are digging in on and trying to break out of is the hottest part of the front right now."

Samuel had at least a limited grasp of what is often dubbed the big picture. But in war, no matter how brilliant the general may be, at the molecular level anybody and everybody's big picture condenses down to individual bodies on their own individual-sized pieces of bloody ground and into individual stories of heroism and fear, pain and numbness, life, blood, and death. All big stories in military history books boil down to the stories of individuals whose stories go on or else stop forever in the nameless random places where their stories are brought to an end. The girl had been familiar with that principle of hard life, both at home and away from home, before Samuel had become acquainted with it.

"The Germans have whipped all opposition to the drive so far. We're up to bat now."

"And they've been chewing the hell out of us the last few days," Private Hollingsworth said. "Every time I turn around, someone else I know is gone or is splattered all over the ground or all over me. Our unit's down to close to half strength, and there are always more Krauts over the next rise and behind the next tree. One more big fight and we won't have the strength left to break a loaf of French bread, let alone the Kraut lines."

On June 1, the Second Division formed a line across the road the Germans were using as their main avenue of advance. The marine brigade was in the center. The Germans attacked the next day. As part of their training, marines had been drilled in shooting accurately at long range. The Germans learned a lesson in rifle fire, that it can kill at eight hundred yards. For three days the Germans pressed their attack, but they could not push the US lines back significantly. Then on June 6, the Second Division counterattacked on the German flank. In front of the marines stretched the patchwork combination of cultivated plots and hunting preserve called Belleau Wood. The Germans had extracted a price from the marines in getting them from the open to the edge of the woods as the marines had extracted a price from the German advance in the open at Château-Thierry. Ahead of the marines now lay the thickness of an unknown woods with an unknown network of defenses, manned by an unknown number of German troops. The number of troops was unknown. The reputation of the particular troops they were facing was better known.

Without raising up to look over the lip of the trench, Private Hollingsworth glanced in the direction of the German trench line. But all he could see was the side of the trench they were hunkered down in.

"How many men do they have in the trenches over there?"

"Enough to make trouble for anyone trying to get at them," Samuel answered in a flat tone. "The Gerrys are getting worn down as much as we are. I don't know how many men they have left in the immediate area. I don't know how many men they've got in there. In our case, it's not the numbers so much as who it is we're up against. … I think those are Prussian Guards in the trench on the other side. In Germany the Prussian Guards are considered an elite unit. They're some of the best troops they've got."

Samuel realized again that he might be discouraging the boy. He figured he should offer some encouragement to counter what he had said about their facing an elite enemy force. All he could offer was relative encouragement because relative encouragement was all there was to offer.

"At least they're some of the tallest troops they've got. You've got to be a minimum of six feet tall to be a Prussian Guard. By itself, being tall doesn't make you a better shot. But if you stand up, it does make you a bigger target. Being tall just makes it easier for someone to cut you down."

Samuel stopped there and changed directions, if only for his own good. In a backhanded way he was putting the hex on himself. In the next few minutes he would be the tall one running exposed across open ground.

"Don't go thinking about how big their reputation is supposed to be. Just think of how big of a target they'll make. They'll look a whole lot smaller when you're looking down on them from the top of the trench and they're pissing in their pants, looking down the barrel of your rifle. They think they're some kind of German gods. They think they're better than everyone else in the world. They're used to swaggering around. But those who swagger with their heads full don't know when to keep their heads down. One shot will take the swagger out of them. Their brains will splatter as fast and far as those of the smallest peewee when you draw down and unload on them."

Samuel knew something about how far the brains of a swaggering bastard who thought he was better than other, little people fly when someone fires into his face at close range.

"So don't think about how tall they may stand. Just keep yourself low going at them. Don't think about anything but doing what you've got to do. You're a farmer. You know what it's like. There ain't no use in complaining when you've got a job to do. You just do what has to be done without thinking about it."

Samuel was talking faster. His words ran on in no particular direction. As the jumping-off time approached, in other parts of the trench other men were talking faster. That's the way it often went just before the start of a battle. Some men talked faster; others fell into total silence.

"The Krauts are probably stretched as thin as we are. I don't think they have any reserves to bring up. Like I said, at least it's not totally open ground. The woods will give us some cover. We made it past this trench. We can make it past the one out there."

"But there's always more damned woods and another damned trench beyond," Private Hollingsworth said.

A midsized German shell, an Austrian 88 by the sound of it, exploded with an ear- and teeth-jarring bang on the soil several yards from the edge of the trench section Samuel and his squad were crouched down in. Only in Hollywood movies do shells explode with a low-pitched, throaty, drawn-out rumble. In real life and real war, a high-velocity explosive packed tight inside a metal casing detonates with an instantaneous bang that can kill by concussion as much as by anything else. If one is close enough, the single pulse blast can rupture the eardrums, even if one is not hit by the high-velocity steel fragments from the shell casing.

Heavy barrages involving an enormous number of shells intended to collapse trenches and cut apart barbed wire had been launched by both sides in innumerable offensives. They had proven of little effect against the simple earthen ramparts. Most soldiers in trenches under bombardment had survived, leaving more than sufficient numbers to rise up and mow down the oncoming attackers, who had thought they were going to simply walk over the shattered corpses of their enemies in the rubble of their collapsed trenches. The earth that had sustained Samuel's family as farmers also worked to sustain the lives of soldiers, that is, until they emerged into the open space of no-man's-land to charge enemy trenches and be mowed down row upon row. The earth embraced the dead of all sides in an egalitarian manner, though their remains would often lay exposed for years before being gathered for final interment.

To those in the trenches, the war seemed to have been going on forever. But in the end it was the soil that continued eternally. Though combat and killing wasn't all that new, to Samuel, mechanized war on the scale they all were experiencing was relatively new. But to Samuel the land had always been old. As a farmer, Samuel knew that generations passed, but the land went on.

Samuel glanced down the line of the trench. He saw the company commander on his feet, crouched down behind the rim of the trench. With one hand, the captain had his service pistol drawn. He was looking intently at his watch on his other wrist. The protective barrage was scheduled to stop at a preset time. When the barrage stopped, their frontal assault would begin. The moment their shelling stopped, they would scramble out of their trench and swarm toward the German trenches without the danger of being hit by friendly artillery fire. The moment their protective fire stopped and they emerged onto the open ground between the opposing trench lines would probably be the same moment the Germans would double the rate of their shelling.

The double reminder of approaching mortality in the form of the close shell hit and the sight of the company commander about to order a charge prompted Private Hollingsworth to remind Samuel of what he had asked him to do for him in case the coming mortality of the day included him.

"Do you still have that piece of paper I gave you with my parents' name on it?" Private Hollingsworth asked.

"Yes," Samuel answered. It was a bit of a lie. He didn't have the paper on him. It was in his backpack. But he had abandoned his backpack behind the lines before the series of engagements had begun days earlier. He and the other soldiers had dropped everything that would slow them down when crossing open ground. The shotgun in his hands was the only extraneous weight he allowed himself. Unlike his backpack which would be unnecessary weight every step of the way, even at the end, the shotgun could provide help at a critical moment.

"Like I asked you then, if you make it and I don't, please stop by my parents' house and tell them that you knew me and that I was thinking of them when I died. If I die all torn up in some bad way, don't tell them how I died; just tell them that I loved them and that I missed them. If my girl is around, say the same to her."

Samuel nodded his head. "I'll remember," he said in order to reassure the boy. He didn't tell him that wasn't sure when he would ever get to Iowa.

The boy's request reminded Samuel of something. He reached into his pocket and brought out a folded piece of paper of his own, which he handed to the private.

"Here's the name of my parents," Samuel said. "Do the same for me as you asked me to do for you. If I don't make it and you do, tell them the same thing, that I loved them and missed them and was thinking about them."

"Back on the ship, you told me both your parents were dead," Private

Hollingsworth said with a confused look on his face. Another shell exploded elsewhere.

"That's the story I've been telling everyone," Samuel said. "They're still alive. Far as I know, at least. Their last name is different from the one I'm using. I come from a different state from what I said. It's a long story. I don't have time to go into details. … Remember that girl, the one who I said had died?"

"Yes," Private Hollingsworth answered, growing more confused by the mention of the additional character.

"Well, she didn't die," Samuel said. As another shell burst on the landscape farther down the trench line, Private Hollingsworth figured there had been some kind of earlier breakup between the corporal and his sweetheart. He figured that she was back home and that Samuel wanted him to tell her that he still loved her.

"A bastard murdered her. I tracked him down." Samuel touched the carrying strap of the shotgun. "I was carrying a shotgun with me that day too. Hated him more then than I hate Krauts now. Blew his head to pieces with it. After I killed him, I had to run away and change my name to get distance between me and the law. Got caught up in a lot of fights, before and after I came to be in the marines."

Battlefield confessions were becoming a motif for Samuel. He nodded toward the piece of paper the private had put in his pocket. "She called herself Clarinda. She made up the name. I never knew her real name. She was a hooker, but I loved her like she was a princess. I put the name she went by on her grave. Her grave is in the cemetery in my hometown. I can't go back home to her grave any more than I can go back to my hometown. If I catch it here or somewhere else, go to my hometown and put some flowers on her grave for me. I don't think anyone in town but me thought very highly of her in life. They probably don't think much more highly of her now that she's dead. Other than her working sisters in the bordello she worked out of, there probably aren't many people who would tend her grave. I asked my sister to, but I don't know if she did. Maybe you could plant a single flower on her grave for me. That would mean more to me than any general saying an amen over my grave."

Private Hollingsworth was learning that there was a lot more to the corporal than he had imagined. But then he was learning a lot more about war than he had ever expected. Samuel looked away from the lad, out toward the direction in which they would soon charge.

Another German shell went off between where the first and second ones had landed, throwing another spray of dirt over the top of the trench. Samuel and the private stopped talking. There really wasn't a whole lot more to be said and no time left to say it.

Well, girl, this may be it for me, Samuel thought to himself. *Both our stories may come to an end far from where they began, under a different name than the ones we both started out with. I guess we're not so different after all. For all I know, I may be coming to see you. If I am, wait down by the river for me in the place where we once said goodbye. Maybe we can work it out right in eternity.*

The sound of the more remote explosions of their bombardment of the German trenches ceased. The captain looked up from his watch. He raised his service pistol in air.

"*Company!*" the captain shouted.

"*Platoon!*" the sergeants shouted.

"*Squad!*" Samuel and the other corporals shouted. "On your feet!"

Samuel and all the other men in the trench stood up, bending over to keep their heads down behind the top of the trench. All conversation ceased. All reminiscences were pushed back into the past from which they had emerged. All the past was put in suspension. The future was put in suspension. The only future, the only fate awaiting, the only universe ahead, the only universe in existence to be seen, was the strip of ground between their trench and the enemy trench. As universes go, to many of the men about to cross it, the space between the trenches looked as wide as the visible universe does to an astronomer. To many it would be the door to a wider, final universe.

The captain raised his pistol the rest of the way and fired a single shot into the air.

"That's it. We're up to bat. Let's go!" Samuel shouted to the men nearest him. He started to scramble up the makeshift wooden ladder out of the trench.

The blood was drying and turning black on the bodies of their compatriots and on the ground of the wheat field they had left behind them. A washing infusion of fresh red blood would soon further mottle the dappled color of the floor of the forest ahead of them. In the wider world, all pretense of a brotherhood of civilized and genteel advanced nations had blown apart in 1914. In the occasional gentlemen's hunting preserve of Belleau Wood, there would be little occasion for gentlemanly thinking or behavior. All civilization was dead. All gods were dead. Only the gyrating furies held the ground and moved on it. All faith in and respect for humankind was dead. Respect for the dead themselves was gone.

The trench erupted with men scrambling up and out. As they gained their footing, they trampled with their knees and feet over the dead Germans they had thrown out of the trench following the battle the day before. Samuel wasn't looking at the ground. He was focusing hard on the edge of the woods a few short yards away. As he leapt off the ladder and onto the ground, his left foot landed on the back of a dead German soldier lying facedown on the ground where he had been thrown. Samuel's right foot and boot came down on the smooth and rounded back surface of the man's helmet. It was like stepping on an unseen slippery rock below the surface of the river back home. His foot slipped, and he almost fell. For a second he swayed unsteadily as he fought to regain balance. Throwing his body forward in a crouching run, he regained his balance and headed for the woods. As he ran, he unslung the shotgun off his shoulder and carried it with the barrel held forward like a rifle.

"Get out of the open!" Samuel called out to the members of his squad following behind him. "Get into the woods!"

Like an animated litho drawing of the time showing soldiers with fierce growls on their faces, advancing with bayonets lowered, the lines of marines rushed toward the edge of the woods with rifles held out forward, their two-foot bayonets extending the length. The bayonets didn't glisten in the sun. Gleaming bayonets may be a staple image in military adventure stories, but they tend to give away one's position and offer the enemy an easy range-finding advantage. The marines' bayonets had been painted black to prevent such position-revealing reflections.

In short order they had crossed the open ground separating the forest from the trench between it and the wheat field. As the advancing troops reached the edge of the forest, the drab brown of their uniforms merged into the drab green and brown of the woods like they were melting into a dull greenish-brown fogbank. After the carnage of the day before when crossing the open wheat field under fire, the woods they were rushing into offered some cover and camouflage. The trees and brush might obscure their advance and break up any clear field of fire for the Germans in the unseen trench line they were advancing toward, but rifle and machine-gun bullets can shred through leaves and twigs as thoroughly as they can move through the cloth of soldiers' uniforms.

"Don't bunch up!" Platoon Sergeant MacKensie shouted. "They'll take us all out with one machine-gun volley." With his left hand he waved left. "First squad, spread out to the left." With his right hand he waved to Samuel and his squad. "Second squad, spread out and take the right flank."

Samuel barked his own set of directional orders on the run. With the shotgun, he waved toward the right and moved off at a shallow angle. The members of his squad followed, spreading out as they went. This put Samuel and his squad on the extended far-right flank of the attack. In latter-day war movies, it would be the right flank that often got hammered or that ran into the hornet's nest.

As he ran forward, Samuel pushed and stumbled through the underbrush of the woods. Branches of trees and tall brush lashed his face, which still had small pieces of dirt embedded in it from the near miss of the artillery shell that had killed the two men to his side the day before. He held the shotgun up at an angle in front of his face to deflect the brush and keep from being hit by branches. He had to leap over the trunks of dead and fallen trees.

In its own way, the woods he was rushing hell-bent deeper into weren't all that different-looking from the two woods he had rushed himself and the girl deep into in a rush to get himself deep into the girl. Those days he had looked forward to the grappling confrontation to come.

The coming encounter that day would hardly make for extended romantic memories. But Samuel wasn't thinking in terms of romance on any horizon, present or past, near or distant. His lover of the past was dead. For Samuel, all lovers and all thoughts of love were dead. Along with the shotgun, the decidedly less than romantic formulation he carried with him as he closed on the German trench line was the same one he had carried the night he had closed on Harold Ethridge with a shotgun in his hands. It was the same one he had carried in his mind when he had charged the trench the day before and the day he had stood on the strike line watching the strikebreakers closing in on his position. To Samuel, what applied to men who broke girls' necks and who tried to beat women to death with an iron pipe applied on the geopolitical scale to Kaiser Bill's Huns: You can't talk madness into being becoming saintly. You can only close with it and pulverize it. The killers of women and children in Belgium by gun and bayonet, the killers of civilians in Paris by long-range artillery fire and in London by aerial bombing by zeppelins, the killers of his buddies in the field behind him, were just ahead of him in the trees they were charging. He ran with a different shotgun in his hands than the one he had carried when he had gone after Ethridge. Otherwise he went at the Germans with the same thought he had gone after Ethridge with. He would run over them or die in the process.

As he charged headlong across the open ground and into the brush and the trees, charging headlong into a woods of France that looked like the woods of home, Samuel's life hung in the balance. But it had hung in the balance when he had gone out after Harold Ethridge to avenge the girl. It had hung in the balance when he had stood on the strike line at the packinghouse gate to defend his fellow workers. At his moment of full movement, he wasn't thinking of his life so much as evening the score for the little people of the world. To Samuel, all the arrogant strutting Harold Ethridges of Europe were in the trenches ahead of him, wearing their arrogant pointy Prussian helmets. He had left the arrogance of Harold Ethridge a crumpled heap in the dirt of his hog barn. If he could, he intended to leave the arrogance of the Prussian Guards a crumpled heap in the dirt of their trenches.

In the trench ahead, a German officer in a nonpointy standard rounded German army-issue helmet barked hasty, almost panicky-sounding directions into a field telephone.

Around the now empty trench line they had just abandoned, the explosions of shells stopped. The German officer's hurried call had been to the artillery battery that had been backing them up behind their lines, telling the gunners to adjust their angle of fire and to drop their ordnance into the woods in front of the trench the marines were rushing toward.

Artillery shells exploded on the forest floor. The patch of ground they exploded on would disappear in an instantaneous orange flash, which was followed by a dark vortex of dirt and smoke shooting upward in an expanding *V*. The deeper the shell penetrated the ground before exploding, the narrower the geyser of dirt and torn vegetation. The ear- and teeth-cracking shock and blast of the explosions threw shredded in a circle and ripped upward, tearing leaves and branches off any trees near to the epicenter. Occasionally an explosion would throw a man end over end, spinning like a rag doll in a whirling dog's mouth. Just as often, and with even more ease, a shell explosion would send dismembered arms and legs flying out from the center of the debris cloud. The tree trunks offered a modicum of protection against flying shrapnel, but only if they were in a precise straight line between the man and the exploding shell.

The explosion of a shell in the upper reaches of a tree removed the blast, taking it up high and away from being directly under a man's feet. In that sense, the forest canopy protected the advancing soldiers from the close-quarter shock and deadly spray of shrapnel. But detonating above ground only spread the shrapnel in a wider arc, sending it downward in a wider circumference. The explosion of shells in the tree also sent saberlike shards of splintered wood out at nearly the same velocity as the shrapnel the shells sprayed. A shell blasting a tree in two halfway up the trunk could drop the whole top of the tree straight down on a man who had taken refuge under it.

Waving his service pistol in the air, the captain yelled at the soldiers to keep moving. It wasn't out of suicidal bravado or glory-seeking that he directed them to stay on their feet and keep advancing. The natural instinct under an artillery barrage was to duck and cover and throw oneself on the ground. But that would only leave them motionless, waiting for a random shell to land next to them. The only real protection from the shells lay below the ground in the trenches ahead. It was just necessary to evict the current occupants.

Samuel thought his life had begun when the girl had spontaneously made love to him in the woods on the shore of Gustafson Lake. His life might come to an end any second in a woods on the other side of the world. *If so, then so be it* was the only thought Samuel had for himself. For what Samuel considered his opinion to be worth, his life had ended when the girl's life had ended. His past was behind him, over a horizon that couldn't be breached. For all he knew, there might be no horizon for him beyond the woods. The only horizon line Samuel could see was the black gash of the trench that ran horizontally across the floor of the vertical green woods.

The charging leathernecks burst through the partial camouflage and concealment of the woods and into fuller view in front of the trench line that the Germans had cleared out in front. As they did so, the German trench commander grabbed the handset of the field telephone, yelling into it for the artillery gunners behind the line to pull in their fire even closer to the trench line. As he finished yelling into the phone, with the handset still up to his mouth, the German commander yelled to the soldiers down the line to open fire.

Bullets passing in the air don't whizz or whistle. The supersonic speed of high-velocity bullets makes a cracking sound as the bullets pass. Bullets cracked around Samuel, passing at different distances. One passed close by his ear. Another passed between his legs. Bullets ripped through the leaves and thin branches of bushes and smacked into the trunks of trees. As if the forest floor were being hit by the rainfall of the devil's spit, geysers of dirt, dead leaves, and twigs leapt upward into the air around them. Behind and to the side, Samuel heard Private Hollingsworth scream. Out of the corner of his eye, he saw him go down.

The other men in his squad dived for cover behind trees and for concealment behind bushes. More dirt sprays shot into the air off the forest floor. Along with the machine gun, the individual riflemen at the end of the trench line were firing at them. Exposed between the trees, Samuel dropped to a half crouch and quickly looked back and to his side. Private Hollingsworth had rolled over on his back on open ground, grimacing in extreme pain and grabbing his leg. Even with the distance between them, Samuel could see the wide and ugly crater gash in the middle of his left leg where the knee should have been. The bloodred gouge stood out bright against the drab brown of his uniform. It looked like a mass of bloody, mangled cauliflower. Private Hollingsworth's right leg thrashed and withered on the ground. The lower half of his left leg flapped around like a disjointed rag doll. It seemed attached only by flesh.

With his rifle slung over his shoulder and his shotgun still in hand, Samuel burst back up out of his crouch and sprinted over to the fallen private. Without slowing, he grabbed the private by the center of his fatigue shirt and dragged him to a tree, behind which he dropped him down on the ground.

"Stay down!" Samuel shouted to the lad as he sprinted off to the side to draw fire away from him. As he moved away, a bullet cranged at a shallow angle off the top of his flat-shaped Tin Hat doughboy's helmet.

Samuel dived and rolled into some brush. He flattened himself on the ground behind it. The brush offered minimal concealment, but it wouldn't stop a bullet.

More geysers of dirt sprayed into the air. The fronts and sides of trees shattered and sprayed bark as they were hit. A bullet hit the ground near Samuel's head, sending a small shower of dirt through the brush at his face. Another bullet hit near the fingers of his outstretched hand.

From behind the brush, Samuel looked quickly around. The other members of his squad who were farthest forward were firing their weapons at the trench ahead of them. Dirt sprays danced off the tops of the frontal trench mound. The fire was ineffectual against the German soldiers protected by the trench, but at least the marines had the range.

Samuel looked at the trench. From his position he could see fresh-turned dirt. Samuel was a farm boy. He recognized fresh-turned dirt when he saw it. Then he saw why it was fresh. The trench stopped not far beyond the position they were pinned down in. The Germans had been trying to extend the trench, but they hadn't had time. From the mean streets of Packingtown to the strike line at the slaughterhouse, Samuel had the ability to quickly size up a coming street fight. In the fields and forests of France, he had developed the ability to size up a military situation quickly.

"We can't stay here!" Samuel shouted over the din of the German guns and the din of their own weapons. "There's no cover. If we stay here, they'll pick us off one at a time. If we try to run back, they'll nail us before we've gone ten yards. We've got to take that trench and knock out as many of their guns as we can, or they'll shoot the hell out of our guys coming up the middle."

Samuel pointed at one man and then waved his hand forward. "Haskell, take your machine gun and move up behind that tree." He looked at the other men close by. "Lindholm, Barker, Crenshaw, take up position on the right of him. Watch for my signal. When I give you the word, open up on them. Try to keep their heads down. While you've got them distracted, the rest of us are going to rush the far end of the trench. We'll distract them for you. When we get there, you rush them straight from here."

The nearest machine gun on the German line swept another volley through the brush where the marines had taken cover. Another rapid sprint of dirt geysers flew off the ground, ripping between them, missing some men by only a foot or so. The body of the tripod-mounted gun was visible at the top of the trench berm. Samuel looked at Private Haskell and pointed to the machine gun in his hands and then to the German machine gun that was strafing them with bullets. "Try to hit that gun. See if you can put it out of commission." The cranky French-made Chauchat machine guns his unit had been equipped with had been poorly designed. The open-frame magazines easily picked up dirt, which would cause the gun to jam. Samuel hoped the weapons would work when called upon. He hoped the same for himself and his men.

Samuel rolled over to the wounded Private Hollingsworth. When he arrived at the fallen lad, he dragged up the rifle he had dropped when he had been hit and laid it down beside him.

"Chester, I'm going to need you too," Samuel said. "When they start shooting, I want you to open up on them. I know you're hurt, but we're going to need everyone who can shoot to help keep them busy so that the rest of us can get at them. Just keep shooting. When the rest of us go in, you stay here. After we clean out the Krauts, someone will come back for you, I promise."

The boy nodded. He rolled over painfully on his stomach and brought up his rifle. From the way he moved and from the sight Samuel caught of the boy's mangled knee, Samuel could see the boy's leg had been hit bad enough that he wouldn't be able to charge the trench or even hobble toward it. Whether he would ever be able to use the leg again was something that Samuel didn't have time to think about.

Samuel jumped up and sprinted the short distance to the side of where the rest of his squad had taken cover. As he moved, he heard the crack of bullets passing in front of him and behind. A bullet chopped a small, low-hanging branch off a tree ahead of him. The shots missed him, but they were high enough that they would have hit him in the chest if the shooters had been quicker. Or luckier.

As if coming back to home plate ahead of a forced throw, Samuel slid on his side into the brush in the midst of the rest of his squad on the outer-right flank.

"When they start blasting, the rest of us are going to hit the end of the trench," Samuel said in a command voice. "I'll go for the end of the trench itself and try to engage them and keep them off of you. While I'm keeping them busy, the rest of you try to come around the end of the trench and get in behind them. When you come around, go after the machine guns. They're what's going to kill most of our guys in the center."

Samuel raised up and looked at the men of his squad he had just come from. The German machine guns firing at them had turned to fire at the main body of marines closing in from the front.

"See you at the general's victory ball," Samuel said. All the men of his squad were looking toward him. Samuel raised his hand in the air.

"Open up!" Samuel shouted at the members of his squad for whom he had set out to give covering fire.

The men started shooting rapid fire at the trench only about one hundred feet away from them. The riflemen worked the bolts on their Springfield rifles the way they had been taught to rapid fire in boot camp. The French-made Chauchat machine gun in Private Haskell's hands blasted out a clumsy chunking staccato of fire. It hadn't jammed. So far. Private Hollingsworth was firing as Samuel had asked him. The pain slowed down his speed, but he kept firing.

Little dust devils of dirt splattered off the top edge of the trench ridge. The German soldiers behind the earthwork ducked lower for protection. Samuel looked at the men nearest him.

"Let's go!" Samuel shouted to the men on his right. "Down their throats. And don't stop till you come out the back of their asses!"

Samuel and the rest of his squad jumped to their feet out of the brush that had partially concealed them. They rushed forward, angling off toward the far end of the German trench line as Samuel had directed. The whole operation had taken little more than a minute, from conception to jumping off, for Samuel to set up and initiate. A lot of eternities hung on that one minute in the woods.

Trench lines of the Great War were divided into sections, isolated from each other by short angles cut in the trenches themselves. The object of the design was to confine the blast and the flying shrapnel of a shell landing directly in a trench to that one section alone. It also prevented one man with a machine gun from jumping into the trench and mowing down the whole trench complement by firing in a straight line down the trench with no intervening barriers.

They say that men in battle live an eternity even in short-duration attacks. That's understandable given that they're facing eternity. Samuel couldn't remember how many eternities, good and bad, he had lived since the night he had met the girl.

As Samuel charged the German line, in his charging mind he killed Harold Ethridge and saved the girl again. As he rushed the German line, in his mind he imagined himself rushing in a screaming charge to save the girl as Ethridge was attempting to break her neck. As he carried his rifle and shotgun in his hands toward the Germans, in his imagination he wasn't carrying the shotgun he had in his hands; he was carrying the shotgun he had taken to Harold Ethridge's barn. The pumping anger of his thoughts of killing in the past added spring to his step and carried him toward those who were trying to kill him and his buddies in the present.

As he broke through the last of the underbrush into the full open space in front of the trench, Samuel's mind snapped back to the immediate present. He found himself less than twenty feet in front of the trench without even the thin cover and concealment of the brush. As he ran toward the trench, he saw the helmeted heads of soldiers sticking above the trench wall. At the same time he saw rifle barrels swinging toward him. In that instant Samuel knew that if he stopped at the front edge of the trench to try to fire down into it, he would be cut down before he could get off a shot.

The base-stealing Samuel Martin drove himself into a double-time sprint toward the trench. At the edge of the trench, he vaulted into a leap that carried him completely over it. He moved too fast for the soldiers in the trench to swing their rifles out ahead of him. The one shot that was fired passed two feet behind him. Samuel landed on his feet on the far side of the trench.

In a flash, the fast-moving Samuel disappeared from sight behind the upper side of the ground. Samuel's move threw the soldiers in the trench into confusion. They weren't sure what to do next or which way to turn. Some of the soldiers looked in the direction Samuel had gone. They were down too far in the trench and looking up at too steep of an angle to see more than a short distance at a high angle beyond the trench wall. They lowered their rifles partway. The others turned to look toward the second group of soldiers, who had risen up out of the woods and were coming at them from the front.

Beyond the far side of the trench, Samuel dropped on the side of his legs and slid to a stop as if he were sliding into home plate on a sandlot baseball field. After he stopped, he jumped back up and rushed back toward the trench from the rear. As he did so, he cocked the hammer on the shotgun.

As quickly as he had disappeared, Samuel sprang back into sight of the soldiers in the trench. He stopped just two feet from the edge of the trench, standing at an oblique angle to it, the barrel of his shotgun lowered. As the surprised soldiers started to raise their rifles, Samuel fired. The first man in line in the trench went down.

The M97 military shotgun could be fired in rapid succession by holding the trigger back and firing as fast as the slide could be pumped. Samuel held his right arm pressed to his side, the gun straight out ahead of him. He held the trigger back all the way. Using his left hand, he pumped the slide of the gun, firing it almost as fast as he could have fired an automatic rifle. In the narrow confines of the trench, the German soldiers were not able to scatter to the sides. They went down one after the other in straight-line order. The Trench Broom was living up to its name.

One of the soldiers near the back of the line raised his rifle and got off a shot. The bullet sliced between Samuel's right side and the arm he held next to his side, gouging a gash in both. Samuel fired, and the man went down. The last man standing in the trench threw his rifle up hastily. As Samuel ducked to the side, the man fired. Samuel's move threw off the man's aim. The bullet went a foot and a half over Samuel's left shoulder. As the soldier worked the bolt on his rifle, Samuel leveled the shotgun and pulled the trigger. Only a hollow click came from the gun.

Samuel threw himself flat on the ground, down at a low position, to keep the ground between him and the rifleman in the trench. He hastily reached into his pocket and shoved shells into the magazine of the empty gun. Any second he expected to see the barrel of a rifle appear over the edge of the trench and be pushed across the ground to fire at him almost at point-blank range. The next second could be his last on earth.

With the time constraint, which could turn into eternity in his mind, Samuel didn't fill the magazine all the way. He pumped a round into the chamber and quickly low crawled to the side of the trench.

Instead of leaping up to where he could have gotten a clear shot at Samuel, the soldier in the trench made the mistake of crouching and keeping his head down, waiting for Samuel to reappear. When Samuel got to the edge of the trench, he pushed himself up quickly with his left arm, holding the gun with his right hand as if it were an extended pistol. When the German soldier saw Samuel's head appear above the top of the trench and the gun extended in his hand, he fired his rifle at Samuel's face. The bullet struck the lip of the trench. The near miss splattered dirt in Samuel's face. Samuel pointed the shotgun down at the soldier and fired. The spread-out shot hit the man in the chest. He dropped his rifle and fell backward. But the man was still alive. As Samuel pumped another round into the chamber, the man rolled over and tried to crawl fast toward the angle of the trench wall that separated the end section from the next section in line. Samuel leveled the gun and fired. It looked to Samuel that he had hit the man in the back of the head at the base of the neck. The man dropped the rest of the way to the ground. It may not have been the most sporting shot, but the war was on. Out in the field in front of the trench, his buddies were being killed. The men firing in the other sections of the trench were killing them. He had to clean out as much of the trench as he could. He might not have been able to do much more, but the life of someone he had known and served with longer than he had known and been with the girl might depend on what he did or didn't do next.

Samuel neither paused to pin a marksman medal on himself nor to pour opprobrium on his soul for shooting the man in the back. No one moved at the bottom of the trench section, but the rest of the line was still alive and firing at the advancing men of his battalion. He had to do something, and it had to be done fast.

Samuel jumped down into the trench. In a combat crouch, he sprinted over the dead Germans he had cut down. As he moved, he looked intently for anyone coming around the angle that divided the trench sections. No one appeared.

In the din of battle, the other Germans in the adjoining section had not heard what had been going on to the side. No one down the line had seen Samuel assault the trench section next to them. The sound of their own firing had drowned out the battle one section over.

Samuel moved quickly into the zigzag that separated the sections. Where the protective angle ended, he flattened his back against the trench wall. From there he cautiously leaned out and looked around the corner. One glance told the story and gave him the picture. German riflemen were facing forward, firing at the advancing marines, out of sight beyond the trench wall. In the middle of the section was the tripod-mounted machine gun that had fired on them earlier. The gunner was swinging the gun from side to side, sweeping fire straight outward in the direction of his advancing company. There were other machine guns on the line, but this one had already smashed the leg of the farm boy Samuel had promised to protect. Samuel didn't know how many men the gunner had wounded and killed so far. He didn't know how many men he would kill. But he was extracting enough of a toll. It just might be enough to break the assault. At that moment Samuel felt he had even fewer options than he had had with Harold Ethridge. All he knew was that the gun had to be silenced.

The distance was too great for a shotgun. Samuel pushed himself back against the trench wall and dropped the shotgun. He quickly unslung his rifle off his back and switched the safety off. It might be the last shot he would fire in the war and in life. In all probability he would be cut apart by a volley of fire immediately afterward. But from down in the bottom of the enemy trench, Samuel had no idea how many of his friends would die if he didn't fire it.

For a second or two Samuel leaned back against the trench wall and steadied himself. "Wish me luck, girl," Samuel said to himself. "If I'm coming home, save me a spot next to you. We can sit by the river together again." They had made energetic love by the river. The girl had waved a knife at him by the river when they had broken up. They had never really sat quietly by the river together.

Samuel bolted the two steps around the corner of the protective jog in the trench and stopped in the middle of the opening to the next section. None of the German soldiers saw Samuel coming. They were too distracted facing the charge of the marines. The closest German soldier was only a few yards away from him. Standing in the middle of the trench section, Samuel leveled his rifle, aiming past the nearer German soldiers at the machine gunner in the middle of the section. For a short moment he steadied his aim. Then he pulled the trigger. The shot hit the gunner square in the side and caused him to tumble away from the gun. The deadly blasting rattle of the gun stopped.

Even in the roar of battle, it was hard to miss something like that. The German soldiers between Samuel and the machine gun whirled around in alarm at a danger coming over their shoulder that was even more clear and present than the soldiers closing in on their position. Samuel quickly worked the bolt on his rifle, ejecting the empty shell and closing the breech. The German soldier nearest him in the trench was busy trying to clear a spent cartridge from his own rifle as he swung it around. Samuel fired from a range of no more than six feet, and the man doubled over.

Samuel jumped out of sight, back behind the cover of the angle of the trench wall, where he dropped down on one knee. But it wasn't to beseech any deity for forgiveness. With a fresh shell in the rifle's chamber, he snapped the rifle around the corner of the trench wall. Keeping his head halfway behind the wall, he started firing down the trench line. Six years earlier Samuel had been the sharpshooter who broke lines of clay pipes and knocked over small metal ducks to win the girl a teddy bear. It's easy enough to shoot ducks in a row when they're lined up in front of you. It's even easier when the ducks are as big as you and they're in front of you in a straight line. It's a bit trickier when the ducks are shooting back at you with live ammunition.

Samuel duplicated the feat he had performed in the first trench section with the shotgun. He had the advantage of the partial cover of the wall angle. The Germans were exposed in the narrow trench, which had turned from a protective cleft in the earth to a linear death trap. Working the bolt of his rifle fast, Samuel knocked German soldiers down one after the other in series as if they were tenpins. The Germans fired back at him, but their shots just blasted showers of dirt off the inside trench wall close to his head. The flying dirt obscured Samuel's view occasionally, but not enough to throw off his aim. The important thing to him was that he had the enemy firing at him and not at his fellow soldiers advancing in front. Samuel kept on firing, taking down one man per shot, until the rifle clicked empty.

Samuel ducked back behind the wall angle. He opened the breech on his rifle and grabbed another stripper clip of ammunition off his army belt. Working fast, he pushed the shells down into the magazine and closed the bolt. When he had the rifle reloaded, he steadied himself again and then whipped it and the side of his head around the wall angle. Down the trench line, near the now abandoned machine gun, he saw a soldier in a crouching position pointing a rifle at him. Before the man could fire, Samuel fired. The man crumpled down backward.

As Samuel was working the rifle bolt, he suddenly saw a man on the ground in front of the one he had just shot. The man was wounded, but he wasn't dead. He had a rifle raised and pointing at Samuel. The man had thrown himself down on the ground in a prone firing position. Samuel had been thinking and looking higher up. In the haste of battle, in the second he had to think and act, Samuel had taken the prone shooter for a dead man. He had shot the soldier behind him instead of the one drawing a bead on him. His missed clue had given the man on the ground extra time to aim.

Samuel quickly pushed the bolt of his rifle closed. As he did so, the soldier on the ground in the trench fired his Mauser rifle at the half of Samuel's head he could see. The bullet sliced his jaw down to the bone at a nearly flat angle and ricocheted off, tearing a gouge line along the right side of Samuel's jaw. The impact of the bullet jarred Samuel's head to the side. The jolt of being hit caused Samuel's hand to jerk and fire the rifle. The shot missed the man high, splattering dirt harmlessly off the trench wall. Samuel pulled his head back behind the corner and worked the bolt. The German soldier already had another shell in the breech of his rifle, ready to go.

Samuel leaned back against the trench wall. His head was spinning as if he had been hit by a line drive baseball or a right-cross punch from a prizefighter. He held the position, waiting for his head to clear. He could have slipped back around the bend in the trench, but he knew that he had to go up against the soldier again. It wasn't personal revenge against the man who had chopped up his profile, and it wasn't bravado. The only thought in Samuel's spinning head was that if he retreated the way he had come and let the soldier go, the soldier would probably take over the machine gun Samuel had just silenced.

Samuel raised his rifle to a ready position. He didn't ask Clarinda to wish him luck again. At the moment there was nothing he had to say to the girl.

Samuel brought the rifle around the corner with his head behind it in the aiming position. He had the advantage of being behind cover. The German soldier's advantage was the fact that Samuel had been partially stunned by the shot that grazed his jaw. Samuel's aim and reaction time had been degraded. The German soldier also had the advantage that he had marked the spot where Samuel's head would appear. He knew where to aim and had already drawn a bead on the spot. As Samuel's head came around the corner of the trench wall, he saw the prone soldier waiting in firing position. The man's rifle was pointed dead at him. Samuel knew that in the next moment or two, he or the man would be dead. Samuel wasn't kneeling. The advantage belonged to the prone rifleman. Samuel was well aware that the moment he exposed himself could be the last moment of his life. He wondered if the girl could see and if she knew it too.

At that moment, the ground around the German soldier erupted in a quick march stream of geysers of dirt flying straight up into the air. The soldier's body erupted in red geysers of spraying blood. In the same instant, Samuel heard from above the blasting, clanking rattle of a machine gun. Samuel spun his damaged head around and looked up quickly in the direction from which his deliverance had come. Half blocked from view, at the top of the trench, Samuel saw the figure of Private Haskell firing his Chauchat machine gun down into the trench. As Samuel watched, Private Haskell raised the angle of his aim and swept the stream of bullets farther away down the trench. The members of his squad he had left behind to give covering fire had made it to the trench.

In his peripheral vision, movement off to the other side caught Samuel's eye. Over the top of the trench on the other side, Samuel saw the heads of the members of his squad whom he had sent to flank the trench moving past and away from him on the ground behind the trench. They too were firing down into the trench.

Still partially stunned by the hit to his jaw, Samuel stood up on his feet, his rifle still in his hands. As he moved, he felt as if he were moving in a dreamlike state. His body didn't seem to want to move as fast as his mind was telling it to. He stood in the angle of the trench wall and watched.

The two opposing lines closed and merged into one like an explosive-lined zipper being drawn shut. Farther down the line, the whole trench was erupting in swirling confusion and unchoreographed mayhem. Marines were rushing up to the top edge of the trench. The rattle of the remaining machine guns stopped. The marines had the advantage of momentum and the high ground. They fired their rifles down into the trenches. Germans fired back with rifles and pistols. The troops above also fired back with their own drawn service automatics. For a short but decisive duration, the guns of the closing line of men above and the trapped and spinning line of men below blasted downward and upward toward each other and past each other. German soldiers threw their wood-handled potato masher grenades. Marines threw their own pineapple grenades. Samuel heard the crump of grenades going off outside the trench and inside. Marines leapt into the trench. Both sides lunged with their three-foot-long bayonets. Samuel heard the screams that issued when such implements were employed.

As Samuel watched, a German soldier scrambled up out of the trench and ran toward the rear. Samuel did not fire at him. He never found out whether the man made it or not. Other Germans threw their hands up in surrender. As if they were a rainwater flash flood filling a roadside ditch, marines flowed over the forward side of the trench, filling it. For a short while the only sound of firing came from down inside the trench.

Almost as fast as it had started, the firing came to a stop. As Samuel looked down the trench line, instead of surprised or angry German faces under dark helmets in their darker uniforms raising weapons at him, he saw only the familiar brown uniforms and the faces of the men of his battalion. The gash in the earth that a minute ago had been an enemy lair was now populated by faces he had known longer than he had known the girl's face.

The German artillery stopped firing. The firing in the trench ceased. In the relative quiet that followed, Samuel could hear the ringing in his ears caused by the blow to the jaw from the bullet that had hit him. In a half-numb state, Samuel looked for familiar faces and tried to count noses to see who was there and who wasn't. In his half-dazed state, he knew he couldn't take credit for the victory. His unit had overrun the German line on the strength of their own training and spirit. They would have won without him. But by taking out the one machine gun and diverting so many of the Germans in the trench, Samuel had probably saved the lives of an unknown number of his fellow soldiers. Samuel had no way of knowing the identity of those he might have saved. He would congratulate himself later. At the moment there were more pressing considerations.

The marines had carried the trench. They had carried the day, but they hadn't carried the final day. There were many such days and trenches ahead that had to be carried. Samuel had carried himself through once more. He had crossed the German trench line, but he wouldn't be crossing over to the girl that day. But Samuel wasn't thinking about the girl. In his mind he had heard her screams while was charging the line. Now he was starting to hear the moans and cries of the dying in the trench and from the woods in front. He had to know who among his fellow soldiers had made it and who hadn't. Though wounded himself, he had to help the wounded of his unit.

With his head still buzzing, the bloodied Samuel reached down and picked up the shotgun. He walked around the zag in the trench. Out of the corner of his eye, Private Barker saw him coming. He spun around and raised his rifle.

"Don't shoot," Samuel said, waving his hand. His voice sounded thick to him, but he could still talk. At least his vocal cords were still in working order. "I've already had a bad day at the office. Having you kill me would ruin the day totally for me." He did not want to be sent off to the girl with a bullet from a friend between his eyes.

"Are you okay?" Private Barker asked, looking at Samuel's face. Samuel could feel blood running down the side of his neck.

"Do I have a have a jaw left?" Samuel asked. His fear wasn't misplaced. They were all well aware of the men whose faces had been reduced to human gargoyles by being shot in the face by high-velocity projectiles. Reconstructive surgery was in its infancy. Untold numbers of men with mutilated faces would wear masks for the rest of their lives.

Private Barker looked at Samuel's jaw. "Looks like it's all there and in one piece," he said. "It's sliced open pretty bad. Can you still move it?"

Samuel wiggled his jaw around. He was starting to feel pain. "Yeah, it moves," he said. "I just won't be able to eat solid food for a year." It was a bit of a moot point at the moment. They hadn't eaten anything for almost two days.

Samuel looked down the trench, searching for other familiar faces. "Any other guys in our squad get it?" he asked.

"I don't know," Private Barker said.

Samuel pointed with the shotgun down the trench. The private turned in the direction Samuel indicated he wanted to go, and the two of them walked down the trench, walking over the dead littering the narrow ground. The bloodied Samuel rejoined the rest of his bloodied unit.

"Okay, gentlemen," the captain said as he moved down the trench crowded with the living milling about and littered with the unmoving dead, "you can pat yourselves on the back and buy each other beer in a pub in London when we get back. But this isn't over. We're not out of the woods yet."

He just had to say "Not out of the woods yet," Samuel thought to himself. Samuel still had fond memories of his times in the woods with the girl. On the killing fields of France, he had had enough of anybody's woods for one day.

"The Krauts consider this to be their real estate. They're going to want it back real bad. We've got to prepare for a counterattack. I don't know how much time we've got before they come at us. We've got to get organized and get our perimeter set. We can't afford to kick back and waste any time. We've got a lot to do to get ready."

The captain motioned to a group of soldiers standing near to him and then pointed to the dispirited-looking Germans they had under guard. "You guys run these prisoners to the back of the lines and turn them over to the MPs. We don't need them in our hair in the middle of a close-quarter fight." He motioned to another corporal. "Take your squad and go back to the rear lines and bring up the machine guns. We may be needing them before the day is over. While you're there, send the medical corpsmen up with every stretcher they have. We've got a lot of wounded to evacuate."

The corporal nodded and motioned to his men. The captain started walking down the line again, coming toward where Samuel was standing in the trench. Samuel's head had stopped buzzing, but his jaw was starting to ache. He wondered if it was broken. The captain came up to Samuel and stopped in front of him.

"From what they say, you practically cleaned out this end of the German line singlehandedly," the captain said. "Good work."

"That's what the corps is paying me to do," Samuel said in a flat and self-effacing country tone. "Father always taught me that if someone is paying you to do a job, you should give them a good day's work for a day's pay. It wasn't all my work. The rest of my squad had a hand in it too."

The captain looked at the gouge in Samuel's jaw and then down to the butterfly-shaped bloodstain that had spread out and seeped into the cloth of his fatigue uniform where the single bullet had sliced open both his arm and his side. "Are you hit bad?" the captain asked.

"They're just scratches," Samuel answered. Compared to the seemingly endless spectrum of old-style and new-style wounds that afflicted men in the war, they were scratches. But they were a lot deeper and more painful than the scratches he had gotten on his hands helping his mother tend her roses, or the ones he had gotten on his legs chasing the girl naked around the shore of Gustafson Lake. "They won't slow me down."

"That's good, because I need you bad," the captain said. He waved his finger up and down the two sections of trench that Samuel and his squad had cleared out. "Take your platoon and spread them out through here. I doubt Fritz is going to take the black eye we gave him lying down. Get set for the counterattack they'll probably launch. You did such a good job cleaning out this end of the trench, I'm setting you and your platoon to hold it."

"My platoon, sir?" Samuel said. "Sergeant MacKenzie is the platoon leader. Where's the sergeant?"

"MacKenzie bought the farm," the captain answered. He pointed at Samuel. "You're the sergeant now. Get things cleaned up and ready. If the Krauts hold true to form, they'll regroup and hit us tomorrow morning. But they could come back at us any minute or any hour. We've got to be ready at a moment's notice."

Samuel realized that he would be leaving the woods with another rank insignia on his arm—provided he left the woods alive. He still wouldn't be able to sew his real name on his uniform.

"We're hurting pretty bad," Samuel said. "The company's probably down to half strength, maybe less when we count noses. If they hit us full strength, we may not be able to hold. We're going to need the reserves."

"I've already sent in a request for them," the captain said. "It depends on how badly they're needed elsewhere. If they can't spare them to our sector, we're going to have to depend on ourselves no matter how thin of a margin we've been cut down to. We took this trench understrengthed. If we can do that against the odds, we've got the mettle to hold it even if we're going on thinner odds. If the rest are anything like you, we'll have no problem giving the Krauts another broken nose if they come at us. Carry on."

Officers always seem to say "Carry on" when they don't have any answers and/or when they know the odds aren't in their favor.

The captain turned in a crisp military manner and walked away, going back down the trench. The rank-enhanced Samuel watched him walk away.

You just had to say "bought the farm," didn't you? Samuel said to himself. When a serviceman was killed in the line of duty, the government would pay the surviving family members ten thousand dollars. In those days, ten thousand dollars was just enough to buy a small farm or pay off the mortgage on one. Therefore the soldier slain was said to have bought the farm for his family. Samuel was reacting more to the knowledge that even if he lived through the war, he would never return to the farm of his birth.

"Okay, just like the last trench," Brevet Sergeant Samuel Martin, a.k.a. Sergeant Martin Heisner, USMC, said. "Let's get these dead Germans out of here so we won't be tripping over them."

The Germans had piled the dirt they had dug out when they cut the trench in front of the ditch to give them enhanced cover on what had been their front of the line. The back of the trench, which was now the new front, was lower and offered less protection. The dead German soldiers would partially make up for the absence of earthworks.

The men of the platoon followed Samuel's instructions and started throwing the bodies of the dead German soldiers out of the trench in a line along the back. Who were they to argue with the new company sergeant and the new company hero? A good number of the dead soldiers to be heaved out of the end segments of the trench were Samuel's handiwork.

After they had cleared the inner section, Samuel led the men into the end section of the trench. He put his hand on the shoulder of the first soldier nearest to the angle of the trench wall. As Samuel rolled the man over, the man took a raspy breath.

The startled Samuel looked down at the soldier. His eyes were open.

The man looked upward in no direction in particular. He was still breathing, but his breaths were shallow. Other than the movement of his chest, the man didn't move at all. It was the same soldier whom Samuel had shot in the back of the neck with the shotgun as he had tried to crawl to safety after he had shot him in the chest. Apparently one or more of the pellets in the load had severed the man's spinal column at the neck and had paralyzed him.

Looking at the man struggling for what might be his last few short breaths, Samuel had a vision of the dying girl gasping out her final wrenched breaths in the river, her lungs filling with water, unable to move because she was paralyzed from her neck's being broken. The soldier at his feet didn't look like a Hun to Samuel. Neither did he look like one of the grotesque half-human apelike caricatures in a pointed helmet portrayed stomping over the bodies of dead women and children in the anti-German propaganda posters of the time. The man looked to Samuel to be about his age, even younger. He looked about as ordinary as they come. He was probably just another joe like himself. For all Samuel knew, he was a German farm boy, a farm boy with a family waiting for him back home somewhere in German farming country, a family he might never get back to or to whom he might go back to as an inert lump, paralyzed from the neck down.

Knowing it was his handiwork that had put the man in the condition he was in, Samuel felt a wave of sorrow. His efforts had probably saved many of his friends in his unit. He didn't regret that. He just wished that when he had brought the man down, he had done something different. He just didn't know what that something different might have been. But then again, since the night he had gotten into the saloon fight over the girl back in his hometown, Samuel had spent the inner moments of his life wishing he had done things differently.

Hands reached down to take the limbs of the fallen soldier and throw him out of the trench.

"This guy's still alive," Samuel said, stopping the soldiers from picking the man up. "I think his neck's broken. If you move him, it will only make it worse. Throw the others out if they're dead. Leave this guy here. The corpsmen can pick him up when they come for our wounded."

The soldiers moved on to the next body. Samuel bent down closer to the man. "Just lie quiet and don't try to move," he said. "We'll get a doctor to you as soon as we can, I promise." Samuel didn't know whether the man understood English or even if he was conscious enough to hear him at all.

At that moment, Samuel remembered another promise he had made to come back and be there for someone. It wasn't the girl he was thinking of. Samuel stood up and looked around.

"Where the hell are those corpsmen?!" Samuel growled out loud. "We've got men dying in this trench and spread out all over the woods, and they're off scratching their crotches somewhere."

Samuel scrambled up the side of the trench. "Finish up here," he said to the men in the trench as he climbed out and stood up on the ground. "If the captain wants to know where I am, tell him I went out to bring in wounded."

Samuel headed out on a run in the direction from which he had charged the trench. If the captain wanted to court-martial him for desertion, Samuel didn't particularly care.

When he got into the thicker woods, Samuel had to stop and get his bearings. The area wasn't all that big, but the brush and trees all looked alike. In the speed of the attack, he hadn't made a mental picture of the directions from which he had come or the spot from which they had launched their final assault. Samuel looked at the trees, trying to remember which one it had been, but he hadn't been looking at them when they had taken shelter behind them while under fire from the trench. Looking for patterns of battle damage didn't help either. Most all the trees Samuel saw were punctured up front and shredded on the sides by bullets. He didn't know if they would survive the damage done to them or not. At the moment he was far more concerned with the survival of one damaged friend he had promised to come back for. He just had to find the one tree he had left him under.

Samuel looked around the area he estimated to be the place where he had left the wounded Private Hollingsworth, but he couldn't see him or see any movement. He didn't know if the wound to the lad's leg was bad enough to cause an unattended man to bleed out and die, but it hadn't looked good.

They had been pushing right when they had attacked. From his starting position, Samuel moved to the right. He stopped where he estimated he had dived to the ground when they had been strafed by machine-gun fire from the trench, but he couldn't see anything that looked any different from the rest of the woods. At that point, a metallic glint caught his eye. Under a tree, off to the side, Samuel spotted a pile of empty shells and an open-frame ammunition clip. He went over to the spot. From their shape, the spent shell casings looked like the 8 mm label cartridges used by the French military. Samuel realized that was the spot where Private Haskell had fired his French-made Chauchat machine gun at the Germans. Samuel realized he had been looking far to the left. They had started farther right than where he was standing. In only a few steps more, Samuel found Private Hollingsworth lying under the tree where he had left him and told him to stay down.

As Samuel came up alongside the friend he had met on the ship coming over to France, he got a better look at the wound to his leg. The familiar profile of the knee was gone. In its place was a formless mangled knot of flesh. The red of the twisted tissue and cartilage stood out in contrast to the brown of the pants leg of his uniform, the black dirt of the forest floor, and the green of the woods. The still attached leg lay at a twisted, unnatural angle to the side. Private Hollingsworth had a groggy and half-conscious look on his face as Samuel approached. For a moment Samuel thought the boy might be slipping into unconsciousness from shock and loss of blood, but he turned his head toward Samuel as he approached. Before the boy could say anything, Samuel dropped to his knees alongside him.

"Okay, I'm getting you outta here," Samuel said in a quick and direct military voice. Not knowing how conscious the boy was, he tried to keep his instructions clear and simple so the lad could understand him through the fog in his head. "We can't wait for the corpsmen to find us. I'm going to walk you to the rear lines. You're going to have to help me. I'm going to need you to walk on your good leg for me." Samuel shook Private Hollingsworth's right leg with his hand. "This is your good leg. Don't try to walk on the other one."

"Am I going to lose that leg?" Private Hollingsworth asked in a quietly plaintive voice.

Samuel wasn't a doctor, but it didn't look good to him. He just didn't want to say anything. "I'm not a doctor," Samuel said. "But it's the million-dollar wound that's going to get you out of this war. My job is to get you to the back of the line. You'll be in an American field hospital by the end of the day and a French hospital in the next day or so. But we don't have time to discuss it."

Samuel pulled the boy's right arm up and wrapped it over his shoulder. He had once helped a member of his high school baseball team off the field the same way when he had sprained his ankle during a game.

"Let's go. Leave your rifle here. It's just extra weight."

With the strength of the wrestling team captain he had been, Samuel pulled the boy up off the ground. He waited a second while the boy gained his footing with his good leg. Then he started off with the boy, who was hobbling along on one leg.

There were bodies in the woods off to the sides of the path Samuel was taking back out of the woods. Some of them were moving. Some of them weren't. Samuel looked straight ahead. In his mind he marked the spots where other soldiers of his battalion lay. He would come back for them later. But for the moment his concentration was fixed on getting to safety the boy he had instructed on the transport ship to follow him. The boy had followed him. Now the price of having followed him might be the boy's leg. The same thing, maybe worse, could have happened on some other part of the line. But the boy had been following him. In the hyperbole in his mind, Samuel was determined to get the boy to safety and medical treatment if he had to lug him all the way to Paris.

As they moved, the boy grunted and grimaced at the pain in his smashed leg. Samuel tried to hold a straight-line course to minimize the boy's pain and keep from doing more damage to his leg, but there were trees and shell craters they had to walk around. On the way out, two groups soldiers came running through the woods, heading toward the trench they had just captured. They carried with them the Browning tripod-mounted machine guns the captain had called for. After dropping Private Hollingsworth off at an ambulance, Samuel would be following the men with the machine guns back to where the guns would be set up, facing the counterattacking Germans. The lad would be out of whatever battle came later. At the end of the day the boy might only have half a leg to stand on. After the counterattack that might come the next day, none of those left on the line might be found standing among the living.

Outside the woods, not far from the trench they had started, Samuel spotted two corpsmen heading toward the woods. They were easy to recognize by the red medical crosses on their helmets.

"Hey you!" Samuel shouted to the corpsmen. "Over here. Get this guy to an evacuation ambulance."

The corpsmen changed their direction and came over to where Samuel had stopped. Samuel noticed they weren't carrying a stretcher with them. "Where's your stretcher?" he asked as the medics came up to him.

"We don't have any stretchers," one of the men said to him. He held up a folded blanket. "All we have to carry with are blankets."

"Oh, great, another thing there's a shortage of," Samuel said as the other medic helped him lower Private Hollingsworth to the ground. "Food, water, guns, and bullets. Now it's stretchers. We're short of everything no matter which way you turn. This war has been screwed up from day one."

A lot of men living and dead who had been in the war a lot longer than Samuel would agree with the assessment. Yet the marines had gone into the war better prepared and better armed than the army.

As Samuel held the boy up, the medical corpsmen spread a blanket on the ground. Between the three of them, they managed to position the boy on the blanket doubling as a makeshift stretcher. The corpsmen took a corner of the blanket in each hand and prepared to lift. It would be an awkward carry, probably as painful for the boy as walking had been. But he was on his way to the back of the line and out of the war.

"Okay, you're on your way home," Samuel said as the medics prepared to lift the boy. "We probably won't see each other again. The next time you're on your front porch watching the sunset and your crop is high, think of me."

The boy reached into his pocket and pulled out the piece of paper Samuel had given him with his parents' name and address and the location of the girl's grave on it. He handed it to Samuel. "Maybe you'd better take this," he said. "I don't think they can kill you, but if you're alive and I die and they find this on me, with what you told me, it could be trouble for you."

Samuel took the piece of paper. "You're not going to die," Samuel said. "Not in the field, not on the operating table, not in France. You'll probably die seventy years from now, walking your fields back home on the farm in

Iowa. You'll be buried where you started out. No matter how hard to kill I may be, you'll always be one up on me in that respect."

Samuel turned to the corpsmen. "Get going," he said in his sergeant's command voice. "Get him out of here and back to an ambulance. Then get your butts back here on the double, and bring some others with you. We've got a lot more where he came from lying all over the ground in there."

The medics started to carry the boy away, heading for the safety of the rear lines. For a minute Samuel watched them tromp away, carrying the boy on the blanket stretched between them. From the looks of the boy's leg, Samuel had a nasty feeling that when it came to sitting around estimating crop yields and watching sunsets, the boy would be sitting on his porch wearing a wooden leg. His leg might clunk a bit when he crossed the porch, but he would be walking the floor of his own house and the fields and crop rows of his own land.

As an honorable way out of the war, the boy's shattered leg was a stiff price to pay. After a field surgeon had potentially completed his work with scalpel and bone saw, it could prove to be an even stiffer price. But a large number of men and their families had paid a far stiffer price. At least the boy was going home to family. Even with a wooden leg, he would have what Samuel knew he could never have. Despite the boy's complimenting him on being indestructible, Samuel knew that the next day or any day after he could pay the final price for his life in war.

He never saw the boy again, just like he never saw Rufus or the Kraznapolskis again.

Samuel fingered the piece of paper. The one tenuous link who would inform his family if he was subsequently killed was gone. He wasn't sure if he could trust anyone else with what he had revealed to the boy. If he ended up paying the final price, just how his family would ever learn his fate was something Samuel didn't know. He felt himself not only on another continent but also in another world removed from home.

Back in the woods, their dead and wounded still littered the forest floor. Probably all of the remaining wounded were in worse shape than the boy. They had won that day's battle of the trenches. Samuel had received a promotion. But at that moment, Samuel felt as far removed from military glory as he felt himself removed from home. His face and side were starting to hurt more. He stuffed the piece of paper in his pocket and headed back into the woods at a run.

"Load a new belt before they come at us again!" Samuel half shouted in his newly appointed sergeant voice. Even though the belt wasn't fully depleted, there were only about a dozen cartridges left on the end of the belt hanging from the side of gun. The momentary and relative respite in the German assault gave them a short minute to reload the gun with a full belt. If they had to pause to reload in the middle of a fast-paced charge, the delay could spell the difference between surviving and being overrun.

The soldier to the left of Samuel tossed the empty ammunition box down into the trench. Samuel threw a canister with a full belt up onto the ground next to the machine gun. In quick and practiced order, Samuel pulled the nearly expended belt out of the gun. As Samuel ejected the cartridge in the chamber, the soldier fed the lead strap of the ammunition belt into the open breech of the machine gun. Samuel pulled the end through, then he slammed the breech closed, setting the first round in the chamber.

Samuel, newly charged to be the platoon sergeant, looked down the water-jacketed barrel of the recharged and ready machine gun. His sense of foresight hadn't particularly served him well back home where the girl had been concerned. But under fire in a trench in France, his preparations had been right on the money and right in time. As if the forest were being consumed by a mudslide of black dirt, ahead of him the green of the forest was turning a darker hue as the gray of German uniforms pushed through in a wave. It was yet another charge by a determined and hardened enemy. Mr. Kraznapolski had once said that Samuel couldn't take on the whole world with a gun. Since he had joined the marines, that was all he had been doing.

His ancestors had been some of the first pioneers in the area where his father's farm stood. Though swarming with men bound and determined to kill him, the woods they were emerging from reminded Samuel of the woods by Gustafson Lake where he had made love to the girl. In his mind, Samuel sang the pioneering song his father had taught him, the song he had sung to the girl when he had made love to her by the river:

Come, come, there's a wondrous land
For a hopeful heart and a willing hand.
Come, come, come away with me,
And I'll build you a home in the meadow.

The wave of German soldiers broke through the brush, rushing hard toward the trench Samuel was in. The baseball-coordinated Samuel, well versed in how to throw a baseball past a runner for the baseman to catch and tag the runner out, swung the machine gun in an sweeping arc. He pulled the trigger and held it.

The sunset was turning red on the western horizon behind her. But Mrs. Martin wasn't looking to the west. When she paused in the circles she was turning in, she looked to the darkening horizon to the east. All the horizons in all directions around her seemed to have dissolved into grim landscapes of gnawing fear. That fear was overlaid with her feeling of helplessness to go anywhere and do anything to help the one her fear was for. Samuel's mother's fear hadn't been triggered by a sudden and specific premonition that had come out of the blue, saying her son was about to die. She hadn't had a sudden clairvoyant vision of Samuel lying dead on the ground, the lifeblood draining out of him. But Samuel's mother was sure that she had the instinct she believed all mothers have, the telepathic knowing beyond sense that comes out of the ether and spans the globe to tell them when their child is in mortal danger. Many people would consider that type of quasi-mystical motherly instinct to be superstitious country legend and an old wives' tale. But Mrs. Martin was an old country wife and a mother.

Mrs. Martin was religious, but she wasn't country superstitious. Her deep connection with her son had begun the moment she had first seen him after giving birth to him in the upstairs room of the house behind her. Her maternal connection had continued unbroken after her only son had been forced to flee home under danger of arrest for murder. The connection had continued unbroken, unchanged, and undiminished during the nearly six years she had not seen him. In the twilight of his absence, in the twilight of the life they had known together, in the twilight of the day, Samuel's mother had the feeling that the connection to her son and the final connection to the old world she had known her son in was about to be broken forever on the other side of the world.

Skeptics would say that what Samuel's mother was feeling as she looked away from the sunset to the other side of the world, where the sun was poised above the carnage of battle, was perfectly understandable and explainable, not in terms of telepathy and clairvoyance but in terms of a mother's natural fear. After all, she had read the day's newspaper accounts of how US forces were engaged in fierce fighting with mainline units of the kaiser's army. Like everyone else in town, she knew from the news service what was happening across the ocean. From the letters her son had sent to his sister, pretending to be a distant cousin, Samuel's mother knew he was in the military. She also knew he was in France. It was only logical and natural that the open knowledge that her son was probably in the midst of the very real danger in the fighting would reach down into the subconscious of a superstitious country woman to produce a false sense of telepathic awareness that her child was in imminent peril. Then again, people of the land may, in some deep mystic way, be connected to all the land everywhere.

Mrs. Martin walked back and forth between the farmhouse and the tree in the middle of the yard. She would alternately stop pacing and then start up again. As she paced, she held her hands gripped together in a tight knot below her heart.

She stopped pacing again. Again she looked toward the east, looking in the direction from which he had left the yard of the house when her husband had driven him away from home.

"Oh, Sam," she said quietly as she looked in the direction where the darkness was gathering. Samuel's mother brought her hands up to her mouth. She bit down on the knotted fingers.

On a rattling trolley passing down the streets of Berlin, another mother was focused on her fingers. But she wasn't chewing on them. To all the world, the woman seemed to be locked in impenetrable concentration. With the index finger of one hand, she counted the open fingers of her other hand.

"Eins, zwei, drei, vier, fünf"—German for one, two, three, four, five—she said repeatedly. By the sound of her voice and the blank look on her face, she seemed to be oblivious to any other world except the one in her head and the other at her fingertips.

"Eins, zwei, drei, vier, fünf. Eins, zwei, drei, vier, fünf. Eins, zwei, drei, vier, fünf," the woman intoned at the same unbroken pace.

"Why does she do that?" said a somewhat annoyed-sounding man in a seat across the center aisle of the trolley to the woman's husband, who was sitting next to her.

The woman's husband turned to the man. When he answered, his voice didn't sound annoyed or angered. The tone of his voice sounded as if it were coming from an empty dimension far removed from all the petty annoyances of life.

"You must forgive my poor wife," the man said. "All five of our sons have been killed in the war. Her mind has broken. I'm taking her to the asylum."

When he had bowed his head to pray in church back home, Samuel had often touched his forehead to the back of the pew in front of him. He had done this as a way of grabbing a quick snatch of rest as if out of reverence for the Almighty or because he had been driven to the point of prostrating himself in repentance by Pastor Russell's sermon. In the now quiet trench, Samuel leaned his head forward until his forehead rested on the back of the machine gun just above his hands. He was still gripping the trigger assembly.

"Come, come ye all to me, and I'll dig you a grave in the meadow," Samuel said under his breath.

In the woods in front of the trench, the sounds of moaning were undistinguishable from the sounds that had come from behind the trench when it had been their wounded spread out on the ground. Only when the cries resolved into formed words was it possible to distinguish nationality. Gasps and pleas of "Mein Gott" and "Muttar" issued from the strip of open ground behind the trench that was now the front of the trench. The sounds drifted out of the woods from unspecified directions from men lying unseen on the forest floor. The soldiers of Samuel's unit stood tense and unmoving in the trench, in the same positions they had taken when the attack had begun. However moved or unmoved individual soldiers were by the cries of the wounded they had put down, they had beaten back the German charges. Samuel's understrengthed unit had taken the trench they were in. The even more understrengthed unit had held out against a determined counterattack.

With fingers wrapped around triggers just short of the firing point, the bloodied marines of Samuel's unit squinted down the sights of their weapons, waiting for any next round of human wave that might come at them from out of the woods. No wind waved the tops of the trees with their bullet-shredded trunks. No birds sang in the trees. The only sounds were the moans and cries of the wounded German soldiers spread out to an unknown depth in the woods in front of them.

"Somebody get out there and pick those guys up," Samuel said, raising his head up from the machine gun. "Get the corpsmen working on them to patch them up, or else they'll bleed to death."

"If anybody goes out there now, the Krauts will just pick them right off," one of the soldiers in Samuel's now expanded unit answered. "They'll send their own corpsmen in to pick up their wounded."

Samuel realized the man was right and countered his directive. It would not be an auspicious beginning for his new rank if he were to send men under his command out to be shot by snipers.

"When the German medics come out, hold your fire unless they try something," Samuel said. It was a needlessly redundant instruction. Firing on enemy medics would be an intolerable violation of marine honor.

Samuel looked out into the woods for any sign of movement that would indicate another attack wave was coming or that the Germans were trying to infiltrate from closer up.

Suspended in the trees, Samuel thought he saw the face of the girl. The face was half hidden in the jumbled and broken-up background of the woods. Samuel wasn't fully sure it was the girl he was seeing. His main focus of concentration was on trying to spot movement in the brush. The dead girl would just have to wait in more ways than one.

I see you're still with me, Samuel said to himself, knowing the girl was in his mind and not in the forests of France. *It looks like I've managed to survive for another day. Are you here because you're grateful that I'm still alive, or are you disappointed that I'm not on my way to you? Apparently I won't be coming to you today. But stick around. That could change at any minute of any day. Especially in this war. Pick yourself a shady spot on the shore of Gustafson Lake or down by the river in front of Mrs. Richardson's house, and wait for me there. I may arrive soon enough. You may not even have to wait beyond tomorrow.*

Samuel didn't see the face of the girl in the woods again. There were enough images of death around on all sides to suffice.

The Germans did not come at them again, either charging out of the woods or emerging through the girl's face. Samuel's unit finally received supplies of much-needed food and water. A field medic was able to treat the gash in Samuel's face; he did so by swabbing it with disinfectant and sewing it up, all without the benefit of anesthetic. The pain was almost intolerable, but a true marine doesn't cry or wince. When he later looked at his face in a small shiny metal hand mirror, Samuel felt that the plain-looking Katherine Clarke was better-looking than he was. In his now scarred state, he didn't think that Katherine Clarke would marry him.

After being reinforced by what reserves could be spared, Samuel's unit moved deeper into the woods. Instead of more frontal assaults, the unit re-formed into small combat groups and adopted guerilla-style tactics more suited for combat in the brush. But having ambushed Harold Ethridge in his own barn, Samuel had come to the woods already well versed in guerilla tactics and surprising the enemy on his own turf.

Deeper in the woods with his new rank, Samuel was able to further hone his killing skill with shotgun and rifle. With his heightening and hardening skill as a warrior and leader, Samuel was able to keep some of his men alive who would have otherwise been killed. But his skill as hunter and killer brought only a certain degree of protection. Men die in war under the best of commanders. More of the men he had known were killed around him. After a week's fighting, the marines held most of the woods. Having suffered more than 50 percent casualties, Samuel's unit was pulled out for a week's rest in the middle of June that year and then sent back in to finish the job. The marines had won, but the victory had not come easily. More marines were killed at Belleau Wood and related offensives than would die on Iwo Jima.

The Germans tried one more offensive on July 15 of that year. The French responded with a counterattack of their own. The Second Division had been loaned to the French. On July 18, the Second Division went into action southeast of Soissons. By nightfall, the Fifth Marines had taken the village of Vierzy. The following morning, the Sixth Marines, the brother unit of Samuel's Fifth Marines, continued the attack. They crossed an open field behind a thin line of French tanks. The two days of fighting cost the marines another two thousand dead and wounded. But when the smoke cleared, they found they had broken the German lines and blunted the offensive the Germans had counted on to turn the tide of battle.

After recovering from their losses at Soissons, Samuel's unit went into action again during the Allied attack on Saint-Mihiel on September 12 as part of the newly formed US First Army. By nightfall on the fifteenth, Samuel's brigade held its objective.

Samuel's Fourth Marine Brigade finally received significant reinforcement in the form of the Fifth Marine Brigade, which arrived in France in September of 1918. After the Saint-Mihiel offensive, the Second Division moved over and joined with the French Fourth Army for the Meuse–Argonne offensive. The marines were assigned the task of taking Mont Blanc, French for White Mountain. The position and the attack was key to cracking the German lines. The Sixth Marines led off the attack on October 3, followed by the Fifth Marines. In three days, amid some of the heaviest fighting in the war, the marines seized Mont Blanc.

Following the Mont Blanc engagement, the Second Division joined up with the American First Army's V Corps for what would become the final drive of the war. On November 1, the division attacked on a narrow two-kilometer front. In hard fighting, they pierced the Hindenburg Line, Germany's last main line of prepared defenses defending the German heartland.

Sour and egotistical Prussians are not easily impressed, but the marines duly impressed the forces of Kaiser Bill. Even before the war had ended, the marines discovered they had a new nickname bestowed upon them: Teufel Hunden, German for Devil Dogs. The name meant all the more to the marines because it had been conveyed upon them not by a military recruiting poster or by the editor of a yellow journalistic newspaper but by an otherwise formidable enemy they had impressed with their fighting ability. In time, the nickname Devil Dogs would come to equal the word *leathernecks* or *gyrenes* in the pantheon of names the marines liked to call themselves.

In the late fall of that year, the exhausted Imperial Germany Army launched one more desperate general offensive. For a few days they gained some ground, more ground than either side had gained during four years of static trench warfare. The Allies fell back strategically, letting the German Army extend itself beyond its lines of supply. When the German offensive stalled from lack of supplies and failing morale, the Allies, led by the French, launched a massive counterattack. The dispirited German Army, exhausted and out of food and ammunition, with no fighting spirit left, collapsed. Tens of thousands surrendered. Back in Germany, German society collapsed into dissension and social insurrection. Kaiser Wilhelm and his family fled into exile in Holland, and the German Republic was formed and sued for peace. Instead of ceasing fire then and there, a formal time for the cessation of hostilities and the commencement of the armistice was agreed upon. For that they chose a time everyone could easily remember. On the eleventh hour of the eleventh day of the eleventh month of 1918, the guns fell silent, though both sides continued to fire away at each other at an undiminished clip until the last minute literally arrived.

The day after the cease-fire, Samuel's unit was sent to Paris to take part in a victory parade. To the tune of stirring martial music played by French military bands, the soldiers marched down the Champs-Élysées and through the Arc de Triomphe with the Eiffel Tower in the background. This was the first time Samuel had seen the famous and imperiled city that he had fought to defend and that so many of his compatriots, whom he had soldiered with for longer than he had known the girl, had died for and been wounded for to deliver it from the menace of the Huns. It was also the first time since he had slipped in through the back door of Chicago that Samuel found himself walking the streets of a large metropolitan city. Some of the buildings impressed him, but as a whole the city didn't appear any cleaner or less congested than Chicago had. The Seine river was wider than the river that flowed past his hometown, the river that the girl had met her end in.

Where the Seine river flowed through Paris, it was an open-air sewer. From what Samuel could see of it, the river didn't seem any cleaner or less muddy than the one back home. The one back in his hometown didn't smell as bad.

The crowds lining the streets of Paris cheered and waved. They seemed appreciative enough. Paris was supposed to be the proverbial city of love and romance. The gash in Samuel's face hadn't yet fully healed. As he marched through Paris that day, Samuel figured that with his chopped-up face, he probably didn't cut a particularly romantic-looking figure for the young belles of France to look at.

Not that there wasn't a goodly number of potential romantic mates to be had in postwar France. Four years of war, comprised mainly of meat grinder battles, had decimated the population of young males in the country. A whole generation of young men in France had been nearly wiped out. The situation wasn't much different in Britain and Germany. There were more than enough young French widows mourning the loss of their husbands. There were just as many young French women mourning the loss of active sweethearts and the general loss of men their age. The guns of the trenches had shifted the balance of the sexes and created an appreciable surplus of marriageable young women. There were plenty of sad and lonely women for romantically inclined young men like Samuel to pick up on.

That aspect wasn't going through Samuel's mind as he marched in rank and file through the streets of Paris that day. No real thought of making France his new home was going through Samuel's mind that day as the shops and crowds of Paris went by. Now that the war was over, he was busy in his mind trying to restart and reformulate his plan for slipping back and living close to his home in Ohio. As it would prove to be, any possible romantic encounter leading to a tête-à-tête between Samuel and a lonely Frenchwoman was circumvented before it could start. Not long after the parade, Samuel's unit would march eastward out of France to do occupation duty in Germany.

Corporal Martin Heisner, now Sergeant Heisner, had come out of the war one step in rank above that of a disgruntled German corporal by the name of Adolf Hitler. Sergeant Samuel and Corporal Hitler would never meet. If they had met, they wouldn't have had much to talk about. They could have exchanged war stories and described how they had been wounded. But though Samuel's wound was as readily visible as a Heidelberg dueling scar, Mr. Hitler's wound wasn't immediately visible. He had been sent to a hospital suffering from temporary blindness caused by gas, but it might have been hysterical blindness brought on by his knowing Germany was going to lose the war. The two wouldn't even have been able to talk wistfully of the homes they would be returning to. Samuel didn't know how close he would ever be able to get to the happy home of his past. Mr. Hitler had never had much in the way of a happy home life.

Samuel was thinking of home in terms of a shining light in the distance, a light beyond his reach. Though his sociopolitical views hadn't yet taken final shape, Mr. Hitler was thinking of home in terms of fatherland, and racial superiority, and national and personal destiny denied. Samuel was thinking of home and family in mournful terms of a dream he had forfeited. Mr. Hitler was thinking in growing angry terms of a dream betrayed.

Along with the other soldiers in the parade, Samuel's unit marched through Paris and out the far side. Twenty-two-some years later, the Germans would march the other way down the same Paris street in the cakewalk that Samuel and the men of his unit had helped deny them. At the time, Samuel's dream of returning to the home he had known would seem impossibly far out beyond the horizon. At the same time it would seem to Mr. Hitler that his dream was falling into his hands. Samuel's deferred dream would remain a warm, sad memory out beyond the horizon of a world he could not return to. Mr. Hitler's dream, when brought to full fruition, would set the world and his beloved Germany on fire.

After marching in triumph through the streets of Paris, Samuel's unit was sent on a long march on foot into Germany for occupation duty in the American sector around the Rhine bridgehead at Koblenz. As Samuel and his platoon crossed over the bridge over the Rhine, he looked up and once again caught a glimpse of the face of the girl in the sky between the girders of the bridge he was on.

"Well, Clarinda, it looks like I won't be crossing over to your side of the river anytime soon after all," Samuel remarked to himself and the absent girl while he was on the bridge above the middle of the river. "You'll just have to wait for me a bit longer than both of us figured. Whatever river of eternity you're walking the shore of, sit down, count the daisies, comb your hair, look to the horizon, and wait for me to appear. I'll be along soon enough. I'm just not sure when."

Occupation duty passed dull and uneventfully, though the sound of the backfiring motor of a rattletrap vehicle would send Samuel diving for a foxhole that wasn't there. The German civilians Samuel met in his unit's zone of occupation weren't the slavering gargoyles he had seen in propaganda posters. They seemed friendly and reasonable enough. After having been gouged by French shopkeepers who overcharged them, some soldiers started wondering if they had fought for the wrong people.

The women of Germany had the same problem as the women of France. So many young men had been killed that there was a deficit of marriageable men for younger women. Samuel saw many attractive young fräuleins. A goodly number of them had rounded chests of Wagnerian proportions that rivaled the girl's figure. Though the pointed outlines of the frontal portions of their womanliness sometimes showed through their dresses, none of them wore pointed helmets.

The young women of postwar Germany caught the eye of many a US soldier. Samuel had grown up hard, fast, and far on the battlefield, but in his body he was still a young man. Though he had sworn off women on the train leaving Chicago, as the German spring approached, his thoughts turned again to home and love on home ground. He didn't make any attempt to chat up any of the buxom blonde German women he saw. It wasn't that the dark-haired Clarinda had spoiled him for blondes. For one thing, he didn't speak the language. For another, Samuel knew he would be mustered out of the service and sent home soon enough. He still didn't know what he was going to do when he returned home—home to the United States, that is, not home to the farm. He couldn't take up the life he had left behind. He didn't even know if he could safely take up the state he had left when he had fled from home.

Samuel's unit was pulled out of Europe in the summer of 1919 and shipped back to the States. He went home with the others of his outfit on a transport ship that was as plodding and crowded as the one he had come over on. At least they didn't have to observe the strict blackout procedures that had been in place when he was inbound and the U-boats had been on the prowl. Samuel was able to walk the deck later into the evening. No scared young farm boys came up to him, asking him what it was like to be in combat. Like so many soldiers grateful to have survived, he was being sent home. To Samuel, home still seemed as far away as it had seemed in France or in Chicago.

Samuel and his unit had not quite seen the last of triumphal marching. Not long after arriving home, on the twelfth of August 1919, the Fourth Brigade of marines marched in review down Pennsylvania Avenue past the White House in Washington, DC. It was the first time Samuel had ever seen the city that was the capital of the nation he had fought for and came close to dying for on the fields of France. His brief passage would be the last time he would see the city. Samuel and the men of his platoon wore their best clean and starched uniforms that day, not the sweat-soaked uniforms with dirt ground into them that they had slogged through the trenches, fields, and forests of France wearing.

Samuel had left behind more friends dead than he cared to remember. The usual convention would be to say that Samuel had left his youth and innocence behind him on the blood-soaked fields of France. But he had already left callow youth and innocence behind on the floor of Harold Ethridge's barn, in the gutters of the streets of Chicago, and on the bloody ground at the packinghouse gate.

As a platoon leader, Samuel marched at the head of his unit on the right side. The sun shone on the crisp chevron angles of Samuel's sergeant's stripes. The same sun shone on the irregular-shaped scar that ran most of the length of his lower right jaw. Pennsylvania Avenue was wide enough that even people on the right side of the road might not see the scar and be left uneasy, thinking about the human cost. The direction of the march took them past the reviewing stand in front of the White House on their left. The laceration on Samuel's face was hidden from the official types by Samuel's having his left side to the reviewing stand and by his being on the right, outside of the columns of men.

The marines hadn't slighted the country in war. In return, the government hadn't slighted them that day by sending out only low-level functionaries as a condescending token of appreciation. The officialdom on display for the marching heroes extended all the way up to the president himself.

Samuel knew the president and other important personages were supposed to be in attendance. The marines had been instructed to look sharp and step sharp. To Samuel, the reviewing stand that held the dignitaries he and the men of his unit marched in front of that day seemed large enough to hold half of Congress. Some of the people in the reviewing stand were women. Since there were no female legislators in that day, Samuel figured that they had to be wives of the really top-level dignitaries in the stand. Samuel was marching on the outside, the side away from the reviewing stand. With the rest of his unit between him and the stand, he couldn't get a clear view of who was in attendance on the stand, or what agency of government they worked for, or what branch of Congress they might be members of.

For all Samuel knew, the other men on the reviewing platform might have been congressmen from the House of Representatives or senators from the Senate. But Samuel wouldn't know any members of Congress by sight if he tripped over them on the street in front of the Capitol dome. He hadn't seen any pictures of the contentious men of Congress who had scuttled the president's plan to have the United States join the League of Nations.

Samuel had seen pictures of President Woodrow Wilson in the newspaper and on campaign posters. As his platoon passed in front of the reviewing stand, out of the corner of his eye, through the other soldiers to his side, Samuel caught sight of a long, thin, careworn face. He assumed it to be the president.

President Woodrow Wilson had returned to the United States after months spent hammering out the conditions of the Treaty of Versailles. The treaty, hammered out in a way not to Wilson's liking, boiled down to hammering the German people with punitive reparations for having started the war. The costly reparations would help drive the German economy into hyperinflation and leave the German people broken and in poverty. Mr. Hitler would later play on the resentment created by the heavy-handedness of the treaty to hone his demagoguery and solidify his hold on power, enough to launch a second wave of madness, worse than the one that had left him temporarily blinded.

The heavy-handedness and backstabbing of the treaty process would leave President Wilson broken in his own way. President Wilson had gone to the conference with an idealistic set of principles he called his Twelve Points, which outlined his views of human rights, national sovereignty, and anticolonialism and his definitions of progressive, enlightened rule. His Twelve Points had been sloughed off, ignored at best or treated with scorn at worst, as the victors jockeyed to sort out who got whose colonies, who got what part of whose territory at home, and how much of the reparations money they would get. Self-satisfied men who had not fought a day in the war sat around with tea and cakes to redraw the boundaries of nations and set the destinies of millions.

Against this backdrop, President Wilson had thrown himself and battered his head and the ideals he carried within his head. In the end, President Wilson had come home, driven to the point of nervous breakdown by an impenetrable legacy of European hatreds, by the jockeying for the self-interest of nations, and by Allied vengefulness toward the defeated Germany. In the not so distant future, Mr. Hitler, stewing out of sight in the faraway wings as Samuel's unit marched past the reviewing stand, would hand the vengefulness of the delegates of the victors back to them in spades, along with an added measure of his own spontaneous madness. Twenty years later, his vengeful madness would set Europe and the world on fire in a wider and worse way than anyone had known up to that point. It would totally derail the peaceable future and human rights agenda that President Wilson had tried to build. Though not aware of the details of the postwar territorial jockeying going on behind the scenes, Samuel knew how uncontrolled vengefulness could derail the future.

From his position on the outside of the column, away from the reviewing stand, Samuel could not get a good look at the president. The gaunt man on the reviewing stand was not the same vigorous patrician figure who had bested two other candidates, including Samuel's hero Teddy Roosevelt, to win the presidency. The man was a fading shadow of himself. Wilson's Twelve Points had already faded and withered to nothing in the scorn of the vengeful and opportunistic victors at Versailles. His idealistically conceived and intricately wrought and detailed creedal outline of human rights lay in tattered ribbons on the ground as they were swept off the floor and out of the ornately appointed halls of European arrogance and duplicity.

As quickly as they had come up to be reviewed by the dignitaries on the reviewing stand, Samuel and his unit marched smartly past and away. At the end of the parade, Samuel's unit would be returned to their barracks at the marine base at Quantico, Virginia. In the next few days beyond that, his unit was scheduled to be demobilized.

The march took them past the White House. The line of the march wasn't on Samuel's mind, but the road ahead was. The White House and the reviewing stand fell away behind them. They were marching to the north up Pennsylvania Avenue. The sun was behind them.

Over Samuel's shoulder the sun had turned orange on the horizon. The fading vista it illuminated was the rifle range at the marine base at Quantico, Virginia. Samuel was alone. There were no crowds. No one was around. Looking out across the open range was like looking out over an empty field that had been recently plowed.

Samuel walked slowly down the firing line, looking out over the empty rifle range at sunset. He wasn't on the rifle range because he was gung-ho or because he had any particular desire to relive his days on the live-fire ranges of Europe when he had been the target. He had come to the rifle range because he needed a quiet and open place to think. He had often gone walking in the fields of his farm when he had wanted to think. Samuel had always felt that he could think better when he was on open ground.

In the next two days, his unit would stand down and be officially demobilized. For all those who had survived the war, for those not remaining in the corps, it meant they would be going home at last. For many it would be a joyous occasion. For a few it would be a bittersweet occurrence. Some of them had left pieces of their bodies on the fields of France. Others had left pieces of their minds embedded in the wreckage of the war. Others would carry pieces of the war embedded in their bodies and in their minds for the rest of their lives.

With the sunset behind him, Samuel's one organizing hope of returning home faded with the setting sun. As he stood alone on the empty rifle range, running the calculations around in his mind, he found they weren't adding up to his going home. It had been almost seven years since he had gunned down Harold Ethridge back in his hometown. But by Samuel's estimate, not enough time had passed for the memory to have faded enough for him to return home. Samuel had always known that he would never be able to return home to the house and the town of his birth. The town's memory of what he had done would never fade.

As the sun dropped out of sight behind the landscape of Virginia, Samuel's long-held hope and plan of returning home dropped below the horizon. Until more time had passed, he calculated that returning and living as close to home as he had wanted and planned would be too risky. It wasn't just a risk to him. If he were caught and it was discovered that he had been visiting his parents, they could possibly be put in legal jeopardy. He had been keeping in touch with his parents by corresponding with his sister, Beth, under the guise of being a distant cousin. If it were to be revealed that she had been withholding information from the police, she could find herself in legal trouble as an accessory after the fact. Beth could face possible arrest and jail tie for aiding and abetting a fugitive just as she was starting her life as a young wife and mother. By easing back to the borders of home too early, he wouldn't just be putting himself in danger; he could be putting the family he loved and wanted to return home to in legal peril.

In that moment of full realization, Samuel knew he couldn't subject them to that kind of possible trouble. By his thoughtlessness, he had already brought so much hurt to those who loved him and to those he had loved and wanted to love. By his reckless act of violence, he had driven Clarinda away from him and toward death at the hands of Harold Ethridge. He had made himself an outcast and fugitive by his heedless vengeance upon Ethridge. He couldn't put the remaining family he loved in danger by committing the emotional and irresponsible act of trying to come home to them before it was safe to do so. The war had burned into him concern for his men above concern for himself. The orange of the sunset over the rifle range seemed to burn concern into him for the danger he might put his family in because of his sentimental desire to slip back home.

Samuel was determined this time not to decide things in the irresponsible and reckless manner with which he had hurt so many people before.

There and then, Samuel cast the second-largest die of his life. When his unit would be mustered out of service, he would reenlist in the marines. Maybe after one more enlistment, enough time would have passed that it would then be safe to move back closer to home.

Samuel drew his foot in a random line across the dirt behind the firing line of the rifle range, setting the lines he would cross and would not cross. As much as he loved his family and wanted to see them again, both he and they would have to wait until it was safer for all of them. Until in his estimate the situation had died down with the passage of time, or at least once Constable Harkness had died or retired, Samuel would continue to live his scattered life apart from his family. But with his sister's marriage and her moving away to her own home, his family was already starting to scatter. Just how far they would be scattered before he could get back closer to them was something Samuel didn't know.

In his mind, Samuel settled his career path. For the time being, he would stay in the marines. Other US veterans of the Great War would follow in his path and stay in the military, men with names like Eisenhower, Patton, and MacArthur. General Pershing would retire with accolades following him. A little-known artillery officer by the name of Harry Truman would leave the service and, for a while, go back to selling hats. Later he would go into politics and find far more success than he had found as a milliner.

As far as the career and life path of another veteran of the Great War would go, over in Germany, after failing as an artist and wallpaper hanger, Adolf Hitler would go into politics. There he would rise fast and far. For Herr Hitler, it would be a destiny dream come true. For others, it would spell the beginnings of an engulfing nightmare.

For Samuel, the end of the war would spell another endless length down the long and narrow corridor he had been walking since he had left home.

Chapter 35

With casual indifference to stated emphatic injunctions, a soldier lit up a cigarette, took a puff, and exhaled. As he was taking a second puff, the cigarette was brusquely yanked out of his mouth and thrown on the ground. A boot stomped the cigarette out. The next thing the private saw was the glowering face and stripes of Marine Staff Sergeant Martin Heisner pressing into his face.

"I told you no smoking!" the sergeant growled. He pointed away, toward the dark lumped forms, peaks, and recesses of the mountains of Nicaragua, not far from the Honduran border. "You think those guys out there are stupid hicks just because they're uneducated peasants? Most of them have probably never been more than twenty miles from where they were born. But they know those mountains like the backs of their hands. They know every sight in the woods. Every sound. Every smell." He grabbed the soldier's hand that held the cigarette pack and held it up. "They can smell one of these from a mile away." He grabbed the soldier's other hand, which held the cigarette lighter he had lit the cigarette with. "From up in the mountains, the flash made by one of these can be seen from twenty miles away across the valley. You may have given away our position!" He looked around at the platoon of men. "But that might work in our favor. If they have spotted us, hopefully they'll think we'll hold position here for the night."

Samuel, known to the men under his command as Staff Sergeant Heisner, pivoted his head as he swept a glance over the men around him. "But we're going to steal a march on them. We're going to take a page out of their playbook, go where they don't expect us to go, and be waiting for them where they don't expect us to be. We're already in their backyard." He pointed up into the nearby mountains, growing gold in the late afternoon setting sun. "I intend us to get even deeper into their backyard. Maybe it's instinct. Maybe I'm flattering myself thinking I have instinct or that I know the way they think. But I think they're going to hit the United Fruit Company plantation tonight. They're overdue to hit it. Instead of chasing after them all over the mountains, following their dust after they've hit and pulled out before we can get our pants on. That's the way it's been going. This time, instead of us stumbling around chasing the wind after it's blown through and gone, we're going to be there waiting for them when they come down. We're going to be in their faces and be gone before the ones left standing even see our faces. I know a thing or two about setting up ambushes. What worked in Haiti can work here."

He didn't mention that he had originally become proficient at setting up ambushes in barns in Ohio.

"But we've got to get into position before they come out. It may be a long wait. They may not come out at all. We may be there all night for nothing. Just like the corps: Hurry up and wait. You may get hungry waiting. Just keep in mind that the insurgents are a lot harder case than you candy-asses think you are. They're hardened to the point that they can exist on short rations of just a handful of beans. Their diet would have you chewing on your knapsacks for something more to fill your stomachs. If you get hungry waiting, chew on a candy bar or on your belt. But be quiet about it. You can get your steak and eggs and smoke your weeds back at base when it's over. Out here we do it their way and we do it better than them. So let's move out."

Samuel hoisted his BAR. "Don't underestimate them. Don't overestimate them. Don't over estimate yourselves. Don't get clumsy or careless."

Throwing his arm through the strap, Samuel shouldered his BAR. He waved at the others to follow, and took the point lead.

"Follow me. Stay in the trees and off the main paths. They've got them booby-trapped with tin can bombs filled with dynamite and nails. We disarmed one of them. We're going to give it back to them, the hard way. Bring our own charges, the detonators, and the battery. Watch out for trip wires. Watch out for snakes. But don't holler if one bites you. Just cut incisions around the bite holes and suck out the poison. Keep your wits about you. Keep your mouths shut and your eyes busy looking all around for the slightest sign of movement. Keep your ears open. Don't get lazy. This is far from any place to get lazy and overconfident. Don't underestimate them, and maybe you'll get back to base to write your girl back home about how exciting and glamorous life in the corps can be."

In the mid-1920s, Nicaraguan insurgents were engaged in a guerilla war against the tin-pot dictatorship government of Nicaragua and against the plantations and fruit-packing plants of the US-owned United Fruit Company, which they saw as being in league with the government. Along the lines of the interventions in Haiti and the Dominican Republic, the United States sent in a legation guard to help quell the unrest. The legation guard left the country in 1925, but continuing unrest brought the marines back the next year. The Second Marine Brigade under Brigadier General Logan Feland created and trained a Nicaraguan Guardia Nacional along the same lines of the guards that had been established in Haiti and the Dominican Republic. After that he stayed on to supervise reasonably free elections.

Augusto César Sandino, the fieriest leader of the Nicaraguan insurgents, did not agree with the arrangements. He took his men up into the mountains near the Honduran border and continued to carry on the war. For the next six years, the marines and the Guardia fought him, sometimes in good-sized pitched battles. They were all part of the Banana Wars as they were called at the time.

But most of the fighting was patrol actions of the kind Samuel's unit was engaged in that day. Samuel's squad was part of the larger unit led by Captain Merritt A. "Red Mike" Edson, who led sensational patrols in native boats up the wild Coco River along the Nicaraguan border with Honduras. Though the river was bigger than the one that ran by his hometown, riding in the boats on the river had made Samuel think about that river, the river next to which he had made love to Clarinda, the river she had been found dead in. As he had ridden in the boats, there had been memories in mind, but no thoughts or echoes of love came out of the jungle to ease his memories of the girl he had left behind dead and the home he had left equally far behind.

That evening, far from the river, farther from the river that ran past his hometown, there were no boats to sit in and ride. Whatever encounter was to come, whatever fate might await them, they would get there by foot all the way. Hurry up, bear down, and hump it.

"Okay, spread out along this side of the road," Samuel said in a hushed near-whisper to the men in the platoon. "Don't bunch up. At least ten feet between you. If you're too close together, that will make it easier for them to hightail it out of the ambush when the shooting starts. They also may outnumber us. I want to get them all the way into the ambush before we spring it."

"Why do you want us on only one side?" a soldier asked. "Wouldn't it be more effective of an ambush if we were spread out on both sides? Catch them in a crossfire?"

"If we did that," Samuel said, "at this close-quarter-range distance, we'd end up shooting each other in the face. We don't have any trenches to hunker down in for protection. I want our fire directed in one direction so we don't nail each other. I don't want anybody in this unit killing anyone else in the unit. I don't want any friendly fire casualties."

Having said that, he turned to another soldier. "Swanson, take your squad and set up on the other side at the far end of the ambush facing up the path. Stretch the trip wire to the rattle can about a foot off the ground. Use black string so they won't see it in the dark, especially if they're not looking for it. When they trip the rattle can, we open up from the side. You shoot up the path in the direction they're coming from." What he was setting up was an L-shaped ambush. Decades hence, the Viet Cong would use the same tactic to effect in their backhand war. "If they jump off the path on your side, you can nail them before they get away into the jungle."

He pointed to another soldier. "Set out their booby trap can on the other side of the path about fifty feet up the path from Swanson's position. Lay the detonator wire on the ground over to this side. The black wire won't show in the dark. Keep the detonator switch in your hand, but don't get nervous and squeeze it before they're in place. When they trip over the wire to the rattle can, hit the detonator switch."

Samuel did know a thing or two about setting ambushes. But an ambush works better when you can see what you're shooting at.

He pointed to another soldier. "Climb up in these trees and set the flares. Trail the wires down behind the trees so they don't show. Wire them up to the hand detonators, but keep your hands loose on the detonator switch. When you hear them coming, don't get nervous and set them off too soon. Wait till I give you the word. Until then, keep your mouths shut. Do everything right, and we might be able to put a lot of them down and get away before they know what hit them and gain the ability to rally. If we give them a taste of their own hit and run, maybe they won't want to come back to these parts."

The marines under Samuel's command went quickly about following his directions. Some of them were not sure why they were in Nicaragua. Others weren't sure it was the right war at the right time to be in. The more immediate thinkers weren't sure what would happen if it came down to shots fired. But they had confidence in Samuel. They figured that any man who could survive a face-to-face firefight in the trenches with the storm troopers of Kaiser Bill and had faced down and put down insurgents in Haiti and the Dominican Republic probably had a good handle on what he was doing. It gave them more confidence that he would never lead them in an impetuous and reckless manner. But Samuel had never told them about the girl and the manner in which he had dealt with Harold Ethridge.

The preparations having been completed, Samuel and the marines of his contingent hunkered down in the dark of a jungle night and waited. Back to hurry up and wait. It always seemed to come down to that—that and long hours of boredom punctuated by moments of sheer terror. For their part, the men under Samuel's command didn't know what, if anything, the rest of the night might bring. For his part, Samuel figured it might very well come down to nothing at all. His guess that the insurgents would come out that night might prove to be very wrong. In the morning they would take down their explosive devices, leave their positions, and trudge back to their base camp. Another night they would hurry up, wait, and do it all over again.

After a wait that seemed interminably long but had been only about two hours, the shuffle of multiple feet approaching, coming down the path toward their position, came to them, low-pitched and distant at first, growing louder as the walkers drew closer. Whoever was coming wasn't sneaking silently but was being careful not to make any noise. They seemed to be walking at a normal pace, seemingly sure they had the jungle path to themselves and were in no danger. Apparently they were assured that the marines in their area were ensconced in their base camp, filling up on military rations and smoking American cigarettes, and would otherwise pose no problem for them. Samuel figured they figured they could hit the United Fruit Company plantation with ease and be long gone before the marines got there.

Samuel silently flipped off the safety switch on his BAR. He put his hand on the shoulder of the man lying prone next to him.

The company of insurgents moved past them down the path in the dark, more felt than seen. The fire discipline that Samuel had instilled in his men held. No one panicked. No one fired early. The line of insurgents moved past them in the dark, maintaining their own discipline with regard to noise. None of them talked, laughed, joked, or smoked. Their peasant sandals made only soft swishing sounds as they walked down the path coming down from out of their mountain redoubt—the path they thought they owned.

The relative silence was suddenly broken by the rattling sound of the loose pebbles in the rattle can, rattling as the insurgent on point lead tripped the string connected to the rattle can.

"Hit the flares!" Samuel shouted to the marine with his hand on the trigger switch. The electrically triggered flares tied to the side of a tree erupted in a stream of blinding white light that revealed a line of startled armed insurgents dressed in peasant garb and carrying a variety of weapons. Some of them carried lever-action Winchesters, the classic Wild West rifle. Others carried what looked like bolt-action rifles, most likely Spanish Mausers.

"Hit the dynamite can!" Samuel said to the man whose shoulder he had his hand on.

Before the insurgents could take cover, the booby trap can packed with dynamite, nails, and other pieces of sharp metal, the booby trap that had been intended for them, exploded with a sharp bang. It had been set at a spacing from the far end of the ambush, set to catch the middle of the insurgent column. At that close range, the blast was almost deafening. Men screamed as the improvised shrapnel tore into them.

"Open fire!" Samuel shouted.

From along the line of ambush and from the far end of the ambush, firing erupted, aimed at the standing men outlined in the harsh light of the flares. Samuel swung his BAR down the line of insurgents, firing it tipped on its side, allowing the kick of the weapon to help swing it in an sweeping arc. His was the only automatic weapon in the platoon. The other marines fired with their bolt-action 1903 Springfield rifles, working the bolts as fast as they could.

Some of the insurgents fired back inaccurately and ineffectively. With the harsh light of the flares blinding them, they could not see where to shoot. The marines, spread out on the ground in prone firing positions, were not looking into the flares. The insurgents outlined in the light of the flares were easy targets. Those who fired back were quickly cut down. Men who were hit screamed and fell where they stood. Others ran off into the jungle. Many of them were cut down before they could get very far. The firing continued unabated until no more motion was seen. It had not been a drawn-out fight like the attack at Belleau Wood or the fight at the Packingtown plant gate. In less than one punctuated minute, it was all over.

"Cease fire," Samuel said. He listened carefully to the restored silence of the jungle but could hear nothing. The surviving insurgents had moved out of hearing range. One man lay moaning on the ground on the path.

"Okay," Samuel said in a quick command voice, "pick up their rifles. No need to leave them around for the other insurgents to pick back up. After that, let's get out of here. I don't want to be around in case they come back with reinforcements looking to get even for their buddies."

They quickly picked up the fallen insurgents' weapons.

"What are we going to with him?" one of his platoon said, indicating the wounded insurgent groaning on the ground. "Should I shoot him?"

"Marines don't shoot wounded prisoners," Samuel said gruffly. "Just pick up his gun and leave him. His buddies will come back for him. They don't leave a man behind any more than marines do. I don't want to be around when they come back looking for him and us."

He looked around at his men as they picked up the dead insurgents' rifles. The flares were beginning to burn out. The light was fading.

"We bloodied them pretty good tonight. Hopefully they'll take a clue, move away, and not operate in this area again. But we're not going to make book on it by hanging around here with our asses hanging out where they know we're at. So let's hurry up and roll."

They picked up the insurgents' weapons and moved out orderly but quickly, headed back to their base camp. It had been neither a stirring triumphal victory nor a disheartening defeat. It was what it was. The dead were dead. Samuel and the marines of his platoon were alive—alive to write letters home to the girlfriends they had left behind. Samuel was still alive to remember the girl and see visions of her face in the sky. He had not joined her that night. He wondered if he ever would.

Samuel's estimate that things were not over for him or the marines in Nicaragua proved more accurate than even he had imagined. In July of 1927, in one of the stiffest actions in the Nicaraguan war, thirty-eight marines, including Samuel's unit, and forty-eight *guardias* defended the mountain town of Ocotal against a determined siege by Augusto Sandino. The fight was far more intense and drawn out than the ambush on the mountain path.

The action at Ocotal was a primitive prefiguring of the urban fighting of World War Two. In a primitive prefiguring of action in wars to come, the defending marines were given air cover in the form of close-in bombing raids by marine DH.4 De Havilland bombers. After the successful defense and more losses among his forces, Sandino retreated. The marine victors celebrated with a triumphal victory picture, after which they went back to pack it, lift it, carry it, hump it, and move out.

Life in the corps didn't appreciably change for Samuel Martin, a.k.a. Martin Heisner, after the battle. Like the French (and a whole lot of others) say, the more things change, the more they remain the same. The future still remained unseen and unknown to him out over the horizon. While his future remained unseen, his past dropped away from him, deeper and more irretrievable. The biggest loss of all the sequential losses that had piled up for him and upon him since he had left home came in the form of a letter delivered to him in camp in Nicaragua. By the handwriting on the envelope, Samuel could tell without opening the letter that it had come from his sister. The handwriting was delicate and frilly enough that it was obvious it came from a female source. Though the letter addressed him as her cousin, the other marines in his unit suspected she was really a secret girlfriend. Many of them had the proverbial girl they had left behind waiting for them back home. They suspected he had one too. Samuel would just shake his head and quietly say she was his cousin as the salutation on the letterhead indicated. Nothing in the letter to see or talk about.

Getting the letter from Beth in camp soon after the engagement in the hills was one small gratification to be had in the remote camp between remote mountains in a remote and unfamiliar country, engaged in a remote war that probably all the familiar names in his hometown and most Americans weren't even aware of. Her letters were the only source of information about his family. He carefully opened the letter with the blade of a jackknife, as he did with all letters from home, so as to keep the envelope intact so the letters could be saved from ruin by rough travel in a knapsack and read again. A bayonet would have ripped the letter mortally. The sun had set behind the mountains. Darkness had come on and was deepening. Out of sight of the others, Samuel sat by a lantern. He unfolded the letter and started to read:

Dear Cousin,

I do so much hate to be the bearer of bad tidings to you so far away in a land of bad tidings. But I must say what must be said and get it past me.

As for sorrowful passings, I regret to inform you that my father passed away recently.

Samuel froze with the letter in his hand. It was his father as well as hers she was talking about. She just felt that even under the circumstance, she had to continue with the relationship deception of being his cousin on the chance that military censors might read her letter and figure out that Samuel had enlisted under a false name. That would be enough trouble for him, but it could lead to an investigation of him that might reveal his true identity and lead to his arrest for the killing of Harold Ethridge in their hometown.

> Father apparently had a heart seizure while plowing in the field. He fell off the riding plow he had been working from. Our hired hand became worried when the team returned to the barn alone, still hitched to the plow. He went out into the field and found Father lying between the rows of standing corn. If there is anything fortunate to be found in this, fortunately he seems to have died quickly and didn't suffer in his passing. He also died doing what he had done all his life, namely, farming the land. He died living the way he wanted to live, doing the work he wanted to do. He loved the land. Now he will enter into and become part of the land. I am making the funeral arrangements as Mother is too distraught to handle it. He will be interred with his parents in the family plot in the local cemetery. When Mother dies, she will be interred next to him.

It was a code phrase for the same cemetery where his grandparents had been buried. His father would now be buried next to them in line, in the cemetery where the girl had been buried under the headstone Samuel had had carved for her, buried under the name she had given herself, the name she had died without ever revealing it to him or anyone.

> Mother is terribly broken up about the passing of the only man she had ever loved. She has become mournful, morose, and languid. She hardly talks anymore, even to me. She sits all day, either in the front room or on the outside porch, and stares out vacantly across the room or across the land. It is not as if she is trying to see the future but is trying to see the past again and to reach it.

She doesn't seem to see a future. I don't know if she sees any future for herself. She may eventually pull out of her disjunction from life and her lassitude. But I don't think she will or can return all the way to a hopeful vision or even an ongoing one in this life.

Father will be buried in the family plot next to and in line with Grandmother and Grandfather. In the fullness of time, when my and my husband's lives have run their course, I and he will be buried in his family plot in the town we live in now. If you do not come home to be buried next in line to your parents, your family line and name will cease with their graves.

It always seemed to come down to names, names real and false, names uncertain, a name unshared. It had started with the girl and her dogged refusal to state her last name or give him her real first name. Samuel had wanted to give her his last name. At the time he had known the girl, it just hadn't quite fully dawned on him that her rejection of her real name was a deeper sign of her rejection of all names and her desire not to be pinned down under any name other than the one she had given herself. Her rejection of names had been part and parcel of her way of not getting pulled into a life she didn't set for herself.

My mother is not physically, emotionally, or financially able to maintain a farm on her own, no matter how much she loves it and considers it home. Nor does she have the stamina, physical or emotional, to do so. Neither does she have the business sense and acumen to manage a farm. Father always handled that. Mother kept the house well when Father was alive and I was there, but now there is no one there to keep it for. I, my husband, and my family have taken my mother into our house to live with us on our farm. The farm she lived on and worked in the house of will be sold and the proceeds dedicated to her keeping. If more is needed, like the Good Samaritan, we will make

917

up the difference as if she were a member of our own house, which she will become.

I can understand how my unwelcome news might hit you hard. You and my father were very close. In some ways you were as close as father and son. You visited often. We all spent a lot of time together in each other's company. When you lived in the same world as us, you spent a lot of time with us. You were always welcome in our house. You were like a son to my parents and a brother to me. Since you went far away, we have missed your presence and hope you will be able to return to us someday.

Samuel's hand closed on the letter, crumpling it partially. Return to whom? Return to what? His mother and sister were still alive, but the farm he had grown up on and had loved was gone. His sister and mother had gone to another family. He smoothed out the letter and went on reading.

I am starting to break down. My chest is becoming heavy and tight with pain and sorrow. I cannot bring myself to write any more at this time. I will write to you again. Do not fail to write to me, no matter how far away you are or on what far side of the world you might be on.

Again it pains me to be the bearer of the news that my father is now far away from both of us. His parting has hurt me grievously. Your parting from us hurt us both. But I do not believe that partings on this earth are partings forever. I'm sure that we will all stand together once again on that bright shore far away.

Your cousin,
Beth

Samuel folded the letter and held it in a tight, straining grip. Tears started to form in his eyes. He didn't try to hold them back or quickly wipe them away. It was too dark and he was too far away from the others to be seen crying. Besides, marines aren't supposed to cry.

His father was dead. He would not see him again in life. The idea he had carried in his mind for so long to slip back close to home and visit his parents in secret dissolved in his mind and disappeared into the darkness shadowing and concealing the Nicaraguan mountains.

At that moment, Samuel, the farm boy who had never wanted to be anyone but a farmer on his land, felt like he was being ripped in two. He felt ripped apart not only over his father's passing and the knowledge that the home he wanted to return to and live in the periphery of was finally and fully removed from him but also by the feeling that he was far removed from the land of his youth, in a foreign land, fighting not for the United States and democracy like he had done in France in the Great War, but fighting for the US-business-owned United Fruit Company, an ally to Nicaragua, that was protected by the corrupt Nicaraguan government against insurgents who had formerly been simple farmers like him and had been forced off their land and were now trying to regain sway over the land that had once been in their family—had been in their family for generations—as the farm he had never planned to leave had been in his family for generations. At that piercing moment, Samuel felt like a skulking traitor to the land and to all farmers on the land.

Samuel could no longer believe in his mission or in himself on the mission. A marine who cannot believe in his mission or in himself is dead. Samuel felt dead inside. He did not know if he would ever feel alive again. The feeling was nothing new. He had felt the same way when he had seen the girl lying dead on the table in the basement of the station house in his hometown. He had felt the same way on the train leaving Chicago. He would continue to do his duty and go on with his mission, though he no longer believed in his mission or particularly believed in himself.

At that moment of piercing light, all that was left to Samuel was to wonder what he was there for, whether any good would or could come of it for him or for either country, and whether he would survive. Decades later, a good number of other American soldiers would wonder the same thing about their mission in an even farther-away land called Vietnam.

Samuel looked up into the sky. In the darkened sky he saw the face of Clarinda floating above and away from him. The look on her face was neither sorrowful nor sensual. Nor was it optimistic. Her expression was flat, distant, and uncertain in what emotion it expressed. He didn't think the girl had any answers to the questions that had haunted him since she died, but he intended to have a word with her.

"I see you're back to haunt me," Samuel said under his breath, directing his words at the face in his mind in the sky. "And you're here at the time when I'm most haunted by memories of the happiness that was between me and my family and the happiness I hoped would exist between you and me, the happiness that didn't come to be between us. The happiness you didn't believe in."

Samuel steadied himself and went on with his silent soliloquy directed at the silent face in the sky.

"In one way I'm angry with you. None of what has happened would have happened if you had run to me and not away from me. If you had joined yourself and your life to my life, you might be swimming naked with me in Gustafson Lake and not be floating high above me where I can't reach you. I would be home with the family I grew up with. Father would be gone, but at least I would have been close by when he died. He wouldn't have died alone in the field, the field I loved as much as I loved him. My sister would still be married and living in the next town over. But it would be an easy thing to visit her. Mother would still be sorrowful about father's death, but she would have her son and daughter-in-law with her in the home she knew and loved for so long."

Samuel looked at the vision of the girl suspended in the sky. The vision held its place in his mind.

"I suppose I can't be angry with you. It wasn't your fault that you died. You didn't ask to be killed. But then again, it was your fault. If you had come to me and joined with me—joined with me in heart and soul as well as in your practiced physical way of joining—and if you had married me, if you had run to me and run with me instead of running away from me, we might be together there in the town where it all began. ... You were also running from a name you didn't want to hear spoken again. Even when you were not in motion, you were still running. In your mind and soul, you were never at rest. I tried to catch up with you, but I couldn't. I couldn't get near to you, really near to you, on your endless run. Trying to catch you was like trying to catch the wind."

Samuel looked away from the vision of the girl.

"Are you at rest where you are, or are you still running? Do you feel sorry for yourself? Do you feel sorrow for the life you never had, the life that was ripped from you, ripped from you by those you knew before you came to my town, by the one who ripped your life from you in my hometown? Or are you beyond sorrow, beyond in a land that knows no pain? Is it a land of light and rejoicing like the pastor spoke of? Or is it a limbo of waiting, waiting for your life to be validated in some manner by a higher Life than yours? I can't tell what you're thinking or feeling by the look on your face. But then again, it was always hard to tell what you were really thinking and feeling on the inside by looking at the expression you held on your face."

Samuel paused a moment in his reflection. Without looking up at the reflection in his mind, he went on, this time speaking silently.

Like you, I'm on a run of my own. I started my running just after your time ran out. One way or the other, through one fight or the other, I've been running since. … Whatever dimension or world beyond that you inhabit now, does it make you happy that I'm a runner like you were? Are you looking for me to come and join you in your run through eternity? That may happen any day now. But so far I've proven pretty resilient. You may have a long time to wait before I catch up to you.

Samuel looked back up. His vision of the girl was gone. He saw only the empty dark sky of Nicaragua and the mountains concealed by the darkness.

"Well, that was a short visit on your part. I see you're gone again. But while you were alive, you spent as much of your time with your soul gone from me as you spent with me. Why should this night be any different? Does your leaving me now mean you have no answers for me, not even from out in the beyond? You never had any real answers for me while you were alive and next to me in the town and the life we briefly shared. Did you ever have any real answers for yourself there or anywhere? Did you ever even pause in the run that was your life to ask yourself any questions? But you never got yourself to the answer stage. I'm no closer to those answers down here than I was standing outside your door in Mrs. Richardson's house."

Samuel looked at the flickering light of the lantern. He didn't see any more answers or any view of the future in it than he had seen in the girl's face in the sky.

For his actions and leadership in Nicaragua, Staff Sergeant E-6 Martin Heisner was promoted to sergeant first class E-7. He was later reassigned to a marine base in California. It was there that he learned in another letter from his sister that his mother had died, her death possibly partially caused by her lingering sorrow and the emptiness brought on by the death of her husband, whose passing she had never gotten over and didn't want to get over. People with depth of heart often hold dearly to the love and memory of the one person who was special to them beyond all, whether that person was a man who was the salt of the earth or a willful, frightened girl on the run.

FDR brought the marines out of Nicaragua at the beginning of 1933. Though the marines in the expeditionary force had bloodied his forces, they had not caught Sandino. A year after they left, Sandino was lured out of the hills by promises of amnesty and political reform of the government and the social system of the country. Instead of ever seeing the promised reforms, he was assassinated by the director of the Guardia Nacional and future president, Colonel Anastasio "Tacho" Somoza Garcia. Somoza would make himself dictator and go on to rule and trouble Nicaragua for decades, until he was overthrown and later assassinated himself by the partisan descendants of Sandino, who named themselves Sandinistas after their spiritual father Augusto Sandino.

Several years afterward, Samuel was promoted to master sergeant and was reassigned to a marine unit stationed near Pearl Harbor, Hawaii. Whether you were in the army, navy, marines, or coast guard, Pearl Harbor was considered to be a choice posting, even idyllic. But most of that was lost on Samuel. To him, Hawaii was a remote place far away from the home he had grown up in, as far on the opposite side of the world he had never particularly wanted to see as he had been from home when he had been in the trenches of France. Hawaii was just another place far removed from the world and the home of his past.

Over the intervening years, the situation evolved from a threat to the United Fruit Company into a threat to all of Europe, including England;

to the United States; and beyond that, through the alliances of madmen, to most of the world. It also evolved into a threat to democracy, to freedom, to tolerance, and to sanity itself. Madness arose in Germany that made the madness of Kaiser Wilhelm seem like reasoned coolness by comparison. On the opposite side of the globe, the Imperial Japanese Empire had been on the move for some time, longer than Hitler and Germany had been on the march, invading neighboring countries and assassinating moderate members of their own government in Japan. Presently they were marching faster and farther afield. In the final extension, the range of their marching would stretch across all of Southeast Asia. From there it would move through the length of Burma to the border of India, before eventually being halted. On both sides of the world, the once seemingly inexorable and unstoppable rush of Fascism of all kinds would eventually be stopped hard at the battles of Moscow, Kurtz, Stalingrad, El Alamain, Midway, Guadalcanal, Iwo Jima, and Okinawa and the beaches of Normandy. From there on out, the mad tyrants and their crews of killers would not move forward again, only backward to defeat and the grave.

On their march through China, the Imperial Japanese had committed spontaneous atrocities of a kind that the Nazis would later take to a higher and more organized systematic level. Though the United States had not yet been swept into the war, on the day that Samuel had arrived on the island that would be his last posting, for the United States, the situation from over the far horizon in Europe to the equally far horizon of the Far East, the world had grown steadily darker and more savage and had slid more into madness, cruelty, and genocide with the mortal danger of the United States being drawn into all the theaters of the all-out war going on on both sides of the globe. The horizon was closing in on the United States and on Samuel.

At the same time, the distant horizons of his home and memories slowly faded and grew more distant. The only horizon of his past that remained clear and present in memory was his memory of the girl.

As the threats from both sides of the world ratcheted up, Samuel was pulled from his choice position in Hawaii, a position he had not considered choice because of the distance involved from his home and memories. From there he was sent to the dicier proposition of the island fortress of Corregidor, guarding the entrance to Manila Bay. Samuel was an experienced and battle-tested soldier. Such men were needed there on what could easily become the flash point and first assault target of a war in the Pacific. His military skills went with him to the remote island that few people in the United States were aware of, let alone had even heard the name of. His memories went with him to the fortress island. His remembrance of the home now gone from him, he found that his remembrance of his parents, whom he would and could never see again in this life, went with him. His visions of the girl went with him. Once there, he found that the added distance didn't cause his memories or his visions of home or of her to fade. If anything, the distance sharpened them.

When the Japanese bombed Pearl Harbor, catapulting the United States into the war, a wall of fire and steel came down around the farthest-removed outpost of the United States, trapping Samuel, a.k.a. Marine Sergeant Martin Heisner, on the island along with the men he served with. The way to any home of his past, except his newfound home in the marines, was closed.

Chapter 36

"Eat it raw, Tojo!" the sergeant growled. He looked over at the soldier next to him in the shallow trench. "Hit it!" he called to the soldier. As they all ducked below the top of the trench, the soldier pressed the firing lever on the firing box wired to the gun.

Samuel had always likened the apocalyptic roar of the big guns to the thundering voice of God calling down on Judgment Day. While it might not have been the voice of Jehovah, the unchecked blast of the gun could cause flesh to quake and spirit to quail. If you stood too close, the blast felt as if it was going to rip the flesh off your skull, collapse your chest, and crush your intestines. The massive seventy-two-ton siege mortars mounted on twenty-foot-wide ground-level pivoting turntables could fire a thousand-pound twelve-inch projectile eight miles in any direction. The weapons had initially been set up to pulverize any enemy ship that tried to enter Manila Bay. Now they dueled with the shore batteries of the Japanese army, which pounded them daily and at night.

At the pressing of the firing lever, the gun's judgment thundered out. The short, stubby barrel absorbed or moderated little of the explosive blast. Even from within the relative protection of the trench, the heavy blast felt like a bank vault door being slammed on their chests. If one was standing anywhere near the gun when it was fired, he had to stand with his legs spread and his knees flexed or the concussion would knock him off his feet. One also had to stand with his hands over his ears and his mouth open to equalize pressure, or else the concussion could damage tissue in the cranial cavity.

On the mainland, the shell landed square in the line of Japanese light artillery firing on the island. The volcanic blast of the shell, as heavy as a battleship shell, sent one of the lighter artillery pieces flying into the air end over end, the gun blown off its mount. The gun crew was also sent flying into the air, some of them in pieces themselves. It was a right good shot. But it was the big gun's last hurrah.

Samuel looked up from the trench. One glance told his practiced military eye that the configuration was off-kilter.

"Something's wrong," Samuel said. He jumped out of the trench and raced to the gun. With Japanese shells landing in random locations around, the others in the trench followed him, flinching at the blast of shells landing close enough for them to feel the jolt, spraying them with small pieces of flying dirt and the rattle of spent shrapnel falling on the movable metal plate the gun was mounted on.

At the gun, the others could spot what Samuel had seen from the distance. Though it had only two feet of recoil distance to recover from, the barrel of the gun had not returned to its firing position. It was still pressed full length backward.

"She's jammed up," Samuel said. He looked around at the other artillerymen. "Get the sledge," he called out over the deafening blast of exploding shells. One of the soldiers ran back to the trench and returned with the sledgehammer. Samuel took it and started hammering on the ends of the four large recoil cylinders that acted as shock absorbers to the blast of the gun's firing. Samuel hoped the jam was only a minor one and that hitting the recoil cylinders would cause it to loosen and release.

"Remember the Marine Corps motto," Samuel shouted over the explosions. "If at first you don't succeed, get a bigger hammer." The quip, delivered under fire, was Samuel's attempt to interject a little humor into a grim and dicey situation, a situation made grimmer and dicier by the fact that they had lost the last useful of the biggest guns on the island.

All Samuel's pounding was to no avail. The barrel did not budge.

"She's jammed up tight," he said. "I don't know what's wrong inside or how bad it is, but it probably needs a lot more than an oil job."

A random shell exploded several hundred yards away.

"We can't fix it under fire. No use hanging our asses out. Back to the trench. When the shelling lets up, head out back to the tunnel."

They ran back to the trench. As they jumped into the trench, a shell whistled high overhead. But it's not the ones you hear that get you. It's the ones you don't hear.

A close-in shell they didn't hear coming burst on the ground not far from the trench. The explosion rang in their ears and shook the walls of the trench. Pieces of dirt showered down on them as they pressed themselves against the bottom of the trench.

"Another glorious day in the corps," Samuel said.

Chapter 37

Four days after the Christmas that hadn't been Christmas for anyone, the sergeant stood on the North Mine Wharf, surveying the damage. He had been instructed by the major, who had been instructed by the commanding general, to see if it could be used to offload supplies in case any were able to get through to them. His inspection seemed a useless gesture to the sergeant. He knew as well as everyone on the island that there was no resupply or reinforcements in the pipeline and that the Japanese navy had the pipeline and all approaches to the island blocked. The pipeline that had nothing in it was otherwise bottled up. No GI rumor mill had informed Samuel or anyone else. Every person of every rank on the island was able to read the grim logistical and strategic situation for themselves.

It is said that there is no logic to war. Actually there is logic to war. It's just that the logic is tinged with varying degrees of perverseness, ranging from reasonable and often necessary perverseness to total raging madness and savagery—madness and savagery delivered on macro levels where the combatants cover and comfort themselves with the thought that they are just doing their duty, down to the individual level, where the individual soldier brings personal madness, vengeance, and zest to his killing, both in the field and off it. The Nazis and Imperial Japanese had perfected this on a greater scale as their operational policy to grind under those they considered inferior. The individual German soldier had hardened himself to the madness that had sent him into the field in his country's grand cause of suppressing inferiors. Hardened to the madness surrounding him and coming from above him, the individual soldier of the Reich hardened himself and perfected his own madness and perverse logic as he forced Jews and other lessers into trenches and shot them there en masse. He would perfect his madness further by forcing other Jews and inferiors into sealed chambers to be gassed, or by torturing and killing them outside for sport and dragging them into demonic medical facilities where horrific medical experiments were performed on them.

The Imperial Japanese had perfected their own savage, perverse logic of death and killing as sport where they shot prisoners and civilians in China and other conquered territory, used prisoners for bayonet and sword practice, and slashed open the wombs of pregnant women, killing both the woman and her child.

At that moment, another installment of the logic of war appeared overhead in the form of a flight of Japanese twin-engine bombers. Air-raid sirens blew. Men scrambled for cover. The sergeant rushed off the dock as fast as he could run. Exposed in the open on a wharf that was a prime target was not the best situation to be in. Instead of heading toward the tunnel entrance, which was still the main target of the Japanese bombers, after he got off the wharf, the sergeant went in the opposite direction and jumped into a bomb crater. From there he looked up.

As the Japanese planes came, antiaircraft fire erupted from several directions on the island. The gunners had the range and altitude on the money. From his vantage point, the sergeant could see the antiaircraft shells exploding in the middle of the formation. The planes jinked and twisted around, trying to throw off the gunners, but their maneuvers didn't work. A plane was hit hard. A gas tank exploded. The wing erupted in flames and broke off. The stricken plane fell out of formation, spiraling downward, fire trailing thick from the broken wing root. The sergeant pushed himself up out of the bomb crater and watched as the plane fell, spinning downward at an increasingly steep angle, out of control. It arched over the narrow part of the island above the tunnel entrance. No parachutes came out of the plane. The centrifugal force of the spin must have been too great for the crew to bail out. The sergeant wasn't even sure whether the Japanese even gave their fliers parachutes. He figured samurai fliers were expected to die with their planes rather than bail out and suffer the humiliation of being captured. He watched the plane fall to where it dived vertically and crashed headlong into Manila Bay, throwing up a tall geyser of water. No one could have possibly survived the crash.

"Burn for your emperor!" the sergeant said as flames from burning gasoline from the plane's ruptured fuel tanks roiled from the surface of the water and rose up into the sky.

That morning five Japanese planes went over. Three came back. It was good shooting on the part of the antiaircraft gunners. Later that afternoon, nine Japanese planes went over. Only four came back. It was better shooting. The Japanese airmen may have considered themselves to be the sons of heaven, but they were having trouble in the skies over Corregidor. Still, the number of planes they lost was just a drop in the bucket against the number of planes they had. And they were bringing in more.

As the bombs from the other planes started to hit the ground, the sergeant pressed himself back into the crater, covered his face with his helmet, and rolled over. Whether it was lack of precision bombsights or whether the Japanese were also trying to catch and kill men caught out in the open, only a few bombs landed close to the tunnel entrance. The rest were spread out in a saturation pattern in front of the tunnel opening. One bomb landed twenty yards from the crater the sergeant was pressing himself into. Even below ground level, the blast and concussion was terrific. Dirt showered down on the sergeant's back.

"Another outstanding day in the corps," he muttered to himself.

When the all-clear sounded, the sergeant jumped out of the crater and headed quickly toward the tunnel entrance. But it wasn't to get himself to better cover. He wanted to check on and help with any casualties. There had been casualties. One man had both his feet blown off. Only bloody stumps remained. He was already being carried into the tunnel when the sergeant arrived.

The story that day was the same as the usual story with casualties. Half the injuries involved arms and legs blown off and deep gashes ripped into bodies by flying shrapnel. Both the wounded and the dead were carried into the tunnel and laid out on the floor in separate rows. The medical corpsmen who tended them could do little more for the wounded than try to make them comfortable. They were simply not fully prepared for trauma on that sort of epic scale. The wounded laid out on the floor would moan continuously in pain. Others would quietly give up the ghost and join the ghosts of Corregidor. If their spirits hovered over the landscape along with the spirit of the girl, then the airspace above the island was getting crowded. The sergeant didn't think anyone on Corregidor would ever go to hell because they had their share of it on a daily basis.

That night the sergeant sat in the tunnel listening to broadcasts coming in from the United States on a portable shortwave radio receiver. Earlier news broadcasts had had an optimistic, if surreal, quality about them. The news had always been good: Valiant US and Filipino forces on Bataan were slaughtering Japanese attackers by the thousands or counterattacking with equal results. Japanese troops had often launched fanatical mass charges at US and Filipino forces on Bataan and had suffered heavy casualties. As quasi propaganda, it sounded great. But in fact the US and Filipino forces were ravaged by disease, near-starvation, and lack of supplies. They had held on for as long as they had only through incomparable spirit. Before being finally forced to surrender, they had adopted a sour and ironic poem to describe themselves: "We're the battling bastards of Bataan. No mother. No father. No Uncle Sam."

Some of the soldiers on Bataan had made it to Corregidor before the rest were forced to surrender. Eighty thousand of them were sent off to prison camps on the infamous Bataan Death March. Ten thousand died along the way from starvation, abuse, and murder. Those who made it to Corregidor only delayed their final surrender. Some of them were killed on the island by bombing and shelling.

The shortwave broadcast from stateside that night brought them familiar music from home. The news didn't mention that the battling holdouts of Corregidor weren't in much better shape than their compatriots on Bataan, who had been ground down and forced to surrender. Nor did it say what everyone on the island knew, namely that their time and parallel fate wasn't all that far off, nor could it be delayed forever. Forever, at least the good kind, was in short supply on the island.

Chapter 38

The major sat at his rickety wooden desk shuffling papers that, given the deteriorated and further deteriorating situation, were fast becoming irrelevant. The papers couldn't do much of anything to reverse or even moderate the disorder in the tunnel or the greater disorder outside it. They couldn't do anything to prevent the final disorder that would envelop and submerge them any day now. The major couldn't even get the irrelevant papers off the island.

In the dim light of the tunnel, the major felt the approaching presence of the sergeant as much as he saw him. The sergeant wasn't heavy or hulking, but he had a solid presence about him. Everyone in the tunnel knew the profile of his body. The sentries at the tunnel entrance had made out the profile of his body as he had approached out of the dark. There had been no need to challenge him to give identification before he had come into the light. The figure of MSG Martin Heisner, US Marine Corps, coming into the light was a reassuring presence on an island where reassurance had otherwise vanished into the dark. The major didn't know why the sergeant was coming to him at that particular time.

"What can I do for you, Sergeant?" the major said.

"Nothing for me," the sergeant said. "I'm sticking around till the last shot is fired. I'll fire it myself if I'm still alive. But I was hoping to get an evacuation going for the wounded. I've got men ripped and shredded by shrapnel. I've got men with arms and legs blown off. They need to be in a hospital. They're dying by the day because our medical supplies are all but gone. They can't fight. The Japanese don't think much of prisoners. They think even less of wounded. If they overrun us, they won't treat the wounded. They'll just shoot them where they lie. Or they'll bayonet them or use their swords on them. These are the same people who use live Chinese for bayonet practice. … Like I say, I'll stick around as long as I'm able. I'll stay even if I'm wounded. Just set me up with a gun in a sitting position. As long as I'm mad at them, which is forever, and as long as I've got ammunition, I'll take as many of them with me as I can. When they close in on me, I'll take myself and some more of them out with a grenade."

The major knew the sergeant well enough by reputation and association to know that he wasn't talking shallow bravado.

"I'll go out fighting to the last bit of spit in me. But the wounded can't do anything but lie there and be butchered by those slant-eyed baboons. They'll die for nothing. That's why I want to get an evac going before it's too late and they come down the tunnel, shouting like the demons they are."

"General Wainwright would evacuate this island in a minute if he could," the major said. "We can't hold it, and even if we could, it wouldn't make any difference. But we can't evacuate because we don't have anything to evacuate with. We can't fly anybody off. Most of our air force out here was destroyed on the first day of attack, transport planes included. We can't do an evacuation by sea."

"What the hell?" the sergeant snapped. "They got MacArthur and the civilian dependents who were here off on a PT boat."

"And those boats were the last bottoms in the area that can go anywhere over open water and can move fast enough to get away. The Japs have all the Philippines sewn up by now. And they've got the sea-lanes locked up tight. They've got destroyers, cruisers, and battleships waiting like buzzards outside the harbor, outside the range of our guns to give them covering fire. Any slow-moving transport ship that tried to get to us would be shredded to junk. We might be able to get a sub in here. They might be able to ferry a handful of wounded out. But the subs were withdrawn with the rest of the fleet, to be regrouped and reorganized."

"Can they put together a task force?" the sergeant asked.

"A task force of what?" the major said. "All our battleships got whacked at Pearl. I don't think there's one that isn't sitting at the bottom of the harbor. Fortunately our carriers weren't in port at the time. They're still intact."

"Can the navy put together a carrier task force?" the sergeant asked.

"We've only got three big carriers, the *Lexington*, the *Saratoga*, and the *Yorktown*," the major said. "They're old and getting obsolete. The *Wasp* and *Hornet* are small and underpowered. Our first carrier, the old *Langley*, is a coal boat they slapped a flight deck on. It was built when they were still flying Wright Brothers biplanes. The navy can't do very much with an obsolete barge like that."

Neither the major nor the sergeant knew that by that time the *Langley* was already at the bottom of the Timor Sea, a victim of Japanese carrier planes. Any help from the *Langley* was a moot point in a situation that was a conglomeration of moot points.

"The Japs have a crackerjack fleet. They have maybe four carriers to each one of ours. If CINCPAC sends a carrier task force this deep into Japanese waters, it would be a suicide mission. We'd lose every carrier we have. The navy will most likely hold the few carries they have back and keep them as a defense and delay force to keep the Japs off-balance and hold them away from the West Coast while the War Department builds a whole new fleet, one five times bigger than the Jap fleet on its best day. We can do it. There are probably more factories in New Jersey alone than in all of Japan. Every factory we have can be converted over to war production. But it's going to take time to get the country on a war footing. That may take two years. We can count ourselves lucky if we've got two weeks left out here."

The sergeant didn't answer. He was as good of a strategic analyst as the major, possibly better. He could judge the situation as accurately without a microscope and without rose-colored glasses. He already knew that the handwriting was on the wall for them, and the handwriting was in Japanese.

"If there isn't anything you can do for me, is there anything I can do for you?" the sergeant said.

"You can tell me if we can get the last big gun back in operation," the major said.

"That's the other thing I was coming to see you about," the sergeant answered. "It's still jammed. We've beaten on it with sledgehammers from all angles. It won't loosen up. It won't budge. It wouldn't make much, if any, difference if we could get it working. It was built to counter battleships entering the harbor. It fires too slow to be of much use against a fast-moving landing force in small landing craft. Besides, we're almost out of shells for it. We used up most of them trying to knock out the Japanese guns on shore. We did some good with it. We knocked out some of their guns. But they kept bringing up more. If there's a landing, we'd be off better counting on the smaller coastal defense guns. They can fire faster. But we're low on shells for them too."

"Then all I can have you do is keep working on firming up the coastal defenses," the major said. "If they try to land and we hit them hard enough and drive them back, maybe they'll think twice about trying it again. It could buy us the time we need."

The major laid down the stack of irrelevant papers he was holding. The sergeant turned and left without saying anything. They both knew that the optimism expressed wasn't in the realm of reasonable possibility or anywhere near it.

The sergeant walked in silence to the entrance of the tunnel. He stepped outside into the dark and looked up. The cordite and smoke from the shelling and bombing of the day had blown away. The night sky was cloudless. The stars were clear and bright above the island. As the sergeant looked up into the sky, he saw the face of the girl floating there. The look on her face was the same distant, uncertain look he had seen on her face in the sky above the North Atlantic and in the night sky of Nicaragua. He didn't startle or jump at the vision. He knew he wasn't actually seeing the girl's spirit come to haunt him. He believed in the afterlife, but he never had particularly believed in ghosts. The girl had once been the most real thing in the world to him. He knew what he was seeing wasn't really the girl, but he still wanted to talk to her.

"Well, hello again," the sergeant said quietly to himself, not loud enough for anyone to hear. "I haven't see you for some time. I think the last time I saw you like this, when I was awake and not dreaming, was in Nicaragua. Since then I've seen you in dreams. I've seen you in more dreams than I can add up. You were all I once dreamed about when you were alive. It's been years since I last saw you in a waking dream. Maybe in all those years, somewhere along the line, I lost the ability to dream. But here you are. I see I haven't lost the ability to remember."

The sergeant paused and mused.

"It seems to me like I've seen you in the sky this way before, from the sky above my hometown, the town that was my hometown and briefly your hometown too. As I remember, I've seen you in the sky over the North Atlantic and the mountains of Nicaragua. You are a far-flung girl. You do get around. But even when you were lying in my arms, quiet and unmoving, you were always in motion in your mind. Your thoughts were always of moving on. I enjoyed most every minute you were close to me. But did your thoughts back then ever include any thought of staying with me? Or were all your long thoughts strung out on the road? Did your thoughts ever circle back around to me?"

The sergeant paused in his inaudible recitation.

"Seems to me like I've had this one-way conversation with you before, over the North Atlantic, over Nicaragua. You didn't have any ready answers for me back then. From your silence, I see you don't have any answers for me now. But why should this night be any different from all the other times you didn't have any answers for me or yourself?"

The sergeant looked down from the sky and out across the dark shapes of the blacked-out fortress island of Corregidor.

"You came into our town on the run. Even when you were in the safety of Mrs. Richardson's house, in your mind you were still on the run. Since you went away, I've become a runner myself. I left my hometown on the run. I've been running ever since. I've run through more countries and more wars than I care to remember. Are you still running where you are? Do the patterns we set for ourselves in life end when we die, or do the patterns we set in life go on and carry on in death? Does running cease in the great beyond, or does running go on? Do you run so far and so long that you forget why you started running, but still you keep on running? I would have run with you through life, but I never could catch up with you. You were always out ahead of me. … If you're running in death, wait for me to catch up with you. I'll probably be along shortly. I'll run with you. I'll run with you through eternity."

The sergeant looked back up into the sky. The image of the girl was gone.

"I see you're gone. Are you off running again, or are you just hanging back in the shadows, watching and waiting for whatever is going to happen down here to unfold? We can't hold this island. You can go if you want. I won't try to hold you to me as I once did. I never could hold you, no more than I could catch up with you. I would have held you in my arms. I would have held you in my life and my love forever. But you didn't want either of them from me. Have you rethought what you felt then? Is that why you're here, to tell me that from your new perspective in the great beyond, having thought it over and after having had a change of heart, that now you wish you had joined me together in life? Or is that wishful thinking on my part? I had hoped to give you good memories to cover all the bad memories you carried within you. I had hoped I could soothe your soul. In the end my impulsiveness only riled you up and set you running again. I had hoped to draw you to me and bring you close to me, but my reckless actions only drove you farther away. That knowledge has been the millstone I've carried around in my mind and soul since the day you died."

Inside the tunnel, medical corpsmen picked up the body of a wounded man who had quietly died. They quietly moved him to the ranks of the dead. At least one death on the island had been a quiet one.

"Can you see what's happening here, or is this world a faint blur when seen from that far out in the beyond? Is this world a single point of distant light, a dim star far away and removed? Can you see me from where you are? Can you hear me where you are? Or is this world just a mute, silent blank far away on the far side of the beyond? Do people out in the beyond know what's going on back on earth? Do the ones who died leaving lovers and loved ones behind wonder about what's happening to the ones they departed from? Do they think of them? Do you think of me out in the beyond? I've thought about you just about every day since you were killed. Do you remember me? I've never been able to forget you, even during the times I was mad at you and wanted to forget you. Can you read my mind from out there? If you can, you'll know that I loved you. Is my mind an open book to you now? I didn't keep my mind and the way I felt about you a mystery to you. I made it plain to you that I loved you. It just never seemed to break through the wall around your heart."

The sergeant looked up into the empty sky again.

"That you didn't believe I loved you was probably as much my fault as it was yours. But even before that, you hid yourself from me. I never hid myself from you. I was no mystery to you. Your mind and your heart were always a mystery to me as much as you were. You were as distant as you were close. I was never sure if that was just the way you were or if it was the way you wanted it. My heart belonged to you. Your heart always belonged to you. You held your heart closer to you than you ever held my heart. You took your heart with you when you left this world. I had given you my heart. Along with your heart, you took my heart with you when you left. It hasn't come back to me since. Are you holding it there with you as a souvenir or a keepsake? Do you now hold my heart as a reminder, or do you hold it as a treasure? Will we get our hearts back in eternity? Will we meet again in heaven? Will we know each other in eternity?"

The sergeant looked out over the darkened landscape of Corregidor. Instead of the shrieking of shells going overhead, he heard only the low stirring of the wind and the distant sound of waves. It was a peaceful moment in a violent world.

At the present, fleeting moment of peace in the world, in his corner of the South Pacific on the war-scarred island of Corregidor, it was distant worlds, worlds separated by distance, time, memory, and his thoughts of what might be there for him in the waning days of his life and what might be there for him in the beyond, that was on his mind. The world he was in was becoming as irrelevant to him as the papers in the major's hands. He assumed he would probably be leaving the world soon enough. He would not be sad to leave the world. The world held little for him. It had held little for him for a long time. What little it held was fading into something beyond. Even his memories were growing thin and empty.

"I thought I knew you, but I never really did know you. Did you ever really know yourself? Do you know yourself now? Do you know me now? Do people in the great beyond know all truth and know it clearly? Do they know each other with certainty? In the beyond, do we know each other without the masks we wear and the lies we tell? Or does the uncertainty and confusion and lie telling of life in this world go on in confusion and uncertainty over there forever?"

A quick and distant small streak of light went through a partial arc in the sky. Thinking it was an incoming shell, the sergeant instinctively started to duck. But the streak disappeared without drawing closer. The sergeant realized that it was a shooting star that had burned up in the upper atmosphere—cosmic shellfire that would not reach them. The sergeant went back to his silent free association with worlds, love, and a lover long gone.

"When we meet again in the great beyond as I pray we will, will you finally tell me what your real name was? I knew you by no other name than the name you gave yourself, but it was never real to me. The name you gave yourself was just another way of hiding yourself from me and from everybody. Will you hide from me there, or will you be open with me the way you weren't in life? Will you tell me your real name then? But, out in the beyond, knowing what your real name was in life might not mean anything. Maybe in eternity all names are meaningless. In eternity only the heart has any meaning. I didn't know your full heart in life. Will I know your heart in eternity?"

Samuel paused and looked out again over the darkened island. A deep twinge replaced the casual words he had been speaking.

I will remember you forever, he said silently. *If we don't meet again but memory goes on in eternity, remember for all time and all remembrance that I loved you.*

The sergeant turned and looked into the tunnel. The lights were on, but there was no light at the end of the tunnel.

Chapter 39

"Okay, Tojo, step right up and get what's coming to you, you slimy, bucktoothed, grinning, strutting pigs," the sergeant said over the muttering of the landing barges drawing nearer. "Our time may be up, but your time in the fire is just beginning."

As he watched and spoke, he held the field telephone up at his shoulder. "There are a lot of dead Americans at Pearl Harbor that you need to be paid back for. There are a lot more than that number of dead Chinese, Korean, and Malaysian men, women, and children killed by your bombs and shells. There are probably just as many weak innocents chopped up by your swords and pinned to the ground by your bayonets and killed by you for sport. But we're not them. We're not innocent about war, and we're not the weaklings you like to shoot and carve up. You may eventually kill all of us here, but you're going to pay for every inch of this island with your own blood. It will be a small taste of what's going to be coming your way. You may be on a roll now, but when America gets rolling, we're going to roll you all the way back to Tokyo. From there we'll roll right down your throat and up your emperor's nose. You and your Nazi bedmates may think you can win and rule by fear, but when we and the rest of the world get going, we're going to teach you the meaning of fear like you don't think it can exist. You call yourselves sons of heaven. You sons of heaven are going to swim the length of hell. You'll catch a taste of it here before you get there. You like to put your steel to those you make cower before you. The steel will be put to you. You like to burn women and children. Before you die, you'll see your country burn. You're brave enough when it comes to sticking a sword through the stomach of a mother and the child she's holding to her chest, but I know something about killing thugs who like to kill women."

Fighting the current, the landing craft closed in on the beach at an angle.

"Tell the batteries to commence firing," the major said.

"Open fire!" the sergeant shouted into the field telephone. "Fire at will. And don't ask me which one is Will."

From the main part of the island, the remaining serviceable artillery pieces that hadn't been knocked out of commission by Japanese artillery fire coming from the surrounding shores of Manila Bay unloosened what they had left to contribute, sending billowing balls of orange flame out to dissolve and disappear into the night sky, and sending out shells glowing a dull red and flying away at high speed on arcs heading out toward the beach the Japanese landing barges were closing in on. The guns were nearly out of ammunition and were firing blind, but the six-inch shells, as heavy in caliber as the naval shells of a light cruiser, packed a good amount of explosive power. Most of the shells fired at random missed. They sent geysers of water flying up into the night sky to a height where the tops couldn't be seen by the troops pressing themselves down onto the floor of the landing craft they were in. One shell landed a few feet from a landing barge and went off under water. The explosion tossed the barge up and flipped it over as if it were a pancake, spilling the men in the craft into deep water, still wearing their heavy military backpacks. Another shell landed and exploded under water just off the stern of a landing barge. The concussion of the explosion shattered the back end of the barge, and the craft started to settle by the stern. Yet another shell scored a direct hit on a landing barge. The explosion completely demolished the flimsy wooden craft, sending pieces of shattered wood and pieces of shattered bodies into the air to vanish in the dark sky and into the dark water.

The major had positioned himself and his adjutant sergeant off to the side, where he could get a linear panoramic view of the battle and the landing as he thought it would unfold on the optimal beach where he assumed the Japanese would land. But the Japanese miscalculation of the strength of the current was bringing them right in front of his position.

"Tell the gunners to target the beach," the major said as the landing barges progressed beyond the area zeroed in on by the guns. The sergeant barked new coordinates into the field phone. It would bring the fire perilously close to them, but they were begging for any advantage, and beggars can't be choosers. Neither can dead men walking or crouching in trenches.

"Tell the batteries to redirect fire down the beachline and unload with everything you've got!" the major shouted to the sergeant as the first landing craft hit the shore and ground its square front into the beach. The sergeant barked the directions into the field telephone. There was a moment's pause while sight settings were adjusted on the artillery pieces. Then the beach erupted in heavy orange flashes, followed almost immediately by thundering blasts.

"Open fire!" the major shouted down the trench line.

From all along the line of battle, a makeshift array of weapons opened up. Most of the troops were armed with the First World War vintage bolt-action 1903 30.06 Springfield rifle. The classic faster-firing semiautomatic M1 rifle, which would become the workhorse military rifle on all fronts of the Second World War and through Korea, hadn't come on line yet. There were a handful BARs available. Some soldiers had only pistols. The sergeant had a forty-five-caliber Thompson shoulder-fired machine gun with a sixty-round drum magazine. It was the classic gangster gun favored by the underworld, but it was comparatively underpowered and short ranged. But the sergeant knew how to get the most effect out of short-range weapons like shotguns and derringers.

The only more effective rapid-fire weapons the defenders had were tripod-mounted, belt-fed Browning machine guns. But they were thirty-caliber trench defense guns, also holdovers from World War I. They were water-cooled brutes with a big water cylinder surrounding the barrel it was designed to keep cool. The coolant water was supplied by a separate water can connected to the water jacket by a hose. The weapons were separate sectioned, heavy, and awkward to move. They were fixed-position guns not designed to be grabbed and transported quickly by two men in the heat of a flowing, shifting battle. They sent out a stream of lead as deadly as any machine gun, but they could not be grabbed and moved at a running pace if the Japanese troops succeeded in swarming the positions they were being fired from. Like the men firing them, these weapons were prisoners of the limited terrain they were trapped on. They couldn't go any farther forward, and they couldn't readily go backward.

To Samuel, a.k.a. Marine Sergeant Martin Heisner, the situation he found himself in was a metaphor for his life. He had started his run on the option that had been made available to him to leave home and go forward. The option to stay where he was hadn't been available, and it hadn't become available. The present military option to go forward was blocked by the ocean beyond the beach, the beach about to be swarmed by Japanese troops. The option to go backward ended at the tunnel. As the landing craft pushed the few remaining yards to the beach and the cacophony of firing swelled, Samuel wondered if the girl had felt her options to be equally limited. He wondered again how she had felt when she found her options cut off from her by Harold Ethridge. He wondered again if this was the place that the delayed end of his options had finally caught up with him and had run out. But he had no time to reflect on any question, and he had few places to run.

Machine-gun and rifle fire ripped and raked the incoming landing craft. The intense Japanese preparatory bombardment had knocked out no more than one of the machine guns. Enough were left to do damage. Samuel unloaded with his Thompson as soon as the first front gate on the landing craft opened. Soldiers fell backward into the landing barges as they tried to rush out when the front gates had been dropped. Other Japanese soldiers tried to hunker down behind the sides of their landing craft for protection, but the machine-gun and rifle fire ripped through the plywood sides of the landing craft. Many troops were killed or wounded before they could exit their barges and rush the beach for cover. Others jumped over the sides into the water but were pulled under and drowned by the weight of their backpacks in the unexpectedly deep water. The slope of the shore was shallow and provided little in the way of cover. Those who made it onto the beach were pinned down and raked by fire from higher up on the shore. The six-inch shells from the remaining coastal defense guns landed among the soldiers who were trying to find cover that wasn't there to be found. The bone-jarring blasts of the shells threw sand, gravel, coral, seashell fragments, flotsam, and the occasional body into the night air. But another wave of landing craft was on the way.

Only a third of the initial Japanese landing force reached the beach at North Point. But successive waves followed. They got on shore without suffering as bad of a fate as the first wave. Their numbers built up. The defenders were stretched thin. They were low on ammunition, and they had no reserves to call out. The Japanese juggernaut flexed and started to push inland. Some were cut down, but in short order the survivors reached the defenders' positions. Hand-to-hand fighting broke out.

It was clear to the major that they couldn't hold the position and that the Japanese would break through the full length of the line. If the Japanese wiped them out there on the shore, there would no one left even to slow them down. It would be a leisurely stroll for them to get to the tunnel, where there would be no one to take them on except for the wounded piling up inside. The thin-spread line at the beach could not hold. A more concentrated line in a narrower position was needed.

"Back to the tunnel!" the major shouted. The shout was relayed up and down the length of the line.

The now even more ragged, ragtag, and bloodied defenders scrambled out of their improvised trenches and started streaming down the post road that wound past the single runway of Kindley airfield and Monkey Point beyond.

Without waiting for orders and without saying anything, the sergeant allowed the major to go ahead. He fell behind and stopped any able-bodied man with a weapon in order to form up a rear guard to counter the Japanese pursuit he was sure would be following hot on their heels. He positioned his hastily assembled force in an ambush on either side of the road and waited for the rush of bloodthirsty Japanese soldiers with their swords drawn and bayonets fixed whom he was sure would appear any moment, swarming out of the dark shadows on the road, shouting "Banzai!" or some such demon howl used to work themselves up into a killing lather.

But the immediate rush the sergeant anticipated did not materialize out of the dark. After a due interval, the sergeant surmised that the reason the Japanese were not following in hot pursuit was that they were biding their time, gathering their forces, organizing themselves, and bringing more men and equipment ashore on the beach they now controlled, all in preparation for the final push that would squeeze the combined marine and army forces back into the tunnel, where they could be wiped out. The sergeant figured that the Japanese figured that they had the US forces cornered, which they did; that the US troops had no avenue or way of escape, which they didn't; and that the Japanese could roll them up and wipe them out, which they could. The sergeant figured that the Japanese were waiting for the daylight to launch the final phase of their assault—a plan that involved the killing of every last man on the island unless they all surrendered. The sergeant also suspected that the Japanese intended to kill every last man on the island even if they did surrender.

Given that they apparently had until daylight to prepare, the sergeant turned to his last-ditch contingent. "It looks like they're going to come at us in the daylight," he said. "They're probably too nearsighted to see us in the dark. But in the light of day, they'll see us where we are now. We'll lose the element of surprise. We're too exposed on this road. We need a better location with more concealment."

Given that he was good at arranging ambushes, the sergeant gathered up his ambush force and moved them to a better ambush location in a swath of jungle at a narrower neck of the island between Ordnance Point and the eastern entrance to the Malinta Hill tunnel complex. His hope was to hit the advancing Japanese hard enough and bloody them enough that they might pause to regroup. That delay could give the tunnel defenders a long enough time to dig in and be better prepared to meet the attack. If properly prepared, the ambush might delay the Japanese advance long enough that the rest of the defenders might be able to firm up their position enough to blunt the attack. It might allow them the ability to hold out until relief arrived, if it ever did.

The sergeant reasoned that if he and his men had to be a sacrifice to buy time for the rest, he would be that sacrifice. The sacrifice of his life to avenge the dead girl hadn't worked all that well for his earlier life. Maybe this time he could sell his life better, to greater effect for the living. As reasoning goes, it was limited. But reason is usually in short supply in war.

As hope went, it was a limited hope, but every hope on the island had been limited since day one.

Having only a limited number of soldiers under his impromptu command, the sergeant positioned them concealed in the jungle on both sides of the road the confident Japanese were likely to come swaggering down. The position they took up was not far from MacArthur House, where General MacArthur stayed when in residence on the island. At that time, General MacArthur was safely in residence in Australia. He had left, promising to return. The sergeant took him at his word. He just didn't think he would make it back in the next half hour.

After he positioned himself and had hunkered out of sight in the foliage, the sergeant took the two remaining drum magazines out of his backpack and laid them close by, where he could pick them up in a hurry. Concealed in the jungle, the sergeant listened for the sound of approaching movement in the dark the way he had listened for the sound of danger approaching in the dark of Haiti, France, Nicaragua, and a barn in Ohio. He looked up toward the canopy of the jungle, concealed in the darkness. It was often in times of uncertainty that he had seen the face of the girl floating above and away from him in the dark. But he had always seen visions of her face in the open sky. He didn't see her face in the canopy of jungle above. Instead, he listened for the sound of her voice. She had never spoken to him in any of the visitations he had had from her before. He wasn't sure he would recognize the sound of her voice even if she did speak to him. After all the time that had gone by, he had kind of forgotten how her voice sounded. He remembered only that she had a hillbilly accent and that there had been an undertone of pain in her voice whenever she spoke, the pain he had tried to heal but hadn't been able to heal or even approach. He remembered the sound of pleasure she had made when they made love. He remembered the sound of fear and biting anger in her voice when she had threatened him with a knife on the bank of the river that ran past his hometown in front of Mrs. Richardson's establishment. As he looked up into the jungle growth blocking the sky above Corregidor, he neither saw her face nor heard her voice. She had spoken love to him when they had been together in his hometown, but her words of love hadn't brought her to him in a life together—a life together with him she hadn't wanted. At the end, her words had been angry and as sharp as the knife she had waved at him.

But the girl neither appeared to him nor spoke to him out of the dark. Samuel wondered why she neither spoke nor showed her face to him that night, the night that could be the closing night of his life. He wondered if the reason she neither appeared nor spoke was that she knew they would soon enough be speaking face-to-face in another world.

Of course Samuel knew that the visions he had had of the girl all the years that had gone by, as well as the one he had had of her on the island, were just creations of his mind. But he would have liked to have one last vision of the girl before all visions of this world and his life in it were summarily cut off. Though he couldn't see her from his vantage point at the edge of battle, Samuel wondered again if the girl could see him from where she was on the cusp of eternity. She hadn't been able to change the course of her life in the past. He doubted she could change the course of the battle to come. She could only watch over what happened to him as he had watched over what had happened to her.

From out over the island, from out in the beyond, the girl would watch over his death as it unfolded, unable to do anything about it, as he had watched over her life as it had proceeded to her death and had not been able to alter the trajectory of her life. Whether she would watch what happened to him in sorrow or mute acceptance, Samuel didn't know.

Samuel listened again to see if he could hear the voice of the girl. From out of the dark jungle came the low rustle of fronds and leaves in the night breeze. From out of his past came only silence.

Chapter 40

The sergeant had spent the night listening with concentrated intensity for any sound that might indicate the approach of Japanese troops. He had also listened for the sound of the girl's voice, but he hadn't heard as much as a single word from her. In all the years gone by since she had died, he had seen an endless number of visions of her face floating above him, but she hadn't spoken a single word. Apparently she wasn't prepared to break her silence. The sergeant wondered why he had thought this day would be any different from any of the other days since her death that she hadn't spoken to him.

If the coming day was going to be the day he was going to die and the girl somehow knew it, he thought she might have at least a few words of farewell for him. If not that, then a simple statement that they would soon be together again. But the whole night had passed without a single vision of her or a single word from her. If she was watching and was able to communicate across the deep gulf of death, maybe she figured that it wouldn't change anything he would do in the coming fight. Maybe she just knew him.

Through the silence of the jungle, a sound started coming toward them, and it wasn't the soft melodious sound of the voice of a girl who was a practiced seducer. The sound was a creaking, clanking metallic sound punctuated by the rumble of motors.

"Oh shit, they've got tanks," the soldier nearest to Samuel said, speaking what Samuel already knew.

Now the sergeant knew why the Japanese had delayed their pursuit of them as they had retreated from the beach. Not only had they been regrouping and reinforcing their ranks with troops to replace those killed, but also they had been landing tanks to put heavy throw weight behind their final assault on the tunnel and its last-ditch defenders. The tanks were moving down the road toward the entrance to the tunnel, which contained the able-bodied soldiers left as well as the wounded and the dead.

"We've got nothing that can stop a tank," the soldier said.

Japanese tanks of the Second World War were light, relatively thinly armored affairs that mounted a comparatively small gun. They were nowhere near as formidable as the heavy-gunned monster German Panzer and Tiger tanks. They weren't even up to the relatively junky US Sherman tanks available at the start of the war. But the defenders had little that could be brought up to stop the tanks. The sergeant didn't think there was a single bazooka on the island that could be brought to bear on them. They didn't even have improvised Molotov cocktail gasoline firebombs in whiskey bottles to throw at them. The troops of Samuel's improvised ambush force had only small arms and a few hand grenades, none of which could disable a tank. To complicate matters, Japanese infantry were moving through the jungle on either side of the road in a coordinated armored–infantry assault. The Japanese tanks were closing single file down the road, heading unimpeded toward the back entrance to the tunnel.

"What do we do?"

"If you separate tanks from their accompanying infantry, the tanks are vulnerable to being attacked from the sides by your infantry," the sergeant said, reciting one the classic dictums of armored warfare. "If we can take out the infantry cover coming with the tanks, maybe the men at the tunnel can figure out a way to stop the tanks. At least they won't have to fend off an infantry assault at the same time."

Without fully taking his eyes off the advancing Japanese, hidden from their sight in the jungle growth, the sergeant turned his head partway to the soldier next to him.

"Pass the word," the sergeant spoke to his impromptu adjutant. "Hold your positions. Let the tanks go by. When I give the word or when I start firing, everyone open up on the Jap infantry. Give them every bit of what for we've got left."

Keeping low in the jungle to stay out of sight, the man headed off to spread the sergeant's instructions.

Though they were masters of camouflage, the Japanese soldiers were advancing without camouflage, feeling that they probably wouldn't encounter any resistance until they reached the troops they were reasonably sure they had bottled up in the tunnel. The khaki brown of their uniforms appeared out of and disappeared into the green of the jungle growth as they moved through it, heading for the unmoving marine and army troops that Samuel had scraped together, waiting in the ambush the confident Japanese didn't know was there.

The sergeant looked back toward the Japanese troops advancing through the jungle. One could say that the sergeant was brave. But as Eddie Rickenbacker said, "bravery is doing what you're afraid to do." One could say the sergeant was resolute, but resoluteness is doing what must be done, doing the only thing that can be done, doing what should be done, even if you know it won't make any difference. One could say the sergeant was stoic about the situation and about his part in it and his fate in it. Since he had fled his home and family, he had been stoic about an uncountable number of things, but now even stoicism was something apart from him. Stoicism hadn't fully outlined, described, defined, or ordered his life. Stoicism is one-dimensional. Both he and his life had been anything but one-dimensional. His life had traveled in many paths that, while seeming to diverge, had run in parallel. Now all those paths were about to converge and merge into one final line leading to one final vanishing point.

The sergeant knew he was going to die. He knew he was going to die that day. The knowledge did not come as a shock to him. It was not a fearful thing. If anything, it would be a blessed release from life, a life that had too often held him in a crushing grip as the girl's life had held her. It would be just the final turn in a life of unplanned turns, some that had been created for him, others that he had created for himself. But the girl had been the fulcrum that had set the angle and radius of his life. She

951

had set the vortex of his life for all his days after he had met her. Now she would be the unspoken, unknown postscript to his life.

The rumbling of the tanks was off to his side. The rustle of the advancing Japanese troops was coming straight toward him, their position set by the sound of them pushing through the ground-level jungle foliage. They were only about thirty yards away.

Some people say that when you know you're about to die, your life flashes before you. That's not always the case. Sometimes when you're about to die, it is the smallest things that go through your mind—small things attached by tendrils to the largest things. In a momentary flashback similar to the one he had experienced in the trench of World War I, seeing the sight of the jungle before him, Samuel caught flash visions of how he and the girl had made love in the woods along the shore of Gustafson Lake and by the river. They were visions of a world and a life long parted from him. But his visions snapped him back to the present he was in, only to emphasize that he would probably soon be leaving the world and the life he had come a long way through and that he would come out on the other side of eternity.

Though he wasn't fully sure what awaited him on the other side, the sergeant figured that, one way or the other, in one celestial incarnation or the other, he would be seeing the girl again, and probably soon. But as he remembered the church service that day and as the lyrics of the hymn ran through his mind, it more or less dawned on him that there was another celestial dweller in the celestial hall of light he was going to have to pass muster for and stand in front of before he could go to the girl or any lover or loved one from his past.

"Well, Lord, I guess this is finally it," Samuel said. "It's been a long time coming. It's been a long run. My parents are there with You. The girl is already there with You. At least I hope she is. It looks like I'm coming to You as well. I guess I have a lot of explaining and apologizing to do to my parents and to Sis about the pain I brought to them. Beyond that, whether I owe any explanations or apologies to any of those I've taken down and taken out is Your call. As far as further explaining might go, I suppose I have just as much, if not more, explaining to do for the muck I made out of my life. You'll have to forgive me for doing it my way with my headstrong ways instead of Your way. I've kept myself out ahead of a lot of judgments that came my way, but at this point I can't save my soul any more than I can save my ass. You'll have to do the forgiving and saving. You'll have to forgive me for the sorrow I brought to my parents and sister. You have to forgive me for the disappointment I made of my life and for leaving my parents' home, the only home I had then or since."

The sergeant looked out at the jungle, from where the final end of his earthly continuance would probably come.

"I offer no excuses for my life. Excuses didn't save me then. Excuses aren't going to deliver me now. I guess it's way too late to hope for a deliverer outside of Your Son Jesus. But that's in another world and another life. No one's going to deliver what's left of me in what's left of my life in this world."

The bushes deep behind the ones in front of Samuel rustled. Someone was coming through, but it wasn't a deliverer. There were no deliverers coming from the jungle in front of him.

"Forgive me for all the sins I've ever committed, against You, against the girl, against my parents, against my sister, and against all the people I've ever sinned against. I've killed a whole lot of men for many reasons. At the time I killed them, I thought I was doing the right thing. At least in my own light I thought it was the right and just thing. Whether they were righteous kills, I don't know. I don't know how You see what I did in Your light. I may need even more forgiveness than I imagine."

He heard the bushes immediately behind the ones in front of him rustle as soldiers pushed through. The average Japanese soldier of that day was only about five feet three inches tall. The sergeant realized he might be aiming a bit too high. His first burst would go over their heads. He lowered the aim on the machine gun to aim it more directly forward.

"I've made men die, but I've never died for anyone the way Your Son did. I would have died for the girl, but I killed instead. I lived my life out of my headstrong head and with my headstrong ways. I live for myself as much as for anyone. Now it looks like I'm going to die for myself. Your Son Jesus died for the sins of everyone. Jesus, if You're listening, forgive me for my sins. Break through the gloom I've made of my life and take me to Your skies. You'll probably be able to pick me up off the ground right here."

The sergeant moved his thumb and clicked off the safety on his machine gun.

"I don't know if Your Father in heaven sees much of any righteousness in my life. I don't know if He sees whether I did my proper duty in life for my family or the girl. All I can say in my defense on that front is that I loved them all. I don't know how Your Father in heaven sees my duty here and now, but for what it's worth, for what I'm worth, I'm going to do my earthly duty to my last bullet and my last breath. And I'm not about to surrender myself to the likes of men who drive swords through the stomachs of women. I'm going to take as many of them with me, along with men who like to break girls' necks."

In the quiet of the jungle dawn that he knew would erupt into the flame and rage of battle in the light of the day, his finger poised above the trigger of his limited weapon that was inadequate to stop the swarming Japanese attack, and with death probably closing in unseen from only yards away, the sergeant slipped into a quiet, contemplative mental state that matched his quiet, fatalistic mood, the fatalistic mood that had followed him and defined him since he had left home so long ago.

"Since I'll probably be standing before You soon enough, how does my life pass in review to You? A man's life has got to mean something. How does my life stack up to You? I've been all over the board in what my life has been and how I've lived it. What's my life been as You see it? What has the character of my life been as You see it? I've lived in the midst of violence and meanness the better part of my life. I've practiced meanness and violence and vengeance throughout the later times of my life. I suppose You're not too crazy about that on my part as You're not too crazy about violence in general. You say in Your Book that love is the greatest and most godly trait of all. I have loved, though to some it may be hard to see where. I loved my parents. I loved my sister, even though she could be a snot at times. Will I get to see them up there? I loved the farm. Does any of the love I felt in my early days balance out the meanness of my life that came after those days?"

The sergeant paused again in his train of thought, his finger still poised over the trigger.

"You say the greatest of gifts is love. I have loved as deep and real as I have killed. How do the two sides of my life stack up to You? You must weigh the good against the bad, the tenderness I felt for those I loved against the meanness I brought to those I hated."

The focus of his thoughts shifted from third person to God, to the first person behind his reverie.

"I loved you, girl. Whether the love I had for you was good love or bad love, I loved you like I had never loved before and have never loved since. I loved you like there was no other. I loved you like there was no tomorrow. In the end, my love for you foreclosed all my tomorrows from the day I met you onward. Some people may fault you that you didn't love me back. I faulted you in my own way for that. But maybe you can't be faulted. Like Sis said of you, maybe your heart was so torn up that you couldn't give love or even receive it."

Samuel could hear rustling in the jungle close in front of him.

"Are you out there, still unable to love, or are you waiting for me, holding love for me, the love you weren't able to bring out of your heart in life? Have you found your way in eternity? Are you walking in eternity in peace, or are you still running as scared as you were on earth?"

His focus on eternity shifted back to the Author of eternity.

"Will I see her again out there, Lord? Will our lives be revealed to have meant something in eternity? Will anything both of us went through mean anything in heaven? Will the relationships and loves we find in this world and bring to our lives and the lives of those around us continue unbroken and now be unbreakable in heaven? Will anything that any of us do in this life carry on and carry forward in heaven? Or is heaven so far beyond anything of this world that nothing of this world applies? Can we start all over again, on the right path, with no pain and crippling remembrances lingering from our lives on earth to throw us off the paths of heaven? I've asked myself the same questions more times than I can remember. I never got an answer out of myself. I still don't have an answer for my life. Maybe when it's all over, I'll get an answer for my life from heaven."

As Samuel pulled his finger closer to the trigger, he pulled the girl closer to him in his heart.

"Maybe it was all your fault that we never came together in a real way, girl. Maybe it was all my fault. Maybe it was the evenly shared fault of both of us. Given the horizon-to-horizon difference in the ways we thought, maybe there was never any possible way that we ever could come together. Whatever way it may have been, I guess now it doesn't matter anymore."

The rustling in the jungle bushes drew closer.

"I never really knew what you thought of me in life, but I've thought of you pretty much every day of my life since you lost yours. I'm thinking of you. My last thoughts will probably be of you."

The rustling in the bushes in front of him grew louder.

"If those who loved in life can find those they loved in eternity, seek me out as I'll seek you out. We can come together in a land where there is no parting. If the Lord is willing, we can be together again. There we can walk along the river hand in hand once more."

As the sergeant's hand tightened on the pistol grip of the Thompson and his finger pressed more firmly on the trigger, the thing that came to his mind as full and bright as the day he had first heard it in the church of his hometown were the lyrics of the hymn that they had been singing the day and the moment that he had resolved to marry the girl:

> Hold Thou Thy cross before my closing eyes.
> Shine through the gloom and point me to the skies.
> Heaven's morning breaks, and earth's vain shadows flee.
> In life, in death, O Lord, abide with me.

"Wherever you are in death, O girl, wait there for me," Samuel said in a low voice.

The bushes directly in front of Samuel's position started to part. The dull brown of a Japanese infantry uniform appeared in the gap in the green foliage. Samuel pulled the trigger and fired off a disciplined burst. A shower of shredded green leaves mixed with sprays of bright red blood from where the heavy-caliber bullets fired at close-quarter range, tearing holes into the chest of the soldier who was emerging through the parting jungle foliage. Samuel never fully saw the man's face. The man fell backward, dead, and dropped out of sight. His long-barreled Arisaka Type 38 rifle, taller than the man was when the bayonet was fixed, too long and impractical for jungle fighting, fell next to him, bayonet fixed.

"There's one for the woman with the sword through her stomach." The sergeant spit in anger at the fallen man. "There's one for the likes of all of you bucktooth sons-of-heaven devils." He glanced quickly up toward heaven. "There's another one for the likes of the man who killed you, girl."

From along the thinly manned US line, firing erupted. Maybe a dozen

Japanese soldiers fell dead or wounded. Samuel sprayed the jungle in front of him, trying to add to the dead and wounded, in the hope that if his side inflicted enough carnage, the Japanese would beat a hasty retreat. In short order he had exhausted the magazine in his gun. He quickly ejected the spent drum magazine and inserted another. As he did so, he realized it was the last magazine he had.

Instead of fleeing or retreating in an orderly manner, the Japanese soldiers rushed the line, yelling some kind of Japanese war cry. The frontal assault met much the same fate as the ones they had launched on Bataan. Numbers of Japanese soldiers were cut down. But driven on by whatever contrived warrior code or patriotic lie about the honor and defense of Japan they had been inculcated with, the Japanese came on, firing as they went. The US line was stretched and thin, and the defenders were running out of ammunition.

"We can't hold them!" the sergeant shouted. "Fall back to the tunnel and form up there. I'll try to slow them up."

The soldiers on the improvised line jumped up and started moving through the jungle toward the tunnel entrance, turning to fire as they went. The sergeant stood up. Swinging his Thompson machine gun, he fired off bursts in the directions the Japanese troops were coming from. He hit another soldier and made the rest duck, slowing them in their pursuit as he had hoped. The delay the sergeant had created gave the retreating men an extra measure of time to put enough extra distance between them and the Japanese troops that they were able to reach the tunnel.

The sergeant's machine gun went silent in his hands. He was out of ammunition, and he didn't have another drum to reload with. He didn't know if there were more drums back at the tunnel. He didn't know if there were any serviceable machine guns at the tunnel, but there were rifles and other weapons he could use.

He had one more weapon at his immediate disposal. Holding his empty machine gun in one hand, he drew his Colt .45 service automatic out of his holster. Still standing exposed, he fired the pistol at the advancing Japanese troops.

Like his machine gun, the sergeant's pistol fell silent as the clip ran out of bullets and the last shot was fired. He didn't have another clip.

With nothing further that could be done, and with bullets whizzing around him, the sergeant turned quickly and started on a run, following his men back toward the tunnel. He held on to both his empty machine gun and his empty pistol. Guns were at a premium and weren't to be thrown away, not even in a desperate flight for life. As he started running, the sergeant calculated how long it would take him to reach the tunnel. The tunnel was a relatively short distance away, but he felt as if it would take an eternity to get there.

As Samuel was running, a Japanese soldier dropped into a prone firing position. Aiming, the soldier let off a long burst with his Type 96 light machine gun. He could see small spurts where several shots hit the man's back. The man stumbled forward and went down. He did not get back up. A short time later, another soldier approached the fallen figure lying motionless. Using the nearly three-foot bayonet at the end of his rifle, the soldier rolled the fallen figure over. He would have lunged with the bayonet if the man had shown any sign of life. But Samuel Martin was already dead.

For Marine Sergeant Martin Heisner, a.k.a. Samuel Martin, farm boy, baseball player, devoted son, son of the soil, big brother to his snotty but loved little sister, lover of the lost girl, lover of older women needful of love, defender of women, barroom brawler, striker, professional soldier, avenger, gunman, killer of killers, and runner from the law, the final reveille had blown. His run through life had come to its end. One more run awaited him.

Fearing a massacre, General Wainwright, the overall commander after General MacArthur's departure, surrendered the garrison. The massacre that Samuel feared would fall on all those who surrendered never happened. The survivors became prisoners of war of the Japanese. They were removed from the island and taken ashore to the main island of Luzon. There would be no US presence on the island again for the next three years. While spared the horrors of the Bataan Death March, the prisoners suffered the privations and mistreatment the Imperial Japanese inflicted on all their prisoners.

World War II marched on for four more years in two hemispheres and across the multiple oceans of the world, fought in swirling offensives over vistas vast and wide and in tight corners of hell and misery. But the war was not through with the island of Corregidor.

In February of 1945, the 503rd Parachute Regimental Combat Team, including units of the 34th and 151st Infantry regiments, assaulted the island. They lost 210 men. True to their fanatic devotion to the Imperial Japanese cause and their emperor, thinking surrender to be dishonorable, the Japanese garrison of an estimated fifty-two hundred fought to near extinction for their dishonorable cause. They also died wasting their lives for the vile militarists who had sent them out to conquer other lands and torment other peoples for the aggrandizement of the militarists, and for their milquetoast emperor who had never once challenged the militarists' megalomania. The militarists probably would have assassinated him if he had.

Fewer than fifty of the Japanese garrison who had occupied Corregidor survived. In the end, the massacre Samuel had feared would fall upon the Americans on the island fell instead upon the Japanese garrison—but only because of their misguided, suicidal devotion to their homeland, to which the militarists had brought war by bringing war to others to build themselves an empire; by their devotion to their wimp emperor, who never summoned the courage to challenge the warmongers who dominated the Japanese governing Diet; and by their devotion to the vile militarists themselves, who had commanded them to march forth to conquer, kill, and die in order to build an empire for Japan and the militarists. The slavish devotion of the Japanese of that era to their perverted sense of duty, honor, and country would, in the end, be broken, not by a dawning sense of shame and guilt at the atrocities they had committed in the name of their sense of superiority and in the name of their martial codes, but by massive carpet bombings culminating in two nuclear bombs.

In the sunset of their empire, the presumption, arrogance, and inhumanity of the Japanese militarists would be carried away on the winds of defeat along with the clouds of smoke that would rise over Tokyo and other Japanese cities and by the radioactive clouds that would rise over Hiroshima and Nagasaki. The smoke of burning Japanese cities would rise and mingle in the upper atmosphere with the smoke of the cities they had burned and the cities their Nazi soul mates had burned and with the smoke of the innocent burned in Nazi crematoria. It would be men like Sergeant Heisner who, through their heroism, sacrifice, and blood, would pound down the evil of all the militarists who had started the war and drive their madness and brutality back down to hell where it had come from.

At the final drawn-out end, Hitler would kill himself in his bunker. Many German and Japanese fanatics would kill themselves, not able to imagine a world not ruled by their madness and their mad leaders. Many of the militarists who had launched the most destructive war in human history on two continents would go to the gallows. This included not only Nazis but also a good number of the Japanese militarists and war criminals, Tojo included, who had brought the fire to others and finally down upon their own country. Their star would be gone from the heavens. The Rising Sun would set. The US flag would be raised again on the still standing flagpole on the parade ground of the bombed-out Topside Barracks.

In later years, the already war-ruined buildings would fall into further disrepair and neglect. Yet the spirit of the memorial the abandoned buildings represented remains in the lines inscribed on one of the walls:

> Sleep, my sons.
> Sleep in the silent depths of the sea,
> Or in your bed of hallowed sod,
> Until you hear at dawn
> The low, clear reveille of God.

The smoke from the fires of battle that hung over Corregidor faded away, to be replaced in subsequent years by the smoke and fire that rose over the battles fought on other islands of the Philippines. The fire that the Imperial Japanese and warlord militarists had brought to others would be brought back upon Japanese cities in a hell of consuming flames. The last of that consuming fire would be atomic.

The immediate question of the day that remained and that would hang suspended for four years was whether or not the flamboyant MacArthur would keep his promise to return. He did, but instead of landing on Corregidor, he landed on the Philippine island of Leyte, wading onto the shore from a landing craft, getting his feet wet in the process. Wet socks and posturing notwithstanding, he and the United States had kept their promise to return.

From the deserts of North Africa, to the mountains of Italy, to the beaches of Normandy, to the mile markers on the road to Berlin, to the endless islands of the Pacific, there were many fathers, sons, husbands, and lovers who did not return. Many of them were buried near the places where they fell. Many were returned halfway home to cemeteries like the Cemetery of the Pacific, the Punchbowl Crater cemetery in Hawaii, and Arlington National Cemetery. A few of the hallowed dead did manage to make it all the way back to where their stories had started.

Chapter 41

"Well, I guess we're done here, ma'am," the cemetery manager said to the woman as the gravediggers walked away, their work done. The man looked at the fresh and crisp words carved into the flat, raised gray granite stone that the woman had delivered to the cemetery to be placed and which they had cemented to the support block just below the surface of the ground. The two-stone system would not sink very far into the ground. The words carved into the hard stone would endure for millennia:

> MSG Samuel Martin
> Fourth Brigade USMC
> Killed in action 1942
> Beloved son, beloved brother
> Returned home for burial by his sister

"I'm curious," the man said to the older woman who had directed the burial and specified that the headstone be placed across from the far older stone with the involved carved epitaph that ended with the following mournful words:

I died alone far from my home.
Nobody knows from where I came.
This stone at my head will say I am dead
And know me by no other name.

"You're not from this town. You're from the next town over. If these are your brother's remains, why are you burying him here and not in your hometown?"

"This town was our hometown once," the woman said. "My family is originally from here. My brother and I both grew up in this town. Our parents are buried down in the main section in the middle of the cemetery in the plot where the members of my family have been buried since my great-grandfather's time. The male line of our family came to an end when my brother was killed in the war. He left no descendants. Our family came to an end with him."

"If the rest of your ancestors are buried down there, why don't you want your brother buried there too?" the man asked. He looked over at the ornately lettered gravestone, bigger than the modest stone the woman had chosen to bury her brother's returned remains under. The thirty-year difference in the dates of death was a bit confusing.

"Why did you specify that you wanted him buried across from her? Was there a connection between them?"

"There was a connection," the woman said, "a deep and abiding connection. More abiding on his part than hers, but a connection. A connection that changed my brother's life entirely. Unfortunately that connection did not change her life enough to save it. That connection was broken in this world. I only hope it has been reestablished and honored in heaven."

The woman said no more. The man didn't ask further. For all he knew, there was a painful family memory involved.

"The war has been over for two years," the man said. "Why did it take the army so long to bring his remains back home here?"

"He was a marine, not army," the woman said. "The marines have their own ways of doing things. As for why it took them so long, I guess they had to find where the Japanese had buried the dead Americans they killed. They just buried them in pits and didn't mark any of them. I guess they had to identify the remains first. They identified my brother by his dog tags. I don't know how they did it. I'm just glad it was done. I would hate to think of him lying somewhere I don't know under a stone that says 'Unknown.'"

"If he's a bona fide war hero, you could have him interred at Arlington National Cemetery," the man said. "Why did you chose to have him buried here?"

"This is where it all started out for him," Beth Martin Howard said. "I wanted to bring him back here to his home …" She glanced at the older grave across from her brother's newly turned grave. "I had you place him here where they could face each other on Resurrection Day."

Her business completed, the woman started to walk away. The cemetery manager followed her.

"He did his duty to the end for all those he did duty for," Beth said as they walked down the shallow slope, heading toward the main road of the cemetery. "He protected those he could protect. He wasn't always successful, but he stood his ground to the end. He never ran backward. He only ran forward to protect those he stood his ground to help. He stood up for and tried to protect a girl who had come into town on a run. Her run came to an end a long time ago. Now his run has reached its end. He can stop running now."

Samuel Martin sprang up and started running through the jungle. No shouts in Japanese followed him. No bullets whizzed past him. He heard no gunshots. There was no sound of battle going on anywhere around him. He pushed out of the jungle and back on the road leading to the east end of the Malinta Tunnel. As he raced down the road, picking up speed as he went, no shots rang out around him. No soldiers appeared, Japanese or American. The road was deserted. He was the only runner on the road. On the way to the tunnel entrance, he left the MacArthur house behind. He did not look at it.

At the entrance to the Malinta Tunnel, no defensive perimeter had been drawn up. There were no trenches or bulwarks in evidence. No hastily assembled defensive ramparts blocked the entrance to the tunnel.

He entered the tunnel at a run without slowing down. He was not weakened by the speed at which he was running. If anything, he seemed to be picking up speed and strength. Inside the tunnel there was litter on the floor. Chairs and tables were there where they had been left, but no soldiers, Japanese or American, were in the tunnel. No medics were in residence treating wounded. The walkway through the tunnel was as deserted as the road leading up to it. There was no activity in any of the numerous side tunnels.

Samuel dashed through the tunnel and came out the west end. From there, instead of following the coastal road, he took one of the serpentine inner roads that wound through the inner reaches of the main island. He passed the parade ground and the post headquarters. He did not look at them. Behind him and to the side was Battery Way. He ran by Battery Hearn, where he had directed fire at the Japanese guns on the far shore of Manila Bay. The huge barrels of the massive siege guns pointed skyward, mute and unmoving.

As he drew close to the west end of the island, he left the road and started sprinting through the jungle again. By now unexpected energy was coursing through him. He no longer felt like a professional soldier worn and callused by long years spent in the military, ragged from wars he had stopped counting. He felt not like a teenager but like a young man in the prime of energetic life.

He pushed his way through the jungle growth. It did not slow him down. At the far end of the island where the water of Manila Bay started again, he pushed through the last of the jungle and came out where the lumberyard sat, just inside the town boundary by the bridge where the town began. There was no one walking the main street or any of the side streets. There were no shoppers looking into store windows or walking with packages in hand. There were no parents leading their children by hand down the sidewalk. No voices were heard. No dogs were barking. The town was deserted.

Samuel sprinted the short distance down the main street of the town and turned onto the road that wound along the river. He followed the road to where it came to Mrs. Richardson's establishment. From there he cut in front of the Richardson house. No one was in the yard, back or front. There were no girls walking on the lawn, or sitting on the grass, or sitting in open windows displaying their bodily wares. The house was as deserted as the town.

On the side of the house facing the river, Samuel turned and came to the edge of the bluff, where he looked down. At the base of the bluff, standing on the sand of the river shore, he saw the girl trying futilely to climb the embankment. She had been trying for an hour to climb it and get to the safety of Mrs. Richardson's house, which had been a place of refuge and safety for her. But every time she tried to climb the clay of the embankment, she just kept sliding back. In her frustration, she could not understand why she was unable to climb the embankment.

To Samuel she seemed even more beautiful than she had appeared the first time he had seen her in the parlor of Mrs. Richardson's house. The same hint of fear he had seen in her eyes that night was in her eyes in the daylight.

"Clarinda! Clarinda!" Samuel shouted down toward the girl. Startled by the voice, the girl looked up and saw Samuel standing at the edge of the bluff. When she saw him, she startled and drew back. She turned and ran out onto the shallow sand in the middle of the river, where she stopped and turned around to look at him, her feet in the water.

Samuel slid quickly down the bank. Sprinting to where she had stopped in the shallow water, he turned around. As he approached, she reached into the pocket of her dress and pulled out the folding knife she always carried when away from the house. She snapped out the blade and held the knife out at him, her eyes filled with fear and uncertainty. Samuel strode up to where she was standing. With a wide backhand stroke, he drove the knife from the girl's hand. It fell into the river with a splash and disappeared. Samuel threw his arms around the girl and pulled her to him in a tight embrace. The girl grabbed his shoulders and pulled herself against him as tightly as he was pulling her to him. Her fear gone, her running complete, the girl buried her head in his shoulder and clung to him tightly, crying softly.

The water of the river of eternity flowed around their feet, heading past and away.

About the Book

Samuel Martin is not afflicted with the wanderlust that teenage boys growing into young men in isolated areas in isolated times so often are. Samuel has no desire to break out of the isolation of the remote rural farm town he was born in and go see the world. He wants nothing more than to be the third-generation patriarch on the farm of his ancestors, living on the land he loves in company with the family he loves. He is just facing the problem of finding the one girl he wants to share his love and his life with. He thinks he has found that girl in the form of the beautiful, enigmatic young prostitute who hides her early life and hides herself behind a flowery contrived name. The girl shares her body with him but never shares her real name. Neither does she share the love she is incapable of returning.

However socially problematic loving a prostitute may be in the conservative small town he grew up in and the conservative era he lives in, Samuel is ready to give his heart to the girl in the fullness of his love for her and the fullness of love for a lifetime. He is sure he can win her heart to his heart. He just is not aware how closed off and shut down her heart is, locked up hard and tight behind a barrier of painful memory, hurt, and fear.

Not realizing how deep the tortured depth of her soul runs, Samuel loves the nameless girl beyond reason, logic, and caution. He just doesn't realize that loving beyond reason can invert, disrupt, overturn, and shatter one's life as much as anything pursued beyond reason. When his lover is murdered, Samuel's raging vengeance rips apart her killer. It also rips apart his life and forces him to flee, leaving him to survive a hard life far from home over a distant horizon of loneliness and violence. In the dissolution of his life and home, he learns the hard adage: "Life is what happens to you when you are making other plans."